Mrs. Radcliffe's Novels. the Italian, the
Romance of the Forest, the Mysteries of
Udolpho

MRS. RADCLIFFE'S

NOVELS

THE ITALIAN
THE ROMANCE OF THE FOREST
THE MYSTERIES OF UDOLPHO

LONDON AND NEW YORK
GEORGE ROUTLEDGE AND SONS

THE ITALIAN

OR

THE CONFESSIONAL OF THE BLACK PENITENTS

A ROMANCE

BY

ANN RADCLIFFE

AUTHOR OF "THE MYSTERIES OF UDOLPHO" AND "THE ROMANCE OF THE FOREST

He, wrapt in clouds of mystery and silence,
Broods o'er his passions, bodies them in deeds,
And sends them forth on wings of Fate to others:
Like the invisible Will, that guides us,
Unheard, unknown, unsearchable !

LONDON AND NEW YORK
GEORGE ROUTLEDGE AND SONS
1877

THE ITALIAN.

ABOUT the year 1764, some English travellers in Italy, during one of their excursions in the environs of Naples, happened to stop before the portico of the Santa Maria del Pianto, a church belonging to a very ancient convent of the order of the Black Penitents. The magnificence of this portico, though impaired by time, excited so much admiration that the travellers were curious to survey the structure to which it belonged, and with this intention they ascended the marble steps that led to it.

Within the shade of the portico, a person with folded arms, and eyes directed towards the ground, was pacing behind the pillars the whole extent of the pavement, and was apparently so engaged by his own thoughts as not to observe that strangers were approaching. He turned, however, suddenly, as if startled by the sound of steps, and then, without further pausing, glided to a door that opened into the church, and disappeared

There was something too extraordinary in the appearance of this man, and too singular in his conduct, to pass unnoticed by the visitors. He was of a tall thin figure, bending forward from the shoulders ; of a sallow complexion and harsh features, and had an eye which, as it looked up from the cloak that muffled the lower part of his countenance, seemed expressive of uncommon ferocity.

The travellers, on entering the church, looked round for the stranger who had passed thither before them ; but he was nowhere to be seen, and, through all the shade of the long aisles, only one other person appeared. This was a friar of the adjoining convent, who sometimes pointed out to visitors the objects in the church which were most worthy of attention, and who now, with this design, approached the party that had just entered.

The interior of this edifice had nothing of the showy ornament and general splendour which distinguish the churches of Italy, and particularly those of Naples ; but it exhibited a simplicity and grandeur of design considerably more interesting to persons of taste, and a solemnity of light and shade much more suitable to promote the sublime elevation of devotion.

When the party had viewed the different shrines and whatever had been judged worthy of observation, and were returning through an obscure aisle towards the portico, they perceived the person who had appeared upon the steps, passing towards a confessional on the left, and, as he entered it, one of the party pointed him out to the friar and inquired who he was. The friar, turning to look after him, did not immediately reply ; but, on the question being repeated, he inclined his head, as in a kind of obeisance, and calmly replied, " He is an assassin."

" An assassin ! " exclaimed one of the Englishmen ; " an assassin, and at liberty! "

An Italian gentleman, who was of the party, smiled at the astonishment of his friend.

" He has sought sanctuary here," replied the friar ; " within these walls he may not be molested."

" Do your altars, then, protect the murderer ? " said the Englishman.

" He could find shelter nowhere else," answered the friar, meekly.

" This is astonishing ! " said the Englishman ; " of what avail are your laws, if the most atrocious criminal may thus find shelter from them ? But how does he contrive to exist here ? He is at least in danger of being starved."

" Pardon me," replied the friar, " there are always people willing to assist those who cannot assist themselves ; and, as the criminal may not leave the church in search of food, they bring it to him here."

" Is this possible ? " said the Englishman, turning to his Italian friend.

" Why, the poor wretch must not starve," replied the friend ; " which he inevitably would do if food were not brought to him. But have you never, since your arrival in Italy, happened to see a person in the situation of this man ? It is by no means an uncommon one."

" Never," answered the Englishman, " and I can scarcely credit what I see now ! "

" Why, my friend," observed the Italian, " assassinations are so frequent that if we were to show no mercy to such unfortunate persons, our cities would be half depopulated."

In notice of this profound remark the Englishman could only gravely bow.

" But observe yonder confessional," added the Italian, " that beyond the pillars on the left of the aisle, below a painted window. Have you discovered it ? The colours of the glass throw, instead of light, a shade over that part of the church, which, perhaps, prevents your distinguishing what I mean."

The Englishman looked whither his friend pointed, and observed a confessional of oak, or some very dark wood, adjoining the wall, and remarked also that it was the same which the assassin had just entered. It consisted of three compartments, covered with a black canopy. In the central division was the chair of the confessor, elevated by several steps above the pavement of the church ; and on either hand was a small closet or box, with steps leading up to a grated partition, at which the penitent might kneel, and, concealed from observation, pour into the ear of the confessor the consciousness of crimes that lay heavy on his heart.

"You observe it ?" said the Italian.

"I do," replied the Englishman ; "it is the same which the assassin has passed into, and I think it one of the most gloomy spots I ever beheld ; the view of it is enough to strike a criminal with despair."

"We in Italy are not so apt to despair," replied the Italian, smilingly.

"Well, but what of this confessional ?" inquired the Englishman. "The assassin entered it."

"He has no relation with what I am about to mention," said the Italian ; "but I wish you to mark the place, because some very extraordinary circumstances belong to it."

"What are they ?" said the Englishman.

"It is now several years since the confession which is connected with them was made at that very confessional," added the Italian ; "the view of it, and the sight of this assassin, with your surprise at the liberty which is allowed him, led me to a recollection of the story. When you return to the hotel I will communicate it to you, if you have no pleasanter way of engaging your time."

"I have a curiosity to hear it," replied the Englishman ; "cannot you relate it now ?"

"It is much too long to be related now— that would occupy a week. I have it in writing, and will send you the volume. A young student of Padua, who happened to be at Naples soon after this horrible confession became public ——"

"Pardon me," interrupted the Englishman ; "that is surely very extraordinary. I thought confessions were always held sacred by the priest to whom they were made."

"Your observation is reasonable," rejoined the Italian. "The faith of the priest is never broken except by an especial command from a higher power ; and the circumstances must even then be very extraordinary to justify such a departure from the law. But when you read the narrative, your surprise on this head will cease. I was going to tell you that it was written by a student of Padua, who, happening to be here soon after the affair became public, was so much struck with the facts that, partly as an exercise and partly in return for some trifling services I had rendered him, he committed them to paper for me. You will perceive from the work, that this student was very young as to the arts of composition ; but the facts are what you require, and from these he has not deviated. But come, let us leave the church."

"After I have taken another view of this solemn edifice," replied the Englishman, "and particularly of the confessional you have pointed to my notice."

While the Englishman glanced his eye over the high roofs and along the solemn perspectives of the Santa del Pianto, he perceived the figure of the assassin stealing from the confessional across the choir ; and, shocked on again beholding him, he turned his eyes and hastily quitted the church.

The friends then separated, and the Englishman, soon after returning to his hotel, received the volume. He read as follows :—

CHAPTER I.

IT was in the church of San Lorenzo at Naples, in the year 1758, that Vincentio di Vivaldi first saw Ellena Rosalba. The sweetness and fine expression of her voice attracted his attention to her figure, which had a distinguished air of delicacy and grace ; but her face was concealed in her veil. So much, indeed, was he fascinated by the voice that a most painful curiosity was excited as to her countenance, which he fancied must express all the sensibility of character that the modulation of her tones indicated. He listened to their exquisite expression with a rapt attention, and hardly withdrew his eyes from her person till the matin service had concluded, when he observed her leave the church with an aged lady, who leaned upon her arm and who appeared to be her mother.

Vivaldi immediately followed their steps, determined to obtain, if possible, a view of Ellena's face, and to observe the home to which she should retire. They walked quickly, looking neither to the right nor left, and as they turned into the Strada di Toledo he had nearly lost them, but quickening his pace, and relinquishing the cautious distance he had hitherto kept, he overtook them as they entered on the Terrazzo Nuovo, which runs along the bay of Naples and leads towards the Gran Corso. He overtook them ; but the fair unknown still held her veil close, and he knew not how to introduce himself to her notice or to obtain a view of the features which excited his curiosity. He was embarrassed by a respectful timidity that mingled with his admiration, and which kept him silent, notwithstanding his wish to speak.

In descending the last steps of the Terrazzo, however, the foot of the elder lady faltered ; and while Vivaldi hastened to assist her the breeze from the water caught the veil, which Ellena had no longer a hand sufficiently disengaged to confine, and, wafting it partially aside, disclosed to him a countenance more touchingly beautiful than he had dared to image. Her features were of the Grecian outline, and though they expressed the tranquillity of an elegant mind, her dark blue eyes sparkled with intelligence. She was assisting her companion so anxiously as not immediately to observe the admiration she had inspired; but the moment her eyes met those of Vivaldi, she became conscious of the effect and hastily drew her veil.

The old lady was not materially hurt by her fall, but as she walked with difficulty, Vivaldi seized the opportunity thus offered and insisted that she should accept his arm. She refused this with many acknowledgments, but he pressed the offer so repeatedly and respectfully that at length she accepted it, and they walked towards her residence together.

On the way thither he attempted to converse with Ellena, but her replies were concise, and he arrived at the end of the walk while he was yet considering what he could say that might interest and withdraw her from this severe reserve. From the style of their residence he imagined that they were persons of honourable but moderate independence. The house was small, but exhibited an air of comfort and even of taste. It stood on an eminence, surrounded by a garden and vineyards, which commanded the City and Bay of Naples, an ever-moving picture, and was canopied by a thick grove of pines and majestic date trees, and, though the little portico and colonnade in front were of common marble, the style of architecture was elegant. While they afforded a shelter from the sun, they admitted the cooling breezes that rose from the bay below, and a prospect of the whole scope of its enchanting shores.

Vivaldi stopped at the little gate which led into the garden, where the elder lady repeated her acknowledgments for his care, but did not invite him to enter; and he, trembling with anxiety and sinking with disappointment, remained for a moment gazing upon Ellena, unable to take leave, yet irresolute what to say that might prolong the interview, till the old lady again bade him good-day. He then summoned courage enough to request he might be allowed to inquire after her health, and, having obtained a reluctant permission, his eyes bade adieu to Ellena, who, as they were parting, ventured to thank him for the care he had taken of her aunt. The sound of her voice and this acknowledgment of obligation made him less willing to go than before, but at length he tore himself away. The beauty of her countenance haunting his imagination, and the touching accents of her voice still vibrating on his heart, he descended to the shore below her residence, pleasing himself with the consciousness of being near her though he could no longer behold her; and

sometimes hoping that he might again see her, however distantly, in a balcony of the house, where the silk awning seemed to invite the breeze from the sea. He lingered hour after hour, stretched beneath the umbrageous pines that waved over the shore, or traversing, regardless of the heat, the base of the cliffs that crowned it, recalling to his fancy the enchantment of her smile, and seeming still to listen to the sweetness of her accents.

In the evening he returned to his father's palace at Naples, thoughtful yet pleased, anxious yet happy, dwelling with delightful hope on the remembrance of the thanks he had received from Ellena, yet not daring to form any plan as to his future conduct. He returned time enough to attend his mother in her evening ride on the Corso, where, in every gay carriage that passed, he hoped to see the object of his constant thought, but she did not appear. His mother, the Marchesa di Vivaldi, observed his anxiety and unusual silence, and asked him some questions, which she meant should lead to an explanation of the change in his manners; but his replies only excited a stronger curiosity, and, though she forbore to press her inquiries, it was, probably, that she might employ a more artful means of renewing them.

Vincentio di Vivaldi was the only son of the Marchese di Vivaldi, a nobleman of one of the most ancient families of the kingdom of Naples, a favourite possessing an uncommon share of influence at Court; a man still higher in power than in rank. His pride of birth was equal to either, but it was mingled with the justifiable pride of a principled mind; it governed his conduct in morals as well as in the jealousy of ceremonial distinctions, and elevated his practice as well as his claims. His pride was at once his vice and his virtue, his safeguard and his weakness.

The mother of Vivaldi, descended from a family as ancient as that of his father, was equally jealous of her importance; but her pride was that of birth and distinction, without extending to morals. She was of violent passions, haughty, vindictive, yet crafty and deceitful; patient in stratagem, and indefatigable in pursuit of vengeance on the unhappy objects who provoked her resentment. She loved her son rather as being the last of two illustrious houses who was to reunite and support the honour of both, than with the fondness of a mother.

Vincentio inherited much of the character of his father, and very little of that of his mother. His pride was as noble and generous as that of the Marchese; but he had somewhat of the fiery passions of the Marchesa, without any of her craft, her duplicity, or vindictive thirst of revenge. Frank in his temper, ingenuous in his sentiments, quickly offended, but easily appeased; irritated by any appearance of disrespect, but melted by a concession, a high sense of honour rendered him no more jealous of offence than a delicate humanity made him ready for reconciliation, and anxious to spare the feelings of others.

On the day following that on which he had seen Ellena, he returned to the Villa Altieri, to use the permission granted him of inquiring after the health of Signora Bianchi. The expectation of seeing Ellena agitated him with impatient joy and trembling hope, which still increased as he approached her residence, till, having reached the garden-gate, he was obliged to rest for a few moments to recover breath and composure.

Having announced himself to an old female servant, who came to the gate, he was soon after admitted to a small vestibule, where he found Bianchi winding balls of silk, and alone; though from the position of a chair, which stood near a frame for embroidery, he judged that Ellena had but just quitted the apartment, Signora Bianchi received him with a reserved politeness, and seemed very cautious in her replies to his inquiries after her niece, who he hoped, every moment, would appear. He lengthened his visit till there was no longer an excuse for doing so; till he had exhausted every topic of conversation, and till the silence of Bianchi seemed to hint that his departure was expected. With a heart saddened by disappointment, and having obtained only a reluctant permission to inquire after the health of that lady on some future day, he then took leave.

On his way through the garden he often paused to look back upon the house, hoping to obtain a glimpse of Ellena at a lattice; and threw a glance around him, almost expecting to see her seated beneath the shade of the luxuriant plantains; but his search was everywhere vain, and he quitted the place with the slow and heavy step of despondency.

The day was employed in endeavours to obtain intelligence concerning the family of Ellena, but of this he procured little that was satisfactory. He was told that she was an orphan, living under the care of her aunt, Signora Bianchi; that her family, which had never been illustrious, was decayed in fortune, and that her only dependence was upon this aunt. But he was ignorant of what was very true, though very secret, that she assisted to support this aged relative, whose sole property was the small estate on which they lived, and that she passed whole days in embroidering silks, which were disposed of to the nuns of a neighbouring convent, who sold them to the Neapolitan ladies that visited their grate, at a very high advantage. He little thought that a beautiful robe which he had often seen his mother wear, was worked by Ellena; nor that some copies from the antique, which ornamented a cabinet of the Vivaldi palace, were drawn by her hand. If he had known these

circumstances, they would only have served to increase the tenderness which, since they were proofs of a disparity of fortune that would certainly render his family repugnant to a connection with hers, it would have been prudent to overcome.

Ellena could have endured poverty, but not contempt: and it was to protect herself from this effect of the narrow prejudices of the world around her, that she had so cautiously concealed from it a knowledge of the industry which did honour to her character. She was not ashamed of poverty, or of the industry which overcame it, but her spirit shrunk from the senseless smile and humiliating condescension which prosperity sometimes gives to indigence. Her mind was not yet strong enough, or her views sufficiently enlarged, to teach her a contempt of the sneer of vicious folly, and to glory in the dignity of virtuous independence. Ellena was the sole support of her aunt's declining years; was patient to her infirmities, and consoling to her sufferings; and repaid the fondness of a mother with the affection of a daughter. Her mother she had never known, having lost her while she was an infant, and from that period Bianchi had practised the kindness of one towards her.

Thus, innocent and happy in the silent performance of her duties and in the veil of retirement, lived Ellena Rosalba, when she first saw Vincentio di Vivaldi. He was not of a figure to pass unobserved when seen, and Ellena had been struck by the spirit and dignity of his air, and by his countenance, so frank, noble, and full of that kind of expression which announces the energies of the soul. But she was cautious of admitting a sentiment more tender than admiration, and endeavoured to dismiss his image from her mind, and, by engaging in her usual occupations, to recover the state of tranquillity which his appearance had somewhat interrupted.

Vivaldi, meanwhile, restless from disappointment, and impatient from anxiety, having passed the greater part of the day in inquiries which repaid him only with doubt and apprehension, determined to return to Villa Altieri when evening should conceal his steps, consoled by the certainty of being near the object of his thoughts, and hoping that chance might favour him once more with a view, however transient, of Ellena.

The Marchesa Vivaldi held an assembly this evening, and a suspicion concerning the impatience he betrayed, induced her to detain him about her person to a late hour, engaging him to select the music for her orchestra, and to superintend the performance of a new piece, the work of a composer whom she had brought into fashion. Her assemblies were among the most brilliant and crowded in Naples, and the nobility who were to be at the palace this evening were divided into two parties as to the merits of the musical genius whom she patronised and those of another candidate for fame. The performance of the evening, it was expected, would finally decide the victory. This, therefore, was a night of great importance and anxiety to the Marchesa, for she was as jealous of the reputation of her favourite composer as of her own, and the welfare of her son did but slightly divide her cares.

The moment he could depart unobserved he quitted the assembly, and muffling himself in his cloak, hastened to Villa Altieri, which lay at a short distance to the west of the city. He reached it unobserved, and, breathless with impatience, traversed the boundary of the garden; where, free from ceremonial restraint, and near the object of his affection, he experienced for the few first moments a joy as exquisite as her presence could have inspired. But this delight faded with its novelty, and in a short time he felt as forlorn as if he was separated for ever from Ellena, in whose presence he but lately almost believed himself.

The night was far advanced, and, no light appearing from the house, he concluded the inhabitants had retired to rest, and all hope of seeing her vanished from his mind. Still, however, it was sweet to be near her, and he anxiously sought to gain admittance to the gardens, that he might approach the window where it was possible she reposed. The boundary, formed of trees and thick shrubs, was not difficult to be passed, and he found himself once more in the portico of the villa.

It was nearly midnight, and the stillness that reigned was rather soothed than interrupted by the gentle dashing of the waters of the bay below, and by the hollow murmurs of Vesuvius, which threw up at intervals its sudden flame on the horizon, and then left it to darkness. The solemnity of the scene accorded with the temper of his mind, and he listened in deep attention for the returning sounds, which broke upon the ear like distant thunder muttering imperfectly from the clouds. The pauses of silence that succeeded each groan of the mountain, when expectation listened for the rising sound, affected the imagination of Vivaldi at this time with particular awe; and wrapt in thought, he continued to gaze upon the sublime and shadowy outline of the shores, and on the sea just discerned beneath the twilight of a cloudless sky. Along its grey surface many vessels were pursuing their silent course, guided over the deep waters only by the polar star, which burned with steady lustre. The air was calm, and rose from the bay with most balmy and refreshing coolness; it scarcely stirred the heads of the broad pines that overspread the villa; and bore no sounds but of the waves and the groans of the far-off mountain—till a chaunting of deep voices swelled from a distance. The solemn character of the strain engaged his attention; he perceived that it was a requiem, and he endeavoured to discover from what quarter it came. It advanced though distantly, and then passed away on the air. The circumstance struck him; he knew it was usual in some parts of Italy to chaunt this strain over the bed of the dying; but here the mourners seemed to walk the earth, or the air. He was not doubtful as to the strain itself; once before he had heard it, and attended with circumstances which made it impossible that he should ever forget it. As he now listened to the choral voices softening into distance, a few pathetic notes brought full upon his remembrance the divine melody he had heard Ellena utter in the church of San Lorenzo. Overcome by the recollection, he started away, and, wandering over the garden, reached another side of the villa, where he soon heard the voice of Ellena herself, performing the midnight hymn to the Virgin, and accompanied by a lute, which she touched with most affecting and delicate expression. He stood for a moment entranced, and scarcely daring to breathe, lest he should lose any note of that meek and holy strain, which seemed to flow from a devotion almost saintly. Then looking round to discover the object of his admiration, a light issuing from among the bowery foliage of a clematis led him to a lattice, and showed him Ellena. The lattice had been thrown open to admit the cool air, and he had a full view of her and the apartment. She was rising from a small altar where she had concluded the service; the glow of devotion was still upon her countenance as she raised her eyes, and with a rapt earnestness fixed them on the heavens. She still held the lute, but no longer awakened it, and seemed lost for a moment to every surrounding object. Her fine hair was negligently bound up in a silk net, and some tresses that had escaped it played on her neck and round her beautiful countenance, which now was not even partially concealed by a veil. The light drapery of her dress, her whole figure, air, and attitude, were such as might have been copied for a Grecian nymph.

Vivaldi was perplexed and agitated between the wish of seizing an opportunity, which might never again occur, of pleading his love, and the fear of offending by intruding upon her retirement at so sacred an hour. While he thus hesitated she placed herself in a chair, and, touching her lute in sweet symphony, presently accompanied it with her voice in a little air beautiful for its simplicity and pathos. When she had concluded, he heard her sigh, and then, with a sweetness peculiar to her accent, pronounce his name. During the trembling anxiety with which he listened to what might follow this mention of his name he disturbed the clematis that surrounded the lattice, and she turned her eyes towards the window : but Vivaldi was entirely concealed by the foliage. She, however, rose to close the lattice, when, as she approached it, Vivaldi, unable any longer to command himself, appeared before her. She stood fixed for an instant, while her countenance changed to an ashy paleness ; and then, with trembling haste clo-ing the lattice, quitted the apartment. Vivaldi felt as if all his hopes had vanished with her.

After lingering in the garden for some time without perceiving a light in any other part of the building, or hearing a sound proceed from it, he took his melancholy way to Naples. He now began to ask himself some questions which he ought to have urged before, and to inquire wherefore he sought the dangerous pleasure of seeing Ellena, since her family was of such a condition as rendered the consent of his parents to a marriage with her unattainable.

He was lost in reverie on this subject, sometimes half resolved to seek her no more, and then shrinking from a conduct which seemed to strike him with the force of despair, when, as he emerged from the dark arch of a ruin that extended over the road, his steps were crossed by a person in the habit of a monk whose face was shrouded by his cowl still more than by the twilight. The stranger, addressing him by his name, said, " Signor, your steps are watched ; beware how you revisit Altieri !" Having uttered this he disappeared, before Vivaldi could return the sword he had half drawn into the scabbard, or demand an explanation of the words he had heard. He called loudly and repeatedly, conjuring the unknown person to appear, and lingered near the spot for a considerable time; but the vision came no more.

Vivaldi arrived at home with a mind occupied by this incident, and tormented by the jealousy to which it gave rise ; for, after indulging various conjectures, he concluded with believing the notice, of which he had been warned, to be that of a rival, and that the danger which menaced him was from the poniard of jealousy. This belief discovered to him at once the extent of his passion, and of the imprudence which had thus readily admitted it ; yet so far was this new conviction from restraining his impetuosity, that, stung with a torture more exquisite than he had ever known, he resolved at every event to declare his love, and sue for the hand of Ellena. Unhappy young man, he knew not the fatal error into which passion was precipitating him !

On his arrival at the Vivaldi palace he learned that the Marchesa had observed his absence, had repeatedly inquired for him, and had given orders that the time of his return should be mentioned to her. She had, however, retired to rest ; but the Marchese, who had attended the King on an excursion to one of the royal villas on the bay, did not return home till after Vincentio, when he met his son with looks of unusual displeasure, but avoided saying anything which either explained or alluded to the subject of it ; and after a short conversation they separated.

Vivaldi shut himself in his apartment to deliberate, if that may deserve the name of deliberation in which a conflict of passions rather than an exertion of judgment prevailed. For several hours he traversed his suite of rooms, alternately tortured by the remembrance of Ellena, fired with jealousy, and alarmed for the consequence of the imprudent step which he was about to take. He knew the temper of his father, and some traits of the character of his mother, sufficiently to fear that their displeasure would be irreconcilable concerning the marriage he meditated ; yet, when he considered that he was their only son, he was inclined to admit a hope of forgiveness, notwithstanding the weight which the circumstance must add to their disappointment. These reflections were frequently interrupted by fears lest Ellena had already disposed of her affections to this imaginary rival. He was, however, somewhat consoled by remembering the sigh she had uttered, and the tenderness with which she had immediately pronounced his name. Yet, even if she were not averse to his suit, how could he solicit her hand and hope it would be given him when he should declare that this must be in secret? He scarcely dared to believe that she would condescend to enter a family who were unwilling to receive her ; and again despondency overcame him.

The morning found him as distracted as the night had left him. His determination, however, was fixed ; and this was to sacrifice what he now considered as a delusive pride of birth to a choice which he believed would ensure the happiness of his life. But before he ventured to declare himself to Ellena, it appeared necessary to ascertain whether he held an interest in her heart, or whether she had devoted it to the rival of his love, and who this rival really was. It was so much easier to wish for such information than to obtain it, that, after forming a thousand projects, either the delicacy of his respect for Ellena, or his fear of offending her, or an apprehension of discovery from his family before he had secured an interest in her affections, constantly opposed his views of an inquiry.

In this difficulty he opened his heart to a friend who had long possessed his confidence, and whose advice he solicited with somewhat more anxiety and sincerity than is usual on such occasions. It was not a sanction of his own opinion that he required, but the im partial judgment of another mind. Bonarmo, however little he might be qualified for the office of an adviser, did not scruple to give his advice. As a means of judging whether Ellena was disposed to favour Vivaldi's addresses, he proposed that, according to the custom of the country, a serenade should be given. He maintained that if she was not disinclined towards him, some sign of approbation would appear; and if otherwise, that she would remain silent and invisible. Vivaldi objected to this coarse and inadequate mode of expressing a love so sacred as his; and he had too lofty an opinion of Ellena's mind and delicacy to believe that the trifling homage of a serenade would either flatter her self-love or interest her in his favour; nor, if it did, could he venture to believe that she would display any sign of approbation.

His friend laughed at his scruples and at his opinion of what he called such romantic delicacy, that his ignorance of the world was his only excuse for having cherished them. But Vivaldi interrupted this raillery, and would neither suffer him for a moment to speak thus of Ellena or to call such delicacy romantic. Bonarmo, however, still urged the serenade as at least a possible means of discovering her disposition towards him before he made a formal avowal of his suit; and Vivaldi, perplexed and distracted with apprehension and impatience to terminate his present state of suspense, was at length so far overcome, by his own difficulties rather than by his friend's persuasion, that he consented to make the adventure of a serenade on the approaching night. This was adopted rather as a refuge from despondency than with a hope of success, for he still believed that Ellena would not give any hint which might terminate his uncertainty.

Beneath their cloaks, when the day had closed, they carried musical instruments, and muffling up their faces so that they could not be known, they proceeded in thoughtful silence on the way to Villa Altieri. Already they had passed the arch in which Vivaldi was stopped by the stranger on the preceding night, when he heard a sudden sound near him, and raising his head from his cloak, he perceived the same figure! Before he had time for exclamation the stranger crossed him again. "Go not to Villa Altieri," said he, in a solemn voice, "lest you meet the fate you ought to dread."

"What fate?" demanded Vivaldi, stepping back. "Speak, I conjure you!"

But the monk was gone, and the darkness of the hour baffled observation as to the way of his departure.

"*Dio mi guardi!*" exclaimed Bonarmo; "this is almost beyond belief. But let us return to Naples; this second warning ought to be obeyed."

"It is almost beyond endurance," exclaimed Vivaldi. "Which way did he pass?"

"He glided by me," replied Bonarmo, "and he was gone before I could cross him!"

"I will tempt the worst at once," said Vivaldi. "If I have a rival, it is best to meet him. Let us go on."

Bonarmo remonstrated, and represented the serious danger that threatened from so rash a proceeding. "It is evident that you have a rival," said he, "and your courage cannot avail you against hired bravos."

Vivaldi's heart swelled at the mention of a rival. "If you think it dangerous to proceed, I will go alone," he rejoined.

Hurt by this reproof, Bonarmo accompanied his friend in silence, and they reached without interruption the boundary of the villa. Vivaldi led to the place by which he had entered on the preceding night, and they passed unmolested into the garden.

"Where are these terrible bravos of whom you warned me?" said Vivaldi, with taunting exultation.

"Speak cautiously," replied his friend; "we may, even now, be within their reach."

"They also may be within ours," observed Vivaldi.

At length these adventurous friends came to the orangery, which was near the house, when, tired by the ascent, they rested to recover breath and to prepare their instruments for the serenade. The night was still, and they now heard for the first time murmurs as of a distant multitude, and then the sudden splendour of fireworks broke upon the sky. These arose from a villa on the western margin of the bay, and were given in honour of the birth of one of the royal princes. They soared to an immense height, and, as their lustre broke silently upon the night, it lightened on the thousand upturned faces of the gazing crowd, illumined the waters of the bay, with all the shipping and every little boat that skimmed its surface, and showed distinctly the whole sweep of its rising shores, the stately city of Naples on the strand below, and, spreading far among the hills, its terraced roofs crowded with spectators, and the Corso, tumultuous with carriages and blazing with torches.

While Bonarmo surveyed this magnificent scene, Vivaldi turned his eyes to the residence of Ellena, part of which looked out from among the trees, with a hope that the spectacle would draw her to a balcony; but she did not appear, nor was there any light that might indicate her approach.

While they still rested on the turf of the orangery they heard a sudden rustling of the leaves as if the branches were disturbed by some person who endeavoured to make his way between them, when Vivaldi demanded who passed. No answer was returned, and a long silence followed.

"We are observed," said Bonarmo at length, "and are even now, perhaps, almost beneath the poniard of the assassin. Let us be gone."

"Oh, that my heart were as secure from the darts of love, the assassin of my peace," exclaimed Vivaldi, "as yours is from those of bravos. My friend, you have little to interest you, since your thoughts have so much leisure for apprehension."

"My fear is that of prudence, not of weakness," retorted Bonarmo, with acrimony. "You will find, perhaps, that I have none when you most wish me to possess it."

"I understand you," replied Vivaldi; "let us finish this business and you shall receive reparation, since you believe yourself injured. I am as anxious to repair an offence as jealous of receiving one."

"Yes," replied Bonarmo, "you would repair the injury you have done your friend with his blood."

"Oh, never! never!" said Vivaldi, falling on his neck. "Forgive my hasty violence! allow for the distraction of my mind!"

Bonarmo returned the embrace. "It is enough," said he; "no more, no more, I hold again my friend to my heart."

While this conversation passed they had quitted the orangery and reached the walls of the villa, where they took their station under a balcony that overhung the lattice through which Vivaldi had seen Ellena on the preceding night. They tuned their instruments and opened the serenade with a duet.

Vivaldi's voice was a fine tenor, and the same susceptibility which made him passionately fond of music, taught him to modulate its cadence with exquisite delicacy and to give his emphasis with the most simple and pathetic expression. His soul seemed to breathe in the sounds—so tender, so imploring, yet so energetic. On this night enthusiasm inspired him with the highest eloquence, perhaps, which music is capable of attaining. What might be its effect on Ellena he had no means of judging, for she did not appear either at the balcony or the lattice, nor give any hint of applause. No sounds stole on the stillness of the night except those of the serenade, nor did any light from within the villa break upon the obscurity without: once, indeed, in a pause of the instruments, Bonarmo fancied he distinguished voices near him as of persons who feared to be heard, and he listened attentively, but without ascertaining the truth. Sometimes they seemed to sound heavily in his ear, and then a death-like silence prevailed. Vivaldi affirmed the sound to be nothing more than the confused murmur of the distant multitude on the shore, but Bonarmo was not thus easily convinced.

The musicians, unsuccessful in their first endeavour to attract attention, removed to the opposite side of the building and placed themselves in front of the portico, but with as little success; and after having exercised their powers of harmony and of patience for above an hour, they resigned all further effort to win upon the obdurate Ellena. Vivaldi, notwithstanding the feebleness of his first hope of seeing her, now suffered an agony of disappointment; and Bonarmo, alarmed for the consequence of his despair, was as anxious to persuade him that he had no rival as he had lately been pertinacious in affirming that he had one.

At length they left the gardens, Vivaldi protesting that he would not rest till he had discovered the stranger who so wantonly destroyed his peace and had compelled him to explain his ambiguous warnings; and Bonarmo remonstrating on the imprudence and difficulty of the search, and representing that such conduct would probably be the means of spreading a report of his attachment where most he dreaded it should be known.

Vivaldi refused to yield to remonstrance or considerations of any kind. "We shall see," said he, "whether this demon in the garb of a monk will haunt me again at the accustomed place; if he does, he shall not escape my grasp, and if he does not, I will watch as vigilantly for his return as he seems to have done for mine. I will lurk in the shade of the ruin and wait for him, though it be till death."

Bonarmo was particularly struck by the vehemence with which he pronounced the last words, but he no longer opposed his purpose, and only bade him consider whether he was well armed. "For," he added, "you may have need of arms there, though you had no use for them at Altieri. Remember that the stranger told you that your steps were watched."

"I have my sword," replied Vivaldi, "and the dagger which I usually wear. But I ought to inquire, what are your weapons of defence?"

"Hush!" said Bonarmo, as they turned the foot of a rock that overhung the road, "we are approaching the spot, yonder is the arch!" It appeared duskily in the perspective, suspended between two cliffs, where the road wound from sight; on one of which were the ruins of the Roman fort it belonged to, and on the other, shadowing pines and thickets of oak that tufted the rock to its base.

They proceeded in silence, treading lightly, and often throwing a suspicious glance around, expecting every instant that the monk would steal out upon them from some recess of the cliffs. But they passed on unmolested to the archway. "We are here before him, however," said Vivaldi, as they entered the darkness. "Speak low, my friend," said Bonarmo; "others besides ourselves may be shrouded in this obscurity. I like not the place."

"Who but ourselves would choose so dismal a retreat?" whispered Vivaldi, "unless indeed it were banditti; the savageness of the spot would in truth suit their humour, and it suits well also with my own."

"It would suit their purpose too, as well as their humour," observed Bonarmo. "Let us remove from this deep shade into the more open road, where we can as closely observe who passes."

Vivaldi objected that in the road they might themselves be observed. "And if we are seen by my unknown tormentor our design is defeated, for he comes upon us suddenly or not at all, lest we should be prepared to detain him."

Vivaldi, as he said this, took his station within the thickest gloom of the arch, which was of considerable depth, and near a flight of steps that was cut in the rock, and ascended to the fortress. His friend stepped close to his side. After a pause of silence, during which Bónarmo was meditating and Vivaldi was impatiently watching, "Do you really believe," said the former, "that any effort to detain him would be effectual. He glided past me with a strange facility; it was surely more than human!"

"What is it you mean?" inquired Vivaldi.

"Why, I mean that I could be superstitious. This place perhaps infects my mind with congenial gloom, for I find that at this moment there is scarcely a superstition too dark for my credulity."

Vivaldi smiled. "And you must allow," added Bonarmo, "that he has appeared under circumstances somewhat extraordinary. How should he know your name, by which you say he addressed you at the first meeting? How should he know from whence you came, or whether you designed to return? By what magic could he become acquainted with your plans?"

"Nor am I certain that he is acquainted with them," observed Vivaldi; "but if he is, there was no necessity for superhuman means to obtain such knowledge."

"The result of this evening surely ought to convince you that he is acquainted with your designs," said Bonarmo. "Do you believe it possible that Ellena could have been insensible to your attentions if her heart had not been pre-engaged, and that she would have forborne to show herself at a lattice?"

"You do not know Ellena," replied Vivaldi, "and therefore I once more pardon you the question. Yet had she been disposed to accept my addresses, surely some sign of approbation——" He checked himself.

"The stranger warned you not to go to Villa Altieri," resumed Bonarmo; "he seemed to anticipate the reception which awaited you, and to know a danger which hitherto you have happily escaped."

"Yes, he anticipated too well that reception," said Vivaldi, losing his prudence in passionate exclamation; "and he is himself perhaps the rival whom he has taught me to suspect. He has assumed a disguise only the more effectually to impose upon my credulity and to deter me from addressing Ellena. And shall I tamely lie in wait for his approach? Shall I lurk like a guilty assassin for this rival?"

"For Heaven's sake!" said Bonarmo, "moderate these transports; consider where you are. This surmise of yours is in the highest degree improbable."

He gave his reasons for thinking so, and these convinced Vivaldi, who was prevailed upon to be once more patient.

They had remained watchful and still for a considerable time, when Bonarmo saw a person approach the end of the archway nearest to Altieri. He heard no step, but he perceived a shadowy figure station itself at the entrance of the arch, where the twilight of this brilliant climate was for a few paces admitted. Vivaldi's eyes were fixed on the road leading towards Naples, and he therefore did not perceive the object of Bonarmo's attention, who, fearful of his friend's precipitancy, forbore to point out immediately what he observed, judging it more prudent to watch the motions of this unknown person, that he might ascertain whether it really were the monk. The size of the figure and the dark drapery in which it seemed wrapped induced him at length to believe that this was the expected stranger, and he seized Vivaldi's arm to direct his attention to him, when the form, gliding forward, disappeared in the gloom of the arch, but not before Vivaldi had understood the occasion of his friend's gesture and significant silence. They heard no footstep pass them, and being convinced that this person, whatever he was, had not left the archway, they kept their station in watchful stillness. Presently they heard a rustling, as of garments, near them, and Vivaldi, unable longer to command his impatience, started from his concealment, and, with arms extended to prevent any one from escaping, demanded who was there.

The sound ceased, and no reply was made. Bonarmo drew his sword, protesting he would stab the air till he found the person who lurked there; but that if the latter would discover himself he should receive no injury. This assurance Vivaldi confirmed by his promise. Still no answer was returned; but as they listened for a voice they thought something passed them, and the avenue was not narrow enough to have prevented such a circumstance. Vivaldi rushed forward, but did not perceive any person issue from the arch into the highway, where the stronger twilight must have discovered him.

"Somebody certainly passed," whispered Bonarmo, "and I think I hear a sound from yonder steps that lead to the fortress."

"Let us follow," cried Vivaldi, and he began to ascend.

"Stop, for Heaven's sake, stop!" said Bonarmo; "consider what you are about. Do not brave the utter darkness of these ruins; do not pursue the assassin to his den."

"It is the monk himself!" exclaimed Vivaldi, still ascending; "he shall not escape me."

Bonarmo paused a moment at the foot of the steps, and his friend disappeared. He hesitated what to do, till, ashamed of suffering him to encounter danger alone, he sprang to the flight, and, not without difficulty, surmounted the rugged steps.

Having reached the summit of the rock, he found himself on a terrace that ran along the top of the archway and had once been fortified; this, crossing the road, commanded the defile each way. Some remains of massy walls, that still exhibited loops for archers, were all that now hinted of its former use. It led to a watch-tower, almost concealed in thick pines, that crowned the opposite cliff, and had thus served not only for a strong battery over the road, but, connecting the opposite sides of the defile, had formed a line of communication between the fort and this outpost.

Bonarmo looked round in vain for his friend, and the echoes of his own voice only, among the rocks, replied to his repeated calls. After some hesitation whether to enter the walls of the main building, or to cross to the watch-tower, he determined on the former, and entered a rugged area, the walls of which, following the declivities of the precipice, could scarcely now be traced The citadel, a round tower of majestic strength, with some Roman arches scattered near, was all that remained of this once important fortress; except. indeed, a mass of ruins near the edge of the cliff, the construction of which made it difficult to guess for what purpose it had been designed.

Bonarmo entered the immense walls of the citadel, but the utter darkness within checked his progress, and contenting himself with calling loudly on Vivaldi, he returned to the open air.

As he approached the mass of ruin, whose singular form had interested his curiosity, he thought he distinguished the low accents of a human voice, and while he listened in anxiety, a person rushed forth from a doorway of the ruin, carrying a drawn sword. It was Vivaldi himself. Bonarmo sprang to meet him; he was pale and breathless, and some moments elapsed before he could speak, or appeared to hear the repeated inquiries of his friend.

"Let us go," said Vivaldi; "let us leave this place!"

"Most willingly," replied Bonarmo; "but where have you been, and who have you seen, that you are thus affected?"

"Ask me no more questions; let us go," repeated Vivaldi.

They descended the rock together, and when, having reached the archway, Bonarmo inquired, half sportively, whether they should remain any longer on the watch, his friend answered, "No!" with an emphasis that startled him. They passed hastily on the way to Naples, Bonarmo repeating inquiries which Vivaldi seemed reluctant to satisfy, and wondering no less at the cause of this sudden reserve than anxious to know whom he had seen.

"It was the monk, then," said Bonarmo; "you secured him at last?"

"I know not what to think," replied Vivaldi. "I am more perplexed than ever."

"He escaped you, then?"

"We will speak of this in future," said Vivaldi; "but be it as it may, the business rests not here. I will return in the night of to-morrow with a torch; dare you venture yourself with me?"

"I know not," replied Bonarmo, "whether I ought to do so, since I am not informed for what purpose."

"I will not press you to go," said Vivaldi; "my purpose is already known to you."

"Have you really failed to discover the stranger?—have you still doubts concerning the person you pursued?"

"I have doubts which to-morrow night will, I hope, dissipate."

"This is very strange!" said Bonarmo. "It was but now that I witnessed the horror with which you left the fortress of Paluzzi, and already you speak of returning to it! And why at night?—why not in the day, when less danger would beset you?"

"I know not as to that," replied Vivaldi. "You are to observe that daylight never pierces within the recess to which I penetrated; we must search the place with torches at whatsoever hour we would examine it."

"Since this is necessary," said Bonarmo, "how happens it that you found your way in total darkness?"

"I was too much engaged to know how; I was led on, as by an invisible hand."

"We must, notwithstanding," observed Bonarmo, "go in daytime, if not by daylight, provided I accompany you. It would be little less than insanity to go twice to a place which is probably infested with robbers, and at their own hour of midnight."

"I shall watch again in the accustomed place," replied Vivaldi, "before I use my last resource, and this cannot be done during the day. Besides, it is necessary that I should go at a particular hour—the hour when the monk has usually appeared."

"He did escape you, then," said Bonarmo,

"and you are still ignorant concerning who he is?"

Vivaldi rejoined only with an inquiry whether his friend would accompany him, "If not," he added, "I must hope to find another companion."

B.narmo said that he must consider of the proposal. and would acquaint him with his determination before the following evening.

While this conversation concluded they were in Naples, and at the gates of the Vivaldi palace, where they separated for the remainder of the night.

CHAPTER II.

SINCE Vivaldi had failed to procure an explanation of the words of the monk, he determined to relieve himself from the tortures of suspense respecting a rival, by going to Villa Altieri and declaring his pretensions. On the morning immediately following his late adventures he went thither, and on inquiring for Signora Bianchi, was told that she could not be seen. With much difficulty he prevailed upon the old housekeeper to deliver a request that he might be permitted to wait upon her for a few moments. Permission was granted him, when he was conducted into the very apartment where he had formerly seen Ellena. It was unoccupied, and he was told that Signora Bianchi would be there presently.

During this interval he was agitated at one moment with quick impatience, and at another with enthusiastic pleasure, while he gazed on the altar whence he had seen Ellena rise, and where, to his fancy, she still appeared, and on every object on which he knew her eyes had lately dwelt. These objects, so familiar to her, had in the imagination of Vivaldi acquired somewhat of the sacred character that had impressed upon his heart, and affected him in some degree as her presence would have done. He trembled as he took up the lute she had been accustomed to touch, and, when he awakened the chords, her own voice seemed to speak. A drawing, half-finished, of a dancing nymph remained on a stand, and he immediately understood that her hand had traced the lines. It was a copy from Herculaneum, and, though a copy, was touched with the spirit of original genius. The light steps appeared almost to move, and the whole figure displayed the airy lightness of exquisite grace. Vivaldi perceived this to be one of a set that ornamented the apartment, and observed with surprise that they were the particular subjects which adorned his father's cabinet, and which he had understood to be the only copies permitted from the originals in the Royal Museum.

Every object on which his eyes rested seemed to announce the presence of Ellena ; and the very flowers that so gaily embellished the apartment breathed forth a perfume which fascinated his senses and affected his imagination. Before Signora Bianchi appeared, his anxiety and apprehension had increased so much that, believing he should be unable to support himself in her presence, he was more than once upon the point of leaving the house. At length he heard her approaching step from the hall, and his breath almost forsook him. The figure of Signora Bianchi was not of an order to inspire admiration, and a spectator might have smiled to see the perturbation of Vivaldi, his faltering step and anxious eye, as he advanced to meet this venerable lady, as he bowed upon her faded hand, and listened to her querulous voice. She received him with an air of reserve, and some moments passed before he could recollect himself sufficiently to explain the purpose of his visit ; yet this, when he discovered it, did not apparently surprise her. She listened with composure, though with somewhat of a severe countenance, to his protestations of regard for her niece ; and when he implored her to intercede for him in obtaining the hand of Ellena, she said, " I cannot be ignorant that a family of your rank must be averse to a union with one of mine ; nor am I unacquainted that a full sense of the value of birth is a marking feature in the characters of the Marchese and Marchesa di Vivaldi. This proposal must be disagreeable or, at least, unknown to them : and I am to inform you, signor, that though Signora di Rosalbi is their inferior in rank, she is their equal in pride."

Vivaldi disdained to prevaricate, yet was shocked to own the truth thus abruptly. The ingenuous manner, however, with which he at length did this, and the energy of a passion too eloquent to be misunderstood, somewhat soothed the anxiety of Bianchi, with whom other considerations began to arise. She considered that from her own age and infirmities she must very soon, in the course of nature, leave Ellena a young and friendless orphan, still somewhat dependent upon her own industry, and entirely so on her discretion. With much beauty and little knowledge of the world, the dangers of her future situation appeared in vivid colours to the affectionate mind of Signora Bianchi ; and she sometimes thought that it might be right to sacrifice considerations which in other circumstances would be laudable, to the obtaining for her niece the protection of a husband and a man of honour. If, in this instance, she descended from the lofty integrity which ought to have opposed her consent that Ellena should clandestinely enter any family, a consideration of her parental anxiety may soften the censure she deserved.

But, before she determined upon this subject, it was necessary to ascertain that Vivaldi was worthy of the confidence she might repose in him. To try, also, the constancy of his affection, she gave little present encouragement to his hopes. His request to see Ellena she absolutely refused, till she should have considered further of his proposals : and his inquiry whether he had a rival, and, if he had, whether Ellena was disposed to favour him, she evaded, fearing that a reply would give more encouragement to his hopes than it might hereafter be proper to confirm.

Vivaldi at length took his leave, released, indeed, from absolute despair, but scarcely encouraged to hope : ignorant that he had a rival ; yet doubtful whether Ellena honoured himself with any share of her esteem.

He had received permission to wait upon Signora Bianchi on a future day, but till that day should arrive time appeared motionless, and, since it seemed utterly impossible to endure this interval of suspense, his thoughts on the way to Naples were wholly engaged in contriving the means of concluding it, till he reached the well-known arch, and looked round, though hopelessly, for his mysterious tormentor. The stranger did not appear ; and Vivaldi pursued the road, determined to revisit the spot at night, and also to return privately to Villa Altieri, where he hoped a second visit might procure for him some relief from his present anxiety.

When he reached home he found that the Marchese, his father, had left an order for him to wait his arrival, which he obeyed ; but the day passed without his return. The Marchesa, when she saw him, inquired, with a look that expressed much, how he had engaged himself of late, and completely frustrated his plans for the evening by requiring him to attend her to Portici. Thus he was prevented from receiving Bonarmo's determination, from watching at Paluzzi, and from revisiting Ellena's residence.

He remained at Portici the following evening, and on his return to Naples, the Marchese being again absent, he continued ignorant of the intended subject of the interview. A note from Bonarmo brought a refusal to accompany him to the fortress, and urged him to forbear so dangerous a visit. Being for this night unprovided with a companion for the adventure, and unwilling to go alone, Vivaldi deferred it to another evening ; but no consideration could deter him from visiting Villa Altieri. Not choosing to solicit his friend to accompany him thither, since he had refused his first request, he took his solitary lute, and reached the garden at an earlier hour than usual.

The sun had been set above an hour, but the horizon still retained somewhat of a saffron brilliancy, and the whole dome of the sky had an appearance of transparency, peculiar to this enchanting climate, which seemed to diffuse a more soothing twilight over the reposing world. In the south-east the outline of Vesuvius appeared distinctly, but the mountain itself was dark and silent.

Vivaldi heard only the quick and eager voices of some Lazaroni at a distance on the shore, as they contended at the simple game of morra. From the bowery lattices of a pavilion within the orangery he perceived a light, and the sudden hope which it occasioned of seeing Ellena almost overcame him. It was impossible to resist the opportunity of beholding her, yet he checked the impatient step he was taking, to ask himself whether it was honourable thus to steal upon her retirement, and become an unsuspected observer of her secret thoughts. But the temptation was too powerful for his honourable hesitation ; the pause was momentary, and stepping lightly towards the pavilion, he placed himself near an open lattice, so as to be shrouded from observation by the branches of an orange-tree, while he obtained a full view of the apartment. Ellena was alone, sitting in a thoughtful attitude, and holding her lute, which she did not play. She appeared lost to a consciousness of surrounding objects, and a tenderness was on her countenance which seemed to tell him that her thoughts were engaged by some interesting subject. Recollecting that, when last he had seen her thus, she pronounced his name, his hope revived, and he was going to discover himself and appear at her feet, when she spoke, and he paused.

"Why this unreasonable pride of birth !" said she. "A visionary prejudice destroys our peace. Never would I submit to enter a family averse to receive me ; they shall learn, at least, that I inherit nobility of soul. Oh, Vivaldi ! but for this unhappy prejudice !—"

Vivaldi, while he listened to this, was immovable ; he seemed as if entranced. The sound of her lute and voice recalled him, and he heard her sing the first stanza of the very air with which he had opened the serenade on a former night, and with such sweet pathos as the composer must have felt when he was inspired with the idea.

She paused at the conclusion of the first stanza, when Vivaldi, overcome by the temptation of such an opportunity for expressing his passion, suddenly struck the chords of his lute, and replied to her in the second. The tremor of his voice, though it restrained his tones, heightened its eloquence. Ellena instantly recollected it ; her colour alternately faded and returned ; and, before the verse concluded, she seemed to have lost all consciousness. Vivaldi was now advancing into the pavilion, when his approach recalled her ; she waved him to retire, and before he could spring to her support she rose and would have left the place, had he not interrupted her and implored a few moments' attention.

"It is impossible," said Ellena.

"Let me only hear you say that I am not

hateful to you," rejoined Vivaldi, "that this intrusion has not deprived me of the regard with which but now you acknowledged you honoured me——"

"Oh, never, never!" interrupted Ellena, impatiently. "Forget that I ever made such acknowledgment! forget that you ever heard it! I knew not what I said."

"Ah, beautiful Ellena! do you think it possible I ever can forget it? It will be the solace of my solitary hours, the hope that shall sustain me——"

"I cannot be detained, signor," interrupted Ellena, still more embarrassed, "or forgive myself for having permitted such a conversation." But as she spoke the last words an involuntary smile seemed to contradict their meaning. Vivaldi believed the smile in spite of the words, but before he could express the lightning joy of conviction, she had left the pavilion. He followed through the garden, but she was gone.

From this moment Vivaldi seemed to have arisen into a new existence: the whole world to him was Paradise; that smile seemed impressed upon his heart for ever. In the fulness of present joy he believed it impossible that he could ever be unhappy again, and defied the utmost malice of future fortune. With footsteps light as air he returned to Naples, nor once remembered to look for his old monitor on the way.

The Marchese and his mother being from home, he was left at his leisure to indulge the rapturous recollection that pressed upon his mind, and of which he was impatient of a moment's interruption. All night he either traversed his apartment with an agitation equal to that which anxiety had so lately inflicted, or composed and destroyed letters to Ellena; sometimes fearing that he had written too much, and at others fearing that he had written too little; recollecting circumstances which he ought to have mentioned, and lamenting the cold expression of a passion to which it appeared that no language could do justice.

By the hour when the domestics had risen, he had, however, completed a letter somewhat more to his satisfaction, and he despatched it to Villa Altieri by a confidential person. But the servant had scarcely quitted the gates, when he recollected new arguments which he wished to urge, and expressions to change of the utmost importance to enforce his meaning, and he would have given half the world to have recalled the messenger.

In this state of agitation he was summoned to attend the Marchese, who had been too much engaged of late to keep his own appointment. Vivaldi was not long in doubt as to the subject of this interview.

"I have wished to speak with you," said the Marchese, assuming an air of haughty severity, "upon a subject of the utmost im-portance to your honour and happiness; and I wished, also, to give you an opportunity of contradicting a report which would have occasioned me considerable uneasiness if I could have believed it. Happily I had too much confidence in my son to credit this, and I affirmed that he understood too well what was due to his family and himself to take any step derogatory from the dignity of either. My motive for this conversation, therefore, is merely to afford you a moment for refuting the calumny I shall mention, and to obtain for myself authority for contradicting it to the persons who have communicated it to me."

Vivaldi waited impatiently for the conclusion of this exordium, and then begged to be informed of the subject of the report.

"It is said," resumed the Marchese, "that there is a young woman who is called Ellena Rosalba—I think that is the name—do you know any person of the name?"

"Do I know!" exclaimed Vivaldi—"but pardon me; pray proceed, my lord."

The Marchese paused, and regarded his son with sternness, but without surprise. "It is said that a young person of this name has contrived to fascinate your affections and——"

"It is most true, my lord, that Signora Rosalba has won my affections," interrupted Vivaldi, with honest impatience, "but without contrivance."

"I will not be interrupted," said the Marchese, interrupting in his turn. "It is said that she has so artfully adapted her temper to yours that, with the assistance of a relation who lives with her, she has reduced you to the degrading situation of her devoted suitor."

"Signora Rosalba, my lord, has not yet allowed me to assume that honourable title," said Vivaldi, unable longer to command his feelings. He was proceeding when the Marchese again checked him. "You avow your folly, then?"

"My lord, I glory in my choice."

"Young man," rejoined his father, "as this is the arrogance and romantic enthusiasm of a boy, I am willing to forgive it for once, and, observe me, only for once. If you will acknowledge your error, and instantly dismiss this new favourite——"

"My lord!"

"You must instantly dismiss her," repeated the Marchese, with sterner emphasis: "and to prove that I am more merciful than just, I am willing, on this condition, to allow her a small annuity as some reparation for the depravity into which you have assisted to sink her."

"My lord!" exclaimed Vivaldi, aghast, and scarcely daring to trust his voice, "my lord!—depravity?" struggling for breath. "Who has dared to pollute her spotless fame by insulting your ears with such infamous falsehood? Tell me, I conjure you, instantly tell me, that I may hasten to give him his reward. Depravity!—an annuity!—an annuity! Oh, Ellena! Ellena!" As he pronounced her name tears of tenderness mingled with those of indignation.

"Young man," said the Marchese, who had observed the violence of his emotion with strong displeasure and alarm, "I do not lightly give faith to report, and I cannot suffer myself to doubt the truth of what I have advanced. You are deceived, and your vanity will continue the delusion, unless I condescend to exert my authority, and tear the veil from your eyes. Dismiss her instantly, and I will adduce proof of her former character which will stagger even your faith, enthusiastic as it is."

"Dismiss her!" repeated Vivaldi, with calm yet stern energy, such as his father had never seen him assume. "My lord, you have never yet doubted my word, and I now pledge you that honourable word that Ellena is innocent. Innocent! Oh, Heavens, that it should ever be necessary to affirm so, and, above all, that it should ever be necessary for me to vindicate her!"

"I must indeed lament that it ever should," replied the Marchese, coldly. "You have pledged your word, which I cannot question. I believe, therefore, that you are deceived; that you think her virtuous, notwithstanding your midnight visits to her house. And grant she is, unhappy boy! what reparation can you make her for the infatuated folly which has thus stained her character? What——"

"By proclaiming to the world, my lord, that she is worthy of becoming my wife," replied Vivaldi, with a glow of countenance which announced the courage and the exultation of a virtuous mind.

"Your wife!" said the Marchese, with a look of ineffable disdain, which was instantly succeeded by one of angry alarm. "If I believed you could so far forget what is due to the honour of your house, I would for ever disclaim you as my son."

"Oh! why," exclaimed Vivaldi, in an agony of conflicting passions, "why should I be in danger of forgetting what is due to father, when I am only asserting what is due to innocence—when I am only defending her who has no other to defend her? Why may not I be permitted to reconcile duties so congenial? But, be the event what it may, I will defend the oppressed, and glory in the virtue which teaches me that it is the first duty of humanity to do so. Yes, my lord, if it must be so, I am ready to sacrifice inferior duties to the grandeur of a principle which ought to expand all hearts and impel all actions. I shall best support the honour of my house by adhering to its dictates."

"Where is the principle," said the Marchese, impatiently, "which shall teach you to disobey a father? where is the virtue which shall instruct you to degrade your family?"

"There can be no degradation, my lord, where there is no vice," replied Vivaldi; "and there are instances— pardon me, my lord— there are some few instances in which it is virtuous to disobey even a parent."

"This paradoxical morality," said the Marchese, with increased displeasure, "and this romantic language, sufficiently explain to me the character of your associates, and the innocence of her whom you defend with so chivalric an air. Are you to learn, signor, that you belong to your family, not your family to you—that you are only a guardian of its honour, and not at liberty to dispose of yourself? My patience will endure no more!"

Nor could the patience of Vivaldi endure this repeated attack upon the honour of Ellena. But, while he yet asserted her innocence, he endeavoured to do so with the temper which was due to the presence of a father; and though he maintained the independence of a man, he was equally anxious to preserve inviolate the duties of a son. But unfortunately the Marchese and Vivaldi differed in opinion concerning the limits of these duties; the first extending them to passive obedience, and the latter conceiving them to conclude at a point wherein the happiness of an individual is so deeply concerned as in marriage. They parted mutually inflamed; Vivaldi unable to prevail with his father to mention the name of his infamous informant, or to acknowledge himself convinced of Ellena's innocence; and the Marchese equally unsuccessful in his endeavours to obtain from his son a promise that he would see her no more.

Here then was Vivaldi, who only a few short hours before had experienced a happiness so supreme as to efface all impressions of the past, and to annihilate every consideration of the future; a joy so full that it permitted him not to believe it possible that he could ever again taste of misery; he, who had felt as if that moment was an eternity, rendering him independent of all others— even he was thus soon fallen into the region of time and suffering!

The present conflict of passion appeared endless. He loved his father, and would have been more shocked to consider the vexation he was preparing for him, had he not been resentful of the contempt he expressed for Ellena. He adored Ellena, and, while he felt the impracticability of resigning his hopes, was equally indignant at the slander which affected her name, and impatient to avenge the insult upon the original defamer.

Though the displeasure of the Marchese concerning a marriage with Ellena had been already foreseen, the experience of it was severer and more painful than Vivaldi had imagined; while the indignity offered to Ellena was as unexpected as intolerable. But this circumstance furnished him with additional argument for addressing her, for if it had been possible that his love could have paused, his honour seemed now engaged in her behalf, and since he had been a means of sullying her fame, it became his duty to restore it. Willingly listening to the dictates of a duty so plausible, he determined to persevere in his original design. But his first efforts were directed to discover her slanderer, and recollecting with surprise those words of the Marchese which had confessed a knowledge of his evening visits to Villa Altieri, the doubtful warnings of the monk seemed explained. He suspected that this man was at once the spy of his steps and the defamer of his love, till the inconsistency of such conduct with the seeming friendliness of his admonitions struck Vivaldi, and compelled him to believe the contrary.

Meanwhile, the heart of Ellena had been little less tranquil. It was divided by love and pride; but had she been acquainted with the circumstances of the late interview between the Marchese and Vivaldi, it would have been divided no longer, and a just regard for her own dignity would instantly have taught her to subdue without difficulty this infant affection.

Signora Bianchi had informed her niece of the subject of Vivaldi's visit; but she had softened the objectionable circumstances that attended his proposal, and had, at first, merely hinted that it was not to be supposed his family would approve of a connection with any person so much their inferior in rank as herself. Ellena, alarmed by this suggestion, replied that, since she believed so, she had done right to reject Vivaldi's suit; but her sigh, as she said this, did not escape the observation of Bianchi, who ventured to add that she had not *absolutely* rejected his offers.

While in this and future conversations Ellena was pleased to conceive her secret admiration thus justified by an approbation so indisputable as that of her aunt, and was willing to believe that the circumstance which had alarmed her just pride was not so humiliating as she at first imagined, Bianchi was careful to conceal the real considerations which had induced her to listen to Vivaldi, being well assured that they would have no weight with Ellena, whose generous heart and inexperienced mind would have revolted from mingling any motives of interest with an engagement so sacred as that of marriage. When, however, from further deliberation upon the advantages which such an alliance must secure for her niece, Signora Bianchi determined to encourage his views, and to direct the mind of Ellena, whose affections were already engaged on her side, the opinions of the latter were found less ductile than had been expected. She was shocked at the idea of entering clandestinely the family of Vivaldi. But Bianchi, whose infirmities urged her

wishes, was now so strongly convinced of the prudence of such an engagement for her niece that she determined to prevail over her reluctance, though she perceived that this must be by means more gradual and persuasive than she had believed necessary. On the evening when Vivaldi had surprised from Ellena an acknowledgment of her sentiments, her embarrassment and vexation, on her returning to the house, and relating what had occurred, sufficiently expressed to Signora Bianchi the exact situation of her heart. And when, on the following morning, his letter arrived, written with the simplicity and energy of truth, the aunt neglected not to adapt her remarks upon it to the character of Ellena with her usual address.

Vivaldi, after the late interview with the Marchese, passed the remainder of the day in considering various plans which might discover to him the person who had abused the credulity of his father; and in the evening returned once more to Villa Altieri, not in secret, to serenade the dark balcony of his mistress, but openly, and to converse with Signora Bianchi, who now received him more courteously than on his former visit. Attributing the anxiety in his countenance to the uncertainty concerning the disposition of her niece, she was neither surprised or offended, but ventured to relieve him from a part of it by encouraging his hopes. Vivaldi dreaded lest she should inquire further respecting the sentiments of his family, but she spared both his delicacy and her own on this point; and, after a conversation of considerable length, he left Altieri with a heart somewhat soothed by approbation and lightened by hope, although he had not obtained a sight of Ellena. The disclosure she had made of her sentiments on the preceding evening, and the hints she had received as to those of his family, wrought upon her mind with too much effect to permit an interview.

Soon after his return to Naples, the Marchesa, whom he was surprised to find disengaged, sent for him to her closet, where a scene passed similar to that which had occurred with his father, except that the Marchesa was more dexterous in her questions and more subtle in her whole conduct, and that Vivaldi never for a moment forgot the decorum which was due to a mother. Managing his passions rather than exasperating them, and deceiving him with respect to the degree of resentment she felt from his choice, she was less passionate than the Marchese in her observations and remonstrances, perhaps only because she entertained more hope than he did of preventing the evil she contemplated.

Vivaldi quitted her unconvinced by her arguments, unsubdued by her prophecies, and unmoved in his designs. He was not alarmed, because he did not sufficiently understand her character to apprehend her purposes. Despairing to effect these by open violence, she called in an auxiliary of no mean talents, and whose character and views well adapted him to be an instrument in her hands. It was, perhaps, the baseness of her own heart, not either depth of reflection or keenness of penetration, which enabled her to understand the nature of his, and she determined to modulate that nature to her own views.

There lived in the Dominican convent of the Santo Spirito, at Naples, a man called Father Schedoni; an Italian, as his name imported, but whose family was unknown, and from some circumstances it appeared that he wished to throw an impenetrable veil over his origin. For whatever reason, he was never heard to mention a relative, or the place of his nativity, and he had artfully eluded every inquiry that approached the subject which the curiosity of his associates had occasionally prompted. There were circumstances ,however, which seemed to indicate him a man of birth, and of fallen fortune; his spirit, as it had sometimes looked forth from under the disguise of his manners, appeared lofty; it showed not, however, the aspirings of a generous mind, but rather the gloomy pride of a disappointed one. Some few persons in the convent, who had been interested by his appearance, believed that the peculiarities of his manners, his severe reserve and unconquerable silence, his solitary habits and frequent penances, were the effect of misfortune preying upon a haughty and disordered spirit; while others conjectured them the consequence of some hideous crime gnawing upon an awakened conscience.

He would sometimes abstract himself from the society for whole days together, or when with such a disposition he was compelled to mingle with it, he seemed unconscious where he was, and continued shrouded in meditation and silence till he was again alone. There were times when it was unknown whither he had retired, notwithstanding that his steps had been watched, and his customary haunts examined. No one ever heard him complain. The elder brothers of the convent said that he had talents, but denied him learning; they applauded him for the profound subtlety which he occasionally discovered in argument, but observed that he seldom perceived truth when it lay on the surface; he could follow it through all the labyrinths of disquisition, but overlooked it when it was undisguised before him. In fact, he cared not for truth, nor sought it by bold and broad argument, but loved to exert the wily cunning of his nature in hunting it through artificial perplexities. At length, from a habit of intricacy and suspicion, his vitiated mind could receive nothing for truth which was simple and easily comprehended.

Among his associates no one loved him,

many disliked him, and more feared him. His figure was striking, but not so from grace; it was tall, and, though extremely thin, his limbs were large and uncouth, and as he stalked along, wrapped in the black garments of his order, there was something terrible in its air, something almost superhuman. His cowl, too, as it threw a shade over the livid paleness of his face, increased its severe character, and gave an effect to his large melancholy eye which approached to horror. His was not the melancholy of a sensible and wounded heart, but apparently that of a gloomy and ferocious disposition. There was something in his physiognomy extremely singular, and that cannot easily be defined. It bore the traces of many passions, which seemed to have fixed the features they no longer animated. An habitual gloom and severity prevailed over the deep lines of his countenance; and his eyes were so piercing that they seemed to penetrate, at a single glance, into the hearts of men, and to read their most secret thoughts; few persons could support their scrutiny, or even endure to meet them twice. Yet, notwithstanding all this gloom and austerity, some rare occasions of interest had called forth a character upon his countenance entirely different; and he could adapt himself to the tempers and passions of persons whom he wished to conciliate with astonishing facility, and generally with complete triumph. This monk, this Schedoni, was the confessor and secret adviser of the Marchesa di Vivaldi. In the first effervescence of pride and indignation which the discovery of her son's intended marriage occasioned, she consulted him on the means of preventing it, and she soon perceived that his talents promised to equal her wishes. Each possessed, in a considerable degree, the power of assisting the other. Schedoni had subtlety with ambition to urge it; and the Marchesa had inexorable pride and courtly influence; the one hoped to obtain a high benefice for his services, and the other to secure the imaginary dignity of her house by her gifts. Prompted by such passions, and allured by such views, they concerted in private, and unknown even to the Marchese, the means of accomplishing their general end.

Vivaldi, as he quitted his mother's closet, had met Schedoni in the corridor leading thither. He knew him to be her confessor, and was not much surprised to see him, though the hour was an unusual one. Schedoni bowed his head as he passed, and assumed a meek and holy countenance; but Vivaldi, as he eyed him with a penetrating glance, now recoiled with involuntary emotion, and it seemed as if a shuddering presentiment of what this monk was preparing for him had crossed his mind.

CHAPTER III.

VIVALDI, from the period of his last visit to Altieri, was admitted a frequent visitor to Signora Bianchi, and Ellena was, at length, prevailed upon to join the party, when the conversation was always on indifferent topics. Bianchi, understanding the disposition of her niece's affections, and the accomplished mind and manners of Vivaldi, judged that he was more likely to succeed by silent attentions than by a formal declaration of his sentiments. By such a declaration, Ellena, till her heart was more engaged in his cause, would, perhaps, have been alarmed into an absolute rejection of his addresses, and this was every day less likely to happen, so long as he had an opportunity of conversing with her.

Signora Bianchi had acknowledged to Vivaldi that he had no rival to apprehend ; that Ellena had uniformly rejected every admirer who had hitherto discovered her within the shade of her retirement, and that her present reserve proceeded more from considerations of the sentiments of his family than from disapprobation of himself. He forbore, therefore, to press his suit, till he should have secured a stronger interest in her heart, and in this hope he was encouraged by Bianchi, whose gentle remonstrances in his favour became every day more pleasing and more convincing.

Several weeks passed away in this kind of intercourse, till Ellena, yielding to the representations of her aunt, and to the pleadings of her own heart, received Vivaldi as an acknowledged admirer ; and the sentiments of his family were no longer remembered, or, if remembered, it was with a hope that they might at length be overcome by considerations more favourable to herself.

The lovers, with Signora Bianchi and a Signor Giotto, a distant relation of the latter, frequently made excursions in the delightful environs of Naples ; for Vivaldi was no longer anxious to conceal his attachment, but wished to contradict any report injurious to his love by the publicity of his conduct ; while the consideration that Ellena's name had suffered by his late imprudence contributed, with the unsuspecting innocence and sweetness of her manners towards him, who had been the occasion of her injuries, to mingle a sacred pity with his love, which obliterated all family politics from his mind, and bound her irrecoverably to his heart.

These excursions sometimes led them to Puzzuoli ; and as, on their return, they glided along the moon-lit bay, the melody of Italian strains seemed to give enchantment to the scenery of its shore. At this cool hour the voices of the vine-dressers were frequently heard in trio, as they reposed, after the labour of the day, on some pleasant promontory, under the shade of poplars ; or the brisk music of the dance from fishermen, on the margin of the waves below. The boatmen rested on their oars, while their company listened to voices modulated by sensibility to finer eloquence than it is in the power of art alone to display ; and at others, while they observed the airy natural grace which distinguishes the dance of the fishermen and peasants of Naples. Frequently as they glided round a promontory, whose shaggy masses impended far over the sea, such magic scenes of beauty unfolded, adorned by these dancing groups on the bay beyond, as no pencil could do justice to. The deep, clear waters reflected every image of the landscape ; the cliffs, branching into wild forms, crowned with groves, whose rough foliage often spread down their steeps in picturesque luxuriance ; the ruined villa on some bold point, peeping through the trees ; peasants' cabins hanging on the precipices, and the dancing figures on the strand—all touched with the silvery tint and soft shadows of moonlight. On the other hand, the sea, trembling with a long line of radiance, and showing in the clear distance the sails of vessels stealing in every direction along its surface, presented a prospect as grand as the landscape was beautiful.

One evening that Vivaldi sat with Ellena and Signora Bianchi, in the very pavilion where he had overheard that short but interesting soliloquy which assured him of her regard, he pleaded with more than his usual earnestness for a speedy marriage. Bianchi did not oppose his arguments ; she had been unwell for some time, and, believing herself to be declining fast, was anxious to have their nuptials concluded. She surveyed with languid eyes the scene that spread before the pavilion. The strong effulgence which a setting sun threw over the sea, showing innumerable gaily-painted ships, and fishing-boats returning from Santa Lucia into the port of Naples, had no longer power to cheer her. Even the Roman tower that terminated the mole below, touched as it was with the slanting rays, and the various figures of fishermen, who lay smoking beneath its walls in the long shadow, or who stood in sunshine on the beach, watching the approaching boats of their comrades, combined a picture which was no longer interesting. "Alas !" said she, breaking from meditative silence, "this sun so glorious, which lights up all the various colouring of these shores, and the glow of those majestic mountains—alas ! I feel that it will not long shine for me—my eyes must soon close upon the prospect for ever !"

To Ellena's tender reproach for this melancholy suggestion Bianchi replied only by expressing an earnest wish to witness the certainty of her being protected ; adding that this must be soon, or she should not live to see it. Ellena, extremely shocked both by this presage of her aunt's fate, and by the direct reference made to her own condition in the presence of Vivaldi, burst into tears, while he, supported by the wishes of Signora Bianchi, urged his suit with increased interest.

"This is not a time for fastidious scruples," said Bianchi, "now that a solemn truth calls out to us. My dear girl, I will not disguise my feelings; they assure me I have not long to live. Grant me then the only request I have to make, and my last hours will be comforted."

After a pause she added, as she took the hand of her niece, "This will, no doubt, be an awful separation to us both; and it must also be a mournful one, signor," turning to Vivaldi, "for she has been as a daughter to me, and I have, I trust, fulfilled to her the duties of a mother. Judge, then, what will be her feelings when I am no more. But it will be your care to soothe them."

Vivaldi looked with emotion at Ellena, and would have spoken; her aunt, however, proceeded. "My own feelings would now be little less poignant if I did not believe that I was confiding her to a tenderness which cannot diminish; that I should prevail with her to accept the protection of a husband. To you, signor, I commit the legacy of my child. Watch over her future moments, guard her from inquietude as vigilantly as I have done, and, if possible from misfortune! I have yet much to say, but my spirits are exhausted."

While he listened to this sacred charge, and recollected the injury Ellena had already sustained for his sake by the cruel obloquy which the Marchese had thrown upon her character, he suffered a degree of generous indignation, of which he scarcely could conceal the cause, and a succeeding tenderness that almost melted him to tears; and he secretly vowed to defend her fame and protect her peace at the sacrifice of every other consideration.

Bianchi, as she concluded her exhortation, gave Ellena's hand to Vivaldi, who received it with emotion such as his countenance only could express, and with solemn fervour raising his eyes to heaven, vowed that he never would betray the confidence thus reposed in him, but would watch over the happiness of Ellena with a care as tender, as anxious, and as unceasing as her own; that from this moment he considered himself bound by ties not less sacred than those which the Church confers to defend her as his wife, and would do so to the latest moment of his existence. As he said this, the truth of his feelings appeared in the energy of his manner.

Ellena, still weeping, and agitated by various considerations, spoke not, but withdrawing the handkerchief from her face, she looked at him through her tears with a smile so meek, so affectionate, so timid, yet so confiding, as expressed all the mingled emotions of her heart, and appealed more eloquently to his than the most energetic language could have done.

Before Vivaldi left the villa, he had some further conversation with Signora Bianchi, when it was agreed that the nuptials should be solemnized in the following week, if Ellena could be prevailed on to confirm her consent so soon; and that when he returned the next day, her determination would probably be made known to him.

He departed for Naples once more with the lightly-bounding steps of joy, which, however, when he arrived there, was somewhat alloyed by a message from the Marchese, demanding to see him in his cabinet. Vivaldi anticipated the subject of the interview, and obeyed the summons with reluctance.

He found his father so absorbed in thought that he did not immediately perceive him. On raising his eyes from the floor, where discontent and perplexity seemed to have held them, he fixed a stern regard on Vivaldi. "I understand," said he, "that you persist in the unworthy pursuit against which I warned you. I have left you thus long to your own discretion, because I was willing to afford you an opportunity of retracting with grace the declaration which you have dared to make me of your principles and intentions; but your conduct has not therefore been the less observed. I am informed that your visits have been as frequent at the residence of the unhappy young woman who was the subject of our former conversation as formerly, and that you are as much infatuated."

"If it is Signora Rosalba whom your lordship means," said Vivaldi, "she is not unhappy; and I do not scruple to own that I am as sincerely attached to her as ever. Why, my dear father," continued he, subduing the feelings which this degrading mention of Ellena had aroused, "why will you persist in opposing the happiness of your son? and above all, why will you continue to think unjustly of her who deserves your admiration as much as my love?"

"As I am not a lover," replied the Marchese, "and the age of boyish credulity is past with me, I do not wilfully close my mind against examination, but am directed by proof and yield only to conviction."

"What proof is it, my lord, that has thus easily convinced you?" said Vivaldi. "Who is it that persists in abusing your confidence, and in destroying my peace?"

The Marchese haughtily reproved his son for such doubts and questions, and a long conversation ensued, which failed to alter the interests or the opinions of either party. The Marchese persisted in accusation and menace; and Vivaldi in defending Ellena, and in affirming that his affections and intentions were irrecoverable.

Not any art of persuasion could prevail with the Marchese to adduce his proofs, or deliver up the name of his informer; nor any menace awe Vivaldi into a renunciation of Ellena; and they parted mutually dissatisfied. The Marchese had failed on this occasion to act with his usual policy, for his menaces and accusations had aroused spirit and indignation, when kindness and gentle remonstrance would certainly have awakened filial affection, and might have occasioned a contest in the breast of Vivaldi. Now, no struggle of opposing duties divided his resolution. He had no hesitation on the subject of dispute; but, regarding his father as a haughty oppressor, who would rob him of his most sacred right, and as one who did not scruple to stain the name of the innocent and the defenceless, when his interest required it, upon the doubtful authority of a base informer, he suffered neither pity nor remorse to mingle with the resolution of asserting the freedom of his nature, and was even more anxious than before to conclude a marriage which he believe would secure his own happiness, and the reputation of Ellena.

He returned, therefore. on the following morning, to Villa Altieri with increased impatience to learn the result of Signora Bianchi's further conversation with her niece, and the day on which the nuptials might be solemnized. On the way thither, his thoughts were wholly occupied by Ellena, and he proceeded mechanically, and without observing where he was, till the shade which the well-known arch threw over the road recalled him to local circumstances, and a voice instantly arrested his attention. It was the voice of the monk, whose figure again passed before him. "Go not to Altieri," it said, solemnly, "for death is in the house!"

Before Vivaldi could recover from the dismay into which this abrupt assertion and sudden appearance had thrown him the stranger was gone. He had escaped in the gloom of the place, and seemed to have retired into the obscurity from which he had so suddenly emerged, for he was not seen to depart from under the arch. Vivaldi pursued him with his voice, conjuring him to appear, and demanding who was dead; but no voice replied.

Believing that the stranger could not have passed unseen from the arch by any way but that leading to the fortress above, Vivaldi began to ascend the steps, when considering that the more certain means of understanding this awful assertion would be, to go immediately to Altieri, he left this portentous ruin, and hastened thither.

An indifferent person would perhaps have understood the words of the monk to allude to Signora Bianchi, whose infirm state of health rendered her death, though sudden, not improbable; but to the affrighted fancy of Vivaldi the dying Ellena only appeared. His fears, however probabilities might sanction,

or the event justify them, were natural to ardent affection; but they were accompanied by a presentiment as extraordinary as it was horrible: it occurred to him, more than once, that Ellena was murdered. He saw her wounded and bleeding to death; saw her ashy countenance, and her wasting eyes, from which the spirit of life was fast departing, turned piteously on himself, as if imploring him to save her from the fate that was dragging her to the grave. And when he reached the boundary of the garden, his whole frame trembled so with horrible apprehension that he rested a while, unable to venture further towards the truth. At length he summoned courage to dare it, and unlocking a private gate, of which he had lately received the key, because it spared him a considerable distance of the road to Naples, he approached the house. All around it was silent and forsaken; many of the lattices were closed, and, as he endeavoured to collect from every trivial circumstance some conjecture, his spirits still sank as he advanced, till, having arrived within a few paces of the portico, all his fears were confirmed. He heard from within a feeble sound of lamentation, and then a few notes of that solemn and peculiar kind of recitative which is in some parts of Italy the requiem of the dying. The sounds were so low and distant that they only murmured on his ear; but, without pausing for information, he rushed into the portico, and knocked loudly at the folding doors, now closed against him.

After repeated summonses, Beatrice, the old housekeeper, appeared. She did not wait for Vivaldi's inquiries. "Alas! signor," said she, "alas-a-day! who would have thought it! who would have expected such a change as this! It was only yester-evening that you was here—she was then as well as I am; who would have thought that she would be dead to-day?"

"She *is* dead, then!" exclaimed Vivaldi, struck to the heart; "she *is* dead!" staggering towards a pillar of the hall, and endeavouring to support himself against it. Beatrice, shocked at his condition, would have gone for assistance, but he waved her to stay. "When did she die?" said he, drawing breath with difficulty; "how and where?"

"Alas! here in the villa, signor," replied Beatrice, weeping. "Who would have thought that I should live to see this day? I hoped to have laid down my old bones in peace."

"What has caused her death?" interrupted Vivaldi, impatiently; "and when did she die?"

"About two of the clock this morning, signor, about two o'clock. Oh, miserable day, that I should live to see it!"

"I am better," said Vivaldi, raising himself. "Lead me to her apartment—I must see her. Do not hesitate; lead me on."

"Alas! signor, it is a dismal sight; why should you wish to see her? Be persuaded; do not go, signor; it is a woeful sight!"

"Lead me on," repeated Vivaldi, sternly; "or if you refuse, I will find the way myself."

Beatrice, terrified by his look and gesture, no longer opposed him, begging only that he would wait until she had informed her lady of his arrival: but he followed her closely up the staircase, and along a corridor that led round the west side of the house, which brought him to a suite of chambers darkened by the closed lattices, through which he passed towards the one where the body lay. The requiem had ceased, and no sound disturbed the awful stillness that prevailed in these deserted rooms. At the door of the last apartment, where he was compelled to stop, his agitation was such that Beatrice, expecting every instant to see him sink to the floor, made an effort to support him with her feeble aid, but he gave a signal for her to retire. He soon recovered himself, and passed into the chamber of death, the solemnity of which might have affected him in any other state of his spirits; but these were now too severely pressed upon by real suffering to feel the influence of local circumstances. Approaching the bed on which the corpse was laid, he raised his eyes to the mourner who hung weeping over it, and beheld—Ellena! who, surprised by this sudden intrusion, and by the agitation of Vivaldi, repeatedly demanded the occasion of it. But he had neither power nor inclination to explain a circumstance which must deeply wound the heart of Ellena, since it would have told that the same event which excited her grief had accidentally inspired his joy.

He did not long intrude upon the sacredness of sorrow, and the short time he remained was employed in endeavours to command his own emotion and to soothe hers.

When he left Ellena, he had some conversation with Beatrice as to the death of Signora Bianchi, and understood that she had retired to rest on the preceding night apparently in her usual state of health.

"It was about one in the morning, signor," continued Beatrice, "I was waked out of my first sleep by a noise in my lady's chamber. It is a grievous thing to me, signor, to be waked from my first sleep; and I, Santa Maria forgive me! was angry at being disturbed. So I would not get up, but laid my head upon the pillow again, and tried to sleep; but presently I heard the noise again. Nay, now, says I, somebody must be up in the house, that's certain. I had scarcely said so, signor, when I heard my young lady's voice calling 'Beatrice! Beatrice!' Ah! poor young lady, she was indeed in a sad

fright, as well she might be. She was at my door in an instant, and looked as pale as death, and trembled so. 'Beatrice,' said she, 'rise this moment; my aunt is dying.' She did not stay for my answer, but was gone directly. Santa Maria protect me! I thought I should have swooned outright."

"Well, but your lady?" said Vivaldi, whose patience the tedious circumlocution of old Beatrice had exhausted.

"Ah! my poor lady, signor; I thought I never should have been able to reach her room; and when I got there I was scarcely more alive than herself. There she lay on her bed! Oh, it was a grievous sight to see! There she lay, looking so piteously; I saw she was dying. She could not speak, though she tried often; but she was sensible, for she would look so at Signora Ellena, and then try again to speak; it almost broke one's heart to see her. Something seemed to lie upon her mind, and she tried almost to the last to tell it; and as she grasped Signora Ellena's hand, she would still look up in her face with such doleful expression as no one who had not a heart of stone could bear. My poor young mistress was quite overcome by it, and cried as if her heart would break. Poor young lady! she has lost a friend indeed; such a one as she must never hope to see again."

"But she shall find one as firm and affectionate as the last!" exclaimed Vivaldi, fervently.

"The good saint grant it may prove so," replied Beatrice, doubtingly. "All that could be done for our dear lady," she continued, "was tried, but with no avail. She could not swallow what the doctor offered her. She grew fainter and fainter, yet would often utter such deep sighs, and would then grasp my hand so hard! At last she turned her eyes from Signora Ellena, and they grew duller and fixed, and she seemed not to see what was before her. Alas! I knew then she was going; her hand did not press mine, as it had done a minute or two before, and a deadly coldness was upon it. Her face changed so, too, in a few minutes. This was about two o'clock, and she died before her confessor could administer."

Beatrice ceased to speak, and wept; Vivaldi almost wept with her, and it was some time before he could command his voice sufficiently to inquire what were the symptoms of Signora Bianchi's disorder, and whether she had ever been thus suddenly attacked before.

"Never, signor!" replied the old housekeeper; "and though, to be sure, she has long been very infirm, and going down, as one may say, yet——"

"What is it you mean?" said Vivaldi.

"Why, signor, I do not know what to think about my lady's death. To be sure, there is nothing certain; and I may only get scoffed at if I speak my mind abroad, for nobody would believe me—it is so strange—yet I must have my own thoughts, for all that."

"Do speak intelligibly," said Vivaldi; "you need not apprehend censure from me."

"Not from you, signor, but if the report should get abroad, and it was known that I had set it going."

"That shall never be known from me," said Vivaldi, with increased impatience; "tell me, without fear, all that you conjecture."

"Well then, signor, I will own that I do not like the suddenness of my lady's death; no, nor the manner of it, nor her appearance after death!"

"Speak explicitly and to the point," said Vivaldi.

"Nay, signor, there are some folks that will not understand if you speak ever so plain; I am sure I speak plain enough. If I might tell my mind—I do not believe she came fairly by her death at last!"

"How!" said Vivaldi. "Your reasons?"

"Nay, signor, I have given them already; I said I did not like the suddenness of her death, nor her appearance after, nor ——"

"Good heaven!" interrupted Vivaldi. "You mean poison!"

"Hush, signor, hush! I do not say that; but she did not seem to die naturally."

"Who has been at the villa lately?" said Vivaldi, in a tremulous voice.

"Alas! signor, nobody has been here; she lived so privately that she saw nobody."

"Not one person?" said Vivaldi. "Consider well, Beatrice; had she no visitor?"

"Not of a long while, signor; no visitors but yourself and her cousin Signor Giotto. The only other person that has been within these walls for many weeks, to the best of my remembrance, is a sister of the convent, who comes for silks my young lady embroiders."

"Embroiders! What convent?"

"The Santa Maria della Pieta, yonder, signor; if you will step this way to the window, I will show it you. Yonder, among the woods on the hill-side, just above those gardens that stretch down to the bay. There is an olive ground close beside it; and observe, signor, there is a red and yellowish ridge of rocks rises over the woods higher still, and looks as if it would fall down upon those old spires. Have you found it, signor?"

"How long is it since this sister came here?" said Vivaldi.

"Three weeks, at least, signor."

"And you are certain that no other person has called within that time?"

"No other, signor, except the fisherman and the gardener, and a man who brings macaroni, and such sort of things; for it is such a long way to Naples, signor, and I have so little time."

"Three weeks, say you? You said three weeks, I think! Are you certain as to this?"

"Three weeks, signor! Santa della Pieta! Do you believe, signor, that we could fast for three weeks? Why, they call almost every day."

"I speak of the nun," said Vivaldi.

"Oh, yes, signor," replied Beatrice; "it is that, at least, since she was here."

"This is strange," said Vivaldi, musing; "but I will talk with you some other time. Meanwhile, I wish you could contrive that I should see the face of your deceased lady without the knowledge of Signora Ellena. And, observe me, Beatrice, be strictly silent as to your surmises concerning her death: do not suffer any negligence to betray your suspicions to your young mistress. Has she any suspicions herself of the same nature?"

Beatrice replied that she believed Signora Ellena had none; and promised faithfully to observe his injunctions.

He then left the villa, meditating on the circumstances he had just learned, and on the prophetic assertion of the monk, between whom and the cause of Bianchi's sudden death he could not forbear surmising there was some connection; and it now occurred to him, and for the first time, that this monk, this mysterious stranger, was no other than Schedoni, whom he had observed of late going more frequently than usual to his mother's apartment. He almost started in horror of the suspicion to which this conjecture led, and precipitately rejected it as a poison that would destroy his own peace for ever. But though he instantly dismissed the suspicion, the conjecture returned to his mind, and he endeavoured to recollect the voice and figure of the stranger, that he might compare them with those of the confessor. The voices were, he thought, of a different tone, and the persons of a different height and proportion. This comparison, however, did not forbid him to surmise that the stranger was an agent of the confessor's; that he was, at least, a secret spy upon his actions, and the defamer of Ellena; while both, if indeed there were two persons concerned, appeared to be at the command of his parents. Fired with indignation at the unworthy arts that he believed to have been employed against him, and impatient to meet the slanderer of Ellena, he determind to attempt some decisive step towards a discovery of the truth; and either to compel the confessor to reveal it to him, or to search out his agent, who, he fancied, was occasionally a resident within the ruins of Paluzzi.

The inhabitants of the convent which Beatrice had pointed out, did not escape his consideration; but no reason appeared for supposing them the enemies of his Ellena, who, on the contrary, he understood, had been for some years amicably connected

with them. The embroidered silks, of which
the old servant had spoken, sufficiently explained the nature of the connection ; and
discovering more fully the circumstances of
Ellena's fortune, her conduct heightened the
tender admiration with which he had hitherto
regarded her.

The hints for suspicion which Beatrice had
given respecting the cause of her mistress's
decease incessantly recurred to him ; and it
appeared extraordinary, and sometimes in the
highest degree improbable, that any person
could be sufficiently interested in the death of
a woman apparently so blameless as to administer poison to her. What motive could
have prompted so horrible a deed was still
more inexplicable. It was true that she had
long been in a declining state ; yet the suddenness of her departure, and the singularity
of some circumstances preceding as well as
some appearances that had followed it, compelled Vivaldi to doubt as to the cause. He
believed, however, that, after having seen the
corpse, his doubts must vanish ; and Beatrice
had promised that, if he could return in the
evening, when Ellena had retired to rest, he
should be permitted to visit the chamber of
the deceased. There was something repugnant to his feelings in going thus secretly, or,
indeed, at all, to the residence of Ellena at
this delicate period, yet it was necessary he
should introduce there some medical professor
on whose judgment he could rest respecting
the occasion of Bianchi's death ; and as he
believed he should so soon acquire the right
of vindicating the honour of Ellena, that
consideration did not so seriously affect him
as otherwise it would have done. The inquiry which called him thither was, besides,
of a nature too solemn and important to be
lightly resigned ; he had therefore, told
Beatrice he would be punctual to the hour
she appointed. His intention to search for
the monk was thus again interrupted.

CHAPTER IV.

WHEN Vivaldi returned to Naples, he
inquired for the Marchesa, of whom
he wished to ask some questions concerning
Schedoni, which, though he scarcely expected
they would be explicitly answered, might yet
lead to part of the truth he sought for.

The Marchesa was in her closet, and
Vivaldi found the confessor with her. "This
man crosses me like my evil genius," said he
to himself as he entered ; "but I will know
whether he deserves my suspicions before I
leave the room."

Schedoni was so deeply engaged in conversation that he did not immediately perceive
Vivaldi, who stood for a moment examining
his countenance, and tracing subjects for
curiosity in its deep lines. His eyes, while he
spoke, were cast downward, and his features

were fixed in an expression at once severe and
crafty. The Marchesa was listening with
deep attention, her head inclined towards
him, as if to catch the lowest murmur of his
voice, and her face picturing the anxiety and
vexation of her mind. This was evidently a
conference, not a confession.

Vivaldi advancing, the monk raised his
eyes ; his countenance suffered no change
as they met those of Vivaldi. He rose, but
did not take leave, and returned the slight and
somewhat haughty salutation of Vivaldi with
an inclination of the head that indicated a
pride without pettishness, and a firmness bordering on contempt.

The Marchesa, on perceiving her son, was
somewhat embarrassed, and her brow, before
slightly contracted by vexation, now frowned
with resentment. Yet it was an involuntary
emotion, for she endeavoured to chase the
expression of it with a smile. Vivaldi liked
the smile still less than the frown.

Schedoni seated himself quietly, and began,
with almost the ease of a man of the world,
to converse on general topics. Vivaldi, however, was reserved and silent : he knew not
how to begin a conversation which might
lead to the knowledge he desired, and the
Marchesa did not relieve him from the difficulty. His eye and his ear assisted him to
conjecture, at least, if not to obtain, the information he wished ; and, as he listened to
the deep tones of Schedoni's voice, he became
almost certain that they were not the accents
of his unknown adviser; though he considered,
at the same moment, that it was not difficult
to disguise or to feign a voice. His stature
seemed to decide the question more reasonably ; for the figure of Schedoni appeared
taller than that of the stranger : and though
there was something of resemblance in their
air which Vivaldi had never observed before,
he again considered that the habit of the
same order, which each wore, might easily
occasion an artificial resemblance. Of the
likeness, as to countenance, he could not
judge, since the stranger's had been so much
shrouded by his cowl that Vivaldi had never
distinctly seen a single feature. Schedoni's
hood was now thrown back, so that he could
not compare even the hair of their heads under similar circumstances ; but as he remembered to have seen the confessor on a former
day approaching his mother's closet with the
cowl shading his face, the same gloomy severity
seemed to characterise both, and nearly the
same terrible portrait was drawn on his fancy.
Yet this again might be only an artificial
effect, a character which the cowl only gave
to the head ; and any face seen imperfectly
beneath its dark shade might have appeared
equally severe. Vivaldi was still extremely
perplexed in his opinion. One circumstance,
however, seemed to throw some light on his
judgment. The stranger had appeared in the

habit of a monk, and, if Vivaldi's transient observation might be trusted, he was of the very same order with that of Schedoni. Now if he were Schedoni, or his agent, it was not probable that he would have shown himself in a dress that might lead to a discovery of his person. That he was anxious for concealment, his manner had strongly proved; it seemed, then, that this habit of a monk was only a disguise, assumed for the purpose of misleading conjecture. Vivaldi, however, determined to put some questions to Schedoni, and at the same time to observe their effect on his countenance. He took occasion to notice some drawings of ruins, which ornamented the cabinet of the Marchesa, and to say that the fortress of Paluzzi was worthy of being added to her collection.

"You have seen it lately, perhaps, reverend father," added Vivaldi, with a penetrating glance.

"It is a striking relic of antiquity," replied the confessor.

"That arch," resumed Vivaldi, his eye still fixed on Schedoni, "that arch suspended between two rocks, the one overtopped by the towers of the fortress, the other shadowed with pine and broad oak, has a fine effect. But a picture of it would want human figures. Now either the grotesque shapes of banditti lurking within the ruin, as if ready to start out upon the traveller, or a friar rolled up in his black garments, just stealing forth from under the shade of the arch, and looking like some supernatural messenger of evil, would finish the piece."

The features of Schedoni suffered no change during these remarks. "Your picture is complete," said he, "and I cannot but admire the facility with which you have classed the monks together with banditti."

"Your pardon, holy father," said Vivaldi; "I did not draw a parallel between them."

"Oh, no offence, signor," replied Schedoni, with a smile somewhat ghastly.

During the latter part of this conversation, if conversation it may be called, the Marchesa had followed a servant, who had brought her a letter, out of the apartment, and as the confessor appeared to await her return, Vivaldi determined to press his inquiry. "It appears, however," said he, "that Paluzzi, if not haunted by robbers, is at least frequented by ecclesiastics; for I have seldom passed it without seeing one of the order, and that one has appeared so suddenly, and vanished so suddenly, that I have been almost compelled to believe he was literally a spiritual being!"

"The convent of the Black Penitents is not far distant," observed the confessor.

"Does the dress of this convent resemble that of your order, reverend father? For I observed that the monk I speak of was habited like yourself; aye, and he was about your stature, and very much resembled you."

"That well may be, signor," replied the confessor calmly; "there are many brethren who, no doubt, resemble each other : but the brothers of the Black Penitents are clothed in sackcloth, and the death's head on the garment, the peculiar symbol of this order, would not have escaped your observation ; it could not, therefore, be a member of their society whom you have seen."

"I am not inclined to think that it was," said Vivaldi; "but be it who it may, I hope soon to be better acquainted with him and to tell him truths so strong that he shall not be permitted even to affect the misunderstanding of them."

"You will do right, if you have cause of complaint against him," observed Schedoni.

"And *only* if I have cause of complaint, holy father? Are strong truths to be told only when there is direct cause of complaint? Is it only when we are injured that we are to be sincere?" He believed that he had now detected Schedoni, who seemed to have betrayed a consciousness that Vivaldi had reason for complaint against the stranger.

"You will observe, reverend father, that I have said I am injured," he added. "If you know that I am, this must be by other means than by my words ; I have not even expressed resentment."

"Except by your voice and eye, signor," replied Schedoni, drily. "When a man is vehement and disordered, we usually are inclined to suppose he feels resentment, and that he has cause of complaint, either real or imaginary. As I have not the honour of being acquainted with the subject you allude to, I cannot decide to which of the two your cause belongs."

"I have never been in doubt as to that," said Vivaldi, haughtily ; "and if I have, you will pardon me, holy father, but I should not have requested your decision. My injuries are, alas ! too real ; and I now think it is also too certain to whom I may attribute them. The secret adviser, who steals into the bosom of a family only to poison its repose, the informer, the base asperser of innocence, stand revealed in one person."

Vivaldi delivered these words with a tempered energy, at once dignified and pointed, which seemed to strike directly to the heart of Schedoni : but whether it was his conscience or his pride that took the alarm, did not certainly appear. Vivaldi believed the former. A dark malignity overspread the features of the monk, and at that moment Vivaldi thought he beheld a man whose passions might impel him to the perpetration of almost any crime, how hideous soever. He recoiled from him as if he had suddenly seen a serpent in his path, and stood gazing on his face with an attention so wholly occupied as to be unconscious that he did so.

Schedoni almost instantly recovered himself; his features relaxed from their first expression, and that portentous darkness passed away from his countenance; but, with a look that was still stern and haughty, he said, "Signor, however ignorant I may be of the subject of your discontent, I cannot misunderstand that your resentment is, to some extent or other, directed against myself as the cause of it. Yet I will not suppose, signor, I say I will not suppose," raising his voice significantly, "that you have dared to brand me with the ignominious titles you have just uttered; but——"

"I have applied them to the author of my injuries," interrupted Vivaldi; "you, father, can best inform me whether they applied to yourself."

"I have then nothing to complain of," said Schedoni, adroitly, and with a sudden calmness that surprised Vivaldi. "If you directed them against the author of your injuries, whatever they may be, I am satisfied."

The cheerful complacency with which he spoke this renewed the doubts of Vivaldi, who thought it nearly impossible that a man conscious of guilt could assume, under the very charge of it, the tranquil and dignified air which the confessor now displayed. He began to accuse himself of having condemned him with passionate rashness, and gradually became shocked at the indecorum of his conduct towards a man of Schedoni's age and sacred profession. Those expressions of countenance which had so much alarmed him, he was now inclined to think the effect of a jealous and haughty honour; and he almost forgot the malignity which had mingled with Schedoni's pride, in sorrow for the offence that had provoked it. Thus, not less precipitate in his pity than his anger, and credulous alike to the passion of the moment, he was now as eager to apologise for his error as he had been hasty in committing it. The frankness with which he apologised and lamented the impropriety of his conduct would have won an easy forgiveness from a generous heart. Schedoni listened with apparent complacency and secret contempt. He regarded Vivaldi as a rash boy, who was swayed only by his passions; but while he suffered deep resentment for the evil in his character, he felt neither respect nor kindness for the good, for the sincerity, the love of justice, the generosity, which threw a brilliancy even on his foibles. Schedoni, indeed, saw only evil in human nature.

Had the heart of Vivaldi been less generous, he would now have distrusted the satisfaction which the confessor assumed, and have discovered the contempt and malignity that lurked behind the smile thus imperfectly masking his countenance. The confessor perceived his power, and the character of Vivaldi lay before him as a map. He saw, or fancied he saw, every line and feature of

its plan, and the relative proportions of every energy and weakness of its nature. He believed, also, he could turn the very virtues of this young man against himself; and he exulted, even while the smile of good-will was yet upon his countenance, in anticipating the moment that should avenge him for the past outrage, and which, while Vivaldi was ingenuously lamenting it, he had apparently forgotten.

Schedoni was thus ruminating evil against Vivaldi, and Vivaldi was considering how he might possibly make Schedoni atonement for the affront he had offered him, when the Marchesa returned to the apartment, and perceived in the honest countenance of Vivaldi some symptoms of the agitation which had passed over it; his complexion was flushed, and his brow slightly contracted. The aspect of Schedoni told nothing but complacency, except that now and then when he looked at Vivaldi it was with half-shut eyes, that indicated treachery, or, at least, cunning, trying to conceal exasperated pride.

The Marchesa, with displeasure directed against her son, inquired the reason of his emotion; but he, stung with consciousness of his conduct towards the monk, could neither endure to explain it or to remain in her presence; and, saying that he would confide his honour to the discretion of the holy father, who would speak only too favourably of his fault, he abruptly left the room.

When he had departed, Schedoni gave, with seeming reluctance, the explanation which the Marchesa required, but was cautious not to speak too favourably of Vivaldi's conduct, which, on the contrary, he represented as much more insulting than it really was; and, while he aggravated the offensive part of it, he suppressed all mention of the candour and self-reproach which had followed the charge. Yet this he managed so artfully that he appeared to extenuate Vivaldi's errors, to lament the hastiness of his temper, and to plead for a forgiveness from his irritated mother. "He is very young," added the monk, when he perceived that he had sufficiently exasperated the Marchesa against her son; "he is very young, and youth is warm in its passions and precipitate in its judgments. He was, besides, jealous, no doubt, of the friendship, with which you are pleased to honour me; and it is natural that a son should be jealous of the attention of such a mother."

"You are too good, father," said the Marchesa; her resentment increasing towards Vivaldi in proportion as Schedoni displayed his artificial candour and meekness.

"It is true," continued the confessor, "that I perceive all the inconveniences to which my attachment, I should say my duty, to your family exposes me; but I willingly submit to these, while it is yet possible that my advice may be a means of preserving the honour of your house unsullied, and of saving this inconsiderate young man from future misery and unavailing repentance."

During the warmth of this sympathy in resentment, the Marchesa and Schedoni mutually and sincerely lost their remembrance of the unworthy motives by which each knew the other to be influenced, as well as that disgust which those who act together to the same bad end can seldom escape from feeling towards their associates. The Marchesa, while she commended the fidelity of Schedoni, forgot his views and her promises as to a rich benefice ; while the confessor imputed her anxiety for the splendour of her son's condition to a real interest in his welfare, not a care of her own dignity. After mutual compliments had been exchanged, they proceeded to a long consultation concerning Vivaldi, and it was agreed that their efforts for what they termed his preservation should no longer be confined to remonstrances.

CHAPTER V.

VIVALDI, when his first feelings of pity and compunction for having insulted an aged man, the member of a sacred profession, were past, and when he looked with a more deliberate eye upon some circumstances of the confessor's conduct, perceived that suspicion was again gathering on his mind. But, regarding this as a symptom of his own weakness, rather than as a hint of truth, he endeavoured, with a magnanimous disdain, to reject every surmise that boded unfavourably of Schedoni.

When evening arrived, he hastened towards Villa Altieri, and having met, without the city, according to appointment, a physician upon whose honour and judgment he thought he might rely, they proceeded on their way together. Vivaldi had forgotten, during the confusion of his last interview with Ellena, to deliver up the key of the garden-gate, and he now entered it as usual, though he could not entirely overcome the reluctance which he felt on thus visiting, in secret and at night, the dwelling of Ellena. Under no other circumstances, however, could the physician, whose opinion was so necessary to his peace, be introduced without betraying a suspicion which must render her unhappy, perhaps for ever.

Beatrice, who had watched for them in the portico, led the way to the chamber where the corpse was laid out ; and Vivaldi, though considerably affected when he entered, soon recovered composure enough to take his station on one side of the bed, while the physician placed himself on the other. Unwilling to expose his emotion to the observation of a servant, and desirous also of some private conversation with the physician, he took the lamp from Beatrice, and dismissed her. As the light glared on the livid face of the corpse, Vivaldi gazed with melancholy surprise ; and an effort of reason was necessary to convince him that this was the same countenance which only one evening preceding was animated like his own ; which had looked upon him in tears, while, with anxiety the most tender, Bianchi had committed the happiness of her niece to his care, and had, alas ! too justly predicted her approaching dissolution. The circumstances of that scene now appeared to him like a vision, and touched every fibre of his heart. He was fully sensible of the importance of the trust committed to him, and as he now hung over the pale and deserted form of Bianchi, he silently renewed his solemn vows to Ellena, to deserve the confidence of her departed guardian.

Before Vivaldi had courage enough to ask the opinion of the physician, who was still viewing the face of the deceased with very earnest attention and a disapproving countenance, his own suspicions strengthened from some circumstances of her appearance ; and particularly from the black tint that prevailed over her complexion, it seemed to him that her death had been by poison. He feared to break a silence which prolonged his hope of the contrary, feeble though it was ; and the physician, who probably was apprehensive of the consequence of delivering his real thought, did not speak.

"I read your opinion," said Vivaldi, at length ; "it coincides with my own."

"I know not as to that, signor," replied the physician ; "though I think I perceive what is yours. Appearances are unfavourable, yet I will not take upon me to decide from them that it is as you suspect. There are other circumstances under which similar appearances might occur." He gave his reasons for this assertion, which were plausible even to Vivaldi, and concluded by requesting to speak with Beatrice. "For I wish to understand," said he, "what was the exact situation of this lady for some hours previous to her decease."

After a conversation of some length with Beatrice, whatever might be the opinion resulting from his inquiries, he adhered nearly to his former assertions ; pronouncing that so many contradictory circumstances appeared as rendered it impossible for him to decide whether Bianchi had died from poison or otherwise. He stated, more fully than he had done before, the reasons which must render the opinion of any medical person on this subject doubtful. But whether it was that he feared to be responsible for a decision which would accuse some person of murder, or that he really was inclined to believe that Bianchi died naturally, it is certain he seemed disposed to adopt the latter opinion, and that he was very anxious to quiet the suspicions of Vivaldi. He so far succeeded, indeed, as to convince him that it would be unavailing to pursue the inquiry, and at length almost compelled him to believe that she had departed according to the common course of nature.

Vivaldi, having lingered awhile over the death-bed of Bianchi, and taken a last farewell of her silent form, quitted the chamber and the house as softly as he had approached, and unobserved, as he believed, by Ellena or any other person. The morning dawned over the sea when he returned into the garden, and a few fishermen, loitering on the beach or putting off their little boats from the shore, were the only persons visible at this early hour. The time, however, was past for renewing the inquiry he had purposed at Paluzzi, and the brightening dawn warned him to retire. To Naples, therefore, he returned, with spirits somewhat soothed by a hope that Bianchi had not fallen prematurely, and by the certainty that Ellena was well. On the way thither he passed the fort without interruption, and, having parted with the physician, was admitted into his father's mansion by a confidential servant.

CHAPTER VI.

ELLENA, on thus suddenly losing her aunt, her only relative, the friend of her whole life, felt as if left alone in the world. But it was not in the first moments of affliction that this feeling occurred. Her own forlorn situation was not even observed, while affection, pity, and irresistible grief for Bianchi occupied her heart.

Bianchi was to be interred in the church belonging to the convent of Santa Maria della Pieta. The body, attired according to the custom of the country, and decorated with flowers, was carried on an open bier to the place of interment, attended only by priests and torch-bearers. But Ellena could not endure thus lightly to part with the relics of a beloved friend, and being restrained by custom from following the corpse to the grave, she repaired first to the convent to attend the funeral service. Her sorrow did not allow her to join in the choral symphonies of the nuns, but their sacred solemnity was soothing to her spirits, and the tears she shed while she listened to the lengthening notes assuaged the force of grief.

When the service concluded, she withdrew to the parlour of the Lady Abbess, who mingled with her consolations many entreaties that Ellena would make the convent her present asylum ; and her affliction required little persuasion on this subject. It was her wish to retire hither, as to a sanctuary, which was not only suitable to her particular circumstances, but especially adapted to the present state of her spirits. Here she believed that she should sooner acquire resignation, and regain tranquillity, than in a place less consecrated to religion ; and before she took leave of the Abbess it was agreed that she should be received as a boarder. To acquaint Vivaldi with her intention was, indeed, her chief motive for returning to Villa Altieri, after this her resolution had been taken. Her affection and esteem had been gradual in their progress, and had now attained a degree of strength which promised to decide the happiness or misery of her whole life. The sanction given by her aunt to this choice, and particularly the very solemn manner in which, on the evening preceding her death, she bequeathed Ellena to Vivaldi's care, had still more endeared him to her heart, and imparted a sacredness to the engagement which made her consider him as her guardian and only surviving protector. The more tenderly she lamented her deceased relative, the more tenderly she thought of Vivaldi ; and her love for the one was so intimately connected with her affection for the other that each seemed strengthened and exalted by the union.

When the funeral was over they met at Altieri.

He was neither surprised nor averse to her withdrawing awhile to a convent ; for there was a propriety in retiring, during the period of her grief, from a home where she had no longer a guardian, which delicacy seemed to demand. He only stipulated that he might be permitted to visit her in the parlour of the convent, and to claim, when decorum should no longer object to it, the hand which Bianchi had resigned to him.

Notwithstanding that he yielded to this arrangement without complaining, it was not entirely without repining ; but being assured by Ellena of the worthiness of the Abbess of La Pieta, he endeavoured to silence the secret murmurs of his heart with the conviction of his judgment.

Meanwhile, the deep impression made by his unknown tormentor, the monk, and especially by the prediction of the death of Bianchi, remained upon his mind, and he once more determined to ascertain, if possible, the true nature of the portentous visitant, and what were the motives which induced him thus to haunt his footsteps and interrupt his peace. He was awed by the circumstances which had attended the visitations of the monk, if monk it was ; by the suddenness of his appearance and departure, by the truth of his prophecies, and, above all, by the solemn event which had verified his last warning ; and his imagination, thus elevated by wonder and painful curiosity, was prepared for something above the reach of common conjecture, and beyond the accomplishment of human agency. His understanding was sufficiently clear and strong to teach him to detect many errors of opinion that prevailed around him, as well as to despise the common superstitions of his country; and, in the usual state of his mind, he probably would not have hesitated for a moment on the subject before him; but his passions were now interested and his fancy awakened, and though he was unconscious of this propensity, he would, perhaps, have been somewhat disappointed to have descended suddenly from the region of fearful sublimity, to which he had soared—the world of terrible shadows!—to the earth on which he daily walked, and to an explanation simply natural.

He designed to visit again, at midnight, the fortress of Paluzzi, and not to watch for the appearance of the stranger, but to carry torches into every recess of the ruin, and discover, at least, whether it was haunted by any other human being than himself. The chief difficulty which had hitherto delayed him was that of finding a person in whom he could confide, to accompany him in the search, since his former adventure had warned him never to renew it alone. Signor Bonarmo persisted absolutely, and, perhaps, wisely, to refuse his request on this subject; and as Vivaldi had no other acquaintance to whom he chose to give so much explanation of the affair as might induce compliance, he at length determined to take with him Paulo, his own servant.

On the evening previous to the day of Ellena's departure to La Pieta, Vivaldi went to Altieri to bid her adieu. During this interview his spirits were more than usually depressed; and, though he knew that her retirement was only for a short period, and had as much confidence in the continuance of her affection as is, perhaps, possible to a lover, Vivaldi felt as if he was parting with her for ever. A thousand vague and fearful conjectures, such as he had never till this moment admitted, assailed him, and amongst them it appeared probable that the arts of the nuns might win her from the world, and sacrifice her to the cloister. In her present state of sorrow this seemed to be even more than probable, and not all the assurances which Ellena gave him—and in these parting moments she spoke with less reserve than she had hitherto done—could reanimate his mind. "It should seem, Ellena, by these boding ears," said he, imprudently, "that I am parting with you for ever; I feel a weight upon my heart which I cannot throw off. Yet I consent that you shall withdraw awhile to this convent, convinced of the propriety of the step; and I ought, also, to know that you will soon return, that I shall soon take you from its walls as my wife, never more to leave me, never more to pass from my immediate care and tenderness. I ought to feel assured of all this; yet so apt are my fears that I cannot confide in what is probable, but rather apprehend what is possible. And is it then possible that I yet may lose you; and is it only probable that you may be mine for ever? How, under such circumstances, could I weakly consent to your retirement? Why did I not urge you to bestow immediately those indissoluble bands which no human force can burst asunder? How could I leave the destiny of all my peace within the reach of a possibility which it was once in my power to have removed! Which it *was* in my power! It is, perhaps, still in my power. O Ellena! let the severities of custom yield to the security of my happiness. If you do go to La Pieta, let it be only to visit its altar?"

Vivaldi delivered this expostulation with a rapidity that left no pause for Ellena to interrupt him. When, at length, he concluded, she gently reproached him for doubting the continuance of her regard, and endeavoured to soothe his apprehension of misfortune, but would not listen to his request. She represented that not only the state of her spirits required retirement, but that respect to the memory of her aunt demanded it; and added, gravely, that if he had so little confidence in the steadiness of her opinions as to doubt the constancy of her affection, and for so short a period, unless her vows were secured to him, he had done imprudently to elect her for the companion of his whole life.

Vivaldi, then ashamed of the weakness he had betrayed, besought her forgiveness, and endeavoured to appease apprehensions which passion only made plausible, and which reason reproved; notwithstanding which, he could recover neither tranquillity nor confidence: nor could Ellena, though her conduct was supported and encouraged by justness of sentiment, entirely remove the oppression of spirits she had felt from almost the first moment of this interview. They parted with many tears; and Vivaldi, before he finally took his leave, frequently returned to claim some promise, or to ascertain some explanation; till Ellena remarked, with a forced smile, that these resembled eternal adieus, rather than those only of a few days: an observation which renewed all his alarm, and furnished an excuse for again delaying his departure. At length he tore himself away, and left Villa Altieri; but as the time was yet too early to suit his purposed inquiry at Paluzzi, he returned to Naples.

Ellena, meanwhile, endeavouring to dissipate melancholy recollections by employment, continued busied in preparation for her departure on the following day till a late hour of the night. In the prospect of quitting, though only for so short a period, the home where she had passed almost every day since the dawn of her earliest remembrance, there was something melancholy, if not solemn.

In leaving these well-known scenes, where, it might be said, the shade of her deceased relative seemed yet to linger, she was quitting all vestige of her late happiness, all note of former years and of present consolation ; and she felt as if going forth into a new and homeless world. Her affection for the place increased as the passing time diminished, and it seemed as if the last moment of her stay would be precisely that in which the Villa Alteri would be most valued.

In her favourite apartments she lingered for a considerable time ; and in the room where she had supped on the night immediately preceding the death of Signora Bianchi, she indulged many tender and mournful recollections, and probably would have continued to indulge them much longer, had not her attention been withdrawn by a sudden rustling of the foliage that surrounded the window ; when, on raising her eyes, she thought she perceived some person pass quickly from before it. The lattices had, as usual, been left open to admit the fresh breeze from the bay below, but she now rose with some alarm to close them, and had scarcely done so when she heard a distant knocking from the portico, and in the next instant the screams of Beatrice in the hall.

Alarmed for herself, Ellena had, however, the courage to hasten to the assistance of her old servant ; when, on entering the passage leading to the hall, three men, masked and muffled up in cloaks, appeared, advancing from the opposite extremity. While she retreated, they pursued her to the apartment she had quitted. Her breath and her courage were gone, yet she struggled to sustain herself, and endeavoured to ask with calmness what was their errand. They gave no reply, but threw a veil over her face, and, seizing her arms, led her almost unresisting, but supplicating, towards the portico.

In the hall, Ellena perceived Beatrice bound to a pillar, and another ruffian, who was also masked, watching over and menacing her, not by words but gestures. Ellena's shrieks seemed to recall the almost lifeless Beatrice, for whom she supplicated as much as for herself ; but entreaty was alike unavailing for each, and Ellena was borne from the house and through the garden. All consciousness had now forsaken her. On recovering, she perceived herself in a carriage, which was driven with great rapidity, and that her arms were within the grasp of some persons whom, when her recollection returned more fully, she believed to be the men who had carried her from the villa. The darkness prevented her from observing their figures, and to all her questions and entreaties a deathlike silence was observed.

During the whole night the carriage proceeded rapidly, stopping only while the horses were changed, when Ellena endeavoured to interest by her cries the compassion of the people at the post-houses, and by her cries only, for the blinds were closely drawn. The postilions, no doubt, imposed on the credulity of these people, for they were insensible to her distress, and her immediate companions soon overcame the only means that had remained by which she could make it known.

For the first hours a tumult of terror and amazement occupied her mind ; but as this began to subside, and her understanding to recover its clearness, grief and despondency mingled with her fears. She saw herself separated from Vivaldi, probably for ever, for she apprehended that the strong and invisible hand which governed her course would never relinquish its grasp till it had placed her irrecoverably beyond the reach of her lover. A conviction that she should see him no more came at intervals with such overwhelming force that every other consideration and emotion disappeared before it ; and at these moments she lost all anxiety as to the place of her destination, and all fear as to her personal safety.

As the morning advanced and the heat increased, the blinds were let down a little to admit air ; and Ellena then perceived that only two of the men who had appeared at Villa Altieri were in the carriage, and that they were still disguised in cloaks and visors. She had no means of judging through what part of the country she was travelling, for above the small openings which the blinds left she could see only the towering tops of mountains, or sometimes the veiny precipices and tangled thickets that closely impended over the road.

About noon, as she judged from the excessive heat, the carriage stopped at a post-house, and ice-water was handed through the window ; when, as the blind was lowered to admit it, she perceived herself on a wild and solitary plain surrounded by mountains and woods. The people at the door of the post-house seemed "unused to pity or be pitied." The lean and sallow countenance of poverty stared over their gaunt bones, and habitual discontent had fixed the furrows of their cheeks. They regarded Ellena with only a feeble curiosity, though the affliction in her looks might have interested almost any heart that was not corroded by its own sufferings ; nor did the masked faces of her companions excite a much stronger attention.

Ellena accepted the cool refreshment offered her, the first she had taken on the road. Her companions, having emptied their glasses, drew up the blind, and, notwithstanding the almost intolerable heat of noon, the carriage proceeded. Fainting under its oppression, Ellena entreated that the windows might be open, when the men, probably in compliance with their own necessity rather than with her request, lowered the blinds, and she had a glimpse of the lofty region of the mountains, but of no object that could direct her conjecture concerning where she was. She saw only pinnacles and vast precipices of various-tinted marbles, intermingled with scanty vegetation, such as stunted pinasters, dwarf-oak and holly, which gave dark touches to the many coloured cliffs, and sometimes stretched in shadowy masses to the deep valleys, that, winding into obscurity, seemed to invite curiosity to explore the scenes beyond. Below these bold precipices extended the gloomy region of olive-trees, and lower still other rocky steeps sunk towards the plains, bearing terraces crowned with vines, and where often the artificial soil was propped by thickets of Indian-fig, pomegranate, and oleander.

Ellena, after having been so long shut in darkness, and brooding over her own alarming circumstances, found temporary, though feeble, relief in once more looking upon the face of nature ; till, her spirits being gradually revived and elevated by the grandeur of the images around her, she said to herself, " If I am condemned to misery, surely I could endure it with more fortitude in scenes like these than amidst the tamer landscapes of nature ! Here, the objects seem to impart somewhat of their own force, their own sublimity, to the soul. It is scarcely possible to yield to the pressure of misfortune while we walk, as with the Deity, amidst his most stupendous works ! "

But soon after, the idea of Vivaldi glancing athwart her memory, she melted into tears ; the weakness, however, was momentary, and during the rest of the journey she preserved a strenuous equality of mind.

It was when the heat and the light were declining that the carriage entered a rocky defile, which showed, as through a telescope reversed, distant plains and mountains opening beyond, lighted up with all the purple splendour of the setting sun. Along this deep and shadowy perspective, a river, which was seen descending among the cliffs of a mountain, rolled with impetuous force, fretting and foaming amidst the dark rocks in its descent, and then flowing in a limpid lapse to the brink of other precipices, whence again it fell with thundering strength to the abyss, throwing its misty clouds of spray high in the air, and seeming to claim the sole empire of this solitary wild. Its bed took up the whole breadth of the chasm which some strong convulsion of the earth seemed to have formed, not leaving space even for a road along its margin. The road, therefore, was carried high among the cliffs, that impended over the river, and seemed as if suspended in air ; while the gloom and vastness of the precipices which towered above and sunk below it, together with the amazing force and uproar of the falling waters, combined to render the pass more terrific than the pencil could describe, or language may express. Ellena ascended it, not with indifference, but with calmness ; she experienced somewhat of a dreadful pleasure in looking down upon the irresistible flood ; but this emotion was heightened into awe when she perceived that the road led to a slight bridge, which, thrown across the chasm at an immense height, united two opposite cliffs, between which the whole cataract of the river descended. The bridge, which was defended only by a slender railing, appeared as if hung amidst the clouds. Ellena, while she was crossing it, almost forgot her misfortunes. Having reached the opposite side of the glen, the road gradually descended the precipices for about half a mile, when it opened to extensive prospects over plains and towards distant mountains—the sunshine landscape which had long appeared to bound this shadowy pass. The transition was as the passage through the vale of death to the bliss of eternity ; but the idea of its resemblance did not long remain with Ellena. Perched high among the cliffs of a mountain, which might be said to terminate one of the jaws of this terrific defile, and which was one of the loftiest of a chain that surrounded the plains, appeared the spires and long terraces of a monastery ; and she soon understood that her journey was to conclude there.

At the foot of this mountain her companions alighted, and obliged her to do the same, for the ascent was too steep and irregular to admit of a carriage. Ellena followed unresistingly, like a lamb to the sacrifice, up a path that wound among the rocks, and was coolly overshadowed by thickets of almond-trees, figs, broad-leaved myrtle, and ever-green rose-bushes, intermingled with the strawberry tree, beautiful in fruit and blossoms, the yellow jasmine, the delightful *acacia mimosa*, and a variety of other fragrant plants. These bowers frequently admitted glimpses of the glowing country below, and sometimes opened to expansive views bounded by the snowy mountains of Abruzzo. At every step were objects which would have afforded pleasure to a tranquil mind ; the beautifully variegated marbles that formed the cliffs immediately above, their fractured masses embossed with mosses and flowers of every vivid hue that paints the rainbow ; the elegance of the shrubs that tufted, and the majestic grace of the palms which waved over them, would have charmed almost any other eye than Ellena's, whose spirit was wrapt in care, or than those of her companions, whose hearts were dead to feeling. Partial features of the vast edifice she was approaching appeared now and then between the trees ; the tall west window of the cathedral, with the spires that overtopped it ; the narrow pointed roofs of the cloisters ; angles of the insurmountable walls which fenced the garden from the precipices below, and. the dark portal leading into the chief court ; each of these, seen at intervals beneath the gloom of cypress and spreading cedar, seemed as if menacing the unhappy Ellena with hints of future suffering. She passed several shrines and images half hid among the shrubs and the cliffs ; and, when she drew near the monastery, her companions stopped at a little chapel which stood beside the path, where, after examining some papers, an act which she observed with surprise, they drew aside, as if to consult respecting herself. Their conversation was delivered in voices so low that she could not catch a single tone distinctly, and it is probable that if she could, this would not have assisted her in conjecturing who they were ; yet the profound silence they had hitherto observed had much increased her curiosity now that they spoke.

One of them soon after quitted the chapel and proceeded alone to the monastery, leaving Ellena in the custody of his comrade, whose pity she now made a last, though almost hopeless, effort to interest. He replied to all her entreaties only by a waving of the hand, and an averted face ; and she endeavoured to meet with fortitude and to endure with patience the evil which she could neither avoid nor subdue. The spot where she awaited the return of the ruffian, was not of a character to promote melancholy, except, indeed. that luxurious and solemn kind of melancholy which a view of stupendous objects inspires. It overlooked the whole extent of plains, of which she had before caught partial scenes, with the vast chain of mountains, which seemed to form an insurmountable rampart to the rich landscape at their feet. Their towering and fantastic summits, crowding together into dusky air, like flames tapering to a point, exhibited images of peculiar grandeur, while each minuter line and feature withdrawing at this evening hour from observation, seemed to resolve itself into the more gigantic masses, to which the dubious tint, the solemn obscurity, that began to prevail over them gave force and loftier character. The silence and deep repose of the landscape served to impress this character more awfully on the heart; and while Ellena sat wrapt in the thoughtfulness it promoted, the vesper-service of the monks, breathing softly from the cathedral above, came to her ear.; it was a music which might be said to win on silence, and was in perfect unison with her feelings ; solemn, deep, and full, it swelled in holy peals, and rolled away .in murmurs, which attention pursued to the last faint note that melted into air. Ellena's heart owned the power of this high minstrelsy ; and while

she caught for a moment the sweeter voices of the nuns mingling in the choral response, she indulged a hope that they would not be wholly insensible to her sufferings, and that she should receive some consolation from sympathy as soft as these tender-breathing strains appeared to indicate.

She had rested nearly half an hour on the turfy slope, before the chapel, when she perceived through the twilight two monks descending from the monastery towards the spot where she sat. As they drew near, she distinguished their dress of grey stuff, the hood, the shaven head, where only a coronet of white hair was left, and other ensigns of their particular order. On reaching the chapel, they accosted her companion, with whom they retired a few paces and conversed. Ellena heard, for the first time, the sound of her conductor's voice, and though this was but faintly, she marked it well. The other ruffian did not yet appear, but it seemed evident that these friars had left the convent in consequence of his information ; and sometimes, when she looked upon the taller of the two, she fancied she saw the person of the very man whose absence she had remarked, a conjecture which strengthened while she more accurately noticed him. The portrait had certainly much resemblance in height and bulk ; and the same gaunt awkwardness, which even the cloak of the ruffian had not entirely shrouded, obtruded itself from under the folded garments of the recluse. If countenance, too, might be trusted, this same friar had a ruffian's heart, and his keen and cunning eye seemed habitually upon the watch for prey. His brother of the order showed nothing strongly characteristic, either in his face or manner.

After a private conversation of some length, the friars approached Ellena, and told her that she must accompany them to the convent ; when her disguised conductor, having resigned her to them, immediately departed, and descended the mountain.

Not a word was uttered by either of the party as they pursued the steep tract leading to the gates of this secluded edifice, which were opened to them by a lay-brother, and Ellena entered a spacious court. Three sides of this were inclosed by· lofty buildings lined with ranges of cloisters ; the fourth opened to a garden, shaded with avenues of melancholy cypress, that extended to the cathedral, whose fretted windows and ornamented spires appeared to close the perspective. Other large and .detached buildings skirted the gardens on the left, while, on the right, spacious olive-grounds aud vineyards spread to the cliffs that formed a barrier to all this side of the domain of the convent.

The friar, her conductor, crossed the court to the north wing, and there, ringing a bell, a door was opened by a nun, into whose hands Ellena was given. A significant look was exchanged between the devotees, but no words; the friar departed, and the nun, still silent, conducted her through many solitary passages, where not even a distant footfall echoed, and whose walls were roughly painted with subjects indicatory of the severe superstitions of the place, tending to inspire melancholy awe. Ellena's hope of pity vanished, as her eyes glanced over these symbols of the disposition of the inhabitants, and on the countenance of the recluse, characterised by a gloomy malignity which seemed ready to inflict upon others some portion of the unhappiness she herself suffered. As she glided forward with soundless step, her white drapery floating along these solemn avenues, and her hollow features touched with the mingled light and shadow which the partial rays of a taper she held occasioned, she seemed like a spectre newly risen from the grave, rather than a living being. These passages terminated in the parlour of the abbess, where the nun paused, and, turning to Ellena, said, "It is the hour of vespers; you will wait here till our lady of the convent leaves the church; she would speak with you."

"To what saint is the convent dedicated?" said Ellena: "and who, sister, presides over it?"

The nun gave no reply, and after having eyed the forlorn stranger for a moment with inquisitive ill-nature, quitted the room. The unhappy Ellena had not been left long to her own reflections, when the abbess appeared— a stately lady, apparently occupied with opinions of her own importance, and prepared to receive her guest with rigour and supercilious haughtiness. This abbess, who was herself a woman of some distinction. believed that of all possible crimes, next to that of sacrilege, offences against persons of rank were least pardonable. It is not surprising, therefore, that, supposing Ellena, a young woman of no family, to have sought clandestinely to unite herself with the noble house of Vivaldi, she should feel for her not only disdain, but indignation, and that she should readily consent not only to punish the offender, but, at the same time, to afford means of preserving the ancient dignity of the offended.

"I understand," said the abbess, on whose appearance the alarmed Ellena had arisen, "I understand," said she, without making any signal for her to be seated, "that you are the young person who is arrived from Naples."

"My name is Ellena di Rosalba," said her auditor, recovering some degree of courage from the manner which was designed to depress her.

"I know nothing of your name," replied the superior; "I am informed only that you are sent here to acquire a knowledge of your-self and of your duties. Till the period shall be passed for which you are given into my charge, I shall scrupulously observe the obligations of the troublesome office which my regard for the honour of a noble family has induced me to undertake."

By these words the author and the motives of this extraordinary transaction were at once revealed to Ellena, who was for some moments almost overwhelmed by the sudden horrors that gathered on her mind, and she stood silent and motionless. Fear, shame, and indignation alternately assailed her; and the sting of offended honour, on being suspected, and thus accused, of having voluntarily disturbed the tranquillity, and sought the alliance of any family, and especially of one who disdained her, struck forcibly to her heart; till the pride of conscious worth gradually reviving her courage and fortifying her patience, she demanded by whose will she had been torn from her home, and by whose authority she was now detained, as it appeared, a prisoner.

The abbess, unaccustomed to have her power opposed, or her words questioned, was for a moment too indignant to reply; and Ellena observed, but no longer with dismay, the brooding tempest ready to burst over her head. "It is I only who am injured," said she to herself; "and shall the guilty oppressor triumph, and the innocent sufferer sink under the shame that belongs only to guilt! Never will I yield to a weakness so contemptible. The consciousness of deserving well shall recall my presence of mind, which, permitting me to estimate the characters of my oppressors by their actions, will enable me also to despise their power."

"I must remind you," said the abbess, at length, "that the questions you make are unbecoming in your situation; and that contrition and humility are the best extenuations of error. You may withdraw."

"Most true," replied Ellena, bowing with dignity to the superior; "and I most willingly resign them to my oppressors."

Ellena forbore to make further inquiry or remonstrance; and perceiving that resistance would not only be useless, but degrading, she immediately obeyed the mandate of the abbess, determined, since she must suffer, to suffer, if possible, with firmness and dignity.

She was conducted from the parlour by the recluse who had admitted her, and as she passed through the refectory where the nuns, just returned from vespers, were assembled, their inquisitive glances, their smiles and busy whispers told her that she was not only an object of curiosity, but of suspicion; and that little sympathy could be expected from hearts which even the offices of hourly devotion had not purified from the malignant envy that taught them to exalt themselves upon the humiliation of others,

B

The little room to which Ellena was led, and where, to her great satisfaction, she was left alone, rather deserved the denomination of a cell than of a chamber; since, like those of the nuns, it had only one small lattice, and a mattress, one chair, and a table, with a crucifix and a prayer-book, were all its furniture. Ellena, as she surveyed her melancholy habitation, suppressed a rising sigh, but she could not remain unaffected by recollections, which, on this view of her altered state, crowded to her mind; nor think of Vivaldi far away, perhaps for ever, and, probably, even ignorant of her destination, without bitter tears. But she dried them, as the idea of the Marchesa obtruded on her thoughts, for other emotions than those of grief possessed her. It was to the Marchesa that she especially attributed her present situation; and it now appeared that the family of Vivaldi had not been reluctant only, but positively averse to a connection with hers, contrary to a suggestion of Signora Bianchi, who had represented that it might be supposed only, from their known character, that they would disapprove of the alliance, but of course be reconciled to an event which their haughtiest displeasure never could revoke. This discovery of their absolute rejection awakened all the proper pride which the mistaken prudence of her aunt and her affection for Vivaldi had lulled to rest; and she now suffered the most acute vexation and remorse for having yielded her consent to enter clandestinely into any family. The imaginary honours of so noble an alliance vanished when the terms of obtaining them were considered; and now that the sound mind of Ellena was left to its own judgment, she looked with infinitely more pride and preference upon the industrious means which had hitherto rendered her independent, than on all distinction which might be reluctantly given. The consciousness of worth, which had supported her in the presence of the superior, began to falter. "Her accusation was partly just!" said Ellena, "and I deserve punishment, since I could even for a moment submit to the humiliation of consenting to an alliance which I knew would be unwillingly conferred. But it is not yet too late to retrieve my own esteem by asserting my independence, and resigning Vivaldi for ever. By resigning him! by abandoning him who loves me—abandoning him to misery! Him whom I cannot think of without tears,—to whom my vows have been given,—who may claim me by the sacred remembrance of my dying friend,—him to whom my whole heart is devoted! Oh, miserable alternative!—that I can no longer act justly, but at the expense of all my future happiness! Justly! and would it then be just to abandon him who is willing to resign everything for me,—abandon him to ceaseless sorrow that the prejudices of his family may be gratified?"

Poor Ellena perceived that she could not obey the dictates of a laudable pride without such opposition from her heart as she had never experienced before. Her affections were now too deeply engaged to permit her to act with firmness, at the price of long-suffering. The consideration of resigning Vivaldi was so very grievous that she could scarcely endure to pause upon it for a moment; yet, on the other hand, when she thought of his family, it appeared that she never could consent to make a part of it. She would have blamed the erroneous judgment of Signora Bianchi, whose persuasions had so much assisted in reducing her to the present alternative, had not the tenderness with which she cherished her memory rendered this impossible. All that now remained for her was to endeavour patiently to endure present evils, which she could not conquer; for, to forsake Vivaldi at the price of liberty, should liberty be offered to her on such terms, or to accept him in defiance of honourable pride, should he ever effect her release, appeared to her distracted thoughts almost equally impracticable. But as the probability of his never being able to discover her abode returned to her consideration, the anguish she suffered showed how much more she dreaded to lose than to accept Vivaldi, and that love was, after all, the most powerful affection of her heart.

CHAPTER VII.

VIVALDI, meanwhile ignorant of what had occurred at Villa Altieri, repaired, as he had purposed, to Paluzzi, attended by his servant Paulo. It was deep night before he left Naples, and so anxious was he to conceal himself from observation, that though Paulo carried a torch, he did not permit it to be lighted till after he should have remained some time within the archway, thinking it most prudent to watch a while in secret for his unknown adviser, before he proceeded to examine the fort.

His attendant, Paulo, was a true Neapolitan—shrewd, inquisitive, insinuating, adroit; possessing much of the spirit of intrigue, together with a considerable portion of humour, which displayed itself, not so much in words, as in his manner and countenance, in the archness of his dark, penetrating eye, and in the exquisite adaptation of his gesture to his idea. He was a distinguished favourite with his master, who, if he had not humour himself, had a keen relish of it in others, and who certainly did possess wit, with all its lively accompaniments, in an eminent degree. Vivaldi had been won by the *naïveté* and humour of this man, to allow him an unusual degree of familiarity in conversation; and, as they now walked together towards Paluzzi, he unfolded to Paulo as much of his former adventure there as he judged necessary to interest his curiosity and excite his vigilance. The relation did both. Paulo, however, naturally courageous, was incredulous to superstition of any kind; and, having quickly perceived that his master was not altogether indisposed to attribute to a supernatural cause the extraordinary occurrences at Paluzzi, he began, in his manner, to rally him. But Vivaldi was not in a temper to endure jesting; his mood was grave, even to solemnity, and he yielded, though reluctantly, to the awe which at intervals returned upon him with the force of a magical spell, binding up all his faculties to sternness, and fixing them in expectation. While he was nearly regardless of defence against human agency, his servant was, however, preparing for that alone, and very properly represented the imprudence of going to Paluzzi in darkness. Vivaldi observed that they could not watch for the monk otherwise than in darkness, since the torch which lighted them would also warn him, and he had very particular reasons for watching before he proceeded to examine. He added that after a certain time had elapsed the torch might be lighted at a neighbouring cottage. Paulo objected that, in the meanwhile, the person for whom they watched might escape; and Vivaldi compromised the affair. The torch was lighted, but concealed within a hollow of the cliffs that bordered the road; and the sentinels took their station in darkness within the deep arch, near the spot where Vivaldi had watched with Bonarmo. As they did this, the distant chime of a convent informed Vivaldi that midnight was turned. The sound recalled to his mind the words of Schedoni concerning the vicinity of the convent of the *Black Penitents* to Paluzzi, and he asked Paulo whether this was the chime of that convent. Paulo replied that it was, and that a remarkable circumstance had taught him to remember the *Santa dell Pianto* or *Our Lady of Tears*. "The place, signor, would interest you," said Paulo, "for there are some odd stories told of it; and I am inclined to think that this unknown monk must be one of that society, his conduct is so strange."

"You believe, then, that I am willing to give faith to wonderful stories," said Vivaldi, smiling. "But what have you heard that is so extraordinary respecting this convent? Speak low, or we may be discovered."

"Why, signor, the story is not generally known," said Paulo, in a whisper. "I half promised never to reveal it."

"If you are under any promise of secrecy," interrupted Vivaldi, "I forbid you to tell this wonderful tale, which, however, seems somewhat too big to rest within your brain."

"The story would fain expand itself to yours, signor," said Paulo; "and, as I did

not absolutely promise to conceal it, I am very willing to tell it."

"Proceed, then," said Vivaldi; "but let me once more caution you to speak low."

"You are obeyed, signor. You must know, then, *maestro*, that it was on the eve of the festival of *Santo Marco*, and about six years since——"

"Peace!" said Vivaldi. They were silent; but everything remaining still, Paulo, after some time, ventured to proceed, though in a yet lower whisper. "It was on the eve of the *Santo Marco*, and when the last bell had rung, that a person——" He stopped again, for a rustling sound passed near him.

"You are too late," said a sudden voice beside Vivaldi, who instantly recognised the thrilling accents of the monk. "It is past midnight; she departed an hour ago. Look to your steps!"

Though thrilled by this well-known voice, Vivaldi scarcely yielded to his feelings for a moment, but, checking the question which would have asked "Who departed?" he, by a sudden spring, endeavoured to seize the intruder, while Paulo, in the first hurry of his alarm, fired a pistol, and then hastened for the torch. So certainly did Vivaldi believe himself to have leaped upon the spot whence the voice proceeded that, on reaching it, he instantly extended his arms, and, searching around, expected every moment to find his enemy in his grasp. Darkness again baffled his attempt.

"You are known," cried Vivaldi; "you shall see me at the *Santa dell Pianto!* What, ho! Paulo, the torch!—the torch!"

Paulo, swift as the wind, appeared with it. "He passed up those steps in the rock, signor; I saw the skirts of his garments ascending!"

"Follow me, then," said Vivaldi, mounting the steps. "Away, away, *maestro!*" rejoined Paulo, impatiently; "but, for Heaven's sake, name no more the convent of the *Santa dell Pianto*; our lives may answer it!"

He followed to the terrace above, where Vivaldi, holding high the torch, looked round for the monk. The place, however, as far as his eye could penetrate, was forsaken and silent. The glare of the torch enlightened only the rude walls of the citadel, somepoints of the cliff below, and some tall pines that waved over them, leaving in doubtful gloom many a recess of the ruin, and many a tangled thicket that spread among the rocks beyond.

"Do you perceive any person, Paulo?" said Vivaldi, waving the torch in the air to rouse the flame.

"Among those arches on the left, signor, those arches that stand duskily beyond the citadel, I thought I saw a shadowy sort of a figure pass. He might be a ghost, by his silence, for aught I know, *maestro*; but he seems to have a good mortal instinct in taking care of himself, and to have as swift a pair of heels to assist in carrying him off as any lazaro in Naples need desire."

"Fewer words, and more caution!" said Vivaldi, lowering the torch, and pointing it towards the quarter which Paulo had mentioned. "Be vigilant, and tread lightly."

"You are obeyed, signor; but their eyes will inform them, though their ears refuse, while we hold a light to our own steps."

"Peace with this buffoonery!" said Vivaldi, somewhat sternly; "follow in silence, and be on your guard."

Paulo submitted, and they proceeded towards the range of arches which communicated with the building, whose singular structure had formerly arrested the attention of Bonarmo, and whence Vivaldi himself had returned with such unexpected precipitancy and consternation.

On perceiving the place he was approaching he suddenly stopped, and Paulo, observing his agitation, and probably not relishing the adventure, endeavoured to dissuade him from further research. "For we know not who may inhabit this gloomy place, signor, or their numbers, and we are only two of us after all. Besides, signor, it was through that door, yonder," and he pointed to the very spot whence Vivaldi had formerly issued, "through that door that I fancied just now I saw something pass."

"Are you certain as to this?" said Vivaldi, with increased emotion. "What was its form?"

"It was so dusky thereabouts, maestro, that I could not distinguish."

Vivaldi's eyes were fixed upon the building, and a violent conflict of feeling seemed to shake his soul. A few seconds decided it. "I will go on," said he, "and terminate, at any hazard, this state of intolerable anxiety. Paulo, pause a moment, and consider well whether you can depend on your courage, for it may be severely tried. If you can, descend with me in silence, and I warn you to be wary; if you cannot, I will go alone."

"It is too late now, signor, to ask myself that question," replied Paulo, with a submissive air; "and if I had not settled it long ago, I should not have followed you thus far. My courage, signor, you never doubted before."

"Come on then," said Vivaldi. He drew his sword, and, entering the narrow doorway, the torch, which he had now resigned to Paulo, showed a stone passage, that was, however, interminable to the eye.

As they proceeded, Paulo observed that the walls were stained in several places with what appeared to be blood, but prudently forbore to point this out to his master, observing the strict injunction of silence he had received.

Vivaldi stepped cautiously, and often paused to listen, after which he went on with a quicker pace, making signs only to Paulo to follow and be vigilant. The passage terminated in a staircase that seemed to lead to vaults below. Vivaldi remembered the light which had formerly appeared there; and, as recollections of the past gathered on his mind, he faltered in his purpose.

Again he paused, looked back upon Paulo, but was once more going forward, when Paulo himself seized him by the arm. "Stop! signor," said he in a low voice. "Do you not distinguish a figure standing yonder in the gloom?"

Vivaldi, looking forward, perceived, indistinctly, something as of human form, but motionless and silent. It stood at the dusky extremity of the avenue, near the staircase. Its garments, if garments they were, were dark; but its whole figure was so faintly traced to the eye, that it was impossible to ascertain whether this was the monk. Vivaldi took the light, and held it forward, endeavouring to distinguish the object before he ventured further; but the inquiry was useless, and, resigning the torch to Paulo, he rushed on. When he reached the head of the staircase, however, the form, whatever it might be, was gone. Vivaldi had heard no footstep. Paulo pointed out the exact spot where it had stood, but no vestige of it appeared. Vivaldi called loudly upon the monk, but he heard only the lengthening echoes of his own voice revolving among the chambers below; and, after hesitating a while on the head of the stairs, he descended.

Paulo had not followed down many steps when he called out, "It is there, signor; I see it again! and now it flits away through the door that opens to the vaults!"

Vivaldi pursued so swiftly that Paulo could scarcely follow fast enough with the light; and as at length he rested to take breath, he perceived himself in the same spacious chamber to which he had formerly descended. At this moment Paulo observed his countenance change. "You are ill, signor," said he. "In the name of our holy saint, let us quit this hideous place! Its inhabitants can be nothing good, and no good can come of our remaining here."

Vivaldi made no reply; he drew breath with difficulty, and his eyes remained fixed on the ground, till a noise, like the creaking of a heavy hinge, rose in a distant part of the vault. Paulo turned his eyes, at the same instant, towards the place whence it came, and they both perceived a door in the wall slowly opened and immediately closed again, as if the person within had feared to be discovered. Each believed, from the transient view he had of it, that this was the same figure which had appeared on the staircase, and that it was the monk himself. Reanimated by this belief, Vivaldi's nerves were instantly rebraced, and he sprang to the door, which was unfastened, and yielded immediately to his impetuous hand. "You shall not deceive me now," cried he, as he entered; "Paulo, keep guard at the door!"

He looked round the second vault in which he now found himself, but no person appeared; he examined the place, and particularly the walls, without discovering any aperture, either of door or window, by which the figure could have quitted the chamber; a strongly-grated casement, placed near the roof, was all that admitted air, and probably light. Vivaldi was astonished! "Have you seen anything pass?" said he to Paulo.

"Nothing, *maestro*," replied the servant.

"This is almost incredible," exclaimed Vivaldi. "'Tis certain this form can be nothing human!"

"If so, signor," observed Paulo, "why should it fear us? as surely it does; or why should it have fled?"

"That is not so certain," rejoined Vivaldi; "it may have fled only to lead us into evil. But bring hither the torch; here is something in the wall which I would examine."

Paulo obeyed. It was merely a ruggedness in the stones, not the partition of a door, that had excited his curiosity. "This is inexplicable!" exclaimed Vivaldi, after a long pause. "What motive could any human being have for thus tormenting me?"

"Or any being superhuman, either, my signor?" said Paulo.

"I am warned of evils that await me," continued Vivaldi, musing; "of events that are regularly fulfilled; the being who warns me crosses my path perpetually, yet, with the cunning of a demon, as constantly eludes my grasp, and baffles my pursuit! It is incomprehensible by what means he glides thus away from my eye, and fades, as if into air, at my approach! He is repeatedly in my presence, yet is never to be found!"

"It is most true, signor," said Paulo, "that he is never to be found, and therefore let me entreat you to give up the pursuit. This place is enough to make one believe in the horrors of purgatory! Let us go, signor."

"What but spirit could have quitted this vault so mysteriously?" continued Vivaldi, not attending to Paulo. "What but spirit——"

"I would fain prove," said the servant, "that substance can quit it as easily; I would fain evaporate through that door myself."

He had scarcely spoken the words when the door closed with a thundering clap that echoed through all the vaults. Vivaldi and Paulo stood for a moment aghast, and then both hastened to open it, and to leave the place. Their consternation may be easily conceived when they found that all their efforts at the door were ineffectual. The thick wood was inlaid with solid bars of iron,

and was of such unconquerable strength that it evidently guarded what had been designed for a prison, and appeared to be the keep or dungeon of the ancient fort.

"Ah, signor *mio!*" said Paulo, "if this was a spirit, 'tis plain he knew we were not so, by his luring us hither. Would we could exchange natures with him for a moment; for I know not how, as mere mortal men, we can ever squeeze ourselves out of this scrape. You must allow, *maestro*, that this was not one of the evils he warned you of; or, if he did, it was through my organs, for I entreated you——"

"Peace, good Signor *Buffo!*" said Vivaldi. "A truce with this nonsense, and assist in searching for some means of escape."

Vivaldi again examined the walls, and as unsuccessfully as before; but in one corner of the vault lay an object which seemed to tell the fate of one who had been confined here, and to hint his own: it was a garment covered with blood. Vivaldi and his servant discovered it at the same instant; and a dreadful foreboding of their own destiny fixed them, for some moments, to the spot. Vivaldi first recovered himself, when, instead of yielding to despondency, all his faculties were aroused to devise some means for escaping; but Paulo's hopes seemed buried beneath the dreadful vestments upon which he still gazed. "Ah, my signor!" said he, at length, in a faltering accent, "who shall dare to raise that garment? What if it should conceal the mangled body whose blood has stained it?"

Vivaldi shudderingly turned to look on it again.

"It moves!" exclaimed Paulo. "I see it move!" as he said which, he started to the opposite side of the chamber. Vivaldi stepped a few paces back, and as quickly returned; when, determined to know the event at once, he raised the garment upon the point of his sword, and perceived, beneath, other remains of dress, heaped high together, while even the floor below was stained with gore.

Believing that fear had deceived the eyes of Paulo, Vivaldi watched this horrible spectacle for some time, but without perceiving the least motion; when he became convinced that not any remains of life were shrouded beneath it, and that it contained only articles of dress which had belonged to some unfortunate person who had probably been decoyed hither for plunder, and afterwards murdered. This belief, and the repugnance he felt to dwell upon the spectacle, prevented him from examining further, and he turned away to a remote part of the vault. A conviction of his own fate, and of his servant's, filled his mind for a while with despair. It appeared that he had been ensnared by robbers; till, as he recollected the circumstances which had attended his entrance, and the several peculiar occurrences connected with the archway, this conjecture seemed highly improbable. It was unreasonable that robbers should have taken the trouble to decoy, when they might at first have seized him; still more so that they would have persevered so long in the attempt; and most of all, that when he had formerly been in their power, they should have neglected their opportunity, and suffered him to leave the ruin unmolested. Yet granting that all this, improbable as it was, were, however, possible, the solemn warnings and predictions of the monk, so frequently delivered and so faithfully fulfilled, could have no connection with the schemes of banditti. It appeared, therefore, that Vivaldi was not in the hands of robbers; or, if he were, that the monk, at least, had no connection with them: yet it was certain that he had just heard the voice of this monk beneath the arch; that his servant had said he saw the vestments of one ascending the steps of the fort; and that they had both reason afterward to believe it was his shadowy figure which they had pursued to the very chamber where they were now confined.

As Vivaldi considered all these circumstances, his perplexity increased, and he was more than ever inclined to believe that the form which had assumed the appearance of a monk was something superhuman.

"If this being had *appeared only*," said he to himself, "I should, perhaps, have thought it the perturbed spirit of him who doubtless has been murdered here, and that it led me hither to discover the deed, that his bones might be removed to holy ground; but this monk, or whatever it is, was neither silent nor apparently anxious concerning himself; he spoke only of events connected with my peace, and predicted of the future, as well as reverted to the past. If he had either hinted of himself or had been wholly silent, his appearance and manner of eluding pursuit are so extraordinary that I should have yielded for once, perhaps, to the tales of our grandfathers, and thought he was the spectre of a murdered person."

As Vivaldi expressed his incredulity, however, he returned to examine the garment once more, when, as he raised it, he observed, what had before escaped his notice, black drapery mingled with the heap beneath; and, on lifting this also with the point of his sword, he perceived part of the habiliment of a monk! He started at the discovery as if he had seen the apparition which had so long been tempting his credulity. Here were the vest and scapulary, rent and stained with blood! Having gazed for a moment, he let them drop upon the heap, when Paulo, who had been silently observing him, exclaimed:

"Signor! that should be the garment of the demon who led us hither. Is it a winding-sheet for us, *maestro?* or was it one for the body he inhabited while on earth?"

"Neither, I trust," replied Vivaldi, endeavouring to command the perturbation he suffered, and turning from the spectacle, "therefore we will try once more to regain our liberty."

This was a design, however, beyond his accomplishment; and, having again attacked the door, raised Paulo to the grated window, and vociferated for release with his utmost strength, in which he was very ably seconded by Paulo, he abandoned for the present all further attempts, and, weary and desponding, threw himself on the ground of the dungeon.

Paulo bitterly lamented his master's rashness in penetrating to this remote spot, and bewailed the probability of their being famished.

"For, supposing, signor, that we were not decoyed hither for plunder and butchery, and supposing we are not surrounded by malicious spirits—which San Januarius forbid I should take upon me to affirm is impossible!—supposing all this, signor, yet still there remains almost a certainty of our being starved to death; for how is it possible that anybody can hear our cries in a place so remote from all resort, and buried, as one may say, underground, as this is?"

"Thou art an excellent comforter," said Vivaldi, groaning.

"You must allow, signor, that you are even with me," replied Paulo, "and that you are as excellent a conductor."

Vivaldi gave no answer, but lay on the ground, abandoned to agonising thought. He had now leisure to consider the late words of the monk, and to conjecture, for he was in a mood for conjecturing the worst, that they not only alluded to Ellena, but that his saying "she had departed an hour ago," was a figurative manner of telling that she had died then. This was a conjecture which dispelled almost all apprehension for himself. He started from the ground, and paced his prison with quick and unequal steps; it was now no longer a heavy despondency that oppressed him, but an acute anxiety that stung him, and, with the tortures of suspense, brought also those of passionate impatience and horror concerning the fate of Ellena. The longer he dwelt upon the possibility of her death, the more probable it appeared. This monk had already forewarned him of the death of Bianchi; and when he recollected the suspicious circumstances which had attended it, his terrors for Ellena increased. The more he yielded to his feelings, the more violent they became, till, at length, his ungovernable impatience and apprehension arose almost to frenzy.

Paulo forgot, for a while, his own situation in the superior sufferings of his master, and now, at least, endeavoured to perform the offices of a comforter, for he tried to calm Vivaldi's mind by selecting the fairest circumstances for hope which the subject admitted, and he passed without noticing, or, if noticing, only lightly touched upon, the most prominent possibilities of evil. His master, however, was insensible to all he said, till he mentioned again the Convent dell' Pianto; and this subject, as it seemed connected with the monk, who had hinted the fate of Ellena, interested the unhappy Vivaldi, who withdrew awhile from his own reflections to listen to a recital which might assist his conjectures.

Paulo complied with his command, but not without reluctance. He looked round the empty vault, as if he feared that some person might be lurking in the obscurity who would overhear and even answer him.

"We are tolerably retired here, too, signor," said he, recollecting himself; "one may venture to talk secrets with little danger of being discovered. However, maestro, it is best to make matters quite sure; and, therefore, if you will please to take a seat on the ground, I will stand beside you and relate all I know of the convent of *Our Lady of Tears*, which is not much after all."

Vivaldi having seated himself and bidden Paulo do the same, the servant began in a low voice—"It was on the vigil of *San Marco*, just after the last vesper-bell had tolled—you never were at *Santa Maria dell' Pianto*, signor, or you would know what a gloomy old church it has—it was in a confessional in one of the side aisles of this church, and just after the last bell had ceased, that a person, so muffled up that neither face nor shape could be distinguished, came and placed himself on the steps of one of the boxes adjoining the confessional chair; but if he had been as airily dressed as yourself, signor, he might have been just as well concealed; for that dusky aisle is lighted only by one lamp, which hangs at the end next the painted window, except when the tapers at the shrine of San Antonio happen to be burning at the other extremity, and even then the place is almost as gloomy as this vault. But that is, no doubt, contrived for the purpose that people may not blush for the sins they confess; and, in good faith, this is an accommodation which may bring more money to the poor-box, for the monks have a shrewd eye that way, and ——"

"You have dropped the thread of your story," said Vivaldi.

"True, signor, let me recollect where I lost it—oh! at the steps of the confessional. The stranger knelt down upon them, and for some time poured such groans into the ear of the confessor as were heard all along the aisle. You are to know, signor, that the brothers of the *Santa dell' Pianto* are of the order of *Black Penitents*; and people who have more than their ordinary to confess

sometimes go there to consult with the grand penitentiary what is to be done. Now it *happened* that Father Ansaldo, the grand penitentiary himself, was in the chair, as is *customary* on the vigil of the *Santo Marco*; and he gently reproved the penitent for bewailing so loud, and bade him take comfort; when the other replied only by a groan deeper than before, but it was not so loud, and then proceeded to confess. But what he did confess, signor, I know not; for the confessor, you know, never must divulge, except, indeed, on very extraordinary occasions. It was, however, something so very strange and horrible that the grand penitentiary suddenly quitted the chair, and before he reached the cloisters he fell into strong convulsions. On recovering himself, he asked the people about him whether the penitent who had visited such a confessional, naming it, was gone; adding, that if he was still in the church it was proper he should be detained. He described, at the same time, as well as he could, the sort of figure he had dimly seen approaching the confessional just before he had received the confession, at recollecting which he seemed ready to go off again into his convulsions. One of the fathers, who had crossed the aisle, on his way to the cloisters, upon the first alarm of Ansaldo's disorder, remembered that a person such as was described had passed him hastily. He had seen a tall figure, muffled up in the habit of a white friar, gliding swiftly along the aisle, towards the door which opened into the outer court of the convent; but he was himself too much engaged to notice the stranger particularly. Father Ansaldo thought this must be the person; and the porter was summoned, and asked whether he had observed such a one pass. He affirmed that he had not seen any person go forth from the gate within the last quarter of an hour; which might be true enough, you know, signor, if the rogue had been off his post. But he further said that no one had entered, during the whole evening, habited in white, as the stranger was described to be; so the porter proved himself to be a vigilant watchman; for he must have been fast asleep too, or how could this personage have entered the convent, and left it again, without being seen by him?"

"In white, was he?" said Vivaldi. "If he had been in black, I should have thought this must have been the monk, my tormentor."

"Why, you know, signor, that occurred to me before," observed Paulo; "and a man might easily change his dress, if that were all."

"Proceed," said Vivaldi.

"Hearing this account from the porter," continued Paulo, "the fathers believed, one and all, that the stranger must be secreted within the walls · and the convent, with every part of the precincts, was searched; but no person was found!"

"This must certainly be the monk," said Vivaldi, "notwithstanding the difference of his habit; there surely cannot be two beings in the world who would conduct themselves in this same mysterious manner!"

Vivaldi was interrupted by a low sound, which seemed, to his distracted fancy, to proceed from a dying person. Paulo also heard it; he started, and they both listened with intense and almost intolerable expectation.

"Ah!" said Paulo, at length, "it was only the wind."

"It was no more," said Vivaldi; "proceed therefore."

"From the period of this strange confession," resumed Paulo, "Father Ansaldo was never properly himself, he ——"

"Doubtless the crime confessed related to himself," observed Vivaldi.

"Why, no, signor, I never heard that that was the case; and some remarkable circumstances which followed seemed to prove it otherwise. About a month after the time I have mentioned, on the evening of a sultry day, when the monks were retiring from the last service ——"

"Hark!" cried Vivaldi.

"I hear whispers," said Paulo, whispering himself.

"Be still!" said Vivaldi.

They listened attentively, and heard a murmuring, as of voices; but could not ascertain whether they came from the adjoining vault, or arose from beneath the one in which they were. The sound returned at intervals; and the persons who conversed, whatever they were, seemingly restrained their voices, as if they feared to be heard. Vivaldi considered whether it were better to discover himself, and call for assistance, or to remain still.

"Remember, signor," said Paulo, "what a chance we have of being starved, unless we venture to discover ourselves to these people, or whatever they are."

"Venture!" exclaimed Vivaldi. "What has such a wretch as I to do with fear! Oh, Ellena, Ellena!"

He instantly called loudly to the persons whom he believed he had heard, and was seconded by Paulo; but their continued vociferations availed them nothing; no answer was returned; and even the indistinct sounds which had awakened their attention were heard no more.

At length, exhausted by their efforts, they laid down on the floor of the dungeon, abandoning all other attempts at escape till the morning light might assist them.

Vivaldi had no further spirits to inquire for the remainder of Paulo's narrative. Almost despairing for himself, he could not feel an interest concerning strangers; for he had already perceived that it could not afford him information connected with Ellena; and Paulo, who had roared himself hoarse, was very willing to be silent.

CHAPTER VIII.

DURING several days after Ellena's arrival at the monastery of San Stefano she was not permitted to leave her room. The door was locked upon her, and not any person appeared except a nun, who brought her a scanty portion of food, and who was the same that had first admitted her into that part of the convent appropriated to the abbess.

On the fourth day, when, probably, it was believed that her spirits were subdued by confinement, and by her experience of the suffering she had to expect from resistance, she was summoned to the parlour. The abbess was alone, and the air of austerity with which she regarded Ellena prepared the latter to endure.

After an exordium on the heinousness of her offence, and the necessity there was for taking measures to protect the peace and dignity of a noble family, which her late conduct had nearly destroyed, the superior informed her that she must determine either to accept the veil, or the person whom the Marchesa di Vivaldi had, of her great goodness, selected for her husband.

"You never can be sufficiently grateful," added the abbess, "for the generosity the Marchesa displays in allowing you a choice on the subject. After the injury you have endeavoured to inflict upon her and her family, you could not expect that any indulgence would be shown you. It was natural to suppose that the Marchesa would have punished you with severity; instead of which, she allows you to enter into our society; or, if you have not strength of mind sufficient to enable you to renounce a sinful world, she permits you to return into it, and gives you a suitable partner to support you through its cares and toils,—a partner much more according with your circumstances than him to whom you had the temerity to lift your eye."

Ellena blushed at this coarse appeal to her pride, and persevered in a disdainful silence. Thus to give to injustice the colouring of mercy, and to acts most absolutely tyrannical the softening tints of generosity, excited her honest indignation. She was not, however, shocked by a discovery of the designs formed against her, since, from the moment of her arrival at San Stefano, she had expected something terribly severe, and had prepared her mind to meet it with fortitude; for she believed that, so supported, she should weary the malice of her enemies, and finally triumph over misfortune. It was only when she thought of Vivaldi that her courage failed, and that the injuries she endured seemed too heavy to be long sustained.

"You are silent," said the abbess, after a pause of expectation. "Is it possible, then, that you can be ungrateful for the generosity of the Marchesa? But, though you may at present be insensible to her goodness, I will forbear to take advantage of this insensibility, and will still allow you liberty of choice. You may retire to your chamber, to consider and to decide. But remember that you must abide by the determination you shall avow; and that you will be allowed no appeal from the alternatives which are now placed before you. If you reject the veil, you must accept the husband who is offered you."

"It is unnecessary," said Ellena, with an air of dignified tranquillity, "that I should withdraw for the purposes of considering and deciding. My resolution is already taken, and I reject each of the offered alternatives. I will neither condemn myself to a cloister, or to the degradation with which I am threatened on the other hand. Having said this, I am prepared to meet whatever suffering you shall inflict upon me; but be assured that my own voice never shall sanction the evils to which I may be subjected, and that the immortal love of justice, which fills all my heart, will sustain my courage no less powerfully than the sense of what is due to my own character. You are now acquainted with my sentiments and my resolutions; I shall repeat them no more."

The abbess, whose surprise had thus long suffered Ellena to speak, still fixed upon her a stern regard, as she said, "Where is it that you have learned these heroics, and acquired the rashness which thus prompts you to avow them?—the boldness which enables you to insult your superior, a priestess of your holy religion, even in her sanctuary!"

"The sanctuary is profaned," said Ellena, mildly, but with dignity: "it is become a prison. It is only when the superior ceases to respect the precepts of that holy religion, the precepts which teach her justice and benevolence, that she herself is no longer respected. The very sentiment which bids us revere its mild and beneficent laws, bids us also reject the violators of them: when you command me to reverence my religion, you urge me to condemn yourself."

"Withdraw!" said the abbess, rising impatiently from her chair; "your admonition, so becomingly delivered, shall not be forgotten."

Ellena willingly obeyed, and was led back to her cell, where she sat down pensively, and reviewed her conduct. Her judgment approved of the frankness with which she had asserted her rights, and of the firmness with which she had reproved a woman who had dared to demand respect from the very victim

of her cruelty and oppression. She was the more satisfied with herself because she had never, for an instant, forgotten her own dignity so far as to degenerate into the vehemence of passion, or to falter with the weakness of fear. Her conviction of the abbess's unworthy character was too clear to allow Ellena to feel abashed in her presence; for she regarded only the censure of the good, to which she had ever been as tremblingly alive as she was obdurately insensible to that of the vicious.

Ellena, having now asserted her resolutions, determined to avoid, if possible, all repetitions of scenes like the last, and to repel, by silence only, whatever indignity might be offered her. She knew that she must suffer, and she resolved to endure. Of the three evils which were placed before her, that of confinement, with all its melancholy accompaniments, appeared considerably less severe than either the threatened marriage or a formal renunciation of the world; either of which would devote her, during life, to misery, and that by her own act. Her choice, therefore, had been easy, and the way was plain before her. If she could support with calmness the hardships which she could not avoid, half their weight would be unfelt; and she now most strenuously endeavoured to attain the strength of mind which was necessary for the practice of such equanimity.

For several days after the late interview with the abbess she was kept a close prisoner; but on the fifth evening she was permitted to attend vespers. As she walked through the garden to the chapel, the ordinary freshness of the open air and the verdure of the trees and shrubs were luxuries to her who had so long been restricted from the blessings of nature. She followed the nuns to a chapel where they usually performed their religious duties, and was there seated among the novices. The solemnity of the service, and particularly of those parts which were accompanied by music, touched all her heart, and soothed and elevated her spirit.

Among the voices of the choir was one whose expression immediately fixed her attention; it seemed to speak a loftier sentiment of devotion than the others, and to be modulated by the melancholy of a heart that had long since taken leave of this world. Whether it swelled with the high peal of the organ, or mingled in low and trembling accents with the sinking chorus, Ellena felt that she understood all the feelings of the breast from which it flowed; and she looked to the gallery where the sisters were assembled, to discover a countenance that might seem to accord with the sensibility expressed in the voice. As no strangers were admitted to the chapel, some of the devotees had thrown back their veils, and she saw little that interested her in

their various faces ; but the figure and attitude of a nun, kneeling in a remote part of
the gallery, beneath a lamp which threw its
rays aslant her head, perfectly agreed with
the idea she had formed of the singer, and
the sound seemed to approach immediately
from that direction. Her face was concealed
by a black veil, whose transparency, however,
permitted the fairness of her complexion to
appear ; but the air of her head and the
singularity of her attitude, for she was the
only person who remained kneeling, sufficiently indicated the superior degree of fer-
vency and penitence which the voice had
expressed.

When the hymn had ceased she rose from
her knees, and Ellena, soon after, observing
her throw back her veil, discovered, by the
lamp, which shed its full light upon her features, a countenance that instantly confirmed
her conjecture. It was touched with a melancholy kind of resignation ; yet grief seemed
still to occasion the paleness and the air of
languor that prevailed over it, and which disappeared only when the momentary energy
of devotion seemed to lift her spirit above
this world, and to impart to it somewhat of a
seraphic grandeur.   At those moments her
blue eyes were raised towards Heaven with
such meek, yet fervent love, such sublime enthusiasm as the heads of Guido sometimes
display, and which renewed with Ellena all
the enchanting effect of the voice she had
just heard.

While she regarded the nun with a degree
of interest which rendered her insensible to
every other object in the chapel, she fancied
she could perceive the calmness in her countenance to be that of despair, rather than of
resignation ; for, when her thoughts were not
elevated in prayer, there was frequently a
fixedness in her look too energetic for common suffering, or for the temper of mind
which may lead to perfect resignation. It
had, however, much that attached the sympathy of Ellena, and much that seemed to
speak a similarity of feeling. Ellena was not
only soothed, but in some degree comforted,
while she gazed upon her ; a selfishness which
may, perhaps, be pardoned, when it is considered that she thus knew there was one
human being, at least, in the convent who
must be capable of feeling pity and willing
to administer consolation. Ellena endeavoured to meet her eye, that she might inform
her of the regard she had inspired, and
express her own unhappiness ; but the recluse
was so entirely devoted that she did not
succeed.

As they left the chapel, however, the sister
passed close by Ellena, who threw back her
veil and fixed upon her a look so supplicating
and expressive that the nun paused, and in
her turn regarded the novice, not with surprise only, but with a mixture of curiosity and

compassion. A faint blush crossed her cheek,
her spirits seemed to falter, and she was unwilling to withdraw her eyes from Ellena :
but it was necessary that she should continue
in the procession, and, bidding her farewell
by a smile of ineffable pity, she passed on to
the court, while Ellena followed with attention still fixed upon the nun, who soon disappeared beyond the doorway of the abbess's
apartment, and Ellena had nearly reached
her own before her thoughts were sufficiently
disengaged to permit her to inquire the name
of the stranger.

"It is sister Olivia whom you mean, perhaps," said her conductress.

"She is very handsome," said Ellena.

"Many of the sisters are so," replied Margaritone, with an air of pique.

"Undoubtedly," said Ellena ; "but she
whom I mean has a most touching countenance—frank, noble, and full of sensibility ;
and there is a gentle melancholy in her eye
which cannot but interest all who observe
her."

Ellena was so [fascinated by this interesting nun that she forgot she was describing
her to a person whose callous heart rendered
her insensible to the influence of any countenance except, perhaps, the commanding one
of the lady abbess, and to whom, therefore,
a description of the fine traits which Ellena
felt, was as unintelligible as would have been
an Arabic inscription.

"She is past the bloom of youth," continued Ellena, still anxious to be understood ;
"but she retains all its interesting graces, and
adds to them the dignity of ——"

"If you mean that she is of middle age,"
interrupted Margaritone, peevishly, "it is
sister Olivia you mention, for we are all
younger than she is."

Ellena, raising her eyes almost unconsciously as the nun spoke this, fixed them
upon a face sallow, meagre, seemingly near
fifty years an inhabitant of this world ; and
she could scarcely conceal the surprise she
felt on perceiving such wretched vanity lingering among the chilled passions of so repulsive a frame, and within the sequestered
shade of a cloister. Margaritone, still jealous
of the praise bestowed on Olivia, repelled all
further inquiry, and having attended Ellena
to her cell locked her up for the night.

On the following evening Ellena was again
permitted to attend vespers, and, on the way
to the chapel, the hope of seeing her interesting favourite reanimated her spirits. In the
same part of the gallery as on the preceding
night she again appeared, and kneeling as
before beneath the lamp in private orison, for
the service was not begun.

Ellena endeavoured to subdue the impatience she felt to express her regard and to
be noticed by the holy sister till she should
have finished. When the nun rose and ob-

served Ellena, she lifted her veil, and, fixing on her the same inquiring eye, her countenance brightened into a smile so full of compassion and intelligence that Ellena, forgetting the decorum of the place, left her seat to approach her; it seemed as if the soul which beamed forth in that smile had long been acquainted with hers. As she advanced, the nun dropped her veil, a reproof which she immediately understood, and she withdrew to her seat: but her attention remained fixed on the recluse during the whole service.

At the conclusion, when they left the chapel, and she saw Olivia pass without noticing her, Ellena could scarcely restrain her tears; she returned in deep dejection to her room. The regard of this nun was not only delightful, but seemed necessary to her heart, and she dwelt, with fond perseverance, on the smile that had expressed so much, and which threw one gleam of comfort even through the bars of her prison.

Her reverie was soon interrupted by a light step that approached her cell, and in the next moment the door was unlocked, and Olivia herself appeared. Ellena rose with emotion to meet her; the nun held forth her hand to receive hers.

"You are unused to confinement," said she, mournfully, and placing on the table a little basket containing refreshment, "and our hard fare ——"

"I understand you," said Ellena, with a look expressive of her gratitude. "You have a heart that can pity, though you inhabit these walls; you have suffered too, and know the delicate generosity of softening the sorrows of others by any attention that may tell them your sympathy. Oh! if I could express how much the sense of this affects me!"

Tears interrupted her. Olivia pressed her hand, looked steadily upon her face, and was somewhat agitated; but she soon recovered apparent tranquillity, and said, with a serious smile. "You judge rightly, my sister, respecting my sentiments, however you may err concerning my sufferings. My heart is not insensible to pity, nor to you, my child. You were designed for happier days than you may hope to find within these cloisters."

She checked herself, as if she had allowed too much, and then added, "But you may, perhaps, be peaceful; and since it consoles you to know that you have a friend near you, believe me that friend—but believe it in silence. I will visit you when I am permitted —but do not inquire for me; and if my visits are short, do not press me to lengthen them."

"How good this is!" said Ellena, in a tremulous voice. "How sweet too it is! You will visit me, and I am pitied by you!"

"Hush!" said the nun, expressively; "no more; I may be observed. Good night, my sister; may your slumbers be light!"

Ellena's heart sank. She had not spirits to say "Good night!" but her eyes, covered with tears, said more. The nun turned her own away suddenly, and pressing her hand in silence, left the cell. Ellena, firm and tranquil under the insults of the abbess, was now melted into tears by the kindness of a friend. These gentle tears were refreshing to her long-oppressed spirits, and she indulged them. Of Vivaldi she thought with more composure than she had done since she left Altieri; and something like hope began to revive in her heart, though reflection offered little to support it.

On the following morning, she perceived that the door of her cell had not been closed. She rose impatiently, and, not without a hope of liberty, immediately passed it. The cell, opening upon a short passage, which communicated with the main building, and which was shut up by a door, was secluded, and almost insulated from every other chamber; and this door being now secured Ellena was as truly a prisoner as before. It appeared, then, that the nun had omitted to fasten the cell only for the purpose of allowing her the convenience of walking in the passage, and she was grateful for the attention. Still more she was so, when, having traversed it, she perceived one extremity terminate in a narrow staircase that appeared to lead to other chambers.

She ascended the winding steps hastily, and found they led only to a door, opening into a small room, where nothing remarkable appeared till she approached the windows, and beheld thence a horizon, and a landscape spread below, whose grandeur awakened all her heart. The consciousness of her prison was lost while her eyes ranged over the wide and really sublime scene without. She perceived that this chamber was within a small turret, projecting from an angle of the convent over the walls, and suspended, as in air, above the vast precipices of granite that formed part of the mountain. These precipices were broken into cliffs, which, in some places, impended far above their base, and in others rose, in nearly perpendicular lines, to the walls of the monastery, which they supported. Ellena, with a dreadful pleasure, looked down them, shagged as they were with larch, and frequently darkened by lines of gigantic pine bending along the rocky ledges, till her eye rested on the thick chestnut woods that extended over their winding base, and which, softening to the plains, seemed to form a gradation between the variegated cultivation there and the awful wildness of the rocks above. Round these extensive plains were tumbled the mountains, of various shape and attitude, which Ellena admired on her approach to San Stefano ; some shaded with forests of olive and almond trees, but the greater part abandoned to the flocks, which in summer feed on their aromatic herbage, and on the approach of winter descend to the sheltered plains of the *Tavogliere di Puglia.*

On the left opened the dreadful defile which she had traversed, and the thunder of whose waters now murmured at a distance. The accumulation of overtopping points, which the mountains of this dark perspective exhibited, presented an image of grandeur superior to anything she had seen while within the pass itself.

To Ellena, whose mind was capable of being highly elevated or sweetly soothed by scenes of nature, the discovery of this little turret was an important circumstance. Hither she could come, and her soul, refreshed by the views it afforded, would acquire strength to bear her with equanimity through the persecutions that might await her. Here, gazing upon the stupendous imagery around her, looking as it were beyond the awful veil which obscures the features of the Deity, and conceals him from the eyes of his creatures—dwelling as with a present God in the midst of his sublime works—with a mind thus elevated, how insignificant would appear to her the transactions, and the sufferings of the world ! How poor, too, the boasted power of man, when the fall of a single cliff from these mountains would with ease destroy thousands of his race assembled on the plains below ! How would it avail them that they were accoutred for battle, armed with all the instruments of destruction that human invention ever fashioned ? Thus man, the giant who held her in captivity, would shrink to the diminutiveness of a fairy; and she would experience that his utmost force was unable to enchain her soul, or compel her to fear him, while he was destitute of virtue.

Ellena's attention was recalled from the scene without by a sound from the gallery below, and she then heard a key turning in the door of the passage. Fearing that it was sister Margaritone who approached, and who, informed by her absence of the consolatory turret she had discovered, would perhaps debar her from ever returning to it, Ellena descended with a palpitating heart, and found that nun in the cell. Surprise and severity were on her countenance when she inquired by what means she had unclosed the door, and whither she had been.

Ellena answered, without any prevarication, that she had found the door unfastened, and that she had visited the turret above ; but she forbore to express a wish to return thither, judging that such an expression would certainly exclude her in future. Margaritone, after sharply rebuking her for prying beyond the passage, and having set down the break-

fast she had brought, left the room, the door of which she did not forget to secure. Thus Ellena was at once deprived of so innocent a means of consolation as her pleasant turret had promised.

During several days she only saw the austere nun, except when she attended vespers ; where, however, she was so vigilantly observed that she feared to speak with Olivia, even by her eyes. Olivia's were often fixed upon her face, and with a kind of expression which Ellena, when she did venture to look at her, could not perfectly interpret. It was not only of pity, but of anxious curiosity, and of something also like fear. A blush would sometimes wander over her cheek, which was succeeded by an extreme paleness, and by an air of such universal languor as precedes a fainting fit ; but the exercises of devotion seemed frequently to recall her fleeting spirits, and to elevate them with hope and courage.

When she left the chapel Ellena saw Olivia no more that night ; but on the following morning she came with breakfast to the cell. A character of peculiar sadness was on her brow.

"Oh ! how glad I am to see you," said Ellena ; "and how much I have regretted your long absence ! I was obliged to remember constantly what you had enjoined, to forbear inquiring after you."

The nun replied with a melancholy smile, " I come in obedience to our lady abbess," said she, as she seated herself on Ellena's mattress.

"And did you not wish to come?" said Ellena, mournfully.

" I did wish it," replied Olivia ; "but ——" and she hesitated.

"Whence then this reluctance ?" inquired Ellena.

Olivia was silent a moment.

"You are a messenger of evil news !" said Ellena. "You are only reluctant to afflict me."

"It is as you say," rejoined the nun ; "I am only reluctant to afflict you ; and I fear you have too many attachments to the world to allow you to receive, without sorrow, what I have to communicate. I am ordered to prepare you for the vows, and to say that, since you have rejected the husband which was proposed to you, you are to accept the veil ; that many of the customary forms are to be dispensed with ; and that the ceremony of taking the black veil will follow without delay that of receiving the white one."

The nun paused, and Ellena said, "You are an unwilling bearer of this cruel message ; and I reply only to the lady abbess, when I declare that I never will accept either ; that force may send me to the altar, but that it never shall compel me to utter vows which my heart abhors ; and if I am constrained to appear there, it shall be only to protest against her tyranny, and against the form intended to sanction it."

To Olivia this answer was so far from being displeasing that it appeared to give her satisfaction.

"I dare not applaud your resolution," said she ; "but I will not condemn it. You have, no doubt, connections in the world which would render a seclusion from it afflicting. You have relations, friends, from whom it would be dreadful to part ?"

"I have neither," said Ellena, sighing.

"No ! Can that be possible ? and yet you are so unwilling to retire !"

"I have only one friend," replied Ellena, "and it is of him they would deprive me !"

"Pardon, my love, the abruptness of these inquiries," said Olivia ; "yet, while I entreat your forgiveness, I am inclined to offend again, and to ask your name."

"That is a question I will readily answer. My name is Ellena di Rosalba."

"How ?" said the nun, with an air of deliberation. "Ellena di ——"

"Di Rosalba," repeated her companion. "And permit me to ask your motive for the inquiry : do you know any person of my name ?"

"No," replied the sister, mournfully; "but your features have some resemblance to those of a friend I once had."

As she spoke this, her agitation was apparent, and she rose to go. "I must not lengthen my visit, lest I should be forbidden to repeat it," said she. "What answer shall I give to the abbess ? If you are determined to reject the veil, allow me to advise you to soften your refusal as much as possible. I am, perhaps, better acquainted with her character than you are ; and oh, my sister ! I would not see you pining away your existence in this solitary cell."

"How much I am obliged by the interest you express for my welfare," said Ellena, "and by the advice you offer ! I will yield my judgment in this instance to yours ; you shall modulate my refusal as you think proper : but remember that it must be absolute, and beware lest the abbess should mistake gentleness for irresolution."

"Trust me, I will be cautious in all that relates to you," said Olivia. "Farewell ! I will visit you, if possible, in the evening. In the meantime the door shall be left open, that you may have more air and prospect than this cell affords. That staircase leads to a pleasant chamber."

"I have visited it already," replied Ellena, "and have to thank you for the goodness which permitted me to do so. To go thither will greatly soothe my spirits ; if I had some books, and my drawing-instruments, I could almost forget my sorrows there."

"Could you so ?" said the nun, with an affectionate smile. "Adieu ! I will endea-vour to see you in the evening. If sister Margaritone returns, be careful not to inquire for me ; nor once ask her for the little indulgence I give you."

Olivia withdrew, and Ellena retired to the chamber above, where she lost for a while all sense of sorrow amidst the great scenery which its window exhibited.

At noon the step of Margaritone summoned Ellena from her retreat, and she was surprised that no reproof followed this second discovery of her absence. Margaritone only said that the abbess had the goodness to permit Ellena to dine with the novices, and that she came to conduct her to their table.

Ellena did not rejoice in this permission, preferring to remain in her solitary turret to the being exposed to the examining eyes of strangers; and she followed dejectedly through the silent passages to the apartment where they were assembled. Here she was not less surprised than embarrassed to observe, in the manners of young people residing in a convent, an absence of that decorum which includes beneath its modest shade every grace that ought to adorn the female character, like the veil which gives dignity to their air and softness to their features. When Ellena entered the room, the eyes of the whole company were immediately fixed upon her ; the young ladies began to whisper and smile, and showed, by various means, that she was the subject of conversation, not otherwise than censorious. No one advanced to meet and to encourage her, to welcome her to the table, or displayed one of those nameless graces with which a generous and delicate mind delights to reanimate the modest and the unfortunate.

Ellena took a chair in silence, and, though she had at first felt forlorn and embarrassed by the impertinent manners of her companions, a consciousness of innocence gradually revived her spirits, and enabled her to resume an air of dignity which repressed this rude presumption.

Ellena returned to her cell, for the first time, with eagerness. Margaritone did not fasten the door of it, but she was careful to secure that of the passage ; and even this small indulgence she seemed to allow with a surly reluctance, as if compelled to obey the command of a superior. The moment she was gone, Ellena withdrew to her pleasant turret, where, after having suffered from the coarse manners of the novices, her gratitude was the more lively when she perceived the delicate attention of her beloved nun. It appeared that she had visited the chamber in Ellena absence, and had caused to be brought thither a chair and a table, on which were placed some books and a knot of fragrant flowers. Ellena did not repress the grateful tears which the generous feelings of Olivia excited ; and she forbore for some moments to examine the books, that the pleasing emotions she experienced might not be interrupted.

On looking into these books, however, she perceived that some of them treated of mystical subjects, which she laid aside with disappointment; but in others she observed a few of the best Italian poets, and a volume or two of Guicciardini's history. She was somewhat surprised that the poets should have found their way to the library of a nun, but was too much pleased with the discovery to dwell on the inquiry.

Having arranged her books, and set her little room in order, she seated herself at a window, and, with a volume of Tasso, endeavoured to banish every painful remembrance from her mind. She continued wandering in the imaginary scenes of the poet till the fading light recalled her to those of reality. The sun was set, but the mountain-tops were still lighted up by his beams, and a tint of glorious purple coloured all the west, and began to change the snowy points on the horizon. The silence and repose of the vast scene promoted the tender melancholy that prevailed in her heart; she thought of Vivaldi, and wept—of Vivaldi, whom she might, perhaps, never see again, though she doubted not that he would be indefatigable in searching for her. Every particular of their last conversation, when he had so lamented the approaching separation, even while he allowed of its propriety, came to her mind; and while she witnessed, in imagination, the grief and distraction which her mysterious departure and absence must have occasioned him, the fortitude with which she had resisted her own sufferings yielded to the picture of his.

The vesper-bell at length summoned her to prepare for mass, and she descended to her cell to await the arrival of her conductress. It was Margaritone, who soon appeared; but in the chapel she, as usual, saw Olivia, who, when the service had concluded, invited her into the garden of the convent. There, as she passed beneath the melancholy cedars that, ranged on either side the long walks, formed a majestic canopy, almost excluding the evening twilight, Olivia conversed with her on serious but general topics, carefully avoiding any mention of the abbess, and of the affairs of Ellena. The latter, anxious to learn the effect of her repeated objection to the veil, ventured to make some inquiries, which the nun immediately discouraged, and as cautiously checked the grateful effusions of her young friend for the attentions she had received.

Olivia accompanied Ellena to her cell, and there no longer scrupled to relieve her from uncertainty. With a mixture of frankness and discretion, she related as much of the conversation that had passed between herself and the abbess as it seemed necessary for Ellena to know, from which it appeared that the former was as obstinate as the latter was firm.

"Whatever may be your resolution," added the nun, "I earnestly advise you, my sister, to allow the superior some hope of compliance, lest she proceed to extremities."

"And what extremity can be more terrible," replied Ellena, "than either of those to which she would now urge me? Why should I descend to practise dissimulation?"

"To save yourself from undeserved sufferings," said Olivia, mournfully.

"Yes, but I should then incur deserved ones," observed Ellena, "and forfeit such peace of mind as my oppressors never could restore to me." As she said this, she looked at the nun with an expression of gentle reproach and disappointment.

"I applaud the justness of your sentiment," replied Olivia, regarding her with tenderest compassion. "Alas! that a mind so ingenuous should be subjected to the power of injustice and depravity!"

"Not subjected," said Ellena, with a noble pride; "do not say subjected. I have accustomed myself to contemplate those sufferings; I have chosen the least of such as were given to my choice, and I will endure them with fortitude; and can you then say that I am subjected?"

"Alas, my sister! you know not what you promise," rejoined Olivia; "you do not comprehend the sufferings which may be preparing for you."

As she spoke her eyes filled with tears, and she withdrew them from Ellena, who, surprised at the extreme concern on her countenance, entreated she would explain herself.

"I am not certain, myself, as to this point," added Olivia; "and if I were, I should not dare to explain it."

"Not dare!" repeated Ellena, mournfully. "Can benevolence like yours know fear when courage is necessary to prevent evil?"

"Inquire no further," said the nun; but no blush of conscious duplicity stained her cheek. "It is sufficient that you understand the consequence of open resistance to be terrible, and that you consent to avoid it."

"But how avoid it, my beloved friend, without incurring a consequence which, in my apprehension, would be yet more dreadful? How avoid it, without either subjecting myself to a hateful marriage or accepting the vows? Either of these events would be more terrible to me than anything with which I may otherwise be menaced."

"Perhaps not," observed the nun. "Imagination cannot draw the horrors of ——. But, my sister, let me repeat that I would save you, oh! how willingly save you, from the evils preparing! and that the only chance of doing so is by prevailing with you to abandon at least the appearance of resistance."

"Your kindness deeply affects me," said Ellena; "and I am fearful of appearing insensible of it when I reject your advice; yet I cannot adopt it. The very dissimulation which I should employ in self-defence might be a means of involving me in destruction."

As Ellena concluded, and her eyes glanced upon the nun, unaccountable suspicion occurred to her that Olivia might be insincere, and that, at this very moment, when she was advising dissimulation, she was endeavouring to draw Ellena into some snare which the abbess had laid. She sickened at this dreadful supposition, and dismissed it without suffering herself to examine its probability. That Olivia, from whom she had received so many attentions, whose countenance and manners announced so fair a mind, and for whom she had conceived so much esteem and affection, should be cruel and treacherous, was a suspicion that gave her more pain than the actual imprisonment in which she suffered; and when she looked again upon her face, Ellena was consoled by a clear conviction that she was utterly incapable of perfidy.

"If it were possible that I could consent to practise deceit," resumed Ellena, after a long pause, "what could it avail me? I am entirely in the power of the abbess, who would soon put my sincerity to the proof when a discovery of my duplicity would only provoke her vengeance, and I should be punished even for having sought to avoid injustice."

"If deceit is at any time excusable," replied Olivia, reluctantly, "it is when we practise it in self-defence. There are some rare situations when it may be resorted to without our incurring ignominy, and yours is one of those. But I will acknowledge, that all the good I expect is from the delay which temporising may procure you. The superior, when she understands there is a probability of obtaining your consent to her wishes, may be willing to allow you the usual time of preparation for the veil, and meanwhile something may occur to rescue you from your present situation."

"Ah! could I but believe so!" said Ellena; "but, alas! what power can rescue me? And I have not one relative remaining even to attempt my deliverance. To what possibility do you allude?"

"The Marchesa may relent."

"Does, then, your possibility of good rest with her, my dear friend? If so, I am in despair again; for such a chance of benefit, there would certainly be little policy in forfeiting one's integrity."

"There are also other possibilities, my sister," said Olivia; "but hark! what bell is that? It is the chime which assembles the nuns in the apartment of the abbess, where she dispenses her evening benediction. My absence will be observed. Good-night, my sister. Reflect on what I have advised; and remember, I conjure you, to consider that the consequence of your decision must be solemn, and may be fatal."

The nun spoke this with a look and emphasis so extraordinary that Ellena at once wished and dreaded to know more; but before she had recovered from her surprise Olivia had left the room.

CHAPTER IX.

THE adventurous Vivaldi and his servant Paulo, after passing the night of Ellena's departure from Villa Altieri in one of the subterraneous chambers of the fort of Paluzzi, and yielding, at length, to exhausted nature, awoke in terror and utter darkness, for the flambeau had expired. When a recollection of the occurrences of the preceding evening returned, they renewed their efforts for liberty with ardour. The grated window was again examined, and being found to overlook only a confined court of the fortress, no hope appeared of escaping.

The words of the monk returned with Vivaldi's first recollections, to torture him with apprehension that Ellena was no more; and Paulo, unable either to console or to appease his master, sat down dejectedly beside him. Paulo had no longer a hope to suggest or a joke to throw away; and he could not forbear seriously remarking that to die of hunger was one of the most horrible means of death, or lamenting the rashness which had made them liable to so sad a probability.

He was in the midst of a very pathetic oration, of which, however, his master did not hear a single word, so wholly was his attention engaged by his own melancholy thoughts, when on a sudden he became silent, and then, starting to his feet, exclaimed, "Signor, what is yonder? Do you see nothing?"

Vivaldi looked round.

"It is certainly a ray of light," continued Paulo; "and I will soon know where it comes from."

As he said this he sprang forward, and his surprise almost equalled his joy when he discovered that the light issued through the door of the vault, which stood a little open. He could scarcely believe his senses, since the door had been strongly fastened on the preceding night, and he had not heard its ponderous bolts undrawn. He threw it widely open, but, recollecting himself, stopped to look into the adjoining vault before he ventured forth; when Vivaldi darted past him and, bidding him follow him instantly, ascended to the day. The courts of the fortress were

silent and vacant, and Vivaldi reached the
archway, without having observed a single
person, breathless with speed and scarcely
daring to believe he had regained his liberty.

Beneath the arch he stopped to recover
breath, and to consider whether he should
take the road to Naples or to Altieri, for
it was yet early morning, and at an hour
when it appeared improbable that Ellena's
family would be risen. The apprehension of
her death had vanished as Vivaldi's spirits
revived, which this pause of hesitation sufficiently announced : but even this was the
pause only of an instant ; a strong anxiety
concerning her determined him to proceed to
Villa Altieri, notwithstanding the unsuitable-
ness of the hour, since he could at least reconnoitre her residence, and await till some
sign of the family having arisen should
appear.

" Pray, signor," said Paulo, while his master was deliberating, " do not let us stop
here, lest the enemy should appear again ;
and do, signor, take the road which is nearest
to some house where we may get breakfast,
for the fear of starving has taken such hold
upon me that it has nearly anticipated the
reality of it already."

Vivaldi immediately departed for the villa.
Paulo, as he danced joyfully along, expressed
all the astonishment that filled his mind as to
the cause of their late imprisonment and
escape ; but Vivaldi, who had now leisure to
consider the subject, could not assist him in
explaining it. The only certain point was
that he had not been confined by robbers ;
and what interest anyone could have in im-
prisoning him for the night and suffering him
to escape in the morning did not appear.

On entering the garden at Altieri he was
surprised to see that several of the lower
lattices were open at this early hour, but surprise changed to terror when, on reaching the
portico, he heard a moaning of distress from
the hall, and when, after loudly calling, he was
answered by the piteous cries of Beatrice.
The hall-door was fastened, and Beatrice
being unable to open it, Vivaldi, followed by
Paulo, sprang through one of the unclosed
lattices ; when on reaching the hall he found
the housekeeper bound to a pillar, and learned
that Ellena had been carried off during the
night by armed men.

For a moment he was almost stupefied by
the shock of this intelligence, and then asked
Beatrice a thousand questions concerning the
affair, without allowing her time to answer
one of them. When, however, he had patience
to listen, he learned that the ruffians were
four in number ; that they were masked ; that
two of them had carried Ellena through the
garden, while the others, after binding Beatrice
to a pillar, threatening her with death if she
made any noise, and watching over her till
their comrades had secured their prize, left

her a prisoner. This was all the information
she could give respecting Ellena.

Vivaldi, when he could think coolly, believed he had discovered the instigators and
the design of the whole affair, and the cause
also of his late confinement. It appeared
that Ellena had been carried off by order of
his family, to prevent the intended marriage,
and that he had been decoyed into the fort of
Paluzzi, and kept a prisoner there, to secure
him from interrupting the scheme, which his
presence at the villa would effectually have
done. He had himself spoken of his former
adventure at Paluzzi ; and it was now evident
that his family had taken advantage of the
curiosity he had expressed to lead him into
the vaults. The event of this design had
been the more probable, since, as the fort lay
in the direct road to Altieri, Vivaldi could not
go thither without being observed by the
creatures of the Marchesa, who, by an artful
manoeuvre, might make him their prisoner
without employing violence.

As he considered these circumstances, it
appeared almost certain that father Schedoni
was in truth the monk who had so long
haunted his steps ; that he was the secret adviser of his mother, and one of the authors of
the predicted misfortunes which it seemed he
possessed a too infallible means of fulfilling.
Yet Vivaldi, while he admitted the probability
of all this, reflected with new astonishment on
the conduct of Schedoni during his interview
with him in the Marchesa's cabinet—the air
of dignified innocence with which he had repressed accusation ; the apparent simplicity
with which he had pointed out circumstances
respecting the stranger that seemed to make
against himself ; and Vivaldi's opinion of the
confessor's duplicity began to waver. " Yet
what other person," said he; " could be so
intimately acquainted with my concerns, or
have an interest sufficiently strong for thus
indefatigably thwarting me, except this confessor, who is, no doubt, well rewarded for
his perseverance ? The monk can be no
other than Schedoni ; yet it is strange that he
should have forborne to disguise his person,
and should appear in this mysterious office in
the very habit he usually wears !"

Whatever might be the truth as to Schedoni, it was evident that Ellena had been
carried away by order of Vivaldi's family,
and he immediately returned towards Naples
with an intention of demanding her at their
hands, not with any hope of their compliance,
but believing that they might accidentally
afford him some light on the subject. If,
however, he should fail to obtain any hint
that might assist him in tracing the route she
had been carried, he determined to visit Schedoni, accuse him of perfidy, urge him to a
full explanation of his conduct, and, if possible, obtain from him a knowledge of Ellena's place of confinement.

When at length he obtained an interview with the Marchese, and, throwing himself at his feet, supplicated that Ellena might be restored to her home, the unexpected surprise of his father overwhelmed him with astonishment and despair. The look and manner of the Marchese could not be doubted; Vivaldi was convinced that he was absolutely ignorant of any step that had been taken against Ellen.

"However ungraciously you have conducted yourself," said the Marchese, "my conduct towards you has never yet been sullied by duplicity ; however I may have wished to break the unworthy connection you have formed, I should disdain to employ artifice as the means. If you really design to marry this person, I shall make no other effort to prevent such a measure than by telling you the consequence you are to expect : from thenceforth I will disown you for my son."

The Marchese quitted the apartment when he had said this, and Vivaldi made no attempt to detain him. His words expressed little more than they had formerly done, yet Vivaldi was shocked by the absolute menace now delivered. The stronger passion of his heart, however, soon overcame their effect ; and this moment, when he began to fear that he had irrecoverably lost the object of his dearest affections, was not the time in which he could long feel remoter evils, or calculate the force of misfortunes which never might arrive. The nearer interest pressed solely upon his mind, and he was conscious only to the loss of Ellena.

The interview which followed with his mother was of a different character from that which had occurred with the Marchese. The keen dart of suspicion, however, sharpened as it was by love and by despair, pierced beyond the veil of her duplicity ; and Vivaldi as quickly detected her hypocrisy as he had yielded his conviction to the sincerity of the Marchese. But his power rested here : he possessed no means of awakening her pity or actuating her justice, and could not obtain even a hint that might guide him in his search of Ellena.

Schedoni yet remained to be tried. Vivaldi had no longer a doubt as to his having caballed with the Marchesa, and that he had been an agent in removing Ellena. Whether, however, he was the person who haunted the ruins of Paluzzi was still questionable ; for, though several circumstances seemed to declare in the affirmative, others not less plausible asserted the contrary.

On leaving the Marchesa's apartment, Vivaldi repaired to the convent of the Spirito Santo, and enquired for father Schedoni. The lay brother who opened the gate informed him that he was in his cell, and Vivaldi stepped impatiently into the court, requesting to be shown thither.

"I dare not leave the gate, signor," said the brother, " but if you cross the court, and ascend that staircase which you see yonder beyond the doorway on your right, it will lead you to a gallery, and the third door you will come to is father Schedoni's."

Vivaldi passed on without seeing another human being, and not a sound disturbed the silence of this sanctuary, till, as he ascended the stairs, a feeble note of lamentation proceeded from the gallery, and he concluded it was uttered by some penitent at confession.

He stopped, as he had been directed, at the third door, when, as he gently knocked, the sound ceased, and the same profound silence returned. Vivaldi repeated his summons but receiving no answer, he ventured to open the door. In the dusky cell within no person appeared, but he still looked round, expecting to discover someone in the dubious gloom. The chamber contained little more than a mattress, a chair, a table, and a crucifix ; some books of devotion were upon the table, one or two of which were written in unknown characters ; several instruments of torture lay beside them. Vivaldi shuddered as he hastily examined these, though he did not comprehend the manner of their application, and he left the chamber without noticing any other object, and returned to the court. The porter said that since father Schedoni was not in his cell, he was probably either in the church or in the gardens, for that he had not passed the gates during the morning.

"Did he pass yester-evening?" said Vivaldi, eagerly.

"Yes, he returned to vespers," replied the brother, with surprise.

"Are you certain as to that, my friend?" rejoined Vivaldi. "Are you certain that he slept in the convent last night?"

"Who is it that asks the question?" said the lay brother, with displeasure ; "and what right has he to make it? You are ignorant of the rules of our house, signor, or you would perceive such questions to be unnecessary. Any member of our community is liable to be severely punished if he sleeps a night without these walls, and father Schedoni would be the last among us so to trespass. He is one of the most pious of the brotherhood ; few, indeed, have courage to imitate his severe example. His voluntary sufferings are sufficient for a saint. He pass the night abroad ! Go, signor ; yonder is the church ; you will find him there, perhaps."

Vivaldi did not linger to reply. "The hypocrite !" said he to himself as he crossed to the church, which formed one side of the quadrangle ; "but I will unmask him."

The church which he entered was vacant and silent, like the court. "Whither can the inhabitants of this place have withdrawn themselves?" said he. "Wherever I go I hear only the echoes of my own footsteps ; it seems as if death reigned here over all. But, perhaps it is one of the hours of general meditation, and the monks have only retired to their cells."

As he paced the long aisles he suddenly stopped to catch the startling sound that murmured through the lofty roof; but it seemed to be only the closing of a distant door. Yet he often looked forward into the sacred gloom which the painted windows threw over the remote perspective, in the expectation of perceiving a monk. He was not long disappointed; a person appeared, standing silently in an obscure part of the cloister clothed in the habit of this society, and he advanced towards him.

The monk did not avoid Vivaldi, or even turn to observe who was approaching, but remained in the same attitude, fixed like a statue. This tall and gaunt figure had, at a distance, reminded him of Schedoni, and Vivaldi, as he now looked under the cowl, discovered the ghastly countenance of the confessor.

"Have I found you at last?" said Vivaldi. "I would speak with you, father, in private. This is not a proper place for such discourse as we must hold."

Schedoni made no reply, and Vivaldi, once again looking at him, observed that his features were fixed, and his eyes bent towards the ground. The words of Vivaldi seemed not to have reached his understanding, nor even to have made any impression on his senses.

He repeated them in a louder tone, but still not a single line of Schedoni's countenance acknowledged their influence. "What means this mummery?" said he, his patience exhausted, and his indignation aroused. "This wretched subterfuge shall not protect you; you are detected: your stratagems are known! Restore Ellena di Rosalba to her home, or confess where you have concealed her."

Schedoni was still silent and unmoved. A respect for his age and profession withheld Vivaldi from seizing and compelling him to answer; but the agony of impatience and indignation which he suffered formed a striking contrast to the death-like apathy of the monk. "I now also know you," continued Vivaldi, "for my tormentor at Paluzzi, the prophet of evils which you too well practised the means of fulfilling, the predictor of the death of Signora Bianchi." Schedoni frowned. "The forewarner of Ellena's departure; the phantom who decoyed me into the dungeons of Paluzzi; the prophet and the artificer of all my misfortunes."

The monk raised his eyes from the ground, and fixed them with terrible expression upon Vivaldi, but was still silent.

"Yes, father," added Vivaldi, "I know and will proclaim you to the world. I will strip you of the holy hypocrisy in which you shroud

yourself, announce to all your society the despicable artifices you have employed, and the misery you have occasioned. Your character shall be announced aloud."

While Vivaldi spoke the monk had withdrawn his eyes, and fixed them again on the ground. His countenance had resumed its usual expression.

"Wretch! restore to me Ellena di Rosalba!" cried Vivaldi, with the sudden anguish of renewed despair. "Tell me at least where she may be found, or you shall be compelled to do so. Whither—whither have you conveyed her?"

As he pronounced this in loud and passionate accents several ecclesiastics entered the cloisters, and were passing on to the body of the church, when his voice arrested their attention. They paused, and perceiving the singular attitude of Schedoni and the frantic gesticulations of Vivaldi, hastily advanced towards them. "Forbear!" said one of the strangers, as he seized the cloak of Vivaldi. "Do you not observe!"

"I observe a hypocrite," replied Vivaldi, stepping back and disengaging himself. "I observe a destroyer of the peace it was his duty to protect. I——"

"Forbear this desperate conduct," said the priest, "lest it provoke the just vengeance of Heaven! Do you not observe also the holy office in which he is engaged?" pointing to the monk. "Leave the church while you are permitted to do so in safety; you suspect not the punishment you may provoke."

"I will not quit the spot till you answer my inquiries," said Vivaldi to Schedoni, without deigning even to look upon the priest. "Where, I repeat, is Ellena di Rosalba?"

The confessor was still silent and unmoved. "This is beyond all patience, and all belief," continued Vivaldi. "Speak! Answer me, or dread what I may unfold. Yet silent! Do you know the Convent *del Pianto?* Do you know the confessional of the *Black Penitents?*"

Vivaldi thought he perceived the countenance of the monk suffer some change. "Do you remember that terrible night," he added, "when, on the steps of that confessional a tale was told,——"

Schedoni raised his eyes, and fixing them once more on Vivaldi with a look that seemed intended to strike him to the dust, "Avaunt!" cried he in a tremendous voice; "avaunt, sacrilegious boy! Tremble for the consequence of thy desperate impiety!"

As he concluded he started from his position, and gliding with the silent swiftness of a shadow along the cloister, vanished in an instant. Vivaldi, when attempting to pursue him, was seized by the surrounding monks. Insensible to his sufferings, and exasperated by his assertions, they threatened that if he did not immediately leave the convent he should be confined, and undergo the severe punishment to which he had become liable for having disturbed and even insulted one of their holy order while performing an act of penance.

"He has need of such acts," said Vivaldi; "but when can they restore the happiness his treachery has destroyed? Your order is disgraced by such a member, reverend fathers; your ——"

"Peace!" cried a monk; "he is the pride of our house; he is severe in his devotion, and in self-punishment terrible beyond the reach of ——. But I am throwing away my commendations; I am talking to one who is not permitted to value or to understand the sacred mysteries of our exercises."

"Away with him to the *Padre Abbate!*" cried an enraged priest; "away with him to the dungeon!"

"Away! away!" repeated his companions, and they endeavoured to force Vivaldi through the cloisters. But with the sudden strength which pride and indignation lent him, he burst from their united hold, and, quitting the church by another door, escaped into the street.

Vivaldi returned home in a state of mind that would have engaged the pity of any heart which prejudice or self-interest had not hardened. He avoided his father, but sought the Marchesa, who, however, triumphant in the success of her plan, was still insensible to the sufferings of her son.

When the Marchesa had been informed of his approaching marriage, she had, as usual, consulted with her confessor on the means of preventing it, who had advised the scheme she adopted, a scheme which was the more easily carried into effect, since the Marchesa had early in life been acquainted with the abbess of San Stefano, and knew, therefore, enough of her character and disposition to confide without hesitation the management of this important affair to her discretion. The answer of the abbess to her proposal was not merely acquiescent but zealous, and it appeared that she too faithfully justified the confidence placed in her. After this plan had been so successfully prosecuted, it was not to be hoped that the Marchesa would be prevailed upon to relinquish it by the tears, the anguish, or all the varied sufferings of her son. Vivaldi now reproved the easiness of his own confidence in having hoped it, and quitted her cabinet with a despondency that almost reached despair.

The faithful Paulo, when he obeyed the hasty summons of his master, had not succeeded in obtaining intelligence of Ellena; and Vivaldi, having dismissed him again on the same inquiry, retired to his apartment, where the excess of grief, and a feeble hope of devising some successful mode of remedy, alternately agitated and detained him.

In the evening, restless and anxious for change, though scarcely knowing whither to bend his course, he left the palace and strolled down to the sea-beach. A few fishermen and lazzaroni only were loitering along the strand, waiting for the boats from St. Lucia. Vivaldi, with folded arms and his hat drawn over his face to shade his sorrow from observation, paced the edge of the waves, listening to their murmur as they broke gently at his feet, and gazing upon their undulating beauty, while all consciousness was lost in melancholy reverie concerning Ellena. Her late residence appeared at a distance rising over the shore. He remembered how often from thence they had together viewed this lovely scene! Its features had now lost its charm; they were colourless and uninteresting, or impressed only mournful ideas. The sea, fluctuating beneath the setting sun, the long mole and its lighthouse tipped with the last rays, fishermen reposing in the shade, little boats skimming over the smooth waters, which their oars scarcely dimpled: these were images that brought to his recollection the affecting evening when he had last seen this picture from Villa Altieri, when, seated in the orangery with Ellena and Bianchi on the night preceding the death of the latter, Ellena herself had so solemnly been given to his care, and had so affectingly consented to the dying request of her relative. The recollection of that scene came to Vivaldi with all the force of contrast, and renewed all the anguish of despair; he paced the beach with quicker steps, and long groans burst from his heart. He accused himself of indifference and inactivity for having been thus long unable to discover a single circumstance which might direct his search; and, though he knew not whither to go, he determined to leave Naples immediately and return no more to his father's mansion till he should have rescued Ellena.

Of some fishermen who were conversing together upon the beach, he inquired whether they could accommodate him with a boat, in which he meant to coast the bay; for it appeared probable that Ellena had been conveyed from Altieri by water to some town or convent on the shore, the privacy and facility of such a mode of conveyance being suitable to the designs of her enemies.

"I have but one boat, signor," said a fisherman, "and that is busy enough in going to and fro between here and Santa Lucia, but my comrade, here, perhaps can serve you. What, Carlo, can you help the signor to your little skiff? the other, I know, has enough to do in the trade."

His comrade, however, was too much engaged with a party of three or four men, who were listening in deep attention round him, to reply. Vivaldi, advancing to urge the question, was struck by the eagerness with which he delivered his narrative, as well as the uncouthness of his gesticulation ; and he paused a moment in attention. One of the auditors seemed to doubt of something that had been asserted. " I tell you," replied the narrator, " I used to carry fish there two and three times a week, and very good sort of people they were ; they have laid out many a ducat with me in their time. But as I was saying, when I got there, and knocked upon the door, I heard, all of a sudden, a huge groaning, and presently I heard the voice of the old housekeeper herself roaring out for help ; but I could give her none, for the door was fastened ; and, while I ran away for assistance to old Bartoli—you know old Bartoli, he lives by the road side as you go to Naples ; well, while I ran to him, comes a signor, and jumps through the window and sets her at liberty at once. So then I heard the whole story ——"

" What story ? " said Vivaldi, " and of whom do you speak ? "

" All in good time, *maestro,* you shall hear," said the fisherman, who, looking at him for a moment, added, " Why, signor, it should be you I saw there ; you should be the very signor that let old Beatrice loose."

Vivaldi, who had scarcely doubted before that it was Altieri of which the man had spoken, now asked a thousand questions respecting the route the ruffians had taken Ellena, but obtained no relief to his anxiety,

" I should not wonder," said a lazzaro, who had been listening to the relation, " I should not wonder if the carriage that passed Bracelli early on the same morning, with the blinds drawn up, though it was so hot that people could scarcely breathe in the open air, should prove to be it which carried off the lady ! "

This hint was sufficient to reanimate Vivaldi, who collected all the information the lazzaro could give, which was, however, little more than that a carriage, such as he described, had been seen by him driving furiously through Bracelli, early on the morning mentioned as that of Signora di Rosalba's departure. Vivaldi had now little doubt as to its being the one which conveyed her away, and he determined to set out immediately for that place, where he hoped to obtain from the postmaster further intelligence concerning the road she had pursued.

With this intention he returned once more to his father's mansion, not to acquaint him with his purpose, or to bid him farewell, but to await the return of his servant Paulo, who he meant should accompany him in the search. Vivaldi's spirits were now animated with hope, slender as were the circumstances that supported it ; and, believing his design to be wholly unsuspected by those who would be disposed to interrupt it, he did not guard either against the measures which might impede his departure from Naples, or those which might overtake him on his journey.

CHAPTER X.

THE Marchesa, alarmed at some hints dropped by Vivaldi in the late interview between them, and by some circumstances of his latter conduct, summoned her constant adviser, Schedoni. Still suffering with the insult he had received in the church of the *Spirito Santo,* he obeyed with sullen reluctance, yet not without a malicious hope of discovering some opportunity for retaliation. That insult, which had pointed forth his hypocrisy and ridiculed the solemn abstraction he assumed, had sunk deep in his heart, and, fermenting the direst passions of his nature, he meditated a terrible revenge. It had subjected him to mortifications of various kinds. Ambition, it has already appeared, was one of his strongest motives of action, and he had long since assumed a character of severe sanctity, chiefly for the purposes of lifting him to promotion. He was not beloved in the society of which he was a member ; and many of the brotherhood, who had laboured to disappoint his views and to detect his errors, who hated him for his pride and envied him for his reputed sanctity, now gloried in the mortification he had received, and endeavoured to turn the circumstance to their own advantage. They had not scrupled already to display by insinuation and pointed sneers their triumph, and to menace his reputation ; and Schedoni, though he deserved contempt, was not of a temper to endure it.

But, above all, some hints respecting his past life which had fallen from Vivaldi, and which occasioned him so abruptly to leave the church, alarmed him. So much terror, indeed, had they excited that it is not improbable that he would have sealed his secret in death, devoting Vivaldi to the grave, had he not been restrained by the dreaded vengeance of the Vivaldi family. Since that hour he had known no peace, and had never slept ; he had taken scarcely any food, and was almost continually on his knees upon the steps of the high altar. The devotees who beheld him paused and admired ; such of the brothers as disliked him sneered and passed on. Schedoni appeared alike insensible to each ; lost to this world, and preparing for a higher.

The torments of his mind and the severe penance he had observed had produced a surprising change in his appearance, so that he resembled a spectre rather than a human being. His visage was wan and wasted, his eyes were sunk and become nearly motionless, and his whole air and attitudes exhibited the wild energy of something not of this earth.

When he was summoned by the Marchesa,

his conscience whispered this to be the consequence of circumstances which Vivaldi had revealed, and at first he had determined not to attend her ; but, considering that if it was so his refusal would confirm suspicion, he resolved to trust once more to the subtlety of his address for deliverance.

With these apprehensions, tempered by this hope, he entered the Marchesa's closet. She almost started on observing him, and could not immediately withdraw her eyes from his altered visage, while Schedoni was unable wholly to conceal the perturbation which such earnest observation occasioned. "Peace rest with you, daughter !" said he, and he seated himself, without lifting his eyes from the floor.

"I wished to speak with you, father, upon affairs of moment," said the Marchesa gravely, "which are probably not unknown to you." She paused, and Schedoni bowed his head, awaiting in anxious expectation what was to follow.

"You are silent, father," resumed the Marchesa. "What am I to understand by this?"

"That you have been misinformed," replied Schedoni, whose apt conscience betrayed his discretion.

"Pardon me," said the Marchesa, "I am too well informed, and should not have requested your visit if any doubt had remained upon my mind."

"Signora ! be cautious of what you credit," said the confessor, imprudently ; "you know not the consequences of a hasty credulity."

"Would that mine were a rash credulity !" replied the Marchesa ; "but—we are betrayed."

"We ?" repeated the monk, beginning to revive. "What has happened ?"

The Marchesa informed him of Vivaldi's absence, and inferred from its length, for it was now several days since his departure, that he had certainly discovered the place of Ellena's confinement, as well as the authors of it.

Schedoni differed from her, but hinted that the obedience of youth was hopeless unless severer measures were adopted.

"Severer !" exclaimed the Marchesa ; "good father, is it not severe enough to confine her for life?"

"I mean severer with respect to your son, lady," replied Schedoni. "When a young man has so far overcome all reverence for an holy ordinance as publicly to insult its professor, and yet more, when that professor is in the very performance of his duties, it is time he should be controlled with a strong hand. I am not in the practice of advising such measures, but the conduct of Signor Vivaldi is such as calls aloud for them. Public decency demands it. For myself,

indeed, I should have endured patiently the indignity which has been offered me, receiving it as a salutary mortification, as one of those inflictions that purify the soul from the pride which even the holiest men may unconsciously cherish. But I am no longer permitted to consider myself ; the public good requires that an example should be made of the horrible impiety of which your son—it grieves me, daughter, to disclose it ! —your son, unworthy of such a mother, has been guilty."

It is evident that in the style, at least, of this accusation, Schedoni suffered the force of his resentment to prevail over the usual subtlety of his address, the deep and smooth insinuation of his policy.

"To what do you allude, righteous father ?" inquired the astonished Marchesa ; "what indignity, what impiety has my son to answer for? I entreat you will speak explicitly, that I may prove I can lose the mother in the strict severity of the judge."

"That is spoken with the grandeur of sentiment which has always distinguished you, my daughter ! Strong minds perceive that justice is the highest of the moral attributes ; mercy is only the favourite of weak ones."

Schedoni had a view in this commendation beyond that of confirming the Marchesa's present resolution against Vivaldi. He wished to prepare her for measures which might hereafter be necessary to accomplish the revenge he meditated, and he knew that by flattering her vanity he was most likely to succeed. He praised her, therefore, for qualities he wished her to possess, encouraged her to reject general opinions by admiring, as the symptoms of a superior understanding, the convenient morality upon which she had occasionally acted ; and, calling sternness justice, extolled that for strength of mind which was only callous insensibility.

He then described to her Vivaldi's late conduct in the church of the *Spirito Santo,* exaggerated some offensive circumstances of it, invented others, and formed of the whole an instance of monstrous impiety and unprovoked insult.

The Marchesa listened to the relation with no less indignation than surprise, and her readiness to adopt the confessor's advice allowed him to depart with renovated spirits and most triumphant hopes.

Meanwhile, the Marchese remained ignorant of the subject of the conference with Schedoni. His opinions had formerly been sounded, and having been found decidedly against the dark policy it was thought expedient to practise, he was never afterwards consulted respecting Vivaldi. Parental anxiety and affection began to revive as the lengthened absence of his son was observed. Though jealous of his rank, he loved Vivaldi ; and, though he had never positively believed that he designed to enter into a secret engagement with a person whom the Marchese considered to be so much his inferior as Ellena, he had suffered doubts which gave him considerable uneasiness. The present extraordinary absence of Vivaldi renewed his alarm. He apprehended that if she was discovered at this moment, when the fear of losing her for ever, and the exasperation which such complicated opposition occasioned, had awakened all the passions of his son, this rash young man might be prevailed upon to secure her for his own by the indissoluble vow. On the other hand, he dreaded the effect of Vivaldi's despair should he fail in the pursuit; and thus, fearing at one moment that for which he wished in the next, the Márchese suffered a tumult of mind inferior only to his son's.

The instructions which he delivered to the servants whom he sent in pursuit of Vivaldi were given under such distraction of thought that scarcely any person perfectly understood his commission; and, as the Marchesa had been careful to conceal from him her knowledge of Ellena's abode, he gave no direction concerning the route to San Stefano.

While the Marchese at Naples was thus employed, and while Schedoni was forming further plans against Ellena, Vivaldi was wandering from village to village, and from town to town, in pursuit of her whom all his efforts had hitherto been unsuccessful to recover. From the people at the post-house at Bracelli he had obtained little information that could direct him; they only knew that a carriage, such as had been described to Vivaldi, with the blinds drawn up, changed horses there on the morning which he remembered to be that of Ellena's departure, and had proceeded on the road to Morgagni.

When Vivaldi arrived thither all trace of Ellena was lost; the master of the post could not recollect a single circumstance connected with the travellers, and even if he had noticed them it would have been insufficient for Vivaldi's purpose, unless he had also observed the road they followed, for at this place several roads branched off into opposite quarters of the country. Vivaldi, therefore, was reduced to choose one of these as chance or fancy directed; and as it appeared probable that the Marchese had conveyed Ellena to a convent, he determined to make inquiries at every one on his way.

He had now passed over some of the wildest tracts of the Apennine, among scenes which seemed abandoned by civilised society to the banditti who haunted their recesses. Yet even here, amidst wilds that were inaccessible, convents, with each its small dependent hamlet, were scattered, and, shrouded from the world by woods and mountains, enjoyed unsuspectedly many of its luxuries, and displayed unnoticed some of its elegance. Vi-

valdi, who had visited several of these in search of Ellena, had been surprised at the refined courtesy and hospitality with which he was received.

It was on the seventh day of his journey, and near sunset, that he was bewildered in the woods of Rugieri. He had received a direction for the road he was to take at a village some leagues distant, and had obeyed it confidently till now, when the path was lost in several tracts that branched out among the trees. The day was closing, and Vivaldi's spirits began to fail, but Paulo, light of heart and ever gay, commended the shade and pleasant freshness of the woods, and observed that if his master did lose his way, and was obliged to remain here for the night, it would not be so very unlucky, for they could climb up among the branches of a chestnut-tree, and find more neat and airy lodging than any inn had yet afforded them.

While Paulo was thus endeavouring to make the best of what might happen, and his master was sunk in a reverie, they suddenly heard the sound of instruments and voices from a distance. The gloom which the trees threw around prevented their distinguishing objects afar off, and not a single human being was visible, nor any trace of his art, beneath the shadowy scene. They listened to ascertain from what direction the sounds approached, and heard a chorus of voices, accompanied by a few instruments, performing the evening service.

"We are near a convent, signor," said Paulo, "listen! they are at their devotions.'

"It is as you say," replied Vivaldi; "and we will make the best of our way towards it."

"Well, signor! I must say, if we find as good doings here as we had at the Capuchin's, we shall have no reason to regret our beds *al fresco* among the chestnut branches."

"Do you perceive any walls or spires beyond the trees?" said Vivaldi, as he led the way.

"None, signor," replied Paulo; "yet we draw nearer the sounds. Ah, signor! do you hear that note? How it dies away! And those instruments just touched in symphony! This is not the music of peasants; a convent must be near, though we do not see it."

Still, as they advanced, no walls appeared, and soon after the music ceased; but other sounds led Vivaldi forward to a pleasant part of the woods, where he perceived a party of pilgrims seated on the grass. They were laughing and conversing with much gaiety, as each spread before him the supper which he drew from his scrip; while he who appeared to be the *Father-director* of the pilgrimage sat with a jovial countenance in the midst of the company, dispensing jokes and merry stories, and receiving in return a tribute from every scrip. Wines of various sorts were ranged before him, of which he drank abundantly, and seemed not to refuse any dainty that was offered.

Vivaldi, whose apprehensions were now quieted, stopped to observe the group, as the evening rays, glancing along the skirts of the wood, threw a gleam upon their various countenances, showing, however, in each a spirit of gaiety that might have characterised the individuals of a party of pleasure, rather than those of a pilgrimage. The *Father-director* and his flock seemed perfectly to understand each other; the Superior willingly resigned the solemn austerity of his office, and permitted the company to make themselves as happy as possible, in consideration of receiving plenty of the most delicate of their viands; yet somewhat of dignity was mingled with his condescensions, that compelled them to receive even his jokes with a degree of deference, and perhaps they laughed at them less for their spirit than because they were favours.

Addressing the Superior, Vivaldi requested to be directed how he might regain his way. The father examined him for a moment before he replied; but observing the elegance of his dress and a certain air of distinction, and perceiving also that Paulo was his servant, he promised his services, and invited him to take a seat at his right hand and partake of the supper.

Vivaldi, understanding that the party was going his road, accepted the invitation; when Paulo, having fastened the horses to a tree, soon became busy with the supper. While Vivaldi conversed with the father, Paulo engrossed all the attention of the pilgrims near him; they declared he was the merriest fellow they had ever seen, and often expressed a wish that he was going as far with them as to the shrine in a convent of Carmelites, which terminated their pilgrimage. When Vivaldi understood that this shrine was in the church of a convent, partly inhabited by nuns, and that it was little more than a league and a half distant, he determined to accompany them, for it was as possible that Ellena might be confined there as in any other cloister; and of her being imprisoned in some convent he had less doubt the more he considered the character and views of his mother. He set forward, therefore, with the pilgrims, and on foot, having resigned his horse to the weary *Father-director.*

Darkness closed over them long before they reached the village where they designed to pass the night; but they beguiled the way with songs and stories, now and then only stopping, at command of the father, to repeat some prayer or sing a hymn. But, as they drew near a village, at the base of the mountain on which the shrine stood, they halted to arrange themselves in procession; and the Superior, having stopped short in the midst of one of his best jokes, dismounted

Vivaldi's horse, placed himself at their head, and, beginning a loud strain, they proceeded in full chorus of melancholy music.

The peasants, hearing their sonorous voices, came forth to meet and conduct them to their cabins. The village was already crowded with devotees, but these poor peasants, looking up to them with love and reverence, made every possible contrivance to accommodate all who came: notwithstanding which, when Paulo soon after turned into his bed of straw, he had more reasons than one to regret his chestnut mattress.

Vivaldi passed an anxious night, waiting impatiently for the dawning of that day which might possibly restore to him Ellena. Considering that a pilgrim's habit would not only conceal him from suspicion, but allow him opportunities for observation, which his own dress would not permit, he employed Paulo to provide him one. The address of the servant, assisted by a single ducat, easily procured it, and at an early hour he set forward on his inquiry.

CHAPTER XI.

A FEW devotees only had begun to ascend the mountain, and Vivaldi kept aloof even from these, pursuing a lonely track, for his thoughtful mind desired solitude. The early breeze, sighing among the foliage that waved high over the path, and the hollow dashing of distant waters, he listened to with complacency, for these were sounds which soothed yet promoted his melancholy mood; and he sometimes rested to gaze upon the scenery around him, for this too was in harmony with the temper of his mind. Disappointment had subdued the wilder energy of the passions, and produced a solemn and lofty state of feeling; he viewed with pleasing sadness the dark rocks and precipices, the gloomy mountains and vast solitudes, that spread around him; nor was the convent he was approaching a less sacred feature of the scene, as its grey walls and pinnacles appeared beyond the dusky groves. "Ah! if it should enclose her!" said Vivaldi, as he caught a first glimpse of its hall. "Vain hope! I will not invite your illusions again, I will not expose myself to the agonies of new disappointment; I will search, but not expect. Yet, if she should be there!"

Having reached the gates of the convent, he passed with hasty steps into the court; where his emotion increased as he paused a moment and looked round its silent cloisters. The porter only appeared, when Vivaldi, fearful lest he should perceive him to be other than a pilgrim, drew his hood over his face, and, gathering up his garments still closer in his folded arms, passed on without speaking, though he knew not which of the avenues before him led to the shrine. He advanced, however, towards the church, a stately edifice detached and at some little distance from the other parts of the convent. Its highly-vaulted aisles, extending in twilight perspective, where a monk or a pilgrim only now and then crossed, whose dark figures, passing without sound, vanished like shadows; the universal stillness of the place, the gleam of tapers from the high altar, and of lamps, which gave a gloomy pomp to every shrine in the church—all these circumstances conspired to impress a sacred awe upon his heart.

He followed some devotees through a side aisle to a court that was overhung by a tremendous rock, in which was a cave, containing the shrine of *our Lady of Mount Carmel*. This court was enclosed by the rock, and by the choir of the church, except that to the south a small opening led the eye to a glimpse of a landscape below, which, seen beyond the dark jaws of the cliff, appeared free and light, and gaily coloured, melting away into blue and distant mountains.

Vivaldi entered the cave, where, enclosed within a filigree screen of gold, lay the image of the saint, decorated with flowers and lighted up by innumerable lamps and tapers. The steps of the shrine were thronged with kneeling pilgrims, and Vivaldi, to avoid singularity, kneeled also; till a high peal of the organ, at a distance, and the deep voices of choristers announced that the first mass was begun. He left the cave, and, returning into the church, loitered at an extremity of the aisles, where he listened awhile to the solemn harmony pealing along the roofs, and softening away in distance. It was such full and entrancing music as frequently swells in the high festivals of the Sicilian Church, and is adapted to inspire that sublime enthusiasm which sometimes elevates its disciples. Vivaldi, unable to endure long the excess of feeling which this harmony awakened, was leaving the church, when suddenly it ceased, and the tolling of a bell sounded in its stead. This seemed to be the knell of death, and it occurred to him, that a dying person was approaching to receive the last sacrament; when he heard remotely a warbling of female voices, mingling with the deeper tones of the monks, and with the hollow note of the bell, as it struck at intervals. So sweetly, so plaintively did the strain grow on the air that those who listened, as well as those who sung, were touched with sorrow, and seemed equally to mourn for a departing friend.

Vivaldi hastened to the choir, the pavement of which was strewn with palm branches and fresh flowers. A pall of black velvet lay upon the steps of the altar, where several priests were silently attending. Everywhere appeared the ensigns of solemn pomp and ceremony, and in every countenance the stillness and observance of expectation. Meanwhile the sounds drew nearer, and Vivaldi perceived a procession of nuns approaching from a distant aisle.

As they advanced, he distinguished the lady abbess leading the train, dressed in her pontifical robes, with the mitre on her head; and well he marked her stately step, moving in time to the slow minstrelsy, and the air of proud yet graceful dignity with which she characterized herself. Then followed the nuns, according to their several orders, and last came the novices, carrying lighted tapers, and surrounded by other nuns, who were distinguished by a particular habit.

Having reached a part of the church appropriated for their reception, they arranged themselves in order. Vivaldi with a palpitating heart inquired the occasion of this ceremony, and was told that a nun was going to be professed.

"You are informed, no doubt, brother," added the friar who gave him this intelligence, "that on the morning of our high festival, our *Lady's* day, it is usual for such as devote themselves to heaven to receive the veil. Stand by a while, and you will see the ceremony."

"What is the name of the novice who is now to receive it?" said Vivaldi, in a voice whose tremulous accents betrayed his emotion.

The friar glanced an eye of scrutiny upon him, as he replied, "I know not her name, but if you will step a little this way, I will point her out to you."

Vivaldi, drawing his hood over his face, obeyed in silence.

"It is she on the right of the abbess," said the stranger, "who leans on the arm of a nun; she is covered with a white veil, and is taller than her companions."

Vivaldi observed her with a fearful eye, and, though he did not recognise the person of Ellena, whether it was that his fancy was possessed with her image, or that there was truth in his surmise, he thought he perceived a resemblance of her. He inquired how long the novice had resided in the convent, and many other particulars, to which the stranger either could not or dared not reply.

With what anxious solicitude did Vivaldi endeavour to look through the veils of the several nuns, in search of Ellena, whom he believed the barbarous policy of his mother might already have devoted to the cloister. With a solicitude still stronger, he tried to catch a glimpse of the features of the novices, but their faces were shaded by hoods, and their white veils, though thrown half back, were disposed in such artful folds that they concealed them from observation as effectually as did the pendant lawn the features of the nuns.

The ceremony began with the exhortation of the *Father-Abbot*, delivered with solemn energy; then the novice kneeling before him made her profession, for which Vivaldi listened with intense attention, but it was delivered in such low and trembling accents, that he could not ascertain even the tone. But during the anthem that mingled with the ensuing part of the service, he thought he distinguished the voice of Ellena—that touching and well-known voice, which in the church of San Lorenzo had first attracted his attention. He listened, scarcely daring to draw breath, lest he should lose a note; and again he fancied her voice spoke in a part of the plaintive response delivered by the nuns.

Vivaldi endeavoured to command his emotion, and to await with patience some further unfolding of the truth; but when the priest prepared to withdraw the white veil from the face of the novice, and throw the black one over her, a dreadful expectation that she was Ellena seized him, and he with difficulty forbore stepping forward and discovering himself on the instant.

The veil was at length withdrawn, and a very lovely face appeared, but not Ellena's. Vivaldi breathed again, and waited with tolerable composure for the conclusion of the ceremony; till, in the solemn strain that followed the putting on of the black veil, he heard again the voice, which he was now convinced was her's. Its accents were low, and mournful, and tremulous, yet his heart acknowledged instantaneously their magic influence.

When this ceremony had concluded another began, and he was told it was that of a noviciation. A young woman, supported by two nuns, advanced to the altar, and Vivaldi thought he beheld Ellena. The priest was beginning the customary exhortation, when she lifted her half-veil, and, showing a countenance where meek sorrow was mingled with heavenly sweetness, raised her blue eyes, all bathed in tears, and waved her hand as if she would have spoken. It was Ellena herself.

The priest attempted to proceed.

"I protest in the presence of this congregation," said she, solemnly, "that I am brought hither to pronounce vows which my heart disclaims. I protest——"

A confusion of voices interrupted her, and at the same time she perceived Vivaldi rushing towards the altar. Ellena gazed for a moment, and then, stretching forth her supplicating hands towards him, closed her eyes, and sank into the arms of some persons round her, who vainly endeavoured to prevent him from approaching and assisting her. The anguish with which he bent over her lifeless form and called upon her name excited the commiseration even of the nuns, and especially of Olivia, who was most assiduous in efforts to revive her young friend.

When Ellena unclosed her eyes, and, looking up, once more beheld Vivaldi, the expression with which she regarded him told that her heart was unchanged, and that she was unconscious of the miseries of imprisonment while he was with her. She desired to withdraw, and, assisted by Vivaldi and Olivia, was leaving the church, when the abbess ordered that she should be attended by the nuns only; and, retiring from the altar, she gave directions that the young stranger should be conducted to the parlour of the convent.

Vivaldi, though he refused to obey an imperious command, yielded to the entreaties of Ellena, and to the gentle remonstrances of Olivia; and, bidding Ellena farewell for a while, he repaired to the parlour of the abbess. He was not without some hope of awakening her to a sense of justice or of pity; but he found that her notions of right were inexorably against him, and that pride and resentment usurped the influence of every other feeling. She began her lecture with expressing the warm friendship she had so long cherished for the Marchesa, his mother; proceeded to lament that the son of a friend whom she so highly esteemed should have forgotten his duty to his parents, and the observance due to the dignity of his house, so far as to seek connection with a person of Ellena di Rosalba's inferior station; and concluded with a severe reprimand for having disturbed the tranquillity of her convent and the decorum of the church by his intrusion.

Vivaldi listened with submitting patience to this mention of morals and decorum from a person who, with the most perfect self-applause, was violating some of the plainest obligations of humanity and justice; who had conspired to tear an orphan from her home, and who designed to deprive her for life of liberty, with all the blessings it inherits. But, when she proceeded to speak of Ellena with the caustic of severe reprobation, and to hint at the punishment which her public rejection of the vows had incurred, the patience of Vivaldi submitted no longer; indignation and contempt rose high against the Superior, and he exhibited a portrait of herself in the strong colours of truth. But the mind which compassion could not persuade, reason could not appal—selfishness had hardened it alike to the influence of each; her pride only was affected, and she retaliated the mortification she suffered by menace and denunciation.

Vivaldi, on quitting her apartment, had no other resource than an application to the *Abate*, whose influence, at least, if not his authority, might assuage the severity of her power. In this Abate a mildness of temper and a gentleness of manner were qualities of less value than is usually and deservedly imputed to them; for, being connected with feebleness of mind, they were but the pleasing merits of easy times, which in an hour of difficulty never assumed the character of virtues, by inducing him to serve those for whom he might feel. And thus, with a temper and disposition directly opposite to those of the severe and violent abbess, he was equally selfish and almost equally culpable; since, by permitting evil, he was nearly as injurious in his conduct as those who planned it. Indolence and timidity—the consequence of want of clear perception—deprived him of all energy of character; he was prudent rather than wise, and so fearful of being thought to do wrong that he seldom did right.

To Vivaldi's temperate representations and earnest entreaties that he would exert some authority towards liberating Ellena, he listened with patience; acknowledged the hardships of her situation; lamented the unhappy divisions between Vivaldi and his family, and then declined advancing a single step in so delicate an affair. Signora di Rosalba, he said, was in the care of the abbess, over whom he had no right of control in matters relative to her domestic concerns. Vivaldi then supplicated, that though he possessed no authority, he would at least intercede or remonstrate against so unjust a procedure as that of detaining Ellena a prisoner, and assist in restoring her to the home from which she had been forcibly carried.

"And this, again," replied the Abate, "does not come within my jurisdiction; and I make it a rule never to encroach upon that of another person."

"And can you endure, holy father," said Vivaldi, "to witness a flagrant act of injustice and not endeavour to counteract it; not even step forward to rescue the victim when you perceive the preparation for the sacrifice?"

"I repeat, that I never interfere with the authority of others," replied the Superior; "having asserted my own, I yield to them, in their sphere, the obedience which I require in mine."

"Is power then," said Vivaldi, "the infallible test of justice? Is it morality to obey where the command is criminal? The whole world have a claim upon the fortitude, the active fortitude of those who are placed, as you are, between the alternative of confirming a wrong by your consent, or preventing it by your resistance. Would that your heart expanded towards that world, reverend father!"

"Would that the whole world were wrong that you might have the glory of setting it right!" said the Abate, smiling. "Young man! you are an enthusiast, and I pardon you. You are a knight of chivalry, who would go about the earth fighting with everybody, by way of proving your right to do good; it is unfortunate you are born somewhat too late."

"Enthusiasm in the cause of humanity" —said Vivaldi, but he checked himself; and

despairing of touching a heart so hardened by selfish prudence, and indignant at beholding an apathy so vicious in its consequence, he left the Abate without other effort. He perceived that he must now have recourse to further stratagem, a recourse which his frank and noble mind detested; but he had already tried, without success, every other possibility of rescuing the innocent victim of the Marchesa's prejudice and pride.

Ellena meanwhile had retired to her cell, agitated by a variety of considerations, and contrary emotions, of which, however, those of joy and tenderness were long predominant. Then came anxiety, apprehension, pride, and doubt, to divide and torture her heart. It was true that Vivaldi had discovered her prison, but if it were possible that he could release her, she must consent to quit it with him; a step from which a mind so tremblingly jealous of propriety as her's recoiled with alarm, though it would deliver her from captivity. And how, when she considered the haughty character of the Marchese di Vivaldi, the imperious and vindictive nature of the Marchesa, and, still more, their united repugnance to a connection with her, how could she endure to think, even for a moment of intruding herself into such a family! Pride, delicacy, good sense seemed to warn her against a conduct so humiliating and vexatious in its consequences, and to exhort her to preserve her own dignity by independence; but the esteem, the friendship, the tender affection, which she had cherished for Vivaldi made her pause and shrink with emotions of little less than horror, from the eternal renunciation which so dignified a choice required. Though the encouragement, which her deceased relative had given to this attachment seemed to impart to it a sacred character, that considerably soothed the alarmed delicacy of Ellena, the approbation thus implied had no power to silence her own objections and she would have regretted the mistaken zeal which had contributed to lead her into the present distressing situation, had she revered the memory of her aunt or loved Vivaldi less. Still, however, the joy, which his presence had occasioned, and which the consciousness that he was still near her had prolonged, was not subdued, though it was frequently obscured by such anxious considerations. With jealous and indiscreet solicitude, she now recollected every look and the accent of every word which had told that his affection was undiminished; thus seeking, with inconsistent zeal, for a conviction of the very tenderness which but a moment before she had thought it would be prudent to lament, and almost necessary to renounce.

She awaited with extreme anxiety the appearance of Olivia, who might probably know the result of Vivaldi's conference with the abbess, and whether he was yet in the convent.

In the evening Olivia came, a messenger of evil ; and Ellena, informed of the conduct of the abbess, and the consequent departure of Vivaldi, perceived all her courage, and all the half-formed resolutions which a consideration of his family had suggested, falter and expire. Sensible only of grief and despondency, she ascertained, for the first time, the extent of her affection and the severity of her situation. She perceived, also, that the injustice which his family had exercised towards her, absolved her from all consideration of their displeasure, otherwise than as it might affect herself; but this was a conviction which it were now probably useless to admit.

Olivia not only expressed the tenderest interest in her welfare, but seemed deeply affected with her situation ; and, whether it was that the nun's misfortunes bore some resemblance to Ellena's, or from whatever cause, it is remarkable that her eyes were often filled with tears, while she regarded her young friend, and she betrayed so much emotion that Ellena noticed it with surprise. She was, however, too delicate to hint any curiosity on the subject ; and too much engaged by a nearer interest to dwell long upon the circumstance.

When Olivia withdrew, Ellena retired to her turret, to soothe her spirits with a view of serene and majestic nature, a resource which seldom failed to elevate her mind and soften the asperities of affliction. It was to her like sweet and solemn music, breathing peace over the soul—like the oaten stop of Milton's spirit.

While she sat before a window, observing the evening light beaming up the valley, and touching all the distant mountains with misty purple, a reed as sweet, though not as fanciful, sounded from among the rocks below. The instrument and the character of the strain were such as she had been unaccustomed to hear within the walls of San Stefano, and the tone diffused over her spirits a pleasing melancholy that rapt all her attention. The liquid cadence, as it trembled and sunk away, seemed to tell the dejection of no vulgar feelings ; and the exquisite taste with which the complaining notes were again swelled almost convinced her that the musician was Vivaldi.

On looking from the lattice, she perceived a person perched on a point of the cliff below, whither it appeared almost impracticable for any human step to have climbed, and preserved from the precipice only by some dwarf shrubs that fringed the brow. The twilight did not permit her immediately to ascertain whether it was Vivaldi, and the situation was so dangerous that she hoped it was not he. Her doubts were removed when, looking up, she perceived Ellena and she heard his voice.

Vivaldi had learned from a lay-brother of the convent, whom Paulo had bribed, and who, when he worked in the garden, had sometimes seen Ellena at the window, that she frequented this remote turret ; and, at the hazard of his life, he had now ventured thither, with a hope of conversing with her.

Ellena, alarmed at his tremendous situation, refused to listen to him, but he would not leave the spot till he had communicated a plan concerted for her escape; and, intreating that she would confide herself to his care, assured her she would be conducted to wherever she judged proper. It appeared that the brother had consented to assist his views, in consideration of an ample reward, and to admit him within the walls on this evening, when, in his pilgrim's habit, he might have an opportunity of again seeing Ellena. He conjured her to attend, if possible, in the convent parlour during supper ; explaining, in a few words, the motive for this request, and the substance of the following particulars :

The lady-abbess, in observance of the custom upon high festivals, gave a collation to the *padre abate* and such of the priests as had assisted at vesper-service. A few strangers of distinction and pilgrims were also to partake of the entertainments of this night, among which was included a concert to be performed by the nuns. At the collation was to be displayed a profusion of delicacies, arranged by the sisters, who had been busy in preparing the pastry and confectionery during several days, and who excelled in these articles no less than in embroidery and other ingenious arts. This supper was to be given in the abbess's outer parlour, while she herself, attended by some nuns of high rank, and a few favourites, was to have a table in the inner apartment, where, separated only by the grate, she could partake of the conversation of the holy fathers. The tables were to be ornamented with artificial flowers, and a variety of other fanciful devices upon which the ingenuity of the sisters had been long employed; who prepared for these festivals with as much vanity, and expected them to dissipate the gloomy monotony of their usual life with as much eagerness of delight, as a young beauty anticipates a first ball.

On this evening, therefore, every member of the convent would be engaged either by amusement or business ; and to Vivaldi, who had been careful to inform himself of these circumstances, it would be easy, with the assistance of the brother, to obtain admittance, and mingle himself among the spectators, disguised in his pilgrim's habit. He entreated, therefore, that Ellena would contrive to be in the abbess's apartment this evening, when he would endeavour to convey to her some further particulars of the plan of escape, and would have mules in waiting at the foot of the mountain, to conduct her to Villa Altieri, or to the neighbouring convent of the Santa della Pieta. Vivaldi secretly hoped that she might be prevailed with to give him her hand on quitting San Stefano, but he forbore to mention this hope, lest it should be mistaken for a condition, and that Ellena might be either reluctant to accept his assistance, or, accepting it, might consider herself bound to grant a hasty consent.

To his mention of escape she listened with varying emotion, at one moment attending to it with hope and joy, as promising her only chance of liberation from an imprisonment which was probably intended to last for her life, and of restoring her to Vivaldi ; and at another, recoiling from the thought of departing with him while his family was so decidedly averse to their marriage. Thus, unable to form any instant resolution on the subject, and intreating that he would leave his dangerous station before the thickening twilight should increase the hazard of his descent, Ellena added that she would endeavour to obtain admittance to the apartment of the abbess, and to acquaint him with her final determination. Vivaldi understood all the delicacy of her scruples, and though they afflicted him, he honoured the good sense and just pride that suggested them.

He lingered on the rock till the last moments of departing light, and then, with a heart fluttering with hopes and fears, bade Ellena farewell, and descended : while she watched his progress through the silent gloom, faintly distinguishing him gliding along ledges of the precipice, and making his adventurous way from cliff to cliff, till the winding thickets concealed him from her view. Still anxious, she remained at the lattice, but he appeared no more ; no voice announced disaster ; and, at length, she returned to her cell, to deliberate on the subject of her departure.

Her considerations were interrupted by Olivia, whose manner indicated something extraordinary ; the usual tranquillity of her countenance was gone, and an air of grief mingled with apprehension appeared there. Before she spoke, she examined the passage and looked round the cell. "It is as I feared," said she abruptly ; "my suspicions are justified, and you, my child, are sacrificed, unless it were possible for you to quit the convent this night."

"What is it that you mean ?" said the alarmed Ellena.

"I have just learned," resumed the nun, "that your conduct this morning, which is understood to have thrown a premeditated insult upon the abbess, is to be punished with what they *call* imprisonment ; alas ! why should I soften the truth,—with what I believe is death itself, for who ever returned alive from that hideous chamber ! "

"With death ! " said Ellena, aghast ; " oh, heavens ! how have I deserved death ?"

"That is not the question, my daughter ; but how you may avoid it. Within the deepest recesses of our convent is a stone chamber, secured by doors of iron, to which such of the sisterhood as have been guilty of any heinous offence have, from time to time, been consigned. This condemnation admits of no reprieve ; the unfortunate captive is left to languish in chains and darkness, receiving only an allowance of bread and water just sufficient to prolong her sufferings, till nature, at length, sinking under their intolerable pressure, obtains refuge in death. Our records relate several instances of such horrible punishment, which has generally been inflicted upon nuns who, weary of the life which they had chosen under the first delusions of the imagination, or which they had been compelled to accept by the rigour or avarice of parents, have been detected in escaping from the convent."

The nun paused, but Ellena remaining wrapt in silent thought, she resumed : " One miserable instance of this severity has occurred within my memory. I saw the wretched victim enter that apartment—never more to quit it alive ! I saw, also, her poor remains laid at rest in the convent garden ! During nearly two years she languished upon a bed of straw, denied even the poor consolation of conversing through the grate with such of the sisters as pitied her ; and who of us was there that did not pity her ! A severe punishment was threatened to those who should approach with any compassionate intention ; thank God ! I incurred it, and I endured it, also, with secret triumph."

A gleam of satisfaction passed over Olivia's countenance as she spoke this ; it was the sweetest that Ellena had ever observed there. With a sympathetic emotion, she threw herself on the bosom of the nun and wept ; for some moments they were both silent. Olivia, at length, said, " Do you not believe, my child, that the officious and offended abbess will readily seize upon the circumstance of your disobedience as a pretence for confining you in that fatal chamber? The wishes of the Marchesa will thus surely be accomplished without the difficulty of exacting your obedience to the vows. Alas ! I have received proof too absolute of her intention, and that to-morrow is assigned as the day of your sacrifice ; you may, perhaps, be thankful that the business of the festival has obliged her to defer executing the sentence even till to-morrow."

Ellena replied only with a groan, as her head still drooped upon the shoulder of the nun ; she was not now. hesitating whether to accept the assistance of Vivaldi, but desponding lest his utmost efforts for her deliverance should be vain.

Olivia, who mistook the cause of her silence, added, "Other hints I could give, which are strong as they are dreadful, but I will forbear. Tell me how it is possible I may assist you; I am willing to incur a second punishment, in endeavouring to relieve a second sufferer."

Ellena's tears flowed fast at this new instance of the nun's generosity. "But if they should discover you in assisting me to leave the convent!" she said, in a voice convulsed by her gratitude, "Oh! if they should discover you!——"

"I can ascertain the punishment," Olivia replied with firmness, "and do not fear to meet it."

"How nobly generous this is!" said the weeping Ellena; "I ought not to suffer you to be thus careless of yourself!"

"My conduct is not wholly disinterested," the nun modestly replied; "for I think I could endure any punishment with more fortitude than the sickening anguish of beholding such sufferings as I have witnessed. What are bodily pains in comparison with the subtle, the exquisite tortures of the mind! Heaven knows I can support my own afflictions, but not the view of those of others when they are excessive. The instruments of torture I believe I could endure, if my spirit was invigorated with the consciousness of a generous purpose; but pity touches upon a nerve that vibrates instantly to the heart, and subdues resistance. Yes, my child, the agony of pity is keener than any other, except that of remorse, and even in remorse it is, perhaps, the mingling unavailing pity that points the sting. But while I am indulging this egotism, I am, perhaps, increasing your danger of the suffering I deprecate."

Ellena, thus encouraged by the generous sympathy of Olivia, mentioned Vivaldi's purposed visit of this evening; and consulted with her on the probability of procuring admittance for herself to the abbess's parlour. Reanimated by this intelligence, Olivia advised her to repair not only to the supper-room, but to attend the previous concert, to which several strangers would be admitted, among whom might probably be Vivaldi. When, to this, Ellena objected her dread of the abbess's observation, and of the immediate seclusion that would follow, Olivia soothed her fears of discovery by offering her the disguise of a nun's veil, and promising not only to conduct her to the apartment, but to afford every possible assistance towards her escape.

"Among the crowd of nuns who will attend in that spacious apartment," Olivia added, "it is improbable you would be distinguished, even if the sisters were less occupied by amusement, and the abbess were at leisure to scrutinise. As it is, you will hazard little danger of discovery; the superior, if she thinks of you at all, will believe you are still a prisoner in your cell;

but this is an evening of too much importance to her vanity for any consideration distinct from that emotion to divide her attention. Let hope, therefore, support you, my child, and do you prepare a few lines to acquaint Vivaldi with your consent to his proposal, and with the urgency of your circumstances; you may, perhaps, find an opportunity of conveying them through the grate."

They were still conversing on this subject, when a particular chime sounded, which Olivia said summoned the nuns to the concert-room; and she immediately hastened for a black veil, while Ellena wrote the few lines that were necessary for Vivaldi.

CHAPTER XII.

WRAPT in Olivia's veil, Ellena descended to the music-room and mingled with the nuns who were assembled within the grate. Among the monks and pilgrims without it were some strangers in the usual dress of the country, but she did not perceive any person who resembled Vivaldi; and she considered that, if he were present, he would not venture to discover himself, while her nun's veil concealed her as effectually from him as from the lady abbess. It would be necessary, therefore, to seek an opportunity of withdrawing it for a moment at the grate, an expedient which must, however, expose her to the notice of strangers.

On the entrance of the lady abbess, Ellena's fear of observation rendered her insensible to every other consideration; she fancied that the eyes of the Superior were particularly directed upon herself. The veil seemed an insufficient protection from their penetrating glances, and she almost sank with the terror of instant discovery.

The abbess, however, passed on, and, having conversed for a few moments with the *padre abate* and some visitors of distinction, took her chair; and the performance immediately opened with one of those solemn and impressive airs which the Italian nuns know how to give with so much taste and sweetness. It rescued even Ellena for a moment from a sense of danger, and she resigned herself to the surrounding scene, of which the *coup d'œil* was striking and grand. In a vaulted apartment of considerable extent, lighted by innumerable tapers, and where even the ornaments, though pompous, partook of the solemn character of the institution, were assembled about fifty nuns, who, in the interesting habit of their order, appeared with graceful plainness. The delicacy of their air, and their beauty, softened by the lawn that thinly veiled it, were contrasted by the severe majesty of the lady abbess, who, seated on an elevated chair, apart from the audience, seemed the empress of the scene;

and by the venerable figures of the father
abate and his attendant monks, who were
arranged without that screen of wire-work,
extending the whole breadth of the apartment, which is called the grate. Near the
holy father were placed the strangers of distinction, dressed in the splendid Neapolitan
habit, whose gay colouring and airy elegance
opposed well with the dark drapery of the
ecclesiastics ; their plumed hats loftily overtopping the half-cowled heads and grey locks
of the monks. Nor was the contrast of
countenances less striking ; the grave, the
austere, the solemn, and the gloomy inter-
mingling with the light, the blooming, and
the debonnaire, expressed all the various tempers that render life a blessing or a burden,
and, as with the spell of magic, transform
this world into a transient paradise or purgatory. In the background of the picture stood
some pilgrims, with looks less joyous and
more demure than they had worn on the road
the preceding day ; and among them were
some inferior brothers and attendants of the
convent. To this part of the chamber Ellena
frequently directed her attention, but did not
distinguish Vivaldi ; and, though she had
taken a station near the grate, she had not
courage indecorously to withdraw her veil
before so many strangers. And thus, if he
even were in the apartment, it was not probable he would venture to come forward.

The concert concluded without his having
been perceived by Ellena, and she withdrew
to the apartment where the collation was
spread, and where the abbess and her guests
soon after appeared. Presently she observed
a stranger in a pilgrim's habit station himself
near the grate ; his face was partly muffled in
his cloak, and he seemed to be a spectator
rather than a partaker of the feast.

Ellena, who understood this to be Vivaldi,
was watchful for an opportunity of approaching, unseen by the abbess, the place where
he had fixed himself. Engaged in conversation with the ladies around her, the Superior
soon favoured Ellena's wish, who, having
reached the grate, ventured to lift her veil for
one instant. The stranger, letting his cloak
fall, thanked her with his eyes for her condescension, and she perceived that he was
not Vivaldi ! Shocked at the interpretation
which might be given to a conduct apparently so improper, as much as by the disappointment which Vivaldi's absence occasioned,
she was hastily retiring, when another stranger
approached with quick steps, whom she instantly knew, by the grace and spirit of his
air, to be Vivaldi ; but, determined not to be
exposed a second time to the possibility of a
mistake, she awaited silently for some further
signal of his identity. His eyes were fixed
upon her in earnest attention before he drew
aside the cloak from his face. But he soon
did so ;—and it was Vivaldi himself.

Ellena, perceiving that she was known,
did not raise her veil, but advanced a few
steps towards the grate. Vivaldi there deposited a small folded paper, and before she
could venture to deliver her own billet, he
had retired among the crowd. As she stepped
forward to secure his letter, she observed a
nun hastily approach the spot where he had
laid it, and she paused. The garment of the
recluse wafted it from the place where it had
been partly concealed ; and when Ellena perceived the nun's foot rest upon the paper,
she with difficulty disguised her apprehensions.

A friar, who from without the grate addressed the sister, seemed with much earnestness, yet with a certain air of secrecy, communicating some important intelligence. The
fears of Ellena suggested that he had observed the action of Vivaldi, and was making
known his suspicions ; and she expected every
instant to see the nun lift up the paper and
deliver it to the abbess.

From this immediate apprehension, however, she was released when the sister pushed
it gently aside without examination, a circumstance that not less surprised than relieved her. But, when the conference broke
up, and the friar, hastily retreating among
the crowd, disappeared from the apartment,
and the nun approached and whispered the
Superior, all her terrors were renewed. She
scarcely doubted that Vivaldi was detected,
and that his letter was designedly left where
it had been deposited for the purpose of
alluring her to betray herself. Trembling,
dismayed, and almost sinking with apprehension, she watched the countenance of
the abbess while the nun addressed her, and
thought she read her own fate in the frown
that appeared there.

Whatever might be the intentions or the
directions of the Superior, no active measure
was at present employed ; the recluse,
having received an answer, retired quietly
among the sisters, and the abbess resumed
her usual manner. Ellena, however, supposing she was now observed, did not dare to
seize the paper, though she believed it contained momentous information ; and feared
that the time was now escaping which might
facilitate her deliverance. Whenever she
ventured to look round, the eyes of the
abbess seemed pointed upon her, and she
judged from the position of the nun, for the
veil concealed her face, that she also was
vigilantly regarding her.

Above an hour had elapsed in this state of
anxious suspense when the collation concluded, and the assembly broke up, during
the general bustle of which Ellena ventured
to the grate and secured the paper. As she
concealed it in her robe, she scarcely dared
to inquire by a hasty glance whether she had
been observed, and would have withdrawn

immediately to examine the contents, had she not perceived, at the same instant, the abbess quitting the apartment. On looking round for the nun, Ellena discovered that she was gone.

Ellena followed distantly in the abbess's train; and, as she drew nearer to Olivia, gave a signal, and passed on to her cell. There, once more alone, and having secured the door, she sat down to read Vivaldi's billet, trying to command her impatience, and to understand the lines, over which her sight rapidly moved, when, in the eagerness of turning over the paper, the lamp dropped from her trembling hand and expired. Her distress now nearly reached despair. To go forth into the convent for a light was utterly impracticable, since it would betray that she was no longer a prisoner, and not only would Olivia suffer from a discovery of the indulgence she had granted, but she herself would be immediately confined. Her only hope rested upon Olivia's arrival before it might be too late to practise the instructions of Vivaldi, if, indeed, they were still practicable; and she listened with intense solicitude for an approaching footstep, while she yet held, ignorant of its contents, the billet that probably would decide her fate. A thousand times she turned about the eventful paper, endeavoured to trace the lines with her fingers, and to guess their import, thus enveloped in mystery; while she experienced all the various torture that the consciousness of having in her very hand the information on a timely knowledge of which her life, perhaps, depended, without being able to understand it, could inflict.

Presently she heard advancing steps, and a light gleamed from the passage before she considered they might be some other than Olivia's, and that it was prudent to conceal the billet she held. The consideration, however, came too late to be acted upon; for, before the rustling paper was disposed of, a person entered the cell, and Ellena beheld her friend. Pale, trembling, and silent, she took the lamp from the nun, and eagerly running over Vivaldi's note, learned that at the time it was written brother Jerohimo was in waiting without the gate of the nuns' garden, where Vivaldi designed to join him immediately, and conduct her by a private way beyond the walls. He added that horses were stationed at the foot of the mountain to convey her wherever she should judge proper; and conjured her to be expeditious, since other circumstances, besides the universal engagement of the recluses, were at that moment particularly favourable to an escape.

Ellena, desponding and appalled, gave the paper to Olivia, requesting she would read it hastily, and advise her how to act. It was now an hour and a half since Vivaldi had said that success depended upon expedition, and that he had probably watched at the appointed place; in such an interval how many circumstances might have occurred to destroy every possibility of a retreat, which it was certain the engagement of the abbess and sisters no longer favoured!

The generous Olivia, having read the billet, partook of all her young friend's distress, and was as willing as Ellena was anxious to dare every danger for the chance of obtaining deliverance.

Ellena could feel gratitude for such goodness even at this moment of agonising apprehension. After a pause of deep consideration, Olivia said, "In every avenue of the convent we are now liable to meet some of the nuns; but my veil, though thin, has hitherto protected you, and we must hope it may still assist your purpose. It will be necessary, however, to pass through the refectory, where such of the sisters as did not partake of the collation are assembled at supper and will remain so till the first matin calls them to the chapel. If we wait till then, I fear it will be to no purpose to go at all."

Ellena's fears perfectly agreed with those of Olivia; and entreating that another moment might not be lost in hesitation, and that she would lead the way to the nuns' garden, they quitted the cell together.

Several of the sisters passed them as they descended to the refectory, but without particularly noticing Ellena, who, as she drew near that alarming apartment, wrapt her veil closer and leaned with heavier pressure upon the arm of her faithful friend. At the door they were met by the abbess, who had been overlooking the nuns assembled at supper, and missing Olivia, had inquired for her. Ellena shrank back to elude observation, and to let the Superior pass; but Olivia was obliged to answer to the summons. Having, however, unveiled herself, she was permitted to proceed; and Ellena, who had mingled with the crowd that surrounded the abbess, and thus escaped detection, followed Olivia, with faltering steps, through the refectory. The nuns were, luckily, too much engaged by the entertainment at this moment to look round them, and the fugitive reached, unsuspected, an opposite door.

In the hall to which they descended the adventurers were frequently crossed by servants bearing dishes from the refectory to the kitchen; and, at the very moment when they were opening the door that led into the garden, a sister, who had observed them, demanded whether they had yet heard the matin-bell, since they were going towards the chapel. Terrified at this critical interruption, Ellena pressed Olivia's arm, in signal of silence, and was hastening forward, when the latter, more prudent, paused, and calmly answering the question, was then suffered to proceed.

As they crossed the garden towards the gate, Ellena's anxiety lest Vivaldi should have been compelled to leave it, increased so much that she had scarcely power to proceed. "Oh, if my strength should fail before I reach it!" she said softly to Olivia, "or if I should reach it too late!"

Olivia tried to cheer her, and pointed out the gate, on which the moonlight fell. "At the end of this walk only," said Olivia; "see!—where the shadows of the trees open is your goal."

Encouraged by the view of it, Ellena fled with lighter steps along the alley; but the gate seemed to mock her approach, and to retreat before her. Fatigue overtook her in this long avenue before she could overtake the spot so anxiously sought, and, breathless and exhausted, she was once more compelled to stop, and once more in the agony of terror exclaimed, "Oh, if my strength should fail before I reach it!—Oh, if I should drop even while it is within my view!"

The pause of a moment enabled her to proceed, and she stopped not again till she arrived at the gate; when Olivia suggested the prudence of ascertaining who was without, and of receiving an answer to the signal which Vivaldi had proposed, before they ventured to make themselves known. She then struck upon the wood, and, in the anxious pause that followed, whispering voices were distinctly heard from without, but no signal spoke in reply to the nun's.

"We are betrayed!" said Ellena, softly; "but I will know the worst at once," and she repeated the signal, when, to her unspeakable joy, it was answered by three smart raps upon the gate. Olivia, more distrustful, would have checked the sudden hope of her friend till some further proof had appeared that it was Vivaldi who waited without, but the precaution came too late; a key already grated in the lock; the door opened, and two persons, muffled in their garments, presented themselves. Ellena was hastily retreating, when a well-known voice recalled her, and she perceived, by the rays of a half-hooded lamp which Jeronimo held, Vivaldi.

"Oh, Heavens!" he exclaimed, in a voice tremulous with joy, as he took her hand, "is it possible that you are again my own! If you could but know what I have suffered during this last hour!" Then observing Olivia, he drew back, till Ellena expressed her deep sense of obligation to the nun.

"We have no time to lose," said Jeronimo, sullenly; "we have stayed too long already, as you will find, perhaps."

"Farewell, dear Ellena!" said Olivia; "may the protection of Heaven never leave you!"

The fears of Ellena now gave way to affectionate sorrow, as, weeping on the bosom of the nun, she said "Farewell! oh, farewell, my dear, my tender friend! I must never,

never see you more, but I shall always love you; and you have promised that I shall hear from you. Remember the Convent della Pieta!"

"You should have settled this matter within," said Jeronimo; "we have been here these two hours already."

"Ah, Ellena!" said Vivaldi, as he gently disengaged her from the nun, "do I then hold only the second place in your heart?"

Ellena, as she dismissed her tears, replied with a smile more eloquent than words; and when she had again and again bade adieu to Olivia, she gave him her hand and quitted the gate.

"It is moonlight," observed Vivaldi to Jeronimo; "your lamp is useless, and may betray us."

"It will be necessary in the church," replied Jeronimo, "and in some circuitous avenues we must pass, for I dare not lead you out through the great gates, signor, as you well know."

"Lead on, then," replied Vivaldi, and they reached one of the cypress walks that extended to the church; but before they entered it, Ellena paused and looked back to the garden gate, that she might see Olivia once again. The nun was still there, and Ellena perceived her faintly in the moonlight, waving her hand in signal of a last adieu. Ellena's heart was full; she wept, and lingered, and returned the signal, till the gentle violence of Vivaldi withdrew her from the spot.

"I envy your friend those tears," said he, "and feel jealous of the tenderness that excites them. Weep no more, my Ellena."

"If you knew her worth," replied Ellena, "and the obligations I owe her!" Her voice was lost in sighs, and Vivaldi only pressed her hand in silence.

As they traversed the gloomy walk that led to the church, Vivaldi said, "Are you certain, father, that not any of the brothers are doing penance at the shrines in our way?"

"Doing penance on a festival, signor! They are more likely, by this time, to be taking down the ornaments."

"That would be equally unfortunate for us," said Vivaldi; "cannot we avoid the church, father?"

Jeronimo assured him that this was impossible; and they immediately entered one of its lonely aisles, where he unhooded the lamp, for the tapers, which had given splendour at an earlier hour to the numerous shrines, had expired, except those at the high altar, which were so remote that their rays faded into twilight long before they reached the part of the church where the fugitives passed. Here and there, indeed, a dying lamp shot a tremulous gleam upon the shrine below, and vanished again, serving to mark the distances in the long perspective of arches rather than to enlighten the gloomy solitude;

but no sound, not even of a whisper, stole along the pavement.

They crossed to a side door communicating with the court, and with the rock which enshrined the image of *Our Lady of Mount Carmel.* There the sudden glare of tapers issuing from the cave alarmed the fugitives, who had begun to retreat, when Jeronimo, stepping forward to examine the place, assured them there was no symptom of any person being within, and that lights burned day and night around the shrine.

Revived by this explanation, they followed into the cave, where their conductor opened a part of the wire-work enclosing the saint, and led them to the extremity of the vault, sunk deep within which appeared a small door. While Ellena trembled with apprehension, Jeronimo applied a key, and they perceived, beyond the door, a narrow passage winding away into the rock. The monk was leading on, but Vivaldi, who partook of the suspicions of Ellena, paused at the entrance, and demanded whither he was conducting them.

"To the place of your *destination*," replied the brother, in a hollow voice; an answer which alarmed Ellena, and did not satisfy Vivaldi. "I have given myself to your guidance," he said, "and have confided to you what is dearer to me than existence. Your life," pointing to the short sword concealed beneath his pilgrim's vest, "your life, you may rely upon my word, shall answer for your treachery. If your purpose is evil, pause a moment, and repent, or you shall not quit this passage alive."

"Do you menace me?" replied the brother, his countenance darkening. "Of what service would be my death to you? Do you know that every brother in the convent would rise to avenge it?"

"I know only that I will make sure of one traitor, if there be one," said Vivaldi, "and defend this lady against your host of monks; and, since you also know this, proceed accordingly."

At this instant, it occurring to Ellena that the passage in question probably led to the prison-chamber which Olivia had described as situated within some deep recess of the convent, and that Jeronimo had certainly betrayed them, she refused to go further. "If your purpose is honest," said she, "why do you not conduct us through some direct gate of the convent? why are we brought into these subterraneous labyrinths?"

"There is no direct gate but that of the portal," Jeronimo replied, "and this is the only other avenue leading beyond the walls."

"And why can we not go out through the portal?" Vivaldi asked.

"Because it is beset with pilgrims and lay brothers," replied Jeronimo, "and though you might pass them safely enough, what is to

become of the lady? But all this you knew before, signor; and were willing enough to trust me then. The passage we are entering opens upon the cliffs, at some distance. I have run hazard enough already, and will waste no more time; so if you do not choose to go forward, I will leave you, and you may act as you please."

He concluded with a laugh of derision, and was re-locking the door, when Vivaldi, alarmed for the probable consequence of his resentment and somewhat reassured by the indifference he discovered as to their pursuing the avenue or not, endeavoured to appease him, as well as to encourage Ellena; and he succeeded in both.

As he followed in silence through the gloomy passage, his doubts were, however, not so wholly vanquished but that he was prepared for attack, and while he supported Ellena with one hand, he held his sword in the other.

The avenue was of considerable length, and before they reached its extremity they heard music from a distance, winding along the rocks. "Hark!" cried Ellena, "whence come those sounds? Listen!"

"From the cave we have left," replied Jeronimo, "and it is midnight by that; it is the last chaunt of the pilgrims at the shrine of our Lady. Make haste, signor; I shall be called for."

The fugitives now perceived that all retreat was cut off, and that, if they had lingered a few moments longer in the cave, they should have been surprised by those devotees, some one of whom, however, it appeared possible, might wander into this avenue, and still interrupt their escape. When Vivaldi told his apprehensions, Jeronimo, with an arch sneer, affirmed there was no danger of that, "for the passage," he added, "is known only to the brothers of the convent."

Vivaldi's doubts vanished when he further understood that the avenue led only from the cliffs without to the cave, and was used for the purpose of conveying secretly to the shrine such articles as were judged necessary to excite the superstitious wonder of the devotees.

While he proceeded in thoughtful silence, a distant chime sounded hollowly through the chambers of the rock. "The matin-bell strikes!" said Jeronimo, in seeming alarm. "I am summoned. Signora, quicken your steps!" an unnecessary request, for Ellena already passed with her utmost speed; and she now rejoiced on perceiving a door in the remote winding of the passage, which she believed would emancipate her from the convent. But, as she advanced, the avenue appeared extending beyond it; and the door, which stood a little open, allowed her a glimpse of a chamber in the cliff, duskily lighted.

Vivaldi, alarmed by the light, inquired,

C

when he had passed, whether any person was in the chamber, and received an equivocal answer from Jeronimo, who, however, soon after pointed to an arched gate that terminated the avenue. They proceeded with lighter steps, for hope now cheered their hearts, and, on reaching the gate, all apprehension vanished. Jeronimo gave the lamp to Vivaldi, while he began to unbar and unlock the door, and Vivaldi had prepared to reward the brother for his fidelity, before they perceived that the door refused to yield. A dreadful imagination seized on Vivaldi. Jeronimo, turning round, coolly said, "I fear we are betrayed; the second lock is shot! I have only the key of the first."

"We *are* betrayed," said Vivaldi in a resolute tone; "but do not suppose that your dissimulation conceals you. I understand by whom we are betrayed. Recollect my late assertion, and consider once more whether it is your interest to intercept us."

"My signor," replied Jeronimo, "I do not deceive you when I protest by our holy saint that I have not caused this gate to be fastened, and that I would open it if I could. The lock which holds it was not shot an hour ago. I am the more surprised at what has happened because this place is seldom passed, even by the holiest footstep; and I fear whoever has passed now has been led hither by suspicion, and comes to intercept your flight."

"Your wily explanation, brother, may serve you for an inferior occasion, but not on this," replied Vivaldi; "either, therefore, unclose the gate, or prepare for the worst. You are not now to learn that, however slightly I may estimate my own life, I will never abandon this lady to the horrors which your community have already prepared for her."

Ellena, summoning her fleeting spirits, endeavoured to calm the indignation of Vivaldi, and to prevent the consequence of his suspicions, as well as to prevail with Jeronimo to unfasten the gate. Her efforts were, however, followed by a long altercation; but, at length, the art or the innocence of the brother appeased Vivaldi, who now endeavoured to force the gate, while Jeronimo in vain represented its strength, and the certain ruin that must fall upon himself if it should be discovered that he had concurred in destroying it.

The gate was immovable; but, as no other chance of escaping appeared, Vivaldi was not easily prevailed with to desist; all possibility of retreating too was gone, since the church and the cave were now crowded with devotees attending the matin service.

Jeronimo, however, seemingly did not despair of effecting their release, but he acknowledged that they would probably be compelled to conceal themselves in this gloomy avenue all night, and perhaps the next day. At length it was agreed that he should return to the church, to examine whether a possibility remained of the fugitives passing unobserved to the great portal; and, having conducted them back to the chamber, of which they had taken a passing glimpse, he proceeded to the shrine.

For a considerable time after his departure they were not without hope; but, their confidence diminishing as his delay increased, their uncertainty at length became terrible; and it was only for the sake of Vivaldi, from whom she scrupulously concealed all knowledge of the particular fate which she was aware must await her in the convent, that Ellena appeared to endure it with calmness. Notwithstanding the plausibility of Jeronimo, suspicion of his treachery returned upon her mind. The cold and earthy air of this chamber was like that of a sepulchre; and when she looked round, it appeared exactly to correspond with the description given by Olivia of the prison where the nun had languished and expired. It was walled and vaulted with the rock, and had only one small grated aperture in the roof to admit air, and contained no furniture, except one table, a bench, and the lamp, which dimly showed the apartment. That a lamp should be found burning in a place so remote and solitary, amazed her still more when she recollected the assertion of Jeronimo—that even holy steps seldom passed this way; and when she considered also, that he had expressed no surprise at a circumstance, according to his own assertion, so unusual. Again it appeared that she had been betrayed into the very prison designed for her by the Abbess; and the horror occasioned by this supposition was so great that she was on the point of disclosing it to Vivaldi; but an apprehension of the destruction into which his desperate courage might precipitate him restrained her.

While these considerations occupied Ellena, and it appeared that any certainty would be less painful than this suspense, she frequently looked round the chamber in search of some object which might contradict or confirm her suspicion that this was the death-room of the unfortunate nun. No such circumstance appeared, but as her eyes glanced with almost frenzied eagerness, she perceived something shadowy in a remote corner of the floor; and, on approaching, discovered what seemed a dreadful hieroglyphic—a mattress of straw, in which she thought she beheld the death-bed of the miserable recluse; nay, more, that the impression it still retained was that which her form had left there.

While Vivaldi was yet entreating her to explain the occasion of the horror she betrayed, the attention of each was withdrawn by a hollow sigh that rose near them. Ellena caught unconsciously the arm of Vivaldi, and listened, aghast, for a return of the sound, but all remained still.

"It surely was not fancied!" said Vivaldi, after a long pause ; "you heard it also!"

"I did!" replied Ellena.

"It was a sigh, was it not?" he added.

"Oh, yes, and such a sigh!"

"Some person is concealed near us," observed Vivaldi, looking round ; "but be not alarmed, Ellena ; I have a sword."

"A sword! alas! you know not —— But hark! there, again!"

That was very near us!" said Vivaldi. "This lamp burns so sickly!"—and he held it high, endeavouring to penetrate the furthest gloom of the chamber. "Hah! who goes there?" he cried, and stepped suddenly forward ; but no person appeared, and a silence, as of the tomb, returned.

"If you are in sorrow, speak!" Vivaldi at length said ; "from fellow-sufferers you will meet with sympathy. If your designs are evil —tremble, for you shall find I am desperate."

Still no answer was returned, and he carried forward the lamp to the opposite end of the chamber, where he perceived a small door in the rock. At the same instant he heard, from within, a low tremulous sound, as of a person in prayer or in agony. He pressed against the door, which, to his surprise, yielded immediately, and discovered a figure kneeling before a crucifix, with an attention so wholly engaged as not to observe the presence of a stranger till Vivaldi spoke. The person then rose from his knees, and turning, showed the silvered temples and pale features of an aged monk. The mild and sorrowful character of the countenance, and the lambent lustre of eyes which seemed still to retain somewhat of the fire of genius, interested Vivaldi, and encouraged Ellena, who had followed him.

An unaffected surprise appeared in the air of the monk ; but Vivaldi, notwithstanding the interesting benignity of his countenance, feared to answer his inquiries, till the father hinted to him that an explanation was necessary even to his own safety. Encouraged by his manner, rather than intimidated by this hint, and perceiving that his situation was desperate, Vivaldi confided to the friar some partial knowledge of his embarrassment.

While he spoke, the father listened with deep attention, looked with compassion alternately upon him and Ellena ; and some harassing objection seemed to contend with the pity which urged him to assist the strangers. He inquired how long Jeronimo had been absent, and shook his head significantly when he learned that the gate of the avenue was fastened by a double lock. "You are betrayed, my children" said he ; "you have trusted with the simplicity of youth, and the cunning of age has deceived you."

This terrible conviction affected Ellena to tears ; and Vivaldi, scarcely able to command the indignation, which a view of such treachery excited, was unable to offer her any consolation.

"You, my daughter, I remember to have seen in the church this morning," observed the friar. "I remember, too, that you protested against the vows you were brought thither to seal. Alas! my child, were you aware of the consequence of such a proceeding?"

"I had only a choice of evils," Ellena replied.

"Holy father," said Vivaldi, "I will not believe that you are one of those who either assisted in or approved the persecution of innocence. If you were acquainted with the misfortunes of this lady, you would pity and save her, but there is now no time for detail ; and I can only conjure you, by every sacred consideration, to assist her to leave the convent. If there were leisure to inform you of the unjustifiable means which have been employed to bring her within these walls—if you knew that she was taken, an orphan, from her home at midnight—that armed ruffians brought her hither—and at the command of strangers—that she has not a single relation surviving to assert her right of independence, or reclaim her of her persecutors. Oh! holy father, if you knew all this ——" Vivaldi was unable to proceed.

The friar again regarded Ellena with compassion, but still in thoughtful silence. "All this may be very true," at length he said, "but——" and he hesitated.

"I understand you, father," said Vivaldi—"you require proof ; but how can proof be adduced here? You must rely upon the honour of my word. And, if you are inclined to assist us, it must be immediately!—while you hesitate, we are lost. Even now I think I hear the footsteps of Jeronimo."

He stepped softly to the door of the chamber, but all was yet still. The friar, too, listened, but he also deliberated ; while Ellena, with a look of eager supplication and terror, awaited his decision.

"No one is approaching," said Vivaldi, "it is not yet too late!—Good father! if you would serve us, despatch."

"Poor innocent!" said the friar, half to himself, "in this chamber—in this fatal place——"

"In this chamber!" exclaimed Ellena, anticipating his meaning. "It was in this chamber, then, that a nun was suffered to perish ; and I, no doubt, am conducted hither to undergo a similar fate!"

"In this chamber!" re-echoed Vivaldi, in a voice of desperation. "Holy father, if you are indeed disposed to assist us, let us act this instant ; the next, perhaps, may render your best intentions unavailing."

The friar, who had regarded Ellena while she mentioned the nun with the utmost surprise, now withdrew his attention ; a few

Tears fell on his cheek, but he hastily dried them, and seemed struggling to overcome some grief that was deep in his heart.

Vivaldi, finding that entreaty had no power to hasten his decision, and expecting every moment to hear the approach of Jeronimo, paced the chamber in agonising perturbation, now pausing at the door to listen, and then calling, though almost hopelessly, upon the humanity of the friar; while Ellena, looking round the room in shuddering horror, repeatedly exclaimed, "On this very spot! in this very chamber! Oh, what sufferings have these walls witnessed! what are they yet to witness!"

Vivaldi now endeavoured to soothe the spirits of Ellena, and again urged the friar to employ this critical moment in saving her. "Oh, heaven!" said he, "if she is now discovered her fate is certain!"

"I dare not say what that fate would be," interrupted the father, "or what my own, should I consent to assist you; but, though I am old, I have not quite forgotten to feel for others. They may oppress the few remaining years of my age, but the blooming days of youth should flourish; and they shall flourish, my children, if my power can aid you. Follow me to the gate; we will see whether my key cannot unfasten all the locks that hold it."

Vivaldi and Ellena immediately followed the feeble steps of the old man, who frequently stopped to listen whether Jeronimo or any of the brothers, to whom the latter might have betrayed Ellena's situation, were approaching; but not an echo wandered along the lonely avenue till they reached the gate, when distant footsteps beat upon the ground.

"They are approaching, father," whispered Ellena. "Oh, if the key should not open these locks instantly, we are lost! Hark! now I hear their voices—they call upon my name! Already they have discovered we have left the chamber."

While the friar, with trembling hands, applied the key, Vivaldi endeavoured at once to assist him and to encourage Ellena.

The locks gave way, and the gate opened at once upon the moonlight mountains. Ellena heard once more, with the joy of liberty, the midnight breeze passing among the pensile branches of the palms that loftily overshadowed a rude platform before the gate, and rustling with fainter sound among the pendent shrubs of the surrounding cliffs.

"There is no leisure for thanks, my children," said the friar, observing they were about to speak. "I will fasten the gate, and endeavour to delay your pursuers, that you may have time to escape. My blessing go with you."

Ellena and Vivaldi had scarcely a moment to bid him "farewell" before he closed the door, and Vivaldi, taking her arm, was hastening towards the spot where he had ordered Paulo to wait with the horses, when, on turning an angle of the convent wall, they perceived a long train of pilgrims issuing forth from the portal at a little distance.

Vivaldi drew back; yet, dreading every moment that he lingered near the monastery to hear the voice of Jeronimo or other persons from the avenue, he was sometimes inclined to proceed at any hazard. The only practicable path leading to the base of the mountain, however, was now occupied by these devotees, and to mingle with them was little less than certain destruction. A bright moonlight showed distinctly every figure that moved in the scene, and the fugitives kept within the shadow of the walls, till, warned by an approaching footstep, they crossed to the feet of the cliffs that rose beyond some palmy hillocks on the right, whose dusky recesses promised a temporary shelter. As they passed with silent steps along the winding rocks, the tranquillity of the landscape below afforded an affecting contrast with the tumult and alarm of their minds.

Being now at some distance from the monastery, they rested under the shade of the cliffs till the procession of devotees, which was traced descending among the thickets and hollows of the mountain, should be sufficiently remote. Often they looked back to the convent, expecting to see lights issue from the avenue or the portal, and attended in mute anxiety for the sullen murmurs of pursuit; but none came on the breeze, nor did any gleaming lamp betray the steps of a spy.

Released, at length, from immediate apprehension, Ellena listened to the matin-hymn of the pilgrims, as it came upon the still air and descended towards the cloudless heavens. Not a sound mingled with the holy strain, and even in the measured pause of voices only the trembling of the foliage above was distinguished. The responses, as they softened away in distance, and swelled again on the wasting breeze, appeared like the music of spirits, watching by night upon the summits of the mountains, and answering each other in celestial airs, as they walk their high boundary and overlook the sleeping world.

"How often, Ellena, at this hour," said Vivaldi, "have I lingered round your dwelling, consoled by the consciousness of being near you! Within those walls, I have said, she reposes; they enclose my world; all without is to me a desert. Now, I am in your presence! Oh, Ellena! now that you are once more restored to me, suffer not the caprice of possibility again to separate us! Let me lead you to the first altar that will confirm our vows."

Vivaldi forgot, in the anxiety of a stronger interest, the delicate silence he had resolved to impose upon himself till Ellena should be in a place of safety.

"This is not a moment," she replied, with hesitation, "for conversation. Our situation is yet perilous ; we tremble on the very brink of danger."

Vivaldi immediately rose. "Into what imminent danger," said he, "had my selfish folly nearly precipitated you ! We are lingering in this alarming neighbourhood, when that feeble strain indicates the pilgrims to be sufficiently remote to permit us to proceed !"

As he spoke, they descended cautiously among the cliffs, often looking back to the convent, where, however, no light appeared; except what the moon shed over the spires and tall windows of its cathedral. For a moment, Ellena fancied she saw a taper in her favourite turret, and a belief that the nuns, perhaps the abbess herself, were searching for her there, renewed her terror and her speed. But the rays were only those of the moon striking through opposite casements of the chamber ; and the fugitives reached the base of the mountain without further alarm, where Paulo appeared with horses. "Ah ! signor *mio*," said the servant, "I am glad to see you alive and merry ; I began to fear, by the length of your stay, that the monks had clapped you up to do penance for life. How glad I am to see you, *maestro !*

"Not more so than I am to see you, good Paulo. But where is the pilgrim's cloak I bade you provide?"

Paulo displayed it, and Vivaldi having wrapped it round Ellena, and placed her on horseback, they took the road towards Naples, Ellena designing to take refuge in the Convent della Pieta. Vivaldi, however, apprehending that their enemies would seek them on this road, proposed leaving it as soon as practicable, and reaching the neighbourhood of Villa Altieri by a circuitous way.

They soon after arrived at the tremendous pass through which Ellena had approached the monastery, and whose horrors were considerably heightened at this dusky hour, for the moonlight fell only partially upon the deep barriers of the defile, and frequently the precipice, with the road on its brow, was entirely shadowed by other cliffs and woody points that rose above it. But Paulo, whose spirits seldom owned the influence of local scenery, jogged merrily along, frequently congratulating himself and his master on their escape, and carolling briskly to the echoes of the rocks, till Vivaldi, apprehensive for the consequence of this loud gaiety, desired him to desist.

"Ah, signor *mio !* I must obey you," said he, "but my heart was never so full in my life ; and I would fain sing to unburden it of some of its joy. That scrape we got into in the dungeon there, at what's the name of the place ? was bad enough, but it was nothing to this, because here I was left out of it ; and

you, *maestro*, might have been murdered again and again, while I, thinking of nothing at all, was quietly airing myself on the mountain by moonlight.

"But what is that yonder in the sky, signor ? It looks for all the world like a bridge ; only it is perched so high that nobody would think of building one in such an out-of-the-way place, unless to cross from cloud to cloud, much less would take the trouble of clambering up after it, for the pleasure of going over."

Vivaldi looked forward, and Ellena perceived the Alpine bridge she had formerly crossed with so much alarm in the moonlight perspective, airily suspended between tremendous cliffs, with the river far below, tumbling down the rocky chasm. One of the supporting cliffs, with part of the bridge, was in deep shade, but the other, feathered with foliage, and the rising surges at its foot, were strongly illumined ; and many a thicket, wet with the spray, sparkled in contrast to the dark rock it overhung. Beyond the arch the long-drawn prospect faded into misty light.

"Well, to be sure ! " exclaimed Paulo, "to see what curiosity will do ! If there are not some people have found their way up to the bridge already."

Vivaldi now perceived figures upon the slender arch, and, as their indistinct forms glided into the moonshine, other emotions than those of wonder disturbed him, lest these might be pilgrims going to the shrine of our Lady and who would give information of his route. No possibility, however, appeared of avoiding them, for the precipices that rose immediately above, and fell below, forbade all excursion, and the road itself was so narrow, as scarcely to admit of two horses passing each other.

"They are all off the bridge now, and without having broken their necks, perhaps ! " said Paulo ; "where, I wonder, will they go next ! Why, surely, signor, this road does not lead to the bridge yonder ; we are not going to pick our way in the air too. The roar of these waters has made my head dizzy already ; and the rocks here are as dark as midnight, and seem ready to tumble upon one ; they are enough to make one despair to look at them. You need not have checked my mirth, signor."

"I would fain check your loquacity," replied Vivaldi. "Do, good Paulo, be silent and circumspect ; those people may be near us, though we do not yet see them."

"The road does lead to the bridge then, signor," said Paulo, dolorously. "And see, there they are again, winding round that cliff, and coming towards us."

"Hush, they are pilgrims," whispered Vivaldi ; "we will linger under the shade of these rocks while they pass. Remember, Paulo, that a single indiscreet word may be fatal; and that if they hail us, I alone am to answer."

"You are obeyed, signor."

The fugitives drew up close under the cliffs, and proceeded slowly, while the words of the devotees, as they advanced, became audible.

"It gives one some comfort," said Paulo, "to hear cheerful voices in such a place as this. Bless their merry hearts! theirs seems a pilgrimage of pleasure; but they will be demure enough, I warrant, by-and-by. I wish I ——"

"Paulo, have you so soon forgot?" said Vivaldi, sharply.

The devotees, on perceiving the travellers, became suddenly silent; till he who appeared to be the father-director, as they passed, said "Hail! in the name of Our Lady of Mount Carmel!" and they repeated the salutation in chorus.

"Hail!" replied Vivaldi; "the first mass is over," and he passed on.

"But if you make haste you may come in for the second," said Paulo, jogging after.

"You have just left the shrine, then?" said one of the party, "and can tell us ——"

"Poor pilgrims, like yourselves," replied Paulo, "and can tell as little. Good morrow, fathers; yonder peeps the dawn."

He came up with his master, who had hurried forward with Ellena, and who now severely reproved his indiscretion; while the voices of the Carmelites, singing the matin-hymn, sank away among the rocks, and the quietness of solitude returned.

"Thank heaven, we are quit of this adventure," said Vivaldi.

"And now we have only the bridge to get over," rejoined Paulo, "and I hope we shall all be safe."

They were now at the entrance of it. As they passed the trembling planks, and looked up the defile, a party of people appeared advancing on the road the fugitives had left, and a chorus of other voices than those of the Carmelites were heard mingling with the hollow sound of the waters.

Ellena, again alarmed, hastened forward, and Vivaldi, though he endeavoured to appease her apprehension of pursuit, encouraged her speed.

"These are nothing but more pilgrims, signora," said Paulo, "or they would not send such loud shouts before them; they must needs think we can hear."

The travellers proceeded as fast as the broken road would permit, and were soon beyond the reach of the voices; but as Paulo turned to look whether the party was within sight, he perceived two persons, wrapped in cloaks, advancing under the brow of the cliffs, and within a few paces of his horse's heels. Before he could give notice to his master, they were at his side.

"Are you returning from the shrine of Our Lady?" said one of them.

Vivaldi, startled by the voice, looked round, and demanded who asked the question.

"A brother pilgrim," replied the man; "one who has toiled up these steep rocks till his limbs will scarcely bear him further. Would that you would take compassion on him, and give him a ride."

However compassionate Vivaldi might be to the sufferings of others, this was not a moment when he could indulge his disposition without endangering the safety of Ellena; and he even fancied the stranger spoke in a voice of dissimulation. His suspicions were strengthened when the traveller, not repulsed by a refusal, inquired the way he was going, and proposed to join his party. "For these mountains, they say, are infested with banditti," he added, "and a large company is less likely to be attacked than a small one."

"If you are so very weary, my friend," said Vivaldi, "how is it possible you can keep pace with our horses? though I acknowledge you have done wonders in overtaking them."

"The fear of these banditti," replied the stranger, "urged us on."

"You have nothing to apprehend from robbers," said Vivaldi, "if you will only moderate your pace; for a large company of pilgrims are on the road, who will soon overtake you."

He then put an end to the conversation by clapping spurs to his horse, and the strangers were soon left far behind. The inconsistency of their complaints with their ability, and the whole of their manner, were serious subjects of alarm to the fugitives; but when they had lost sight of them, they lost also their apprehensions; and having at length emerged from the pass, they quitted the high road to Naples, and struck into a solitary one that led westward towards Aquila.

CHAPTER XIII.

FROM the summit of a mountain the morning light showed the travellers the distant lake of Celano, gleaming at the feet of other lofty mountains of the Apennine far in the south. Thither Vivaldi judged it prudent to direct his course, for the lake lay so remote from the immediate way to Naples, and from the neighbourhood of San Stefano, that its banks promised a secure retreat. He considered, also, that among the convents scattered along those delightful banks might easily be found a priest who would solemnize their nuptials, should Ellena consent to an immediate marriage.

The travellers descended among olive woods, and soon after were directed by some peasants at work into a road that leads from Aquila to the town of Celano, one of the very few roads which intrude among the wild mountains that on every side sequester the lake. As they approached the low grounds the scent of orange blossoms breathed upon the morning air, and the spicy myrtle sent forth all its fragrance from among the cliffs which it thickly tufted. Bowers of lemon and orange spread along the valley, and among the cabins of the peasants who cultivated them Vivaldi hoped to obtain repose and refreshment for Ellena.

The cottages, however, at which Paulo inquired were unoccupied, the owners being all gone forth to their labour: and the travellers, again ascending, found themselves soon after among mountains inhabited by the flocks, where the scent of the orange was exchanged for the aromatic perfume of the pasturage.

"My signor," said Paulo, "is not that a shepherd's horn sounding at a distance? If so, the signora may yet obtain some refreshment."

While Vivaldi listened, a hautboy and a pastoral drum were heard considerably nearer.

They followed the sound over the turf, and came within view of a cabin, sheltered from the sun by a tuft of almond trees. It was a dairy-cabin belonging to some shepherds, who at a short distance were watching their flocks, and, stretched beneath the shade of chestnuts, were amusing themselves by playing upon these rural instruments: a scene of Arcadian manners frequent at this day upon the mountains of Abruzzo. The simplicity of their appearance, approaching to wildness, was tempered by a hospitable spirit. A venerable man, the chief shepherd, advanced to meet the strangers, and learning their wants, conducted them into his cool cabin, where cream, cheese made of goat's milk, honey extracted from the delicious herbage of the mountains, and dried figs, were quicklyplaced before them.

Ellena, overcome with the fatigue of anxiety, rather than that of travelling, retired, when she had taken breakfast, for an hour's repose, while Vivaldi rested on the bench before the cottage, and Paulo, keeping watch, discussed his breakfast, together with the circumstances of the late alarm, under the shade of the almond trees.

When Ellena again appeared, Vivaldi proposed that they should rest here during the intense heat of the day; and, since he now considered her to be in a place of temporary safety, he ventured to renew the subject nearest his heart; to represent the evils that might overtake them, and to urge an immediate solemnisation of their marriage. Thoughtful and dejected, Ellena attended for some time in silence to the arguments and pleadings of Vivaldi. She secretly acknowledged the justness of his representations, but she shrunk, more than ever, from the in-

delicacy, the degradation, of intruding herself into his family ; a family, too, from whom she had not only received proofs of strong dislike, but had suffered terrible injustice and been menaced with still severer cruelty. These latter circumstances, however, released her from all obligations of delicacy or generosity, so far as concerned only the authors of her suffering ; and she had now but to consider the happiness of Vivaldi and herself. Yet she could not decide thus precipitately on a subject which so solemnly involved the fortune of her whole life ; nor forbear reminding Vivaldi, affectionately, gratefully, as she loved him, of the circumstances which withheld her decision.

"Tell me yourself," added she, "whether I ought to give my hand, while your family —your mother"——She paused, and blushed, and burst into tears.

"Spare me the view of those tears," said Vivaldi, "and a recollection of the circumstances that excite them. Oh, let me not think of my mother, while I see you weep ! Let me not remember that her injustice and cruelty destined you to perpetual sorrow !"

Vivaldi's features became agitated while he spoke ; he rose, paced the room with quick steps, and then quitted it and walked under the shade of the trees in front of the cabin.

In a few moments, however, he commanded his emotion and returned. Again he placed himself on the bench beside Ellena, and taking her hand, said solemnly, and in a voice of extreme sensibility, "Ellena, you have long witnessed how dear you are to me ; you cannot doubt my love ; you have long since also promised, solemnly promised, in the presence of her who is now no more, but whose spirit may even at this moment look down upon us, —of her, who bequeathed you to my tenderest care—to be mine for ever. By these sacred truths, by these affecting recollections ! I conjure you, abandon me not to despair, nor, in the energy of a just resentment, sacrifice the son to the cruel and mistaken policy of the mother ! You, nor I, can conjecture the machinations which may be spread for us, when it shall be known that you have left San Stefano. If we delay to exchange our vows, I know, and I feel—that you are lost to me for ever !"

Ellena was affected, and for some moments unable to reply. At length, drying her tears, she said tenderly, "Resentment can have no influence on my conduct towards you ; I think I feel none towards the Marchesa—for she is your mother. But pride, insulted pride, has a right to dictate, and ought to be obeyed ; and the time is now, perhaps, arrived when, if I would respect myself, I must renounce you——"

"Renounce me !" interrupted Vivaldi, "renounce me ! And is it, then, possible you could renounce me?" he repeated, his eyes still fixed upon her face with eagerness and consternation. "Tell me at once, Ellena, is it possible?"

"I fear it is not," she replied.

"You fear, alas! if you *fear*, it is too possible, and I have lost you already! Say, oh, say but that you *hope* it is not, and I, too, will hope again!"

The anguish with which he uttered this awakened all her compassion, and, forgetting the reserve she had imposed upon herself, and every half-formed resolution, she said, with a smile of ineffable sweetness, "I will neither fear nor hope in this instance: I will obey the dictates of gratitude, of affection, and will *believe* that I never can renounce you, while you are unchanged."

"Believe!" repeated Vivaldi, "will you only believe? And why that mention of gratitude? and why that unnecessary reservation? Yet even this assurance, feebly as it sustains my hopes, is extorted; you see my misery, and from pity, from *gratitude*, not affection, would assuage it. Besides, you will neither fear nor hope. Ah, Ellena! did love ever exist yet without fear, and without hope? Oh, never, never! I fear and hope with such rapid transition; every assurance, every look of yours, gives such force either to the one or the other, that I suffer unceasing anxiety. Why, too, that cold, that heart-breaking mention of gratitude? No, Ellena, it is too certain that you do not love me! My mother's cruelty has estranged your heart from me!"

"How much you mistake!" said Ellena. "You have already received sacred testimonies of my regard; if you doubt their sincerity, pardon me if I so far respect myself as to forbear entreating you will believe them."

"How calm, how indifferent, how circumspect, how prudent!" exclaimed Vivaldi in tones of mournful reproach. "But I will not distress you; forgive me for renewing this subject at this time. It was my intention to be silent till you should have reached a place of more permanent security than this; but how was it possible, with such anxiety pressing upon my heart, to persevere in that design? And what have I gained by departing from it? increase of anxiety, of doubt, of fear!"

"Why will you persist in such self-inflictions?" said Ellena. "I cannot endure that you should doubt my affection, even for a moment. And how can you suppose it possible that I ever can become insensible of yours: that I can ever forget the imminent danger you have voluntarily incurred for my release; or, remembering it, can cease to feel the warmest gratitude?"

"That is the very word which tortures me beyond all others!" said Vivaldi. "Is it, then, only a sense of obligation you own for me? Oh! rather say you hate me than suffer me to deceive my hopes with assurances of a sentiment so cold, so circumscribed, so dutiful as that of gratitude!"

"With me the word has a very different acceptation," replied Ellena, smiling. "I understand it to imply all that is tender and generous in affection; and the sense of duty which you say it includes is one of the sweetest and most sacred feelings of the human heart."

"Ah, Ellena! I am too willing to be deceived to examine your definition rigorously; yet I believe it is your smile, rather than the accuracy of your explanation, that persuades me to a confidence in your affection; and I will trust that the gratitude *you* feel is thus tender and comprehensive. But, I beseech you, name the word no more! Its sound is like the touch of the Torpedo; I perceive my confidence chilled even while I listen to my own pronunciation of it."

The entrance of Paulo interrupted the conversation, who, advancing with an air of mystery and alarm, said in a low voice,

"Signor! as I kept watch under the almond trees, who should I see mounting up the road from the valley yonder, but the two bare-footed Carmelites, that overtook us in the pass of Chiari! I lost them again behind the woods, but I daresay they are coming this way; for, the moment they spy out this dairy-hut, they will guess something good is to be had here; and the shepherds would believe their flocks would all die, if ——"

"I see them at this moment emerging from the woods," said Vivaldi, "and now they are leaving the road and crossing this way. Where is our host, Paulo?"

"He is without, at a little distance, signor. Shall I call him?"

"Yes," replied Vivaldi, "or, stay; I will call him myself. Yet, if they see me ——"

"Aye, signor; or, for that matter, if they see me! But we cannot help ourselves now; for if we call the host, we shall betray ourselves, and, if we do not call him, he will betray us; so they must find us out, be it as it may."

"Peace! peace! let me think a moment," said Vivaldi. While Vivaldi undertook to think, Paulo was peeping about for a hiding place, if occasion should require one.

"Call our host immediately," said Vivaldi, "I must speak with him."

"He passes the lattice at this instant," observed Ellena.

Paulo obeyed, and the shepherd entered the cabin.

"My good friend," said Vivaldi, "I must entreat that you will not admit those friars, whom you see coming this way, nor suffer them to know what guests you have. They have been very troublesome to us already on the road; I will reward you for any loss their sudden departure may occasion you."

"Nay, for that matter, friend," said Paulo,

"It is their visit only that can occasion you loss, begging the signor's pardon; their departure never occasioned loss to anybody. And to tell you the truth, for my master will not speak out, we were obliged to look pretty sharply about us while they bore us company, or we have reason to think our pockets would have been the lighter. They are designing people, friend, take my word for it; banditti, perhaps, in disguise. The dress of a Carmelite would suit their purpose, at this time of the pilgrimage. So be pretty blunt with them, if they want to come in here; and you will do well, when they go, to send somebody to watch which way they take, and see them clear off, or you may lose a stray lamb, perhaps."

The old shepherd lifted up his eyes and hands, "To see how the world goes!" said he. "But thank you, maestro, for your warning: they shall not come within my threshold, for all their holy seeming, and it's the first time in my life I ever said nay to one of their garb, and mine has been a pretty long one, as you may guess, perhaps, by my face. How old, signor, should you take me to be? I warrant you will guess short of the matter though; for on these high mountains ——"

"I will guess when you have dismissed the travellers," said Vivaldi, "after having given them some hasty refreshment without; they must be almost at the door by this time. Despatch, friend."

"If they should fall foul upon me, for refusing them entrance," said the shepherd, "you will come out to help me, signor? for my lads are at some distance."

Vivaldi assured him that they would, and he left the cabin.

Paulo ventured to peep at the lattice, on what might be going forward without. "They are gone round to the door, signor, I fancy," said he, "for I see nothing of them this way. If there was but another window! What foolish people to build a cottage with no window near the door! But I must listen." He stepped on tiptoe to the door, and bent his head in attention.

"They are certainly spies from the monastery," observed Ellena to Vivaldi, "they follow us so closely! If they were pilgrims, it is improbable, too, that their way should lie through this unfrequented region, and still more so that they should not travel in a larger party. When my absence was discovered, these people were sent, no doubt, in pursuit of me; and, having met the devotees whom we passed, they were enabled to follow our route."

"We shall do well to act upon this supposition," replied Vivaldi, "but, though I am inclined to believe them emissaries from San Stefano, it is not improbable that they are only Carmelites returning to some convent on the lake of Celano."

"I cannot hear a syllable, signor," said Paulo. "Pray do listen yourself! and there is not a single chink in this door to afford one consolation. Well! if ever I build a cottage there shall be a window near ——"

"Listen!" said Vivaldi.

"Not a single word, signor!" cried Paulo after a pause, "I do not even hear a voice! But now I hear steps, and they are coming to the door, too; they shall find it no easy matter to open it, though," he added, placing himself against it. "Ay, ay, you may knock, friend, till your arm aches, and kick and lay about you—no matter for that."

"Silence! let us know who it is," said Vivaldi; and the old shepherd's voice was heard without.

"They are gone, signors," said he, "you may open the door."

"Which way did they go?" asked Vivaldi when the man entered.

"I cannot say as to that, signor, because I did not happen to see them at all; and I have been looking all about, too."

"Why, I saw them myself, crossing this way from the wood yonder," said Paulo.

"And there is nothing to shelter them from our view between the wood and this cottage, friend," added Vivaldi. "What can they have done with themselves?"

"For that matter, gone into the wood again, perhaps," said the shepherd.

Paulo gave his master a significant look, and added, "It is likely enough, friend; and you may depend upon it, they are lurking there for no good purpose. You will do well to send somebody to look after them; your flocks will suffer for it else. Depend upon it they design no good."

"We are not used to such sort of folks in these parts," replied the shepherd; "but if they mean any harm they shall find we can help ourselves." As he spoke he took down a horn from the roof, and blew a shrill blast that made the mountains echo; when immediately the younger shepherds were seen running from various quarters towards the cottage.

"Do not be alarmed, friend," said Vivaldi; "these travellers mean you no harm, I daresay, whatever they may design against us. But, as I think them suspicious persons, and should not like to overtake them on the road, I will reward one of your lads if you will let him go a little way towards Celano, and examine whether they are lurking on that route."

The old man consented, and, when the shepherds came up, one of them received directions from Vivaldi.

"And be sure you do not return till you have found them," added Paulo.

"No, master," replied the lad, "and I will bring them safe here, you may trust me."

"If you do, friend, you will get your head

broke for your trouble. You are only to discover where they are, and to watch where they go," said Paulo.

Vivaldi at length made the lad comprehend what was required of him, and he departed, while the old shepherd went out to keep guard.

The time of his absence was passed in various conjectures by the party in the cabin concerning the Carmelites. Vivaldi still inclined to believe they were honest people returning from a pilgrimage, but Paulo was decidedly against this opinion. "They are waiting for us on the road, you may depend upon it, signor," said the latter. "You may be certain they have some *great design* in hand, or they would never have turned their steps from this dairy-house when once they had spied it ; and that they did spy it we are sure."

"But if they have in hand the great design you speak of, Paulo," said Vivaldi, "it is probable that they have spied us also, by their taking this obscure road. Now it must have occurred to them, when they saw a dairy-hut in so solitary a region, that we might probably be found within—yet they have not examined. It appears, therefore, they have no design against us. What can you answer to this, Paulo? I trust the apprehensions of Signora di Rosalba are unfounded."

"Why! do you suppose, signor, they would attack us when we were safe housed, and had these good shepherds to lend us a helping hand? No, signor, they would not even have shown themselves if they could have helped it ; and being once sure we were here, they would skulk back to the woods and lurk for us in the road they knew we must go, since, as it happens, there is only one."

"How is it possible," said Ellena, "that they can have discovered us here, since they did not approach the cabin to inquire?"

"They came near enough for their purpose, signora, I daresay ; and, if the truth were known, they spied my face looking at them through the lattice."

"Come, come," said Vivaldi, "you are an ingenious tormentor, indeed, Paulo. Do you suppose they saw enough of thy face last night by moonlight, in that dusky glen, to enable them to recollect it again at a distance of forty yards? Revive, my Ellena, I think every appearance is in our favour."

"Would I could think so too !" said she, with a sigh.

"Oh ! for that matter, signora," rejoined Paulo, "there is nothing to be afraid of ; they should find tough work of it, if they thought proper to attack us, lady."

"It is not an open attack that we have to fear," replied Ellena, "but they may surround us with their snares, and defy resistance."

However Vivaldi might accede to the truth of this remark, he would not appear to do so ; but tried to laugh away her apprehensions ; and Paulo was silenced for a while by a significant look from his master.

The shepherd's boy returned much sooner than they had expected, and he probably saved his time that he might spare his labour, for he brought no intelligence of the Carmelites. "I looked for them among the woods, along the roadside in the hollow yonder, too," said the lad, "and then I mounted the hill further on, but I could see nothing of them far or near, nor of a single soul, except our goats, and some of them do stray wide enough sometimes ; they lead me a fine dance often. They sometimes, signor, have wandered as far as Monte Nuvola, yonder, and got to the top of it, up among the clouds, and the crags, where I should break my neck if I climbed ; and the rogues seemed to know it, too, for when they have seen me coming, scrambling up, puffing and blowing, they ceased their capering, and stood peeping over a crag so sly, and so quiet, it seemed as if they were laughing at me ; as much as to say, ' Catch us if you can.' "

Vivaldi, who during the latter part of this speech had been consulting with Ellena whether they should proceed on their way immediately, asked the boy some further questions concerning the Carmelites ; and becoming convinced that they had either not taken the road to Celano, or, having taken it, were at a considerable distance, he proposed setting out, and proceeding leisurely, "For I have now little apprehension of these people," he added, "and a great deal lest night should overtake us before we reach the place of our destination, since the road is mountainous and wild, and further, we are not perfectly acquainted with it."

Ellena approving the plan, they took leave of the good shepherd, who with difficulty was prevailed with to accept any recompense for his trouble, and who gave them some further directions as to the road ; and their way was long cheered by the sound of the tabor and the sweetness of the hautboy, wafted over the wild.

When they descended into the woody hollow mentioned by the boy, Ellena sent forth many an anxious look beneath the deep shade ; while Paulo, sometimes silent, and at others whistling and singing loudly, as if to overcome his fears, peeped under every bough that crossed the road, expecting to discover his friends, the Carmelites, lurking within its gloom.

Having emerged from this valley, the road lay over mountains covered with flocks ; for it was now the season when they had quitted the plains of Apulia, to feed upon the herbage for which this region is celebrated ; and it was near sunset, when, from a summit to which the travellers had long been ascending, the whole lake of Celano, with its vast circle of mountains, burst at once upon their view.

"Ah, signor!" exclaimed Paulo, "what a prospect is here! It reminds me of home; it is almost as pleasant as the bay of Naples! I should never love it like that though, if it were a hundred times finer."

The travellers stopped to admire the scene, and to give their horses rest, after the labour of the ascent. The evening sun, shooting athwart a clear expanse of water, between eighteen and twenty leagues in circumference, lighted up all the towns and villages, and towered castles and spiry convents, that enriched the rising shores, brought out all the various tints of cultivation, and coloured with beamy purple the mountains, which on every side formed the majestic background of the landscape. Vivaldi pointed out to Ellena the gigantic Velino in the north, a barrier mountain between the territories of Rome and Naples. Its peaked head towered far above every neighbouring summit, and its white precipices were opposed to the verdant points of the Majella, snow-crowned, however, and next in altitude, loved by the flocks. Westward, near woody hills, and rising immediately from the lake, appeared Monte Salviano, covered with wild sage, as its name imports, and once pompous with forests of chestnut; a branch from the Appenine extended to meet it. "See," said Vivaldi, "where Monte Corno stands like a ruffian, huge, scared, threatening, and horrid!—and in the south, where the sullen mountain of San Nicola shoots up, barren and rocky! From thence, mark how other overtopping ridges of the mighty Appenine darken the horizon far along the east, and circle to approach the Velino in the north!"

"Mark too," said Ellena, "how sweetly the banks and undulating plains repose at the feet of the mountains; what an image of beauty and elegance they oppose to the awful grandeur that overlooks and guards them. Observe, too, how many a delightful valley, opening from the lake, spreads its rice and corn fields, shaded with groves of the almond, far among the winding hills; how gaily vineyards and olives alternately chequer the acclivities, and how gracefully the lofty palms bend over the higher cliffs!"

"Ay, signora!" exclaimed Paulo, "and have the goodness to observe how like are the fishing boats that sail towards the hamlet below, to those one sees upon the bay of Naples. They are worth all the rest of the prospect, except indeed this huge sheet of water, which is almost as good as the bay, and that mountain, with its sharp head, which is almost as good as Vesuvius—if it would but throw out fire!"

"We must despair of finding a mountain in this neighbourhood so *good* as to do that,

Paulo," said Vivaldi, smiling at this stroke of nationality; "though, perhaps, many that we now see have once been volcanic."

"I honour them for that, signor, and look at them with double satisfaction; but *our* mountain is the only mountain in the world. Oh! to see it of a dark night! what a blazing it makes! and what a height it will shoot to! and what a light it throws over the sea! No other mountain can do so. It seems as if the waves were all on fire. I have seen the reflection as far off as Capri, trembling all across the gulf, and showing every vessel as plain as at noon day; ay, and every sailor on the deck. You never saw such a sight, signor."

"Why, you do, indeed, seem to have forgotten that I ever did, Paulo, and also that a volcano can do any mischief. But let us return, Ellena, to the scene before us. Yonder, a mile or two within the shore, is the town of Celano, whither we are going."

The clearness of an Italian atmosphere permitted him to discriminate the minute though very distant features of the landscape; and on an eminence rising from the plains of a valley, opening to the west, he pointed out the modern Alba, crowned with the ruins of its ancient castle, still visible upon the splendour of the horizon, the prison and tomb of many a Prince, who "fallen from his high estate," was sent from Imperial Rome to finish here the sad reverse of his days; to gaze from the bars of his tower upon solitudes, where beauty or grandeur administered no assuaging feelings to him, whose life had passed amidst the intrigues of the world and the feverish contentions of disappointed ambition; to him, with whom reflection brought only remorse, and anticipation despair; whom "no horizontal beam enlivened in the crimson evening of life's dusty day."

"And to such a scene as this," said Vivaldi, "a Roman Emperor came, only for the purpose of witnessing the most barbarous exhibition! to indulge the most savage delights! Here Claudius celebrated the accomplishment of his arduous work, an aqueduct to carry the overflowing waters of the Celano to Rome, by a naval fight, in which hundreds of wretched slaves perished for his amusement! Its pure and polished surface was stained with human blood, and roughened by the plunging bodies of the slain, while the gilded galleys of the Emperor floated gaily around, and these beautiful shores were made to echo with applauding yells, worthy of the furies!"

"We scarcely dare to trust the truth of history, in some of its traits of human nature," said Ellena.

"Signor," cried Paulo, "I have been thinking that while we are taking the air so much at our ease here, those Carmelites may be spying at us from some hole or corner that we know nothing of, and may swoop upon us all of a sudden, before we can help ourselves. Had we not better go on, signor?"

"Our horses are, perhaps, sufficiently rested," replied Vivaldi, "but, if I had not long since dismissed all suspicion of the evil intention of those strangers, I should not willingly have stopped for a moment."

"But pray let us proceed," said Ellena.

"Ay, signora, it is best to be of the safe side," observed Paulo. "Yonder, below, is Celano ; and I hope we shall get safe housed there before it is quite dark, for here we have no mountain that will light us on our way if we should happen to be-benighted ! Ah ! if we were but within twenty miles of Naples, now—and it was an *illumination* night ! "

As they descended the mountain, Ellena, silent and dejected, abandoned herself to reflection. She was too sensible of the difficulties of her present situation, and too apprehensive of the influence which her determination must have on all her future life, to be happy, though escaped from the prison of San Stefano, and in the presence of Vivaldi, her beloved deliverer and protector. He observed her dejection with grief, and, not understanding all the finer scruples that distressed her, interpreted her reserve into indifference towards himself. But he forbore to disturb her again with a mention of his doubts or fears ; and he determined not to urge the subject of his late entreaties, till he should have placed her in some secure asylum, where she might feel herself at perfect liberty to accept or to reject his proposal. By acting with an honour so delicate, he unconsciously adopted a certain means of increasing her esteem and gratitude, and deserved them the more since he had to endure the apprehension of losing her by the delay thus occasioned to their nuptials.

They reached the town of Celano before the evening closed ; when Vivaldi was requested by Ellena to inquire for a convent, where she might be lodged for the night. He left her at the inn, with Paulo for her guard, and proceeded on his search. The first gate he knocked upon belonged to a society of Carmelites. It appeared probable that the pilgrims of that order who had occasioned him so much disquietude were honest brothers of this house ; but, as it was also probable that if they were emissaries of the Abbess of San Stefano, and came to Celano, they would take up their lodging with a community of their own class in preference to that of any other, Vivaldi thought it prudent to retire from their gates without making himself known. He passed on, therefore, and soon after arrived at a convent of Dominicans, where he learned that there were only two houses of nuns in Celano, and that these admitted no other boarders than permanent ones.

Vivaldi returned with this information to Ellena, who endeavoured to reconcile herself to the necessity of remaining where she was ; but Paulo, ever active and zealous, soon brought intelligence that at a little fishing town at some distance, on the bank of the lake, was a convent of Ursalines, remarkable for their hospitality to strangers. The obscurity of so remote a place was another reason for preferring it to Celano; and Vivaldi proposing to remove thither, if Ellena was not too weary to proceed, she readily assented, and they immediately set off.

"It happens to be a fine night," said Paulo, on leaving Celano, "and as for that matter, our nights generally are, so, signor, we cannot well lose our way ; besides, they say there is but one. The town we are going to lies yonder, on the edge of the lake, about a mile and a half off. I think I can see a grey steeple or two a little to the right of that wood, where the water gleams so."

"No, Paulo," replied Vivaldi, after looking attentively, " I perceive what you mean ; but those are not the points of steeples, they are only the tops of some tall cypresses."

" Pardon me, signor, they are too tapering for trees ; that must surely be the town. This road, however, will lead us right, for there is no other to puzzle us, as they say."

"This cool and balmy air revives me," said Ellena, "and what a soothing shade prevails over the scene. How softened, yet how distinct, is every near object ; how sweetly dubious the more removed ones ; while the mountains beyond character themselves sublimely upon the still glowing horizon."

"Observe, too," added Vivaldi, "how their broken summits, tipped with the beams that have set to our lower region, exhibit the portraiture of towers and castles and embattled ramparts, which appear designed to guard them against the enemies that may come by the clouds."

"Yes," replied Ellena, "the mountains themselves display a sublimity that seems to belong to a higher world ; their besiegers ought not to be of this earth : they can be only spirits of the air."

"They can be nothing else, signora," said Paulo, "for nothing of this earth can reach them. See, lady, they have some of the qualities of your spirits, too ; see how they change their shapes and colours, as the sunbeams sink. And now, how grey and dim they grow. See but how fast they vanish ! "

"Everything reposes," observed Vivaldi. " Who would willingly travel in the day, when Italy has such nights as this ! "

"Signor, that *is* the town before us," said Paulo, "for now I can discern, plain enough, the spires of convents ; and there goes a light ! Ha ! ha ! and there is a bell, too, chiming from one of the spires ! The monks are going to mass: would we were going to supper, signor!"

"That chime is nearer than the place you point to, Paulo, and I doubt whether it comes from the same quarter."

"Hark! signor, the air wafts the sound, and now it is gone again."

"Yes, I believe you are right, Paulo, and that we have not far to go."

The travellers descended the gradual slopes towards the shore; and Paulo some time after exclaimed, "See, signor, where another light glides along. See, it is reflected on the lake."

"I hear the faint dashing of waves now," said Ellena, "and the sound of oars, too. But observe, Paulo, the light is not in the town, it is in the boat that moves yonder."

"Now it retreats, and trembles in a lengthening line upon the dark waters," added Vivaldi. "We have been too ready to believe what we wish, and have yet far to go."

The shore they were approaching formed a spacious bay for the lake immediately below. Dark woods seemed to spread along the banks and ascend among the cultivated slopes towards the mountains; except where, here and there, cliffs bending over the water were distinguished through the twilight by the whiteness of their limestone precipices. Within the bay the town became gradually visible; lights twinkled between the trees, appearing and vanishing like the stars of a cloudy night; and at length was heard the melancholy song of boatmen, who were fishing near the shore.

Other sounds soon after struck the ear. "Oh, what merry notes!" exclaimed Paulo; "they make my heart dance. See! signora, there is a group footing it away so gaily on the bank of the lake yonder, by those trees where the water glimmers! Oh, what a merry set! Would I were among them; that is, I mean, if you, *maestro*, and the signora were not here."

"Well corrected, Paulo."

"It is a festival, I fancy," observed Vivaldi. "These peasants of the lake can make the moments fly as gaily as the voluptuaries of the city, it seems."

"Oh! what merry music!" repeated Paulo. "Ah! how often I have footed it as joyously on the beach at Naples, after sunset of a fine night like this, with such a pleasant fresh breeze to cool one. Ah! there are none like the fishermen of Naples for a dance by moonlight; how lightly do they trip it! Oh! if I was but there now! That is, I mean, if you, *maestro*, and the signora were there too. Oh! what merry notes!"

"We thank you, good Signor Paulo," said Vivaldi, "and I trust we shall all be there soon, when you shall trip it away with as joyous a heart as the best of them."

The travellers now entered the town, which

consisted of one street straggling along the margin of the lake; and having inquired for the Ursaline convent, were directed to its gates. The porteress appeared immediately upon the ringing of the bell, and carried a message to the abbess, who, returning an invitation to Ellena, she alighted, and followed the porteress to the parlour, while Vivaldi remained at the gate till he should know whether she approved of her new lodging. A second invitation induced him also to alight. He was admitted to the grate, and offered refreshment, which, however, he declined staying to accept, as he had yet a lodging to seek for the night. The abbess, on learning this circumstance, courteously recommended him to a neighbouring society of Benedictines, and desired him to mention her name to the abbot.

Vivaldi then took leave of Ellena, and, though it was only for a few hours, he left her with dejection, and with some degree of apprehension for her safety, which, though circumstances could not justify him in admitting, he could not entirely subdue. She shared his dejection, but not his fears, when the door closed after him, and she found herself once more among strangers. The forlornness of her feelings could not be entirely overcome by the attentions of the abbess; and there was a degree of curiosity and even of scrutiny expressed in the looks of some of the sisters which seemed more than was due to a stranger. From such examination she eagerly escaped to the apartment allotted for her, and to the repose from which she had so long been withheld.

Vivaldi, meanwhile, had found an hospitable reception with the Benedictines, whose sequestered situation made the visit of a stranger a pleasurable novelty to them. In the eagerness of conversation, and, yielding to the satisfaction which the mind receives from exercising ideas that have long slept in dusky indolence, and to the pleasure of admitting new ones, the abbot and a few of the brothers sat with Vivaldi to a late hour. When, at length, the traveller was suffered to retire, other subjects than those which had interested his host engaged his thoughts; and he revolved the means of preventing the misery that threatened him in a serious separation from Ellena. Now that she was received into a respectable asylum, every motive for silence upon this topic was done away. He determined, therefore, that on the following morning he would urge all his reasons and entreaties for an immediate marriage; and among the brothers of the Benedictine, he had little doubt of prevailing with one to solemnize the nuptials, which he believed would place his happiness and Ellena's peace beyond the influence of malignant possibilities.

CHAPTER XIV.

WHILE Vivaldi and Ellena were on the way from San Stefano, the Marchese di Vivaldi was suffering the utmost vexation respecting his son ; and the Marchesa felt not less apprehension that the abode of Ellena might be discovered ; yet this fear did not withhold her from mingling in all the gaieties of Naples. Her assemblies were, as usual, among the most brilliant of that voluptuous city, and she patronised, as jealously as formerly, the strains of her favourite composer. But, notwithstanding this perpetual dissipation, her thoughts frequently withdrew themselves from the scene, and dwelt on gloomy forebodings of disappointed pride.

A circumstance which rendered her particularly susceptible to such disappointment at this time was, that overtures of alliance had been lately made to the Marchese by the father of a lady who was held suitable, in every consideration, to become his daughter; and whose wealth rendered the union particularly desirable, at a time when the expenses of such an establishment as was necessary to the vanity of the Marchesa considerably exceeded his income, large as it was.

The Marchesa's temper had been thus irritated by the contemplation of her son's conduct in an affair which so materially affected the fortune, and, as she believed, the honour of his family ; when a courier from the Abbess of San Stefano brought intelligence of the flight of Ellena with Vivaldi. She was in a disposition which heightened disappointment into fury ; and she forfeited, by the transports to which she yielded, the degree of pity that otherwise was due to a mother who believed her only son to have sacrificed his family and himself to an unworthy passion. She understood that he was now married, and irrecoverably lost. Scarcely able to endure the agony of this conviction, she sent for her ancient adviser, Schedoni, that she might, at least, have the relief of expressing her motions, and of examining whether there remained a possibility of dissolving these long dreaded nuptials. The frenzy of passion, however, did not so far overcome her circumspection as to compel her to acquaint the Marchese with the contents of the abbess's letter before she had consulted with her confessor. She knew that the principles of her husband were too just, upon the grand points of morality, to suffer him to adopt the measures she might judge necessary ; and she avoided informing him of the marriage of his son, until the means of counteracting it should have been suggested and accomplished, however desperate such means might be.

Schedoni was not to be found. Trifling circumstances increase the irritation of a mind in such a state as was hers. The delay of an opportunity for unburthening her heart to Schedoni was hardly to be endured ; another and another messenger were despatched to her confessor.

"My mistress has committed some great sin, truly," said the servant, who had been twice to the convent within the last half-hour. "It must lie heavy on her conscience, in good truth, since she cannot support it for one half-hour. Well ! the rich have this comfort, however, that, let them be never so guilty, they can buy themselves innocent again, in the twinkling of a ducat. Now a poor man might be a month before he recovered his innocence, and that, too, not till after many a bout of hard flogging."

In the evening Schedoni came, but it was only to confirm her worst fear. He, too, had heard of the escape of Ellena, as well as that she was on the lake of Celano, and was married to Vivaldi. How he had obtained this information he did not choose to disclose; but he mentioned so many minute circumstances in confirmation of its truth, and appeared to be so perfectly convinced of the facts he related, that the Marchesa believed them as implicitly as himself ; and her passion and despair transgressed all bounds of decorum.

Schedoni observed, with dark and silent pleasure, the turbulent excess of her feelings, and perceived that the moment was now arrived when he might command them to his purpose, so as to render his assistance indispensable to her repose, and, probably, so as to accomplish the revenge he had long meditated against Vivaldi, without hazarding the favour of the Marchesa. So far was he from attempting to soothe her sufferings, that he contrived to irritate her resentment and exasperate her pride ; effecting this, at the same time, with such consummate art that he appeared only to be palliating the conduct of Vivaldi and endeavouring to console his distracted mother.

"This is a rash step, certainly," said the confessor; "but he is young, very young, and therefore does not foresee the consequences to which it leads. He does not perceive how seriously it will affect the dignity of his house; how much it will depreciate his consequence with the Court, with the nobles of his own rank, and even with the plebeians with whom he has condescended to connect himself. Intoxicated with the passions of youth, he does not weigh the value of those blessings which wisdom and the experience of maturer age know how to estimate. He neglects them only because he does not perceive their influence in society, and that lightly to resign them is to degrade himself in the view of almost every mind. Unhappy young man ! he is to be pitied fully as much as blamed."

"Your excuses, reverend father," said the tortured Marchesa, "prove the goodness of your heart; but they illustrate, also, the degeneracy of his mind, and detail the full extent of the effects which he has brought upon his family. It affords me no consolation to know that this degradation proceeds from his head rather than his heart; it is sufficient that he has incurred it, and that no possibility remains of throwing off the misfortune."

"Perhaps that is affirming too much," observed Schedoni.

"How, father!" said the Marchesa.

"Perhaps a possibility does remain," he added.

"Point it out to me, good father! I do not perceive it."

"Nay, my lady," replied the subtle Schedoni, correcting himself, "I am by no means assured that such possibility does exist. My solicitude for your tranquillity, and for the honour of your house, makes me so unwilling to relinquish hope, that, perhaps, I only imagine a possibility in your favour. Let me consider.——Alas! the misfortune, severe as it is, must be endured; there remain no means of escaping from it."

"It was cruel of you, father, to suggest a hope which you could not justify," observed the Marchesa.

"You must accuse my extreme solicitude, then," replied the confessor. "But how is it possible for me to see a family of your ancient estimation brought into such circumstances; its honours blighted by the folly of a thoughtless boy, without feeling sorrow and indignation, and looking round for even some desperate means of delivering it from disgrace." He paused.

"Disgrace!" exclaimed the Marchesa, "father, you—you—disgrace!—The word is a strong one, but —— It is, alas! justly applied. And shall we submit to this?—Is it possible we *can* submit to it?"

"There is no remedy," said Schedoni, coldly.

"Good God!" said the Marchesa, "that there should be no law to prevent, or, at least, to punish such criminal marriages!"

"It is much to be lamented," replied Schedoni.

"The woman who obtrudes herself upon a family, to dishonour it," continued the Marchesa, deserves a punishment nearly equal to that of a state criminal, since she injures those who best support the state. She ought to suffer ——."

"Not nearly, but quite equal," interrupted the confessor, "she deserves —— death!"

He paused, and there was a moment of profound silence, till he added—"for death only can obviate the degradation she has occasioned; her death alone can restore the original splendour of the line she would have sullied."

He paused again, but the Marchesa still remaining silent, he added, "I have often marvelled that our lawgivers should have failed to perceive the justness, nay the necessity, of such punishment!"

"It is astonishing," said the Marchesa, thoughtfully, "that a regard for their own honour did not suggest it."

"Justice does not the less exist, because her laws are neglected," observed Schedoni. "A sense of what she commands lives in every breast: and when we fail to obey that sense, it is to weakness, not to virtue, that we yield."

"Certainly," replied the Marchesa, "that truth never yet was doubted."

"Pardon me, I am not so certain as to that," said the confessor. "When justice happens to oppose prejudice, we are apt to believe it virtuous to disobey her. For instance, though the law of justice demands the death of this girl, yet because the law of the land forbears to enforce it, you, my daughter, even you! though possessed of a man's spirit, and his clear perceptions, would think that virtue bade her live, when it was only fear!"

"Hah!" exclaimed the Marchesa, in a low voice, "What is it that you mean? You shall find I have a man's courage also."

"I speak without disguise," replied Schedoni; "my meaning requires none."

The Marchesa mused, and remained silent.

"I have done my duty," resumed Schedoni, at length. "I have pointed out the only way that remains for you to escape dishonour. If my zeal is displeasing —— but I have done."

"No, good father, no," said the Marchesa, "you mistake the cause of my emotion. New ideas, new prospects, open!—they confuse, they distract me! My mind has not yet attained sufficient strength to encounter them; some woman's weakness, too, still lingers at my heart."

"Pardon my inconsiderate zeal," said Schedoni, with affected humility, "I have been to blame. If yours is a weakness, it is, at least, an amiable one, and, perhaps, deserves to be encouraged rather than conquered."

"How, father! If it deserves encouragement it is not a weakness but a virtue."

"Be it so," said Schedoni, coldly, "the interest I have felt on this subject has perhaps misled my judgment, and has rendered me unjust. Think no more of it, or if you do, let it be only to pardon the zeal I have testified."

"It does not deserve pardon, but thanks," replied the Marchesa; "not thanks only, but reward. Good father, I hope it will some time be in my power to prove the sincerity of my words."

The confessor bowed his head.

"I trust that the services you have rendered me shall be gratefully repaid — rewarded, I dare not hope, for what benefit could possibly reward a service so vast as it may, perhaps, be in your power to confer upon my family! What recompense could be balanced against the benefit of having rescued the honour of an ancient house!"

"Your goodness is beyond my thanks, or my desert," said Schedoni, and he was again silent.

The Marchesa wished him to lead her back to the point from which she herself had deviated, and he seemed determined that she should lead him thither. She mused and hesitated. Her mind was not yet familiar with atrocious guilt, and the crime which Schedoni had suggested somewhat alarmed her. She feared to think, and still more to name it; yet, so acutely susceptible was her pride, so stern her indignation, and so profound her desire of vengeance, that her mind was tossed as on a tempestuous ocean, and these terrible feelings threatened to overwhelm the residue of humanity in her heart. Schedoni observed all its progressive movements, and, like a gaunt tiger, lurked in silence, ready to spring forward at the moment of opportunity.

"It is your advice, then, father," resumed the Marchesa, after a long pause—"it is your opinion that this Ellena ——" She hesitated, desirous that Schedoni should anticipate her meaning; but he chose to spare his own delicacy rather than that of the Marchesa.

"You think, then, that this insidious girl deserves ——" She paused again; but the confessor, still silent, seemed to wait with submission for what the Marchesa should deliver.

"I repeat, father, that it is your opinion this girl deserves severe punishment ——."

"Undoubtedly," replied Schedoni. "Is it not also your own?"

"That not any punishment can be too severe?" continued the Marchesa. "That justice, equally with necessity, demands—— her life? Is not this your opinion, too?"

"Oh! pardon me," said Schedoni. "I may have erred; that only *was* my opinion; and when I formed it I was probably too much under the influence of zeal to be just. When the heart is warm, how is it possible that the judgment can be cool?"

"It is *not*, then, your opinion, holy father," said the Marchesa, with displeasure.

"I do not absolutely say that," replied the confessor. "But I leave it to your better judgment to decide upon its justness."

As he said this he rose to depart. The Marchesa was agitated and perplexed, and requested he would stay; but he excused himself by alleging that it was the hour when he must attend a particular mass.

"Well, then, holy father, I will occupy no more of your valuable moments at present;

but you know how highly I estimate your advice, and will not refuse when I shall at some future time request it."

"I cannot refuse to accept an honour," replied the confessor, with an air of meekness; "but the subject you allude to is delicate——"

"And therefore I must value and require your opinion upon it," rejoined the Marchesa.

"I would wish you to value your own," replied Schedoni; "you cannot have a better director."

"You flatter, father."

"I only reply, my daughter."

"On the evening of to-morrow," said the Marchesa, gravely, "I shall be at vespers in the church of San Nicola; if you should happen to be there, you will probably see me, when the service is over and the congregation is departed, in the north cloister. We can there converse on the subject nearest my heart, and without observation. Farewell!"

"Peace be with you, daughter! and wisdom counsel your thoughts!" said Schedoni, "I will not fail to visit San Nicola."

He folded his hands upon his breast, bowed his head, and left the apartment, with the silent footsteps that indicates wariness and conscious duplicity.

The Marchesa remained in her closet, shaken by ever-varying passions, and ever-fluctuating opinions; meditating misery for others, and inflicting it only upon herself.

CHAPTER XV.

THE Marchesa repaired, according to her appointment, to the church of San Nicola; and, ordering her servants to remain with the carriage at a side door, entered the choir, attended only by her woman.

When vespers had concluded, she lingered till nearly every person had quitted the choir, and then walked through the solitary aisles to the north cloister. Her heart was as heavy as her step; for when is it that peace and evil passions dwell together? as she slowly paced the cloister, she perceived a monk passing between the pillars, who, as he approached, lifted his cowl, and she knew him to be Schedoni.

He instantly observed the agitation of her spirits, and that her purpose was not yet determined according to his hope. But, though his mind became clouded, his countenance remained unaltered; it was grave and thoughtful. The sternness of his vulture-like eye was, however, somewhat softened, and its lids were contracted by subtlety.

The Marchesa bade her woman walk apart while she conferred with her confessor.

"This unhappy boy," said she, when the attendant was at some distance, "How much suffering does his folly inflict upon his family!

My good father, I have need of all your advice and consolation. My mind is perpetually haunted by a sense of my misfortune; it has no respite; awake or in my dream, this ungrateful son alike pursues me! The only relief my heart receives is when conversing with you—my only counsellor, my only disinterested friend."

The confessor bowed. "The Marchese is, no doubt, equally afflicted with yourself," said he; "but he is, notwithstanding, much more competent to advise you on this delicate subject than I am."

"The Marchese has prejudices, father, as you well know; he is a sensible man, but he is sometimes mistaken, and he is incorrigible in error. He has the faults of a mind that is merely well disposed; he is destitute of the discernment and the energy which would make it great. If it is necessary to adopt a conduct that departs in the smallest degree from those common rules of morality which he has cherished, without examining them, from his infancy, he is shocked and shrinks from action. He cannot discriminate the circumstances that render the same action virtuous or vicious. How then, father, are we to suppose he would approve of the bold inflictions we meditate?"

"Most true!" said the artful Schedoni, with an air of admiration.

"We, therefore, must not consult him," continued the Marchesa, "lest he should now, as formerly, advance and maintain objections to which we cannot yield. What passes in conversation with you, father, is sacred, it goes no further."

"Sacred as a confession!" said Schedoni, crossing himself.

"I know not,"—resumed the Marchesa, and hesitated; "I know not,"—she repeated in a yet lower voice, "how this girl may be disposed of; and this it is which distracts my mind."

"I marvel much at that," said Schedoni. "With opinions so singularly just, with a mind so accurate, yet so bold as you have displayed, is it possible that you can hesitate as to what is to be done! You, my daughter, will not prove yourself one of those ineffectual declaimers, who can think vigorously, but cannot act so? One way, only, remains for you to pursue, in the present instance; it is the same which your superior sagacity pointed out, and taught me to approve. Is it necessary for me to *persuade her*, by whom I am *convinced*! There is only one way."

"And on that I have been long meditating," replied the Marchesa, "and, shall I own my weakness? I cannot yet decide."

"My daughter! can it be possible that you should want courage to soar above vulgar prejudice, in action, though not in opinion!" said Schedoni, who, perceiving that his assistance was necessary to fix her fluctuating mind, gradually began to steal forth from the prudent reserve in which he had taken shelter.

"If this person was condemned by the law," he continued, "you would pronounce her sentence to be just; yet you dare not, I am humbled while I repeat it, you dare not dispense justice yourself!"

The Marchesa, after some hesitation, said, "I have not the shield of the law to protect me, father: and the boldest virtue may pause when it reaches the utmost verge of safety."

"Never!" replied the confessor, warmly; "virtue never trembles; it is her glory and sublimest attribute to be superior to danger, to despise it. The best principle is not virtue till it reaches this elevation."

A philosopher might, perhaps, have been surprised to hear two persons seriously defining the limits of virtue, at the very moment in which they meditated the most atrocious crime; a man of the world would have considered it to be mere hypocrisy: a supposition which might have disclosed his general knowledge of manners, but would certainly have betrayed his ignorance of the human heart.

The Marchesa was for some time silent and thoughtful, and then repeated deliberately, "I have not the shield of the law to protect me."

"But you have the shield of the Church," replied Schedoni; "you should not only have protection, but absolution."

"Absolution!—Does virtue—justice, require absolution, father?"

"When I mentioned absolution for the action which you perceive to be so just and necessary," replied Schedoni, I accommodated my speech to vulgar prejudice, and to vulgar weakness. And, forgive me, that since you, my daughter, descended from the loftiness of your spirit to regret the shield of the law, I endeavoured to console you, by offering a shield to conscience. But enough of this; let us return to argument. This girl is put out of the way of committing more mischief, of injuring the peace and dignity of a distinguished family; she is sent to an eternal sleep before her time. Where is the crime, where is the evil of this? On the contrary, you perceive, and you have convinced me, that it is only strict justice, only self-defence."

The Marchesa was attentive, and the confessor added, "She is not immortal; and the few years more that might have been allotted her she deverves to forfeit, since she would have employed them in cankering the honour of an illustrious house."

"Speak low, father," said the Marchesa, though he spoke almost in a whisper; "the cloister appears solitary, yet some person may lurk behind those pillars. Advise me how this business may be managed; I am ignoran of the particular means."

"There is some hazard in the accomplishment of it, I grant," rejoined Schedoni ; "I know not in whom you may confide.—The men who make a trade of blood ——"

"Hush!" said the Marchesa, looking round through the twilight—"a step!"

"It is the Friar's, yonder, who crosses to the choir," observed Schedoni.

They were watchful for a few moments, and then he resumed the subject. "Mercenaries ought not be trusted——"

"Yet who but mercenaries"—interrupted the Marchesa, and instantly checked herself. But the question thus implied, did not escape the confessor.

"Pardon my astonishment," said he, "at the inconsistency, or, what shall I venture to call it? of your opinions! After the acuteness you have displayed on some points, is it possible you can doubt that principle may both prompt and perform the deed? Why should we hesitate to do what we judge to be right?"

"Ah! reverend father," observed the Marchesa, with emotion, "but where shall we find another like yourself—another who not only can perceive with justness, but will act with energy?"

Schedoni was silent.

"Such a friend is above all estimation; but where shall we seek him?"

"Daughter!" said the monk, emphatically, "my zeal for your family is also above all calculation."

"Good father," replied the Marchesa, comprehending his full meaning, "I know not how to thank you."

"Silence is sometimes eloquence," said Schedoni, significantly.

The Marchesa mused; for her conscience also was eloquent. She tried to overcome its voice, but it would be heard; and sometimes such starts of horrible conviction came over her mind that she felt as one who, awaking from a dream, opens his eyes only to measure the depth of the precipice on which he totters. In such moments she was astonished that she had paused for an instant upon a subject so terrible as that of murder. The sophistry of the confessor, together with the inconsistencies which he had betrayed, and which had not escaped the notice of the Marchesa, even at the time they were uttered, though she had been unconscious of her own, then became more strongly apparent, and she almost determined to suffer the poor Ellena to live. But returning passion, like a wave that has recoiled from the shore, afterwards came with re-collected energy, and swept from her feeble mind the barriers which reason and conscience had began to rear.

"The confidence with which you have thought proper to honour me," resumed Schedoni, "this affair, so momentous"——

"Aye, this affair," interrupted the Marchesa, in a hurried manner,—"but when, and where, good father? Being once convinced, I am anxious to have it settled."

"That must be as occasion offers," replied the monk, thoughtfully.—"On the shore of the Adriatic, in the province of Apulia, not far from Manfredonia, is a house that might suit the purpose. It is a lone dwelling on the beach, and concealed from travellers, among the forests which spread for many miles along the coast."

"And the people?" said the Marchesa.

"Aye, daughter, or why travel so far as Apulia? It is inhabited by one poor man, who sustains a miserable existence by fishing. I know him, and could unfold the reason of his solitary life ;—but no matter, it is sufficient that *I know him.*

"And would trust him, father?"

"Aye, lady, with the life of this girl—though scarcely with my own."

"How! If he is such a villain he may not be trusted! think further. But now, you objected to a mercenary, yet this man is one!"

"Daughter, he may be trusted; when it is in such a case, he is safe and sure. I have reason to know him."

"Name your reasons, father."

The confessor was silent, and his countenance assumed a very peculiar character; it was more terrible than usual, and overspread with a dark cadaverous hue of mingled anger and guilt. The Marchesa started involuntarily as, passing by a window, the evening gleam that fell there discovered it; and for the first time she wished that she had not committed herself so wholly to his power. But the die was now cast; it was too late to be prudent; and she again demanded his reasons.

"No matter," said Schedoni, in a stifled voice, "she dies!"

"By his hands?" asked the Marchesa, with strong emotion. "Think, once more, father."

They were both again silent and thoughtful. The Marchesa at length said, "Father, I rely upon your integrity and prudence;" and she laid a very flattering emphasis upon the word integrity. "But I conjure you to let this business be finished quickly, suspense is to me the purgatory of this world, and not to trust the accomplishment of it to a second person." After a momentary pause she added, "I would not willingly owe so vast a debt of obligation to any other than yourself."

"Your request, daughter, that I would not confide this business to a second person," said Schedoni, with displeasure, "cannot be accorded to. Can you suppose that I, myself——"

"Can I doubt that principle may both prompt and perform the deed?" interrupted the Marchesa with quickness, and anticipating his meaning, while she retorted upon him his former words, "Why should we hesitate to do what we judge to be right?"

The silence of Schedoni alone indicated his

displeasure, which the Marchesa immediately understanding —

"Consider, good father," she added significantly, "how painful it must be to me to owe so infinite an obligation to a stranger, or to any other than so highly valued a friend as yourself."

Schedoni, while he detected her meaning, and persuaded himself that he despised the flattery with which she so thinly veiled it, unconsciously suffered his self-love to be soothed by the compliment. He bowed his head in signal of consent to her wish.

"Avoid violence, if that be possible," she added, immediately comprehending him, "but let her die quickly! The punishment is due to the crime."

The Marchesa happened, as she said this, to cast her eyes upon the inscription over a confessional, where appeared in black letters these awful words, "*God hears thee!*" It appeared an awful warning. Her countenance changed; it had struck upon her heart. Schedoni was too much engaged by his own thoughts to observe or understand her silence. She soon recovered herself, and, considering that this was a common inscription for confessionals, disregarded what she had at first considered as a peculiar admonition; yet some moments elapsed, before she had courage to renew the subject.

"You were speaking of a place, father, resumed the Marchesa; "you mentioned a——"

"Aye," muttered the confessor, still musing; "in a chamber of that house there is ——"

"What noise is that?" said the Marchesa, interrupting him. They listened. A few low and querulous notes of the organ sounded at a distance, and stopped again.

"What mournful music is that?" inquired the Marchesa in a tremulous voice; "it was touched by a fearful hand! Vespers were over long ago!"

"Daughter," observed Schedoni, somewhat sternly, "you said you had a man's courage. Alas! you have a woman's heart."

"Excuse me, father; I know not why I feel this agitation, but I will command it. That chamber——"

"In that chamber," resumed the confessor, "is a secret door, constructed long ago——"

"And for what purpose constructed?" said the impatient Marchesa.

"Pardon me, daughter; 'tis sufficient that it is there; we will make a good use of it. Through that door—in the night—when she sleeps——"

"I comprehend you," said the Marchesa, "I comprehend you. But why—you have your reasons, no doubt—but why the necessity of a secret door in a house which you say is so lonely—inhabited by only one person?"

"A passage leads to the sea," continued Schedoni, without replying to the question. "There, on the shore, when darkness covers it; there, plunged amidst the waves, no stain shall hint of——"

"Hark!" interrupted the Marchesa, starting; "that note again!"

The organ sounded faintly from the choir, and paused, as before. In the next moment, a slow chanting of voices was heard, mingling with the rising peal, in a strain particularly melancholy and solemn.

"Who is dead?" said the Marchesa, changing countenance; "it is a requiem!"

"Peace be with the departed!" exclaimed Schedoni, and crossed himself; "peace rest with his soul!"

"Hark to that chant!" said the Marchesa, in a faltering voice; "it is a first requiem; the soul has but just quitted the body!"

They listened in silence. The Marchesa was much affected; her complexion varied at every instant; her breathings were short and interrupted, and she even shed a few tears, but they were those of despair rather than of sorrow. "That body is now cold," said she to herself, "which but an hour ago was warm and animated! Those fine senses are closed in death! And to this condition would I reduce a being like myself! Oh, wretched, wretched mother! to what has the folly of a son reduced thee!"

She turned from the confessor, and walked alone in the cloister. Her agitation increased; she wept without restraint, for her veil and the evening gloom concealed her, and her sighs were lost amidst the music of the choir.

Schedoni was scarcely less disturbed, but his were emotions of apprehension and contempt. "Behold, what is woman!" said he. "The slave of her passions, the dupe of her senses! When pride and revenge speak in her breast, she defies obstacles and laughs at crimes! Assail but her senses; let music, for instance, touch some feeble chord of her heart, and echo to her fancy and lo! all her perceptions change: she shrinks from the act she had but an instant before believed meritorious, yields to some new emotion, and sinks—the victim of a sound! Oh, weak and contemptible being!"

The Marchesa, at least, seemed to justify his observations. The desperate passions which had resisted every remonstrance of reason and humanity were vanquished only by other passions; and, her senses touched by the mournful melody of music, and her superstitious tears awakened by the occurrence of a requiem for the dead at the very moment when she was planning murder, she yielded, for a while, to the united influence of pity and terror. Her agitation did not subside; but she returned to the confessor.

"We will converse on this business at some

future time," said she ; "at present my spirits are disordered. Good night, father. Remember me in your orisons."

"Peace be with you, lady ! " said the confessor, bowing gravely, "You shall not be forgotten. Be resolute, and yourself."

The Marchesa beckoned her woman to approach, when, drawing her veil closer, and leaning upon the attendant's arm, she left the cloister. Schedoni remained for a moment on the spot, looking after her, till her figure was lost in the gloom of the long perspective ; he then, with thoughtful steps, quitted the cloister by another door. He was disappointed, but he did not despair.

CHAPTER XVI.

WHILE the Marchesa and the monk were thus meditating conspiracies against Ellena, she was still in the Ursaline convent on the lake of Celano. In this obscure sanctuary, indisposition, the consequence of the long and severe anxiety she had suffered, compelled her to remain. A fever was on her spirits, and a universal lassitude prevailed over her frame, which became the more effectual from her very solicitude to conquer it. Every approaching day she hoped she should be able to pursue her journey homeward, yet every day found her as incapable of travelling as the last ; and the second week was already gone before the fine air of Celano, and the tranquillity of her asylum, began to revive her. Vivaldi, who was her daily visitor at the grate of the convent—and who, watching over her with intense solicitude, had hitherto forbore to renew a subject which, by agitating her spirits, might affect her health—now that her health strengthened, ventured gradually to mention his fears lest the place of her retreat should be discovered, and lest he yet might irrecoverably lose her, unless she would approve of their speedy marriage. At every visit he now urged the subject, represented the dangers that surrounded them, and repeated his arguments and entreaties ; for now, when he believed that time was pressing forward fatal evils, he could no longer attend to the delicate scruples that bade him be sparing in entreaty. Ellena, had she obeyed the dictates of her heart, would have rewarded his attachment and his services by a frank approbation of his proposal ; but the objections which reason exhibited against such a concession she could neither overcome or disregard.

Vivaldi, after he had again represented their present dangers, and claimed the promise of her hand, received in the presence of her deceased relative, Signora Bianchi, gently ventured to remind her that an event as sudden as lamentable had first deferred their nuptials, and that if Bianchi had lived, Ellena would have bestowed, long since, the vows now solicited. Again he entreated her, by every sacred and tender recollection, to conclude the fearful uncertainty of their fate, and to bestow upon him the right to protect her before they ventured forth from this temporary asylum.

Ellena immediately admitted the sacredness of the promise which she had formerly given, and assured Vivaldi that she considered herself as indissolubly bound by that promise as if it had been given at the altar ; but she objected to a confirmation of it till his family should seem willing to acknowledge her for their daughter ; when, forgetting the injuries she had received from them, she would no longer refuse their alliance. Ellena added that Vivaldi ought to be more jealous of the dignity of the woman whom he honoured with his esteem than to permit her making a greater concession.

Vivaldi felt the full force of this appeal ; he recollected, with anguish, circumstances of which she was happily ignorant, but which served to strengthen with him the justness of her reproof. And as the aspersions which the Marchesa had thrown upon her name crowded to his memory, pride and indignation swelled his heart, and so far overcame all apprehensions of hazard that he formed a momentary resolution to abandon every other consideration to that of asserting the respect which was due to Ellena, and to forbear claiming her for his wife till his family should make acknowledgment of their error, and willingly admit her in the rank of their child. But this resolution was as transient as plausible ; other considerations, and former fears, pressed upon him. He perceived the strong improbability that they would ever make a voluntary sacrifice of their pride to his love ; or yield mistakes, nurtured by prejudice and by willing indulgence, to truth and a sense of justice. In the meantime, the plans which would be formed for separating him from Ellena might succeed, and he should lose her for ever. Above all, it appeared that the best, the only, method which remained for confuting the daring aspersions that had affected her name was by proving the high respect he himself felt for her, and presenting her to the world in the sacred character of his wife. These considerations quickly determined him to persevere in his suit ; but it was impossible to urge them to Ellena, since the facts they must unfold would not only shock her delicacy and afflict her heart but would furnish the proper pride she cherished with new arguments against approaching a family who had thus grossly insulted her.

While these considerations occupied him, the emotion they occasioned did not escape Ellena's observation ; it increased as he reflected on the impossibility of urging them to her, and on the hopelessness of prevailing with her unless he could produce new arguments in his favour. His unaffected distress awakened all her tenderness; she asked herself whether she ought any longer to assert her own rights, when, by doing so, she sacrificed the peace of him who had incurred so much danger for her sake, who had rescued her from severe oppression, and had so long and so well proved the strength of his affection.

As she applied these questions, she appeared to herself an unjust and selfish being, unwilling to make any sacrifice for the tranquillity of him who had given her liberty even at the risk of his life. Her very virtues, now that they were carried to excess, seemed to her to border upon vices; her sense of dignity appeared to be narrow pride; her delicacy, weakness; her moderated affection, cold ingratitude; and her circumspection, little less than prudence degenerated into meanness.

Vivaldi, as apt in admitting hope as fear, immediately perceived her resolution beginning to yield, and he urged again every argument which was likely to prevail over it. But the subject was too important for Ellena, to be immediately decided upon; he departed with only a faint assurance of encouragement, and she forbade him to return till the following day, when she would acquaint him with her final determination.

This interval was, perhaps, the most painful he had ever experienced. Alone, and on the banks of the lake, he passed many hours in alternate hope and fear: in endeavouring to anticipate the decision on which seemed suspended all his future peace, and abruptly recoiling from it as often as imagination represented it to be adverse.

Of the walls that enclosed her, he scarcely ever lost sight; the view of them seemed to cherish his hopes, and, while he gazed upon their rugged surface, Ellena alone was pictured on his fancy; till his anxiety to learn her disposition towards him arose to agony, and he would abruptly leave the spot. But an invisible spell still seemed to attract him back again, and evening found him pacing slowly beneath the shade of those melancholy boundaries that concealed his Ellena.

Her day was not more tranquil. Whenever prudence and decorous pride forbade her to become a member of the Vivaldi family, as constantly did gratitude, affection, irresistible tenderness, plead the cause of Vivaldi. The memory of past times returned; and the very accents of the deceased seemed to murmur from the grave, and command her to fulfil the engagement which had soothed the dying moments of Bianchi.

On the following morning, Vivaldi was at the gates of the convent long before the appointed hour, and he lingered in torturing impatience till the clock struck the signal for his entrance.

Ellena was already in the parlour; she was alone, and rose in disorder on his approach. His steps faltered, his voice was lost, and his eyes only, which he fixed with earnestness on hers, had power to inquire her resolution. She observed the paleness of his countenance and his emotion with a mixture of concern and approbation. At that moment he perceived her smile and hold out her hand to him; and fear, care, and doubt vanished at once from his mind. He was incapable of thanking her, but sighed deeply as he pressed her hand, and, overcome with joy, supported himself against the grate that separated them.

"You are, then, indeed my own!" said Vivaldi, at length recovering his voice. "We shall be no more parted—you are mine for ever! But your countenance changes! Oh, heaven! surely I have not mistaken! Speak! I conjure you, Ellena; relieve me from these terrible doubts!"

"I am yours, Vivaldi," replied Ellena, faintly; "oppression can part us no more."

She wept, and drew her veil over her eyes.

"What mean those tears?" said Vivaldi, with alarm. "Ah! Ellena," he added in a softened voice, "should tears mingle with such moments as these! Should your tears fall upon my heart now! They tell me that your consent is given with reluctance—with grief; that your love is feeble, your heart—yes, Ellena! that your whole heart is no longer mine!"

"They ought rather to tell you," replied Ellena, "that it is all your own; that my affection never was more powerful than now, when it can overcome every consideration with respect to your family, and urge me to a step which must degrade me in their eyes—and, I fear, in my own."

"Oh, retract that cruel assertion!" interrupted Vivaldi. "Degrade you in your own! —degrade you in your eyes!" He was much agitated; his countenance was flushed, and an air of more than usual dignity dilated his figure, while he added with energy:

"The time shall come, my Ellena, when they shall understand your worth, and acknowledge your excellence. Oh! that I were an emperor, that I might show to all the world how much I love and honour you!"

Ellena gave him her hand, and, withdrawing her veil, smiled on him through her tears with gratitude and reviving courage.

Before Vivaldi retired from the convent, he obtained her consent to consult with an aged Benedictine, whom he had engaged in his interest, as to the hour at which the marriage might be solemnized with least observation. The priest informed him that at the conclusion of the vesper service he should be disengaged; and that, as the first hour after sunset was more solitary than almost any other, the brotherhood being then assembled in the refectory, he would meet Vivaldi and Ellena at that time in a chapel on the edge of the lake, a short distance from the Benedictine convent to which it belonged, and celebrate their nuptials.

With this proposal Vivaldi immediately returned to Ellena ; when it was agreed that the party should assemble at the hour mentioned by the priest. Ellena, who had thought it proper to mention her intention to the abbess of the Ursalines, was, by her permission, to be attended by a lay-sister ; and Vivaldi was to meet her without the walls and conduct her to the altar. When the ceremony was over, the fugitives were to embark in a vessel hired for the purpose, and, crossing the lake, proceed towards Naples. Vivaldi again withdrew to engage a boat, and Ellena to prepare for the continuance of her journey.

As the appointed hour drew near, her spirits sunk, and she watched, with melancholy foreboding, the sun retiring amidst stormy clouds, and his rays fading from the highest points of the mountains, till the gloom of twilight prevailed over the scene. She then left her apartment, took a grateful leave of the hospitable abbess, and, attended by the lay-sister, quitted the convent.

Immediately without the gate she was met by Vivaldi, whose look, as he put her arm within his, gently reproached her for the dejection of her air.

They walked in silence towards the chapel of San Sebastian. The scene appeared to sympathise with the spirits of Ellena. It was a gloomy evening, and the lake, which broke in dark waves upon the shore, mingled its hollow sounds with those of the wind that bowed the lofty pines, and swept in gusts among the rocks. She observed with alarm the heavy thunderclouds that rolled along the sides of the mountains, and the birds circling swiftly over the waters and scudding away to their nests among the cliffs, and she noticed to Vivaldi that, as a storm seemed approaching, she wished to avoid crossing the lake. He immediately ordered Paulo to dismiss the boat, and to be in waiting with a carriage, that, if the weather should become clear, they might not be detained longer than was otherwise necessary.

As they approached the chapel, Ellena fixed her eyes on the mournful cypresses which waved over it, and sighed. "Those," she said, " are funeral mementoes—not such as should grace the altar of marriage ! Vivaldi, I could be superstitious. Think you not they are portentous of future misfortune? But forgive me ; my spirits are weak."

Vivaldi endeavoured to soothe her mind, and tenderly reproached her for the sadness she indulged. Thus they entered the chapel. Silence, and a kind of gloomy sepulchral

light prevailed within. The venerable Benedictine, and a brother who was to serve as guardian to the bride, were already there, but they were kneeling and engaged in prayer.

Vivaldi led the trembling Ellena to the altar, where they waited till the Benedictines should have finished, and these were moments of great emotion. She often looked round the dusky chapel, in fearful expectation of discovering some lurking observer ; and though she knew it to be very improbable that any person in this neighbourhood could be interested in interrupting the ceremony, her mind involuntarily admitted the possibility of it. Once, indeed, as her eyes glanced over a casement, Ellena fancied she distinguished a human face laid close to the glass, as if to watch what was passing within ; but when she looked again, the apparition was gone. Notwithstanding this, she listened with anxiety to the uncertain sounds without, and sometimes started as the surges of the lake dashed over the rock below, almost believing she heard the steps and whispering voices of men in the avenues of the chapel. She tried, however, to subdue apprehension, by considering that, if this were true, a harmless curiosity might have attracted some inhabitants of the convent hither ; and her spirits became more composed, till she observed a door open a little way, and a dark countenance looking from behind it, In the next instant it retreated, and the door was closed.

Vivaldi, who perceived Ellena's complexion change as she laid her hand on his arm, followed her eyes to the door ; but no person appearing, he inquired the cause of her alarm.

" We are observed," said Ellena ; " some person appeared at that door ! "

"And if we are observed, my love," replied Vivaldi, " who is there in this neighbourhood whose observation we can have reason to fear? Good father, despatch," he added, turning to the priest, " you forget that we are waiting."

The officiating priest made a signal that he had nearly concluded his orison ; but the other brother rose immediately and spoke with Vivaldi, who desired that the doors of the chapel might be fastened to prevent intrusion.

" We dare not bar the gates of this holy temple," replied the Benedictine ; "it is a sanctuary, and never may be closed."

" But you will allow me to repress idle curiosity," said Vivaldi, " and to inquire who watches beyond that door? The tranquillity of this lady demands thus much."

The brother assented, and Vivaldi stepped to the door ; but, perceiving no person in the obscure passage beyond it, he returned with lighter steps to the altar, from which the officiating priest now rose.

"My children,' said he, "I have made you

wait ; but an old man's prayers are not less important than a young man's vows, though this is not a moment when you will admit that truth."

"I will allow whatever you please, good father," replied Vivaldi, "if you will administer those vows without further delay ; time presses."

The venerable priest took his station at the altar, and opened the book. Vivaldi placed himself on his right hand, and with looks of anxious love, endeavoured to encourage Ellena, who, with a dejected countenance, which her veil but ill concealed, and eyes fixed on the ground, leaned on her attendant sister. The figure and homely features of this sister ; the tall stature and harsh visage of the brother, clothed in the grey habit of his order ; the silvered head and placid physiognomy of the officiating priest, enlightened by a gleam from the lamp above, opposed to the youthful grace and spirit of Vivaldi, and the milder beauty and sweetness of Ellena, formed altogether a group worthy of the pencil.

The priest had begun the ceremony, when a noise from without again alarmed Ellena, who observed the door once more cautiously opened, and a man bend forward his gigantic figure from behind it. He carried a torch, and its glare, as the door gradually unclosed, discovered other persons in the passage beyond, looking forward over his shoulder into the chapel. The fierceness of their air, and the strange peculiarity of their dress, instantly convinced Ellena that they were not inhabitants of the Benedictine convent, but some terrible messengers of evil. Her half-stifled shriek alarmed Vivaldi, who caught her before she fell to the ground ; but as he had not faced the door, he did not understand the occasion of her terror, till the sudden rush of footsteps made him turn, when he observed several men armed and very singularly habited, advancing towards the altar.

"Who is he that intrudes upon this sanctuary ?" he demanded, sternly, while he half rose from the ground where Ellena had sunk.

"What sacrilegious footsteps," cried the priest, "thus rudely violate this holy place ?"

Ellena was now insensible ; and the men continuing to advance, Vivaldi drew his sword to protect her.

The priest and Vivaldi now spoke together, but the words of neither could be distinguished, when a voice, tremendous from its loudness, like bursting thunder, dissipated the cloud of mystery.

"You, Vincentio di Vivaldi, and of Naples," it said, "and you, Ellena di Rosalba, of Villa Altieri, we summon you to surrender, in the name of the most holy Inquisition !"

"The Inquisition !" exclaimed Vivaldi, scarcely believing what he heard. "Here is some mistake !"

The official repeated the summons without deigning to reply.

Vivaldi, yet more astonished, added, "Do not imagine you can so far impose upon my credulity as that I can believe myself to have fallen within the cognizance of the Inquisition."

"You may believe what you please, signor," replied the chief officer ; "but you and that lady are our prisoners."

"Begone, impostor !" said Vivaldi, springing from the ground, where he had supported Ellena, "or my sword shall teach you to repent your audacity !"

"Do you insult an officer of the Inquisition !" exclaimed the ruffian. "That holy community will inform you what you incur by resisting its mandate."

The priest interrupted Vivaldi's retort. "If you are really officers of that tremendous tribunal," he said, "produce some proof of your office. Remember this place is sanctified, and tremble for the consequence of imposition. You do wrong to believe that I will deliver up to you persons who have taken refuge here, without an unequivocal demand from that dread power."

"Produce your form of summons," demanded Vivaldi, with haughty impatience.

"It is here," replied the official, drawing forth a black scroll, which he delivered to the priest. "Read, and be satisfied !"

The Benedictine started the instant he beheld the scroll, but he received and deliberately examined it. The kind of parchment, the impression of the seal, the particular form of words, the private signals, understood only by the initiated—all seemed to announce this a true instrument of arrestation from the *Holy Office.* The scroll dropped from his hand, and he fixed his eyes, with surprise and unutterable compassion, upon Vivaldi, who stooped to reach the parchment, when it was snatched by the official.

"Unhappy young man !" said the priest, "it is too true : you are summoned by that awful power to answer for your crime, and I am spared from the commission of a terrible offence !"

Vivaldi appeared thunderstruck. "For what crime, holy father, am I called upon to answer ? This is some bold and artful imposture, since it can delude even you ! What crime ?—what offence ?"

"I did not think you had been thus hardened in guilt !" replied the priest. "Forbear ! add not the audacity of falsehood to the headlong passions of youth. You understand too well your crime."

"Falsehood !" retorted Vivaldi. "But your years, old man, and those sacred vestments protect you. For these ruffians, who have dared to implicate that innocent victim," pointing to Ellena, "in the charge, they shall have justice from my vengeance."

"Forbear! forbear!" said the priest, seizing his arm; "have pity on yourself and on her. Know you not the punishment you incur from resistance?"

"I know nor care not," replied Vivaldi; "but I will defend Ellena di Rosalba to the last moment. Let them approach if they dare."

"It is on her, on her who lies senseless at your feet," said the priest, "that they will wreak their vengeance for these insults; on her—the partner of your guilt."

"The partner of my guilt!" exclaimed Vivaldi, with mingled astonishment and indignation; "of my guilt!"

"Rash young man! does not the very veil she wears betray it? I marvel how it could pass my observation!"

"You have stolen a nun from her convent," said the chief officer, "and must answer for the crime. When you have wearied yourself with these heroics, signor, you must go with us; our patience is wearied already."

Vivaldi observed, for the first time, that Ellena was shrouded in a *nun's* veil; it was the one which Olivia had lent, to conceal her from the notice of the abbess, on the night of her departure from San Stefano, and which, in the hurry of that departure, she had forgotten to leave with the recluse. During this interval, her mind had been too entirely occupied by cares and apprehension to allow her once to notice that the veil she wore was other than her usual one; but it had been too well observed by some of the Ursaline sisters.

Though he knew not how to account for the circumstance of the veil, Vivaldi began to perceive others which gave colour to the charge brought against him, and to ascertain the wide circumference of the snare that was spread around him. He fancied, too, that he perceived the hand of Schedoni employed upon it, and that his dark spirit was now avenging itself for the exposure he had suffered in the church of the Spirito Santo, and for all the consequent mortifications. As Vivaldi was ignorant of the ambitious hopes which the Marchesa had encouraged in Father Schedoni, he did not see the improbability that the confessor would have dared to hazard her favour by this arrest of her son; much less could he suspect that Schedoni, having done so, had secrets in his possession which enabled him safely to defy her resentment, and bind her in silence to his decree.

With the conviction that Schedoni's was the master-hand that directed the present manœuvre, Vivaldi stood aghast, and gazing in silent unutterable anguish on Ellena, who, as she began to revive, stretched forth her helpless hands, and called upon him to save her. "Do not leave me," said she, in accents the most supplicating; "I am safe while you are with me,"

At the sound of her voice he started from his trance; and, turning fiercely upon the ruffians, who stood in sullen watchfulness around, bade them depart or prepare for his fury. At the same instant they all drew their swords; and the shrieks of Ellena, and the supplications of the officiating priest, were lost amidst the tumult of the combatants.

Vivaldi, most unwilling to shed blood, stood merely on the defensive, till the violence of his antagonists compelled him to exert all his skill and strength. He then disabled one of the ruffians; but his skill was insufficient to repel the other two, and he was nearly overcome, when steps were heard approaching, and Paulo rushed into the chapel. Perceiving his master beset, he drew his sword, and came furiously to his aid. He fought with unconquerable audacity and fierceness, till, nearly at the moment when his adversary fell, other ruffians entered the chapel, and Vivaldi, with his faithful servant, was wounded, and at length disarmed.

Ellena, who had been withheld from throwing herself between the combatants, now, on observing that Vivaldi was wounded, renewed her efforts for liberty, accompanied by such agony of supplication and complaint as almost moved to pity the hearts of the surrounding ruffians.

Disabled by his wounds, and also held by his enemies, Vivaldi was compelled to witness her distress and danger without a hope of rescuing her. In frantic accents he called upon the old priest to protect her.

"I dare not oppose the orders of the Inquisition," replied the Benedictine, "even if I had sufficient strength to defy its officials. Know you not, unhappy young man, that it is death to resist them?"

"Death!" exclaimed Ellena; "death!"

"Ay, lady, too surely so!"

"Signor, it would have been well for you," said one of the officers, "if you had taken my advice; you will pay dearly for what you have done," pointing to the ruffian who lay severely wounded on the ground.

"My master will not have that to pay for, friend," said Paulo, "for if you must know, that is a piece of my work; and if my arms were now at liberty, I would try if I could not match it among one of you, though I am so slashed."

"Peace, good Paulo! the deed was mine," said Vivaldi; then addressing the official, "For myself I care not, I have done my duty —but for her! Can you look upon her, innocent and helpless as she is, and not relent? Can you, will you, barbarians, drag her also to destruction, upon a charge too so daringly false?"

"Our relenting would be of no service to her," replied the official; "we must do our duty. Whether the charge is true or false, she must answer to it before her judges."

" What charge?" demanded Ellena.

" The charge of having broken your nun's vow," replied the priest.

Ellena raised her eyes to heaven. " Is it even so!" she exclaimed.

" You hear—she acknowledges the crime," said one of the ruffians.

" She acknowledges no crime," replied Vivaldi ; " she only perceives the extent of the malice that persecutes her. Oh! Ellena, must I then abandon you to their power? leave you for ever!"

The agony of this thought reanimated him with momentary strength ; he burst from the grasp of the officials, and once more clasped Ellena to his bosom, who, unable to speak, wept with the anguish of a breaking heart, as her head sunk upon his shoulder. The ruffians around them so far respected their grief that, for a moment, they did not interrupt it.

Vivaldi's exertion was transient ; faint from sorrow, and from loss of blood, he became unable to support himself, and was compelled again to relinquish Ellena.

" Is there no help?" said she, with agony ; " will you suffer him to expire on the ground?"

The priest directed that he should be conveyed to the Benedictine convent, where his wounds might be examined, and medical aid administered. The disabled ruffians were already carried thither ; but Vivaldi refused to go, unless Ellena might accompany him. It was contrary to the rules of the place that a woman should enter it ; and before the priest could reply, his Benedictine brother eagerly said that they dared not transgress the law of the convent.

Ellena's fears for Vivaldi entirely overcoming those for herself, she entreated that he would suffer himself to be conveyed to the Benedictines : but she could not be prevailed with to leave her. The officials, however, prepared to separate them. Vivaldi in vain urged the useless cruelty of dividing him from Ellena, if, as they had hinted, she also was to be carried to the Inquisition ; and as ineffectually demanded whither they really designed to take her.

" We shall take good care of her, signor," said an officer ; " that is sufficient for you. It signifies nothing whether you are going the same way ; you must not go together."

" Why, did you ever hear, signor, of arrested persons being suffered to remain in company?" said another ruffian. " Fine plots they would lay! I warrant they would not contradict each other's evidence a little."

" You shall not separate me from my master, though," vociferated Paulo. " I demand to be sent to the Inquisition with him, or to the devil, but all is one for that."

" Fair and softly," replied the officer ; " you shall be sent to the Inquisition first,

and to the devil afterwards ; you must be tried before you are condemned."

" But waste no more time," he added to his followers, and pointing to Ellena, " away with her."

As he said this, they lifted Ellena in their arms. " Let me loose!" cried Paulo, when he saw they were carrying her from the place, " let me loose, I say!" and the violence of his struggles burst asunder the cords which held him ; a vain release, for he was instantly seized again.

Vivaldi, already exhausted by the loss of blood and the anguish of his mind, made, however, a last effort to save her ; he tried to raise himself from the ground, but a sudden film came over his sight, and his senses forsook him, while yet the name of Ellena faltered on his lips.

As they bore her from the chapel, she continued to call upon Vivaldi, and alternately to supplicate that she might once more behold him, and take one last adieu. The ruffians were inexorable, and she heard his voice no more, for he no longer heard—no longer was able to reply to hers.

" Oh! once again!" she cried in agony. " One word, Vivaldi! Let me hear the sound of your voice yet once again!" But it was silent.

As she quitted the chapel, with eyes still bent towards the spot where he lay, she exclaimed, in the piercing accents of despair, " Farewell, Vivaldi! Oh! for ever—ever, farewell!"

The tone in which she pronounced the last " farewell!" was so touching that even the cold heart of the priest could not resist it ; but he impatiently wiped away the few tears that rushed into his eyes before they were observed. Vivaldi heard it—it seemed to arouse him from death!—he heard her mournful voice for the last time, and, turning his eyes, saw her veil floating away through the portal of the chapel. All suffering, all effort, all resistance was vain ; the ruffians bound him, bleeding as he was, and conveyed him to the Benedictine convent, together with the wounded Paulo, who unceasingly vociferated on the way thither, " I demand to be sent to the Inquisition! I demand to be sent to the Inquisition!"

_____

CHAPTER XVII.

THE wounds of Vivaldi and of his servant were pronounced, by the Benedictine who had examined and dressed them, to be not dangerous, but those of one of the ruffians were declared doubtful. Some few of the brothers displayed much compassion and kindness towards the prisoners ; but the greater part seemed fearful of expressing any degree of sympathy for persons who had fallen within the cognizance of the Holy Office, and even kept aloof from the chamber in which they were confined. To this self-restriction, however, they were not long subjected ; for Vivaldi and Paulo were compelled to begin their journey as soon as some short rest had sufficiently revived them. They were placed in the same carriage, but the presence of two officers prevented all interchange of conjecture as to the destination of Ellena, and with respect to the immediate occasion of their misfortune. Paulo, indeed, now and then hazarded a surmise, and did not scruple to affirm that the abbess of San Stefano was their chief enemy ; that the Carmelite friars, who had overtaken them on the road, were her agents ; and that, having traced their route, they had given intelligence where Vivaldi and Ellena mi ght be found.

" I guessed we never should escape the abbess," said Paulo, "though I would not disturb you, signor *mio*, nor the poor lady Ellena, by saying so. But your abbesses are as cunning as Inquisitors, and are so fond of governing that they had rather, like them, send a man to the devil than send him nowhere."

Vivaldi gave Paulo a significant look, which was meant to repress his imprudent loquacity, and then sank again into silence and the abstractions of deep grief. The officers, meanwhile, never spoke, but were observant of all that Paulo said, who perceived their watchfulness ; but because he despised them as spies, he thoughtlessly despised them also as enemies, and was so far from concealing opinions which they might repeat to his prejudice, that he had a pride in exaggerating them and in daring the worst which the exasperated tempers of these men, shut up in the same carriage with him, and compelled to hear whatever he chose to say against the institution to which they belonged, could effect. Whenever Vivaldi, recalled from his abstraction by some bold assertion, endeavoured to check his imprudence, Paulo was contented to solace his conscience, instead of protecting himself, by saying, " It is their own fault ; they would thrust themselves into my company ; let them have enough of it ; and, if ever they take me before their reverences the Inquisitors, *they* shall have enough of it too. I will play up such a tune in the Inquisition as is not heard there every day. I will jingle all the bells on their fools' caps, and tell them a little honest truth, if they make me smart for it ever so."

Vivaldi, aroused once more, and seriously alarmed for the consequences which honest Paulo might be drawing upon himself, now insisted on his silence, and was obeyed.

They travelled during the whole night, stopping only to change horses. At every post-house Vivaldi looked for a carriage that might enclose Ellena, but none appeared, nor any sound of wheels told him that she followed. With the morning light he perceived the dome of St. Peter appearing faintly over the plains that surround Rome, and he understood, for the first time, that he was going to the prisons of the Inquisition in that city. The travellers descended upon the Campania, and then rested for a few hours at a small town on its borders.

When they again set forward, Vivaldi perceived that the guard was changed, the officer who had remained with him in the apartment of the inn only appearing among the new faces which surrounded him. The dress and manners of these men differed considerably from those of the other. Their conduct was more temperate, but their countenances expressed a darker cruelty, mingled with a sly demureness, and a solemn self-importance that announced them at once as belonging to the Inquisition. They were almost invariably silent ; and when they did speak, it was only in a few sententious words. To the abounding questions of Paulo, and the few earnest entreaties of his master to be informed of the place of Ellena's destination, they made not the least reply ; and listened to all the flourishing speeches of the servant against Inquisitors and the Holy Office with the most profound gravity.

Vivaldi was struck with the circumstance of the guard being changed, and still more with the appearance of the party who now composed it. When he compared the manners of the late, with those of the present, guard, he thought he discovered in the first the mere ferocity of ruffians ; but in the latter, the principles of cunning and cruelty which seemed particularly to characterise Inquisitors. He was inclined to believe that a stratagem had enthralled him, and that now, for the first time, he was in the custody of the *Holy Office*.

It was near midnight when the prisoners entered Porto del Popolo, and found themselves in the midst of the Carnival at Rome. The Corso, through which they were obliged to pass, was crowded with gay carriages and masks, with processions of musicians, monks, and mountebanks ; was lighted up with innumerable tapers and flambeaux, and resounded with the heterogeneous rattling of wheels, the music of serenaders, and the jokes and laughter of the revellers, as they sportively threw about their sugar-plums. The heat of the weather made it necessary to have the windows of the coach open ; and the prisoners therefore, saw all that passed without. It was a scene which contrasted cruelly with the feelings and circumstances of Vivaldi ; torn as he was from her he most loved, in dreadful uncertainty as to her fate, and himself about to be brought before a tribunal whose mysterious and terrible proceedings appalled even the bravest spirits. Altogether this was one of the most striking examples which the chequer-work of human life could show, or human feelings endure. Vivaldi sickened as he looked upon the splendid crowd, while the carriage made its way slowly with it ; but Paulo, as he gazed, was reminded of the Corso of Naples, such as it appeared at the time of Carnival ; and, comparing the present scene with his native one, he found fault with everything he beheld. The dresses were tasteless, the equipages without splendour, the people without spirit ; yet, such was the propensity of his heart to sympathise with whatever was gay, that for some moments he forgot that he was a prisoner on his way to the Inquisition ; almost forgot that he was a Neapolitan ; and while he exclaimed against the dulness of a Roman Carnival, would have sprung through the carriage window to partake of its spirit, if his fetters and his wounds had not withheld him. A deep sigh from Vivaldi recalled his wandering imagination ; and when he noticed again the sorrow in his master's look, all his lightly joyous spirits fled.

"My *maestro*, my dear *maestro !*" he said, and knew not how to finish what he wished to express.

At that moment they passed the theatre of San Carlo, the doors of which were thronged with equipages, where Roman ladies in their gala habits, courtiers in their fantastic dresses and masks of all descriptions, were hastening to the opera. In the midst of this gay bustle, where the carriage was unable to proceed, the officials of the Inquisition looked on in solemn silence, not a muscle of their features relaxing in sympathy or yielding a single wrinkle of the self-importance that lifted their brows ; and, while they regarded with secret contempt those who could be thus lightly pleased, the people, in return, more wisely, perhaps, regarded with contempt the proud moroseness that refused to partake of innocent pleasures because they were trifling, and shrunk from countenances furrowed with the sternness of cruelty. But, when their office was distinguished, part of the crowd pressed back from the carriage in affright while another part advanced with curiosity ; though, as the majority retreated, space was left for the coach to move on. After quitting the Corso it proceeded for some miles through dark and deserted streets, where only here and there a lamp, hung on high before the image of a saint, shed its glimmering light, and where a melancholy and universal silence prevailed. At intervals, indeed, the moon, as the clouds passed away, showed for a moment some of those mighty monuments of Rome's eternal name, those sacred ruins, those gigantic skeletons which once enclosed a soul whose energies governed a world ! Even Vivaldi could not behold with indifference the grandeur of these relics, as the rays fell upon the hoary walls and columns ; or pass among those scenes of ancient story without feeling a melancholy awe, a sacred enthusiasm, that withdrew him from himself.

But the illusion was transient ; his own misfortunes pressed too heavily upon him to be long unfelt, and his enthusiasm vanished like the moonlight.

A returning gleam lighted up, soon after, the rude and extensive area which the carriage was crossing. It appeared, from its desolation, and the ruins scattered distantly along its skirts, to be a part of the city entirely abandoned by the modern inhabitants to the remains of its former grandeur. Not one shadow of a human being crossed the waste, nor any building appeared which might be supposed to shelter an inhabitant. The deep tone of a bell, however, rolling on the silence of the night, announced the haunts of man to be not far off ; and Vivaldi then perceived in the distance, to which he was approaching, an extent of lofty walls and towers that, as far as the gloom would permit his eye to penetrate, bounded the horizon. He judged these to be the prisons of the Inquisition. Paulo pointed them out at the same moment. "Ah, signor !" said he, despondingly, "that is the place ! what strength ! If, my lord, the old Marchese were but to see where we are going ! Ah ——"

He concluded with a deep sigh, and sunk again into the state of apprehension and mute expectation which he had suffered from the moment that he quitted the Corso.

The carriage, having reached the walls, followed their bendings to a considerable extent. These walls, of immense height, and strengthened by innumerable massy bulwarks, exhibited neither window nor grate, but a vast and dreary blank ; a small round tower only, perched here and there upon the summit, breaking their monotony.

The prisoners passed what seemed to be the principal entrance, from the grandeur of its portal and the gigantic loftiness of the towers that rose over it ; and soon after the carriage stopped at an archway in the walls, strongly barricadoed. One of the escort alighted, and, having struck upon the bars, a folding door within was immediately opened, and a man bearing a torch appeared behind the barricado, whose countenance, as he looked through it, might have been copied for the "Grim-visaged comfortless despair" of the poet.

No words were exchanged between him and the guard ; but on perceiving who were without, he opened the iron gate, and the prisoners, having alighted, passed with the two officials beneath the arch, the guard following with a torch. They descended a flight of broad steps, at the foot of which another iron gate admitted them to a kind of hall ; such, however, it at first appeared to Vivaldi, as his eyes glanced through its gloomy extent, imperfectly ascertaining it by the lamp which hung from the centre of the roof. No person appeared, and a deathlike silence prevailed ;

for neither the officials nor the guard yet spoke ; nor did any distant sound contradict the notion, which soon occurred, that they were traversing the chambers of the dead. To Vivaldi it appeared that this was one of the burial vaults of the victims who suffered in the Inquisition, and his whole frame thrilled with horror. Several avenues, opening from the apartment, seemed to lead to distant quarters of this immense fabric, but still no footstep whispering along the pavement, or voice murmuring through the arched roofs, indicated it to be the residence of the living.

Having entered one of the passages, Vivaldi perceived a person clothed in black, and who bore a lighted taper, crossing silently in the remote perspective ; and he understood too well from his habit that he was a member of this dreadful tribunal.

The sound of footsteps seemed to reach the stranger, for he turned, and paused while the officers advanced. They then made signs to each other, and exchanged a few words, which neither Vivaldi nor his servant could understand, when the stranger, pointing with his taper along another avenue, passed away. Vivaldi followed him with his eyes till a door at the extremity of the passage opened, and he saw the Inquisitor enter an apartment whence a great light proceeded, and where several other figures, habited like himself, appeared waiting to receive him. The door immediately closed ; and, whether the imagination of Vivaldi was affected, or that the sounds were real, he thought, as it closed, he distinguished half stifled groans, as of a person in agony.

The avenue, through which the prisoners passed, opened, at length, into an apartment gloomy like the first they had entered, but more extensive. The roof was supported by arches, and long arcades branched off from every side of the chamber, as from a central point, and were lost in the gloom, which the rays of the small lamps, suspended in each, but feebly penetrated.

They rested here, and a person soon after advanced, who appeared to be the gaoler, into whose hands Vivaldi and Paulo were delivered. A few mysterious words having been exchanged, one of the officials crossed the hall and ascended a wide staircase, while the other, with the gaoler and the guard, remained below, as if awaiting his return.

A long interval elapsed, during which the stillness of the place was sometimes interrupted by a closing door, and, at others, by indistinct sounds, which yet appeared to Vivaldi like lamentations and extorted groans. Inquisitors, in their long black robes, issued from time to time from the passages, and crossed the hall to other avenues. They eyed the prisoners with curiosity, but without pity. Their visages, with few exceptions, seemed stamped with the characters of demons. Vivaldi could not look upon the grave cruelty or the ferocious impatience their countenances severally expressed without reading in them the fate of some fellow-creature, the fate which these men seemed going even at this moment to confirm ; and, as they passed with soundless steps, he shrunk from observation, as if their very looks possessed some supernatural power and could have struck death. But he followed their fleeting figures, as they proceeded on their work of horror, to where the last glimmering ray faded into darkness, expecting to see other doors of other chambers open to receive them. While meditating upon these horrors, Vivaldi lost every selfish consideration in astonishment and indignation at the sufferings which the frenzied wickedness of man prepares for man, who, even at the moment of infliction, insults his victim with assertions of the justice and necessity of such procedure. "Is this possible?" said Vivaldi, internally. "Can this be in human nature? Can such horrible perversion of right be permitted? Can man, who calls himself endowed with reason, and immeasurably superior to every other created being, argue himself into the commission of such horrible folly, such inveterate cruelty, as exceeds all the acts of the most irrational and ferocious brute? Brutes do not deliberately slaughter their species ; it remains for man only, man, proud of his prerogative of reason, and boasting of his sense of justice, to unite the most terrible extremes of folly and wickedness !".

Vivaldi had been no stranger to the existence of this tribunal ; he had long understood the nature of the establishment, and had often received particular accounts of its customs and laws ; but, though he had believed before, it was now only that conviction appeared to impress his understanding. A new view of human nature seemed to burst at once upon his mind, and he could not have experienced greater astonishment if this had been the first moment in which he had heard of the institution. But when he thought of Ellena, considered that she was in the power of this tribunal, and that it was probable she was at this moment within the same dreadful walls, grief, indignation, and despair irritated him almost to frenzy. He seemed suddenly animated with supernatural strength, and ready to attempt impossibilities for her deliverance. It was by a strong effort of self-command that he forbore bursting the bonds which held him, and making a desperate attempt to seek her through the vast extent of these prisons. Reflection, however, had not so entirely forsaken him but that he saw the impossibility of succeeding in such an effort the moment he had conceived it, and he forbore to rush upon the certain destruction to which it must have led. His passions, thus restrained, seemed to become virtues, and to display themselves in the energy of his courage and his fortitude. His soul became stern and vigorous in despair, and his manner and countenance assumed a calm dignity which awed, in some degree, even his guards. The pain of his wounds was no longer felt; it appeared as if the strength of his intellectual self had subdued the infirmities of the body, and, perhaps, in these moments of elevation, he could have endured the torture without shrinking.

Paulo, meanwhile, mute and grave, was watchful of all that passed; he observed the revolutions in his master's mind with grief first and then with surprise, but he could not imitate the noble fortitude which now gave weight and steadiness to Vivaldi's thoughts. And when he looked on the power and gloom around him, and on the visages of the passing Inquisitors, he began to repent that he had so freely delivered his opinion of this tribunal in the presence of its agents, and to perceive that, if he played up the kind of tune he had threatened, it would probably be the last he should ever be permitted to perform in this world.

At length the chief officer descended the staircase, and immediately bade Vivaldi to follow him. Paulo was accompanying his master, but was withheld by the guard, and told he was to be disposed of in a different way. This was the moment of his severest trial; he declared he would not be separated from his master.

"What did I demand to be brought here for," he cried, "if it was not that I might go shares with the signor in all his troubles? This is not a place to come to for pleasure, I warrant; and I can promise ye, gentlemen, I would not have come within a hundred miles of you if it had not been for my master's sake."

The guards roughly interrupted him, and were carrying him away, when Vivaldi's commanding voice interrupted them. He returned to speak a few words of consolation to his faithful servant, and, since they were to be separated, to take leave of him.

Paulo embraced his knees, and, while he wept, and his words were almost stifled by sobs, declared that no force should drag him from his master while he had life; and repeatedly appealed to the guards with—"What did I demand to be brought here for? Did ever anybody come here to seek pleasure? What right have you to prevent my going shares with my master in his troubles?"

"We do not intend to deny you that pleasure, friend," replied one of the guards.

"Don't you? Then heaven bless you!" cried Paulo, springing from his knees, and shaking the man by the hand with a violence that would nearly have dislocated the shoulder of a person less robust.

"So come with us," added the guard, dragging him away from Vivaldi. Paulo now became outrageous, and, struggling with the guards, burst from them, and again fell at the feet of his master, who raised and embraced him, endeavouring to prevail with him to submit quietly to what was inevitable, and to encourage him with hope.

"I trust that our separation will be short," said Vivaldi; "and that we shall meet again in happier circumstances. My innocence must soon appear."

"We shall never, never meet again, signor mio, in this world," said Paulo, sobbing violently, "so don't make me hope so. That old abbess knows what she is about too well to let us escape, or she would not have catched us up so cunningly as she did; so what signifies innocence! Oh, if my old lord, the Marchese, did but know where we are!"

Vivaldi interrupted him, and turning to the guards, said, "I recommend my faithful servant to your compassion; he is innocent. It will some time, perhaps, be in my power to recompense you for any indulgence you may allow him, and I shall value it a thousand times more highly than any you could show to myself! Farewell, Paulo—farewell! Officer, I am ready."

"Oh stay! signor, for one moment—stay!" said Paulo.

"We can wait no longer," said the guard, and again drew Paulo away, who, looking piteously after Vivaldi, alternately repeated, "Farewell, dear *maestro!* farewell, dear, dear *maestro!*" and "What did I demand to be brought here for? What did I demand to be brought here for?—what was it for, if not to go shares with my *maestro?*" till Vivaldi was beyond the reach of sight and of hearing.

Vivaldi, having followed the officer up the staircase, passed through a gallery to an antechamber, where, being delivered into the custody of some persons in waiting, his conductor disappeared beyond a folding door that led to an inner apartment. Over this door was an inscription in Hebrew characters, traced in blood-colour. Dante's inscription on the entrance of the infernal regions would have been suitable to a place where every circumstance and feature seemed to say, "*Hope, that comes to all, comes not here!*"

Vivaldi conjectured that in this chamber they were preparing for him the instruments which were to extort a confession; and, though he knew little of the regular proceedings of this tribunal, he had always understood that the torture was inflicted upon the accused person till he made confession of the crime of which he was suspected. By such a mode of proceeding, the innocent were certain of suffering longer than the guilty; for, as they had nothing to confess, the Inquisitor, mistaking innocence for obstinacy, persevered in his inflictions, and it frequently happened that he compelled the innocent to become criminal, and assert a falsehood, that they might be released from anguish which they could no longer sustain. Vivaldi considered this circumstance undauntedly ; every faculty of his soul was bent up to firmness and endurance. He believed that he understood the extent of the charge which would be brought against him, a charge as false as a specious confirmation of it would be terrible in its consequence both to Ellena and himself. Yet every art would be practised to bring him to an acknowledgment of having carried off a nun, and he knew also that since the prosecutor and the witnesses are never confronted with the prisoner in cases of severe accusation, and since their very names are concealed from him, it would be scarcely possible for him to prove his innocence. But he did not hesitate an instant whether to sacrifice himself for Ellena, determining rather to expire beneath the merciless inflictions of the Inquisitors than to assert a falsehood which must involve her in destruction.

The officer at length appeared, and having beckoned Vivaldi to advance, uncovered his head, and bared his arms. He then led him forward through the folding door into the chamber ; having done which, he immediately withdrew, and the door, which shut out Hope, closed after him.

Vivaldi found himself in a spacious apartment, where only two persons were visible, who were seated at a large table that occupied the centre of the room. They were both habited in black ; the one, who seemed by his piercing eye, and extraordinary physiognomy, to be an Inquisitor, wore on his head a kind of black turban, which heightened the natural ferocity of his visage ; the other was uncovered and his arms bared to the elbows. A book, with some instruments of singular appearance lay before him. Round the table were several unoccupied chairs, on the backs of which appeared figurative signs ; at the upper end of the apartment a gigantic crucifix stretched nearly to the vaulted roof ; and at the lower end, suspended from an arch in the wall, was a dark curtain, but whether it veiled a window, or shrouded some object or person necessary to the designs of the Inquisitor, there were little means of judging. It was, however, suspended from an arch such as sometimes contains a casement, or leads to a deep recess.

The Inquisitor called on Vivaldi to advance, and, when he had reached the table, put a book into his hands, and bade him swear to reveal the truth and keep for ever secret whatever he might see or hear in the apartment. Vivaldi hesitated to obey so unqualified a command. The Inquisitor reminded him, by a look not to be mistaken, that he was absolute here ; but Vivaldi still hesitated. "Shall I consent to my own condemnation ?" said he to himself. "The malice of demons like these may convert the most innocent circumstances into matter of accusation for my destruction, and I must answer whatever questions they choose to ask. And shall I swear, also, to conceal whatever I may witness in this chamber, when I know that the most diabolical cruelties are hourly practised here ?"

The Inquisitor, in a voice which would have made a heart less fortified than was Vivaldi's tremble, again commanded him to swear ; at the same time, he made a signal to the person who sat at the opposite end of the table, and who appeared to be an inferior officer.

Vivaldi was still silent, but he began to consider that, unconscious as he was of crime, it was scarcely possible for his words to be tortured into a self-accusation ; and that, whatever he might witness, no retribution would be prevented, no evil withheld, by the oath which bound him to secrecy, since his most severe denunciation could avail nothing against the supreme power of this tribunal. As he did not perceive any good which could arise from refusing the oath, and saw much immediate evil from resistance, he consented to receive it. Notwithstanding this, when he put the book to his lips, and uttered the tremendous vow prescribed to him, hesitation and reluctance returned upon his mind, and an icy coldness struck to his heart. He was so much affected that circumstances, apparently the most trivial, had at this moment influence upon his imagination. As he accidentally threw his eyes upon the curtain, which he had observed before without emotion, and now thought it moved, he almost started in expectation of seeing some person, an Inquisitor, perhaps, as terrific as the one before him, or an accuser as malicious as Schedoni, steal from behind it.

The Inquisitor having administered the oath, and the attendant having noted it in his book, the examination began. After demanding, as is usual, the names and titles of Vivaldi and his family and his place of residence, to which he fully replied, the Inquisitor asked whether he understood the nature of the accusation on which he had been arrested.

"The order for my arrestation informed me," replied Vivaldi.

"Look to your words," said the Inquisitor, "and remember your oath. What was the ground of accusation ?"

"I understood," said Vivaldi, "that I was accused of having stolen a nun from her sanctuary."

A faint degree of surprise appeared on the brow of the Inquisitor. "You confess it, then ?" he said, after the pause of a moment, and making a signal to the secretary, who immediately noted Vivaldi's words.

"I solemnly deny it," replied Vivaldi. "The accusation is false and malicious."

"Remember the oath you have taken!" repeated the Inquisitor. "Learn also, that mercy is shown to such as make full confession; but that the torture is applied to those who have the folly and the obstinacy to withhold the truth."

"If you torture me till I acknowledge the justness of this accusation," said Vivaldi, "I must expire under your inflictions, for suffering never shall compel me to assert a falsehood. It is not the truth which you seek; it is not the guilty whom you punish; the innocent, having no crimes to confess, are the victims of your cruelty, or, to escape from it, become criminal, and proclaim a lie."

"Recollect yourself," said the Inquisitor, sternly. "You are not brought hither to accuse, but to answer accusation. You say you are innocent, yet acknowledge yourself to be acquainted with the subject of the charge which is to be urged against you! How could you know this, but from the voice of conscience?"

"From the words of your own summons," replied Vivaldi, "and from those of your officials who arrested me."

"How!" exclaimed the Inquisitor. "Note that," pointing to the secretary; "he says by the words of our summons: now, we know that you never read that summons. He says also by the words of our officials; it appears, then, he is ignorant that death would follow such a breach of confidence."

"It is true I never did read the summons," replied Vivaldi, "and as true that I never asserted I did; the friar, who read it, told of what it accused me, and your officials confirmed the testimony."

"No more of this equivocation!" said the Inquisitor. "Speak only to the question."

"I will not suffer my assertions to be misrepresented," replied Vivaldi, "or my words to be perverted against myself. I have sworn to speak the truth only; since you believe I violate my oath, and doubt my direct and simple words, I will speak no more."

The Inquisitor half rose from his chair, and his countenance grew paler. "Audacious heretic!" he said, "will you dispute, insult, and disobey the commands of our most holy tribunal! You will be taught the consequence of your desperate impiety. To the torture with him!"

A stern smile was on the features of Vivaldi: his eyes were calmly fixed on the Inquisitor, and his attitude was undaunted and firm. His courage, and the cool contempt which his looks expressed, seemed to touch his examiner, who perceived that he had not a common mind to operate upon. He abandoned, therefore, for the present, terrific

measures, and, resuming his usual manner, proceeded in the examination.

"Where were you arrested?"

"At the chapel of San Sebastian, on the lake of Celano."

"You are certain as to this?" asked the Inquisitor; "you are sure it was not at the village of Legano, on the high road between Celano and Rome?"

Vivaldi, while he confirmed his assertion, recollected with some surprise that Legano was the place where the guard had been changed, and he mentioned the circumstance. The Inquisitor, however, proceeded in his questions without appearing to notice it. "Was any person arrested with you?"

"You cannot be ignorant," replied Vivaldi, "that Signora di Rosalba was seized at the same time, upon the false charge of being a nun who had broken her vows and eloped from her convent; nor that Paulo Mendrico, my faithful servant, was also made a prisoner, though upon what pretence he was arrested I am utterly ignorant."

The Inquisitor remained for some moments in thoughtful silence, and then inquired slightly concerning the family of Ellena and her usual place of residence. Vivaldi, fearful of making some assertion that might be prejudicial to her, referred him to herself; but the inquiry was repeated.

"She is now within these walls," replied Vivaldi, hoping to learn from the manner of his examiner whether his fears were just, "and can answer these questions better than myself."

The Inquisitor merely bade the notary write down her name, and then remained for a few moments meditating. At length he said, "Do you know where you now are?"

Vivaldi, smiling at the question, replied, "I understand that I am in the prisons of the Inquisition, at Rome."

"Do you know what are the crimes that subject persons to the cognizance of the Holy Office?"

Vivaldi was silent.

"Your conscience informs *you*, and your silence confirms *me*. Let me admonish you, once more, to make a full confession of your guilt; remember that this is a merciful tribunal, and shows favour to such as acknowledge their crimes."

Vivaldi smiled sarcastically; the Inquisitor proceeded.

"It does not resemble some severe, yet just, courts, where immediate execution follows the confession of a criminal. No! it is merciful; and though it punishes guilt, it never applies the torture but in cases of necessity, when the obstinate silence of the prisoner requires such a measure. You see, therefore, what you may avoid, and what you may expect."

"But if the prisoner has nothing to confess?" said Vivaldi. "Can your tortures make him guilty? They may indeed force a weak mind to be guilty of falsehood; and to escape present anguish, a man may unwarily condemn himself to the death! But you will find that I am not such a one."

"Young man," replied the Inquisitor, "you will understand too soon that we never act but upon sure authority; and will wish, too late, that you had made an honest confession. Your silence cannot keep from us a knowledge of your offences; we are in possession of facts, and your obstinacy can neither wrest from us the truth nor pervert it. Your most secret offences are already written on the tablets of the Holy Office; your conscience cannot reflect them more justly. Tremble, therefore, and revere. But understand that though we have sufficient proof of your guilt, we require you to confess; and that the punishment of obstinacy is as certain as that of any other offence."

Vivaldi made no reply, and the Inquisitor, after a momentary silence, added, "Were you ever in the church of the Spirito Santo, at Naples?"

"Before I answer the question," said Vivaldi, "I require the name of my accuser."

"You are to recollect that you have no right to demand anything in this place," observed the Inquisitor, "nor can you be ignorant that the name of the informer is always kept sacred from the knowledge of the accused. Who would venture to do his duty, if his name was arbitrarily to be exposed to the vengeance of the criminal against whom he informs? It is only in a particular process that the accuser is brought forward."

"The names of the witnesses?" demanded Vivaldi. "The same justice conceals them also from the knowledge of the accused," replied the Inquisitor.

"And is no justice left for the accused?" said Vivaldi. "Is he to be tried and condemned without being confronted with either his prosecutor or the witnesses?"

"Your questions are too many," said the Inquisitor, "and your answers too few. The informer is not also the prosecutor; the Holy Office, before which the information is laid, is the prosecutor and the dispenser of justice; its public accuser lays the circumstances and the testimonies of the witnesses before the court. But too much of this."

"How," exclaimed Vivaldi, "is the tribunal at once the prosecutor, witness, and judge? What can private malice wish for more than such a court of *justice*, at which to arraign its enemy? The stiletto of the assassin is not so sure or so fatal to innocence. I now perceive that it avails me nothing to be guiltless; a single enemy is sufficient to accomplish my destruction."

"You have an enemy, then?" observed the Inquisitor.

Vivaldi was too well convinced that he had one, but there was not sufficient proof as to the person of this enemy to justify him in asserting that it was Schedoni. The circumstance of Ellena having been arrested would have compelled him to suspect another person as being at least accessory to the designs of the confessor, had not credulity started in horror from the supposition that a mother's resentment could possibly betray her son into the prisons of the Inquisition, though this mother had exhibited a temper of remorseless cruelty towards a stranger who had interrupted her views for that son.

"You have an enemy, then," repeated the Inquisitor.

"That I am here sufficiently proves it," replied Vivaldi. "But I am so little any man's enemy, that I know not who to call mine."

"It is evident, then, that you have no enemy," observed the subtle Inquisitor, "and that this accusation is brought against you by a respecter of truth and a faithful servant of the Roman interest."

Vivaldi was shocked to perceive the insidious art by which he had been betrayed into a declaration apparently so harmless, and the cruel dexterity with which it had been turned against him. A lofty and contemptuous silence was all that he opposed to the treachery of his examiner, on whose countenance appeared a smile of triumph and self-congratulation, the life of a fellow-creature being, in his estimation, of no comparative importance with the self-applauses of successful art; the art, too, upon which he most valued himself—that of his profession.

The Inquisitor proceeded, "You persist, then, in withholding the truth?" He paused, but Vivaldi making no reply, he resumed.

"Since it is evident, from your own declaration, that you have no enemy whom private resentment might have instigated to accuse you, and, from other circumstances which have occurred in your conduct that you are conscious of more than you have confessed, it appears that the accusation which has been urged against you is not a malicious slander. I exhort you, therefore, and once more conjure you, by our holy faith, to make an ingenuous confession of your offences, and to save yourself from the means which must of necessity be enforced to obtain a confession before your trial commences. I adjure you, also, to consider that by such open conduct only can mercy be won to soften the justice of this most righteous tribunal!"

Vivaldi, perceiving that it was now necessary for him to reply, once more solemnly asserted his innocence of the crime alleged against him in the summons, and of the consciousness of any act which might lawfully subject him to the notice of the Holy Office.

The Inquisitor again demanded what was

the crime alleged, and Vivaldi having repeated the accusation, he again bade the secretary note it; as he did which, Vivaldi thought he perceived upon his features something of a malignant satisfaction, for which he knew not how to account. When the secretary had finished, Vivaldi was ordered to subscribe his name and quality to the depositions, and he obeyed.

The Inquisitor then bade him consider of the admonition he had received, and prepare either to confess on the morrow or to undergo the question. As he concluded, he gave a signal, and the officer who had conducted Vivaldi into the chamber immediately appeared.

"You know your orders," said the Inquisitor; "receive your prisoner, and see that they are obeyed."

The official bowed, and Vivaldi followed him from the apartment in melancholy silence.

CHAPTER XVIII.

ELLENA, meanwhile, when she had been carried from the chapel of San Sebastian, was placed upon a horse in waiting, and, guarded by the two men who had seized her, commenced a journey which continued with little interruption during two nights and days. She had no means of judging whither she was going, and listened in vain expectation for the feet of horses and the voice of Vivaldi, who, she had been told, was following on the same road.

The steps of travellers seldom broke upon the silence of these regions, and, during the journey she was met only by some market-people passing to a neighbouring town, or now and then by the vine-dressers or labourers in the olive grounds; and she descended upon the vast plains of Apulia, still ignorant of her situation. An encampment, not of warriors, but of shepherds, who were leading their flocks to the mountains of Abruzzo, enlivened a small tract of these levels, which were shadowed on the north and east by the mountainous ridge of the Garganus, stretching from the Appennine far into the Adriatic.

The appearance of the shepherds was nearly as wild and savage as that of the men who conducted Ellena; but their pastoral instruments of flageolets and tabors spoke of more civilised feelings, as they sounded sweetly over the desert. Her guards rested, and refreshed themselves with goat's milk, barley cakes, and almonds; and the manners of these shepherds, like those she had formerly met with on the mountains, proved to be more hospitable than their air had indicated.

After Ellena had quitted this pastoral camp no vestige of a human residence appeared

for several leagues, except here and there the towers of a decayed fortress perched upon the lofty acclivities she was approaching, and half concealed in the woods. The evening of the second day was drawing on when her guards drew near the forest, which she had long observed in the distance, spreading over the many rising steeps of the Garganus. They entered by a track, a road it could not be called, which led among oaks and gigantic chestnuts, apparently the growth of centuries, and so thickly interwoven that their branches formed a canopy which seldom admitted the sky. The gloom which they threw around, and the thickets of cystus, juniper, and lenticus which flourished beneath the shade, gave a character of fearful wildness to the scene.

Having reached an eminence where the trees were more thinly scattered, Ellena perceived the forests spreading on all sides among hills and valleys, and descending towards the Adriatic, which bounded the distance in front. The coast, bending into a bay, was rocky and bold. Lofty pinnacles, wooded to their summits, rose over the shores, and cliffs of naked marble, of such gigantic proportions that they were awful even at a distance, obtruded themselves far into the waves, breasting their eternal fury. Beyond the margin of the coast, as far as the eye could reach, appeared pointed mountains, darkened with forests, rising ridge over ridge in many successions. Ellena, as she surveyed this wild scenery, felt as if she was going into eternal banishment from society. She was tranquil, but it was with the quietness of exhausted grief, not of resignation; and she looked back upon the past, and awaited the future, with a kind of outbreathed despair.

She had travelled for some miles through the forest, her guards only now and then uttering to each other a question, or an observation concerning the changes which had taken place in the bordering scenery since they last passed it, when night began to close in upon them.

Ellena perceived her approach to the sea only by the murmurs of its surge upon the rocky coast, till, having reached an eminence which was, however, no more than the base of two woody mountains that towered closely over it, she saw dimly its grey surface spreading in the bay below. She now ventured to ask how much further she was to go, and whether she was to be taken on board one of the little vessels, apparently fishing-smacks, that she could just discern at anchor.

"You have not far to go now," replied one of the guards, surlily; "you will soon be at the end of your journey, and at rest."

They descended to the shore, and presently came to a lonely dwelling, which stood so near the margin of the sea as almost to be washed

D

by the waves. No light appeared at any of the lattices ; and, from the silence that reigned within, it seemed to be uninhabited. The guard had probably reason to know otherwise, for they halted at the door and shouted with all their strength. No voice, however, answered to their call, and while they persevered in efforts to rouse the inhabitants, Ellena anxiously examined the building as exactly as the twilight would permit. It was of an ancient and peculiar structure, and, though scarcely important enough for a mansion, had evidently never been designed for the residence of peasants.

The walls, of unhewn marble, were high, and strengthened by bastions ; and the edifice had turretted corners, which, with the porch in front, and the sloping roof, were falling fast into numerous symptoms of decay. The whole building, with its dark windows and soundless avenues, had an air strikingly forlorn and solitary. A high wall surrounded the small court in which it stood, and probably had once served as a defence to the dwelling ; but the gates, which should have closed against intruders, could no longer perform their office ; one of the folds had dropped from its fastenings; and lay on the ground almost concealed in a deep bed of weeds, and the other creaked on its hinges to every blast, at each swing seeming ready to follow the fate of its companion.

The repeated calls of the guard were at length answered by a rough voice from within, when the door of the porch was lazily unbarred and opened by a man whose visage was so misery-struck that Ellena could not look upon it with indifference, though wrapped in misery of her own. The lamp he held threw a gleam athwart it, and showed the gaunt ferocity of famine, to which the shadow of his hollow eyes added a terrific wildness. Ellena shrunk while she gazed. She had never before seen villainy and suffering so strongly pictured on the same face, and she observed him with a degree of thrilling curiosity which for a moment excluded from her mind all consciousness of the evils to be apprehended from him.

It was evident that this house had not been built for his reception ; and she conjectured that he was the servant of some cruel agent of the Marchesa di Vivaldi.

From the porch she followed into an old hall, ruinous, and destitute of any kind of furniture. It was not extensive, but lofty, for it seemed to ascend to the roof of the edifice, and the chambers above opened around it into a corridor.

Some half-sullen salutations were exchanged between the guard and the stranger, whom they called Spalatro, as they passed into a chamber where it appeared that he had been sleeping on a mattrass laid in a corner. All the other furniture of the place were two or three broken chairs and a table. He eyed Ellena with a shrewd contracted brow, and then looked significantly at the guard, but was silent, till he desired them all to sit down, adding that he would dress some fish for supper. Ellena discovered that this man was the master of the place ; it appeared also that he was the only inhabitant ; and when the guard soon after informed her their journey concluded here, her worst apprehensions were confirmed. The efforts she made to sustain her spirits were no longer successful. It seemed that she was brought hither by ruffians to a lonely house on the sea-shore, inhabited by a man who had "villain" engraved in every line of his face, to be the victim of inexorable pride and an insatiable desire of revenge. After considering these circumstances, and the words which had just told her she was to go no further, conviction struck like lightning upon her heart ; and, believing she was brought hither to be assassinated, horror chilled all her frame, and her senses forsook her.

On recovering, she found herself surrounded by the guard and the stranger, and she would have supplicated for their pity but that she feared to exasperate them by betraying her suspicions. She complained of fatigue, and requested to be shown to her room. The men looked upon one another, hesitated, and then asked her to partake of the fish that was preparing. But Ellena having declined the invitation with as good a grace as she could assume, they consented that she should withdraw. Spalatro, taking the lamp, lighted her across the hall to the corridor above ; where he opened the door of a chamber, in which he said she was to sleep.

"Where is my bed?" said the afflicted Ellena, fearfully, as she looked round.

"It is there—on the floor," replied Spalatro, pointing to a miserable mattrass, over which hung the tattered curtains of what had once been a canopy. "If you want the lamp," he added, "I will leave it, and come for it in a minute or two."

"Will you not let me have a lamp for the night ?" she said, in a supplicating and timid voice.

"For the night !" said the man, gruffly. "What ! to set fire to the house."

Ellena still entreated that he would allow her the comfort of a light.

"Ay, ay," replied Spalatro, with a look she could not comprehend, "it would be a great comfort to you, truly ! You do not know what you ask."

"What is it that you mean ?" said Ellena, eagerly. "I conjure you, in the name of our holy church, to tell me !"

Spalatro stepped suddenly back and looked upon her with surprise, but without speaking.

"Have mercy on me !" said Ellena, greatly

alarmed by his manner; "I am friendless, and without help!"

"What do you fear," said the man, recovering himself; and then, without waiting her reply, added, "Is it such an unmerciful deed to take away a lamp?"

Ellena, who again feared to betray the extent of her suspicions, only replied that it would be merciful to leave it, for that her spirits were low, and she required light to cheer them in a new abode.

"We do not stand upon such conceits here," replied Spalatro; "we have other matters to mind. Besides, it's the only lamp in the house, and the company below are in darkness while I am losing time here. I will leave it for two minutes, and no more." Ellena made a sign for him to put down the lamp; and, when he left the room, she heard the door barred upon her.

She employed these two minutes in examining the chamber, and the possibility it might afford of an escape. It was a large apartment, unfurnished, and unswept of the cobwebs of many years. The only door she discovered was the one by which she had entered, and the only window a lattice, which was grated. Such preparation for preventing escape seemed to hint how much there might be to escape from.

Having examined the chamber, without finding a single circumstance to encourage hope, tried the strength of the bars, which she could not shake, and sought in vain for an inside fastening for her door, she placed the lamp beside it, and awaited the return of Spalatro. In a few moments he came, and offered her a cup of sour wine with a slice of bread, which, being somewhat soothed by this attention, she did not think proper to reject.

Spalatro then quitted the room, and the door was again barred. Left once more alone, she tried to overcome apprehension by prayer; and after offering up her vespers with a fervent heart, she became more confiding and composed.

But it was impossible that she could so far forget the dangers of her situation as to seek sleep, however wearied she might be, while the door of her room remained unsecured against the intrusion of the ruffians below; and, as she had no means of fastening it, she determined to watch during the whole night. Thus left to solitude and darkness, she seated herself upon the mattress to await the return of morning, and was soon lost in sad reflection. Every minute occurrence of the past day, and of the conduct of her guards, moved in review before her judgment; and combining these with the circumstances of her present situation, scarcely a doubt as to the fate designed for her remained. It seemed highly improbable that the Marchesa di Vivaldi had sent her hither merely for imprisonment, since she might have confined her in a convent with much less trouble; and still more so, when Ellena considered the character of the Marchesa, such as she had already experienced it. The appearance of this house, and of the man who inhabited it, with the circumstance of no woman being found residing here, each and all these signified that she was brought hither, not for long imprisonment, but for death. Her utmost efforts for fortitude or resignation could not overcome the cold tremblings, the sickness of heart, the faintness and universal horror that assailed her. How often, with tears of mingled terror and grief, did she call upon Vivaldi—Vivaldi, alas! far distant—to save her; how often exclaim in agony that she should never, never see him more!

She was spared, however, the horror of believing that he was an inhabitant of the Inquisition. Having detected the imposition which had been practised towards herself, and that she was neither on the way to the Holy Office nor conducted by persons belonging to it, she concluded that the whole affair of Vivaldi's arrest had been planned by the Marchesa merely as a pretence for confining him till she should be placed beyond the reach of his assistance. She hoped, therefore, that he had only been sent to some private residence belonging to his family, and that, when her fate was decided, he would be released, and she be the only victim. This was the sole consideration that afforded any degree of assuagement to her sufferings.

The people below sat till a late hour. She listened often to their distant voices, as they were distinguishable in the pauses of the surge that broke loud and hollow on the shore; and every time the creaking hinges of their room door moved, apprehended they were coming to her. At length it appeared they had left the apartment, or had fallen asleep there, for a profound stillness reigned whenever the murmur of the waves sank. Doubt did not long deceive her, for, while she yet listened, she distinguished footsteps ascending to the corridor. She heard them approach her chamber, and stop at the door; she heard, also, the low whisperings of their voices, as they seemed consulting what was to be done, and she scarcely ventured to draw breath, while she intensely attended to them. Not a word, however, distinctly reached her, till, as one of them was departing, another called out in a half-whisper, "It is below on the table, in my girdle; make haste." The man came back, and said something in a lower voice, to which the other replied, "She sleeps," or Ellena was deceived by the hissing consonants of some other words. He then descended the stairs; and in a few minutes she perceived his comrade also pass away from the door; she listened to his retreating steps till the roaring of the sea was alone heard in their stead.

Ellena's terrors were relieved only for a moment. Considering the import of the words, it appeared that the man who had descended was gone for the stiletto of the other, such an instrument being usually worn in the girdle ; and, from the assurance "she sleeps," he seemed to fear that his words had been overheard ; and she listened again for their steps, but they came no more.

Happily for Ellena's peace, she knew not that her chamber had a door, so contrived as to open without sound, by which assassins might enter unsuspectedly at any hour of the night. Believing that the inhabitants of this house had now retired to rest, her hopes and her spirits began to revive ; but she was yet sleepless and watchful. She measured the chamber with unequal steps, often starting as the old boards shook and groaned where she passed ; and often pausing to listen whether all was yet still in the corridor. The gleam which a rising moon threw between the bars of her window now began to show many shadowy objects in the chamber, which she did not recollect to have observed while the lamp was there. More than once she fancied she saw something glide along towards the place where the mattress was laid, and, almost congealed with terror, she stood still to watch it ; but the illusion, if such it was, disappeared where the moonlight faded, and even her fears could not give shape to it beyond. Had she not known that her chamber door remained strongly barred, she would have believed this was an assassin stealing to the bed where it might be supposed she slept. Even now the thought occurred to her, and, vague as it was, had power to strike an anguish almost deadly through her heart, while she considered that her immediate situation was nearly as perilous as the one she had imaged. Again she listened, and scarcely dared to breathe, but not the lightest sound occurred in the pauses of the waves, and she believed herself convinced that no person except herself was in the room. That she was deceived in this belief, appeared from her unwillingness to approach the mattress while it was yet involved in shade. Unable to overcome her reluctance, she took her station at the window till the strengthening rays should allow a clearer view of the chamber, and in some degree restore her confidence ; and she watched the scene without as it gradually became visible. The moon, rising over the ocean, showed its restless surface spreading to the wide horizon ; and the waves, which broke in foam upon the rocky beach below, retiring in long white lines far upon the waters. She listened to their measured and solemn sound, and, somewhat soothed by the solitary grandeur of the view, remained at the lattice till the moon had risen high into the heavens ; and even till the morning began to dawn upon the sea, and purple the eastern clouds.

Reassured by the light that now pervaded her room, she returned to the mattress, where anxiety at length yielded to her weariness, and she obtained a short repose.

CHAPTER XIX.

ELLENA was awakened from profound sleep by a loud noise at the door of her chamber ; when, starting from her mattress, she looked around her with surprise and dismay as imperfect recollections of the past began to gather on her mind. She distinguished the undrawing of iron bars, and then the countenance of Spalatro at her door, before she had a clear remembrance of her situation—that she was a prisoner in a house on a lonely shore, and that this man was her gaoler. Such sickness of the heart returned with these convictions, such faintness and terror, that, unable to support her trembling frame, she sank again upon the mattress without demanding the reason of this abrupt intrusion.

"I have brought you some breakfast," said Spalatro, "if you are awake to take it ; but you seem to be asleep yet. Surely you have had sleep sufficient for one night ; you went to rest soon enough."

Ellena made no reply, but, deeply affected with a sense of her situation, looked with beseeching eyes at the man, who advanced holding forth an oaten cake and a basin of milk. "Where shall I set them," said he ; "you must needs be glad of them since you had no supper."

Ellena thanked him, and desired he would place them on the floor, for there was neither table nor chair in the room. As he did this, she was struck with the expression of his countenance, which exhibited a strange mixture of archness and malignity. He seemed congratulating himself upon his ingenuity, and anticipating some occasion of triumph ; and she was so much interested that her observation never quitted him while he remained in the room. As his eyes accidentally met hers he turned them away with the abruptness of a person who is conscious of evil intentions, and fears lest they should be detected, nor once looked up till he was hastily quitting the chamber, and she then heard the door secured as formerly.

The impression which his look had left on her mind so wholly engaged her in conjecture that a considerable time elapsed before she remembered that he had brought the refreshment she so much required ; but, as she now lifted it to her lips, a horrible suspicion arrested her hand ; it was not, however, before she had swallowed a small quantity of the milk. The look of Spalatro, which had occasioned her surprise, had accompanied the setting down of the breakfast ; and it occurred to her that poison was infused in this liquid.

She was thus compelled to refuse the sustenance which was become necessary to her, for she feared to taste even of the oaten cake, since Spalatro had offered it; but the little milk she had unwarily taken was so very small that she had no apprehension concerning it.

The day, however, was passed in terror, and almost in despondency. She could neither doubt the purpose for which she had been brought hither nor discover any possibility of escaping from her persecutors; yet that propensity to hope, which buoys up the human heart even in the severest moments of trial, sustained, in some degree, her fainting spirits.

During these miserable hours of solitude and suspense, the only alleviation to her suffering arose from a belief that Vivaldi was safe at least from danger though not from grief; but she now understood too much of the dexterous contrivances of the Marchesa, his mother, to think it was practicable for him to escape from her designs and again restore her to liberty.

All day Ellena either leaned against the bars of her window, lost in reverie, while her unconscious eyes were fixed upon the ocean, whose murmurs she no longer heard, or she listened for some sound from within the house that might assist her conjectures as to the number of persons below, or what might be passing there. The house, however, was profoundly still, except when now and then a footstep sauntered along a distant passage, or a door was heard to close; but not the hum of a single voice was heard from the lower rooms, nor any symptom of there being more than one person beside herself in the dwelling. Though she had not heard her former guards depart, it appeared certain that they were gone and that she was left alone in this place with Spalatro. What could be the purport of such a proceeding Ellena could not imagine; if her death was designed, it seemed strange that one person only should be left to the hazard of the deed, when three must have rendered the completion of it certain. But this surprise vanished when her suspicion of poison returned, for it was probable that these men had believed their scheme to be already nearly accomplished, and had abandoned her to die alone in a chamber from whence escape was impracticable, leaving Spalatro to dispose of her remains. All the incongruities she had separately observed in their conduct seemed now to harmonize and unite in one plan; and her death, designed by poison, and that poison to be conveyed in the disguise of nourishment, appeared to have been the object of it. Whether it was that the strength of this conviction affected her fancy or that the cause was real, Ellena, remembering at this moment that she had tasted the milk, was seized with a universal shuddering, and thought she felt that the poison had been sufficiently potent to affect her, even in the inconsiderable quantity she might have taken.

While she was thus agitated she distinguished footsteps loitering near her door, and, attentively listening, became convinced that some person was in the corridor. The steps moved softly, sometimes stopping for an instant as if to allow time for listening, and soon after passed away.

"It is Spalatro!" said Ellena; "he believes that I have taken the poison, and he comes to listen for my dying groans! Alas! he is only come somewhat too soon, perhaps!"

As this horrible supposition occurred, the shuddering returned with increased violence, and she sank, almost fainting, on the mattress; but the fit was not of long continuance. When it gradually left her and recollection revived, she perceived, however, the prudence of suffering Spalatro to suppose she had taken the liquid he brought her, since such belief would at least procure some delay of further schemes, and every delay afforded some possibility for hope to rest upon. Ellena therefore poured through the bars of her window the milk which she believed Spalatro had designed should be fatal in its consequence.

It was evening when she again fancied footsteps were lingering near her door, and the suspicion was confirmed when, on turning her eyes, she perceived a shade on the floor underneath it as of some person stationed without. Presently the shadow glided away, and at the same time she distinguished departing steps treading cautiously.

"It is he!" said Ellena; "he still listens for my moans!"

This further confirmation of his designs affected her nearly as much as the first; when, anxiously turning her looks towards the corridor, the shadow again appeared beneath the door, but she heard no step. Ellena watched it with intense solicitude and expectation; fearing every instant that Spalatro would conclude her doubts by entering the room. "And oh! when he discovers that I live," thought she, "what may I not expect during the first moments of his disappointment! What less than immediate death!"

The shadow, after remaining a few minutes stationary, moved a little, and then glided away as before. But it quickly returned, and a low sound followed, as of some person endeavouring to unfasten bolts without noise. Ellena heard one bar gently undrawn, and then another; she observed the door begin to move, and then to give way, till it gradually unclosed, and the face of Spalatro presented itself from behind it. Without immediately entering, he threw a glance round the chamber, as if he wished to ascertain some circumstance before he ventured further. His look was more than usually haggard as it rested upon Ellena, who apparently reposed on her mattress.

Having gazed at her for an instant, he ventured towards the bed with quick and unequal steps ; his countenance expressed at once impatience, alarm, and the consciousness of guilt. When he was within a few paces Ellena raised herself, and he started back as if a sudden spectre had crossed him. The more than usual wildness and wanness of his looks, with the whole of his conduct, seemed to confirm all her former terror ; and when he roughly asked her how she did, Ellena had not sufficient presence of mind to answer that she was ill. For some moments he regarded her with an earnest and sullen attention, and then a sly glance of scrutiny which he threw round the chamber told her that he was inquiring whether she had taken the poison. On perceiving that the basin was empty, he lifted it from the floor, and Ellena fancied a gleam of satisfaction passed over his visage.

"You have had no dinner," said he, "I forgot you ; but supper will soon be ready, and you may walk upon the beach till then, if you will."

Ellena, extremely surprised and perplexed by this offer of a seeming indulgence, knew not whether to accept or reject it. She suspected that some treachery lurked within it. The invitation appeared to be only a stratagem to lure her to destruction, and she determined to decline accepting it ; when again she considered that, to accomplish this, it was not necessary to withdraw her from the chamber, where she was already sufficiently in the power of her persecutors. Her situation could not be more desperate than it was at present, and almost any change might make it less so.

As she descended from the corridor, and passed through the lower part of the house, no person appeared but her conductor ; and she ventured to inquire whether the men who had brought her hither were departed. Spalatro did not return an answer, but led the way in silence to the court, and, having passed the gates, he pointed toward the west, and said she might walk that way.

Ellena bent her course towards the "many sounding waves," followed at a short distance by Spalatro, and, wrapt in thought, pursued the windings of the shore, scarcely noticing the objects around her ; till, on passing the foot of a rock, she lifted her eyes to the scene that unfolded beyond, and observed some huts scattered at a considerable distance, apparently the residence of fishermen. She could just distinguish the dark sails of some skiffs turning the cliffs, and entering the little bay, where the hamlet margined the beach ; but, though she saw the sails lowered

as the boats approached the shore, they were too far off to allow the figures of the men to appear. To Ellena, who had believed that no human habitation, except her prison, interrupted the vast solitudes of these forests and shores, the view of the huts, remote as they were, imparted a feeble hope, and even somewhat of joy. She looked back to observe whether Spalatro was near ; he was already within a few paces ; and, casting a wistful glance forward to the remote cottages, her heart sunk again.

It was a lowering evening, and the sea was dark and swelling ; the screams of the sea-birds too, as they wheeled among the clouds, and sought their high nests in the rocks, seemed to indicate an approaching storm. Ellena was not so wholly engaged by selfish sufferings but that she could sympathise with those of others, and she rejoiced that the fishermen, whose boats she had observed, had escaped the threatening tempest and were safely sheltered in their little homes, where, as they heard the loud waves break along the coast, they could look with keener pleasure upon the social circle and the warm comforts around them. From such considerations, however, she returned again to a sense of her own forlorn and friendless situation.

"Alas !" said she, "I have no longer a home, a circle to smile welcomes upon me ! I have no longer even one friend to support, to rescue me ! I—a miserable wanderer on a distant shore ! tracked, perhaps, by the footsteps of the assassin, who at this instant eyes his victim with silent watchfulness, and awaits the moment of opportunity to sacrifice her !"

Ellena shuddered as she said this, and turned again to observe whether Spalatro was near. He was not within view ; and while she wondered, and congratulated herself on a possibility of escaping, she perceived a monk walking silently beneath the dark rocks that overbrowed the beach. His black garments were folded round him ; his face was inclined towards the ground, and he had the air of a man in deep meditation.

"His, no doubt, are worthy musings !" said Ellena, as she observed him with mingled hope and surprise. "I may address myself, without fear, to one of his order. It is probably as much his wish, as it is his duty, to succour the unfortunate. Who could have hoped to find on this sequestered shore so sacred a protector ! his convent cannot be far off."

He approached, his face still bent towards the ground, and Ellena advanced slowly, and with trembling steps, to meet him. As he drew near, he viewed her askance, without lifting his head ; but she perceived his large eyes looking from under the shade of his cowl, and the upper part of his peculiar countenance. Her confidence in his protection began to fail, and she faltered, unable to speak, and scarcely daring to meet his eyes. The monk stalked past her in silence, the lower part of his visage still muffled in his drapery, and as he passed her looked neither with curiosity nor surprise.

Ellena paused, and determined, when he should be at some distance, to endeavour to make her way to the hamlet and throw herself upon the humanity of its inhabitants, rather than solicit the pity of this forbidding stranger. But in the next moment she heard a step behind her, and, on turning, saw the monk again approaching. He stalked by as before, surveying her, however, with a sly and scrutinising glance from the corners of his eyes. His air and countenance were equally repulsive, and still Ellena could not summon courage enough to attempt engaging his compassion, but shrank as from an enemy. There was something also terrific in the silent stalk of so gigantic a form; it announced both power and treachery He passed slowly on to some distance, and disappeared among the rocks.

Ellena turned once more with an intention of hastening towards the distant hamlet, before Spalatro should observe her, whose strange absence she had scarcely time to wonder at; but she had not proceeded far, when suddenly she perceived the monk again at her shoulder. She started, and almost shrieked while he regarded her with more attention than before. He paused a moment, and seemed to hesitate; after which he again passed on in silence. The distress of Ellena increased; he was gone the way she had designed to run, and she feared almost equally to follow him, and to return to her prison. Presently he turned, and passed her again, and Ellena hastened forward. But when, fearful of being pursued, she again looked back, she observed him conversing with Spalatro. They appeared to be in consultation while they slowly advanced, till, probably observing her rapid progress, Spalatro called on her to stop, in a voice that echoed among all the rocks. It was a voice which would not be disobeyed. She looked hopelessly at the still distant cottages, and slackened her steps. Presently the monk again passed before her, and Spalatro had again disappeared. The frown with which the former now regarded Ellena was so terrific, that she shrank trembling back, though she knew him not for her persecutor since she had never consciously seen Schedoni. He was agitated, and his look became darker.

"Whither go you?" said he in a voice that was stifled by emotion.

"Who is it, father that asks the question?" said Ellena, endeavouring to appear composed.

"Whither go you, and who are you?" repeated the monk more sternly.

"I am an unhappy orphan," replied Ellena, sighing deeply; "if you are, as your habit denotes, a friend to the charities, you will regard me with compassion."

Schedoni was silent, and then said, "Who and what is it that you fear?"

"I fear—even for my life," replied Ellena, with hesitation. She observed a darker shade pass over his countenance.

"For your life!" said he, with apparent surprise; "who is there that would think it worth the taking?"

Ellena was struck with these words.

"Poor insect!" added Schedoni, "who would crush thee?"

Ellena made no reply; she remained with her eyes fixed in amazement upon his face. There was something in his manner of pronouncing this yet more extraordinary than in the words themselves. Alarmed by his manner, and awed by the increasing gloom, and swelling surge, that broke in thunder on the beach, she at length turned away, and again walked towards the hamlet, which was yet very remote.

He soon overtook her, when, rudely seizing her arm, and gazing earnestly on her face, "Who is it that you fear?" said he; "say, who?"

"That is more than I dare say," replied Ellena, scarcely able to sustain herself.

"Hah! is it even so!" said the monk with increasing emotion. His visage now became so terrible that Ellena struggled to liberate her arm, and supplicated that he would not detain her. He was silent, and still gazed upon her, but his eyes, when she had ceased to struggle, assumed the fixed and vacant glare of a man whose thoughts have retired within themselves, and who is no longer conscious to surrounding objects.

"I beseech you to release me!" repeated Ellena; "it is late, and I am far from home."

"That is true," muttered Schedoni, still grasping her arm, and seeming to reply to his own thoughts rather than to her words—"that is very true."

"The evening is closing fast," continued Ellena, "and I shall be overtaken by the storm."

Schedoni still mused, and then muttered—"The storm, say you? Why, aye, let it come."

As he spoke he suffered her arm to drop, but still held it, and walked slowly towards the house. Ellena, thus compelled to accompany him, and yet more alarmed both by his looks, his incoherent answers, and his approach to her prison, renewed her supplications and her efforts for liberty in a voice of piercing distress, adding, "I am far from home, father; night is coming on. See how the rocks darken! I am far from home, and shall be waited for."

"That is false!" said Schedoni, with emphasis; "and you know it to be so."

"Alas! I do," replied Ellena, with mingled shame and grief. "I have no friends to wait for me!"

"What do those deserve who deliberately utter falsehoods," continued the monk, "who deceive, and flatter young men to their destruction?"

"Father!" exclaimed the astonished Ellena.

"Who disturb the peace of families—who trepan, with wanton arts, the heirs of noble houses—who—hah! what do such deserve?"

Overcome with astonishment and terror, Ellena remained silent. She now understood that Schedoni, so far from being likely to prove a protector, was an agent of her worst, and, as she had believed, her only enemy; and an apprehension of the immediate and terrible vengeance which such an agent seemed willing to accomplish subdued her senses; she tottered, and sank upon the beach. The weight which strained the arm Schedoni held, called his attention to her situation.

As he gazed upon her helpless and faded form he became agitated. He quitted it, and traversed the beach in short turns and with hasty steps; came back again, and bent over it—his heart seemed sensible to some touch of pity. At one moment he stepped towards the sea, and taking water in the hollows of his hands, threw it upon her face; at another, seeming to regret that he had done so, he would stamp with sudden fury upon the shore, and walk abruptly to a distance. The conflict between his design and his conscience was strong, or, perhaps, it was only between his passions. He who had hitherto been insensible to every tender feeling, who, governed by ambition and resentment, had contributed, by his artful instigations, to fix the baleful resolution of the Marchesa di Vivaldi, and who was come to execute her purpose—even he could not now look upon the innocent, the wretched Ellena, without yielding to the momentary weakness, as he termed it, of compassion.

While he was yet unable to baffle the new emotion by evil passions, he despised that which conquered him. "And shall the weakness of a girl," said he, "subdue the resolution of a man? Shall the view of her transient sufferings unnerve my firm heart, and compel me to renounce the lofty plans I have so ardently, so laboriously imagined, at the very instant when they are changing into realities? Am I awake? Is one spark of the fire which has so long smouldered within my bosom, and consumed my peace, alive? Or am I tame and abject as my fortunes? hah! as my fortunes! Shall the spirit of my family yield for ever to circumstances? The question rouses it, and I feel its energy revive within me."

He stalked with hasty steps towards Ellena, as if he feared to trust his resolution with a second pause. He had a dagger concealed beneath his monk's habit; as he had also an assassin's heart shrouded by his garments. He had a dagger—but he hesitated to use it; the blood which it might spill would be observed by the peasants of the neighbouring hamlet, and might lead to a discovery. It would be safer, he considered, and easier, to lay Ellena, senseless as she was, in the waves; their coldness would recal her to life only at the moment before they would suffocate her.

As he stooped to lift her, his resolution faltered again on beholding her innocent face, and in that moment she moved. He started back, as if she could have known his purpose, and, knowing it, could have avenged herself. The water which he had thrown upon her face had gradually revived her; she unclosed her eyes, and, on perceiving him, shrieked and attempted to rise. His resolution was subdued, so tremblingly fearful is guilt in the moment when it would execute its atrocities. Overcome with apprehensions, yet agitated with shame and indignation against himself for being so, he gazed at her for an instant in silence, and then abruptly turned away his eyes and left her. Ellena listened to his departing steps, and, raising herself, observed him retiring among the rocks that led towards the house. Astonished at his conduct, and surprised to find that she was alone, Ellena renewed all her efforts to sustain herself till she should reach the hamlet so long the object of her hopes; but she had proceeded only a few paces, when Spalatro again appeared swiftly approaching. Her utmost exertion availed her nothing; her feeble steps were soon overtaken, and Ellena perceived herself again his prisoner. The look with which she resigned herself awakened no pity in Spalatro, who uttered some taunting jest upon the swiftness of her flight as he led her back to her prison and proceeded in sullen watchfulness. Once again, then, she entered the gloomy walls of that fatal mansion, never more, she now believed, to quit them with life, a belief which was strengthened when she remembered that the monk, on leaving her, had taken the way hither; for, though she knew not how to account for his late forbearance, she could not suppose that he would long be merciful. He appeared no more, however, as she passed to her chamber, where Spalatro left her again to solitude and terror, and she heard that fateful door again barred upon her. When his retreating steps had ceased to sound, a stillness as of the grave prevailed in the house, like the dead calm which sometimes precedes the horrors of a tempest.

CHAPTER XX.

SCHEDONI had returned from the beach to the house in a state of perturbation that defied the control of even his own stern will. On the way thither he met Spalatro, whom, as he despatched him to Ellena, he strictly commanded not to approach his chamber till he should be summoned.

Having reached his apartment, he secured the door, though not any person except himself was in the house, nor anyone expected but those whom he knew would not dare to intrude upon him. Had it been possible to have shut out all consciousness of himself, also, how willingly would he have done so! He threw himself into a chair, and remained for a considerable time motionless and lost in thought, yet the emotions of his mind were violent and contradictory. At the very instant when his heart reproached him with the crime he had meditated, he regretted the ambitious views he must relinquish if he failed to perpetrate it, and regarded himself with some degree of contempt for having hitherto hesitated on the subject. He considered the character of his own mind with astonishment, for circumstances had drawn forth traits, of which, till now, he had no suspicion. He knew not by what doctrine to explain the inconsistencies, the contradictions he experienced; and, perhaps, it was not one of the least, that in these moments of direful and conflicting passions his reason could still look down upon their operations, and lead him to a cool though brief examination of his own nature. But the subtlety of self-love still eluded his inquiries, and he did not detect that pride was, even at this instant of self-examination and of critical import, the master-spring of his mind. In the earliest dawn of his character this passion had displayed its predominancy whenever occasion permitted, and its influence had led to some of the chief events of his life.

The Count di Marinella, for such had formerly been the title of the confessor, was the younger son of an ancient family, who resided in the duchy of Milan, and near the feet of the Tyrolean Alps, on such estates of their ancestors as the Italian wars of a former century had left them. The portion which he had received at the death of his father was not large, and Schedoni was not of a disposition to improve his patrimony by slow diligence, or to submit to the restraint and humiliation which narrow finances would have imposed. He disdained to acknowledge an inferiority of fortune to those with whom he considered himself equal in rank; and, as he was destitute of generous feeling and of sound judgment, he had not that loftiness of soul which is ambitious of true grandeur. On the contrary, he was satisfied with an ostentatious display of pleasures and of power; and, thoughtless of the consequence of dissipation, was contented with the pleasures of the moment till his exhausted resources compelled him to pause and to reflect. He perceived, too late for his advantage, that it was necessary for him to dispose of part of his estate and to confine himself to the income of the remainder. Incapable of submitting with grace to the reduction which his folly had rendered expedient, he endeavoured to obtain by cunning the luxuries that his prudence had failed to keep, and which neither his genius nor his integrity could command. He withdrew, however, from the eyes of his neighbours, unwilling to submit his altered circumstances to their observation.

Concerning several years of his life, from this period, nothing was generally known; and when he was next discovered, it was in the Spirito Santo convent at Naples, in the habit of a monk, and under the assumed name of Schedoni. His air and countenance were as much altered as his way of life; his looks had become gloomy and severe, and the pride which had mingled with the gaiety of their former expression occasionally discovered itself under the disguise of humility, but more frequently in the austerity of silence and in the barbarity of penance.

The person who discovered Schedoni would not have recollected him had not his remarkable eyes first fixed his attention and then revived remembrance. As he examined his features he traced the faint resemblance of what Marinella had been, to whom he made himself known.

The confessor affected to have forgotten his former acquaintance, and assured him that he was mistaken respecting himself, till the stranger so closely urged some circumstances that the former was no longer permitted to dissemble. He retired in some emotion with the stranger, and, whatever might be the subject of their conference, he drew from him, before he quitted the convent, a tremendous vow to keep secret from the brotherhood his knowledge of Schedoni's family, and never to reveal, without those walls, that he had seen him. These requests he had urged in a manner that at once surprised and awed the stranger, and which, at the same time that it manifested the weight of Schedoni's fears, bade the former tremble for the consequence of disobedience; and he shuddered even while he promised to obey. Of the first part of the promise he was probably strictly observant; whether he was equally so of the second does not appear; it is certain that, after this period, he was never more seen or heard of at Naples.

Schedoni, ever ambitious of distinction, adapted his manners to the views and prejudices of the society with whom he resided, and became one of the most exact observers of their outward forms, and almost a prodigy for self-denial and severe discipline. He was pointed out by the fathers of the convent to the juniors as a great example, who was, however, rather to be looked up to with reverential admiration than with a hope of emulating his sublime virtues. But with such panegyrics their friendship for Schedoni concluded. They found it convenient to applaud the austerities which they declined to practise; it procured them a character for sanctity, and saved them the necessity of earning it by mortifications of their own; but they both feared and hated Schedoni for his pride and his gloomy austerities too much to gratify his ambition by anything further than empty praise. He had been several years in the society without obtaining any considerable advancement, and with the mortification of seeing persons who had never emulated his severity raised to high offices in the Church. Somewhat too late he discovered that he was not to expect any substantial favour from the brotherhood; and then it was that his restless and disappointed spirit first sought preferment by other avenues. He had been some time confessor to the Marchesa di Vivaldi, when the conduct of her son awakened his hopes by showing him that he might render himself not only useful but necessary to her by his counsels. It was his custom to study the characters of those around him, with a view of adapting them to his purposes; and, having ascertained that of the Marchesa, these hopes were encouraged. He perceived that her passions were strong, her judgment weak; and he understood that, if circumstances should ever enable him to be serviceable in promoting the end at which any one of those passions might aim, his fortune would be established.

At length, he so completely insinuated himself into her confidence, and became so necessary to her views, that he could demand his own terms, and this he had not failed to do, though with all the affected delicacy and finesse that his situation seemed to require. An office of high dignity in the Church, which had long vainly excited his ambition, was promised him by the Marchesa, who had sufficient influence to obtain it; her condition was that of his preserving the honour of her family, as she delicately termed it, which she was careful to make him understand could be secured only by the death of Ellena. He acknowledged, with the Marchesa, that the death of this fascinating young woman was the only means of preserving that honour, since, if she lived, they had every evil to expect from the attachment and character of Vivaldi, who would discover and extricate her from any place of confinement, however obscure or difficult of access, to which she might be conveyed. How long and how arduously the confessor had aimed to oblige the Marchesa, has already appeared. The last scene was now arrived, and he was on the eve of committing that atrocious act which was to secure the pride of her house,

and to satisfy at once his ambition and his desire of vengeance, when an emotion, new and surprising to him, had arrested his arm and compelled his resolution to falter. But this emotion was transient, it disappeared almost with the object that awakened it; and now, in the silence and retirement of his chamber, he had leisure to re-collect his thoughts, to review his schemes, to reanimate his resolution, and to wonder again at the pity which had almost won him from his purpose. The ruling passion of his nature once more resumed its authority, and he determined to earn the honour which the Marchesa had in store for him.

After some cool, and more of tumultuous, consideration, he resolved that Ellena should be assassinated that night, while she slept, and afterwards conveyed through a passage of the house communicating with the sea, into which the body might be thrown, and buried, with her sad story, beneath the waves. For his own sake he would have avoided the danger of shedding blood, had this appeared easy; but he had too much reason to know she had suspicions of poison, to trust to a second attempt by such means; and again his indignation rose against himself, since, by yielding to a momentary compassion, he had lost the opportunity afforded him of throwing her unresistingly into the surge.

Spalatro, as has already been hinted, was a former confidant of the confessor, who knew too truly, from experience, that he could be trusted, and had, therefore, engaged him to assist on this occasion. To the hands of this man he consigned the fate of the unhappy Ellena, himself recoiling from the horrible act he had willed; and intending by such a step to involve Spalatro more deeply in the guilt, and thus more effectually to secure his secret.

The night was far advanced before Schedoni's final resolution was taken, when he summoned Spalatro to his chamber to instruct him in his office. He bolted the door by which the man had entered, forgetting that themselves were the only persons in the house, except the poor Ellena, who, unsuspicious of what was conspiring, and her spirits worn out by the late scene, was sleeping peacefully on her mattress above. Schedoni moved softly from the door he had secured, and, beckoning Spalatro to approach, spoke in a low voice, as if he feared to be overheard. "Have you perceived any sound from her chamber lately?" said he. "Does she sleep, think you?"

"No one has moved there for this hour past, at least," replied Spalatro. "I have been watching in the corridor till you called, and should have heard if she had stirred, the old floor shakes so with every step."

"Then hear me, Spalatro," said the confessor. "I have tried, and found thee faithful, or I should not trust thee in a business of confidence like this. Recollect all I said to thee in the morning, and be resolute and dexterous, as I have ever found thee."

Spalatro listened in gloomy attention, and the monk proceeded, "It is late; go, therefore, to her chamber; be certain that she sleeps. Take this," he added, "and this," giving him a dagger and a large cloak. "You know how you are to use them."

He paused, and fixed his penetrating eyes on Spalatro, who held up the dagger in silence, examined the blade, and continued to gaze upon it with a vacant stare, as if he was unconscious of what he did.

"You know your business," repeated Schedoni, authoritatively, "dispatch! time wears, and I must set off early."

The man made no reply.

"The morning dawns already," said the confessor, still more urgently, "Do you falter? do you tremble? Do I not know you?"

Spalatro put up the poniard in his bosom without speaking, threw the cloak over his arm, and moved with a loitering step towards the door.

"Dispatch!" repeated the confessor, "why do you linger?"

"I cannot say I like this business, signor," said Spalatro, surlily. "I know not why I should always do the most, and be paid the least."

"Sordid villain!" exclaimed Schedoni, "you are not satisfied then!"

"No more a villain than yourself, signor," retorted the man, throwing down the cloak, "I only do your business; and 'tis you that are sordid, for you would take all the reward, and I would only have a poor man have his dues. Do the work yourself, or give me the greater profit."

"Peace!" said Schedoni, "dare no more to insult me with the mention of reward. Do you imagine I have sold myself! 'Tis my will that she dies; this is sufficient; and for you — the price you have asked has been granted."

"It is too little," replied Spalatro, "and besides, I do not like the work. What harm has she done me?"

"Since when is it that you have taken upon you to moralize?" said the confessor, "and how long are these cowardly scruples to last? This is not the first time you have been employed; what harm had others done you? You forget that I know you, you forget the past."

"No, signor, I remember it too well, I wish I could forget; I remember it too well. I have never been at peace since. The bloody hand is always before me! and often of a night, when the sea roars and storms shake the house, *they* have come, all gashed as I left them, and stood before my bed! I have got up, and ran out upon the shore for safety!"

"Peace!" repeated the confessor, "where is this frenzy of fear to end? To what are these visions, painted in blood, to lead. I thought I was talking with a man, but find I am speaking only to a baby possessed with his nurse's dreams! Yet I understand you—you shall be satisfied."

Schedoni, however, had for once misunderstood this man, when he could not believe it possible that he was really averse to execute what he had undertaken. Whether the innocence and beauty of Ellena had softened his heart, or that his conscience did torture him for his past deeds, he persisted in refusing to murder her. His conscience, or his pity, was of a very peculiar kind, however; for, though he refused to execute the deed himself he consented to wait at the foot of a back staircase that communicated with Ellena's chamber, while Schedoni accomplished it, and afterward to assist in carrying the body to the shore. "This is a compromise between conscience and guilt, worthy of a demon," muttered Schedoni, who appeared to be insensible that he had made the same compromise with himself not an hour before; and whose extreme reluctance at this moment, to perpetrate with his own hand what he had willingly designed for another, ought to have reminded him of that compromise.

Spalatro, released from the immmediate office of an executioner, endured silently the abusive yet half-stifled indignation of the confessor, who also bade him remember that, though he now shrunk from the most active part of this transaction, he had not always been restrained, in offices of the same nature, by equal compunction; and that not only his means of subsistence but his very life itself was at his mercy. Spalatro readily acknowledged that it was so; and Schedoni knew too well the truth of what he had urged, to be restrained from his purpose by any apprehension of the consequence of a discovery from this ruffian.

"Give me the dagger, then," said the confessor, after a long pause, "take up the cloak, and follow to the staircase. Let me see whether your valour will carry you thus far."

Spalatro resigned the stiletto, and threw the cloak again over his arm. The confessor stepped to the door, and, trying to open it, "It is fastened!" said he in alarm, "some person has got into the house—it is fastened!"

"That well may be, signor," replied Spalatro, calmly, "for I saw you bolt it yourself, after I came into the room."

"True," said Schedoni, recovering himself; "that is true."

He opened it and proceeded along the silent passages, towards the private staircase, often pausing to listen, and then stepping more lightly; the terrific Schedoni, in this moment of meditative guilt, feared even the feeble Ellena. At the foot of the staircase, he again stopped to listen, "Do you hear anything?" said he in a whisper.

"I hear only the sea," replied the man.

"Hush! it is something more!" said Schedoni; "that is the murmur of voices!"

They were silent. After a pause of some length, "It is, perhaps, the voice of the spectres I told you of, signor," said Spalatro, with a sneer.

"Give me the dagger," said Schedoni.

Spalatro, instead of obeying, now grasped the arm of the confessor, who, looking at him for an explanation of this extraordinary action, was still more surprised to observe the paleness and horror of his countenance. His starting eyes seemed to follow some object along the passage, and Schedoni, who began to partake of his feelings, looked forward to discover what occasioned this dismay, but could not perceive anything that justified it. "What is it you fear?" said he at length.

Spalatro's eyes were still moving in horror. "Do you see nothing!" said he, pointing. Schedoni looked again, but did not distinguish any object in the remote gloom of the passage whither Spalatro's sight was now fixed.

"Come, come," said he, ashamed of his own weakness, "this is not a moment for such fancies. Awake from this idle dream."

Spalatro withdrew his eyes, but they retained all their wildness. "It was no dream," said he, in the voice of a man who is exhausted by pain and begins to breathe somewhat more freely again. "I saw it as plainly as I now see you."

"Dotard! what did you see?" inquired the confessor.

"It came before my eyes in a moment, and showed itself distinctly and outspread."

"What showed itself?" repeated Schedoni.

"And then it beckoned—yes, it beckoned me, with that blood-stained finger! and glided away down the passage, still beckoning—till it was lost in the darkness."

"This is very frenzy!" said Schedoni, excessively agitated. "Arouse yourself, and be a man!"

"Frenzy! would it were, signor. I saw that dreadful hand—I see it now—it is there again!—there!"

Schedoni, shocked, embarrassed, and once more infected with the strange emotions of Spalatro, looked forward expecting to discover some terrific object; but still nothing was visible to him, and he soon recovered himself sufficiently to endeavour to appease the fancy of this conscience-struck ruffian. But Spalatro was insensible to all he could urge, and the confessor, fearing that his voice, though weak and stifled, would awaken Ellena, tried to withdraw him from the spot to the apartment they had quitted.

"The wealth of San Loretto should not make me go that way, signor," replied he,

shuddering—"that was the way it beckoned, it vanished that way!"

Every emotion now yielded with Schedoni to that of apprehension lest Ellena, being awakened, should make his task more horrid by a struggle; and his embarrassment increased at each instant, for neither command, menace, nor entreaty could prevail with Spalatro to retire, till the monk luckily remembered a door which opened beyond the staircase and would conduct them by another way to the opposite side of the house. The man consented so to depart, when Schedoni, unlocking a suite of rooms of which he had always kept the keys, they passed in silence through an extent of desolate chambers till they reached the one which they had lately left.

Here, relieved from apprehension respecting Ellena, the confessor expostulated more freely with Spalatro; but neither argument nor menace could prevail, and the man persisted in refusing to return to the staircase, though protesting at the same time that he would not remain alone in any part of the house; till the wine, with which the confessor abundantly supplied him, began to overcome the terrors of his imagination. At length his courage was so much re-animated that he consented to resume his station and await at the foot of the stairs the accomplishment of Schedoni's dreadful errand, with which agreement they returned thither by the way they had lately passed. The wine with which Schedoni also had found it necessary to strengthen his own resolution, did not secure him from severe emotion when he found himself again near Ellena; but he made a strenuous effort for self-subjection as he demanded the dagger of Spalatro.

"You have it already, signor," replied the man.

"True," said the monk; "ascend softly, or our steps may awaken her."

"You said I was to wait at the foot of the stairs, signor, while you"——

"True, true, true!" muttered the confessor, and had begun to ascend, when his attendant desired him to stop. "You are going in darkness, signor, you have forgotten the lamp. I have another here."

Schedoni took it angrily, without speaking, and was again ascending, when he hesitated, and once more paused. "The glare will disturb her," thought he, "it is better to go in darkness. Yet——." He considered that he could not strike with certainty without light to direct his hand, and he kept the lamp, but returned once more to charge Spalatro not to stir from the foot of the stairs till he called, and to ascend to the chamber upon the first signal.

"I will obey, signor, if you, on your part, will promise not to give the signal till all is over."

" I do promise," replied Schedoni. " No more ! "

Again he ascended, nor stopped till he reached Ellena's door, where he listened for a sound ; but all was as silent as if death already reigned in the chamber. This door was from long disuse, difficult to be opened ; formerly it would have yielded without sound but now Schedoni was fearful of noise from every effort he made to move it. After some difficulty, however, it gave way, and he perceived, by the stillness within the apartment, that he had not disturbed Ellena. He shaded the lamp with the door for a moment, while he threw an inquiring glance forward, and, and when he did venture further, held part of his dark drapery before the light, to prevent the rays from spreading through the room.

As he approached the bed, her gentle breathings informed him that she still slept, and the next moment he was at her side. she lay in deep and peaceful slumber, and seemed to have thrown herself upon the mattress, after having been wearied by her griefs ; for, though sleep pressed heavily on her eyes, their lids were yet wet with tears.

While Schedoni gazed for a moment upon her innocent countenance, a faint smile stole over it. He stepped back. " She smiles in her murderer's face ! " said he, shuddering, " I must be speedy."

He searched for the dagger, and it was some time before his trembling hand could disengage it from the folds of his garment ; but, having done so, he again drew near, and prepared to strike. Her dress perplexed him ; it would interrupt the blow, and he stooped to examine whether he could turn her robe aside, without waking her. As the light passed over her face, he perceived that the smile had vanished—the visions of her sleep were changed, for tears stole from beneath her eyelids, and her features suffered a slight convulsion. She spoke ! Schedoni, apprehending that the light had disturbed her, suddenly drew back, and, again irresolute, shaded the lamp, and concealed himself behind the curtain, while he listened. But her words were inward and indistinct, and convinced him that she still slumbered.

His agitation and repugnance to strike increased with every moment of delay, and, as often as he prepared to plunge the poniard in her bosom, a shuddering horror restrained him. Astonished at his own feelings, and indignant at what he termed a dastardly weakness, he found it necessary to argue with himself, and his rapid thoughts said, " Do I not feel the necessity of this act. Does not what is dearer to me than existence—does not my consequence depend on the execution of it ? Is she not also beloved by the young Vivaldi ? —have I already forgotten the church of the Spirito Santo ? " This consideration re-ani-

mated him ; vengeance nerved his arm, and drawing aside the lawn from her bosom, he once more raised it to strike ; when, after gazing for an instant, some new cause of horror seemed to seize all his frame, and he stood for some moments aghast and motionless like a statue. His respiration was short and laborious, chilly drops stood on his forehead, and all his faculties of mind seemed suspended. When he recovered, he stooped to examine again the miniature which had occasioned this revolution, and which had lain concealed beneath the lawn that he withdrew. The terrible certainty was almost confirmed, and forgetting, in his impatience to know the truth, the imprudence of suddenly discovering himself to Ellena at this hour of the night, and with a dagger at his feet, he called loudly " Awake ! awake ! Say, what is your name ? Speak ! speak quickly ! "

Ellena, aroused by a man's voice, started from her mattress, when, perceiving Schedoni, and by the pale glare of the lamp, his haggard countenance, she shrieked, and sank back on the pillow. She had not fainted ; and believing that he came to murder her, she now exerted herself to plead for mercy. The energy of her feelings enabled her to rise and throw herself at his feet, " Be merciful, Oh father ! be merciful ! " said she, in a trembling voice.

" Father ! " interrupted Schedoni, with earnestness ; and then, seeming to restrain himself, he added, with unaffected surprise, " Why are you thus terrified ? " for he had lost, in new interests and emotions, all consciousness of evil intention, and of the singularity of his situation. " What do you fear ? " he repeated.

" Have pity, holy father ! " exclaimed Ellena in agony.

" Why do you not say whose portrait that is ? " demanded he, forgetting that he had not asked the question before.

" Whose portrait ? " repeated the confessor in a loud voice.

" Whose portrait ! " said Ellena, with extreme surprise.

" Ay, how came you by it ? Be quick—whose resemblance is it ? "

" Why should you wish to know ? " said Ellena.

" Answer my question," repeated Schedoni, with increasing sternness.

" I cannot part with it, holy father," replied Ellena, pressing it to her bosom ; " you do not wish me to part with it ? "

" Is it impossible to make you answer my question ! " said he, in extreme perturbation, and turning away from her ; " has fear utterly confounded you ? " Then, again stepping towards her, and seizing her wrist, he repeated the demand in a tone of desperation.

" Alas ! he is dead ! or I should not now

want a protector," replied Ellena, shrinking from his grasp, and weeping.

"You trifle," said Schedoni, with a terrible look; "I once more demand an answer—whose picture?——"

Ellena lifted it, gazed upon it for a moment, and then pressing it to her lips said, "This was my father."

"Your father!" he repeated in an inward voice, "your father!" and shuddering, turned away.

Ellena looked at him with surprise. "I never knew a father's care," she said, "nor till lately did I perceive the want of it. But now——"

"His name?" interrupted the confessor.

"But now" continued Ellena, "if you are not as a father to me, to whom can I look for protection?"

"His name?" repeated Schedoni, with sterner emphasis.

"It is sacred," replied Ellena, "for he was unfortunate!"

"His name?" demanded the confessor, furiously.

"I have promised to conceal it, father."

"On your life, I charge you tell it; remember, on your life!"

Ellena trembled, was silent, and with supplicating looks implored him to desist from inquiry; but he urged the question more irresistibly. "His name then," said she, "was Marinella."

Schedoni groaned and turned away; but in a few seconds, struggling to command the agitation that shattered his whole frame, he returned to Ellena, and raised her from her knees, on which she had thrown herself to implore mercy.

"The place of his residence?" said the monk.

"It was far from hence," she replied; but he demanded an unequivocal answer, and she reluctantly gave one.

Schedoni turned away as before, groaned heavily, and paced the chamber without speaking; while Ellena, in her turn, inquired the motive of his questions, and the occasion of his agitation. But he seemed not to notice any thing she said, and wholly given up to his feelings, was inflexibly silent, while he stalked, with measured steps, along the room, and his face, half hid by his cowl, was bent towards the ground.

Ellena's terror began to yield to astonishment, and this emotion increased, when, Schedoni approaching her, she perceived tears swell in his eyes, which were fixed on hers, and his countenance soften from the wild disorder that had marked it. Still he could not speak. At length he yielded to the fulness of his heart, and Schedoni, the stern Schedoni, wept and sighed! He seated himself on the mattress beside Ellena, took her hand, which she, affrighted, attempted to

withdraw, and when he could command his voice, said, "unhappy child!—— behold your more unhappy father!" As he concluded, his voice was overcome by groans, and he drew the cowl entirely over his face.

"My father!" exclaimed the astonished and doubting Ellena—"my father!" and fixed her eyes upon him

He gave no reply, but when, a moment after, he lifted his head, "Why do you reproach me with those looks!" said the conscious Schedoni.

"Reproach you!—reproach my father!" repeated Ellena, in accents softening into tenderness, "why should I reproach my father!"

"Why!" exclaimed Schedoni, starting from his seat.

As he moved he stumbled over the dagger at his foot; at that moment it might be said to strike into his heart. He pushed it hastily from sight. Ellena had not observed it; but she observed his labouring breast, his distracted countenance, and quick steps, as he again walked to and fro in the chamber; and she asked, with the most soothing accents of compassion, and looks of anxious gentleness, what made him so unhappy, and tried to assuage his sufferings. They seemed to increase with every wish she expressed to dispel them; at one moment he would pause to gaze upon her, and in the next would quit her with a frenzied start.

"Why do you look so piteously upon me, father?" Ellena said; "why are you so unhappy? Tell me, that I may comfort you."

This appeal renewed all the violence of remorse and grief, and he pressed her to his bosom, and wetted her cheeks with his tears. Ellena wept to see him weep, till her doubts began to take alarm. Whatever might be the proofs that had convinced Schedoni of the relationship between them, he had not explained these to her, and however strong was the eloquence of nature which she witnessed, it was not sufficient to justify an entire confidence in the assertion he had made, or to allow her to permit his caresses without trembling. She shrunk, and endeavoured to disengage herself; when, immediately understanding her, he said, "Can you doubt the cause of these emotions? these signs of paternal affection?"

"Have I not reason to doubt," replied Ellena, timidly, "since I never witnessed them before?"

He withdrew his arms, and fixing his eyes earnestly on hers, regarded her for some moments in expressive silence. "Poor Innocent!" said he at length, "you know not how much your words convey!—It is too true, you never have known a father's tenderness till now!"

His countenance darkened while he spoke, and he rose again from his seat. Ellena, meanwhile, astonished, terrified and oppressed by a variety of emotions, had no power to demand his reasons for the belief that so much agitated him, or any explanation of his conduct; but she appealed to the portrait, and endeavoured, by tracing some resemblance between it and Schedoni, to decide her doubts. The countenance of each was as different in character as in years. The miniature displayed a young man, rather handsome, of a gay and smiling countenance; yet the smile expressed triumph rather than sweetness, and his whole air and features were distinguished by a consciousness of superiority that rose even to haughtiness.

Schedoni, on the contrary, advanced in years, exhibited a severe physiognomy, furrowed by thought no less than by time, and darkened by the habitual indulgence of morose passions. He looked as if he had never smiled since the portrait was drawn; and it seemed as if the painter, prophetic of Schedoni's future disposition, had arrested and embodied that smile, to prove hereafter that cheerfulness had once played upon his features.

Though the expression was so different between the countenance which Schedoni formerly owned and that he now wore, the same character of haughty pride was visible in both; and Ellena did trace a resemblance in the bold outline of the features, but not sufficient to convince her, without further evidence, that each belonged to the same person, and that the confessor had ever been the young cavalier in the portrait. In the first tumult of her thoughts she had not had leisure to dwell upon the singularity of Schedoni's visiting her at this deep hour of the night, or to urge any questions, except vague ones, concerning the truth of her relationship to him. But now that her mind was somewhat recollected, and that his looks were less terrific, she ventured to ask a fuller explanation of these circumstances, and his reasons for the late extraordinary assertion. "It is past midnight, father," said Ellena; "you may judge then how anxious I am to learn what motive led you to my chamber at this lonely hour?"

Schedoni made no reply.

"Did you come to warn me of danger?" she continued; "had you discovered the cruel designs of Spalatro? Ah! when I supplicated for your compassion on the shore this evening, you little thought what perils surrounded me, or you would ——"

"You say true!" interrupted he, in a hurried manner, "but name the subject no more. Why will you persist in returning to it?"

His words surprised Ellena, who had not even alluded to the subject till now; but the returning wildness of his countenance made her fearful of dwelling upon the topic, even so far as to point out his error.

Another deep pause succeeded, during which

Schedoni continued to pace the room, sometimes stopping for an instant to fix his eyes on Ellena, and regarding her with an earnestness that seemed to partake of frenzy, and then gloomily withdrawing his regards, and sighing heavily as he turned away to a distant part of the room. She, meanwhile, agitated with astonishment at his conduct, as well as at her own circumstances, and with the fear of offending him by further questions, endeavoured to summon courage to solicit the explanation which was so important to her tranquillity. At length she asked how she might venture to believe a circumstance so surprising as that of which he had just assured her, and to remind him that he had not yet disclosed his reason for admitting the belief.

The confessor's feelings were eloquent in reply; and when at length they were sufficiently subdued to permit him to talk coherently, he mentioned some circumstances concerning Ellena's family that proved him at least to have been intimately acquainted with it; and others, which she believed were known only to Bianchi and herself, that removed every doubt of his identity.

This, however, was a period of his life too big with remorse, horror, and the first pangs of parental affection to allow him to converse long; deep solitude was necessary for his soul. He wished to plunge where no eye might restrain his emotions or observe the overflowing anguish of his heart. Having obtained sufficient proof to convince him that Ellena was indeed his child, and assured her that she should be removed from this house on the following day, and be restored to her home, he abruptly left the chamber.

As he descended the staircase, Spalatro stepped forward to meet him with the cloak which had been designed to wrap the mangled form of Ellena when it should be carried to the shore. "Is it done?" said the ruffian, in a stifled voice. "I am ready!" and he spread forth the cloak and began to ascend.

"Hold! villain, hold!" said Schedoni, lifting up his head for the first time. "Dare to enter that chamber, and your life shall answer for it."

"What!" exclaimed the man, shrinking back astonished—"will not *hers* satisfy you?"

He trembled for the consequence of what he had said when he observed the changing countenance of the confessor. But Schedoni spoke not; the tumult in his breast was too great for utterance, and he pressed hastily forward. Spalatro followed. "Be pleased to tell me what I am to do," said he, again holding forth the cloak.

"Avaunt!" exclaimed the other, turning fiercely upon him; "leave me."

"How!" said the man, whose spirit was now aroused; "has *your* courage failed too, signor? If so, I will prove myself no dastard, though you called me one ; I'll do the business myself."

"Villain ! fiend !" cried Schedoni, seizing the ruffian by the throat with a grasp that seemed intended to annihilate him ; when, recollecting that the fellow was only willing to obey the very instructions he had himself but lately delivered to him, other emotions succeeded to that of rage. He slowly liberated him, and in accents broken, and softening from sternness, bade him retire to rest. "To-morrow," he added, "I will speak further with you. As for this night—I have changed my purpose. Begone !"

Spalatro was about to express the indignation which astonishment and fear had hitherto overcome, but his employer repeated his command in a voice of thunder, and closed the door of his apartment with violence, as he shut out a man whose presence had become hateful to him. He felt relieved by his absence, and began to breathe more freely, till, remembering that this accomplice had just boasted that he was no dastard, he dreaded lest, by way of proving the assertion, he should attempt to commit the crime from which he had lately shrunk. Terrified at the possibility, and even apprehending that it might already have become a reality, he rushed from the room, and found Spalatro in the passage leading to the private staircase ; but, whatever might have been his purpose, the situation and looks of the latter were sufficiently alarming. At the approach of Schedoni he turned his sullen and malignant countenance towards him, without answering the call or the demand as to his business there ; and with slow steps obeyed the order of his master, that he should withdraw to his room. Thither Schedoni followed, and having locked him in it for the night, he repaired to the apartment of Ellena, which he secured from the possibility of intrusion. He then returned to his own, not to sleep, but to abandon himself to the agonies of remorse and horror ; and he yet shuddered, like a man who has just recoiled from the brink of a precipice, and who still measures the gulf with his eye.

CHAPTER XXI.

ELLENA, when Schedoni had left her, recollected all the particulars which he had thought proper to reveal concerning her family, and, comparing them with such circumstances as the late Bianchi had related on the same subject, she perceived nothing that was contradictory between the two accounts. But she knew not even yet enough of her own story to understand why Bianchi had been silent as to some particulars which had just been disclosed. From Bianchi she had always understood that her mother had married a

nobleman of the duchy of Milan, and of the house of Marinella ; that the marriage had been unfortunate ; and that she herself, even before the death of the Countess, had been committed to the care of Bianchi, the only sister of that lady. Of this event, or of her mother, Ellena had no remembrance ; for the kindness of Bianchi had obliterated from her mind the loss and the griefs of her early infancy ; and she recollected only the accident which had discovered to her, in Bianchi's cabinet, after the death of the latter, the miniature and the name of her father. When she had inquired the reason of this injunction, Bianchi replied that the degraded fortune of her house rendered privacy desirable ; and answered her further questions concerning her father by relating that he had died while she was an infant. The picture which Ellena had discovered, Bianchi had found among the trinkets of the departed Countess, and designed to present it at some future period to Ellena, when her discretion might be trusted with a knowledge of her family. This was the whole of what Signora Bianchi had judged it necessary to explain, though in her last hours it appeared that she wished to reveal more ; but it was then too late.

Though Ellena perceived that many circumstances of the relations given by Schedoni and by Signora Bianchi coincided, and that none were contradictory except that of his death, she could not yet subdue her amazement at this discovery, or even the doubts which occasionally recurred to her as to its truth. Schedoni, on the contrary, had not even appeared surprised when she assured him that she always understood her father had been dead many years ; though, when she asked if her mother too was living, both his distress and his assurances confirmed the relation made by Bianchi.

When Ellena's mind became more tranquil she noticed again the singularity of Schedoni's visit to her apartment at so sacred an hour ; and her thoughts glanced back involuntarily to the scene of the preceding evening on the sea-shore, and the image of her father appeared in each in the terrific character of an agent of the Marchesa di Vivaldi. The suspicions, however, which she had formerly admitted respecting his designs were now impatiently rejected, for she was less anxious to discover truth than to release herself from horrible suppositions ; and she willingly believed that Schedoni, having misunderstood her character, had only designed to assist in removing her beyond the reach of Vivaldi. The ingenuity of hope suggested also that having just heard from her conductors, or from Spalatro, some circumstances of her story, he had been led to a suspicion of the relationship between them, and that, in the first impatience of parental anxiety, he had disregarded the hour, and come, though at midnight, to her apartment to ascertain the truth.

While she soothed herself with this explanation of a circumstance which had occasioned her considerable surprise, she perceived on the floor the point of a dagger peeping from beneath the curtain! Emotions almost too horrible to be sustained followed this discovery; she took the instrument, and gazed upon it aghast and trembling, for a suspicion of the real motive of Schedoni's visit glanced upon her mind. But it was only for a moment; such a supposition was too terrible to be willingly endured; she again believed that Spalatro alone had meditated her destruction, and she thanked the confessor as her deliverer, instead of shrinking from him as an assassin. She now understood that Schedoni, having discovered the ruffian's design, had rushed into the chamber to save a stranger from his murderous poniard, and had unconsciously rescued his own daughter, when the portrait at her bosom informed him of the truth. With this conviction Ellena's eyes overflowed with gratitude, and her heart was hushed to peace.

Schedoni, meanwhile, shut up in his chamber, was agitated by feelings of a very opposite nature. When their first excess was exhausted, and his mind was calm enough to reflect, the images that appeared on it struck him with solemn wonder. In pursuing Ellena at the criminal instigation of the Marchesa di Vivaldi, it appeared that he had been persecuting his own child; and in thus consenting to conspire against the innocent, he had in the event been only punishing the guilty, and preparing mortification for himself on the exact subject to which he had sacrificed his conscience. Every step that he had taken with a view of gratifying his ambition was retrograde, and while he had been wickedly intent to serve the Marchesa and himself, by preventing the marriage of Vivaldi and Ellena, he had been laboriously counteracting his own fortune. An alliance with the illustrious house of Vivaldi was above his loftiest hope of advancement, and this event he had himself nearly prevented by the very means which had been adopted, at the expense of every virtuous consideration, to obtain an inferior promotion. Thus, by a singular retribution, his own crimes had recoiled upon himself.

Schedoni perceived the many obstacles which lay between him and his newly awakened hopes, and that much was to be overcome before those nuptials could be publicly solemnized, which he was now still more anxious to promote than he had lately been to prevent. The approbation of the Marchesa was, at least, desirable, for she had much at her disposal, and without it, though his daughter might be the wife of Vivaldi, he himself would be no otherwise benefited at present than by the honour of the connection. He had some particular reasons for believing that her consent might be obtained, and, though there was hazard in delaying the nuptials till such an experiment had been made, he resolved to encounter it rather than forbear to solicit her concurrence. But, if the Marchesa should prove inexorable, he determined to bestow the hand of Ellena without her knowledge, and in doing so he well knew that he incurred little danger from her resentment, since he had secrets in his possession the consciousness of which must awe her into a speedy neutrality. The consent of the Marchese, as he despaired of obtaining it, he did not mean to solicit, and the influence of the Marchesa was such that Schedoni did not regard that as essential.

The first steps, however, to be taken were those that might release Vivaldi from the Inquisition, the tremendous prison into which Schedoni himself, little foreseeing that he should so soon wish for his liberation, had caused him to be thrown. He had always understood, indeed, that if the informer forbore to appear against the accused in this court, the latter would of course be liberated; and he also believed that Vivaldi's freedom could be obtained whenever he should think proper to apply to a person at Naples, whom he knew to be connected with the *Holy Office* of Rome. How much the confessor had suffered his wishes to deceive him may appear hereafter. His motives for having thus confined Vivaldi were partly those of self-defence. He dreaded the discovery and the vengeance which might follow the loss of Ellena should Vivaldi be at liberty immediately to pursue his inquiries. But he believed that all trace of her must be lost after a few weeks had elapsed, and that Vivaldi's sufferings from confinement in the Inquisition would have given interests to his mind which must weaken the one he felt for Ellena. Yet, though in this instance self-defence had been a principal motive with Schedoni, a desire of avenging the insult he had received in the church of the Spirito Santo, and all the consequent mortifications he experienced, had been a second; and such was the blackness of his hatred, and the avarice of his revenge, that he had not considered the suffering which the loss of Ellena would occasion Vivaldi as sufficient retaliation.

In adopting a mode of punishment so extraordinary as that of imprisonment in the Inquisition, it appears, therefore, that Schedoni was influenced partly by the difficulty of otherwise confining Vivaldi during the period for which confinement was absolutely necessary to the success of his own schemes, and partly by a desire of inflicting the tortures of terror. He had also been encouraged by his discovery of this opportunity for conferring new obligations on the Marchesa. The very conduct that must have appeared to the first glance of an honest mind fatal to his interests, he thought might be rendered beneficial to them, and that his dexterity could so command the business as that the Marchesa should eventually thank him as the deliverer of her son, instead of discovering and execrating him as his accuser—a scheme favoured by the unjust and cruel rule enacted by the tribunal he approached, which permitted anonymous informers.

To procure the arrestation of Vivaldi, it had been only necessary to send a written accusation, without a name, to the *Holy Office*, with a mention of the place where the accused person might be seized. But the suffering in consequence of such information did not always proceed further than the *question :* since, if the informer failed to discover himself to the Inquisitors, the prisoner, after many examinations, was released, unless he happened unwarily to criminate himself. Schedoni, as he did not intend to prosecute, believed, therefore, that Vivaldi would of course be discharged after a certain period, and supposing it utterly impossible that he could ever discover his accuser, the confessor determined to appear anxious and active in effecting his release. This character of a deliverer he knew he should be the better enabled to support by means of a person officially connected with the *Holy Office*, who had already unconsciously assisted his views. In the apartment of this man, Schedoni had accidentally seen a formula of arrestation against a person suspected of heresy, the view of which had not only suggested to him the plan he had since adopted, but had in some degree assisted him to carry it into effect. He had seen the scroll only for a short time, but his observations were so minute, and his memory so clear, that he was able to copy it with at least sufficient exactness to impose upon the Benedictine priest, who had, perhaps, seldom or never seen a real instrument of this kind. Schedoni had employed this artifice for the purpose of immediately securing Vivaldi, apprehending that, while the Inquisitors were slowly deliberating upon his arrest, he might quit Celano and elude discovery. If the deception succeeded, it would enable him also to seize Ellena, and to mislead Vivaldi respecting her destination. The charge of having carried off a nun might appear to be corroborated by many circumstances, and Schedoni would probably have made these the subject of real denunciation, had he not foreseen the danger and the trouble in which it might implicate himself; and that, as the charge could not be substantiated, Ellena would finally escape. As far as his plan now went, it had been successful; some of the bravoes whom he hired to personate officials had conveyed Vivaldi to the town where the real officers of the Inquisition were appointed to receive him; while the others carried Ellena to the shore of the Adriatic. Schedoni had much applauded his own ingenuity, in thus contriving, by the matter of the forged accusation, to throw an impenetrable veil over the fate of Ellena, and to secure himself from the suspicions or vengeance of Vivaldi, who, it appeared, would always believe that she had died or was still confined in the unsearchable prisons of the Inquisition.

Thus he had betrayed himself in endeavouring to betray Vivaldi, whose release, however, he yet supposed could be easily obtained ; but how much his policy had, in this instance, outrun his sagacity now remained to be proved.

The subject of Schedoni's immediate perplexity was the difficulty of conveying Ellena back to Naples ; since, not choosing to appear at present in the character of her father, he could not decorously accompany her thither himself, nor could he prudently entrust her to the conduct of any person whom he knew in this neighbourhood. It was, however, necessary to form a speedy determination, for he could neither endure to pass another day in a scene which must continually impress him with the horrors of the preceding night, nor that Ellena should remain in it ; and the morning light already gleamed upon his casements.

After some further deliberation, he resolved to be himself her conductor, as far, at least, as through the forests of the Garganus ; and, at the first town where conveniences could be procured, to throw aside his monk's habit, and, assuming the dress of a layman, accompany her in this disguise towards Naples, till he should either discover some secure means of sending her forward to that city, or a temporary asylum for her in a convent on the way.

His mind was scarcely more tranquil after having formed this determination than before, and he did not attempt to repose himself even for a moment. The circumstances of the late discovery were almost perpetually recurring to his affrighted conscience, accompanied by a fear that Ellena might suspect the real purpose of his midnight visit ; and he alternately formed and rejected plausible falsehoods that might assuage her curiosity and delude her apprehension.

The hour arrived, however, when it was necessary to prepare for departure, and found him still undecided as to the explanation he should form.

Having released Spalatro from his chamber, and given him directions to procure horses and a guide immediately from the neighbouring hamlet, he repaired to Ellena's room to prepare her for this hasty removal. On approaching it, a remembrance of the purpose with which he had last passed through these same passages and staircase appealed so powerfully to his feelings that he was unable to proceed, and he turned back to his own apartment to recover some command over himself. A few moments restored to him his usual address, though not his tranquillity, and he again approached the chamber; it was now, however, by way of the corridor. As he unbarred the door, his hand trembled; but, when he entered the room, his countenance and manner had resumed their usual solemnity, and his voice only would have betrayed, to an attentive observer, the agitation of his mind.

Ellena was considerably affected on seeing him again, and he examined with a jealous eye the emotions he witnessed. The smile with which she met him was tender, but he perceived it pass away from her features, like the aerial colouring that illumines a mountain's brow; and the gloom of doubt and apprehension again overspread them. As he advanced, he held forth his hand for her's, when, suddenly perceiving the dagger he had left in the chamber, he involuntarily withdrew his proffered courtesy, and his countenance changed. Ellena, whose eyes followed his to the object that attracted them, pointed to the instrument, took it up, and, approaching him, said, "This dagger I found last night in my chamber! Oh, my father!"

"That dagger!" said Schedoni with affected surprise.

"Examine it," continued Ellena, while she held it up. "Do you know to whom it belongs and who brought it hither?"

"What is it you mean?" asked Schedoni, betrayed by his feelings.

"Do you know, too, for what purpose it was brought?" said Ellena, mournfully.

The confessor made no reply, but irresolutely attempted to seize the instrument.

"Oh yes, I perceive you know too well," continued Ellena. "Here, my father, while I slept ——"

"Give me the dagger," interrupted Schedoni, in a frightful voice.

"Yes, my father, I will give it as an offering of my gratitude," replied Ellena; but as she raised her eyes, filled with tears, his look and fixed attitude terrified her, and she added, with a still more persuasive tenderness, "Will you not accept the offering of your child, for having preserved her from the poniard of an assassin?"

Schedoni's looks became yet darker; he took the dagger in silence, and threw it with violence to the farthest end of the chamber, while his eyes remained fixed on hers. The force of the action alarmed her. "Yes, it is in vain that you would conceal the truth," she added, weeping unrestrainedly, "your goodness cannot avail; I know the whole."

The last words aroused Schedoni again from his trance, his features became convulsed, and his look furious. "What do you know?" he demanded, in a subdued voice that seemed ready to burst in thunder.

"All that I owe you," replied Ellena, "that last night, while I slept upon this mattress, unsuspicious of what was designed against me, an assassin entered the chamber with that instrument in his hand, and ——"

A stifled groan from Schedoni checked Ellena; she observed his rolling eyes, and trembled; till, believing that his agitation was occasioned by indignation against the assassin, she resumed, "Why should you think it necessary to conceal the danger which has threatened me, since it is to you that I owe my deliverance from it? Oh, my father! do not deny me the pleasure of shedding tears of gratitude, do not refuse the thanks which are due to you! While I slept upon that couch, while a ruffian stole upon my slumber—it was you, yes! can I ever forget that it was my father who saved me from his poniard!"

Schedoni's passions were changed, but they were not less violent; he could scarcely control them, while he said in a tremulous tone, "It is enough, say no more;" and he raised Ellena, but turned away without embracing her.

His strong emotion, as he paced in silence the farthest end of the apartment, excited her surprise, but she then attributed it to a remembrance of the perilous moment from which he had rescued her.

Schedoni, meanwhile, to whom her thanks were daggers, was trying to subdue the feelings of remorse that tore his heart; and was so enveloped in a world of his own as to be for some time unconscious of all around him. He continued to stalk in gloomy silence along the chamber, till the voice of Ellena, entreating him rather to rejoice that he had been permitted to save her, than so deeply to consider dangers which were past, again touched the chord that vibrated to his conscience, and recalled him to a sense of his situation. He then bade her prepare for immediate departure, and abruptly quitted the room.

Vainly hoping that in flying from the scene of his meditated crime he should leave with it the acuteness of remembrance and the agonising stings of remorse, he was now more anxious than ever to leave the place. Yet he should still be accompanied by Ellena, and her innocent looks, her affectionate thanks, inflicted an anguish which was scarcely endurable. Sometimes, thinking that her hatred, or what to him would be still severer, her contempt, must be more tolerable than this gratitude, he almost resolved to undeceive her respecting his conduct, but as constantly and impatiently repelled the thought with horror, and finally determined to suffer her to account for his late extraordinary visit in the way she had chosen.

Spalatro, at length, returned from the hamlet with horses, but without having procured a guide to conduct the travellers through a tract of the long-devolving forests of the Garganus which it was necessary for them to pass. No person had been willing to undertake so arduous a task ; and Spalatro, who was well acquainted with all the labyrinths of the way, now offered his services.

Schedoni, though he could scarcely endure the presence of this man, had no alternative but to accept him, since he had dismissed the guide who had conducted him hither. Of personal violence Schedoni had no apprehension, though he too well understood the villainy of his proposed companion ; for he considered that he himself should be well armed, and he determined to ascertain that Spalatro was without weapons ; he knew also that in case of a contest his own superior stature would easily enable him to overcome such an antagonist.

Everything being now ready for departure, Ellena was summoned, and the confessor led her to his own apartment, where a slight breakfast was prepared.

Her spirits being revived by the speed of this departure, she would again have expressed her thanks, but he peremptorily interrupted her and forbade any further mention of gratitude.

On entering the court where the horses were in waiting, and perceiving Spalatro, Ellena shrank and put her arm within Schedoni's for protection. "What recollections does the presence of that man revive ?" said she. "I can scarcely venture to believe myself safe even with you when he is here."

Schedoni made no reply till the remark was repeated. "You have nothing to fear from him," muttered the confessor while he hastened her forward, "and we have no time to lose in vague apprehension."

"How !" exclaimed Ellena. "Is not he the assassin from whom you saved me? I cannot doubt that you know him to be such, though you would spare me the pain of believing so."

"Well, well, be it so," replied the confessor. "Spalatro, lead the horses this way."

The party were soon mounted, when, quitting this eventful mansion and the shore of the Adriatic, as Ellena hoped, for ever, they entered upon the gloomy wilderness of the Garganus. She often turned her eyes back upon the house with emotions of inexpressible awe, astonishment, and thankfulness, and gazed while a glimpse of its turreted walls could be caught beyond the dark branches which, closing over it, at length shut it from her view. The joy of this departure, however, was considerably abated by the presence of Spalatro, and her fearful countenance inquired of Schedoni the meaning of his being suffered to accompany them. The confessor was reluctant to speak concerning a man of whose very existence he would willingly have ceased to think. Ellena guided her horse still closer to Schedoni's, but, forbearing to urge the inquiry otherwise than by looks, she received no reply, and endeavoured to quiet her apprehensions by considering that he would not have permitted this man to be their guide unless he had believed he might be trusted. This consideration, though it relieved her fears, increased her perplexity respecting the late designs of Spalatro and her surprise that Schedoni, if he had really understood them to be evil, should endure his presence. Every time she stole a glance at the dark countenance of this man, rendered still darker by the shade of the trees, she thought "assassin" was written in each line of it, and she could scarcely doubt that he, and not the people who had conducted her to the mansion, had dropped the dagger in her chamber. Whenever she looked round through the deep glades and on the forest-mountains that on every side closed the scene and seemed to exclude all cheerful haunt of man, and then regarded her companions, her heart sank, notwithstanding the reasons she had for believing herself in the protection of a father. Nay, the very looks of Schedoni himself, more than once reminding her of his appearance on the sea-shore, renewed the impressions of alarm and even of dismay which she had there experienced. At such moments it was scarcely possible for her to consider him as her parent, and, in spite of every late appearance, strange and unaccountable doubts began to gather on her mind.

Schedoni, meanwhile, lost in thought, broke not by a single word the deep silence of the solitudes through which they passed. Spalatro was equally mute, and equally engaged with his reflections on the sudden change in Schedoni's purpose, and by wonder as to the motive which could have induced him to lead Ellena in safety from the very spot whither she was brought by his express command to be destroyed. He, however, was not so wholly occupied as to be unmindful of his situation, or unwatchful of an opportunity of serving his own interests, and retaliating upon Schedoni for the treatment he had received on the preceding night.

Amongst the various subjects that distracted the confessor, the difficulty of disposing of Ellena, without betraying at Naples that she was his relative, was not the least distressing. Whatever might be the reason which could justify such feelings, his fears of a premature discovery of the circumstance to the society with whom he lived were so strong as to often produce the most violent effect upon his countenance ; and it was, perhaps, when he was occupied by this subject, that its terrific expression revived with Ellena the last scene upon the shore. His embarrassment was not less as to the excuse to be offered the Marchesa, for having failed to fulfil his engagement, and respecting the means by which he might interest her in favour of Ellena, and even dispose her to approve the marriage before she should be informed of the family of this unfortunate young woman. Perceiving all the necessity for ascertaining the probabilities of such consent before he ventured to make an avowal of her origin, he determined not to reveal himself till he should be perfectly sure that the discovery would be acceptable to the Marchesa. In the meantime, as it would be necessary to say something of Ellena's birth, he meant to declare that he had discovered it to be noble, and her family worthy in every respect of a connection with that of the Vivaldi.

An interview with the Marchesa was almost equally wished for and dreaded by the confessor. He shuddered at the expectation of meeting a woman who had instigated him to the murder of his own child, which, though he had been happily prevented from committing it, was an act that would still be wished for by the Marchesa. How could he endure her reproaches when she should discover that he had failed to accomplish her will! How conceal the indignation of a father, and dissimulate all a father's various feelings, when, in reply to such reproaches, he must form excuses and act humility from which his whole soul would revolt! Never could his arts of dissimulation have been so severely tried, not even in the late scenes with Ellena, never have returned upon himself in punishment so severe, as in that which awaited him with the Marchesa; and from its approach the cool and politic Schedoni often shrank in such horror that he almost determined to avoid it at any hazard, and secretly to unite Vivaldi and Ellena without even soliciting the consent of the Marchesa.

A desire, however, of the immediate preferment, so necessary to his pride, constantly checked this scheme, and finally made him willing to subject every honest feeling, and submit to any meanness, however vicious, rather than forego the favourite object of his erroneous ambition. Never, perhaps, was the paradoxical union of pride and abjectness more strongly exhibited than on this occasion.

While thus the traveller silently proceeded, Ellena's thoughts often turned to Vivaldi, and she considered, with trembling anxiety, the effect which the late discovery was likely to have upon their future lives. It appeared to her that Schedoni must approve of a connection thus flattering to the pride of a father, though he would probably refuse his consent to a private marriage. And, when she further considered the revolution which a knowledge of her family might occasion towards herself in the minds of the Vivaldi, her prospects seemed to brighten and her cares began to dissipate. Judging that Schedoni

must be acquainted with the present situation of Vivaldi, she was continually on the point of mentioning him, but was as constantly restrained by timidity; though, had she suspected him to be an inhabitant of the Inquisition, her scruples would have vanished before an irresistible interest. As it was, believing that he, like herself, had been imposed upon by the Marchesa's agents in the disguise of officials, she concluded, as has before appeared, that he now suffered a temporary imprisonment, by order of his mother, at one of the family villas. When, however, Schedoni, awaking from his reverie, abruptly mentioned Vivaldi, her spirits fluttered with impatience to learn his exact situation, and she inquired respecting it.

"I am no stranger to your attachment," said Schedoni, evading the question, "but I wish to be informed of some circumstances relative to its commencement."

Ellena, confused, and not knowing what to reply, was for a moment silent, and then repeated her inquiry.

"Where did you first meet?" said the confessor, still disregarding her question. Ellena related that she had first seen Vivaldi when attending her aunt from the church of San Lorenzo. For the present she was spared the embarrassment of further explanation by Spalatro, who, riding up to Schedoni, informed him they were approaching the town of Zanti. On looking forward, Ellena perceived houses peeping from among the forest-trees at a short distance, and presently heard the cheerful bark of a dog—that sure herald and faithful servant of man.

Soon after the travellers entered Zanti, a small town surrounded by the forest, where, however, the poverty of the inhabitants seemed to forbid a longer stay than was absolutely necessary for repose and a slight refreshment. Spalatro led the way to a cabin, in which the few persons who journeyed this road were usually entertained. The appearance of the people who owned it was, as wild as their country, and the interior of the dwelling was so dirty and comfortless that, Schedoni preferring to take his repast in the open air, a table was spread under the luxuriant shade of the forest-trees at a little distance. Here, when the host had withdrawn and Spalatro had been despatched to examine the post-horses and to procure a lay habit for the confessor, the latter, once more alone with Ellena, began to experience again somewhat of the embarrassments of conscience: and Ellena, whenever her eyes glanced upon him, suffered a solemnity of fear that rose almost to terror. He at length terminated his emphatic silence by renewing his mention of Vivaldi and his command that Ellena should relate the history of their affection. Not daring to refuse, she obeyed, but with as much brevity as possible, and Schedoni did

not interrupt her by a single observation.
However eligible their nuptials now appeared
to him, he forbore to give any hint of approbation, till he should have extricated the object
of her regards from his perilous situation.
But, with Ellena, this silence implied the
very opinion it was meant to conceal, and,
encouraged by the hope it imparted, she ventured once more to ask by whose order Vivaldi had been arrested ; whither he had been
conveyed, and the circumstances of his present situation.

Too politic to intrust her with a knowledge
of his actual condition, the confessor spared
her the anguish of learning that Vivaldi was
a prisoner in the Inquisition. He affected
ignorance of the late transaction at Celano,
but ventured to believe that both Vivaldi and
herself had been arrested by order of the
Marchesa, who, he conjectured, had thrown
him into temporary confinement, a measure
which she, no doubt, had meant to enforce
also towards Ellena.

"And you, my father?" observed Ellena,
"what brought you to my prison—you who
were not informed of the Marchesa's designs?
What accident conducted you to that remote
solitude, just at the moment when you could
save your child?"

"Informed of the Marchesa's designs!" said
Schedoni, with embarrassment and displeasure. "Have you ever imagined that I could
be accessory—that I could consent to assist, I
mean could consent to be a confidant of such
atrocious——" Schedoni, bewildered, confounded, and half-betrayed, restrained himself.

"Yet you have said the Marchesa meant
only to confine me?" observed Ellena ; "was
that design so atrocious? Alas! my father,
I know too well that her plan was more atrocious, and since you also had too much reason
to know this, why do you say that imprisonment only was intended for me? But your
solicitude for my tranquillity leads you to——"

"What means," interrupted the suspicious
Schedoni, "can I particularly have of understanding the Marchesa's schemes? I repeat,
that I am not her confidant ; how then is it
to be supposed I should know that they extended further than to imprisonment?"

"Did you not save me from the arm of the
assassin," said Ellena, tenderly ; "did not
you wrench the very dagger from his grasp!"

"I had forgotten, I had forgotten," said the
confessor, yet more embarrassed.

"Yes, good minds are ever thus apt to forget the benefits they confer," replied Ellena.
"But you shall find, my father, that a grateful heart is more watchful to remember them ;
it is the indelible register of every act that is
dismissed from the memory of the benefactor."

"Mention no more of benefits," said Schedoni, impatiently ; "let silence on this subject

henceforth indicate your wish to oblige
me."

He rose, and joined the host, who was at
the door of his cabin. Schedoni wished to
dismiss Spalatro as soon as possible, and he
inquired for a guide to conduct him through
that part of the forest which remained to be
traversed. In this poor town a person willing to undertake that office was easily to be
found, but the host went in quest of a neighbour whom he had recommended.

Meanwhile Spalatro returned without having succeeded in his commission. Not any
lay-habit could be procured, upon so short a
notice, that suited Schedoni. He was oblig·d,
therefore, to continue his journey, to the next
town at least, in his own dress ; but the
necessity was not very serious to him, since it
was improbable that he should be known in
this obscure region.

Presently the host appeared with his neighbour, when Schedoni, having received satisfactory answers to his questions, engaged him
for the remainder of the forest-road, and
dismissed Spalatro. The ruffian departed
with sullen reluctance and evident ill-will,
circumstances which the confessor scarcely
noticed while occupied by the satisfaction of
escaping from the presence of the atrocious
partner of his conscience. But Ellena, as he
passed her, observed the malignant disappointment of his look, and it served only to heighten
the thankfulness his absence occasioned her.

It was afternoon before the travellers proceeded. Schedoni had calculated that they
could easily reach the town at which he
designed to pass the night before the close
of evening, and he had been in no haste to
set forward during the heat of the day.
Their track now lay through a country less
savage, though scarcely less wild, than that
they had passed in the morning. It emerged
from the interior towards the border of the
forest ; they were no longer inclosed by impending mountains ; the withdrawing shades
were no longer impenetrable to the eye, but
now and then opened to gleams of sunshine,
landscape, and blue distances ; and, in the
immediate scene, many a green glade spread
its bosom to the sun. The grandeur of the
trees, however, did not decline ; the plane,
the oak, and the chestnut still threw a pomp
of foliage round these smiling spots, and
seemed to consecrate the mountain streams
that descended beneath their solemn shade.

To the harassed spirits of Ellena the
changing scenery was refreshing, and she
frequently yielded her cares to the influence
of majestic nature. Over the gloom of Schedoni no scenery had, at any moment, power ;
the shape and paint of external imagery gave
neither impression nor colour to his fancy.
He contemned the sweet illusions to which
other spirits are liable, and which often
confer a delight more exquisite, and not

less innocent, than any which deliberative reason can bestow.

The same thoughtful silence that had wrapt him at the beginning of the journey he still preserved, except when occasionally he asked a question of the guide concerning the way, and received answers too loquacious for his humour. This loquacity, however, was not easily repressed, and the peasant had already begun to relate some terrible stories of murder committed in these forests upon people who had been hardy enough to venture into them without a guide, before the again abstracted Schedoni even noticed that he spoke. Though Ellena did not give much credit to these narratives, they had some effect upon her fears when, soon after, she entered the deep shades of a part of the forest that lay along a narrow defile, whence every glimpse of cheerful landscape was again excluded by precipices which towered on either side. The stillness was not less effectual than the gloom, for no sounds were heard, except such as seemed to characterize solitude, and impress its awful power more deeply on the heart—the hollow dashing of torrents descending distantly, and the deep sighings of the wind, as it passed among trees which threw their broad arms over the cliffs and crowned the highest summits. Onward through the narrowing windings of the defile, no living object appeared ; but, as Ellena looked fearfully back, she thought she distinguished a human figure advancing beneath the dusky umbrage that closed the view. She communicated her suspicion to Schedoni, though not her fears, and they stopped for a moment to observe further. The object advanced slowly, and they perceived the stature of a man, who, having continued to approach, suddenly paused, and then glided away behind the foliage that crossed the perspective, but not before Ellena fancied she discriminated the figure of Spalatro. None but a purpose the most desperate, she believed, could have urged him to follow into this pass, instead of returning, as he had pretended, to his home. Yet it appeared improbable that he alone should be willing to attack two armed persons, for both Schedoni and the guide had weapons of defence. This consideration afforded her only a momentary respite from apprehension, since it was possible that he might not be alone, though only one person had yet been seen among the shrouding branches of the woods. "Did you not think he resembled Spalatro?" said Ellena to the confessor ; "was he not of the same stature and air? You are well armed, or I should fear for you as well as for myself."

"I did not observe a resemblance," replied Schedoni, throwing a glance back ; "but whosoever he is, you have nothing to apprehend from him, for he has disappeared."

"Yes, signor, so much the worse," observed the guide, "so much the worse, if he means us any harm, for he can steal along the rocks behind these thickets, and strike out upon us before we are aware of him. Or, if he knows the path that runs among those old oaks yonder on the left, where the ground rises, he has us sure at the turning of the next cliff."

"Speak lower," said Schedoni, "unless you mean that he should benefit by your instructions."

Though the confessor said this without any suspicion of evil intention from the guide, the man immediately began to justify himself, and added, "I'll give him a hint of what he may expect, however, if he attacks us." As he spoke he fired his trombone in the air, when every rock reverberated the sound, and the faint and fainter thunder retired in murmurs through all the windings of the defile. The eagerness with which the guide had justified himself produced an effect upon Schedoni contrary to what he designed ; and the confessor, as he watched him suspiciously, observed that, after he had fired, he did not load his piece again. "Since you have given the enemy sufficient intimation where to find us," said Schedoni, "you will do well to prepare for his reception ; load again, friend. I, too, have arms, and they are ready."

While the man sullenly obeyed, Ellena, again alarmed, looked back in search of the stranger, but not any person appeared beneath the gloom, and no footstep broke upon the stillness. When, however, she suddenly heard a rustling noise, she looked to the bordering thickets, almost expecting to see Spalatro break from among them, before she perceived that it was only the sounding pinions of birds, which, startled by the report of the trombone from their high nests in the cliffs, winged their way from danger.

The suspicions of the confessor had, probably, been slight, for they were transient ; and when Ellena next addressed him, he had again retired within himself. He was ruminating upon an excuse to be offered the Marchesa which might be sufficient both to assuage her disappointment and baffle her curiosity, and he could not, at present, fabricate one that might soothe her resentment without risk of betraying his secret.

Twilight had added its gloom to that of the rocks before the travellers distinguished the town at which they meant to pass the night. It terminated the defile, and its grey houses could scarcely be discerned from the precipice upon which they hung, or from the trees that embosomed them. A rapid stream rolled below, and over it a bridge conducted the wanderers to the little inn at which they were to take up their abode. Here, quietly lodged, Ellena dismissed all present apprehension of Spalatro, but she still believed she had seen him, and her suspicions as to the motive of his extraordinary journey were not appeased.

As this was a town of ampler accommodation than the one they had left, Schedoni easily procured a lay habit that would disguise him for the remainder of the journey, and Ellena was permitted to lay aside the nun's veil for one of a more general fashion ; but, in thus dismissing it, she did not forget that it had been the veil of Olivia, and she preserved it as a sacred relic of her favourite recluse.

The distance between this town and Naples was still that of several days' journey according to the usual mode of travelling ; but the most dangerous part of the way was now overcome, the road having emerged from the forests ; and when Schedoni, on the following morning, was departing, he would have discharged the guide, had not the host assured him he would find one still necessary in the open, but wild, country through which he must pass. Schedoni's distrust of this guide had never been very serious, and, as the result of the preceding evening proved favourable, he had restored him so entirely to his confidence as willingly to engage him for the present day. In this confidence, however, Ellena did not perfectly coincide.   She had observed the man while he loaded the trombone on Schedoni's order, and his evident reluctance had almost persuaded her that he was in league with some person who designed to attack them ; a conjecture, perhaps, the most readily admitted while her mind was suffering from the impression of having seen Spalatro.   She now ventured to hint her distrust to the confessor, who paid little attention to it, and reminded her that sufficient proof of the man's honesty had appeared in their having been permitted to pass in safety a defile so convenient for the purpose of rapine as that of yesterday.   To a reply apparently so reasonable, Ellena could oppose nothing, had she even dared to press the topic ; and she recommenced the journey with gayer hopes.

CHAPTER XXII.

ON this day Schedoni was more communicative than on the preceding one. While they rode apart from the guide, he conversed with Ellena on various topics relative to herself, but without once alluding to Vivaldi, and even condescended to mention his design of disposing of her in a convent at some distance from Naples till it should be convenient for him to acknowledge her for his daughter. But the difficulty of finding a suitable situation embarrassed him, and he was disconcerted by the awkwardness of introducing her himself to strangers, whose curiosity would be heightened by a sense of their interest.

These considerations induced him the more easily to attend to the distress of Ellena, on her learning that she was again to be placed at a distance from her home, and among strangers ; and the more willingly to listen to the account she gave of the Convent della Pieta, and to her request of returning thither. But in whatever degree he might be inclined to approve, he listened without consenting, and Ellena had only the consolation of perceiving that he was not absolutely determined to adopt his first plan.

Her thoughts were too deeply engaged upon her future prospects to permit leisure for present fears, or probably she would have suffered some return of those of yesterday in traversing the lonely plains and rude valleys through which the road lay. Schedoni was thankful to the landlord who had advised him to keep the guide, the road being frequently obscured amongst the wild heaths that stretched around, and the eye often sweeping over long tracts of country without perceiving a village or any human dwelling. During the whole morning they had not met one traveller, and they continued to proceed beneath the heat of noon, because Schedoni had been unable to discover even a cottage in which shelter and repose might be obtained.

It was late in the day when the guide pointed out the grey walls of an edifice which crowned the acclivity they were approaching. But this was so shrouded among woods that no feature of it could be distinctly seen, and it did but slightly awaken their hopes of discovering a convent which might receive them with hospitality.

The high banks, overshadowed with thickets, between which the road ascended, soon excluded even a glimpse of the walls ; but, as the travellers turned the next projection, they perceived a person on the summit of the road, crossing as if towards some place of residence, and concluded that the edifice they had seen was behind the trees among which he had disappeared.

A few moments brought them to the spot, where, retired at a short distance among the woods that browed the hill, they observed the extensive remains of what seemed to have been a villa, and which, from the air of desolation it exhibited, Schedoni would have judged to be wholly deserted, had he not already seen a person enter. Wearied and exhausted, he determined to ascertain whether any refreshment could be procured from the inhabitants within, and the party alighted before the portal of a deep and broad avenue of arched stone, which seemed to have been the grand approach to the villa. Over this majestic portal rose the light boles and tall heads of aloes ; while the Indian fig threw its broad leaves in many a luxuriant cluster among the capitals and rich ornaments below.

The entrance was obstructed by fragments of columns, and by the underwood that had taken root amongst them. The travellers, however, easily overcame these interruptions; but, as the avenue was of considerable extent, and as its only light proceeded from the portal, except what a few narrow loops in the walls admitted, they soon found themselves involved in an obscurity that rendered the way difficult, and Schedoni endeavoured to make himself heard by the person he had seen. The effort was unsuccessful, but, as they proceeded, a bend in the passage showed a distant glimmering of light, which served to guide them to the opposite entrance, where an arch opened immediately into a court of the villa. Schedoni paused here in disappointment, for every object seemed to bear evidence of abandonment and desolation; and he looked, almost hopelessly, round the light colonnade which ran along three sides of the court, and to the palmetos that waved over the fourth, in search of the person who had been seen from the road. No human figure stole upon the vacancy; yet the apt fears of Ellena almost imaged the form of Spalatro gliding behind the columns, and she started as the air shook over the wild plants that wreathed them, before she discovered that it was not the sound of steps. At the extravagance of her suspicions, however, and the weakness of her terrors, she blushed, and endeavoured to resist that propensity to fear which nerves long pressed upon had occasioned in her mind.

Schedoni meanwhile stood in the court like the evil spirit of the place, examining its desolation, and endeavouring to ascertain whether any person lurked in the interior of the building. Several doorways in the colonnade appeared to lead to chambers of the villa, and, after a short hesitation, Schedoni, having determined to pursue his inquiry, entered one of them, and passed through a marble hall to a suite of rooms whose condition told how long it was since they had been inhabited. The roofs had entirely vanished, and even portions of the walls had fallen, and lay in masses amongst the woods without.

Perceiving that it was as useless as difficult to proceed, the confessor returned to the court, where the shade of the palmetos at least offered a hospitable shelter to the wearied travellers. They reposed themselves beneath the towering branches on some fragments of a marble fountain, whence the court opened to the extensive landscape, now mellowed by the evening beams, and partook of the remains of a repast which had been deposited in the wallet of the guide.

"This place appears to have suffered from an earthquake, rather than from time," said Schedoni, "for the walls, though shattered, do not seem to have decayed, and much that has been strong lies in ruin, while what is comparatively slight remains uninjured; these

are certainly symptoms of partial shocks of the earth. Do you know anything of the history of this place, friend?"

"Yes, signor," replied the guide.

"Relate it, then."

"I shall never forget the earthquake that destroyed it, s'gnor, for it was felt all through the Garganus. I was then about sixteen, and I remember it was near an hour before midnight that the great shock was felt. The weather had been almost stifling for several days, scarcely a breath of air had stirred, and slight tremblings of the ground were noticed by many people. I had been out all day, cutting wood in the forest with my father, and tired enough we were, when ——"

"This is the history of yourself," said Schedoni, interrupting him. "Who did this place belong to?"

"Did any person suffer here?" asked Ellena.

"The Baróne di Cambrusca lived here," replied the guide.

"Hah! the Baróne!" repeated Schedoni, and sank into one of his customary fits of abstraction.

"He was a signor little loved in the country," continued the guide, "and some people said it was a judgment upon him for ——"

"Was it not rather a judgment upon the country?" interrupted the confessor, lifting up his head, and then sinking again into silence.

"I know not for that, signor, but he had committed crimes enough to make one's hair stand on end. It was here that he —— "

"Fools are always wondering at the actions of those above them," said Schedoni, testily. "Where is the Baróne now?"

"I cannot tell, signor, but most likely where he deserves to be, for he has never been heard of since the night of the earthquake, and it is believed he was buried under the ruins."

"Did any other person suffer?" repeated Ellena.

"You shall hear, signora," replied the peasant. "I happen to know something about the matter, because a cousin of ours lived in the family at the time, and my father has often told me all about it, as well as of the late lord's goings-on. It was near midnight when the great shock came, and the family, thinking of nothing at all, had supped and been asleep some time. Now it happened that the Baróne's chamber was in the tower of the old building, at which people often wondered, because, said they, why should he choose to sleep in the old part when there are so many fine rooms in the new villa?— but so it was."

"Come, despatch your meal," said Schedoni, awaking from his deep musing; "the sun is setting, and we have yet far to go."

"I will finish the meal and the story together, signor, with your leave," replied the guide. Schedoni did not notice what he said, and as the man was not forbidden, he proceeded with his relation.

"Now it happened that the Baróne's chamber was in that old tower—if you will look this way, signora, you will see what is left of it."

Ellena turned her attention to where the guide pointed, and perceived the shattered remains of a tower rising beyond the arch through which she had entered the court.

"You see that corner of a window-case left in the highest part of the wall, signora," continued the guide; "just by that fig-tree, which grows out of the stone?"

"I observe," said Ellena.

"Well, that was one of the windows of the very chamber, signora, and, you see, scarcely anything else is left of it. Yes, there is the door-case, too, but the door itself is gone ; that little staircase that you see beyond it led up to another story, which nobody now would guess had ever been ; for roof, and flooring, and all are fallen. I wonder how that little staircase in the corner happened to hold so fast ! "

"Have you almost done ?" inquired Schedoni, who had not apparently attended to anything the man said, and now alluded to the refreshment he was taking.

"Yes, signor, I have not a great deal more to tell, or to eat either, for that matter," replied the guide ; "but you shall hear. Well, yonder was the very chamber, signora ; at that door-case, which is still in the wall, the Baróne came in. Ah ! he little thought, I warrant, that he should never more go out at it ! How long he had been in the room I do not know, nor whether he was asleep or awake, for there is nobody that can tell ; but when the great shock came, it split the old tower at once, before any other part of the buildings. You see that heap of ruins, yonder, on the ground, signora ; there lie the remains of the chamber ; the Baróne, they say, was buried under them ! "

Ellena shuddered while she gazed upon this destructive mass. A groan from Schedoni startled her, and she turned towards him, but, as he appeared shrouded in meditation, she again directed her attention to this awful memorial. As her eye passed upon the neighbouring arch, she was struck with the grandeur of its proportions, and with its singular appearance, now that the evening rays glanced upon the overhanging shrubs, and darted a line of partial light athwart the avenue beyond. But what was her emotion when she perceived a person gliding away in the perspective of the avenue, and, as he crossed where the gleam fell, distinguished the figure and countenance of Spalatro ! She had scarcely power faintly to exclaim, "Steps go there ! " before he had disappeared ; and when Schedoni looked round the vacuity and silence of solitude everywhere prevailed.

Ellena now did not scruple positively to affirm that she had seen Spalatro, and Schedoni, fully sensible that, if her imagination had not deluded her, the purpose of his thus tracing their route must be desperate, immediately rose, and, followed by the peasant, pass-d into the avenue to ascertain the truth, leaving Ellena alone in the court. He had scarcely disappeared before the danger of his adventuring into that obscure passage, where an assassin might strike unseen, forcibly occurred to Ellena, and she loudly conjured him to return. She listened for his voice, but heard only his retreating steps ; when, too anxious to remain where she was, she hastened to the entrance of the avenue. But all was now hushed ; neither voice nor steps were distinguished. Awed by the gloom of the place, she feared to venture further, yet almost equally dreaded to remain alone in any part of the ruin while a man so desperate as Spalatro was hovering about it.

As she yet listened at the entrance of the avenue, a faint cry, which seemed to issue from the interior of the villa, reached her. The first dreadful surmise that struck Ellena was that they were murdering her father, who had probably been decoyed by another passage back into some chamber of the ruin ; when, instantly forgetting every fear for herself, she hastened towards the spot whence she judged the sound to have issued. She entered the hall which Schedoni had noticed, and passed on through a suite of apartments beyond. Everything here, however, was silent, and the place apparently deserted. The suite terminated in a passage that seemed to lead to a distant part of the villa, and Ellena, after a momentary hesitation, determined to follow it.

She made her way with difficulty between the half-demolished walls, and was obliged to attend so much to her steps that she scarcely noticed whither she was going, till, the deepening shade of the place recalling her attention, she perceived herself among the ruins of the tower whose history had been related by the guide ; and, on looking up, observed she was at the foot of the stair-case which still wound up the wall that had led to the chamber of the Baróne.

At a moment less anxious the circumstance would have affected her ; but now she could only repeat her calls upon the name of Schedoni, and listen for some signal that he was near. Still receiving no answer, nor hearing any further sound of distress, she began to hope that her fears had deceived her, and having ascertained that the passage terminated here, she quitted the spot.

On regaining the first chamber, Ellena rested for a moment to recover breath ; and, while she leaned upon what had once been a window opening to the court, she heard a distant report of firearms. The sound swelled, and seemed to revolve along the avenue through which Schedoni had disappeared. Supposing that the combatants were engaged at the furthest entrance, Ellena was preparing to go thither, when a sudden step moved near her, and, on turning, she discovered, with a degree of horror that almost deprived her of recollection, Spalatro himself stealing along the very chamber in which she was.

That part of the room which she stood in, fell into a kind of recess; and whether it was this circumstance that prevented him from immediately perceiving her, or that, his chief purpose being directed against another object, he did not choose to pause here, he passed on with skulking steps; and, before Ellena had determined whether to go, she observed him cross the court before her, and enter the avenue. As he passed he looked up at the window: and it was certain he then saw her, for he instantly faltered, but in the next moment proceeded swiftly, and disappeared in the gloom.

It seemed that he had not yet encountered Schedoni, but it also occurred to Ellena that he was gone into the avenue for the purpose of awaiting to assassinate him in the darkness. While she was meditating some means of giving the confessor a timely alarm of his danger, she once more distinguished his voice. It approached from the avenue, and Ellena, immediately calling aloud that Spalatro was there, entreated him to be on his guard. In the next instant a pistol was fired there.

Among the voices that succeeded the report Ellena thought she distinguished groans. Schedoni's voice was in the next moment heard again, but it seemed faint and low. The courage which she had before exerted was now exhausted; she remained fixed to the spot, unable to encounter the dreadful spectacle that probably awaited her in the avenue, and almost sinking beneath the expectation of it.

All was now hushed; she listened for Schedoni's voice, and even for a footstep—in vain. To endure this state of uncertainty much longer was scarcely possible, and Ellena was endeavouring to collect fortitude to meet a knowledge of the worst, when suddenly a feeble groaning was again heard. It seemed near, and to be approaching still nearer. At that moment, Ellena, on looking towards the avenue, perceived a figure, covered with blood, pass into the court. A film which drew over her eyes prevented her noticing further. She tottered a few paces back, and caught at the fragment of a pillar, by which she supported herself. The weakness was, however, transient; immediate assistance appeared necessary to the wounded person, and pity soon predominating over horror, she recalled her spirits, and hastened to the court.

When, on reaching it, she looked round in search of Schedoni, he was nowhere to be seen; the court was again solitary and silent, till she awakened all its echoes with the name of *father.* While she repeated her calls, she hastily examined the colonnade, the separated chamber which opened immediately from it, and the shadowy ground beneath the palmetos, but without discovering any person.

As she turned towards the avenue, however, a track of blood on the ground told her too certainly where the wounded person had passed. It guided her to the entrance of a narrow passage that seemingly led to the foot of the tower; but here she hesitated, fearing to trust the obscurity beyond. For the first time Ellena conjectured that not Schedoni, but Spalatro, might be the person she had seen, and that, though he was wounded, vengeance might give him strength to strike his stiletto at the heart of whomsoever approached him, while the duskiness of the place would favour the deed.

She was yet at the entrance of the passage, fearful to enter, and reluctant to leave it, listening for a sound, and still hearing at intervals swelling though feeble groans, when quick steps were suddenly heard advancing up the grand avenue, and presently her own name was repeated loudly in the voice of Schedoni. His manner was hurried as he advanced to meet her, and he threw an eager glance round the court. "We must be gone," said he, in a low tone, and taking her arm within his. "Have you seen anyone pass?"

"I have seen a wounded man enter the court," replied Ellena, "and feared he was yourself."

"Where?—Which way did he go?" inquired Schedoni, eagerly, while his eyes glowed, and his countenance became fell.

Ellena, instantly comprehending his motive for the question, would not acknowledge that she knew whither Spalatro had withdrawn; and, reminding him of the danger of their situation, she entreated that they might quit the villa immediately.

"The sun is already set," she added. "I tremble at what may be the perils of this place at such an obscure hour, and even at what may be those of our road at a later!"

"You are sure he was wounded?" said the confessor.

"Too sure," replied Ellena, faintly.

"Too sure!" sternly exclaimed Schedoni.

"Let us depart, my father; oh, let us go this instant!" repeated Ellena.

"What is the meaning of all this?" asked Schedoni, with anger. "You cannot, surely, have the weakness to pity this fellow!"

"It is terrible to see anyone suffer," said Ellena. "Do not, by remaining here, leave me a possibility of grieving for you. What anguish it would occasion you to see me bleed; judge, then, what must be mine, if you are wounded by the dagger of an assassin."

Schedoni stifled the groan which swelled from his heart, and abruptly turned away.

"You trifle with me," he said, in the next moment. "You do not know that the villain is wounded. I fired at him, it is true, at the instant I saw him enter the avenue, but he has escaped me. What reason have you for your supposition?"

Ellena was going to point to the track of blood on the ground at a little distance, but restrained herself, considering that this might guide him on to Spalatro; and again she entreated they might depart, adding, "Oh! spare yourself, and him!"

"What! spare an assassin!" said Schedoni, impatiently.

"An assassin! He *has*, then, attempted your life?" exclaimed Ellena.

"Why, no, not absolutely that," replied Schedoni, recollecting himself, "but—what does the fellow do here? Let me pass; I will find him."

Ellena still hung upon his garment, while, with persuasive tenderness, she endeavoured to awaken his humanity. "Oh! if you had ever known what it was to expect instant death," she continued, "you would pity this man now, as he, perhaps, has sometimes pitied others! I have known such suffering, my father, and can, therefore, feel even for him."

"Do you know for *whom* you are pleading?" said the distracted Schedoni, while every word she had uttered seemed to have penetrated his heart. The surprise which this question awakened in Ellena's countenance recalled him to a consciousness of his imprudence; he recollected that Ellena did not certainly know the office with which Spalatro had been commissioned against her: and when he considered that this very Spalatro, whom Ellena had with such simplicity supposed to have, at some time, spared a life through pity, had in truth spared her own, and, yet more, had been eventually a means of preventing him from destroying his own child, the confessor turned in horror from his design; all his passions changed, and he abruptly quitted the court, nor paused till he reached the furthest extremity of the avenue, where the guide was in waiting with the horses.

A recollection of the conduct of Spalatro respecting Ellena had thus induced Schedoni to spare him: but this was all; it did not prevail with him to inquire into the condition of this man, or to mitigate his punishment; and, without remorse, he now left him to his fate.

With Ellena it was otherwise. Though she was ignorant of the obligation she owed him,

she could not know that any human being was left under such circumstances of suffering and solitude without experiencing very painful emotion; but, considering how expeditiously Spalatro had been able to remove himself, she endeavoured to hope that his wound was not mortal.

The travellers, mounting their horses in silence, left the ruin, and were for some time too much engaged by the impression of the late occurrences to converse together. When, at length, Ellena inquired the particulars of what had passed in the avenue, she understood that Schedoni, on pursuing Spalatro, had seen him there only for a moment. Spalatro had escaped by some way unknown to the confessor, and had regained the interior of the ruin while his pursuers were yet following the avenue. The cry which Ellena had imagined to proceed from the interior was uttered, as it now appeared, by the guide, who, in his haste, had fallen over some fragments of the wall that lay scattered in the avenue. The first report of arms had been from the trombone, which Schedoni had discharged on reaching the portal; and the last when he fired a pistol, on perceiving Spalatro passing from the court.

"We have had trouble enough in running after this fellow," said the guide, "and could not catch him at last. It is strange that, if he came to look for us, he should run away so when he had found us! I do not think he meant us any harm after all, else he might have done it easily enough in the dark passage; instead whereof he only took to his heels!"

"Silence!" said Schedoni; "fewer words, friend."

"Well, signor, he's peppered now, however; so we need not be afraid. His wings are clipped for one while, so he cannot overtake us. We need not be in such a hurry, signor; we shall get to the inn in good time yet. It is upon a mountain yonder, whose top you may see upon that red streak in the west. He cannot come after us; I myself saw his arm was wounded."

"Did you so?" said Schedoni, sharply; "and pray where were you when you saw so much? It was more than I saw."

"I was close at your heels, signor, when you fired the pistol."

"I do not remember to have heard you there," observed the confessor; "and why did not you come forward, instead of retreating? And where, also, did you hide yourself while I was searching for the fellow, instead of assisting me in the pursuit?"

The guide gave no answer, and Ellena, who had been attentively observing him during the whole of this conversation, perceived that he was now considerably embarrassed; so that her former suspicions as to his integrity began to revive, notwithstanding the several circumstances which had occurred to render them improbable. There was, however, at present no opportunity for further observation, Schedoni having, contrary to the advice of the guide, immediately quickened his pace, and the horses continuing on the full gallop till a steep ascent compelled them to relax their speed.

Contrary to his usual habit, Schedoni now, while they slowly ascended, appeared desirous of conversing with this man, and asked him several questions relative to the villa they had left ; and whether it was that he really felt an interest on the subject or that he wished to discover if the man had deceived him in the circumstances he had already narrated, from which he might form a judgment as to his general character, he pressed his inquiries with a patient minuteness that somewhat surprised Ellena. During this conversation, the deep twilight would no longer permit her to notice the countenance of either Schedoni or the guide ; but she gave much attention to the changing tones of their voices, as different circumstances and emotions seemed to affect them. It is to be observed that during the whole of this discourse the guide rode at the side of Schedoni.

While the confessor appeared to be musing upon something which the peasant had related respecting the Baróne di Cambrusca, Ellena inquired as to the fate of the other inhabitants of the villa.

"The falling of the old tower was enough for them," replied the guide ; "the crash waked them all directly, and they had time to get out of the new buildings before the second and third shocks laid them also in ruins. They ran out into the woods for safety, and found it too, for they happened to take a different road from the earthquake. Not a soul suffered except the Baróne, and he deserved it well enough. Oh ! I could tell such things that I have heard of him ——"

"What became of the rest of the family ?" interrupted Schedoni.

"Why, signor, they were scattered here and there and everywhere ; and they none of them ever returned to the old spot. No ! no ! they had suffered enough there already, and might have suffered to this day, if the earthquake had not happened."

"If it had *not* happened ?" repeated Ellena.

"Aye, signora, for that put an end to the Baróne. If those walls could but speak, they could tell strange things, for they have looked upon sad doings ; and that chamber which I showed you, signora, nobody ever went into it but himself, except the servant to keep it in order, and that he would scarcely suffer and always stayed in the room the while."

"He had probably treasure secreted there," observed Ellena.

"No, signora, no treasure ! He had

always a lamp burning there, and sometimes in the night he has been heard—once, indeed, his valet happened to ——"

"Come on," said Schedoni, interrupting him ; "keep pace with me. What idle dream are you relating now ?"

"It is about the Baróne di Cambrusca, signor," replied the guide, raising his voice ; "him that you were asking me so much about just now. I was saying what strange ways he had, and how that on one stormy night in December, as my cousin Francisca told my father, who told me, and he lived in the family at the time it happened ——"

"What happened ?" said Schedoni, hastily.

"What I am going to tell, signor. My cousin lived there at the time ; so, however *unbelievable* it may seem, you may depend upon it, it is all true. My father knows I would not believe it myself till ——"

"Enough of this," said Schedoni ; "no more. What family had this Baróne—had he a wife at the time of this destructive shock ?"

"Yes, truly, signor, he had, as I was going to tell if you would but condescend to have patience."

"The Baróne had more need of that, friend. I have no wife."

"The Baróne's wife had most need of it, signor, as you shall hear. A good soul, they say, was the Baronessa ; but luckily she died many years before. He had a daughter also, and, young as she was, she had lived too long but for the earthquake, which set her free."

"How far is it to the inn ?" said the confessor, roughly.

"When we get to the top of this hill, signor, you will see it on the next if any light is stirring, for there will only be the hollow between us. But do not be frightened, signor, the fellow we left cannot overtake us. Do you know much about him, signor ?"

Schedoni inquired whether the trombone was charged, and, discovering that it was not, ordered the man to load immediately.

"Why, signor, if you knew as much of him as I do you could not be more afraid !" said the peasant, while he stopped to obey the order.

"I understood that he was a stranger to you !" observed the confessor, with surprise.

"Why, signor, he is and he is not ; I know more about him than he thinks for."

"You seem to know a vast deal too much of other persons' affairs," said Schedoni, in a tone that was meant to silence him.

"Why, that is just what he would say, signor ; but bad deeds will out, whether people like them to be known or not. This man comes to our town sometimes to market, and nobody knew where he came from for a long while ; so they set themselves to work, and found it out at last."

"We shall never reach the summit of this hill," said Schedoni, testily.

"And they found out, too, a great many strange things about him," continued the guide.

Ellena, who had attended to this discourse with a degree of curiosity that was painful, now listened impatiently for what might be further mentioned concerning Spalatro, but without daring to invite, by a single question, any discovery on a subject which appeared to be so intimately connected with Schedoni.

"It was many years ago," rejoined the guide, "that this man came to live in that strange house on the sea-shore. It had been shut up ever since——"

"What are you talking of now?" interrupted the confessor, sharply.

"Why, signor, you never will let me tell you. You always snap me up so short at the beginning, and then ask what I am talking about! I was going to begin the story, and it is a pretty long one. But first of all, signor, who do you suppose this man belonged to? And what do you think the people determined to do when the report was first set a-going? only they could not be sure it was true, and anybody would be unwilling enough to believe such a shocking——"

"I have no curiosity on the subject," replied the confessor sternly interrupting him, "and desire to hear no more concerning it."

"I meant no harm, signor," said the man; "I did not know it concerned you."

"And who says that it does concern me?"

"Nobody, signor, only you seemed to be in a bit of a passion, and so I thought—— But I meant no harm, signor; only, as he happened to be your guide part of the way, I guessed you might like to know something of him."

"All that I desire to know of my guide is that he does his duty," replied Schedoni, "that he conducts me safely, and understands when to be silent."

To this the man replied nothing, but slackened his pace, and slunk behind his reprover.

The travellers, reaching soon after the summit of this long hill, looked out for the inn of which they had been told; but darkness now confounded every object, and no domestic light twinkling, however distantly, through the gloom gave signal of security and comfort. They descended dejectedly into the hollow of the mountains, and found themselves once more immerged in woods. Schedoni again called the peasant to his side, and bade him keep abreast of him; but he did not discourse, and Ellena was too thoughtful to attempt conversation. The hints which the guide had thrown out respecting Spalatro had increased her curiosity on that subject; but the conduct of Schedoni, his impatience, his embarrassment, and the decisive manner in which he had put an end to the talk of the peasant, excited a degree of surprise that bordered on astonishment. As she had, however, no clue to lead her conjectures to any point, she was utterly bewildered in surmise, understanding only that Schedoni had been much more deeply connected with Spalatro than she had hitherto believed.

The travellers, having descended into the hollow, and commenced the ascent of the opposite height, without discovering any symptoms of a neighbouring town, began again to fear that their conductor had deceived them. It was now so dark that the road, though the soil was a limestone, could scarcely be discerned, the woods on either side forming a "close dungeon of innumerable boughs," that totally excluded the twilight of the stars.

While the confessor was questioning the man with some severity, a faint shouting was heard from a distance; and he stopped the horses to listen from what quarter it came.

"That comes the way we are going, signor," said the guide.

"Hark!" exclaimed Schedoni; "those are strains of revelry!"

A confused sound of voices, laughter, and musical instruments was heard; and, as the air blew stronger, tambourines and flutes were distinguished.

"Oh! oh! we are near the end of our journey!" said the peasant; "all this comes from the town we are going to. But what makes them all so merry, I wonder!"

Ellena, revived by this intelligence, followed with alacrity the sudden speed of the confessor; and presently reaching a point of the mountain where the woods opened, a cluster of lights on another summit, a little higher, more certainly announced the town.

They soon after arrived at the ruinous gates, which had formerly led to a place of some strength, and passed at once from darkness and desolated walls into a marketplace blazing with light and resounding with the multitude. Booths, fantastically hung with lamps, and filled with merchandise of every kind, disposed in the gayest order, were spread on all sides, and peasants in their holiday clothes, and parties of masks, crowded every avenue. Here was a band of musicians, and there a group of dancers; on one spot the *outré* humour of a zanni provoked the never-failing laugh of an Italian rabble; in another the *improvisatore*, by the pathos of his story and the persuasive sensibility of his strains, was holding the attention of his auditors as in the bands of magic. Further on was a stage raised for a display of fireworks, and near this a theatre, where a mimic opera, the "shadow of a shade," was exhibiting, whence the roar of laughter, excited by the principal *buffo* within, mingled with the heterogeneous voices of the vendors of ice, macaroni, sherbet, and diavoloni without.

The confessor looked upon this scene with disappointment and ill-humour, and bade the guide go before him, and show the way to the best inn; an office which the latter undertook with great glee, though he made his way with difficulty. "To think I should not know it was the time of the fair!" said he; "though, to say truth, I never was at it but once in my life, and then I was only three months old, so it was not so surprising, signor."

"Make way through the crowd," said Schedoni.

"After jogging on so long in the dark, signor, with nothing at all to be seen," continued the man, without attending to the direction, "then to come, all of a sudden, to such a place as this, why, it is like coming out of purgatory into paradise. Well, signor, you have forgot all your quandaries now; you think nothing now about that old ruinous place where we had such a race after the man that would not murder us; but that shot I fired did his business."

"You fired!" said Schedoni, aroused by the assertion.

"Yes, signor, as I was looking over your shoulder. I should have thought you must have heard it!"

"I should have thought so too, friend."

"Aye, signor, this fine place has put all that out of your head, I warrant, as well as what I said about that same fellow; but, indeed, signor, I did not know he was related to you when I talked so of him. But, perhaps, for all that, you may not know the piece of his story I was going to tell you when you cut me off so short, though you are better acquainted with one another than I guessed for; so, when I come in from the fair, signor, if you please, I will tell it to you; and it is a pretty long history, for I happen to know the whole of it; though, where you cut me short, when you were in one of those quandaries, was only just at the beginning, but no matter for that, I can begin it again, for——"

"What is all this?" said Schedoni, again recalled from one of the thoughtful moods in which he had so habitually indulged that even the bustle around him had failed to interrupt the course of his mind. He now bade the peasant be silent; but the man was too happy to be tractable, and proceed to express all he felt as they advanced slowly through the crowd. Every object here was to him new and delightful; and, nothing doubting that it must be equally so to every other person, he was continually pointing out to the proud and gloomy confessor the trivial subjects of his own admiration. "See! signor, there is Punchinello; see how he eats the hot macaroni! And look there, signor! there is a juggler! Oh, good signor, stop one minute

to look at his tricks. See! he has turned a monk into a devil already, in the twinkling of an eye!"

"Silence! and proceed," said Schedoni.

"That is what I say, signor, silence! for the people make such a noise that I cannot hear a word you speak. Silence, there!"

"Considering that you could not hear, you have answered wonderfully to the purpose," said Ellena.

"Ah! signor, is not this better than those dark woods and hills? But what have we here? Look, signor, here is a fine sight!"

The crowd, which was assembled round a stage on which some persons grotesquely dressed were performing, now interrupting all further progress, the travellers were compelled to stop at the foot of the platform. The people above were acting what seemed to have been intended for a tragedy, but what their strange gestures, uncouth recitation, and incongruous countenances had transformed into a comedy.

Schedoni, thus obliged to pause, withdrew his attention from the scene; Ellena consented to endure it, and the peasant, with gaping mouth and staring eyes, stood like a statue, yet not knowing whether he ought to laugh or cry, till suddenly turning round to the confessor, whose horse was of necessity close to his, he seized his arm, and pointing to the stage, called out, "Look! signor, see! signor, what a scoundrel! what a villain! see, he has murdered his own daughter!"

At these terrible words the indignation of Schedoni was done away by other emotions; he turned his eyes upon the stage, and perceived that the actors were performing the story of Virginia. It was at the moment when she was dying in the arms of her father, who was holding up the poniard with which he had stabbed her. The feelings of Schedoni at this instant inflicted a punishment almost worthy of the crime he had meditated.

Ellena, struck with the action, and with the contrast which it seemed to offer to what she believed to have been the late conduct of Schedoni towards herself, looked at him with most expressive tenderness, and as his glance met hers she perceived with surprise the changing emotions of his soul and the inexplicable character of his countenance. Stung to the heart, the confessor furiously spurred his horse that he might escape from the scene, but the poor animal was too spiritless and jaded to force its way through the crowd; and the peasant, vexed at being hurried from a place where, almost for the first time in his life, he was suffering under the strange delights of artificial grief, and half angry to observe an animal of which he had the care ill treated, loudly remonstrated, and seized the bridle of Schedoni, who, still more incensed, was applying the whip to the shoulders of the guide, when the crowd suddenly fell back and opened a way through which the travellers passed, and arrived with little further interruption at the door of the inn.

Schedoni was not in a humour which rendered him fit to encounter difficulties, and still less the vulgar squabbles of a place already crowded with guests; yet it was not without much opposition that he at length obtained a lodging for the night. The peasant was not less anxious for the accommodation of his horses; and when Ellena heard him declare that the animal which the confessor had so cruelly spurred should have a double feed, and a bed of straw as high as his head, if he himself went without one, she gave him, unnoticed by Schedoni, the only ducat she had left.

CHAPTER XXIII.

SCHEDONI passed the night without sleep. The incident of the preceding evening had not only renewed the agonies of remorse, but excited those of pride and apprehension. There was something in the conduct of the peasant towards him which he could not clearly understand, though his suspicions were sufficient to throw his mind into a state of the utmost perturbation. Under the air of extreme simplicity, this man had talked of Spalatro, had discovered that he was acquainted with much of his history, and had hinted that he knew by whom he had been employed; yet at the same time appeared unconscious that Schedoni's was the master-hand which had directed the principal actions of the ruffian. At other times his behaviour had seemed to contradict the supposition of his ignorance on this point; from some circumstances he had mentioned it appeared impossible but that he must have known who Schedoni really was, and even his own conduct had occasionally seemed to acknowledge this, particularly when, being interrupted in his history of Spalatro, he attempted an apology, by saying he did not know it concerned Schedoni; nor could the conscious Schedoni believe that the very pointed manner in which the peasant had addressed him at the representation of Virginia was merely accidental. He wished to dismiss the man immediately, but it was first necessary to ascertain what he knew concerning him, and then to decide on the measures to be taken. It was, however, a difficult matter to obtain this information without manifesting an anxiety which might betray him if the guide had, at present, only a general suspicion of the truth, and no less difficult to determine how to proceed towards him if it should be evident that his suspicions rested on Spalatro. To take him forward to Naples was to bring an informer to his home; to suffer him to return with his discovery, now that he probably knew the place of Schedoni's

residence, was little less hazardous. His death only could secure the secret.

After a night passed in the tumult of such considerations, the confessor summoned the peasant to his chamber, and, with some short preface, told him he had no further occasion for his services, adding carelessly that he advised him to be on his guard as he repassed the villa, lest Spalatro, who might yet lurk there, should revenge upon him the injury he had received. "According to your account of him, he is a very dangerous fellow," added Schedoni, "but your information is, perhaps, erroneous."

The guide began testily to justify himself for his assertions, and the confessor then endeavoured to draw from him what he knew on the subject. But, whether the man was piqued by the treatment he had lately received, or had other reasons for reserve, he did not at first appear so willing to communicate as formerly.

"What you hinted of this man," said Schedoni, "has, in some degree, excited my curiosity. I have now a few moments of leisure, and you may relate, if you will, something of the wonderful history you talked of."

"It is a long story, signor, and you would be tired before I got to the end of it," replied the peasant; "and, craving your pardon, signor, I don't much like to be snapped up so."

"Where did this man live?" said the confessor. "You mentioned something of a house at the seaside."

"Aye, signor, there is a strange history belonging to that house too; but this man, as I was saying, came there all of a sudden, nobody knew how; and the place had been shut up ever since the Marchese ——"

"The Marchese!" said Schedoni, coldly; "what Marchese, friend?"

"Why, I mean the Baróne di Cambrusca, signor, to be sure, as I was going to have told you of my own accord, if you would only have let me. Shut up ever since the Baróne —I left off there, I think?"

"I understood that the Baróne was dead," observed the confessor.

"Yes, signor," replied the peasant, fixing his eyes on Schedoni; "but what has his death to do with what I was telling? This happened before he died."

Schedoni, somewhat disconcerted by this unexpected remark, forgot to resent the familiarity of it. "This man, then—this Spalatro—was connected with the Baróne di Cambrusca?" said he.

"It was pretty well guessed so, signor."

"How! no more than guessed?"

"No, signor, and that was more than enough for the Baróne's liking, I warrant. He took too much care for anything certain to appear against him, and he was wise so to do, for if it had, it would have been worse for him. But I was going to tell you the story, signor."

"What reasons were there for believing this was an agent of the Baróne di Cambrusca, friend?"

"I thought you wished to hear the story, signor."

"In good time; but, first, what were your reasons?"

"One of them is enough, signor; and, if you would only have let me gone straight on with the story, you would have found it out by this time, signor."

Schedoni frowned, but did not otherwise reprove the impertinence of the remark.

"It was reason enough, signor, to my mind," continued the peasant, "that it was such a crime as nobody but the Baróne di Cambrusca could have committed; there was nobody wicked enough in our parts to have done it but him. Why, is not this *reason* enough, signor? What makes you look at me so? Why, the Baróne himself could hardly have looked worse if I had told him as much."

"Be less prolix," said the confessor, in a restrained voice.

"Well then, signor, to begin at the beginning. It is a good many years ago that Marco came first to our town. Now the story goes, that one stormy night ——"

"You may spare yourself the trouble of relating the story," said Schedoni, abruptly. "Did you ever see the Baróne you were speaking of, friend?"

"Why did you bid me tell it, signor, since you knew it already? I have been here all this while, just a-going to begin it, and all for nothing!"

"It is very surprising," resumed the artful Schedoni, without having noticed what had been said, "that if this Spalatro was known to be the villain you say he is, not any step should have been taken to bring him to justice; how happened that? But, perhaps, all this story was nothing more than a report."

"Why, signor, it was everybody's business, and nobody's, as one may say; then, besides, nobody could prove what they had heard, and though everybody believed the story just the same as if they had seen the whole, yet that, they said, would not do in law, but that they should be made to prove it. Now it is not one time in ten, signor, that anything can be proved, signor, as you well know, yet we none of us believe it the less for that!"

"So, then, you would have had this man punished for a murder which, probably, he never committed!" said the confessor.

"A murder!" repeated the peasant.

Schedoni was silent, but in the next instant said, "Did you not say it was a murder?"

"I have not told you so, signor!"

"What was the crime, then?" resumed Schedoni, after another momentary pause;

"you said it was atrocious, and what more so than—murder?" His lip quivered as he pronounced the last word.

The peasant made no reply, but remained with his eyes fixed upon the confessor, and at length repeated, "Did I say it was murder, signor?"

"If it was not that, say what it was," demanded the confessor, haughtily; "but let it be in two words."

"As if a story could be told in two words, signor!"

"Well, well, be brief."

"How can I, signor, when the story is so long?"

"I will waste no more time," said Schedoni, going.

"Well, signor, I will do my best to make it short. It was one stormy night in December that Marco Torma had been out fishing. Marco, signor, was an old man that lived in our town when I was a boy; I can but just remember him, but my father knew him well and loved old Marco, and used often to say ——"

"To the story!" said Schedoni.

"Why, I am telling it, signor, as fast as I can. This old Marco did not live in our town at the time it happened, but in some place, I have forgot the name of it, near the sea shore. What can the name be? it is something like ——"

"Well, what happened to this old dotard?"

"You are out there, signor, he was no old dotard; but you shall hear. At that time, signor, Marco lived in this place that I have forgot the name of, and was a fisherman, but better times turned up afterwards, but that is neither here nor there. Old Marco had been out fishing; it was a stormy night, and he was glad enough to get on shore, I warrant. It was quite dark—as dark, signor, I suppose, as it was last night—and he was making the best of his way, signor, with some fish along the shore, but it being so dark he lost his way notwithstanding. The rain beat and the wind blew, and he wandered about a long while, and could see no light nor hear anything but the surge near him, which sometimes seemed as if it was coming to wash him away. He got as far off it as he could, but he knew there were high rocks over the beach, and he was afraid he should run his head against them if he went too far, I suppose. However, at last he went up close to them, and as he got a little shelter he resolved to try no further for the present. I tell it you, signor, just as my father told it me, and he had it from the old man himself."

"You need not be so particular," replied the confessor; "speak to the point."

"Well, signor, as old Marco lay snug under the rocks, he thought he heard somebody coming, and he lifted up his head, I warrant, poor old soul! as if he could have seen who it was;

E

However, he could hear, though it was so dark, and he heard the steps coming on; but he said nothing yet, meaning to let them come close up to him before he discovered himself. Presently he sees a little moving light, and it comes nearer and nearer, till it was just opposite to him, and then he saw the shadow of a man on the ground, and then he spied the man himself, with a dark lantern, passing along the beach."

"Well, well, to the purpose," said Schedoni.

"Old Marco, signor, my father says, was never stout-hearted, and he took it into his head this might be a robber, because he had the lantern, though, for that matter he would have been glad enough of a lantern himself, and so he lay quiet. But, presently, he was in a rare fright, for the man stopped to rest the load he had upon his back on a rock near him, and old Marco saw him throw off a heavy sack, and heard him breathe hard, as if he was hugely tired. I tell it, signor, just as my father does."

"What was in the sack?" said Schedoni, coolly.

"All in good time, signor; perhaps old Marco never found it out; but you shall hear. He was afraid, when he saw the sack, to stir a limb, for he thought it held booty. But, presently, the man, without saying a word, heaved it on his shoulders again, and staggered away with it along the beach, and Marco saw no more of him."

"Well! what has he to do with your story, then?" said the confessor. "Was this Spalatro?"

"All in good time, signor; you put me out. When the storm was down a little, Marco crept out, and thinking there must be a village, or a hamlet, or a cottage at no great distance, since this man had passed, he thought he would try a little further. He had better have stayed where he was, for he wandered about a long while, and could see nothing, and what was worse, the storm came on louder than before, and he had no rocks to shelter him now. While he was in this quandary, he sees a light at a distance, and it came into his head this might be the lantern again, but he determined to go on notwithstanding, for if it was he could stop short, and if it was not he should get shelter, perhaps; so on he went, and I suppose I should have done the same, signor."

"Well! this history never will have an end!" said Schedoni.

"Well, signor, he had not gone far when he found out that it was no lantern, but a light at a window. When he came up to the house he knocked softly at the door, but nobody came."

"What house?" inquired the confessor, sharply.

"The rain beat hard, signor, and I war-rant poor old Marco waited a long time before he knocked again, for he was main patient, signor. Oh! how I have seen him listen to a story, let it be ever so long!"

"I have need of his patience!" said Schedoni.

"When he knocked again, signor, the door gave way a little, and he found it was open, and so, as nobody came, he thought fit to walk in of his own accord."

"The dotard! what business had he to be so curious?" exclaimed Schedoni.

"Curious, signor, he only sought shelter! He stumbled about in the dark for a good while, and could find nobody, nor make nobody hear, but; at last he came to a room where there was some fire, not quite out, upon the hearth, and he went up to it to warm himself till somebody should come."

"What! was there nobody in the house?" said the confessor.

"You shall hear, signor. He had not been there, he said, no, he was sure not above two minutes, when he heard a strange sort of a noise in the very room where he was, but the fire gave such a poor light he could not see whether anybody was there."

"What was the noise?"

"You put me out, signor. He said he did not much like it, but what could he do? So he stirred up the fire, and tried to make it blaze a little, but it was as dusky as ever; he could see nothing. Presently, however, he heard somebody coming, and saw a light, and then a man coming towards the room where he was, so he went up to ask shelter."

"Who was this man?" said Schedoni.

"Ask shelter. He says the man, when he came to the door of the room, turned as white as a sheet, as well he might to see a stranger—to find a stranger there at that time of night. I suppose I should have done the same myself. The man did not seem very willing to let him stay, but asked what he did there, and such like; but the storm was very loud, and so Marco did not let a little matter daunt him, and when he showed the man what a fine fish he had in his basket, and said he was welcome to it, he seemed more willing."

"Incredible!" exclaimed Schedoni; "the blockhead!"

"He had wit enough, for that matter, signor; Marco says he appeared to be main hungry——"

"Is that any proof of his wit?" said the confessor, peevishly.

"You never will let me finish, signor; main hungry, for he put more wood on the fire directly to dress some of the fish. While he was doing this, Marco says, his heart somehow misgave him that this was the man he saw on the beach, and he looked at him pretty hard, till the other asked him, crossly, what he stared at him so for; but Marco took care not to tell. While he was busy making ready the fish, however, Marco had an opportunity of eyeing him the more; and every time the man looked round the room, which happened to be pretty often, he had a notion it was the same."

"Well, and if it was the same?" said Schedoni.

"But when Marco happened to spy the sack lying in a corner, he had no doubt about the matter. He says his heart then misgave him sadly, and he wished himself safe out of the house, and determined in his own mind, to get away as soon as he could, without letting the man suspect what he thought of him. He now guessed, too, what made the man look round the room so often; and, though Marco thought before it was to find out if he had brought anybody with him, he now believed it was to see whether his treasure was safe."

"Aye, likely enough," observed Schedoni.

"Well, old Marco sat not much at his ease, while the fish was preparing, and thought it was 'out of the frying-pan into the fire' with him; but what could he do?"

"Why get up and walk away, to be sure," said the confessor, "as I shall do, if your story lasts much longer."

"You shall hear, signor; he would have done so, if he had thought this man would have let him; but——"

"Well, this man was Spalatro, I suppose," said Schedoni, impatiently, "and this was the house on the shore you formerly mentioned."

"How well you have guessed it, signor! though, to say truth, I have been expecting you to find it out for this half-hour."

Schedoni did not like the significant look which the peasant assumed while he said this, but he bade him proceed.

"At first, signor, Spalatro hardly spoke a word; but he came to by degrees, and by the time the fish was nearly ready he was talkative enough."

Here the confessor rose with some emotion and paced the room.

"Poor old Marco, signor, began to think better of him; and when he heard the rain at the casements he was loath to think of stirring. Presently Spalatro went out of the room for a plate to eat the fish——."

"Out of the room?" said Schedoni, and checked his steps.

"Yes, signor, but he took care to carry the light with him. However, Marco, who had a great deal of curiosity to——"

"Yes, he appears to have had a great deal, indeed!" said the confessor, and, turning away, renewed his pace.

"Nay, signor, I am not come to that yet; he has shown none yet;—a great deal of curiosity to know what was in the sack, before he consented to let himself stay much longer, thought this a good opportunity for

looking, and as the fire was now pretty bright, he determined to see. He went up to the sack, therefore, signor, and tried to lift it, but it was too heavy for him, though it did not seem full."

Schedoni again checked his steps, and stood fixed before the peasant.

"He raised it, however, a little, signor; but it fell from his hands, and with such a heavy weight upon the floor that he was sure it held no common booty. Just then, he says, he thought he heard Spalatro coming, and the sound of the sack was enough to have frightened him, and so Marco quitted it; but he was mistaken, and he went to it again. But you don't seem to hear me, signor, for you look as you do when you are in those quandaries, so busy a-thinking, and I——"

"Proceed," said Schedoni, sternly, and renewed his steps; "I hear you."

"Went to it again," resumed the peasant, cautiously taking up the story at the last words he had dropped. "He untied the string, signor, that held the sack, and opened the cloth a little way; but think, signor, what he must have thought when he felt cold flesh? Oh, signor! and when he saw by the light of the fire the face of the corpse within! Oh, signor!"

The peasant, in the eagerness with which he related this circumstance, had followed Schedoni to the other end of the chamber; and he now took hold of his garment as if to secure his attention to the remainder of the story. The confessor, however, continued his steps, and the peasant kept pace with him, still loosely holding his garment.

"Marco," he resumed, "was so terrified, as my father says, that he hardly knew where he was; and I warrant, if one could have seen him, he looked as white, signor, as you do now."

The confessor abruptly withdrew his garment from the peasant's grasp, and said, in an inward voice, "If I am shocked at the mere mention of such a spectacle, no wonder he was who beheld it!" After the pause of a moment, he added, "But what followed?"

"Maroo says he had no power to tie up the cloth again, signor; and when he came to his thoughts, his only fear was lest Spalatro should return—though he had hardly been gone a minute—before he could get out of the house, for he cared nothing about the storm now. And sure enough he heard him coming; but he managed to get out of the room into a passage another way from that Spalatro was in. And luckily, too, it was the same passage he had come in by, and it led him out of the house. He made no more ado, but ran straight off, without stopping to choose his way, and many perils and dangers he got into among the woods that night, and——"

"How happened it that this Spalatro was

not taken up after this discovery?" said Schedoni. "What was the consequence of it?"

"Why, signor, old Marco had like to have caught his death that night; what with the wet and what with the fright, he was laid up with a fever and was light-headed, and raved such strange things that people would not believe anything he said when he came to his senses."

"Aye," said Schedoni. the narrative resembles a delirious dream more than a reality; "I perfectly accord with them in their opinion of this feverish old man."

"But you shall hear, signor. After a while they began to think better of it, and there was some stir made about it; but what could poor folks do, for nothing could be proved! The house was searched, but the man was gone, and nothing could be found! From that time the place was shut up, till, many years after this, Spalatro appeared; and old Marco then said he was pretty sure he was the man, but he could not swear it and so nothing could be done."

"Then it appears after all that you are not certain that this long history belongs to this Spalatro!" said the confessor; "nay, not even that the history itself is anything more than the vision of a distempered brain!"

"I do not know, signor, what you may call certain; but I know what we all believe. But the strangest part of the story is to come yet, and that which nobody would believe, hardly, if——"

"I have heard enough," said Schedoni; "I will hear no more!"

"Well but, signor, I have not told you half yet; and I am sure when I heard it myself it so terrified me——"

"I have listened too long to this idle history," said the confessor; "there seems to be no rational foundation for it. Here is what I owe you; you may depart."

"Well, signor, tis plain you know the rest already, or you never would go without it. But you don't know, perhaps, signor, what an unaccountable—I am sure it made my hair stand on end to hear of it, what an unaccountable——"

"I will hear no more of this absurdity," interrupted Schedoni, with sternness. "I reproach myself for having listened so long to such a gossip's tale, and have no further curiosity concerning it. You may withdraw, and bid the host attend me."

"Well, signor, if you are so easily satisfied," replied the peasant, with disappointment, "there is no more to be said, but——"

"You may stay, however, while I caution you," said Schedoni, "how you pass the villa, where this Spalatro may yet linger; for, though I can only smile at the story you have related——"

"Related, signor! why I have not told it half; and if you would only please to be patient ——"

"Though I can only smile at that simple narrative," repeated Schedoni, in a louder tone ——

"Nay, signor, for that matter, you can frown at it too, as I can testify," muttered the guide.

"Listen to me!" said the confessor, in a yet more insisting voice. "I say, that though I give no credit to your curious history, I think this same Spalatro appears to be a desperate fellow, and, therefore, I would have you be on your guard. If you see him, you may depend upon it that he will attempt your life in revenge of the injury I have done him. I give you, therefore, in addition to your trombone, this stiletto to defend you."

Schedoni, while he spoke, took an instrument from his bosom, but it was not the one he usually wore, or, at least, that he was seen to wear. He delivered it to the peasant, who received it with a kind of stupid surprise, and then gave him some directions as to the way in which it should be managed.

"Why, signor," said the man, who had listened with much attention, "I am kindly obliged to you for thinking about me; but is there anything in this stiletto different from others, that it is to be used so?"

Schedoni looked gravely at the peasant for an instant, and then replied, "certainly not, friend; I would only instruct you to use it to the best advantage; farewell!"

"Thank you kindly, signor, but—but I think I have no need of it; my trombone is enough for me."

"This will defend you more adroitly," replied Schedoni, refusing to take back the stiletto; "and moreover, while you were loading the trombone your adversary might use his poniard to advantage. Keep it, therefore, friend; it will protect you better than a dozen trombones. Put it up."

Perhaps it was Schedoni's particular look, more than his argument, that convinced the guide of the value of his gift. He received it submissively, though with a stare of stupid surprise; probably it had been better if it had been suspicious surprise. He thanked Schedoni again, and was leaving the room when the confessor called out, "Send the landlord to me immediately; I shall set off for Rome without delay."

"Yes, signor," replied the peasant; "you are at the right place—the road parts here; but I thought you was going for Naples."

"For Rome," said Schedoni.

"For Rome, signor! Well, I hope you will get safe, signor, with all my heart," said the guide, and quitted the chamber.

While this dialogue had been passing between Schedoni and the peasant, Ellena, in solitude, was considering on the means of prevailing on the confessor to allow her to return either to Altieri or to the neighbouring cloister of Our Lady of Pity, instead of placing her at a distance from Naples, till he should think proper to acknowledge her. The plan which he had mentioned seemed to her long-harassed mind to exile her for ever from happiness, and all that was dear to her affections. It appeared like a second banishment to San Stefano ; and every abbess, except that of La Pieta, came to her imagination in the portraiture of an inexorable gaoler. While this subject engaged her she was summoned to attend Schedoni, whom she found impatient to enter the carriage which at this town they had been able to procure. Ellena, on looking out for the guide, was informed that he had already set off for his home, a circumstance for the suddenness of which she knew not how to account.

The travellers immediately proceeded on their journey. Schedoni, reflecting on the late conversation, said little ; and Ellena read not in his countenance anything that might encourage her to introduce the subject of her own intended solicitation. Thus separately occupied they advanced during some hours on the road to Naples, for thither Schedoni had designed to go, notwithstanding his late assertion to the guide, whom it appears, for whatever reason, he was anxious to deceive as to the place of his actual residence.

They stopped to dine at a town of some consideration, and, when Ellena heard the confessor inquire concerning the numerous convents it contained, she perceived that it was necessary for her no longer to defer her petition. She therefore represented immediately what must be the forlornness of her state, and the anxiety of her mind, if she were placed at a distance from the scenes and the people which affection and early habit seemed to have consecrated ; especially at this time, when her spirits had scarcely recovered from the severe pressure of long-suffering, and when, to soothe and renovate them, not only quiet but the consciousness of security were necessary ; a consciousness which it was impossible, and especially so soon after her late experience, that she could acquire amongst strangers till they should cease to be such.

To these pleadings Schedoni thoughtfully attended, but the darkness of his aspect did not indicate that his compassion was touched ; and Ellena proceeded to represent, secondly, that which, had she been more artful, or less disdainful of cunning, she would have urged the first. As it was, she had begun with the mention of circumstances which, though she felt to be most important to herself, were the least likely to prevail with Schedoni ; and she concluded with representing that which was most interesting to him. Ellena suggested that her residence in the neighbourhood of Altieri might be so managed that his secret would be as effectually preserved as if she were at a hundred miles from Naples.

It may appear extraordinary that a man of Schedoni's habitual coolness and exact calculation should have suffered fear on this occasion to obscure his perceptions ; and this instance strongly proved the magnitude of the cause which could produce so powerful an effect. While he now listened to Ellena, he began to perceive circumstances that had eluded his own observation ; and he, at length, acknowledged that it might be safer to permit her to return to Villa-Altieri, and that she should from thence go, as she had formerly intended, to La Pieta, than to place her in any convent, however remote, where it would be necessary for himself to introduce her. His only remaining objection to the neighbourhood of Naples now rested on the chance it would offer the Marchesa di Vivaldi of discovering Ellena's abode before he should judge it convenient to disclose to her any hint respecting his family ; and his knowledge of the Marchesa justified his most horrible suspicion as to the consequence of such a premature discovery.

Something, however, it appeared, must be risked in any situation he might choose for Ellena : and her residence at the Santa della Pieta, a large convent, well secured, and where, as she had been known to them from her infancy, the abbess and the sisters might be supposed to be not indifferent concerning her welfare, seemed to promise security against any actual violence from the malice of the Marchesa—against her artful duplicity every place would be almost equally insufficient. Here, as Ellena would appear in the character she had always been known in, no curiosity could be excited or suspicion awakened as to her family ; and here, therefore, Schedoni's secret would more probably be preserved than elsewhere. As this was at present the predominant subject of his anxiety, to which, however unnatural it may seem, even the safety of Ellena was secondary, he finally determined that she should return to La Pieta ; and she thanked him almost with tears for a consent which she received as a generous indulgence, but which was in reality little more than an effect of selfish apprehensions.

The remainder of the journey, which was of some days, passed without any remarkable occurrence. Schedoni, with only short intervals, was still enveloped in gloom and silence ; and Ellena, with thoughts engaged by the one subject of her interest—the present situation and circumstances of Vivaldi—willingly submitted to this prolonged stillness.

As at length she drew near Naples, her emotions became more various and powerful ; and when she distinguished the top of Vesuvius peering over every intervening summit, she wept as her imagination charactered all the well-known country it overlooked. But when, having reached an eminence, that scenery was exhibited to her senses; when the Bay of Naples, stretching into remotest distance, was spread out before her; when every mountain of that magnificent horizon which enclosed her native landscape, that country which she believed Vivaldi to inhabit, stood unfolded, how affecting, how overwhelming were her sensations! Every object seemed to speak of her home, of Vivaldi, and of happiness that was passed; and so exquisitely did regret mingle with hope, the tender grief of remembrance with the interest of expectation, that it were difficult to say which prevailed.

Her expressive countenance disclosed to the confessor the course of her thoughts and of her feelings—feelings which, while he contemned, he believed he perfectly comprehended, but of which, having never in any degree experienced them, he really understood nothing. The callous Schedoni, by a mistake not uncommon, especially to a mind of his order, substituted words for truths; not only confounding the limits of neighbouring qualities, but mistaking their very principles. Incapable of perceiving their nice distinctions, he called the persons who saw them merely fanciful; thus making his very incapacity an argument for his superior wisdom. And, while he confounded delicacy of feeling with fatuity of mind, taste with caprice, and imagination with error, he yielded, when he most congratulated himself on his sagacity, to illusions not less egregious because they were less brilliant than those which are incident to sentiment and feeling.

The better to escape observation, Schedoni had contrived to avoid reaching Naples till the close of evening, and it was entirely dark before the carriage stopped at the gate of the Villa-Altieri. Ellena, with a mixture of melancholy and satisfaction, viewed once more her long-deserted home; and while she waited till a servant should open the gate, remembered how often she had thus waited when there was a beloved friend within to welcome her with smiles, which were now gone for ever. Beatrice, the old housekeeper, at length, however, appeared, and received her with an affection as sincere, if not as strong, as that of the relative for whom she mourned.

Here Schedoni alighted, and, having dismissed the carriage, entered the house for the purpose of relinquishing also his disguise, and resuming his monk's habit. Before he departed, Ellena ventured to mention Vivaldi, and to express her wish to hear of his exact situation; but, though Schedoni was too well enabled to inform her of it, the policy which had hitherto kept him silent on this subject still influenced him; and he replied only

that if he should happen to learn the circumstances of his condition, she should not remain ignorant of them.

This assurance revived Ellena, for two reasons: it afforded her a hope of relief from her present uncertainty, and it also seemed to express a degree of approbation of the object of her affection, such as the confessor had never yet disclosed. Schedoni added that he should see her no more till he thought proper to acknowledge her for his daughter; but that, if circumstances made it necessary, he should in the meantime write to her; and he now gave her a direction by which to address him under a fictitious name, and at a place remote from his convent. Ellena, though assured of the necessity for this conduct, could not yield to such disguise without an aversion that was strongly expressed in her manner, but of which Schedoni took no notice. He bade her, as she valued her existence, watchfully to preserve the secret of her birth; and to waste not a single day at Villa-Altieri, but to retire to La Pietà; and these injunctions were delivered in a manner so solemn and energetic as not only deeply to impress upon her mind the necessity of fulfilling them but to excite some degree of amazement.

After a short and general direction respecting her further conduct, Schedoni bade her farewell, and, privately quitting the villa in his ecclesiastical dress, repaired to the Dominican convent, which he entered as a brother returned from a distant pilgrimage. He was received as usual by the society, and found himself once more the austere father Schedoni of the Spirito Santo.

The cause of his first anxiety was the necessity for justifying himself to the Marchesa di Vivaldi, for ascertaining how much he might venture to reveal of the truth, and for estimating what would be her decision were she informed of the whole. His second step would be to obtain the release of Vivaldi; and, as his conduct in this instance would be regulated, in a great degree, by the result of his conference with the Marchesa, it would be *only* the second. However painful it must be to Schedoni to meet her, now that he had discovered the depth of the guilt in which she would have involved him, he determined to seek this eventful conference on the following morning: and he passed this night partly in uneasy expectation of the approaching day, but chiefly in inventing circumstances and arranging arguments that might bear him triumphantly towards the accomplishment of his grand design.

CHAPTER XXIV.

SCHEDONI, on his way to the Vivaldi palace, again reviewed and arranged every argument, or rather specious circumstance, which might induce the Marchesa's consent to the nuptials he so much desired. His family was noble. though no longer wealthy, and he believed that, as the seeming want of descent had hitherto been the chief objection to Ellena, the Marchesa might be prevailed with to overlook the wreck of his fortune.

At the palace he was told that the Marchesa was at one of her villas on the bay; and he was too anxious not to follow her thither immediately. This delightful residence was situated on an airy promontory that overhung the water, and was nearly embosomed among the woods that spread far along the heights, and descended, with great pomp of foliage and colouring, to the very margin of the waves. It seemed scarcely possible that misery could inhabit so enchanting an abode; yet the Marchesa was wretched amidst all these luxuries of nature and art, which would have perfected the happiness of an innocent mind! Her heart was possessed by evil passions, and all her perceptions were distorted and discoloured by them, which, like a dark magician, had power to change the fairest scenes into those of gloom and desolation.

The servants had orders to admit father Schedoni at all times, and he was shown into a saloon in which the Marchesa was alone. Every object in this apartment announced taste, and even magnificence. The hangings were of purple and gold; the vaulted ceiling was designed by one of the first painters of the Venetian school; the marble statues that adorned the recesses were not less exquisite, and the whole symmetry and architecture, airy, yet rich—gay, yet chastened—resembled the palace of a fairy, and seemed to possess almost equal fascinations. The lattices were thrown open to admit the prospect, as well as the air loaded with fragrance from an orangery that spread before them. Lofty palms and plantains threw their green and refreshing tint over the windows, and on the lawn that sloped to the edge of the precipice a shadowy perspective, beyond which appeared the ample waters of the gulf, where the light sails of feluccas, and the spreading canvas of larger vessels, glided upon the scene, and passed away, as in a camera obscura. Vesuvius and the city of Naples were seen on the coast beyond, with many a bay and lofty cape of that long tract of bold and gaily-coloured scenery which extends towards Cape Campanella, crowned by fading ranges of mountains, lighted up with all the magic of Italian sunshine. The Marchesa reclined on a sofa before an open lattice; her eyes were fixed upon the prospect without, but her attention was wholly occupied by the visions that evil passions painted to her imagination. On her still beautiful features was the langour of discontent and indisposition; and though her manners, like her dress, displayed the

elegant negligence of the graces, they concealed the movements of a careful and even a tortured heart. On perceiving Schedoni a faint smile lightened up her countenance, and she held forth her hand to him, at the touch of which he shuddered.

"My good father, I rejoice to see you," said the Marchesa; "I have felt the want of your conversation much, and at this moment of indisposition especially."

She waved to the attendant to withdraw: while Schedoni, stalking to a window, could with difficulty conceal the perturbation with which he now, for the first time, consciously beheld the willing destroyer of his child. Some further compliment from the Marchesa recalled him; he soon recovered all his address, and, approaching her, said:

"Daughter! you always send me away a worse Dominican than I come. I approach you with humility, but depart elated with pride, and am obliged to suffer much from self-infliction before I can descend to my proper level."

After some other flatteries had been exchanged, a silence of several moments followed, during which neither of the parties seemed to have sufficient courage to introduce the subjects that engaged their thoughts, subjects upon which their interests were now so directly and unexpectedly opposite. Had Schedoni been less occupied by his own feelings, he might have perceived the extreme agitation of the Marchesa, the tremor of her nerves, the faint flush that crossed her cheek, the wanness that succeeded, the languid movement of her eyes, and the laborious sighs that interrupted her breathing, while she wished, yet dared not ask, whether Ellena was no more, and averted her regards from him whom she almost believed to be a murderer.

Schedoni, not less affected, though apparently tranquil, as sedulously avoided the face of the Marchesa, whom he considered with a degree of contempt almost equal to his indignation: his feelings had reversed, for the present, all his opinion on the subject of their former arguments, and had taught him, for once, at least, to think justly. Every moment of silence increased his embarrassment and his reluctance even to name Ellena. He feared to tell that she lived, yet despised himself for suffering such fear, and shuddered at a recollection of the conduct which had made any assurance concerning her life necessary. The insinuation that he had discovered her family to be such as would not degrade that of the Marchesa, he knew not how to introduce with such delicacy of graduation as might win upon the jealousy of her pride and soothe her disappointment; and he was still meditating how he could lead to this subject, when the Marchesa herself broke the silence.

"Father," she said, with a sigh, "I always look to you for consolation, and am seldom disappointed. You are too well acquainted with the anxiety which has long oppressed me; may I understand that the cause of it is removed?" She paused, and then added. "May I hope that my son will no longer be led from the observance of his duty?"

Schedoni, with his eyes fixed on the ground, remained silent, but at length said, "The chief occasion for your anxiety is certainly removed!" and he was again silent.

"How!" exclaimed the Marchesa, with the quick-sightedness of suspicion, while all her dissimulation yielded to the urgency of her fear. "Have you failed? Is she not dead?"

In the earnestness of the question she fixed her eyes on Schedoni's face, and, perceiving there symptoms of extraordinary emotion, added, "Relieve me of my apprehensions, good father, I entreat; tell me that you have succeeded, and that she has paid the debt of justice."

Schedoni raised his eyes to the Marchesa, but instantly averted them; indignation had lifted them, and disgust and stifled horror turned them away. Though very little of these feelings appeared, the Marchesa perceived such expression as she had never been accustomed to observe in his countenance; and her surprise and impatience increasing, she repeated the question, and with a yet more insisting air than before.

"I have not failed in the grand object," replied Schedoni; "your son is no longer in danger of forming a disgraceful alliance."

"In what, then, have you failed?" asked the Marchesa; "for I perceive that you have not been completely successful."

"I ought not to say that I have failed in any respect," replied Schedoni, with emotion, "since the honour of your house is preserved, and—a life is spared."

His voice faltered as he pronounced the last words, and he seemed to experience again the horror of that moment when, with an uplifted poniard in his grasp, he had discovered Ellena for his daughter.

"Spared!" repeated the Marchesa, doubtingly. "Explain yourself, good father."

"She lives," replied Schedoni; "but you have nothing, therefore, to apprehend."

The Marchesa, surprised no less by the tone in which he spoke than shocked at the purport of his words, changed countenance, while she said, impatiently, "You speak in enigmas, father."

"Lady! I speak plain truth—she lives."

"I understand that sufficiently," said the Marchesa; "but when you tell me I have nothing to apprehend ——"

"I tell you truth, also," rejoined the confessor; "and the benevolence of your nature may be permitted to rejoice, for justice no longer has forbidden the exercise of mercy."

"That is all very well in its place," said the Marchesa, betrayed by the vexation she suffered. "Such sentiments and such compliments are. like gala suits, to be put on in fine weather. My day is cloudy; let me have a little plain sense: inform me of the circumstances which have occasioned this change in the course of your observations, and, good father, be brief."

Schedoni then unfolded, but with reserve and his usual art, such particulars relative to the family of Ellena as he hoped would soften the aversion of the Marchesa to the connection, and incline her, in consideration of her son's tranquillity, finally to approve it; with which disclosure he mingled a plausible relation of the way in which the discovery had been made, without, however, betraying by the most distant hint how nearly this discovery affected himself.

The Marchesa's patience would scarcely await the conclusion of his narrative, or her disappointment submit to the curb of discretion. When at length he had finished his history. "Is it possible," said she, with fretful displeasure, "that you have suffered yourself to be deceived by the plausibility of a girl who might have been expected to utter any falsehood which should appear likely to protect her? Has a man of your discernment given faith to this idle and improbable tale? Say rather, father, that your resolution failed in the critical moment, and that you are now anxious to form excuses to yourself for a conduct so pusillanimous."

"I am not apt to give an easy faith to appearances," replied Schedoni, gravely, "and still less to shrink from the performance of any act which I judge to be necessary and just. To the last intimation I make no reply; it does not become my character to vindicate myself from an implication of falsehood."

The Marchesa, perceiving that her passion had betrayed her into imprudence, condescended to apologise for that which she termed an effect of her extreme anxiety as to what might follow from an act of such indiscreet indulgence; and Schedoni as willingly accepted the apology, each believing the assistance of the other necessary to success.

Schedoni then informed her that he had better authority for what he had advanced than the assertion of Ellena; and he mentioned some circumstances which proved him to be more anxious for the reputation than the truth of his words. Believing that his origin was entirely unknown to the Marchesa, he ventured to disclose some further particulars of Ellena's family, without apprehending that it could lead to a suspicion of his own.

The Marchesa, though neither appeased nor convinced, commanded her feelings so far as to appear tranquil, while the confessor represented, with the most delicate address, the unhappiness of her son, and the satisfaction which must finally result to herself from all acquiescence with his choice, since the object of it was known to be worthy of his alliance. He added that, while he had believed the contrary, he had proved himself as strenuous to prevent as he was now sincere in approving their marriage; and concluded with gently blaming her for suffering prejudice and some remains of resentment to obscure her excellent understanding. "Trusting to the natural clearness of your perceptions," he added, "I doubt not that when you have maturely considered the subject, every objection will yield to a consideration of your son's happiness."

The earnestness with which Schedoni pleaded for Vivaldi excited some surprise; but the Marchesa, without condescending to reply either to his argument or remonstrance, inquired whether Ellena had a suspicion of the design with which she had been carried into the forest of the Garganus, or concerning the identity of her persecutor. Schedoni, immediately perceiving to what these questions tended, replied, with the facility with which he usually accommodated his conscience to his interest, that Ellena was totally ignorant as to who were her immediate persecutors, and equally unsuspicious of any other evil having been intended her than that of a temporary confinement.

The last assertion was admitted by the Marchesa to be probable till the boldness of the first made her doubt the truth of each, and occasioned her new surprise and conjecture as to the motive which could induce Schedoni to venture these untruths. She then inquired where Ellena was now disposed of, but he had too much prudence to disclose the place of her retreat, however plausible might be the air with which the inquiry was urged; and he endeavoured to call off her attention to Vivaldi. The confessor did not, however, venture, at present, to give a hint as to the pretended discovery of his situation in the Inquisition, but reserved to a more favourable opportunity such mention, together with a zealous offer of his services to extricate the prisoner. The Marchesa, believing that her son was still engaged in pursuit of Ellena, made many inquiries concerning him, but without expressing any solicitude for his welfare, resentment appearing to be the only emotion she retained towards him. While Schedoni replied with circumspection to her questions, he urged inquiries of his own as to the manner in which the Marchese endured the long absence of Vivaldi, thus endeavouring to ascertain how far he might hereafter venture to appear in any efforts for liberating him, and how shape his conduct respecting Ellena. It seemed that the Marchese was not indifferent as to his son's absence; and, though he had at first believed the search for Ellena to have occasioned it, other apprehensions now disturbed him, and taught him the

feelings of a father. His numerous avocations and interests, however, seemed to prevent such anxiety from preying upon his mind; and, having dismissed persons in search of Vivaldi, he passed his time in the usual routine of company and the court. Of the actual situation of his son it was evident that neither he nor the Marchesa had the least apprehension, and this was a circumstance which the confessor was very careful to ascertain.

Before he took leave he ventured to renew the mention of Vivaldi's attachment, and gently to plead for him. The Marchesa, however, seemed inattentive to what he represented, till at length awakening from her reverie, she said, "Father, you have judged ill——" and before she concluded the sentence, she relapsed again into thoughtful silence. Believing that he anticipated her meaning, Schedoni began to repeat his own justification respecting his conduct towards Ellena.

"You have judged erroneously, father," resumed the Marchesa, with the same considering air, "in placing the girl in such a situation; my son cannot fail to discover her there."

"Nor wherever she may be," replied the confessor, believing that he understood the Marchesa's aim. "It may not be possible to conceal her long from his search."

"The neighbourhood of Naples ought at least to have been avoided," observed the Marchesa.

Schedoni was silent, and she added, "So near also to his own residence! How far is La Pieta from the Vivaldi palace?"

Though Schedoni had thought that the Marchesa, while displaying a pretended knowledge of Ellena's retreat, was only endeavouring to obtain a real one, this mention of the place of her actual residence startled him; but he replied almost immediately, "I am ignorant of the distance, for till now I was unacquainted that there is a convent of the name you mention. It appears, however, that La Pieta is the place of all others which ought to have been avoided. How could you suspect me, lady, of imprudence thus extravagant!"

While Schedoni spoke, the Marchesa regarded him attentively, and then replied, "I may be allowed, good father, to suspect you of indiscretion in this instance, since you have just given me so unequivocal a proof of it in another."

She would then have changed the subject, but Schedoni, believing this inclination to be the consequence of her having assured herself that she had actually discovered Ellena's asylum, and too reasonably suspecting the dreadful uses she designed to make of the discovery, endeavoured to unsettle her opinion and mislead her as to the place of Ellena's abode. He not only contradicted the fact of her present residence at La Pieta, but, without scruple, made a positive assertion that she was at a distance from Naples, naming, at the same time, a fictitious place, whose obscurity, he added, would be the best protection from the pursuit of Vivaldi.

"Very true, father," observed the Marchesa, "I believe that my son will not readily discover the girl in the place you have named."

Whether the Marchesa believed Schedoni's assertion or not, she expressed no further curiosity on the subject, and appeared considerably more tranquil than before. She now chatted with ease on general topics, while the confessor dared no more to urge the subject of his secret wishes; and, having supported, for some time, a conversation most dissonant with his temper, he took his leave, and returned to Naples. On the way thither he reviewed, with exactness, the late behaviour of the Marchesa, and the result of this examination was a resolution never to renew the subject of their conversation, but to solemnize without her consent the nuptials of Vivaldi and Ellena.

The Marchesa, meanwhile, on the departure of Schedoni, remained for some time in the very attitude in which he had left her, and absorbed by the interest which his visit excited. The sudden change in his conduct no less astonished and perplexed than disappointed her. She could not explain it by the supposition of any principle or motive. Sometimes it occurred to her that Vivaldi had bribed him with rich promises to promote the marriage which he contributed to thwart; but when she considered the high expectations she had herself encouraged him to cherish, the improbability of the conjecture was apparent. That Schedoni, from whatever cause, was no longer to be trusted in this business, was sufficiently clear, but she endeavoured to console herself with a hope that a confidential person might yet be discovered. A part of Schedoni's resolution she also adopted, which was never again to introduce the subject of their late interview. But while she should silently pursue her own plans, she determined to conduct herself towards the confessor in every other respect as usual, not suffering him to suspect that she had withdrawn her confidence, but inducing him to believe that she had relinquished all further designs against Ellena.

CHAPTER XXV.

ELLENA, obedient to the command of Schedoni, withdrew from her home on the day that followed her arrival there to La Pieta. The Superior, who had known her from her infancy, and from the acquaintance which such long observation afforded both esteemed and loved her, received Ellena with a degree of satisfaction proportionate to the concern she had suffered when informed of her disastrous removal from Villa Altieri.

Among the quiet groves of this convent, however, Ellena vainly endeavoured to moderate her solicitude respecting the situation of Vivaldi; for, now that she had a respite from immediate calamity, she thought with more intense anxiety as to what might be his sufferings, and her fears and impatience increased as each day disappointed her expectation of intelligence from Schedoni.

If the soothings of sympathy and the delicate art of benevolence could have restored the serenity of her mind, Ellena would now have been peaceful; for all these were offered her by the abbess and the sisters of the Santa della Pieta. They were not acquainted with the cause of her sorrow, but they perceived that she was unhappy, and wished her to be otherwise. The society of Our Lady of Pity was such as a convent does not often shroud; to the wisdom and virtue of the Superior the sisterhood was principally indebted for the harmony and happiness which distinguished them. This lady was a shining example to governesses of religious houses, and a striking instance of the influence which a virtuous mind may acquire over others, as well as of the extensive good that it may thus diffuse. She was dignified without haughtiness, religious without bigotry, and mild, though decisive and firm. She possessed penetration to discover what was just, resolution to adhere to it, and temper to practise it with gentleness and grace; so that even correction from her assumed the winning air of courtesy: the person whom she admonished, wept in sorrow for the offence, instead of being secretly irritated by the reproof, and loved her as a mother, rather than feared her as a judge. Whatever might be her failings, they were effectually concealed by the general benevolence of her heart and the harmony of her mind; a harmony not the effect of torpid feelings, but the accomplishment of correct and vigilant judgment. Her religion was neither gloomy or bigoted; it was the sentiment of a grateful heart offering itself up to a deity who delights in the happiness of his creatures; and she conformed to the customs of the Roman Church without supposing a faith in all of them to be necessary to salvation. This opinion, however, she was obliged to conceal, lest her very virtue should draw upon her the punishment of a crime from some fierce ecclesiastics, who contradicted in their practice the very essential principles which the Christianity they professed would have taught them.

In her lectures to the nuns she seldom touched upon points of faith, but explained and enforced the moral duties, particularly such as were most practicable in the society to which she belonged; such as tended to soften and harmonize the affections, to impart that repose of mind which persuades to the practice of sisterly kindness, universal charity, and the most pure and elevated devotion. When she spoke of religion, it appeared so interesting, so beautiful, that her attentive auditors revered and loved it as a friend, a refiner of the heart; a sublime consoler; and experienced somewhat of the meek and holy ardour which may belong to angelic natures,

The society appeared like a large family, of which the lady abbess was the mother, rather than an assemblage of strangers; and particularly when, gathered round her, they listened to the evening sermon, which she delivered with such affectionate interest, such persuasive eloquence, and sometimes with such pathetic energy as few hearts could resist.

She encouraged in her convent every innocent and liberal pursuit which might sweeten the austerities of confinement, and which were generally rendered instrumental to charity. The Daughters of Pity particularly excelled in music; not in those difficulties of the art which display florid graces and intricate execution, but in such eloquence of sound as steals upon the heart and awakens its sweetest and best affections. It was probably the well-regulated sensibility of their own minds that enabled these sisters to diffuse through their strains a character of such finely tempered taste as drew crowds of visitors, on every festival, to the church of the Santa della Pietà.

The local circumstances of this convent were scarcely less agreeable than the harmony of its society was interesting. These extensive domains included olive-grounds, vineyards, and some corn-land; a considerable tract was devoted to the pleasures of the garden, whose groves supplied walnuts, almonds, oranges, and citrons, in abundance, and almost every kind of fruit and flower which this luxurious climate nurtured. These gardens hung upon the slope of a hill about a mile within the shore, and afforded extensive views of the country round Naples, and of the gulf. But from the terraces, which extended along a semicircular range of rocks that rose over the convent and formed a part of the domain, the prospects were infinitely finer. They extended on the south to the Isle of Capri, where the gulf expands into the sea; in the west appeared the island of Ischia, distinguished by the white pinnacles of the lofty mountain Epomeo; and near it Profida, with its many-coloured cliffs, rose out of the waves. Overlooking several points towards Puzzuoli, the eye caught, beyond other promontories, and others further still to the north, a glimpse of the sea, that bathes the now desolate shores of Baiæ; with Capua, and all the towns and villas that speckle the garden-plains between Caserta and Naples.

In the nearer scene were the rocky heights of Pausilippo, and Naples itself, with all its crowded suburbs ascending among the hills, and mingling with vineyards and overtopping cypress; the castle of San Elmo, conspicuous on its rock, overhanging the magnificent monastery of the Chartreux; while in the scene below appeared the Castel Nuovo, with its clustered towers, the long-extended Corso, the mole, with its tall pharos, and the harbour, gay with painted shipping, busy with vessels of all nations continually arriving and departing, and full to the brim with the blue waters of the bay. Beyond the hills of Naples, the whole horizon to the north and east was bounded by the mountains of the Apennine, an amphitheatre proportioned to the grandeur of the plain, which the gulf spread out below.

These terraces, shaded with acacias and plane-trees, were the favourite haunt of Ellena. Between the opening branches, she looked down upon Villa Altieri, which brought to her remembrance the affectionate Bianchi, with all the sportive years of her childhood, and where some of her happiest hours had been passed in the society of Vivaldi. Along the windings of the coast, too, she could distinguish many places rendered sacred by affection, to which she had made excursions with her lamented relative and Vivaldi; and, though sadness mingled with the recollections a view of them restored, they were precious to her heart. Here, alone and unobserved, she frequently yielded to the melancholy which she endeavoured to suppress in society; and, at other times, tried to deceive, with books and the pencil, the lingering moments of uncertainty concerning the state of Vivaldi; for day after day still elapsed without bringing any intelligence from Schedoni. Whenever the late scenes connected with the discovery of her family recurred to Ellena, she was struck with almost as much amazement as if she was gazing upon a vision, instead of recalling realities. Contrasted with the sober truth of her present life, the past appeared like romance; and there were moments when she shrunk from the relationship of Schedoni with unconquerable affright. The first emotions his appearance had excited were so opposite to those of filial tenderness that she perceived it was now nearly impossible to love and revere him as her father; and she endeavoured, by dwelling upon all the obligations which she believed he had lately conferred upon her, to repay him in gratitude what was withheld in affection.

In such melancholy considerations she often lingered under the shade of the acacias till the sun had sunk behind the far-distant promontory of Miseno, and the last bell of vespers summoned her to the convent below.

Among the nuns Ellena had many favourites, but not one that she admired and loved equally with Olivia of San Stefano, the remembrance of whom was always accompanied with a fear lest she should have suffered from her generous compassion, and a wish that she had taken up her abode with the happy society of the Daughters of Pity instead of being subjected to the tyranny of the abbess of San Stefano. To Ellena, the magnificent scenes of La Pieta seemed to open a secure and, perhaps, a last asylum; for, in her present circumstances, she could not avoid perceiving how menacing and various were the objections to her marriage with Vivaldi, even should Schedoni prove propitious to it. The character of the Marchesa di Vivaldi, such as it stood unfolded by the late occurrences, struck her with dismay; for her designs appeared sufficiently atrocious, whether they had extended to the utmost limit of Ellena's suspicions or had stopped where the affected charity of Schedoni had pointed out. In either case, the pertinacity of her aversion and the vindictive violence of her nature were obvious.

In this view of her character, however, it was not the inconvenience threatened to those who might become connected with her that principally affected Ellena, but the circumstance of such a woman being the mother of Vivaldi; and, to alleviate so afflicting a consideration, she endeavoured to believe all the palliating suggestions of Schedoni respecting the Marchesa's late intentions. But, if Ellena was grieved on discovering crime in the character of Vivaldi's parent, what would have been her suffering had she suspected the nature of Schedoni?—what if she had been told that he was the adviser of the Marchesa's plans?—if she had known that he had been the partner of her intentional guilt? From such suffering she was yet spared, as well as from that which a knowledge of Vivaldi's present situation, and of the result of Schedoni's efforts to procure a release from the perils among which he had precipitated him, would have inflicted. Had she known this, it is possible that in the first despondency of her mind she would have relinquished what is called the world, and sought a lasting asylum with the society of the holy sisters. Even as it was, she sometimes endeavoured to look with resignation upon the events which might render such a step desirable; but it was an effort that seldom soothed her, even with a temporary self-delusion. Should the veil, however, prove her final refuge, it would be by her own choice; for the lady abbess of La Pieta employed no art to win a recluse, nor suffered the nuns to seduce votaries to the order.

CHAPTER XXVI.

WHILE the late events had been passing in the Garganus and at Naples, Vivaldi and his servant Paulo remained imprisoned in distinct chambers of the Inquisition. They were again separately interrogated. From the servant no information could be obtained; he asserted only his master's innocence, without once remembering his own; clamoured, with more justness than prudence, against the persons who had occasioned his arrest; and, seriously endeavouring to convince the inquisitors that he himself had *no other motive* in having demanded to be brought to these prisons than that he might comfort his master, he gravely remonstrated on the injustice of separating them, adding that he was sure when they knew the rights of the matter, they would order him to be carried to the prison of Signor Vivaldi.

"I do assure your Serenissimo Illustrissimo," continued Paulo, addressing the chief inquisitor with profound gravity, "that this is the last place I should have thought of coming to on any other account; and if you will only condescend to ask your officials who took my master up, they will tell you *as good*. They knew well enough all along what I came here for; and if they had known it would be all in vain, it would have been but civil of them to have told me as much, and not have brought me; for this is the last place in the world I would have come to, otherwise, of my own accord."

Paulo was permitted to harangue in his own way, because his examiners hoped that his prolixity would be a means of betraying circumstances connected with his master. By this view, however, they were misled, for Paulo, with all his simplicity of heart, was both vigilant and shrewd in Vivaldi's interest. But, when he perceived them really convinced that his sole motive for visiting the Inquisition was that he might console his master, yet still persisting in the resolution of separately confining him, his indignation knew no bounds. He despised alike their reprehension, their thundering menaces, and their more artful exhibitions; told them of all they had to expect both here and hereafter, for their cruelty to his dear master, and said they might do what they would with him; he defied them to make him more miserable than he was.

It was not without difficulty that he was removed from the chamber; where he left his examiners in a state of astonishment at his rashness, and indignation of his honesty, such as they had, probably, never experienced before.

When Vivaldi was again called up to the table of the Holy Office, he underwent a longer examination than on a former occasion. Several inquisitors attended, and every art was employed to induce him to confess crimes of which he was suspected, and to draw from him a discovery of others which might have eluded even suspicion. Still the examiners cautiously avoided informing him of the subject of the accusation on which he had been arrested; and it was, therefore, only on the former assurances of the Benedictine and the officials in the chapel of San Sebastian, that Vivaldi understood he was accused of having carried off a nun. His answers on the present occasion were concise and firm, and his whole deportment undaunted. He felt less apprehension for himself than indignation of the general injustice and cruelty which the tribunal was permitted to exercise upon others; and this virtuous indignation gave a loftiness, a calm heroic grandeur to his mind, which never for a moment forsook him, except when he conjectured what might be the sufferings of Ellena. Then his fortitude and magnanimity failed, and his tortured spirit rose almost to frenzy.

On this, his second examination, he was urged by the same dark questions, and replied to them with the same open sincerity, as during the first. Yet the simplicity and energy of truth failed to impress conviction on minds which, no longer possessing the virtue themselves, were not competent to understand the symptoms of it in others. Vivaldi was again threatened with the torture, and again dismissed to his prison.

On the way to this dreadful abode, a person passed him in one of the avenues, of whose air and figure he thought he had some recollection; and as the stranger stalked away, he suddenly knew him to be the prophetic monk who had haunted the ruins of Paluzzi. In the first moment of surprise, Vivaldi lost his presence of mind so far that he made no attempt to interrupt him. In the next instant, however, he paused and looked back, with an intention of speaking; but this mysterious person was already at the extremity of the avenue. Vivaldi, however, called and besought him to stop; when, without either speaking or turning his head, he immediately disappeared beyond a door that opened at his approach. Vivaldi, on attempting to take the way of the monk, was withheld by his guards; and when he inquired who was the stranger he had seen, the officials asked, in their turn, what stranger he alluded to.

" He who has just passed us," replied Vivaldi.

The officials seemed surprised. " Your spirits are disordered, signor," observed one of them, " I saw no person pass ! "

" He passed so closely," said Vivaldi, " that it was hardly possible you could avoid seeing him ! "

" I did not even hear a footstep ! " added the man.

" I do not recollect that I did," answered Vivaldi, " but I saw his figure as plainly as I now see yours; his black garments almost touched me ! Was he an inquisitor ? "

The official appeared astonished; and, whether his incredulity was real, or affected

for the purpose of concealing his knowledge of the person alluded to, his embarrassment and awe seemed natural. Vivaldi observed, with almost equal curiosity and surprise, the fear which his face expressed; but perceived also that it would avail nothing to repeat his questions.

As they proceeded along the avenue, a kind of half-stifled groan was sometimes audible from a distance. " Whence come those sounds ? " said Vivaldi ; " they strike to my heart ! "

" They should do so," replied the guard.

" Whence come they ? " repeated Vivaldi, more impatiently, and shuddering.

" From the place of torture," said the official.

" Oh, God ! oh, God ! " exclaimed Vivaldi, with a deep groan.

He passed with hasty steps the door of that terrible chamber, and the guard did not attempt to stop him. The officials had brought him, in obedience to the customary orders they had received, within hearing of those doleful sounds, for the purpose of impressing upon his mind the horrors of the punishment with which he was threatened, and of inducing him to confess without incurring them.

On this same evening Vivaldi was visited in his prison by a man whom he had never consciously seen before. He appeared to be between forty and fifty ; was of a grave and observant physiognomy, and of manners which, though somewhat austere, were not alarming. The account he gave of himself and of his motive for this visit was curious. He said that he also was a prisoner in the Inquisition, but, as the ground of accusation against him was light, he had been favoured so far as to be allowed some degree of liberty within certain bounds; that having heard of Vivaldi's situation, he had asked and obtained leave to converse with him, which he had done in compassion, and with a desire of assuaging his sufferings, so far as an expression of sympathy and commiseration might relieve them.

While he spoke, Vivaldi regarded him with deep attention, and the improbability that these pretensions should be true did not escape him ; but the suspicion which they occasioned he prudently concealed. The stranger conversed on various subjects. Vivaldi's answers were cautious and concise ; but not even long pauses of silence wearied the compassionate patience of his visitor. Among other topics he at length introduced that of religion.

" I have myself been accused of heresy," said he, " and know how to pity others in the same situation."

" It is of heresy, then, that I am accused ! " observed Vivaldi, " of heresy ! "

" It availed me nothing that I asserted my

innocence," continued the stranger, without noticing Vivaldi's exclamation, "I was condemned to the torture. My sufferings were too terrible to be endured! I confessed my offence ——"

"Pardon me," interrupted Vivaldi, "but allow me to remark that, since your sufferings were so severe—yours, against whom the ground of accusation was light, what may be the punishment of those whose offences are more serious?"

The stranger was somewhat embarrassed. "My offence was slight," he continued, without giving a full answer.

"Is it possible," said Vivaldi, again interrupting him, "that heresy can be considered as a slight offence before the tribunal of the Inquisition?"

"It was only a slight degree of heresy," replied the visitor, reddening with displeasure, "of which I was suspected, and ——"

"Does, then, the Inquisition allow of degrees in heresy?" said Vivaldi.

"I confessed my offence," added the stranger, with a louder emphasis, "and the consequence of this confession was a remission of punishment. After a trifling penance I shall be dismissed, and probably in a few days leave the prison. Before I left it I was desirous of administering some degree of consolation to a fellow-sufferer; if you have any friends whom you wish to inform of your situation, do not fear to confide their names and your message to me."

The latter part of the speech was delivered in a low voice, as if the stranger feared to be overheard. Vivaldi remained silent, while he examined with closer attention the countenance of his visitor. It was of the utmost importance to him that his family should be made acquainted with his situation; yet he knew not exactly how to interpret, or to confide in, this offer. Vivaldi had heard that informers sometimes visited the prisoners, and, under the affectation of kindness and sympathy, drew from them a confession of opinions, which were afterwards urged against them; and obtained discoveries relative to their connections and friends, who were, by these insidious means, frequently involved in their destruction. Vivaldi, conscious of his own innocence, had, on the first examination, acquainted the inquisitor with the names and residence of his family; he had, therefore, nothing new to apprehend from revealing them to this stranger; but he perceived that if it should be known he had attempted to convey a message, however concise and harmless, the discovery would irritate the jealous inquisitors against him, and might be urged as a new presumption of his guilt. These considerations, together with the distrust which the inconsistency of his visitor's assertions and the occasional embarrassment of his manner had excited, determined Vi-

valdi to resist the temptation now offered to him; and the stranger, having received his thanks, reluctantly withdrew, observing, however, that should any unforeseen circumstance detain him in the Inquisition longer than he had reason to expect, he should beg leave to pay him another visit. In reply to this, Vivaldi only bowed; but he remarked that the stranger's countenance altered, and that some dark brooding appeared to cloud his mind as he quitted the chamber.

Several days elapsed, during which Vivaldi heard no more of his new acquaintance. He was then summoned to another examination, from which he was dismissed as before; and some weeks of solitude and of heavy uncertainty succeeded, after which he was a fourth time called up to the table of the Holy Office. It was then surrounded by inquisitors, and a more than usual solemnity appeared in the proceedings.

As proofs of Vivaldi's innocence had not been obtained, the suspicions of his examiners, of course, were not removed; and as he persisted in denying the truth of the charge which he understood would be exhibited against him, and refused to make any confession of crimes, it was ordered that he should, within three hours, be put to the *question*. Till then Vivaldi was once more dismissed to his prison-chamber. His resolution remained unshaken, but he could not look unmoved upon the horrors which might be preparing for him. The interval of expectation between the sentence and the accomplishment of this preliminary punishment was indeed dreadful. The seeming ignominy of his situation, and his ignorance as to the degree of torture to be applied, overcame the calmness he had before exhibited, and as he paced his cell, cold damps, which hung upon his forehead, betrayed the agony of his mind. It was not long, however, that he suffered from a sense of ignominy; his better judgment showed him that innocence cannot suffer disgrace from any situation or circumstance; and he once more resumed the courage and the firmness which belong to virtue.

It was about midnight that Vivaldi heard footsteps approaching, and a murmur of voices at the door of his cell. He understood by these that persons were coming to summon him to the torture. The door was unbarred, and two men, habited in black, appeared at it. Without speaking they advanced, and, throwing over him a singular kind of mantle, led him from the chamber.

Along the galleries and other avenues through which they passed, not any person was seen, and, by the profound stillness that reigned, it seemed as if death had already anticipated his work in these regions of horror, and had condemned alike the tortured and the torturer.

They descended to the large hall, where

Vivaldi had waited on the night of his entrance, and thence through an avenue and down a long flight of steps that led to subterranean chambers. His conductors did not utter a syllable during the whole progress; Vivaldi knew too well that questions would only subject him to greater severity, and he asked none.

The doors through which they passed regularly opened at the touch of an iron rod, carried by one of the officials, and without the appearance of any person. The other man bore a torch, and the passages were so dimly lighted that the way could scarcely have been found without one. They crossed what seemed to be a burial vault, but the extent and obscurity of the place did not allow it to be ascertained; and, having reached an iron door, they stopped. One of the officials struck upon it three times with the rod, but it did not open as the others had done. While they waited, Vivaldi thought he heard, from within, low intermitting sounds, as of persons in their last extremity, but, though within, they appeared to come from a distance. His whole heart was chilled, not with fear, for at that moment he did not remember himself, but with horror.

Having waited a considerable time, during which the official did not repeat the signal, the door was partly opened by a figure whom Vivaldi could not distinguish in the gloom beyond, and with whom one of his conductors communicated by signs; after which the door was closed.

Several minutes had elapsed when tones of deep voices aroused the attention of Vivaldi. They were loud and hoarse, and spoke in a language unknown to him. At the sounds, the official immediately extinguished his torch. The voices drew nearer, and, the door again unfolding, two figures stood before Vivaldi, which, shown by a glimmering light within, struck him with astonishment and dismay. They were clothed, like his conductors, in black, but in a different fashion, for their habits were made close to the shape. Their faces were entirely concealed beneath a very peculiar kind of cowl which descended from the head to the feet; and their eyes only were visible through small openings contrived for the sight. It occurred to Vivaldi that these men were torturers; their appearance was worthy of demons. Probably they were thus habited that the persons whom they afflicted might not know them; or, perhaps, it was only for the purpose of striking terror upon the minds of the accused, and thus compelling them to confess without further difficulty. Whatever motive might have occasioned their horrific appearance, and whatever was their office, Vivaldi was delivered into their hands, and in the same moment heard the iron door shut, which enclosed him with them in a narrow passage,

gloomily lighted by a lamp suspended from the arched roof. They walked in silence on each side of their prisoner, and came to a second door which admitted them instantly into another passage. A third door, at a short distance, admitted them to a third avenue, at the end of which one of his mysterious guides struck upon a gate, and they stopped. The uncertain sounds that Vivaldi had fancied he heard were now more audible, and he distinguished, with inexpressible horror, that they were uttered by persons suffering.

The gate was, at length, opened by a figure habited like his conductors, and two other doors of iron, placed very near each other, being also unlocked, Vivaldi found himself in a spacious chamber, the walls of which were hung with black, duskily lighted by lamps, that gleamed in the lofty vault. Immediately on his entrance, a strange sound ran along the walls, and echoed among other vaults, that appeared, by the progress of the sound, to extend far beyond this.

It was not immediately that Vivaldi could sufficiently recollect himself to observe any object before him; and even when he did so, the gloom of the place prevented his ascertaining many appearances. Shadowy countenances and uncertain forms seemed to flit through the dusk, and many instruments, the application of which he did not comprehend, struck him with horrible suspicions. Still he heard, at intervals, half-suppressed groans, and was looking round to discover the wretched people from whom they were extorted, when a voice from a remote part of the chamber called on him to advance.

The distance, and the obscurity of the spot whence the voice issued, had prevented Vivaldi from noticing any person there, and he was now slowly obeying; when, on a second summons, his conductors seized his arms, and hurried him forward.

In a remote part of this extensive chamber he perceived three persons seated under a black canopy, on chairs raised several steps from the floor, and who appeared to preside there in the office of either judges or examiners, or directors of the punishments. Below, at a table, sat a secretary, over whom was suspended the only lamp, that could enable him to commit to paper what should occur during the examination. Vivaldi now understood that the three persons who composed the tribunal were the vicar-general, or grand inquisitor, the advocate of the exchequer, and an ordinary inquisitor, who was seated between the other two, and who appeared more eagerly to engage in the duties of his cruel office. A portentous obscurity enveloped alike their persons and their proceedings.

At some distance from the tribunal stood a large iron frame, which Vivaldi conjectured to be the rack; and near it another, resembling in shape a coffin; but happily he could not distinguish, through the remote obscurity, any person undergoing actual suffering. In the vaults beyond, however, the diabolical decrees of the inquisitors seemed to be fulfilling; for, whenever a distant door opened for a moment, sounds of lamentation issued forth; and men, whom he judged to be familiars, habited like those who stood beside him, were seen passing to and fro within.

Vivaldi almost believed himself in the infernal regions; the dismal aspect of this place, the horrible preparation for punishment, and, above all, the disposition and appearance of the persons that were ready to inflict it, confirmed the resemblance. That any human being should willingly afflict a fellow-being who had never injured or even offended him; that, unswayed by passion, he should deliberately become the means of torturing him, appeared to Vivaldi nearly incredible. But, when he looked at the three persons who composed the tribunal, and considered that they had not only voluntarily undertaken the cruel office they fulfilled, but had probably long regarded it as the summit of their ambition, his astonishment and indignation were unbounded.

The grand inquisitor, having again called on Vivaldi by name, admonished him to confess the truth, and avoid the suffering that awaited him.

As Vivaldi had on former examinations spoken the truth, which was not believed, he had no chance of escaping present suffering but by asserting falsehood: in doing so, to avoid such monstrous injustice and cruelty, he might, perhaps, have been justified, had it been certain that such assertion could affect himself alone; but since he knew that the consequence must extend to others, and, above all, believed that Ellena di Rosalba must be involved in it, he did not hesitate for an instant to dare whatever torture his firmness might provoke. But, even if morality could have forgiven falsehood in such extraordinary circumstances as these, policy, after all, would have forbidden it; since a discovery of the artifice would probably have led to the final destruction of the accused person.

Of Ellena's situation he would now have asked, however desperate the question; would again have asserted her innocence, and supplicated for compassion, even to inquisitors, had he not perceived that, in doing so, he should only furnish them with a more exquisite means of torturing him than any other they could apply; for if, when all the terrors of his soul concerning her were understood, they should threaten to increase her sufferings, as the punishment of what was termed his obstinacy, they would, indeed, become the masters of his integrity, as well as of his person.

The tribunal again, and repeatedly, urged Vivaldi to confess himself guilty; and the inquisitor, at length concluded with saying, that the judges were innocent of whatever consequence might ensue from his obstinacy; so that, if he expired beneath his sufferings, himself only, not they, would have occasioned his death.

"I am innocent of the charges which I understand are urged against me," said Vivaldi, with solemnity; "I repeat that I am innocent. If, to escape the horrors of these moments, I could be weak enough to declare myself guilty, not all your racks could alter truth, and make me so, except in that assertion. The consequence of your tortures therefore, be upon your own heads!"

While Vivaldi spoke the vicar-general listened with attention, and when he had ceased to speak, appeared to meditate; but the inquisitor was irritated by the boldness of his speech, instead of being convinced by the justness of his representation; and made a signal for the officers to prepare for the *question*. While they were obeying, Vivaldi observed, notwithstanding the agitation he suffered, a person cross the chamber, whom he immediately knew to be the same that had passed him in the avenue of the Inquisition on a former night, and whom he had then fancied to be the mysterious stranger of Paluzzi. Vivaldi now fixed his eyes upon him, but his own peculiar situation prevented his feeling the interest he had formerly suffered concerning him.

The figure, air, and stalk, of this person were so striking, and so strongly resembled those of the monk of Paluzzi, that Vivaldi had no longer a doubt as to their identity. He pointed him out to one of the officials, and inquired who he was. While he spoke, the stranger was passing forward, and before any reply was given, a door leading to the further vaults shut him from view. Vivaldi, however, repeated the inquiry, which the official appeared unable to answer, and a reproof from the tribunal reminded him that he must not ask questions there. Vivaldi observed that it was the grand inquisitor who spoke, and that the manner of the official immediately changed.

The familiars, who were the same that had conducted Vivaldi into the chamber, having made ready the instrument of torture, approached him, and, after taking off his cloak and vest, bound him with strong cords. They threw over his head the customary black garment, which entirely enveloped his figure, and prevented his observing what was further preparing. In this state of expectation he was again interrogated by the inquisitor.

"Were you ever in the church of the Spirito Santo, at Naples?" said he.

"Yes," replied Vivaldi.

"Did you ever express there a contempt of the Catholic faith?"

"Never," said Vivaldi.

"Neither by word nor action?" continued the inquisitor.

"Never, by either!"

"Recollect yourself," added the inquisitor. "Did you never insult there a minister of our most holy Church?"

Vivaldi was silent: he began to perceive the real nature of the charge which was to be urged against him, and that it was too plausible to permit his escape from the punishment which is adjudged for heresy. Questions so direct and minute had never yet been put to him: they had been reserved for a moment when it was believed he could not evade them; and the real charge had been concealed from him that he might not be prepared to elude it.

"Answer!" repeated the inquisitor. "Did you ever insult a minister of the Catholic faith in the church of the Spirito Santo, at Naples?"

"Did you not insult him while he was performing an act of holy penance?" said another voice.

Vivaldi started, for he instantly recollected the well-known tones of the monk of Paluzzi.

"Who asks the question?" demanded Vivaldi.

"It is you who are to answer here," resumed the inquisiter. "Answer to what I have required."

"I have offended a minister of the Church," replied Vivaldi, "but never could intentionally insult our holy religion. You are not acquainted, fathers, with the injuries that provoked——"

"Enough!" interrupted the inquisitor; "speak to the question. Did you not, by insult and menace, force a pious brother to leave unperformed the act of penance in which he had engaged himself? Did you not compel him to quit the church, and fly for refuge to his convent?"

"No," replied Vivaldi. "'Tis true, he left the church, and that in consequence of my conduct there; but the consequence was not necessary; if he had only replied to my inquiry, or promised to restore her of whom he had treacherously robbed me, he might have remained quietly in the church till this moment, had that depended upon my forbearance."

"What!" said the vicar-general, "would you have compelled him to speak when he was engaged in silent penance? You confess that you occasioned him to leave the church. That is enough."

"Where did you first see Ellena di Rosalba?" said the voice which had spoken once before.

"I demand again, who gives the question?" answered Vivaldi.

"Recollect yourself," said the inquisitor; "a criminal may not make a demand."

"I do not perceive the connection between your admonition and your assertion," observed Vivaldi.

"You appear to be rather too much at your ease," said the inquisitor. "Answer to the question which was last put to you, or the familiars shall do their duty."

"Let the same person ask it," replied Vivaldi.

The question was repeated in the former voice.

"In the church of San Lorenzo, at Naples," rejoined Vivaldi, with a heavy sigh, "I first beheld Ellena di Rosalba."

"Was she then professed!" asked the vicar-general.

"She never accepted the veil," replied Vivaldi, "nor ever intended to do so."

"Where did she reside at that period?"

"She lived with a relative at Villa Altieri, and would yet reside there, had not the machinations of a monk occasioned her to be torn from her home, and confined in a convent, from which I had just assisted to release her, when she was again seized, and upon a charge most false and cruel. Oh, reverend fathers! I conjure, I supplicate——" Vivaldi restrained himself, for he was betraying to inquisitors all the feelings of his heart.

"The name of the monk?" said the stranger earnestly.

"If I mistake not," replied Vivaldi, "you are already acquainted with it. The monk is called Father Schedoni. He is of the Dominican convent of the Spirito Santo, in Naples: the same who accuses me of having insulted him in the church of that name."

"How did you know him for your accuser?" asked the same voice.

"Because he is my only enemy," replied Vivaldi.

"Your enemy!" observed the inquisitor; "a former deposition says you were unconscious of having one! You are inconsistent in your replies.

"You were warned not to visit Villa Altieri," said the unknown person. "Why did you not profit by the warning?"

"I was warned by yourself," answered Vivaldi. "Now I know you well?"

"By me!" said the stranger, in a solemn tone.

"By you!" repeated Vivaldi: "you, who also foretold the death of Signora Bianchi; and you are that enemy—that father Schedoni by whom I am accused."

"Whence come these questions?" demanded the vicar-general. "Who has been authorised thus to interrogate the prisoner?"

No reply was made. A busy hum of voices from the tribunal succeeded the silence. At length, the murmuring subsided, and the monk's voice was heard again.

"I will declare thus much," it said, addressing Vivaldi; "I am not father Schedoni."

The peculiar tone and emphasis with which this was delivered, more than the assertion itself, persuaded Vivaldi that the stranger spoke truth ; and though he still recognised the voice of the monk of Paluzzi, he did not know it to be that of Schedoni. Vivaldi was astonished ! He would have torn the veil from his eyes, and once more viewed this mysterious stranger, had his hands been at liberty. As it was, he could only conjure him to reveal his name and the motives for his former conduct.

"Who is come amongst us?" said the vicar-general, in the voice of a person who means to inspire others with the awe he himself suffers.

"Who is come amongst us?" he repeated, in a louder tone. Still no answer was returned ; but again a confused murmur sounded from the tribunal, and a general consternation seemed to prevail. No person spoke with sufficient pre-eminence to be understood by Vivaldi ; something extraordinary appeared to be passing, and he waited the issue with all the patience he could command. Soon after he heard doors opened, and the noise of people quitting the chamber. A deep silence followed ; but he was certain that the familiars were still beside him, waiting to begin their work of torture.

After a considerable time had elapsed, Vivaldi heard footsteps advancing, and a person give orders for his release, that he might be carried back to his cell.

When the veil was removed from his eyes, he perceived that the tribunal was dissolved, and that the stranger was gone. The lamps were dying away, and the chamber appeared more gloomily terrific than before.

The familiars conducted him to the spot at which they had received him ; whence the officers who had led him thither guarded him to his prison. There, stretched upon his bed of straw, in solitude and in darkness, he had leisure enough to reflect upon what had passed, and to recollect with minute exactness every former circumstance connected with the stranger. By comparing those with the present, he endeavoured to draw a more certain conclusion as to the identity of this person, and his motives for the very extraordinary conduct he had pursued. The first appearance of this stranger among the ruins of Paluzzi, when he had said that Vivaldi's steps were watched, and had cautioned him against returning to Villa Altieri, was recalled to his mind. Vivaldi reconsidered, also, his second appearance on the same spot, and his second warning ; the circumstances which had attended his own adventures within the fortress, the monk's prediction of Bianchi's death, and his evil tidings respecting Ellena at the very hour when she had been seized and carried from her home. The longer he considered these several instances, as they

were now connected in his mind, with the certainty of Schedoni's evil disposition towards him, the more he was inclined to believe, notwithstanding the voice of seeming truth which had just affirmed the contrary, that the unknown person was Schedoni himself, and that he had been employed by the Marchesa to prevent Vivaldi's visits to Villa Altieri. Being thus an agent in the events of which he had warned Vivaldi, he was too well enabled to predict them. Vivaldi paused upon the remembrance of Signora Bianchi's death ; he considered the extraordinary and dubious circumstances that had attended it, and shuddered as a new conjecture crossed his mind. The thought was too dreadful to be permitted, and he dismissed it instantly.

Of the conversation, however, which he had afterwards held with the confessor in the Marchesa's cabinet he recollected many particulars that served to renew his doubts as to the identity of the stranger ; the behaviour of Schedoni when he was obliquely challenged for the monk of Paluzzi still appeared that of a man unconscious of disguise ; and, above all, Vivaldi was struck with the seeming candour of his having pointed out a circumstance which removed the probability that the stranger was a brother of the Santa del Pianto.

Some particulars, also, of the stranger's conduct did not agree with what might have been expected from Schedoni, even though the confessor had really been Vivaldi's enemy ; a circumstance which the latter was no longer permitted to doubt. Nor did those particular circumstances accord, as he was inclined to believe, with the manner of a being of this world ; and, when Vivaldi considered the suddenness and mystery with which the stranger had always appeared and retired, he felt disposed to adopt again one of his earliest conjectures, which undoubtedly the horrors of his present abode disposed his imagination to admit, as those of his former situation in the vaults of Paluzzi, together with a youthful glow of curiosity concerning the marvellous, had before contributed to impress upon his mind.

He concluded his present reflections as he had begun them—in doubt and perplexity ; but at length found a respite from thought and from suffering in sleep.

Midnight had been passed in the vaults of the Inquisition ; but it was probably not yet two o'clock when he was imperfectly awakened by a sound, which he fancied proceeded from within his chamber. He raised himself to discover what had occasioned the noise ; it was, however, impossible to discern any object, for all was dark, but he listened for a return of the sound. The wind only was heard moaning among the inner buildings of the prison, and Vivaldi concluded that his dream had mocked him with a mimic voice.

Satisfied with this conclusion, he again laid his head on his pillow of straw, and soon sank into a slumber. The subject of his waking thoughts still haunted his imagination, and the stranger, whose voice he had this night recognised as that of the prophet of Paluzzi, appeared before him. Vivaldi, on perceiving the figure of this unknown, felt, perhaps, nearly the same degree of awe, curiosity, and impatience that he would have suffered had he beheld the substance of this shadow. The monk, whose face was still shrouded, he thought advanced, till, having come within a few paces of Vivaldi, he paused, and, lifting the awful cowl that had hitherto concealed him, disclosed, not the countenance of Schedoni, but one which Vivaldi did not recollect ever having seen before! It was not less interesting to curiosity than striking to the feelings. Vivaldi, at the first glance, shrunk back—something of that strange and indescribable air which we attach to the idea of a supernatural being prevailed over the features, and the intense and fiery eyes resembled those of an evil spirit rather than of a human character. He drew a poniard from beneath a fold of his garment, and, as he displayed it, pointed with a stern frown to the spots which discoloured the blade; Vivaldi perceived they were of blood! He turned away his eyes in horror; and, when he again looked round in his dream, the figure was gone.

A groan awakened him; but what were his feelings when, on looking up, he perceived the same figure standing before him! It was not, however, immediately that he could convince himself the appearance was more than the phantom of his dream strongly impressed upon an alarmed fancy. The voice of the monk, for his face was as usual concealed, recalled Vivaldi from his error; but his emotion cannot easily be conceived, when the stranger, slowly lifting that mysterious cowl, discovered to him the same awful countenance which had characterised the vision in his slumber. Unable to inquire the occasion of this appearance, Vivaldi gazed in astonishment and terror, and did not immediately observe that, instead of a dagger, the monk held a lamp, which gleamed over every deep furrow of his features, yet left their shadowy markings to hint the passions and the history of an extraordinary life.

"You are spared for this night," said the stranger, "but for to-morrow"——he paused.

"In the name of all that is most sacred," said Vivaldi, endeavouring to re-collect his thoughts, "who are you, and what is your errand?"

"Ask no questions," replied the monk, solemnly; "but answer me."

Vivaldi was struck by the tone with which he said this, and dared not to urge the inquiry at the present moment.

"How long have you known father Schedoni?" continued the stranger; "Where did you first meet?"

"I have known him about two years, as my mother's confessor," replied Vivaldi. "I first saw him in a corridor of the Vivaldi palace; it was evening, and he was returning from the Marchesa's closet."

"Are you certain as to this? said the monk, with peculiar emphasis. "It is of consequence that you should be so."

"I am certain," repeated Vivaldi.

"It is strange," observed the monk, after a pause, "that a circumstance which must have appeared trivial to you at the moment, should have left so strong a mark on your memory! In two years we have time to forget many things!" He sighed as he spoke.

"I remember the circumstance," said Vivaldi, "because I was struck with his appearance; the evening was far advanced—it was dusk, and he came upon me suddenly. His voice startled me; as he passed he said to himself—"It is for vespers." At the same time I heard the bell of the Spirito Santo."

"Do you know who he is?" resumed the stranger solemnly.

"I know only what he appears to be," replied Vivaldi.

"Did you never hear any report of his past life?"

"Never," answered Vivaldi.

"Never anything extraordinary concerning him?" added the monk.

Vivaldi paused a moment; for he now recollected the obscure and imperfect story which Paulo had related while they were confined in the dungeon of Paluzzi, respecting a confession made in the church of the Black Penitents; but he could not presume to affirm that it concerned Schedoni. He remembered also the monk's garments, stained with blood, which he had discovered in the vaults of that fort. The conduct of the mysterious being, who now stood before him, with many other particulars of his own adventures there, passed like a vision over his memory. His mind resembled the glass of a magician, on which the apparitions of long-buried events arise, and as they fleet away, point portentously to shapes half veiled in the duskiness of futurity. An unusual dread seized upon him; and a superstition, such as he had never before admitted in an equal degree, usurped his judgment. He looked up to the shadowy countenance of the stranger; and almost believed he beheld an inhabitant of the world of spirits.

The monk spoke again, repeating in a severer tone, "Did you never hear anything extraordinary concerning father Schedoni?"

"Is it reasonable," said Vivaldi, re-collecting his courage, "that I should answer the questions, the minute questions, of a person who refuses to tell me even his name?"

"My name is passed away—it is no more remembered," replied the stranger, turning from Vivaldi. "I leave you to your fate."

"What fate?" asked Vivaldi, "and what is the purpose of this visit? I conjure you, in the tremendous name of the Inquisition, to say!"

"You will know full soon; have mercy on yourself!"

"What fate?" repeated Vivaldi.

"Urge me no further," said the stranger; "but answer to what I shall demand. Schedoni——"

"I have told all that I certainly know concerning him," interrupted Vivaldi; "the rest is only conjecture."

"What is that conjecture? Does it relate to a confession made in the church of the Black Penitents of the Santa Maria del Pianto?"

"It does!" replied Vivaldi, with surprise.

"What was that confession?"

"I know not," answered Vivaldi.

"Declare the truth," said the stranger, sternly.

"A confession," replied Vivaldi, "is sacred, and for ever buried in the bosom of the priest to whom it is made. How, then, is it to be supposed that I can be acquainted with the subject of this?"

"Did you never hear that father Schedoni had been guilty of great crimes, which he endeavours to erase from his conscience by the severity of penance?"

"Never!" said Vivaldi.

"Did you never hear that he had a wife—a brother?"

"Never!"

"Nor the means he used—no hint of—murder, of——"

The stranger paused, as if he wished Vivaldi to fill up his meaning. Vivaldi was silent and aghast.

"You know nothing, then, of Schedoni," resumed the monk, after a deep pause—"nothing of his past life?"

"Nothing, except what I have mentioned," replied Vivaldi.

"Then listen to what I shall unfold," continued the monk, with solemnity. "To-morrow night you will be again carried to the place of torture; you will be taken to a chamber beyond that in which you were this night. You will there witness many extraordinary things, of which you have not now any suspicion. Be not dismayed; I shall be there, though, perhaps, not visible."

"Not visible!" exclaimed Vivaldi.

"Interrupt me not, but listen. When you are asked of father Schedoni, say that he has lived for fifteen years in the disguise of a monk, a member of the Dominicans of the Spirito Santo, at Naples. When you are asked who he is, reply, 'Ferando Count di Bruno.' You will be asked the motive for such disguise. In reply to this, refer them to the Black Penitents of the Santa Maria del Pianto, near that city; bid the inquisitors summon before their tribunal one father Ansaldo di Rovalli, the grand penitentiary of the society, and command him to divulge the crimes confessed to him in the year 1752, on the evening of the twenty-fourth of April, which was then the vigil of San Marco, in a confessional of the Santa del Pianto."

"It is probable he may have forgotten such confession, at this distance of time," observed Vivaldi.

"Fear not but he will remember," replied the stranger.

"But will his conscience suffer him to betray the secrets of a confession?" said Vivaldi.

"The tribunal command, and his conscience is absolved," answered the monk. "He may not refuse to obey. You are further to direct your examiners to summon father Schedoni, to answer for the crimes which Ansaldo shall reveal."

The monk paused, and seemed waiting the reply of Vivaldi, who, after a momentary consideration, said,

"How can I do all this, and upon the instigation of a stranger? Neither conscience nor prudence will suffer me to assert what I cannot prove. It is true that I have reason to believe Schedoni is my bitter enemy, but I will not be unjust even to him. I have no proof that he is the Count di Bruno, nor that he is the perpetrator of the crimes you allude to, whatever those may be; and I will not be made an instrument to summon any man before a tribunal where innocence is no protection from ignominy, and where suspicion alone may inflict death."

"You doubt, then, the truth of what I assert?" said the monk, in a haughty tone.

"Can I believe that of which I have no proof?" replied Vivaldi.

"Yes, there are cases which do not admit of proof; under your peculiar circumstances, this is one of them; you can act only upon assertion. I attest," continued the monk, raising his hollow voice to a tone of singular solemnity, "I attest the powers which are beyond this earth to witness to the truth of what I have delivered!"

As the stranger uttered this adjuration, Vivaldi observed, with emotion, the extraordinary expression of his eyes. Vivaldi's presence of mind, however, did not forsake him; and, in the next moment, he said, "But who is he that thus attests? It is upon the assertion of a stranger that I am to rely, in defect of proof! It is a stranger who calls upon me to bring solemn charges against a man of whose guilt I know nothing!"

"You are not required to bring charges; you are only to summon him who will."

"I should still assist in bringing forward accusations which may be founded in error," replied Vivaldi. "If you are convinced of their truth, why do not you summon Ansaldo yourself!"

"I shall do more," said the monk.

"But why not summon also?" urged Vivaldi.

"I shall *appear*," said the stranger, with emphasis.

Vivaldi, though somewhat awed by the manner which accompanied these words, still urged his inquiries: "As a witness?" said he.

"Aye, as a dreadful witness!" replied the monk.

"But may not a witness summon persons before the tribunal of the Inquisition?" continued Vivaldi, falteringly.

"He may."

"Why, then," observed Vivaldi, "am I, a stranger to you, called upon to do that which you could perform yourself?"

"Ask no further," rejoined the monk, "but answer whether you will deliver the summons?"

"The charges which must follow," replied Vivaldi, "appear to be of a nature too solemn to justify my promoting them. I resign the task to you."

"When *I* summon," said the stranger, "*you* shall obey!"

Vivaldi, again awed by his manner, again justified his refusal, and concluded with repeating his surprise that he should be required to assist in this mysterious affair; "Since I neither know you, father," he added, "nor the Penitentiary Ansaldo, whom you bid me admonish to appear."

"You shall know me hereafter," said the stranger, frowningly; "and he drew from beneath his garment a dagger!

Vivaldi remembered his dream.

"Mark those spots," said the monk.

Vivaldi looked, and beheld blood!

"This blood," added the stranger, pointing to the blade, "would have saved yours! Here, at least, is some print of truth! To-morrow night you will meet me in the chambers of death!"

As he spoke, he turned away; and before Vivaldi had recovered from his consternation the light disappeared. Vivaldi knew that the stranger had quitted the prison only by the silence which prevailed there.

He remained sunk in thought till, at the dawn of day, the man on watch unfastened the door of his cell, and brought, as usual, a jug of water, and some bread. Vivaldi inquired the name of the stranger who had visited him in the night. The sentinel looked surprised, and Vivaldi repeated the question before he could obtain an answer.

"I have been on guard since the first

hour," said the man, "and no person in that time has passed through this door!"

Vivaldi regarded the sentinel with attention while he made this assertion, and did not perceive in his manner any consciousness of falsehood; yet he knew not how to believe what he had affirmed. "Did you hear no noise either?" said Vivaldi. "Has all been silent during the night?"

"I have heard only the bell of San Dominico strike upon the hour," replied the man, "and the watch word of the sentinels."

"This is incomprehensible!" exclaimed Vivaldi. "What! no footsteps, no voice?"

The man smiled contemptuously. "None, but of the sentinels," he replied.

"How can you be certain you heard only the sentinels, friend?" added Vivaldi.

"They speak only to pass the watch word, and the clash of their arms is heard at the same time."

"But their footsteps!—how are they distinguished from those of other persons!"

"By the heaviness of their tread; our sandals are braced with iron. But why these questions, signor?"

"You have kept guard at the door of this chamber?" said Vivaldi.

"Yes, signor."

"And you have not once heard, during the whole night, a voice from within it?"

"None, signor."

"Fear nothing from discovery, friend; confess that you have slumbered."

"I had a comrade," replied the sentinel, angrily, "has he too slumbered! and if he had, how could admittance be obtained without our keys?"

"And those might easily have been procured, friend, if you were overcome with sleep. You may rely upon my promise of secrecy."

"What!" said the man; "have I kept guard for three years in the Inquisition, to be suspected by a heretic of neglecting my duty?"

"If you were suspected by a heretic," replied Vivaldi, "you ought to console yourself by recollecting that his opinions are considered to be erroneous."

"We were watchful every minute of the night," added the sentinel, going.

"This is incomprehensible!" said Vivaldi. "By what means could the stranger have entered my prison?"

"Signor, you still dream!" replied the sentinel, pausing. "No person has been here."

"*Still* dream!" repeated Vivaldi, "how do you know that I have dreamed at all?" His mind deeply affected by the extraordinary circumstances of the dream, and the yet more extraordinary incident that had followed, Vivaldi gave a meaning to the words of the sentinel which did not belong to them.

"When people sleep, they are apt to dream," replied the man, drily. "I suppose you had slept, signor."

"A person, habited like a monk, came to me in the night," resumed Vivaldi ; and he described the appearance of the stranger. The sentinel, while he listened, became grave and thoughtful.

"Do you know any person resembling the one I have mentioned," said Vivaldi.

"No !" replied the guard.

"Though you have not seen him enter my prison," continued Vivaldi, "you may perhaps recollect such a person, as an inhabitant of the Inquisition."

"San Dominico forbid !"

Vivaldi, surprised at this exclamation, inquired the reason for it.

"I know him not," replied the sentinel, with emotion, and he abruptly left the prison. Whatever consideration might occasion this sudden departure, his assertion that he had been for three years a guard of the Inquisition could scarcely be credited, since he had held so long a dialogue with a prisoner, and was apparently insensible of the danger he incurred by so doing.

CHAPTER XXVII.

AT about the same hour as on the preceding night Vivaldi heard persons approaching his prison, and the door unfolding, his former conductors appeared. They threw over him the same mantle as before, and in addition, a black veil, that completely muffled his eyes ; after which they led him from the chamber. Vivaldi heard the door shut on his departure, and the sentinels followed his steps, as if their duty was finished, and he was to return thither no more. At this moment he remembered the words of the stranger when he had displayed the poniard, and Vivaldi apprehended the worst from having thwarted the designs of a person apparently so malignant : but he exulted in the rectitude which had preserved him from debasement ; and, with the magnanimous enthusiasm of virtue, he almost welcomed sufferings which would prove the firmness of his justice towards an enemy ; for he determined to brave everything rather than impute to Schedoni circumstances the truth of which he possessed no means of ascertaining.

While Vivaldi was conducted, as on the preceding night, through many passages, he endeavoured to discover by their length, and the abruptness of their turnings, whether they were the same he had traversed before. Suddenly one of his conductors cried "Steps !" It was the first word Vivaldi had ever heard him utter. He immediately perceived that the ground sank, and he began to descend ; as he did which, he tried to count the number of the steps, that he might form some judg-

ment whether this was the flight he had passed before. When he had reached the bottom, he inclined to believe that it was not so ; and the care which had been observed in blinding him seemed to indicate that he was going to some new place.

He passed through several avenues, and then ascended ; soon after which he again descended a very long staircase, such as he had not any remembrance of, and they passed over a considerable extent of level ground. By the hollow sound which his steps returned, he judged that he was walking over vaults. The footsteps of the sentinels who had followed from the cell were no longer heard, and he seemed to be left with his conductors only. A second flight appeared to lead him into subterraneous chambers, for he perceived the air change, and felt a damp vapour wrap round him. The menace of the monk, that he should meet him in the chambers of death, frequently occurred to Vivaldi.

His conductors stopped in this vault, and seemed to hold a consultation, but they spoke in such low accents that their words were not distinguishable, except a few unconnected ones that hinted of more than Vivaldi could comprehend. He was at length again led forward, and soon after he heard the heavy grating of hinges, and perceived that he was passing through several doors, by the situation of which, judging they were the same he had entered the night before, he concluded that he was going to the hall of the tribunal.

His conductors stopped again, and Vivaldi heard the iron rod strike three times upon a door ; immediately a strange voice spoke from within, and the door was unclosed. He passed on, and imagined that he was admitted into a spacious vault ; for the air was freer, and his steps sounded to a distance.

Presently a voice, as on the preceding night, summoned him to come forward, and Vivaldi understood that he was again before the tribunal. It was the voice of the inquisitor who had been his chief examiner.

"You, Vincentio di Vivaldi," it said, "answer to your name, and to the questions which shall be put to you, without equivocation, on pain of the torture."

As the monk had predicted, Vivaldi was asked what he knew of father Schedoni, and, when he replied, as he had formerly done to his mysterious visitor, he was told that he knew more than he acknowledged.

"I *know* no more," replied Vivaldi.

"You equivocate," said the inquisitor. "Declare what you have heard, and remember that you formerly took an oath to that purpose."

Vivaldi was silent, till a tremendous voice from the tribunal commanded him to respect his oath.

"I do respect it," said Vivaldi ; "and I conjure you to believe that I also respect truth when I declare that what I am going to relate is a report to which I give no confidence, and concerning even the probability of which I cannot produce the smallest proof."

"Respect truth!" said another voice from the tribunal, and Vivaldi fancied he distinguished the tones of the monk. He paused a moment, and the exhortation was repeated. Vivaldi then related what the stranger had said concerning the family of Schedoni, and the disguise which the father had assumed in the convent of the Spirito Santo; but forbore even to name the penitentiary Ansaldo, and any circumstances connected with the extraordinary confession. Vivaldi concluded with again declaring that he had not sufficient authority to justify a belief in those reports.

"On what authority do you repeat them?" said the vicar-general.

Vivaldi was silent.

"On what authority?" inquired the inquisitor.

Vivaldi, after a momentary hesitation, replied, "What I am about to declare, holy fathers, is so extraordinary ———".

"Tremble," said a voice close to his ear, which he instantly knew to be the monk's, and the suddenness of which electrified him. He was unable to conclude the sentence.

"What is your authority for the reports?" demanded the inquisitor.

"It is unknown, even to myself," answered Vivaldi.

"Do not equivocate," said the vicar-general.

"I solemnly protest," rejoined Vivaldi, "that I know not either the name or the condition of my informer, and that I never even beheld his face till the period when he spoke of father Schedoni."

"Tremble!" repeated the same low but emphatic voice in his ear. Vivaldi started, and turned involuntarily towards the sound, though his eyes could not assist his curiosity.

"You did well to say that you had something extraordinary to add," observed the inquisitor. "'Tis evident, also, that you expected something extraordinary from your judges, since you supposed they would credit these assertions."

Vivaldi was too proud to attempt the justifying himself against so gross an accusation, or to make any reply.

"Why do you not summon father Ansaldo?" said the voice. "Remember my words!"

Vivaldi, again awed by the voice, hesitated for an instant how to act, and in that instant his courage returned.

"My informer stands beside me!" said Vivaldi, boldly. "I know his voice! Detain him; it is of consequence."

"Whose voice?" demanded the inquisitor. "No person spoke but myself."

"Whose voice?" said the vicar-general.

"The voice was close beside me," replied Vivaldi. "It spoke low, but I knew it well."

"This is either the cunning or the frenzy of despair!" observed the vicar-general.

"Not any person is now beside you, except the familiars," said the inquisitor, "and they wait to do their office, if you shall refuse to answer the questions put to you."

"I persist in my assertion," replied Vivaldi; "and I supplicate that my eyes may be unbound, that I may know my enemy."

The tribunal, after a long private consultation, granted the request; the veil was withdrawn, and Vivaldi perceived beside him—only the familiars. Their faces, as is usual, were concealed. It appeared that one of these torturers must be the mysterious enemy who pursued him, if, indeed, that enemy was an inhabitant of the earth! and Vivaldi requested that they might be ordered to uncover their features. He was sternly rebuked for so presumptuous a requisition, and reminded of the inviolable law and faith which the tribunal had pledged, that persons appointed to their awful office should never be exposed to the revenge of the criminal whom it might be their duty to punish.

"Their duty!" exclaimed Vivaldi, thrown from his guard by strong indignation. "And is faith held sacred with demons?"

Without awaiting the order of the tribunal, the familiars immediately covered Vivaldi's face with the veil, and he felt himself again in their grasp. He endeavoured, however, to disentangle his hands, and, at length, shook these men from their hold, and again unveiled his eyes; but the familiars were instantly ordered to replace the veil.

The inquisitor bade Vivaldi to recollect in whose presence he then was, and to dread the punishment which his resistance had incurred, and which would be inflicted without delay unless he could give some instance that might tend to prove the truth of his late assertions.

"If you expect that I should say more," replied Vivaldi, "I claim, at least, protection from the unbidden violence of the men who guard me. If they are suffered, at their pleasure, to sport with the misery of their prisoner, I will be inflexibly silent; and, since I must suffer, it shall be according to the laws of the tribunal."

The vicar-general, or, as he is called, the grand inquisitor, promised Vivaldi the degree of protection he claimed; and demanded, at the same time, what were the words he had just heard.

Vivaldi considered that, though justice bade him avoid accusing an enemy of suspicious circumstances concerning which he had no proof, yet, that neither justice nor common sense required he should make a sacrifice of himself to the dilemma in which he was placed; he therefore, without further scruple, acknowledged that the voice had bidden him require of the tribunal to summon one father Ansaldo, the grand penitentiary of the Santa del Pianto, near Naples, and also father Schedoni, who was to answer to extraordinary charges which would be brought against him by Ansaldo. Vivaldi anxiously and repeatedly declared that he knew not the nature of the charges, nor that any just grounds for them existed.

These assertions seemed to throw the tribunal into new perplexity. Vivaldi heard their busy voices in low debate, which continued for a considerable time. In this interval he had leisure to perceive the many improbabilities that either of the familiars should be the stranger who so mysteriously haunted him; and among these was the circumstance of his having resided so long at Naples.

The tribunal, after some time had elapsed in consultation, proceeded on the examination, and Vivaldi was asked what he knew of father Ansaldo. He immediately replied that Ansaldo was an utter stranger to him, and that he was not even acquainted with a single person residing in the Santa del Pianto or who had any knowledge of the penitentiary.

"How!" said the grand inquisitor, "You forget that the person who bade you require of this tribunal to summon Ansaldo has knowledge of him."

"Pardon me, I do not forget," replied Vivaldi; and I request it may be remembered that I am not acquainted with that person. If, therefore, he had given me any account of Ansaldo, I could not have relied upon its authenticity." Vivaldi again required of the tribunal to understand that he did not summon Ansaldo, or any other person, before them, but had merely obeyed their command to repeat what the stranger had said.

The tribunal acknowledged the justness of this injunction, and exculpated him from any harm that should be the consequence of the summons. But this assurance of safety for himself was not sufficient to appease Vivaldi, who was alarmed lest he should be the means of bringing an innocent person under suspicion. The grand inquisitor again addressed him, after a general silence had been commanded in the court.

"The account you have given of your informer," said he, "is so extraordinary that it would not deserve credit, but that you have discovered the utmost reluctance to reveal the charge he gave you; from which it appears, that on your part, at least, the summons is not malicious. But are you certain that you have not deluded yourself, and that the voice beside you was not an imaginary one, conjured up by your agitated spirits?"

"I am certain," replied Vivaldi, with firmness.

"It is true," resumed the grand inquisitor, "that several persons were near you when you exclaimed that you heard the voice of your informer; yet no person heard it besides yourself?"

"Where are those persons now?" demanded Vivaldi.

"They are dispersed; alarmed at your accusation."

"If you will summon them," said Vivaldi, "and order that my eyes may be uncovered, I will point out to you without hesitation the person of my informer, should he remain among them."

The tribunal commanded that they should appear, but new difficulties arose. It was not remembered of whom the crowd consisted; a few individuals only were recollected, and these were summoned.

Vivaldi, in solemn expectation, heard steps and the hum of voices gathering round him, and impatiently awaited for the words that would restore him to sight, and perhaps release him from uncertainty. In a few moments he heard the command given; the veil was once more removed from his eyes, and he was ordered to point out the accuser. Vivaldi threw a hasty glance upon the surrounding strangers.

"The lights burn dimly," said he, "I cannot distinguish these faces."

It was ordered that a lamp should be lowered from the roof, and that the strangers should arrange themselves on either side of Vivaldi. When this was done, and he glanced his eyes again upon the crowd, "He is not here!" said Vivaldi; not one of these countenances resembles the monk of Paluzzi. Yet, stay; who is he that stands in the shade behind those persons on the left? Bid him lift his cowl!"

The crowd fell back, and the person to whom Vivaldi had pointed was left alone within the circle.

"He is an officer of the Inquisition," said a man near Vivaldi, "and he may not be compelled to discover his face, unless by an express command from the tribunal."

"I call upon the tribunal to command it!" said Vivaldi.

"Who calls!" exclaimed a voice, and Vivaldi recognised the tones of the monk, but he knew not exactly whence they came.

"I, Vincentio di Vivaldi," replied the prisoner, "I claim the privilege that has been awarded me, and bid you unveil your countenance."

There was a pause of silence in the court, except that a dull murmur ran through the tribunal. Meanwhile, the figure within the circle stood motionless, and remained veiled.

"Spare him," said the man who had before addressed Vivaldi; "he has reasons for wishing to remain unknown, which you cannot conjecture. He is an officer of the Inquisition, and not the person you apprehend."

"Perhaps I *can* conjecture his reasons," replied Vivaldi, who, raising his voice, added, "I appeal to this tribunal, and command you who stand alone within the circle, you in black garments, to unveil your features!"

Immediately a loud voice issued from the tribunal, and said,

"We command you, in the name of the most holy Inquisition, to reveal yourself?"

The stranger trembled, but, without presuming to hesitate, uplifted his cowl. Vivaldi's eyes were eagerly fixed upon him; but the action disclosed, not the countenance of the monk, but of an official whom he recollected to have seen once before, though exactly on what occasion he did not now remember.

"This is not my informer!" said Vivaldi, turning from him with deep disappointment, while the stranger dropped his cowl, and the crowd closed upon him. At the assertion of Vivaldi, the members of the tribunal looked upon each other doubtingly, and were silent, till the grand inquisitor, waving his hand, as if to command attention, addressed Vivaldi.

"It appears, then, that you *have* formerly seen the face of your informer!"

"I have already declared so," replied Vivaldi.

The grand inquisitor demanded when and where he had seen it.

"Last night, and in my prison," answered Vivaldi.

"In your prison!" said the ordinary inquisitor, contemptuously, who had before examined him, "and in your dreams, too, no doubt!"

"In your prison!" exclaimed several members of the lower tribunal.

"He dreams still!" observed an inquisitor. "Holy fathers! he abuses your patience, and the frenzy of terror has deluded his credulity. We neglect the moments."

"We must inquire further into this," said another inquisitor. "Here is some deception. If you, Vincentio di Vivaldi have asserted a falsehood—tremble!"

Whether Vivaldi's memory still vibrated with the voice of the monk, or that the tone in which this same word was now pronounced did resemble it, he almost started when the inquisitor had said *tremble!* and he demanded who spoke then.

"It is ourself," answered the inquisitor.

After a short conversation among the members of the tribunal, the grand inquisitor gave orders that the sentinels who had watched on the preceding night at the prison door of Vivaldi should be brought into the hall of justice. The persons who had been lately summoned into the chamber were now

bidden to withdraw, and all further examination was supended till the arrival of the sentinels. Vivaldi heard only the low voices of the inquisitors, as they conversed privately together, and he remained silent, thoughtful, and amazed.

When the sentinels appeared, and were asked who had entered the prison of Viva'di during the last night, they declared, without hesitation or confusion, that not any person had passed through the door after the hour when the prisoner had returned from examination till the following morning, when the guard had carried in the usual allowance of bread and water. In this assertion they persisted, without the least equivocation, notwithstanding which they were ordered into confinement till the affair should be cleared up.

The doubts, however, which were admitted as to the integrity of these men, did not contribute to dissipate those which had prevailed over the opposite side of the question. On the contrary, the suspicions of the tribunal, augmenting with their perplexity, seemed to fluctuate equally over every point of the subject before them, till, instead of throwing any light upon the truth they only served to involve the whole in deeper obscurity. More doubtful than before of the honesty of Vivaldi's extraordinary assertions, the grand inquisitor informed him that if, after further inquiry into this affair, it should appear he had been trifling with the credulity of his judges, he would be severely punished for his audacity; but that, on the other hand, should there be reason to believe that the sentinels had failed in their duty, and that some person had entered his prison during the night, the tribunal would proceed in a different manner.

Vivaldi, perceiving that, to be believed, it was necessary he should be more circumstantial, described with exactness the person and appearance of the monk, without, however, mentioning the poniard which had been exhibited. A profound silence reigned in the chamber while he spoke; it seemed a silence not merely of attention, but of astonishment. Vivaldi himself was awed, and, when he had concluded, almost expected to hear the voice of the monk uttering defiance or threatening vengeance; but all remained hushed, till the inquisitor who had first examined him said in a solemn tone,

"We have listened with attention to what you have delivered, and will give the case a full inquiry. Some points on which you have touched excite our amazement, and call for particular regard. Retire whence you came, and sleep this night without fear; *you will soon know more.*"

Vivaldi was immediately led from the chamber, and, still blindfolded, re-conducted to the prison to which he had supposed it was designed he should return no more. When the veil was withdrawn, he perceived that his guard was changed.

Again left to the silence of his cell, he reviewed all that had passed in the chamber of justice : the questions which had been put to him ; the different manners of the inquisitors ; the occurrence of the monk's voice ; and the similarity which he had fancied he perceived between it and that of an inquisitor, when the latter pronounced the word tremble ; but the consideration of all these circumstances did not in any degree relieve him from his perplexity. Sometimes he was inclined to think that the monk was an inquisitor, and the voice had more than once appeared to proceed from the tribunal ; but he remembered also that, more than once, it had spoken close to his ear, and he knew that a member of this tribunal might not leave his station during the examination of a prisoner ; and that, even if he had dared to do so, his singular dress would have pointed him out to notice, and consequently to suspicion, at the moment when Vivaldi had exclaimed that he heard the voice of his informer.

Vivaldi, however, could not avoid meditating, with surprise, on the last words which the inquisitor who had been his chief examiner had addressed to him, when he was dismissed from before the tribunal. These were the more surprising, because they were the first from him that had in any degree indicated a wish to console or quiet the alarm of the prisoner ; and Vivaldi even fancied that they betrayed some foreknowledge that he would not be disturbed this night by the presence of his awful visitor. He would entirely have ceased to apprehend, though not to expect, had he been allowed a light and any weapon of defence ; if, in truth, the stranger was of a nature to fear a weapon ; but to be thus exposed to the designs of a mysterious and powerful being, whom he was conscious of having offended, to sustain such a situation without suffering anxiety required somewhat more than courage or less than reason.

CHAPTER XXVIII.

IN consequence of what had transpired at the last examination of Vivaldi, the grand penitentiary Ansaldo, together with the father Schedoni, were cited to appear before the table of the holy office.

Schedoni was arrested on his way to Rome, whither he was going privately to make further efforts for the liberation of Vivaldi, whose release he had found it more difficult to effect than his imprisonment : the person upon whose assistance the confessor relied in the first instance having boasted of more influence than he possessed, or perhaps thought it prudent to exert. Schedoni had been the more anxious to procure an immediate release

for Vivaldi, lest a report of his situation should reach his family notwithstanding the precautions which are usually employed to throw an impenetrable shroud over the prisoners of this dreadful tribunal, and bury them for ever from the knowledge of their friends. Such premature discovery of Vivaldi's circumstances Schedoni apprehended might include also a discovery of the persecutor, and draw down upon himself the abhorrence and the vengeance of a family whom it was now more than ever his wish and his interest to conciliate. It was still his intention that the nuptials of Vivaldi and Ellena should be privately solemnized immediately on the release of the prisoner, who, even if he had reason to suspect Schedoni for his late persecutor, would then be interested in concealing his suspicions for ever, and from whom, therefore, no evil was to be apprehended.

How little did Vivaldi foresee that, in repeating to the tribunal the stranger's summons of father Schedoni, he was deferring or, perhaps, wholly preventing his own marriage with Ellena di Rosalba. How little, also, did he apprehend what would be the further consequences of a disclosure, which the peculiar circumstances of his situation had hardly permitted him to withhold ; though, could he have understood the probable event of it, he would have braved all the terrors of the tribunal, and death itself, rather than incur the remorse of having promoted it.

The motive for his arrestation was concealed from Schedoni, who had not the remotest suspicion of its nature but attributed the arrest to a discovery which the tribunal had made of his being the accuser of Vivaldi. This disclosure he judged to be the consequence of his own imprudence in having stated, as an instance of Vivaldi's contempt for the Catholic faith, that he had insulted a priest while doing penance in the church of the Spirito Santo. But by what art the tribunal had discovered that he was the priest alluded to, and the author of the accusation, Schedoni could by no means conjecture. He was willing to believe that this arrest was only for the purpose of obtaining proof of Vivaldi's guilt ; and the confessor knew that he could so conduct himself in evidence as in all probability to exculpate the prisoner, from whom, when he should explain himself, no resentment on account of his former conduct was to be apprehended. Yet Schedoni was not perfectly at ease : for it was possible that a knowledge of Vivaldi's situation, and of the author of it, had reached his family, and had produced his own arrest. On this head, however, his fears were not powerful ; since, the longer he dwelt upon the subject, the more improbable it appeared that such a disclosure, at least so far as it related to himself, could have been affected.

Vivaldi, from the night of his late examination, was not called upon till Schedoni and father Ansaldo appeared together in the hall of the tribunal. The two latter had already been separately examined, and Ansaldo had privately stated, the particulars of the confession, he had received on the vigil of San Marco, in the year 1752, for which disclosure he had received formal absolution. What had passed at that examination does not appear; but on this, his second interrogation, he was required to repeat the subject and the circumstances of the confession. This was probably with a view of observing its effect on Schedoni and on Vivaldi, which would direct the opinion of the tribunal as to the guilt of the confessor and the veracity of the young prisoner.

On this night a very exact inquiry was made concerning every person who had obtained admission into the hall of justice; such officials as were not immediately necessary to assist in the ceremonies of the tribunal were excluded, together with every other person belonging to the Inquisition not material to the evidence, or to the judges. When this scrutiny was over, the prisoners were brought in, and their conductors ordered to withdraw. A silence of some moments prevailed in the hall; and, however different might be the reflections of the several prisoners, the degree of anxious expectation was in each, probably, nearly the same.

The grand-vicar having spoken a few words in private to a person on his left hand, an inquisitor rose.

"If any person in this court," said he, "is known by the name of father Schedoni, belonging to the Dominican society of the Spirito Santo at Naples, let him appear."

Schedoni answered to the summons. He came forward with a firm step, and, having crossed himself and bowed to the tribunal, awaited in silence its commands.

The penitentiary Ansaldo was next called upon. Vivaldi observed that he faltered as he advanced, and that his obedience to the tribunal was more profound than Schedoni's had been. Vivaldi himself was then summoned; his air was calm and dignified, and his countenance expressed the solemn energy of his feelings, but nothing of dejection.

Schedoni and Ansaldo were now, for the first time, confronted. Whatever might be the feelings of Schedoni on beholding the penitentiary of the Santa del Pianto, he effectually concealed them.

The grand-vicar himself opened the examination: "You, father Schedoni, of the Spirito Santo," he said, "answer and say whether the person who now stands before you, bearing the title of grand penitentiary of the order of the Black Penitents, and presiding over the convent of the Santa Maria del Pianto at Naples, is known to you."

To this requisition Schedoni replied with firmness in the negative.

"You have never, to your knowledge, seen him before this hour?"

"Never!". said Schedoni.

"Let the oath be administered," added the grand-vicar. Schedoni having accepted it, the same questions were put to Ansaldo concerning the confessor, when, to the astonishment of Vivaldi and of the greater part of the court, the penitentiary denied all knowledge of Schedoni. His negative was given, however, in a less decisive manner than that of the confessor, and when the usual oath was offered, Ansaldo declined to accept it.

Vivaldi was next called upon to identify Schedoni: he declared that the person who was then pointed out to him he had never known by any other denomination than that of father Schedoni, and that he had always understood him to be a monk of the Spirito Santo; but Vivaldi was at the same time careful to repeat that he knew nothing further relative to his life.

Schedoni was somewhat surprised at this apparent candour of Vivaldi towards himself; but accustomed to impute an evil motive to all conduct which he could not clearly comprehend, he did not scruple to believe that some latent mischief was directed against him in this seemingly honest declaration.

After some further preliminary forms had passed, Ansaldo was ordered to relate the particulars of the confession which had been made to him on the eve of San Marco. It must be remembered that this was still what is called in the Inquisition a *private* examination.

After he had taken the customary oath to relate neither more nor less than the truth of what had passed before him, Ansaldo's depositions were written down nearly in the following words, to which Vivaldi listened with almost trembling attention, for, besides the curiosity which some previous circumstances had excited respecting them, he believed that his own fate in a great measure depended upon a discovery of the fact to which they led. What, if he had surmised how much! and that the person whom he had been in some degree instrumental in citing before this tremendous tribunal was the father of his Ellena di Rosalba!

Ansaldo, having again answered to his name and titles, gave his deposition as follows :—

"It was on the eve of the twenty-fifth of April, in the year 1752, that as I sat, according to my custom, in the confessional of San Marco, I was alarmed by deep groans, which came from the box on my left hand."

Vivaldi observed that the date now mentioned agreed with that recorded by the stranger, and he was thus prepared to believe what might follow, and to give his confidence to this extraordinary and unseen personage.

Ansaldo continued, "I was the more alarmed by these sounds because I had not been prepared for them; I knew not that any person was in the confessional, nor had even observed anyone pass along the aisle—but the duskiness of the hour may account for my having failed to do so; it was after sunset, and the tapers at the shrine of San Antonio as yet burn-d feebly in the twilight."

"Be brief, holy father," said the inquisitor who had formerly been most active in examining Vivaldi; "speak closely to the point."

"The groans would sometimes cease," resumed Ansaldo, "and long pauses of silence follow; they were those of a soul in agony, struggling with the consciousness of guilt, yet wanting resolution to confess it. I tried to encourage the penitent, and held forth every hope of mercy and forgiveness which my duty would allow, but for a considerable time without effect — the enormity of the sin seemed too big for utterance, yet the penitent appeared equally unable to endure the concealment of it. His heart was bursting with the secret, and required the comfort of absolution, even at the price of the severest penance."

"Facts!" said the inquisitor, "these are only surmises."

"Facts will come full soon!" replied Ansaldo, and bowed his head; "the mention of them will petrify you, holy fathers! as they did me, though not for the same reasons. While I endeavoured to encourage the penitent, and assured him that absolution should follow the acknowledgment of his crimes, however heinous those crimes might be, if accompanied by sincere repentance, he more than once began his confession, and abruptly dropped it. Once, indeed, he quitted the confessional; his agitated spirit required liberty; and it was then, as he walked with perturbed steps along the aisle, that I first observed his figure. He was in the habit of a white friar, and, as nearly as I can recollect, was about the stature of him, the father Schedoni, who now stands before me."

As Ansaldo delivered these words, the attention of the whole tribunal was turned upon Schedoni, who stood unmoved, and with his eyes bent towards the ground.

"His face," continued the penitentiary, "I did not see; he was, with good reason, careful to conceal it; other resemblance, therefore, than the stature, I cannot point out between them. The voice indeed, the voice of the penitent, I think I shall never forget; I should know it again at any distance of time."

"Has it not struck your ear since you came within these walls?" said a member of the tribunal.

"Of that hereafter," observed the inquisitor, "you wander from the point, father."

The vicar-general remarked that the circumstances just related were important, and ought not to be passed over as irrelevant. The inquisitor submitted to this opinion, but objected that they were not pertinent to the moment: and Ansaldo was again bidden to repeat what he had heard at confession.

"When the stranger returned to the steps of the confessional, he had acquired sufficient resolution to go through with the task he had imposed upon himself, and a thrilling voice spoke through the grate the facts I am about to relate."

Father Ansaldo paused, and was somewhat agitated; he seemed endeavouring to recollect courage to go through with what he had begun. During this pause the silence of expectation wrapt the court, and the eyes of the tribunal were directed alternately to Ansaldo and Schedoni, who certainly required something more than human firmness to support unmoved the severe scrutiny, and the yet severer suspicions, to which he stood exposed. Whether, however, it was the fortitude of conscious innocence or the hardihood of atrocious vice that protected the confessor, he certainly did not betray any emotion. Vivaldi, who had unceasingly observed him from the commencement of the depositions, felt inclined to believe that he was not the penitent described. Ansaldo, having at length recollected himself, proceeded as follows:

"'I have been through life,' said the penitent, 'the slave of my passions, and they have led me into horrible excesses. I had once a brother——' He stopped, and deep groans again told the agony of his soul; at length he added, 'That brother had a wife! Now listen, father, and say whether guilt like mine may hope for absolution! She was beautiful—I loved her; she was virtuous, and I despaired. You, father,' he continued, in a frightful tone, 'never knew the fury of despair! It overcame or communicated its own force to every other passion of my soul, and I sought to release myself from its tortures by any means. My brother died!' The penitent paused again," continued Ansaldo. "I trembled while I listened; my lips were sealed. At length, I bade him proceed, and he spoke as follows: 'My brother died at a distance from home.' Again the penitent paused, and the silence continued so long that I thought it proper to inquire of what disorder the brother had expired. 'Father, I was his murderer!' said the penitent, in a voice which I never can forget; it sank into my heart."

Ansaldo appeared affected by the remembrance, and was for a moment silent. At the last words Vivaldi had particularly noticed Schedoni, that he might judge by their effect upon him whether he was guilty; but he remained in his former attitude, and his eyes were still fixed upon the ground.

"Proceed, father," said the inquisitor. "What was your reply to this confession?"

"'I was silent," said Ansaldo; "but at length I bade the penitent go on. 'I contrived,' said he, 'that my brother should die at a distance from home; and I so conducted the affair that his widow never suspected the cause of his death. It was not till long after the usual time of mourning had expired that I ventured to solicit her hand. But she had not yet 'orgotten my brother, and she rejected me. My passion would no longer be trifled with. I caused her to be carried from her house, and she was afterwards willing to retrieve her honour by the marriage vow. I had sacrificed my conscience without having found happiness; she did not even condescend to conceal her disdain. Mortified, exasperated by her conduct, I began to suspect that some other emotion than resentment occasioned this disdain; and, last of all, jealousy—jealousy came to crown my misery—to light up all my passions into madness!'

"The penitent," added Ansaldo, "appeared by the manner in which he uttered this to be nearly frantic at the moment, and convulsive sobs soon stifled his words. When he resumed his confession, he said : ' I soon found an object for my jealousy. Among the few persons who visited us in the retirement of our country residence was a gentleman who, I fancied, loved my wife. I fancied, too, that whenever he appeared an air of particular satisfaction was visible on her countenance. She seemed to have pleasure in conversing with and showing him distinction. I even sometimes thought she had pride in displaying to me the preference she entertained for him, and that an air of triumph, and even of scorn, was addressed to me, whenever she mentioned his name. Perhaps I mistook resentment for love, and she only wished to punish me by exciting my jealousy. Fatal error ! she punished herself also !'

"Be less circumstantial, father," said the inquisitor.

Ansaldo bowed his head, and proceeded.

"'One evening,' continued the penitent, 'that I returned home unexpectedly, I was told that a visitor was with my wife ! As I approached the apartment where they sat I heard the voice of Sacchi ; it seemed mournful and supplicating. I stopped to listen, and distinguished enough to fire me with vengeance. I restrained myself, however, so far as to step softly to a lattice that opened from the passage, and overlooked the apartment. The traitor was on his knee before her. Whether she had heard my step, or observed my face through the high lattice, or that she resented his conduct, I know not, but she rose immediately from her chair. I did not pause to question her motive; but, seizing my stiletto, I rushed into the room with an intent to strike it to the villain's heart. The supposed assassin of my honour escaped into the garden, and was heard of no more.' ' But

your wife?' said I. 'Her bosom received the poniard !' replied the penitent."

Ansaldo's voice faltered as he repeated this part of the confession, and he was utterly unable to proceed. The tribunal, observing his condition, allowed him a chair, and, after a struggle of some moments, he added, "Think, holy fathers, oh, think ! what must have been my feelings* at that 'instant ! I was myself the lover of the woman whom he confessed himself to have murdered."

"Was she innocent ?" said a voice ; and Vivaldi, whose attention had lately been fixed upon Ansaldo, now, on looking at Schedoni, perceived that it was he who had spoken. At the sound of his voice, the penitentiary turned instantly towards him. There was a pause of general silence, during which Ansaldo's eyes were earnestly fixed upon the accused. At length he spoke, "She was innocent ! " he replied, with solemn emphasis, "she was most virtuous ! "

Schedoni had shrunk back within himself ; he asked no further. A murmur ran through the tribunal, which rose by degrees till it broke into audible conversation ; at length the secretary was directed to note the question of Schedoni.

"Was that the voice of the penitent which you have just heard ?" demanded the inquisitor of Ansaldo. "Remember, you have said that you should know it again !"

"I think it was," replied Ansaldo; "but I cannot swear to that."

"What infirmity of judgment is this ! " said the same inquisitor, who himself was seldom troubled with the modesty of doubt upon any subject. Ansaldo was bidden to resume the narrative.

"On this discovery of the murder," said the penitentiary, "I quitted the confessional, and my senses forsook me before I could deliver orders for the detention of the assassin. When I recovered, it was too late ; he had escaped ! From that hour to the present I have never seen him, nor dare I affirm that the person now before me is he."

The inquisitor was about to speak, but the grand-vicar waved his hand as a signal for attention, and, addressing Ansaldo, said, " Although you may be unacquainted with Schedoni, the monk of the Spirito Santo, reverend father, can you not recollect the person of the Count di Bruno, your former friend ? ".

Ansaldo again looked at Schedoni with a scrutinising eye ; he fixed it long, but the countenance of Schedoni suffered no change.

"No ! " said the penitentiary, at length, "I dare not take upon me to assert that this is the Count di Bruno. If it is he, years have wrought deeply on his features. That the penitent was the Count di Bruno I have proof ; he mentioned my name as his visitor, and particular circumstances known only to the Count and myself ; but that father Schedoni was the penitent, I repeat it, I dare not affirm."

"But that I dare!" said another voice; and Vivaldi, turning towards it, beheld the mysterious stranger advancing, his cowl now thrown back, and an air of menace overspreading every terrific feature. Schedoni, in the instant that he perceived him, seemed agitated: his countenance, for the first time, suffered some change.

The tribunal was profoundly silent, but surprise, and a kind of restless expectation, marked every brow. Vivaldi was about to exclaim, "That is my informer!" when the voice of the stranger checked him.

"Dost thou know me?" said he, sternly, to Schedoni, and his attitude became fixed.

Schedoni gave no reply.

"Dost thou know me?" repeated his accuser, in a steady, solemn voice.

"Know thee!" uttered Schedoni, faintly.

"Dost thou know this?" cried the stranger, raising his voice as he drew from his garment what appeared to be a dagger. "Dost thou know these indelible stains?" said he, lifting the poniard, and, with an outstretched arm, pointing it towards Schedoni.

The confessor turned away his face; it seemed as if his heart sickened.

"With this dagger was thy brother slain!" said the terrible stranger. "Shall I declare myself?"

Schedoni's courage forsook him, and he sank against a pillar of the hall for support.

The consternation was now general; the extraordinary appearance and conduct of the stranger seemed to strike the greater part of the tribunal, a tribunal of the Inquisition itself! with dismay. Several of the members rose from their seats; others called aloud for the officials who kept guard at the doors of the hall, and inquired who had admitted the stranger, while the vicar-general and a few inquisitors conversed privately together, during which they frequently looked at the stranger and at Schedoni, as if they were the subjects of the discourse. Meanwhile the monk remained with the dagger in his grasp, and his eyes fixed on the confessor, whose face was still averted, and who yet supported himself against the pillar.

At length, the vicar-general called upon the members who had arisen to return to their seats, and ordered that the officials should withdraw to their posts.

"Holy brethren!" said the vicar, "we recommend to you, at this important hour, silence and deliberation. Let the examination of the accused proceed; and hereafter let us inquire as to the admittance of the accuser. For the present, suffer him also to have a hearing, and the father Schedoni to reply."

"We suffer him," answered the tribunal, and bowed their heads.

Vivaldi, who during the tumult had in-effectually endeavoured to make himself heard, now profited by the pause which followed the assent of the inquisitors to claim attention; but, the instant he spoke, several members impatiently bade the examination should proceed, and the grand-vicar was again obliged to command silence, before the request of Vivaldi could be understood. Permission to speak being granted him, "That person," said he, pointing to the stranger, "is the same who visited me in my prison: and the dagger the same he then displayed! It was he who commanded me to summon the penitentiary Ansaldo and the father Schedoni. I have acquitted myself, and have nothing further to do in this struggle."

The tribunal was again agitated, and the murmurs of private conversation again prevailed. Meanwhile Schedoni appeared to have recovered some degree of self-command; he raised himself, and, bowing to the tribunal, seemed preparing to speak; but waited till the confusion of sound that filled the hall should subside. At length he could be heard, and, addressing the tribunal, he said—

"Holy fathers, the stranger who is now before you is an impostor! I will prove that my accuser was once my friend—you may see how much the discovery of his perfidy affects me. The charge he brings is both false and malicious!"

"Once thy friend!" replied the stranger, with peculiar emphasis, "and what has made me thy enemy! View these spots," he continued, pointing to the blade of the poniard. "Are they also false and malicious? are they not, on the contrary, reflected on thy conscience?"

"I know them not," replied Schedoni, "my conscience is unstained."

"A brother's blood has stained it!" said the stranger, in a hollow voice.

Vivaldi, whose attention was now fixed upon Schedoni, observed a livid hue overspread his complexion, and that his eyes were averted from this extraordinary person with horror: the spectre of his deceased brother could scarcely have called forth a stronger expression. It was not immediately that he could command his voice; when he could, he again appealed to the tribunal.

"Holy fathers," said he, "suffer me to defend myself."

"Holy fathers," said the accuser, with solemnity, "hear! hear what I shall unfold!"

Schedoni, who seemed to speak by a strong effort only, again addressed the inquisitors; "I will prove," said he, "that this evidence is not to be trusted."

"I will bring such proof to the contrary!" said the monk. "And here," pointing to Ansaldo, "is sufficient testimony that the Count di Bruno did confess himself guilty of murder."

The court commanded silence, and upon

the appeal of the stranger to Ansaldo, the penitentiary was asked whether he knew him. He replied that he did not.

"Recollect yourself," said the grand inquisitor; "it is of the utmost consequence that you should be correct on this point."

The penitentiary observed the stranger with deep attention, and then repeated his assertion.

"Have you never seen him before?" said an inquisitor.

"Never, to my knowledge!" replied Ansaldo.

The inquisitors looked upon each other in silence.

"He speaks the truth," said the stranger.

This extraordinary fact did not fail to strike the tribunal and to astonish Vivaldi. Since the accuser confirmed it, Vivaldi was at a loss to understand the means by which he could have become acquainted with the guilt of Schedoni, who, it was not to be supposed, would have acknowledged crimes of such magnitude as those contained in the accusation to any person, except indeed to his confessor, and this confessor, it appeared, was so far from having betrayed his trust to the accuser, that he did not even know him. Vivaldi was no less perplexed as to what would be the nature of the testimony, with which the accuser designed to support his charges: but the pause of general amazement which had permitted Vivaldi these considerations was now at an end; the tribunal resumed the examination, and the grand inquisitor called aloud—

"You, Vincentio di Vivaldi, answer with exactness to the questions that shall be put to you."

He was then asked some questions relative to the person who had visited him in prison. In his answers Vivaldi was clear and concise, constantly affirming that the stranger was the same who now accused Schedoni.

When the accuser was interrogated, he acknowledged, without hesitation, that Vivaldi had spoken the truth. He was then asked his motive for that extraordinary visit.

"It was," replied the monk, "that a murderer might be brought to justice."

"This," observed the grand inquisitor, "might have been accomplished by fair and open accusation. If you had known the charge to be just, it is probable that you would have appealed directly to this tribunal, instead of endeavouring insidiously to obtain an influence over the mind of a prisoner, and urging him to become the instrument of bringing the accused to punishment."

"Yet I have not shrunk from discovery," observed the stranger, calmly; "I have voluntarily appeared."

At these words, Schedoni seemed again much agitated, and even drew his hood over his eyes.

"That is just," said the grand inquisitor, addressing the stranger; "but you have neither declared your name, nor whence you come!"

To this remark the monk made no reply; but Schedoni, with reviving spirit, urged the circumstance in evidence of the malignity and falsehood of the accuser.

"Wilt thou compel me to reveal my proof?" said the stranger. "Darest thou to do so?"

"Why should I fear thee?" answered Schedoni.

"Ask thy conscience!" said the stranger, with a terrible frown.

The tribunal again suspended the examination, and consulted in private together.

To the last exhortation of the monk Schedoni was silent. Vivaldi observed that during this short dialogue the Confessor had never once turned his eyes towards the stranger, but apparently avoided him as an object too affecting to be looked upon. He judged from this circumstance, and from some other appearances in his conduct, that Schedoni was guilty; yet the consciousness of guilt alone did not perfectly account, he thought, for the strong emotions with which he avoided the sight of his accuser—unless, indeed, he knew that accuser to have been, not only an accomplice in his crime, but the actual assassin. In this case it appeared natural even for the stern and subtle Schedoni to betray his horror on beholding the person of the murderer with the very instrument of crime in his grasp. On the other hand, Vivaldi could not but perceive it to be highly improbable that the very man who had really committed the deed should come voluntarily into a court of justice for the purpose of accusing his employer; that he should dare publicly to accuse him whose guilt, however enormous, was not more so than his own.

The extraordinary manner also in which the accuser had proceeded in the commencement of the affair engaged Vivaldi's consideration; his apparent reluctance to be seen in this process, and the artful and mysterious plan by which he had caused Schedoni to be summoned before the tribunal, and had endeavoured that he should be there accused by Ansaldo, indicated, at least to Vivaldi's apprehension, the fearfulness of guilt, and still more, that malice and a thirst of vengeance had instigated his conduct in the prosecution. If the stranger had been actuated only by a love of justice, it appeared that he would not have proceeded towards it in a way thus dark and circuitous, but have sought it by the usual process, and have produced the proofs, which he even now asserted he possessed, of Schedoni's crimes. In addition to the circumstances, which seemed to strengthen a supposition of the guiltlessness of Schedoni, was that of the accuser's avoiding to acknowledge who he was and whence he came. But Vivaldi paused again upon this point; it appeared to be inexplicable, and he could not imagine why the accuser had adopted a style of secrecy which, if he persisted in it, must probably defeat the very purpose of the accusation; for Vivaldi did not believe that the tribunal would condemn a prisoner upon the testimony of a person who, when called upon, should publicly refuse to reveal himself even to them. Yet the accuser must certainly have considered this circumstance before he ventured into court; notwithstanding which, he had appeared!

These reflections led Vivaldi to various conjectures relative to the visit he had himself received from the monk, the dream that had preceded it, the extraordinary means by which he had obtained admittance to the prison, the declaration of the sentinels that not any person had passed the door, and many other unaccountable particulars; and, while Vivaldi now looked upon the wild physiognomy of the stranger, he almost fancied, as he had formerly done, that he beheld something not of this earth.

"I have heard of the spirit of the murdered," said he, to himself, "restless for justice, becoming visible in our world——" But Vivaldi checked the imperfect thought, and though his imagination inclined him to the marvellous and to admit ideas which, filling and expanding all the faculties of the soul, produce feelings that partake of the sublime, he now resisted the propensity, and dismissed, as absurd, a supposition which had begun to thrill his every nerve with horror. He awaited, however, the result of the examination, and what might be the further conduct of the stranger, with intense expectation.

When the tribunal had, at length, finally determined on the method of their proceedings, Schedoni was first called upon, and examined as to his knowledge of the accuser. It was the same inquisitor who had formerly interrogated Vivaldi that now spoke. "You, father Schedoni, a monk of the Spirito Santo convent, at Naples, otherwise Ferando Count di Bruno, answer to the questions which shall be put to you. Do you know the name of this man who now appears as your accuser?"

"I answer not to the title of Count di Bruno," replied the confessor, "but I will declare that I know this man. His name is Nicola di Zampari."

"What is his condition?"

"He is a monk of the Dominican convent of the Spirito Santo," replied Schedoni. "Of his family I know little."

"Where have you seen him?"

"In the city of Naples, where he has resided during some years, beneath the same roof with me, which I was of the convent of San Angiolo, and since that time in the Spirito Santo."

"You have been a resident at the San Angiolo?" said the inquisitor.

"I have," replied Schedoni; "and it was there that we first lived together in the confidence of friendship."

"You now perceive how ill placed was that confidence," said the inquisitor, "and repent, no doubt, of your imprudence?"

The wary Schedoni was not entrapped by this observation.

"I must lament a discovery of ingratitude," he replied, calmly, "but the subjects of my confidence were too pure to give occasion for repentance."

"This Nicola di Zampari was ungrateful, then? You had rendered him services?" said the inquisitor.

"The cause of his enmity I can well explain," observed Schedoni, evading, for the present, the question.

"Explain," said the stranger, solemnly.

Schedoni hesitated; some sudden consideration seemed to occasion him perplexity.

"I call upon you, in the name of your deceased brother," said the accuser, "to reveal the cause of my enmity!"

Vivaldi, struck by the tone in which the stranger spoke this, turned his eyes upon him, but knew not how to interpret the emotion visible on his countenance.

The inquisitor commanded Schedoni to explain himself; the latter could not immediately reply, but, when he recovered a self-command, he added,

"I promised this accuser, this Nicola di Zampari, to assist his preferment with what little interest I possessed; it was but little. Some succeeding circumstances encouraged me to believe that I could more than fulfil my promise. His hopes were elevated, and, in the fulness of expectation, he was disappointed, for I was myself deceived by the person in whom I had trusted. To the disappointment of a choleric man I am to attribute this unjust accusation."

Schedoni paused, and an air of dissatisfaction and anxiety appeared upon his features. His accuser remained silent, but a malicious smile announced his triumph.

"You must declare also the services," said the inquisitor, "which merited the reward promised."

"Those services were inestimable to me," resumed Schedoni, after a momentary hesitation, "though they cost Di Zampari little; they were the consolations of sympathy, the intelligence of friendship, which he administered, and which gratitude told me never could be repaid."

"Of sympathy! of friendship!" said the grand-vicar. "Are we to believe that a man who brings false accusation of so dreadful a nature as the one now before us is capable of bestowing the consolations of sympathy and of friendship? You must either acknowledge that services of a less disinterested nature won your promises of reward, or we must conclude that your accuser's charge is just. Your assertions are inconsistent, and your explanation too trivial to deceive for a moment."

"I have declared the truth," said Schedoni haughtily.

"In which instance?" asked the inquisitor; "for your assertions contradict each other!"

Schedoni was silent. Vivaldi could not judge whether the pride which occasioned his silence was that of innocence or of remorse.

"It appears, from your own testimony," said the inquisitor, "that the ingratitude was yours, not your accuser's, since he consoled you with kindness, which you have never returned him! Have you anything further to say?"

Schedoni was still silent.

"This, then, is your only explanation?" added the inquisitor.

Schedoni bowed his head. The inquisitor then, addressing the accuser, demanded what he had to reply.

"I have nothing to reply," said the stranger, with malicious triumph; "the accused has replied for me."

"We are to conclude, then, that he has spoken truth when he asserted you to be a monk of the Spirito Santo, at Naples?" said the inquisitor.

"You, holy father," said the stranger, gravely, appealing to the inquisitor, "can answer for me, whether I am."

Vivaldi listened with emotion.

The inquisitor rose from his chair, and with solemnity replied, "I answer, then, that you are not a monk of Naples."

"By that reply," said the vicar-general, in a low voice to the inquisitor, "I perceive you think father Schedoni is guilty."

The rejoinder of the inquisitor was delivered in so low a tone that Vivaldi could not understand it. He was perplexed to interpret the answer given to the appeal of the stranger. He thought that the inquisitor would not have ventured an assertion thus positive if his opinion had been drawn from inference only; and that he should know the accuser, while he was conducting himself towards him as a stranger, amazed Vivaldi no less than if he had understood the character of an inquisitor to be as artless as his own. On the other hand, he had so frequently seen the stranger at Paluzzi, and in the habit of a monk, that he could hardly question the assertion of Schedoni as to his identity.

The inquisitor, addressing Schedoni, said, "Your evidence we know to be in part erroneous; your accuser is not a monk of Naples,

but a servant of the most holy Inquisition. Judging from this part of your evidence, we must suspect the whole."

"A servant of the Inquisition!" exclaimed Schedoni, with unaffected surprise. "Reverend father! your assertion astonishes me. You are deceived, however strange it may appear; trust me, you are deceived! You doubt the credit of my word; I therefore will assert no more. But inquire of Signor Vivaldi; ask him whether he has not often, and lately, seen my accuser at Naples, and in the habit of a monk."

"I have seen him at the ruins of Paluzzi, near Naples, and in the ecclesiastical dress," replied Vivaldi, without waiting for the regular question, "and under circumstances no less extraordinary than those which have attended him here. But, in return for this frank acknowledgment, I require of you, father Schedoni, to answer some questions which I shall venture to suggest to the tribunal. By what means were you informed that I have often seen the stranger at Paluzzi, and were you interested or not in his mysterious conduct towards me there?"

To these questions, though formally delivered from the tribunal, Schedoni did not deign to reply.

"It appears, then," said the vicar-general, "that the accuser and the accused were once accomplices."

The inquisitor objected that this did not certainly appear; and that, on the contrary, Schedoni seemed to have given his last questions in despair; an observation which Vivaldi thought extraordinary from an inquisitor.

"Be it *accomplices*, if it so please you," said Schedoni, bowing to the grand-vicar, without noticing the inquisitor; "you may call us accomplices, but I say that we were *friends*. Since it is necessary to my own peace that I should more fully explain some circumstances attending our intimacy, I will own that my accuser was occasionally my agent, and assisted in preserving the dignity of an illustrious family at Naples, the family of the Vivaldi. And there, holy father," added Schedoni, pointing to Vincentio, "is the son of that ancient house for whom I have attempted so much!"

Vivaldi was almost overwhelmed by this confession of Schedoni, though he had already suspected a part of the truth. In the stranger he believed he saw the slanderer of Ellena, the base instrument of the Marchesa's policy, and of Schedoni's ambition; and the whole of his conduct at Paluzzi, at least, seemed now intelligible. In Schedoni he beheld his secret accuser, and the inexorable enemy whom he believed to have occasioned the imprisonment of Ellena. At this latter consideration, all circumspection, all prudence forsook him: he declared with energy that from what Schedoni had just acknowledged to be his conduct, he

F

knew him for his secret accuser, and the accuser of Ellena di Rosalba ; and he called upon the tribunal to examine into the confessor's motives for the accusation, and afterwards to give hearing to what he would himself unfold.

To this the grand-vicar replied that Vivaldi's appeal would be taken into consideration ; and he then ordered that the present business should proceed.

The inquisitor, addressing Schedoni, said, " The disinterested nature of your friendship is now sufficiently explained, and the degree of credit which is due to your late assertions understood. Of you we ask no more, but turn to father Nicola di Zampari, and demand what he has to say in support of his accusation. What are your proofs, Nicola di Zampari, that he who calls himself father Schedoni is Ferando Count di Bruno ; and that he has been guilty of murder, the murder of his brother, and of his wife ? Answer to our charge ! "

" To your first question," said the monk, " I reply that he has himself acknowledged to me, on an occasion which it is not necessary to mention, that he was the Count di Bruno ; to the last I produce the poniard, which I received with the dying confession of the assassin whom he employed."

" Still, these are not proofs but assertions," observed the vicar-general, " and the first forbids our confidence in the second. If, as you declare, Schedoni himself acknowledged to you that he was Count di Bruno, you must have been to him the intimate friend he has declared you were, or he would not have confided to you a secret so dangerous to himself. And, if you were that friend, what confidence ought we to give to your assertions repecting the dagger ? Since, whether your accusations be true or false, you prove yourself guilty of treachery in bringing them forward at all."

Vivaldi was surprised to hear such candour from an inquisitor.

" Here is my proof," said the stranger, who now produced a paper, containing what he asserted to be the dying confession of the assassin. It was signed by a priest of Rome, as well as by himself, and appeared from the date to have been given only a very few weeks before. The priest, he said, was living, and might be summoned. The tribunal issued an order for the apprehension of this priest, and that he should be brought to give evidence on the following evening ; after which the business of this night proceeded without further interruption towards its conclusion.

The vicar-general spoke again. " Nicola di Zampari, I call upon you to say why, if your proof of Schedoni's guilt is so clear, as the confession of the assassin himself must make it,—why you thought it necessary to summon father Ansaldo to attest the criminality of the Count di Bruno ? The dying confession of the assassin is certainly of more weight than any other evidence."

" I summoned the father Ansaldo," replied the stranger, " as a means of proving that Schedoni is the Count di Bruno. The confession of the assassin sufficiently proves the Count to have been the instigator of the murder, but not that Schedoni is the Count."

" But that is more than I will engage to prove," replied Ansaldo. " I know it was the Count di Bruno who confessed to me ; but I do not know that the father Schedoni who is now before me was the person who so confessed."

" Conscientiously observed ! " said the vicar-general, interrupting the stranger, who was about to reply ; " but you, Nicola di Zampari, have not on this head been sufficiently explicit. How do you know that Schedoni is the penitent who confessed to Ansaldo on the vigil of San Marco ? "

" Reverend father, that is the point I was about to explain," replied the monk. " I myself accompanied Schedoni, on the eve of San Marco, to the church of the Santa Maria del Pianto, at the very hour when the confession is said to have been made. Schedoni told me he was going to confession ; and, when I observed to him his unusual agitation, his behaviour implied a consciousness of extraordinary guilt ; he even betrayed it by some words which he dropped in the confusion of his mind. I parted with him at the gates of the church. He was then of an order of white friars, and habited as father Ansaldo has described. Within a few weeks after this confession he left his convent, for what reason I never could learn, though I have often surmised it, and came to reside at the Spirito Santo, whither I also had removed."

" Here is no proof," said the vicar-general ; " other friars of that order might confess at the same hour in the same church."

" But here is strong presumption for proof," observed the inquisitor. " Holy father, we must judge from probabilities, as well as from proof."

" But probabilities themselves," replied the vicar-general, " are strongly against the evidence of a man who would betray another by means of words dropped in the unguarded moments of powerful emotion."

" Are these the sentiments of an inquisitor ! " said Vivaldi to himself. " Can such glorious candour appear amidst the tribunal of an Inquisition ! " Tears fell fast upon Vivaldi's cheek while he gazed upon this just judge, whose candour had it been exerted in his cause, could not have excited more powerful sensations of esteem and admiration. " An inquisitor ! " he repeated to himself, " an inquisitor ! "

The inferior inquisitor, however, was so far

from possessing any congeniality of character with his superior, that he was evidently disappointed by the appearance of liberality which the vicar-general discovered, and immediately said, "Has the accuser anything further to urge in evidence, that the father Schedoni is the penitent who confessed to the penitentiary Ansaldo?"

"I have," replied the monk, with asperity. "When I had left Schedoni in the church, I lingered without the walls for his return, according to appointment. But he appeared considerably sooner than I expected, and in a state of disorder such as I had never witnessed in him before. In an instant he passed me, nor could my voice arrest his progress. Confusion seemed to reign within the church and the convent, and when I would have entered, for the purpose of inquiring the occasion of it, the gates were suddenly closed, and all entrance forbidden. It has since appeared that the monks were then searching for the penitent. A rumour afterwards reached me that a confession had caused this disturbance; that the father-confessor, who happened at that time to be the grand-penitentiary Ansaldo, had left the chair in horror of what had been divulged from the grate, and had judged it necessary that a search should be made for the penitent, who was a white friar. This report, reverend fathers, excited general attention; with me it did more—for I thought I knew the penitent. When on the following day I questioned Schedoni as to his sudden departure from the church of the Black Penitents, his answers were dark, but emphatic; and he extorted from me a promise, thoughtless that I was! never to disclose his visit of the preceding evening to the Santa del Pianto. I then certainly discovered who was the penitent."

"Did he then confess to you also?" said the vicar-general.

"No, father. I understood him to be the penitent to whom the report alluded, but I had no suspicion of the nature of his crimes till the assassin began his confession, the conclusion of which clearly explained the subject of Schedoni's; it explained also his motive for endeavouring ever after to attach me to his interest."

"You have now," said the vicar-general, "you have now confessed yourself a member of the convent of the Spirito Santo at Naples, and an intimate of the father Schedoni; one whom for many years he had endeavoured to attach to him. Not an hour has passed since you denied all this; the negative to the latter circumstance was given; it is true, by implication only; but to the first a direct and absolute denial was pronounced!"

"I denied that I *am* a monk of Naples," replied the accuser, "and I appealed to the inquisitor as to the truth of my denial. He has

said that I am now a servant of the most holy Inquisition."

The vicar-general, with some surprise, looked at the inquisitor for explanation; other members of the tribunal did the same; the rest appeared to understand more than they had thought it necessary to avow. The inquisitor who had been called upon, rose and replied:

"Nicola di Zampari has spoken the truth. It is not many weeks since he entered the holy office. A certificate from his convent at Naples bears testimony to the truth of what I advance, and procured him admittance here."

"It is extraordinary that you should not have disclosed your knowledge of this person before!" said the vicar-general.

"Holy father, I had reasons," replied the inquisitor, "you will recollect that the accused was present, and you will understand them."

"I comprehend you," said the vicar-general, "but I do neither approve of, nor perceive any necessity for, your countenancing the subterfuge of this Nicola di Zampari relative to his identity. But more of this in private."

"I will explain all there," answered the inquisitor.

"It appears then," resumed the vicar-general, speaking aloud, "that this Nicola di Zampari was formerly the friend and confidant of father Schedoni, whom he now accuses. The accusation is evidently malicious; whether it be also false remains to be decided. A material question naturally arises out of the subject—Why was not the accusation brought forward before this period?"

The monk's visage brightened with the satisfaction of anticipated triumph, and he immediately replied:

"Most holy father! as soon as I ascertained the crime, I prepared to prosecute the perpetrator of it. A short period only has elapsed since the assassin gave his confession. In this interval I discovered, in these prisons, signor Vivaldi, and immediately comprehended by whose means he was confined. I knew enough, both of the accuser and the accused, to understand which of these was innocent, and had then a double motive for causing Schedoni to be summoned; I wished equally to deliver the innocent and to punish the criminal. The question as to the motive for my becoming the enemy of him who was once my friend, is already answered—it was a sense of justice, not a suggestion of malice."

The grand-vicar smiled, but asked no further; and this long examination concluded with committing Schedoni again into close custody, till full evidence should be obtained of his guilt, or his innocence should appear. Respecting the manner of his wife's death, there was yet no other evidence than that which was asserted to be his own confession, which, though perhaps sufficient to condemn a criminal before the tribunal of the Inquisition, was not enough to satisfy the present vicar-general, who gave direction that means might be employed towards obtaining proof of each article of the accusation; in order that, should Schedoni be acquitted of the charge of having murdered his brother, documents might appear for prosecuting him respecting the death of his wife.

Schedoni, when he withdrew from the hall, bowed respectfully to the tribunal, and whether, notwithstanding late appearances, he were innocent, or that subtlety enabled him to reassume his usual address, it is certain his manner no longer betrayed any symptom of conscious guilt. His countenance was firm and even tranquil, and his air dignified. Vivaldi, who during the greater part of his examination had been convinced of his criminality, now only doubted his innocence. Vivaldi was himself reconducted to his prison, and the sitting of the tribunal was dissolved.

CHAPTER XXIX.

WHEN the night of Schedoni's trial arrived, Vivaldi was again summoned to the hall of the tribunal. Every circumstance was now arranged according to the full ceremonies of the place; the members of the tribunal were more numerous than formerly at the examinations; the chief inquisitors wore habits of a fashion different from those which before distinguished them, and their turbans, of a singular form and larger size, seemed to give an air of sterner ferocity to their features. The hall, as usual, was hung with black, and every person who appeared there, whether inquisitor, official, witness, or prisoner, was habited in the same dismal hue, which, together with the kind of light diffused through the chamber from lamps hung high in the vaulted roof, and from torches held by parties of officials who kept watch at the several doors and in different parts of this immense hall, gave a character of gloomy solemnity to the assembly which was almost horrific.

Vivaldi was situated in a place whence he beheld the whole of the tribunal, and could distinguish whatever was passing in the hall. The countenance of every member was now fully displayed to him by the torchmen, who, arranged at the steps of the platform on which the three chief inquisitors were elevated extended in a semicircle on either hand of the place occupied by the inferior members. The glare which the torches threw upon the latter certainly did not soften the expression of faces for the most part sculptured by passions of dark malignity, or fiercer cruelty: and Vivaldi could not bear even to examine them long.

Before the bar of the tribunal he distinguished Schedoni, and little did he suspect that in him, a criminal brought thither to answer for the guilt of murder—the murder of a brother, and of a wife, he beheld the parent of Ellena di Rosalba!

Near Schedoni was placed the penitentiary Ansaldo, the Roman priest, who was to be a principal witness, and father Nicola di Zampari, upon whom Vivaldi could not even look without experiencing somewhat of the awe which had prevailed over his mind when he was inclined to consider the stranger rather as a vision of another world than as a being of this. The same wild and indescribable character still distinguished his air, his every look and movement, and Vivaldi could not but believe that something in the highest degree extraordinary would yet be discovered concerning him.

The witnesses being called over, Vivaldi understood that he was placed among them, though he had only repeated the words which father Nicola had spoken, and which, since Nicola himself was present as a witness against Schedoni, he did not perceive could be in the least material on the trial.

When Vivaldi had, in his turn, answered to his name, a voice, bursting forth from a distant part of the hall, exclaimed, "It is my master! my *dear* master!" and on directing his eyes whence it came, he perceived the faithful Paulo struggling with his guard. Vivaldi called to him to be patient, and to forbear resistance; an exhortation, however, which served only to increase the efforts of the servant for liberty, and in the next instant he broke from the grasp of the officials, and darting towards Vivaldi, fell at his feet, sobbing, and clasping his knees, and exclaiming, "Oh, my master! my master! have I found you at last?"

Vivaldi, as much affected by this meeting as Paulo, could not immediately speak. He would, however, have raised and embraced his affectionate servant, but Paulo, still clinging to his knees and sobbing, was so much agitated that he scarcely understood anything said to him; and to the kind assurances and gentle remonstrances of Vivaldi, constantly replied as if to the officers, whom he fancied to be forcing him away.

"Remember your situation, Paulo," said Vivaldi; "consider mine also, and be governed by prudence."

"You shall not force me hence!" cried Paulo; "you can take my life only once! if I must die, it shall be here."

"Recollect yourself, Paulo, and be composed. Your life, I trust, is in no danger."

Paulo looked up, and again bursting into a passion of tears, repeated, "Oh, my master! my master! where have you been all this while? are you indeed alive? I thought I never should see you again! I have dreamt a hundred times that you were dead and buried!

and I wished to be dead and buried with you. I thought you were gone out of this world into the next. I feared you were gone to heaven, and so believed we should never meet again. But now I see you once more, and know that you live! Oh, my master! my master!"

The officers who had followed Paulo, now endeavouring to withdraw him, he became more outrageous.

"Do your worst at once," said he; "but you shall find tough work of it, if you try to force me from hence, so you had better be contented with killing me here."

The incensed officials were laying violent hands upon him, when Vivaldi interposed. "I entreat, I supplicate you," said he, "that you will suffer him to remain near me."

"It is impossible," replied an officer, "we dare not."

"I will promise that he shall not even speak to me, if you will only allow him to be near," added Vivaldi.

"Not speak to you, master!" exclaimed Paulo, "but I will stay by you, and speak to you, as long as I like, till my last gasp. Let them do their worst at once; I defy them all, and all the devils of inquisitors at their heels, too, to force me away. I can die but once, and they ought to be satisfied with that,—so what is there to be afraid of? Not speak!"

"He knows not what he says," said Vivaldi to the officials, while he endeavoured to silence Paulo with his hand. "I am certain that he will submit to whatever I shall require of him, and will be entirely silent; or, if he does speak now and then, it shall only be in a whisper."

"A whisper!" said an officer, sneeringly, "do you suppose, signor, that any person is suffered to speak in a whisper here?"

"A whisper!" shouted Paulo, "I scorn to speak in a whisper. I will speak so loud that every word I say shall ring in the ears of all those old black devils on the benches yonder; aye, and those on that mountebank stage too, that sit there looking so grim and angry, as if they longed to tear us in pieces. They ——"

"Silence," said Vivaldi with emphasis, "Paulo, I command you to be silent."

"They shall know a bit of my mind," continued Paulo, without noticing Vivaldi, "I will tell them what they have to expect for all their cruel usage of my poor master. Where do they expect to go when they die, I wonder? Though, for that matter, they cannot go to a worse place than they are in already, and I suppose it is knowing that which makes them not afraid of being ever so wicked. They shall hear a little plain truth for once in their lives, however, they shall hear ——"

During the whole of this harangue Vivaldi, alarmed for the consequence of such imprudent, though honest indignation, had been

using all possible effort to silence him, and was the more alarmed since the officials made no further attempt to interrupt Paulo, a forbearance which Vivaldi attributed to malignity, and to a wish that Paulo might be entrapped by his own act. At length he made himself heard.

"I entreat," said Vivaldi.

Paulo stopped for a moment.

"Paulo!" rejoined Vivaldi, earnestly, "do you love your master?"

"Love my master!" said Paulo, resentfully, without allowing Vivaldi to finish his sentence, "have I not gone through fire and water for him? or, what is as good, have I not put myself into the Inquisition, and all on his account? and now to be asked 'Do I love my master!' If you believe, signor, that anything else made me come here, into these dismal holes, you are quite entirely out; and when they have made an end of me, as I suppose they will do, before all is over, you will, perhaps, think better of me than to suspect that I came here for my own pleasure."

"All that may be as you say, Paulo," replied Vivaldi, coldly, while he with difficulty commanded his tears, "but your immediate submission is the only conduct that can convince me of the sincerity of your professions. I entreat you to be silent."

"Entreat me!" said Paulo. "Oh, my master! what have I done that it should come to this? Entreat me!" he repeated, sobbing.

"You will, then, give me this proof of your attachment?" asked Vivaldi.

"Do not use such a heart-breaking word again, master," replied Paulo, while he dashed the tears from his cheek, "such a heart-breaking word, and I will do anything."

"You submit to what I require then, Paulo?"

"Aye, signor, if—if it is even to kneel at the feet of that devil of an inquisitor, yonder."

"I shall only require you to be silent," replied Vivaldi, "and you may then be permitted to remain near me."

"Well, signor, well; I will do as you bid me, then, and only just say——"

"Not a syllable, Paulo," interrupted Vivaldi.

"Only just say, master——"

"Not a word, I entreat you!" added Vivaldi, "or you will be removed immediately."

"His removal does not depend on that," said one of the officials, breaking from his watchful silence, "he must go, and that without more delay."

"What! after I have promised not to open my lips!" said Paulo; "do you pretend to break your agreement?"

"There is no pretence, and there was no

agreement," replied the man, sharply, "so obey directly, or it will be the worse for you."

The officials were provoked, and Paulo became still more enraged and clamorous, till at length the uproar reached the tribunal at the other end of the hall, and silence having been commanded, an inquiry was made into the cause of the confusion. The consequence of this was an order that Paulo should withdraw from Vivaldi; but as at this moment he feared no greater evil, he gave his refusal to the tribunal with as little ceremony as he had done before to the officials.

At length, after much difficulty, a sort of compromise was made, and Paulo being soothed by his master into some degree of compliance, was suffered to remain within a short distance of him.

The business of the trial soon after commenced. Ansaldo, the penitentiary, and father Nicola appeared as witnesses, as did also the Roman priest who had assisted in taking the depositions of the dying assassin. He had been privately interrogated, and had given clear and satisfactory evidence as to the truth of the paper produced by Nicola. Other witnesses also had been subpoenaed, whom Schedoni had no expectation of meeting.

The deportment of the confessor, on first entering the hall, was collected and firm; it remained unchanged when the Roman priest was brought forward; but, on the appearance of another witness, his courage seemed to falter. Before this evidence was, however, called for, the depositions of the assassin were publicly read. They stated with the closest conciseness the chief facts, of which the following is a somewhat more dilated narrative.

It appeared that about the year 1742 the late Count di Bruno had passed over into Greece, a journey which his brother, the present confessor, having long expected, had meditated to take advantage of. Though a lawless passion had first suggested to the dark mind of Schedoni the atrocious act which should destroy a brother, many circumstances and considerations had conspired to urge him towards its accomplishment. Among these was the conduct of the late Count towards himself, which, however reasonable, as it had contradicted his own selfish gratifications, and added strong reproof to opposition, had excited his most inveterate hatred. Schedoni, who, as a younger brother of his family, bore at that time the title of Count di Marinella, had dissipated his small patrimony at a very early age; but though suffering might then have taught him prudence, it had only encouraged him in duplicity, and rendered him more eager to seek a temporary refuge in the same habits of extravagance which had led to it. The Count

di Bruno, though his fortune was very limited, had afforded frequent supplies to his brother; till, finding that he was incorrigible, and that the sums which he himself spared with difficulty from his family were lavished without remorse by Marinella, instead of being applied with economy to his support, he refused further aid than was sufficient for his absolute necessities.

It would be difficult for a candid mind to believe how a conduct so reasonable could possibly excite hatred in any breast, or that the power of selfishness could so far warp any understanding as to induce Marinella, whom we will in future again call Schedoni, to look upon his brother with detestation, because he had refused to ruin himself that his kinsman might revel! Yet it is certain that Schedoni, terming the necessary prudence of di Bruno to be meanness and cold insensibility to the comfort of others, suffered full as much resentment towards him from system as he did from passion, though the meanness and the insensibility he imagined in his brother's character were not only real traits in his own, but were displaying themselves in the very arguments he urged against them.

The rancour thus excited was cherished by innumerable circumstances, and ripened by envy, that meanest and most malignant of human passions; by envy of di Bruno's blessings, of an unencumbered estate, and of a beautiful wife, he was tempted to perpetrate the deed which might transfer those blessings to himself. Spalatro, whom he employed to this purpose, was well known to him, and he did not fear to confide the conduct of the crime to this man, who was to purchase a little habitation on the remote shore of the Adriatic, and, with a certain stipend, to reside there. The ruinous dwelling to which Ellena had been carried, as its solitary situation suited Schedoni's views, was taken for him.

Schedoni, who had good intelligence of all di Bruno's movements, acquainted Spalatro, from time to time, with his exact situation; and it was after di Bruno, on his return, had crossed the Adriatic, from Ragusi to Manfredonia, and was entering upon the woods of the Garganus, that Spalatro, with his comrade, overtook him. They fired at the Count and his attendants, who were only a valet and a guide of the country; and, concealed among the thickets, they securely repeated the attack. The shot did not immediately succeed, and the Count, looking round to discover his enemy, prepared to defend himself, but the firing was so rapidly sustained that, at length, both di Bruno and his servant fell, covered with wounds. The guide fled.

The unfortunate travellers were buried by their assassins on the spot; but whether the suspicion which attends upon the consciousness of guilt prompted Spalatro to guard against every possibility of being betrayed by the accomplice of his crime, or whatever was the motive, he returned to the forest alone, and, shrouded by night, removed the bodies to a pit which he had prepared under the flooring of the house where he lived, thus displacing all proof should his accomplice hereafter point out to justice the spot in which he had assisted to deposit the mangled remains of di Bruno.

Schedoni contrived a plausible history of the shipwreck of his brother upon the Adriatic, and of the loss of the whole crew ; and as no persons but the assassins were acquainted with the real cause of his death, the guide, who had fled, and the people at the only town he had passed through since he landed, being ignorant even of the name of di Bruno, there was not any circumstance to contradict the falsehood. It was universally credited, and even the widow of the Count had, perhaps, never doubted its truth ; or if, after her compelled marriage with Schedoni, his conduct did awaken a suspicion, it was too vague to produce any serious consequence.

During the reading of Spalatro's confession, and particularly at the conclusion of it, the surprise and dismay of Schedoni were too powerful for concealment ; and it was not the least considerable part of his wonder that Spalatro should have come to Rome for the purpose of making these depositions ; but further consideration gave him a conjecture of the truth.

The account which Spalatro had given of his motive for this journey to the priest was that, having lately understood Schedoni to be resident at Rome, he had followed him thither with an intention of relieving his conscience by an acknowledgment of his own crimes and a disclosure of Schedoni's. This, however, was not exactly the fact. The design of Spalatro was to extort money from the guilty confessor ; a design from which the latter believed he had protected himself, as well as from every other evil consequence, when he misled his late accomplice respecting his place of residence, little foreseeing that the very artifice which should send this man in search of him to Rome, instead of Naples, would be the means of bringing his crimes before the public.

Spalatro had followed the steps of Schedoni as far as the town at which he slept on the first night of his journey ; and, having there passed him, had reached the Villa di Cambrusca, when, perceiving the confessor approaching, he had taken shelter from observation within the ruin. The motive which before made him shrink from notice had contributed, and still did so, to a suspicion that he aimed at the life of Schedoni, who, in wounding him, believed he had saved

himself from an assassin. The wounds, however, of Spalatro did not so much disable him but that he proceeded towards Rome from the town whence the parting road had conducted his master to Naples.

The fatigue of a long journey, performed chiefly on foot, in Spalatro's wounded condition, occasioned a fever that terminated together his journey and his life ; and in his last hours he had unburdened his conscience by a full confession of his guilt. The priest who, on this occasion, had been sent for, alarmed by the importance of the confession, since it implicated a living person, called in a friend as witness to the depositions. This witness was father Nicola, the former intimate of Schedoni, and who was of a character to rejoice in any discovery which might punish a man from whose repeated promises he had received only severe disappointments.

Schedoni now perceived that all his designs against Spalatro had failed, and he had meditated more than have yet been fully disclosed. It may be remembered that on parting with the peasant, his conductor, the confessor gave him a stiletto, to defend him, as he said, from the attack of Spalatro in case of encountering him on the road. The point of this instrument was tipped with poison, so that a scratch from it was sufficient to inflict death. Schedoni had for many years secretly carried about him such an envenomed instrument, for reasons known only to himself. He had hoped that, should the peasant meet Spalatro, and be provoked to defend himself, this stiletto would terminate the life of his accomplice, and relieve him from all probability of discovery, since the other assassin whom he employed had been dead several years. The expedient failed in every respect. The peasant did not even see Spalatro ; and, before he reached his home, he luckily lost the fatal stiletto, which, as he had discovered himself to be acquainted with some circumstances connected with the crimes of Schedoni, the confessor would have wished him to keep, from the chance that he might some time injure himself in using it. The poniard, however, as he had no proper means of fastening it to his dress, had fallen, and was carried away by the torrent he was crossing at that moment.

But if Schedoni had been shocked by the confession of the assassin, his dismay was considerably greater when a new witness was brought forward, and he perceived an ancient domestic of his house. This man identified Schedoni for Ferando, Count di Bruno, with whom he had lived as a servant after the death of the Count his brother. And not only did he bear testimony to the person of Schedoni, but to the death of the Countess, his wife. Giovanni declared himself to be one of the domestics who had assisted in conveying her to her apartment after she had been struck by the poniard of Schedoni, and who had afterwards attended her funeral in the church of the Santa del Miracoli, a convent near the late residence of di Bruno. He further affirmed that the physicians had reported her death to be in consequence of the wound she had received, and he bore witness to the flight of his master previous to the death of the Countess, and immediately upon the assassination, and that he had never publicly appeared upon his estate since that period.

An inquisitor asked whether any measures had been taken by the relations of the deceased lady toward a prosecution of the Count.

The witness replied that a long search had been made for the Count for such a purpose, but that he had wholly eluded discovery, and that, of course, no further step had been taken in the affair. This reply appeared to occasion dissatisfaction. The tribunal was silent, and seemed to hesitate ; the vicar-general then addressed the witness.

" How can you be certain that the person now before you, calling himself father Schedoni, is the Count di Bruno, your former master, if you have never seen him during the long interval of years you mention ? "

Giovanni, without hesitation, answered that, though years had worn the features of the Count, he recollected them the moment he beheld him ; and not the Count only, but the person of the penitentiary, Ansaldo, whom he had seen a frequent visitor at the house of di Bruno, though his appearance also was considerably changed by time, and by the ecclesiastical habit which he now wore.

The vicar-general seemed still to doubt the evidence of this man, till Ansaldo himself, on being called upon, remembered him to have been a servant of the Count, though he could not identify the Count himself.

The grand inquisitor remarked that it was extraordinary he should recollect the face of the servant, yet forget that of the master, with whom he had lived in habits of intimacy. To this Ansaldo replied that the stronger passions of Schedoni, together with his particular habits of life, might reasonably be supposed to have wrought a greater change upon the features of the Count than the character and circumstances of Giovanni's could have effected on his.

Schedoni, not without reason, was appalled on the appearance of this servant, whose further testimony gave such clearness and force to some other parts of the evidence that the tribunal pronounced sentence upon Schedoni as the murderer of the Count his brother, and as this, the first charge, was sufficient for his condemnation to death, they did not proceed upon the second, that which related to his wife.

The emotion betrayed by Schedoni on the appearance of the last witness, and during the delivery of the evidence, disappeared when his fate became certain, and when the dreadful sentence of the law was pronounced it made no visible impression on his mind. From that moment, his firmness, or his hardihood, never forsook him.

Vivaldi, who witnessed this condemnation, appeared infinitely more affected by it than himself ; and though in revealing the circumstance of father Nicola's summons, which had eventually led to the discovery of Schedoni's crimes, he had not been left a choice in his conduct, he felt, at this moment, as miserable as if he had actually borne witness against the life of a fellow being. What, then, would have been his feelings had he been told that this Schedoni, thus condemned, was the father of Ellena di Rosalba ! But, whatever these might be, he was soon condemned to experience them. One of the most powerful of Schedoni's passions appeared even in this last scene ; and as, in quitting the tribunal, he passed near Vivaldi, he uttered these few words : "In me you have murdered the father of Ellena di Rosalba ! "

Not with any hope that the intercession of Vivaldi, himself also a prisoner, could in the least mitigate a sentence pronounced by the Inquisition, did he say this, but for the purpose of revenging himself for the evil which Vivaldi's evidence had contributed to produce, and inflicting the exquisite misery such information must give. The attempt succeeded too well.

At first, indeed, Vivaldi judged this to be only the desperate assertion of a man who believed his last chance of escaping the rigour of the law to rest with him ; and, at the mention of Ellena, forgetting every precaution, he loudly demanded to know her situation. Schedoni, throwing upon him a horrible smile of triumph and derision, was passing forward without replying, but Vivaldi, unable to support this state of uncertainty, asked permission of the tribunal to converse for a few moments with the prisoner, a request which was granted with extreme reluctance, and only on condition that the conversation should be public.

To Vivaldi's questions as to the situation of Ellena, Schedoni only replied that she was his daughter, and the solemnity which accompanied these repeated assertions, though it failed to convince Vivaldi of this truth, occasioned him agonizing doubt and apprehension ; but when the confessor, perceiving the policy of disclosing her place of residence to Vivaldi, softened from his desire of vengence to secure the interest of his family, and named the Santa della Pieta as her present asylum, the joy of such intelligence overcame, for a time, every other consideration.

To this dialogue, however, the officials put a speedy conclusion. Schedoni was led back to his cell, and Vivaldi was soon after ordered to his former close confinement.

But Paulo became again outrageous when he was about to be separated from his master, till the latter, having petitioned the tribunal that his servant might accompany him to his prison, and received an absolute refusal, endeavoured to calm the violence of his depair. He fell at his master's feet and shed tears, but he uttered no further complaints. When he rose, he turned his eyes in silence upon Vivaldi, and they seemed to say, "Dear master! I shall never see you more!" and with this sad expression he continued to gaze on him till he had left the hall.

Vivaldi, notwithstanding the various subjects of his distress, could not bear to meet the piteous looks of this poor man, and he withdrew his eyes; yet, at every other step he took, they constantly returned to his faithful servant, till the doors folded him from sight.

When he had quitted the hall, Vivaldi pleaded, however hopelessly, to the officials in favour of Paulo, entreating that they would speak to the persons who kept guard over him, and prevail with them to show him every allowable indulgence.

"No indulgence can be allowed him," replied one of the men, "except bread and water, and the liberty of walking in his cell."

"No *other!*" said Vivaldi.

"None," repeated the official. "This prisoner has been near getting one of his guards into a scrape already, for somehow or other he so talked him over and won upon him (for he is but a young one here) that the man let him have a light, and a pen and ink; but, luckily, it was found out before any harm was done."

"And what became of this honest fellow?" inquired Vivaldi.

"Honest! he was none so honest, either, signor, if he could not mind his duty."

"Was he punished, then?"

"No, signor," replied the man, pausing, and looking back upon the long avenue they were passing, to inquire whether he was observed to hold this conversation with a prisoner; "no, signor, he was a younker, so they let him off for once, and sent him to guard a man who was not so full of his coaxing ways."

"Paulo made him merry, perhaps?" asked Vivaldi. "What were the coaxing ways you spoke of?"

"Merry, signor! no; he made him cry, and that was as bad."

"Indeed!" said Vivaldi. "The man must have been here, then, a very short time."

"Not more than a month or so, signor."

"But the coaxing ways you talked of," repeated Vivaldi "what were they?—a ducat or so?"

"A ducat!" exclaimed the man "No! not a paolo!"

"Are you *sure* of that?" cried Vivaldi, shrewdly.

"Aye, sure enough, signor. This fellow is not worth a ducatin the world."

"But his master is, friend," observed Vivaldi, in a very low voice, while he put some money into his hand.

The officer made no answer, but concealed the money, and nothing further was said.

Vivaldi had given this as a bribe to procure some kindness for his servant, not from any consideration of himself, for his own critical situation had ceased at this time to be a subject of anxiety with him. His mind was at present strangely agitated between emotions the most opposite in their nature, the joy which a discovery of Ellena's safety inspired, and the horrible suspicion that Schedoni's assurances of relationship occasioned. That his Ellena was the daughter of a murderer, that the father of Ellena should be brought to ignominious death, and that he himself, however unintentionally, should have assisted to this event, were considerations almost too horrible to be sustained! Vivaldi sought refuge from them in various conjectures as to the motive which might have induced Schedoni to assert a falsehood in this instance, but that of revenge alone appeared plausible; and even this surmise was weakened when he considered that the confessor had assured him of Ellena's safety, an assurance which, as Vivaldi did not detect the selfish policy connected with it, he believed Schedoni would not have given had his general intent towards him been malicious. But it was possible that this very information, on which all his comfort reposed, might be false, and had been given only for the purpose of inflicting the anguish a discovery of the truth must lead to. With an anxiety so intense as almost to overcome his faculty of judging, he examined every minute probability relative to this po nt, and concluded with believing that Schedoni had, in this last instance at least, spoken honestly.

Whether he had done so in his first assertion was a question which had raised in Vivaldi's mind a tempest of conjecture and of horror; for, while the subject of it was too astonishing to be fully believed, it was also too dreadful not to be apprehended even as a possibility.

CHAPTER XXX.

WHILE these events were passing in the prisons of the Inquisition at Rome, Ellena, in the sanctuary of Our Lady of Pity, remained ignorant of Schedoni's arrest and of Vivaldi's situation. She understood that the confessor was preparing to acknowledge her for his daughter, and believed that she comprehended also the motive for his absence; but, though he had forbidden her to expect a visit from him till his arrangement should be completed, he had promised to write in the meantime, and inform her of all the present circumstances of Vivaldi. His unexpected silence had excited, therefore, apprehensions as various, though not so terrible, as those which Vivaldi had suffered for her ; nor did the silence of Vivaldi himself appear less extraordinary.

"His confinement must be severe indeed," said the afflicted Ellena, "since he cannot relieve my anxiety by a single line of intelligence. Or, perhaps, harassed by unceasing opposition, he has submitted to the command of his family, and, has consented to forget me. Ah ! why did I leave the opportunity for that command to his family ; why did I not enforce it myself !"

Yet, while she uttered this self-reproach, the tears she shed contradicted the pride which had suggested it ; and a conviction lurking in her heart that Vivaldi could not so resign her soon dissipated those tears. But other conjectures recalled them ; it was possible that he was ill—that he was dead.

In such vague and gloomy surmise her days passed away ; employment could no longer withdraw her from herself, nor music, even for a moment, charm away the sense of sorrow. Yet she regularly partook of the various occupations of the nuns, and was so far from permitting herself to indulge in any useless expression of anxiety, that she had never once disclosed the sacred subject of it ; so that, though she could not assume an air of cheerfulness, she never appeared otherwise than tranquil. Her most soothing, though perhaps most melancholy, hour was when about sunset she could withdraw unnoticed to the terrace among the rocks that overlooked the convent and formed a part of its domain. There, alone and relieved from all the ceremonial restraints of the society, her very thoughts seemed more at liberty. As from beneath the light foliage of the acacias, or the more majestic shade of the plane trees that waved their branches over the many coloured cliffs of this terrace, Ellena looked down upon the magnificent scenery of the bay, it brought back to memory, in sad yet pleasing detail, the many happy days she had passed on those blue waters, or on the shores, in the society of Vivaldi and her departed relative, Bianchi ; and every point of the prospect marked by such remembrance, which the veiling distance stole, was rescued by affection, and pictured by imagination in tints more animated than hose of brightest nature.

One evening Ellena had lingered on the terrace later than usual. She had watched the rays retiring from the highest points of the horizon, and the fading imagery of the lower scene, till the sun having sunk into the waves, all colouring was withdrawn, except an empurpling and reposing hue, which overspread the waters and the heavens, and blended in soft confusion every feature of the landscape. The roofs and slender spires of the Santa della Pieta, with a single tower of the church rising loftily over every other part of the buildings that composed the convent, were fading fast from the eye ; but the solemn tint that invested them accorded so well with their style that Ellena was unwilling to relinquish this interesting object. Suddenly she perceived through the dubious light an unusual number of moving figures in the court of the great cloister, and, listening, fancied she could distinguish the murmuring of many voices. The white drapery of the nuns rendered them conspicuous as they moved, but it was impossible to ascertain who were the individuals engaged in this bustle. Presently the assemblage dispersed ; and Ellena, curious to understand the occasion of what she had observed, prepared to descend to the convent.

She had left the terrace, and was about to enter a long avenue of chestnuts that extended to a part of the convent communicating immediately with the great court, when she heard approaching steps, and, on turning into the walk, perceived several persons advancing in the shady distance. Among the voices, as they drew nearer, she distinguished one whose interesting tone engaged all her attention, and began also to awaken memory. She listened, wondered, doubted, hoped, and feared. It spoke again ! Ellena thought she could not be deceived in those tender accents, so full of intelligence, so expressive of sensibility and refinement. She proceeded with quicker steps, yet faltered as she drew near the group, and paused to inquire whether among them was any figure that might accord with the voice and justify her hopes.

The voice spoke again. It pronounced her name, pronounced it with the tremblings of tenderness and impatience, and Ellena scarcely dared to trust her senses when she beheld Olivia, the nun of San Stefano, in the cloisters of La Pieta !

Ellena could find no words to express her joy and surprise on beholding her preserver in safety, and in these quiet groves ; but Olivia repaid all the affectionate caresses of her young friend, and, while she promised to explain the circumstances that had led to her present appearance here, she, in her turn, made numerous inquiries relative to Ellena's adventures after she had quitted San Stefano. They were now, however, surrounded by too many auditors to allow of unreserved conversation. Ellena, therefore, led the nun to her apartment, and Olivia then explained her reasons for having left the convent of San Stefano, which were indeed sufficient to justify, even with the most rigid devotee, her conduct as to the change. This unfortunate recluse, it appeared, persecuted by the suspicions of the abbess, who understood that she had assisted in the liberation of Ellena, had petitioned the bishop of her diocese for leave to remove to La Pieta. The abbess had not proof to proceed formally against her, as an accomplice in the escape of a novice, for though Jeronimo could have supplied the requisite evidence, he was too deeply implicated in this adventure to do so without betraying his own conduct. From his having withheld such proof, it appears, however, that accident rather than design had occasioned his failure on the evening of Ellena's departure from the monastery. But, though the abbess had not testimony enough for legal punishment, she was acquainted with circumstances sufficient to justify suspicion, and had both the inclination and the power to render Olivia very miserable.

In her choice of La Pieta, the nun was influenced by many considerations, some of which were the consequence of conversations she had held with Ellena respecting the state of that society. Her design she had been unable to disclose to her friend, lest, by a discovery of such correspondence, the abbess of San Stefano should obtain grounds on which to proceed against her. Even in her appeal to the bishop the utmost caution and secrecy had been necessary, till the order for her removal, procured not without considerable delay and difficulty, arrived, and when it came, the jealous anger of the superior rendered an immediate departure necessary.

Olivia, during many years, had been unhappy in her local circumstances, but it is probable she would have concluded her days within the walls of San Stefano, had not the aggravated oppression of the abbess aroused her courage and activity, and dissipated the despondency with which severe misfortune had obscured her views.

Ellena was particular in her inquiries whether any person of the monastery had suffered for the assistance they had given her; and learning that not one, except Olivia, had been even suspected of befriending her, she understood that the venerable friar, who had dared to unfasten the gate which restored her, with Vivaldi, to liberty, had not been involved by his kindness.

"It is an embarrassing and rather an unusual circumstance," concluded Olivia, "to change one's convent; but you perceive the strong reasons which determined me upon a removal. I was, however, perhaps the more impatient of severe treatment since you, my sister, had described to me the society of Our Lady of Pity, and since I believed it possible that you might form a part of it. When, on my arrival here, I learnt that my wishes had not deceived me on this point, I was impatient to see you once more, and as

soon as the ceremonies attending an introduction to the superior were over, I requested to be conducted to you, and was in search of you when we met in the avenue. It is unnecessary for me to insist upon the satisfaction which this meeting gives me; but you may not, perhaps, understand how much the manners of our lady abbess, and of the sisterhood in general, as far as a first interview will allow me to judge of them, have reanimated me. The gloom which has long hung over my prospects seems now to open, and a distant gleam promises to light up the evening of my stormy day."

Olivia paused, and appeared to recollect herself. This was the first time she had made so direct a reference to her own misfortunes; and while Ellena silently remarked it, and observed the dejection which was already stealing upon the expressive countenance of the nun, she wished, yet feared, to lead her back towards the subject of them.

Endeavouring to dismiss some painful remembrance, and assuming a smile of languid gaiety, Olivia said, "Now that I have related the history of my removal, and sufficiently indulged my egotism, will you let me hear what adventures have befallen you, my young friend, since the melancholy adieu you gave me in the gardens of San Stefano?"

This was a task to which Ellena's spirits, though revived by the presence of Olivia, were still unequal. Over the scenes of her past distress Time had not yet drawn his shadowing veil; the colours were all too fresh and garish for the meek dejection of her eye, and the subject was too intimately connected with that of her present anxiety to be reviewed without very painful feelings. She therefore requested Olivia to spare her from a detail of particulars, which she could not recollect but with extreme reluctance; and, scrupulously observing the injunction of Schedoni, she merely mentioned her separation from Vivaldi upon the banks of the Celano, and that a variety of distressing circumstances had intervened before she could regain the sanctuary of Della Pieta.

Olivia understood too well the kind of feelings from which Ellena was desirous of escaping to willingly subject her to a renewal of them, and felt too much generous compassion for her sufferings not to endeavour to soothe the sense of them by an exertion of those delicate and nameless arts which, while they mock detection, fascinate the weary spirit as by a charm of magic.

The friends continued in conversation till a chime from a chapel of the convent summoned them to the last vespers; and when the service had concluded they separated for the night.

With the society of La Pieta Olivia had thus found an asylum such as till lately she had never dared to hope for, but, though she frequently expressed her sense of this blessing, it was seldom without tears ; and Ellena observed with some surprise and more disappointment, within a very few days after her arrival, a cloud of melancholy spreading again over her mind.

But a nearer interest soon withdrew Ellena's attention from Olivia to fix it upon Vivaldi ; and when she saw her infirm old servant, Beatrice, enter a chamber of the convent, she anticipated that the knowledge of some extraordinary, and probably unhappy event had brought her. She knew too well the circumspection of Schedoni to believe that Beatrice came commissioned from him ; and as the uncertain situation of Vivaldi was so constantly the subject of her anxiety, she immediately concluded that her servant came to announce some evil relative to him—his indisposition ; perhaps his actual confinement in the Inquisition, which lately she had sometimes been inclined to think might not have been a mere menace to Vivaldi, though it had proved to be no more to herself ; or possibly she came to tell of his death—his death in those prisons ! This last was a possibility that almost incapacitated her for inquiring what was the errand of Beatrice.

The old servant, trembling and wan, either from the fatigue of her walk or from a consciousness of disastrous intelligence, seated herself without speaking, and some moments elapsed before she could be prevailed with to answer the repeated inquiries.

"Oh, signora !" said she, at length, "you do not know what it is to walk up hill such a long way, at my age ! Well, heaven protect you ; I hope you never will !"

"I perceive you bring ill news," said Ellena. "I am prepared for it, and you need not fear to tell me all you know."

"Holy San Marco !" exclaimed Beatrice ; "if death be ill news, you have guessed right, signora, for I do bring news of that, it is certain. How came you, lady, to know my errand? They have been beforehand with me, I see, though I have not walked so fast up hill this many a day, as I have now, to tell you what has happened."

She stopped on observing the changing countenance of Ellena, who tremulously called upon her to explain what had happened—who was dead ; and entreated her to relate the particulars as speedi'y as possible.

"You said you were prepared, signora," said Beatrice ; "but your looks tell another tale."

"What is the event you would disclose? " said Ellena, almost breathless. "When did it happen ?—be brief."

"I cannot tell exactly when it happened, signora ; but it was an own servant of the Marchese that I had it from."

"The Marchese ?" interrupted Ellena, in a faltering voice.

"Aye, lady ; you will say that is pretty good authority."

"Death ! and in the Marchese's family ! " exclaimed Ellena.

"Yes, signora ; I had it from his own servant. He was passing by the garden-gate just as I happened to be speaking to the macaroni-man. But you are ill, lady ! "

"I am very well, if you will but proceed," replied Ellena, faintly, while her eyes were fixed upon Beatrice as if they only had power to enforce her meaning.

"'Well, dame,' he says to me, 'I have not seen you of a long time.' 'No,' says I, 'that is a great grievance truly ; for old women nowadays are not much thought of ; out of sight, out of mind with them, nowadays —— '"

"I beseech you to the purpose," interrupted Ellena. "Whose death did he announce?" She had not courage to pronounce Vivaldi's name.

"You shall hear, signora. I saw he looked in a sort of a bustle, so I asked him how all did at the Palazzo ; so he answers, 'Bad enough, signora Beatrice ; have not you heard?' 'Heard,' says I ; 'what should I have heard?' 'Why,' says he, 'of what has just happened in our family.'"

"Oh, heavens ! " exclaimed Ellena, "he is dead ! Vivaldi is dead ! "

"You shall hear, signora," continued Beatrice.

"Be brief ! " said Ellena ; "answer me simply yes or no."

"I cannot, till I come to the right place, signora ; if you will but have a little patience you shall hear all. But if you fluster me so, you will put me quite out."

"Grant me patience ! " said Ellena, endeavouring to calm her spirits.

"With that, signora, I asked him to walk in and rest himself, and tell me all about it. He answered, he was in a great hurry, and could not stay a moment, and a great deal of that sort ; but I, knowing that whatever happened in that family, signora, was something to you, would not let him go off so easily ; and so, when I asked him to refresh himself with a glass of lemon-ice, he forgot all his business in a minute, and we had a long chat."

And Beatrice might now have continued her circumlocution, perhaps, as long as she had pleased, for Ellena had lost all power to urge inquiry, and was scarcely sensible of what was said. She neither spoke, nor shed a tear ; the one image that possessed her fancy, the image of Vivaldi dead, seemed to hold all her faculties as by a spell.

"So when I asked him," added Beatrice, "again what had happened, he was ready enough to tell all about it. 'It is near a month ago,' said he, 'since she was first taken ; the Marchese had been —— '"

"The Marchesa!" repeated Ellena, with whom that one word had dissolved the spell of terror—"the Marchesa!"

"Yes, signora, to be sure. Who else did I say it was?"

"Go on, Beatrice. The Marchesa?—

"What makes you look so glad all of a sudden, signora? I thought just now you was very sorry about it. What I I warrant you was thinking about my young lord, Vivaldi."

"Proceed," said Ellena.

"Well," added Beatrice, "it was about a month ago that the Marchesa was first taken, continued the varlet. 'She had seemed poorly a long time, but it was from a conversazione at the di Voglio Palazzo that she came home so ill. It is supposed she had been in a bad state of health, but nobody thought her so near her end, till the doctors were called together; and then matters looked very bad indeed. They found out that she had been dying, or as good, for many years, though nobody else had suspected it, and the Marchesa's own physician was blamed for not finding it out before. But he,' added the rogue, 'had a regard for my lady. He was very obstinate too, for he kept saying, almost to the last, there was no danger, when everybody else saw how it was going. The other doctors soon made their words good, and my lady died."

"And her son," said Ellena; "was he with the Marchesa when she expired?"

"What, Signor Vivaldi, lady? No, the signor was not there."

"This is very extraordinary!" observed Ellena, with emotion. "Did the servant mention him?"

"Yes, signora; he said what a sad thing it was that he should be out of the way at that time, and nobody know where!"

"Are his family then ignorant where he is?" asked Ellena, with increased emotion.

"To be sure they are, lady, and have been for these many weeks. They have heard nothing at all of the signor, nor of one Paulo Mendrico, his servant, though the Marchese's people have been riding post after them from one end of the kingdom to the other all the time."

Shocked with the conviction of a circumstance which, till lately, she scarcely believed was possible, the imprisonment of Vivaldi in the Inquisition, Ellena lost for a while all power of further inquiry; but Beatrice proceeded.

"The Lady Marchesa seemed to lay something much to heart, as the man told me, and often inquired for Signor Vincentio."

"The Marchesa, you are sure then, was ignorant where he was?" said Ellena, with new astonishment and perplexity as to the person who, after betraying him into the Inquisition, could yet have suffered her, though arrested at the same time, to escape,

"Yes, signora, for she wanted sadly to see him. And when she was dying, she sent for her confessor, one father Schedoni, I think they call him, and —— '

"What of him," said Ellena, incautiously.

"Nothing, signora, for he could not be found."

"Not be found!" repeated Ellena.

"No, signora, not just then. He was confessor, I warrant, to other people beside the Marchesa, and I dare say they had sins enough to confess; so he could not get away in a hurry."

Ellena recollected herself sufficiently to ask no further of Schedoni; and, when she considered the probable cause of Vivaldi's arrest, she was again consoled by a hope: that he had not fallen into the power of real officials, since the comrades of the men who had arrested him had proved themselves otherwise, and she thought it highly probable that, while undiscovered by his family, he had been and was still engaged in searching for the place of her confinement.

"But I was saying," proceeded Beatrice, "what a bustle there was when my lady the Marchesa was dying. As this father Schedoni was not to be found, another confessor was sent for, and shut up with her for a long while indeed. And then my Lord Marchese was called in, and there seemed to be a deal going forward, for my lord was heard every now and then, by the attendants in the antechamber, talking loud, and sometimes my Lady Marchesa's voice was heard too, though she was so ill! At last all was silent, and after some time my lord came out of the room, and he seemed very much flustered, they say, that is, very angry and yet very sorrowful. But the confessor remained with my lady for a long while after; and, when he departed, my lady appeared more unhappy than ever. She lived all that night and part of the next day, and something seemed to lie very heavy at her heart, for she sometimes wept, but oftener groaned, and would look so that it was piteous to see her. She frequently asked for the Marchese, and when he came the attendants were sent away, and they held long conferences by themselves. The confessor also was sent for again, just at the last, and they were all shut up together. After this, my lady appeared more easy in her mind, and not long after, she died."

Ellena, who had attended closely to this little narrative, was prevented for the present from asking the few questions which it had suggested by the entrance of Olivia, who, on perceiving a stranger, was retiring, but Ellena, not considering these inquiries as important, prevailed with the nun to take a chair at the embroidery frame she had lately quitted.

After conversing for a few moments with Olivia, she returned to a consideration of her own interests. The absence of Schedoni still appeared to her as something more than accidental; and, though she could not urge any inquiry with Beatrice concerning the monk of the Spirito Santo, she ventured to ask whether she had lately seen the stranger who had restored her to Altieri, for Beatrice knew him only in the character of Ellena's deliverer.

"No, signora," replied Beatrice, rather sharply; "I have never seen his face since he attended you to the villa, though, for that matter, I did not see much of it there; and then how he contrived to let himself out of the house that night without my seeing him, I cannot divine, though I have thought of it often enough since! I am sure he need not have been ashamed to have shown his face to me, for I should only have blessed him for bringing you safe home again!"

Ellena was somewhat surprised to find that Beatrice had noticed a circumstance apparently so trivial, and replied that she had herself opened the door for her protector.

While Beatrice spoke, Olivia, raising her eyes from the embroidery, had fixed them upon the old servant, who respectfully withdrew here; but, when the nun was again engaged on her work, she resumed her observation. Ellena fancied she perceived something extraordinary in this mutual examination, although the curiosity of strangers towards each other might have accounted for it.

Beatrice then received directions from Ellena as to some drawings which she wished to have sent to the convent, and when the servant spoke in reply, Olivia again raised her eyes, and fixed them on her face with intense curiosity.

"I certainly ought to know that voice," said the nun with great emotion, "though I dare not judge from your features. Is it—can it be possible!—is it Beatrice Olca to whom I speak? So many years have passed—"

Beatrice, with equal surprise, answered, "It is. signora; you are right in my name. But, lady, who are you that know me?"

While she earnestly regarded Olivia, there was an expression of dismay in her look which increased Ellena's perplexity. The nun's complexion varied every instant, and her words failed when she attempted to speak. Beatrice meanwhile exclaimed, "My eyes deceive me! yet there is a strange likeness, Santa della Pieta! how it has fluttered me! my heart beats still—you are so like her, lady, yet you are very different too."

Olivia, whose regards were now entirely fixed upon Ellena, said, in a voice that was scarcely articulate, while her whole frame seemed sinking beneath some irresistible feeling. "Tell me, Beatrice, I conjure you quickly say, who is this——" She pointed to Ellena, and the sentence died on her lips.

Beatrice, wholly occupied by interests of her own, gave no reply, but exclaimed, "It is in truth the Lady Olivia! It is herself! In the name of all that is sacred, how came you here? Oh! how glad you must have been to find one another out!" She looked, still gasping with astonishment, at Olivia, while Ellena, unheard, repeatedly inquired the meaning of her words, and in the next moment found herself pressed to the bosom of the nun, who seemed better to have understood them, and who, weeping, trembling, and almost fainting, held her there in silence.

Ellena, after some moments had thus passed, requested an explanation of what she witnessed, and Beatrice at the same time demanded the cause of all this emotion. "For can it be that you did not know one another?" she added.

"What new discovery is this?" said Ellena, fearfully, to the nun. "It is but lately that I have found my father! Oh, tell me by what tender name I am to call you?"

"Your father!" exclaimed Olivia.

"Your father, lady!" echoed Beatrice.

Ellena, betrayed by strong emotion into this premature mention of Schedoni, was embarrassed, and remained silent.

"No, my child!" said Olivia, softening from amazement into tones of ineffable sorrow, while she again pressed Ellena to her heart—"no!—thy father is in the grave!"

Ellena no longer returned her caresses; surprise and doubt suspended every tender emotion; she gazed upon Olivia with an intenseness that partook of wildness. At length she said slowly, "It is my mother then whom I see! When will these discoveries end?"

"It is your mother!" replied Olivia, solemnly; "a mother's blessing rests with you!"

The nun endeavoured to soothe the agitated spirits of Ellena, though she was herself nearly overwhelmed by the various and acute feelings this disclosure occasioned. For a considerable time they were unable to speak but in short sentences of affectionate exclamation, but joy was evidently a more predominant feeling with the parent than with the child. When, however, Ellena could weep, she became more tranquil, and by degrees was sensible to a degree of happiness such as she had perhaps never experienced.

Meanwhile Beatrice seemed lost in amazement, mingled with fear. She expressed no pleasure, notwithstanding the joy she witnessed, but was uniformly grave and obedient.

Olivia, when she recovered some degree of composure, inquired for her sister Bianchi. The silence and sudden dejection of Ellena indicated the truth. On this mention of her late mistress, Beatrice recovered the use of speech.

"Alas! lady," said the old servant, "she is now where I believed you were; and I should as soon have expected to see my dear mistress here as yourself!"

Olivia, though affected by this intelligence, did not feel it with the acuteness she would have done probably at any other moment. After she had indulged her tears, she added that, from the unusual silence of Bianchi, she had suspected the truth, and particularly since not any answer had been returned to the letter she had sent to Altieri upon her arrival at the Santa della Pieta.

"Alas!" said Beatrice, "I wonder much my lady abbess failed to tell you the sad news, for she knew it too well! My dear mistress is buried in the church here; as for the letter, I have brought it with me for Signora Ellena to open."

"The lady abbess is not informed of our relationship," replied Olivia, "and I have particular reasons for wishing that at present she should remain ignorant of it. Even you, my Ellena, must appear only as my friend, till some inquiries have been made which are essential to my peace."

Olivia asked an explanation of Ellena's late extraordinary assertion respecting her father, but this was a request made with emotions very different from those which hope or joy inspire. Ellena, believing that the same circumstances which had deceived herself during so many years as to his death had also misled Olivia, was not surprised at the incredulity her mother had shown, but she was considerably embarrassed how to answer her inquiries. It was now too late to observe the promise of secrecy extorted from her by Schedoni; the first moments of surprise had betrayed her; yet, while she trembled further to transgress his injunction, she perceived that a full explanation was now unavoidable. And since Ellena considered that, as Schedoni could not have foreseen her present peculiar situation, his command had no reference to her mother, her scruples on this head disappeared. When, therefore, Beatrice had withdrawn, Ellena repeated her assertion that her father still lived; which, though it increased the amazement of Olivia, did not vanquish her incredulity. Olivia's tears flowed fast while, in contradiction to this assurance, she mentioned the year in which the Count di Bruno died, with some circumstances relative to his death, which, however, as Ellena understood that her mother had not witnessed it, she still believed not happened. To confirm her late assertion, Ellena then related a few particulars of her second interview with Schedoni, and, as some confirmation that he lived, offered to produce the portrait which he had claimed as his own. Olivia, in great agitation, requested to see the miniature, and Ellena left the apartment in search of it.

Every moment of her absence was to Olivia's expectation lengthened to an hour; she paced the room, listened for a footstep, endeavoured to tranquillise her spirits, and still Ellena did not return. Some strange mystery seemed to lurk in the narrative she had just heard, which she wished, yet dreaded, to develop; and when, at length, Ellena appeared with the miniature, she took it in trembling eagerness, and having gazed upon it for an instant, her complexion faded and she fainted.

Ellena had now no doubt respecting the truth of Schedoni's declaration, and blamed herself for not having more gradually prepared her mother for the knowledge of a circumstance which she believed had overwhelmed her with joy. The usual applications, however, soon restored Olivia, who, when she was again alone with her daughter, desired to behold once more the portrait. Ellena, attributing the strong emotion with which she still regarded it to surprise, and fear lest she was admitting a fallacious hope, endeavoured to comfort her by renewed assurances that not only the Count di Bruno yet existed, but that he lived at this very time in Naples, and, further, that he would probably be in her presence within the hour. "When I quitted the room for the miniature," added Ellena, "I despatched a person with a note, requesting to see my father immediately, being impatient to realise the joy which such a meeting between my long-lost parents must occasion."

In this instance Ellena had certainly suffered her generous sympathy to overcome her discretion, for, though the contents of the note to Schedoni could not positively have betrayed him, had he even been in Naples at this time, her sending it to the Spirito Santo, instead of the place which he had appointed for his letters, might have led to a premature discovery respecting herself.

While Ellena had acquainted Olivia that Schedoni would probably be with them soon, she watched eagerly for the joyful surprise she expected would appear on her countenance; how severe, then, was her disappointment when only terror and dismay were expressed there, and when, in the next moment, her mother uttered exclamations of distress and even of despair!

"If he sees me," said Olivia, "I am irrecoverably lost! Oh, unhappy Ellena! your precipitancy has destroyed me. The original of this portrait is not the Count di Bruno, my dear lord, nor your parent, but his brother, the cruel husband——"

Olivia left the sentence unfinished, as if she was betraying more than was at present discreet; but Ellena, whom astonishment had kept silent, now entreated that she would explain her words and the cause of her distress.

"I know not," said Olivia, "by what

means that portrait has been conveyed to you, but it is the resemblance of the Count Ferando di Bruno, the brother of my lord, and my——'' second husband, she should have said, but her lips refused to honour him with the title.

She paused and was much affected, but presently added :

'' I cannot at present explain the subject more fully, for it is to me a very distressing one. Let me rather consider the means of avoiding an interview with di Bruno, and even of concealing, if possible, that I exist.''

Olivia was, however, soothed when she understood that Ellena had not named her in the note, but had merely desired to see the confessor upon a very particular occasion.

While they were consulting upon the excuse it would be necessary to form for this imprudent summons, the messenger returned with the note unopened, and with information that father Schedoni was abroad on a pilgrimage, which was the explanation the brothers of the Spirito Santo chose to give of his absence, judging it prudent, for the honour of their convent, to conceal his real situation.

Olivia, thus released from her fears, consented to explain some points of the subject so interesting to Ellena ; but it was not till several days after this discovery that she could sufficiently command her spirits to relate the whole of her narrative. The first part of it agreed perfectly with the account delivered in the confession to the penitentiary, Ansaldo ; that which follows was known only to herself, her sister Bianchi, a physician, and one faithful servant, who had been considerably entrusted with the conduct of the plan.

It may be recollected that Schedoni left his house immediately after the act which was designed to be fatal to the Countess his wife, and that she was carried senseless to her chamber. The wound, as appears, was not mortal. But the atrocity of the intent determined her to seize the opportunity thus offered by the absence of Schedoni, and her own peculiar circumstances, to release herself from his tyranny without having recourse to a court of justice, which would have covered with infamy the brother of her first husband. She withdrew, therefore, from his house for ever, and, with the assistance of the three persons before mentioned, retired to a remote part of Italy, and sought refuge in the convent of San Stefano, while at home the report of her death was confirmed by a public funeral. Bianchi remained for some time after the departure of Olivia in her own residence near the Villa di Bruno, having taken under her immediate care the daughter of the Countess and of the first Count di Bruno, as well as an infant daughter of the second.

After some time had elapsed, Bianchi withdrew with her young charge, but not to the

neighbourhood of San Stefano. The indulgence of a mother's tenderness was denied to Olivia, for Bianchi could not reside near the convent without subjecting her to the hazard of a discovery, since Schedoni, though he now believed the report of her death, might be led to doubt it by the conduct of Bianchi, whose steps would probably be observed by him. She chose a residence, therefore, at a distance from Olivia, though not yet at Altieri. At this period, Ellena was not two years old ; the daughter of Schedoni was scarcely as many months, and she died before the year concluded. It was this his child for whom the confessor, who had too well concealed himself to permit Bianchi to acquaint him with her death, had mistaken Ellena, and to which mistake his own portrait, affirmed by Ellena to be that of her father, had contributed. This miniature she had found in the cabinet of Bianchi after her aunt's decease, and, observing it inscribed with the title of Count di Bruno, she had worn it with a filial fondness ever since that period.

Bianchi, when she had acquainted Ellena with the secret of her birth, was withheld, both by prudence and humanity, from entrusting her with a knowledge that her mother lived ; but this, no doubt, was the circumstance she appeared so anxious to disclose on her death-bed, when the suddenness of her disorder had deprived her of the power. The abruptness of that event had thus contributed to keep the mother and daughter unknown to each other, even when they afterwards accidentally met, to which concealment the name of Rosalba, given to Ellena from her infancy by Bianchi, for the purpose of protecting her from discovery by her uncle, had assisted. Beatrice, who was not the domestic entrusted with the escape of Olivia, had believed the report of her death, and thus, though she knew Ellena to be the daughter of the Countess di Bruno, she could never have been a means of discovering them to each other, had it not happened that Olivia recognised this ancient servant of Bianchi while Ellena was present.

When Bianchi came to reside in the neighbourhood of Naples, she was unsuspicious that Schedoni, who had never been heard of since the night of the assassination, inhabited there, and she so seldom left her house that it is not surprising she should never happen to meet him, at least, consciously, for her veil, and the monk's cowl, might easily have concealed them from each other if they had met.

It appears to have been the intention of Bianchi to disclose to Vivaldi the family of Ellena before their nuptials were solemnised ; since, on the evening of their last conversation, she had declared, when her spirits were exhausted by the exertion she had made, that much remained for her to say, which weakness obliged her to defer till another opportunity. Her unexpected death prevented any future meeting. That she had not sooner intended to make a communication which might have removed, in a considerable degree, the objection of the Vivaldi to a connection with Ellena appears extraordinary, till other circumstances of her family than that of its nobility are considered. Her present indigence, and, yet more, the guilt attached to an individual of the di Bruno, it was reasonable to suppose would operate as a full antidote to the allurement of rank, however jealous of birth the Vivaldi had proved themselves.

Ferando di Bruno had contrived, even in the short interval between the death of his brother and the supposed decease of his wife, again to embarrass his affairs, and soon after his flight the income arising from what remained of his landed property had been seized upon by his creditors—whether lawfully or not, he was then in a situation which did not permit him to contest—and Ellena was thus left wholly dependent upon her aunt. The small fortune of Bianchi had been diminished by the assistance she afforded Olivia, for whose admittance into the convent of San Stefano it had been necessary to advance a considerable sum ; and her original income was afterwards reduced by the purchase of the Villa Altieri. This expenditure, however, was not an imprudent one, since she preferred the comforts and independence of a pleasant home with industry to the indulgence of an indolence which must have confined her to an inferior residence, and was acquainted with the means of making this industry profitable without being dishonourable. She excelled in many elegant and ingenious arts; and the productions of her pencil and needle were privately disposed of to the nuns of La Pieta. When Ellena was of an age to assist her she resigned much of the employment and the profit to her niece, whose genius having unfolded itself, the beauty of her designs and the elegance of her execution, both in drawings and embroidery, were so highly valued by the purchasers at the grate of the convent that Bianchi committed to Ellena altogether the exercise of her art.

Olivia, meanwhile, had dedicated her life to devotion in the monastery of San Stefano, a choice which was willingly made while her mind was yet softened by grief for the death of her first lord, and wearied by the cruelty she had afterwards experienced. The first years of her retirement were passed in tranquillity, except when the remembrance of her child, whom she did not dare to see at the convent, awakened a parental pang. With Bianchi she, however, corresponded as regularly as opportunity would allow, and had at least the consolation of knowing that the object most dear to her lived, till, within a short period of Ellena's arrival at the very asylum

chosen by her mother, her apprehensions were in some degree excited by the unusual silence of Bianchi.

When Olivia had first seen Ellena in the chapel of San Stefano, she was struck with a slight resemblance she bore to the late Count di Bruno, and had frequently afterwards examined her features with a most painful curiosity ; but, circumstanced as she was, Olivia could not reasonably suspect the stranger to be her daughter. Once, however, a sense of this possibility so far overcame her judgment as to prompt an inquiry for the surname of Ellena ; but the mention of Rosalba had checked all further conjecture. What would have been the feelings of the nun had she been told, when her generous compassion was assisting a stranger to escape from oppression, that she was preserving her own child ! It may be worthy of observation that the virtues of Olivia, exerted in a general cause, had thus led her unconsciously to the happiness of saving her daughter ; while the vices of Schedoni had as unconsciously urged him nearly to destroy his niece, and had always been preventing, by the means they prompted him to employ, the success of his constant aim.

CHAPTER XXXI.

THE Marchesa di Vivaldi, of whose death Beatrice had given an imperfect account, struck with remorse for the crime she had meditated against Ellena, and with terror of the punishment due to it, had sent, when on her death-bed, for a confessor, to whom she unburthened her conscience, and from whom she hoped to receive in return an alleviation of her despair. This confessor was a man of good sense and humanity ; and when he fully understood the story of Vivaldi and Ellena di Rosalba, he declared that her only hope of forgiveness, both for the crime she had meditated and the undeserved sufferings she had occasioned, rested upon her willingness to make those now happy whom she had formerly rendered miserable. Her conscience had already given her the same lesson ; and now that she was sinking to that grave which levels all distinctions, and had her just fear of retribution no longer opposed by her pride, she became as anxious to promote the marriage of Vivaldi with Ellena as she had ever been to prevent it. She sent, therefore, for the Marchese ; and having made an avowal of the arts she had practised against the peace and reputation of Ellena, without, however, confessing the full extent of her intended crimes, she made it her last request that he would consent to the happiness of his son.

The Marchese, however, shocked as he was at this discovery of the duplicity and cruelty of his wife, had neither her terror of the future, nor remorse for the past, to overcome his objection to the rank of Ellena; and he resisted all her importunity till the anguish of her last hours vanquished every consideration but that of affording her relief. He then gave a solemn promise, in the presence of the confessor, that he would no longer oppose the marriage of Vivaldi and Ellena, should the former persist in his attachment to her. This promise was sufficient for the Marchesa, and she died with some degree of resignation. It did not, however, appear probable. that the Marchese would soon be called upon to fulfil the engagements into which he had so willingly entered, every inquiry after Vivaldi having been hitherto ineffectual.

During the progress of this fruitless search for his son, and while the Marchese was almost lamenting him as dead, the inhabitants of the Vivaldi palace were one night aroused from sleep by a violent knocking at the great gate of the court. The noise was so loud and incessant that, before the porter could obey the summons, the Marchese, whose apartment looked upon the court, was alarmed, and he sent an attendant from his ante-room to inquire the occasion of it.

Presently a voice was heard from the first ante-chamber, exclaiming, "I must see my Lord Marchese directly; he will not be angry to be waked, when he knows all about it," and before the Marchese could order that no person, on whatever pretence, should be admitted, Paulo, haggard, ragged, and covered with dirt, was in the chamber. His wan and affrighted countenance, his disordered dress, and his very attitude, as on entering he half turned to look back upon the ante-rooms, like one who, just escaped from bondage, listens to the fancied sounds of pursuit, were altogether so striking and terrific that the Marchese, anticipating some dreadful news of Vivaldi, had scarcely power to inquire for him. Paulo, however, rendered questions unnecessary, for without any circumlocution or preface he immediately informed the Marchese that the signor, his dear master, was in the prisons of the Inquisition at Rome, if, indeed, they had not put an end to him before that time.

"Yes, my lord," said Paulo, "I am just got out myself, for they would not let me be with the signor, so it was of no use to stay there any longer. Yet it was a hard matter with me to go away and leave my dear master within those dismal walls; and nothing should have persuaded me to do so, but that I hoped, when your lordship knew where the signor was, you might be able to get him out. But there is not a minute to be lost, my lord, for when once a gentleman has got within the claws of those inquisitors, there is no knowing how soon they may take it in their heads

to tear him in pieces. Shall I order horses for Rome, my lord? I am ready to set off again directly."

The suddenness of such intelligence, concerning an only son, might have agitated stronger nerves than those of the Marchese; and so much was he shocked by it that he could not immediately determine how to proceed, or give any answer to Paulo's repeated questions. When, however, he became sufficiently recollected to make further inquiry into the situation of Vivaldi, he perceived the necessity of an immediate journey; but first it would be prudent to consult with some friends, whose connections at Rome might be a means of greatly facilitating the important purpose which led him thither, and this could not be done till the following morning. Yet he gave orders that preparation should be made for his setting out at a moment's notice; and, having listened to as full an account as Paulo could give of the past and present circumstances of Vivaldi, he dismissed him to repose for the remainder of the night.

Paulo, however, though much in want of rest, was in too great an agitation of spirits either to seek or to find it; and the fear he had indicated. on entering the Marchese's apartment, proceeded from the hurry of his mind rather than from any positive apprehension of new evil. For his liberty he was indebted to the young sentinel who had on a former occasion been removed from the door of his prison, but who, by means of the guard to whom Vivaldi had given money as he returned one night from the tribunal, had since been able to communicate with him. This man, of a nature too humane for his situation, was become wretched in it, and he determined to escape from his office before the expiration of the time for which he had been engaged. He thought that to be a guard over prisoners was nearly as miserable as being a prisoner himself. "I see no difference between them," said he, "except that the prisoner watches on one side of the door, and the sentinel on the other."

With the resolution to release himself, he conferred with Paulo, whose good nature and feeling heart, among so many people of a contrary character, had won his confidence and affection, and he laid his plan of escape so well that it was on the point of succeeding, when Paulo's obstinacy in attempting an impossibility had nearly counteracted the whole. It went to his heart, he said, to leave his master in prison while he himself was to march off in safety, and he would run the risk of his neck rather than have such a deed upon his head. He proposed, therefore, as Vivaldi's guards were of too ferocious a nature to be tampered with, to scale a wall of the court into which a grate of Vivaldi's dungeon looked. But had this lofty wall been practicable, the grate was not; and the attempt had nearly cost Paulo not only his liberty but his life.

When, at length, he had made his way through the perilous avenues of the prison, and was fairly beyond the walls, he could hardly be prevailed upon by his companion to leave them. For near an hour, he wandered under their shade, weeping and exclaiming, and calling upon his dear master, at the evident hazard of being retaken ; and probably would have remained there much longer, had not the dawn of morning rendered his companion desperate. Just, however, as the man was forcing him away, Paulo fancied he distinguished, by the strengthening light, the roof of that particular building in whose dungeon his master was confined, and the appearance of Vivaldi himself could scarcely have occasioned a more sudden burst of joy ; succeeded by one of grief. "It is the roof, it is the very roof !" exclaimed Paulo, vaulting from the ground and clapping his hands ; "it is the roof, the roof ! Oh, my master, my master ! the roof, the roof !" He continued alternately to exclaim, "My master ! the roof ! my master ! the roof !" till his companion began to fear he was frantic, while tears streamed down his cheeks, and every look and gesture expressed the most extravagant and whimsical union of joy and sorrow. At length the absolute terror of discovery compelled his companion to force him from the spot; when, having lost sight of the building which enclosed Vivaldi, he set off for Naples with a speed that defied all interruption, and arrived there in the condition which has been mentioned, having taken no sleep, and scarcely any sustenance, since he left the Inquisition. Yet, though in this exhausted state, the spirit of his affection remained unbroken; and when, on the following morning, the Marchese quitted Naples, neither his weariness, nor the imminent danger to which this journey must expose him, could prevent his attending him to Rome.

The rank of the Marchese and the influence he was known to possess at the court of Naples were circumstances that promised to have weight with the Holy Office, and to procure Vivaldi a speedy release ; but yet more than these were the high connections which the Count di Maro, the friend of the Marchese, had in the Church of Rome.

The applications, however, which were made to the inquisitors were not so soon replied to as the wishes of the Marchese had expected, and he had been above a fortnight in that city before he was even permitted to visit his son. In this interview affection predominated on both sides over all remembrance of the past. The condition of Vivaldi, his faded appearance, to which the wounds he had received at Celano, and from which he was scarcely recovered, had con-

tributed, and his situation in a melancholy and terrible prison, were circumstances that awakened all the tenderness of the father ; his errors were forgiven, and the Marchese felt disposed to consent to all that might restore him to happiness, could he but be restored to liberty.

Vivaldi, when informed of his mother's death, shed bitter tears of sorrow and remorse for having occasioned her so much uneasiness. The unreasonableness of her claims was forgotten, and her faults were extenuated ; happily, indeed, for his peace, the extent of her criminal designs he had never understood ; and when he learned that her dying request had been intended to promote his happiness, the cruel consciousness of having interrupted her's occasioned him severe anguish, and he was obliged to recollect her former conduct towards Ellena at San Stefano before he could become reconciled to himself.

CHAPTER XXXII.

NEAR three weeks had elapsed since the Marchese's arrival at Rome, and not any decisive answer was returned by the Inquisition to his application, when he and Vivaldi received at the same time a summons to attend father Schedoni in his dungeon. To meet the man who had occasioned so much suffering to his family was extremely painful to the Marchese, but he was not allowed to refuse the interview ; and at the hour appointed he called at the chamber of Vivaldi, and, followed by two officials, they passed on together to that of Schedoni.

While they waited at the door of the prison-room till the numerous bars and locks were unfastened, the agitation which Vivaldi had suffered on receiving the summons returned with redoubled force, now that he was about to behold, once more, that wretched man who had announced himself to be the parent of Ellena di Rosalba. The Marchese suffered emotions of a different nature, and with his reluctance to see Schedoni was mingled a degree of curiosity as to the event which had occasioned this summons.

The door being thrown open the officials entered first, and the Marchese and Vivaldi, on following, discovered the confessor lying on a mattress. He did not rise to receive them ; but, as he lifted his head and bowed it in obeisance, his countenance, upon which the little light admitted through the triple grate of his dungeon gleamed, seemed more than usually ghastly ; his eyes were hollow, and his shrunk features appeared as if death had already touched them. Vivaldi, on perceiving him, groaned and averted his face ; but, soon recovering a command of himself, he approached the mattress.

The Marchese, suppressing every expres-

curred, the torch of one of the sentinels who watched in the dark avenue without was brought in its stead, and this discovered to Schedoni the various figures assembled in his dusky chamber, and to them the emaciated form and ghastly visage of the confessor. As Vivaldi now beheld him by the stronger light of the torch, he again fancied that death was in his aspect.

Every person was now ready for the declaration of Schedoni; but he himself seemed not fully prepared. He remained for some moments reclining on his pillow in silence, with his eyes shut, while the changes in his features indicated the strong emotion of his mind. Then, as if by a violent effort, he half raised himself and made an ample confession of the arts he had practised against Vivaldi. He declared himself to be the anonymous accuser who had caused him to be arrested by the Holy Office, and that the charge of heresy which he had brought against him was false and malicious.

At the moment when Vivaldi received this confirmation of his accuser, he discovered more fully that the charge was not what had been stated to him at the chapel of San Sebastian, in which Ellena was implicated; and he demanded an explanation of this circumstance. Schedoni acknowledged that the persons who had there arrested him were not officers of the Inquisition; and that the instrument of arrest, containing the charge of elopement with a nun was forged by himself for the purpose of empowering the ruffians to carry off Ellena without opposition from the inhabitants of the convent, in which she was then lodged.

To Vivaldi's inquiry, why it had been thought necessary to employ stratagem in the removal of Ellena, since, if Schedoni had only claimed her for his daughter, he might have removed her without any; the confessor replied, that he was then ignorant of the relationship which existed between them. But to the further inquiries, with what design, and whither Ellena had been removed, and the means by which he had discovered her to be his daughter, Schedoni was silent; and he sank back, overwhelmed by the recollections they awakened.

The depositions of Schedoni, having been taken down by the secretary, were formally signed by the inquisitor and the officials present: and Vivaldi thus saw his innocence vindicated by the very man who had thrown him among the perils of the Inquisition. But the near prospect of release now before him failed to affect him with joy, while he understood that Ellena was the daughter of Schedoni, the child of a murderer, whom he himself had been in some degree instrumental in bringing to a dreadful and ignominious death. Still, however, willing to hope that Schedoni had not spoken the truth concern-

ing his relationship to Ellena, he claimed, in consideration of the affection he had so long cherished for her, a full explanation of the circumstances connected with the discovery of her family.

At this public avowal of his attachment, a haughty impatience appeared on the countenance of the Marchese, who forbade him to make further inquiry on the subject and was immediately retiring from the chamber.

"My presence is no longer necessary," he added; "the prisoner has concluded the only detail which I could be interested to hear from him; and, in consideration of the confession he has made as to the innocence of my son, I pardon him the suffering which his false charge has occasioned to me and my family. The paper containing his depositions is given to your responsibility, holy father," addressing the inquisitor; "and you are required to lay it upon the table of the Holy Office, that the innocence of Vincentio di Vivaldi may appear, and that he may be released from these prisons without further delay. But, first, I demand a copy of those declarations, and that the copy also shall be signed by the present witnesses."

The secretary was now bidden to copy them, and, while the Marchese waited to receive the paper (for he would not leave the chamber till he had secured it), Vivaldi was urging his claim for an explanation respecting the family of Ellena, with unconquerable perseverance. Schedoni, no longer permitted to evade the inquiry, could not, however, give a circumstantial explanation without partly disclosing also the fatal designs which had been meditated by him and the late Marchesa di Vivaldi, of whose death he was ignorant; he related, therefore, little more respecting Ellena than that a portrait, which she wore as being her father's, had first led to the discovery of her family.

While the confessor had been giving this brief explanation, Nicola, who was somewhat withdrawn from the circle, stood gazing at him with the malignity of a demon. His glowing eyes just appeared beneath the edge of his cowl, while, rolled up in his dark drapery, the lower features of his face were muffled; but the intermediate part of his countenance, receiving the full glare of the torch, displayed all its speaking and terrific lines. Vivaldi, as his eye glanced upon him, saw again the very monk of Paluzzi, and he thought he beheld also a man capable of the very crimes of which he had accused Schedoni. At this instant, he remembered the dreadful garment that had been discovered in a dungeon of the fortress; and, yet more, he remembered the extraordinary circumstances attending the death of Bianchi, together with the immediate knowledge which the monk had displayed of that event. Vivaldi's suspicions respecting the cause of her death being thus revived, he determined to obtain, if possible, either a relief from, or a confirmation of them; and he solemnly called upon Schedoni, who, already condemned to die, had no longer anything to fear from a disclosure of the truth, whatever it might be, to declare all that he knew on the subject. As he did so, he looked at Nicola, to observe the effect of this demand, whose countenance was now, however, so much shrouded, that little of its expression could be seen; and Vivaldi remarked that, while he had spoken, the monk drew his garment closer over the lower part of his face, and that he had immediately turned his eyes from him upon the confessor.

With most solemn protestations, Schedoni declared himself to be both innocent and ignorant of the cause of Bianchi's death.

Vivaldi then demanded by what means his agent, Nicola, had obtained such immediate information, as the warning he had delivered at Paluzzi proved him to have, of an event in which it appeared that he could be little interested; and why that warning had been given.

Nicola did not attempt to anticipate the reply of Schedoni, who, after a momentary silence, said "That warning, young man, was given to deter you from visiting Altieri, as was every circumstance of advice or intelligence which you received beneath the arch of Paluzzi."

"Father," replied Vivaldi, "you have never loved, or you would have spared yourself the practice of artifices so ineffectual to mislead or to conquer a lover. Did you believe that an anonymous adviser could have more influence with me than my affection, or that I could be terrified by such stratagems into the renunciation of its object?"

"I believed," rejoined the confessor, "that the disinterested advice of a stranger might have some weight with you; but I trusted more to the impression of awe which the conduct and seeming foreknowledge of that stranger were adapted to inspire in a mind like yours, and I thus endeavoured to avail myself of your prevailing weakness."

"And what do you term my prevailing weakness?" said Vivaldi, blushing.

"A susceptibility which renders you especially liable to superstition," replied Schedoni.

"What! does a monk call superstition a weakness?" rejoined Vivaldi. "But grant he does, on what occasion have I betrayed such weakness?"

"Have you forgotten a conversation which I once held with you on invisible spirits?" said Schedoni.

As he asked this, Vivaldi was struck with the tones of his voice; he thought it was different from what he had remembered ever to have heard from him, and he looked at Schedoni more intently, that he might be certain it was he who had spoken. The confessor's eyes were fixed upon him, and he repeated slowly in the same tone, "Have you forgotten?"

"I have not forgotten the conversation to which you allude," replied Vivaldi, "and I do not recollect that I then disclosed any opinion that may justify your assertion."

"The opinions you avowed were rational," said Schedoni, "but the ardour of your imagination was apparent; and what ardent imagination ever was contented to trust to plain reasoning, or to the evidence of the senses? It may not willingly confine itself to the dull truths of this earth, but, eager to expand its faculties, to fill its capacity, and to experience its own peculiar delights, soars after new wonders into a world of its own!"

Vivaldi blushed at this reproof, now conscious of its justness; and was surprised that Schedoni should so well have understood the nature of his mind, while he himself, with whom conjecture had never assumed the stability of opinion on the subject to which the confessor alluded, had been ignorant even of its propensities.

"I acknowledge the truth of your remark," said Vivaldi, "as far as it concerns myself. I have, however, inquiries to make on a point less abstracted, and towards explaining which the evidence of my senses themselves have done little. To whom belonged the bloody garments I found in the dungeon of Paluzzi, and what became of the person to whom they had pertained?"

Consternation appeared for an instant on the features of Schedoni. "What garments?" said he.

"They appeared to be those of a person who had died by violence," replied Vivaldi, "and they were discovered in a place frequented by your avowed agent, Nicola, the monk."

As he concluded the sentence, Vivaldi looked at Nicola, upon whom the attention of every person present was now directed.

"They were my own," said this monk.

"Your own! and in that condition!" exclaimed Vivaldi. "They were covered with gore!"

"They were my own," repeated Nicola. "For their condition I have to thank you—the wound your pistol gave me occasioned it."

Vivaldi was astonished at this apparent subterfuge. "I had no pistol," he rejoined, "my sword was my only weapon."

"Pause a moment," said the monk.

"I repeat that I had no firearms," replied Vivaldi.

"I appeal to father Schedoni," rejoined Nicola, "whether I was not wounded by a pistol shot."

"To me you have no longer any right of

appeal," said Schedoni. "Why should I save you from suspicions that may bring you to a state like this to which you have reduced me!"

"Your crimes have reduced you to it," replied Nicola. "I have only done my duty, and that which another person could have effected without my aid—the priest to whom Spalatro made his last confession."

"It is, however, a duty of such a kind," observed Vivaldi, "as I would not willingly have upon my conscience. You have betrayed the life of your former friend, and have compelled me to assist in the destruction of a fellow-being."

"You, like me, have assisted to destroy a destroyer," replied the monk. "He has taken life, and deserves, therefore, to lose it. If, however, it will afford you consolation to know that you have not materially assisted in his destruction, I will hereafter give you proof for this assurance. There were other means of showing that Schedoni was the Count di Bruno than the testimony of Ansaldo, though I was ignorant of them when I bade you summon the penitentiary."

"If you had sooner avowed this," said Vivaldi, "the assertion would have been more plausible. Now I can only understand that it is designed to win my silence, and prevent my retorting upon you your own maxim— that he who has taken the life of another, deserves to lose his own.—To whom did those garments belong?"

"To myself, I repeat," replied Nicola, "Schedoni can bear testimony that I received at Paluzzi a pistol wound."

"Impossible," said Vivaldi, "I was armed only with my sword!"

"You had a companion," observed the monk; "had not he firearms?"

Vivaldi, after a momentary consideration, recollected that Paulo had pistols, and that he had fired one beneath the arch of Paluzzi, on the first alarm occasioned by the stranger's voice. He immediately acknowledged the recollection. "But I heard no groan, no symptom of distress!" he added. "Besides, the garments were at a considerable distance from the spot where the pistol was fired! How could a person, so severely wounded as those garments indicated, have silently withdrawn to a remote dungeon, or having done so, is it probable he would have thrown aside his dress!"

"All that is nevertheless true," replied Nicola. "My resolution enabled me to stifle the expression of my anguish; I withdrew to the interior of the ruin to escape from you, but you pursued me even to the dungeon where I threw off my discoloured vestments, in which I dared not return to my convent, and departed by a way which all your ingenuity failed to discover. The people who were already in the fort, for the purpose of assisting

to confine you and your servant during the night on which Signora Rosalba was taken from Altieri, procured me another habit and relief for my wound. But, though I was unseen by you during the night I was not entirely unheard for my groans reached you more than once from an adjoining chamber, and my companions were entertained with the alarm which your servant testified.—Are you now convinced?"

The groans were clearly remembered by Vivaldi; and many other circumstances of Nicola's narration accorded so well with others which he recollected to have occurred on the night alluded to, that he had no longer a doubt of its veracity. The suddenness of Bianchi's death, however, still occasioned him suspicions as to its cause; yet Schedoni had declared not only that he was innocent but ignorant of its cause, which, it appeared from his unwillingness to give testimony in favour of his agent, he would not have affirmed had he been conscious that the monk was in any degree guilty in this instance. That Nicola could have no inducement for attempting the life of Bianchi other than a reward offered him by Schedoni, was clear; and Vivaldi, after more fully considering these circumstances, became convinced that her death was in consequence of some incident of natural decay.

While this conversation was passing, the Marchese, impatient to put a conclusion to it, and to leave the chamber, repeatedly urged the secretary to despatch; and while he now earnestly renewed his request, another voice answered for the secretary, that he had nearly concluded. Vivaldi thought that he had heard the voice on some former occasion, and on turning his eyes upon the person who had spoken, discovered the stranger to be the same who had first visited him in prison. Perceiving by his dress that he was an officer of the Inquisition, Vivaldi now understood too well the purport of his former visit, and that he had come with a design to betray him by affected sympathy into a confession of some heretical opinions. Similar instances of treachery Vivaldi had heard were frequently practised upon accused persons, but he had never fully believed such cruelty possible till now that it had been attempted towards himself.

The visit of this person bringing to his recollection the subsequent one he had received from Nicola, Vivaldi inquired whether the sentinels had really admitted him to his cell, or he had entered it by other means; a question to which the monk was silent, but the smile on his features, if so strange an expression deserved to be called a smile, seemed to reply, "Do you believe that I, a servant of the Inquisition, will betray its secrets?"

Vivaldi, however, urged the inquiry, for he

wished to know whether the guard, who appeared to be faithful to their office, had escaped the punishment that was threatened.

"They were honest," replied Nicola, "seek no further."

"Are the tribunal convinced of their integrity?"

Nicola smiled again in derision, and replied. "They never doubted it."

"How!" said Vivaldi. "Why were these men put under arrest, if their faithfulness was not even suspected?"

"Be satisfied with the knowledge which experience has given you of the secrets of the Inquisition," replied Nicola, solemnly; "seek to know no more!"

"It has terrible secrets!" said Schedoni, who had been long silent. "Know, young man, that almost every cell of every prisoner has a concealed entrance, by which the ministers of death may pass unnoticed to their victims. This Nicola is now one of those dreadful summoners, and is acquainted with all the secret avenues that lead to murder."

Vivaldi shrunk from Nicola in horror, and Schedoni paused; but while he had spoken, Vivaldi had again noticed the extraordinary change in his voice, and shuddered at its sound no less than at the information it had given. Nicola was silent; but his terrible eyes were fixed in vengeance on Schedoni.

"His office has been short," resumed the confessor, turning his heavy eyes upon Nicola "and his task is almost done!" As he pronounced the last words his voice faltered, but they were heard by the monk, who, drawing nearer to the bed, demanded an explanation of them. A ghastly smile triumphed in the features of Schedoni. "Fear not but that an explanation will come full soon," said he.

Nicola fixed himself before the confessor, and bent his brows upon him as if he would have searched into his very soul. When Vivaldi again looked at Schedoni he was shocked on observing the sudden alteration of his countenance, yet still a faint smile of triumph lingered there. But while Vivaldi gazed, the features suddenly became agitated; in the next instant his whole frame was convulsed, and heavy groans laboured from his breast. Schedoni was now evidently dying.

The horror of Vivaldi and of the Marchese, who endeavoured to leave the chamber, was equalled only by the general confusion that reigned there; every person present seemed to feel, at least, a momentary compassion, except Nicola, who stood unmoved beside Schedoni and looked steadfastly upon his pangs, while a smile of derision marked his countenance. As Vivaldi observed with detestation this expression, a slight spasm darted over Nicola's face, and his muscles also seemed to labour with sudden contraction; but the affection was transient, and vanished as abruptly as it had appeared. The monk, however, turned from the miserable spectacle before him, and as he turned he caught involuntarily at the arm of a person near him, and leaned on his shoulder for support. His manner appeared to betray that he had not been permitted to triumph in the sufferings of his enemy without participating at least in their horror.

Schedoni's struggles now began to abate, and in a short time he lay motionless. When he unclosed his eyes, death was in them. He was still nearly insensible, but presently a faint gleam of recollection shot from them, and gradually lighting them up, the character of his soul appeared there; the expression was indeed feeble, but it was true. He moved his lips as if he would have spoken, and looked languidly round the chamber, seemingly in search of some person. At length he uttered a sound, but he had not yet sufficient command of his muscles to modulate that sound into a word, till, by repeated efforts, the name of Nicola became intelligible. At the call, the monk raised his head from the shoulder of the person on whom he had reclined, and, turning round, Schedoni, as was evident from the sudden change of expression in his countenance, discovered him; his eyes, as they settled on Nicola, seemed to re-collect all their wonted fire, and the malignant triumph, lately so prevalent in his physiognomy, again appeared as in the next moment he pointed to him. His glance seemed suddenly impowered with the destructive fascination attributed to that of the basilisk, for while it now met Nicola's, that monk seemed as if transfixed to the spot, and unable to withdraw his eyes from the glare of Schedoni's; in their expression he read the dreadful sentence of his fate, the triumph of revenge and cunning. Struck with this terrible conviction a pallid hue overspread his face, at the same time an involuntary motion convulsed his features, cold trembling seized upon his frame, and, uttering a deep groan, he fell back, and was caught in the arms of the people near him. At the instant of his fall, Schedoni uttered a sound so strange and horrible, so convulsed and so loud, so exulting, yet so unlike any human voice, that every person in the chamber, except those who were assisting Nicola, struck with irresistible terror, endeavoured to make their way out of it. This, however, was impracticable, for the door was fastened until a physician, who had been sent for, should arrive, and some investigation could be made into this mysterious affair. The consternation of the Marchese and of Vivaldi, compelled to witness this scene of horror, cannot easily be imagined.

Schedoni, having uttered that demoniacal sound of exultation, was not permitted to repeat it, for the pangs he had lately suffered returned upon him, and he was again in strong convulsions when the physician entered the chamber. The moment he beheld Schedoni he declared him to be poisoned, and he pronounced a similar opinion on father Nicola, affirming also that the drug, as appeared from the violence of the effect, was of too subtle and inveterate a nature to allow of antidote. He was, however, willing to administer the medicine usual in such cases.

While he was giving orders to an attendant with respect to this, the violence of Schedoni's convulsions once more relaxed ; but Nicola appeared in the last extremity. His sufferings were incessant, his senses never for a moment returned, and he expired before the medicine which had been sent for could be brought. When it came, however, it was administered with some success to Schedoni, who recovered not only his recollection, but his voice ; and the first word he uttered was, as formerly, the name of Nicola.

" Does he live ? " added the confessor, with the utmost difficulty, and after a long pause. The persons around him were silent, but the truth which this silence indicated seemed to revive him.

The inquisitor who had attended, perceiving that Schedoni had recovered the use of his intellects, now judged it prudent to ask some questions relative to his present condition, and to the cause of Nicola's death.

" Poison," replied Schedoni, readily.

" By whom administered ?" said the inquisitor ; " consider that, while you answer, you are on your death-bed."

" I have no wish to conceal the truth," rejoined Schedoni, " nor the satisfaction,"— he was obliged to pause, but presently added, " I have destroyed him who would have destroyed me, and—and I have escaped an ignominious death."

He paused again ; it was with difficulty that he had said thus much; and he was now overcome by the exertions he had made. The secretary, who had not been permitted to leave the chamber, was ordered to note Schedoni's words.

" You avow, then, "continued the inquisitor, " that the poison was administered, both in the case of father Nicola and in your own, by yourself ?"

Schedoni could not immediately reply ; but when he did, he said, " I avow it."

He was asked by what means he had contrived to procure the poison, and was bidden to name his accomplice.

" I had no accomplice," replied Schedoni.

" How did you procure the poison, then ?"

Schedoni, slowly and with difficulty, replied, " It was concealed in my vest."

" Consider that you are dying," said the inquisitor, " and confess the truth. We cannot believe what you have last asserted. It

is improbable that you should have had an opportunity of providing yourself with poison after your arrest, and equally improbable that you should have thought such provision necessary before that period. Confess who is your accomplice."

This accusation of falsehood recalled the spirit of Schedoni, which contending with and conquering, for a moment, corporeal suffering, he said in a firmer tone, " It was the poison in which I dip my poniard, the better to defend me."

The inquisitor smiled in contempt of this explanation, and Schedoni, observing him, desired a particular part of his vest might be examined, where would be found some remains of the drug concealed, as he had affirmed. He was indulged in his request, and the poison was discovered within a broad hem of his garment.

Still it was inconceivable how he had contrived to administer it to Nicola, who, though he had been for some time alone with him on this day, would scarcely have so far confided in an enemy as to have accepted any seeming sustenance that might have been offered by him. The inquisitor, still anxious to discover an accomplice, asked Schedoni who had assisted to administer the drug to Nicola ; but the confessor was no longer in a condition to reply. Life was now sinking apace ; the gleam of spirit and of character that had returned to his eyes was departed, and left them haggard and fixed ; and presently a livid corpse was all that remained of the once terrible Schedoni !

While this awful event had been accomplishing, the Marchese, suffering under the utmost perturbation, had withdrawn to the distant grate of the dungeon, where he conversed with an official as to what might be the probable consequence of his present situation to himself ; but Vivaldi, in an agony of horror, had been calling incessantly for the medicine, which might possibly afford some relief to the anguish he witnessed ; and when it was brought, he had assisted to support the sufferers.

At length, now that the worst was over, and when the several witnesses had signed to the last avowal of Schedoni, every person in the chamber was suffered to depart ; and Vivaldi was re-conducted to his prison, accompanied by the Marchese, where he was to remain till the decision of the Holy Office respecting his innocence, as asserted by the deposition of Schedoni, should be known. He was too much affected by the late scene to give the Marchese any explanation at present respecting the family of Ellena di Rosalba ; and the Marchese, having remained for some time with his son, withdrew to the residence of his friend.

CHAPTER XXXIII.

IN consequence of the dying confession of Schedoni, an order was sent from the Holy Office for the release of Vivaldi within a few days after the death of the confessor, and the Marchese conducted his son from the prisons of the Inquisition to the mansion of his friend, the Count di Maro, with whom he had resided since his arrival at Rome.

While they were receiving the ceremonious congratulations of the Count, and of some nobles assembled to welcome the emancipated prisoner, a loud voice was heard from the ante-chamber, exclaiming, "Let me pass! It is my master; let me pass! May all those who attempt to stop me be sent to the Inquisition themselves!"

In the next instant Paulo burst into the saloon, followed by a group of lacqueys, who, however, paused at the door, fearful of the displeasure of their lord, yet scarcely able to stifle a laugh; while Paulo, springing forward, had nearly overset some of the company, who happened at that moment to be bowing with profound joy to Vivaldi.

"It is my master! it is my dear master!" cried Paulo; and, sending off a nobleman with each elbow, as he made his way between them, he hugged Vivaldi in his arms, repeating, "Oh, my master! my master!" till a passion of joy and affection overcame his voice, and he fell at his master's feet and wept.

This was a moment of finer satisfaction to Vivaldi than he had known since his meeting with his father; and he was too much interested by his faithful servant to have leisure to apologize fo the astonished company for his rudeness. While the lacqueys were repairing the mischief Paulo had occasioned, were picking up the rolling snuff-boxes he had jerked away in his passage, and wiping the snuff from the soiled clothes, Vivaldi was participating in all the delight and returning all the affection of his servant, and was so wholly occupied by these pleasurable feelings as scarcely to be sensible that any persons besides themselves were in the room. The Marchese, meanwhile, was making a thousand apologies for the disasters Paulo had occasioned; was alternately calling upon him to recollect in whose presence he was, and to quit the apartment immediately, explaining to the company that he had not seen Vivaldi since they were together in the Inquisition, and remarking profoundly that he was much attached to his master. But Paulo, insensible to the repeated commands of the Marchese, and to the endeavours of Vivaldi to raise him, was still pouring forth his whole heart at his master's feet. "Ah! nay signor," said he, "if you could but know how miserable I was when I got out of the Inquisition——"

"He raves!" observed the Count to the Marchese; "you perceive that joy has rendered him delirious!"

"How I wandered about the walls half the night, and what it cost me to leave them! But when I lost sight of them, signor, oh, San Dominico! I thought my heart would have broke. I had a great mind to have gone back again and given myself up; and, perhaps, I should too, if it had not been for my friend, the sentinel, who escaped with me, and I would not do him an injury, poor fellow! for he meant nothing but kindness when he let me out. And, sure enough, as it proved, it was all for the best; for now I am here, too, signor, as well as you, and can tell you all I felt when I believed I should never see you again."

The contrast of his present joy to his remembered grief again brought tears into Paulo's eyes; he smiled and wept and sobbed and laughed with such rapid transition that Vivaldi began to be alarmed for him; when, suddenly becoming calm, he looked up in his master's face, and said gravely, but with eagerness, "Pray, signor, was not the roof of your little prison peaked, and was there not a little turret stuck up at one corner of it? and was there not a battlement round the turret? and was there not ——" Vivaldi, after regarding him for a moment, replied smilingly, "Why, truly, my good Paulo, my dungeon was so far from the roof that I never had an opportunity of observing it."

"That is very true, signor," replied Paulo; "very true indeed; but I did not happen to think of that. I am certain, though, it was as I say, and I was sure of it at the time. Oh, signor! I thought that roof would have broke my heart. Oh, how I did look at it! and now to think that I am here, with my dear master once again!".

As Paulo concluded, his tears and sobs returned with more violence than before; and Vivaldi, who could not perceive any necessary connection between this mention of the roof of his late prison and the joy his servant expressed on seeing him again, began to fear that his senses were bewildered, and desired an explanation of his words. Paulo's account, rude and simple as it was, soon discovered to him the relation of these apparently heterogeneous circumstances to each other; when Vivaldi, overcome by this new instance of the power of Paulo's affection, embraced him with his whole heart, and, compelling him to rise, presented him to the assembly as his faithful friend and chief deliverer.

The Marchese, affected by the scene he had witnessed, and with the truth of Vivaldi's words, condescended to give Paulo a hearty shake by the hand, and to thank him warmly for the bravery and fidelity he had displayed in his master's interest. "I never can fully reward your attachment," added the Marchese, "but what remains for me to do shall be done. From this moment I make you independent, and promise, in the presence of this noble company, to give you a thousand sequins, as some acknowledgment of your services."

Paulo did not express all the gratitude for this gift which the Marchese expected. He stammered, and bowed, and blushed, and at length burst into tears; and when Vivaldi inquired what distressed him, he replied, "Why, signor, of what use are the thousand sequins to me, if I am to be independent? what use, if I am not to stay with you?"

Vivaldi cordially assured Paulo that he should always remain with him, and that he should consider it as his duty to render his future life happy. "You shall henceforth," added Vivaldi, "be placed at the head of my household, the management of my servants and the whole conduct of my domestic concerns shall be committed to you, as a proof of my entire confidence in your integrity and attachment, and because this is a situation which will allow you to be always near me."

"Thank you, my signor," replied Paulo, in a voice rendered almost inarticulate by his gratitude; "thank you with my whole heart! If I stay with you, that is enough for me; I ask no more. But I hope my Lord Marchese will not think me ungrateful for refusing to accept of the thousand sequins he was so kind as to offer me if I would but be independent, for I thank him as much as if I had received them, and a great deal more too."

The Marchese, smiling at Paulo's mistake, rejoined, "As I do not perceive, my good friend, how your remaining with your master can be a circumstance to disqualify you from accepting a thousand sequins, I command you, on pain of my displeasure, to receive them; and whenever you marry, I shall expect that you will show your obedience to me again, by accepting another thousand from me with your wife as her dower."

"This is too much, signor," said Paulo, sobbing—"too much to be borne!" and ran out of the saloon. But amidst the murmur of applause which his conduct drew from the noble spectators, for Paulo's warm heart had subdued even the coldness of their pride, a convulsive sound from the ante-chamber betrayed the excess of emotion which he had thus abruptly withdrawn himself to conceal.

In a few hours the Marchese and Vivaldi took leave of their friends, and set out for Naples, where they arrived, without any interruption, on the fourth day. But it was a melancholy journey to Vivaldi, notwithstanding the joy of his late escape; for the Marchese, having introduced the mention of his attachment to Ellena di Rosalba, informed him that under the present unforseen circumstances he could not consider his late engagement to the Marchesa on that subject as binding, and that Vivaldi must relinquish

Ellena if it should appear that she really was the daughter of the late Schedoni.

Immediately on his arrival at Naples, however, Vivaldi, with a degree of impatience to which his utmost speed was inadequate, and with a revived joy so powerful as to overcome every fear and every melancholy consideration which the late conversation with his father had occasioned, hastened to the Santa della Pieta.

Ellena heard his voice from the grate inquiring for her of a nun who was in the parlour, and in the next instant they beheld each other yet once again.

In such a meeting, after the long uncertainty and terror which each had suffered for the fate of the other, and the dangers and hardships they had really incurred, joy was exalted almost to agony. Ellena wept, and some minutes passed before she could answer to Vivaldi's few words of tender exclamation; it was long ere she was tranquil enough to observe the alteration which severe confinement had given to his appearance. The animated expression of his countenance was unchanged; yet, when the first glow of joy had faded from it, and Ellena had leisure to observe its wanness, she understood too certainly that he had been a prisoner in the Inquisition.

During this interview he related, at Ellena's request, the particulars of his adventures since he had been separated from her in the chapel of San Sebastian; but when he came to that part of the narration where it was necessary to mention Schedoni he paused in unconquerable embarrassment, and a distress not unmingled with horror. Vivaldi could scarcely endure even to hint to Ellena any part of the unjust conduct which the confessor had practised towards him, yet it was impossible to conclude his account without expressing much more than hints; nor could he bear to afflict her with a knowledge of the death of him whom he believed to be her parent, however the dreadful circumstances of that event might be concealed. His embarrassment became obvious, and was still increased by Ellena's inquiries.

At length, as an introduction to the information it was necessary to give, and to the fuller explanation he wished to receive upon a subject which, though it was the one that pressed most anxiously upon his mind, he had not yet dared to mention, Vivaldi ventured to declare his knowledge of her having discovered her parent to be living. The satisfaction immediately apparent upon Ellena's countenance heightened his distress and his reluctance to proceed, believing, as he did, that the event he had to communicate must change her gladness to grief.

Ellena, however, upon this mention of a topic so interesting to them both, proceeded to express the happiness she had received from the discovery of a parent whose virtues had even won her affection long before she understood her own interest in them. It was with some difficulty that Vivaldi could conceal his surprise at such an avowal of prepossession, the manners of Schedoni, of whom he believed her to speak, having certainly never been adapted to inspire tenderness. But his surprise soon changed its object when Olivia, who had heard that a stranger was at the grate, entered the parlour, and was announced as the mother of Ellena di Rosalba.

Before Vivaldi left the convent, a full explanation as to family was given on both sides, when he had the infinite joy of learning that Ellena was not the daughter of Schedoni; and Olivia had the satisfaction to know that she had no future evil to apprehend from him who had hitherto been her worst enemy. The manner of his death, however, with all the circumstances of his character, as unfolded by the late trial, Vivaldi was careful to conceal.

When Ellena had withdrawn from the room, Vivaldi made a full acknowledgment to Olivia of his long attachment to her daughter, and supplicated for her consent to their marriage. To this application, however, Olivia replied that, though she had been no stranger to their mutual affection, or to the several circumstances which had both proved its durability and tried their fortitude, she never could consent that her daughter should become a member of any family whose principal was either insensible of her value or unwilling to acknowledge it, and that in this influence it would be necessary to Vivaldi's success, not only that he, but that his father, should be a suitor, on which condition only she allowed him to hope for her acquiescence.

Such a suspicion scarcely chilled the hopes of Vivaldi, now that Ellena was proved to be the daughter, not of the murderer Schedoni, but of a Count di Bruno, who had been no less respectable in character than in rank, and he had little doubt that his father would consent to fulfil the promise he had given to the dying Marchesa.

In this belief he was not mistaken. The Marchese, having attended to Vivaldi's account of Ellena's family, promised that, if it should appear there was no second mistake on the subject, he would no longer oppose the wishes of his son.

The Marchese immediately caused a private inquiry to be made as to the identity of Olivia, the present Countess di Bruno; and, though this was not pursued without difficulty, the physician, who had assisted in the plan of her escape from the cruelty of Ferando di Bruno, and who was living, as well as Beatrice, who clearly remembered the sister of her late mistress, at length rendered Olivia's identity unquestionable. Now, therefore, that the Marchese's every doubt was removed, he paid a visit to La Pieta, and solicited in due form Olivia's consent to the nuptials of Vivaldi with Ellena, which she granted him with an entire satisfaction. In this interview the Marchese was so much fascinated by the manners of the Countess, and pleased with the delicacy and sweetness which appeared in those of Ellena, that his consent was no longer a constrained one, and he willingly relinquished the views of superior rank and fortune, which he had formerly looked to for his son, for those of virtue and permanent happiness that were now unfolded to him.

On the twentieth of May, the day on which Ellena completed her eighteenth year, her nuptials with Vivaldi were solemnized in the church of the Santa Maria della Pieta, in the presence of the Marchese and of the Countess di Bruno. As Ellena advanced through the church, she recollected when on a former occasion she had met Vivaldi at the altar, and the scenes of San Sebastian rising to her memory, the happy character of those which her present situation opposed to them drew tears of tender joy and gratitude to her eyes. Then, irresolute, desolate, surrounded by strangers, and ensnared by enemies, she had believed she saw Vivaldi for the last time; now, supported by the presence of a beloved parent, and by the willing approbation of the person who had hitherto so strenuously opposed her, they were met to part no more; and, as a recollection of the moment when she had been carried from the chapel glanced upon her mind, that moment when she had called upon him for succour, supplicated even to hear his voice once more, and when a blank silence, which, as she believed, was that of death, had succeeded—as the anguish of that moment was now remembered, Ellena became more than ever sensible of the happiness of the present.

Olivia, in thus relinquishing her daughter so soon after she had found her, suffered some pain; but she was consoled by the fair prospect of happiness that opened to Ellena, and cheered by considering that, though she relinquished she should not lose her, since the vicinity of Vivaldi's residence to La Pieta would permit a frequent intercourse with the convent.

As a testimony of singular esteem, Paulo was permitted to be present at the marriage of his master; when, as perched in a high gallery of the church he looked down upon the ceremony, and witnessed the delight in Vivaldi's countenance, the satisfaction in that of my "old lord Marchese," the pensive happiness in the Countess di Bruno's, and the tender complacency of Ellena's, which her veil, partly undrawn, allowed him to observe, he could scarcely refrain from expressing the joy he felt, and shouting aloud, *"Oh, giorno felice! Oh, giorno felice!"*

CHAPTER XXXIV.

THE fete which, some time after the nuptials, was given by the Marchese in celebration of them was held at a delightful villa belonging to Vivaldi, a few miles distant from Naples, upon the border of the gulf, and on the opposite shore to that which had been the frequent abode of the Marchesa. The beauty of its situation and its interior elegance induced Vivaldi and Ellena to select it as their chief residence. It was, in truth, a scene of fairyland. The pleasure grounds extended over a valley which opened to the bay, and the house stood at the entrance of this valley, upon a gentle slope that margined the water, and commanded the whole extent of its luxuriant shores, from the lofty cape of Miseno to the bold mountains of the south, which, stretching across the distance, appeared to rise out of the sea, and divided the gulf of Naples from that of Salerno.

The marble porticoes and arcades of the villa were shadowed by groves of the beautiful magnolia, flowering ash, cedrati, camellias, and majestic palms; and the cool and airy halls, opening on two opposite sides to a colonnade, admitted beyond the rich foliage all the seas and shores of Naples from the west; and to the east, views of the valley of the domain, withdrawing among winding hills wooded to their summits, except where cliffs of various-coloured granites, yellow, green, and purple, lifted their tall heads, and threw gay gleams of light amidst the umbrageous landscape.

The style of the gardens, where lawns and groves and woods varied the undulating surface, was that of England, and of the present day, rather than of Italy, except "where a long alley peeping on the main" exhibited such gigantic loftiness of shade, and grandeur of perspective as characterize the Italian taste.

On this jubilee, every avenue and grove and pavilion was richly illuminated. The villa itself, where each airy hall and arcade was resplendent with lights, and lavishly decorated with flowers and the most beautiful shrubs, whose buds seemed to pour all Arabia's perfumes on the air—this villa resembled a fabric called up by enchantment, rather than a structure of human art.

The dresses of the higher rank of visitors were as splendid as the scenery, of which Ellena was, in every respect, the queen. But this entertainment was not given to persons of distinction only, for both Vivaldi and Ellena had wished that all the tenants of the domain should partake of it, and share the abundant happiness which themselves possessed; so that the grounds, which were extensive enough to accommodate each rank, were relinquished to a general gaiety. Paulo was, on this occasion, a sort of master of the revels, and, surrounded by a party of his own particular associates, danced once more, as he had so often wished, upon the moonlight shore of Naples.

As Vivaldi and Ellena were passing the spot which Paulo had chosen for the scene of his festivity, they paused to observe his strange capers and extravagant gesticulations as he mingled in the dance, while every now and then he shouted forth, though half breathless with the heartiness of the exercise, "Oh, giorno felice! Oh, giorno felice!".

On perceiving Vivaldi, and the smiles with which he and Ellena regarded him, he quitted his sports, and advancing, "Ah! my dear master," said he, "do you remember the night when we were travelling on the banks of the Celano, before that diabolical accident happened in the chapel of San Sebastian? don't you remember how those people, who were tripping it away so joyously by moonlight, reminded me of Naples and the many merry dances I had footed on the beach here?"

"I remember it well," replied Vivaldi.

"Ah! signor mio, you said at the time that you hoped we should soon be here, and that then I should frisk it away with as glad a heart as the best of them. The first part of your hope, my dear master, you were out in, for, as it happened, we had to go through purgatory before we could reach paradise; but the second part is come at last, for here I am, sure enough! dancing by moonlight in my own dear bay of Naples, with my own dear master and mistress, in safety, and as happy almost as myself, and with that old mountain yonder, Vesuvius, which I, forsooth, thought I was never to see again, spouting up fire, just as it used to do before we got ourselves put into the Inquisition! Oh! who could have foreseen all this! Oh, giorno felice! Oh, giorno felice!"

"I rejoice in your happiness, my good Paulo," said Vivaldi, "almost as much as in my own; though I do not entirely agree with you as to the comparative proportion of each."

"Paulo," said Ellena, "I am indebted to you beyond any ability to repay; for to your intrepid affection your master owes his present safety. I will not attempt to thank you for your attachment to him; my care of your welfare shall prove how well I know it; but I wish to give to all your friends this acknowledgment of your worth, and of my sense of it."

Paulo bowed, and stammered, and writhed and blushed, and was unable to reply; till at length, giving a sudden and lofty spring from the ground, the emotion which had nearly stifled him, burst forth in words, and "Oh, giorno felice! Oh, giorno felice!" flew from his lips with the force of an electric shock. They communicated his enthusiasm to the whole company; the words passed like lightning from one individual to another, till Vivaldi and Ellena withdrew amidst a choral shout, and all the woods and strands of Naples re-echoed with, "*Oh, giorno felice! Oh, giorno felice!*"

"You see," said Paulo, when they had departed, and he came to himself again, "you see how people get through their misfortunes, if they have but a heart to bear up against them, and do nothing that can lie on their conscience afterwards; and how suddenly one comes to be happy, just, perhaps, when one is beginning to think one never is to be happy again! Who would have guessed that my dear master and I, when we were clapped up in that diabolical place, the Inquisition, should ever come out again into this world! Who would have guessed, when we were taken before those old devils of inquisitors, sitting there all of a row in a place under ground, hung with black, and nothing but torches all around, and faces grinning at us that looked as black as the gentry aforesaid, and when I was not so much as suffered to open my mouth—no! they would not let me open my mouth to my master!—who, I say, would have guessed we should ever be let loose again! Who would have thought we should ever know what it is to be happy! Yet here we are all abroad once more! All at liberty!

And may run, if we will, straight forward, from one end of the earth to the other, and back again without being stopped! May fly in the sea, or swim in the sky, or tumble over head and heels into the moon! For remember, my good friends, we have no lead in our consciences to keep us down!"

"You mean swim in the sea and fly in the sky, I suppose," observed a grave personage near him; "but as for tumbling over head and heels into the moon, I don't know what you mean by that!"

"Pshaw!" replied Paulo, "who can stop at such a time as this to think about what he means! I wish that all those who on this night are not merry enough to speak before they think may ever after be grave enough to think before they speak! But you, none of you, no, not one of you, I warrant, ever saw the roof of a prison when your master happened to be below in the dungeon, nor know what it is to be forced to run away and leave him behind to die by himself! Poor souls! But no matter for that—you can be tolerably happy, perhaps, notwithstanding; but as for guessing how happy I am, or knowing anything about the matter—— Oh! it's quite beyond what you can understand. *Oh, giorno felice! Oh, giorno felice!*" repeated Paulo, as he bounded forward to mingle in the dance, and "*Oh, giorno felice!*" was again shouted in chorus by his joyful companions.

THE END.

J. OGDEN AND CO., PRINTERS, 172, ST. JOHN STREET, E.C.

THE

ROMANCE OF THE FOREST

INTERSPERSED WITH

SOME PIECES OF POETRY

BY

ANN RADCLIFFE

AUTHOR OF "THE ITALIAN," "THE MYSTERIES OF UDOLPHO"

LONDON AND NEW YORK

GEORGE ROUTLEDGE AND SONS

1877

THE ROMANCE OF THE FOREST.

CHAPTER I.

"WHEN once sordid interest seizes on the heart, it freezes up the source of every warm and liberal feeling ; it is an enemy alike to virtue and to taste—*this* it perverts and *that* it annihilates. The time may come, my friend, when death shall dissolve the sinews of Avarice, and Justice be permitted to resume her rights."

Such were the words of the Advocate Nemours to Pierre de la Motte, as the latter stepped at midnight into the carriage which was to bear him far from Paris, from his creditors, and the persecution of the laws. De la Motte thanked him for this last instance of his kindness, the assistance he had given him in escape, and, when the carriage drove away, uttered a sad adieu. The gloom of the hour, and the peculiar emergency of his circumstances, sunk him in silent reverie.

Whoever has read Guyot de Pitaval, the most faithful of those writers who record the proceedings in the Parliamentary Courts of Paris during the seventeenth century, must surely remember the striking story of Pierre de la Motte, and the Marquis Philippe de Montalt : let all such, therefore, be informed that the person here introduced to their notice was that individual Pierre de la Motte.

As Madame de la Motte leaned from the coach window, and gave a last look to the walls of Paris—Paris, the scene of her former happiness, and the residence of many dear friends—the fortitude which had till now supported her yielded to the force of grief. "Farewell all !" sighed she, "this last look —and we are separated for ever !" Tears followed her words, and, sinking back, she resigned herself to the stillness of sorrow. The recollection of former times pressed heavily upon her heart : a few months before and she was surrounded by friends, fortune, and consequence ; now she was deprived of all, a miserable exile from her native place, without home, without comfort—almost without hope. It was not the least of her afflictions that she had been obliged to quit Paris without bidding adieu to her only son, who was now on duty with his regiment in Germany ; and such had been the precipitancy of this removal, that had she even known where he was stationed, she had no time to inform him of it, or of the alteration in his father's circumstances.

Pierre de la Motte was a gentleman descended from an ancient house of France. He was a man whose passions often overcame his reason, and, for a time, silenced his conscience ; but though the image of virtue, which Nature had impressed upon his heart, was sometimes obscured by the passing influence of vice, it was never wholly obliterated. With strength of mind sufficient to have withstood temptation, he would have been a good man ; as it was, he was always a weak, and sometimes a vicious member of society : yet his mind was active, and his imagination vivid, which, co-operating with the force of passion, often dazzled his judgment and subdued principle. Thus he was a man infirm in purpose and visionary in virtue ; in a word, his conduct was suggested by feeling, rather than principle ; and his virtue, such as it was, could not stand the pressure of occasion.

Early in life he had married Constance Valentia, a beautiful and elegant woman, attached to her family and beloved by them. Her birth was equal, her fortune superior, to his ; and their nuptials had been celebrated under the auspices of an approving and flatter-

ing world. Her heart was devoted to La
Motte, and, for some time she found in him
an affectionate husband; but, allured by the
gaieties of Paris, he was soon devoted to its
luxuries, and in a few years his fortune and
affection were equally lost in dissipation. A
false pride had still operated against his interest, and withheld him from honourable
retreat while it was yet in his power; the
habits which he had acquired, enchained him
to the scene of his former pleasure; and thus
he had continued an expensive style of life
till the means of prolonging it were exhausted.
He at length awoke from this lethargy of
security; but it was only to plunge into new
error, and to attempt schemes for the reparation of his fortune which served to sink him
deeper in destruction. The consequence of a
transaction in which he thus engaged now
drove him, with the small wreck of his property, into dangerous and ignominious exile.

It was his design to pass into one of the
southern provinces, and there seek, near the
borders of the kingdom, an asylum in some
obscure village. His family consisted of his
wife and two faithful domestics, a man and
woman who followed the fortunes of their
master.

The night was dark and tempestuous, and,
at about the distance of three leagues from
Paris, Peter, who now acted as postillion,
having drove for some time over a wild
heath where many ways crossed, stopped, and
acquainted De la Motte with his perplexity.
The sudden stopping of the carriage roused
the latter from his reverie, and filled the whole
party with the terror of pursuit; he was unable to supply the necessary direction, and
the extreme darkness made it dangerous to
proceed without one. During this period of
distress, a light was perceived at some distance, and after much doubt and hesitation,
La Motte, in the hope of obtaining assistance,
alighted and advanced towards it; he proceeded slowly from the fear of unknown pits.
The light issued from the window of a small
and ancient house, which stood alone on the
heath, at the distance of half a mile.

Having reached the door, he stopped for
some moments, listening in apprehensive
anxiety; no sound was heard but that of the
wind, which swept in hollow gusts over the
waste. At length he ventured to knock, and,
having waited some time, during which he indistinctly heard several voices in conversation,
someone within inquired what he wanted? La
Motte answered that he was a traveller who
had lost his way, and desired to be directed to
the nearest town. "That," said the person,
"is seven miles off, and the road bad enough,
even if you could see it; if you only want a
bed, you may have it here, and had better
stay."

The "pitiless pelting" of the storm, which
at this time beat with increasing fury upon

La Motte, inclined him to give up the attempt
of proceeding farther till daylight; but, desirous of seeing the person with whom he conversed before he ventured to expose his family
by calling up the carriage, he asked to be
admitted. The door was now opened by a
tall figure with a light, who invited La Motte
to enter. He followed the man through a
passage into a room almost unfurnished, in
one corner of which a bed was spread upon
the floor. The forlorn and desolate aspect of
his apartment made La Motte shrink involuntarily, and he was turning to go out when the
man suddenly pushed him back, and he heard
the door locked upon him; his heart failed,
yet he made a desperate though vain effort
to force the door, and called loudly for release.
No answer was returned, but he distinguished
the voices of men in the room above, and not
doubting but their intention was to rob and
murder him, his agitation at first nearly overcame his reason. By the light of some almost
expiring embers he perceived a window, but
the hope which this discovery revived was
quickly lost, when he found the aperture
guarded by strong iron bars. Such preparation of security surprised him, and confirmed
his worst apprehensions. Alone, unarmed,
beyond the chance of assistance, he saw himself in the power of people whose trade was
apparently rapine—murder their means! After
revolving every possibility of escape, he endeavoured to await the event with fortitude;
but La Motte could boast of no such virtue.

The voices had ceased, and all remained
still for a quarter of an hour, when, between
the pauses of the wind, he thought he distinguished the sobs and moaning of a female;
he listened attentively and became confirmed
in his conjecture; it was too evidently the
accent of distress. At this conviction the
remains of his courage forsook him, and a
terrible surmise darted with the rapidity of
lightning across his brain. It was probable
that his carriage had been discovered by the
people of the house, who, with a design of
plunder, had secured his servant, and brought
hither Madame de la Motte. He was the
more inclined to believe this by the stillness
which had for some time reigned in the house
previous to the sounds he now heard. Or
it was possible that the inhabitants were not
robbers, but persons to whom he had been
betrayed by his friend or servant, and who
were appointed to deliver him into the hands
of justice. Yet he hardly dared to doubt
the integrity of his friend, who had been
entrusted with the secret of his flight and the
plan of his route, and had procured him the
carriage in which he had escaped. "Such
depravity," exclaimed La Motte, "cannot
surely exist in human nature; much less in
the heart of Nemours!"

This ejaculation was interrupted by a noise
in the passage leading to the room; it ap-

proached—the door was unlocked—and the man who had admitted La Motte into the house, entered, leading, or rather forcibly dragging along, a beautiful girl, who appeared to be about eighteen. Her features were bathed in tears, and she seemed to suffer the utmost distress. The man fastened the lock and put the key in his pocket. He then advanced to La Motte, who had before observed other persons in the passage, and pointing a pistol to his breast, "You are wholly in our power," said he, "no assistance can reach you; if you wish to save your life, swear that you will convey this girl where I may never see her more; or rather consent to take her with you, for your oath I would not believe, and I can take care you shall not find me again. Answer quickly, you have no time to lose."

He now seized the trembling hand of the girl, who shrunk aghast with terror, and hurried her towards La Motte, whom surprise still kept silent. She sunk at his feet, and, with supplicating eyes that streamed with tears, implored him to have pity on her. Notwithstanding his present agitation, he found it impossible to contemplate the beauty and distress of the object before him with indifference. Her youth, her apparent innocence, the artless energy of her manner, forcibly assailed his heart, and he was going to speak, when the ruffian, who mistook the silence of astonishment for that of hesitation, prevented him. "I have a horse ready to take you from hence," said he, "and I will direct you over the heath. If you return within an hour, you die; after then, you are at liberty to come here when you please."

La Motte, without answering, raised the lovely girl from the floor, and was so much relieved from his own apprehensions that he had leisure to attempt dissipating hers. "Let us be gone," said the ruffian, "and have no more of this nonsense; you may think yourself well off it's no worse. I'll go and get the horse ready."

The last words roused La Motte and perplexed him with new fears; he dreaded to mention his carriage, lest it might tempt the banditti to plunder; and to depart on horseback with this man might produce a consequence yet more to be dreaded. Madame la Motte, wearied with apprehension, would probably send for her husband to the house, when all the former danger would be incurred, with the additional evil of being separated from his family, and the chance of being detected by the emissaries of justice in endeavouring to recover them. As these reflections passed over his mind in tumultuous rapidity, a noise was again heard in the passage, an uproar and scuffle ensued, and in the same moment he could distinguish the voice of his servant, who had been sent by Madame La Motte in search of him. Being now determined to disclose what could not long be concealed, he exclaimed aloud that a horse was unnecessary, that he had a carriage at some distance which would convey them from the heath, and declared the man who was seized to be his servant.

The ruffian, speaking through the door, bid him be patient awhile, and he should hear more from him. La Motte now turned his eyes upon his unfortunate companion, who, pale and exhausted, leaned for support against the wall. Her features, which were delicately beautiful, had gained from distress an expression of captivating sweetness: she had

> An eye,
> As when the blue sky trembles thro' a cloud
> Of purest white.

A habit of gray camlet, with short slashed sleeves, showed, but did not adorn, her figure; it was thrown open at the bosom, upon which part of her hair had fallen in disorder, while the light veil hastily thrown on, had, in her confusion, been suffered to fall back. Every moment of further observation heightened the surprise of La Motte, and interested him more warmly in her favour. Such elegance and apparent refinement, contrasted with the desolation of the house, and the savage manners of its inhabitants, seemed to him like a romance of imagination rather than an occurrence of real life. He endeavoured to comfort her, and his sense of compassion was too sincere to be misunderstood. Her terror gradually subsided into gratitude and grief. "Ah, sir!" said she, "Heaven has sent you to my relief, and will surely reward you for your protection; I have no friend in the world if I do not find one in you."

La Motte assured her of his kindness, when he was interrupted by the entrance of the ruffian. He desired to be conducted to his family. "All in good time," replied the latter; "I have taken care of one of them, and will of you, please St. Peter; so be comforted." These *comfortable* words renewed the terror of La Motte, who now earnestly begged to know if his family were safe. "Oh! as for that matter they are safe enough, and you will be with them presently; but don't stand *parlying* here all night. Do you choose to go or stay? you know the conditions?" They now bound the eyes of La Motte and of the young lady, whom terror had hitherto kept silent, and then placed them on two horses, a man mounted behind each, and they immediately galloped off. They had proceeded in this way near half an hour, when La Motte entreated to know whither he was going; "You will know that by-and-by," said the ruffian, "so be at peace." Finding interrogatories useless, La Motte resumed silence till the horse stopped. His conductor then hallooed, and being answered by voices at some distance, in a few moments the sound of carriage wheels was heard and, soon after, the words of a man directing Peter which way to drive. As the carriage approached, La Motte called, and to his inexpressible joy was answered by his wife.

" You are now beyond the borders of the heath, and may go which way you will," said the ruffian ; " if you return within an hour you will be welcomed by a brace of bullets." This was a very unnecessary caution to La Motte, whom they now released. The young stranger sighed deeply, as she entered the carriage ; and the ruffians, having bestowed upon Peter some directions and more threats, waited to see him drive off. They did not wait long.

La Motte immediately gave a short relation of what had passed at the house, including an account of the manner in which the young stranger had been introduced to him. During this narrative, her deep convulsive sighs frequently drew the attention of Madame La Motte, whose compassion became gradually interested in her behalf, and who now endeavoured to tranquillise her spirits. The unhappy girl answered her kindness in artless and simple expressions, and then relapsed into tears and silence. Madame forebore for the present to ask any questions that might lead to a discovery of her connections, or seem to require an explanation of the late adventure, which now furnishing her with a new subject of reflection, the sense of her own misfortunes pressed less heavily upon her mind. The distress even of La Motte was for awhile suspended ; he ruminated on the late scene, and it appeared like a vision, or one of those extravagant fictions that sometimes are exhibited in romance ; he could reduce it to no principle of probability, or render it comprehensible by any endeavour to analyse it. The present charge, and the chance of future trouble brought upon him by this adventure, occasioned some dissatisfaction ; but the beauty and seeming innocence of Adeline, united with the pleadings of humanity in her favour, and he determined to protect her.

The tumult of emotions which had passed in the bosom of Adeline, began now to subside ; terror was softened into anxiety, and despair into grief. The sympathy so evident in the manners of her companions, particularly in those of Madame La Motte, soothed her heart, and encouraged her to hope for better days.

Dismally and silently the night passed on; for the minds of the travellers were too much occupied by their several sufferings to admit of conversation. The dawn, so anxiously watched for, at length appeared, and introduced the strangers more fully to each other. Adeline derived comfort from the look of Madame La Motte, who gazed frequently and attentively at her, and thought she had seldom seen a countenance so interesting, or a form so striking. The languor of sorrow

threw a melancholy grace upon her features that appealed immediately to the heart ; and there was a penetrating sweetness in her blue eyes, which indicated an intelligent and amiable mind.

La Motte now looked anxiously from the coach window, that he might judge of his situation, and observe whether he was followed. The obscurity of the dawn confined his views, but no person appeared. The sun at length tinted the eastern clouds and the tops of the highest hills, and soon after burst in full splendour on the scene. The terror of La Motte began to subside, and the grief of Adeline to soften. They entered upon a lane confined by high banks, and overarched by trees on whose branches appeared the first green buds of spring glittering with dews. The fresh breeze of the morning animated the spirits of Adeline, whose mind was delicately sensible to the beauties of nature, and as she viewed the flowery luxuriance of the turf, and the tender green of the trees, or caught, between the opening banks, a glimpse of the varied landscape, rich with wood, and fading away in blue and distant mountains, her heart expanded in momentary joy. With Adeline the charms of external nature were heightened by those of novelty ; she had seldom seen the grandeur of an extensive prospect, or the magnificence of a wide horizon — and not often the picturesque beauties of more confined scenery. Her mind had not lost, by long oppression, that elastic energy which resists calamity ; else, however susceptible might have been her original taste, the beauties of nature would no longer have charmed her thus easily even to temporary repose.

The road at length wound down the side of a hill, and La Motte, again looking anxiously from the window, saw before him an open champaign country, through which the road, wholly unsheltered from observation, extended almost in a direct line. The danger of these circumstances alarmed him, for his flight might without difficulty be traced for many leagues from the hills he was now descending. Of the first peasant that passed he inquired for a road among the hills, but heard of none. La Motte now sunk into his former terrors. Madame, notwithstanding her own apprehensions, endeavoured to reassure him, but finding her efforts ineffectual, she also retired to the contemplation of her misfortunes. Often, as they went on, did La Motte look back upon the country they had passed, and often did imagination suggest to him the sounds of distant pursuit.

The travellers stopped to breakfast in a village where the road was at length obscured by woods, and La Motte's spirits again revived. Adeline appeared more tranquil than she had yet been, and La Motte now asked for an explanation of the scene he had witnessed on the preceding night. The inquiry renewed all her distress, and with tears she entreated for the present to be spared on the subject. La Motte pressed it no further, but he observed that for the greater part of the day she seemed to remember it in melancholy and dejection. They now travelled among the hills, and were, therefore, in less danger of observation ; but La Motte avoided the great towns, and stopped in obscure ones no longer than to refresh the horses. About two hours after noon the road wound into a deep valley, watered by a rivulet, and overhung with wood. He now called to Peter, and ordered him to drive to a thickly-embowered spot that appeared on the left. Here he alighted with his family, and Peter having spread the provisions on the turf, they seated themselves and partook of a repast which, in other circumstances, would have been thought delicious. Adeline endeavoured to smile, but the languor of grief was now heightened by indisposition. The violent agitation of mind and fatigue of body which she had suffered for the last twenty-four hours, had overpowered her strength, and, when La Motte led her back to the carriage her whole frame trembled with illness ; but she uttered no complaint, and, having long observed the dejection of her companions, she made a feeble effort to enliven them.

They continued to travel during the day without any accident or interruption, and about three hours after sunset arrived at Monville, a small town, where La Motte determined to pass the night. Repose was, indeed, necessary to the whole party, whose pale and haggard looks, as they alighted from the carriage, were but too obvious to pass unobserved by the people of the inn. As soon as beds could be prepared, Adeline withdrew to her chamber, accompanied by Madame La Motte, whose concern for the fair stranger made her exert every effort to soothe and console her. Adeline wept in silence, and taking the hand of Madame, pressed it to her bosom. These were not merely tears of grief—they were mingled with those which flow from the grateful heart when, unexpectedly, it meets with sympathy. Madame La Motte understood them. After some momentary silence, she renewed her assurances of kindness, and entreated Adeline to confide in her friendship ; but she carefully avoided any mention of the subject which had before so much affected her. Adeline at length found words to express her sense of this goodness, which she did in a manner so natural and sincere, that Madame, finding herself much affected, took leave of her for the night.

In the morning La Motte rose at an early hour, impatient to be gone. Everything was prepared for his departure, and the breakfast had been waiting some time, but

Adeline did not appear. Madame La Motte went to her chamber, and found her sunk in a disturbed slumber. Her breathing was short and irregular—she frequently started or sighed, and sometimes she muttered an incoherent sentence. While Madame gazed with concern upon her languid countenance, she awoke, and, looking up, gave her hand to Madame La Motte, who found it burning with fever. She had passed a restless night, and, as she now attempted to rise, her head, which beat with intense pain, became giddy, her strength failed, and she sunk back.

Madame was much alarmed, being at once convinced that it was impossible she could travel, and that a delay might prove fatal to her husband. She went to inform him of the truth, and his distress may be more easily imagined than described. He saw all the inconvenience and danger of delay, yet he could not so far divest himself of humanity as to abandon Adeline to the care, or rather to the neglect, of strangers. He sent immediately for a physician, who pronounced her to be in a high fever, and said a removal in her present state must be fatal. La Motte now determined to wait the event, and endeavoured to calm the transports of terror which, at times, assailed him. In the meanwhile, he took such precautions as his situation admitted of, passing the greater part of the day out of the village, in a spot from whence he had a view of the road for some distance ; yet to be exposed to destruction by the illness of a girl, whom he did not know, and who had actually been forced upon him, was a misfortune to which La Motte had not philosophy enough to submit with composure.

Adeline's fever continued to increase during the whole day, and at night, when the physician took his leave, he told La Motte the event would very soon be decided. La Motte received this hint of her danger with real concern. The beauty and innocence of Adeline had overcome the disadvantageous circumstances under which she had been introduced to him, and he now gave less consideration to the inconvenience she might hereafter occasion him than to the hope of her recovery.

Madame La Motte watched over her with tender anxiety and observed, with admiration her patient sweetness and mild resignation. Adeline amply repaid her, though she thought she could not. "Young as I am," she would say, "and deserted by those upon whom I have a claim for protection, I can remember no connection to make me regret life so much as that I hope to form with you. If I live, my conduct will best express my sense of your goodness—words are but feeble testimonies."

The sweetness of her manners so much attracted Madame La Motte that she watched the crisis of her disorder with a solicitude which precluded every other interest. Adeline passed a very disturbed night, and when the physician appeared in the morning he gave orders that she should be indulged with whatever she liked, and answered the inquiries of La Motte with a frankness that left him nothing to hope.

In the meantime his patient, after drinking profusely of some mild liquids, fell asleep, in which she continued for several hours, and so profound was her repose, that her breath alone gave sign of existence. She awoke free from fever, and with no other complaint than weakness, which in a few days she overcame so well as to be able to set out with La Motte for B——, a village out of the great road, which he thought it prudent to quit. There they passed the following night, and early the next morning commenced their journey upon a wild and woody tract of country. They stopped about noon at a solitary village, where they took refreshments and obtained directions for passing the vast forest of Fontanville, upon the borders of which they now were. La Motte wished at first to take a guide, but he apprehended more evil from the disclosure he might make of his route, than he hoped for benefit from assistance in the wilds of this uncultivated tract.

La Motte now designed to pass on to Lyons, where he could either seek concealment in its neighbourhood, or embark on the Rhone for Geneva, should the emergency of his circumstances hereafter require him to leave France. It was about twelve o'clock at noon, and he was desirous to hasten forward that he might pass the forest of Fontanville, and reach the town on its opposite borders before nightfall. Having deposited a fresh stock of provisions in the carriage, and received such directions as were necessary concerning the roads, they again set forward, and in a short time entered upon the forest. It was now the latter end of April, and the weather was remarkably temperate and fine. The balmy freshness of the air, which breathed the first pure essence of vegetation, and the gentle warmth of the sun, whose beams vivified every hue of nature and opened every floweret of spring, revived Adeline, and inspired her with life and health. As she inhaled the breeze, her strength seemed to return, and, as her eyes wandered through the romantic glades that opened into the forest, her heart was gladdened with complacent delight; but when from these objects she turned her regard upon Monsieur and Madame La Motte, to whose tender attentions she owed her life, and in whose looks she now read esteem and kindness, her bosom glowed with sweet affections, and she experienced a force of gratitude which might be called sublime.

For the remainder of the day they continued to travel, without seeing a hut or meeting a human being. It was now near sunset, and the prospect being closed on all sides by the forest, La Motte began to have apprehensions that his servant had mistaken the way. The road, if a road it could be called, which afforded only a slight track upon the grass, was sometimes overrun by luxuriant vegetation, and sometimes obscured by the deep shades, and Peter at length stopped, uncertain of the way. La Motte, who dreaded being benighted in a scene so wild and solitary as this forest, and whose apprehension of banditti were very sanguine, ordered him to proceed at any rate, and, if he found no track, to endeavour to gain a more open part of the forest. With these orders, Peter again set forwards; but having proceeded some way, and his view being still confined by woody glades and forest walks, he began to despair of extricating himself, and stopped for further orders. The sun was now set; but as La Motte looked anxiously from the window, he observed upon the vivid glow of the western horizon, some dark towers from among the trees at a little distance, and ordered Peter to drive towards them. "If they belong to a monastery," said he, "we may probably gain admittance for the night."

The carriage drove along under the shade of "melancholy boughs," through which the evening twilight, which yet coloured the air, diffused a solemnity that vibrated in thrilling sensations upon the hearts of the travellers. Expectation kept them silent. The present scene recalled to Adeline a remembrance of the late terrific circumstances, and her mind responded but too easily to the apprehension of new misfortunes. La Motte alighted at the foot of a green knoll, where the trees, again opening to light, permitted a nearer though imperfect view of the edifice.

CHAPTER II.

What awful silence! how these antique towers,
And vacant courts, chill the suspended soul!
Till e: pectation wears the face of fear;
And fear, half ready to become devotion,
Mutters a kind of mental orison,
It knows not wherefore. What a kind of being
Is circumstance!   HORACE WALPOLE.

HE approached, and perceived the Gothic remains of an abbey: it stood on a kind of rude lawn, overshadowed by high and spreading trees, which seemed coeval with the building, and diffused a romantic gloom around. The greater part of the pile appeared to be sinking into ruins, and that which had withstood the ravages of time showed the remaining features of the fabric more awful in decay. The lofty battlements, thickly enwreathed with ivy, were half demolished and become the residence of birds of prey. Huge fragments of the eastern tower, which was almost demolished, lay scattered amid the high grass that waved slowly to the breeze. "The thistle shook its lonely head ; the moss whistled to the wind." A Gothic gate, richly ornamented with fretwork, which opened into the main body of the edifice but which was now obstructed with brushwood, remained entire. Above the vast and magnificent portal of this gate arose a window of the same order, whose pointed arches still exhibited fragments of stained glass, once the pride of monkish devotion. La Motte, thinking it possible it might yet shelter some human being, advanced to the gate and lifted a massy knocker. The hollow sounds rung through the emptiness of the place. After waiting a few minutes he forced back the gate, which was heavy with iron-work and creaked harshly on its hinges.

He entered what appeared to have been the chapel of the abbey, where the hymn of devotion had once been raised, and the tear of penitence had once been shed ; sounds which could now only be recalled by imagination—tears of penitence, which had been long since fixed in fate. La Motte paused a moment, for he felt a sensation of sublimity rising into terror—a suspension of mingled astonishment and awe ! He surveyed the vastness of the place, and as he contemplated its ruins fancy bore him back to past ages. "And these walls," said he, "where once superstition lurked and austerity anticipated an earthly purgatory, now tremble over the mortal remains of the beings who reared them !"

The deepening gloom reminded La Motte that he had no time to lose, but curiosity prompted him to explore farther, and he obeyed the impulse. As he walked over the broken pavement, the sound of his steps ran in echoes through the place, and seemed like the mysterious accents of the dead, reproving the sacrilegious mortal who thus dared to disturb their holy precincts.

From this chapel he passed into the nave of the great church, of which one window, more perfect than the rest, opened upon a long vista of the forest, and through this was seen the rich colouring of evening, melting by imperceptible gradations into the solemn gray of upper air. Dark hills, whose outline appeared distinctly upon the vivid glow of the horizon, closed the perspective. Several of the pillars which had once supported the roof remained, the proud effigies of sinking greatness, and seemed to nod at every murmur of the blast over the fragments of those that had fallen a little before them. La Motte sighed. The comparison between himself and the gradation of decay which these columns exhibited, was but too obvious and affecting. "A few years," said he, "and I shall become like the mortals on whose

relics I now gaze, and, like them too, I may be the subject of meditation to a succeeding generation, which shall totter but a little while over the object they contemplate, ere they also sink into the dust."

Retiring from the scene he walked through the cloisters, till a door which communicated with a lofty part of the building attracted his curiosity. He opened this and perceived, across the foot of a staircase, another door ; but now, partly checked by fear and partly by the recollection of the surprise his family might feel in his absence, he returned with hasty steps to his carriage, having wasted some of the precious moments of twilight and gained no information.

Some slight answer to Madame La Motte's inquiries, and a general direction to Peter to drive carefully on and look for a road, was all that his anxiety would permit him to utter. The night shade fell thick around, which, deepened by the gloom of the forest, soon rendered it dangerous to proceed. Peter stopped, but La Motte persisting in his first determination, ordered him to go on. Peter ventured to remonstrate, Madame La Motte entreated, but La Motte reproved, commanded, and at length repented ; for the hind wheel, rising upon the stump of an old tree which the darkness had prevented Peter from observing, the carriage was in an instant overturned.

The party, as may be supposed, were much terrified, but no one was materially hurt ; and having disengaged themselves from their perilous situation, La Motte and Peter endeavoured to raise the carriage. The extent of this misfortune was now discovered, for they perceived that the wheel was broken. Their distress was reasonably great, for not only was the coach disabled from proceeding but it could not even afford a shelter from the cold dews of the night, it being impossible to preserve it in an upright situation. After a few moments' silence, La Motte proposed that they should return to the ruins they had just quitted, which lay at a very short distance, and pass the night in the most habitable part of them ; that when morning dawned, Peter should take one of the coach-horses, and endeavour to find a road and a town, from whence assistance could be procured for repairing the carriage. This proposal was opposed by Madame La Motte, who shuddered at the idea of passing so many hours of darkness in a place so forlorn as the monastery. Terrors which she neither endeavoured to examine or combat overcame her, and she told La Motte she had rather remain exposed to the unwholesome dews of night than encounter the desolation of the ruins. La Motte had at first felt an equal reluctance to return to this spot, but having subdued his own feelings, he resolved not to yield to those of his wife.

The horses being now disengaged from the carriage, the party moved towards the edifice. As they proceeded, Peter, who followed them, struck a light, and they entered the ruins by the flame of sticks which he had collected. The partial gleams thrown across the fabric seemed to make its desolation more solemn, while the obscurity of the greater part of the pile heightened its sublimity, and led fancy on to scenes of horror. Adeline, who had hitherto remained silent, now uttered an exclamation of mingled admiration and fear. A kind of pleasing dread thrilled her bosom and filled all her soul. Tears started to her eyes; she wished yet feared to go on; she hung upon the arm of La Motte, and looked at him with a sort of hesitating interrogation.

He opened the door of the great hall, and they entered; its extent was lost in gloom. "Let us stay here," said Madame La Motte, "I will go no farther." La Motte pointed to the broken roof, and was proceeding, when he was interrupted by an uncommon noise which passed along the hall. They were all silent—it was the silence of terror. Madame La Motte spoke first. "Let us quit this spot," said she, "almost any evil is preferable to the feeling which now oppresses me. Let us retire instantly." The stillness had for some time remained undisturbed, and La Motte, ashamed of the fear he had involuntarily betrayed, now thought it necessary to affect a boldness which he did not feel. He therefore opposed ridicule to the terror of Madame, and insisted upon proceeding. Thus compelled to acquiesce, she traversed the hall with trembling steps. They came to a narrow passage, and Peter's sticks being nearly exhausted, they awaited here while he went in search of more.

The almost expiring light flashed faintly upon the walls of the passage, showing the recess more horrible. Across the hall, the greater part of which was concealed in shadow, the feeble ray spread a tremulous gleam, exhibiting the chasm in the roof, while many nameless objects were seen imperfectly through the dusk. Adeline, with a smile, inquired of La Motte if he believed in spirits. The question was ill-timed, for the present scene impressed its terrors upon La Motte, and in spite of endeavour he felt a superstitious dread stealing upon him. He was now, perhaps, standing over the ashes of the dead. If spirits were ever permitted to revisit the earth, this seemed the hour and the place most suitable for their appearance. La Motte remained silent. Adeline said: "Were I inclined to superstition——" She was interrupted by a return of the noise which had been lately heard; it sounded down the passage, at whose entrance they stood, and sunk gradually away. Every heart palpitated, and they remained listening in silence. A

new subject of apprehension seized La Motte —the noise might proceed from banditti; and he hesitated whether it would be safe to go on. Peter now came with a light. Madame refused to enter the passage. La Motte was not much inclined to it; but Peter, in whom curiosity was more prevalent than fear, readily offered his services. La Motte, after some hesitation, suffered him to go, while he awaited at the entrance the result of the inquiry. The extent of the passage soon concealed Peter from view, and the echoes of his footsteps were lost in a sound which rushed along the avenue, and became fainter and fainter till it sunk into silence. La Motte now called aloud to Peter, but no answer was returned; at length they heard the sound of a distant footstep, and Peter soon after appeared, breathless and pale with fear.

When he came within hearing of La Motte, he called out, "An' please, your honour, I've done for them, I believe, but I've had a hard bout. I thought I was fighting with the devil."

"What are you speaking of?" said La Motte.

"They were nothing but owls and rooks after all," continued Peter; "but the light brought them all about my ears, and they made such a confounded clapping with their wings, that I thought at first I had been beset with a legion of devils. But I have drove them all out, master, and you have nothing to fear now."

The latter part of the sentence, intimating a suspicion of his courage, La Motte could have dispensed with, and to retrieve in some degree his reputation he made a point of proceeding through the passage. They now moved on with alacrity, for, as Peter said, "they had nothing to fear."

The passage led into a large area, on one side of which, over a range of cloisters, appeared the west tower and a lofty part of the edifice; the other side was open to the woods. La Motte led the way to a door of the tower, which he now perceived was the same he had formerly entered; but he found some difficulty in advancing, for the area was overgrown with brambles and nettles, and the light which Peter carried afforded only an uncertain gleam. When he unclosed the door, the dismal aspect of the place revived the apprehensions of Madame La Motte, and extorted from Adeline an inquiry whither they were going. Peter held up the light to show the narrow staircase that wound round the tower; but La Motte, observing the second door, drew back the rusty bolts, and entered a spacious apartment, which, from its style and condition, was evidently of a much later date than the other part of the structure; though desolate and forlorn, it was very little impaired by time; the walls were damp, but not decayed; and the glass was yet firm in the windows.

They passed on to a suite of apartments resembling the first they had seen, and expressed their surprise at the incongruous appearance of this part of the edifice with the mouldering walls they had left behind. These apartments conducted them to a winding passage that received light and air through narrow cavities placed high in the wall, and was at length closed by a door barred with iron, which being with some difficulty opened they entered a vaulted room. La Motte surveyed it with a scrutinising eye, and endeavoured to conjecture for what purpose it had been guarded by a door of such strength, but he saw little within to assist his curiosity. The room appeared to have been built in modern times upon a Gothic plan. Adeline approached a large window that formed a kind of recess raised by one step over the level of the floor ; she observed to La Motte that the whole floor was inlaid with Mosaic work ; which drew from him a remark that the style of this apartment was not strictly Gothic. He passed on to a door, which appeared on the opposite side of the room, and, unlocking it, found himself in the great hall by which he had entered the fabric.

He now perceived, what the gloom had before concealed, a spiral staircase which led to a gallery above ; and which from its present condition seemed to have been built with the more modern part of the fabric, though this also affected the Gothic mode of architecture. La Motte had little doubt that these stairs led to apartments corresponding with those he had passed below, and hesitated whether to explore them ; but the entreaties of Madame, who was much fatigued, prevailed with him to defer all further examination. After some deliberation in which of the rooms they should pass the night, they determined to return to that which opened from the tower.

A fire was kindled on a hearth, which it is probable had not for many years before afforded the warmth of hospitality ; and Peter having spread the provision he had brought from the coach, La Motte and his family, encircling the fire, partook of a repast which hunger and fatigue made delicious. Apprehension gradually gave way to confidence, for they now found themselves in something like a human habitation, and they had leisure to laugh at their late terrors ; but as the blast shook the doors, Adeline often started and threw a fearful glance around. They continued to laugh and talk cheerfully for a time, yet their merriment was transient, if not affected, for a sense of their peculiar and distressed circumstances pressed upon their recollection, and sunk each individual into languor and pensive silence. Adeline felt the forlornness of her condition with energy ; she reflected upon the past with astonishment, and anticipated the future with fear. She found

herself, wholly dependent upon strangers, with no other claim than what distress demands from the common sympathy of kindred beings ; sighs swelled her heart, and the frequent tear started to her eye ; but she checked it ere it betrayed on her cheek the sorrow which she thought it would be ungrateful to reveal.

La Motte at length broke this meditative silence by directing the fire to be renewed for the night and the door to be secured ; this seemed a necessary precaution, even in this solitude, and was effected by means of large stones piled against it, for other fastening there was none. It had frequently occurred to La Motte that this apparently forsaken edifice might be a place of refuge to banditti. Here was solitude to conceal them, and a wild and extensive forest to assist their schemes of rapine, and to perplex with its labyrinths those who might be bold enough to attempt pursuit. These apprehensions, however, he hid within his own bosom, saving his companions from a share of the uneasiness they occasioned. Peter was ordered to watch at the door, and having given the fire a rousing stir, our desolate party drew round it, and sought in sleep a short oblivion of care.

The night passed on without disturbance. Adeline slept, but uneasy dreams flitted before her fancy, and she awoke at an early hour ; the recollection of her sorrows rose upon her mind, and, yielding to their pressure, her tears flowed silently and fast. That she might indulge them without restraint, she went to a distant window that looked upon an open part of the forest ; all without was gloom and silence ; she stood for some time viewing the shadowy scene.

The first tender tints of morning now appeared on the verge of the horizon, stealing upon the darkness ;—so pure, so fine, so ethereal ! it seemed as if heaven was opening to the view. The dark mists were seen to roll off to the west, as the tints of light grew stronger, deepening the obscurity of that part of the hemisphere, and involving the features of the country below ; meanwhile, in the east, the hues became more vivid, darting a trembling lustre far around, till a ruddy glow, which fired all that part of the heavens, announced the rising sun. At first a small line of inconceivable splendour emerged on the horizon, which, quickly expanding, the sun appeared in all his glory, unveiling the whole face of nature, vivifying every colour of the landscape, and sprinkling the dewy earth with glittering light. The low and gentle responses of birds, awakened by the morning ray, now broke the silence of the hour : their soft warbling rising by degrees till they swelled the chorus of universal gladness. Adeline's heart swelled too with gratitude and adoration.

The scene before her soothed her mind and exalted her thoughts to the Great Author of Nature; she uttered an involuntary prayer: "Father of Good, who made this glorious scene! I resign myself to Thy hands; Thou wilt support me under my present sorrows, and protect me from future evil."

Thus confiding in the benevolence of God, she wiped the tears from her eyes, while the sweet unison of conscience and reflection rewarded her trust; and her mind, losing the feelings which had lately oppressed it, became tranquil and composed.

La Motte awoke soon after, and Peter prepared to set out on his expedition. As he mounted his horse, "An' please you, master," said he, "I think we had as good look no farther for an habitation till better times turn up; for nobody will think of looking for us here; and when one sees the place by daylight, it's none so bad but what a little patching up would make it comfortable enough." La Motte made no reply, but he thought of Peter's words. During the intervals of the night, when anxiety had kept him waking, the same idea had occurred to him; concealment was his only security, and this place afforded it. The desolation of the spot was repulsive to his wishes; but he had only a choice of evils—a forest with liberty was not a bad home for one who had too much reason to expect a prison. As he walked through the apartments and examined their condition more attentively, he perceived they might easily be made habitable; and now, surveying them under the cheerfulness of morning, his design strengthened, and he mused upon the means of accomplishing it, which nothing seemed so much to obstruct as the apparent difficulty of procuring food.

He communicated his thoughts to Madame La Motte, who felt repugnance to the scheme. La Motte, however, seldom consulted his wife till he had determined how to act; and he had already resolved to be guided in this affair by the report of Peter. If he could discover a town in the neighbourhood of the forest, where provisions and other necessaries could be procured, he would seek no farther for a place of rest.

In the meantime he spent the anxious interval of Peter's absence in examining the ruin and walking over the environs; they were sweetly romantic, and the luxuriant woods with which they abounded seemed to sequester this spot from the rest of the world. Frequently a natural vista would yield a view of the country, terminated by hills, which, retiring in distance, faded into the blue horizon. A stream, various and musical in its course, wound at the foot of the lawn on which stood the abbey; here it silently glided beneath the shades, feeding the flowers that bloomed on its banks, and diffusing dewy freshness around; there it spread in broad expanse to-day, reflecting the sylvan scene and the wild deer that tasted its waves. La Motte observed everywhere a profusion of game; the pheasants scarcely flew from his approach, and the deer gazed mildly at him as he passed. They were strangers to man!

On his return to the abbey, La Motte ascended the stairs that led to the tower. About half way up, a door appeared in the wall; it yielded without resistance to his hand, but a sudden noise within, accompanied by a cloud of dust, made him step back and close the door. After waiting a few minutes, he again opened it, and perceived a large room of the more modern building. The remains of tapestry hung in tatters upon the walls, which were become the residence of birds of prey, whose sudden flight, on the opening of the door, had brought down a quantity of dust and occasioned the noise. The windows were shattered and almost without glass; but he was surprised to observe some remains of furniture—chairs, whose fashion and condition bore the date of their antiquity; a broken table and an iron grate almost consumed by rust.

On the opposite side of the room was a door, which led to another apartment, proportioned like the first, but hung with arras somewhat less tattered. In one corner stood a small bedstead, and a few shattered chairs were placed round the walls. La Motte gazed with a mixture of wonder and curiosity. "'Tis strange," said he, "that these rooms, and these alone, should bear the marks of inhabitation; perhaps some wretched wanderer like myself may have here sought refuge from a persecuting world; and here, perhaps, laid down the load of existence; perhaps, too, I have followed his footsteps but to mingle my dust with his!" He turned suddenly and was about to quit the room, when he perceived a door near the bed; it opened into a closet which was lighted by one small window, and was in the same condition as the apartments he had passed, except that it was destitute even of the remains of furniture. As he walked over the floor, he thought he felt one part of it shake beneath his steps, and, examining, found a trap-door. Curiosity prompted him to explore farther, and with some difficulty he opened it; it disclosed a staircase which terminated in darkness. La Motte descended a few steps, but was unwilling to trust the abyss; and after wondering for what purpose it was so secretly constructed, he closed the trap, and quitted this suite of apartments.

The stairs in the tower above were so much decayed that he did not attempt to ascend them; he returned to the hall, and by the spiral staircase which he had observed the evening before reached the gallery, and found another suite of apartments entirely unfurnished, very much like those below.

He renewed with Madame La Motte his former conversation respecting the abbey, and she exerted all her endeavours to dissuade him from his purpose, acknowledging the solitary security of the spot, but pleading that other places might be found equally well adapted for concealment and more for comfort. This La Motte doubted; besides the forest abounded with game, which would at once afford him amusement and food; a circumstance, considering his small stock of money, by no means to be overlooked; and he had suffered his mind to dwell so much upon the scheme that it was become a favourite one. Adeline listened in silent anxiety to the discourse, and waited with impatience the issue of Peter's report.

The morning passed, but Peter did not return. Our solitary party took their dinner of the provision they had fortunately brought with them, and afterwards walked forth into the woods. Adeline, who never suffered any good to pass unnoticed because it came attended with evil, forgot for a while the desolation of the abbey in the beauty of the adjacent scenery. The pleasantness of the shades soothed her heart, and the varied features of the landscape amused her fancy; she almost thought she could be contented to live here. Already she began to feel an interest in the concerns of her companions, and for Madame La Motte she felt more; it was the warm emotion of gratitude and affection.

The afternoon wore away, and they returned to the abbey. Peter was still absent, and his absence now began to excite surprise and apprehension. The approach of darkness also threw a gloom upon the hopes of the wanderers; another night must be passed under the same forlorn circumstances as the preceding one; and, what was still worse, with a very scanty stock of provisions. The fortitude of Madame La Motte now entirely forsook her, and she wept bitterly. Adeline's heart was as mournful as Madame's; but she rallied her drooping spirits, and gave the first instance of her kindness by endeavouring to revive those of her friend.

La Motte was restless and uneasy, and leaving the abbey, he walked alone the way which Peter had taken. He had not gone far when he perceived him between the trees, leading his horse. "What news, Peter?" hallooed La Motte. Peter came on, panting for breath, and said not a word till La Motte repeated the question in a tone of somewhat more authority. "Ah, bless you, master," said he, when he had taken breath to answer, "I am glad to see you; I thought I should never have got back again; I've met with a world of misfortunes."

"Well, you may relate them hereafter; let me hear whether you have discovered——"

"Discovered!" interrupted Peter, "yes, I am discovered with a vengeance! If your honour will look at my arms, you'll see how I am discovered!"

"Discoloured! I suppose you mean," said La Motte; "but how came you in this condition?"

"Why, I'll tell you how it was, sir; your honour knows I learned a smack of boxing of that Englishman that used to come with his master to our house?"

"Well, well—tell me where you have been."

"I scarcely know myself, master; I've been where I got a sound drubbing, but then it was in your business, and so I don't mind. But if ever I meet with that rascal again!"

"You seem to like your first drubbing so well, that you want another, and unless you speak more to the purpose, you shall soon have one."

Peter was now frightened into method, and endeavoured to proceed: "When I left the old abbey," said he, "I followed the way you directed, and turning to the right of that grove of trees yonder, I looked this way and that to see if I could see a house or a cottage, or even a man, but not a soul of them was to be seen; and so I jogged on, near the value of a league, I warrant, and then I came to a track; 'Oh! oh!' says I, 'we have you now; this will do; paths can't be made without feet.' However, I was out in my reckoning, for the devil a bit of a soul could I see, and, after following the track this way and that way for the third of a league, I lost it, and had to find out another."

"Is it impossible for you to speak to the point?" said La Motte; "omit these foolish particulars, and tell whether you have succeeded."

"Well then, master, to be short, for that's the nearest way after all, I wandered a long while at random, I did not know where, all through a forest like this, and I took special care to note how the trees stood, that I might find my way back. At last I came to another path, and was sure I should find something now, though I had found nothing before, for I could not be mistaken twice; so, peeping between the trees, I spied a cottage, and I gave my horse a lash that sounded through the forest, and I was at the door in a minute. They told me there was a town about half a league off, and bade me follow the track and it would bring me there; so I did; and my horse, I believe, smelt the corn in the manger by the rate he went at. I inquired for a wheelwright, and was told there was but one in the place, and he could not be found. I waited and waited, for I knew it was in vain to think of returning without doing my business. The man at last came home from the country, and I told him how long I had waited; 'For,' says I, 'I knew it was in vain to return without my business.'"

"Do be less tedious," said La Motte, "if it is in thy nature."

"It is in my nature," answered Peter, "and if it was more in my nature your honour should have it all. Would you think it, sir, the fellow had the impudence to ask a louis-d'or for mending the coach-wheel? I believe in my conscience he saw I was in a hurry, and could not do without him. 'A louis-d'or!' says I, 'my master shall give no such price; he sha'n't be imposed upon by no such rascal as you.' Whereupon the fellow looked glum, and gave me a dose o' the chops; with this I up with my fist and gave him another, and should have beat him presently if another man had not come in, and then I was obliged to give up."

"And so you are returned as wise as you went?"

"Why, master, I hope I have too much spirit to submit to a rascal, or let you submit to one either; besides, I have bought some nails, to try if I can't mend the wheel myself, I had always a hand at carpentry."

"Well, I commend your zeal in my cause, but on this occasion it was rather ill-timed. And what have you got in that basket?"

"Why, master, I bethought me that we could not get away from this place till the carriage was ready to draw us; 'And in the meantime,' says I, 'nobody can live without victuals, so I'll e'en lay out the little money I have, and take a basket with me.'"

"That's the only wise thing you have done yet, and this, indeed, redeems your blunders."

"Why now, master, it does my heart good to hear you speak; I knew I was doing for the best all the while; but I've had a hard job to find my way back; and here's another piece of ill-luck, for the horse has got a thorn in his foot."

La Motte made inquiries concerning the town, and found it was capable of supplying him with provisions, and what little furniture was necessary to render the abbey habitable. This intelligence almost settled his plans, and he ordered Peter to return on the following morning and make inquiries concerning the abbey. If the answers were favourable to his wishes, he commissioned him to buy a cart, and load it with some furniture, and some materials necessary for repairing the modern apartments. Peter stared: "What, does your honour mean to live here?"

"Why, suppose I do?"

"Why then your honour has made a wise determination, according to my hint; for your honour knows I said——"

"Well, Peter, it is not necessary to repeat what you said; perhaps I had determined on the subject before."

"Egad, master, you're in the right, and I'm glad of it, for, I believe, we shall not quickly be disturbed here, except by the rooks and owls. Yes, yes—I warrant I'll make it a place fit for a king; and as for the town, one may get anything there, I'm sure of that; though they think no more about this place than they do about India, or England, or any of those places."

They now reached the abbey, where Peter was received with great joy; but the hopes of his mistress and Adeline were repressed when they learned that he returned without having executed his commission, and heard his account of the town. La Motte's orders to Peter were heard with almost equal concern by Madame and Adeline; but the latter concealed her uneasiness, and used all her efforts to overcome that of her friend. The sweetness of her behaviour, and the air of satisfaction she assumed, sensibly affected Madame, and discovered to her a source of comfort which she had overlooked. The affectionate attentions of her young friend promised to console her for the want of other society, and her conversation to enliven the hours which might otherwise be passed in painful regret.

The remarks and general behaviour of Adeline already bespoke a good understanding and an amiable heart, but she had yet more—she had genius. She was now in her nineteenth year; her figure of the middling size, and turned to the most exquisite proportion; her hair was dark auburn, her eyes blue, and whether they sparkled with intelligence or melted with tenderness they were equally attractive; her form had the airy lightness of a nymph, and, when she smiled, her countenance might have been drawn for the younger sister of Hebe: the captivations of her beauty were heightened by the grace and simplicity of her manners, and confirmed by the intrinsic value of a heart

> That might be shrin'd in crystal,
> And have all its movements scan'd.

Annette now kindled the fire for the night: Peter's basket was opened, and supper prepared. Madame La Motte was still pensive and silent, which Adeline observing, she said cheerfully, "There is scarcely any condition so bad but we may, one time or other, wish we had not quitted it. Honest Peter, when he was bewildered in the forest, or had two enemies to encounter instead of one, confesses he wished himself at the abbey. And I am certain there is no situation so destitute but comfort may be extracted from it. The blaze of this fire shines yet more cheerfully from the contrasted dreariness of the place, and this plentiful repast is made yet more delicious from the temporary want we have suffered. Let us enjoy the good and forget the evil."

"You speak, my dear," replied Madame La Motte, "like one whose spirits have not been often depressed by misfortune" (Adeline sighed), "and whose hopes are, therefore, vigorous."

"Long suffering," said La Motte, "has subdued in our minds that elastic energy which repels the pressure of evil and dances to the bound of joy. But I speak in rhapsody, though only from the remembrance of such a time. I once, like you, Adeline, could extract comfort from most situations."

"And may now, my dear sir," said Adeline; "still believe it possible, and you will find it so."

"The illusion is gone—I can no longer deceive myself."

"Pardon me, sir, if I say it is now only you deceive yourself, by suffering the cloud of sorrow to tinge every object you look upon."

"It may be so," said La Motte; "but let us leave the subject."

After supper the doors were secured, as before, for the night, and the wanderers resigned themselves to repose.

On the following morning, Peter again set out for the little town of Auboine, and the hours of his absence were again spent by Madame La Motte and Adeline in much anxiety and some hope; for the intelligence he might bring concerning the abbey might yet release them from the plans of La Motte. Towards the close of day he was descried coming slowly on; and the cart, which accompanied him, too certainly confirmed their fears. He brought materials for repairing the place, and some furniture.

Of the abbey he gave an account of which the following is the substance: It belonged, together with a large part of the adjacent forest, to a nobleman who now resided with his family on a remote estate. He inherited it, in right of his wife, from his father-in-law, who had caused the more modern apartments to be erected, and had resided in them some part of every year for the purposes of shooting and hunting. It was reported that some person was, soon after it came to the present possessor, brought secretly to the abbey and confined in these apartments; who or what he was had never been conjectured, and what became of him nobody knew. The report died gradually away, and many persons entirely disbelieved the whole of it. But, however this affair might be, certain it was the present owner had visited the abbey only two summers since his succeeding to it; and the furniture, after some time, was removed.

This circumstance had at first excited surprise, and various reports arose in consequence, but it was difficult to know what ought to be believed. Among the rest, it was said that strange appearances had been observed at the abbey, and uncommon noises heard; and though this report had been ridiculed by sensible persons as the idle superstition of ignorance, it had fastened so strongly upon the minds of the common people, that for the last seventeen years none of the peasantry had ventured to approach the spot. The abbey was now, therefore, abandoned to decay.

La Motte ruminated upon this account. At first it called up unpleasant ideas, but they were soon dismissed, and considerations more interesting to his welfare took place: he congratulated himself that he had now found a spot where he was not likely to be either discovered or disturbed; yet it could not escape him that there was a strange coincidence between one part of Peter's narrative and the condition of the chambers that opened from the tower above-stairs. The remains of furniture, of which the other apartments were void—the solitary bed—the number and connection of the rooms, were circumstances that united to confirm his opinion. This, however, he concealed in his own breast, for he already perceived that Peter's account had not assisted in reconciling his family to the necessity of dwelling at the abbey.

But they had only to submit in silence, and whatever disagreeable apprehension might intrude upon them, they now appeared willing to suppress the expression of it. Peter, indeed, was exempt from any evil of this kind; he knew no fear, and his mind was now wholly occupied with his approaching business. Madame La Motte, with a placid kind of despair, endeavoured to reconcile herself to that which no effort of understanding could teach her to avoid, and which an indulgence in lamentation could only make more intolerable. Indeed, though a sense of the immediate inconveniences to be endured at the abbey had made her oppose the scheme of living there, she did not really know how their situation could be improved by removal; yet her thoughts often wandered towards Paris, and reflected the retrospect of past times, with the images of weeping friends left, perhaps, for ever. The affectionate endearments of her only son, whom, from the danger of his situation and the obscurity of hers, she might reasonably fear never to see again, arose upon her memory and overcame her fortitude. "Why, why was I reserved for this hour?" would she say, "and what will be my years to come?"

Adeline had no retrospect of past delight to give emphasis to present calamity—no weeping friends—no dear regretted objects to point the edge of sorrow, and throw a sickly hue upon her future prospects; she knew not yet the pangs of disappointed hope, or the acuter sting of self-accusation; she had no misery but what patience could assuage, or fortitude overcome.

At the dawn of the following day Peter arose to his labour: he proceeded with alacrity, and, in a few days, two of the lower apartments were so much altered for the better that La Motte began to exult, and his family to perceive that their situation would

B

not be so miserable as they had imagined. The furniture Peter had already brought was disposed in these rooms, one of which was the vaulted apartment. Madame La Motte furnished this as a sitting-room, preferring it for its large Gothic window, that descended almost to the floor, admitting a prospect of the lawn and the picturesque scenery of the surrounding woods.

Peter having returned to Auboine for a further supply, all the lower apartments were in a few weeks not only habitable but comfortable. These, however, being insufficient for the accommodation of the family, a room above-stairs was prepared for Adeline; it was the chamber that opened immediately from the tower, and she preferred it to those beyond, because it was less distant from the family, and the windows fronting an avenue of the forest afforded a more extensive prospect. The tapestry that was decayed and hung loosely from the walls, was now nailed up and made to look less desolate; and, though the room had still a solemn aspect from its spaciousness and the narrowness of the windows, it was not uncomfortable.

The first night that Adeline retired hither she slept little; the solitary air of the place affected her spirits; the more so, perhaps, because she had, with friendly consideration, endeavoured to support them in the presence of Madame La Motte. She remembered the narrative of Peter, several circumstances of which had impressed her imagination in spite of her reason, and she found it difficult wholly to subdue apprehension. At one time terror so strongly seized her mind that she had even opened the door with an intention of calling Madame La Motte; but, listening for a moment on the stairs of the tower, everything seemed still; at length, she heard the voice of La Motte speaking cheerfully, and the absurdity of her fears struck her forcibly; she blushed that she had for a moment submitted to them, and returned to her chamber wondering at herself.

CHAPTER III.

Are not these woods
More free from peril than the envious court?
Here feel we but the penalty of Adam,
The seasons' difference, as the icy fang
And churlish chiding of the winter's wind.
SHAKSPEARE.

LA MOTTE arranged his little plan of living. His mornings were usually spent in shooting or fishing, and the dinner thus provided by his industry he relished with a keener appetite than had ever attended him at the luxurious tables of Paris. The afternoons he passed with his family; sometimes he would select a book from the few he had brought with him,

and endeavour to fix his attention to the words his lips repeated; but his mind suffered little abstraction from its own cares, and the sentiment he pronounced left no trace behind it. Sometimes he conversed, but oftener sat in gloomy silence, musing upon the past, or anticipating the future.

At these moments Adeline, with a sweetness almost irresistible, endeavoured to enliven his spirits and to withdraw him from himself. Seldom she succeeded, but when she did the grateful looks of Madame La Motte, and the benevolent feelings of her own bosom, realised the cheerfulness she had at first only assumed. Adeline's mind had the happy art, or, perhaps, it were more just to say the happy nature, of accommodating itself to her situation. Her present condition, though forlorn, was not devoid of comfort, and this comfort was confirmed by her virtues. So much she won upon the affections of her protectors, that Madame La Motte loved her as her child, and La Motte himself, though a man little susceptible of tenderness, could not be insensible to her solicitudes. Whenever he relaxed from the sullenness of misery, it was at the influence of Adeline.

Peter regularly brought a weekly supply of provision from Auboine, and, on those occasions, always quitted the town by a route contrary to that leading to the abbey. Several weeks having passed without molestation, La Motte dismissed all apprehension of pursuit, and at length became tolerably reconciled to the complexion of his circumstances. As habit and effort strengthened the fortitude of Madame La Motte, the features of misfortune appeared to soften. The forest, which at first seemed to her a frightful solitude, had lost its terrific aspect; and that edifice, whose half-demolished walls and gloomy desolation had struck her mind with the force of melancholy and dismay, was now beheld as a domestic asylum and a safe refuge from the storms of power.

She was a sensible and highly-accomplished woman, and it became her chief delight to form the rising graces of Adeline, who had, as has been already shown, a sweetness of disposition which made her quick to repay instruction with improvement and indulgence with love. Never was Adeline so pleased as when she anticipated her wishes, and never so diligent as when she was employed in her business. The little affairs of the household she overlooked and managed with such admirable exactness, that Madame La Motte had neither anxiety nor care concerning them. And Adeline formed for herself in this barren situation many amusements that occasionally banished the remembrance of her misfortunes. La Motte's books were her chief consolation. With one of these she would frequently ramble into the forest, to where the river, winding through a glade, diffused coolness, and with its murmuring accents invited repose; there she would seat herself, and, resigned to the illusions of the page, pass many hours in oblivion of sorrow.

Here, too, when her mind was tranquillised by the surrounding scenery, she wooed the gentle muse and indulged in ideal happiness. The delight of these moments she commemorated in the following address :—

TO THE VISIONS OF FANCY.

Dear, wild illusions of creative mind,
  Whose varying hues arise to Fancy's art,
And by her magic force are swift combin'd
  In forms that please and scenes that touch the
     heart—
Oh! whether at her voice ye soft assume
  The pensive grace of sorrow drooping low ;
Or rise sublime on Terror's lofty plume,
  And shake the soul with wildly-thrilling woe ;
Or, sweetly bright, your gayer tints ye spread,
  Bid scenes of pleasure steal upon my view,
Love wave his purple pinions o'er my head,
  And wake the tender thought to passion true ;
Oh still—ye shadowy forms—attend my lonely hours,
Still chase my real cares with your illusive powers !

Madame La Motte had frequently expressed curiosity concerning the events of Adeline's life, and by what circumstances she had been thrown into a situation so perilous and mysterious as that in which La Motte had found her. Adeline had given a brief account of the manner in which she had been brought thither, but had always, with tears, entreated to be spared for that time from a particular relation of her history. Her spirits were not then equal to retrospection, but now that they were soothed by quiet and strengthened by confidence, she one day gave Madame La Motte the following narration :

"I am the only child," said Adeline, "of Louis de St. Pierre, a chevalier of family, but of small fortune, who for many years resided at Paris. Of my mother I have a faint remembrance ; I lost her when I was only seven years old, and this was my first misfortune. At her death my father gave up housekeeping, boarded me in a convent, and quitted Paris. Thus was I, at this early period of my life, abandoned to strangers. My father came sometimes to Paris ; he then visited me, and I well remember the grief I used to feel when he bade me farewell. On these occasions, which wrung my heart with grief, he appeared unmoved ; so that I often thought he had little tenderness for me. But he was my father, and the only person to whom I could look up for protection and love.

"In this convent I continued till I was twelve years old. A thousand times I had entreated my father to take me home ; but at first motives of prudence, and afterwards of avarice, prevented him. I was now removed from this convent and placed in another, where I learned my father intended I should take the veil. I will not attempt to express my surprise and grief on this occasion. Too long I had been immured in the walls of a cloister, and too much had I seen of the sullen misery of its votaries not to feel horror and disgust at the prospect of being added to their number.

"The lady abbess was a woman of rigid decorum and severe devotion ; exact in the observance of every detail of form, and never forgave an offence against ceremony. It was her method, when she wanted to make converts to her order, to denounce and terrify, rather than to persuade and allure. Hers were the arts of cunning practised upon fear, not those of sophistication upon reason. She employed numberless stratagems to gain me to her purpose, and they all wore the complexion of her character. But in the life to which she would have devoted me I saw too many forms of real terror to be overcome by the influence of her ideal host, and was resolute in rejecting the veil. Here I passed several years of miserable resistance against cruelty and superstition. My father I seldom saw ; when I did, I entreated him to alter my destination, but he objected that his fortune was insufficient to support me in the world, and at length denounced vengeance on my head, if I persisted in disobedience.

"You, my dear madam, can form little idea of the wretchedness of my situation, condemned to perpetual imprisonment, and imprisonment of the most dreadful kind, or to the vengeance of a father from whom I had no appeal. My resolution relaxed—for some time I paused upon the choice of evils—but at length the horrors of a monastic life rose so fully to my view, that fortitude gave way before them. Excluded from the cheerful intercourse of society—from the pleasant view of nature—almost from the light of day—condemned to silence—rigid formality—abstinence and penance—condemned to forego the delights of a world which imagination painted in the gayest and most alluring colours, and whose hues were, perhaps, not the less captivating because they were only ideal ;—such was the state to which I was destined. Again my resolution was invigorated ; my father's cruelty subdued tenderness and roused indignation. 'Since he can forget,' said I, 'the affection of a parent, and condemn his child without remorse to wretchedness and despair—the bond of filial and parental duty no longer subsists between us—he has himself dissolved it, and I will yet struggle for liberty and life.'

"Finding me unmoved by menace, the lady abbess had now recourse to more subtle measures ; she condescended to smile, and even to flatter ; but hers was the distorted smile of cunning, not the gracious emblem of kindness ; it provoked disgust, instead of inspiring affection. She painted the character of a vestal in the most beautiful tints of art—

B 2

its holy innocence—its mild dignity—its sublime devotion. I sighed as she spoke. This
she regarded as a favourable symptom, and
proceeded on her picture with more animation. She described the serenity of a monastic
life—its security from the seductive charms,
restless passions, and sorrowful vicissitudes of
the world—the rapturous delights of religion,
and the sweet, reciprocal affection of the
sisterhood.

"So highly she finished the piece, that the
lurking lines of cunning would, to an inexperienced eye, have escaped detection. Mine
was too sorrowfully informed. Too often had
I witnessed the secret tear and bursting sigh
of vain regret, the sullen pinings of discontent,
and the mute anguish of despair. My silence
and my manner assured her of my incredulity,
and it was with difficulty that she preserved a
decent composure.

"My father, as may be imagined, was
highly incensed at my perseverance, which
he called obstinacy; but, what will not be so
easily believed, he soon after relented, and
appointed a day to take me from the convent.
Oh judge of my feelings when I received this
intelligence! The joy it occasioned awakened
all my gratitude; I forgot the former cruelty
of my father, and that the present indulgence
was less the effect of his kindness than of my
resolution. I wept that I could not indulge
his every wish.

"What days of blissful expectation were
those that preceded my departure! The world,
from which I had been hitherto secluded—
the world, in which my fancy had been so
often delighted to roam—whose paths were
strewn with fadeless roses — whose every
scene smiled in beauty and invited to delight
—where all the people were good, and all the
good happy — ah! then that world was
bursting upon my view. Let me catch the
rapturous remembrance before it vanish! It
is like passing lights of autumn, that gleam
for a moment on a hill and then leave it to
darkness. I counted the days and hours
that withheld me from this fairy land. It
was in the convent only that people were
deceitful and cruel: it was there only that
misery dwelt. I was quitting it all! How I
pitied the poor nuns that were to be left behind.
I would have given half that world I prized so
much, had it been mine, to have taken them
out with me.

"The long-wished-for day at last arrived.
My father came, and for a moment my joy
was lost in the sorrow of bidding farewell
to my poor companions, for whom I had
never felt such warmth of kindness as at this
instant. I was soon beyond the gates of the
convent. I looked around me and viewed
the vast vault of heaven, no longer bounded
by monastic walls, and the green earth extended in hill and dale to the round verge of
the horizon! My heart danced with delight,

tears swelled in my eyes, and for some
moments I was unable to speak. My
thoughts rose to Heaven in sentiments of
gratitude to the Giver of all good.

"At length I turned to my father. 'Dear
sir,' said I, 'how I thank you for my deliverance, and how I wish I could do everything
to oblige you.'

"'Return, then, to your convent,' said he,
in a harsh accent. I shuddered; his look
and manner jarred the tone of my feelings;
they struck discord upon my heart, which
had before responded only to harmony. The
ardour of joy was in a moment repressed,
and every object around me was saddened
with the gloom of disappointment. It was
not that I suspected my father would take me
back to the convent; but that his feelings
semed so very dissonant to the joy and
gratitude which I had but a moment before
felt and expressed to him. Pardon, madam,
a relation of these trivial circumstances; the
strong vicissitudes of feeling which they
impressed upon my heart make me think
them important, when they are, perhaps,
only disgusting."

"No, my dear," said Madame La Motte,
"they are interesting to me; they illustrate
little traits of character which I love to
observe. You are worthy of all my regards,
and from this moment I give my tenderest
pity to your misfortunes, and my affection to
your goodness."

These words melted the heart of Adeline;
she kissed the hand which Madame held out,
and remained a few minutes silent. At
length she said: "May I deserve this goodness! and may I ever be thankful to God,
who, in giving me such a friend, has raised
me to comfort and hope!

"My father's house was situated a few
leagues on the other side of Paris, and, in
our way to it, we passed through that city.
What a novel scene! Where were now the
solemn faces, the demure manners, I had
been accustomed to see in the convent?
Every countenance was here animated, either
by business or pleasure; every step was airy,
and every smile was gay. All the people
appeared like friends; they looked and
smiled at me; I smiled again, and wished to
have told them how pleased I was. 'How
delightful,' said I, 'to live surrounded by
friends!'

"What crowded streets! What magnificent hotels! What splendid equipages! I
scarcely observed that the streets were
narrow or the way dangerous. What bustle,
what tumult, what delight! I could never
be sufficiently thankful that I was removed
from the convent. Again I was going to express my gratitude to my father, but his looks
forbade me, and I was silent. I am too
diffuse; even the faint forms which memory
reflects of past delight are grateful to the

heart. The shadow of pleasure is still gazed upon with a melancholy enjoyment, though the substance is fled beyond our reach.

"Having quited Paris, which I left with many sighs, and gazed upon till the towers of every church dissolved in distance from my view, we entered upon a gloomy and unfrequented road. It was evening when we reached a wild heath; I looked round in search of a human dwelling, but could find none; and not a human being was to be seen. I experienced something of what I used to feel in the convent; my heart had not been so sad since I left it. Of my father, who still sat in silence, I inquired if we were near home; he answered in the affirmative. Night came on, however, before we reached the place of our destination; it was a lone house on the waste; but I need not describe it to you, madam. When the carriage stopped, two men appeared at the door and assisted us to alight; so gloomy were their countenances, and so few their words, I almost fancied myself again in the convent. Certain it is I had not seen such melancholy faces since I quitted it. 'Is this a part of the world I have so fondly contemplated?' said I.

"The interior appearance of the house was desolate and mean; I was surprised that my father had chosen such a place for his habitation, and also that no woman was to be seen; but I knew that inquiry would only produce reproof, and was therefore silent. At supper, the two men I had before seen sat down with us; they said little, but seemed to observe me much. I was confused and displeased, which, my father noticing, frowned at them with a look which convinced me he meant more than I comprehended. When the cloth was drawn, my father took my hand and conducted me to the door of my chamber; having set down the candle and wished me good-night, he left me to my own solitary thoughts.

"How different were they from those I had indulged a few hours before! Then expectation, hope, delight, danced before me; now melancholy and disappointment chilled the ardour of my mind and discoloured my future prospect. The appearance of everything around conduced to depress me. On the floor lay a small bed without curtains or hangings; two old chairs and a table were all the remaining furniture in the room. I went to the window, with an intention of looking out upon the surrounding scene, and found it was grated. I was shocked at this circumstance, and, comparing it with the lonely situation and the strange appearance of the house, together with the countenances and behaviour of the men who had supped with us, I was lost in a labyrinth of conjecture.

"At length I lay down to sleep; but the anxiety of my mind prevented repose;

gloomy, unpleasing images flitted before my fancy, and I fell into a sort of waking dream; I thought that I was in a lonely forest with my father; his looks were severe, and his gestures menacing. He upbraided me for leaving the convent, and, while he spoke, drew from his pocket a mirror, which he held before my face; I looked in it and saw—my blood now thrills as I repeat it—I saw myself wounded, and bleeding profusely. Then I thought myself in the house again, and suddenly heard these words, in accents so distinct that, for some time after I awoke, I could scarcely believe them ideal: 'Depart this house, destruction hovers here.'

"I was awakened by a footstep on the stairs; it was my father retiring to his chamber; the lateness of the hour surprised me, for it was past midnight.

"On the following morning, the party of the preceding evening assembled at breakfast, and were as gloomy and silent as before. The table was spread by a boy of my father's; but the cook and the housemaid, whatever they might be, were invisible.

"The next morning I was surprised, on attempting to leave my chamber, to find the door locked. I waited a considerable time before I ventured to call; when I did, no answer was returned; I then went to the window, and called more loudly, but my own voice was still the only sound I heard. Near an hour passed in a state of surprise and terror not to be described. At length I heard a person coming upstairs, and I renewed the call. I was answered that my father had that morning set off for Paris, whence he would return in a few days; in the meanwhile he had ordered me to be confined in my chamber. On my expressing surprise and apprehension at this circumstance, I was assured I had nothing to fear, and that I should live as well as if I was at liberty.

"The latter part of this speech seemed to contain an odd kind of comfort; I made little reply, but submitted to necessity. Once more I was abandoned to sorrowful reflection; what a day was the one I now passed! alone, and agitated with grief and apprehension. I endeavoured to conjecture the cause of this harsh treatment; and at length concluded it was designed by my father as a punishment for my former disobedience. But why abandon me to the power of strangers, to men whose countenances bore the stamp of villany so strongly as to impress even my inexperienced mind with terror! Surmise involved me only deeper in perplexity, yet I found it impossible to forbear pursuing the subject; and the day was divided between lamentation and conjecture. Night at length came, and such a night! Darkness brought new terrors; I looked round the chamber for some means of fastening my door on the inside, but could perceive none; at last I contrived to place the back of a chair in an oblique direction, so as to render it secure.

"I had scarcely done this, and laid down upon my bed in my clothes—not to sleep, but to watch—when I heard a rap at the door of the house, which was opened and shut so quickly that the person who had knocked seemed only to deliver a letter or message. Soon after, I heard voices at intervals in a room below-stairs, sometimes speaking very low, and sometimes rising all together, as if in dispute. Something more excusable than curiosity made me endeavour to distinguish what was said, but in vain; now and then a word or two reached me, and once I heard my name repeated, but no more.

"Thus passed the hours till midnight, when all became still. I had lain for some time in a state between fear and hope, when I heard the lock of my door gently moved backward and forward; I started up and listened; for a moment it was still, then the noise returned, and I heard a whispering without; my spirits died away, but I was yet sensible. Presently an effort was made at the door, as if to force it; I shrieked aloud, and immediately heard the voices of the men I had seen at my father's table; they called loudly for the door to be opened, and on my returning no answer, uttered dreadful execrations. I had just strength sufficient to move to the window, in the desperate hope of escaping thence; but my feeble efforts could not even shake the bars. Oh! how can I recollect these moments of horror, and be sufficiently thankful that I am now in safety and comfort!

"They remained some time at the door, then they quitted it, and went downstairs. How my heart revived at every step of their departure! I fell upon my knees, thanked God that he had preserved me this time, and implored His further protection. I was rising from this short prayer, when suddenly I heard a noise in a different part of the room; and, on looking round, I perceived the door of a small closet open and two men enter the chamber.

"They seized me, and I sunk senseless in their arms; how long I remained in this condition I know not; but on reviving, I perceived myself again alone, and heard several voices from below-stairs. I had presence of mind to run to the door of the closet, which afforded the only chance of escape—but it was locked! I then recollected it was possible that the ruffians might have forgot to turn the key of the chamber-door, which was held by the chair; but here also I was disappointed. I clasped my hands in an agony of despair, and stood for some time immovable.

"A violent noise from below roused me, and soon after I heard people ascending the stairs; I now gave myself up for lost. The steps approached, the door of the closet was again unlocked. I stood calmly, and again saw the men enter the chamber; I neither spoke nor resisted: the faculties of my soul were wrought up beyond the power of feeling, as a violent blow on the body stuns for a while the sense of pain. They led me downstairs—the door of a room below was thrown open, and I beheld a stranger. It was then that my senses returned; I shrieked and resisted, but was forced along. It is unnecessary to say that this stranger was Monsieur La Motte, or to add that I shall for ever bless him as my deliverer."

Adeline ceased to speak; Madame La Motte remained silent. There were some circumstances in Adeline's narrative which raised all her curiosity. She asked if Adeline believed her father to be a party in this mysterious affair. Adeline—though it was impossible to doubt that he had been principally and materially concerned in some part of it—thought, or said she thought, he was innocent of any intention against her life.

"Yet what motive," said Madame La Motte, "could there be for a degree of cruelty so apparently unprofitable?"

Here the inquiry ended; and Adeline confessed she had pursued it till her mind shrunk from all further research.

The sympathy which such uncommon misfortune excited Madame La Motte now expressed without reserve, and this expression of it strengthened the bond of mutual friendship. Adeline felt her spirits relieved by the disclosure she had made to Madame La Motte, and the latter acknowledged the value of the confidence, by an increase of affectionate attentions.

CHAPTER IV.

My May of life
Is fall'n into the sear, the yellow leaf.
SHAKSPEARE.

Full oft unknowing and unknown
He wore his endless noons alone,
Amid th' autumnal wood;
Oft was he wont, in hasty fit,
Abrupt the social board to quit.
WARTON.

LA MOTTE had now passed above a month in this seclusion; and his wife had the pleasure to see him recover tranquillity, and even cheerfulness. In this pleasure Adeline warmly participated; and she might justly have congratulated herself as one cause of his restoration—her cheerfulness and delicate attention had effected what Madame La Motte's greater anxiety had failed to accomplish. La Motte did not seem regardless of her amiable disposition, and sometimes thanked her in a manner more earnest than was usual with him. She in her turn considered him as her only protector, and now felt towards him the affection of a daughter.

The time she had spent in this peaceful retirement had softened the remembrance of past events, and restored her mind to its natural tone ; and when memory brought back to her view her former short and romantic expectations of happiness, though she gave a sigh to the rapturous illusion, she less lamented the disappointment than rejoiced in her present security and comfort.

But the satisfaction which La Motte's cheerfulness diffused around him was of short continuance — he became suddenly gloomy and reserved—the society of his family was no longer grateful to him ; and he would spend whole hours in the most secluded parts of the forest, devoted to melancholy and secret grief. He did not, as formerly, indulge the humour of his sadness without restraint in the presence of others ; he now endeavoured to conceal it, and affected a cheerfulness that was too artificial to escape detection.

His servant Peter, either impelled by curiosity or kindness, sometimes followed him unseen into the forest. He observed him frequently retire to one particular spot in a remote part, which having gained he always disappeared before Peter—who was obliged to follow at a distance—could exactly notice where. All his endeavours, now prompted by wonder and invigorated by disappointment, were unsuccessful, and he was still compelled to endure the tortures of unsatisfied curiosity.

This change in the manners and habits of her husband was too conspicuous to pass unobserved by Madame La Motte, who endeavoured by all the stratagems which affection could suggest or female invention supply, to win him to her confidence. He seemed insensible to the influence of the first, and withstood the wiles of the latter. Finding all her efforts insufficient to dissipate the glooms which overhung his mind, or to penetrate their secret cause, she desisted from further attempt and endeavoured to submit to this mysterious distress.

Week after week elapsed and the same unknown cause sealed the lips and corroded the heart of La Motte. The place of his visitation in the forest had not been traced. Peter had frequently examined round the spot where his master disappeared, but had never discovered any recess which could be supposed to conceal him. The astonishment of the servant was at length raised to an insupportable degree, and he communicated to his mistress the subject of it.

The emotion which this information excited she disguised from Peter, and reproved him for the means he had taken to gratify his curiosity. But she revolved this circumstance in her thoughts, and, comparing it with the late alteration in his temper, her uneasiness was renewed and her perplexity considerably increased. After much consideration, being unable to assign any other motive for his conduct, she began to attribute it to the influence of illicit passion ; and her heart, which now outran her judgment, confirmed the supposition, and roused all the torturing pangs of jealousy.

Comparatively speaking she had never known affliction till now ; she had abandoned her dearest friends and connections — had relinquished the gaieties, the luxuries, and almost the necessaries of life—fled with her family into exile, an exile the most dreary and comfortless—experiencing the evils of reality and those of apprehension united—all these she had patiently endured, supported by the affection of him for whose sake she suffered. Though that affection indeed had for some time appeared to be abated, she had borne its decrease with fortitude ; but the last stroke of calamity, hitherto withheld, now came with irresistible force—the love of which she lamented the loss she now believed was transferred to another.

The operation of strong passion confuses the powers of reason, and warps them to its own particular direction. Her usual degree of judgment, unopposed by the influence of her heart, would probably have pointed out to Madame La Motte some circumstances upon the subject of her distress, equivocal if not contradictory to her suspicions. No such circumstances appeared to her, and she did not long hesitate to decide that Adeline was the object of her husband's attachment. Her beauty out of the question, who else indeed could it be in a spot thus secluded from the world ?

The same cause destroyed, almost at the same moment, her only remaining comfort ; and when she wept that she could no longer look for happiness in the affection of La Motte, she wept also that she could no longer seek solace in the friendship of Adeline. She had too great an esteem for her to doubt at first the integrity of her conduct ; but in spite of reason, her heart no longer expanded to her with its usual warmth of kindness. She shrunk from her confidence ; and, as the secret broodings of jealousy cherished her suspicions, she became less kind to her, even in manner.

Adeline, observing the change, at first attributed it to accident, and afterwards to a temporary displeasure, arising from some little inadvertency in her conduct. She therefore increased her assiduities ; but perceiving, contrary to all expectation, that her efforts to please failed of their usual consequence, and that the reserve of Madame's manner rather increased than abated, she became seriously uneasy, and resolved to seek an explanation. This Madame La Motte as sedulously avoided, and was for some time able to prevent. Adeline, however, too much interested in the event to yield to delicate scruples, pressed the subject so closely that Madame was at first agitated and confused, but at length invented some idle excuse, and laughed off the affair.

She now saw the necessity of subduing all appearance of reserve towards Adeline; and though her heart could not conquer the prejudices of passion, it taught her to assume, with tolerable success, the aspect of kindness. Adeline was deceived, and was again at peace. Indeed, confidence in the sincerity and goodness of others was her weakness. But the pangs of stifled jealousy struck deeper to the heart of Madame La Motte, and she resolved at all events to obtain some certainty upon the subject of her suspicions.

She now condescended to an act of meanness which she had before despised, and ordered Peter to watch the steps of his master, in order to discover, if possible, the place of his visitation. So much did passion win upon her judgment by time and indulgence, that she sometimes ventured even to doubt the integrity of Adeline, and afterwards proceeded to believe it possible that the object of La Motte's rambles might be an assignation with her. What suggested this conjecture was that Adeline frequently took long walks alone in the forest, and sometimes was absent from the abbey for many hours. This circumstance, which Madame La Motte had at first attributed to Adeline's fondness for the picturesque beauties of nature, now operated forcibly upon her imagination, and she could view it in no other light than as affording an opportunity for secret conversation with her husband.

Peter obeyed the orders of his mistress with alacrity, for they were warmly seconded by his own curiosity. All his endeavours were, however, fruitless; he never dared to follow La Motte near enough to observe the place of his last retreat. Her impatience, thus heightened by delay, and her passions stimulated by difficulty, Madame La Motte now resolved to apply to her husband for an explanation of his conduct.

After some consideration concerning the manner most likely to succeed with him, she went to La Motte, but when she entered the room where he sat, forgetting all her concerted address, she fell at his feet, and was for some moments lost in tears. Surprised at her attitude and distress, he inquired the occasion of it, and was answered that it was caused by his own conduct.

"My conduct! What part of it, pray?" inquired he.

"Your reserve, your secret sorrow, and frequent absence from the abbey."

"Is it then so wonderful that a man, who has lost almost everything, should sometimes lament his misfortunes? or so criminal to attempt concealing his grief that he must be blamed for it by those whom he would save from the pain of sharing it?"

Having uttered these words, he quitted the room, leaving Madame La Motte lost in surprise, but somewhat relieved from the pressure of her former suspicions. Still, however, she pursued Adeline with an eye of scrutiny; and the mask of kindness would sometimes fall off, and discover the features of distrust. Adeline, without exactly knowing why, felt less at ease and less happy in her presence than formerly; her spirits drooped, and she would often, when alone, weep at the forlornness of her condition. Formerly, her remembrance of past sufferings was lost in the friendship of Madame La Motte; now, though her behaviour was too guarded to betray any striking instance of unkindness, there was something in her manner which chilled the hopes of Adeline, unable as she was to analyse it. But a circumstance which soon occurred, suspended, for awhile, the jealousy of Madame La Motte, and roused her husband from his state of gloomy stupefaction.

Peter, having been one day to Auboine for the weekly supply of provisions, returned with intelligence that awakened in La Motte new apprehension and anxiety.

"Oh, sir! I've heard something that has astonished me, as well it may," cried Peter; "and so it will you when you come to know it. As I was standing in the blacksmith's shop, while the smith was driving a nail into the horse's shoe (by-the-bye, the horse lost it in an odd way, I'll tell you, sir, how it was)——"

"Nay, prithee, leave it till another time, and go on with your story."

"Why, then, sir, as I was standing in the blacksmith's shop, comes in a man with a pipe in his mouth, and a large pouch of tobacco in his hand——"

"Well—what has the pipe to do with the story?"

"Nay, sir, you put me out; I can't go on, unless you let me tell it my own way. As I was saying—with a pipe in his mouth—I think I was there, your honour?"

"Yes, yes."

"He sets himself down on the bench, and, taking the pipe from his mouth, says to the blacksmith: 'Neighbour, do you know anybody of the name of La Motte hereabouts?' Bless your honour, I turned all of a cold sweat in a minute!—Is not your honour well, shall I fetch you anything?"

"No—but be brief in your narrative."

"'La Motte! La Motte!' said the blacksmith, 'I think I've heard the name.' 'Have you?' said I; 'you're cunning then, for there's no such person hereabouts to my knowledge.'"

"Fool!—why did you say that?"

"Because I did not want them to know your honour was here; and if I had not managed very cleverly, they would have found me out. 'There is no such person hereabouts, to my knowledge,' says I. 'Indeed!' says the blacksmith, 'you know more of the neighbourhood than I do then.' "'Aye,' says the man with the pipe, 'that's very true. How came you to know so much of the neighbourhood? I came here twenty-six years ago, come next St. Michael, and you know more than I do. How came you to know so much?'

"With that he put his pipe in his mouth, and gave a whiff full in my face. Lord! your honour, I trembled from head to foot. 'Nay, as for that matter,' says I, 'I don't know more than other people; but I'm sure I never heard of such a man as that.' 'Pray,' says the blacksmith, staring me full in the face, 'ain't you the man that was inquiring some time since about St. Clair's Abbey?' 'Well, what of that?' says I; 'what does that prove?' 'Why, they say somebody lives in the abbey now,' said the man, turning to the other; 'and for aught I know, it may be this same La Motte.'

"'Aye, for aught I know either,' says the man with the pipe, getting up from the bench, 'and you know more of this than you'll own. I'll lay my life on't, this Monsieur La Motte lives at the abbey.' 'Aye,' says I, 'you are out there, for he does not live at the abbey now.'"

"Confound your folly!" cried La Motte; "but be quick—how did the matter end?"

"'My master does not live there now,' said I. 'Oh, oh!' said the man with the pipe, 'he is your master, then? And pray how long has he left the abbey—and where does he live now?'

"'Hold,' said I, 'not so fast—I know when to speak and when to hold my tongue—but who has been inquiring for him?'

"'What! he expected somebody to inquire for him,' says the man. 'No,' says I, 'he did not; but if he did, what does that prove? —that argues nothing.' With that he looked at the blacksmith, and they went out of the shop together, leaving my horse's shoe undone. But I never minded that, for the moment they were gone, I mounted and rode away as fast as I could. But in my fright, your honour, I forgot to take the roundabout way, and so came straight home."

La Motte, extremely shocked at Peter's intelligence, made no other reply than by cursing his folly, and immediately went in search of Madame, who was walking with Adeline on the banks of the river. La Motte was too much agitated to soften his information by preface: "We are discovered!" said he, "the King's officers have been inquiring for me at Auboine, and Peter has blundered upon my ruin!" He then informed her of what Peter had related, and bade her prepare to quit the abbey.

"But whither can we fly?" said Madame La Motte, scarcely able to support herself.

"Anywhere!" said he, "to stay here is certain destruction. We must take refuge in Switzerland, I think. If any part of France would have concealed me, surely it had been this!"

"Alas, how we are persecuted!" rejoined Madame. "This spot is scarcely made comfortable, before we are obliged to leave it, and go we know not whither."

"I wish we may not know whither," replied La Motte; "that is the least evil that threatens us. Let us escape a prison, and I care not whither we go. But return to the abbey immediately, and pack up what movables you can."

A flood of tears came to the relief of Madame La Motte, and she hung upon Adeline's arm, silent and trembling. Adeline, though she had no comfort to bestow, endeavoured to command her feelings and appear composed.

"Come," said La Motte, "we waste time; let us lament hereafter, but at present prepare for flight. Exert a little of that fortitude which is so necessary for our preservation. Adeline does not weep, yet her state is as wretched as your own, for I know not how long I shall be able to protect her."

Notwithstanding her terror, this reproof touched the pride of Madame La Motte, who dried her tears, but disdained to reply, and looked at Adeline with a strong expression of displeasure. As they moved silently toward the abbey, Adeline asked La Motte if he was sure they were the King's officers who inquired for him.

"I cannot doubt it," he replied; "who else could possibly inquire for me? Besides, the behaviour of the man who mentioned my name puts the matter beyond a question."

"Perhaps not," said Madame La Motte; "let us wait till morning ere we set off. We may then find it will be unnecessary to go."

"We may, indeed; the King's officers would probably by that time have told us as much." La Motte went to give orders to Peter.

"Set off in an hour!" said Peter. "Lord bless you, master! only consider the coach-wheel: it would take me a day at least to mend it, for your honour knows I never mended one in my life."

This was a circumstance which La Motte had entirely overlooked. When they settled at the abbey, Peter had at first been too busy in repairing the apartments to remember the carriage, and afterwards, believing it would not quickly be wanted, he had neglected to do it. La Motte's temper now entirely forsook him, and with many execrations he ordered Peter to go to work immediately; but on searching for the materials formerly bought, they were nowhere to be found, and Peter at length remembered, though he was prudent enough to conceal this circumstance, that he had used the nails in repairing the abbey.

It was now therefore impossible to quit the forest that night, and La Motte had only to consider the most probable plan of concealment, should the officers of justice visit the ruin before the morning, a circumstance which the thoughtlessness of Peter, in returning from Auboine by the straight way, made not unlikely.

At first, indeed, it occurred to him that though his family could not be removed, he might himself take one of the horses and escape from the forest before night. But he thought there would still be some danger of detection in the towns through which he must pass, and he could not well bear the idea of leaving his family unprotected, without knowing when he could return to them or whither he could direct them to follow him. La Motte was not a man of very vigorous resolution, and he was, perhaps, rather more willing to suffer in company than alone.

After much consideration, he recollected the trap-door of the closet belonging to the chambers above ; it was invisible to the eye, and, whatever might be its direction, it would securely shelter *him*, at least, from discovery. Having deliberated further upon the subject, he determined to explore the recess to which the stairs led, and thought it possible that, for a short time, his whole family might be concealed within it. There was little time between the suggestion of the plan and the execution of his purpose, for darkness was spreading around, and, in every murmur of the wind, he thought he heard the voices of his enemies.

He called for a light and ascended alone to the chamber. When he came to the closet, it was some time before he could find the trap-door, so exactly did it correspond with the boards of the floor. At length he found and raised it. The chill damps of long-confined air rushed from the aperture, and he paused for a moment to let them pass ere he descended. As he stood looking down the abyss, he recollected the report which Peter had brought concerning the abbey, and it gave him an uneasy sensation ; but this soon yielded to more pressing interests.

The stairs were steep, and in many places trembled beneath his weight.

Having continued to descend for some time, his feet touched the ground, and he found himself in a narrow passage ; but as he turned to pursue it, the damp vapours curled around him and extinguished the light. He called aloud for Peter, but could make nobody hear, and, after some time, endeavoured to find his way up the stairs. In this, with difficulty, he succeeded, and, passing the chambers with cautious steps, descended the tower.

The security which the place he had just quitted seemed to promise was of too much importance to be slightly rejected, and he determined immediately to make another experiment with the light ; having now fixed it in a lantern, he descended a second time to the passage. The current of vapours occasioned by the opening of the trap-door was abated, and the fresh air thence admitted had begun to circulate ; La Motte passed on unmolested.

The passage was of considerable length, and led him to a door, which was fastened. He placed the lantern at some distance to avoid the current of air, and applied his strength to the door ; it shook under his hand, but did not yield. Upon examining it more closely he perceived the wood round the lock was decayed, probably by the damps, and this encouraged him to proceed. After some time it gave way to his effort, and he found himself in a square stone room.

He stood for some time to survey it. The walls which were dripping with unwholesome dews, were entirely bare, and afforded not even a window. A small iron grate alone admitted the air. At the farther end, near a low recess, was another door. La Motte went towards it, and as he passed looked into the recess. Upon the ground within it stood a large chest, which he went forward to examine, and, lifting the lid he saw the remains of a human skeleton. Horror struck upon his heart, and he involuntarily stepped back. During a pause of some moments his first emotions subsided. That thrilling curiosity which objects of terror often excite in the human mind, impelled him to take a second view of this dismal spectacle.

La Motte stood motionless as he gazed ; the object before him seemed to confirm the report that some person had formerly been murdered in the abbey. At length he closed the chest, and advanced to the second door, which also was fastened, but the key was in the lock. He turned it with difficulty, and then found the door was held by two strong bolts. Having undrawn these, it disclosed a flight of steps, which he descended : they terminated in a chain of low vaults, or rather cells that, from the manner of their construction and present condition, seemed to have been coeval with the most ancient parts of the abbey. La Motte, in his then depressed state of mind, thought them the burial-places of the monks who formerly inhabited the pile above ; but they were more calculated for places of penance for the living than of rest for the dead.

Having reached the extremity of these cells, the way was again closed by a door. La Motte now hesitated whether he should attempt to proceed any farther. The present spot seemed to afford the security he sought.

Here he might pass the night unmolested by apprehension of discovery, and it was most probable that if the officers arrived in the night and found the abbey vacated, they would quit it before morning, or at least before he could have any occasion to emerge from concealment. These considerations restored his mind to a state of greater composure. His only immediate care was to bring his family as soon as possible to this place of security, lest the officers should come unawares upon them ; and while he stood thus musing he blamed himself for delay.

But an irresistible desire of knowing to what this door led arrested his steps, and he turned to open it ; the door, however, was fastened, and as he attempted to force it, he suddenly thought he heard a noise above. It now occurred to him that the officers might already have arrived, and he quitted the cells with precipitation, intending to listen at the trap-door.

"There," said he, " I may wait in security, and perhaps hear something of what passes. My family will not be known, or at least not hurt, and their uneasiness on my account they must learn to endure."

These were the arguments of La Motte, in which, it must be owned, selfish prudence was more conspicuous than tender anxiety for his wife. He had by this time reached the bottom of the stairs, when, on looking up he perceived the trap-door was left open, and ascending in haste to close it, he heard footsteps advancing through the chambers above. Before he could descend entirely out of sight he again looked up, and perceived through the aperture the face of a man looking down upon him.

"Master !" cried Peter.

La Motte was somewhat relieved at the sound of his voice, though angry that he had occasioned him so much terror.

"What brings you here, and what is the matter below ?"

"Nothing, sir, nothing's the matter ; only my mistress sent me to see after your honour."

"There's nobody there then ?" said La Motte, setting his foot upon the step.

"Yes, sir, there is my mistress and Mademoiselle Adeline——"

"Well—well," said La Motte, briskly, "go your ways, I am coming."

He informed Madame La Motte where he had been and of his intention to secrete himself, and deliberated upon the means of convincing the officers, should they arrive, that he had quitted the abbey. For this purpose he ordered all the movable furniture to be conveyed to the cells below. La Motte himself assisted in the business, and every hand was employed for despatch. In a very short time the habitable part of the fabric was left almost as desolate as he had found it.

He then bade Peter take the horses to a distance from the abbey, and turn them loose. After further consideration, he thought it might contribute to mislead the officers if he placed in some conspicuous part of the fabric an inscription, signifying his condition, and mentioning the date of his departure from the abbey. Over the door of the tower, which led to the habitable part of the structure, he therefore cut the following lines :—

Oh ye whom misfortune may lead to this spot,
Learn that there are others as miserable as yourselves.

P . . . L . . . M . . . , a wretched exile, sought within these walls a refuge from persecution on the 27th of April, 1658, and quitted them on the 12th of July in the same year, in search of a more convenient asylum.

After engraving these words with a knife, the small stock of provisions remaining from the week's supply (for Peter, in his fright, had returned unloaded from his last journey) was put into a basket, and La Motte having assembled his family, they all ascended the stairs of the tower, and passed through the chambers to the closet. Peter went first with a light, and with some difficulty found the trap-door. Madame La Motte shuddered as she surveyed the gloomy abyss ; but they were all silent.

La Motte now took the light and led the way ; Madame followed, and then Adeline.

"These old monks loved good wine, as well as other people," said Peter, who brought up the rear ; " I warrant, your honour, now, this was their cellar ; I smell the casks already."

"Peace," said La Motte ; "reserve your jokes for a proper occasion."

"There is no harm in loving good wine, as your honour knows."

"Have done with this buffoonery," said La Motte, in a tone more authoritative, "and go first." Peter obeyed.

They came to the vaulted room. The dismal spectacle he had seen here deterred La Motte from passing the night in this chamber ; and the furniture had, by his own order, been conveyed to the cells below. He was anxious that his family should not perceive the skeleton—an object which would probably excite a degree of horror not to be overcome during their stay. La Motte now passed the chest in haste, and Madame La Motte and Adeline were too much engrossed by their own thoughts to give minute attention to external circumstances.

When they reached the cells Madame La Motte wept at the necessity which condemned her to a spot so dismal. "Alas," said she, "are we indeed thus reduced ! The apartments above formerly appeared to me a deplorable habitation, but they are a palace compared to these."

"True, my dear," said La Motte ; "and

let the remembrance of what you once thought them soothe your discontent now ; these cells are also a palace compared to the Bicêtre or the Bastille, and to the terrors of further punishment which would accompany them. Let the apprehension of the greater evil teach you to endure the less. I am contented if we find here the refuge I seek."

Madame La Motte was silent, and Adeline, forgetting her late unkindness, endeavoured as much as she could to console her ; while her heart was sinking with the misfortunes which she could not but anticipate, she appeared composed and even cheerful. She attended Madame La Motte with the most watchful solicitude, and felt so thankful that La Motte was now secreted within this recess that she almost lost all perception of its glooms and inconveniences.

This she artlessly expressed to him who could not be insensible to the tenderness it discovered. Madame La Motte was also sensible of it, and it renewed a painful sensation. The effusions of gratitude she mistook for those of tenderness.

La Motte returned frequently to the trapdoor to listen if anybody was in the abbey ; but no sound disturbed the stillness of night ; at length they sat down to supper—the repast was a melancholy one.

"If the officers do not come hither to-night," said Madame La Motte, sighing, "suppose, my dear, Peter returns to Auboine to-morrow ; he may there learn something more of this affair ; or at least he might procure a carriage to convey us hence."

"To be sure he might," said La Motte peevishly, "and people to attend it also. Peter would be an excellent person to show the officers the way to the abbey, and to inform them of what they might else be in doubt about—my concealment here."

"How cruel is this irony !" replied Madame La Motte ; "I proposed only what I thought would be for our mutual good ; my judgment was perhaps wrong, but my intention was certainly right."

Tears welled into her eyes as she spoke these words. Adeline wished to console her ; but delicacy kept her silent. La Motte observed the effect of his speech, and something like remorse touched his heart. He approached, and, taking his wife's hand, "You must allow for the perturbation of my mind," said he ; "I did not mean to afflict you thus. The idea of sending Peter to Auboine, where he has already done so much harm by his blunders, teased me, and I could not let it pass unnoticed. No, my dear, our only chance of safety is to remain where we are while our provisions last. If the officers do not come here to-night, they probably will to-morrow ; or perhaps the next day. When they have searched the abbey without finding me they will depart ; we may then emerge

from this recess and take measures for removing to a distant country."

Madame La Motte acknowledged the justness of his remarks, and her mind being relieved by the little apology he had made, she became tolerably cheerful. Supper being ended, La Motte stationed the faithful though simple Peter at the foot of the steps that ascended to the closet, there to keep watch during the night. Having done this he returned to the lower cells, where he had left his little family. The beds were spread, and having mournfully bade each other good-night, they lay down and implored rest.

Adeline's thoughts were too busy to suffer her to repose, and when she believed 'her companions were sunk in slumber, she indulged the sorrow which reflection brought. She also looked forward to the future with the most mournful apprehension.

Should La Motte be seized, what was to become of her ? She would then be a wanderer in the wide world ; without friends to protect or money to support her ; the prospect was gloomy—was terrible !

She surveyed it and shuddered ! The distresses too of Monsieur and Madame La Motte, whom she loved with the most lively affection, formed no inconsiderable part of hers.

Sometimes she looked back to her father, but in him she only saw an enemy from whom she must fly. This remembrance heightened her sorrow ; yet it was not the recollection of the suffering he had occasioned her by which she was so much afflicted, as by the sense of his unkindness ; she wept bitterly. At length, with that artless piety which innocence only knows, she addressed the Supreme Being, and resigned herself to His care. Her mind then gradually became peaceful and reassured, and soon after she sunk to repose.

CHAPTER V.

A SURPRISE—AN ADVENTURE—A MYSTERY.

THE night passed without any alarm ; Peter had remained upon his post and heard nothing that prevented his sleeping. La Motte heard him (long before he saw him) most musically snoring ; though it must be owned there was more of the bass than of any other part of the gamut in his performance. He was soon roused by the *bravura* of La Motte, whose notes sounded discord to his ears and destroyed the torpor of his tranquillity.

"God bless you, master, what's the matter?" cried Peter, waking ; "are they come?"

"Yes, for aught you care, they might be come. Did I place you here to sleep, sirrah?"

"Bless you, master," returned Peter,

"sleep is the only comfort to be had here; I'm sure I would not deny it to a dog in such a place as this."

La Motte sternly questioned him concerning any noise he might have heard in the night, and Peter full as solemnly protested he had heard none—an assertion which was strictly true, for he had enjoyed the comfort of being asleep the whole time.

La Motte then ascended to the trap-door and listened attentively. No sounds were heard, and, as he ventured to lift it, the full light of the sun burst upon his sight, the morning being now far advanced. He walked softly along the chambers and looked through a window; no person was to be seen. Encouraged by his apparent security, he ventured down the stairs of the tower, and entered the first apartment. He was proceeding towards the second, when, suddenly recollecting himself, he first peeped through the crevice of the door, which stood half open. He looked, and distinctly saw a person sitting near the window, upon which his arm rested.

The discovery so much shocked him that for a moment he lost all presence of mind, and was utterly unable to move from the spot. The person, whose back was towards him, arose and turned his head. La Motte now recovered himself, and quitting the apartment as quickly, and, at the same time, as silently as possible, ascended to the closet. He raised the trap-door, but, before he closed it, heard the footsteps of a person entering the outer chamber. Bolts or other fastening to the trap there were none; and his security depended solely upon the exact correspondence of the boards. The outer door of the stone room had no means of defence; and the fastenings of the inner one were on the wrong side to afford him security even till some means of escape could be found.

When he reached this room he paused, and heard distinctly persons walking in the closet above. While he was listening he heard a voice call him by name, and he instantly fled to the cells below, expecting every moment to hear the trap lifted and the footsteps of pursuit; but he was fled beyond the reach of hearing either. Having thrown himself on the ground at the farthest extremity of the vaults, he lay for some time breathless with agitation. Madame La Motte and Adeline, in the utmost terror, inquired what had happened. It was some time before he could speak; when he did it was almost unnecessary, for the distant noises, which sounded from above, informed the family of a part of the truth.

The sounds did not seem to approach, but Madame La Motte, unable to command her terror, shrieked aloud. This redoubled the distress of La Motte.

"You have destroyed me!" cried he; "that shriek has informed them where I am."

He traversed the cells with clasped hands and quick steps. Adeline stood pale and still as death, supporting Madame La Motte, whom with difficulty she prevented from fainting.

"Oh, Dupras! Dupras! you are already avenged!" said he, in a voice that seemed to burst from his heart. There was a pause of silence. "But why should I deceive myself with a hope of escaping?" he resumed; "why do I wait here for their coming? Let me rather end these torturing pangs by throwing myself into their hands at once."

As he spoke he moved towards the door, but the distress of Madame La Motte arrested his steps. "Stay," said she, "for my sake, stay; do not leave me thus, nor throw yourself voluntarily upon destruction!"

"Surely, sir," said Adeline, "you are too precipitate; this despair is useless, as it is ill-founded. We hear no person approaching. If the officers had discovered the trap-door they would certainly have been here before now."

The words of Adeline stilled the tumult of his mind; the agitation of terror subsided, and reason beamed a feeble ray upon his hopes. He listened attentively, and perceiving that all was silent, advanced with caution to the stone room, and thence to the foot of the stairs that led to the trap-door. It was closed; no sound was heard above.

He watched a long time, and, the silence continuing, his hopes strengthened, and at length he began to believe that the officers had quitted the abbey; the day, however, was spent in anxious watchfulness. He did not dare to unclose the trap-door; and he frequently thought he heard distant noises. It was evident, however, that the secret of the closet had escaped discovery, and on this circumstance he justly founded his security. The following night was passed, like the day, in trembling hope and incessant watching.

But the necessities of hunger now threatened them. The provisions, which had been distributed with the nicest economy, were nearly exhausted, and the most deplorable consequences might be expected from their remaining longer in concealment. Thus circumstanced, La Motte deliberated upon the most prudent method of proceeding. There appeared no other alternative than to send Peter to Auboine, the only town from which he could return within the time prescribed by their necessities. There was game, indeed, in the forest; but Peter could neither handle a gun or use a fishing-rod to any advantage.

It was therefore agreed that he should go to Auboine for a supply of provisions, and at the same time bring materials for mending the coach-wheel, that they might have some ready conveyance from the forest. La Motte forbade Peter to ask any questions concerning the people who had inquired for him, or take any methods for discovering whether they had quitted the country, lest his blunders should again betray him. He ordered him to be entirely silent as to these subjects, and to finish his business and leave the place with all possible despatch.

A difficulty yet remained to be overcome—who should first venture abroad into the abbey, to learn whether it was vacated by the officers of justice? La Motte considered that if he was again seen he should be effectually betrayed, which could not be *so* certain, if one of his family was observed, for they were each unknown to the officers. It was necessary, however, that the person he sent should have courage enough to go through with the inquiry, and wit enough to conduct it with caution. Peter, perhaps, had the first; but was certainly destitute of the last. Annette had neither. La Motte looked at his wife, and asked her if, for his sake, she dared to venture. Her heart shrunk from the proposal, yet she was unwilling to refuse, or appear indifferent upon a point so essential to the safety of her husband. Adeline observed in her countenance the agitation of her mind, and, surmounting the fears which had hitherto kept her silent, she offered herself to go.

"They will be less likely to offend me," said she, "than a man." Shame would not suffer La Motte to accept her offer; and Madame, touched by the magnanimity of her conduct, felt a momentary renewal of all her former kindness. Adeline pressed her proposal so warmly, and seemed so much in earnest, that La Motte began to hesitate. "You, sir," said she, "once preserved me from the most imminent danger, and your kindness has since protected me. Do not refuse me the satisfaction of deserving your goodness by a grateful return of it. Let me go into the abbey, and if, by so doing, I should preserve you from evil, I shall be sufficiently rewarded for what little danger I may incur, for my pleasure will be at least equal to yours."

Madame La Motte could scarcely refrain from tears as Adeline spoke; and La Motte, sighing deeply, said, "Well, be it so; go, Adeline, and from this moment consider me as your debtor." Adeline stayed not to reply, but taking a light quitted the cells, La Motte following to raise the trap-door, and cautioning her to look, if possible, into every apartment before she entered it. "If you should be seen," he said, "you must account for your appearance so as not to discover me. Your own presence of mind may assist you, I cannot—God bless you !"

When she was gone, Madame La Motte's admiration of her conduct began to yield to other emotions. Distrust gradually undermined kindness, and jealousy raised suspicions. "It must be a sentiment more powerful than gratitude," thought she, "that

could teach Adeline to subdue her fears. What, but love, could influence her to a conduct so generous !" Madame La Motte, when she found it impossible to account for Adeline's conduct without alleging some interested motive for it, however her suspicions might agree with the practice of the world, had surely forgotten how much she once admired the purity and disinterestedness of her young friend.

Adeline meanwhile ascended to the chambers; the cheerful beams of the sun played once more upon her sight, and reanimated her spirits; she walked lightly through the apartments, nor stopped till she came to the stairs of the tower. Here she stood for some time, but no sounds met her ear, save the sighing of the wind among the trees, and at length she descended. She passed the apartments below without seeing any person, and the little furniture that remained seemed to stand exactly as she had left it. She now ventured to look out from the tower; the only animate objects that appeared were the deer quietly grazing under the shade of the woods. Her favourite little fawn distinguished Adeline, and came bounding towards her with strong marks of joy. She was alarmed lest the animal, being observed, should betray her, and walked swiftly away through the cloisters.

She opened the door that led to the great hall of the abbey, but the passage was so gloomy and dark that she feared to enter it, and started back. It was necessary, however, that she should examine farther, particularly on the opposite side of the ruin, of which she had hitherto had no view ; but her fears returned when she recollected how far it would lead her from her only place of refuge, and how difficult it would be to retreat. She hesitated what to do; but when she recollected her obligations to La Motte, and considered this as perhaps her only opportunity of doing him a service, she determined to proceed.

As these thoughts passed rapidly over her mind, she raised her innocent looks to Heaven, and breathed a silent prayer. With trembling steps she proceeded over fragments of the ruin, looking anxiously around, and often starting as the breeze rustled among the trees, mistaking it for the whisperings of men. She came to the lawn which fronted the fabric, but no person was to be seen, and her spirits revived. The great door of the hall she now endeavoured to open, but suddenly remembering that it was fastened by La Motte's orders, she proceeded to the north end of the abbey, and, having surveyed the prospect around, as far as the thick foliage of the trees would permit, without perceiving any person, she turned her steps to the tower from which she had issued.

Adeline was now light of heart, and returned with impatience to inform La Motte of his security. In the cloisters she was again met by her little favourite, and she stopped for a moment to caress it. The fawn seemed sensible to the sound of her voice, and discovered new joy; but while she spoke, it suddenly started from her hand, and looking up, she perceived the door of the passage, leading to the great hall, open, and a man in the habit of a soldier issue forth.

With the swiftness of an arrow she fled along the cloisters, nor once ventured to look back; but a voice called to her to stop, and she heard steps advancing quick in pursuit. Before she could reach the tower, her breath failed her, and she leaned against a pillar of the cloister, pale and exhausted. The man came up, and gazing at her with a strong expression of surprise and curiosity, he assumed a gentle manner, assured her she had nothing to fear, and inquired if she belonged to La Motte: observing that she still looked terrified and remained silent, he repeated his assurances and his question.

"I know that he is concealed within the ruin," said the stranger; "the occasion of his concealment I also know; but it is of the utmost importance I should see him, and he will then be convinced that he has nothing to fear from me."

Adeline trembled so excessively, that it was with difficulty she could support herself—she hesitated, and knew not what to reply. Her manner seemed to confirm the suspicions of the stranger, and her consciousness of this increased her embarrassment; he took advantage of it to press her farther. Adeline at length replied that "La Motte had some time since resided at the abbey."

"And does still, madam," said the stranger; "lead me to where he may be found—I must see him, and——"

"Never, sir," replied Adeline; "and I solemnly assure you it will be in vain to search for him."

"That I must try," resumed he, "since you, madam, will not assist me. I have already followed him to some chambers above, where I suddenly lost him; thereabouts he must be concealed, and it's plain, therefore, they afford some secret passage."

Without waiting Adeline's reply, he sprung to the door of the tower. She now thought it would betray a consciousness of the truth of his conjecture to follow him, and resolved to remain below. But, on farther consideration, it occurred to her, that he might steal silently into the closet, and possibly surprise La Motte at the door of the trap. She therefore hastened after him, that her voice might prevent the danger she apprehended. He was already in the second chamber when she overtook him; she immediately began to speak aloud.

This room he searched with the most scrupulous care, but finding no private door or other outlet he proceeded to the closet; then it was that it required all her fortitude to conceal her agitation. He continued the search. "Within these chambers I know he is concealed," said he, "though hitherto I have not been able to discover how. It was hither I followed a man, whom I believe to be him, and he could not escape without a passage; I shall not quit the place till I have found it."

He examined the walls and the boards, but without discovering the division of the floor, which, indeed, so exactly corresponded, that La Motte himself had not perceived it by the eye, but by the trembling of the floor beneath his feet. "Here is some mystery," said the stranger, "which I cannot comprehend, and perhaps never shall." He was turning to quit the closet, when, who can paint the distress of Adeline, upon seeing the trap-door gently raised, and La Motte himself appear. "Hah!" cried the stranger, advancing eagerly to him. La Motte sprang forward, and they were locked in each other's arms.

The astonishment of Adeline for a moment surpassed even her former distress; but a remembrance darted across her mind which explained the present scene, and, before La Motte could exclaim, "My son!" she knew the stranger as such. Peter, who stood at the foot of the stairs and heard what passed above, flew to acquaint his mistress with the joyful discovery, and in a few moments she was folded in the embrace of her son. This spot, so lately the mansion of despair, seemed metamorphosed into the palace of pleasure, and the walls echoed only to the accents of joy and congratulation.

The joy of Peter on this occasion was beyond expression: he acted a perfect pantomime—he capered about, clapped his hands —ran to his young master—shook him by the hand, in spite of the frowns of La Motte; ran everywhere without knowing for what, and gave no rational answer to anything that was said to him.

After their first emotions were subsided, La Motte, as if suddenly recollecting himself, resumed his wonted solemnity: "I am to blame," said he, "thus to give way to joy, when I am still perhaps surrounded by danger. Let us secure a retreat while it is yet in our power," continued he; "in a few hours the King's officers may search for me again."

Louis comprehended his father's words, and immediately relieved his apprehensions by the following relation:

"A letter from Monsieur Nemours, containing an account of your flight from Paris, reached me at Peronne, where I was then upon duty with my regiment. He mentioned that you were gone towards the south of France, but as he had not since heard from you, he was ignorant of the place of your refuge. It was about this time that I was despatched into Flanders ; and being unable to obtain further intelligence of you, I passed some weeks of very painful solicitude. At the conclusion of the campaign I obtained leave of absence, and immediately set out for Paris, hoping to learn from Nemours where you had found an asylum.

"Of this, however, he was equally ignorant with myself. He informed me that you had once before written to him from D——, upon your second day's journey from Paris, under an assumed name, as had been agreed upon ; and that you then said the fear of discovery would prevent your hazarding another letter ; he therefore remained ignorant of your abode, but said he had no doubt you had continued your journey to the southward.

"Upon this slender information I quitted Paris in search of you, and proceeded immediately to V——, where my inquiries concerning your farther progress were successful as far as M——. There they told me you had stayed some time, on account of the illness of a young lady, a circumstance which perplexed me much, as I could not imagine what young lady would accompany you. I proceeded, however, to L—— ; but there all traces of you seemed to be lost. As I sat musing at the window of the inn, I observed some scribbling on the glass, and the curiosity of idleness prompted me to read it. I thought I knew the characters, and the lines I read confirmed my conjecture, for I remembered to have heard you often repeat them.

"Here I renewed my inquiries concerning your route, and at length I made the people of the inn recollect you, and traced you as far as Auboine. There I again lost you, till upon my return from a fruitless inquiry in the neighbourhood, the landlord of the little inn where I lodged told me he believed he had heard news of you, and immediately recounted what had happened at a blacksmith's shop a few hours before.

"His description of Peter was so exact, that I had not a doubt it was you who inhabited the abbey ; and as I knew your necessity for concealment, Peter's denial did not shake my confidence. The next morning, with the assistance of my landlord, I found my way hither, and having searched every visible part of the fabric, I began to credit Peter's assertion ; your appearance, however, destroyed this fear, by proving that the place was still inhabited, for you disappeared so instantaneously, that I was not certain it was you whom I had seen. I continued seeking you till near the close of day, and till then scarcely quitted the chambers whence you had disappeared. I called on you repeatedly, believing that my voice might convince you of your mistake. At length I retired, to pass the night at a cottage near the border of the forest.

"I came early this morning to renew my inquiries, and hoped that, believing yourself safe, you would emerge from concealment. But how was I disappointed to find the abbey as silent and solitary as I had left it the previous evening! I was returning once more from the great hall, when the voice of this young lady caught my ear, and effected the discovery I had so anxiously sought."

This little narrative entirely dissipated the first apprehensions of La Motte ; but he now dreaded that the inquiries of his son and his own obvious desire of concealment, might excite a curiosity amongst the people of Auboine and lead to a discovery of his true circumstances. However, for the present he determined to dismiss all painful thoughts, and endeavour to enjoy the comfort which the presence of his son had brought him. The furniture was removed to a more habitable part of the abbey, and the cells were again abandoned to their own glooms.

The arrival of her son seemed to have animated Madame La Motte with new life, and all her afflictions were for the present absorbed in joy. She often gazed silently on him with a mother's fondness, and her partiality heightened every improvement which time had wrought in his person and manner. He was now in his twenty-third year ; his person was manly and his air military ; his manners were unaffected and graceful rather than dignified ; and though his features were irregular, they composed a countenance which, having seen it once, you would seek again.

She made eager inquiries after the friends she had left at Paris, and learned that, within the few months of her absence, some had died and others quitted the place. La Motte also learned that a very strenuous search for him had been prosecuted at Paris ; and though this intelligence was only what he had before expected, it shocked him so much that he now declared it would be expedient to remove to a distant country. Louis did not scruple to say that he thought he would be as safe at the abbey as at any other place ; and repeated what Nemours had said, that the King's officers had been unable to trace any part of his route from Paris.

"Besides," resumed Louis, "this abbey is protected by a supernatural power, and none of the country people dare approach it."

"Please you, my young master," said Peter, who was waiting in the room, "we were frightened enough the first night we came here, and I myself, God forgive me! thought the place was inhabited by devils, but they were only owls and such like after all."

"Your opinion was not asked," said La Motte ; "learn to be silent."

Peter was abashed. When he had quitted the room, La Motte asked his son with seeming carelessness, what were the reports circulated by the country people.

"Oh, sir," replied Louis, "I cannot recollect half of them. I remember, however, they said that many years ago a person (but nobody had ever seen him, so we may judge how far the report ought to be credited) was privately brought to this abbey and confined in some part of it, and that there were strong reasons to believe he came unfairly to his end."

La Motte sighed.

"They further said," continued Louis, "that the spectre of the deceased had ever since watched nightly among the ruins; and, to make the story more wonderful—for the marvellous is the delight of the vulgar—they added that there was a certain part of the ruin from whence no person that had dared to explore it had ever returned. Thus people who have few objects of real interest to engage their thoughts, conjure up for themselves imaginary ones."

La Motte sat musing. "And what were the reasons," said he, at length awaking from his reverie, "they pretended to assign for believing the person confined here was murdered?"

"They did not use a term so positive as that," replied Louis.

"True," said La Motte, recollecting himself, "they only said he came unfairly to his end."

"That is a nice distinction," said Adeline.

"Why, I could not well comprehend what these reasons were," resumed Louis; "the people indeed say that the person who was brought here was never known to depart, but I do not find it certain that he ever arrived; that there was strange privacy and mystery observed while he was here, and that the abbey has never since been inhabited by its owner. There seems, however, to be nothing in all this that deserves to be remembered."

La Motte raised his head as if to reply, when the entrance of Madame turned the discourse upon a new subject, and it was not resumed that day.

Peter was now despatched for provisions, while La Motte and Louis retired to consider how far it was safe for them to continue at the abbey. La Motte, notwithstanding the assurances lately given him, could not but think that Peter's blunders and his son's inquiries might lead to a discovery of his residence. He resolved this in his mind for some time, but at length a thought struck him that the latter of these circumstances might considerably contribute to his security. "If you," said he to Louis, "return to the inn at Auboine from whence you were directed here, and without seeming to intend giving intelligence, do give the landlord an account of your having found the abbey uninhabited, and then add, that you had discovered the residence of the person you sought in some

distant town, it would suppress any reports that may at present exist, and prevent the belief of any in future. And if after all this you can trust yourself for presence of mind and command of countenance so far as to describe some dreadful apparition, I think these circumstances, together with the distance of the abbey and the intricacies of the forest, could entitle me to consider this place as my castle."

Louis agreed to all that his father had proposed, and on the following day executed his commission with such success, that the tranquillity of the abbey may be then said to have been entirely restored.

Thus ended this adventure, the only one that had occurred to disturb the family during their residence in the forest. Adeline, removed from the apprehension of those evils with which the late situation of La Motte had threatened her, and from the depression which her interest in his occasioned her, now experienced a more than usual complacency of mind. She thought, too, that she observed in Madame La Motte a renewal of her former kindness, and this circumstance awakened all her gratitude, and imparted to her a pleasure as lively as it was innocent. The satisfaction with which the presence of her son inspired Madame La Motte, Adeline mistook for kindness to herself, and she exerted her whole attention in an endeavour to become worthy of it.

But the joy which his unexpected arrival had given to La Motte quickly began to evaporate, and the gloom of despondency again settled on his countenance. He returned frequently to his haunt in the forest—the same mysterious sadness tinctured his manner, and revived the anxiety of Madame La Motte, who was resolved to acquaint her son with this subject of distress, and solicit his assistance to discover its source.

Her jealousy of Adeline, however, she could not communicate, though it again tormented her, and taught her to misconstrue with wonderful ingenuity every look and word of La Motte, and often to mistake the artless expressions of Adeline's gratitude and regard for those of warmer tenderness. Adeline had formerly accustomed herself to long walks in the forest, and the design Madame had formed of watching her steps had been frustrated by the late circumstances, and was now entirely overcome by her sense of its difficulty and danger. To employ Peter in the affair would be to acquaint him with her fears, and to follow her herself would most probably betray her scheme by making Adeline aware of her jealousy. Being thus restrained by pride and delicacy, she was obliged to endure the pangs of uncertainty concerning her suspicions.

To Louis, however, she related the mysterious change in his father's temper. He lis-

C

tened to her account with very earnest attention, and the surprise and concern impressed upon his countenance spoke how much his heart was interested. He was, however, involved in equal perplexity with herself upon this subject, and readily undertook to observe the motions of La Motte, believing his interference likely to be of equal service both to his father and his mother. He saw, in some degree, the suspicions of his mother, but as he thought she wished to disguise her feelings, he suffered her to believe that she succeeded.

He now inquired concerning Adeline, and listened to her little history, of which his mother gave a brief relation, with great apparent interest. So much pity did he express for her condition, and so much indignation at the unnatural conduct of her father, that the apprehensions which Madame La Motte began to form of his having discovered her jealousy yielded to those of a different kind. She perceived that the beauty of Adeline had already fascinated his imagination, and she feared that her amiable manners would soon impress his heart. Had her first fondness for Adeline continued, she would still have looked with displeasure upon their attachment as an obstacle to the promotion and the fortune she hoped to see one day enjoyed by her son. On these she rested all her future hopes of prosperity, and regarded the matrimonial alliance which he might form as the only means of extricating his family from their present difficulties. She therefore touched lightly upon Adeline's merit, coolly joined with Louis in compassionating her misfortunes, and, with her censure of the father's conduct, mixed an implied suspicion of that of Adeline's. The means she employed to repress the passions of her son had a contrary effect. The indifference which she expressed towards Adeline increased his pity for her destitute condition, and the tenderness with which she affected to judge the father heightened his honest indignation at his character.

As he quitted Madame La Motte he saw his father cross the lawn and enter the deep shade of the forest on the left. He judged this to be a good opportunity of commencing his plan, and, quitting the abbey, slowly followed at a distance. La Motte continued to walk straight forward, and seemed so deeply wrapt in thought that he looked neither to the right or left, and scarcely lifted his head from the ground. Louis had followed him near half a mile when he saw him suddenly strike into an avenue of the forest which took a different direction from the way he had hitherto gone. He quickened his steps that he might not lose sight of him; but, having reached the avenue, found the trees so thickly interwoven that La Motte was already hid from his view.

He continued, however, to pursue the way

before him; it conducted him through the most gloomy part of the forest he had yet seen, till at length it terminated in an obscure recess, overarched with high trees, whose interwoven branches excluded the direct rays of the sun, and admitted only a sort of solemn twilight. Louis looked around in search of La Motte, but he was nowhere to be seen. While he stood surveying the place, and considering what further should be done, he observed through the gloom an object at some distance, but the deep shadow that fell around prevented his distinguishing what it was.

On advancing he perceived the ruins of a small building, which, from the traces that remained, appeared to have been a tomb. As he gazed upon it, "Here," said he, "are probably deposited the ashes of some ancient monk, once an inhabitant of the abbey—perhaps the founder—who, after having spent a life of abstinence and prayer, sought in heaven the reward of his forbearance upon earth. Peace be to his soul! But did he think a life of mere negative virtue deserved an eternal reward? Mistaken man! Reason, had you trusted to its dictates, would have informed you that the active virtues—the adherence to the golden rule, 'Do as you would be done unto'—could alone deserve the favour of a Deity whose glory is benevolence."

He remained with his eyes fixed upon the spot, and presently saw a figure arise under the arch of the sepulchre. It started, as if on perceiving him, and immediately disappeared. Louis, though unused to fear, felt at that moment an uneasy sensation, but it almost immediately struck him that this was La Motte himself. He advanced to the ruin and called him. No answer was returned, and he repeated the call, but all was yet still as the grave. He then went up to the archway and endeavoured to examine the place where he had disappeared, but the shadowy obscurity rendered the attempt fruitless. He observed, however, a little to the right, an entrance to the ruin, and advanced some steps down a dark kind of passage, when, recollecting that this place might be the haunt of banditti, his danger alarmed him, and he retreated with precipitation.

He walked towards the abbey by the way he came, and finding no person followed him, and believing himself again in safety, his former surmise returned, and he thought it was La Motte he had seen. He mused upon this strange possibility, and endeavoured to assign a reason for so mysterious a conduct, but in vain. Notwithstanding this, his belief of it strengthened, and he entered the abbey under as full a conviction as the circumstances would admit of that it was his father who had appeared in the sepulchre. On entering what was now used as a parlour, he was much surprised to find him quietly seated there with Madame La Motte and Adeline, and conversing as if he had been returned some time.

He took the first opportunity of acquainting his mother with the late adventure, and of inquiring how long La Motte had been returned before him; when, learning that it was near half an hour, his surprise increased, and he knew not what to conclude.

Meanwhile, a perception of the growing partiality of Louis co-operated with the canker of suspicion to destroy in Madame La Motte that affection which pity and esteem had formerly excited for Adeline. Her unkindness was now too obvious to escape the notice of her to whom it was directed, and, being noticed, it occasioned an anguish which Adeline found it very difficult to endure. With the warmth and candour of youth, she sought an explanation of this change of behaviour and an opportunity of exculpating herself from any intention of provoking it. But this Madame La Motte artfully evaded, while at the same time she threw out hints that involved Adeline in deeper perplexity, and served to make her present affliction more intolerable.

"I have lost that affection," she would say, "which was my all. It was my only comfort—yet I have lost it—and this without even knowing my offence. But I am thankful I have not merited unkindness, and though *she* has abandoned *me*, I shall always love *her*."

Thus distressed, she would frequently leave the parlour, and, retiring to her chamber, would yield to a despondency which she had never known till now.

One morning, being unable to sleep, she arose at a very early hour. The faint light of day now trembled through the clouds, and, gradually spreading from the horizon, announced the rising sun. Every feature of the landscape was slowly unveiled, moist with the dews of night, and brightening with the dawn, till at length the sun appeared and shed the full flood of day. The beauty of the hour invited her to walk, and she went forth into the forest to taste the sweets of morning. The carols of new-waked birds saluted her as she passed, and the fresh gale came scented with the breath of flowers, whose tints glowed more vivid through the dewdrops that hung on their leaves.

She wandered on without noticing the distance, and, following the windings of the river, came to a dewy glade, whose woods, sweeping down to the very edge of the water, formed a scene so sweetly romantic that she seated herself at the foot of a tree to contemplate its beauty. These images insensibly soothed her sorrow, and inspired her with that pleasing melancholy so dear to the feeling mind. For some time she sat lost in a reverie, while the flowers that grew on the banks beside her seemed to smile in new life, and drew from her a comparison with her own condition. She mused and sighed, and then in a voice whose charming melody was modulated by the tenderness of her heart, she sung the following words:—

SONNET.

TO THE LILY.

Soft silken flow'r! that in the dewy vale
  Unfolds thy modest beauties to the morn,
And breath'st thy fragrance on her wand'ring gale,
  O'er earth's green hills and shadowy valleys borne:

When day has closed his dazzling eye,
  And dying gales sink soft away;
When eve steals down the western sky,
  And mountains, woods, and vales decay:

Thy tender cups, that graceful swell,
  Droop sad beneath her chilly dews;
Thy odours seek their silken cell,
  And twilight veils thy languid hues.

But soon, fair flow'r! the morn shall rise,
  And rear again thy pensive head;
Again unveil thy snowy dyes,
  Again thy velvet foliage spread.

Sweet child of spring! like thee, in sorrow's shade,
  Full oft I mourn in tears, and droop forlorn:
And, oh! like thine, may light MY gloom pervade,
  And sorrow fly before joy's living morn!

A distant echo lengthened out her tones, and she sat listening to the soft response, till, repeating the last stanza of the sonnet, she was answered by a voice almost as tender, and less distant. She looked round in surprise, and saw a young man in a hunter's dress, leaning against a tree, and gazing on her with that deep attention which marks an enamoured mind.

A thousand apprehensions shot athwart her busy thought; and she now first remembered her distance from the abbey. She rose in haste to be gone, when the stranger respectfully advanced; but observing her timid looks and retiring steps he paused. She pursued her way towards the abbey; and, though many reasons made her anxious to know whether she was followed, delicacy forbade her to look back. When she reached the abbey, finding the family was not yet assembled to breakfast, she retired to her chamber, where her whole thoughts were employed in conjectures concerning the stranger; believing that she was interested on this point no further than as it concerned the safety of La Motte, she indulged, without scruple, the remembrance of that dignified air and manner which so much distinguished the youth she had seen. After revolving the circumstance more deeply, she believed it impossible that a person of his appearance should be engaged in a stratagem to betray a fellow-creature; and though she was destitute of a single circumstance that might assist her surmises of who he was, or what was his business in an unfrequented forest, she rejected, unconsciously, every suspicion injurious to his

character. Upon further deliberation, therefore, she resolved not to mention this little
circumstance to La Motte, well knowing that
though his danger might be imaginary, his
apprehensions would be real, and would renew all the sufferings and perplexity from
which he was but just released. She resolved,
however, to refrain for some time walking
in the forest.

When she came down to breakfast she
observed Madame La Motte to be more than
usually reserved. La Motte entered the room
soon after her, and made some trifling observation on the weather; and, having endeavoured to support an effort at cheerfulness,
sunk into his usual melancholy. Adeline
watched the countenance of Madame with
anxiety; and when there appeared in it a
gleam of kindness, it was as sunshine to her
soul; but she very seldom suffered Adeline
thus to flatter herself. Her conversation was
restrained, and often pointed at something
more than could be understood. The
entrance of Louis was a very seasonable
relief to Adeline, who almost feared to trust
her voice with a sentence, lest its trembling
accents should betray her uneasiness.

"This charming morning drew you early
from your chamber," said Louis, addressing
Adeline.

" You had, no doubt, a pleasant companion
too," said Madame La Motte, "a solitary
walk is seldom agreeable."

" I was alone, madam," replied Adeline.

" Indeed! your own thoughts must be
highly pleasing then."

" Alas!" returned Adeline, a tear, spite of
her efforts, starting to her eye, "there are
now few subjects of pleasure left for them."

" That is very surprising," pursued Madame
La Motte.

" It is indeed surprising, madam, for those
who have lost their last friend to be unhappy?"

Madame La Motte's conscience acknowledged the rebuke, and she blushed. "Well,"
resumed she, after a short pause, " that is not
your situation, Adeline;" looking earnestly at
La Motte.

Adeline, whose innocence protected her from
suspicion, did not regard this circumstance;
but, smiling through her tears, said, "She
rejoiced to hear her say so."

During this conversation, La Motte had remained absorbed in his own thoughts; and
Louis, unable to guess at what it pointed,
looked alternately at his mother and Adeline
for an explanation. The latter he regarded
with an expression so full of tender compassion that it revealed at once to Madame
La Motte the sentiments of his soul; and she
immediately replied to the last words of
Adeline with a very serious air: " A friend
is only estimable when our conduct deserves
one; the friendship that survives the merit of

its object is a disgrace, instead of an honour,
to both parties."

The manner and emphasis with which she
delivered these words again alarmed Adeline,
who mildly said, "She hoped she should
never deserve such censure." Madame was
silent; but Adeline was so much shocked by
what had already passed, that tears sprung
from her eyes, and she hid her face with her
handkerchief.

Louis now arose with some emotion; and
La Motte, roused from his reverie, inquired
what was the matter; but, before he could
receive an answer, he seemed to have forgot
that he had asked a question.

"Adeline may give you her own account.
said Madame La Motte.

"I have not deserved this," said Adeline.
rising; " but since my presence is displeasing.
I will retire."

She moved towards the door, when Louis,
who was pacing the room in apparent
agitation, gently took her hand, saying, "Here
is some unhappy mistake," and would have
led her to her seat; but her spirits were too
much depressed to endure a longer restraint;
and withdrawing her hand, "Suffer me to go,"
said she; "if there is any mistake, I am unable to explain it." Saying this she quitted
the room.

Louis followed her with his eyes to the
door; when, turning to his mother, "Surely,
madam," said he, "you are to blame: my life
on it, she deserves your warmest tenderness."

" You are very eloquent in her cause, sir,"
said Madame: " may I presume to ask what
has interested you thus in her favour?"

" Her own amiable manners," rejoined
Louis, "which no one can observe without
esteeming them."

" But you may presume too much on your
own observations; it is possible these amiable
manners may deceive you."

" Your pardon, madam; I may, without
presumption, affirm they cannot deceive me."

" You have, no doubt, good reasons for
this assertion; and I perceive, by your admiration of this artless innocent, she has
succeeded in her design of entrapping your
heart."

" Without designing it she has won my
admiration, which would not have been the
case had she been capable of the conduct you
mention."

Madame La Motte was going to reply, but
was prevented by her husband, who, again
roused from his reverie, inquired into the cause
of dispute: " Away with this ridiculous behaviour," said he, in a voice of displeasure.
" Adeline has omitted some household duty,
I suppose, and an offence so heinous deserves
severe punishment, no doubt; but let me be
no more disturbed with your petty quarrels:
if you must be tyrannical, madam, indulge
your humour in private."

Saying this he abruptly quitted the room, and Louis immediately following, Madame was left to her own unpleasant reflections. Her ill-humour proceeded from the usual cause. She had heard of Adeline's walk ; and La Motte having gone forth into the forest at an early hour, her imagination, heated by the broodings of jealousy, suggested that they had appointed a meeting. This was confirmed to her by the entrance of Adeline, quickly followed by La Motte ; and her perceptions thus jaundiced by passion, neither the presence of her son nor her usual attention to good manners had been able to restrain her emotions. The behaviour of Adeline in the late scene she considered as a fine piece of art, and the indifference of La Motte as affected. So true it is that

> Trifles light as air,
> Are to the jealous confirmations strong,
> As proof of Holy Writ.

And so ingenious was she " to twist the true cause the wrong way."

Adeline had retired to her chamber to weep. When her first agitation had subsided, she took an ample review of her conduct ; and perceiving nothing of which she could accuse herself, she became more satisfied, deriving her best comfort from the integrity of her intentions. In the moment of accusation, innocence may sometimes be oppressed with the punishment due only to guilt ; but reflection dissolves the illusions of terror, and brings to the aching bosom the consolations of virtue.

When La Motte quitted the room, he had gone into the forest, which Louis observing, he followed and joined him, with an intention of touching upon the subject of his melancholy.

" It is a fine morning, sir," said Louis ; " if you will give me leave, I will walk with you."

La Motte, though dissatisfied, did not object ; and after they had proceeded some way, he changed the course of his walk, striking into a path contrary to that which Louis had observed him take on the foregoing day.

Louis remarked that the avenue they had quitted was " more shady ; and, therefore, more pleasant." La Motte not seeming to notice this remark, " It leads to a singular spot," continued he, " which I discovered yesterday." La Motte raised his head ; Louis proceeded to describe the tomb, and the adventure he had met with. During his relation La Motte regarded him with earnest attention, while his own countenance suffered various changes.

When he had concluded, " You were very daring," said La Motte, " to examine that place, particularly when you ventured down the passage ; I would advise you to be more cautious how you penetrate the depths of this forest. I myself have not ventured beyond a certain boundary, and am therefore uninformed what inhabitants it may harbour. Your account has alarmed me," continued he, " for if banditti are in the neighbourhood I am not safe from their depredations : 'tis true I have but little to lose, except my life."

" And the lives of your family," rejoined Louis.

" Of course," said La Motte.

" It would be well to have more certainty upon that head," rejoined Louis ; " I am considering how we may obtain it."

" 'Tis useless to consider that," said La Motte ; " the inquiry itself brings danger with it ; your life would, perhaps, be paid for the indulgence of your curiosity ; our only chance of safety is by endeavouring to remain undiscovered. Let us move towards the abbey."

Louis knew not what to think, but said no more upon the subject. La Motte soon after relapsed into a fit of musing ; and his son now took occasion to lament that depression of spirits which he had lately observed in him.

" Rather lament the cause of it," said La Motte, with a sigh.

" That I do most sincerely, whatever it may be. May I venture to inquire, sir, what is the cause ? "

" Are, then, my misfortunes so little known to you," rejoined La Motte, " as to make the question necessary ? Am I not driven from my home, from my friends, and almost from my country, and shall it be asked why I am afflicted ? "

Louis felt the justice of this reproof, and was for a moment silent.

" That you are afflicted, sir, does not excite my surprise," resumed he ; " it would, indeed, be strange were you not."

" What, then, does excite your surprise ? "

" The air of cheerfulness you wore when I first came hither."

" You lately lamented that I was afflicted," said La Motte, " and now seem not very well pleased that I once was cheerful. What is the meaning of this ? "

" You much mistake me," said his son ; " nothing could give me so much satisfaction as to see that cheerfulness renewed ; the same cause of sorrow existed at that time, yet you was then cheerful."

" That I was then cheerful," said La Motte, " you might, without flattery, have attributed to yourself ; your presence revived me, and I was relieved, at the same time, from a load of apprehension."

" Why, then, since the same cause exists, are you not still cheerful ? "

" And why do you not recollect that it is your father you thus speak to ? "

" I do, sir ; and nothing but anxiety for my father could have urged me thus far. It is with inexpressible concern I perceive you have some secret cause of uneasiness ; reveal it, sir, to those who claim a share in all your affliction, and suffer them, by participation, to soften its severity."

Louis looked up, and observed the countenance of his father pale as death ; his lips trembled while he spoke.

"Your penetration, however you may rely upon it, has, in the present instance, deceived you. I have no subject of distress but what you are already acquainted with, and I desire this conversation may never be renewed."

"If it is your desire, of course I obey," said Louis ; "but pardon me, sir, if——"

"I will not pardon you, sir," interrupted La Motte ; "let the discourse end here." Saying this, he quickened his steps, and Louis, not daring to pursue, walked quietly on till he reached the abbey.

Adeline passed the greatest part of the day alone in her chamber, where, having examined her conduct, she endeavoured to fortify her heart against the unmerited displeasure of Madame La Motte. This was a task more difficult than that of self-acquaintance. She loved her, and had relied on her friendship, which, notwithstanding the conduct of Madame, still appeared valuable. It was true she had not deserved to lose it, but Madame was so averse to explanation, that there was little probability of recovering it, however ill-founded might be the cause of her dislike. At length she reasoned, or rather, perhaps, persuaded herself into tolerable composure ; for to resign a real good with contentment is less an effort of reason than of temper.

For many hours she busied herself upon a piece of work which she had undertaken for Madame La Motte ; and this she did without the least intention of conciliating her favour, but because she felt there was something in thus repaying unkindness which was suitable to her own temper, sentiments, and pride. Self-love may be the centre round which the human affections move, for whatever motive conduces to self-gratification may be resolved into self-love ; yet some of these affections are in their nature so refined, that though we cannot deny their origin, they almost deserve the name of virtue. Of this species was that of Adeline.

In this employment, and in reading, Adeline passed as much of the day as possible. From books, indeed, she had constantly derived her chief information and amusement ; those belonging to La Motte were few but well chosen, and Adeline could find pleasure in reading them more than once. When her mind was discomposed by the behaviour of Madame La Motte, or by a retrospection of her early misfortunes, a book was the opiate that lulled it to repose. La Motte had several of the best English poets, a language which Adeline had learned in the convent ; their beauties, therefore, she was capable of tast-

ing, and they often inspired her with enthusiastic delight.

At the decline of day she quitted her chamber to enjoy the sweet evening hour, but strayed no farther than an avenue near the abbey, which fronted the west. She read a little, but, finding it impossible any longer to abstract her attention from the scene around, she closed the book, and yielded to the sweet complacent melancholy which the hour inspired. The air was still ; the sun, sinking below the distant hills, spread a purple glow over the landscape, and touched the forest glades with softer light. A dewy freshness was diffused upon the air. As the sun descended, and the dusk came silently on, the scene assumed a solemn grandeur. As she mused, she recollected and repeated the following stanzas :

NIGHT.

Now ev'ning fades ! her pensive step retires,
  And night leads on the dews, and shadowy hours—
Her awful pomp of planetary fires,
  And all her train of visionary powers.

THESE paint with fleeting shapes the dream of sleep,
  THESE swell the waking soul with pleasing dread ;
These through the glooms in forms terrific sweep,
  And rouse the thrilling horrors of the dead !

Queen of the solemn thought—mysterious night
  Whose step is darkness, and whose voice is fear—
Thy shades I welcome with severe delight,
  And hail thy hollow gales, that sigh so drear !

When wrapt in clouds, and riding in the blast,
  Thou roll'st the storm along the sounding shore,
I love to watch the whelming billows, cast
  On rocks below, and listen to the roar.

Thy milder terrors, night, I frequent woo,
  Thy silent lightnings, and thy meteor's glare,
Thy northern fires, bright with ensanguine hue,
  That light in heaven's high vault the fervid air.

But chief I love thee when thy lucid car
  Sheds through the fleecy clouds a trembling gleam,
And shows the misty mountain from afar,
  The nearer forest, and the valley's stream :

And nameless objects in the vale below,
  That, floating dimly, to the musing eye
Assume, at fancy's touch, fantastic show,
  And raise her sweet romantic visions high.

Then let me stand amid thy glooms profound,
  On some wild woody steep, and hear the breeze
That swells in mournful melody around,
  And faintly dies upon the distant trees.

What melancholy charm steals o'er the mind !
  What hallow'd tears the rising rapture greet !
While many a viewless spirit in the wind
  Sighs to the lonely hour in accent sweet !

Ah ! who the dear illusions pleas'd would yield,
  Which fancy wakes from silence and from shades,
For all the sober forms of truth reveal'd,
  For all the scenes that day's bright eye pervades !

On her return to the abbey she was joined by Louis, who after some conversation said : "I am much grieved by the scene to which I was witness this morning, and have longed for an opportunity of telling you so. My mother's behaviour is too mysterious for me to account for, but it is not difficult to perceive she labours under some mistake. What I have to request is that whenever I can be of service to you, you will command me."

Adeline thanked him for his friendly offer, which she felt more sensibly than she chose to express. "I am unconscious," said she, "of any offence that may have deserved Madame La Motte's displeasure, and am therefore totally unable to account for it. I have repeatedly sought an explanation, which she has as anxiously avoided; it is better, therefore, to press the subject no farther. At the same time, sir, suffer me to assure you I have a just sense of your goodness."

Louis sighed and was silent. At length, "I wish you would permit me," resumed he, "to speak with my mother upon this subject. I am sure I could convince her of her error."

"By no means," replied Adeline. "Madame La Motte's displeasure has given me inexpressible concern; but to compel her to an explanation would only increase this displeasure instead of removing it. Let me beg of you not to attempt it."

"I submit to your judgment," said Louis; "but for once it is with reluctance; I should esteem myself most happy if I could be of service to you."

He spoke this with an accent so tender, that Adeline for the first time perceived the sentiments of his heart. A mind more fraught with vanity than hers would have taught her long ago to regard the attentions of Louis as the result of something more than well-bred gallantry. She did not appear to notice his last words, but remained silent, and involuntarily quickened her pace. Louis said no more, but seemed sunk in thought; and this silence remained uninterrupted till they entered the abbey.

CHAPTER VI.

Hence, horrible shadow!
Unreal mockery, hence!
SHAKSPEARE.

NEAR a month elapsed without any remarkable occurrence. The melancholy of La Motte suffered little abatement; and the behaviour of Madame to Adeline, though somewhat softened, was still far from kind. Louis, by numberless little attentions, testified his growing affection for Adeline, who continued to treat them as passing civilities.

It happened one stormy night, as they were preparing for rest, that they were alarmed by the tramping of horses near the abbey. The sound of several voices succeeded, and a loud knocking at the great gate of the hall soon after confirmed the alarm. La Motte had little doubt that the officers of justice had at

length discovered his retreat, and the perturbation of fear almost confounded his senses; he, however, ordered the lights to be extinguished and a profound silence to be observed, unwilling to neglect the slightest possibility of security. There was a chance, he thought, that the persons might suppose the place uninhabited, and believe they had mistaken the object of their search. His orders were scarcely obeyed when the knocking was renewed, and with increased violence. La Motte now repaired to a small grated window in the portal of the gate, that he might observe the number and appearance of the strangers.

The darkness of the night baffled his purpose—he could only perceive a group of men on horseback; but, listening attentively, he distinguished a part of their discourse. Several of the men contended that they had mistaken the place, till a person, who from his authoritative voice appeared to be their leader, affirmed that the lights had issued from this spot, and he was positive there were persons within. Having said this, he again knocked loudly at the gate, and was answered only by hollow echoes. La Motte's heart trembled at the sound, and he was unable to move.

After waiting some time the strangers seemed as if in consultation, but their discourse was conducted in such a low tone of voice that La Motte was unable to distinguish its purport. They withdrew from the gate as if to depart, but he presently thought he heard them amongst the trees on the other side of the fabric, and soon became convinced they had not left the abbey. A few minutes held La Motte in a state of torturing suspense; he quitted the grate, where Louis now stationed himself, for that part of the edifice which overlooked the spot where he supposed them to be waiting.

The storm was now loud, and the hollow blasts which rushed among the trees prevented his distinguishing any other sound. Once, in a pause of the wind, he thought he heard voices, but he was not long left to conjecture, for the renewed knocking at the gate again appalled him; and, regardless of the terrors of Madame La Motte and Adeline, he ran to try his last chance of concealment by means of the trap-door.

Soon after, the violence of the assailants seeming to increase with every gust of the tempest, the gate, which was old and decayed, burst from its hinges and admitted them to the hall. At the moment of their entrance, a scream from Madame La Motte, who stood at the door of an adjoining apartment, confirmed the suspicion of the principal stranger, who continued to advance as fast as the darkness would permit him.

Adeline had fainted, and Madame La Motte was calling loudly for assistance, when Peter entered with lights, and discovered the hall filled with men, and his young mistress senseless upon the floor.

A chevalier now advanced, and soliciting pardon of Madame for the rudeness of his conduct, was attempting an apology, when, perceiving Adeline, he hastened to raise her from the ground; but Louis, who now returned, caught her in his arms and desired the stranger not to interfere.

The person to whom he spoke this wore the star of one of the first orders in France, and had an air of dignity which declared him to be of superior rank. He appeared to be about forty, but perhaps the spirit and fire of his countenance made the impression of time upon his features less perceptible. His softened aspect and insinuating manners, while, regardless of himself, he seemed attentive only to the condition of Adeline, gradually dissipated the apprehensions of Madame La Motte, and subdued the sudden resentment of Louis. Upon Adeline, who was yet insensible, he gazed with an eager admiration which seemed to absorb all the faculties of his mind. She was indeed an object not to be contemplated with indifference.

Her beauty, touched with the languid delicacy of illness, gained from sentiment what it lost in bloom. The negligence of her dress, loosened for the purpose of freer respiration, discovered the graces which her auburn tresses, that fell in profusion over her bosom, shaded, but could not conceal.

There now entered another stranger, a young chevalier, who, having spoken hastily to the elder, joined the general group that surrounded Adeline. He was of a person in which elegance was happily blended with strength, and had a countenance animated, but not haughty; noble, yet expressive of peculiar sweetness. What rendered it at present most interesting was the compassion he seemed to feel for Adeline, who now revived, and saw him—the first object that met her eyes—bending over her in silent anxiety.

On perceiving him a blush of quick surprise passed over her cheek, for she knew him to be the stranger she had seen in the forest. Her countenance instantly changed to the paleness of terror when she observed the room crowded with people. Louis now supported her into another apartment, where the two chevaliers, who followed her, again apologised for the alarm they had occasioned. The elder, turning to Madame La Motte, said:

"You are no doubt, madam, ignorant that I am the proprietor of this abbey." She started. "Be not alarmed, madam, you are safe and welcome. This ruinous spot has been long abandoned by me, and if it has afforded you a shelter, I am happy."

Madame La Motte expressed her gratitude for this condescension, and Louis declared his sense of the politeness of the Marquis de Montalt, for that was the title of the noble stranger.

"My chief residence," said the Marquis, "is in a distant province, but I have a château near the borders of the forest, and in returning from an excursion I have been benighted and lost my way. A light which gleamed through the trees attracted me hither, and such was the darkness without that I did not know it proceeded from the abbey till I came to the door."

The noble deportment of the strangers, the splendour of their apparel, and, above all, this speech, dissipated every remaining doubt of Madame's, and she was giving orders for refreshment to be set before them when La Motte, who had listened, and was now convinced he had nothing to fear, entered the apartment.

He advanced towards the Marquis with a complacent air, but, as he would have spoke, the words of welcome faltered on his lips, his limbs trembled, and a ghastly paleness overspread his countenance. The Marquis was little less agitated, and, in the first moment of surprise, put his hand upon his sword, but, recollecting himself, he withdrew it, and endeavoured to obtain a command of features. A pause of agonising silence ensued. La Motte made some motion towards the door, but his agitated frame refused to support him, and he sunk into a chair, silent and exhausted. The horror of his countenance, together with his whole behaviour, excited the utmost surprise in Madame, whose eyes inquired of the Marquis more than he thought proper to answer; his looks increased instead of explaining the mystery, and expressed a mixture of emotions which she could not analyse. Meanwhile she endeavoured to soothe and revive her husband, but he repressed her efforts, and, averting his face, covered it with his hands.

The Marquis, seeming to recover his presence of mind, stepped to the door of the hall, where his people were assembled, when La Motte, starting from his seat with a frantic air, called on him to return. The Marquis looked back and stopped, but still hesitated whether to proceed; the supplications of Adeline, who was now returned, added to those of La Motte, determined him, and he sat down.

"I request of you, my lord," said La Motte, "that we may converse for a few moments by ourselves."

"The request is bold, and the indulgence, perhaps, dangerous," said the Marquis; "it is more also than I will grant. You can have nothing to say with which your family are not acquainted—speak your purpose and be brief."

La Motte's complexion varied to every sentence of his speech.

"Impossible, my lord!" said he; "my lips

shall close for ever, ere they pronounce before another human being the words reserved for you alone. I entreat, I supplicate of you a few moments' private discourse."

As he pronounced these words, tears welled into his eyes, and the Marquis, softened by his distress, consented, though with evident emotion and reluctance, to his request.

La Motte took a light and led the Marquis to a small room in a remote part of the edifice, where they remained near an hour. Madame, alarmed by the length of their absence, went in quest of them; as she drew near, a curiosity, in such circumstances, perhaps, not unjustifiable, prompted her to listen.

La Motte just then exclaimed, "The frenzy of despair!" Some words followed, delivered in a low tone, which she could not understand. "I have suffered more than I can express," continued he; "the same image has pursued me in my midnight dream, and in my daily wanderings. There is no punishment short of death which I would not have endured to regain the state of mind with which I entered this forest. I again address myself to your compassion."

A loud gust of wind that burst along the passage where Madame La Motte stood overpowered his voice and that of the Marquis, who spoke in reply; but she soon after distinguished these words—"To-morrow, my lord, if you return to these ruins, I will lead you to the spot."

"That is scarcely necessary, and may be dangerous," said the Marquis.

"From you, my lord, I can excuse these doubts," resumed La Motte, "but I will swear whatever you shall propose. Yes," continued he, "whatever may the consequence, I will swear to submit to your decree!"

The rising tempest again drowned the sound of their voices, and Madame La Motte vainly endeavoured to hear those words upon which probably hung the explanation of this mysterious conduct. They now moved towards the door, and she retreated with precipitation to the apartment where she had left Adeline with Louis and the young chevalier.

Hither the Marquis and La Motte soon followed—the first haughty and cool, the latter somewhat more composed than before, though the impression of horror was not yet faded from his countenance. The Marquis passed on to the hall, where his retinue awaited; the storm had not yet subsided, but he seemed impatient to be gone, and ordered his people to be in readiness. La Motte observed a sullen silence, frequently pacing the room with hasty steps, and was sometimes lost in reverie. Meanwhile, the Marquis, seating himself by Adeline, directed to her his whole attention, except when sudden fits of absence came over his mind and suspended him in silence; at these times the young chevalier addressed Adeline, who, with diffidence and some agitation, shrunk from the observance of both.

The Marquis had been near two hours at the abbey, and the tempest still continuing Madame La Motte offered him a bed. A look from her husband made her tremble for the consequence. Her offer, however, was politely declined, the Marquis being evidently as impatient to be gone as his tenant appeared distressed by his presence. He often returned to the hall, and from the gates raised a look of impatience to the clouds. Nothing was to be seen through the darkness of night—nothing heard but the howling of the storm.

The morning dawned before he departed. As he was preparing to leave the abbey, La Motte again drew him aside, and held him for a few moments in close conversation. His impassioned gestures, which Madame La Motte observed from a remote part of the room, added to her curiosity a degree of wild apprehension derived from the obscurity of the subject. Her endeavour to distinguish the corresponding words was baffled by the low voice in which they were uttered.

The Marquis and his retinue at length departed, and La Motte, having himself fastened the broken gates, silently and dejectedly withdrew to his chamber. The moment they were alone, Madame seized the opportunity of entreating her husband to explain the scene she had witnessed.

"Ask me no questions," said La Motte, sternly, "for I will answer none. I have already forbade your speaking to me on this subject."

"What subject?" said his wife.

La Motte seemed to recollect himself. "No matter; I was mistaken; I thought you had repeated these questions before."

"Ah!" said Madame La Motte, "it is then as I suspected; your former melancholy and the distress of this night have the same cause."

"And why should you either suspect or inquire? Am I always to be persecuted with conjectures?"

"Pardon me, I meant not to persecute you; but my anxiety for your welfare will not suffer me to rest under this dreadful uncertainty. Let me claim the privilege of a wife, and share the affliction which oppresses you. Deny me not——"

La Motte interrupted her. "Whatever may be the cause of the emotions which you have witnessed, I swear that I will not now reveal it. A time may come when I shall no longer judge concealment necessary; till then be silent, and desist from importunity; above all, forbear to remark to anyone what you may have seen uncommon in me. Bury your surmise in your own bosom, as you would avoid my curse and my destruction." The determined air with which he spoke this, while his countenance was overspread with a livid hue, made his wife shudder ; and she forbore all reply.

Madame La Motte retired to bed, but not to rest. She ruminated on the past occurrence ; and her surprise and curiosity concerning the words and behaviour of her husband, were but more strongly stimulated by reflection. One truth, however, appeared ; she could not doubt but the mysterious conduct of La Motte, which had for so many months oppressed her with anxiety, and the late scene with the Marquis, originated from the same cause. This belief, which seemed to prove how unjustly she had suspected Adeline, brought with it a pang of self-accusation. She looked forward to the morrow, which would lead the Marquis again to the abbey, with impatience.

Wearied nature at length resumed her rights, and yielded a short oblivion of care.

At a late hour the next day the family assembled to breakfast. Each individual of the party appeared silent and abstracted, but very different was the aspect of their features, and still more the complexion of their thoughts. La Motte seemed agitated by impatient fear, yet the sullenness of despair overspread his countenance. A certain wildness in his eye at times expressed the sudden start of horror, and again his features would sink into the gloom of despondence.

Madame La Motte seemed harassed with anxiety ; she watched every turn of her husband's countenance, and impatiently awaited the arrival of the Marquis. Louis was composed and thoughtful. Adeline seemed to feel her full share of uneasiness. She had observed the behaviour of La Motte on the preceding night with much surprise, and the happy confidence she had hitherto reposed in him was shaken. She feared, also, lest the exigency of his circumstances should precipitate him again into the world, and that he would be either unable or unwilling to afford her a shelter beneath his roof.

During breakfast La Motte frequently rose to the window, from whence he cast many an anxious look. His wife understood too well the cause of his impatience, and endeavoured to repress her own. In these intervals Louis attempted by whispers to obtain some information from his father, but La Motte always returned to the table, where the presence of Adeline prevented further discourse.

After breakfast, as he walked upon the lawn, Louis would have joined him, but La Motte peremptorily declared he intended to be alone, and soon after, the Marquis being not yet arrived, proceeded to a greater distance from the abbey.

Adeline retired into their usual working-room with Madame La Motte, who affected an air of cheerfulness and even of kindness. Feeling the necessity of offering some reason for the striking agitation of La Motte, and

of preventing the surprise which the unexpected appearance of the Marquis would occasion Adeline if she was left to connect it with his behaviour of the preceding night, she mentioned that the Marquis and La Motte had long been known to each other, and that this unexpected meeting, after an absence of many years, and under circumstances so altered and humiliating on the part of the latter, had occasioned him much painful emotion. This had been heightened by a consciousness that the Marquis had formerly misinterpreted some circumstances in his conduct towards him, which had caused a suspension of their intimacy.

This account did not bring conviction to the mind of Adeline, for it seemed inadequate to the degree of emotion the Marquis and La Motte had mutually betrayed. Her surprise was excited and her curiosity awakened by the words which were meant to delude them both, but she forbore to express her thoughts.

Madame, proceeding with her plan, said, "the Marquis was now expected, and she hoped whatever differences remained would be perfectly adjusted."

Adeline blushed, and endeavouring to reply, her lips faltered. Conscious of this agitation, and of the observance of Madame La Motte, her confusion increased, and her endeavours to suppress it served only to heighten it. Still she tried to renew the discourse, and still she found it impossible to collect her thoughts. Shocked lest Madame should apprehend the sentiment which had till this moment been concealed almost from herself, her colour fled, she fixed her eyes on the ground, and for some time found it difficult to respire. Madame La Motte inquired if she was ill, when Adeline, glad of the excuse, withdrew to the indulgence of her own thoughts, which were now wholly engrossed by the expectation of seeing again the young chevalier who had accompanied the Marquis.

As she looked from her room she saw the Marquis on horseback, with several attendants, advancing at a distance, and she hastened to apprise Madame La Motte of his approach. In a short time he arrived at the gates, and Madame and Louis went out to receive him, La Motte being not yet returned. He entered the hall, followed by the young chevalier, and accosting Madame with a sort of stately politeness, inquired for La Motte, whom Louis now went to seek.

The Marquis remained for a few minutes silent, and then asked of Madame La Motte, "how her fair daughter did?"

Madame understood it was Adeline he meant, and having answered his inquiry, and slightly said that she was not related to her, Adeline, upon some indication of the Marquis's wish, was sent for ; she entered the room with a modest blush and a timid air, which seemed to engage all his attention

His compliments she received with a sweet grace; but when the younger chevalier approached, the warmth of his manner rendered hers involuntarily more reserved, and she scarcely dared to raise her eyes from the ground, lest they should encounter his.

La Motte now entered and apologised for his absence, which the Marquis noticed only by a slight inclination of his head, expressing at the same time by his looks both distrust and pride. They immediately quitted the abbey together, and the Marquis beckoned his attendants to follow at a distance. La Motte forbade his son to accompany him, but Louis observed he took the way into the thickest part of the forest. He was lost in a chaos of conjecture concerning this affair, but curiosity and anxiety for his father induced him to follow at some distance.

In the meantime the younger stranger, whom the Marquis had addressed by the name of Theodore, remained at the abbey with Madame La Motte and Adeline. The former, with all her address, could not conceal her agitation during this interval. She moved involuntarily to the door whenever she heard a footstep, and several times she went to the hall-door in order to look into the forest, but as often returned, checked by disappointment. No person appeared. Theodore seemed to address as much of his attention to Adeline as politeness would allow him to withdraw from Madame La Motte. His manners, so gentle, yet dignified, insensibly subdued her timidity, and banished her reserve. Her conversation no longer suffered a painful constraint, but gradually disclosed the beauties of her mind, and seemed to produce a mutual confidence. A similarity of sentiment soon appeared, and Theodore, by the impatient pleasure which animated his countenance, seemed frequently to anticipate the thoughts of Adeline.

To them the absence of the Marquis was short, though long to Madame La Motte, whose countenance brightened when she heard the tramping of horses at the gate.

The Marquis appeared but for a moment, and passed on with La Motte to a private room, where they remained for some time in conference, immediately after which he departed. Theodore took leave of Adeline, who, as well as La Motte and Madame, attended them to the gate with an expression of tender regret, and often, as he went, looked back upon the abbey till the intervening branches entirely excluded it from his view.

The transient glow of pleasure diffused over the cheek of Adeline disappeared with the young stranger, and she sighed as she turned into the hall. The image of Theodore pursued her to her chamber; she recollected with exactness every particular of his late conversation—his sentiments so congenial with her own—his manners so engaging—his countenance so animated, so ingenuous and so noble, in which manly dignity was blended with the sweetness of benevolence; —these and every other grace she recollected, and a soft melancholy stole upon her heart. "I shall see him no more," said she. A sigh that followed told her more of her heart than she wished to know. She blushed and sighed again, and then, suddenly recollecting herself, she endeavoured to divert her thoughts to a different subject. La Motte's connection with the Marquis for some time engaged her attention; but, unable to develop the mystery that attended it, she sought a refuge for her own reflections in the more pleasing ones to be derived from books.

During this time Louis, shocked and surprised at the extreme distress which his father had manifested upon the first appearance of the Marquis, addressed him on the subject. He had no doubt that the Marquis was intimately concerned in the event which made it necessary for La Motte to leave Paris, and he spoke his thoughts without disguise, lamenting at the same time the unlucky chance which had brought him to seek refuge in a place of all others the least capable of affording it—the estate of his enemy. La Motte did not contradict this opinion of his son's, and joined in lamenting the evil fate which had conducted him thither.

The term of Louis' absence from his regiment was now nearly expired, and he took occasion to express his sorrow that he must soon be obliged to leave his father in circumstances so dangerous as the present. "I should leave you, sir, with less pain," continued he, "were I sure I knew the full extent of your misfortunes. At present I am left to conjecture evils which perhaps do not exist. Relieve me, sir, from this state of painful uncertainty, and suffer me to prove myself worthy of your confidence."

"I have already answered you on this subject," said La Motte, "and forbade you to renew it. I am now obliged to tell you I care not how soon you depart, if I am to be persecuted with these inquiries." La Motte walked abruptly away, and left his son to doubt and concern."

The arrival of the Marquis had dissipated the jealous fears of Madame La Motte, and she awoke to a sense of her cruelty towards Adeline. When she considered her orphan state—the uniform affection which had appeared in her behaviour—the mildness and patience with which she had borne her injurious treatment, she was shocked, and took an early opportunity of renewing her former kindness. But she could not explain this seeming inconsistency of conduct without betraying her late suspicions, which she now blushed to remember, nor could she apologise for her former behaviour without giving this explanation.

She contented herself, therefore, with expressing in her manner the regard which was thus revived. Adeline was at first surprised, but she felt too much pleasure at the change to be scrupulous in inquiring the cause.

But notwithstanding the satisfaction which Adeline received from the revival of Madame La Motte's kindness, her thoughts frequently recurred to the peculiar and forlorn circumstances of her condition. She could not help feeling less confidence than she had formerly done in the friendship of Madame La Motte, whose character now appeared less amiable than her imagination had represented it, and seemed strongly tinctured with caprice. Her thoughts often dwelt upon the strange introduction of the Marquis at the abbey, and on the mutual emotions and apparent dislike of La Motte and himself; and, under these circumstances, it equally excited her surprise that La Motte should choose, and that the Marquis should permit him, to remain in his territory.

Her mind returned the oftener, perhaps, to this subject, because it was connected with Theodore; but it returned unconscious of the idea which attracted it. She attributed the interest she felt in the affair to her anxiety for the welfare of La Motte, and for her own future destination, which was now so deeply involved in his. Sometimes, indeed, she caught herself busy in conjecture as to the degree of relationship in which Theodore stood to the Marquis, but she immediately checked her thoughts, and severely blamed herself for having suffered them to stray to an object which she perceived was too dangerous to her peace.

CHAPTER VII.

Present ills
Are less than horrible imaginings.
SHAKSPEARE.

A FEW days after the occurrence related in the preceding chapter, as Adeline sat alone in her chamber, she was roused from a reverie by a tramping of horses near the gate, and, on looking from the casement, she saw the Marquis de Montalt enter the abbey. This circumstance surprised her, and an emotion, whose cause she did not trouble herself to inquire for, made her instantly retreat from the window. The same cause, however, led her thither again as hastily, but the object of her search did not appear, and she was in no haste to retire.

As she stood musing and disappointed the Marquis came out with La Motte, and, immediately looking up, saw Adeline and bowed. She returned his compliment respectfully and withdrew from the window, vexed at having been seen there. They went into the forest, but the Marquis's attendants did not, as before, follow them thither. When they returned, which was not till after a considerable time, the Marquis immediately mounted his horse and rode away.

For the remainder of the day La Motte appeared gloomy and silent, and was frequently lost in thought. Adeline observed him with particular attention and concern; she perceived that he was always more melancholy after an interview with the Marquis, and was now surprised to hear that the latter had appointed to dine the next day at the abbey.

When La Motte mentioned this he added some high eulogium on the character of the Marquis, and particularly praised his generosity and nobleness of soul. At this instant Adeline recollected the anecdotes she had formerly heard concerning the abbey, and they threw a shadow over the brightness of that excellence which La Motte now celebrated. The account, however, did not appear to deserve much credit, a part of it, as far as a negative will admit of demonstration, having been already proved false; for it had been reported that the abbey was haunted, and no supernatural appearance had ever been observed by the present inhabitants.

Adeline, however, ventured to inquire whether it was the present Marquis of whom those injurious reports had been raised?

La Motte answered her with a smile of ridicule: "Stories of ghosts and hobgoblins have always been admired and cherished by the vulgar," said he. "I am inclined to rely upon my own experience at least as much as upon the accounts of these peasants. If you have seen anything to corroborate these accounts, pray inform me of it, that I may establish my faith."

"You mistake me, sir," said she, "it was not concerning supernatural agency that I would inquire; I alluded to a different part of the report, which hinted that some person had been confined here by order of the Marquis, who was said to have died unfairly. This was alleged as a reason for the Marquis's having abandoned the abbey."

"All the mere coinage of idleness," said La Motte—"a romantic tale to excite wonder: to see the Marquis is alone sufficient to refute this; and if we credit half the number of those stories that spring from the same source we prove ourselves little superior to the simpletons who invent them. Your good sense, Adeline, I think, will teach you the merit of disbelief."

Adeline blushed and was silent; but La Motte's defence of the Marquis appeared much warmer and more diffuse than was consistent with his own disposition or required by the occasion. His former conversation with Louis occurred to her, and she was the more surprised at what passed at present.

She looked forward to the morrow with a mixture of pain and pleasure, the expectation of seeing again the young chevalier occupying her thoughts and agitating them with a various emotion. Now she feared his presence, and now she doubted whether he would come. At length she observed this, and blushed to find how much he engaged her attention.

The morrow arrived. The Marquis came—but he came alone; and the sunshine of Adeline's mind was clouded, though she was able to wear her usual air of cheerfulness. The Marquis was polite, affable, and attentive; to manners the most easy and elegant was added the refinement of polished life. His conversation was lively, amusing, sometimes even witty, and discovered great knowledge of the world, or, what is often mistaken for it, an acquaintance with the higher circles, and with the topics of the day.

Here La Motte was also qualified to converse with him, and they entered into a discussion of the characters and manners of the age with great spirit and some humour. Madame La Motte had not seen her husband so cheerful since they left Paris, and sometimes she could almost fancy she was there. Adeline listened till the cheerfulness which she had at first only assumed became real. The address of the Marquis was so insinuating and affable that her reserve insensibly gave way before it, and her natural vivacity resumed its long-lost empire.

At parting, the Marquis told La Motte he rejoiced at having found so agreeable a neighbour. La Motte bowed. " I shall sometimes visit you," continued he, "and I lament that I cannot at present invite Madame La Motte and her fair friend to my château, but it is undergoing some repairs, which make it but an uncomfortable residence."

The vivacity of La Motte disappeared with his guest, and he soon relapsed into fits of silence and abstraction.

" The Marquis is a very agreeable man," said Madame La Motte.

" Very agreeable," replied he.

" And seems to have an excellent heart," she resumed.

" An excellent one," said La Motte.

" You seem discomposed, my dear; what has disturbed you ? "

" Not in the least. I was only thinking that with such agreeable talents, and such an excellent heart, it was a pity the Marquis should——"

" What, my dear ? " said Madame with impatience.

" That the Marquis should—should suffer this abbey to fall into ruins," replied La Motte.

" Is that all ! " said Madame with disappointment.

" That is all, upon my honour," said La Motte, and left the room.

Adeline's spirits, no longer supported by the animated conversation of the Marquis, sunk into languor, and when he departed she walked pensively into the forest. She followed a little romantic path that wound along the margin of the stream, and was overhung with deep shades. The tranquillity of the scene, which autumn now touched with her sweetest tints, softened her mind to a tender kind of melancholy, and she suffered a tear which, she knew not wherefore, had stolen into her eye, to tremble there unchecked. She came to a lonely recess, formed by high trees; the wind sighed mournfully among the branches, and as it waved their lofty heads scattered their leaves to the ground. She seated herself on a bank beneath, and indulged the melancholy reflections that pressed to her mind.

"Oh, could I dive into futurity and behold the events which await me ! " said she, " I should perhaps, by constant contemplation, be enabled to meet them with fortitude. An orphan in this wide world—thrown upon the friendship of strangers for comfort, and upon their bounty for the very means of existence —what but evil have I to expect ! Alas, my father ! how could you thus abandon your child—how could you leave her to the storms of life— to sink perhaps beneath them ? Alas, I have no friend ! "

She was interrupted by a rustling among the fallen leaves; she turned her head, and perceiving the Marquis's young friend, arose to depart.

" Pardon this intrusion," said he, "your voice attracted me hither, and your words detained me. My offence, however, brings with it its own punishment; having learned your sorrows—how can I help feeling them myself ? Would that my sympathy, or my suffering, could rescue you from them ! " He hesitated. "Would that I could deserve the title of your friend, and be thought worthy of it by yourself ! "

The confusion of Adeline's thoughts would scarcely permit her to reply; she trembled, and gently withdrew her hand, which he had taken while he spoke.

"You have perhaps heard, sir, more than is true : I am indeed not happy, but a moment of dejection has made me unjust, and I am less unfortunate than I have represented. When I said I had no friend, I was ungrateful to the kindness of Monsieur and Madame La Motte, who have been more than friends— have been as parents to me."

" If so, I honour them," cried Theodore with warmth; "and if I did not feel it to be presumption, I would ask why you are unhappy? But——" He paused. Adeline, raising her eyes, saw him gazing upon her with intense and eager anxiety, and her looks were again fixed upon the ground. " I have pained you," said Theodore, "by an improper request. Can you forgive me, and also when I add that it was an interest in your welfare which urged my inquiry?"

"Forgiveness, sir, it is unnecessary to ask. I am certainly obliged by the compassion you express. But the evening is cold; if you please, we will walk towards the abbey."

As they moved on, Theodore was for some time silent. At length, "It was but lately that I solicited your pardon," said he, "and I shall now, perhaps, have need of it again; but you will do me the justice to believe that I have a strong, and, indeed, a pressing reason, to inquire how nearly you are related to Monsieur La Motte."

"We are not at all related," said Adeline; "but the service he has done me I can never repay, and I hope my gratitude will teach me never to forget it."

"Indeed!" said Theodore, surprised; "and may I ask how long you have known him?"

"Rather, sir, let me ask, why these questions should be necessary?"

"You are just," said he, with an air of self-condemnation; "my conduct has deserved this reproof; I should have been more explicit."

He looked as if his mind was labouring with something which he was unwilling to express.

"But you know not how delicately I am circumstanced," continued he, "yet I will aver that my questions are prompted by the tenderest interest in your happiness, and even by my fears for your safety."

Adeline started.

"I fear you are deceived," said he; "I fear there's danger near you."

Adeline stopped, and, looking earnestly at him, begged he would explain himself. She suspected that some mischief threatened La Motte, and, Theodore continuing silent, she repeated her request.

"If La Motte is concerned in this danger," said she, "let me entreat you to acquaint him with it immediately. He has but too many misfortunes to apprehend."

"Excellent Adeline!" cried Theodore, "that heart must be adamant that would injure you. How shall I hint what I fear is too true, and how forbear to warn you of your danger without——"

He was interrupted by a step among the trees, and presently after saw La Motte cross into the path they were in. Adeline felt confused at being thus seen with the chevalier, and was hastening to join La Motte, but Theodore detained her, and entreated a moment's attention.

"There is now no time to explain myself," said he, "yet what I would say is of the utmost consequence to yourself. Promise, therefore, to meet me in some part of the forest at about this time to-morrow evening; you will then, I hope, be convinced that my conduct is directed neither by common circumstances nor common regard."

Adeline shuddered at the idea of making an appointment. She hesitated, and at length entreated Theodore not to delay till to-morrow an explanation which appeared to be so important, but to follow La Motte and inform him of his danger immediately.

"It is not with La Motte I would speak," replied Theodore; "I know of no danger that threatens him—but he approaches—be quick, lovely Adeline, and promise to meet me."

"I do promise," said Adeline, in a faltering voice; "I will come to the spot where you found me this evening, an hour earlier to-morrow."

Saying this she withdrew her trembling hand, which Theodore had pressed to his lips in token of acknowledgment, and he immediately disappeared.

La Motte now approached Adeline, who, fearing that he had seen Theodore, was in some confusion.

"Whither is Louis gone so fast?" said La Motte.

She rejoiced to find his mistake, and suffered him to remain in it. They walked pensively towards the abbey, where Adeline, too much occupied by her own thoughts to bear company, retired to her chamber. She ruminated upon the words of Theodore, and the more she considered them the more she was perplexed. Sometimes she blamed herself for having made an appointment, doubting whether he had not solicited it for the purpose of pleading a passion; and now delicacy checked this thought, and made her vexed that she presumed upon having inspired one. She recollected the serious earnestness of his voice and manner, when he entreated her to meet him; and, as they convinced her of the importance of the subject, she shuddered at a danger which she could not comprehend, looking forward to the morrow with anxious impatience.

Sometimes, too, a remembrance of the tender interest he had expressed for her welfare, and of his correspondent look and air, would steal across her memory, awakening a pleasing emotion and a latent hope that she was not indifferent to him. From reflections like these she was roused by a summons to supper. The repast was a melancholy one, it being the last evening of Louis's stay at the abbey. Adeline, who esteemed him, regretted his departure, while his eyes were often bent on her with a look which seemed to express that he was about to leave the object of his affection. She endeavoured, by her cheerfulness, to reanimate the whole party, and especially Madame La Motte, who frequently shed tears.

"We shall soon meet again," said Adeline ; "I trust in happier circumstances."

La Motte sighed. The countenance of Louis brightened at her words.

"Do you wish it?" said he, with peculiar emphasis.

"Most certainly I do," she replied ; "can you doubt my regard for my best friends?"

"I cannot doubt anything that is good of you," said he.

"You forget you have left Paris," said La Motte to his son, while a faint smile crossed his face; "such a compliment would there be in character with the place—in these solitary woods it is quite *outre.*"

"The language of admiration is not always that of compliment, sir," said Louis.

Adeline, willing to change the discourse, asked to what part of France he was going. He replied that his regiment was now at Peronne, and he should go immediately thither. After some mention of indifferent subjects, the family withdrew for the night to their several chambers.

The approaching departure of her son occupied the thoughts of Madame La Motte, and she appeared at breakfast with eyes swollen with weeping. The pale countenance of Louis seemed to indicate that he had rested no better than his mother. When breakfast was over Adeline retired for awhile, that she might not interrupt by her presence their last conversation. As she walked on the lawn before the abbey she returned in thought to the occurrence of yesterday evening, and her impatience for the appointed interview increased. She was soon joined by Louis.

"It was unkind of you to leave us," said he, "in the last moments of my stay. Could I hope that you would sometimes remember me when I am far away, I should depart with less sorrow."

He then expressed his concern at leaving her, and, though he had hitherto armed himself with resolution to forbear a direct avowal of an attachment which must be fruitless, his heart now yielded to the force of passion, and he told what Adeline every moment feared to hear.

"This declaration," said Adeline, endeavouring to overcome the agitation it excited, "gives me inexpressible concern."

"Oh, say not so!" interrupted Louis, "but give me some slender hope to support me in the miseries of absence. Say that you do not hate me—say——"

"That I do most readily say," replied Adeline in a tremulous voice ; "if it will give you pleasure to be assured of my esteem and friendship, receive this assurance : as the son of my best benefactors, you are entitled to——"

"Name not benefits," said Louis, "your merits outrun them all ; and suffer me to hope for a sentiment less cool than that of friendship, as well as to believe that I do not owe your approbation of me to the actions of others. I have long borne my passion in silence, because I foresaw the difficulties that would attend it—nay, I have even dared to endeavour to overcome it ; I have dared to believe it possible—forgive the supposition—that I could forget you—and——"

"You distress me," interrupted Adeline ; "this is a conversation which I ought not to hear. I am above disguise, and therefore assure you that, though your virtues will always command my esteem, you have nothing to hope for my love. Were it even otherwise, our circumstances would effectually decide for us. If you are really my friend, you will rejoice that I am spared the struggle between affection and prudence. Let me hope also that time will teach you to reduce love within the limits of friendship."

"Never!" cried Louis vehemently ; "were this possible my passion would be unworthy of its object." While he spoke Adeline's favourite fawn came towards her. This circumstance affected Louis even to tears. "This little animal," said he, after a short pause, "first conducted me to you ; it was a witness to that happy moment when I first saw you, surrounded by attractions too powerful for my heart ; that moment is now fresh in my memory, and the creature comes even to witness this sad one of my departure." Grief interrupted his utterance.

When he recovered his voice, he said, "Adeline! when you look upon your little favourite and caress it, remember the unhappy Louis, who will then be far, far from you. Do not deny me the poor consolation of believing this!"

"I shall not require such a monitor," said Adeline, with a smile ; "your excellent parents and your own merits have sufficient claim upon my remembrance. Could I see your natural good sense resume its influence over passion, my satisfaction would equal my esteem for you."

"Do not hope," said Louis, "nor will I wish it—for passion here is virtue." As he spoke, he saw La Motte turn round an angle of the abbey. "The moments are precious," said he ; "I am interrupted. Oh! Adeline, farewell! and say that you will sometimes think of me."

"Farewell," said Adeline, who was affected by his distress, "farewell! and peace attend you. I will think of you with the affection of a sister."

He sighed deeply, and pressed her hand ; when La Motte, winding round another projection of the ruin, again appeared. Adeline left them together; and withdrew to her chamber, oppressed by the scene. Louis's passion and her esteem were too sincere not to inspire her with a strong degree of pity for his unhappy attachment. She remained in her chamber till he had quitted the abbey, unwilling to subject him or herself to the pain of a formal parting.

As evening and the hour of appointment drew nigh Adeline's impatience increased ; yet, when the time arrived, her resolution failed, and she faltered from her purpose. There was something of indelicacy and dissimulation in an appointed interview, on her part, that shocked her. She recollected the tenderness of Theodore's manner, and several little circumstances which indicated that his heart was not unconcerned in the event. Again she was inclined to doubt whether he had not obtained her consent to this meeting upon some groundless suspicion ; and she almost determined not to go ; yet it was possible that Theodore's assertion might be sincere, and her danger real ; the chance of this made her delicate scruples appear ridiculous ; she wondered that she had for a moment suffered them to weigh against so serious an interest, and blaming herself for the delay they had occasioned, hastened to the place of appointment.

The little path which led to this spot was silent and solitary, and when she reached the recess, Theodore had not arrived. A transient pride made her unwilling he should find that she was more punctual to his appointment than himself, and she turned from the recess into a track which wound among the trees to the right. Having walked some way, without seeing any person or hearing a footstep, she returned ; but he was not come, and she again left the place. A second time she came back, and Theodore was still absent. Recollecting the time at which she had quitted the abbey she grew uneasy, and calculated that the hour appointed was now exceeded. She was vexed and perplexed ; but she seated herself on the turf, and was resolved to wait the event. After remaining here till the fall of twilight in fruitless expectation, her pride became more alarmed ; she feared that he had discovered something of the partiality he had inspired, and believing that he now treated her with purposed neglect, she quitted the place with disgust and self-accusation.

When these emotions subsided, and reason resumed its influence, she blushed for what she termed this childish effervescence of self-love. She recollected, as if for the first time, these words of Theodore : " I fear you are deceived, and that some danger is near you." Her judgment now acquitted the offender, and she saw only the friend. The import of these words, whose truth she no longer doubted, again alarmed her. Why did he trouble himself to come from the château, on purpose to hint her danger, if he did not wish to preserve her ? And if he wished to preserve her, what but necessity could have withheld him from the appointment ?

These reflections decided her at once. She

resolved to repair on the following day at the same hour to the recess, whither the interest which she believed him to take in her fate would no doubt conduct him in the hope of meeting her. That some evil hovered over her she could not disbelieve, but what it might be she was unable to guess. Monsieur and Madame La Motte were her friends, and who else, removed as she now thought herself beyond the reach of her father, could injure her ? But why did Theodore say she was deceived ? She found it impossible to extricate herself from the labyrinth of conjecture, but endeavoured to command her anxiety till the following evening. In the meantime she engaged herself in efforts to amuse Madame La Motte, who required some relief, after the departure of her son.

Thus oppressed by her own cares, and interested by those of Madame La Motte, Adeline retired to rest. She soon lost her recollection, but it was only to fall into harassed slumbers, such as but too often haunt the couch of the unhappy. At length her perturbed fancy suggested the following dream :

She thought she was in a large old chamber belonging to the abbey, more ancient and desolate, though in part furnished, than any she had yet seen. It was strongly barricaded, yet no person appeared. While she stood musing and surveying the apartment she heard a low voice call her, and, looking towards the place whence it came, she perceived by the dim light of a lamp a figure stretched on a bed that lay on the floor. The voice called again, and approaching the bed, she distinctly saw the features of a man who appeared to be dying. A ghastly paleness overspread his countenance, yet there was an expression of mildness and dignity in it, which strongly interested her.

While she looked on him his features changed, and seemed convulsed in the agonies of death. The spectacle shocked her, and she started back, but he suddenly stretched forth his hand, and seizing hers, grasped it with violence. She struggled in terror to disengage herself, and again looking on his face, saw a man who appeared to be about thirty, with the same features, but in full health and of a most benign countenance. He smiled tenderly upon her and moved his lips as if to speak, when the floor of the chamber suddenly opened and he sank from her view. The effort she made to save herself from following awoke her. This dream had so strongly impressed her fancy that it was some time before she could overcome the terror it occasioned, or even be perfectly convinced she was in her own apartment. At length, however, she composed herself to sleep : again she fell into a dream.

She thought she was bewildered in some winding passages of the abbey, that it was almost dark, and that she wandered about a considerable time without being able to find a door. Suddenly she heard a bell toll from above, and soon after a confusion of distant voices. She redoubled her efforts to extricate herself. Presently all was still, and, at length, wearied with the search, she sat down on a step that crossed the passage. She had not been long here when she saw a light glimmer at a distance on the walls, but a turn in the passage, which was very long, prevented her seeing from what it proceeded. It continued to glimmer faintly for some time, and then grew stronger, when she saw a man enter the passage, habited in a long black cloak, like those usually worn by the attendants at funerals, and bearing a torch. He called to her to follow him, and led her through a long passage to the foot of a staircase. Here she feared to proceed, and was running back, when the man suddenly turned to pursue her, and with the terror which this occasioned she awoke.

Shocked by these visions, and more so by their seeming connection, which now struck her, she endeavoured to continue awake, lest their terrific images should again haunt her mind; after some time, however, her harassed spirits again sank into slumber, though not to repose.

She now thought herself in a large old gallery, and saw at one end of it a chamber door standing a little open, and a light within. She went towards it, and perceived the man she had before seen, standing at the door, and beckoning her towards him. With the inconsistency so common in dreams, she no longer endeavoured to avoid him, but, advancing, followed him into a suite of very ancient apartments, hung with black, and lighted up as if for a funeral. Still he led her on, till she found herself in the same chamber she remembered to have seen in her former dream. A coffin, covered with a pall, stood at the farther end of the room; some lights, and several persons, surrounded it, who appeared to be in great distress.

Suddenly she thought these persons were all gone, and that she was left alone, that she went up to the coffin, and while she gazed upon it she heard a voice speak, as if from within, but saw nobody. The man she had before seen soon after stood by the coffin, and, lifting the pall, she saw beneath it a dead person, whom she thought to be the dying chevalier she had seen in her former dream; his features were sunk in death, but they were yet serene. While she looked at him a stream of blood gushed from his side, and descending to the floor, the whole chamber was overflowed; at the same time some words were uttered in the voice she heard before; but the horror of the scene so entirely overcame her that she started and awoke.

When she had recovered her recollection, she raised herself in the bed, to be convinced it was a dream she had witnessed, and the agitation of her spirits was so great that she feared to be alone, and almost determined to call Annette. The features of the deceased person, and the chamber where he lay, were strongly impressed upon her memory, and she still thought she heard the voice and saw the countenance which her dream represented. The longer she considered these dreams the more she was surprised—they were so very terrible, returned so often, and seemed to be so connected with each other, that she could scarcely think them accidental, yet why they should be supernatural she could not tell. She slept no more that night.

CHAPTER VIII.

When these prodigies
Do so conjointly meet, let not men say:
These are their reasons; they are natural;
For I believe they are portentous things.
SHAKSPEARE.

WHEN Adeline appeared at breakfast, her harassed and languid countenance struck Madame La Motte, who inquired if she was ill. Adeline, forcing a smile upon her features, said she had not rested well, for that she had had very disturbed dreams; she was about to describe them, but a strong and involuntary impulse prevented her. At the same time La Motte ridiculed her concern so unmercifully, that she was almost ashamed to have mentioned it, and tried to overcome the remembrance of its cause.

After breakfast, she endeavoured to employ her thoughts by conversing with Madame La Motte; but they were really engaged by the incidents of the last two days; the circumstance of her dreams, and her conjectures concerning the information to be communicated to her by Theodore. They had thus sat for some time, when a sound of voices arose from the great gate of the abbey; and on going to the casement, Adeline saw the Marquis and his attendants on the lawn below. The portal of the abbey concealed several people from her view, and among these it was possible might be Theodore, who had not yet appeared. She continued to look for him with great anxiety till the Marquis entered the hall with La Motte and some other persons, soon after which Madame La Motte went to receive him, and Adeline retired to her own apartment.

A message from La Motte, however, soon called her to join the party, where she vainly hoped to find Theodore. The Marquis arose as she approached; and having paid her some general compliments, the conversation took a very lively turn. Adeline, finding it impossible to counterfeit cheerfulness, while her heart was sinking with anxiety and disappointment, took little part in it. Theodore

D

was not once named. She would have asked concerning him, had it been possible to inquire with propriety ; but she was obliged to content herself with hoping, first, that he would arrive before dinner ; and then, before the departure of the Marquis.

Thus the day passed in expectation and disappointment. The evening was now approaching, and she was condemned to remain in the presence of the Marquis, apparently listening to a conversation which in truth she scarcely heard, while the opportunity was perhaps escaping that would decide her fate. She was suddenly relieved from this state of torture, and thrown into one, if possible, still more distressing.

The Marquis inquired for Louis, and being informed of his departure, mentioned that Theodore Peyrou had that morning set out for his regiment in a distant province. He lamented the loss he should sustain by his absence ; and expressed some very flattering praise of his talents. The shock of this intelligence overpowered the long-agitated spirits of Adeline ; the blood forsook her cheeks, and a sudden faintness came over her, from which she recovered only to a consciousness of having betrayed her emotion, and the danger of relapsing into a second fit.

She retired to her chamber, where, being once more alone, her oppressed heart found relief from tears, in which she freely indulged. Ideas crowded so fast upon her mind that it was long ere she could arrange them so as to produce anything like reasoning. She endeavoured to account for the abrupt departure of Theodore. "Is it possible," said she, "that he should take an interest in my welfare, and yet leave me exposed to the full force of a danger which he himself foresaw ? Or am I to believe that he has trifled with my simplicity for an idle frolic, and has now left me to the wondering apprehension he has raised ? Impossible ! A countenance so noble and manners so amiable could never disguise a heart capable of forming so despicable a design. No ! whatever is reserved for me, let me not relinquish the pleasure of believing that he is worthy of my esteem."

She was awakened from thoughts like these by a peal of distant thunder, and now perceived that the gloominess of evening was deepened by the coming storm ; it rolled onward, and soon after the lightning began to flash along the chamber. Adeline was superior to the affectation of fear, and was not apt to be terrified ; but she now felt it unpleasant to be alone, and, hoping that the Marquis might have left the abbey, she went down to the sitting-room ; but the threatening aspect of the heavens had hitherto detained him, and now the evening tempest made him rejoice that he had not quitted a shelter.

The storm continued and night came on. La Motte pressed his guest to take a bed at the abbey, and he at length consented—a circumstance which threw Madame La Motte into some perplexity as to the accommodation to be afforded him. After some time she arranged the affair to her satisfaction, resigning her own apartment to the Marquis, and that of Louis to two of his superior attendants ; Adeline, it was further settled, should give up her room to Monsieur and Madame La Motte, and remove to an inner chamber, where a small bed, usually occupied by Annette, was placed for her.

At supper the Marquis was less gay than usual ; he frequently addressed Adeline, and his look and manner seemed to express the tender interest which her indisposition, for she still appeared pale and languid, had excited. Adeline, as usual, made an effort to forget her anxiety and appear happy, but the veil of assumed cheerfulness was too thin to conceal the features of sorrow, and her feeble smiles only added a peculiar softness to her air. The Marquis conversed with her on a variety of subjects, and displayed an elegant mind. The observations of Adeline, which, when called upon, she gave with modest reluctance, in words at once simple and forcible, seemed to excite his admiration, which he sometimes betrayed by an apparently inadvertent expression.

Adeline retired early to her room, which adjoined on one side to Madame La Motte's, and on the other to the closet formerly mentioned. It was spacious and lofty, and what little furniture it contained was falling to decay ; but perhaps the present tone of her spirits might contribute more than these circumstances to give that air of melancholy which seemed to reign in it. She was unwilling to go to bed, lest the dreams that had lately pursued her should return, and determined to sit up till she found herself oppressed by sleep, when it was probable her rest would be profound. She placed the light on a small table, and, taking a book, continued to read for above an hour, till her mind refused any longer to abstract itself from its own cares, and she sat for some time leaning pensively on her arm.

The wind was high, and as it whistled through the desolate apartment and shook the feeble doors she often started, and sometimes even thought she heard sighs in the pauses of the gust ; but she checked these illusions, which the hour of the night and her own melancholy imagination conspired to raise.

As she sat musing, her eyes fixed on the opposite wall, she perceived the arras with which the room was hung wave backwards and forwards ; she continued to observe it for some minutes, and then rose to examine it further. It was moved by the wind, and she blushed at the momentary fear it had excited; but she observed that the tapestry was more strongly agitated in one particular place than elsewhere, and a noise that seemed something more than that of the wind issued thence. The old bedstead which La Motte had found in this apartment had been removed to accommodate Adeline, and it was behind the place where this had stood that the wind seemed to rush with particular force. Curiosity prompted her to examine still further. She felt about the tapestry, and perceiving the wall behind shake under her hand, she lifted the arras and discovered a small door, whose loosened hinges admitted the wind, and occasioned the noise she had heard.

The door was held only by a bolt, having undrawn which, and brought the light, she descended by a few steps into another chamber. She instantly remembered her dreams. The chamber was not much like that in which she had seen the dying chevalier, and afterwards the bier, but it gave her a confused remembrance of one through which she had passed. Holding up the light to examine it more fully, she was convinced by its structure that it was part of the ancient foundation. A shattered casement, placed high from the floor, seemed to be the only opening to admit light. She observed a door on the opposite side of the apartment, and, after some moments of hesitation, gained courage, and determined to pursue the inquiry. "A mystery seems to hang over these chambers," said she, "which it is perhaps my lot to develop; I will at least see to what that door leads."

She stepped forward, and having unclosed it, proceeded with faltering steps along a suite of apartments, resembling the first in style and condition, and terminating in one exactly like that where her dream had represented the dying person. The remembrance struck so forcibly upon her imagination, that she was in danger of fainting; and looking round the room, almost expected to see the phantom of her dream.

Unable to quit the place, she sat down on some old lumber to recover herself, while her spirits were nearly overcome by a superstitious dread such as she had never felt before. She wondered to what part of the abbey these chambers belonged, and that they had so long escaped detection. The casements were all too high to afford any information from without. When she was sufficiently composed to consider the direction of the rooms, and the situation of the abbey, there appeared not a doubt that they formed an interior part of the original building.

As these reflections passed over her mind, a sudden gleam of moonlight fell upon some object without the casement. Being now sufficiently composed to wish to pursue the inquiry, and believing this object might afford her some means of learning the situation of these rooms, she combated her remaining terrors, and in order to distinguish it more clearly, removed the light to an outer chamber; but before she could return a heavy cloud was driving over the face of the moon, and all without was perfectly dark; she stood for some moments waiting a returning gleam, but the obscurity continued. As she went softly back for the light her foot stumbled over something on the floor, and while she stooped to examine it the moon again shone, so that she could distinguish through the casement the eastern towers of the abbey. This discovery confirmed her former conjectures concerning the interior situation of these apartments. The obscurity of the place prevented her discovering what it was that had impeded her steps, but having brought the light forward, she perceived on the floor an old dagger: with a trembling hand she took it up, and upon a closer view perceived that it was spotted and stained with rust.

Shocked and surprised, she looked round the room for some object that might confirm or destroy the dreadful suspicion which now rushed upon her mind; but she saw only a great chair, with broken arms, that stood in one corner of the room, and a table in a condition equally shattered, except that in another part lay a confused heap of things which appeared to be old lumber. She went up to it, and perceived a broken bedstead, with some decayed remnants of furniture, covered with dust and cobwebs, and which seemed, indeed, as if they had not been moved for many years. Desirous, however, of examining further, she attempted to raise what appeared to have been part of the bedstead, but it slipped from her hand, and rolling to the floor, brought with it some of the remaining lumber. Adeline started aside and saved herself, and when the noise it made had ceased, she heard a small rustling sound, and as she was about to leave the chamber, saw something falling gently among the lumber.

It was a small roll of paper, tied with a string and covered with dust. Adeline took it up, and opening it perceived a handwriting. She attempted to read it, but the part of the manuscript she looked at was so much obliterated that she found this difficult, though what few words were legible impressed her with curiosity and terror, and induced her to return with it immediately to her chamber.

Having reached her own room, she fastened the private door, and let the arras fall over it as before. It was now midnight. The stillness of the hour, interrupted only at intervals by the hollow sighings of the blast, heightened the solemnity of Adeline's feelings. She wished she was not alone, and before she proceeded to look into the manuscript, listened whether Madame La Motte was yet in her chamber: not the least sound was heard, and she gently opened the door. The profound silence within almost convinced her that no person was there; but willing to be farther satisfied, she brought the light and found the room empty. The lateness of the hour made her wonder that Madame La Motte was not in her chamber, and she proceeded to the top of the tower stairs to hearken if any person was stirring.

She heard the sound of voices from below, and amongst the rest that of La Motte speaking in his usual tone. Being now satisfied that all was well, she turned towards her room, when she heard the Marquis pronounce her name with unusual emphasis. She paused. "I adore her," pursued he, "and by heaven"—He was interrupted by La Motte: "My Lord, remember your promise."

"I do," replied the Marquis, "and I will abide by it. But we trifle. To-morrow I will declare myself, and I shall then know both what to hope and how to act."

Adeline trembled so excessively that she could scarcely support herself; she wished to return to her chamber: yet she was too much interested in the words she had heard not to be anxious to have them more fully explained. There was an interval of silence, after which they conversed in a lower tone. Adeline remembered the hints of Theodore, and determined, if possible, to be relieved from the terrible suspense she now suffered. She stole softly down a few steps that she might catch the accents of the speakers; but they were so low, that she could only now and then distinguish a few words.

"Her father, say you?" said the Marquis. "Yes, my lord, her father. I am well informed of what I say."

Adeline shuddered at the mention of her father; a new terror seized her, and with increasing eagerness she endeavoured to distinguish their words, but for some time found this to be impossible.

"Here is no time to be lost," said the Marquis; "to-morrow then."

She heard La Motte rise, and believing it was to leave the room, she hurried up the steps, and having reached her chamber, sank almost lifeless in a chair.

It was her father only of whom she thought. She doubted not that he had pursued and discovered her retreat, and though this conduct appeared very inconsistent with his former behaviour in abandoning her to strangers, her fears suggested it would terminate in some new cruelty. She did not hesitate to pronounce this the danger of which Theodore had warned her; but it was impossible to surmise how he had gained his knowledge of it, or how he had become sufficiently acquainted with her story, except through La Motte, her apparent friend and protector, whom she was thus, though unwillingly, led to suspect of treachery. Why, indeed, should La Motte conceal from her only his knowledge of her father's intention, unless he designed to deliver her into his hands? Yet it was long ere she could bring herself to believe this conclusion possible. To discover depravity in those whom we have loved, is one of the most exquisite tortures to a virtuous mind, and the conviction is often rejected before it is finally admitted.

The words of Theodore, which told her he was fearful she was deceived, confirmed this painful apprehension of La Motte, with another more distressing, that Madame La Motte was also united against her. This thought for a moment subdued terror and left her only grief; she wept bitterly. "Is this human nature?" cried she. "Am I doomed to find everybody deceitful?" An unexpected discovery of vice in those whom we have admired, inclines us to extend our censure of the individual to the species: we henceforth contemn appearances, and too hastily conclude that no person is to be trusted.

Adeline determined to throw herself at the feet of La Motte on the following morning, and implore his pity and protection. Her mind was now too much agitated by her own interests to permit her to examine the manuscript, and she sat musing in her chair, till she heard the steps of Madame La Motte when she retired to bed. La Motte soon after came up to his chamber, and Adeline—the mild, persecuted Adeline, who had now passed two days of torturing anxiety, and one night of terrific visions—endeavoured to compose her mind to sleep. In the present state of her spirits she quickly caught alarm, and she had scarcely fallen into a slumber, when she was roused by a loud and uncommon noise. She listened, and thought the sound came from the apartments below, but in a few minutes there was a hasty knocking at the door of La Motte's chamber.

La Motte having just fallen asleep was not easily to be roused; but the knocking increased with such violence, that Adeline, extremely terrified, arose and went to the door that opened from her chamber into his, with a design to call him. She was stopped by the voice of the Marquis, which she now clearly distinguished at the outer door. He called not La Motte to arise immediately, and Madame La Motte endeavoured at the same time to rouse her husband, who at length awoke in much alarm, and soon after joining the Marquis, they went downstairs together. Adeline now dressed herself, as well as her trembling hands would permit, and went into the adjoining chamber, where she found Madame La Motte extremely surprised and terrified.

The Marquis in the meantime told La Motte, with great agitation, that he recollected having appointed some persons to meet him upon business of importance early in the morning, and it was therefore necessary for him to set off for his château immediately. As he said this, and desired that his servants might be called, La Motte could not help observing the ashy paleness of his countenance, or expressing some apprehension that his lordship was ill. The Marquis assured him he was perfectly well, but desired that he might set out immediately. Peter was now ordered to call the other servants; and the Marquis having refused to take any refreshment, bade La Motte a hasty adieu, and, as soon as his people were ready, left the abbey.

La Motte returned to his chamber, musing on the abrupt departure of his guest, whose emotion appeared much too strong to proceed from the cause assigned. He appeased the anxiety of Madame La Motte, and at the same time excited her surprise by acquainting her with the occasion of the late disturbance. Adeline, who had retired from the chamber on the approach of La Motte, looked out from her window on hearing the tramping of horses. It was the Marquis and his people who just then passed at a little distance. Unable to distinguish who the persons were, she was alarmed by observing such a party about the abbey at that hour, and, calling to inform La Motte of the circumstance, was made acquainted with what had passed. At length she retired to bed, and her slumbers were this night undisturbed by dreams.

When she arose in the morning she observed La Motte walking alone in the avenue below, and she hastened to seize the opportunity which now offered of pleading her cause. She approached him with faltering steps, while the paleness and timidity of her countenance discovered the disorder of her mind. Her first words, without entering upon any explanation, implored his compassion. La Motte stopped, and looking earnestly in her face, inquired whether any part of his conduct towards her merited the suspicion which her request implied. Adeline for a moment blushed that she had doubted his integrity, but the words she had overheard returned to her memory.

"Your behaviour, sir," said she, "I acknowledge to have been kind and generous, beyond what I had a right to expect, but——" and she paused. She knew not how to mention what she blushed to believe. La Motte continued to gaze on her in silent expectation, and at length desired her to proceed and explain her meaning. She entreated that he would protect her from her father. La Motte looked surprised and confused.

"Your father!" said he.

"Yes, sir," replied Adeline. "I am not ignorant that he has discovered my retreat. I have everything to dread from a parent who has treated me with such cruelty as you were witness of; and I again implore that you will save me from his hands."

La Motte stood fixed in thought, and Adeline continued her endeavours to interest his pity. "What reason have you to suppose, or rather, how have you learned that your father pursues you?"

The question confused Adeline, who blushed to acknowledge how she had overheard his discourse, and disdained to invent or utter a falsity; at length she confessed the truth. The countenance of La Motte instantly changed to a savage fierceness, and sharply rebuking her for conduct, to which she had been rather tempted by chance than prompted by design, he inquired what she had overheard that could so much alarm her. She faithfully repeated the substance of the incoherent sentences that had met her ear. While she spoke he regarded her with a fixed attention.

"And was this all you heard? Is it from these few words that you draw such a positive conclusion? Examine them, and you will find they do not justify it."

She now perceived what the fervour of her fears had not permitted her to observe before, that the words, unconnectedly as she heard them, imported little, and that her imagination had filled up the void in the sentences, so as to suggest the evil apprehended. Notwithstanding this, her fears were little abated.

"Your apprehensions are doubtless now removed," resumed La Motte; "but to give you a proof of the sincerity which you have ventured to question, I will tell you they were just. You seem alarmed, and with reason. Your father has discovered your residence, and has already demanded you. It is true that from a motive of compassion I have refused to resign you, but I have neither authority to withhold or means to defend you. When he comes to enforce his demand, you will perceive this. Prepare yourself, therefore, for the evil which you see is inevitable."

Adeline for some time could speak only by her tears. At length, with a fortitude which despair had roused, she said: "I resign myself to the will of heaven!" La Motte gazed on her in silence, and a strong emotion appeared on his countenance. He forbore, however, to renew the discourse, and withdrew to the abbey, leaving Adeline in the avenue absorbed in grief.

A summons to breakfast hastened her to the parlour, where she passed the morning in conversation with Madame La Motte, to whom she told all her apprehensions and expressed all her sorrow. Pity and superficial consolation were all that Madame La Motte could offer, though apparently much affected by Adeline's discourse. Thus the hours passed heavily away, while the anxiety of

" If, for instance, the Marquis should hereafter avow a serious passion for you, and offer you his hand, would no petty resentment, no lurking prepossession for some more happy lover, prompt you to refuse it ? "

Adeline blushed, and fixed her eyes on the ground. " You have indeed, sir, named the only means I should reject of evincing my sincerity. The Marquis I can never love, nor, to speak sincerely, ever esteem. I confess the peace of one's whole life is too much to sacrifice, even to gratitude."

La Motte looked displeased. " 'Tis as I thought," he said, " these delicate sentiments make a fine appearance in speech, and render the person who utters them infinitely amiable ; but bring them to the test of action, and they dissolve into air, leaving only the wreck of vanity behind."

This unjust sarcasm brought tears to her eyes. " Since your safety, sir, depends upon my conduct," said she, " resign me to my father. I am willing to return to him, since my stay here must not involve you in new misfortunes. Let me not prove myself unworthy of the protection I have hitherto experienced, by preferring my own welfare to yours. When I am gone you will have no reason to apprehend the Marquis's displeasure, which you may probably incur if I stay here ; for I feel it impossible that I could ever consent to receive his addresses, however honourable were his views."

La Motte seemed hurt and alarmed. " This must not be," said he ; " let us not harass ourselves by stating *possible* evils, and then, to avoid them, fly to those which are *certain*. No, Adeline, though you are ready to sacrifice yourself to my safety, I will not suffer you to do so. I will not yield you to your father but upon compulsion. Be satisfied therefore upon this point. The only return I ask is a civil deportment towards the Marquis."

" I will endeavour to obey you, sir," said Adeline.

Madame La Motte now entered the room, and this conversation ceased. Adeline passed that evening in melancholy thoughts, and retired as soon as possible to her chamber, eager to seek in sleep a refuge for sorrow.

CHAPTER IX.

Full many a melancholy night
  He watched the slow return of light,
And sought the powers of sleep ;
  To spread a momentary gloom
  O'er his sad couch, and in the balm
Of bland oblivion's dews his burning eyes to steep.
                                        WARTON.

THE MS. found by Adeline the preceding night, had several times occurred to her recollection in the course of the day, but she had then been either too much interested by the events of the moment, or too apprehensive of interruption, to attempt a perusal of it. She now took it from the drawer in which it had been deposited, and intending only to look cursorily over the few first pages, sat down with it by her bedside.

She opened it with an eagerness of inquiry which the discoloured and almost obliterated ink but slowly gratified. The first words on the page were entirely lost, but those that appeared to commence the narrative were as follow :

" Oh ! ye, whoever ye are, whom chance or misfortune may hereafter conduct to this spot—to ye I speak—to ye reveal the story of my wrongs, and ask you to avenge them. Vain hope ! yet it imparts some comfort to believe it possible that what I now write may one day meet the eye of a fellow-creature ; that the words which tell my sufferings, may one day draw pity from the feeling heart.

" Yet stay your tears—your pity now is useless ; long since have the pangs of misery ceased ; the voice of complaining is passed away. It is weakness to wish for compassion which cannot be excited till I shall sink in the repose of death, and taste, I hope, the happiness of eternity.

" Know then, that on the night of the 12th of October, in the year 1642, I was arrested on the road to Caux, and on the very spot where a column is erected to the memory of the immortal Henry, by four ruffians, who, after disabling my servant, bore me through wilds and woods to this abbey. Their demeanour was not that of common banditti, and I soon perceived they were employed by a superior power to perpetrate some dreadful purpose. Entreaties and bribes were vainly offered them to discover their employer and abandon their design : they would not reveal even the least circumstance of their intentions.

" But when, after a long journey they arrived at this edifice, their base employer was at once revealed, and his horrid scheme but too well understood. What a moment was that ! All the thunders of heaven seemed launched at this defenceless head ! Oh ! fortitude ! nerve my heart to——"

Adeline's light was now expiring in the socket, and the paleness of the ink, so feebly shone upon, baffled her effort to discriminate the letters ; it was impossible to procure a light from below without discovering that she was yet up, a circumstance which would excite surprise, and lead to explanations such as she did not wish to enter upon. Thus compelled to suspend the inquiry, which so many attendant circumstances had rendered awfully interesting, she retired to her humble bed.

What she had read of the MS. awakened a dreadful interest in the fate of the writer, and called up terrific images to her mind. "In these apartments!" said she, and she shuddered and closed her eyes. At length she heard Madame La Motte enter her chamber, and the phantoms of fear beginning to dissipate, left her to repose.

In the morning she was awakened by Madame La Motte, and found, to her disappointment, that she had slept so much beyond her usual time, as to be unable to renew the perusal of the MS. La Motte appeared uncommonly gloomy, and Madame wore an air of melancholy, which Adeline attributed to the concern she felt for her. Breakfast was scarcely over when the sound of horses' feet announced the arrival of a stranger; and Adeline, from the oriel recess of the hall, saw the Marquis alight. She retreated with precipitation, and forgetting the request of La Motte, was hastening to her chamber; but the Marquis was already in the hall, and seeing her leaving it, turned to La Motte with a look of inquiry. La Motte called her back, and by a frown too intelligent reminded her of her promise. She summoned all her spirits to her aid, but advanced, notwithstanding, in visible emotion, while the Marquis addressed her as usual, the same easy gaiety playing upon his countenance and directing his manner.

Adeline was surprised and shocked at this careless confidence, which, however, by awakening her pride, communicated to her an air of dignity that abashed him. He spoke with hesitation, and frequently appeared abstracted from the subject of discourse. At length arising, he begged Adeline would favour him with a few moments' conversation. Monsieur and Madame La Motte were now leaving the room, when Adeline, turning to the Marquis, told him, "she would not hear any conversation except in the presence of her friends." But she said this in vain, for they were gone; and La Motte, as he withdrew, expressed by his looks, how much an attempt to follow would displease him.

She sat for some time in silence and trembling expectation.

"I am sensible," said the Marquis, at length, "that the conduct to which the ardour of my passion lately betrayed me, has injured me in your opinion, and that you will not easily restore me to your esteem; but, I trust, the offer which I now make you, both of my *title* and fortune, will sufficiently prove the sincerity of my attachment, and atone for the transgression which love only occasioned."

After this specimen of commonplace verbosity, which the Marquis seemed to consider as a prelude to triumph, he attempted to impress a kiss upon the hand of Adeline, who, withdrawing it hastily, said:

"You are already, my lord, acquainted with my sentiments upon this subject, and it is almost unnecessary for me now to repeat, that I cannot accept the honour you offer me."

"Explain yourself, lovely Adeline! I am ignorant that till now I ever made you this offer."

"Most true, sir," said Adeline, "and you do well to remind me of this, since, after having heard your former proposal, I can listen for a moment to any other." She rose to quit the room.

"Stay, madam," said the Marquis, with a look in which offended pride struggled to conceal itself; "do not suffer an extravagant resentment to operate against your true interests; recollect the dangers that surround you, and consider the value of an offer, which may afford you at least an honourable asylum."

"My misfortunes, my lord, whatever they are, I have never obtruded upon you; you will therefore excuse my observing that your present mention of them conveys a much greater appearance of insult than compassion."

The Marquis, though with evident confusion, was going to reply; but Adeline would not be detained, and retired to her chamber. Destitute as she was, her heart revolted from the proposal of the Marquis, and she determined never to accept it. To her dislike of his general disposition, and the aversion excited by his late offer, were added indeed the influence of a prior attachment, and of a remembrance which she found it impossible to erase from her heart.

The Marquis stayed to dine, and in consideration of La Motte, Adeline appeared at table; where the former gazed upon her with such frequent and silent earnestness, that her distress became insupportable, and when the cloth was drawn, she instantly retired. Madame La Motte soon followed, and it was not till evening that she had an opportunity of returning to the MS. When Monsieur and Madame La Motte were in their chamber, and all was still, she drew forth the narrative, and trimming her lamp, sat down to read as follows:

"The ruffians unbound me from my horse, and led me through the hall up the spiral staircase of the abbey: resistance was useless, but I looked around in the hope of seeing some person less obdurate than the men who brought me hither; some one who might be sensible to pity, or capable at least of civil treatment. I looked in vain; no person appeared: and this circumstance confirmed my worst apprehensions. The secrecy of the beginning foretold a horrible conclusion. Having passed some chambers, they stopped in one hung with old tapestry. I inquired why we did not go on, and was told I should soon know.

"At that moment I expected to see the

instrument of death uplifted, and I silently recommended myself to God. But death was not then designed for me; they raised the arras, and discovered a door, which they then opened. Seizing my arms, they led me through a suite of dismal chambers beyond. Having reached the farthest of these, they again stopped; the horrid gloom of the place seemed congenial to murder, and inspired deadly thoughts. Again I looked round for the instrument of destruction, and again I was respited. I supplicated to know what was designed me; it was now unnecessary to ask who was the author of the design. They were silent to the question, but at length told me this chamber was my prison. Having said this, and set down a jug of water, they left the room, and I heard the door barred upon me.

"Oh sound of despair! Oh moment of unutterable anguish! The pang of death itself is surely not superior to that I then suffered. Shut out from day, from friends, from life—for such I must foretell it—in the prime of my years, in the height of my transgressions, and left to imagine horrors more terrible than any, perhaps, which certainty could give—I sink beneath the——"

Here several pages of the manuscript were decayed with damp, and totally illegible. With much difficulty Adeline made out the following lines:

"Three days have now passed in solitude and silence; the horrors of death are ever before my eyes; let me endeavour to prepare for the dreadful change! When I awake in the morning I think I shall not live to see another night; and when night returns, that I must never unclose my eyes on the morning. Why am I brought hither—why confined thus rigorously—but for death? Yet what action of my life has deserved this at the hand of a fellow-creature! Of——

*   *   *   *   *

"Oh my children! Oh friends far distant! I shall never see you more—never more perceive the parting look of kindness—never bestow·a parting blessing! Ye know not my wretched state—alas! you cannot know it by human means. Ye believe me happy, or ye would fly to my relief. I know that what I now write cannot avail me, yet there is comfort in pouring forth my griefs, and I bless that man, less savage than his fellows, who has supplied me these means of recording them. Alas! he knows full well, that from this indulgence he has nothing to fear. My pen can call no friends to succour me, nor reveal my danger ere it is too late. Oh! ye who may hereafter read what I now write, give a tear to my sufferings. I have wept often for the distresses of my fellow-creatures!"

Adeline paused. Here the wretched writer appealed directly to her heart; he spoke in the energy of truth, and, by a strong illusion of fancy, it seemed as if his past sufferings were at this moment present. She was for some time unable to proceed, and sat in musing sorrow.

"In these very apartments," said she, "this poor sufferer was confined: here he——"

Adeline started, and thought she heard a sound, but the stillness of night was undisturbed.

"In these very chambers," said she, "these lines were written—these lines, from which he then derived a comfort in believing they would hereafter be read by some pitying eye. This time is now come. Your miseries, oh injured being! are lamented, where they were endured. Here, where you suffered, I weep for your sufferings!"

Her imagination was now strongly impressed, and, to her distempered senses the suggestions of a bewildered mind appeared with the force of reality. Again she started and listened, and thought she heard "Here," distinctly repeated by a whisper immediately behind her. The terror of the thought, however, was but momentary, she knew it could not be; convinced that her fancy had deceived her, she took up the MS. and again began to read:

"For what am I reserved; why this delay? If I am to die, why not quickly? Three weeks have I now passed within these walls, during which time no look of pity has softened my afflictions, no voice save my own has met my ear. The countenances of the ruffians who attend me are stern and inflexible, and their silence is obstinate. This stillness is dreadful! Oh, ye who have known what it is to live in the depths of solitude, who have passed your dreary days without one sound to cheer you, ye, and ye only, can tell what I feel now, and ye may know how much I would endure to hear the accents of a human voice!

"Oh dire extremity! Oh state of living death! What dreadful stillness! All around me is dead, and do I really exist, or am I but a statue? Is this a vision? Are these things real? Alas, I am bewildered!—this death-like and perpetual silence—this dismal chamber—the dread of further sufferings have disturbed my fancy. Oh for some friendly breast to lay my weary head on, some cordial accents to revive my soul!

*   *   *   *   *

I write by stealth. He who furnished me with the means I fear has suffered for some symptoms of pity he may have discovered for me. I have not seen him for several days, perhaps he is inclined to help me, and for that reason is forbid to come. Oh, that hope!

but how vain! Never more must I quit these walls while life remains. Another day is gone and yet I live; at this time to-morrow night my sufferings may be sealed in death. I will continue my journal nightly till the hand that writes shall be stopped by death—when the journal ceases the reader will know I am no more. Perhaps these are the last lines I shall ever write."

* * * * *

Adeline paused, while her tears fell fast. "Unhappy man!" she exclaimed, "and was there no pitying soul to save thee? Great God! thy ways are wonderful!"

While she sat musing, her fancy, which now wandered in the regions of terror, gradually subdued reason. There was a glass before her upon the table, and she feared to raise her looks towards it, lest some other face than her own should meet her eyes. Other dreadful ideas and strange images of fantastic thought now crossed her mind.

A hollow sigh seemed to pass near her.

"Holy Virgin, protect me!" cried she, and threw a fearful glance round the room; "this is surely something more than fancy."

Her fears so far overcame her that she was several times upon the point of calling up part of the family, but unwillingness to disturb them and a dread of ridicule withheld her. She was also afraid to move and almost to breathe. As she listened to the wind that murmured at the casements of her lonely chamber, she again thought she heard a sigh. Her imagination refused any longer the control of reason, and, turning her eyes, a figure, whose exact form she could not distinguish, appeared to pass along an obscure part of the chamber; a dreadful chillness came over her, and she sat fixed in her chair. At length a deep sigh somewhat relieved her oppressed spirits, and her senses seemed to return.

All remaining quiet, after some time she began to question whether her fancy had not deceived her, and she so far conquered her terror as to desist from calling Madame La Motte; her mind was, however, so much disturbed, that she did not venture to trust herself that night again with the MS., but, having spent some time in prayer, and in endeavouring to compose her spirits, she retired to bed.

When she awoke in the morning the sunbeams played upon the casements, and dispelled the illusions of darkness; her mind, soothed and invigorated by sleep, rejected the mystic and turbulent promptings of imagination. She arose refreshed and thankful, but, upon going down to breakfast, this transient gleam of peace fled upon the appearance of the Marquis, whose frequent visits at the abbey, after what had passed, not only displeased but alarmed her. She saw that he

was determined to persevere in addressing her, and the boldness and insensibility of this conduct, while it excited her indignation, increased her disgust. In pity to La Motte she endeavoured to conceal these emotions, though she now thought that he required too much from her complaisance, and began seriously to consider how she might avoid the necessity of continuing it. The Marquis behaved to her with the most respectful attention, but Adeline was silent and reserved, and seized the first opportunity to withdraw.

As she passed up the spiral staircase Peter entered the hall below, and seeing Adeline, he stopped and looked earnestly at her; she did not observe him, but he called her softly, and she then saw him make a signal as if he had something to communicate. In the next instant La Motte opened the door of the vaulted room, and Peter hastily disappeared. She proceeded to her chamber, ruminating on this signal, and the cautious manner in which Peter had given it.

But her thoughts soon returned to their wonted subjects. Three days were now passed, and she heard no intelligence of her father; she began to hope that he had relented from the violent measures hinted at by La Motte, and that he meant to pursue a milder plan; but when she considered his character, this appeared improbable, and she relapsed into her former fears. Her residence at the abbey was now become painful from the perseverance of the Marquis and the conduct which La Motte obliged her to adopt; yet she could not think, without dread, of quitting it to return to her father.

The image of Theodore often intruded upon her busy thoughts, and brought with it a pang, which his strange departure occasioned. She had a confused notion that his fate was somehow connected with her own, and her struggles to prevent the remembrance of him served only to show how much her heart was his.

To divert her thoughts from these subjects, and gratify the curiosity so strongly excited on the preceding night, she now took up the MS., but was hindered from opening it by the entrance of Madame La Motte, who came to tell her the Marquis was gone. They passed their morning together in work and general conversation, La Motte not appearing till dinner, when he said little, and Adeline less. She asked him, however, if he had heard from her father.

"I have not heard from him," said La Motte; "but there is good reason, as I am informed by the Marquis, to believe he is not far off."

Adeline was shocked, yet she was able to reply, with becoming firmness:

"I have already, sir, involved you too much in my distress, and now see that resistance will destroy you without serving me; I am, therefore, contented to return to my father, and thus spare you further calamity."

"This is a rash determination," replied La Motte, "and if you pursue it I fear you will severely repent. I speak to you as a friend, Adeline, and desire you will endeavour to listen to me without prejudice. The Marquis, I find, has offered you his hand. I know not which circumstance most excites my surprise—that a man of his rank and consequence should solicit a marriage with a person without fortune or ostensible connections, or that a person so circumstanced should even for a moment reject the advantages thus offered her. You weep, Adeline; let me hope that you are convinced of the absurdity of this conduct, and will no longer trifle with your good fortune. The kindness I have shown you must convince you of my regard, and that I have no motive for offering you this advice but your advantage. It is necessary, however, to say that, should your father not insist upon your removal, I know not how long my circumstances may enable me to afford even the humble pittance you receive here. Still you are silent."

The anguish which this speech excited suppressed her utterance, and she continued to weep. At length she said:

"Suffer me, sir, to go back to my father; I should, indeed, make an ill return for the kindness you mention could I wish to stay after what you now tell me, and to accept the Marquis I feel to be impossible." The remembrance of Theodore arose to her mind, and she wept aloud.

La Motte sat for some time musing. "Strange infatuation!" said he. "Is it possible that you can persist in this heroism of romance, and prefer a father so inhuman as yours to the Marquis de Montalt? a destiny so full of danger to a life of splendour and delight?"

"Pardon me," said Adeline, "a marriage with the Marquis would be splendid, but never happy. His character excites my aversion, and I entreat, sir, that he may now no more be mentioned."

CHAPTER X.

Nor are those empty-hearted, whose low sound
Reverbs no hollowness.   SHAKSPEARE.

THE conversation related in the last chapter was interrupted by the entrance of Peter, who, as he left the room, looked significantly at Adeline, and almost beckoned. She was anxious to know what he meant, and soon after went into the hall, where she found him loitering. The moment he saw her he made a sign of silence, and beckoned her into the recess.

"Well, Peter, what is it you would say?" said Adeline.

"Hush, ma'amselle; for heaven's sake speak lower : if we should be overheard, we are all blown up."

Adeline begged him to explain what he meant.

"Yes, ma'amselle, this is what I have wanted all day long. I have watched and watched for an opportunity, and looked and looked, till I was afraid my master himself would see me; but all would not do; you would not understand."

Adeline entreated he would be quick.

"Yes, ma'am, but I am so afraid we shall be seen; but I would do much to serve such a good young lady, for I could not bear to think of what threatened you without telling you of it."

"For God's sake," said Adeline, "speak quickly, or we shall be interrupted."

"Well, then; but you must first promise by the Holy Virgin never to say it was I that told you. My master would—"

"I do, I do!" said Adeline.

"Well, then—on Monday evening as I—hark! did not I hear a step? Do, ma'amselle, just step this way to the cloisters. I would not for the world we should be seen. I'll go out at the hall door, and you can go through the passage. I would not for the world we should be seen."

Adeline was much alarmed by Peter's words, and hurried to the cloisters. He quickly appeared, and looking cautiously around resumed his discourse.

"As I was saying, ma'amselle, Monday night, when the Marquis slept here, you know he sat up very late, and I can guess, perhaps, the reason of that. Strange things came out, but it is not my business to tell all I think."

"Pray do speak to the purpose," said Adeline impatiently; "what is this danger which you say threatens me? Be quick, or we shall be observed."

"Danger enough, ma'amselle," replied Peter, "if you knew all; and when you do, what will it signify, for you can't help yourself. But that's neither here nor there; I was resolved to tell you, though I may repent it."

"Or rather you are resolved not to tell me," said Adeline, "for you have made no progress towards an explanation yet! But what do you mean? You were speaking of the Marquis."

"Hush, ma'am, not so loud. The Marquis, as I said, sat up very late, and my master sat up with him. One of his men went to bed in the oak room, and the other stayed to undress his lord. So as we were sitting together—Lord have mercy! it made my hair stand on end! I tremble yet. So as we were sitting together—but as sure as I live yonder is my master : I caught a glimpse of him between the trees; if he sees me it is all over with us. I'll tell you another time,"

So saying he hurried into the abbey, leaving Adeline in a state of alarm, curiosity, and vexation. She walked out into the forest, ruminating upon Peter's words, and endeavouring to guess to what they alluded ; there Madame La Motte joined her, and they conversed on various topics till they reached the abbey.

Adeline watched in vain through that day for an opportunity of speaking with Peter. While he waited at supper she occasionally observed his countenance with great anxiety, hoping that it might afford her some degree of intelligence on the subject of her fears. When she retired Madame La Motte accompanied her to her chamber, and continued to converse with her for a considerable time, so that she had no means of obtaining an interview with Peter.

Madame La Motte appeared to labour under some great affliction ; and when Adeline, noticing this, entreated to know the cause of her dejection, tears started into her eyes, and she abruptly left the room.

This behaviour of Madame La Motte concurred, with Peter's discourse, to alarm Adeline, who sat pensively upon her bed, given up to reflection, till she was roused by the sound of a clock which stood in the room below, and which now struck twelve. She was preparing for rest, when she recollected the MS. and was unable to conclude the night without reading it. The first words she could distinguish were the following :

"Again I return to this poor consolation—again I have been permitted to see another day. It is now midnight ! My solitary lamp burns beside me ; the time is awful, but to me the silence of noon is as the silence of midnight : a deeper gloom is all in which they differ. The still, unvarying hours are numbered only by my sufferings ! Great God ! when shall I be released !

* * * * *

" But whence this strange confinement ! I have never injured him. If death is designed me, why this delay ; and for what but death am I brought hither? This abbey—alas ! "

Here the MS. was again illegible, and for several pages Adeline could only make out disjointed sentences.

" Oh bitter draught ! when, when shall I have rest? Oh my friends ! will none of ye fly to aid me ; will none of ye avenge my sufferings ? Ah ! when it is too late—when I am gone for ever, ye will endeavour to avenge them.

* * * * *

" Once more is night returned to me. Another day has passed in solitude and misery. I have climbed to the casement, thinking the view of nature would refresh my soul, and somewhat enable me to support these afflictions. Alas ! even this small comfort is denied me, the windows open towards inner parts of this abbey, and admit only a portion of that day which I must never more fully behold ! Last night ! last night ! Oh scene of horror ! "

* * * * *

Adeline shuddered. She feared to read the coming sentence, yet curiosity prompted her to proceed. Still she paused ; an unaccountable dread came over her.

" Some horrid deed has been done here," said she, " the reports of the peasants are true. Murder has been committed."

The idea thrilled her with horror. She recollected the dagger which had impeded her steps in the secret chamber, and this circumstance served to confirm her most terrible conjectures. She wished to examine it, but it lay in one of these chambers, and she feared to go in quest of it.

" Wretched, wretched victim ! " she exclaimed, " could no friend rescue thee from destruction ! Oh that I had been near ! yet what could I have done to save thee? Alas ! nothing. I forget that even now, perhaps, I am, like thee, abandoned to dangers, from which I have no friend to succour me. Too surely I guess the author of my miseries ! "

She stopped, for she thought she heard a sigh, such as on the preceding night had passed along the chamber. Her blood was chilled, and she sat motionless. The lonely situation of her room—remote from the rest of the family (she was now in her own apartment, from which Madame La Motte had removed), who were almost beyond call, struck so forcibly upon her imagination, that she with difficulty preserved herself from fainting. She sat for a considerable time, but all was still. When she was somewhat recovered her first design was to alarm the family, but further reflection withheld her.

She endeavoured to compose her spirits, and addressed a short prayer to that Being who had hitherto protected her in every danger. While she was thus employed her mind gradually became elevated and reassured, a sublime complacency filled her heart, and she sat down once more to pursue the narrative.

Several lines that immediately followed were obliterated.

* * * * *

"He had told me I should not be permitted to live long, not more than three days, and bade me choose whether I would die by poison or the sword. Oh the agonies of that moment ! Great God, thou seest my sufferings ! I often viewed with a momentary hope of escaping the high-grated windows of my prison. All things within the compass of possibility I was resolved to try, and with an eager desperation I climbed towards the casements, but my foot slipped, and, falling back to the floor, I was stunned by the blow. On recovering, the first sounds I heard were the steps of a person entering my prison. A recollection of the past returned, and deplorable was my condition. I shuddered at what was to come. The same man approached. He looked at me first with pity, but his countenance soon recovered its natural ferocity. Yet he did not then come to execute the purpose of his employer. I am reserved to another day. Great God, thy will be done!"

Adeline could not go on. All the circumstances that seemed to corroborate the fate of this unhappy man crowded upon her mind—the reports concerning the abbey, the dreams which had forerun her discovery of the private apartments, the singular manner in which she had found the MS., and the apparition, which she now believed she had really seen. She blamed herself for having not yet mentioned the discovery of the manuscript and chambers to La Motte, and resolved to delay the disclosure no longer than the following morning. The immediate cares that had occupied her mind, and a fear of losing the manuscript before she had read it, had hitherto kept her silent.

Such a combination of circumstances she believed could only be produced by some supernatural power, operating for the retribution of the guilty. This reflection filled her mind with a degree of awe, which the loneliness of the large old chamber in which she sat, and the hour of the night, soon heightened into terror. She had never been superstitious, but circumstances so uncommon had hitherto conspired in this affair, that she could not believe them accidental. Her imagination, wrought upon by these reflections, again became sensible to every impression; she feared to look round, lest she should again see some dreadful phantom, and she almost fancied she heard voices swell in the storm which now shook the fabric.

Still, she tried to command her feelings so as to avoid disturbing the family; but they became so painful, that even the dread of La Motte's ridicule had hardly power to prevent her quitting the chamber. Her mind was now in such a state that she found it impossible to pursue the story in the MS. through; to avoid the tortures of suspense she had attempted it. She laid it down again, and tried to soothe herself to composure.

"What have I to fear?" said she; "I am at least innocent, and I shall not be punished for the crime of another."

A violent gust of wind, that now rushed through the whole suite of apartments, shook the door that led from her late bedchamber to the private rooms so forcibly, that Adeline, unable to remain longer in doubt, ran to see from whence the noise issued. The arras which concealed the door, was violently agitated, and she stood for a moment observing it in indescribable terror, till, believing it was swayed by the wind, she made a sudden effort to overcome her feelings, and stooped to raise it. At that instant she thought she heard a voice. She stopped and listened, but everything was still; yet apprehension so far overcame her, that she had no power either to examine or to leave the chamber.

In a few moments the voice returned: she was now convinced she had not been deceived, for, though low, she heard it distinctly, and was almost sure it repeated her own name. So much was her fancy affected, that she even thought it was the same voice she had heard in her dreams. This conviction entirely subdued the small remains of her courage, and, sinking into a chair, she lost all recollection.

How long she remained in this state she knew not, but when she recovered, she exerted all her strength and reached the winding staircase, where she called aloud. No one heard her, and she hastened, as fast as her feebleness would permit, to the chamber of Madame La Motte. She tapped gently at the door, and was answered by Madame, who was alarmed at being awakened at so unusual an hour, and believed that some danger threatened her husband. When she understood that it was Adeline, and that she was unwell, she quickly came to her relief. The terror that was yet visible in Adeline's countenance excited her inquiries, and the occasion of it was explained to her.

Madame was so much discomposed by the relation that she called La Motte from his bed, who, more angry at being disturbed than interested for the agitation he witnessed, reproved Adeline for suffering her fancies to overcome her reason. She now mentioned the discovery she had made of the inner chambers and the manuscript, circumstances which roused the attention of La Motte so much, that he desired to see the MS. and resolved to go immediately to the apartments described by Adeline.

Madame La Motte endeavoured to dissuade him from his purpose; but La Motte, with whom opposition had always an effect contrary to the one designed, and who wished to throw further ridicule upon the terrors of Adeline, persisted in his intention. He called to Peter to attend with a light, and insisted that Madame La Motte and Adeline should accompany him; Madame desired to be excused, and Adeline at first declared she would not go; but he would be obeyed.

They ascended the tower, and entered the first chamber together, for each of the party was reluctant to be the last; in the second chamber all was quiet and in order. Adeline presented the MS. and pointed to the arras which concealed the door. La Motte lifted the arras and opened the door, but Madame La Motte and Adeline entreated to go no farther. Again he called to them to follow. All was quiet in the first chamber; he expressed his surprise that the rooms should so long have remained undiscovered, and was proceeding to the second, but suddenly stopped.

"We will defer our examination till to-morrow," said he, "the damps of these apartments are unwholesome at any time; but they strike one more sensibly at night. I am chilled. Peter, remember to throw open the windows early in the morning that the air may circulate."

"Lord bless your honour," said Peter, "don't you see I can't reach them? Besides, I don't believe they are made to open; see what strong iron bars there are; the room looks for all the world like a prison. I suppose this is the place the people meant when they said nobody that had been in ever came out."

La Motte, who during this speech had been looking attentively at the high windows, which, if he had seen them at first, he had certainly not observed, now interrupted the eloquence of Peter, and bade him carry the light before them. They all willingly quitted these chambers, and returned to the room below, where a fire was lighted, and the party remained together for some time.

La Motte, for reasons best known to himself, attempted to ridicule the discovery and fears of Adeline, till she, with a seriousness that checked him, entreated he would desist. He was silent, and soon after Adeline, encouraged by the return of daylight, ventured to her chamber, and for some hours experienced the blessings of undisturbed repose.

On the following day, Adeline's first care was to obtain an interview with Peter, whom she had some hopes of seeing as she went downstairs; he, however, did not appear, and she proceeded to the sitting-room, where she found La Motte apparently much disturbed. Adeline asked him if he had looked at the MS.

"I have run my eye over it," said he, "but it is so much obscured by time that it can scarcely be deciphered. It exhibits a strange romantic story; and I do not wonder that after you had suffered its terrors to impress your imagination, you fancied you saw spectres and heard wondrous noises."

Adeline thought La Motte did not choose to be convinced, and she therefore forbore reply. During breakfast, she often looked at Peter, who waited, with anxious inquiry; and, from his countenance, was still more assured that he had something of importance to communicate. In the hope of some conversation with him, she left the room as soon as possible, and repaired to her favourite avenue, where she had not long remained when he appeared.

"God bless you, ma'amselle!" said he, "I am sorry I frightened you so last night."

"Frightened me!" said Adeline, "how were you concerned in that?"

He then informed her, that when he thought Monsieur and Madame La Motte were asleep he had stolen to her chamber-door, with an intention of giving her the sequel of what he had begun in the morning; that he had called several times as loud as he dared, but receiving no answer, he believed she was asleep, or did not choose to speak with him, and he had therefore left the door. This account of the voice she had heard relieved Adeline's spirits; she was even surprised that she did not know it, till remembering the perturbation of her mind for some time preceding, this surprise disappeared.

She entreated Peter to be brief in explaining the danger with which she was threatened.

"If you'll let me go on my own way, ma'am, you'll soon know it; but if you hurry me, and ask me questions here and there, out of their places, I don't know what I am saying."

"Be it so," said Adeline, "only remember that we may be observed."

"Yes, ma'amselle, I am as much afraid of that as you are, for I believe I should be almost as ill off; however, that is neither here nor there; but I'm sure if you stay in this old abbey another night it will be worse for you; for, as I said before, I know all about it."

"What mean you, Peter?"

"Why, about this scheme that's going on."

"What, then, is my father——?"

"Your father!" interrupted Peter. "Lord bless you, that is all fudge to frighten you; your father *nor nobody* else has ever sent after you; I daresay he knows no more of you than the Pope does—not he."

Adeline looked displeased. "You trifle," said she; "if you have anything to tell, say it quickly; I am in haste."

"Bless you, young lady, I meant no harm; I hope you're not angry; but I'm sure you can't deny that your father is cruel. But, as I was saying, the Marquis de Montalt likes you, and he and my master (Peter looked round) have been laying their heads together about you."

Adeline turned pale; she comprehended a part of the truth, and eagerly entreated him to proceed.

"They have been laying their heads together about you. This is what Jacques, the Marquis's man, tells me. Says he, 'Peter, you little know what is going on—I could tell all if I chose it, but it is not for those who are trusted to tell again. I warrant now your master is close enough with you.' Upon which I was piqued, and resolved to make him believe I could be trusted as well as he. 'Perhaps not,' says I; 'perhaps I know as much as you, though I do not choose to brag on't;' and I winked. 'Do you so?' says he; 'then you are closer than I thought for. She is a fine girl,' says he, meaning you, ma'amselle; 'but she is nothing but a poor foundling, after all, so it does not much signify.' I had a mind to know further what he meant, so I did not knock him down. By seeming to know as much as he, I at last made him discover all, and he told me—but you look pale, ma'amselle; are you ill?"

"No," said Adeline, in a tremulous accent, and scarcely able to support herself; "pray proceed."

"And he told me that the Marquis had been courting you a good while, but you would not listen to him, and had even pretended he would marry you, and all would not do. 'As for marriage,' says I, 'I suppose she knows the Marchioness is alive; and I'm sure she is not one for his turn upon other terms.'"

"The Marchioness is really living, then?" said Adeline.

"Oh yes, ma'amselle! we all know that, and I thought you had known it too. 'We shall see that,' replies Jacques; 'at least, I believe that our masters will outwit her.' I stared; I could not help it. 'Aye,' says he, 'you know your master has agreed to give her up to my lord.'"

"Good God! what will become of me?" exclaimed Adeline.

"Aye, ma'amselle, I am sorry for you; but hear me out. When Jacques said this I quite forgot myself. 'I'll never believe it,' said I; 'I'll never believe my master would be guilty of such a base action; he'll not give her up, or I'm no Christian.' 'Oh!' said Jacques; 'for that matter, I thought you'd known all, else I should not have said a word about it. However, you may soon satisfy yourself by going to the parlour-door, as I have done; they're in consultation about it now, I daresay.'"

"You need not repeat any more of this conversation," said Adeline; "but tell me the result of what you heard from the parlour."

"Why, ma'amselle, when he said this, I took him at his word and went to the door, where, sure enough, I heard my master and the Marquis talking about you. They said a great deal which I could make nothing of, but at last I heard the Marquis say: 'You know the terms—on these terms only will I consent to bury the past in ob—ob—oblivion'—that was the word. Monsieur La Motte then told the Marquis, if he would return to the abbey upon such a night—meaning this very night, ma'amselle—everything should be prepared according to his wishes; 'Adeline shall then be yours, my lord,' said he—'you are already acquainted with her chamber.'"

At these words Adeline clasped her hands and raised her eyes to heaven in silent despair.

Peter went on: "When I heard this I could not doubt what Jacques had said. 'Well,' said he, 'what do you think of it now?' 'Why, that my master's a rascal,' says I. 'It's well you don't think mine one too,' says he. 'Why, as for that matter,' says I——'"

Adeline, interrupting him, inquired if he had heard anything further.

"Just then," said Peter, "we heard Madame La Motte come out from another room, and so we made haste back to the kitchen."

"She was not present at this conversation, then?" said Adeline.

"No, ma'amselle, but my master has told her of it, I warrant."

Adeline was almost as much shocked by this apparent perfidy of Madame La Motte as by a knowledge of the destruction that threatened her. After musing a few moments in extreme agitation, "Peter," said she, "you have a good heart, and feel a just indignation at your master's treachery—will you assist me to escape?"

"Ah, ma'amselle!" said he, "how can I assist you? Besides, where can we go? I have no friends about here, no more than yourself."

"Oh!" replied Adeline, in extreme emotion, "we fly from enemies! strangers may prove friends. Assist me but to escape from this forest, and you will claim my eternal gratitude; I have no fears beyond it."

"Why, as for this forest," replied Peter, "I am weary of myself; though, when we first came, I thought it would be fine living here—at least, I thought it was very different from any life I had ever lived before. But these ghosts that haunt the abbey—I am no more a coward than other men, but I don't like them; and then there is so many strange reports abroad, and my master—I thought I could have served him to the end of the world, but now I care not how soon I leave him, for his behaviour to you, ma'amselle."

"You consent, then, to assist me in escaping?" said Adeline with eagerness.

"Why, as to that, ma'amselle, I would willingly if I knew where to go. To be sure I have a sister lives in Savoy, but that is a great way off; and I have saved a little money out of my wages, but that won't carry us such a long journey."

"Regard not that," said Adeline; "if I was once beyond this forest I would then endeavour to take care of myself, and repay you for your kindness."

"Oh! as for that, madam——"

"Well, well, Peter, let us consider how we

may escape. This night, say you, this night —the Marquis is to return?"

"Yes, ma'amselle, to-night about dark. I have just thought of a scheme. My master's horses are grazing in the forest; we may take one of them, and send it back from the first stage; but how shall we avoid being seen? Besides, if we go off in the daylight, he will soon pursue and overtake us; and if we stay till night the Marquis will be come, and then there is no chance. If they miss us both at the same time, too, they'll guess how it is, and set off directly. Could you not contrive to go first, and wait for me till the hurly-burly's over? Then, while they're searching in the place underground for you, I can slip away, and we shall be out of their reach before they think of pursuing us."

Adeline agreed to the truth of all this, and was somewhat surprised at Peter's sagacity. She inquired if he knew of any place in the neighbourhood of the abbey where she could remain concealed till he came with a horse.

"Why, yes, madam, there is a place, now I think of it, where you may be safe enough, for nobody goes near; but they say it's haunted, and perhaps you would not like to go there."

Adeline, remembering the last night, was somewhat startled at this intelligence; but a sense of her present danger pressed again upon her mind, and overcame every other apprehension. "Where is this place?" said she; "if it will conceal me, I shall not hesitate to go."

"It is an old tomb that stands in the thickest part of the forest, about a quarter of a mile off the nearest way, and almost a mile the other. When my master used to hide himself so much in the forest, I have followed him somewhere thereabouts, but I did not find out the tomb till t'other day. However, that's neither here nor there; if you dare venture to it, ma'amselle, I'll show you the nearest way." So saying he pointed to a winding path on the right. Adeline having looked round without perceiving any person near, directed Peter to lead her to the tomb. They pursued the path till, turning into a gloomy, romantic part of the forest, almost impervious to the rays of the sun, they came to the spot whither Louis had formerly traced his father.

The stillness and solemnity of the scene struck awe upon the heart of Adeline, who paused, and surveyed it for some time in silence. At length Peter led her into the interior part of the ruin, to which they descended by several steps. "Some old abbot," said he, "was formerly buried here, as the Marquis's people say; and it's like enough that he belonged to the abbey yonder. But I don't see why he should take it in his head to walk; he was not murdered, surely?"

"I hope not," said Adeline.

"That's more than can be said for all that lies buried at the abbey, though——"

Adeline interrupted him. "Hark! surely I hear a noise," said she. "Heaven protect us from discovery!" They listened, but all was still, and they went on. Peter opened a low door, and they entered upon a dark passage, frequently obstructed by loose fragments of stone, and along which they moved with caution.

"Whither are we going?" said Adeline.

"I scarcely know myself," said Peter, "for I never was so far before; but the place seems quiet enough." Something obstructed his way; it was a door, which yielded to his hand, and discovered a kind of cell, obscurely seen by the twilight admitted through a grate above. A partial gleam shot athwart the place, leaving the greater part of it in shadow.

Adeline sighed as she surveyed it. "This is a frightful spot," said she; "but if it will afford me a shelter it is a palace. Remember, Peter, that my peace and honour depend upon your faithfulness; be both discreet and resolute. In the dusk of the evening I can pass from the abbey with the least danger of being observed, and in this cell I will wait your arrival. As soon as Monsieur and Madame La Motte are engaged in searching the vaults, you will bring here a horse; three knocks upon the tomb shall inform me of your arrival. For Heaven's sake be cautious, and be punctual!"

"I will, ma'amselle, let come what may."

They reascended to the forest, and Adeline, fearful of observation, directed Peter to run first to the abbey, and invent some excuse for his absence if he had been missed. When she was again alone, she yielded to a flood of tears, and indulged the excess of her distress. She saw herself without friends, without relations, forlorn, destitute, and abandoned to the worst of evils. Betrayed by the very persons to whose comfort she had so long administered, whom she had loved as her protectors, and revered as her parents! These reflections touched her heart with the most afflicting sensations, and the sense of her immediate danger was for a while absorbed in the grief occasioned by a discovery of such guilt in others.

At length she roused all her fortitude, and turning towards the abbey, endeavoured to await with patience the hour of evening, and to sustain an appearance of composure in the presence of Monsieur and Madame La Motte. For the present she wished to avoid seeing either of them, doubting her ability to disguise her emotions. Having reached the abbey, she therefore passed on to her chamber. Here she endeavoured to direct her attention to indifferent subjects, but in vain; the danger of her situation, and the severe

E

disappointment she had received in the character of those whom she had so much esteemed, and even loved, pressed hard upon her thoughts. To a generous mind, few circumstances are more afflicting than a discovery of perfidy in those whom we have trusted, even though it may fail of any absolute inconvenience to ourselves. The behaviour of Madame La Motte in thus, by concealment, conspiring to her destruction, particularly shocked her.

"How has my imagination deceived me!" said she, "what a picture did it draw of the goodness of the world! And must I then believe that everybody is cruel and deceitful? No; let me still be deceived, and still suffer, rather than be condemned to a state of such wretched suspicion."

She now endeavoured to extenuate the conduct of Madame La Motte, by attributing it to a fear of her husband.

"She dare not oppose his will," said she, "else she would warn me of my danger and assist me to escape from it. No; I will never believe her capable of conspiring my ruin. Terror alone keeps her silent."

Adeline was somewhat comforted by this thought. The benevolence of her heart taught her, in this instance, to sophisticate. She perceived not that by ascribing the conduct of Madame La Motte to terror she only softened the degree of her guilt, imputing it to a motive less depraved, but not less selfish. She remained in her chamber till summoned to dinner, when, drying her tears, she descended with faltering steps and a palpitating heart to the parlour. When she saw La Motte, in spite of all her efforts, she trembled and grew pale; she could not behold, even with apparent indifference, the man who she knew had destined her to destruction. He observed her emotion, and, inquiring if she was ill, she saw the danger to which her agitation exposed her. Fearful lest La Motte should suspect its true cause, she rallied all her spirits, and, with a look of complacency, answered she was well.

During dinner she preserved a degree of composure that effectually concealed the varied anguish of her heart. When she looked at La Motte, terror and indignation were her predominant feelings, but when she regarded Madame La Motte it was otherwise. Gratitude for her former tenderness had long been confirmed into affection, and her heart now swelled with the bitterness of grief and disappointment. Madame La Motte appeared depressed, and said little. La Motte seemed anxious to prevent thought, by assuming a fictitious and unnatural gaiety; he laughed and talked, and threw off frequent bumpers of wine—it was the mirth of desperation.

Madame became alarmed, and would have restrained him, but he persisted in his libations to Bacchus, till reflection seemed to be almost overcome.

Madame La Motte, fearful that in the carelessness of the present moment he might betray himself, withdrew with Adeline to another room. Adeline recollected the happy hours she once passed with her, when confidence banished reserve, and sympathy and esteem dictated the sentiments of friendship. Now those hours were gone for ever, she could no longer unbosom her griefs to Madame La Motte, no longer esteem her. Yet, notwithstanding all the danger to which she was exposed by the criminal silence of the latter, she could not converse with her consciously for the last time, without feeling a degree of sorrow, which wisdom may call weakness, but to which benevolence will allow a softer name.

Madame La Motte, in her conversation, appeared to labour under an almost equal oppression with Adeline. Her thoughts were abstracted from the subject of discourse, and there were long and frequent intervals of silence. Adeline more than once caught her gazing with a look of tenderness upon her, and saw her eyes fill with tears. By this circumstance she was so much affected, that she several times upon the point of throwing herself at her feet, and imploring her pity and protection. Cooler reflection showed her the extravagance and danger of this conduct. She suppressed her emotions, but they at length compelled her to withdraw from the presence of Madame La Motte.

CHAPTER X.

Thou! to whom the world unknown
With all its shadowy shapes is shown;
Who seest appall'd th' unreal scene,
While fancy lifts the veil between;
Ah, Fear! ah, frantic Fear!
I see, I see thee near!
I know thy hurry'd step, thy haggard eye!
Like thee I start, like thee disorder'd fly!
　　　　　　　　　　　　COLLINS.

ADELINE anxiously watched from her chamber window the sun set behind the distant hills, and the time of her departure draw nigh. It set with uncommon splendour, and threw a fiery gleam athwart the woods, and upon some scattered fragments of the ruins, which she could not gaze upon with indifference.

"Never, probably, again shall I see the sun sink below these hills," said she, "or illumine this scene! Where shall I be when next it sets—where this time to-morrow? sunk, perhaps, in misery!" She wept at the thought. "A few hours," resumed Adeline, "and the Marquis will arrive—a few hours, and this abbey will be a scene of confusion and tumult: every eye will be in search of me, every recess will be explored."

These reflections inspired her with new terror, and increased her impatience to be gone.

Twilight gradually came on, and she now thought it sufficiently dark to venture forth; but, before she went, she kneeled down and addressed herself to Heaven. She implored support and protection, and committed herself to the care of the God of Mercies. Having done this, she quitted her chamber, and passed with cautious steps down the winding staircase. No person appeared, and she proceeded through the door of the tower into the forest. She looked around; the gloom of evening obscured every object.

With a trembling heart she sought the path, pointed out by Peter, which led to the tomb; having found it, she · passed along forlorn and terrified. Often did she start as the breeze shook the light leaves of the trees, or as the bat flitted by, gamboling in the twilight; and often, as she looked back towards the abbey, thought she distinguished, amid the deepening gloom, the figures of men. Having proceeded some way, she suddenly heard the feet of horses, and soon after a sound of voices, among which she distinguished that of the Marquis; they seemed to come from the quarter she was approaching, and evidently advanced. Terror for some minutes arrested her steps; she stood in a state of dreadful hesitation; to proceed was to run into the hands of the Marquis; to return was to fall into the power of La Motte.

After remaining for some time uncertain whither to fly, the sounds suddenly took a different direction, and the party wheeled towards the abbey. Adeline had a short cessation of terror. She now understood that the Marquis had passed this spot only in his way to the abbey, and she hastened to secrete herself in the ruin. At length, after much difficulty, she reached it, the deep shades almost concealing it from her search. She paused at the entrance, awed by the solemnity that reigned within, and the utter darkness of the place; at length she determined to watch without till Peter should arrive. "If any person approaches," said she, "I can hear them before they can see me, and I can then secrete myself in the cell."

She leaned against a fragment of the tomb in trembling expectation, and, as she listened, no sound broke the silence of the hour. The state of her mind can only be imagined, by considering that upon the present time turned the crisis of her fate. "They have now," thought she, "discovered my flight; even now they are seeking me in every part of the abbey. I hear their dreadful voices call me; I see their eager looks." The power of imagination almost overcame her. While she yet looked around, she saw lights moving at a distance; sometimes they glimmered between the trees, and sometimes they totally disappeared.

They seemed to be in a direction with the abbey; and she now remembered, that in the morning she had seen a part of the fabric through an opening in the forest. She had, therefore, no doubt that the lights proceeded from people in search of her; who, she feared, not finding her at the abbey, might direct their steps towards the tomb. Her place of refuge now seemed too near her enemies to be safe, and she would have fled to a more distant part of the forest, but recollected that Peter would not know where to find her.

While these thoughts passed over her mind, she heard distant voices in the wind, and was hastening to conceal herself in the cell, when she observed the lights suddenly disappear. All was soon after hushed in silence and darkness, yet she endeavoured to find the way to the cell. She remembered the situation of the outer door and of the passage, and having passed these, she unclosed the door of the cell. Within, it was utterly dark. She trembled violently, but entered; and, having felt about the walls, at length seated herself on a projection of stone.

She here again addressed herself to Heaven, and endeavoured to reanimate her spirits till Peter should arrive. Above half an hour elapsed in this gloomy recess, and no sound foretold his approach. Her spirits sank, she feared some part of their plan was discovered or interrupted, and that he was detained by La Motte. This conviction operated sometimes so strongly upon her fears as to urge her to quit the cell alone and seek in flight her only chance of escape.

While this design was fluctuating in her mind, she distinguished through the grate above a clattering of hoofs. The noise approached, and at length stopped at the tomb. In the succeeding moment she heard three strokes of a whip; her heart beat, and for some moments her agitation was such that she made no effort to quit the cell. The strokes were repeated; she now roused her spirits, and stepping forward, ascended to the forest. She called "Peter!" for the deep gloom would not permit her to distinguish either man or horse. She was quickly answered, "Hush! ma'amselle, our voices will betray us."

They mounted and rode off as fast as the darkness would permit. Adeline's heart revived at every step they took. She inquired what had passed at the abbey, and how he had contrived to get away.

"Speak softly, ma'amselle; you'll know all by-and-by, but I can't tell you now."

He had scarcely spoke ere they saw lights move along at a distance; and coming now to a more open part of the forest, he set on a full gallop, and continued the pace till the horse could hold it no longer. They looked back, and no lights appearing, Adeline's terror subsided. She inquired again what had passed at the abbey when her flight was discovered.

"You may speak without fear of being heard," said she; "we are gone beyond their reach, I hope."

"Why, ma'amselle," said he, "you had not been gone long before the Marquis arrived, and Monsieur La Motte then found out you had fled. Upon this a great rout there was, and he talked a great deal with the Marquis."

"Speak louder," said Adeline; "I cannot hear you."

"I will, ma'amselle."

"Oh, heavens!" interrupted Adeline, "what voice is this? It is not Peter's. For God's sake tell me who you are, and whither I am going?"

"You'll know that soon enough, young lady," answered the stranger, for it was indeed not Peter; "I am taking you where my master ordered."

Adeline, not doubting it was the Marquis's servant, attempted to leap to the ground, but the man, dismounting, bound her to the horse. One feeble ray of hope at length beamed upon her mind; she endeavoured to soften the man to pity, and pleaded with all the genuine eloquence of distress; but he understood his interest too well to yield, even for a moment, to the compassion which, in spite of himself, her artless supplication inspired. She now resigned herself to despair, and, in passive silence, submitted to her fate. They continued thus to travel till a storm of rain, accompanied by thunder and lightning, drove them to the covert of a thick grove. The man believed this a safe situation, and Adeline was too careless of life to attempt convincing him of his error. The storm was violent and long; but as soon as it abated they set off on a full gallop; and having continued to travel for about two hours, came to the borders of the forest, and soon after to a high lonely wall, which Adeline could just distinguish by the moonlight, which now streamed through the parting clouds.

Here they stopped; the man dismounted, and having opened a small door in the wall, he unbound Adeline, who shrieked, though involuntarily and in vain, as he took her from the horse. The door opened upon a narrow passage, dimly lighted by a lamp that hung at the farther end. He led her on till they came to another door, which opened and disclosed a magnificent saloon, splendidly illuminated, and fitted up in the most airy and elegant taste. The walls were painted in fresco, representing scenes from Ovid, and hung above with silk drawn up in festoons, and richly fringed. The sofas were of a silk to suit the hangings. From the centre of the ceiling,

which exhibited a scene from the Armida of Tasso, descended a silver lamp of Etruscan form; it diffused a blaze of light, that, reflected from large pier glasses, completely illuminated the saloon. Busts of Horace, Ovid, Anacreon, Tibullus, and Petronius Arbiter adorned the recesses, and stands of flowers, placed in Etruscan vases, breathed the most delicious perfume. In the middle of the apartment stood a table, spread with a collation of fruits, ices, and liqueurs. No person appeared. The whole seemed the work of enchantment, and rather resembled the palace of a fairy than anything of human conformation.

Adeline was astonished, and inquired where she was; but the man refused to answer her questions, and, having desired her to take some refreshment, left her. She then walked to the windows, from which a gleam of moonlight discovered an extensive garden, where groves, and lawns, and water, glittering in the moonbeam, composed a scenery of varied and romantic beauty. "What can this mean?" said she. "Is this a charm to lure me to destruction?" She endeavoured, with a hope of escaping, to open the windows, but they, as well as the doors, were all fastened.

Perceiving all chance of escape removed, she remained for some time a prey to sorrow and reflection; but was at length drawn from her reverie by the notes of soft music, breathing such dulcet and entrancing sounds as suspended grief, and waked the soul to tenderness and pensive pleasure. Adeline listened in surprise, and insensibly became soothed and interested; a tender melancholy stole upon her heart, and subdued every harsher feeling; but the moment the strain ceased, the enchantment dissolved, and she returned to a sense of her situation.

Again the music sounded:

Music such as charmeth sleep.

And again she gradually yielded to its sweet magic. A female voice, accompanied by a lute, a hautboy, and a few other instruments, now gradually swelled into a tone so exquisite, as raised attention into ecstasy. It sunk by degrees, and touched a few simple notes with pathetic softness, when the measure was suddenly changed, and in a gay and airy melody Adeline distinguished the following words:

SONG.

Life's a varied, bright illusion,
  Joy and sorrow—light and shade;
Turn from sorrow's dark suffusion,
  Catch the pleasures ere they fade.

Fancy paints with hues unreal,
  Smile of bliss, and sorrow's mood;
If they both are but ideal,
  Why reject the seeming good?

Hence! no more! 'tis Wisdom calls ye,
Bids ye court Time's present aid,
The future trust not—hope enthrals ye,
Catch the pleasures ere they fade.

The music ceased, but the sounds still vibrated on her imagination, and she was sunk in the pleasing languor they had inspired, when the door opened, and the Marquis de Montalt appeared. He approached the sofa where Adeline sat, and addressed her, but she heard not his voice—she had fainted. He endeavoured to recover her, and at length succeeded; but when she unclosed her eyes, and again beheld him, she relapsed into a state of insensibility, and having in vain tried various methods to restore her, he was obliged to call assistance. Two young women entered, and when she began to revive, he left them to prepare her for his reappearance. When Adeline perceived that the Marquis was gone, and that she was in the care of women, her spirits gradually returned, she looked at her attendants, and was surprised to see so much elegance and beauty.

Some endeavour she made to interest their pity, but they seemed wholly insensible to her distress, and began to talk of the Marquis in terms of the highest admiration. They assured her it would be her own fault if she was not happy, and advised her to appear so in his presence. It was with the utmost difficulty that Adeline forbore to express the disdain which was rising to her lips, and that she listened to their discourse in silence. But she saw the inconvenience and fruitlessness of opposition, and she commanded her feelings.

They were thus proceeding in their praises of the Marquis, when he himself appeared, and, waving his hand, they immediately quitted the apartment. Adeline beheld him with a kind of mute despair, while he approached and took her hand, which she hastily withdrew, and turning to him with a look of unalterable distress, burst into tears. He was for some time silent, and appeared softened by her anguish. But again approaching, and addressing her in a gentle voice, he entreated her pardon for the step which despair, and, as he called it, love had prompted. She was too much absorbed in grief to reply, till he solicited a return of his love, when sorrow yielded to indignation, and she reproached him with his conduct. He pleaded that he had long loved and sought her upon honourable terms, and his offer of those terms he began to repeat; but raising his eyes towards Adeline, he saw in her looks the contempt which he was conscious he deserved.

For a moment he was confused, and seemed to understand both that his plan was discovered and his person despised; but soon resuming his usual command of feature, he again pressed his suit, and solicited her love.

A little reflection showed Adeline the danger of exasperating his pride by an avowal of the contempt which his pretended offer of marriage excited, and she thought it not improper, upon an occasion in which the honour and peace of her life was concerned, to yield somewhat to the policy of dissimulation. She saw that her only chance of escaping his designs depended upon delaying them, and she now wished him to believe her ignorant that the Marchioness was living, and that his offers were delusive.

He observed her pause, and, in the eagerness to turn her hesitation to his advantage, renewed his proposal with increased vehemence.

"To-morrow shall unite us, lovely Adeline —to-morrow you shall consent to become the Marchioness de Montalt. You will then return my love and——"

"You must first deserve my esteem, my lord."

"I will—I do deserve it. Are you not now in my power, and do I not forbear to take advantage of your situation? Do I not make you the most honourable proposals?"

Adeline shuddered.

"If you wish I should esteem you, my lord, endeavour, if possible, to make me forget by what means I came into your power; if your views are, indeed, honourable, prove them so by releasing me from my confinement."

"Can you then wish, lovely Adeline, to fly from him who adores you?" replied the Marquis, with a studied air of tenderness. "Why will you exact so severe a proof of my disinterestedness, a disinterestedness which is not inconsistent with love? No, charming Adeline, let me at least have the pleasure of beholding you till the bonds of the church shall remove every obstacle to my love. To-morrow——"

Adeline saw the danger to which she was now exposed, and interrupted him.

"Deserve my esteem, sir, and then you will obtain it—as a first step towards which, liberate me from a confinement that obliges me to look on you only with terror and aversion. How can I believe your professions of love while you show that you have no interest in my happiness?"

Thus did Adeline, to whom the arts and the practice of dissimulation were hitherto equally unknown, condescend to make use of them in disguising her indignation and contempt. But though these arts were adopted only for the purpose of self-preservation, she used them with reluctance, and almost with abhorrence; for her mind was habitually impregnated with the love of virtue, in thought, word, and action, and, while her end in using them was certainly good, she scarcely believed that end could justify the means.

The Marquis persisted in his sophistry.

"Can you doubt the reality of that love which, to obtain you, has urged me to risk your displeasure? But have I not consulted your happiness even in the very conduct which you condemn? I have removed you from a solitary and desolate ruin to a gay and splendid villa, where every luxury is at your command, and where every person shall be obedient to your wishes."

"My first wish is to go hence," said Adeline; "I entreat, I conjure you, my lord, no longer to detain me. I am a friendless and wretched orphan, exposed to many evils, and, I fear, abandoned to misfortune; I do not wish to be rude, but allow me to say that no misery can exceed that I shall feel in remaining here, or, indeed, in being anywhere pursued by the offers you make me."

Adeline had now forgot her policy; tears prevented her from proceeding, and she turned away her face to hide her emotion.

"By Heaven, Adeline, you do me wrong!" said the Marquis, rising from his seat and seizing her hand; "I love—I adore you, yet you doubt my passion, and are insensible to my vows. Every pleasure possible to be enjoyed within these walls you shall partake, but beyond them you shall not go."

She disengaged her hand, and in silent anguish walked to a distant part of the saloon; deep sighs burst from her heart, and, almost fainting, she leaned on a window-frame for support.

The Marquis followed her. "Why thus obstinately persist in refusing to be happy?" said he; "recollect the proposal I have made you, and accept it while it is yet in your power. To-morrow a priest shall join our hands. Surely, being, as you are, in my power, it must be your interest to consent to this?"

Adeline could answer only by tears; she despaired of softening his heart to pity, and feared to exasperate his pride by disdain. He now led her, and she suffered him, to a seat near the banquet, at which he pressed her to partake of a variety of confectioneries, particularly of some liqueurs, of which he himself drank freely. Adeline accepted only of a peach.

And now the Marquis, who interpreted her silence into a secret compliance with his proposal, resumed all his gaiety and spirit, while the long and ardent regards he bestowed on Adeline overcame her with confusion and indignation. In the midst of the banquet, soft music again sounded the most tender and impassioned airs; but its effect on Adeline. was now lost, her mind being too much embarrassed and distressed by the presence of the Marquis to admit even the soothings of harmony.

A song was now heard, written with that sort of impotent art by which some voluptuous poets believe they can at once conceal and recommend the principles of vice. Adeline received it with contempt and displeasure, and the Marquis, perceiving its effect, presently made a sign for another composition, which, adding the force of poetry to the charms of music, might withdraw her mind from the present scene, and enchant it in sweet delirium.

SONG OF A SPIRIT.

In the sightless air I dwell,
    On the sloping sunbeams play;
Delve the cavern's inmost cell,
    Where never yet did daylight stray.

Dive beneath the green sea waves,
    And gambol in the briny deeps;
Skim every shore that Neptune laves,
    From Lapland's plains to India's steeps.

Oft I mount with rapid force
    Above the wide earth's shadowy zone;
Follow the day-star's flaming course
    Through realms of space to thought unknown,

And listen to celestial sounds
    That swell the air, unheard of men,
As I watch my nightly rounds
    O'er woody steep, and silent glen.

Under the shade of waving trees,
    On the green bank of fountain clear,
At pensive eve I sit at ease,
    While dying music murmurs near.

And oft, on point of airy clift,
    That hangs upon the western main,
I watch the gay tints passing swift,
    And twilight veil the liquid plain.

Then when the breeze has sunk away,
    And ocean scarce is heard to lave,
For me the sea-nymphs softly play
    Their dulcet shells beneath the wave.

Their dulcet shells! I hear them now,
    Slow swells the strain upon mine ear;
Now faintly falls—now warbles low,
    Till rapture melts into a tear.

The ray that silvers o'er the dew,
    And trembles through the leafy shade,
And tints the scene with softer hue,
    Calls me to rove the lonely glade;

Or hie me to some ruin'd tower,
    Faintly shown by moonlight gleam,
Where the lone wanderer owns my power
    In shadows dire that substance seem.

In thrilling sounds that murmur woe,
    And pausing silence makes more dread;
In music breathing from below
    Sad, solemn strains, that wake the dead.

Unseen I move—unknown am fear'd!
    Fancy's wildest dreams I weave;
And oft by bards my voice is heard
    To die along the gales of eve.

When the voice ceased, a mournful strain, played with exquisite expression, sounded from a distant horn; sometimes the notes floated on the air in soft undulations—now they swelled into full and sweeping melody, and now died faintly into silence; when again they rose and trembled in sounds so sweetly tender, as drew tears from Adeline, and exclamations of rapture from the Marquis. He threw his arms around her, and would have pressed her towards him, but she liberated herself from his embrace, and with a look, on which was impressed the firm dignity of virtue, yet touched with sorrow, she awed him to forbearance. Conscious of a superiority, which he was ashamed to acknowledge, and endeavouring to despise the influence which he could not resist, he stood for a moment the slave of virtue, though the votary of vice. Soon, however, he recovered his confidence, and began to plead his love ; when Adeline, no longer animated by the spirit she had lately shown, and sinking beneath the languor and fatigue which the various and violent agitations of her mind produced, entreated he would leave her to repose.

The paleness of her countenance, and the tremulous tone of her voice, were too expressive to be misunderstood ; and the Marquis, bidding her remember *to-morrow*, with some hesitation withdrew. The moment she was alone, she yielded to the bursting anguish of her heart, and was so absorbed in grief, that it was some time before she perceived she was in the presence of the young women who had lately attended her, and had entered the saloon after the Marquis quitted it : they came to conduct her to her apartment. She followed them for some time in silence, till, prompted by desperation, she again endeavoured to awaken their compassion ; but again the praises of the Marquis were repeated, and perceiving that all attempts to interest them in her favour were in vain, she dismissed them. She secured the door through which they had departed, and then, in the languid hope of discovering some means of escape, she surveyed her chamber. The airy elegance with which it was fitted up, and the luxurious accommodations with which it abounded, seemed designed to fascinate the imagination, and to seduce the heart. The hangings were of straw-coloured silk, adorned with a variety of landscapes and historical paintings, the subjects of which partook of the voluptuous character of the owner ; the chimney-piece, of Parian marble, was ornamented with several reposing figures from the antique. The bed was of silk, the colour of the hangings, richly fringed with purple and silver, and the head made in form of a canopy. The steps, which were placed near the bed to assist in ascending it, were supported by Cupids, apparently of solid silver. China vases, filled with perfume, stood in several of the recesses, upon stands of the same structure as the toilet, which was magnificent, and ornamented with a variety of trinkets.

Adeline threw a transient look upon these various objects, and proceeded to examine the windows, which descended to the floor and opened into balconies towards the garden she had seen from the saloon. They were now fastened, and her efforts to move them were ineffectual ; at length she gave up the attempt. A door next attracted her notice, which she found was not fastened ; it opened upon a dressing-closet, to which she descended by a few steps ; two windows appeared, she hastened towards them ; one refused to yield, but her heart beat with sudden joy when the other opened to her touch.

In the transport of the moment she forgot that its distance from the ground might yet deny the escape she meditated. She returned to lock the door of the closet to prevent a surprise, which, however, was unnecessary, that of the bedroom being already secured. She now looked out from the window ; the garden lay before her, and she perceived that the window, which descended to the floor, was so near the ground that she might jump from it with ease. Almost in the moment she perceived this she sprang forward and alighted safely in an extensive garden, resembling more an English pleasure-ground than a series of French parterres.

Thence she had little doubt of escaping, either by some broken fence or low part of the wall ; she tripped lightly along, for hope played round her heart. The clouds of the late storm were now dispersed, and the moonlight, which slept on the lawns and spangled the flowers yet heavy with rain-drops, afforded her a distinct view of the surrounding scenery. She followed the direction of the high wall that adjoined the château, till it was concealed from her sight by a thick wilderness, so entangled with boughs and obscured by darkness that she feared to enter, and turned into a walk on the right ; it conducted her to the margin of a lake overhung with lofty trees.

The moonbeams danced upon the waters that, with gentle undulation, played along the shore, exhibiting a scene of tranquil beauty which would have soothed a heart less agitated than was that of Adeline. She sighed as she tranquilly surveyed it, and passed hastily on in search of the garden wall, from which she had strayed a considerable way. After wandering for some time through alleys and over lawns without meeting with anything like a boundary to the grounds, she again found herself at the lake, and now traversed its borders with the footsteps of despair ; tears rolled down her cheeks. The scene around exhibited only images of peace and delight ; every object seemed to repose ; not a breath waved the foliage, not a sound stole through the air ; it was in her bosom only that tumult and distress prevailed. She still pursued the windings of the shore, till an opening in the woods conducted her up a gentle ascent ; the path now wound along the side of a hill, where the gloom was so deep that it was with some difficulty she found her way ; suddenly, however, the avenue opened to a lofty grove, and she perceived a light issue from a recess at some distance.

She paused, and her first impulse was to retreat ; but listening, and hearing no sound, a faint hope beamed upon her mind that the person to whom the light belonged might be won to favour her escape. She advanced with trembling and cautious steps towards the recess, that she might secretly observe the person before she ventured to enter it. Her emotion increased as she approached, and having reached the bower, she beheld, through an open window, the Marquis reclining on a sofa, near which stood a table covered with fruit and wine. He was alone, and his countenance was flushed with drinking.

While she gazed, fixed to the spot by terror, he looked up towards the casement ; the light gleamed full upon her face, but she stayed not to learn whether he had observed her, for, with the swiftness of sound, she left the place and ran, without knowing whether she was pursued. Having gone a considerable way, fatigue at length compelled her to stop, and she threw herself upon the turf, almost fainting with fear and languor. She knew if the Marquis detected her attempting to escape, he would probably burst the bounds which he had hitherto prescribed to himself, and that she had the most dreadful evils to expect. The palpitations of terror were so strong that she could with difficulty breathe.

She watched and listened in trembling expectation, but no human form met her eye, no sound her ear ; in this state she remained a considerable time. She wept, and the tears she shed relieved her oppressed heart. "Oh my father !" said she, "why did you abandon your child ? If you knew the dangers to which you have exposed her, you would surely pity and relieve her. Alas ! shall I never find a friend ? Am I destined still to trust and be deceived ? Peter, too, could he be treacherous ? " She wept again, and then returned to a sense of her present danger, and to a consideration of the means of escaping it, but no means appeared.

To her imagination the grounds were boundless ; she had wandered from lawn to lawn and from grove to grove without perceiving any termination to the place ; the garden wall she could not find, but she resolved neither to return to the château nor to relinquish her search. As she was rising to depart she perceived a shadow move along the ground at some distance ; she stood still to observe it. It slowly advanced and then disappeared, but presently she saw a person emerge from the gloom and approach the spot where she stood. She had no doubt that the Marquis had observed her, and she ran with all possible speed to the shade of some woods on the left. Footsteps pursued her, and she heard her name repeated, while she in vain endeavoured to quicken her pace.

Suddenly the sound of pursuit turned, and sank away in a different direction. She paused to take breath ; she looked around, and no person appeared. She now proceeded slowly along the avenue, and had almost reached its termination, when she saw the same figure emerge from the woods and dart across the avenue ; it instantly pursued her and approached. A voice called her, but she was gone beyond its reach, for she had sunk senseless upon the ground. It was long before she revived ; when she did, she found herself in the arms of a stranger, and made an effort to disengage herself.

"Fear nothing, lovely Adeline," said he, "fear nothing ; you are in the arms of a friend, who will encounter any hazard for your sake, who will protect you with his life."

He pressed her gently to his heart.

"Have you then forgot me ?" continued he.

She looked earnestly at him, and was now convinced that it was Theodore who spoke. Joy was her first emotion, but, recollecting his former abrupt departure, at a time so critical to her safety, and that he was the friend of the Marquis, a thousand sensations struggled in her breast, and overwhelmed her with mistrust, apprehension, and disappointment.

Theodore raised her from the ground, and while he yet supported her : "Let us immediately fly from this place," said he ; "a carriage waits to receive us ; it shall go wherever you direct, and convey you to your friends."

This last sentence touched her heart.

"Alas, I have no friends ! " said she, "nor do I know whither to go."

Theodore gently pressed her hand between his, and, in a voice of the softest compassion, said :

"My friends, then, shall be yours ; suffer me to lead you to them. But I am in agony while you remain in this place ; let us hasten to quit it."

Adeline was going to reply, when voices were heard among the trees, and Theodore, supporting her with his arm, hurried her along the avenue. They continued their flight till Adeline, panting for breath, could go no farther.

Having paused awhile, and heard no footsteps in pursuit, they renewed their course. Theodore knew that they were now not far from the garden wall, but he was also aware that in the intermediate space several paths wound from remote parts of the grounds into the walk he was to pass, from whence the Marquis's people might issue and intercept him. He, however, concealed his apprehensions from Adeline, and endeavoured to soothe and support her spirits.

At length they reached the wall, and Theodore was leading her towards a low part of it, near which stood the carriage, when again they heard voices in the air. Adeline's spirits and strength were nearly exhausted, but she made a last effort to proceed, and she now saw the ladder at some distance by which Theodore had descended to the garden.

"Exert yourself yet a little longer," said he, "and you will be in safety."

He held the ladder while she ascended: the top of the wall was broad and level, and Adeline, having reached it, remained there till Theodore followed and drew the ladder to the other side.

When they had descended, the carriage appeared in waiting, but without the driver. Theodore feared to call, lest his voice should betray him; he therefore put Adeline into the carriage, and went himself in search of the postillion, whom he found asleep under a tree at some distance. Having awakened him, they returned to the vehicle, which soon drove furiously away. Adeline did not yet dare to believe herself safe, but, after proceeding a considerable time without interruption, joy burst upon her heart, and she thanked her deliverer in terms of the warmest gratitude. The sympathy expressed in the tone of his voice and manner proved that his happiness on this occasion almost equalled her own.

As reflection gradually stole upon her mind, anxiety superseded joy. In the tumult of the late moments she thought only of escape, but the circumstances of her present situation now appeared to her, and she became silent and pensive. She had no friends to whom she could fly, and was going with a young chevalier, almost a stranger to her, she knew not whither. She remembered how often she had been deceived and betrayed where she trusted most, and her spirits sank; she remembered also the former attention which Theodore had shown her, and dreaded lest his conduct might be prompted by a selfish passion. She saw this to be possible, but she disdained to believe it probable, and felt that nothing could give her greater pain than to doubt the integrity of Theodore.

He interrupted her reverie, by recurring to her late situation at the abbey.

"You would be much surprised," said he, "and, I fear, offended, that I did not attend my appointment at the abbey, after the alarming hints I had given you at our last interview. That circumstance has, perhaps, injured me in your esteem, if, indeed, I was ever so happy as to possess it; but my designs were overruled by those of the Marquis de Montalt, and I think I may venture to assert that my distress upon this occasion was, at least, equal to your apprehensions."

Adeline said she had been much alarmed by the hints he had given her, and by his failing to afford further information concerning the subject of her danger; and——

She checked the sentence that hung upon her lips, for she perceived that she was unwarily disclosing the interest he held in her heart. There were a few moments of silence, and neither party seemed perfectly at ease. Theodore at length renewed the conversation:

"Suffer me to acquaint you," said he, "with the circumstances that withheld me from the interview I solicited; I am anxious to exculpate myself."

Without waiting her reply, he proceeded to inform her that the Marquis had, by some inexplicable means, learned or suspected the subject of their last conversation, and, perceiving his designs were in danger of being counteracted, had taken effectual means to prevent her obtaining further intelligence of them. Adeline immediately recollected that Theodore and herself had been seen in the forest by La Motte, who had no doubt suspected their growing intimacy, and had taken care to inform the Marquis how likely he was to find a rival in his friend.

"On the day following that on which I last saw you," said Theodore, "the Marquis, who is my colonel, commanded me to prepare to attend my regiment, and appointed the following morning for my journey. This sudden order gave me some surprise, but I was not long in doubt concerning the motive of it; a servant of the Marquis, who was attached to me, entered my room soon after I had left his lord, and expressing concern at my abrupt departure, dropped some hints respecting it, which excited my surprise. I inquired farther, and was confirmed in the suspicions I had for some time entertained of the Marquis's designs upon you.

"Jacques further informed me that our late interview had been noticed and mentioned to the Marquis. His information had been obtained from a fellow-servant, and it alarmed me so much, that I engaged him to send me intelligence from time to time concerning the proceedings of the Marquis. I now looked forward to the evening which would bring me again to your presence with increased impatience; but the ingenuity of the Marquis effectually counteracted my endeavours and wishes. He had made an engagement to pass the day at the villa of a nobleman some leagues distant, and, notwithstanding all the excuses I could offer, I was obliged to attend him. Thus compelled to obey, I passed a day of more agitation and anxiety than I had ever before experienced. It was midnight before we returned to the Marquis's château. I arose early in the morning to commence my journey, and resolved to seek an interview with you before I left the province.

"When I entered the breakfast-room I was much surprised to find the Marquis there already, who, commending the beauty of the morning, declared his intention of accompanying me as far as Chineau. Thus unexpectedly deprived of my last hope, my countenance, I believe, expressed what I felt, for the scrutinising eye of the Marquis instantly changed from seeming carelessness to displeasure. The distance from Chineau to the abbey was at least twelve leagues; yet I had once some intention of returning from thence when the Marquis should leave me, till I recollected the very remote chance there would even then be of seeing you alone, and also, that if I was observed by La Motte, it would awaken all his suspicions, and caution him against any future plan I might see it expedient to attempt. I therefore proceeded to join my regiment.

"Jacques sent me frequent accounts of the operations of the Marquis; but his manner of relating them was so very confused that they only served to perplex and distress me. His last letter, however, alarmed me so much, that my residence in quarters became intolerable; and, as I found it impossible to obtain leave of absence, I secretly left the regiment, and concealed myself in a cottage about a mile from the château, that I might obtain the earliest intelligence of the Marquis's plans. Jacques brought me daily information, and at last an account of the horrible plot which was laid for the following night.

"I saw little probability of warning you of your danger. If I ventured near the abbey, La Motte might discover me, and frustrate every attempt on my part to serve you; yet I determined to encounter this risk for the chance of seeing you, and towards evening I was preparing to set out for the forest, when Jacques arrived and informed me that you were to be brought to the château. My plan was thus rendered less difficult. I learned, also, that the Marquis, by means of those refinements in luxury with which he is but too well acquainted, designed, now that his apprehension of losing you was no more, to seduce you to his wishes, and impose upon you by a fictitious marriage. Having obtained information concerning the situation of the room allotted you, I ordered a chaise to be in waiting, and, with a design of scaling your window and conducting you thence, I entered the garden at midnight."

Theodore having ceased to speak, "I know not how words can express my sense of the obligations I owe you," said Adeline, "or my gratitude for your generosity."

"Ah! call it not generosity," he replied; "it was love." He paused. Adeline was silent. After some moments of expressive emotion, he resumed: "But pardon this abrupt declaration; yet why do I call it abrupt, since my actions have already disclosed what my lips have never, till this instant, ventured to acknowledge?" He paused again. Adeline was still silent. "Yet do me

the justice to believe that I am sensible of the impropriety of pleading my love at present, and have been surprised into this confession. I promise also to forbear from a renewal of the subject, till you are placed in a situation where you may freely accept or refuse the sincere regards I offer you. If I could, however, now be certain that I possess your esteem, it would relieve me from much anxiety."

Adeline felt surprised that he should doubt her esteem for him, after the signal and generous service he had rendered her; but she was not yet acquainted with the timidity of love. "Do you then," said she, in a tremulous voice, "believe me ungrateful? Is it possible I can consider your friendly interference in my behalf without esteeming you?" Theodore immediately took her hand, and pressed it to his lips in silence. They were both too much agitated to converse, and continued to travel for some miles without exchanging a word.

CHAPTER XI.

And Hope enchanted smil'd, and wav'd her golden
    hair;
And longer had she sung—but with a frown,
Revenge impatient rose.
                                    COLLINS.

THE dawn of morning now trembled through the clouds, when the travellers stopped at a small town to change horses. Theodore entreated Adeline to alight and take some refreshment, and to this she at length consented. But the people of the inn were not yet up, and it was some time before the knocking and roaring of the postillion could rouse them.

Having taken some slight refreshment, Theodore and Adeline returned to the carriage. The only subject upon which Theodore could have spoken with interest, delicacy forbade him at this time to renew; and after pointing out some beautiful scenery on the road, and making other efforts to support a conversation, he relapsed into silence. His mind, though still anxious, was now relieved from the apprehension that had long oppressed it. When he first saw Adeline, her loveliness made a deep impression on his heart; there was a sentiment in her beauty which his mind immediately acknowledged, and the effect of which her manners and conversation had afterwards confirmed. Her charms appeared to him like those since so finely described by an English poet:

Oh! have you seen, bathed in the morning dew,
    The budding rose its infant bloom display?
When first its virgin tints unfold to view,
It shrinks, and scarcely trusts the blaze of day.

So soft, so delicate, so sweet she came,
  Youth's damask glow just dawning on her cheek,
I gaz'd, I sigh'd, I caught the tender flame,
  Felt the fond pang, and droop'd with passion weak.

A knowledge of her destitute condition, and of the dangers with which she was environed, had awakened in his heart the tenderest touch of pity, and assisted the change of admiration into love. The distress he suffered, when compelled to leave her exposed to these dangers, without being able to warn her of them, can only be imagined. During his residence with his regiment, his mind was the constant prey of terrors, which he saw no means of combating but by returning to the neighbourhood of the abbey, where he might obtain early intelligence of the Marquis's schemes, and be ready to give his assistance to Adeline.

Leave of absence he could not request, without betraying his design where most he dreaded it should be known, and, at length, with a generous rashness, which, though it defied the law, was impelled by virtue, he secretly quitted his regiment. The progress of the Marquis's plan he had observed with trembling anxiety, till the night that was to decide the fate of Adeline and himself roused all his mind to action, and involved him in a tumult of hope and fear, horror and expectation.

Never, till the present hour, had he ventured to believe she was in safety. Now, the distance they had gained from the château without perceiving any pursuit, increased his best hopes. It was impossible he could sit by the side of his beloved Adeline, and receive assurances of her gratitude and esteem, without venturing to hope for her love. He congratulated himself as her preserver, and anticipated scenes of happiness when she should be under the protection of his family. The clouds of misery and apprehension disappeared from his mind, and left it to the sunshine of joy. When a shadow of fear would sometimes return, or when he recollected, with compunction, the circumstances under which he had left his regiment, stationed, as it was, upon the frontiers, and in a time of war, he looked at Adeline, and her countenance, with instantaneous magic, beamed peace upon his heart.

But Adeline had a subject of anxiety from which Theodore was exempt; the prospect of her future days was involved in darkness and incertitude. Again she was going to claim the bounty of strangers—again going to encounter the uncertainty of their kindness; exposed to the hardships of dependence, or to the difficulty of earning a precarious livelihood. These anticipations obscured the joy occasioned by her escape, and by the affection which the conduct and avowal of Theodore had exhibited. The delicacy of his behaviour, in forbearing to take advantage of her present situation to plead his love, increased her esteem, and flattered her pride. Adeline was lost in meditation upon subjects like these, when the postillion stopped the carriage, and, pointing to part of the road which wound down the side of a hill they had passed, said there were several horsemen in pursuit. Theodore immediately ordered him to proceed with all possible speed, and to strike out of the great road into the first obscure way that offered. The postillion cracked his whip in the air, and set off as if he was flying for life. In the meanwhile, Theodore endeavoured to reanimate Adeline, who was sinking with terror, and who now thought if she could only escape the Marquis she could defy the future.

Presently they struck into a bye-lane, screened and overshaded by thick trees. Theodore again looked from the window, but the closing boughs prevented his seeing far enough to determine whether the pursuit continued. For his sake Adeline endeavoured to disguise her emotions.

"This lane," said Theodore, "will certainly lead to a town or village, and then we have nothing to apprehend; for though my single arm could not defend you against the number of our pursuers, I have no doubt of being able to interest some of the inhabitants in our behalf."

Adeline appeared to be comforted by the hope this reflection suggested, and Theodore again looked back, but the windings of the road closed his view, and the rattling of the wheels overcame every other sound. At length he called to the postillion to stop, and having listened attentively, without perceiving any sound of horses, he began to hope they were now in safety. "Do you know where this road leads?" said he. The postillion answered that he did not; but he saw some houses between the trees at a distance, and believed it led to them. This was most welcome intelligence to Theodore, who looked forward and perceived the houses. The postillion set off. "Fear nothing, my adored Adeline," said Theodore, "you are now safe; I will part with you but with life."

Adeline sighed, not for herself only, but for the danger to which Theodore might be exposed.

They had continued to travel in this manner for near half-an-hour, when they arrived at a small village, and soon after stopped at an inn, the best the place afforded. As Theodore lifted Adeline from the chaise, he again entreated her to dismiss her apprehensions, and spoke with a tenderness, to which she could reply only by a smile that ill-concealed her anxiety. After ordering refreshments, he went out to speak with the landlord, but had scarcely left the room, when Adeline observed a party of horsemen enter the inn-yard, and she had no doubt these were the persons from whom they fled. The faces of two of them only were turned towards her, but she thought the figure of one of the others not unlike that of the Marquis.

Her heart was chilled, and for some moments the powers of reason forsook her. Her first design was to seek concealment; but while she considered the means, one of the horsemen looked up to the window near which she stood, and speaking to his companions, they entered the inn. To quit the room without being observed was impossible; to remain there, alone and unprotected as she was, would be almost equally dangerous. She paced the room in an agony of terror, often secretly calling on Theodore, and often wondering he did not return. These were moments of indescribable suffering. A loud and tumultuous sound of voices now arose from a distant part of the house, and she soon distinguished the words of the disputants. "I arrest you in the King's name," said one; "and bid you, at your peril, attempt to go from hence, except under a guard."

The next minute Adeline heard the voice of Theodore in reply. "I do not mean to dispute the King's orders," said he, "and give you my word of honour not to go without you; but first unhand me, that I may return to that room; I have a friend there whom I wish to speak with." To this proposal they at first objected, considering it merely as an excuse to obtain an opportunity of escaping; but, after much altercation and entreaty, his request was granted. He sprang forward towards the room where Adeline remained, while a sergeant and corporal followed him to the door; the two soldiers went out into the yard of the inn to watch the windows of the apartment.

With an eager hand he unclosed the door, but Adeline hastened not to meet him, for she had fainted almost at the beginning of the dispute. Theodore called loudly for assistance, and the mistress of the inn soon appeared with her stock of remedies, which were administered in vain to Adeline, who remained insensible, and by breathing alone gave signs of her existence. The distress of Theodore was in the meantime heightened by the appearance of the officers, who, laughing at the discovery of his pretended friend, declared they could wait no longer. Saying this, they would have forced him from the inanimate form of Adeline, over whom he hung in unutterable anguish, when fiercely turning upon them, he drew his sword, and swore no power on earth should force him away before the lady recovered.

The men, enraged by the action and the determined air of Theodore, exclaimed, "Do you oppose the King's orders?" and advanced to seize him; but he presented the point of his sword, and bade them at their peril approach. One of them immediately drew; Theodore kept his guard, but did not advance. "I demand only to wait here till the lady recovers," said he, "you understand the alternative." The man, already exasperated by the opposition of Theodore, regarded the latter part of his speech as a threat, and became determined not to give up the point; he pressed forward, and while his comrade called the men from the yard, Theodore wounded him slightly in the shoulder, and received himself the stroke of a sabre on his head.

The blood gushed furiously from the wound; Theodore, staggering to a chair, sank into it, just as the remainder of the party entered the room, and Adeline unclosed her eyes to see him ghastly pale and covered with blood. She uttered an involuntary scream, and exclaiming, "They have murdered him," nearly relapsed. At the sound of her voice he raised his head, and smiling, held out his hand to her. "I am not much hurt," he said faintly, "and shall soon be better, if indeed you are recovered." She hastened towards him, and gave her hand.

"Is nobody gone for a surgeon?" said she, with a look of agony.

"Do not be alarmed," said Theodore, "I am not so ill as you imagine."

The room was now crowded with people, whom the report of the affray had brought together; among these was a man, who acted as physician, apothecary, and surgeon to the village, and who now stepped forward to the assistance of Theodore.

Having examined the wound, he declined giving his opinion, but ordered the patient to be immediately put to bed, to which the officers objected, alleging that it was their duty to carry him to the regiment. "That cannot be done without great danger to his life," replied the doctor; "and——"

"Oh; his life," said the sergeant, "we have nothing to do with that; we must do our duty."

Adeline, who had hitherto stood in trembling anxiety, could now no longer be silent. "Since the surgeon," said she, "has declared it as his opinion, that this gentleman cannot be removed in his present condition without endangering his life, you will remember that if he dies yours will probably answer it."

"Yes," rejoined the surgeon, who was unwilling to relinquish his patient, "I declare before these witnesses that he cannot be removed with safety; you will do well, therefore, to consider the consequences. He has received a very dangerous wound, which requires the most careful treatment, and the event is even then doubtful; but if he travels a fever may ensue, and the wound will then be mortal."

Theodore heard this sentence with composure, but Adeline could with difficulty conceal the anguish of her heart ; she summoned all her fortitude to suppress the tears that struggled in her eyes ; and though she wished to interest the humanity or to awaken the fears of the men in behalf of the unfortunate prisoner, she dared not trust her voice with utterance.

From this internal struggle she was relieved by the compassion of the people who filled the room, and, becoming clamorous in the cause of Theodore, declared the officers would be guilty of murder if they removed him.

" Why, he must die, at any rate," said the sergeant, "for quitting his post, and drawing upon me in the execution of the King's orders."

A faint sickness came over the heart of Adeline, and she leaned for support against Theodore's chair, whose concern for himself was for a while suspended in his anxiety for her. He supported her with his arm, and forcing a smile, said in a low voice, which she could only hear :

" This is a misrepresentation ; I doubt not, when the affair is inquired into, it will be settled without any serious consequences."

Adeline knew these words were uttered only to console her, and therefore did not give much credit to them, though Theodore continued to repeat similar assurances of his safety. Meanwhile, the mob, whose compassion for him had been gradually excited by the obduracy of the officer, were now roused to pity and indignation by the seeming certainty of his punishment, and the unfeeling manner in which it had been denounced. In a short time they became so much enraged that, partly from a dread of further consequences, and partly from the shame which their charges of cruelty occasioned, the sergeant consented that Theodore should be put to bed till his commanding officer might direct what was to be done. Adeline's joy at this circumstance overcame for a moment the sense of her misfortunes and of her situation.

She waited in an adjoining room the sentence of the surgeon, who was now engaged in examining the wound ; and though the accident would in any other circumstances have severely afflicted her, she now lamented it the more because she considered herself as the cause of it, and because the misfortune, by illustrating more fully the affection of her lover, drew him closer to her heart, and seemed, therefore, to sharpen the poignancy of her affliction. The dreadful assertion that Theodore, should he recover, would be punished with death she scarcely dared to consider, but endeavoured to believe that it was no more than a cruel exaggeration of his antagonist.

Upon the whole, Theodore's present danger,

together with the attendant circumstances, awakened all her tenderness, and discovered to her the true state of her affections. The graceful form, the noble, intelligent countenance, and the engaging manners which she had at first admired in Theodore, became afterwards more interesting by that strength of thought and elegance of sentiment exhibited in his conversation. His conduct since her escape had excited her warmest gratitude, and the danger which he had now encountered in her behalf called forth her tenderness and heightened it into love. The veil was removed from her heart, and she saw, for the first time, its genuine emotions.

The surgeon at length came out of Theodore's chamber into the room where Adeline was waiting to speak with him. She inquired concerning the state of his wound.

" You are a relation of the gentleman's, I presume, madam—his sister, perhaps?"

The question vexed and embarrassed her, and, without answering it, she repeated her inquiry.

" Perhaps, madam, you are more nearly related," pursued the surgeon, seeming also to disregard her question ; "perhaps you are his wife?" Adeline blushed, and was about to reply, but he continued his speech. "The interest you take in his welfare is, at least, very flattering, and I would almost consent to exchange conditions with him, were I sure of receiving such tender compassion from so charming a lady." Saying this, he bowed to the ground.

Adeline, assuming a very reserved air, said :

" Now, sir, that you have concluded your compliment, you will, perhaps, attend to my question ; I have inquired how you left your patient?"

" That, madam, is, perhaps, a question very difficult to be resolved ; and it is likewise a very disagreeable office to pronounce ill news—I fear he will die."

The surgeon opened his snuff-box and presented it to Adeline.

" Die !" she exclaimed in a faint voice. " Die !"

" Do not be alarmed, madam," resumed the surgeon, observing her grow pale, "do not be alarmed. It is possible that the wound may not have reached the——" he stammered ; "in that case the——" stammering again, "is not affected ; and if so, the interior membranes of the brain are not touched : in this case the wound may, perhaps, escape inflammation, and the patient may possibly recover. But if, on the other hand——"

" I beseech you, sir, to speak intelligibly," interrupted Adeline, "and not to trifle with my anxiety. Do you really believe him in danger?"

" In danger, madam !" exclaimed the surgeon, "in danger ! yes, certainly, in very great danger." Saying this, he walked away with an air of chagrin and displeasure.

Adeline remained for some moments in the room in an excess of sorrow, which she found it impossible to restrain, and then drying her tears, and endeavouring to compose her countenance, she went to inquire for the mistress of the inn, to whom she sent a waiter.

After expecting her in vain for some time she rang the bell, and sent another message somewhat more pressing. - Still the hostess did not appear, and Adeline at length went herself downstairs, where she found her, surrounded by a number of people, relating, with a loud voice and various gesticulations, the particulars of the late accident. Perceiving Adeline, she called out, "Oh! here is mademoiselle herself," and the eyes of the assembly were immediately turned upon her. Adeline, whom the crowd prevented from approaching the hostess, now beckoned her, and was going to withdraw; but the landlady, eager in the pursuit of her story, disregarded the signal. In vain did Adeline endeavour to catch her eye; it glanced everywhere but upon her, who was unwilling to attract the further notice of the crowd by calling out.

"It is a great pity, to be sure, that he should be shot," said the landlady, "he's such a handsome man; but they say he certainly will if he recovers. Poor gentleman! he will very likely not suffer though, for the doctor says he will never go out of this house alive." Adeline now spoke to a man who stood near, and desiring he would tell the hostess she wished to speak with her, left the place.

In about ten minutes the landlady appeared. "Alas! mademoiselle," said she, "your brother is in a sad condition; they fear he won't get over it."

Adeline inquired whether there was any other medical person in the town than the surgeon whom she had seen.

"Lord, madam! this is a rare healthy place, we have little need of medicine-people here; such an accident never happened in it before. The doctor has been here ten years, or thereabout; but there's very bad encouragement for his trade; and I believe he's poor enough himself. One of the sort's quite enough for us."

Adeline interrupted her to ask some questions concerning Theodore, whom the hostess had attended to his chamber. She inquired how he had borne the dressing of the wound, and whether he appeared to be easier after the operation; questions to which the hostess gave no very satisfactory answers. She now inquired whether there was any surgeon in the neighbourhood of the town, and was told there was not.

The distress visible in Adeline's countenance seemed to excite the compassion of the landlady, who now endeavoured to console her in the best manner she was able. She advised her to send for her friends, and offered to procure a messenger. Adeline sighed, and said it was unnecessary.

"I don't know, ma'amselle, what you may think necessary," continued the hostess, "but I know I should think it very hard to die in a strange place with no relations near me, and I daresay the poor gentleman thinks so himself; and, besides, who is to pay for his funeral if he dies?"

Adeline begged she would be silent, and, desiring that every proper attention might be given, she promised her a reward for her trouble, and requested pen and ink immediately.

"Aye, to be sure, ma'amselle, that is the proper way. Why, your friends would never forgive you if you did not acquaint them; I know it by myself. And as for taking care of him, he shall have everything the house affords; and I warrant there is never a better inn in the province, though the town is none of the biggest."

Adeline was obliged to repeat her request for pen and ink before the loquacious hostess would quit the room.

The thought of sending for Theodore's friends had, in the tumult of the late scenes, never occurred to her, and she was now somewhat consoled by the prospect of comfort which it opened for him. When the pen and ink were brought she wrote the following note to Theodore:

"In your present condition you have need of every comfort that can be procured you, and surely there is no cordial more valuable in illness than the presence of a friend. Suffer me therefore to acquaint your family with your situation; it will be a satisfaction to me, and, I doubt not, a consolation to you."

In a short time after she had sent the note she received a message from Theodore, entreating most respectfully, but earnestly, to see her for a few minutes. She immediately went to his chamber, where her worst apprehensions were confirmed by the languor expressed in his countenance; and the shock she received, together with the struggle to disguise her emotions, almost overcame her.

"I thank you for this goodness," said he, extending his hand, which she received; and then, sitting down by the bed, she burst into tears.

When her agitation had somewhat subsided, she removed her handkerchief from her eyes, and again looked on Theodore; a smile of the tenderest love expressed his sense of the interest she took in his welfare, and administered a temporary relief to her heart.

"Forgive this weakness," said she, "my spirits have been of late so variously agitated——"

Theodore interrupted her: "These tears are most flattering to my heart. But, for my sake, endeavour to support yourself; I doubt not I shall soon be better, the surgeon——"

"I do not like him," said Adeline, "But tell me how you find yourself."

He assured her that he was now much easier than he had been; and, mentioning her kind note, he led to the subject on account of which he had solicited to see her.

"My family," said he, "reside at a great distance from hence, and I well know their affection is such that, were they informed of my situation, no consideration, however reasonable, could prevent their coming to my assistance; but before they can arrive their presence will probably be unnecessary." Adeline looked earnestly at him. "I should probably be well," pursued he, smiling, "before a letter could reach them; it would therefore occasion them unnecessary pain, and, moreover, a fruitless journey. For your sake, Adeline, I could wish they were here; but a few days will more fully show the consequences of my wound. Let us wait, at least till then, and be directed by circumstances."

Adeline forbore to press the subject further and turned to one more immediately interesting.

"I much wish," said she, "that you had a more able surgeon. You know the geography of the province better than I do: are we in the neighbourhood of any town likely to afford you other advice?"

"I believe not," said he, "and this is an affair of little consequence, for my wound is so inconsiderable that a very moderate share of skill may suffice to cure it. But why, my beloved Adeline, do you give way to this anxiety? Why suffer yourself to be disturbed by this tendency to forbode the worst? I am willing, perhaps, presumptuously so, to attribute it to your kindness, and suffer me to assure you that, while it excites my gratitude it increases my tenderest esteem. Oh Adeline! since you wish my speedy recovery, let me see you composed; while I believe you to be unhappy I cannot be well."

She assured him she would endeavour to be, at least, tranquil; and fearing the conversation, if prolonged, would be prejudicial to him, she left him to repose.

As she turned out of the gallery she met the hostess, upon whom certain words of Adeline had operated as a talisman, transforming neglect and impertinence into officious civility. She came to inquire whether the gentleman above-stairs had everything that he liked, for she was sure it was her endeavour that he should have.

"I have got him a nurse, ma'amselle, to attend him, and I daresay she will do very well; but I will look to that, for I shall not mind helping him myself sometimes. Poor gentleman, how patiently he bears it! One would not think now that he believed he is going to die, yet the doctor told him so himself, or at least as good."

Adeline was extremely shocked at this imprudent conduct of the surgeon, and dismissed the landlady, after ordering a slight dinner.

Towards evening the surgeon again made his appearance, and, having passed some time with his patient, returned to the parlour, according to the desire of Adeline, to inform her of his condition. He answered Adeline's inquiries with great solemnity.

"It is impossible to determine positively at present, madam, but I have reason to adhere to the opinion I gave you this morning. I am not apt, indeed, to form opinions upon uncertain grounds. I will give you a remarkable instance of this.

"It is not above a fortnight since I was sent for to a patient at some leagues' distance. I was from home when the messenger arrived, and the case being urgent, before I could reach the patient another physician was consulted, who had ordered such medicines as he thought proper, and the patient had been apparently relieved by them. His friends were congratulating themselves upon his improvement when I arrived, and had agreed in opinion with the physician that there was no danger in this case. 'Depend upon it,' said I, 'you are mistaken: these medicines cannot have relieved him, the patient is in the utmost danger.' The patient groaned, but my brother physician persisted in affirming that the remedies he had prescribed would not only be certain but speedy, some good effect having been already produced by them. Upon this I lost all patience, and, adhering to my opinion that these effects were fallacious, and the case desperate, I assured the patient himself that his life was in the utmost danger. I am not one of those, madam, who deceive their patients to their last moments; but you shall hear the conclusion.

"My brother physician was, I suppose, enraged by the firmness of my opposition, and he assumed a most angry look, which did not in the least affect me, and turning to the patient, desired he would decide upon which of our opinions to rely, for he must decline acting with me. The patient did me the honour," pursued the surgeon, with a smile of complacency, and smoothing his ruffles, "to think more highly of me than, perhaps, I deserved, for he immediately dismissed my opponent. 'I could not have believed,' said he, as the physician left the room, 'I could not have believed that a man who has been so many years in the profession could be so wholly ignorant of it.'

" 'I could not have believed it either,' said I. 'I am astonished that he was not aware of my danger,' resumed the patient. 'I am astonished likewise,' replied I. I was resolved to do what I could for the patient, for he was a man of understanding, as you perceive, and I had a regard for him. I therefore altered the prescriptions, and myself administered the medicines, but all would not do, my opinion was verified, and he died even before the next morning."

Adeline, who had been compelled to listen to this long story, sighed at the conclusion of it.

"I don't wonder that you are affected, madam," said the surgeon; "the instance I have related is certainly a very affecting one. It distressed me so much that it was some time before I could think or even speak concerning it. But you must allow, madam," continued he, lowering his voice and bowing with a look of self-congratulation, "that this was a striking instance of the infallibility of my judgment."

Adeline shuddered at the infallibility of his judgment, and made no reply.

"It was a shocking thing for the poor man," resumed the surgeon.

"It was, indeed, very shocking," said Adeline.

"It affected me a good deal when it happened," continued he.

"Undoubtedly, sir," said Adeline.

"But time wears away the most painful impressions."

"I think you mentioned it was about a fortnight since it happened."

"Somewhere thereabouts," replied the surgeon, without seeming to understand the observation.

"And will you permit me, sir, to ask the name of the physician who so ignorantly opposed you?"

"Certainly, madam; it is Lafance."

"He lives in the obscurity he deserves, no doubt," said Adeline.

"Why no, madam; he lives in a town of some note at about the distance of four leagues from hence, and affords one instance, among many others, that the public opinion is generally erroneous. You will hardly believe it, but I assure you it is a fact, that this man comes into a great deal of practice, while I am suffered to remain here neglected, and indeed very little known."

During his narrative Adeline had been considering by what means she could discover the name of the physician, for the instance that had been produced to prove his ignorance, and the infallibility of his opponent, had completely settled her opinion concerning them both. She now more than ever wished to deliver Theodore from the hands of the surgeon, and was musing on the possibility when he, with so much self-security, developed the means.

She asked him a few more questions concerning the state of Theodore's wound, and was told it was much as it had been, but that some degree of fever had come on. "But I have ordered a fire to be made in the room," continued the surgeon, "and some additional blankets to be laid on the bed; these, I doubt not, will have a proper effect. In the meantime, they must be careful to keep from him every kind of liquid, except some cordial draughts which I shall send. He will naturally ask for drink, but it must on no account be given to him."

"You do not approve, then, of the method which I have somewhere heard of," said Adeline, "of attending to Nature in these cases?"

"Nature, madam," pursued he, "Nature is the most improper guide in the world. I always adopt a method directly contrary to what she would suggest, for what can be the use of Art if she is only to follow Nature? This was my first opinion on setting out in life, and I have ever since strictly adhered to it. From what I have said, indeed, madam, you may, perhaps, perceive that my opinions may be depended on; what they once are they always are, for my mind is not of that frivolous kind to be affected by circumstances."

Adeline was fatigued by this discourse, and impatient to impart to Theodore her discovery of a physician; but the surgeon seemed by no means disposed to leave her, and was expatiating upon various topics, and adducing new instances of his surprising sagacity, when the waiter brought a message that some person desired to see him. He was, however, engaged upon too agreeable a topic to be easily prevailed on to quit it, and it was not till after a second message that he made his bow to Adeline and left the room. The moment he was gone she sent a note to Theodore, entreating his permission to call in the assistance of a physician.

The conceited manners of the surgeon had by this time given Theodore a very unfavourable opinion of his talents, and the last prescription had so fully confirmed it, that he now readily consented to have other advice. Adeline immediately inquired for a messenger, but recollecting that the residence of the physician was still a secret, she applied to the hostess, who being really ignorant of it, or pretending to be so, gave her no information. What further inquiries she made were equally ineffectual, and she passed some hours in extreme distress, while the disorder of Theodore rather increased than abated.

When supper appeared, she asked the boy who waited if he knew a physician of the name of Lafance in the neighbourhood. "Not in the neighbourhood, madam; but I know Doctor Lafance of Chancy, for I come from the town."

Adeline inquired further, and received very satisfactory answers. But the town was at some leagues' distance, and the delay this circumstance must occasion again alarmed her; she, however, ordered a messenger to be immediately despatched, and, having sent again to inquire concerning Theodore, retired to her chamber for the night.

The continued fatigue she had suffered for the last fourteen hours overcame her anxiety, and her harassed spirits sank to repose. She slept till late in the morning, and was then awakened by the landlady, who came to inform her that Theodore was much worse, and to inquire what should be done. Adeline, finding that the physician was not arrived, immediately arose, and hastened to inquire further concerning Theodore. The hostess informed her that he had passed a very disturbed night, that he had complained of being very hot, and desired that the fire in his room might be extinguished; but that the nurse knew her duty too well to obey him, and had strictly followed the doctor's orders.

She added that he had taken the cordial draught regularly, but had, notwithstanding, continued to grow worse, and at last became light-headed. In the meantime the boy, who had been sent for the physician, was still absent.

"And no wonder," continued the hostess; "why, only consider, it's eight leagues off, and the lad had to find the road, bad as it is, in the dark. But, indeed, ma'amselle, you might as well have trusted our doctor, for we never want anybody else, not we, in the town here; and if I might speak my mind, Jacques had better have been sent off for the young gentleman's friends than for this strange doctor that nobody knows."

After asking some further questions concerning Theodore, the answers to which rather increased than diminished her alarm, Adeline endeavoured to compose her spirits, and await in patience the arrival of the physician. She was now more sensible than ever of the forlornness of her own condition and of the danger of Theodore's, and earnestly wished that his friends could be informed of his situation; a wish which could not be gratified, for Theodore, who alone could acquaint her with their place of residence, was deprived of recollection.

When the surgeon arrived and perceived the situation of his patient, he expressed no surprise; but having asked some questions and given a few general directions, he went down to Adeline. After paying her his usual compliments, he suddenly assumed an air of importance.

"I am sorry, madam," said he, "that it is my office to communicate disagreeable intelligence, but I wish you to be prepared for the event which I fear is approaching."

Adeline comprehended his meaning, and though she had hitherto given little faith to his judgment, she could not hear him hint at the immediate danger of Theodore without yielding to the influence of fear.

She entreated him to acquaint her with all he apprehended; and he then proceeded to say that Theodore was, as he had foreseen, much worse this morning than he had been the preceding night; and the disorder having now affected his head, there was every reason to fear it would prove fatal in a few hours. "The worst consequences may ensue," continued he; "if the wound becomes inflamed there will be very little chance of his recovery."

Adeline listened to this sentence with a dreadful calmness, and gave no utterance to grief either by words or tears.

"The gentleman, I suppose, madam, has friends, and the sooner you inform them of his condition the better. If they reside at any distance, it is indeed too late; but there are other necessary——you are ill, madam!"

Adeline made an effort to speak, but in vain, and the surgeon now called loudly for a glass of water; she drank it, and a deep sigh that she uttered seemed somewhat to relieve her oppressed heart; tears succeeded. In the meantime, the surgeon perceiving she was better, though not well enough to listen to his conversation, took his leave, and promised to return in an hour. The physician was not yet arrived, and Adeline awaited his appearance with a mixture of fear and anxious hope.

About noon he came, and having been informed of the accident by which the fever was produced, and of the treatment which the surgeon had given it, he ascended to Theodore's chamber; in a quarter of an hour he returned to the room where Adeline expected him.

"The gentleman is still delirious," said he, "but I have ordered him a composing draught."

"Is there any hope, sir?" inquired Adeline.

"Yes, madam, certainly there is hope; the case at present is somewhat doubtful, but a few hours may enable me to judge with more certainty. In the meantime, I have directed that he shall be kept quiet, and be allowed to drink freely of some diluting liquids."

He had scarcely, at Adeline's request, recommended a surgeon, instead of the one at present employed, when the latter gentleman entered the room, and, perceiving the physician, threw a glance of mingled surprise and anger at Adeline, who retired with him to another apartment, where she dismissed him with a politeness which he did not deign to return, and which he certainly did not deserve.

Early the following morning the surgeon arrived, but either the medicines or the crisis of the disorder had thrown Theodore into a deep sleep, in which he remained for several

F

hours. The physician now gave Adeline reason to hope for a favourable issue, and every precaution was taken to prevent his being disturbed. He awoke perfectly sensible and free from fever, and his first words inquired for Adeline, who soon learned that he was out of danger.

In a few days he was sufficiently recovered to be removed from his chamber to a room adjoining, where Adeline met him with a joy which she found it impossible to repress; and the observance of this lighted up his countenance with pleasure; indeed, Adeline, sensible to the attachment he had so nobly testified, and softened by the danger he had encountered, no longer attempted to disguise the tenderness of her esteem, and was at length brought to confess the interest his first appearance had impressed upon her heart.

After an hour of affecting conversation, in which the happiness of a young and mutual attachment occupied all their minds, and excluded every idea not in unison with delight, they returned to a sense of their present embarrassments: Adeline recollecting that Theodore was arrested for disobedience of orders, and deserting his post; and Theodore, that he must shortly be torn away from Adeline, who would be left exposed to all the evils from which he had so lately rescued her. This thought overwhelmed his heart with anguish; and, after a long pause, he ventured to propose, what his wishes had often suggested, a marriage with Adeline before he departed from the village. This was the only means of preventing, perhaps, an eternal separation; and though he saw the many dangerous inconveniences to which she would be exposed by a marriage with a man circumstanced like himself, yet these appeared so unequal to those she would otherwise be left to encounter alone, that his reason could no longer scruple to adopt what his affection had suggested.

Adeline was for some time too much agitated to reply; and though she had little to oppose to the arguments and pleadings of Theodore, though she had no friends to control, and no contrariety of interests to perplex her, she could not bring herself to consent thus hastily to a marriage with a man of whom she had little knowledge, and to whose family and connections she had no sort of introduction. At length she entreated he would drop the subject, and the conversation for the remainder of the day was more general, yet still interesting.

That similarity of taste and opinion, which had at first attracted them, every moment now more fully disclosed. Their discourse was enriched by elegant literature, and endeared by mutual regard. Adeline had enjoyed few opportunities of reading, but the books to which she had had access operating upon a mind eager for knowledge, and upon a taste peculiarly sensible of the beautiful and the elegant, had impressed all their excellencies upon her understanding. Theodore had received from nature many of the qualities of genius, and from education all that it could bestow; to these were added, a noble independency of spirit, a feeling heart, and manners which partook of a happy mixture of dignity and sweetness.

In the evening one of the officers, who, upon the representation of the sergeant, was sent by the persons employed to prosecute military criminals, arrived at the village, and entering the apartment of Theodore, from which Adeline immediately withdrew, informed him with an air of infinite importance, that he should set out on the following day for head-quarters. Theodore answered that he was not able to bear the journey, and referred him to his physician; but the officer replied that he should take no such trouble, it being certain that the physician might be instructed what to say, and that he should begin his journey on the morrow. "Here has been delay enough," said he, "already, and you will have sufficient business on your hands when you reach head-quarters; for the sergeant, whom you have severely wounded, intends to appear against you, and this, with the offence you have committed by deserting your post——"

Theodore's eyes flashed fire. "Deserting!" said he, rising from his seat, and darting a look of menace at his accuser, "who dares to brand me with the name of deserter?" But instantly recollecting how much his conduct had appeared to justify the accusation, he endeavoured to stifle his emotions, and, with a firm voice and composed manner, said that when he reached head-quarters, he should be ready to answer whatever might be brought against him, but that till then he should be silent. The boldness of the officer was repressed by the spirit and dignity with which Theodore spoke these words, and muttering a reply that was scarcely audible, he left the room.

Theodore sat musing on the danger of his situation: he knew that he had much to apprehend from the peculiar circumstances attending his abrupt departure from his regiment, it having been stationed in a garrison-town upon the Spanish frontiers, where the discipline was very severe; and from the power of his colonel, the Marquis de Montalt, whom pride and disappointment would now rouse to vengeance, and probably render indefatigable in the accomplishment of his destruction. But his thoughts soon fled from his own danger to that of Adeline, and, in the consideration of this, all his fortitude forsook him; he could not support the idea of leaving her exposed to the evils he foreboded, nor, indeed, of a separation so sudden as that which now threatened him; and when she again entered the room, he renewed his solicitations for a speedy marriage, with all the arguments that tenderness and ingenuity could suggest.

Adeline, when she learned that he was to depart on the morrow, felt as if bereaved of her last comfort. All the horrors of his situation arose to her mind, and she turned from him in unutterable anguish. Considering her silence as a favourable presage, he repeated his entreaties that she should consent to be his, and thus give him a surety that their separation should not be eternal. Adeline sighed deeply at these words. "And who can know that our separation would not be eternal," said she, " even if I could consent to the marriage you propose ? But while you hear my determination, forbear to accuse me of indifference, for indifference towards you would, indeed, be a crime after the services you have rendered me."

"And is a cold sentiment of gratitude all that I am to expect of you ?" said Theodore. "I know that you are going to distress me with a proof of your indifference, which you mistake for the suggestions of prudence, and that I shall be reduced to look, without reluctance, upon the evils that may shortly await me. Ah, Adeline ! if you mean to reject this, perhaps, the last proposal which I can ever make to you, cease, at least, to deceive yourself with the idea that you love me ; that delirium is fading even from my mind."

"Can you, then, so soon forget our conversation of this morning ?" replied Adeline, "and can you think so lightly of me as to believe I would profess a regard which I do not feel ? If, indeed, you can believe this, I shall do well to forget that I ever made such an acknowledgment, and you, that you heard it."

"Forgive me, Adeline, forgive the doubts and inconsistencies I have betrayed ; let the anxieties of love and the emergency of my circumstances plead for me."

Adeline, smiling faintly through her tears, held out her hand, which he seized and pressed to his lips.

"Yet do not drive me to despair by a rejection of my suit," continued Theodore ; "think what I must suffer to leave you here destitute of friends and protection."

"I am thinking how I may avoid a situation so deplorable," said Adeline. "They say there is a convent which receives boarders, within a few miles, and thither I wish to go."

"A convent !" rejoined Theodore ; "would you go to a convent ? Do you know the persecutions you would be liable to, and that if the Marquis should discover you, there is little probability that the Superior would resist his authority, or, at least, his bribes ?"

"All this I have considered," said Adeline, "and am prepared to encounter it rather than enter into an engagement, which, at this time, can be productive only of misery to us both."

"Ah, Adeline ! could you think thus if you truly loved ? I see myself about to be separated, and that, perhaps, for ever, from the object of my tenderest affections, and I cannot but express all the anguish I feel—I cannot forbear to repeat every argument that may afford even the slightest possibility of altering your determination. But *you*, Adeline, *you* look with complacency upon a circumstance which tortures *me* with despair."

Adeline, who had long tried to support her spirits in his presence, while she adhered to a resolution which reason suggested, but which the pleadings of her heart powerfully opposed, was unable longer to command her distress, and burst into tears. Theodore was in the same moment convinced of his error, and shocked at the grief he had occasioned. He drew his chair towards her, and, taking her hand, again entreated her pardon, and endeavoured in the tenderest accents to soothe and comfort her.

"What a wretch was I to cause you this distress, by questioning that regard with which I can no longer doubt you honour me ! Forgive me, Adeline, say but you forgive me, and, whatever may be the pain of this separation, I will no longer oppose it."

"You have given me some pain," said Adeline, "but you have not offended me."

She then mentioned some further particulars concerning the convent. Theodore endeavoured to conceal the distress which the approaching separation occasioned him, and to consult with her on these plans with composure. His judgment by degrees prevailed over his passions, and he now perceived that the plan she suggested would afford her the best chance of security. He considered, what in the first agitation of his mind had escaped him, that he might be condemned upon the charges brought against him, and that his death, should they have been married, would not only deprive her of her protector, but leave her more immediately exposed to the designs of the Marquis, who would doubtless attend his trial, and by this means discover that Adeline was again within his reach. Astonished that he had not noticed this before, and shocked at the unwariness by which he might have betrayed her into so dangerous a situation, he became at once reconciled to the idea of leaving her in a convent. He could have wished to place her in the asylum of his own family, but the circumstances under which she must be introduced were so painful, and, above all, the distance at which they resided would render a journey so highly dangerous for her, that he forbore to propose it. He entreated only that she would allow him to write to her ; but, recollecting that his letters might be a means of betraying the place of her residence to the Marquis, he checked himself.

"I must deny myself even this melancholy pleasure," said he, "lest my letters should betray your abode ; yet how shall I be able to endure the impatience and uncertainty to which prudence condemns me! If you are in danger, I shall be ignorant of it ; though, indeed, did I know it," said he, with a look of despair, "I could not fly to save you. Oh exquisite misery! 'tis now only I perceive all the horrors of confinement, 'tis now only that I understand all the value of liberty."

His utterance was interrupted by the violent agitation of his mind ; he rose from his chair, and walked with quick paces about the room. Adeline sat, overcome by the description which Theodore had given of his approaching situation, and by the consideration that she might remain in the most terrible suspense concerning his fate. She saw him in a prison —pale, emaciated, and in chains ; she saw the vengeance of the Marquis descending upon him ; and this for his exertions in her cause. Theodore, alarmed by the despair expressed in her countenance, threw himself into a chair by hers, and, taking her hand, attempted to speak comfort to her, but the words faltered on his lips, and he could only bathe her hand with tears.

This mournful silence was interrupted by the arrival of a carriage at the inn, and Theodore, arising, went to the window that opened into the yard. The darkness of the night prevented his distinguishing the objects without, but a light now brought from the house showed him a carriage and four, attended by several servants. Presently he saw a gentleman, wrapped up in a roquelaure, alight and enter the inn, and in the next moment he heard the voice of the Marquis.

He had flown to support Adeline, who was sinking with terror, when the door opened, and the Marquis, followed by the officers and several servants, entered. Fury flashed from his eyes as they glanced upon Theodore, who hung over Adeline with a look of fearful solicitude.

"Seize that traitor," said he, turning to the officers ; "why have you suffered him to remain here so long?"

"I am no traitor," said Theodore, with a firm voice, and the dignity of conscious worth, "but a defender of innocence, of one whom the treacherous Marquis de Montalt would destroy."

"Obey your orders," said the Marquis to the officers. Adeline shrieked, held faster by Theodore's arm, and entreated the men not to part them.

"Force only shall effect it," said Theodore, as he looked round for some instrument of defence, but he could see none, and in the same moment they surrounded and seized him.

"Dread everything from my vengeance," said the Marquis to Theodore, as he caught the hand of Adeline, who had lost all power of resistance, and was scarcely sensible of what passed ; "dread everything from my vengeance ; you know you have deserved it."

"I defy your vengeance," cried Theodore, "and dread only the pangs of conscience, which your power cannot inflict upon me, though your vices condemn you to its tortures."

"Take him instantly from the room, and see that he is strongly fettered," said the Marquis ; "he shall soon know what a criminal, who adds insolence to guilt, may suffer."

Theodore, exclaiming, "Oh Adeline! farewell!" was now forced out of the room ; while Adeline, whose torpid senses were roused by his voice and his last looks, fell at the feet of the Marquis, and with tears of agony implored compassion for Theodore ; but her pleadings for his rival seemed only to irritate the pride and exasperate the hatred of the Marquis. He denounced vengeance on his head, and imprecations too dreadful for the spirits of Adeline, whom he compelled to rise ; and then, endeavouring to stifle the emotions of rage which the presence of Theodore had excited, he began to address her with his usual expressions of admiration.

The wretched Adeline, who, regardless of what he said, still continued to plead for her unhappy lover, was at length alarmed by the returning rage which the countenance of the Marquis expressed, and, exerting all her remaining strength, she sprang from his grasp towards the door of the room ; but he seized her hand before she could reach it, and, regardless of her shrieks, bringing her back to her chair, was going to speak, when voices were heard in the passage, and immediately the landlord and his wife, whom Adeline's cries had alarmed, entered the apartment. The Marquis, turning furiously to them, demanded what they wanted ; but not waiting for their answer, he bade them attend him, and quitting the room she heard the door locked upon her.

Adeline now ran to the windows, which were unfastened, and opened into the inn-yard. Without, all was dark and silent. She called aloud for help, but no person appeared, and the windows were so high, that it was impossible to escape unassisted. She walked about the room in an agony of terror and distress, now stopping to listen, and fancying she heard voices disputing below, and now quickening her steps, as suspense increased the agitation of her mind.

She had continued in this state for near half an hour, when she suddenly heard a violent noise in the lower part of the house, which increased till all was uproar and confusion. People passed quickly through the passages, and doors were frequently opened and shut. She called, but received no answer. It immediately occurred to her that Theodore, having heard her screams, had attempted to come to her assistance, and that the bustle had been occasioned by the opposition of the officers. Knowing their fierceness and cruelty, she was seized with fearful apprehensions for the life of Theodore.

A confused uproar of voices now sounded from below, and the screams of women convinced her there was fighting; she even thought she heard the clashing of swords; the image of Theodore, dying by the hands of the Marquis, now rose to her imagination, and the terrors of suspense became almost insupportable. She made a desperate effort to force the door, and again call for help; but her trembling hands were powerless, and every person in the house seemed to be too much engaged even to hear her. A loud shriek now pierced her ears, and amidst the tumult that followed, she clearly distinguished deep groans. This confirmation of her fears deprived her of all her remaining spirits, and growing faint, she sank almost lifeless into a chair near the door. The uproar gradually subsided till all was still, but nobody returned to her. Soon after she heard voices in the yard, but she had no power to walk across the room even to ask the questions she wished, yet feared, to have answered.

About a quarter of an hour elapsed when the door was unlocked, and the hostess appeared with a countenance as pale as death.

"For God's sake," said Adeline, "tell me what has happened? Is he wounded? Is he killed?"

"He is not dead, ma'amselle, but——"

"He is dying then? Tell me where he is —let me go!"

"Stop, ma'amselle," cried the hostess, "you are to stay here; I only want the hartshorn out of the cupboard there."

Adeline tried to escape by the door, but the hostess pushing her aside, locked it, and went downstairs.

Adeline's distress now entirely overcame her, and she sat down motionless, and scarcely conscious that she existed, till roused by the sound of footsteps near the door, which was again opened, and three men whom she knew to be the Marquis's servants entered. She had sufficient recollection to repeat the questions she asked the landlady, but they answered only that she must come with them, and that a chaise was waiting for her at the door. Still she urged her questions.

"Tell me if he lives," cried she.

"Yes, ma'amselle, he is alive, but he is terribly wounded, and the surgeon is just come to him."

As they spoke they hurried her along the passage, and, without noticing her entreaties and supplications to know whither she was going, they had reached the foot of the stairs, when her cries brought several people to the door. To these the hostess related that the lady was the wife of the gentleman just arrived, who had overtaken her in her flight with a gallant; an account which the Marquis's servants corroborated. "'Tis the gentleman who has just fought the duel," added the hostess, "and it was on her account."

Adeline, partly disdaining to take any notice of this artful story, and partly from her desire to know the particulars of what had happened, contented herself with repeating her inquiries; to which one of the spectators at last replied, that the gentleman was desperately wounded. The Marquis's people would now have hurried her into the chaise, but she sank lifeless in their arms, and her condition so much interested the humanity of the spectators that, notwithstanding their belief of what had been said, they opposed the efforts made to carry her, senseless as she was, into the carriage.

She was at length taken into a room, and, by proper application, restored to her senses. There she so earnestly besought an explanation of what had happened, that the hostess acquainted her with some particulars of the late rencounter.

"When the gentleman that was ill heard your screams, madam," said she, "he became quite outrageous, as they tell me, and nothing could pacify him. The Marquis—for they say he is a Marquis, but you know best—was then in the room with my husband and I, and when he heard the uproar he went down to see what was the matter; and when he came into the room where the Captain was he found him struggling with the sergeant. Then the Captain was more outrageous than ever, and notwithstanding he had one leg chained, and no sword, he contrived to get the sergeant's cutlass out of the scabbard and immediately flew at the Marquis, and wounded him desperately; upon which he was secured."

"It is the Marquis then who is wounded," said Adeline; "the other gentleman is not hurt?"

"No, not he," replied the hostess, "but he will smart for it by-and-by, for the Marquis swears he will do for him."

Adeline for a moment forgot all her misfortunes and all her danger in thankfulness for the immediate escape of Theodore; and she was proceeding to make some further inquiries concerning him, when the Marquis's servants entered the room, and declared they could wait no longer. Adeline, now awakened to a sense of the evils with which she was threatened, endeavoured to win the pity of the hostess, who, however, was, or affected to be, convinced of the truth of the Marquis's story, and therefore insensible to all she could urge. Again she addressed his servants, but in vain; they would neither suffer her to remain longer at the inn, nor inform her whither she was going ; but, in presence of several persons, already prejudiced by the injurious assertions of the hostess, Adeline was hurried into the chaise, and her conductors mounting their horses, the whole party was very soon beyond the village.

Thus ended Adeline's share of an adventure, begun with a prospect not only of security, but of happiness ; an adventure which had attached her more closely to Theodore, and shown him to be more worthy of her love ; but which, at the same time, had distressed her by new disappointment, produced the imprisonment of her generous and now adored lover, and delivered both himself and her into the power of a rival, irritated by delay, contempt, and opposition.

CHAPTER XII.

Nor sea, nor shade, nor shield, nor rock, nor cave,
Nor silent deserts, nor the sullen grave,
Where flame-ey'd Fury means to frown—can save.

THE surgeon of the place having examined the Marquis's wound, gave him an immediate opinion upon it, and ordered that he should be put to bed ; but the Marquis, ill as he was, had scarcely any other apprehension than that of losing Adeline, and declared he should be able to begin his journey in a few hours. With this intention, he had begun to give orders for keeping horses in readiness, when the surgeon persisting most seriously, and even passionately, to exclaim that his life would be the sacrifice of his rashness, he was carried to a bed-chamber, where his valet alone was permitted to attend him.

This man, the convenient confidant of all his intrigues, had been the chief instrument in assisting his designs concerning Adeline, and was, indeed, the very person who had brought her to the Marquis's villa on the borders of the forest. To him the Marquis gave his further directions concerning her ; and, foreseeing the inconvenience, as well as the danger, of detaining her at the inn, he had ordered him, with several other servants, to carry her away immediately in a hired carriage. The valet having gone to execute his orders, the Marquis was left to his own reflections, and to the violence of contending passions.

The reproaches and continued opposition of Theodore, the favoured lover of Adeline, had exasperated his pride and roused all his malice. He could not for a moment consider this opposition, which was in some respects successful, without feeling an excess of indignation and inveteracy, such as the prospect of a speedy revenge could alone enable him to support.

When he had discovered Adeline's escape from the villa, his surprise equalled his disappointment ; and, after exhausting the paroxysm of his rage upon his domestics, he despatched them all different ways in pursuit of her, going himself to the abbey, in the faint hope that, destitute as she was of other succour, she might have fled thither. La Motte, however, being as much surprised as himself, and ignorant of the route which Adeline had taken, he returned to the villa, impatient of intelligence, and found some of his servants arrived, without any news of Adeline, and those who came afterwards were as successless as the first.

A few days after, a letter from the lieutenant-colonel of the regiment informed him that Theodore had quitted his company, and had been for some time absent, nobody knew where. This information, confirming a suspicion, which had frequently occurred to him, that Theodore had been, by some means or other, instrumental in the escape of Adeline, all his other passions became, for a time, subservient in his revenge, and he gave orders for the immediate pursuit and apprehension of Theodore ; but Theodore, in the meantime, had been overtaken and secured.

It was in consequence of having formerly observed the growing partiality between him and Adeline, and of intelligence received from La Motte, who had noticed their interview in the forest, that the Marquis had resolved to remove a rival so dangerous to his love and so likely to be informed of his designs. He had therefore told Theodore, in a manner as plausible as he could, that it would be necessary for him to join the regiment—a notice which affected him only as it related to Adeline, and which seemed the less extraordinary as he had already been at the villa a longer time than was usual with the officers invited by the Marquis. Theodore very well knew the character of the Marquis, and had accepted his invitation rather from an unwillingness to show any disrespect to his colonel by a refusal than from a sanguine expectation of pleasure.

From the men who had apprehended Theodore the Marquis received the information which had enabled him to pursue and recover Adeline ; but though he had now effected this, he was internally a prey to the corrosive effects of disappointed passion and exasperated pride. The anguish of his wound was almost forgotten in that of his mind, and every pang he felt seemed to increase his thirst of revenge, and to recoil with new torture upon his heart. While he was in this state he heard the voice of the innocent Adeline imploring protection, but her cries excited in him neither pity nor remorse ; and when, soon after, the carriage drove away, and he was certain both that she was secured and that Theodore was wretched, he seemed to feel some cessation of mental agony.

Theodore, indeed, did suffer all that a virtuous mind, labouring under oppression so severe, could feel ; but he was, at least, free from those inveterate and malignant passions which tore the bosom of the Marquis, and which inflict upon the possessor a punishment more severe than any they can prompt him to imagine for another. What indignation he might feel towards the Marquis was at this time secondary to his anxiety for Adeline. His captivity was painful, as it prevented his seeking a just and honourable revenge ; but it was dreadful, as it withheld him from attempting the rescue of her whom he loved more than life.

When he heard the wheels of the carriage that contained her drive off, he felt an agony of despair which almost overcame his reason. Even the stern hearts of the soldiers who attended him were not wholly insensible to his wretchedness, and by venturing to blame the conduct of the Marquis they endeavoured to console their prisoner. The physician, who had just arrived, entered the room during this paroxysm of his distress, and both feeling and expressing much concern at his condition, inquired with strong surprise why he had been thus precipitately removed to a room so very unfit for his reception.

Theodore explained to him the reason of this, of the distress he suffered, and of the chains by which he was disgraced ; and perceiving the physician listened to him with attention and compassion, he was anxious to acquaint him with some further particulars, for which purpose he desired the soldiers to leave the room. The men, complying with his request, stationed themselves on the outside of the door.

He then related all the particulars of the late transaction, and of his connection with the Marquis. The physician attended to his narrative with deep concern, and his countenance frequently expressed strong agitation. When Theodore concluded, he remained for some time silent and lost in thought, when, awaking from his reverie, he said :

" I fear your situation is desperate. The character of the Marquis is too well known to suffer him either to be loved or respected ; from such a man you have nothing to hope, for he has scarcely anything to fear. I wish it was in my power to serve you, but I see no possibility of it."

" Alas !" said Theodore, " my situation is indeed desperate, and—for that suffering angel "—deep sobs interrupted his voice, and the violence of his agitation would not allow him to proceed.

The physician could only express the sympathy he felt for his distress and entreat him to be more calm, when a servant entered the room from the Marquis, who desired to see the physician immediately. After some time he said he would attend the Marquis ; and

having endeavoured to attain a degree of composure which he found it difficult to assume, he wrung the hand of Theodore and quitted the room, promising to return before he left the house.

He found the Marquis much agitated both in body and mind, and rather more apprehensive for the consequences of the wound than he had expected. His anxiety for Theodore now suggested a plan by the execution of which he hoped he might be able to serve him. Having felt his patient's pulse, and asked some questions, he assumed a serious look, when the Marquis, who watched every turn of his countenance, desired he would, without hesitation, speak his opinion.

" I am sorry to alarm you, my Lord, but here is some reason for apprehension. How long is it since you received the wound ?"

" Good God, there is danger then !" cried the Marquis, adding some bitter execrations against Theodore.

" There certainly is danger," replied the physician ; a few hours may enable me to determine its degree."

" A few hours, sir !" interrupted the Marquis. " A few hours !"

The physician entreated him to be more calm.

" Confusion !" cried the Marquis. " A man in health may, with great composure, entreat a dying man to be calm. Theodore will be broken upon the wheel for it, however."

" You mistake me, sir," said the physician ; " if I believed you a dying man, or, indeed, very near death, I should not have spoken as I did. But it is of consequence I should know how long the wound has been inflicted."

The Marquis's terrors now began to subside, and he gave a circumstantial account of the affray with Theodore, representing that he had been basely used in an affair where his own conduct had been perfectly just and humane. The physician heard this relation with great coolness, and when it concluded—without making any comment upon it—told the Marquis he would prescribe a medicine which he wished him to take immediately.

The Marquis, again alarmed by the gravity of his manner, entreated he would declare most seriously whether he thought him in immediate danger. The physician hesitated, and the anxiety of the Marquis increased : " It is of consequence," said he, " that I should know my exact situation."

The physician then said that if he had any worldly affairs to settle it would be as well to attend to them, for it was impossible to say what might be the event.

He then turned the discourse, and said he had just been with the young officer under arrest, who, he hoped, would not be removed at present, as such a procedure must endanger his life. The Marquis uttered a dreadful oath, and, cursing Theodore for having brought him to his present condition, said he should depart with the guard that very night. Against the cruelty of this sentence the physician ventured to expostulate ; and endeavouring to awaken the Marquis to a sense of humanity, pleaded earnestly for Theodore. But these entreaties and arguments seemed, by displaying to the Marquis a part of his own character, to rouse his resentment and rekindle all the violence of his passions.

The physician at length withdrew in despondency, after promising, at the Marquis's request, not to leave the inn. He had hoped by exaggerating his danger to obtain some advantages, both for Adeline and Theodore ; but the plan had quite a contrary effect, for the apprehension of death—so dreadful to the guilty mind of the Marquis—instead of awakening penitence, increased his desire of vengeance against the man who had reduced him to such a situation. He determined to have Adeline conveyed where Theodore, should he by any accident escape, could never obtain her ; and thus secure to himself, at least, some means of revenge. He knew, however, that when Theodore was once conveyed to his regiment, his destruction was certain ; for should he even be acquitted of the intention of deserting, he would be condemned for having assaulted his superior officer.

The physician returned to the room where Theodore was confined. The violence of his distress was now subsided into a stern despair, more dreadful than the vehemence which had lately possessed him. The guard, in compliance with his request, having left the room, the physician repeated to him some part of his conversation with the Marquis. Theodore, after expressing his thanks, said he had nothing more to hope. For himself he felt little; it was for his family and for Adeline he suffered. He inquired what route she had taken, and though he had no prospect of deriving advantage from the information, desired the physician to assist him in obtaining it. But the landlord and his wife either were, or affected to be, ignorant of the matter ; and it was in vain to apply to any other person.

The sergeant now entered with orders from the Marquis for the immediate departure of Theodore, who heard the message with composure, though the physician could not help expressing his indignation at this precipitate removal, and his dread of the consequences that might attend it. Theodore had scarcely time to declare his gratitude for the kindness of his valuable friend before the soldiers entered the room to conduct him to the carriage n waiting. As he bade him farewell, Theodore slipped his purse into his hand, and, turning abruptly away, told the soldiers to lead on ; but the physician stopped him, and refused the present with such warmth that he was compelled to resume it. He then wrung the hand of his new friend, and, being unable to speak, hurried away. The whole party immediately set off, and the unhappy Theodore was left to the remembrance of his past hopes and sufferings, to his anxiety for the fate of Adeline, the contemplation of his present wretchedness, and the apprehension of what might be reserved for him in future. For himself he saw nothing but destruction ; and was only relieved from total despair by a feeble hope that she whom he loved better than himself might one time enjoy that happiness of which he did not venture to look for a participation.

CHAPTER XIII.

Have you the heart ? When your head did but ache,
I knit my handkercher about your brows,
And with my hand at midnight held your head ;
And, like the watchful minutes to the hour,
Still and anon cheer'd up the heavy time.
SHAKSPEARE.

If the midnight bell
Did with his iron tongue, and brazen mouth,
Sound on unto the drowsy race of night ;
If this same were a churchyard where we stand,
And thou possessed with a thousand wrongs ;
Or if that surly spirit, Melancholy,
Had bak'd thy blood and made it heavy-thick,
Then, in despite of brooded watchful day,
I would into thy bosom pour my thoughts.
SHAKSPEARE.

MEANWHILE the persecuted Adeline continued to travel, with little interruption, all night. Her mind suffered such a tumult of grief, regret, despair, and terror, that she could not be said to think. The Marquis's valet, who had placed himself in the chaise with her, at first seemed inclined to talk ; but her inattention soon silenced him, and left her to the indulgence of her own misery.

They seemed to travel through obscure lanes and by-ways, along which the carriage drove as furiously as the darkness would permit. When the dawn appeared she perceived herself on the borders of a forest, and renewed her entreaties to know whither she was going. The man replied "He had no orders to tell, but she would soon see." Adeline, who had hitherto supposed they were carrying her to the villa, now began to doubt it ; and as every place appeared less terrible to her imagination than that, her despair began to abate, and she thought only of the devoted Theodore, whom she knew to be the victim of malice and revenge.

They now entered upon the forest, and it occurred to her that she was going to the abbey ; for though she had no remembrance of the scenery through which she passed, it was not the less probable that this was the forest of Fontanville, whose boundaries were much too extensive to have come within the circle of her former walks. This conjecture revived a terror little inferior to that occasioned by the idea of going to the villa, for at the abbey she would be equally in the power of the Marquis, and also in that of her enemy La Motte. Her mind revolted at the picture her fancy drew, and as the carriage moved under the shades, she threw from the window a look of eager inquiry for some object which might confirm or destroy her present surmise. She did not long look before an opening in the forest showed her the distant towers of the abbey. "I am indeed lost then!" said she, bursting into tears.

They were soon at the foot of the lawn, and Peter was seen running to open the gate at which the carriage stopped. When he saw Adeline he looked surprised and made an effort to speak; but the chaise now drove up to the abbey, where, at the door of the hall, La Motte himself appeared. As he advanced to take her from the carriage a universal trembling seized her; it was with the utmost difficulty she supported herself, and for some moments she neither observed his countenance nor heard his voice. He offered his arm to assist her into the abbey, which she at first refused, but having tottered a few paces was obliged to accept. They then entered the vaulted room, where, sinking into a chair, a flood of tears came to her relief. La Motte did not interrupt the silence, which continued for some time, but paced the room in seeming agitation. When Adeline was sufficiently recovered to notice external objects, she observed his countenance, and there read the tumult of his soul, while he was struggling to assume a firmness which his better feelings opposed.

La Motte now took her hand and would have led her from the room, but she stopped, and with a kind of desperate courage made an effort to engage him to pity and to save her. He interrupted her: "It is not in my power," said he, in a voice of emotion; "I am not master of myself or my conduct; inquire no further—it is sufficient for you to know that I pity you; more I cannot do." He gave her no time to reply, but taking her hand led her to the stairs of the tower, and from thence to the chamber she had formerly occupied.

"Here you must remain for the present," said he, "in a confinement which is, perhaps, almost as involuntary on my part as it can be on yours. I am willing to render it as easy as possible, and have therefore ordered some books to be brought you."

Adeline made an effort to speak, but he hurried from the room, seemingly ashamed of the part he had undertaken, and unwilling to trust himself with her tears. She heard the door of the chamber locked, and then, looking towards the windows, perceived they were secured; the door that led to the other apartments was also fastened. Such preparation for security shocked her, and hopeless as she had long believed herself, she now perceived her mind sink deeper in despair. When the tears she shed had somewhat relieved her, and her thoughts could turn from the subject of her immediate concern, she was thankful for the total seclusion allotted her, since it would spare her the pain she must feel in the presence of Monsieur and Madame La Motte, and allow the unrestrained indulgence of her own sorrow and reflection—reflection which, however distressing, was preferable to the agony inflicted on the mind when, agitated by care and fear, it is obliged to assume an appearance of tranquillity.

In about a quarter of an hour her chamber door was unlocked, and Annette appeared with refreshments and books; she expressed satisfaction at seeing Adeline again, but seemed fearful of speaking, knowing, probably, that it was contrary to the orders of La Motte, who, she said, was waiting at the bottom of the stairs. When Annette was gone, Adeline took some refreshment, which was indeed necessary, for she had tasted nothing since she had left the inn. She was pleased, but not surprised, that Madame La Motte did not appear, who, it was evident, shunned her from a consciousness of her own ungenerous conduct—a consciousness which offered some presumption that she was not wholly unfriendly to her. She reflected upon the words of La Motte, "I am not master of myself, or of my conduct," and though they afforded her no hope, she derived some comfort, poor as it was, from the belief that he pitied her. After some time spent in miserable reflection and various conjectures, her long-agitated spirits seemed to demand repose, and she laid down to sleep.

Adeline slept quietly for several hours, and awoke with a mind refreshed and tranquillised. To prolong this temporary peace, and to prevent, therefore, the intrusion of her own thoughts, she examined the books La Motte had sent her; among these she found some that, in happier times, had elevated her mind and interested her heart; their effect was now weakened, they were still, however, able to soften for a time the sense of her misfortunes.

But this Lethean medicine to such a mind was but of temporary effect; the entrance of La Motte dissolved the illusions of the page, and awakened her to a sense of her situation. He came with food, and having placed it on the table, left the room without speaking. Again she endeavoured to read, but his appearance had broken the enchantment; bitter reflections returned to her mind, and brought with it the image of Theodore—of Theodore lost to her for ever!

La Motte meanwhile experienced all the terrors that could be inflicted by a conscience not wholly hardened to guilt. He had been led on by passion to dissipation, and from dissipation to vice ; but having once touched the borders of infamy, the progressive steps followed each other fast, and he now saw himself the pander of a villain, and the betrayer of an innocent girl, whom every plea of justice and humanity called upon him to protect. He contemplated his picture—he shrank from it, but he could change its deformity only by an effort too nobly daring for a man already effeminated by habitual indulgence. He viewed the dangerous labyrinth into which he was led, and perceived, as if for the first time, the progression of his guilt ; from this labyrinth he weakly imagined further guilt could alone extricate him. Instead of employing his mind upon the means of saving Adeline from destruction, and himself from being instrumental to it, he endeavoured only to lull the pangs of conscience, and to persuade himself into a belief that he must proceed in the course he had begun. He knew himself to be in the power of the Marquis, and he dreaded that power more than the sure, though distant, punishment that waits upon guilt. The honour of Adeline, and quiet of his own conscience, he consented to barter for a few years of existence.

He was ignorant of the present illness of the Marquis, or he would have perceived that there was a chance of escaping the threatened punishment at a price less enormous than infamy, and would, perhaps, have endeavoured to save Adeline and himself by flight. But the Marquis, foreseeing the possibility of this, had ordered his servants carefully to conceal the circumstance which detained him, and to acquaint La Motte that he should be at the abbey in a few days, at the same time directing his valet to await him there. Adeline, as he expected, had neither inclination nor opportunity to mention it, and thus La Motte remained ignorant of the circumstances which might have preserved him from further guilt, and Adeline from misery.

Most unwillingly had La Motte acquainted his wife with the action which had made him absolutely dependent on the will of the Marquis, but the perturbation of his mind partly betrayed him ; frequently in his sleep he muttered incoherent sentences, and frequently would start from slumber, and call, in passionate language, upon Adeline. These instances of a disturbed mind had alarmed and terrified Madame La Motte, who watched while he slept, and soon gathered from his words a confused idea of the Marquis's designs.

She hinted her suspicions to La Motte, who reproved her for having entertained them ; but his manner, instead of repressing, increased her fears for Adeline ; fears which the conduct of the Marquis soon confirmed. On the night that he slept at the abbey, it had

occurred to her that whatever scheme was in agitation would then most probably be discussed, and anxiety for Adeline made her stoop to a meanness which, in other circumstances, would have been despicable. She quitted her room, and, concealing herself in an apartment adjoining that in which she had left the Marquis and her husband, listened to their discourse. It turned upon the subject she had expected, and disclosed to her the full extent of their designs. Terrified for Adeline, and shocked at the guilty weakness of La Motte, she was for some time incapable of thinking, or determining how to proceed. She knew her husband to be under great obligations to the Marquis, whose territory thus afforded him a shelter from the world, and that it was in the power of the former to betray him into the hands of his enemies. She believed also that the Marquis would do this if provoked, yet she thought, upon such an occasion, La Motte might find some way of appeasing the Marquis, without subjecting himself to dishonour. After some further reflection, her mind became more composed, and she returned to the chamber, where La Motte soon followed. Her spirits, however, were not then in a state to encounter either his displeasure or his opposition, which she had too much reason to expect whenever she should mention the subject of her concern, and she, therefore, resolved not to notice it till the morrow.

On the morrow she told La Motte all he uttered in his dreams, and mentioned other circumstances which convinced him it was in vain any longer to deny the truth of her apprehensions. She then represented to him how possible it was to avoid the infamy into which he was about to plunge, by quitting the territories of the Marquis ; and pleaded so warmly for Adeline that La Motte, in sullen silence, appeared to meditate upon the plan. His thoughts were, however, very differently engaged. He was conscious of having deserved from the Marquis a severe punishment, and knew that if he exasperated him by refusing to acquiesce with his wishes, he had little to expect from flight, for the eye of justice and revenge would pursue him with indefatigable research.

La Motte meditated how to break this to his wife ; for he perceived that there was no other method of counteracting her virtuous compassion for Adeline, and the dangerous consequences to be expected from it, than by opposing it with terror for his safety, and this could be done only by showing her the extent of the evils that must attend the revenge of the Marquis. Vice had not yet so entirely darkened his conscience but that the blush of shame stained his cheek, and his tongue faltered, when he would have told his guilt. At length, finding it impossible to mention particulars, he told her that, on account of an affair which no entreaties should ever induce him to explain, his life was in the power of the Marquis. "You see the alternative," said he; "take your choice of evils, and, if you can, tell Adeline of her danger, and sacrifice my life to save her from a situation which many would be ambitious to obtain."

Madame La Motte, condemned to the horrible alternative of permitting the seduction of innocence or of dooming her husband to destruction, suffered a distraction of thought which defied all control. Perceiving, however, that an opposition to the designs of the Marquis would ruin La Motte, and avail Adeline little, she determined to yield and endure in silence.

At the time when Adeline was planning her escape from the abbey, the significant looks of Peter had led La Motte to suspect the truth, and to watch them more closely. He had seen them separate in the hall in apparent confusion, and had afterwards observed them conversing together in the cloisters. Circumstances so unusual left him not a doubt that Adeline had discovered her danger, and was concerting with Peter some means of escape. Affecting, therefore, to be informed of the whole affair, he charged Peter with treachery towards himself, and threatened him with the vengeance of the Marquis if he did not disclose all he knew. The menace intimidated Peter, and, supposing that all chance of assisting Adeline was gone, he made a detailed confession, and promised not to acquaint Adeline with the discovery of the scheme. In this promise he was seconded by inclination; for he feared to meet the displeasure which Adeline, believing he had betrayed her, might express.

On the evening of the day on which Adeline's intended escape was discovered, the Marquis designed to come to the abbey, and it had been agreed that he should then take Adeline to his villa. La Motte had immediately perceived the advantage of permitting Adeline to repair, in the belief of being undiscovered, to the tomb. It would prevent much disturbance and opposition, and spare himself the pain he must feel in her presence, when she should know that he had betrayed her. A servant of the Marquis might go at the appointed hour to the tomb, and, wrapt in the disguise of night, might take her quietly thence, in the character of Peter. Thus without resistance she would be carried to the villa, nor discover her mistake till it was too late to prevent its consequence.

When the Marquis did arrive, La Motte, who was not so far intoxicated by what he had drank as to forget his prudence, told him of what had happened and what he had planned; and the Marquis approving it, his servant was made acquainted with the signal which betrayed Adeline to his power.

A deep consciousness of the unworthy neutrality she had observed in Adeline's concerns made Madame La Motte anxiously avoid seeing her, now that she was again in the abbey. Adeline understood this conduct, and rejoiced that she was spared the anguish of meeting her as an enemy whom she had once loved as a friend. Several days now passed in solitude, in miserable retrospection and dreadful expectation. The perilous situation of Theodore was almost the constant subject of her thoughts. Often did she breathe an anxious wish for his safety, and look round the sphere of possibility in search of hope. But hope had almost left the horizon of her prospect; and when it did appear, it hovered only over the death of the Marquis, whose vengeance threatened most certain destruction.

The Marquis, meanwhile, lay at the inn at Baux, in a state of very doubtful recovery. The physician and surgeon, neither of whom he would dismiss, nor suffer to leave the village, proceeded upon contrary principles, and the good effect of what one prescribed was frequently counteracted by the injudicious treatment of the other. Humanity alone prevailed on the physician to continue his attendance. The malady of the Marquis was also heightened by the impatience of his temper, the terrors of death, and the irritation of his passions. One moment he believed himself dying, another he could scarcely be prevented from attempting to follow Adeline to the abbey. So various were the fluctuations of his mind, and so rapid the schemes that succeeded each other, that his passions were in a continual state of conflict. The physician attempted to convince him that his recovery greatly depended upon tranquillity, and to prevail upon him to attempt, at least, some command of his feelings; but he was soon silenced, in hopeless disgust, by the impatient answers of the Marquis.

At length the servant who had carried off Adeline returned, and the Marquis, having ordered him into his chamber, asked so many questions in a breath, that the man knew not which to answer. He pulled a folded paper from his pocket, which he said had been dropped in the chaise by Mademoiselle Adeline, and as he thought his lordship would like to see it, he had taken care of it. The Marquis stretched forth his hand with eagerness, and received a note addressed to Theodore. On perceiving the superscription, the agitation of jealous rage for a moment overcame him, and he held it in his hand unable to open it.

He, however, broke the seal, and found it to be a note of inquiry, written by Adeline to Theodore during his illness, and which, by some accident, she had been prevented from sending him. The solicitude it expressed for his recovery stung the soul of the

Marquis, and drew from him a comparison of her feelings on the illness of his rival and that of himself. "She could be solicitous for his recovery," said he, "but not for mine—she only dreads it." As if willing to prolong the pain this little billet had excited, he then read it again. Again he cursed his fate, and execrated his rival, giving himself up, as usual, to the transports of his passion. He was going to throw it from him, when his eyes caught the seal, and he looked earnestly at it. His anger seemed now to have subsided; he deposited the note carefully in his pocket-book, and was, for some time, lost in thought.

After many days of hopes and fears, the strength of his constitution overcame his illness, and he was well enough to write several letters, one of which he immediately sent off to prepare La Motte for his reception. The same policy which had prompted him to conceal his illness from La Motte now urged him to say, what he knew would not happen, that he should reach the abbey on the day after his servant. He repeated his injunction that Adeline should be strictly guarded, and renewed his promises of reward for the future services of La Motte.

La Motte, to whom each succeeding day had brought a new surprise and perplexity concerning the absence of the Marquis, received this notice with uneasiness, for he had began to hope that the Marquis had altered his intentions concerning Adeline, being either engaged in some new adventure, or obliged to visit his estates in some distant province; he would have been willing thus to have got rid of an affair which was to reflect so much dishonour on himself.

This hope now vanished, and he directed Madame to prepare for the reception of the Marquis. Adeline passed these days in a state of suspense, which was now cheered by hope, and now darkened by despair. This delay, so much beyond her expectation, seemed to prove that the illness of the Marquis was dangerous; and when she looked forward to the consequences of his recovery, she could not be sorry that it was so. So odious was the idea of him to her mind, that she would not suffer her lips to utter his name,' nor make the inquiry of Annette which was of such consequence to her peace.

It was about a week after the receipt of the Marquis's letter, that Adeline one day saw from her window a party of horsemen enter the avenue, and knew them to be the Marquis and his attendants. She retired from the window in a state of mind not to be described, and, sinking in a chair, was for some time scarcely conscious of the objects around her. When she had recovered from the first terror which his ap-

pearance excited, she again tottered to the window; the party was not in sight, but she heard the tramping of horses, and knew that the Marquis had wound round to the great gate of the abbey. She addressed herself to heaven for support and protection, and, her mind being now somewhat composed, sat down to wait the event.

La Motte received the Marquis with expressions of surprise at his long absence, and the latter, merely saying he had been detained by illness, proceeded to inquire for Adeline. He was told she was in her chamber, from whence she might be summoned if he wished to see her. The Marquis hesitated, and at length excused himself, but desired she might be strictly watched.

"Perhaps, my lord," said La Motte, smiling, "Adeline's obstinacy has been too powerful for your passion; you seem less interested concerning her than formerly."

"Oh, by no means!" replied the Marquis; "she interests me, if possible, more than ever; so much, indeed, that I cannot have her too closely guarded; and I therefore beg, La Motte, that you will suffer nobody to attend her but when you can observe them yourself. Is the room where she is confined sufficiently secure?"

La Motte assured him it was; but at the same time expressed his wish that she was removed to the villa. "If by any means," said he, "she should contrive to escape, I know what I must expect from your displeasure; and this reflection keeps my mind in continual anxiety."

"This removal cannot be at present," said the Marquis; "she is safer here, and you do wrong to disturb yourself with any apprehension of her escape, if her chamber is really so secure as you represent it."

"I can have no motive for deceiving you, my lord, on this point."

"I do not suspect you of any," said the Marquis; "guard her carefully, and trust me she will not escape. I can rely upon my valet, and if you wish it he shall remain here."

La Motte thought there could be no occasion for him, and it was agreed that the man should go home.

The Marquis, after remaining about half-an-hour in conversation with La Motte, left the abbey, and Adeline saw him depart with a mixture of surprise and thankfulness that almost overcame her. She had waited in momentary expectation of being summoned to appear, and had been endeavouring to arm herself with resolution to support his presence. She had listened to every voice that sounded from below, and at every step that crossed the passage her heart had palpitated with dread lest it should be La Motte coming to lead her to the Marquis. This state of suffering had been prolonged almost beyond her power of enduring it when she heard voices under her window, and rising, saw the Marquis ride away. After giving utterance to the joy and thankfulness that swelled her heart, she endeavoured to account for this circumstance, which, considering what had passed, was certainly very strange. It appeared, indeed, wholly inexplicable, and after much fruitless inquiry she quitted the subject, endeavouring to persuade herself that it could portend only good.

The time of La Motte's usual visitation now drew near, and Adeline expected it in the trembling hope of hearing that the Marquis had ceased his persecution ; but he was, as usual, sullen and silent, and it was not till he was about to quit the room that Adeline had the courage to inquire when the Marquis was expected again. La Motte, opening the door to depart, replied, "On the following day," and Adeline, whom fear and delicacy embarrassed, saw she could obtain no intelligence of Theodore but by a direct question. She looked earnestly, as if she would have spoken, and La Motte stopped, but she blushed and was still silent, till upon his again attempting to leave the room she faintly called him back.

"I would ask," said she, "after that unfortunate chevalier who has incurred the resentment of the Marquis by endeavouring to serve me. Has the Marquis mentioned him ? "

"He has," replied La Motte ; "and your indifference towards the Marquis is now fully explained."

"Since I must feel resentment towards those who injure me," said Adeline, "I may surely be allowed to be grateful to those who serve me ! Had the Marquis deserved my esteem he would probably have possessed it."

"Well, well," said La Motte ; "this young hero, this Theodore, who, it seems, has been brave enough to lift his arm against his colonel, is taken care of, and, I doubt not, will soon be sensible of the value of his quixotism."

Indignation, grief, and fear struggled in the bosom of Adeline ; she disdained to give La Motte an opportunity of again profaning the name of Theodore ; yet the uncertainty under which she laboured urged her to inquire whether the Marquis had heard of him since he left Baux.

"Yes," said La Motte, "He has been safely carried to his regiment, where he is confined till the Marquis can attend to appear against him."

Adeline had neither power nor inclination to inquire further, and La Motte quitting the chamber, she was left to the misery he had renewed. Though this information contained no new circumstance of misfortune (for she now heard confirmed what she had always expected), a weight of new sorrow seemed to fall upon her heart, and she perceived that she had unconsciously cherished a latent hope of Theodore's escape before he reached the place of his destination. All hope was now, however, gone ; he was suffering the miseries of a prison, and the tortures of apprehension both for his own life and her safety. She pictured to herself the dark damp dungeon where he lay loaded with chains, and pale with sickness and grief ; she heard him, in a voice that thrilled her heart, call upon her name, and raise his eyes to heaven in silent supplication ; she saw the anguish of his countenance, the tears that fell slowly on his cheek, and remembering, at the same time, the generous conduct that had brought him to this abyss of misery, and that it was for her sake he suffered, grief resolved itself into despair, her tears ceased to flow, and she sank silently into a state of dreadful torpor.

On the morrow the Marquis arrived and departed as before. Several days then elapsed and he did not appear, till one evening, as La Motte and his wife were in their usual sitting-room, he entered, and conversed for some time upon general subjects, from which, however, he by degrees fell into a reverie, and after a pause of silence, he rose and drew La Motte to the window.

"I would speak with you alone," said he, "if you are at leisure ; if not, some other time will do."

La Motte, assuring him he was perfectly so, would have conducted him to another room ; but the Marquis proposed a walk in the forest. They went out together, and when they had reached a solitary glade, where the spreading branches of the beech and oak deepened the shades of twilight, and threw a solemn obscurity around, the Marquis turned to La Motte and addressed him.

"Your condition, La Motte, is unhappy. This abbey is a melancholy residence for a man like you, fond of society, and like you also qualified to adorn it."

La Motte bowed.

"I wish it was in my power to restore you to the world," continued the Marquis ; "perhaps, if I knew the particulars of the affair which has driven you from it, I might perceive that my interest could effectually serve you. I think I have heard you hint it was an affair of honour."

La Motte was silent.

"I mean not to distress you, however, nor is it common curiosity that prompts this inquiry, but a sincere desire to befriend you. You have already informed me of some particulars of your misfortunes. I think the liberality of your temper led you into expenses which you afterwards endeavoured to retrieve by gaming."

"Yes, my lord," said La Motte ; "'tis true that I dissipated the greater part of an affluent fortune in luxurious indulgences, and that I afterwards took unworthy means to recover it ; but I wish to be spared upon this subject. I would, if possible, lose the remembrance of a transaction which must for ever stain my character, and the rigorous effect of which, I fear, it is not in your power, my lord, to soften."

"You may be mistaken on this point," replied the Marquis ; "my interest at court is by no means inconsiderable. Fear not from me any severity of censure ; I am not at all inclined to judge harshly of the faults of others. I well know how to allow for the emergency of circumstances, and I think, La Motte, you have hitherto found me your friend."

"I have, my lord."

"And when you recollect that I have forgiven a certain transaction of late date——"

"It is true, my lord, and allow me to say I have a just sense of your generosity. The transaction you allude to is by far the worst of my life, and what I have to relate cannot, therefore, lower me in your opinion. When I had dissipated the greater part of my property in habits of voluptuous pleasure, I had recourse to gaming to supply the means of continuing them. A run of good luck for some time enabled me to do this, and encouraging my most sanguine expectations, I continued in the same career of success. Soon after this a sudden turn of fortune destroyed my hopes, and reduced me to the most desperate extremity. In one night my money was lowered to the sum of two hundred louis. These I resolved to stake also, and with them my life, for it was my resolution not to survive their loss. Never shall I forget the horrors of that moment on which hung my fate, nor the deadly anguish that seized my heart when my last stake was gone. I stood for some time in a state of stupefaction, till, roused to a sense of misfortune, my passion made me pour forth execrations on my more fortunate rivals, and act all the frenzy of despair. During this paroxysm of madness, a gentleman, who had been a silent observer of all that passed, approached me. 'You are unfortunate sir,' said he. 'I need not be informed of that. sir,' I replied. 'You have, perhaps, been ill used,' resumed he. 'Yes, sir, I am ruined, and therefore it may be said, I am ill-used.' 'Do you know the people you have played with ?' 'No ; but I have met them in the first circles.' 'Then I am probably mistaken,' said he, and walked away. His last words roused me, and raised a hope that my money had not been fairly lost. Wishing for further information, I went in search of the gentleman, but he had left the room. I, however, stifled my transports, returned to the table where I had lost my money, placed myself behind the chair of one of the persons who had won it, and closely watched the game. For some time I saw nothing that could confirm my suspicions,

but was at length convinced they were just.

"When the game was ended I called one of my adversaries out of the room, and telling him what I had observed, threatened instantly to expose him if he did not restore my property. The man was for some time as positive as myself ; and, assuming the bravo, threatened me with chastisement for my scandalous assertions. I was not, however, in a state of mind to be frightened, and his manner served only to exasperate my temper, already sufficiently inflamed by misfortune. After retorting his threats, I was about to return to the apartment we had left, and expose what had passed, when, with an insidious smile and a softened voice, he begged I would favour him with a few moments' attention, and allow him to speak with the gentleman his partner. To the latter part of his request I hesitated, but, in the meantime, the gentleman himself entered the room. His partner related to him, in a few words, what had passed between us, and the terror that appeared in his countenance sufficiently declared his consciousness of guilt.

"They then drew aside, and remained a few minutes in conversation together, after which they approached me with an offer, as they phrased it, of a compromise. I declared, however, against anything of this kind, and swore nothing less than the whole sum I had lost should content me. 'Is it not possible, monsieur, that you may be offered something as advantageous as the whole ?' I did not understand their meaning ; but after they had continued for some time to give distant hints of the same sort, they proceeded to explain.

"Perceiving their characters to be wholly in my power, they wished to secure my interest to their party, and therefore informing me that they belonged to an association of persons who lived upon the folly and inexperience of others, they offered me a share in their concern. My fortunes were desperate, and the proposal now made me would not only produce an immediate supply, but enable me to return to those scenes of dissipated pleasure to which passion had at first, and long habit afterwards, attached me. I closed with the offer, and thus sank from dissipation into infamy."

La Motte paused as if the recollection of those times filled him with remorse. The Marquis understood his feelings.

"You judge too rigorously of yourself," said he ; "there are few persons, let their appearance of honesty be what it may. who, in such circumstances, would have acted better than you have done. Had I been in your situation I know not how I might have acted. That rigid virtue which shall condemn you may dignify itself with the appellation of wisdom, but I wish not to possess it ; let it still reside where it generally is to be found, in the cold bosoms of those who, wanting feeling to be men, dignify themselves with the title of philosophers. But pray proceed."

"Our success was for some time unlimited, for we held the wheel of fortune, and trusted not to her caprice. Thoughtless and voluptuous by nature, my expenses fully kept pace with my income. An unlucky discovery of the practices of our party was at length made by a young nobleman, which obliged us to act for some time with the utmost circumspection. It would be tedious to relate the particulars which made us at length so suspected, that the distant civility and cold reserve of our acquaintance rendered the frequenting public assemblies both painful and unprofitable. We turned our thoughts to other modes of obtaining money, and a swindling transaction, in which I engaged to a very large amount, soon compelled me to leave Paris. You know the rest, my lord."

La Motte was now silent, and the Marquis continued for some time musing.

"You perceive, my lord," at length resumed La Motte, "you perceive that my case is hopeless."

"It is bad, indeed, but not entirely hopeless. From my soul I pity you ; yet if you should return to the world, and incur the danger of prosecution, I think my interest with the minister might save you from any severe punishment. You seem, however, to have lost all relish for society, and perhaps do not wish to return to it."

"Oh ! my lord, can you doubt this ? But I am overcome with the excess of your goodness ; would to Heaven it were in my power to prove the gratitude it inspires !"

"Talk not of goodness," said the Marquis ; "I will not pretend that my desire of serving you is unalloyed by any degree of self-interest. I will not affect to be more than man, and trust me those who do are less. It is in your power to testify your gratitude, and bind me to your interest for ever."

He paused.

"Name but the means," cried La Motte, "name but the means, and if they are within the compass of possibility they shall be executed."

The Marquis was still silent.

"Do you doubt my sincerity, my lord, that you are yet silent ? Do you fear to repose a confidence in the man whom you have already loaded with obligations, who lives by your mercy, and almost by your means ?"

The Marquis looked earnestly at him, but did not speak.

"I have not deserved this of you, my lord ; speak, I entreat you."

"There are certain prejudices attached to the human mind," said the Marquis, in a slow and solemn voice, "which it requires all our wisdom to keep from interfering with our happiness ; certain set notions, acquired in infancy, and cherished involuntarily by age, which grow up and assume a gloss so plausible that few minds, in what is called a civilised country, can afterwards overcome them. Truth is often perverted by education. While the refined Europeans boast a standard of honour and a sublimity of virtue which often leads them from pleasure to misery, and from nature to error, the simple, uninformed American follows the impulse of his heart, and obeys the inspiration of wisdom."

The Marquis paused, and La Motte continued to listen in eager expectation.

"Nature, uncontaminated by false refinement," resumed the Marquis, "everywhere acts alike in the great occurrences of life. The Indian discovers his friend to be perfidious, and he kills him ; the wild Asiatic does the same ; the Turk, when ambition fires, or revenge provokes, gratifies his passion at the expense of life, and does not call it murder. Even the polished Italian, directed by jealousy, or tempted by a strong circumstance of advantage, draws his stiletto and accomplishes his purpose. It is the first proof of a superior mind to liberate itself from prejudices of country or of education. You are silent, La Motte ; are you not of my opinion ?"

"I am attending, my lord, to your *reasoning*."

"There are, I repeat it," said the Marquis, "people of minds so weak as to shrink from acts they have been accustomed to hold wrong, however advantageous. They never suffer themselves to be guided by circumstances, but fix for life upon a certain standard, from which they will on no account depart. Self-preservation is the great law of nature ; when a reptile hurts us, or an animal of prey threatens us, we think no further, but endeavour to annihilate it. When my life, or what may be essential to my life, requires the sacrifice of another, or even if some passion, wholly unconquerable, requires it, I should be a madman to hesitate. La Motte, I think I may confide in you—there are ways of doing certain things—you understand me. There are times, and circumstances, and opportunities—you comprehend my meaning."

"Explain yourself, my lord."

"Kind services that——in short, there are services which excite all our gratitude, and which we can never think repaid. It is in your power to place me in such a situation."

"Indeed, my lord ! name the means."

"I have already named them. This abbey well suits the purpose ; it is shut up from the eye of observation ; any transaction may be concealed within its walls ; the hour of midnight may witness the deed, and the morning shall not dawn to disclose it ; these woods tell no tales. Ah, La Motte ! am I right in trusting this business with you ? May I believe you are desirous of serving me, and of preserving yourself?"

The Marquis paused and looked steadfastly at La Motte, whose countenance was almost concealed by the gloom of evening.

"My lord, you may trust me in anything; explain yourself more fully."

"What security will you give me for your faithfulness?"

"My life, my lord; is it not already in your power?"

The Marquis hesitated, and then said:

"To-morrow, about this time, I shall return to the abbey, and will then explain my meaning, if, indeed, you shall not already have understood it. You, in the meantime, will consider your own powers of resolution, and be prepared either to adopt the purpose I shall suggest, or to declare you will not."

La Motte made some confused reply.

"Farewell till to-morrow," said the Marquis; "remember that freedom and affluence are now before you."

He moved towards the abbey, and, mounting his horse, rode off with his attendants. La Motte walked slowly home, musing on the late conversation.

CHAPTER XIV.

Danger, whose limbs of giant mould
What mortal eye can fix'd behold?
Who stalks his round, in hideous form!
Howling amidst the midnight storm!
And with him thousand phantoms join'd,
Who prompt to deeds accursed, the mind,
On whom that raving brood of Fate,
Who lap the blood of Sorrow, wait;
Who, Fear! this ghastly train can see,
And look not madly wild like thee!
COLLINS.

THE Marquis was punctual to the hour. La Motte received him at the gate, but he declined entering, and said he preferred a walk in the forest. Thither, therefore, La Motte attended him. After some general conversation:

"Well," said the Marquis, "have you considered what I said, and are you prepared to decide?"

"I have, my lord, and will quickly decide when you shall further explain yourself. Till then I can form no resolution."

The Marquis appeared dissatisfied, and was a moment silent.

"Is it then possible," he at length resumed, "that you do not understand? This ignorance is surely affected. La Motte, I expect sincerity. Tell me, therefore, is it necessary I should say more?"

"It is, my lord," said La Motte immediately. "If you fear to confide in me freely, how can I fully accomplish your purpose?"

"Before I proceed farther," said the Marquis," "let me administer some oath which

shall bind you to secrecy. But this is scarcely necessary; for, could I even doubt your word of honour, the remembrance of a certain transaction would point out to you the necessity of being as silent yourself as you must wish me to be." There was now a pause of silence, during which, both the Marquis and La Motte betrayed some confusion. "I think, La Motte," said he, "I have given you sufficient proof that I can be grateful; the services you have already rendered me with respect to Adeline have not been unrewarded."

"True, my lord, I am ever willing to acknowledge this, and am sorry it has not been in my power to serve you more effectually. Your further views respecting her I am ready to assist."

"I thank you. Adeline——" the Marquis hesitated.

"Adeline," rejoined La Motte, eager to anticipate his wishes, "has beauty worthy of your pursuit. She has inspired a passion, of which she ought to be proud, and, at any rate, she shall soon be yours. Her charms are worthy of——"

"Yes, yes," interrupted the Marquis; "but——" he paused.

"But they have given you too much trouble in the pursuit," said La Motte; "and to be sure, my lord, it must be confessed they have; but this trouble is all over—you may now consider her as your own."

"I would do so," said the Marquis, fixing an eye of earnest regard upon La Motte; "I would do so."

"Name your hour, my lord; you shall not be interrupted. Beauty, such as Adeline's——"

"Watch her closely," rejoined the Marquis, "and on no account suffer her to leave her apartment. Where is she now?"

"Confined in her chamber."·

"Very well. But I am impatient."

"Name your time, my lord——to-morrow night?"

"To-morrow night," said the Marquis; "to-morrow night. Do you understand me now?"

"Yes, my lord, this night, if you wish it so. But had you not better dismiss your servants, and remain yourself in the forest? You know the door that opens upon the woods from the west tower. Come thither about twelve—I will be there to conduct you to her chamber. Remember, then, my lord, that to-night——"

"Adeline dies!" interrupted the Marquis, in a low voice, scarcely human. "Do you understand me now?"

La Motte shrunk aghast. "My lord!"

"La Motte!" said the Marquis. There was a silence of several minutes, in which La Motte endeavoured to recover himself. "Let me ask, my lord, the meaning of this," said he, when he had breath to speak. "Why should you wish the death of Adeline —of Adeline whom so lately you loved?"

"Make no inquiries for my motive," said the Marquis ; "but it is as certain as that I live that she you name must die. This is sufficient."

The surprise of La Motte equalled his horror.

"The means are various," resumed the Marquis. "I could have wished that no blood might be spilt ; and there are drugs sure and speedy in their effect, but they cannot be soon or safely procured. I also wish it over—it must be done quickly—this night."

"This night, my lord?"

"Aye, this night, La Motte ; if it is to be, why not soon? Have you no convenient drug at hand?"

"None, my lord."

"I feared to trust a third person, or I should have been provided," said the Marquis. "As it is, take this poniard ; use it as occasion offers, but be resolute."

La Motte received the poniard with a trembling hand, and continued to gaze upon it for some time, scarcely knowing what he did.

"Put it up," said the Marquis, "and endeavour to recollect yourself."

La Motte obeyed, but continued to muse in silence.

He saw himself entangled in the web which his own crimes had woven. Being in the power of the Marquis, he knew he must either consent to the commission of a deed from the enormity of which, depraved as he was, he shrank in horror, or sacrifice fortune, freedom, probably life itself, to the refusal. He had been led on by slow gradations from folly to vice, till he now saw before him an abyss of guilt which startled even the conscience that so long had slumbered. The means of retreating were desperate—to proceed was equally so.

When he considered the innocence and the helplessness of Adeline, her orphan state, her former affectionate conduct, and her confidence in his protection, his heart melted with compassion for the distress he had already occasioned her, and shrank in terror from the deed he was urged to commit. But when, on the other hand, he contemplated the destruction that threatened him from the vengeance of the Marquis, and then considered the advantages that were offered him of favour, freedom, and probably fortune— terror and temptation contributed to overcome the pleadings of humanity, and silence the voice of conscience. In this state of tumultuous uncertainty he continued for some time silent, until the voice of the Marquis roused him to a conviction of the necessity of at least appearing to acquiesce in his designs.

"Do you hesitate?" said the Marquis.

"No, my lord, my resolution is fixed—I will obey you. But methinks it would be better to avoid bloodshed. Strange secrets have been revealed by——"

"Aye, but how avoid it?" interrupted the Marquis. "Poison I will not venture to procure. I have given you one sure instrument of death. You also may find it dangerous to inquire for a drug."

La Motte perceived that he could not purchase poison without subjecting himself to very dangerous suspicion, and he immediately replied, "You are right, my lord, and I will follow your orders implicitly."

The Marquis now proceeded, in broken sentences, to give further directions concerning this dreadful scheme.

"In her sleep," said he, "at midnight ; the family will then be at rest."

Afterwards they planned a story, which was to account for her disappearance, and by which it was to seem that she had sought an escape in consequence of her aversion to the addresses of the Marquis. The doors of her chamber and of the west tower were to be left open to corroborate this account, and many other circumstances were to be contrived to confirm the suspicion. They further consulted how the Marquis was to be informed of the event ; and it was agreed that he should come as usual to the abbey on the following day. "*To-night, then,*" said the Marquis, "I may rely upon your resolution?"

"You may, my lord."

"Farewell, then. When we meet again—"

"When we meet again," said La Motte, "it will be done." He followed the Marquis to the abbey, and having seen him mount his horse, and wished him a good night, he retired to his chamber, where he shut himself up.

Adeline, meanwhile, in the solitude of her prison, gave way to the despair which her condition inspired. She tried to arrange her thoughts, and to argue herself into some degree of resignation ; but reflection, by representing the past, and reason, by anticipating the future, brought before her mind the full picture of her misfortunes, and she sank in despondency. Of Theodore, who, by a conduct so noble, had testified his attachment and involved himself in ruin, she thought with a degree of anguish infinitely superior to what she had felt upon any other occasion.

That the very exertions which had deserved all her gratitude and awakened all her tenderness should be the cause of his destruction was a circumstance so much beyond the ordinary bounds of misery that her fortitude sank at once before it. The idea of Theodore suffering — Theodore dying — was for ever present to her imagination, and frequently

G

excluding the sense of her own danger, made her conscious only of his. Sometimes the hope he had given her of being able to vindicate his conduct, or at least to obtain a pardon, would return; but it was like the faint beam of an April morn, transient and cheerless. She knew that the Marquis, stung with jealousy, and exasperated to revenge, would pursue him with unrelenting malice.

Against such an enemy what could Theodore oppose? Conscious rectitude would not avail him to ward off the blow which disappointed passion and powerful pride directed. Her distress was considerably heightened by reflecting that no intelligence of him could reach her at the abbey, and that she must remain she knew not how long in the most dreadful suspense concerning his fate. From the abbey she saw no possibility of escaping. She was a prisoner in a chamber enclosed at every avenue, she had no opportunity of conversing with any person who could afford her even a chance of relief, and she saw herself condemned to wait in passive silence the impending destiny—infinitely more dreadful to her imagination than death itself.

Thus circumstanced, she yielded to the pressure of her misfortunes, and would sit for hours motionless and given up to thought. "Theodore!" she would frequently exclaim, "you cannot hear my voice, you cannot fly to help me—yourself a prisoner and in chains!" The picture was too horrid. The swelling anguish of her heart would subdue her utterance, tears bathed her cheeks, and she became insensible to everything but the misery of Theodore.

On this evening her mind had been remarkably tranquil; and as she watched from her window, with a still and melancholy pleasure, the setting sun, the fading splendour of the western horizon, and the gradual approach of twilight, her thoughts bore her back to the time when, in happier circumstances, she had viewed the same appearances. She recollected also the evening of her temporary escape from the abbey, when from this same window she had watched the declining sun, how anxiously she had awaited the fall of twilight, how much she had endeavoured to anticipate the events of her future life, with what trembling fear she had descended from the tower and ventured into the forest. These reflections produced others that filled her heart with anguish and her eyes with tears.

While she was lost in her melancholy reverie she saw the Marquis mount his horse and depart from the gates. The sight of him revived, in all its force, a sense of the misery he inflicted on her beloved Theodore, and a consciousness of the evils which more immediately threatened herself. She withdrew from the window in an agony of tears, which continuing for a considerable time, her frame was at length quite exhausted, and she retired early to rest.

La Motte remained in his chamber till supper obliged him to descend. At table his wild and haggard countenance, which, in spite of all his endeavours, betrayed the disorder of his mind, and his long and frequent fits of abstraction, surprised as well as alarmed Madame La Motte. When Peter left the room she tenderly inquired what had disturbed him, and he with a distorted smile tried to be gay, but the effort was beyond his art, and he quickly relapsed into silence; when Madame La Motte spoke, and he strove to conceal the absence of his thoughts, he answered so entirely from the purpose that his abstraction became still more apparent. Observing this, Madame La Motte appeared to take no notice of his present temper, and they continued to sit in uninterrupted silence till the hour of rest, when they retired to their chamber.

La Motte lay in a state of disturbed watchfulness for some time, and his frequent starts awoke Madame, who, however, being pacified by some trifling excuse, soon went to sleep again. This agitation continued till near midnight, when, recollecting that the time was now passing in idle reflection which ought to be devoted to action, he stole silently from his bed, wrapped himself in his night-gown, and, taking the lamp which burned nightly in his chamber, passed up the spiral staircase. As he went he frequently looked back, and often started and listened to the hollow sighings of the blast.

His hand shook so violently when he attempted to unlock the door of Adeline's chamber that he was obliged to set the lamp on the ground and apply both his hands. The noise he made with the key induced him to suppose he must have awakened her; but when he opened the door, and perceived the stillness that reigned within, he was convinced she was asleep. When he approached the bed he heard her gently breathe and soon after sigh, and he stopped, but, silence returning, he again advanced, and then heard her sing in her sleep. As he listened he distinguished some notes of a melancholy little air which, in her happier days, she had often sung to him. The low and mournful accent in which she now uttered them expressed too well the tone of her mind.

La Motte now stepped hastily towards the bed, when, breathing a deep sigh, she was again silent. He undrew the curtain, and saw her lying in a profound sleep, her cheek, yet wet with tears, resting upon her arm. He stood a moment looking at her; and, as he viewed her innocent and lovely countenance, pale in grief, the light of the lamp, which shone strong upon her eyes, awoke her, and perceiving a man she uttered a scream. Her recollection returning, she knew him to be La Motte, and it instantly recurring to her that the Marquis was at hand, she raised herself in bed and implored pity and protection. La Motte stood looking eagerly at her, but without replying.

The wildness of his looks and the gloomy silence he preserved increased her alarm, and with tears of terror she renewed her supplication.

"You once saved me from destruction," cried she; "oh save me now! Have pity upon me—I have no protector but you."

"What is it you fear?" said La Motte, in a tone scarcely articulate.

"Oh save—save me from the Marquis!"

"Rise then," said he, "and dress yourself quickly; I shall be back again in a few minutes."

He lighted a candle that stood on the table and left the chamber. Adeline immediately arose and endeavoured to dress, but her thoughts were so bewildered that she scarcely knew what she did, and her whole frame was so violently agitated that it was with the utmost difficulty she preserved herself from fainting. She threw her clothes hastily on, and then sat down to await the return of La Motte. A considerable time elapsed, yet he did not appear, and having in vain endeavoured to compose her spirits, the pain of suspense at length became so insupportable, that she opened the door of her chamber, and went to the top of the staircase to listen. She thought she heard voices below; but, considering that if the Marquis was there, her appearance could only increase her danger, she checked the step she had almost involuntarily taken to descend. Still she listened, and still thought she distinguished voices. Soon after she heard a door shut, and then footsteps, and she hastened back to her chamber.

Near a quarter of an hour elapsed and La Motte did not appear; when again she thought she heard a murmur of voices below, and also passing steps, and at length her anxiety not suffering her to remain in her room, she moved through the passage that communicated with the spiral staircase; but all was now still. In a few moments, however, a light flashed across the hall, and La Motte appeared at the door of the vaulted room. He looked up, and, seeing Adeline in the gallery, beckoned her to descend.

She hesitated and looked towards her chamber; but La Motte now approached the stairs, and, with faltering steps, she went to meet him.

"I fear the Marquis may see me," said she, whispering; "where is he?"

La Motte took her hand and led her on, assuring her she had nothing to fear from the Marquis. The wildness of his looks, however, and the trembling of his hand, seemed to contradict this assurance, and she inquired whither he was leading her.

"To the forest," said La Motte, "that you may escape from the abbey; a horse waits for you without. I can save you by no other means."

New terror seized her. She could scarcely believe that La Motte, who had hitherto conspired with the Marquis, and had so closely confined her, should now himself undertake her escape, and she at this moment felt a dreadful presentiment which it was impossible to account for, that he was leading her out to murder her in the forest. Again shrinking back, she supplicated his mercy. He assured her he meant only to protect her, and desired she would not waste time.

There was something in his manner that spoke sincerity, and she suffered him to conduct her to a side door that opened into the forest, where she could just distinguish through the gloom a man on horseback. This brought to her remembrance the night in which she had quitted the tomb, when, trusting to the person who appeared, she had been carried to the Marquis's villa. La Motte called, and was answered by Peter, whose voice somewhat reassured Adeline.

He then told her that the Marquis would return to the abbey on the following morning, and that this could be her only opportunity of escaping his designs; that she might rely upon his (La Motte's) word, that Peter had orders to carry her wherever she chose; but as he knew the Marquis would be indefatigable in search after her, he advised her by all means to leave the kingdom, which she might do with Peter, who was a native of Savoy, and would convey her to the house of his sister. There she might remain till La Motte himself, who did not now think it would be safe to continue much longer in France, should join her. He entreated her, whatever might happen, never to mention the events which had passed at the abbey.

"To save you, Adeline, I have risked my life; do not increase my danger and your own by any unnecessary discoveries. We may never meet again, but I hope you will be happy; and remember, when you think of me, that I am not quite so bad as I have been tempted to be."

Having said this he gave her some money, which he told her would be necessary to defray the expenses of her journey. Adeline could no longer doubt his sincerity, and her transports of joy and gratitude would scarcely permit her to thank him. She wished to have bid Madame La Motte farewell, and indeed earnestly requested it; but he again told her she had no time to lose, and, having wrapped her in a large cloak, he lifted her on the horse. She bade him adieu with tears of gratitude, and Peter set off as fast as the darkness would permit.

When they were got some way, "I am glad, with all my heart, ma'amselle," said he,

" to see you again. Who would have thought, after all, that my master himself would have bid me take you away? Well, to be sure, strange things come to pass; but I hope we shall have better luck this time." Adeline, not choosing to reproach him with the treachery of which she feared he had been formerly guilty, thanked him for his good wishes, and said she hoped they should be more fortunate; but Peter, in his usual strain of eloquence, proceeded to undeceive her in this point, and to acquaint her with every circumstance which his memory, and it was naturally a strong one, could furnish.

Peter expressed such an artless interest in her welfare, and such concern for her former disappointment, that she could no longer doubt his faithfulness; and this conviction not only strengthened her confidence in the present undertaking, but made her listen to his conversation with kindness and pleasure. " I should never have stayed at the abbey till this time," said he, "if I could have got away; but my master frightened me about the Marquis, and I had not enough money to carry me into my own country, so that I was forced to stay. It's well we have got some solid louis-d'ors now; for I question, ma'amselle, whether the people on the road would have taken those trinkets you formerly talked of for money."

" Possibly not," said Adeline; "I am thankful to Monsieur La Motte that we have more certain means of procuring conveniences. What route shall you take when we leave the forest, Peter?" Peter mentioned very correctly a great part of the road to Lyons; "and then," said he, "we can easily get to Savoy, and that will be nothing. My sister, God bless her! I hope is living; I have not seen her many a year, but if she is not, all the people will be glad to see me, and you will easily get a lodging, ma'amselle, and everything you want."

Adeline resolved to go with him to Savoy. La Motte, who knew the character and designs of the Marquis, had advised her to leave the kingdom, and had told her, what her fears might have suggested, that the Marquis would be indefatigable in search of her. His motive for this advice must be a desire of serving her; why else, when she was already in his power, should he remove her to another place, and even furnish her with money for the expenses of a journey?

At Lelencourt, where Peter said he was well known, she would be most likely to meet with protection and comfort, even should his sister be dead; and its distance and solitary situation were circumstances that pleased her. These reflections would have pointed out to her the prudence of proceeding to Savoy, had she been less destitute of resources in France; in her present situation they proved it to be necessary.

She inquired further concerning the route they were to take, and whether Peter was sufficiently acquainted with the road. "When once I get to Thiers, I know it well enough," said Peter, " for I have gone it many a time in my younger days, and anybody will tell us the way there." They travelled for several hours in darkness and silence, and it was not till they emerged from the forest that Adeline saw the morning light streak the eastern clouds. The sight cheered and revived her; and as she travelled silently along, her mind revolved the events of the past night, and meditated plans for the future. The present kindness of La Motte appeared so very different from his former conduct, that it astonished and perplexed her, and she could only account for it by attributing it to one of those sudden impulses of humanity which sometimes operate even upon the most depraved hearts.

But when she recollected his former words, "that he was not master of himself," she could scarcely believe that mere pity should induce him to break the bonds which had hitherto so strongly held him; and then, considering the altered conduct of the Marquis, she was inclined to think that she owed her liberty to some change in his sentiments towards her; yet the advice La Motte had given her to quit the kingdom, and the money with which he had supplied her for that purpose, seemed to contradict this opinion, and involved her again in doubt.

Peter now got directions to Thiers, which place they reached without any accident, and there stopped to refresh themselves. As soon as Peter thought the horse sufficiently rested, they again set forward, and from the rich plains of the Lyonnois, Adeline, for the first time, caught a view of the distant Alps, whose majestic heads, seeming to prop the vault of heaven, filled her mind with sublime emotions.

In a few hours they reached the vale in which stands the city of Lyons, whose beautiful environs, studded with villas, and rich with cultivation, withdrew Adeline from the melancholy contemplation of her own circumstances and her more painful anxiety for Theodore.

When they reached that busy city, her first care was to inquire concerning the passage of the Rhone; but she forbore to make these inquiries of the people of the inn, considering that if the Marquis should follow her thither they might enable him to pursue her route. She, therefore, sent Peter to the quays to hire a boat, while she herself took a slight repast, it being her intention to embark immediately. Peter presently returned, having engaged a boat and men to take them up the Rhone to the nearest part of Savoy, from whence they were to proceed by land to the village of Lelencourt.

Having taken some refreshment, she ordered

him to conduct her to the vessel. A new and striking scene presented itself to Adeline, who looked with surprise upon the river, gay with vessels, and the quay crowded with busy faces, and felt the contrast which the cheerful objects around bore to herself—to her an orphan, desolate, helpless, and flying from persecution and her country. She spoke with the master of the boat, and having sent Peter back to the inn for the horse (La Motte's gift to Peter, in lieu of some arrears of wages), they embarked.

As they slowly passed up the Rhone, whose steep banks, crowned with mountains, exhibited the most various, wild, and romantic scenery, Adeline sat in pensive reverie. The novelty of the scene through which she floated, now frowning with savage grandeur, and now smiling in fertility, and gay with towns and villages, soothed her mind, and her sorrow gradually softened into a gentle and not unpleasing melancholy. She had seated herself at the head of the boat, where she watched its sides cleave the swift stream, and listened to the dashing of the waters.

The boat, slowly opposing the current, passed along for some hours, and at length the veil of evening was stretched over the landscape. The weather was fine, and Adeline, regardless of the dews that now fell, remained in the open air, observing the objects darken round her, the gay tints of the horizon fade away, and the stars gradually appear, trembling upon the lucid mirror of the waters. The scene was now sunk in deep shadow, and the silence of the hour was broken only by the measured dashing of the oars, and now and then by the voice of Peter speaking to the boatmen. Adeline sat lost in thought; the forlornness of her circumstances came heightened to her imagination.

She saw herself surrounded by the darkness and stillness of night, in a strange place, far distant from any friends, going she scarcely knew whither, under the guidance of strangers, and pursued, perhaps, by an inveterate enemy.

She pictured to herself the rage of the Marquis now that he had discovered her flight, and though she knew it very unlikely he should follow her by water, for which reason she had chosen that manner of travelling, she trembled at the portrait her fancy drew. Her thoughts then wandered to the plan she should adopt after reaching Savoy; and much as her experience had prejudiced her against the manners of a convent, she saw no place more likely to afford her a proper asylum. At length she retired to the little cabin for a few hours' repose.

She awoke with the dawn, and her mind being too much disturbed to sleep again, she rose and watched the gradual approach of day. As she mused, she expressed the feelings of the moment in the following

SONNET.

Morn's beaming eyes at length unclose,
And wake the blushes of the rose,
That all night long, oppress'd with dews,
And veil'd in chilling shade its hues,
Reclin'd, forlorn, the languid head,
And sadly sought its parent bed:
Warmth from her ray the trembling flower derives,
And sweetly blushing through its tears revives.
Morn's beaming eyes at length unclose,
And melt the tears that bend the rose;
But can their charms suppress the sigh,
Or chase the tear from Sorrow's eye?
Can all their lustrous light impart
One ray of peace to Sorrow's heart?
Ah! no; their fires her fainting soul oppress;
Eve's pensive shades more soothe her meek distress!

When Adeline left the abbey, La Motte remained for some time at the gate listening to the steps of the horse that carried her, till the sound was lost in distance; he then turned into the hall with a lightness of heart to which he had long been a stranger. The satisfaction of having thus preserved her, as he hoped, from the designs of the Marquis, overcame for a while all sense of the danger in which this step must involve him. But when he returned entirely to his own situation the terrors of the Marquis's resentment struck their full force upon his mind, and he considered how he might best escape it.

It was now past midnight, the Marquis was expected early on the following day, and in this interval it at first appeared probable to him that he might quit the forest. There was only one horse, but he considered whether it would be best to set off immediately for Auboine, where a carriage might be procured to convey his family and his movables from the abbey, or quietly to await the arrival of the Marquis, and endeavour to impose upon him by a forged story of Adeline's escape.

The time which must elapse before a carriage could reach the abbey would leave him scarcely sufficient to escape from the forest. What money he had remaining from the Marquis's bounty would not carry him far; and when it was expended he must probably be at a loss for subsistence, should he not before then be detected. By remaining at the abbey it would appear that he was unconscious of deserving the Marquis's resentment; and though he could not expect to impress a belief upon him that his orders had been executed, he might make it appear that Peter only had been accessory to the escape of Adeline; an account which would seem the more probable from Peter's having been formerly detected in a similar scheme. He believed also, that if the Marquis should threaten to deliver him into the hands of justice, he might save himself by a menace of disclosing the crime he had commissioned him to perpetrate.

Thus arguing, La Motte resolved to remain

at the abbey, and await the event of the Marquis's disappointment.

When the Marquis did arrive, and was informed of Adeline's flight, the strong workings of his soul, which appeared in his countenance, for awhile alarmed and terrified La Motte. He cursed himself and her in terms of such coarseness and vehemence as La Motte was astonished to hear from a man whose manners were generally amiable, whatever might be the violence and criminality of his passions. To invent and express these terms seemed to give him not only relief, but delight ; yet he appeared more shocked at the circumstance of her escape than exasperated at the carelessness of La Motte ; and recollecting at length that he was wasting time, he left the abbey, and despatched several of his servants in pursuit of her.

When he was gone La Motte, believing his story had succeeded, returned to the pleasure of considering that he had done his duty, and to the hope that Adeline was now beyond the reach of pursuit. This calm was of short continuance. In a few hours the Marquis returned, accompanied by the officers of justice. The affrighted La Motte, perceiving him approach, endeavoured to conceal himself, but was seized and carried to the Marquis, who drew him aside.

"I am not to be imposed upon," said he, "by such a superficial story as you have invented. You know your life is in my hands ; tell me instantly where you have secreted Adeline, or I will charge you with the crime you have committed against me ; but upon your disclosing the place of her concealment, I will dismiss the officers and, if you wish it, assist you to leave the kingdom. You have no time to hesitate, and may know that I will not be trifled with."

La Motte attempted to appease the Marquis, and affirmed that Adeline was really fled he knew not whither. "You will remember, my lord, that your character is also in my power ; and that, if you proceed to extremities, you will compel me to reveal in the face of day that you would have made me a murderer."

"And who will believe you?" said the Marquis. "The crimes that banished you from society will be no testimony of your veracity, and that with which I now charge you will bring with it a sufficient presumption that your accusation is malicious. Officers, do your duty !"

They entered the room and seized La Motte, whom terror had deprived of all power of resistance, could resistance have availed him ; and in the perturbation of his mind he informed the Marquis that Adeline had taken the road to Lyons. This discovery, however, was made too late to serve himself ; the Marquis seized the advantage it offered, but the charge had been given, and, with the anguish of knowing that he had exposed Adeline to danger without benefiting himself, La Motte submitted in silence to his fate. Scarcely allowing time to collect what little effects might easily be carried with him, the officers conveyed him from the abbey ; but the Marquis, in consideration of the extreme distress of Madame La Motte, directed one of his servants to procure a carriage from Auboine, that she might follow her husband.

The Marquis in the meantime, now acquainted with the route Adeline had taken, sent forward his faithful valet to trace her to the place of concealment, and return immediately with intelligence to the villa.

Abandoned to despair, La Motte and his wife quitted the forest of Fontanville, which had for so many months afforded them an asylum, and embarked once more upon the tumultuous world, where justice would meet La Motte in the form of destruction. They had entered the forest as a refuge, rendered necessary by the former crimes of La Motte, and for some time had found in it the security they sought ; but other offences—for even in that sequestered spot there happened to be temptation—soon succeeded ; and his life, already sufficiently marked by the punishment of vice, now afforded him another instance of this great truth, "That where guilt is, there peace cannot enter."

CHAPTER XV.

Hail, awful scenes, that calm the troubled breast,
And woo the weary to profound repose !
                                        BEATTIE.

ADELINE, meanwhile, and Peter proceeded on their voyage without any accident, and landed in Savoy, where Peter placed her upon the horse and himself walked beside her. When he came within sight of his native mountains, his extravagant joy burst forth into frequent exclamations, and he would often ask Adeline if she had ever seen such hills in France.

"No, no," said he, "the hills there are very well for French hills, but they are not to be named on the same day with ours."

Adeline, lost in admiration of the astonishing and tremendous scenery around her, assented very warmly to the truth of Peter's assertion, which encouraged him to expatiate more largely upon the advantages of his country—its disadvantages he totally forgot ; and although he gave away his last sous to the children of the peasantry that ran barefooted by the side of the horse, he spoke of nothing but the happiness and content of the inhabitants.

His native village, indeed, was an exception to the general character of the country, and to the usual effects of an arbitrary government ; it was flourishing, healthy, and happy, and these advantages it chiefly owed to the activity and attention of the benevolent clergyman whose cure it was.

Adeline, who now began to feel the effects of long anxiety and fatigue, much wished to arrive at the end of her journey, and inquired impatiently of Peter concerning it. Her spirits thus weakened, the gloomy grandeur of the scenes which had so lately awakened emotions of delightful sublimity now awed her into terror ; she trembled at the sound of the torrents rolling among the cliffs, and thundering in the vale below, and shrank from the view of the precipices which sometimes overhung the road, and at others appeared beneath it. Fatigued as she was, she frequently dismounted to climb on foot the steep flinty road which she feared to travel on horseback.

The day was closing when they drew near a small village at the foot of the Savoy Alps, and the sun in all his evening splendour, now sinking behind their summits, threw a farewell gleam athwart the landscape, so soft and glowing, as drew from Adeline, languid as she was, an exclamation of rapture.

The romantic situation of the village next attracted her notice. It stood at the foot of several stupendous mountains, which formed a chain round a lake at some little distance, and the woods that swept from their summits almost embosomed the village. The lake, unruffled by the lightest air, reflected the vermeil tints of the horizon with the sublime scenery on its borders, darkening every instant with the falling twilight.

When Peter perceived the village he burst into a shout of joy. "Thank God !" said he, " we are near home. There is my dear native place. It looks just as it did twenty years ago ; and there are the same old trees growing round our cottage, and the huge rock that rises above it. My poor father died there, ma'amselle. Pray heaven my sister be alive ; it's a long while since I saw her."

Adeline listened with a melancholy pleasure to these artless expressions of Peter, who, in retracing the scenes of his former days, seemed to live them over again. As they approached the village he continued to point out various objects of his remembrance.

"And there, too, is the good pastor's château ; look, ma'amselle, that white house, with the smoke curling, that stands on the edge of the lake yonder. I wonder whether he is alive yet. He was not old when I left the place, and as much beloved as ever man was ; but death spares nobody !"

They had now reached the village, which was extremely neat, though it did not promise much accommodation. Peter had hardly advanced ten steps before he was accosted by some of his old acquaintance, who shook hands and seemed not to know how to part with him. He inquired for his sister, and was told she was alive and well. As they

passed on, so many of his old friends flocked round him that Adeline became quite weary of the delay. Many whom he had left in the vigour of life were now tottering under the infirmities of age, while their sons and daughters, whom he had only known in the playfulness of infancy, were grown from his remembrance, and in the pride of youth. At length they approached the cottage, and were met by his sister, who, having heard of his arrival, came and welcomed him with unfeigned joy.

On seeing Adeline she seemed surprised, but assisted her to alight, and conducting her into a neat cottage, received her with a warmth of kindness which would have graced a better situation. Adeline requested to speak with her alone, for the room was now crowded with Peter's friends, and then acquainting her with such particulars of her circumstances as it was necessary to communicate, desired to know if she could be accommodated with lodging in the cottage.

"Yes, ma'amselle," said the good woman, "to such as it is you are heartily welcome ; I am only sorry it is not better. But you seem ill, ma'amselle ; what shall I get you ?"

Adeline, who had been long struggling with fatigue and indisposition, now yielded to their pressure. She said she was indeed ill, but hoped that rest would restore her, and desired a bed might be immediately prepared. The good woman went out to obey her, and soon returning, showed her to a little cabin, where she retired to a bed whose cleanliness was its only recommendation.

But, notwithstanding her fatigue, she could not sleep ; and her mind, in spite of all her efforts, returned to the scenes that were past, or presented gloomy and imperfect visions of the future.

The difference between her own condition and that of other persons, educated as she had been, struck her forcibly, and she wept. "They," said she, "have friends and relations, all striving to save them, not only from what may hurt, but what may displease them, watching not only for their present safety, but for their future advantage, and preventing them even from injuring themselves. But during my whole life I have never known a friend—have been in general surrounded by enemies, and very seldom exempt from some circumstance either of danger or calamity. Yet surely I am not born to be for ever wretched ; the time will come when——" She began to think she might one time be happy ; but recollecting the desperate situation of Theodore, "No," said she, "I can never hope even for peace !"

Early the following morning the good woman of the house came to inquire how she had rested, and found she had slept little, and was much worse than on the preceding night. The uneasiness of her mind contributed to heighten the feverish symptoms that attended her, and in the course of the day her disorder began to assume a serious aspect. She observed its progress with composure, resigning herself to the will of God, and feeling little to regret in life. Her kind hostess did everything in her power to relieve her, and there was neither physician nor apothecary in the village, so that nature was deprived of none of her advantages. Notwithstanding this, the disorder rapidly increased, and on the third day from its first attack she became delirious, after which she sank into a state of stupefaction.

How long she remained in this deplorable condition she knew not, but, on recovering her senses, she found herself in an apartment very different from any she remembered. It was spacious and almost beautiful, the bed and everything around being in one style of elegant simplicity. For some minutes she lay in a trance of surprise, endeavouring to recollect her scattered ideas of the past, and almost fearing to move, lest the pleasing vision should vanish from her eyes.

At length she ventured to raise herself, when she presently heard a soft voice speaking near her, and the bed-curtain on one side was gently undrawn by a beautiful girl. As she leaned forward over the bed, with a smile of mingled tenderness and joy, she inquired of her patient how she did. Adeline gazed in silent admiration upon the most interesting female countenance she had ever seen, in which the expression of sweetness, united with lively sense and refinement, was chastened by simplicity.

Adeline at length recollected herself sufficiently to thank her kind inquirer, and begged to know to whom she was obliged, and where she was.

The lovely girl pressed her hand. "'Tis we who are obliged," said she. "Oh, how I rejoice to find that you have recovered your recollection!"

She said no more, but flew to the door of the apartment and disappeared. In a few minutes she returned with an elderly lady, who, approaching the bed with an air of tender interest, asked concerning the state of Adeline, to which the latter replied as well as the agitation of her spirits would permit, and repeated her desire of knowing to whom she was so greatly obliged.

"You shall know that hereafter," said the lady; "at present be assured that you are with those who will think their care much overpaid by your recovery; submit, therefore, to everything that may conduce to it, and consent to be kept as quiet as possible."

Adeline gratefully smiled, and bowed her head in silent assent. The lady now quitted the room for a medicine, having given which to Adeline, the curtain was closed, and she was left to repose. But her thoughts were too busy to suffer her to profit by the opportunity. She contemplated the past and viewed the present, and, when she compared them, the contrast struck her with astonishment. The whole appeared like one of those sudden transitions so frequent in dreams, in which we pass from grief and despair, we know not how, to comfort and delight. Yet she looked forward to the future with a trembling anxiety that threatened to retard her recovery, and which, when she remembered the words of her generous benefactress, she endeavoured to suppress. Had she better known the disposition of the persons in whose house she now was, her anxiety, as far as it regarded herself, must in a great measure have been done away, for La Luc, its owner, was one of those rare characters to whom misfortune seldom looks in vain, and whose native goodness, confirmed by principle, is uniform and unassuming in its acts. The following little picture of his domestic life, his family and his manners, will more fully illustrate his character; it was drawn from the life, and its exactness will, it is hoped, compensate for its length.

THE FAMILY OF LA LUC.

But half mankind, like Handel's fool, destroy,
Through rage and ignorance, the strain of joy;
Irregularly wild their passions roll
Through Nature's finest instrument—the soul.
While men of sense, with Handel's happier skill,
Correct the taste, and harmonise the will;
Teach their affections, like his notes, to flow,
Nor rais'd too high, nor ever sunk too low;
'Till ev'ry virtue, measur'd and refin'd,
As fits the concert of the master mind,
Melts in its kindred sounds, and pours along
Th' according music of the moral song.
                  CAWTHORNE.

IN the village of Lelencourt, celebrated for its picturesque situation at the foot of the Savoy Alps, lived Arnaud La Luc, a clergyman, descended from an ancient family of France, whose decayed fortunes occasioned them to seek a retreat in Switzerland, in an age when the violence of civil commotion seldom spared the conquered. He was minister of the village, and equally loved for the piety and benevolence of the Christian as respected for the dignity and elevation of the philosopher. His was the philosophy of nature, directed by common sense; he despised the jargon of the modern schools, and the brilliant absurdities of systems, which have dazzled without enlightening, and guided without convincing, their disciples.

His mind was penetrating; his views extensive; and his systems, like his religion, were simple, rational, and sublime. The people of his parish looked up to him as to a father; for while his precepts directed their minds, his example touched their hearts.

In early youth La Luc lost a wife whom he tenderly loved; this event threw a tincture of soft and interesting melancholy over his character, which remained when time had mellowed the remembrance that occasioned it. Philosophy had strengthened, not hardened, his heart ; it enabled him to resist the pressure of affliction, rather than to overcome it.

Calamity taught him to feel with peculiar sympathy the distresses of others. His income from the parish was small, and what remained from the divided and reduced estates of his ancestors did not much increase it ; but though he could not always relieve the necessities of the indigent, his tender pity and holy conversation seldom failed in administering consolation to the mental sufferer. On these occasions, the sweet and exquisite emotions of his heart have often induced him to say, that could the voluptuary be once sensible of these feelings, he would never after forego "the luxury of doing good." "Ignorance of true pleasure," he would say, "more frequently than temptation to that which is false, leads to vice."

La Luc had one son and a daughter, who were too young, when their mother died, to lament their loss. He loved them with peculiar tenderness, as the children of her whom he never ceased to deplore ; and it was for some time his sole amusement to observe the gradual unfolding of their infant minds, and to bend them to virtue. His was the deep and silent sorrow of the heart ; his complaints he never intruded upon others, and very seldom did he even mention his wife. His grief was too sacred for the eye of the vulgar. Often he retired to the deep solitude of the mountains, and amid their solemn and tremendous scenery, would brood over the remembrance of times past, and resign himself to the luxury of grief. On his return from these little excursions, he was always more placid and contented ; a sweet tranquillity, which arose almost to happiness, was diffused over his mind, and his manners were more than usually benevolent. As he gazed on his children, and fondly kissed them, a tear would sometimes steal into his eye, but it was a tear of tender regret, unmingled with the darker qualities of sorrow, and was precious to his heart.

On the death of his wife he received into his house a maiden sister, a sensible, worthy woman, who was deeply interested in the happiness of her brother. Her affectionate attention and judicious conduct anticipated the effect of time in softening the poignancy of his distress; and her unremitted care of his children, while it proved the goodness of her own heart, attracted her more closely to his.

It was with inexpressible pleasure that he traced in the infant features of Clara the resemblance of her mother. The same gentleness of manner, and the same sweetness of disposition, soon displayed themselves ; and as she grew up, her actions often reminded him so strongly of his lost wife, as to fix him in reveries, which absorbed all his soul.

Engaged in the duties of his parish, the education of his children, and in philosophic research, his years passed in tranquillity. The tender melancholy with which affliction had tinctured his mind was, by long indulgence, become dear to him, and he would not have relinquished it for the brightest dream of airy happiness. When any passing incidents disturbed him, he retired for consolation to the idea of her so faithfully loved, and yielding to a gentle, and what the world would call a romantic, sadness, gradually reassumed his composure. This was the secret luxury to which he withdrew from temporary disappointment—the solitary enjoyment which dissipated the cloud of care, and blunted the sting of vexation—which elevated his mind above this world, and opened to his view the sublimity of another.

The spot he now inhabited, the surrounding scenery, the romantic beauties of the neighbouring walks, were dear to La Luc, for they had once been loved by Clara ; they had been the scenes of her tenderness, and of his happiness.

His château stood on the borders of a small lake that was almost environed by mountains of stupendous height, which, shooting into a variety of grotesque forms, composed a scenery singularly solemn and sublime. Dark woods, intermingled with bold projections of rock, sometimes barren, and sometimes covered with the purple bloom of wild flowers, impended over the lake, and were seen in the clear mirror of its waters. The wild and Alpine heights which rose above were either crowned with perpetual snows, or exhibited tremendous crags and masses of solid rock, whose appearance was continually changing as the rays of light were variously reflected on their surface, and whose summits were often wrapt in impenetrable mists. Some cottages and hamlets, scattered on the margin of the lake, or seated in picturesque points of view on the rocks above, were the only objects that reminded the beholder of humanity.

On the side of the lake, nearly opposite to the château, the mountains receded, and a long chain of Alps were seen in perspective. Their innumerable tints and shades, some veiled in blue mists, some tinged with rich purple, and others glittering in partial light, gave luxurious colouring to the scene.

The château was not large, but it was convenient, and was characterised by an air of elegant simplicity and good order. The entrance was a small hall, which, opening by a glass door into the garden, afforded a view of the lake, with the magnificent scenery exhibited on its borders. On the left of the hall was La Luc's study, where he usually passed his mornings ; and adjoining was a small room fitted up with chemical apparatus, astronomical instruments, and other implements of science. On the right was the family parlour, and behind it a room which belonged exclusively to Madame La Luc. Here were deposited various medicines and botanical distillations, together with the apparatus for preparing them. From this room the whole village was liberally supplied with physical comfort ; for it was the pride of Madame to believe herself skilful in relieving the disorders of her neighbours.

Behind the château rose a tuft of pines, and in front a gentle declivity, covered with verdure and flowers, extended to the lake, whose waters flowed even with the grass, and gave freshness to the acacias that waved over its surface. Flowering shrubs, intermingled with mountain-ash, cypress, and evergreen oak, marked the boundary of the garden.

At the return of spring it was Clara's care to direct the young shoots of the plants, to nurse the budding flowers, and to shelter them with the luxuriant branches of the shrubs from the cold blasts that descended from the mountains. In summer she usually rose with the sun, and visited her favourite flowers, while the dew yet hung glittering on their leaves. The freshness of early day, with the glowing colouring which then touched the scenery, gave a pure and exquisite delight to her innocent heart. Born amid scenes of grandeur and sublimity, she had quickly imbibed a taste for their charms, which taste was heightened by the influence of a warm imagination. To view the sun rising above the Alps, tinging their snowy heads with light, and suddenly darting his rays over the whole face of nature—to see the fiery splendour of the clouds reflected in the lake below, and the roseate tints first steal upon the rocks above—were among the earliest pleasures of which Clara was susceptible. From being delighted with the observance of nature, she grew pleased with seeing her finely imitated, and soon displayed a taste for poetry and painting. When she was about sixteen she often selected from her father's library those of the Italian poets most celebrated for picturesque beauty, and would spend the first hours of morning in reading them under the shade of the acacias that bordered the lake. Here she would often attempt rude sketches of the surrounding scenery, and at length, by repeated efforts, assisted by some instruction from her brother, she succeeded so well as to produce twelve drawings in crayon, which were judged worthy of decorating the parlour of the château.

Young La Luc played the flute, and she listened to him with great delight, particu-larly when he stood on the margin of the lake, under her beloved acacias. Her voice was sweet and flexible, but not strong, and she soon learned to modulate it to the instrument. She knew nothing of the intricacies of execution ; her airs were simple, and her style equally so ; but she soon gave them a touching expression, inspired by the sensibility of her heart, which seldom left those of her hearers unaffected.

It was the happiness of La Luc to see his children happy, and in one of his excursions to Geneva, whither he went to visit some relations of his late wife, he brought Clara a lute. She received it with more gratitude than she could express ; and having learned one air, she hastened to her favourite acacias and played it again and again till she forgot everything besides. Her little domestic duties, her books, her drawings, even the hour which her father dedicated to her improvement, when she met her brother in the library, and with him partook of knowledge, even this hour passed unheeded by. La Luc suffered it to pass. Madame was displeased that her niece neglected her domestic duties, and wished to reprove her, but La Luc begged she would be silent. "Let experience teach her her error," said he ; "precept seldom brings conviction to young minds."

Madame objected that experience was a slow teacher. "It is a sure one," replied La Luc, "and is not unfrequently the quickest of all teachers. When it cannot lead us into serious evil it is well to trust to it."

The second day passed with Clara as the first, and the third as the second. She could now play several tunes ; she came to her father and repeated what she had learnt.

At the supper the cream was not dressed, and there was no fruit on the table. La Luc inquired the reason ; Clara recollected it and blushed. She observed that her brother was absent, but nothing was said. Towards the conclusion of the repast he appeared ; his countenance expressed unusual satisfaction, but he seated himself in silence. Clara inquired what had detained him from supper, and learnt that he had been to a sick family in the neighbourhood, with the weekly allowance which her father gave them. La Luc had entrusted the care of this family to his daughter ; and it was her duty to have carried them their little allowance on the preceding day, but she had forgotten everything but music.

"How did you find the woman?" said La' Luc to his son.

"Worse, sir," he replied ; "for her medicines had not been regularly given, and the children had little or no food to-day."

Clara was shocked. "No food to-day!" said she to herself, "and I have been playing all day on my lute under the acacias by the lake!"

Her father did not seem to observe her emotion, but turned to his son.

"I left her better," said the latter; "the medicines I carried eased her pain, and I had the pleasure to see her children make a joyful supper."

Clara, perhaps for the first time in her life, envied him his pleasure; her heart was full, and she sat silent. "No food to-day!" thought she.

She retired pensively to her chamber. The sweet serenity with which she usually went to rest was vanished, for she could no longer reflect on the past day with satisfaction.

"What a pity," said she, "that what is so pleasing should be the cause of so much pain! This lute is my delight and my torment!" This reflection occasioned her much internal debate; but before she could come to any resolution upon the point in question she fell asleep.

She awoke very early the next morning, and impatiently watched the progress of the dawn. The sun at length appearing, she arose, and, determined to make all the atonement in her power for her former neglect, hastened to the cottage.

Here she remained a considerable time, and when she retured to the château her countenance had recovered all its usual serenity; she resolved, however, not to touch her lute that day.

Till the hour of breakfast she busied herself in binding up the flowers and pruning the shoots that were too luxuriant; and she at length found herself, she scarcely knew how, beneath her beloved acacias by the side of the lake. "Ah!" said she with a sigh, "how sweetly would the song I learned yesterday sound now over the waters!" But she remembered her determination, and checked the step she was involuntarily taking towards the château.

She attended her father in the library at the usual hour, and learned from his discourse with her brother on what had been read the two preceding days, that she had lost much entertaining knowledge. She requested her father would inform her to what this conversation alluded; but he calmly replied that she had preferred another amusement at the time when the subject was discussed, and must therefore content herself with ignorance. "You would reap the rewards of study from the amusements of idleness," said he; "learn to be reasonable—do not expect to unite inconsistencies."

Clara felt the justness of this rebuke, and remembered her lute. "What mischief has it occasioned!" sighed she. "Yes, I am determined not to touch it all this day. I will prove that I am able to control my inclinations when I see it necessary so to do." Thus resolving, she applied herself to study with more than usual assiduity.

She adhered to her resolution, and towards the close of day went into the garden to amuse herself. The evening was still, and uncommonly beautiful. Nothing was heard but the faint shivering of the leaves, which returned but at intervals—making silence more solemn—and the distant murmurs of the torrents that rolled among the cliffs. As she stood by the lake and watched the sun slowly sinking below the Alps, whose summits were tinged with gold and purple; as she saw the last rays of light gleam upon the waters, whose surface was not curled by the lightest air, she sighed, "Oh, how enchanting would be the sound of my lute at this moment, on this spot, and when everything is so still around me!"

The temptation was too powerful for the resolution of Clara; she ran to the château, returned with the instrument to her dear acacias, and beneath their shade continued to play till the surrounding objects faded in darkness from her sight. But the moon arose, and, shedding a trembling lustre on the lake, made the scene more captivating than ever.

It was impossible to quit so delightful a spot; Clara repeated her favourite airs again and again. The beauty of the hour awakened all her genius; she never played with such expression before, and she listened with increasing rapture to the tones as they languished over the waters and died away on the distant air. She was perfectly enchanted.

"No! nothing was ever so delightful as to play on the lute beneath her acacias, on the margin of the lake, by moonlight!"

When she returned to the château, supper was over. La Luc had observed Clara, and would not suffer her to be interrupted.

When the enthusiasm of the hour was passed, she recollected that she had broken her resolution, and the reflection gave her pain.

"I prided myself on controlling my inclinations," said she, "and I have weakly yielded to their direction. But what evil have I incurred by indulging them this evening? I have neglected no duty, for I had none to perform. Of what then have I to accuse myself? It would have been absurd to have kept my resolution, and denied myself a pleasure, when there appeared no reason for this self-denial."

She paused, not quite satisfied with this reasoning. Suddenly resuming her inquiry:

"But how," said she, "am I certain that I should have resisted my inclinations if there had been a reason for opposing them? If the poor family whom I neglected yesterday had been unsupplied to-day, I fear I should again have forgotten them while I played on my lute on the banks of the lake."

She then recollected all that her father had

at different times said on the subject of self-command, and she felt some pain.

"No," said she, "if I do not consider that to preserve a resolution which I have once solemnly formed is a sufficient reason to control my inclinations, I fear no other motive would long restrain me. I seriously determined not to touch my lute this whole day, and I have broken my resolution. To-morrow, perhaps, I may be tempted to neglect some duty, for I have discovered that I cannot rely on my own prudence. Since I cannot conquer temptation, I will fly from it."

On the following morning she brought her lute to La Luc, and begged he would receive it again, and at least keep it till she had taught her inclinations to submit to control. The heart of La Luc swelled as she spoke.

"No, Clara," said he, "it is unnecessary that I should receive your lute; the sacrifice you would make proves you worthy of my confidence. Take back the instrument; since you have sufficient resolution to resign it when it leads you from duty, I doubt not that you will be able to control its influence now that it is restored to you."

Clara felt a degree of pleasure and pride at these words, such as she had never before experienced, but she thought that to deserve the commendation they bestowed, it was necessary to complete the sacrifice she had begun. In the virtuous enthusiasm of the moment, the delights of music were forgotten in those of aspiring to well-earned praise; and when she refused the lute thus offered she was conscious only of exquisite sensations.

"Dear sir," said she, tears of pleasure swelling in her eyes, "allow me to deserve the praises you bestow, and then I shall indeed be happy."

La Luc thought she had never resembled her mother so much as at this instant, and, tenderly kissing her, he for some moments wept in silence. When he was able to speak:

"You do already deserve my praises," said he, "and I restore your lute as a reward for the conduct that excites them."

This scene called back recollections too tender for the heart of La Luc, and giving Clara the instrument, he abruptly quitted the room.

La Luc's son, a youth of much promise, was designed by his father for the church, and had received from him an excellent education, which, however, it was thought necessary he should finish at a university—that of Geneva was fixed upon by La Luc. His scheme had been to make his son not a scholar only, he was ambitious that he should also be enviable as a man. From early infancy he had accustomed him to hardihood and endurance, and as he advanced in youth, he encouraged him in manly exercises, and acquainted him with the useful arts as well as with abstract science.

He was high-spirited and ardent in his temper, but his heart was generous and affectionate. He looked forward to Geneva, and to the new world it would disclose, with the sanguine expectations of youth; and in the delight of these expectations was absorbed the regret he would otherwise have felt at a separation from his family.

A brother of the late Madame La Luc, who was by birth an Englishwoman, resided at Geneva with his family. To have been related to his wife was a sufficient claim upon the heart of La Luc, and he had, therefore, always kept up an intercourse with Mr. Audley, though the difference in their characters and manner of thinking would never permit this association to advance into friendship. La Luc now wrote to him, signifying an intention of sending his son to Geneva, and recommending him to his care. To this letter Mr. Audley returned a friendly answer, and, a short time after, an acquaintance of La Luc's being called to Geneva, he determined that his son should accompany him. The separation was painful to La Luc, and almost insupportable to Clara. Madame was grieved, and took care that he should have a sufficient quantity of medicines put in his travelling trunk; she was also at some pains to point out their virtues, and the different complaints for which they were requisite, but she was careful to deliver her lecture during the absence of her brother.

La Luc, with his daughter, accompanied his son on horseback to the next town, which was about eight miles from Leloncourt, and there again enforcing all the advice he had formerly given him respecting his conduct and pursuits, and again yielding to the tender weakness of the father, he bade him farewell. Clara wept, and felt more sorrow at this parting than the occasion could justify; but this was almost the first time she had known grief, and she artlessly yielded to its influence.

La Luc and Clara travelled pensively back, and the day was closing when they came within view of the lake, and soon after the château. Never had it appeared gloomy till now; but now, Clara wandered forlornly through every deserted apartment where she had been accustomed to see her brother, and recollected a thousand little circumstances, which, had he been present, she would have thought immaterial, but on which imagination now stamped a value. The garden, the scenes around, all wore a melancholy aspect, and it was long ere they resumed their natural character, and Clara recovered her vivacity.

Near four years had elapsed since this separation, when one evening, as Madame La Luc and her niece were sitting at work together in the parlour, a good woman in the neighbourhood desired to be admitted. She came to ask for some medicines and the advice of Madame La Luc. "Here is a sad accident happened at our cottage, madam," said she ; " I am sure my heart aches for the poor young creature." Madame La Luc desired she would explain herself ; and the woman proceeded to say, that her brother Peter, whom she had not seen for so many years, was arrived, and had brought a young lady to her cottage, who she verily believed was dying. She described her disorder, and acquainted Madame with what particulars of her mournful story Peter had related, failing not to exaggerate such as her compassion for the unhappy stranger and her love of the marvellous prompted.

The account appeared a very extraordinary one to Madame ; but pity for the forlorn condition of the young sufferer induced her to inquire further into the affair. " Do let me go to her, madam," said Clara, who had been listening with ready compassion to the poor woman's narrative ; " do suffer me to go—she must want comforts, and I wish much to see how she is." Madame asked some further questions concerning her disorder, and then, taking off her spectacles, she arose from her chair and said she would go herself. Clara desired to accompany her. They put on their hats and followed the good woman to the cottage, where, in a very small, close room, on a miserable bed, lay Adeline, pale, emaciated, and unconscious of all around her.

Madame turned to the woman and asked how long she had been in this way, while Clara went up to the bed, and taking the almost lifeless hand that lay on the quilt, looked anxiously in her face. "She observes nothing," said she, " poor creature ! I wish she was at the château ; she would be better accommodated, and I could nurse her there."

The woman told Madame La Luc that the young lady had lain in that state for several hours. Madame examined her pulse, and shook her head. " This room is very close," said she.

" Very close, indeed," cried Clara, eagerly. " Surely she would be better at the château, if she could be moved."

"We will see about that," said her aunt. " In the meantime let me speak to Peter ; it is some years since I saw him." She went to the outer room, and the woman ran out of the cottage to look for him. When she was gone, " This is a miserable habitation for the poor stranger," said Clara ; " she will never be well here ; do, madam, let her be carried to our house ; I am sure my father would wish it. Besides, there is something in her features, even inanimate as they now are, that prejudices me in her favour."

" Shall I never persuade you to give up that romantic notion of judging people by their faces ?" said her aunt. " What sort of a face she has is of very little consequence ; her condition is lamentable, and I am desirous of

amending it, but I wish first to ask Peter a few questions concerning her."

" Thank you, my dear aunt," said Clara ; " she will be removed then !" Madame La Luc was going to reply, but Peter now entered, and, expressing great joy at seeing her again, inquired how Monsieur La Luc and Clara did. Clara immediately welcomed honest Peter to his native place, and he returned her salutation with many expressions of surprise at finding her so much grown. "Though I have so often dandled you in my arms, ma'amselle, I should never have known you again. Young twigs shoot fast, as they say."

Madame La Luc now inquired into the particulars of Adeline's story, and heard as much as Peter knew of it, being only that his late master found her in a very distressed situation, and that he had himself brought her from the abbey to save her from a French marquis. The simplicity of Peter's manner would not suffer her to question his veracity, though some of the circumstances he related excited all her surprise, and awakened all her pity. Tears frequently stood in Clara's eyes during the course of his narrative, and when he concluded she said, "Dear madam, I am sure, when my father learns the history of this unhappy young woman, he will not refuse to be a parent to her, and I will be her sister."

" She deserves it all," said Peter, "for she is very good indeed." He then proceeded in a strain of praise which was very unusual with him. " I will go home and consult with my brother about her," said Madame La Luc, rising ; " she certainly ought to be removed to a more airy room. The château is so near, that I think she may be carried thither without much risk."

" Heaven bless you, madam !" cried Peter, rubbing his hands, " for your goodness to my poor young lady."

La Luc had just returned from his evening walk when they reached the château. Madame told him where she had been, and related the history of Adeline and her present condition. "By all means have her removed hither," said La Luc, whose eyes bore testimony to the tenderness of his heart. " She can be better attended to here than in Susan's cottage."

" I knew you would say so, my dear father," said Clara ; " I will go and order the green bed to be prepared for her."

" Be patient, niece," said Madame La Luc ; " there is no occasion for such haste. Some things are to be considered first, but you are young and romantic." La Luc smiled. " The evening is now closed," resumed Madame, " it will, therefore, be dangerous to remove her before morning. Early to-morrow a room shall be got ready, and she shall be brought here ; in the meantime I will go and make up a medicine, which I hope may be of service to her,". Clara reluctantly assented to this delay, and Madame La Luc retired to her closet.

On the following morning Adeline, wrapped in blankets, and sheltered as much as possible from the air, was brought to the château, where the good La Luc desired she might have every attention paid her, and where Clara watched over her with unceasing anxiety and tenderness. She remained in a state of torpor during the greater part of the day, but towards evening she breathed more freely; and Clara, who still watched by her bed, had at length the pleasure of perceiving that her senses were restored. It was at this moment that she found herself in the situation from which we have digressed to give this account of the venerable La Luc and his family. The reader will find that his virtues and his friendship to Adeline deserved this notice.

CHAPTER XVI.

Still Fancy, to herself unkind,
Awakes to grief the soften'd mind,
And points the bleeding friend.
COLLINS.

ADELINE, assisted by a fine constitution, and the kind attentions of her new friends, was, in a little more than a week, so much recovered as to leave her chamber. She was introduced to La Luc, whom she met with tears of gratitude, and thanked for his goodness in a manner so warm, yet so artless, as interested him still more in her favour. During the progress of her recovery, the sweetness of her behaviour had entirely won the heart of Clara and greatly interested that of her aunt, whose reports of Adeline, together with the praises bestowed by Clara, had excited both esteem and curiosity in the breast of La Luc; and he now met her with an expression of benignity which spoke peace and comfort to her heart. She had acquainted Madame La Luc with such particulars of her story as Peter, either through ignorance or inattention, had not communicated, suppressing only, through a false delicacy, perhaps, an acknowledgment of her attachment to Theodore. These circumstances were repeated to La Luc, who, ever sensible to the sufferings of others, was particularly interested by the singular misfortunes of Adeline.

Near a fortnight had elapsed since her removal to the château, when one morning La Luc desired to speak with her alone. She followed him into his study, and then, in a manner the most delicate, he told her that as he found she was so unfortunate in her father, he desired she would henceforth consider him as her parent, and his house as her home.

"You and Clara shall be equally my daughters," continued he; "I am rich in having such children."

The strong emotions of surprise and gratitude for some time kept Adeline silent.

"Do not thank me," said La Luc; "I know all you would say, and I also know that I am but doing my duty. I thank God that my duty and my pleasures are generally in unison."

Adeline wiped away the tears which his goodness had excited, and was going to speak; but La Luc pressed her hand, and turning away to conceal his emotion, walked out of the room.

Adeline was now considered as a part of the family, and in the parental kindness of La Luc, the sisterly affection of Clara, and the steady and uniform regard of Madame, she would have been happy as she was thankful, had not unceasing anxiety for the fate of Theodore, of whom in this solitude she was less likely than ever to hear, corroded her heart, and embittered every moment of reflection. Even when sleep obliterated for awhile the memory of the past, his image frequently arose to her fancy, accompanied by all the exaggerations of terror. She saw him in chains, and struggling in the grasp of ruffians; or saw him led, amidst the dreadful preparations for execution, into the field; she saw the agony of his look, and heard him repeat her name in frantic accents, till the horrors of the scene overcame her, and she awoke.

A similarity of taste and character attached her to Clara, yet the misery that preyed upon her heart was of a nature too delicate to be spoken of, and she never mentioned Theodore even to her friend. Her illness had yet left her weak and languid, and the perpetual anxiety of her mind contributed to prolong this state. She endeavoured, by strong and almost continual efforts, to abstract her thoughts from their mournful subject, and was often successful. La Luc had an excellent library, and the instruction it offered at once gratified her love of knowledge and withdrew her mind from painful recollections. His conversation, too, afforded her another refuge from misery.

But her chief amusement was to wander among the sublime scenery of the adjacent country, sometimes with Clara, though often with no other companion than a book. There were indeed times when the conversation of her friend imposed a painful restraint, and, when given up to reflection, she would ramble alone through scenes whose solitary grandeur assisted and soothed the melancholy of her heart. Here she would retrace all the conduct of her beloved Theodore, and endeavour to recollect his exact countenance, his air, and manner. Now she would weep at the remembrance, and then, suddenly considering that he had, perhaps, already suffered an ignominious death for her sake, even in consequence of the very action which had proved his love, a dreadful despair would seize her, and, arresting her tears, would threaten to bear down every barrier that fortitude and reason could oppose.

Fearing longer to trust to her own thoughts she would hurry home, and by a desperate effort would try to lose, in the conversation of La Luc, the remembrance of the past. Her melancholy, when he observed it, La Luc attributed to a sense of the cruel treatment she had received from her father; a circumstance which, by exciting his compassion, endeared her strongly to his heart; while that love of rational conversation, which, in her calmer hours, so frequently appeared, opened to him a new source of amusement in the cultivation of a mind eager for knowledge, and susceptible of all the energies of genius. She found a melancholy pleasure in listening to the soft tones of Clara's lute, and would often soothe her mind by attempting to repeat the airs she heard.

The gentleness of her manners, partaking so much of that pensive character which marked La Luc's, was soothing to his heart, and tinctured his behaviour with a degree of tenderness that imparted comfort to her, and gradually won her entire confidence and affection. She saw, with extreme concern, the declining state of his health, and united her efforts with those of the family to amuse and revive him.

The pleasing society of which she partook, and the quietness of the country, at length restored her mind to a state of tolerable composure. She was now acquainted with all the wild walks of the neighbouring mountains, and, never tired of viewing their scenery, she often indulged herself in traversing alone their unfrequented paths, where now and then a peasant from a neighbouring village was all that interrupted the profound solitude. She generally took with her a book, that, if she perceived her thoughts inclined to fix on the one object of her grief, she might force them to a subject less dangerous to her peace. She had become a tolerable proficient in English while at the convent, where she received her education, and the instruction of La Luc, who was well acquainted with the language, now served to perfect her. He was partial to the English; he admired their character and the constitution of their laws, and his library contained a collection of the best authors, particularly of their philosophers and poets.

Adeline found that no species of writing had power so effectually to withdraw her mind from the contemplation of its misery as the higher kinds of poetry, and in these her taste soon taught her to distinguish the superiority of the English over that of the French. The genius of the language, more, perhaps, than the genius of the people—if, indeed, the distinction may be allowed—occasioned this.

She frequently took a volume of Shakspeare or Milton, and having gained some wild eminence, would seat herself beneath the pines, whose low murmurs soothed her heart, and conspired with the visions of the poet to lull her to forgetfulness of grief.

One evening, when Clara was engaged at home, Adeline wandered alone to a favourite spot among the rocks that bordered the lake. It was an eminence which commanded an entire view of the lake, and of the stupendous mountains that environed it. A few ragged thorns grew from the precipice beneath, which descended perpendicularly to the water's edge; and above rose a thick wood of larch, pine, and fir, intermingled with some chestnut and mountain-ash. The evening was fine, and the air so still, that it scarcely waved the light leaves of the trees around, or rippled the broad expanse of the waters below. Adeline gazed on the scene with a kind of still rapture, and watched the sun sinking amid a crimson glow, which tinted the bosom of the lake and the snowy heads of the distant Alps. The delight which the scenery inspired,

> Soothing each gust of passion into peace,
> All but the swellings of the soften'd heart,
> That waken, not disturb, the tranquil mind!

was now heightened by the tones of a French horn, and looking on the lake, she perceived, at some distance, a pleasure-boat. As it was a spectacle rather uncommon in this solitude, she concluded the boat contained a party of foreigners come to view the wonderful scenery of the country, or perhaps of Genevois, who chose to amuse themselves on a lake almost as grand, though much less extensive, than their own; and the latter conjecture was probably just.

As she listened to the mellow and enchanting tones of the horn, which gradually sank away in distance, the scene appeared more lovely than before, and finding it impossible to forbear attempting to paint in language what was so beautiful in reality, she composed the following

STANZAS.

How smooth that lake expands its ample breast!
  Where smiles in soften'd glow the summer sky;
How vast the rocks that o'er its surface rest;
  How wild the scenes its winding shores supply!

Now down the western steep slow sinks the sun,
  And paints with yellow gleam the tufted woods;
While here the mountain-shadows, broad and dun,
  Sweep o'er the crystal mirror of the floods.

Mark how his splendour tips with partial light
  Those shattered battlements! that on the brow
Of yon bold promontory burst to sight
  From o'er the woods that darkly spread below.

In the soft blush of light's reflected power,
  The ridgy rock, the woods that crown its steep,
Th' illumin'd battlement, and darker tower,
  On the smooth wave in trembling beauty sleep.

But lo ! thé sun recalls his fervid ray,
And cold, and dim, the wat'ry visions fail ;
While o'er yon cliff, whose pointed crags decay,
Mild evening draws her thin empurpled veil !

How sweet that strain of melancholy horn !
That floats along the slowly-ebbing wave ;
And up the far-receding mountains borne,
Returns a dying close from Echo's cave !

Hail ! shadowy forms of still, expressive eve ;
Your pensive graces, stealing on my heart,
Bid all the fine-attun'd emotions live,
And Fancy all her loveliest dreams impart.

La Luc, observing how much Adeline was
charmed with the features of the country, and
desirous of amusing her melancholy, which,
notwithstanding her efforts, was often too
apparent, wished to show her other scenes
than those to which her walks were circumscribed. He proposed a party on horseback
to take a nearer view of the glaciers ; to
attempt their ascent was a difficulty and
fatigue to which neither La Luc, in his present
state of health, nor Adeline was equal. She
had not been accustomed to ride single, and
the mountainous road they were to pass made
the experiment rather dangerous ; but she
concealed her fears, and they were not sufficient to make her wish to forego an enjoyment
such as was now offered her.

The following day was fixed for this excursion. La Luc and his party arose at an
early hour, and having taken a slight breakfast,
they set out towards the glacier of Montanvert,
which lay at a few leagues' distance. Peter
carried a small basket of provisions ; and it
was their plan to dine on some spot in the
open air.

It is unnecessary to describe the high
enthusiasm of Adeline, the more complacent
pleasure of La Luc, and the transports of
Clara, as the scenes of this romantic country
shifted to their eyes. Now frowning in dark
and gloomy grandeur, it exhibited only tremendous rocks, and cataracts rolling from the
heights into some deep and narrow valley,
along which their united waters roared and
foamed, and burst away to regions inaccessible
to mortal foot ; and now the scene arose less
fiercely wild ;

The pomp of groves and garniture of fields

were intermingled with the ruder features of
nature, and while the snow froze on the
summit of the mountain, the vine blushed at
its foot.

Engaged in interesting conversation, and
by the admiration which the country excited,
they travelled on till noon, when they looked
round for a pleasant spot where they might
rest and take refreshment. At some little
distance they perceived the ruins of a fabric,
which had once been a castle ; it stood nearly
on a point of rock that overhung a deep
valley ; and its broken turrets, rising from

among the woods that embosomed it, heightened the picturesque beauty of the object.

The edifice invited curiosity, and the shades
repose. La Luc and his party advanced.

Deep struck with awe they mark'd the dome
    o'erthrown,
Where once the beauty bloom'd, the warrior shone ;
They saw the castle's mould'ring tow'rs decay'd,
The loose stone tottering o'er the trembling shade.

They seated themselves on the grass, under
the shade of some high trees, near the ruins.
An opening in the woods afforded a view of
the distant Alps—the deep silence of solitude
reigned. For some time they were lost in
meditation.

Adeline felt a sweet complacency such as
she had long been a stranger to. Looking at
La Luc, she perceived a tear stealing down
his cheek, while the elevation of his mind was
strongly expressed on his countenance. He
turned on Clara his eyes, which were now filled
with tenderness, and made an effort to recover
himself.

"The stillness and total seclusion of this
scene," said Adeline, "those stupendous
mountains, the gloomy grandeur of these
woods, together with that monument of faded
glory on which the hand of time is so emphatically impressed, diffuse a sacred enthusiasm over the mind, and awaken sensations
truly sublime."

La Luc was going to speak ; but Peter,
coming forward, desired to know whether he
had not better open the wallet, as he fancied
his honour and the young ladies must be
main hungry, jogging on so far up-hill and
down before dinner. They acknowledged the
truth of honest Peter's suspicion, and accepted his hint.

Refreshments were spread on the grass, and
having seated themselves under the canopy of
waving woods, surrounded by the sweets of
wild flowers, they inhaled the pure breeze of
the Alps, which might be called spirit of air,
and partook of a repast which these circumstances rendered delicious.

When they arose to depart, "I am unwilling," said Clara, "to quit this charming spot.
How delightful would it be to pass one's life
beneath these shades, with the friends who
are dear to one !" La Luc smiled at the
romantic simplicity of the idea ; but Adeline
sighed deeply at the image of felicity, and of
Theodore, which it recalled, and turned away
to conceal her tears.

They now mounted their horses, and soon
after arrived at the foot of Montanvert. The
emotions of Adeline, as she contemplated in
various points of view the astonishing objects
around her, surpassed all expression ; and the
feelings of the whole party were too strong to
admit of conversation. The profound stillness
which reigned in these regions of solitude

inspired awe, and heightened the sublimity of the scenery to an exquisite degree.

"It seems," said Adeline, "as if we were walking over the ruins of the world, and were the only persons who had survived the wreck. I can scarcely persuade myself that we are not left alone on the globe."

"The view of these objects," said La Luc, "lifts the soul to their Great Author, and we contemplate with a feeling almost too vast for humanity, the sublimity of his nature in the grandeur of his works." La Luc raised his eyes, filled with tears, to heaven, and was for some moments lost in silent adoration.

They quitted these scenes with extreme reluctance, but the hour of the day, and the appearance of the clouds, which seemed gathering for a storm, made them hasten their departure. Adeline almost wished to have witnessed the tremendous effect of a thunderstorm in these regions.

They returned to Lelencourt by a different route, and the shade of the overhanging precipices was deepened by the gloom of the atmosphere. It was evening when they came within view of the lake, which the travellers rejoiced to see. For the storm so long threatened was now fast approaching; the thunder murmured among the Alps, and the dark vapours that rolled heavily along their sides, heightened their dreadful sublimity. La Luc would have quickened his pace, but the road winding down the steep side of a mountain, made caution necessary. The darkening air, and the lightnings that now flashed along the horizon, terrified Clara, but she withheld the expression of her fear in consideration of her father. A peal of thunder, which seemed to shake the earth to its foundations, and was reverberated in tremendous echoes from the cliffs, burst over their heads. Clara's horse took fright at the sound, and, setting off, hurried her with amazing velocity down the mountain towards the lake, which washed its foot. The agony of La Luc, who viewed her progress in the horrible expectation of seeing her dashed down the precipice that bordered the road, is not to be described.

Clara kept her seat, but terror had almost deprived her of sense. Her efforts to preserve herself were mechanical, for she scarcely knew what she did. The horse, however, carried her safely almost to the foot of the mountain, but was making towards the lake when a gentleman, who travelled along the road, caught the bridle as the animal endeavoured to pass. The sudden stopping of the horse threw Clara to the ground, and, impatient of restraint, the animal burst from the hand of the stranger, and plunged into the lake. The violence of the fall deprived her of recollection; but while the stranger endeavoured to support her, his servant ran to fetch water.

She soon recovered, and unclosing her eyes, found herself in the arms of a chevalier, who appeared to support her with difficulty. The compassion expressed in his countenance, while he inquired how she did, revived her spirits, and she was endeavouring to thank him for his kindness, when La Luc and Adeline came up. The terror impressed upon her father's features was perceived by Clara; languid as she was, she tried to raise herself, and said, with a faint smile, which betrayed instead of disguising her sufferings, "Dear sir, I am not hurt." Her pale countenance, and the blood that trickled down her cheek, contradicted her words. But La Luc, to whom terror had suggested the utmost possible evil, now rejoiced to hear her speak; he recalled some presence of mind, and while Adeline applied her salts, he chafed her temples.

When she revived she told him how much she was obliged to the stranger. La Luc endeavoured to express his gratitude, but the former, interrupting him, begged he might be spared the pain of receiving thanks for having followed only an impulse of common humanity.

They were now not far from Lelencourt; but the evening was almost shut in, and the thunder murmured deeply among the hills. La Luc was distressed how to convey Clara home.

In endeavouring to raise her from the ground the stranger betrayed such symptoms of pain, that La Luc inquired concerning it. The sudden jerk which the horse had given the arm of the chevalier in escaping from his hold had violently sprained his shoulder, and rendered his arm almost useless. The pain was exquisite, and La Luc, whose fears for his daughter were now subsiding, was shocked at the circumstance, and pressed the stranger to accompany him to the village, where relief might be obtained. He accepted the invitation, and Clara, being at length placed on a horse led by her father, was conducted to the château.

When Madame, who had been looking out for La Luc some time, perceived the cavalcade approaching she was alarmed, and her apprehensions were confirmed when she saw the situation of her niece. Clara was carried into the house, and La Luc would have sent for a surgeon, but there were none within several leagues of the village, neither were there any of the physical profession within the same distance. Clara was assisted to her chamber by Adeline, and Madame La Luc undertook to examine the wounds. The result restored peace to the family; for though she was much bruised she had escaped material injury; a slight contusion on the forehead had occasioned the bloodshed which at first alarmed La Luc. Madame undertook to restore her niece in a few days, with the assistance of a balsam composed by herself, on the virtues of which she descanted

H

with great eloquence, till interrupted by La Luc, who reminded her of the condition of her patient.

Madame, having bathed Clara's bruises, and given her a cordial of incomparable efficacy, left her, and Adeline watched in the chamber of her friend till she retired to her own for the night.

La Luc, whose spirits had suffered much perturbation, was now tranquillised by the report his sister made of Clara. He introduced the stranger, and having mentioned the accident he had met with, desired that he might have immediate assistance. Madame hastened to her closet, and it is perhaps difficult to determine whether she felt most concern for the sufferings of her guest, or pleasure at the opportunity thus offered of displaying her physical skill. However this might be, she quitted the room with great alacrity, and very quickly returned with a phial containing her inestimable balsam ; and having given the necessary direction for the application of it, she left the stranger to the care of his servant.

La Luc insisted that the chevalier, M. Verneuil, should not leave the château that night, and he very readily submitted to be detained. His manners during the evening were as frank and engaging as the hospitality and gratitude of La Luc were sincere, and they soon entered into interesting conversation. M. Verneuil conversed like a man who had seen much and thought more ; and if he discovered any prejudice in his opinions, it was evidently the prejudice of a mind which, seeing objects through the medium of its own goodness, tinges them with the hue of its predominant quality. La Luc was much pleased, for, in his retired situation, he had not often an opportunity of receiving the pleasure which results from a communion of intelligent minds. He found that M. Verneuil had travelled. La Luc having asked some questions relative to England, they fell into discourse concerning the national characters of the French and English.

"If it is the privilege of wisdom," said M. Verneuil, " to look beyond happiness, I own I had rather be without it. When we observe the English, their laws, writings, and conversation, and at the same time mark their countenances, manners, and the frequency of suicide among them, we are apt to believe that wisdom and happiness are incompatible. If, on the other hand, we turn to their neighbours the French, and see* their wretched policy, their sparkling but sophistical discourse, frivolous occupations, and withal, their gay animated air, we shall be compelled to acknowledge that happiness and folly too often dwell together."

* It must be remembered that this was said in the seventeenth century.

"It is the end of wisdom," said La Luc, "to attain happiness, and I can hardly dignify that conduct or course of thinking which tends to misery with the name of wisdom. By this rule, perhaps, the folly, as we term it, of the French, deserves, since its effect is happiness, to be called wisdom. That airy thoughtlessness, which seems alike to contemn reflection and anticipation, produces all the effect of it, without reducing its subjects to the mortification of philosophy."

Discoursing on the variety of opinions that are daily formed on the same conduct, La Luc observed how much that which is commonly called opinion is the result of passion and temper.

"True," said M. Verneuil, "there is a tone of thought, as there is a key-note in music, that leads all its weaker affections. Thus, where the powers of judging may be equal, the disposition to judge is different at different times, and the actions of men are at least but too often arraigned by whim and caprice, by partial vanity, and the humour of the moment."

Here La Luc took occasion to reprobate the conduct of those writers who, by showing the dark side only of human nature, and by dwelling on the evils only which are incident to humanity, have sought to degrade man in his own eyes, and to make him discontented with life.

"What should we say of a painter," continued La Luc, "who collected in his piece objects of a black hue only, who presented you with a black man, a black horse, a black dog, &c. &c., and tells you that his is a picture of nature, and that nature is black? 'Tis true, you would reply, the objects you exhibit do exist in nature, but they form a very small part of her works. You say that nature is black, and, to prove it, you have collected on your canvas all the animals of this hue that exist. But you have forgotten to paint the green earth, the blue sky, the white man, and objects of all these various hues with which creation abounds."

The countenance of M. Verneuil lightened with peculiar animation during the discourse of La Luc. "To think well of his nature," said he, "is necessary to the dignity and to the happiness of man. There is a decent pride which becomes every mind, and is congenial to virtue. That consciousness of innate dignity, which shows him the glory of his nature, will be his best protection from the meanness of vice. Where this consciousness is wanting," continued M. Verneuil, "there can be no sense of moral honour, and consequently none of the higher principles of action. What can be expected of him who says that it is his nature to be mean and selfish? Or who can doubt that he who thinks thus, thinks from the experience of his own heart, from the tendency of his own inclinations? Let it always be remembered, that he who would persuade men to be good ought to show them that they may be great."

"You speak," said La Luc, "with the honest enthusiasm of a virtuous mind; and, in obeying the impulse of your heart, you utter the truths of philosophy; and, trust me, a bad heart and a truly philosophic head have never yet been united in the same individual. Vicious inclinations not only corrupt the heart, but the understanding, and thus lead to false reasoning. Virtue only is on the side of truth."

La Luc and his guest, mutually pleased with each other, entered upon the discussion of subjects so interesting to them both, that it was late before they parted for the night.

CHAPTER XVII.

'Twas such a scene as gave a kind relief
To memory, in sweetly pensive grief.
                          VIRGIL'S TOMB.
Mine be the breezy hill that skirts the down,
Where a green grassy turf is all I crave,
  With here and there a violet bestrown,
Fast by a brook or fountain's murmuring wave,
And many an evening sun shine sweetly on my
grave.   THE MINSTREL.

REPOSE had so much restored Clara, that when Adeline, anxious to know how she did, went early in the morning to her chamber, she found her already risen and ready to attend the family at breakfast. M. Verneuil appeared also, but his looks betrayed a want of rest, and indeed he had suffered, during the night, a degree of anguish from his arm, which it was an effort of some resolution to endure in silence. It was now swelled and inflamed, and this might in some degree be attributed to the effect of Madame La Luc's balsam, whose restorative qualities had for once failed. The whole family sympathised with his sufferings, and Madame, at the request of M. Verneuil, abandoned her balsam, and substituted an emollient fomentation.

From an application of this he, in a short time, found an abatement of the pain, and returned to the breakfast-table with greater composure. The happiness which La Luc felt at seeing his daughter in safety was very apparent, but the warmth of his gratitude towards her preserver he found it difficult to express. Clara spoke the genuine emotions of her heart, with artless but modest energy, and testified sincere concern for the sufferings which she had occasioned M. Verneuil.

The pleasure received from the company of his guest, and the consideration of the essential service he had rendered him, cooperated with the natural hospitality of La Luc, and he pressed M. Verneuil to remain some time at the château.

"I can never repay the service you have done me," said La Luc; "yet I seek to increase my obligations to you by requesting you will prolong your visit, and thus allow me an opportunity of cultivating your acquaintance."

M. Verneuil, who at the time he met La Luc was travelling from Geneva to a distant part of Savoy, merely for the purpose of viewing the country, being now delighted with his host, and with everything around him, willingly accepted the invitation. In this circumstance prudence concurred with inclination; for to have pursued his journey on horseback, in his present situation, would have been dangerous, if not impracticable.

The morning was spent in conversation, in which M. Verneuil displayed a mind enriched with taste, enlightened by science, and enlarged by observation. The situation of the château, and the features of the surrounding scenery, charmed him, and in the evening he found himself able to walk with La Luc, and explore the beauties of this romantic region. As they passed through the village, the salutations of the peasants, in whom love and respect were equally blended, and their eager inquiries after Clara, bore testimony to the character of La Luc, while his countenance expressed a serene satisfaction, arising from the consciousness of deserving and possessing their love.

"I live surrounded by my children," said he, turning to M. Verneuil, who had noticed their eagerness, "for such I consider my parishioners. In discharging the duties of my office I am repaid, not only by my own conscience, but by their gratitude. There is a luxury in observing their simple and honest love, which I would not exchange for anything the world calls blessings."

"Yet the world, sir, would call the pleasures of which you speak romantic," said M. Verneuil, "for to be sensible of this pure and exquisite delight requires a heart untainted with the vicious pleasures of society—pleasures that deaden its finest feelings, and poison the source of its truest enjoyments."

They pursued their way along the borders of the lake, sometimes under the shade of hanging woods, and sometimes over hillocks of turfs, where the scene opened in all its wild magnificence. M. Verneuil often stopped in raptures to observe and point out the singular beauties it exhibited, while La Luc, pleased with the delight his friend expressed, surveyed with more than usual satisfaction the objects which had so often charmed him before. But there was a tender melancholy in the tone of his voice and his countenance, which arose from the recollection of having often traced these scenes, and partaken of the pleasure they inspired, with her who had long since bade them an eternal farewell.

They presently quitted the lake, and, wind-

H 2

ing up a steep ascent between the woods, came, after an hour's walk, to a green summit, which appeared, among the savage rocks that environed it, like the blossom on the thorn. It was a spot formed for solitary delight, inspiring that soothing tenderness so dear to the feeling mind, and which calls back to memory the images of past regret, softened by distance, and endeared by frequent recollection. Wild shrubs grew from the crevices of the rocks beneath, and the high trees of pine and cedar that waved above afforded a melancholy and romantic shade. The silence of the scene was interrupted only by the breeze as it rolled over the woods, and by the solitary notes of the birds that inhabited the cliffs.

From this point the eye commanded an entire view of those majestic and sublime Alps, whose aspect fills the soul with emotions of indescribable awe, and seems to lift it to a nobler nature. The village and château of La Luc appeared in the bosom of the mountains, a peaceful retreat from the storms that gathered on their tops. All the faculties of M. Verneuil were absorbed in admiration, and he was for some time quite silent ; at length, bursting into a rhapsody, he turned, and would have addressed La Luc, when he perceived him at a distance, leaning against a rustic urn, over which drooped in beautiful luxuriance the weeping birch.

As he approached, La Luc quitted his position and advanced to meet him, while M. Verneuil inquired upon what occasion the urn had been erected. La Luc, unable to answer, pointed to it, and walked silently away, and M. Verneuil, approaching the urn, read the following inscription :

TO

THE MEMORY OF CLARA LA LUC,

THIS URN

IS ERECTED ON THE SPOT WHICH SHE LOVED, IN TESTIMONY OF THE AFFECTION OF

A HUSBAND.

M. Verneuil now comprehended the whole, and feeling for his friend, was hurt that he had not noticed this monument of his grief. He rejoined La Luc, who was standing on the point of the eminence, contemplating the landscape below with an air more placid, and touched with the sweetness of piety and resignation. He perceived that M. Verneuil was somewhat disconcerted, and he sought to remove his uneasiness.

"You will consider it," said he, "as a mark of my esteem, that I have brought you to this spot. It is never profaned by the presence of the unfeeling. They would deride the faithfulness of an attachment which has so long survived its object, and which, in their own breasts, would quickly have been lost amidst the dissipation of general society. I have cherished in my heart the remembrance of a woman whose virtues claimed all my love ; I have cherished it as a treasure to which I could withdraw from temporary cares and vexations, in the certainty of finding a soothing, though melancholy, comfort."

La Luc paused. M. Verneuil expressed the sympathy he felt, but he knew the sacredness of sorrow, and soon relapsed into silence.

"One of the brightest hopes of a future state," resumed La Luc, "is, that we shall meet again those whom we have loved upon earth. And perhaps our happiness may be permitted to consist very much in the society of our friends, purified from the frailties of mortality, with the finer affections more sweetly attuned, and with the faculties of mind infinitely more elevated and enlarged. We shall then be enabled to comprehend subjects which are too vast for human conception ; to comprehend, perhaps, the sublimity of that Deity who first called us into being. These views of futurity, my friend, elevate us above the evils of this world, and seem to communicate to us a portion of the nature we contemplate.

"Call them not the illusions of a visionary brain," proceeded La Luc ; "I trust in their reality. Of this I am certain, that, whether they are illusions or not, a faith in them ought to be cherished for the comfort it brings to the heart, and reverenced for the dignity it imparts to the mind. Such feelings make a happy and important part of our belief in a future existence ; they give energy to virtue, and stability to principle."

"This," said M. Verneuil, "is what I have often felt, and what every ingenuous mind must acknowledge."

La Luc and M. Verneuil continued in conversation till the sun had left the scene. The mountains, darkened by twilight, assumed a sublimer aspect ; while the tops of some of the highest Alps were yet illumined by the sun's rays, and formed a striking contrast to the shadowy obscurity of the world below. As they descended through the woods, and traversed the margin of the lake, the stillness and solemnity of the hour diffused a pensive sweetness over their minds and sunk them into silence.

They found supper spread, as was usual, in the hall, of which the windows opened upon a garden, where the flowers might be said to yield their fragrance in gratitude to the refreshing dews. The windows were embowered with eglantine and other sweet shrubs, which hung in wild luxuriance around, and formed a beautiful and simple decoration. Clara and Adeline loved to pass the evenings in this hall, where they had acquired the first rudiments of astronomy, and from which they had a wide view of the heavens. La Luc pointed out to them the planets and the fixed stars, explained their laws, and from thence—taking occasion to mingle moral with scientific instruction—would often ascend towards that great *First Cause*, whose nature soars beyond the grasp of human comprehension.

"No study," he would sometimes say, "so much enlarges the mind, or impresses it with so sublime an idea of the Deity, as that of astronomy. When the imagination launches into the regions of space, and contemplates the innumerable worlds which are scattered through it, we are lost in astonishment and awe. This globe appears as a mass of atoms in the immensity of the universe, and man a mere insect. Yet how wonderful that man, whose frame is so diminutive in the scale of beings, should have powers which spurn the narrow boundaries of time and space, soar beyond the sphere of his existence, penetrate the secret laws of nature, and calculate their progressive effects! Oh, how expressively does this prove the spirituality of our being! Let the materialist consider it, and blush that he ever doubted."

In this hall the whole family now met at supper; and during the remainder of the evening the conversation turned upon general subjects, in which Clara joined in modest and judicious remark. La Luc had taught her to familiarise her mind to reasoning, and had accustomed her to deliver her sentiments freely. She spoke them with a simplicity extremely engaging, and which convinced her hearers that the love of knowledge, not the vanity of talking, induced her to converse. M. Verneuil evidently endeavoured to draw forth her sentiments; and Clara, interested by the subjects he introduced, a stranger to affectation, and pleased with the opinions he expressed, answered them with frankness and animation. They retired mutually pleased with each other.

M. Verneuil was about six-and-thirty, his figure manly, his countenance frank and engaging. A quick penetrating eye, whose fire was softened by benevolence, disclosed the chief traits of his character; he was quick to discern, but generous to excuse, the follies of mankind; and while no one more sensibly felt an injury, none more readily accepted the concession of an enemy.

He was by birth a Frenchman. A fortune lately devolved to him had enabled him to execute a plan which his active and inquisitive mind had suggested, of viewing the most remarkable parts of the continent of Europe. He was peculiarly susceptible of the beautiful and sublime in nature. To such a taste Switzerland and the adjacent country was, of all others, the most interesting; and he found the scenery it exhibited infinitely surpassing all that his glowing imagination had formed; he saw with the eye of a painter, and felt with the rapture of a poet.

In the habitation of La Luc he met with the hospitality, the frankness, and the simplicity so characteristic of the country. In his venerable host he saw the strength of philosophy united with the finest tenderness of humanity—a philosophy which taught him to correct his feelings, not to annihilate them; in Clara, the bloom of beauty with the most perfect simplicity of heart; and in Adeline, all the charms of elegance and grace, with a genius deserving of the highest culture. In this family picture the goodness of Madame La Luc was not unperceived or forgotten. The cheerfulness and harmony that reigned within the château was delightful; but the philanthropy which, flowing from the heart of the pastor, was diffused through the whole village, and united the inhabitants in the sweet and firm bonds of social compact, was divine. The beauty of its situation conspired with these circumstances to make Lelencourt seem almost a paradise. M. Verneuil sighed that he must so soon quit it. "I ought to seek no farther," said he, "for here wisdom and happiness dwell together."

The admiration was reciprocal; La Luc and his family found themselves much interested in M. Verneuil, and looked forward to the time of his departure with regret. So warmly they pressed him to prolong his visit, and so powerfully his own inclinations seconded theirs, that he accepted the invitation. La Luc omitted no circumstance which might contribute to the amusement of his guest, who having in a few days recovered the use of his arm, they made several excursions among the mountains. Adeline and Clara, whom the care of Madame had restored to her usual health, were generally of the party.

After spending a week at the château, M. Verneuil bade adieu to La Luc and his family; they parted with mutual regret, and the former promised that when he returned to Geneva, he would take Lelencourt in his way. As he said this, Adeline, who had for some time observed with much alarm La Luc's declining health, looked mournfully on his languid countenance, and uttered a secret prayer that he might live to receive the visit of M. Verneuil.

Madame was the only person who did not lament his departure; she saw that the efforts of her brother to entertain his guest were more than his present state of health would admit of, and she rejoiced in the quiet that would now return to him.

But this quiet brought La Luc no respite from illness; the fatigue he had suffered in his late exertions seemed to have increased his disorder, which in a short time assumed the aspect of a consumption. Yielding to the solicitations of his family, he went to Geneva for advice, and was there recommended to try the air of Nice.

The journey thither, however, was of considerable length, and believing his life to be very precarious, he hesitated whether to go. He was also unwilling to leave the duty of his parish unperformed for so long a time as his health might require; but this was an objection which would not have withheld him from Nice, had his faith in the climate been equal to that of his physicians.

His parishioners felt the life of their pastor to be of the utmost consequence to them. It was a general cause, and they testified at once his worth, and their sense of it, by going in a body to solicit him to leave them. He was much affected by this instance of their attachment. Such a proof of regard, conjoined with the entreaties of his own family, and a consideration that for their sakes it was a duty to endeavour to prolong his life, was too powerful to be withstood, and he determined to set out for Italy.

It was settled that Clara and Adeline, whose healths La Luc thought required change of air and scene, should accompany him, attended by the faithful Peter.

On the morning of his departure, a large body of his parishioners assembled round the door to bid him farewell. It was an affecting scene; they might meet no more. At length, wiping the tears from his eyes, La Luc said, "Let us trust in God, my friends; he has power to heal all disorders, both of body and mind. We shall meet again; if not in this world, I hope in a better. Let our conduct be such as to ensure that better."

The sobs of his people prevented any reply. There was scarcely a dry eye in the village; for there was scarcely an inhabitant of it that was not now assembled in the presence of La Luc. He shook hands with them all. "Farewell, my friends," said he, "we shall meet again."

"God grant we may!" said they, with one voice of fervent petition.

Having mounted his horse, and Clara and Adeline being ready, they took a last leave of Madame La Luc, and quitted the château. The people being unwilling to leave La Luc, the greater part of them accompanied him to some distance from the village. As he moved slowly on, he cast a last lingering look at his little home, where he had spent so many peaceful years, and which he now gazed on, perhaps, for the last time, and tears rose in his eyes; but he checked them. Every scene of the adjacent country called up, as he passed, some tender remembrance. He looked towards the spot consecrated to the memory of his deceased wife; the dewy vapours of the morning veiled it. La Luc felt the disappointment more deeply, perhaps, than reason could justify; but those who know from experience how much the imagination loves to dwell on any object, however

remotely connected with that of our tenderness, will feel with him. This was an object round which the affections of La Luc had settled themselves; it was a memorial to the eye, and the view of it awakened more forcibly in the mind every tender idea that could associate with the primary subject of his regard. In such cases fancy gives to the illusions of strong affection the stamp of reality, and they are cherished by the heart with romantic fondness.

His people accompanied him for nearly a mile from the village, and could scarcely then be prevailed on to leave him; at length he once more bade them farewell, and went on his way, followed by their prayers and blessings.

La Luc and his little party travelled slowly on, sunk in pensive silence—a silence too pleasingly sad to be soon relinquished, and which they indulged without fear of interruption. The solitary grandeur of the scenes through which they passed, and the soothing murmur of the pines that waved above, aided this soft luxury of meditation.

They proceeded by easy stages, and after travelling for some days among the romantic mountains and pastoral valleys of Piedmont, they entered the rich country of Nice. The gay and luxuriant views which now opened upon the travellers as they wound among the hills appeared like scenes of fairy enchantment, or those produced by the lovely visions of the poets. While the spiral summits of the mountains exhibited the snowy severity of winter, the pine, the cypress, the olive, and the myrtle shaded their sides with the green tints of spring, and groves of orange, lemon, and citron spread over their feet the full glow of autumn.

As they advanced the scenery became still more diversified, and at length, between the receding heights, Adeline caught a glimpse of the distant waters of the Mediterranean fading into the blue and cloudless horizon. She had never till now seen the ocean, and this transient view of it roused her imagination, and made her watch impatiently for a nearer prospect.

It was towards the close of day when the travellers, winding round that range of Alps which crowns the amphitheatre that environs the city of Nice, looked down upon the green hills that stretch to the shores, on the city and its ancient castle, and on the wide waters of the Mediterranean, with the mountains of Corsica in the farthest distance. Such a sweep of sea and land, so varied with the gay, the magnificent, and the awful, would have fixed any eye in admiration; for Adeline and Clara, novelty and enthusiasm added their charms to the prospect. The soft and salubrious air seemed to welcome La Luc to this smiling region, and the serene atmosphere to promise invariable summer.

They at length descended upon the little plain where stands the city of Nice, and which was the most extensive piece of level ground they had passed since they entered the country. Here, in the bosom of the mountains, sheltered from the north and the east, where the western gales alone seemed to breathe, all the blooms of spring and the riches of autumn were united. Trees of myrtle bordered the road, which wound among groves of orange, lemon, and bergamot, whose delicious fragrance came to the sense mingled with the breath of roses and carnations that blossomed in their shade. The gently-swelling hills that rose from the plain were covered with vines, and crowned with cypresses and date-trees ; beyond, there appeared a range of mountains, whence the travellers had descended, and whence flows the river Paglion, swollen by the snows that melt on their summits, and which, after meandering through the plain, washes the walls of Nice, where it falls into the Mediterranean. In this blooming region Adeline observed that the countenances of the peasants, meagre and discontented, formed a melancholy contrast to the face of the country, and she lamented again the effects of an arbitrary government where the bounties of nature, which were designed for all, are monopolised by a few, and the many are suffered to starve, tantalised by surrounding plenty.

The city lost much of its enchantment on a nearer approach ; its narrow streets and shabby houses but ill answered the expectation which a distant view of its ramparts and its harbour, gay with vessels, seemed to authorise. The appearance of the inn, at which La Luc now alighted, did not contribute to soften his disappointment ; but if he was surprised to find such indifferent accommodation at the inn of a town celebrated as the resort of valetudinarians, he was still more so when he learned the difficulty of procuring furnished lodgings.

After much search, he procured apartments in a small but pleasant château, situated a little way out of the town ; it had a garden, and a terrace which overlooked the sea, and was distinguished by an air of neatness very unusual in the houses of Nice. He agreed to board with the family, whose table likewise accommodated a gentleman and lady, their lodgers, and thus he became a temporary inhabitant of this charming climate.

On the following morning Adeline rose at an early hour, eager to indulge the new and sublime emotion with which a view of the ocean inspired her, and walked with Clara toward the hills that afforded a more extensive prospect. They pursued their way for some time between high embowering banks, till they arrived at an eminence, whence

Heaven, earth, ocean smil'd !

They sat down on a point of rock, overshadowed by lofty palm-trees, to contemplate at leisure the magnificent scene. The sun was just emerged from the sea, over which his rays shed a flood of light, and darted a thousand brilliant tints on the vapours that ascended the horizon, and floated there in light clouds, leaving the bosom of the waters below clear as crystal, except where the white surges were seen to beat upon the rocks, and discovering the distant sails of the fishing-boats, and the far-distant highlands of Corsica, tinted with ethereal blue. Clara, after some time, drew forth her pencil, but threw it aside in despair. Adeline, as they returned home through a romantic glen, when her senses were no longer absorbed in the contemplation of this grand scenery, and when its images floated on her memory only in softened colours, repeated the following lines :

SUNRISE : A SONNET.

Oft let me wander, at the break of day,
  Thro' the cool vale o'erhung with waving woods,
Drink the rich fragrance of the budding May,
  And catch the murmur of the distant floods ;
Or rest on the fresh bank of limpid rill,
  Where sleeps the vi'let in the dewy shade,
Where op'ning lilies balmy sweets distil,
  And the wild musk-rose weeps along the glade ;
Or climb the eastern cliff, whose airy head
Hangs rudely o'er the blue and misty main ;
Watch the fine hues of morn through ether spread,
  And paint with roseate glow the crystal plain.
Oh ! who can speak the rapture of the soul
  When o'er the waves the sun first steals to sight,
And all the world of waters, as they roll,
  And heaven's vast vault unveils in living light !
So life's young hour to man enchanting smiles,
With sparkling health, and joy, and fancy's fairy
  wiles !

La Luc, in his walks, met with some sensible and agreeable companions, who, like himself, came to Nice in search of health. Of these he soon formed a small but pleasant society, among whom was a Frenchman, whose mild manners, marked with a deep and interesting melancholy, had particularly attracted La Luc. He very seldom mentioned himself or any circumstance that might lead to a knowledge of his family, but on other subjects conversed with frankness and much intelligence. La Luc had frequently invited him to his lodgings, but he had always declined the invitation, and this in a manner so gentle as to disarm displeasure, and convince La Luc that his refusal was the consequence of a certain dejection of mind which made him reluctant to meet other strangers.

The description which La Luc had given of this foreigner had excited the curiosity of Clara ; and the sympathy which the unfortunate feel for each other called forth the commiseration of Adeline ; for that he was unfortunate she could not doubt. On their return from an evening walk La Luc pointed out the Chevalier, and quickened his pace to overtake him. Adeline was for a moment impelled to follow, but delicacy checked her steps; she knew how painful the presence of a stranger often is to a wounded mind, and forbore to intrude herself on his notice, for the sake of only satisfying an idle curiosity. She turned therefore into another path; but the delicacy which now prevented the meeting, accident in a few days defeated, and La Luc introduced the stranger. Adeline received him with a soft smile, but endeavoured to restrain the expression of pity which her features had involuntarily assumed; she wished him not to know that she observed he was unhappy.

After this interview he no longer rejected the invitations of La Luc, but made him frequent visits, and often accompanied Adeline and Clara in their rambles. The mild and sensible conversation of the former seemed to soothe his mind, and in her presence he frequently conversed with a degree of animation which La Luc till then had not observed in him. Adeline, too, derived from the similarity of their taste and his intelligent conversation, a degree of satisfaction which contributed, with the compassion his dejection inspired, to win her confidence, and she conversed with an easy frankness rather unusual to her.

His visits soon became more frequent. He walked with La Luc and his family; he attended them on their little excursions to view those magnificent remains of Roman antiquity which enrich the neighbourhood of Nice. When the ladies sat at home and worked, he enlivened the hours by reading to them, and they had the pleasure to observe his spirits somewhat relieved from the heavy melancholy that had oppressed him.

M. Amand was passionately fond of music. Clara had not forgotten to bring her beloved lute; he would sometimes strike the chords in the most sweet and mournful symphonies, but never could be prevailed on to play.

When Adeline or Clara played, he would sit in deep reverie, and lost to every object around him, except when he fixed his eyes in mournful gaze on Adeline, and a sigh would sometimes escape him.

One evening Adeline, having excused herself from accompanying La Luc and Clara in a visit to a neighbouring family, retired to the terrace of the garden which overlooked the sea, and as she viewed the tranquil splendour of the setting sun, and his glories reflected on the polished surface of the waves, she touched the strings of the lute in softest harmony, her voice accompanying it with words which she had one day written, after having read that rich effusion of Shakspeare's genius, "A Midsummer Night's Dream."

TITANIA TO HER LOVE.

Oh! fly with me through distant air
　To isles that gem the western deep!
For laughing Summer revels there,
　And hangs her wreath on every steep.

As through the green transparent sea
　Light floating on the waves we go,
The nymphs shall gaily welcome me,
　Far in their coral caves below.

For oft upon their margin sands,
　When twilight leads the fresh'ning hours,
I come with all my jocund bands
　To charm them from their sea-green bow'rs.

And well they love our sports to view,
And on the ocean's breast to lave;
And oft as we the dance renew,
　They call up music from the wave.

Swift hie we to that splendid clime,
　Where gay Jamaica spreads her scene,
Lifts the blue mountain—wild—sublime!
　And smooths her vales of vivid green.

Where throned high, in pomp of shade,
　The Power of Vegetation reigns,
Expanding wide, o'er hill and glade,
　Shrubs of all growth—fruit of all stains.

She steals the sunbeam's fervid glow,
　To paint her flow'rs of mingling hue;
And o'er the grape the purple throw,
　Breaking from verdant leaves to view.

There myrtle bow'rs, and citron grove,
　O'ercanopy our airy dance;
And there the sea-breeze loves to rove,
　When trembles day's departing glance.

And when the false moon steals away,
　Or o'er the chasing morn doth rise,
Oft, fearless, we our gambols play
　By the fire-worm's radiant eyes.

And suck the honey'd reeds that swell
　In tufted plumes of silver white;
Or pierce the cocoa's milky cell,
　To sip the nectar of delight!

And when the shaking thunders roll,
　And lightnings strike athwart the gloom,
We shelter in the cedar's bole,
　And revel 'mid the rich perfume!

But chief we love beneath the palm,
　Or verdant plantain's spreading leaf,
To hear, upon the midnight calm,
　Sweet Philomela pour her grief.

To mortal sprite such dulcet sound,
　Such blissful hours, were never known!
Oh! fly with me my airy round,
　And I will make them all thine own!

*Adeline ceased to sing, when she immediately heard repeated in a low voice—

To mortal sprite such dulcet sound,
Such blissful hours, were never known!

and turning her eyes whence it came, she saw M. Amand. She blushed and laid down the lute, which he instantly took up, and, with a tremulous hand, drew forth tones

That might create a soul under the ribs of Death.

In a melodious voice that trembled with sensibility, he sang the following

SONNET.

How sweet is Love's first gentle sway,
  When, crown'd with flow'rs, he softly smiles!
  His blue eyes fraught with tearful wiles,
Where beams of tender transport play;
Hope leads him on his airy way,
  And Faith and Fancy still beguiles—
  Faith, quickly tangled in her toils—
Fancy, whose magic forms so gay
  The fair deceiver's self deceive—
How sweet is Love's first gentle sway!
  Ne'er would that heart he bids to grieve
From Sorrow's soft enchantments stray—
  Ne'er—till the god, exulting in his art,
Relentless frowns, and wings th' envenom'd dart!

M. Amand paused; he seemed much oppressed, and at length burst into tears, laid down the instrument, and walked abruptly away to the farther end of the terrace. Adeline, without seeming to observe his agitation, rose and leaned upon the wall, below which a group of fishermen were busily employed in drawing a net. In a few moments he returned with a composed and softened countenance.

"Forgive this abrupt conduct," said he; "I know not how to apologise for it but by owning its cause. When I tell you, madam, that my tears flow to the memory of a lady who strongly resembled you, and who is lost to me for ever, you will know how to pity me."

His voice faltered, and he paused. Adeline was silent.

"The lute," he resumed, "was her favourite instrument, and when you touched it with such melancholy expression, I saw her very image before me. But, alas! why do I distress you with a knowledge of my sorrows! she is gone, never to return! And you, Adeline—you——" He checked his speech, and Adeline, turning on him a look of mournful regard, observed a wildness in his eyes which alarmed her.

"These recollections are too painful," said she, in a gentle voice; "let us return to the house; M. La Luc is probably come home."

"Oh no!" replied M. Amand; "no, this breeze refreshes me. How often at this hour have I talked with her, as I now talk with you! Such were the soft tones of her voice—such the ineffable expression of her countenance."

Adeline interrupted him: "Let me beg of you to consider your health—this dewy air cannot be good for invalids."

He stood with his hands clasped and seemed not to hear her. She took up the lute to go, and passed her fingers lightly over the chords. The sounds recalled his scattered senses; he raised his eyes, and fixed them in long unsettled gaze upon hers.

"Must I leave you here?" said she smiling, and standing in an attitude to depart.

"I entreat you to play again the air I heard just now," said M. Amand, in a hurried voice. "Certainly;" and she immediately began to play. He leaned against a palm-tree in an attitude of deep attention, and as the sounds languished on the air, his features gradually lost their wild expression, and he melted into tears. He continued to weep silently till the song concluded, and it was some time before he recovered voice enough to say:

"Adeline, I sincerely thank you for this goodness. My mind has recovered its bias; you have soothed a broken heart. Increase the kindness you have shown me, by promising never to mention what you have witnessed this evening, and I will endeavour never again to wound your sensibility by a similar offence."

Adeline gave the required promise; and M. Amand, pressing her hand, with a melancholy smile, hurried from the garden, and she saw him no more that night.

La Luc had been nearly a fortnight at Nice, and his health, instead of amending, seemed rather to decline; yet he wished to make a longer experiment of the climate. The air, which failed to restore her venerable friend, revived Adeline; and the variety and novelty of the surrounding scenes amused her mind, though—since they could not obliterate the memory of the past or suppress the pang of present affliction—they were ineffectual to dissipate the sick languor of melancholy. Company, by compelling her to withdraw her attention from the subject of her sorrow, afforded her a transient relief, but the violence of the exertion generally left her more depressed. It was in the stillness of solitude, in the tranquil observance of beautiful nature, that her mind recovered its tone, and indulging the pensive inclination now become habitual to it, was soothed and fortified. Of all the grand objects which nature had exhibited the ocean inspired her with the most sublime admiration. She loved to wander alone on its shores; and, when she could escape so long from the duties or forms of society, she would sit for hours on the beach, watching the rolling waves and listening to their dying murmur, till her softened fancy recalled long-lost scenes and restored the image of Theodore, when tears of despondency too often followed those of pity and regret. But these visions of memory, painful as they were, no longer excited that frenzy of grief they formerly awoke in Savoy; the sharpness of misery was passed, though its heavy influence was not, perhaps, less powerful. To these solitary indulgences generally succeeded calmness, and what Adeline endeavoured to believe was resignation.

She usually rose early, and walked down to the shore to enjoy, in the cool and silent hours of the morning, the cheering beauty of nature, and inhale the pure sea-breeze. Every object then smiled in fresh and lively colours. The blue sea, the brilliant sky, the distant fishing-boats with their white sails, and the voices of the fishermen borne at intervals on the air, were circumstances which reanimated her spirits; and in one of her rambles, yielding to that taste for poetry which had seldom forsaken her, she repeated the following lines:

MORNING ON THE SEA-SHORE.

What print of fairy feet is here
On Neptune's smooth and yellow sands?
What midnight revel's airy dance,
Beneath the moonbeam's trembling glance,
Has blest these shores? What sprightly bands
Have chased the waves unchecked by fear?
Whoe'er they were, they fled from morn,
For now, all silent and forlorn,
These tide-forsaken sands appear:
Return, sweet sprites, the scene to cheer!

In vain the call! Till moonlight's hour
Again diffuse its softer power,
Titania, nor her fairy loves,
Emerge from India's spicy groves.
Then, when the shad'wy hour returns,
When silence reigns o'er air and earth,
And ev'ry star in ether burns,
They come to celebrate their mirth;
In frolic ringlet trip the ground,
Bid music's voice on silence win,
Till magic echoes answer round—
Thus do their festive rites begin.

Oh fairy forms! so coy to mortal ken,
Your mystic steps to poets only shown;
Oh! lead me to the brook or hollow'd glen,
Retiring far, with winding wood o'ergrown!
Where'er ye best delight to rule;
If in some forest's lone retreat,
Thither conduct my willing feet
To the light brink of fountain cool,
Where, sleeping in the midnight dew,
Lie Spring's young buds of ev'ry hue,
Yielding their sweet breath to the air.
To fold their silken leaves from harm,
And their chill heads in moonshine warm,
Is bright Titania's tender care.

There, to the night-bird's plaintive chaunt
Your carols sweet ye love to raise,
With oaten reed and past'ral lays;
And guard with forceful spell her haunt,
Who, when your antic sports are done,
Oft lulls ye in the lily's cell—
Sweet flower! that suits your slumbers well,
And shields ye from the rising sun.
When not to India's steeps ye fly
After twilight and the moon,
In honey-buds ye love to lie,
While reigns supreme light's fervid noon,
Nor quit the cell where peace pervades,
Till night leads on the dews and shades.

E'en now your scenes enchanted meet my sight!
I see the earth unclose, the palace rise,
The high dome swell, and long arcades of light
Glitter among the deep embow'ring woods,
And glance reflecting from the trembling floods!
While to soft lutes the portals wide unfold,
And fairy forms of fine ethereal dyes

Advance with frolic step and laughing eyes,
Their hair with pearl, their garments deck'd with
     gold;
Pearls that in Neptune's briny waves they sought,
And gold from India's deepest caverns brought.
Thus your light visions to my eyes unveil,
Ye sportive pleasures, sweet illusion, hail!
     But ah! at morn's first blush again ye fade!
So from youth's ardent gaze life's landscape gay,
     And forms in fancy's summer hues array'd,
Dissolve at once in air at Truth's resplendent day.

During several days succeeding that on which M. Amand had disclosed the cause of his melancholy, he did not visit La Luc. At length, Adeline met him in one of her solitary rambles on the shore. He was pale and dejected and seemed much agitated when he observed her; she therefore endeavoured to avoid him, but he advanced with quickened steps and accosted her. He said it was his intention to leave Nice in a few days. "I have found no benefit from the climate," added M. Amand. "Alas! what climate can relieve the sickness of the heart? I go to lose, in the variety of new scenes, the remembrance of past happiness; yet the effort is vain; I am everywhere equally restless and unhappy."

Adeline tried to encourage him to hope much from time and change of place. "Time will blunt the sharpest edge of sorrow," said she; "I know it from experience." Yet while she spoke, the tears in her eyes contradicted the assertion of her lips.

"You have been unhappy, Adeline! Yes—I knew it from the first. The smile of pity which you gave me assured me that you knew what it was to suffer." The desponding air with which he spoke renewed her apprehension of a scene similar to the one she had lately witnessed, and she changed the subject, but he soon returned to it. "You bid me hope much from time! My wife! My dear wife!"—his tongue faltered—"it is now many months since I lost her, yet the moment of her death seems but as yesterday."

Adeline faintly smiled. "You can scarcely judge of the effect of time yet; you have much to hope for."

He shook his head. "But I am again intruding my misfortunes on your notice; forgive this perpetual egotism. There is a comfort in the pity of the good, such as nothing else can impart, this must plead my excuse; may you, Adeline, never want it. Ah! those tears——" Adeline hastily dried them. M. Amand forbore to press the subject, and immediately began to converse on different topics. They returned towards the château, but La Luc being from home, M. Amand took leave at the door. Adeline retired to her chamber, oppressed by her own sorrows and those of her amiable friend.

Nearly three weeks had now elapsed at Nice, during which the disorder of La Luc seemed rather to increase than to abate, when his physician very honestly confessed the little hope he entertained from the climate, and advised him more to try the effect of a sea voyage, adding, that if the experiment failed, even the air of Montpellier appeared to him more likely to afford relief than that of Nice. La Luc received this disinterested advice with a mixture of gratitude and disappointment. The circumstances which had made him reluctant to quit Savoy, rendered him more so to protract his absence, and increase his expenses ; but the ties of affection that bound him to his family, and the love of life, which so seldom leaves us, again prevailed over inferior considerations, and he determined to coast the Mediterranean as far as Languedoc, where, if the voyage did not answer his expectations, he would land and proceed to Montpellier.

When M. Amand learned that La Luc designed to quit Nice in a few days, he determined not to leave it before him. During this interval he had not sufficient resolution to deny himself the frequent conversation of Adeline, though her presence, by reminding him of his lost wife, gave him more pain than comfort. He was the second son of a French gentleman of family, and had been married about a year to a lady, to whom he had long been attached, when she died in her lying-in. The infant soon followed its mother, and left the disconsolate father abandoned to grief, which had preyed so heavily on his health, that his physician thought it necessary to send him to Nice. From the air of Nice, however, he had derived no benefit, and he now determined to travel farther into Italy, though he no longer felt any interest in those charming scenes, which in happier days, and with her whom he never ceased to lament, would have offered him the highest degree of mental luxury ; now, he sought only to escape from himself, or rather from the image of her who had once constituted his truest happiness.

La Luc having laid his plan, hired a small vessel, and in a few days embarked with a sick hope, bidding adieu to the shores of Italy and the towering Alps, and seeking on a new element the health which had hitherto mocked his pursuit.

M. Amand took a melancholy leave of his new friends, whom he attended to the sea-side. When he assisted Adeline on board, his heart was too full to suffer him to say farewell ; but he stood long on the beach pursuing with his eyes her course over the waters, and waving his hand, till tears dimmed his sight. The breeze wafted the vessel gently from the coast, and Adeline saw herself surrounded by the undulating waves of the ocean. The shore appeared to recede, its mountains to lessen, the gay colours of its landscape to melt into each other, and in a short time the figure of M. Amand was seen no more ; the town of Nice, with its castle and

harbour, next faded away in distance, and the purple tint of the mountains was at length all that remained on the verge of the horizon. She sighed as she gazed, and her eyes filled with tears.

"So vanished my prospect of happiness," said she, "and my future view is like the waste of waters that surrounds me."

Her heart was full, and she retired from observation to a remote part of the deck, where she indulged her tears as she watched the vessel cut its way through the liquid glass. The water was so transparent that she saw the sunbeams playing at considerable depth, and fish of various colours glance athwart the current. Innumerable marine plants spread their vigorous leaves on the rocks below, and the richness of their verdure formed a beautiful contrast to the glowing scarlet of the coral that branched beside them.

The distant coast, at length, entirely disappeared. Adeline gazed with an emotion the most sublime on the boundless expanse of waters that spread on all sides ; she seemed as if launched into a new world—the grandeur and immensity of the view astonished and overpowered her ; for a moment she doubted the truth of the compass, and believed it to be almost impossible for the vessel to find its way over the pathless waters to any shore. And when she considered that a plank alone separated her from death, a sensation of unmixed terror superseded that of sublimity, and she hastily turned her eyes from the prospect, and her thoughts from the subject.

CHAPTER XVIII.

Is there a heart that music cannot melt ?
Alas ! how is that rugged heart forlorn !
Is there who ne'er that mystic transport felt,
Of solitude and melancholy born?
He need not woo the Muse—he is her scorn.
BEATTIE.

TOWARDS evening the captain, to avoid the danger of encountering a Barbary corsair, steered for the French coast, and Adeline distinguished in the gleam of the setting sun the shores of Provence, feathered with wood, and green with pasturage. La Luc, languid and ill, had retired to the cabin, whither Clara attended him. The pilot at the helm, guiding the tall vessel through the sounding waters, and one solitary sailor, leaning with crossed arms against the mast, and now and then singing parts of a mournful ditty, were all of the crew, except Adeline, that remained upon deck ; and Adeline silently watched the declining sun, which threw a saffron glow upon the waves and on the sails, gently swelling in the breeze that was now dying away. The sun, at length, sank below the ocean, and twilight stole over the scene, leaving the shadowy shores yet visible, and touching with a solemn tint the waters that stretched wide around. She sketched the picture, but it was with a faint pencil.

NIGHT.

O'er the dim breast of Ocean's wave,
Night spreads afar her gloomy wings,
And pensive thought and silence brings,
Save when the distant waters lave.
Or when the mariner's lone voice
Swells faintly in the passing gale,
Or when the screaming sea-gulls poise
O'er the tall mast and swelling sail.
Bounding the gray gleam of the deep,
Where fancied forms arouse the mind,
Dark sweep the shores, on whose rude steep
Sighs the sad spirit of the wind.
Sweet is its voice upon the air
At ev'ning's melancholy close,
When the smooth wave in silence flows !
Sweet, sweet the peace its stealing accents bear !
Blest be thy shades, O Night ! and blest the song
Thy low winds breathe the distant shores along !

As the shadows thickened, the scene sank into deeper repose. Even the sailor's song had ceased ; no sound was heard but that of the waters dashing beneath the vessel, and their fainter murmur on the pebbly coast. Adeline's mind was in unison with the tranquillity of the hour ; lulled by the waves, she resigned herself to a still melancholy, and sat lost in reverie. The present moment brought to her recollection her voyage up the Rhone, when, seeking refuge from the terrors of the Marquis de Montalt, she so anxiously endeavoured to anticipate her future destiny. She then, as now, had watched the fall of evening and the fading prospect, and she remembered what a desolate feeling had accompanied the impressions which those objects made. She had then no friends—no asylum—no certainty of escaping the pursuit of her enemy. Now she had found affectionate friends, a secure retreat, and was delivered from the terrors she then suffered ; but still she was unhappy. The remembrance of Theodore—of Theodore who loved her so truly, who had encountered and suffered so much for her sake, and of whose fate she was now as ignorant as when she traversed the Rhone, was an incessant pang to her heart. She seemed to be more remote than ever from the possibility of hearing of him. Sometimes a faint hope crossed her that he had escaped the malice of his persecutor ; but when she considered the inveteracy and power of the latter, and the heinous light in which the law regards an assault upon a superior officer, even this poor hope vanished, and left her to tears and anguish, such as this reverie, which began with a sensation of only gentle melancholy, now led to. She continued to muse till the moon arose from the bosom of the ocean, and shed her trembling lustre upon the waves, diffusing peace, and making silence more solemn ; beaming a soft light on the white sails, and throwing upon the waters the long shadow of the vessel, which now seemed to glide away unopposed by any current. Her tears had somewhat relieved the anguish of her mind, and she again reposed in placid melancholy, when a strain of such tender and entrancing sweetness stole on the silence of the hour, that it seemed more like celestial than mortal music—so soft, so soothing, it sank upon her ear, that it recalled her from misery to hope and love. She wept again—but these were tears which she would not have exchanged for mirth and joy. She looked round, but perceived neither ship nor boat ; and as the undulating sounds swelled on the distant air, she thought they came from the shore. Sometimes the breeze wafted them away, and again returned them in tones of the most languishing softness. The links of the air thus broken, it was music rather than melody that she caught, till, the pilot gradually steering nearer the coast, she distinguished the notes of a song familiar to her ear. She endeavoured to recollect where she had heard it, but in vain ; yet her heart beat almost unconsciously with a something resembling hope. Still she listened, till the breeze again stole the sounds. With regret she now perceived that the vessel was moving from them, and at length they trembled faintly on the waves, sank away at a distance, and were heard no more. She remained upon deck a considerable time, unwilling to relinquish the expectation of hearing them again, and their sweetness still vibrating on her fancy, and at length retired to the cabin, oppressed by a degree of disappointment which the occasion did not appear to justify.

La Luc grew better during the voyage, his spirits revived, and when the vessel entered that part of the Mediterranean called the Gulf of Lyons, he was sufficiently animated to enjoy from the deck the noble prospect which the sweeping shores of Provence, terminating in the far-distant ones of Languedoc, excited.

Adeline and Clara, who anxiously watched his looks, rejoiced in their amendment ; and the fond wishes of the latter already anticipated his perfect recovery. Disappointment had too often checked the expectations of Adeline, to permit her now to indulge an equal degree of hope with that of her friend, yet she confided much in the effect of this voyage.

La Luc amused himself at intervals with discoursing, and pointing out the situations of considerable ports on the coast, and the mouths of rivers that after wandering through Provence, disembogue themselves into the Mediterranean. The Rhone, however, was the only one of much consequence which he passed. On this object, though it was so distant, that fancy, perhaps, rather than the sense, beheld it, Clara gazed with peculiar pleasure, for it came from the banks of

Savoy ; and the wave which she thought she perceived had washed the feet of her dear native mountains. The time passed with mingled pleasure and improvement, as La Luc described to his attentive pupils the manners and commerce of the different inhabitants of the coast, and the natural history of the country ; or as he traced in imagination the remote wanderings of rivers to their source, and delineated the characteristic beauties of their scenery.

After a pleasing voyage of a few days, the shores of Provence receded, and that of Languedoc, which had long bounded the distance, became the grand object of the scene, and the sailors drew near their port. They landed in the afternoon at a small town situated at the foot of a woody eminence, on the right overlooking the sea, and on the left the rich plains of Languedoc, gay with the purple vine. La Luc determined to defer his journey till the following day, and was directed to a small inn at the extremity of the town, the accommodation of which, such as it was, he endeavoured to be contented with.

In the evening, the beauty of the hour, and the desire of exploring new scenes, invited Adeline to walk. La Luc was fatigued, and did not go out, and Clara remained with him. Adeline took her way to the woods that rose from the margin of the sea, and climbed the wild eminence on which they hung. Often as she went she turned her eyes to catch between the dark foliage the blue waters of the bay, the white sails that flitted by, and the trembling gleam of the setting sun.

When she reached the summit, and looked down over the dark tops of the woods on the wide and various prospect, she was seized with a kind of still rapture impossible to be expressed, and stood unconscious of the flight of time till the sun had left the scene, and twilight threw its solemn shade upon the mountains. The sea alone reflected the fading splendour of the west ; its tranquil surface was partially disturbed by the low wind that crept in tremulous lines along the waters, whence, rising to the woods, it shivered their light leaves, and died away. Adeline, resigning herself to the luxury of sweet and tender emotions, repeated the following lines :

SUNSET.

Soft o'er the mountain's purple brow
  Meek twilight draws her shadows gray ;
From tufted woods and valleys low
  Light's magic colours steal away.
Yet still, amid the spreading gloom,
  Resplendent glow the western waves
  That roll o'er Neptune's coral caves—
A zone of light on evening's dome.
On this lone summit let me rest,
  And view the forms to fancy dear,
Till on the ocean's darkened breast

The stars of ev'ning tremble clear ;
Or the moon's pale orb appear,
Throwing her line of radiance wide,
Far o'er the lightly-curling tide
That seems the yellow sands to chide.
No sounds o'er silence now prevail
  Save of the dying wave below,
Or sailor's song borne on the gale,
  Or oar at distance striking slow.
So sweet ! so tranquil ! may my ev'ning's ray
Set to this world, and rise in future day.

Adeline quitted the heights, and followed a narrow path that wound to the beach below ; her mind was now particularly sensible to fine impressions, and the sweet notes of the nightingale amid the stillness of the woods again awakened her enthusiasm.

TO THE NIGHTINGALE.

Child of the melancholy song !
  Oh, yet that tender strain prolong !
Her lengthened shade when ev'ning slings,
  From mountain-cliffs and forests green,
And sailing slow on silent wings,
  Along the glimm'ring West is seen ;
I love o'er pathless hills to stray,
  Or trace the winding vale remote,
And pause, sweet bird ! to hear thy lay
  While moonbeams on the thin clouds float,
Till o'er the mountain's dewy head
Pale midnight steals to wake the dead.

Far through the heav'n's ethereal blue
  Wafted on Spring's light airs you come,
With blooms, and flowers, and genial dew,
  From climes where Summer joys to roam,
Oh, welcome to your long-lost home !

Child of the melancholy song !
  Who lov'st the lonely woodland-glade
To mourn unseen the boughs among,
  When twilight spreads her pensive shade,
Again thy dulcet voice I hail !
  Oh, pour again the liquid note
That dies upon the ev'ning gale !
For fancy loves the kindred tone,
  Her griefs the plaintive accents own.
  She loves to hear thy music float
At solemn midnight's stillest hour,
  And think on friends for ever lost,
  On joys by disappointment crost,
And weep anew love's charmful power.

Then memory wakes the magic smile,
  Th' impassioned voice, the melting eye,
That wont the trusting heart beguile,
  And wakes again the hopeless sigh !
Her skill the glowing tints revive
  Of scenes that time had bade decay ;
She bids the softened passions live—
  The passions urge again their sway.
Yet o'er the long-regretted scene
  Thy song the grace of sorrow throws—
A melancholy charm serene,
  More rare than all that mirth bestows.
Then hail, sweet bird ! and hail thy pensive tear !
To taste, to fancy, and to virtue dear !

The spreading dusk at length reminded Adeline of her distance from the inn, and that she had her way to find through a wild and lonely wood ; she bade adieu to the siren that had so long detained her, and pursued the path with quick steps. Having followed it for some time, she became bewildered among the thickets, and the increasing darkness did not allow her to judge of the direction she was in. Her apprehensions heightened her difficulties ; she thought she distinguished the voices of men at some little distance, and she increased her speed till she found herself on the sea sands, over which the woods impended.

Her breath was now exhausted ; she paused a moment to recover herself, and fearfully listened, but, instead of the voices of men, she heard faintly swelling in the breeze the notes of mournful music. Her heart, ever sensible to the impressions of melody, melted with the tones, and her fears were for a moment lulled in sweet enchantment. Surprise was soon mingled with delight, when, as the sounds advanced, she distinguished the tone of that instrument, and the melody of that well-known air, she had heard a few preceding evenings from the shores of Provence. But she had no time for conjecture—footsteps approached, and she renewed her speed.

She was now emerged from the darkness of the woods, and the moon, which shone bright, exhibited along the level sands the town and port in the distance. The steps that had followed now came up with her, and she perceived two men, but they passed in conversation without noticing her, and as they passed she was certain she recollected the voice of him who was then speaking. Its tones were so familiar to her ear that she was surprised at the imperfect memory which did not suffer her to be assured by whom they were uttered. Another step now followed, and a rude voice called to her to stop. As she hastily turned her eyes, she saw imperfectly by the moonlight a man in a sailor's habit pursuing, while he renewed the call. Impelled by terror, she fled along the sands, but her steps were short and trembling, those of her pursuer's strong and quick.

She had just strength sufficient to reach the men who had before passed her, and to implore their protection, when her pursuer came up with them, but suddenly turned into the woods on the left and disappeared.

She had no breath to answer the inquiries of the strangers who supported her, till a sudden exclamation, and the sound of her own name, drew her eyes attentively upon the person who uttered them, and in the rays which shone strong upon his features, she distinguished M. Verneuil ! Mutual satisfaction and explanation ensued, and when he learned that La Luc and his daughter were at the inn, he felt an increased pleasure in conducting her thither. He said that he had accidentally met with an old friend in Savoy, whom he now introduced by the name of Mauron, and who had prevailed on him to

change his route and accompany him to the shores of the Mediterranean. They had embarked from the coast of Provence only a few preceding days, and had that evening landed in Languedoc, on the estate of M. Mauron. Adeline had now no doubt that it was the flute of M. Verneuil, and which had so often delighted her at Lelencourt, that she had heard on the sea.

When they reached the inn they found La Luc under great anxiety for Adeline, in search of whom he had sent several people. Anxiety yielded to surprise and pleasure when he perceived her with M. Verneuil, whose eyes beamed with unusual animation on seeing Clara. After mutual congratulations, M. Verneuil observed, and lamented, the very indifferent accommodation which the inn afforded his friends, and M. Mauron immediately invited them to his château, with a warmth of hospitality that overcame every scruple which delicacy or pride could oppose. The woods that Adeline had traversed formed a part of his demesne, which extended almost to the inn ; but he insisted that his carriage should take his guests to the château, and departed to give orders for their reception. The presence of M. Verneuil, and the kindness of his friend, gave to La Luc an unusual flow of spirits ; he conversed with a degree of vigour and liveliness to which he had long been unaccustomed, and the smile of satisfaction that Clara gave to Adeline expressed how much she thought he was already benefited by the voyage. Adeline answered her look with a smile of less confidence, for she attributed his present animation to a more temporary cause.

About half an hour after the departure of M. Mauron a boy, who served as waiter, brought a message from a chevalier then at the inn, requesting permission to speak with Adeline. The man who had pursued her along the sands instantly occurred to her, and she scarcely doubted that the stranger was some person belonging to the Marquis de Montalt, perhaps the Marquis himself, though that he should have discovered her accidentally, in so obscure a place, and so immediately upon her arrival, seemed very improbable. With trembling lips, and a countenance pale as death, she inquired the name of the chevalier. The boy was not acquainted with it. La Luc asked what sort of a person he was, but the boy, who understood little of the art of describing, gave such a confused account of him, that Adeline could only learn he was not large, but of the middle stature. This circumstance, however, convincing her it was not the Marquis de Montalt who desired to see her, she asked whether it would be agreeable to La Luc to have the stranger admitted ? La Luc said, " By all means ! " and the waiter withdrew.

Adeline sat in trembling expectation till the door opened, and Louis de la Motte entered the room. He advanced with an embarrassed and melancholy air, though his countenance had been enlightened with a momentary pleasure when he first beheld Adeline—Adeline, who was still the idol of his heart. After the first salutations were over, all apprehensions of the Marquis being now dissipated, she inquired when Louis had seen Monsieur and Madame La Motte.

"I ought rather to ask you that question," said Louis in some confusion, "for I believe you have seen them since I have; and the pleasure of meeting you thus is equalled by my surprise. I have not heard from my father for some time, owing probably to my regiment being moved to new quarters."

He looked as if he wished to be informed with whom Adeline now was, but, as this was a subject upon which it was impossible she should speak in the presence of La Luc, she led the conversation to general topics, after having said that Monsieur and Madame La Motte were well when she left them. Louis spoke little, and often looked anxiously at Adeline, while his mind seemed labouring under strong oppression. She observed this, and recollecting the declaration he had made her on the morning of his departure from the abbey, she attributed his present embarrassment to the effect of a passion yet unsubdued, and did not appear to notice it.

After he had sat nearly a quarter of an hour under a struggle of feelings which he could neither conquer nor conceal, he rose to leave the room, and as he passed Adeline, said, in a low voice, "Do permit me to speak with you alone for five minutes."

She hesitated in some confusion, and then saying there were none but friends present, begged he would be seated.

"Excuse me," said he, in the same low accent, "what I would say nearly concerns you, and you only. Do favour me with a few moments' attention."

He said this with a look that surprised her, and having ordered candles into another room, she went thither.

Louis sat for some moments silent, and seemingly in great perturbation of mind. At length he said, "I know not whether to rejoice or to lament at this unexpected meeting, though, if you are in safe hands, I ought certainly to rejoice, however hard the task that now falls to my lot. I am not ignorant of the dangers and persecutions you have suffered, and cannot forbear expressing my anxiety to know how you are now circumstanced. Are you indeed with friends?"

"I am," said Adeline; "M. La Motte has informed you."

"No," replied Louis, with a deep sigh, "not my father." He paused. "But I do indeed rejoice," resumed he, "oh! how sincerely rejoice, that you are in safety.

Could you know, lovely Adeline, what I have suffered!" He checked himself.

"I understood you had something of importance to say, sir," said Adeline; "you must excuse me if I remind you that I have not many moments to spare."

"It is indeed of importance," replied Louis, "yet I know not how to mention it—how to soften——. This task is too severe. Alas! my poor friend!"

"Who is it you speak of, sir?" said Adeline with quickness.

Louis rose from his chair, and walked about the room. "I would prepare you for what I have to say," he resumed, "but upon my soul I am not equal to it."

"I entreat you to keep me no longer in suspense," said Adeline, who had a wild suspicion that it was Theodore he would speak of.

Louis still hesitated.

"Is it—oh, is it?—I conjure you tell me the worst at once," said she, in a voice of agony; "I can bear it—indeed I can."

"My unhappy friend!" exclaimed Louis.

"Oh, Theodore! Theodore!" faintly articulated Adeline, "he lives then!"

"He does," said Louis, "but——" He stopped.

"But what?" cried Adeline, trembling violently; "if he is living you cannot tell me worse than my fears suggest. I entreat you, therefore, not to hesitate."

Louis resumed his seat, and endeavouring to assume a collected air, said, "He is living, madam, but he is a prisoner, and—for why should I deceive you?—I fear he has little to hope in this world."

"I have long feared so, sir," said Adeline, in a voice of forced composure; "you have something more terrible than this to relate, and I again entreat you to explain yourself."

"He has everything to apprehend from the Marquis de Montalt," said Louis. "Alas! why do I say to apprehend? His judgment is already fixed—he is condemned to die."

At this confirmation of her fears a deathlike paleness diffused itself over the countenance of Adeline; she sat motionless, and attempted to sigh, but seemed almost suffocated. Terrified at her situation, and expecting to see her faint, Louis would have supported her, but with her hand she waved him from her, unable to speak. He now called for assistance, and La Luc and Clara, with M. Verneuil, informed of Adeline's indisposition, were quickly by her side.

At the sound of their voices she looked up, and seemed to recollect herself, when uttering a heavy sigh she burst into tears. La Luc rejoiced to see her weep, encouraged her tears, which, after some time, relieved her; and when she was able to speak, she desired to go back to La Luc's parlour. Louis attended her thither; when she was better he would have withdrawn, but La Luc begged he would stay.

"You are, perhaps, a relation of this young lady, sir," said he, "and may have brought news of her father?"

"Not so, sir," replied Louis, hesitating.

"This gentleman," said Adeline, who had now recollected her dissipated thoughts, "is the son of M. La Motte, whom you have heard me mention."

Louis seemed shocked to be declared the son of a man that had once acted so unworthily towards Adeline; who, instantly perceiving the pain her words occasioned, endeavoured to soften their effect by saying that La Motte had saved her from imminent danger, and had afforded her an asylum for many months. Adeline sat in a state of dreadful solicitude to know the particulars of Theodore's situation, yet could not acquire courage to renew the subject in the presence of La Luc; she ventured, however, to ask Louis if his own regiment was quartered in the town.

He replied that his regiment lay at Vaceau, a French town on the frontiers of Spain; that he had just crossed a part of the Gulf of Lyons, and was on his way to Savoy, whither he should set out early in the morning.

"We are lately come from thence," said Adeline. "May I ask to what part of Savoy you are going?"

"To Lelencourt," he replied.

"To Lelencourt!" said Adeline, in some surprise.

"I am a stranger in the country," resumed Louis, "but I go to serve my friend. You seem to know Lelencourt."

"I do, indeed," said Adeline.

"You probably know then that M. La Luc lives there, and will guess the motive of my journey."

"Oh heaven! is it possible?" exclaimed Adeline. "Is it possible that Theodore Peyrou is a relation of M. La Luc?"

"Theodore! What of my son?" asked La Luc in surprise and apprehension.

"Your son!" said Adeline in a trembling voice, "your son!"

The astonishment and anguish depicted on her countenance increased the apprehensions of this unfortunate father, and he renewed his question. But Adeline was totally unable to answer him; and the distress of Louis on thus unexpectedly discovering the father of his unhappy friend, and knowing that it was his task to disclose the fate of his son, deprived him for some time of all power of utterance; and La Luc and Clara, whose fears were every instant heightened by this dreadful silence, continued to repeat their questions.

At length a sense of the approaching sufferings of the good La Luc overcoming every other feeling, Adeline recovered strength of

mind sufficient to try to soften the intelligence Louis had to communicate, and to conduct Clara to another room. Here she collected resolution to tell her, and with tender consideration, the circumstances of her brother's situation, concealing only her knowledge of his sentence being already pronounced. This relation necessarily included the mention of their attachment; and in the friend of her heart Clara discovered the innocent cause of her brother's destruction. Adeline also learned the occasion of that circumstance which had contributed to keep her ignorant of Theodore's relationship to La Luc; she was told the former had taken the name of Peyrou with an estate which had been left him about a year before, by a relation of his mother's, upon that condition. Theodore had been designed for the church, but his disposition inclined him to a more active life than the clerical habit would admit of; and on his accession to the estate he entered into the service of the French king.

In the few and interrupted interviews which had been allowed them at Caux, Theodore had mentioned his family to Adeline only in general terms; and thus, when they were so suddenly separated, had, without designing it, left her in ignorance of his father's name and place of residence.

The sacred delicacy of Adeline's grief, which had never permitted her to mention the subject of it even to Clara, had since contributed to deceive her.

The distress of Clara, on learning the situation of her brother, could endure no restraint. Adeline, who, by a strong effort of mind, had commanded her feelings so as to impart this news with tolerable composure, was now almost overwhelmed by her own and Clara's accumulated sufferings. While they wept forth the anguish of their hearts, a scene, if possible, more affecting, passed between La Luc and Louis; who perceived it was necessary to inform him, though cautiously and by degrees, of the full extent of his calamity. He therefore told La Luc that, though Theodore had been first tried for having quitted his post, he was now condemned on a charge of assault made upon his general officer, the Marquis de Montalt, who had brought witnesses to prove that his life had been endangered by the circumstance; and who, having pursued the prosecution with the most bitter rancour, had at length obtained the sentence which the law could not withhold, but which every other officer in the regiment deplored.

Louis added that the sentence was to be executed in less than a fortnight, and that Theodore, being very unhappy at receiving no answers to the letters he had sent his father, wishing to see him once more, and knowing that there was now no time to be lost, had requested him to go to Lelencourt and acquaint his father with his situation.

La Luc received the account of his son's condition with a distress that admitted neither of tears or complaint. He asked where Theodore was, and desiring to be conducted to him, he thanked Louis for all his kindness, and ordered post-horses immediately.

A carriage was soon ready, and this unhappy father, after taking a mournful leave of M. Verneuil, and sending a compliment to M. Mauron, attended by his family, set out for the prison of his son. The journey was a silent one; each individual of the party endeavoured, in consideration of the other, to suppress the expression of grief, but was unable to do more. La Luc appeared calm and complacent; he seemed frequently to be engaged in prayer; but a struggle of resignation and composure was sometimes visible upon his countenance, notwithstanding the efforts of his mind to conceal it.

CHAPTER XIX.

And venom'd with disgrace the dart of Death.
SEWARD.

WE now return to the Marquis de Montalt, who having seen La Motte safely lodged in the prison of D——y, and learning that the trial would not come on immediately, had returned to his villa on the borders of the forest, where he expected to hear news of Adeline. It had been his intention to follow his servants to Lyons; but he now determined to wait a few days for letters, and he had little doubt that Adeline, since her flight had been so quickly pursued, would be overtaken, and probably before she could reach that city. In this expectation he had been miserably disappointed; for his servants informed him that though they traced her thither, they had neither been able to follow her route beyond, nor to discover her at Lyons. This escape she probably owed to having embarked on the Rhone; for it does not appear that the Marquis's people thought of seeking her on the course of that river.

His presence was soon after required at Vaceau, where the court-martial was then sitting; thither, therefore, he went, with passions still more exasperated by his late disappointment, and procured the condemnation of Theodore. The sentence was universally lamented, for Theodore was much beloved in his regiment; and the occasion of the Marquis's personal resentment towards him being known, every heart was interested in his cause.

Louis de la Motte happening at this time to be stationed in the same town, heard an imperfect account of his story, and being convinced that the prisoner was the young chevalier whom he had formerly seen with the Marquis at the abbey, he was induced, partly from compassion, and partly with a hope of hearing of his parents, to visit him. The compassionate sympathy which Louis expressed, and the zeal with which he tendered his services, affected Theodore, and excited in him a warm return of friendship. Louis made him frequent visits, did everything that kindness could suggest to alleviate his sufferings, and a mutual esteem and confidence ensued.

Theodore at length communicated the chief subject of his concern to Louis, who discovered, with inexpressible grief, that it was Adeline whom the Marquis had thus cruelly persecuted, and Adeline for whom the generous Theodore was about to suffer. He soon perceived also that Theodore was his favoured rival; but he generously suppressed the jealous pang this discovery occasioned, and determined that no prejudice of passion should withdraw him from the duties of humanity and friendship. He eagerly inquired where Adeline then resided.

"She is yet, I fear, in the power of the Marquis," said Theodore, sighing deeply. "O God! these chains!" and he threw an agonising glance upon them.

Louis sat silent and thoughtful; at length, starting from his reverie, he said he would go to the Marquis, and immediately quitted the prison. The Marquis was, however, already set off for Paris, where he had been summoned to appear at the approaching trial of La Motte; and Louis, yet ignorant of the late transactions at the abbey, returned to the prison, where he endeavoured to forget that Theodore was the favoured rival of his love, and to remember him only as the defender of Adeline. So earnestly he pressed his offers of service, that Theodore, whom the silence of his father equally surprised and afflicted, and who was very anxious to see him once again, accepted his proposal of going himself to Savoy.

"My letters I strongly suspect to have been intercepted by the Marquis," said Theodore; "if so, my poor father will have the whole weight of his calamity to sustain at once, unless I avail myself of your kindness, and I shall neither see him nor hear from him before I die. Louis! there are moments when my fortitude shrinks from the conflict, and my senses threaten to desert me."

No time was to be lost; the warrant for his execution had already received the king's signature, and Louis immediately set forward to Savoy. The letters of Theodore had, indeed, been intercepted by order of the Marquis, who, in the hope of discovering the asylum of Adeline, had opened and afterwards destroyed them.

But to return to La Luc, who now drew near Vaceau, and who his family observed to be greatly changed in his looks since he had heard the late calamitous intelligence; he uttered no complaint; but it was too obvious that his disorder had made a rapid progress. Louis, who during his journey proved the goodness of his disposition by the delicate attention he paid to this unhappy party, concealed his observation of the decline of La Luc, and, to support Adeline's spirits, endeavoured to convince her that her fears on this subject were groundless. Her spirits did indeed require support, for she was now within a few miles of the town that contained Theodore; and while her increasing perturbation almost overcame her, she yet tried to appear composed. When the carriage entered the town, she cast a timid and anxious glance in search of the prison; but having passed through several streets without perceiving any building which corresponded with her idea of what she looked for, the coach stopped at the inn.

The frequent changes in La Luc's countenance betrayed the violent agitation of his mind, and when he attempted to alight, feeble and exhausted, he was compelled to accept the support of Louis, to whom he faintly said, as he passed to the parlour, "I am indeed sick at heart, but I trust the pain will not be long." Louis pressed his hand without speaking, and hastened back for Adeline and Clara, who were already in the passage. La Luc wiped the tears from his eyes (they were the first he had shed) as they entered the room, "I would go immediately to my poor boy," said he to Louis; "yours, sir, is a mournful office—be so good as to conduct me to him." He rose to go, but feeble and overcome with grief, again sat down. Adeline and Clara united in entreating that he would compose himself, and take some refreshment, and Louis, urging the necessity of preparing Theodore for the interview, prevailed with him to delay it till his son should be informed of his arrival, and immediately quitted the inn for the prison of his friend. When he was gone La Luc, as a duty he owed those he loved, tried to take some support, but the convulsions of his throat would not suffer him to swallow the wine he held to his parched lips, and he was now so much disordered, that he desired to retire to his chamber, where alone, and in prayer, he passed the dreadful interval of Louis's absence.

Clara, on the bosom of Adeline, who sat in calm but deep distress, yielded to the violence of her grief. "I shall lose my dear father too," said she; "I see it; I shall lose my father and my brother together." Adeline wept with her friend for some time in silence; and then attempted to persuade her that La Luc was not so ill as she apprehended.

"Do not mislead me with hope," she replied, "he will not survive the shock of this calamity; I saw it from the first." Adeline knowing that La Luc's distress would be heightened by the observance of his daughter's, and that indulgence would only increase its poignancy, endeavoured to rouse her to an exertion of fortitude, by urging the necessity of commanding her emotion in the presence of her father. "This is possible," added she, "however painful may be the effort. You must know, my dear, that my grief is not inferior to your own, yet I have hitherto been enabled to support my sufferings in silence; for M. La Luc I do, indeed, love and reverence as a parent."

Louis meanwhile reached the prison of Theodore, who received him with an air of mingled surprise and impatience. "What brings you back so soon?" said he; "have you heard news of my father?" Louis now gradually unfolded the circumstances of their meeting, and La Luc's arrival at Vaceau. A various emotion agitated the countenance of Theodore on receiving this intelligence. "My poor father!" said he, "he has then followed his son to this ignominious place! Little did I think when last we parted he would meet me in a prison, under condemnation!" This reflection roused an impetuosity of grief which deprived him for some time of speech. "But where is he?" said Theodore, recovering himself; "now he is come I shrink from the interview I have so much wished for. The sight of his distress will be dreadful to me. Louis, when I am gone, comfort my poor father." His voice was again interrupted by sobs; and Louis, who had been fearful of acquainting him at the same time of the arrival of La Luc, and the discovery of Adeline, now judged it proper to administer the cordial of this latter intelligence.

The glooms of a prison and of calamity vanished for a transient moment; those who had seen Theodore would have believed this to be the instant which gave him life and liberty. When his first emotions subsided, "I will not repine," said he, "since I know that Adeline is preserved, and that I shall once more see my father. I will endeavour to die with resignation." He inquired if La Luc was then in the prison, and was told he was at the inn with Clara and Adeline. "Adeline! Is Adeline there too? This is beyond my hopes. Yet why do I rejoice? I must never see her more; this is no place for Adeline." Again he relapsed into an agony of distress, and again repeated a thousand questions concerning Adeline, till he was reminded by Louis that his father was impatient to see him; when, shocked that he had so long detained his friend, he entreated him to conduct La Luc to the prison, and endeavoured to collect fortitude for the approaching interview.

When Louis returned to the inn La Luc was still in his chamber, and Clara quitting the room to call him, Adeline seized with trembling impatience the opportunity to inquire more particularly concerning Theodore than she chose to do in the presence of his unhappy sister. Louis represented him to be much more tranquil than he really was. Adeline was somewhat soothed by the account, and her tears, hitherto restrained, flowed silently and fast, till La Luc appeared. His countenance had recovered its serenity, but was impressed with a deep and steady sorrow, which excited in the beholder a mingled emotion of pity and reverence. "How is my son, sir?" said he, as he entered the room. "We will go to him immediately."

Clara renewed the entreaties that had been already rejected, to accompany her father, who persisted in a refusal.

"To-morrow you shall see him," added he; "but our first meeting must be alone. Stay with your friend, my dear, she has need of consolation."

When La Luc was gone, Adeline, unable longer to struggle against the force of grief, retired to her chamber and her bed.

La Luc walked silently towards the prison, resting on the arm of Louis. It was now night; a dim lamp that hung above showed them the gates, and Louis rang a bell; La Luc, almost overcome with agitation, leaned against the postern till the porter appeared. He inquired for Theodore, and followed the man; but when he reached the second courtyard he seemed ready to faint, and again stopped. Louis desired the porter would fetch some water, but La Luc, recovering his voice, said he should soon be better, and would not suffer him to go. In a few minutes he was able to follow Louis, who led him through several dark passages, and up a flight of steps to a door, which being unbarred disclosed to him the prison of his son. He was seated at a small table on which stood a lamp that threw a feeble light across the place, sufficient only to show its desolation and wretchedness. When he perceived La Luc, he sprang from his chair, and in the next moment was in his arms. "My father!" said he in a tremulous voice. "My son!" exclaimed La Luc; and they were for some time silent, and locked in each other's embrace.

At length Theodore led him to the only chair the room afforded, and seating himself with Louis at the foot of the bed, had leisure to observe the ravages which illness and calamity had made on the features of his parent. La Luc made several efforts to speak, but, unable to articulate, laid his hand upon his breast and sighed deeply. Fearful of the consequences of so affecting a scene on his shattered frame, Louis endeavoured to call off his attention from the immediate object of his distress, and interrupted the silence; but La Luc, shuddering and complaining he was very cold, sank back in his chair. His condition roused Theodore from the stupor of despair; and while he flew to support his father, Louis ran out for other assistance.

"I shall soon be better, Theodore," said La Luc, unclosing his eyes; "the faintness is already gone off. I have not been well of late, and this sad meeting!"

Unable any longer to command himself, Theodore wrung his hands, and the distress which had long struggled for utterance burst in convulsive sobs from his breast. La Luc gradually revived, and exerted himself to calm the transports of his son; but the fortitude of the latter had now entirely forsaken him, and he could only utter exclamation and complaint. "Ah! little did I think we should ever meet under circumstances so dreadful as the present! But I have not deserved them, my father! The motives of my conduct have still been just!"

"That is my supreme consolation," said La Luc, "and ought to support you in this hour of trial. The Almighty God, who is the judge of hearts, will reward you hereafter. Trust in Him, my son; I look to Him with no feeble hope; with a firm reliance on His justice!" La Luc's voice faltered; he raised his eyes to heaven with an expression of meek devotion, while the tears of humanity fell slowly on his cheek.

Still more affected by his last words, Theodore turned from him, and paced the room with quick steps. The entrance of Louis was a very seasonable relief to La Luc, who, taking a cordial he had brought, was soon sufficiently restored to discourse on the subject most interesting to him. Theodore tried to attain a command of his feelings, and succeeded. He conversed with tolerable composure for above an hour, during which La Luc endeavoured to elevate, by religious hope, the mind of his son, and to enable him to meet with fortitude the awful hour that approached. But the appearance of resignation which Theodore attained always vanished when he reflected that he was going to leave his father a prey to grief, and his beloved Adeline for ever. When La Luc was about to depart, he again mentioned her.

"Afflicting as an interview must be in our present circumstances," said he, "I cannot bear the thought of quitting the world without seeing her once again; yet I know not how to ask her to encounter, for my sake, the misery of a parting scene. Tell her that my thoughts never for a moment leave her; that——"

La Luc interrupted, and assured him that since he so much wished it he should see her, though a meeting could serve only to heighten the mutual anguish of a final separation.

"I know it—I know it too well," said Theodore; "yet I cannot resolve to see her no more, and thus spare her the pain this interview must inflict. Oh, my father! when I think of those whom I must soon leave for ever my heart breaks. But I will indeed try to profit by your precept and example, and show that your paternal care has not been in vain. My good Louis, go with my father—he has need of support. How much I owe this generous friend," added Theodore, "you well know, sir."

"I do, in truth," replied La Luc, "and can never repay his kindness to you. He has contributed to support us all ; but you require comfort more than myself—he shall remain with you—I will go alone."

This Theodore would not suffer ; and La Luc no longer opposing him, they affectionately embraced, and separated for the night.

When they reached the inn, La Luc consulted with Louis on the possibility of addressing a petition to the sovereign in time enough to save Theodore. His distance from Paris, and the short interval before the period fixed for the execution of the sentence, made this design difficult ; but believing it was practicable, La Luc, incapable as he appeared of performing so long a journey, determined to attempt it. Louis, thinking that the undertaking would prove fatal to the father, without benefiting the son, endeavoured, though faintly, to dissuade him from it—but his resolution was fixed. " If I sacrifice the small remains of my life in the service of my child," said he, " I shall lose little ; if I save him, I shall gain everything. There is no time to be lost—I will set off immediately."

He would have ordered post-horses, but Louis, and Clara, who was now come from the bed-side of her friend, urged the necessity of his taking a few hours' repose. He was at length compelled to acknowledge himself unequal to the immediate exertion which parental anxiety prompted, and consented to seek rest.

When he had retired to his chamber, Clara lamented the condition of her father. " He will not bear the journey," said she ; " he is greatly changed within these few days. Louis was so entirely of her opinion, that he could not disguise it, even to flatter her with a hope. She added, what did not contribute to raise his spirits, that Adeline was so much indisposed by her grief for the situation of Theodore, and the sufferings of La Luc, that she dreaded the consequence.

It has been seen that the passion of young La Motte had suffered no abatement from time or absence ; on the contrary, the persecution and the dangers which had pursued Adeline awakened all his tenderness, and drew her nearer to his heart. When he had discovered that Theodore loved her, and was beloved again, he experienced all the anguish of jealousy and disappointment ; for though she had forbade him to hope, he found it too painful an effort to obey her, and had secretly cherished the flame which he ought to have stifled. His heart was, however, too noble to suffer his zeal for Theodore to abate because

he was his favoured rival, and his mind too strong not to conceal the anguish this certainty occasioned. The attachment which Theodore had testified towards Adeline even endeared him to Louis, when he had recovered from the first shock of disappointment ; and that conquest over jealousy which originated in principle, and was pursued with difficulty, became afterwards his pride and his glory. When, however, he again saw Adeline—saw her in the mild dignity of sorrow, more interesting than ever—saw her, though sinking beneath its pressure, yet tender and solicitous to soften the afflictions of those around her—it was with the utmost difficulty he preserved his resolution, and forbore to express the sentiments she inspired. When he further considered that her acute sufferings arose from the strength of her affection, he more than ever wished himself the object of a heart capable of so tender a regard, and Theodore in prison, and in chains, was a momentary object of envy.

In the morning, when La Luc arose from short and disturbed slumbers, he found Louis, Clara, and Adeline, whom indisposition could not prevent from paying him this testimony of respect and affection, assembled in the parlour of the inn to see him depart. After a slight breakfast, during which his feelings permitted him to say little, he bade his friends a sad farewell, and stepped into the carriage, followed by their tears and prayers. Adeline immediately retired to her chamber, which she was too ill to quit that day. In the evening Clara left her friend, and, conducted by Louis, went to visit her brother, whose emotions, on hearing of his father's departure, were various and strong.

CHAPTER XX.

'Tis only when with inbred horror smote,
Of some base act, or done, or to be done,
That the recoiling soul, with conscious dread,
Shrinks back in itself.   MASON.

WE return now to Pierre de la Motte, who, after remaining some weeks in the prison of D——y, was removed to take his trial in the courts of Paris, whither the Marquis de Montalt followed to prosecute the charge. Madame de la Motte accompanied her husband to the prison of the Châtelet. His mind sank under the weight of his misfortunes, nor could all the efforts of his wife rouse him from the torpidity of despair which a consideration of his circumstances occasioned. Should he even be acquitted of the charge brought against him by the Marquis (which was very unlikely) he was now in the scene of his former crimes, and the moment that should liberate him from the walls of his prison would probably deliver him again into the hands of offended justice.

The prosecution of the Marquis was too well founded, and its object of a nature too serious, not to justify the terror of La Motte. Soon after the latter had settled at the Abbey of St. Clair, the small stock of money which the emergency of his circumstances had left him being nearly exhausted, his mind became corroded with the most cruel anxiety concerning the means of his future subsistence. As he was one evening riding alone in a remote part of the forest, musing on his distressed circumstances, and meditating plans to relieve the exigencies which he saw approaching, he perceived among the trees, at some distance, a chevalier on horseback, who was riding deliberately along, and seemed wholly unattended. A thought darted across the mind of La Motte, that he might be spared the evils which threatened him, by robbing this stranger. His former practices had passed the boundary of honesty, fraud was in some degree familiar to him, and the thought was not dismissed. He hesitated—every moment increased the power of temptation—the opportunity was such as might never occur again. He looked round, and as far as the trees opened, saw no person but the chevalier, who seemed to be a man of distinction. Summoning all his courage, La Motte rode forward and attacked him. The Marquis de Montalt, for it was him, was unarmed, but knowing that his attendants were not far off, he refused to yield. While they were struggling for victory, La Motte saw several horsemen enter the extremity of the avenue, and rendered desperate by opposition, he drew from his pocket a pistol (which an apprehension of banditti made him usually carry when he rode to a distance from the abbey) and fired at the Marquis, who staggered, and fell senseless to the ground. La Motte had time to steal from his coat a brilliant star, some diamond rings from his fingers, and to rifle his pockets, before his attendants came up. Instead of pursuing the robber, they all, in their first confusion, flew to assist their lord, and La Motte escaped.

He stopped before he reached the abbey, at a little ruin, the tomb before mentioned, to examine his booty. It consisted of a purse, containing seventy louis-d'ors ; of a diamond star, three rings of great value, and a miniature of the Marquis, set with brilliants, which he had intended as a present for his favourite mistress. To La Motte, who but a few hours before had seen himself nearly destitute, the view of this treasure excited an almost ungovernable transport ; but it was soon checked, when he remembered the means he had employed to obtain it, and that he had paid for the wealth he contemplated the price of blood ! Naturally violent in his passions, this reflection sank him from the summit of exultation to the abyss of despondency. He considered himself a murderer, and startled as one awakened from a dream, would have given half the world, had it been his, to have been as poor, and, comparatively, as guiltless, as he had been a few hours before. On examining the portrait, he discovered the resemblance, and believing he had deprived the original of life, he gazed upon the picture with bitter anguish. To the horrors of remorse succeeded the perplexities of fear. Apprehensive of he knew not what, he lingered at the tomb, where he at length deposited his treasure, believing, that if his offence should awaken justice, the abbey might be searched, and these jewels betray him.

From Madame La Motte it was easy to conceal his increase of wealth ; for, as he had never made her acquainted with the exact state of his finances, she had not suspected the extreme poverty which menaced him ; and, as they continued to live as usual, she believed that their expenses were drawn from the usual supply. But it was not so easy to disguise the workings of remorse and horror. His manner became gloomy and reserved ; and his frequent visits to the tomb, where he went partly to look at his treasure but chiefly to indulge in the dreadful pleasure of contemplating the picture of the Marquis, excited curiosity. In the solitude of the forest, where no variety of objects occurred to renovate his ideas, the horrible one of having committed murder was ever present to him.

When the Marquis arrived at the abbey, the astonishment and terror of La Motte—for at first he scarcely knew whether he beheld the shadow or the substance of a human form—were quickly succeeded by apprehension of the punishment due to the crime he had really committed. When his distress had prevailed on the Marquis to retire, he informed him that he was by birth a chevalier ; he then touched upon such parts of his misfortunes as he thought would excite pity, expressed such abhorrence of his guilt, and uttered such a solemn promise of returning the jewels he had yet in his possession—for he had ventured to dispose only of a small part—that the Marquis at length listened to him with some degree of compassion. This favourable sentiment, seconded by a selfish motive, induced the Marquis to compromise with La Motte. Of quick and inflammable passions, he had observed the beauty of Adeline with an eye of no common regard ; and he resolved to spare the life of La Motte upon no other condition than the sacrifice of this unfortunate girl. La Motte had neither resolution nor virtue sufficient to reject the terms—the jewels were restored, and he consented to betray the innocent Adeline. But as he was too well acquainted with her heart to believe that she would easily be won to the practice of vice, and as he still felt a degree of pity and tenderness for her, he endeavoured to prevail on the Marquis to forbear precipitate measures, and to attempt gradually to undermine her principles by seducing her affections. He approved and adopted this plan. The failure of his first scheme induced him to employ the stratagems he afterwards pursued, and thus to multiply the misfortunes of Adeline.

Such were the circumstances which had brought La Motte to his present deplorable situation. The day of trial was now come, and he was led from prison into the court, where the Marquis appeared as his accuser. When the charge was delivered, La Motte, as is usual, pleaded Not guilty, and the Advocate Nemours, who had undertaken to plead for him, afterwards endeavoured to make it appear that the accusation, on the part of the Marquis de Montalt, was false and malicious. To this purpose he mentioned the circumstance of the latter having attempted to persuade his client to the murder of Adeline; he further urged that the Marquis had lived in habits of intimacy with La Motte for several months immediately preceding his arrest; and that it was not till he had disappointed the designs of his accuser, by conveying beyond his reach the unhappy object of his vengeance, that the Marquis had thought proper to charge La Motte with the crime for which he stood indicted. Nemours urged the improbability of one man's keeping up a friendly intercourse with another from whom he had suffered the double injury of assault and robbery; yet it was certain that the Marquis had observed a frequent intercourse with La Motte for some months following the time specified for the commission of the crime. If the Marquis intended to prosecute, why was it not immediately after his discovery of La Motte? And if not then, what had influenced him to prosecute at so distant a period?

To this nothing was replied on the part of the Marquis; for, as his conduct on this point had been subservient to his designs on Adeline, he could not justify it but by exposing schemes which would betray the darkness of his character and invalidate his cause. He therefore contented himself with producing several of his servants as witnesses of the assault and robbery, who swore, without scruple, to the person of La Motte, though not one of them had seen him otherwise than through the gloom of evening, and riding off at full speed. On a cross-examination most of them contradicted each other; their evidence was of course rejected. But, as the Marquis had yet two other witnesses to produce, whose arrival at Paris had been hourly expected, the event of the trial was postponed, and the court adjourned.

La Motte was reconducted to his prison under the same pressure of despondency with which he had quitted it. As he walked through one of the avenues, he passed a man who stood by to let him proceed, and who regarded him with a fixed and earnest eye. La Motte thought he had seen him before; but the imperfect view he caught of his features through the duskiness of the place made him uncertain as to this, and his mind was in too perturbed a state to suffer him to feel an interest on the subject. When he was gone the stranger inquired of the keeper of the prison who La Motte was; on being told, and receiving answers to some further questions he put, he desired he might be admitted to speak with him.

The request, as the man was only a debtor, was granted; but as the doors were now shut for the night, the interview was deferred till the morrow.

La Motte found Madame, in his room, where she had been waiting for some hours to hear the event of the trial. They now wished more earnestly than ever to see their son; but they were, as he had suspected, ignorant of his change of quarters, owing to the letters which he had, as usual, addressed to them, under an assumed name, remaining at the post-house of Auboine. This circumstance occasioned Madame La Motte to address her letters to the place of her son's late residence, and he had thus continued ignorant of his father's misfortunes and removal. Madame La Motte, surprised at receiving no answer to her letters, sent off another, containing an account of the trial, as far as it had proceeded, and a request that her son would obtain leave of absence, and set out for Paris instantly. As she was still ignorant of the failure of her letters, and, had it been otherwise, would not have known whither to have sent them, she directed them as usual.

Meanwhile his approaching fate was never absent for a moment from the mind of La Motte, which, feeble by nature, and still more enervated by habits of indulgence, refused to support him at this dreadful period.

While these scenes were passing at Paris, La Luc arrived there without any accident, after performing a journey, during which he had been supported almost entirely by the spirit of his resolution. He hastened to throw himself at the feet of his sovereign, and such was the excess of his feeling, on presenting the petition which was to decide the fate of his son, that he could only look silently up, and then fainted. The king received the paper, and giving orders for the unhappy father to be taken care of, passed on. He was carried back to his hotel, where he waited the event of this his final effort.

Adeline, meanwhile, continued at Vaceau, in a state of anxiety too powerful for her long agitated frame, and the illness, in consequence of this, confined her almost wholly to her chamber. Sometimes she ventured to flatter herself with a hope that La Luc's journey would be successful, but these short and illusive intervals of comfort seemed only to heighten, by contrast, the despondency that succeeded, and, in the alternate extremes of feeling, she experienced a state more torturing than that produced either by the sharp sting of unexpected calamity, or the sullen pain of settled despair.

When she was well enough, she came down to the parlour to converse with Louis, who brought her frequent accounts of Theodore, and who passed every moment he could snatch from the duty of his profession in endeavours to support and console his afflicted friends. Adeline and Theodore both looked to him for the little comfort allotted them, for he brought them intelligence of each other, and, whenever he appeared, a transient melancholy kind of pleasure played round their hearts. He could not conceal from Theodore Adeline's indisposition, since it was necessary to account for her not indulging the earnest wish he repeatedly expressed to see her again. To Adeline he spoke chiefly of the fortitude and resignation of his friend, not forgetting to mention the tender affection he constantly expressed for her. Accustomed to derive her sole consolation from the presence of Louis, and to observe his unwearied friendship towards him whom she so truly loved, she found her esteem for him ripen into gratitude and her regard daily increase.

The fortitude with which he had said Theodore supported his calamities was somewhat exaggerated. He could not sufficiently forget those ties which bound him to life to meet his fate with firmness; but though the paroxysms of grief were acute and frequent, he sought, and often attained, in the presence of his friends, a manly composure. From the event of his father's journey he hoped little, yet that little was sufficient to keep his mind in the torture of suspense till the issue should appear.

On the day preceding that fixed for the execution of the sentence, La Luc reached Vaceau. Adeline was at her chamber window when the carriage drew up to the inn; she saw him alight, and, with feeble steps, supported by Peter, enter the house. From the languor of his air she drew no favourable omen, and, almost sinking under the violence of her emotion, she went to meet him. Clara was already with her father when Adeline entered the room. She approached him, but, dreading to receive from his lips a confirmation of the misfortune his countenance seemed to indicate, she looked expressively at him and sat down, unable to speak the question she would have asked. He held out his hand to her in silence, sank back in his chair, and seemed to be fainting under oppression of heart. His manner confirmed all her fears;

at this dreadful conviction her senses failed her, and she sat motionless and stupefied.

La Luc and Clara were too much occupied by their own distress to observe her situation. After some time she breathed a heavy sigh, and burst into tears. Relieved by weeping, her spirits gradually returned, and she at length said to La Luc, "It is unnecessary, sir, to ask the event of your journey, yet when you can bear to mention the subject I wish——"

La Luc waved his hand. "Alas!" said he, "I have nothing to tell but what you already guess too well. My poor Theodore!"

His voice was convulsed with sorrow, and some moments of unutterable anguish followed.

Adeline was the first who recovered sufficient recollection to notice the extreme languor of La Luc, and attend to his support. She ordered him refreshments, and entreated he would retire to his bed, and suffer her to send for a physician, adding that the fatigue he had suffered made repose absolutely necessary.

"Would that I could find it, my dear child," said he; "it is not in this world that I must look for it, but in a better, and that better I trust I shall soon attain. But where is our good friend Louis La Motte? He must lead me to my son."

Grief again interrupted his utterance, and the entrance of Louis was a seasonable relief to them all. Their tears explained the question he would have asked. La Luc immediately inquired for his son, and, thanking Louis for all his kindness to him, desired to be conducted to the prison.

Louis endeavoured to persuade him to defer his visit till the morning, and Adeline and Clara joined their entreaties with his; but La Luc had determined to go that night. "His time is short," said he; "a few hours and I shall see him no more, at least in this world; let me not neglect these precious moments. Adeline! I had promised my poor boy that he should see you once more; you are not now equal to the meeting. I will try to reconcile him to the disappointment; but if I fail, and you are better in the morning, I know you will exert yourself to sustain the interview."

Adeline looked impatient, and attempted to speak. La Luc rose to depart, but could only reach the door of the room, where, faint and feeble, he sat down in a chair. "I must submit to necessity," said he; "I find I am not able to go farther to-night. Go to him, La Motte, and tell him I am somewhat disordered by my journey, but that I will be with him early in the morning. Do not flatter him with a hope; prepare him for the worst." There was a pause of silence; La Luc, at length recovering himself, desired Clara would order his bed to be got ready,

my dear father, would subdue all my fortitude
—would destroy what little composure I may
otherwise be able to attain. Add not to my
sufferings the view of your distress, but leave
me to forget, if possible, the dear parent I
must quit for ever." His tears flowed anew.

La Luc continued to gaze on him in silent
agony; at length he said : "Well, be it so.
If, indeed, my presence would distress you,
I will go." His voice was broken and
interrupted. After a pause of some moments,
he again embraced Theodore. "We must
part," said he, "we must part, but it is only
for a time—we shall soon be reunited in a
higher world. Oh God ! thou seest my heart
—thou seest all its feelings in this bitter
hour !" Grief again overcame him. He
pressed Theodore in his arms; and, at
length, seeming to summon all his fortitude,
he again said : "We must part—Oh ! my
son, farewell for ever in this world ! The
mercy of Almighty God support and bless
you !"

He turned away to leave the prison, but,
quite worn out with grief, sank into a chair
near the door he would have opened. Theodore gazed, with a distracted countenance,
alternately on his father, on Clara, and on
Adeline, whom he pressed to his throbbing
heart, and their tears flowed together. "And
do I then," cried he, "for the last time, look
upon that countenance ? Shall I never—
never more behold it ? Oh ! exquisite misery !
Yet once again—once more," continued he,
pressing her cheek, but it was insensible, and
cold as marble.

Louis, who had left the room soon after
La Luc arrived, that his presence might not
interrupt their farewell grief, now returned.
Adeline raised her head, and perceiving who
entered, it again sank on the bosom of Theodore.

Louis appeared much agitated. La Luc
arose. "We must go," said he. "Adeline,
my love, exert yourself. Clara—my children
—let us depart. Yet one last embrace, and
then——"

Louis advanced and took his hand. "My
dear sir, I have something to say, yet I fear
to tell it."

"What do you mean?" said La Luc, with
quickness ; "no new misfortune can have
power to afflict me at this moment. Do not
fear to speak."

"I rejoice that I cannot put you to the
proof," replied Louis ; "I have seen you
sustain the most trying affliction with fortitude. Can you support the transports of
hope ?"

La Luc gazed eagerly on Louis. "Speak,"
said he, in a faint voice. Adeline raised her
head, and trembling between hope and fear,
looked at Louis as if she would have searched
his soul. He smiled cheerfully upon her.
" Is it—oh, is it possible ? " she exclaimed,

suddenly reanimated; " he lives ! he lives !"
She said no more, but ran to La Luc, who
sank in his chair, while Theodore and Clara,
with one voice, called on Louis to relieve them
from the tortures of suspense.

He proceeded to inform them that he had
obtained from the commanding officer a respite
for Theodore till the king's further pleasure
could be known, and this in consequence of a
letter received that morning from his mother,
Madame La Motte, in which she mentioned
some very extraordinary circumstances that
had appeared in the course of a trial lately
conducted at Paris, and which so materially
affected the character of the Marquis de
Montalt as to render it possible a pardon
might be obtained for Theodore.

These words darted with the rapidity of
lightning upon the hearts of his hearers. La
Luc revived, and that prison, so lately the
scene of despair, now echoed only to the voices
of gratitude and gladness. La Luc, raising
his clasped hands to heaven, said, "Great
God, support me in this moment as thou hast
already supported me ! If my son lives, I die
in peace."

He embraced Theodore, and remembering
the anguish of his last embrace, tears of thankfulness and joy flowed at the contrast. So
powerful, indeed, was the effect of this temporary reprieve, and of the hope it introduced,
that if an absolute pardon had been obtained
it could scarcely, for the moment, have diffused
a more lively joy. But when the first emotions
were subsided, the uncertainty of Theodore's
fate once more appeared. Adeline forbore to
express her sense of this, but Clara, without
scruple, lamented the possibility that her
brother might yet be taken from them, and
all their joy be turned to sorrow. A look
from Adeline checked her. Joy was, however, so much the predominant feeling of the
present moment, that the shade which reflection threw upon their hopes passed away like
the cloud that is dispelled by the strength of
the sunbeam ; and Louis alone was pensive
and abstracted.

When they were sufficiently composed, he
informed them that the contents of Madame
La Motte's letter obliged him to set out for
Paris immediately ; and that the intelligence
he had to communicate intimately concerned
Adeline, who would undoubtedly judge it
necessary to go thither also as soon as her
health would permit. He then related to his
impatient auditors such passages in the letter
as were necessary to explain his meaning ;
but as Madame La Motte had omitted to
mention some circumstances of importance to
be understood, the following is a relation of
the occurrences that had lately happened at
Paris.

It may be remembered that on the first day
of his trial, La Motte, in passing from the
courts to his prison, saw a person whose fea-

tures, though imperfectly seen through the dusk, he thought he recollected ; and that this same person, after inquiring La Motte's name, desired to be admitted to him. On the following day the warder complied with his request, and the surprise of La Motte may be imagined when, in the stronger light of his apartment, he distinguished the countenance of the man from whose hands he had formerly received Adeline.

On observing Madame La Motte in the room, he said he had something of consequence to impart, and desired to be left alone with the prisoner. When she was gone, he told La Motte that he understood he was confined at the suit of the Marquis de Montalt. La Motte assented.

" I know him for a villain," said the stranger boldly. " Your case is desperate. Do you wish for life ? "

" Need the question be asked ? "

" Your trial, I understand, proceeds to-morrow. I am now under confinement in this place for debt ; but if you can obtain leave for me to go with you into the courts, and a condition from the judge that what I reveal shall not criminate myself, I will make discoveries that shall confound the Marquis ; I will prove him a villain ; and it shall then be judged how far his word ought to be taken against you."

La Motte, whose interest was now strongly excited, desired he would explain himself ; and the man proceeded to relate a long history of the misfortunes and consequent poverty which had tempted him to become subservient to the schemes of the Marquis, till he suddenly checked himself, and said :

" When I obtain from the court the promise I require I will explain myself fully ; till then I can say no more."

La Motte could not forbear expressing a doubt of his sincerity, and a curiosity concerning the motive that had induced him to become the Marquis's accuser.

" As to my motive, it is a very natural one," replied the man ; " it is no easy matter to receive ill-usage without resenting it, particularly from a villain whom you have served."

La Motte, for his own sake, endeavoured to check the vehemence with which this was uttered.

" I care not who hears me," continued the stranger, but at the same time he lowered his voice : " I repeat it—the Marquis has used me ill—I have kept his secret long enough. He does not think it worth while to secure my silence or he would relieve my necessities. I am in prison for debt, and have applied to him for relief ; since he does not choose to give it, let him take the consequence. I warrant he shall soon repent that he has provoked me, and 'tis fit he should."

The doubts of La Motte were now dissipated ; the prospect of life again opened upon him, and he assured Du Bosse (which was the stranger's name), with much warmth, that he would commission his advocate to do all in his power to obtain leave for his appearance on the trial, and to procure the necessary condition. After some further conversation, they parted.

CHAPTER XXI.

Drag forth the legal monster into light,
Wrench from his hand oppression's iron rod,
And bid the cruel feel the pangs they give.

LEAVE was at length granted for the appearance of Du Bosse, with a promise that his words should not criminate him, and he accompanied La Motte into court.

The confusion of the Marquis de Montalt on perceiving this man was observed by many persons present, and particularly by La Motte, who drew from this circumstance a favourable presage for himself.

When Du Bosse was called upon he informed the court that, on the night of the twenty-first of April, in the preceding year, one Jean D'Aunoy, a man he had known many years, came to his lodging. After they had discoursed for some time on their circumstances, D'Aunoy said he knew a way by which Du Bosse might change all his poverty to riches, but that he would not say more till he was certain he would be willing to follow it. The distressed state in which Du Bosse then was made him anxious to obtain some means of relief : he eagerly inquired what his friend meant, when D'Aunoy explained himself. He said he was employed by a nobleman (whom he afterwards told Du Bosse was the Marquis de Montalt) to carry off a young girl from a convent, and that she was to be taken to a house a few leagues distant from Paris. " I knew the house he described well," said Du Bosse, " for I have been there many times with D'Aunoy, who lived there to avoid his creditors, though he often passed his nights at Paris. He would not tell me more of the scheme, but said he should want assistants, and if I and my brother, who is since dead, would join him, his employer would grudge no money, and we should be well rewarded. I desired him again to tell me more of the plan, but he was obstinate ; and after I had told him I would consider of what he said, and speak to my brother, he went away.

" When he called the next night for his answer my brother and I agreed to engage, and accordingly we went home with him. He then told us that the young lady he was to bring thither was a natural daughter of the Marquis de Montalt and of a nun belonging to a convent of Ursulines ; that his wife had received the child immediately on its birth, and had been allowed a handsome annuity to bring it up as her own, which she had done till her death, The child was then placed in a convent and designed for the veil, but when she was of an age to receive the vows she had steadily persisted in refusing them. This circumstance had so much exasperated the Marquis that in his rage he ordered that, if she persisted in her obstinacy, she should be removed from the convent and got rid of any way, since, if she lived in the world, her birth might be discovered, and, in consequence of this, her mother, for whom he had yet a regard, would be condemned to expiate her crime by a terrible death."

Du Bosse was interrupted in his narrative by the counsel of the Marquis, who contended that the circumstances alleged tending to criminate his client, the proceeding was both irrelevant and illegal. He was answered that it was not irrelevant, and therefore not illegal, for that the circumstances which threw light upon the character of the Marquis affected his evidence against La Motte. Du Bosse was suffered to proceed.

" D'Aunoy then said that the Marquis had ordered him to despatch her, but that, as he had been used to see her from her infancy, he could not find it in his heart to do it, and wrote to tell him so. The Marquis then commanded him to find those who would, and this was the business for which he wanted us. My brother and I were not so wicked as this came to, and so we told D'Aunoy ; and I could not help asking why the Marquis resolved to murder his own child rather than expose her mother to the risk of suffering death. He said the Marquis had never seen his child, and that, therefore, it could not be supposed he felt much kindness towards it, and still less that he could love it better than he loved its mother."

Du Bosse proceeded to relate how much he and his brother had endeavoured to soften the heart of D'Aunoy towards the Marquis's daughter, and that they prevailed with him to write again and plead for her. D'Aunoy went to Paris to await the answer, leaving them and the young girl at the house on the heath, where the former had consented to remain, seemingly for the purpose of executing the orders they might receive, but really with a design to save the devoted victim from the sacrifice.

It is probable that Du Bosse, in this instance, gave a false account of his motive, since, if he really was guilty of an intention so atrocious as that of murder, he would naturally endeavour to conceal it. However this might be, he affirmed that, on the night of the twenty-sixth of April, he received an order from D'Aunoy for the destruction of the girl, whom he had afterwards delivered into the hands of La Motte.

La Motte listened to this relation in astonishment ; when he knew that Adeline was the daughter of the Marquis, and remembered

the crime to which he had once devoted her, his frame thrilled with horror. He now took up the story, and added an account of what had passed at the abbey between the Marquis and himself concerning a design of the former upon the life of Adeline, urging, as a proof of the present prosecution originating in malice, that it had commenced immediately after he had effected her escape from the Marquis. He concluded, however, with saying that, as the Marquis had immediately sent his people in pursuit of her, it was possible she might have yet fallen a victim to his vengeance.

Here the Marquis's counsel again interfered, and their objections were again overruled by the court. The uncommon degree of emotion which his countenance betrayed during the narrations of Du Bosse and La Motte was generally observed. The court suspended the sentence of the latter, ordered that the Marquis should be put under immediate arrest, and that Adeline (the name given by her foster-mother) and Jean D'Aunoy should be sought for.

The Marquis was accordingly seized at the suit of the Crown, and put under confinement till Adeline should appear, or proof could be obtained that she died by his order, and till D'Aunoy should confirm or destroy the evidence of La Motte.

Madame, who at length obtained intelligence of her son's residence from the town where he was formerly stationed, had acquainted him with his father's situation, and the proceedings of the trial ; and as she believed that Adeline, if she had been so fortunate as to escape the Marquis's pursuit, was still in Savoy, she desired Louis would obtain leave of absence, and bring her to Paris, where her immediate presence was requisite, to substantiate the evidence, and, probably, to save the life of La Motte.

On the receipt of her letter, which happened on the morning appointed for the execution of Theodore, Louis went immediately to the commanding officer, to petition for a respite till the king's further pleasure should be known. He founded his plea on the arrest of the Marquis, and showed the letter he had just received. The commanding officer readily granted a reprieve, and Louis, who, on the arrival of this letter, had forborne to communicate its contents to Theodore, lest it should torture him with false hope, now hastened to him with this comfortable news.

CHAPTER XXII.

Low on his fun'ral couch he lies,
No pitying heart, no eye, afford
A tear to grace his obsequies.
　　　　　　　　　　　　GRAY.

ON learning the purpose of Madame La Motte's letter, Adeline saw the necessity of her immediate departure for Paris. The life of La Motte, who had more than saved hers, the life, perhaps, of her beloved Theodore, depended on the testimony she could give. And she who had so lately been sinking under the influence of illness and despair, who could scarcely raise her languid head, or speak but in the faintest accents, now, reanimated with hope, and invigorated by a sense of the importance of the business before her, prepared to perform a rapid journey of some hundred miles.

Theodore tenderly entreated that she would so far consider her health as to delay this journey for a few days; but with a smile of enchanting tenderness she assured him that she was now too happy to be ill, and that the same cause which would confirm her happiness would confirm her health. So strong was the effect of hope upon her mind, now that it succeeded to the misery of despair, that it overcame the shock she suffered on believing herself a daughter of the Marquis, and every other painful reflection. She did not even foresee the obstacle that circumstance might produce to her union with Theodore, should he at last be permitted to live.

It was settled that she should set off for Paris in a few hours with Louis, and attended by Peter. These hours were passed by La Luc and his family in the prison.

When the time of her departure arrived, the spirits of Adeline again forsook her, and the illusions of joy disappeared. She no longer beheld Theodore as one respited from death, but took leave of him with a mournful presentiment that she should see him no more. So strongly was this presage impressed upon her mind, that it was long before she could summon resolution to bid him farewell; and when she had done so, and even left the apartment, she returned to take of him a last look. As she was once more quitting the room, her melancholy imagination represented Theodore at the place of execution, pale and convulsed in death. She again turned her lingering eyes upon him; but fancy affected her sense, for she thought, as she now gazed, that his countenance changed and assumed a ghastly hue. All her resolution vanished, and such was the anguish of her heart that she resolved to defer her journey till the morrow; though she must by this means lose the protection of Louis, whose impatience to meet his father would not suffer the delay. The triumph of passion, however, was transient; soothed by the indulgence she promised herself, her grief subsided, reason assumed its influence; she again saw the necessity of her immediate departure, and collected sufficient resolution to submit. La Luc would have accompanied her for the purpose of again soliciting the king in behalf of his son, had not the weakness and lassitude to which he was reduced made travelling impracticable.

At length Adeline, with a heavy heart, quitted Theodore, notwithstanding his entreaties that she would not undertake the journey in her present weak state, and was accompanied by Clara and La Luc to the inn. The former parted from her friend with many tears and much anxiety for her welfare, but under a hope of soon meeting again. Should a pardon be granted to Theodore, La Luc designed to fetch Adeline from Paris; but should this be refused, she was to return with Peter. He bade her adieu with a father's kindness, which she repaid with a filial affection; and in her last words conjured him to attend to the recovery of his health. The languid smile he assumed seemed to express that her solicitude was vain, and that he thought his health past recovery.

Thus Adeline quitted the friends so justly dear to her, and so lately found, for Paris; where she was a stranger, almost without protection, and compelled to meet a father who had pursued her with the utmost cruelty in a public court of justice. The carriage, in leaving Vaceau, passed by the prison; she threw an eager look towards it as she passed; its heavy black walls and narrow grated windows seemed to frown upon her hopes; but Theodore was there, and leaning from the window she continued to gaze upon it till an abrupt turning in the street concealed it from her view. She then sank back in the carriage, and, yielding to the melancholy of her heart, wept in silence. Louis was not disposed to interrupt it; his thoughts were anxiously employed on his father's situation, and the travellers proceeded many miles without exchanging a word.

At Paris, whither we shall now return, the search after Jean D'Aunoy was prosecuted without success. The house on the heath, described by Du Bosse, was found uninhabited; and to the places of his usual resort in the city, where the officers of the police awaited him, he no longer came. It even appeared doubtful whether he was living, for he had absented himself from the houses of his customary rendezvous some time before the trial of La Motte; it was therefore certain that his absence was not occasioned by anything which had passed in the courts.

In the solitude of his confinement the Marquis de Montalt had leisure to reflect on the past and to repent of his crimes; but reflection and repentance formed as yet no part of his disposition. He turned with impatience from recollections which produced only pain, and looked forward to the future with an endeavour to avert the disgrace and punishment which he saw impending. The elegance of his manners had so effectually veiled the depravity of his heart that he was a favourite with his sovereign; and on this circumstance he rested his hope of security. He, however, severely repented that he had indulged the hasty spirit of revenge which had urged the prosecution of La Motte, and had thus unexpectedly involved him in a situation dangerous—if not fatal—since, if Adeline could not be found, he would be concluded guilty of her death. But the appearance of D'Aunoy was the circumstance he most dreaded; and to oppose the possibility of this he employed secret emissaries to discover his retreat, and to bribe him to his interest. These were, however, as unsuccessful in their research as the officers of police, and the Marquis at length began to hope the man was really dead.

La Motte meanwhile awaited with trembling impatience the arrival of his son, when he should be relieved, in some degree, from his uncertainty concerning Adeline. On her appearance he rested his only hope of life, since the evidence against him would lose much of its validity from the confirmation she would give of the bad character of his prosecutor; and if the parliament even condemned La Motte, the clemency of the king might yet operate in his favour.

Adeline arrived at Paris after a journey of several days, during which she was chiefly supported by the delicate attention of Louis, whom she pitied and revered, though she could not love. She was immediately visited at the hotel by Madame La Motte; the meeting was affecting on both sides. A sense of her past conduct excited in the latter an embarrassment which the delicacy and goodness of Adeline would willingly have spared her; but the pardon solicited was given with so much sincerity, that Madame gradually became composed and reassured. This forgiveness, however, could not have been thus easily granted, had Adeline believed her former conduct voluntary; a conviction of the restraint and terror under which Madame had acted alone induced her to excuse the past. In this first meeting they forbore dwelling on particular subjects. Madame La Motte proposed that Adeline should remove from the hotel to her lodgings near the Châtelet, and Adeline, for whom a residence at a public hotel was very improper, gladly accepted the offer.

Madame there gave her a circumstantial account of La Motte's situation, and concluded with saying, that as the sentence of her husband had been suspended till some certainty could be obtained concerning the late criminal designs of the Marquis, and Adeline could confirm the chief part of La Motte's testimony, it was probable that, now she was arrived, the court would proceed immediately. She now learnt the full extent of her obligation to La Motte; for she was till now ignorant that when he sent her from the forest, he saved her from death. Her horror of the Marquis, whom she could not bear to consider as her father, and her gratitude to her deliverer, redoubled, and she became impatient to give the testimony so necessary to the hopes of her preserver. Madame then said she believed it was not too late to gain admittance that night to the Châtelet; and as she knew how anxiously her husband wished to see Adeline, she entreated her consent to go thither. Adeline, though much harassed and fatigued, complied. When Louis returned from M. Nemours, his father's advocate, whom he had hastened to inform of her arrival, they all set out for the Châtelet. The view of the prison into which they were now admitted so forcibly recalled to Adeline's mind the situation of Theodore, that she with difficulty supported herself to the apartment of La Motte. When he saw her a gleam of joy passed over his countenance; but again relapsing into despondency, he looked mournfully at her, and then at Louis, and groaned deeply. Adeline, in whom all remembrance of his former cruelty was lost in his subsequent kindness, expressed her thankfulness for the life he had preserved, and her anxiety to serve him in warm and repeated terms. But her gratitude evidently distressed him; instead of reconciling him to himself, it seemed to awaken a remembrance of the guilty designs he had once assisted, and to strike the fangs of conscience deeper in his heart. Endeavouring to conceal his emotions, he entered on the subject of his present danger, and informed Adeline what testimony would be required of her on the trial. After an hour's conversation with La Motte, she returned to the lodgings of Madame, where, languid and ill, she withdrew to her chamber, and tried to obliviate her anxieties in sleep.

The parliament which conducted the trial reassembled in a few days after the arrival of Adeline, and the two remaining witnesses of the Marquis, on whom he now rested his cause against La Motte, appeared. She was led trembling into the court, where almost the first object that met her eyes was the Marquis de Montalt, whom she now beheld with an emotion entirely new to her, and which was strongly tinctured with horror. When Du Bosse saw her he immediately swore to her identity; his testimony was confirmed by her manner; for on perceiving him she grew pale, and a universal tremor seized her. Jean D'Aunoy could nowhere be found, and La Motte was thus deprived of an evidence which essentially affected his interest. Adeline, when called upon, gave her little narrative with clearness and precision; and Peter, who had conveyed her from the abbey, supported the testimony she offered. The evidence produced was sufficient to criminate the Marquis of the intention of murder in the minds of most people present; but it was not sufficient to affect the testimony of his last two witnesses, who positively swore to the robbery, and to the person of La Motte, on whom sentence of death was accordingly pronounced. On receiving this sentence the unhappy criminal fainted, and the compassion of the assembly, whose feelings had been unusually interested in the decision, was expressed in a general groan.

Their attention was quickly called to a new object—it was Jean D'Aunoy, who now entered the court. But his evidence, if it could ever, indeed, have been the means of saving La Motte, came too late. He was reconducted to prison ; but Adeline, who, extremely shocked by his sentence, was much indisposed, received orders to remain in the court during the examination of D'Aunoy. This man had been at length found in the prison of a provincial town, where some of his creditors had thrown him, and from which even the money which the Marquis had remitted to him, for the purpose of satisfying the craving importunities of Du Bosse, had been insufficient to release him. Meanwhile the revenge of the latter had been roused against the Marquis by an imaginary neglect, and the money, which was designed to relieve his necessities, was spent by D'Aunoy in riotous luxury.

He was confronted with Adeline and with Du Bosse, and ordered to confess all he knew concerning this mysterious affair, or to undergo the torture. D'Aunoy, who was ignorant how far the suspicions concerning the Marquis extended, and was conscious that his own words might condemn him, remained for some time obstinately silent ; but when the *question* was administered his resolution gave way, and he confessed a crime, of which he had not even been suspected.

It appeared that, in the year 1642, D'Aunoy, together with one Jacques Martigny and Francis Balliere, had waylaid and seized Henry Marquis de Montalt, half-brother to Philippe ; and after having bound him and bound his servant to a tree; according to the orders they had received, they conveyed him to the Abbey of St. Clair, in the distant forest of Fontanville. Here he was confined for some time, till further directions were received from Philippe de Montalt, the present Marquis, who was then on his estates in a northern province of France. These orders were for death, and the unfortunate Henry was assassinated in his chamber, in the third week of his confinement in the abbey.

On hearing this Adeline grew faint ; she remembered the MS. she had found, together with the extraordinary circumstances that had attended the discovery ; every nerve thrilled with horror, and, raising her eyes, she saw the countenance of the Marquis overspread with the livid paleness of guilt. She endeavoured, however, to arrest her spirits while the man made his confession.

When the murder was perpetrated D'Aunoy had returned to his employer, who gave him

the reward agreed upon, and in a few months after delivered into his hands the infant daughter of the late Marquis, whom he conveyed to a distant part of the kingdom, where, assuming the name of St. Pierre, he brought her up as his own child, receiving from the present Marquis a considerable annuity for his secrecy.

Adeline, no longer able to struggle with the emotions of her heart, uttered a deep sigh and fainted. She was carried from the court, and, when the confusion occasioned by this circumstance subsided, Jean D'Aunoy went on. He related that, on the death of his wife, Adeline was placed in a convent, from whence she was afterwards removed to another, where the Marquis had destined her to receive the vows. That her determined rejection of them had occasioned him to resolve upon her death, and that she had accordingly been removed to the house on the heath. D'Aunoy added that, by the Marquis's order, he had misled Du Bosse with a false story of her birth. Having discovered that his comrades had deceived him concerning her death, D'Aunoy separated from them in enmity ; but they unanimously determined to conceal her escape from the Marquis, that they might enjoy the recompense of their supposed crime. Some months subsequent to this period, however, D'Aunoy received a letter from the Marquis, charging him with the truth, and promising him a large reward if he would confess where he had placed Adeline. In consequence of this letter, he acknowledged that she had been given into the hands of a stranger ; but who he was, or where he lived, was not known.

Upon these depositions Philippe de Montalt was committed to take his trial for the murder of Henry, his brother ; D'Aunoy was thrown into a dungeon of the Châtelet, and Du Bosse was bound to appear as evidence.

The feelings of the Marquis, who, in a prosecution stimulated by revenge, had thus unexpectedly exposed his crimes to the public eye, and betrayed himself to justice, can only be imagined. The passions which had tempted him to the commission of a crime so horrid as that of murder—and what, if possible, heightened its atrocity, the murder of one connected with him by the ties of blood, and by habits of even infantine association— the passions which had stimulated him to so monstrous a deed were ambition and the love of pleasure. The first was more immediately gratified by the title of his brother ; the latter by the riches which would enable him to indulge his voluptuous inclinations.

The late Marquis de Montalt, the father of Adeline, received from his ancestors a patrimony very inadequate to support the splendour of his rank ; but he had married the heiress of an illustrious family, whose fortune amply supplied the deficiency of his own. He had the misfortune to lose her, for she was amiable and beautiful, soon after the birth of a daughter, and it was then that the present Marquis formed the diabolical design of destroying his brother. The contrast of their characters prevented that cordial regard between them which their near relationship seemed to demand. Henry was benevolent, mild, and contemplative. In his heart reigned the love of virtue; in his manners the strictness of justice was tempered, not weakened, by mercy; his mind was enlarged by science and adorned by elegant literature. The character of Philippe has been already delineated in his actions; its nicer shades were blended with some shining tints; but these served only to render more striking, by contrast, the general darkness of the portrait.

He had married a lady who, by the death of her brother, inherited considerable estates, of which the Abbey of St. Clair, and the villa on the borders of the forest of Fontanville, were the chief. His passion for magnificence and dissipation, however, soon involved him in difficulties, and pointed out to him the conveniency of possessing his brother's wealth. His brother and his infant daughter only stood between him and his wishes; how he removed the father has been already related; why he did not employ the same means to secure the child seems somewhat surprising, unless we admit that a destiny hung over him on this occasion, and that she was suffered to live as an instrument to punish the murderer of her parent. When a retrospect is taken of the vicissitudes and dangers to which she had been exposed from her earliest infancy, it appears as if her preservation was the effect of something more than human policy, and affords a striking instance that justice, however long delayed, will overtake the guilty.

While the late unhappy Marquis was suffering at the abbey, his brother, who, to avoid suspicion, remained in the north of France, delayed the execution of his horrid purpose from a timidity natural to a mind not yet inured to enormous guilt. Before he dared to deliver his final orders, he waited to know whether the story he contrived to propagate of his brother's death would veil his crime from suspicion. It succeeded but too well; for the servant, whose life had been spared that he might relate the tale, naturally enough concluded that his lord had been murdered by banditti; and the peasant, who, a few hours after, found the servant wounded, bleeding, and bound to a tree, and knew also that this spot was infested by robbers, as naturally believed him, and spread the report accordingly.

From this period the Marquis, to whom the Abbey of St. Clair belonged, in right of his wife, visited it only twice, and that at distant times, till, after an interval of several years, he accidentally found La Motte its inhabitant. He resided at Paris and on his estate in the north, except that once a year he usually passed a month at his delightful villa on the borders of the forest. In the busy scenes of the court, and in the dissipations of pleasure, he tried to lose the remembrance of his guilt; but there were times when the voice of conscience would be heard, though it was soon again lost in the tumult of the world.

It is probable that, on the night of his abrupt departure from the abbey, the solitary silence and gloom of the hour, in a place which had been the scene of his former crime, called up the remembrance of his brother with a force too powerful for fancy, and awakened horrors which compelled him to quit the polluted spot.

If it were so, it is however certain that the spectres of conscience vanished with the darkness, for on the following day he returned to the abbey, though, it may be observed, he never attempted to pass another night there. But though terror was roused for a transient moment, neither pity nor repentance succeeded, since, when the discovery of Adeline's birth excited apprehension for his own life, he did not hesitate to repeat the crime, and would again have stained his soul with human blood. This discovery was effected by means of a seal, bearing the arms of her mother's family, which was impressed on the note his servant had found and had delivered to him at Caux. It may be remembered that, having read this note, he was throwing it from him in the fury of jealousy, but that, after examining it again, it was carefully deposited in his pocketbook.

The violent agitation which a suspicion of this terrible truth occasioned deprived him for a while of all power to act.

When he was well enough to write he despatched a letter to D'Aunoy, the purport of which has been already mentioned. From D'Aunoy he received the confirmation of his fear. Knowing that his life must pay the forfeiture of his crime should Adeline ever obtain a knowledge of her birth, and not daring again to confide in the secrecy of a man who had once deceived him, be resolved, after some deliberation, on her death. He immediately set out for the abbey, and gave those directions concerning her which terror for his own safety, still more than a desire of retaining her estates, suggested.

As the history of the seal which revealed the birth of Adeline is rather remarkable, it may not be amiss to mention that it was stolen from the Marquis, together with a gold watch, by Jean D'Aunoy; the watch was soon disposed of, but the seal had been kept as a pretty trinket by his wife, and at her death went with Adeline among her clothes to the convent. Adeline had carefully preserved it because it had once belonged to the woman whom she believed to have been her mother,

---

CHAPTER XXIII.

While anxious doubt distracts the tortur'd heart.

WE now return to the course of the narrative and to Adeline, who was carried from the court to the lodging of Madame La Motte. Madame was, however, at the Châtelet with her husband, suffering all the distress which the sentence pronounced against him might be supposed to inflict. The feeble frame of Adeline, so long harassed by grief and fatigue, almost sank under the agitation which the discovery of her birth excited. Her feelings on this occasion were too complex to be analysed. From an orphan, subsisting on the bounty of others, without family, with few friends, and pursued by a cruel and powerful enemy, she saw herself suddenly transformed to the daughter of an illustrious house, and the heiress of great wealth. But she learned also that her father had been murdered—murdered in the prime of his days —murdered by means of his brother, against whom she must now appear, and, in punishing the destroyer of her parent, doom her uncle to death.

When she remembered the manuscript so singularly found, and considered that when she wept to the sufferings it described, her tears had flowed for those of her father, her emotion cannot easily be imagined. The circumstances attending the discovery of these papers no longer appeared to be a work of chance, but of a Power whose designs are great and just. "Oh my father!" she would exclaim, "your last wish is fulfilled—the pitying heart you wished might trace your sufferings shall avenge them."

On the return of Madame La Motte, Adeline endeavoured, as usual, to suppress her own emotions, that she might soothe the affliction of her friend. She related what had passed in the court after the departure of La Motte, and thus caused, even in the sorrowful heart of Madame, a momentary gleam of satisfaction. Adeline determined to recover, if possible, the manuscript. On inquiry, she learned that La Motte, in the confusion of his departure, had left it among other things at the Abbey. This circumstance much distressed her; the more so, because she believed its appearance might be of importance on the approaching trial; she determined, however, if she should recover her rights, to have the manuscript sought for.

In the evening Louis joined this mournful party; he came immediately from his father, whom he left more tranquil than he had been since the fatal sentence was pronounced. After a silent and melancholy supper, they

separated for the night, and Adeline, in the solitude of her chamber, had leisure to meditate on the discoveries of this eventful day. The sufferings of her dead father, such as she had read them recorded by his own hand, pressed most forcibly to her thoughts. The narrative had formerly so much affected her heart and interested her imagination, that her memory now faithfully reflected each particular circumstance they disclosed. But when she considered that she had been in the very chamber where her parent had suffered, where even his life had been sacrificed, and that she had probably seen the very dagger— seen it stained with rust, the rust of blood!— by which he had fallen, the anguish and horror of her mind defied all control.

On the following day Adeline received orders to prepare for the prosecution of the Marquis de Montalt, which was to commence as soon as the requisite witnesses could be collected. Among these were the abbess of the convent, who had received her from the hands of D'Aunoy; Madame La Motte, who was present when Du Bosse compelled her husband to receive Adeline; and Peter, who had not only been witness to this circumstance, but who had conveyed her from the abbey, that she might escape the designs of the Marquis. La Motte and Theodore La Luc were incapacitated, by the sentence of the law, from appearing on the trial.

When La Motte was informed of the discovery of Adeline's birth, and that her father had been murdered at the Abbey of St. Clair, he instantly remembered, and mentioned to his wife, the skeleton he found in the stone-room leading to the subterranean cells. Neither of them doubted, from the situation in which it lay hid in a chest in an obscure room strongly guarded, that La Motte had seen the remains of the late Marquis. Madame, however, determined not to shock Adeline with the mention of this circumstance till it should be necessary to declare it on the trial.

As the time of this trial drew near, the distress and agitation of Adeline increased. Though justice demanded the life of the murderer, and though the tenderness and pity which the idea of her father called forth urged her to avenge his death, she could not without horror consider herself as the instrument of dispensing that justice which would deprive a fellow-being of existence; and there were times when she wished the secret of her birth had never been revealed. If this sensibility was, in her peculiar circumstances, a weakness, it was at least an amiable one, and as such deserves to be reverenced.

The accounts she received from Vaceau of the health of M. La Luc did not contribute to tranquillise her mind. The symptoms described by Clara seemed to say that he was in the last stage of a consumption, and the grief of Theodore and herself on this occasion was expressed in her letters with the lively eloquence so natural to her. Adeline loved and revered La Luc for his own worth and for the parental tenderness he had shown her, but he was still dearer to her as the father of Theodore, and her concern for his declining state was not inferior to that of his children. It was increased by the reflection that she had probably been the means of shortening his life; for she too well knew that the distress occasioned him by the situation in which it had been her misfortune to involve Theodore, had shattered his frame to its present infirmity. The same cause also withheld him from seeking in the climate of Montpellier the relief he had formerly been taught to expect there. When she looked round on the condition of her friends, her heart was almost overwhelmed with the prospect; it seemed as if she was destined to involve all those most dear to her in calamity. With respect to La Motte, whatever were his vices, and whatever the designs in which he had formerly engaged against her, she forgot them all in the service he had finally rendered her, and considered it to be as much her duty as she felt it to be her inclination to intercede for him. This, however, in her present situation she could not do with any hope of success; but if the suit upon which depended the re-establishment of her rank, her fortune, and consequently her influence, should be decided in her favour, she determined to throw herself at the king's feet, and when she pleaded the cause of Theodore, ask the life of La Motte.

A few days preceding that of the trial, Adeline was informed a stranger desired to speak with her, and on going to the room where he was, she found M. Verneuil. Her countenance expressed both surprise and satisfaction at this unexpected meeting, and she inquired, though with little expectation of an affirmative, if he had heard of M. La Luc.

"I have seen him," said M. Verneuil; "I am just come from Vaceau. But I am sorry I cannot give you a better account of his health. He is greatly altered since I saw him before."

Adeline could scarcely refrain from tears at the recollection these words revived of the calamities which had occasioned this lamented change. M. Verneuil delivered her a packet from Clara; as he presented it he said, "Beside this introduction to your notice, I have a claim of a different kind, which I am proud to assert, and which will, perhaps, justify the permission I ask of speaking upon your affairs." Adeline bowed, and M. Verneuil, with a countenance expressive of the most tender solicitude, added, that he had heard of the late proceeding of the parliament of Paris and of the discoveries that so intimately concerned her. "I know not," continued he, "whether I ought to congratulate or condole with you on this trying occasion. That I sincerely

sympathise in all that concerns you, I hope you will believe; and I cannot deny myself the pleasure of telling you that I am related, though distantly, to the late Marchioness, your mother; for that she was your mother I cannot doubt."

Adeline rose hastily, and advanced towards M. Verneuil; surprise and satisfaction re-animated her features. "Do I, indeed, see a relation?" said she in a sweet and tremulous voice, "and one whom I can welcome as a friend?" Tears trembled in her eyes; and she received M. Verneuil's embrace in silence. It was some time before her emotion would permit her to speak.

To Adeline, who from the earliest infancy had been abandoned to strangers—a forlorn and helpless orphan who had never till lately known a relation, and who then found one in the person of an inveterate enemy—to her this discovery was as delightful as unexpected. But after struggling for some time with the various emotions that pressed upon her heart, she begged M. Verneuil's permission to withdraw till she could recover her composure. He would have taken leave, but she entreated him not to go.

The interest which M. Verneuil took in the concerns of La Luc, which was strengthened by his increasing regard for Clara, had drawn him to Vaceau, where he was informed of the family and peculiar circumstances of Adeline. On receiving this intelligence, he immediately set out for Paris, to offer his protection and assistance to his newly-discovered relation, and to aid, if possible, the cause of Theodore.

Adeline in a short time returned, and could then bear to converse on the subject of her family. M. Verneuil offered her his support and assistance, if they should be found necessary. "But I trust," added he, "to the justness of your cause, and hope it will not require any adventitious aid. To those who remember the late Marchioness, your features bring sufficient evidence of your birth. As a proof that my judgment in this instance is not biassed by prejudice, the resemblance struck me when I was in Savoy, though I knew the Marchioness only by her portrait; and I believe I mentioned to M. La Luc that you often reminded me of a deceased relation. You may form some judgment of this yourself," added M. Verneuil, taking a miniature from his pocket; "this was your amiable mother."

Adeline's countenance changed; she received the picture eagerly, gazed on it for a long time in silence, and her eyes filled with tears. It was not the resemblance she studied, but the countenance—the mild and beautiful countenance of her parent; whose blue eyes, full of tender sweetness, seemed bent upon hers, while a soft smile played on her lips. Adeline pressed the picture to hers, and again gazed in silent reverie. At length, with a deep sigh, she said, "This surely *was* my mother. Had she but lived, oh, my poor father! you had been spared." This reflection quite overcame her, and she burst into tears. M. Verneuil did not interrupt her grief, but took her hand and sat by her, without speaking, till she became more composed. Again kissing the picture, she held it out to him with a hesitating look.

"No," said he, "it is already with its true owner."

She thanked him with a smile of ineffable sweetness; and after some conversation on the subject of the approaching trial, on which occasion she requested M. Verneuil would support her by his presence, he withdrew, having begged leave to repeat his visit on the following day.

Adeline now opened her packet, and saw once more the well-known characters of Theodore. For a moment she felt as if in his presence, and the conscious blush overspread her cheek; with a trembling hand she broke the seal, and read the tenderest assurances and solicitudes of his love; she often paused, that she might prolong the sweet emotions which these assurances awakened; but while tears of tenderness stood trembling on her eyelids, the bitter recollection of his situation would return, and they fell in anguish on her bosom.

He congratulated her, and with peculiar delicacy, on the prospects of life which were opening to her; said everything that might tend to animate and support her, but avoided dwelling on his own circumstances except by expressing his sense of the zeal and kindness of his commanding officer, and adding that he did not despair of finally obtaining a pardon.

This hope, though but faintly expressed, and written evidently for the purpose of consoling Adeline, did not entirely fail of the desired effect. She yielded to its enchanting influence, and forgot for a while the many subjects of care and anxiety which surrounded her. Theodore said little of his father's health; what he did say was by no means so discouraging as the accounts of Clara, who, less anxious to conceal a truth that must give pain to Adeline, expressed, without reserve, all her apprehension and concern.

CHAPTER XXIV.

Heaven is just!
And when the measure of his crimes is full,
Will bare its red right arm, and launch its lightnings.
MASON.

THE day of the trial so anxiously awaited, and on which the fate of so many persons depended, at length arrived. Adeline, accompanied by M. Verneuil and Madame La Motte, appeared as the prosecutor of the Marquis de Montalt; and D'Aunoy, Du Bosse, Louis La Motte, and several other persons, as witnesses in her cause. The judges were some of the most distinguished in France; and the advocates on both sides men of eminent abilities. On a trial of such importance, the court, as may be imagined, was crowded with persons of distinction, and the spectacle it presented was strikingly solemn yet magnificent.

When she appeared before the tribunal, Adeline's emotion surpassed all the arts of disguise, but adding to the natural dignity of her air an expression of soft timidity, and to her downcast eyes a sweet confusion, it rendered her an object still more interesting; and she attracted the universal pity and admiration of the assembly. When she ventured to raise her eyes, she perceived that the Marquis was not yet in the court, and while she awaited his appearance in trembling expectation, a confused murmuring rose in a distant part of the hall. Her spirits now almost forsook her; the certainty of seeing immediately and consciously the murderer of her father chilled her with horror, and she was with difficulty preserved from fainting. A low sound now ran through the court, and an air of confusion appeared, which was soon communicated to the tribunal itself. Several of the members arose, some left the hall, the whole place exhibited a scene of disorder, and a report at length reached Adeline that the Marquis de Montalt was dying. A considerable time elapsed in uncertainty; but the confusion continued; the Marquis did not appear; and at Adeline's desire M. Verneuil went in quest of more positive information.

He followed a crowd which was hurrying towards the Châtelet, and with some difficulty gained admittance into the prison; but the porter at the gate, whom he had bribed for a passport, could give him no certain information on the subject of his inquiry, and, not being at liberty to quit his post, furnished M. Verneuil with only a vague direction to the Marquis's apartment. The courts were silent and deserted, but, as he advanced, a distant hum of voices led him on, till, perceiving several persons running towards a staircase which appeared beyond the archway of a long passage, he followed thither, and learned that the Marquis was certainly dying. The staircase was filled with people; he endeavoured to press through the crowd, and, after much struggle and difficulty, he reached the door of an anteroom which communicated with the apartment where the Marquis lay, and whence several persons now issued. Here he learned that the object of his inquiry was already dead. M. Verneuil, however, pressed through the anteroom to the chamber, where lay the Marquis on a bed surrounded by officers of the law and two notaries, who appeared to have been taking

K 2

down depositions. His countenance was suffused with a black and deadly hue, and impressed with the horrors of death. M. Verneuil turned away, shocked by the spectacle, and, on inquiry, heard that the Marquis had died by poison.

It appeared that, convinced he had nothing to hope from his trial, he had taken this method of avoiding an ignominious death. In the last hours of life, while tortured with the remembrance of his crime, he resolved to make all the atonement that remained for him, and having swallowed the potion, he immediately sent for a confessor to take a full confession of his guilt, and two notaries, and thus established Adeline beyond dispute in the rights of her birth, also bequeathing her a considerable legacy.

In consequence of these depositions she was soon after formally acknowledged as the daughter and heiress of Henry Marquis de Montalt, and the rich estates of her father were restored to her. She immediately threw herself at the feet of the king in behalf of Theodore and of La Motte. The character of the former, the cause in which he had risked his life, and the occasion of the late Marquis's enmity towards him, were circumstances so notorious and so forcible that it was more than probable the monarch would have granted his pardon to a pleader less irresistible than was Adeline de Montalt. Theodore La Luc not only received an ample pardon, but, in consideration of his gallant conduct towards Adeline, he was soon after raised to a post of considerable rank in the army.

For La Motte, who had been condemned for the robbery on full evidence, and who had been also charged with the crime which had formerly compelled him to quit Paris, a pardon could not be obtained; but at the earnest supplication of Adeline, and in consideration of the service he had finally rendered her, his sentence was softened from death to banishment. This indulgence, however, would have availed him little had not the noble generosity of Adeline silenced other prosecutions that were preparing against him, and bestowed on him a sum more than sufficient to support his family in a foreign country.

This kindness operated so powerfully upon his heart, which had been betrayed through weakness rather than natural depravity, and awakened so keen a remorse for the injuries he had once meditated against a benefactress so noble, that his former habits became odious to him, and his character gradually recovered the hue which it would probably always have worn, had he never been exposed to the tempting dissipations of Paris.

The passion which Louis had so long owned for Adeline was raised almost to adoration by her late conduct; but he now relinquished even the faint hope which he had hitherto almost unconsciously cherished, and, since the life which was granted to Theodore rendered this sacrifice necessary, he could not repine. He resolved, however, to seek in absence the tranquillity he had lost, and to place his future happiness on that of two persons so deservedly dear to him.

On the eve of his departure La Motte and his family took a very affecting leave of Adeline. He left Paris for England, where it was his design to settle, and Louis, who was eager to fly from her enchantments, set out on the same day for his regiment.

Adeline remained some time at Paris to settle her affairs, where she was introduced by M. V—— to the few and distant relations that remained of her family. Among these were the Count and Countess D—— and M. Amand, who had so much engaged her pity and esteem at Nice. The lady, whose death he lamented, was of the family of De Montalt, and the resemblance which he had traced between her features and those of Adeline, her cousin, was something more than the effect of fancy. The death of his elder brother had abruptly recalled him from Italy, but Adeline had the satisfaction to observe, that the heavy melancholy which formerly oppressed him, had yielded to a sort of placid resignation, and that his countenance was often enlivened by a transient gleam of cheerfulness.

The Count and Countess D——, who were much interested by her goodness and beauty, invited her to make their hotel her residence while she remained at Paris.

Her first care was to have the remains of her parent removed from the Abbey of St. Clair, and deposited in the vault of his ancestors.

D'Aunoy was tried, condemned, and hanged for the murder. At the place of execution he described the spot where the remains of the Marquis were concealed, which was in the stone-room already mentioned, belonging to the abbey. M. V—— accompanied the officers appointed for the search, and attended the ashes of the Marquis to St. Maur, an estate in one of the northern provinces. There they were deposited with the solemn funereal pomp becoming his rank. Adeline attended as chief mourner, and, this last duty paid to the memory of her parent, she became more tranquil and resigned. The MS. that recorded his sufferings had been found at the abbey, and delivered to her by M. V——, and she preserved it with the pious enthusiasm so sacred a relic deserved.

On her return to Paris, Theodore La Luc, who was come from Montpellier, awaited her arrival. The happiness of this meeting was clouded by the account he brought of his father, whose extreme danger had alone withheld him from hastening, the moment he obtained his liberty, to thank Adeline for the life she had preserved. She now received him as the friend to whom she was indebted for her preservation, and as the lover who deserved and possessed her tenderest affection. The remembrance of the circumstances under which they had last met, and of their mutual anguish, rendered more exquisite the happiness of the present moments, when no longer oppressed by the horrid prospect of ignominious death and final separation, they looked forward only to the smiling days that awaited them, when hand in hand they should tread the flowery scenes of life. The contrast which memory gave of the past with the present frequently drew tears of tenderness and gratitude to their eyes, and the sweet smile which seemed struggling to dispel from the countenance of Adeline those gems of sorrow, penetrated the heart of Theodore, and brought to his recollection a little song, which in other circumstances he had formerly sung to her. He took up a lute that lay on the table, and, touching the dulcet chords, accompanied it with the following words :

SONG.

The rose that weeps with morning dew,
  And glitters in the sunny ray,
In tears of smiles resembles you,
  When Love breaks Sorrow's cloud away.

The dews that bend the blushing flow'r,
  Enrich the scent—renew the glow;
So Love's sweet tears exalt his pow'r,
  So bliss more brightly shines by woe

Her affection for Theodore had induced Adeline to reject several suitors, which her goodness, beauty, and wealth had already attracted, and who, though infinitely his superiors in point of fortune, were many of them inferior to him in family, and all of them in merit.

The various and tumultuous emotions which the late events had called forth in the bosom of Adeline, were now subsided ; but the memory of her father still tinctured her mind with a melancholy that time could only subdue ; and she refused to listen to the supplications of Theodore till the period she had prescribed for her mourning should be expired. The necessity of rejoining his regiment obliged him to leave Paris within the fortnight after his arrival ; but he carried with him the assurance of receiving her hand soon after she should lay aside her sable habit, and left therefore with tolerable composure.

M. La Luc's very precarious state was a source of incessant disquietude to Adeline, and she determined to accompany M. V——, who was now the declared lover of Clara, to Montpellier, whither La Luc had immediately gone on the liberation of his son. For this journey she was preparing, when she received from her friend a flattering account of his amendment ; and as some further settlement of her affairs required her presence at Paris, she deferred her design, and M. V—— departed alone.

When Theodore's affairs assumed a more favourable aspect, M. Verneuil had written to La Luc, and communicated to him the secret of his heart respecting Clara. La Luc, who admired and esteemed M. V - - -, and was not ignorant of his family connections, was pleased with the proposed alliance ; Clara thought she had never seen the person whom she was so much inclined to love ; and M. V—— received an answer favourable to his wishes, and which encouraged him to undertake the present journey to Montpellier.

The restoration of his happiness and the climate of Montpellier did all for the health of La Luc that his most anxious friends could wish, and he was at length so far recovered as to visit Adeline at her estate of St. Maur. Clara and M. V—— accompanied him, and a cessation of hostilities between France and Spain soon after permitted Theodore to join this happy party. When La Luc, thus restored to those most dear to him, looked back on the miseries he had escaped, and forward to the blessings that awaited him, his heart dilated with emotions of exquisite joy and gratitude, and his venerable countenance, softened by an expression of complacent delight, exhibited a perfect picture of happy age.

CHAPTER XXV.

Last came Joy's ecstatic trial :
They would have thought who heard the strain,
They saw in Tempe's vale her native maids
Amidst the festal sounding shades,
To some unweary'd minstrel dancing,
While as his flying fingers kiss'd the strings,
Love fram'd with Mirth a gay fantastic roun
                        PASSIONS.

ADELINE, in the society of friends so beloved, lost the impression of that melancholy which the fate of her parent had occasioned; she recovered all her natural vivacity ; and when she threw off the mourning habit which filial piety had required her to assume, she gave her hand to Theodore. The nuptials, which were celebrated at St. Maur, were graced by the presence of the Count and Countess D——, and La Luc had the supreme felicity of confirming on the same day the flattering destinies of both his children. When the ceremony was over, he blessed and embraced them all with tears of fatherly affection. "I thank thee, O God ! that I have been permitted to see this hour," said he ; "whenever it shall please Thee to call me hence, I will depart in peace."

"Long, very long, may you be spared to bless your children," replied Adeline.

Clara kissed her father's hand and wept : "Long, very long !" she repeated in a voice scarcely audible.

La Luc smiled cheerfully, and turned the discourse to a subject less affecting.

But the time now drew nigh when La Luc thought it necessary to return to the duties of his parish, from which he had so long been absent. Madame La Luc, too, who had attended him during the period of his danger at Montpellier, and thence returned to Savoy, complained much of the solitude of her life; and this was with her brother an additional motive for speedy departure. Theodore and Adeline, who could not support the thought of a separation from this venerable parent, endeavoured to persuade him to give up his château, and to reside with them in France; but he was held by strong ties to Lelencourt. For many years he had constituted the comfort and happiness of his parishioners; they revered and loved him as a father, he regarded them with almost parental affection. The attachment they discovered towards him on his departure was not forgotten either; it made a deep impression on his mind, and he could not bear the thought of forsaking them now that heaven had showered on him his abundance. "It is sweet to live for them," said he, "and I will also die amongst them." A sentiment of a still more tender nature (and let not the stoic profane it with the name of weakness, or the world scorn it as unnatural), a sentiment still more tender attracted him to Lelencourt—the remains of his wife reposed there.

Since La Luc would not reside in France, Theodore and Adeline, to whom the splendid gaieties that courted them at Paris were very inferior temptations to the sweet domestic pleasures and refined society which Lelencourt would afford, determined to accompany La Luc and Monsieur and Madame Verneuil abroad. Adeline arranged her affairs so as to render her residence in France unnecessary; and having bade an affectionate adieu to the Count and Countess D——, and to M. Amand, who had recovered a tolerable degree of cheerfulness, she departed with her friends for Savoy.

They travelled leisurely, and frequently turned out of their way to view whatever was worthy of observation. After a long and pleasant journey, they came once more within view of the Swiss mountains, the sight of which revived a thousand interesting recollections in the mind of Adeline. She remembered the circumstances and the sensations under which she had first seen them—when an orphan, flying from persecution to seek shelter among strangers, and lost to the only person on earth whom she loved; she remembered this, and the contrast of the present moment struck with all its force upon her heart.

The countenance of Clara brightened into smiles of the most animated delight as she drew near the beloved scenes of her infant pleasures; and Theodore, often looking from the windows, caught with patriotic enthusiasm the magnificent and changing scenery which the receding mountains successively disclosed.

It was evening when they approached within a few miles of Lelencourt, and the road, winding round the foot of a stupendous crag, presented them a full view of the lake, and of the peaceful dwelling of La Luc. An exclamation of joy from the whole party announced the discovery, and the glance of pleasure was reflected from every eye. The sun's last light gleamed upon the water that reposed in "crystal purity" below, mellowed every feature of the landscape, and touched with purple splendour the clouds that rolled along the mountain-tops.

La Luc welcomed his family to his happy home, and sent up a silent thanksgiving that he was permitted thus to return to it. Adeline continued to gaze upon each well-known object, and again reflecting on the vicissitudes of grief and joy, and the surprising change of ortune, which she had experienced since last she saw them, her heart dilated with gratitude and complacent delight. She looked at Theodore, whom, in these very scenes she had lamented as lost to her for ever; who, when found again, was about to be torn from her by an ignominious death, but who now sat by her side, her secure and happy husband, the pride of his family and herself; and while the sensibility of her heart flowed in tears from her eyes, a smile of ineffable tenderness told him all she felt. He gently pressed her hand, and answered her with a look of love.

Peter, who now rode up to the carriage with a face full of joy and of importance, interrupted a course of sentiment which was become almost too interesting.

"Ah, my dear master!" cried he, "welcome home again. Here is the village, God bless it! It is worth a million such places as Paris. Thank St. Jacques, we are all safe back again!"

The effusion of honest Peter's joy was received and answered with the kindness it deserved. As they drew near the lake music sounded over the water, and they presently saw a large party of the villagers assembled on a green spot that sloped to the very margin of the waves, and dancing in all their holiday finery. It was the evening of a festival. The elder peasants sat under the shade of the trees that crowned this little eminence, eating milk and fruit, and watching their sons and daughters frisk it away to the sprightly notes of the tabor and pipe, which was joined by the softer tones of a mandolin.

The scene was highly interesting, and what added to its picturesque beauty was a group of cattle that stood, some on the brink, some half in the water, and others on the green bank, while several peasant girls, dressed in the neat simplicity of their country, were dispensing the milky feast. Peter now rode on first, and a crowd soon collected round him, who, learning that their beloved master was at hand, went forth to meet and welcome him. Their warm and honest expressions of joy diffused an exquisite satisfaction over the heart of the good La Luc, who met them with the kindness of a father, and who could scarcely forbear shedding tears to this testimony of attachment. When the younger part of the peasants heard of his arrival, the general joy was such, that, led by the tabor and pipe, they danced before his carriage to the château, where they again welcomed him and his family with the enlivening strains of music. At the gate of the château they were received by Madame La Luc, and a happier party never met.

As the evening was uncommonly mild and beautiful, supper was spread in the garden. When the repast was over, Clara, whose heart was all glee, proposed a dance by moonlight. "It will be delicious," said she; "the moonbeams are already dancing on the waters. See what a stream of radiance they throw across the lake, and how they sparkle round that little promontory on the left. The freshness of the hour, too, invites to dancing."

They all agreed to the proposal.

"And let the good people who have so heartily welcomed us home be called in too," said La Luc; "they shall all partake our happiness. There is devotion in making others happy, and gratitude ought to make us devout. Peter, bring more wine, and set some tables under the trees."

Peter flew, and, while chairs and tables were placing, Clara ran for her favourite lute, the lute which had formerly afforded her such delight, and which Adeline had often touched with a melancholy expression. Clara's light hand now ran over the chords, and drew forth tones of tender sweetness, her voice accompanying the following

AIR.

Now, at moonlight's fairy hour,
    When faintly gleams each dewy steep,
And vale and mountain, lake and bow'r,
    In solitary grandeur sleep;

When slowly sinks the evening breeze,
    That lulls the mind in pensive care,
And fancy loftier visions sees,
    Bid music wake the silent air.

Bid the merry, merry tabor sound,
    And with the fays of lawn or glade,
In tripping circlet beat the ground,
    Under the high trees' trembling shade.

Now, at moonlight's fairy hour,
    Shall Music breathe her dulcet voice,
And o'er the waves, with magic pow'r,
    Call on Echo to rejoice.

Peter, who could not move in a sober step, had already spread refreshments under the trees, and in a short time the lawn was encircled with peasantry. The rural pipe and tabor were placed, at Clara's request, under the shade of her beloved acacias on the margin of the lake; the merry notes of music sounded, Adeline led off the dance, and the mountains answered only to the strains of mirth and melody.

The venerable La Luc sat among the elder peasants, and as he surveyed the scene—his children and people thus assembled round him in one grand compact of harmony and joy—the frequent tear bedewed his cheek, and he seemed to taste the fulness of an exalted delight.

So much was every heart roused to gladness that the morning dawn began to peep upon the scene of their festivity, when every cottager returned to his home, blessing the benevolence of La Luc.

After passing some weeks with La Luc, M. Verneuil bought a château in the village of Lelencourt, and as it was the only one not already occupied, Theodore looked out for a residence in the neighbourhood. At the distance of a few leagues, on the beautiful banks of the lake of Geneva, where the waters retire into a small bay, he purchased a villa. The château was characterised by an air of simplicity and taste, rather than of magnificence, which was the chief trait in the surrounding scene. The château was almost encircled with woods, which, forming a grand amphitheatre, swept down to the water's edge, and abounded with wild and romantic walks. Here nature was suffered to sport in all her beautiful luxuriance, except where here and there the hand of art formed the foliage to admit a view of the blue waters of the lake, with the white sail that glided by or of the distant mountains.

In front of the château the woods opened to a lawn, and the eye was suffered to wander over the lake, whose bosom presented an ever-moving picture, while its varied margin, sprinkled with villas, woods, and towns, and crowned beyond with the snowy and sublime Alps, rising point behind point in awful confusion, exhibited a scenery of almost unequalled magnificence.

Here, contemning the splendour of false happiness, and possessing the pure and rational delights of a love, refined into the most tender friendship, surrounded by the friends so dear to them, and visited by a select and enlightened society—here, in the very bosom of felicity, lived Theodore and Adeline La Luc.

The passion of Louis de la Motte yielded at length to the powers of absence and necessity. He still loved Adeline, but it was with the placid tenderness of friendship, and when, at the earnest invitation of Theodore, he visited the villa, he beheld their happiness with a satisfaction unalloyed by any emotion of envy. He afterwards married a lady of some fortune at Geneva, and resigning his commission in the French service, settled on the borders of the lake, and increased the social delights of Theodore and Adeline.

Their former lives afforded an example of trials well endured—and their present, of virtues greatly rewarded; and this reward they continued to deserve—for not to themselves was their happiness contracted, but diffused to all who came within the sphere of their influence. The indigent and unhappy rejoiced in their benevolence, the virtuous and enlightened in their friendship, and their children in parents whose example impressed upon their hearts the precepts offered to their understandings.

CHARLES DICKENS AND EVANS, CRYSTAL PALACE PRESS.

THE

MYSTERIES OF UDOLPHO

A ROMANCE

BY

ANN RADCLIFFE

AUTHOR OF "THE ROMANCE OF THE FOREST" AND "THE ITALIAN"

*

LONDON AND NEW YORK

GEORGE ROUTLEDGE AND SONS

1877

MEMOIRS OF MRS. ANN RADCLIFFE.

In nothing, perhaps, is the contrast between the present and preceding ages more striking, than in the character of British females, who, in our times, have burst those boundaries which the "lords of the creation" had fixed, and boldly contested with them in the fields of Literature. It is true that, in all ages, there have been ladies whose talents raised them to a proud distinction; but their appearance has been like "angels' visits, few and far between." It has, however, been reserved to the present age for woman to maintain her just rank in the creation; to exchange the distaff for the pen; and to wield the latter with as much force, and as much elegance, as had ever been done by the other sex.

It has often been the custom to arraign London as deficient in producing persons of genius; and yet, considering that it is so much a commercial city, it has been prolific in the production of persons of talent.—Among the "worthies," as Fuller would call them, that London has produced, we have to enrol the name of Mrs. Ann Radcliffe, whose maiden name was Ward, and who was born in the metropolis on the 9th of July, 1764. She was collaterally descended from Chesselden, the celebrated surgeon and anatomist. Her parents gave her a good, though not a classical, education; and early in life she discovered much taste for literature, and for contemplating the beauties of nature. At the age of twenty-three, she was married to William Radcliffe, Esq., a graduate at Oxford, who was intended for the bar, and kept several terms at one of the inns of court, but was never called. He afterwards became Editor and Proprietor of a Newspaper.

It was not until after her marriage, that Mrs. Radcliffe astonished the world with those productions which have since been much admired, and translated into almost every European language. Her first production was "The Castles of Athlin and Dunblane," which was soon followed by "The Sicilian Romance," and the "Romance of the Forest." In 1795, she published "A Journey made in the summer of 1793, through Holland, and the Western Frontier of Germany;" to which she added, "Observations made during a Tour to the Lakes of Westmoreland and Cumberland." It was not, however, in the description of matters of fact that Mrs. Radcliffe excelled; it was in wielding the magic wand, and creating regions of her own, where she might rove "a chartered libertine," that her great talents were displayed. Her next work was, of all her writings, the most popular, "The Mysteries of Udolpho," which was followed by her last work, "The Italians."

In all the Romances of Mrs. Radcliffe, there was a great deal of originality ; and she might be said to have founded a new school of fiction. She disdained the ordinary tract of Novelists, and shook the soul by the awe of superstition, and the terrors of guilt. She was, as the elegant author of the "Pursuits of Literature" described her, "a mighty magician, bred and nourished by the Florentine muses, in their sacred, solitary caverns, amid the paler shrines of Gothic superstition, and in all the dreariness of enchantment." The characters in Mrs. Radcliffe's Romances are as original and well-drawn, as the incidents are striking and impressive ; and few writers ever succeeded so well in sustaining the interest of a long tale, as this powerful writer. Her works are also interspersed with several pieces of poetry, which are elegant and fanciful, displaying the riches of a well-cultivated mind.

The popularity of Mrs. Radcliffe's works obtained such prices as had never before been paid for works of fiction. For the "Mysteries of Udolpho" she received £500, and for the "Italians" £800 ; nor were her Publishers the losers, for the sale was such as not only to cover all the expenses, but to repay them well for their liberality.

During the last twelve years of her life, Mrs. Radcliffe suffered under bad health, having been afflicted with a spasmodic asthma. In the autumn of 1822, she visited Ramsgate, which afforded her a temporary relief, but she relapsed at the beginning of the ensuing year. On the 9th of January she was taken very ill, and lingered until the morning of the 7th of February, 1823, when she tranquilly expired ; and was interred in a vault of the Chapel of Ease at Bayswater.

Mrs. Radcliffe, though a giant in intellect, was low in stature, and of a slender form, but exquisitely proportioned : her countenance was beautiful and expressive.

THE MYSTERIES OF UDOLPHO.

CHAPTER I.

. . . . Home is the resort
Of love, of joy, of peace and plenty where,
Supporting and supported, polish'd friends
And dear relations mingle into bliss.

THOMSON.

ON the pleasant banks of the Garonne, in the province of Gascony, stood, in the year 1584, the chateau of Monsieur St. Aubert. From its windows were seen the pastoral landscapes of Guienne and Gascony stretching along the river, gay with luxuriant woods and vine, and plantations of olives. To the south, the view was bounded by the majestic Pyrenees, whose summits veiled in clouds, or exhibiting awful forms, seen, and lost again, as the partial vapours rolled along, were sometimes barren, and gleamed through the blue tinge of air, and sometimes frowned with forests of gloomy pine, that swept downward to their base. These tremendous precipices were contrasted by the soft green of the pastures and woods that hung upon their skirts ; among whose flocks and herds and simple cottages, the eye, after having scaled the cliffs above, delighted to repose. To the north, and to the east, the plains of Guienne and Languedoc were lost in the mist of distance : on the west, Gascony was bounded by the waters of Biscay.

M. St. Aubert loved to wander, with his wife and daughter, on the margin of the Garonne, and to listen to the music that floated on its waves. He had known life in other forms than those of pastoral simplicity, having mingled in the gay and in the busy scenes of the world ; but the flattering portrait of mankind which his heart had delineated in early youth, his experience had too sorrowfully corrected. Yet, amidst the changing visions of life, his principles remained unshaken, his benevolence unchilled ; and he retired from the multitude, more in *pity* than in anger, to scenes of simple nature, to the pure delights of literature, and to the exercise of domestic virtues.

He was a descendant from the younger branch of an illustrious family, and it was designed that the deficiency of his patrimonial wealth should be supplied either by a splendid alliance in marriage, or by success in the intrigues of public affairs. But St. Aubert had too nice a sense of honour to fulfil the latter hope, and too small a portion of ambition to sacrifice what he called happiness, to the attainment of wealth. After the death of his father he married a very amiable woman, his equal in birth, and not his superior in fortune. The late Monsieur St. Aubert's liberality, or extravagance, had so much involved his affairs, that his son found it necessary to dispose of a part of the family domain ; and some years after his marriage he sold it to Monsieur Quesnel, the brother of his wife, and retired to a small estate in Gascony, where conjugal felicity and parental duties divided his attention with the treasures of knowledge and the illuminations of genius.

To this spot he had been attached from his infancy. He had often made excursions to it when a boy ; and the impression of delight given to his mind by the homely kindness of the gray-headed peasant to whom it was intrusted, and whose fruit and cream never failed, had not been obliterated by succeeding circumstances. The green pastures, along which he had so often bounded in the exultation of health and youthful freedom — the woods, under whose refreshing shade he had first indulged that pensive melancholy which afterwards made a strong feature of his character—the wild walks of the mountains, the river, on whose waves he had floated, and the distant plains, which seemed boundless as his early hopes—were never after remembered by St. Aubert but with enthusiasm and regret. At length he disengaged himself from the world, and retired hither, to realise the wishes of many years.

The building, as it then stood, was merely a summer cottage, rendered interesting to a stranger by its neat simplicity, or the beauty of the surrounding scene ; and considerable additions were necessary to make it a comfortable family residence. St. Aubert felt a kind of affection for every part of the fabric, which he remembered in his youth, and would not suffer a stone of it to be removed ; so that the new building, adapted to the style of the old one, formed with it only a simple and elegant residence. The taste of Madame St. Aubert was conspicuous in its internal finishing, where the same chaste simplicity was observable in the furniture, and in the few ornaments of the apartments that characterized the manners of its inhabitants.

The library occupied the west side of the chateau, and was enriched by a collection of the best books in the ancient and modern languages. This room opened upon a grove which stood on the brow of a gentle declivity, that fell towards the river, and the tall trees gave it a melancholy and pleasing shade ; while from the windows the eye caught, beneath the spreading branches, the gay and luxuriant landscape stretching to the west, and overlooked on the left by the bold precipices of the Pyrenees. Adjoining the library was a green-house stored with scarce and beautiful plants ; for one of the amusements of St. Aubert was the study of botany : and among the neighbouring mountains, which afforded a luxurious feast to the mind of the naturalist, he often passed the day in the pursuits of his favourite science. He was sometimes accompanied in these little excursions by Madame St. Aubert, and frequently by his daughter ; when, with a small osier basket to receive plants, and another filled with cold refreshments, such as the cabin of the shepherd did not afford, they wandered away among the most romantic and magnificent scenes, nor suffered the charms of Nature's lowly children to abstract them from the observance of her stupendous works. When weary of sauntering among cliffs that seemed scarcely accessible but to the steps of the enthusiast, and where no track appeared on the vegetation, but what the foot of the lizard had left, they would seek one of those green recesses which so beautifully adorn the bosom of these mountains ; where, under the shade of the lofty larch or cedar, they enjoyed their simple repast, made sweeter by the waters of the cool stream that crept along the turf, and by the breath of wild flowers and aromatic plants that fringed the rocks and inlaid the grass.

Adjoining the eastern side of the greenhouse, looking towards the plains of Languedoc, was a room which Emily called hers, and which contained her books, her drawings, her musical instruments, with some favourite birds and plants. Here she usually exercised herself in elegant arts, cultivated only because they were congenial to her taste, and in which native genius, assisted by the instructions of Monsieur and Madame St. Aubert, made her an early proficient. The windows of this room were particularly pleasant ; they descended to the floor, and, opening upon the little lawn that surrounded the house, the eye

was led between groves of almond, palm-trees, flowering-ash, and myrtle, to the distant landscape, where the Garonne wandered.

The peasants of this gay climate were often seen on an evening, when the day's labour was done, dancing in groups on the margin of the river. Their sprightly melodies, *debonnaire* steps, the fanciful figure of their dances, with the tasteful and capricious manner in which the girls adjusted their simple dress, gave a character to the scene entirely French.

The front of the chateau, which, having a southern aspect, opened upon the grandeur of the mountains, was occupied on the ground-floor by a rustic hall and two excellent sitting-rooms. The first floor, for the cottage had no second story, was laid out in bed-chambers, except one apartment that opened to a balcony, and which was generally used for a breakfast-room.

In the surrounding ground St. Aubert had made very tasteful improvements ; yet such was his attachment to objects he had remembered 'from his boyish days, that he had in some instances sacrificed taste to sentiment. There were two old larches that shaded the building, and interrupted the prospect : St. Aubert had sometimes declared that he believed he should have been weak enough to have wept at their fall. In addition to these larches he planted a little grove of beech, pine, and mountain-ash. On a lofty terrace, formed by the swelling bank of the river, rose a plantation of orange, lemon, and palm-trees, whose fruit in the coolness of evening breathed delicious fragrance. With these were mingled a few trees of other species. Here, under the ample shade of a plane-tree, that spread its majestic canopy towards the river, St. Aubert loved to sit in the fine evenings of summer, with his wife and children, watching beneath its foliage, the setting-sun, the mild splendour of its light fading from the distant landscape, till the shadows of twilight melted its various features into one tint of sober gray. Here, too, he loved to read, and converse with Madame St. Aubert ; or to play with his children, resigning himself to the influence of those sweet affections which are ever attendant on simplicity and nature. He has often said, while tears of pleasure trembled in his eyes, that these were moments infinitely more delightful than any passed amid the brilliant and tumultuous scenes that are courted by the world. His heart was occupied ; it had, what can be so rarely said, no wish for a happiness beyond what it experienced. The consciousness of acting right diffused a serenity over his manners, which nothing else could impart to a man of moral perceptions like his, and which refined his sense of every surrounding blessing.

The deepest shade of twilight did not send him from his favourite plane-tree. He loved the soothing hour, when the last tints of light die away ; when the stars, one by one, tremble through ether, and are reflected on the dark mirror of the waters ; that hour, which, of all others, inspires the mind with pensive tenderness, and often elevates it to sublime contemplation. When the moon shed her soft rays among the foliage, he still lingered, and his pastoral supper of cream and fruits was often spread beneath it. Then, on the stillness of night, came the song of the nightingale breathing sweetness, and awakening melancholy.

The first interruptions to the happiness he had known since his retirement, were occasioned by the death of his two sons. He lost them at that age when infantine simplicity is so fascinating ; and though, in consideration of Madame St. Aubert's distress, he restrained the expression of his own, and endeavoured to bear it, as he meant, with philosophy, he had, in truth, no philosophy that could render him calm to such losses. One daughter was now his only surviving child ; and while he watched the unfolding of her infant character with anxious fondness, he endeavoured with unremitting effort, to counteract those traits in her disposition which might hereafter lead her from happiness. She had discovered in her early years uncommon delicacy of mind, warm affections, and ready benevolence ; but with these was observable a degree of susceptibility too exquisite to admit of lasting peace. As she advanced in youth, this sensibility gave a pensive tone to her spirits, and a softness to her manner, which added grace to beauty, and rendered her a very interesting object to persons of a congenial disposition. But St. Aubert had too much good sense to prefer a charm to a virtue ; and had penetration enough to see that this charm was too dangerous to its possessor to be allowed the character of a blessing. He endeavoured, therefore, to strengthen her mind ; to inure her to habits of self-command ; to teach her to reject the first impulse of her feelings, and to look with cool examination upon the disappointments he sometimes threw in her way. While he instructed her to resist first impressions, and to acquire that steady dignity of mind that can alone counterbalance the passions, and bear us, as far as is compatible with our nature, above the reach of circumstances, he taught himself a lesson of fortitude ; for he was often obliged to witness, with seeming indifference, the tears and struggles which his caution occasioned her.

In person, Emily resembled her mother ; having the same elegant symmetry of form, the same delicacy of features, and the same blue eyes full of tender sweetness. But lovely as was her person, it was the varied expression of her countenance, as conversation awakened the nicer emotions of her mind, that threw such a captivating grace around her :

Those tenderer tints, that shun the careless eye,
And in the world's contagious circle die.

St. Aubert cultivated her understanding with the most scrupulous care. He gave her a general view of the sciences, and an exact acquaintance with every part of elegant literature. He taught her Latin and English, chiefly that she might understand the sublimity of their best poets. She discovered in her early years a taste for works of genius ; and it was St. Aubert's principle, as well as his inclination, to promote every innocent means of happiness. A well-informed mind, he would say, is the best security against the contagion of folly and of vice. The vacant mind is ever on the watch for relief, and ready to plunge into error to escape from the languor of idleness. Store it with ideas, teach it the pleasure of thinking ; and the temptations of the world without will be counteracted by the gratifications derived from the world within. Thought and cultivation are necessary equally to the happiness of a country and a city life ; in the first they prevent the uneasy sensations of indolence, and afford a sublime pleasure in the taste they create for the beautiful and the grand ; in the latter they make dissipation less an object of necessity, and consequently of interest.

It was one of Emily's earliest pleasures to ramble among the scenes of nature ; nor was it in the soft and glowing landscape that she most delighted ; she loved more the wild wood walks that skirted the mountain ; and still more the mountain's stupendous recesses, where the silence and grandeur of solitude impressed a sacred awe upon her heart, and lifted her thoughts to the GOD OF HEAVEN AND EARTH. In scenes like these she would often linger alone, wrapt in a melancholy charm, till the last gleam of day faded from the west ; till the lonely sound of a sheep-bell, or the distant bark of a watch-dog, were all that broke the stillness of the evening. Then, the gloom of the woods ; the trembling of their leaves, at intervals, in the breeze ; the bat, flitting on the twilight ; the cottage-lights, now seen and now lost—were circumstances that awakened her mind into effort, and led to enthusiasm and poetry.

Her favourite walk was to a little fishing-house belonging to St. Aubert, in a woody glen, on the margin of a rivulet that descended from the Pyrenees, and, after foaming among their rocks, wound its silent way beneath the shades it reflected. Above the woods that screened this glen rose the lofty summits of the Pyrenees, which often burst boldly on the eye through the glades below. Sometimes the shattered face of a rock only was seen, crowned with wild shrubs ; or a shepherd's cabin seated on a cliff, overshadowed by dark cypress or waving ash. Emerging from the deep recesses of the woods, the glade opened to the distant landscape, where the rich pastures and vine-covered slopes of Gascony gradually declined to the plains ; and there, on the winding shores of the Garonne, groves, and hamlets, and villas—their outlines softened by distance —melted from the eye into one rich harmonious tint.

This, too, was the favourite retreat of St. Aubert, to which he frequently withdrew from the fervour of noon, with his wife, his daughter, and his books ; or came at the sweet evening hour to welcome the silent dusk, or to listen for the music of the nightingale. Sometimes, too, he brought music of his own, and awakened every fair echo with the tender accents of his oboe ; and often have the tones of Emily's voice drawn sweetness from the waves over which they trembled.

It was in one of her excursions to this spot that she observed the following lines written with a pencil on a part of the wainscot :

SONNET.

Go, pencil ! faithful to thy master's sighs !
  Go —tell the Goddess of this fairy scene,
  When next her light steps wind these wood-walks green,
Whence all his tears, his tender sorrows rise ;

Ah ! paint her form, her soul-illumined eyes,
  The sweet expression of her pensive face,
  The light'ning smile, the animated grace—
The portrait well the lover's voice supplies :

Speaks all his heart must feel, his tongue would say :
  Yet, ah ! not all his heart must sadly feel !
  How oft the floweret's silken leaves conceal
The drug that steals the vital spark away !

And who that gazes on that angel-smile,
Would fear its charm, or think it could beguile !

These lines were not inscribed to any person ; Emily therefore could not apply them to herself, though she was undoubtedly the nymph of these shades. Having glanced round the little circle of her acquaintance without being detained by a suspicion as to whom they could be addressed, she was compelled to rest in uncertainty ; an uncertainty which would have been more painful to an idle mind than it was to hers. She had no leisure to suffer this circumstance, trifling at first, to swell into importance by frequent remembrance : the little vanity it had excited (for the incertitude which forbade her to presume upon having inspired the sonnet, forbade her also to disbelieve it), passed away, and the incident was dismissed from her thoughts amid her books, her studies, and the exercise of social charities.

Soon after this period, her anxiety was awakened by the indisposition of her father, who was attacked with a fever ; which, though not thought to be of a dangerous kind, gave a severe shock to his constitution, Madame St. Aubert and Emily attended him with unremitting care ; but his recovery was very slow, and, as he advanced towards health, Madame seemed to decline.

The first scene he visited, after he was well enough to take the air, was his favourite fish-ing-house. A basket of provisions was sent thither, with books, and Emily's lute ; for fishing-tackle he had no use, for he never could find amusement in torturing or destroying.

After employing himself for about an hour in botanising, dinner was served. It was a repast, to which gratitude for being again permitted to visit this spot gave sweetness ; and family happiness once more smiled beneath these shades. Monsieur St. Aubert conversed with unusual cheerfulness ; every object delighted his senses. The refreshing pleasure from the first view of nature, after the pain of illness and the confinement of a sick chamber, is above the conceptions, as well as the descriptions, of those in health. The green woods and pastures ; the flowery turf ; the balmy air ; the murmur of the limpid stream ; and even the hum of every little insect of the shade, seemed to revivify the soul, and make mere existence bliss.

Madame St. Aubert, reanimated by the cheerfulness and the recovery of her husband, was no longer sensible of the indisposition which had lately oppressed her ; and, as she sauntered along the wood-walks of this romantic glen, and conversed with him and with her daughter, she often looked at them alternately with a degree of tenderness that filled her eyes with tears. St. Aubert observed this more than once, and gently reproved her for the emotion ; but she could only smile, clasp his hand and that of Emily, and weep the more. He felt the tender enthusiasm stealing upon himself in a degree that became almost painful ; his features assumed a serious air, and he could not forbear secretly sighing ' Perhaps I shall some time look back to these moments, as to the summit of my happiness, with hopeless regret. But let me not misuse them by useless anticipation ; let me hope I shall not live to mourn the loss of those who are dearer to me than life.'

To relieve, or perhaps to indulge, the pensive temper of his mind, he bade Emily fetch the lute she knew how to touch with such sweet pathos. As she drew near the fishing-house, she was surprised to hear the tones of the instrument, which were awakened by the hand of taste, and uttered a plaintive air, whose exquisite melody engaged all her attention. She listened in profound silence, afraid to move from the spot, lest the sound of her steps should occasion her to lose a note of the music, or should disturb the musician. Everything without the building was still, and no person appeared. She continued to listen, till timidity succeeded to surprise and delight ; a timidity increased by a remembrance of the pencilled lines she had formerly seen, and she hesitated whether to proceed or to return.

While she paused, the music ceased ; and after a momentary hesitation she re-collected courage to advance to the fishing-house, which she entered with faltering steps, and found unoccupied ! Her lute lay on the table ; everything seemed undisturbed, and she began to believe it was another instrument she had heard, till she remembered that when she followed M. and Madame St. Aubert from this spot her lute was left on the window-seat. She felt alarmed, she knew not wherefore ; the melancholy gloom of evening, and the profound stillness of the place, interrupted only by the light trembling of leaves, heightened her fanciful apprehensions, and she was desirous of quitting the building, but perceived herself grow faint, and sat down. As she tried to recover herself, the pencilled lines on the wainscot met her eye ; she started as if she had seen a stranger ; but endeavouring to conquer the tremour of her spirits, rose and went to the window. To the lines before noticed she now perceived that others were added, in which her name appeared.

Though no longer suffered to doubt that they were addressed to herself, she was as ignorant as before by whom they could be written. While she mused, she thought she heard the sound of a step without the building ; and again alarmed, she caught up her lute and hurried away. Monsieur and Madame St. Aubert she found in a little path that wound along the sides of the glen.

Having reached a green summit, shadowed by palm-trees and overlooking the valleys and plains of Gascony, they seated themselves on the turf ; and while their eyes wandered over the glorious scene, and they inhaled the sweet breath of flowers and herbs that enriched the grass, Emily played and sung several of their favourite airs, with the delicacy of expression in which she so much excelled.

Music and conversation detained them in this enchanting spot till the sun's last light slept upon the plains ; till the white sails that glided beneath the mountains, where the Garonne wandered, became dim, and the gloom of evening stole over the landscape. It was a melancholy but not unpleasing gloom. St. Aubert and his family rose, and left the place with regret : alas ! Madame St. Aubert knew not that she left it for ever.

When they reached the fishing-house she missed her bracelet, and recollected that she had taken it from her arm after dinner, and had left it on the table when she went to walk. After a long search, in which Emily was very active, she was compelled to resign herself to the loss of it. What made this bracelet valuable to her, was a miniature of her daughter to which it was attached, esteemed a striking resemblance, and which had been painted only a few months before. When Emily was convinced that the bracelet was really gone, she blushed, and became thoughtful. That some stranger had been in the fishing-house during her absence, her lute and the additional lines of a pencil already in-

formed her. From the purport of these lines it was not unreasonable to believe that the poet, the musician, and the thief, were the same person. But though the music she had heard, the written lines she had seen, and the disappearance of the picture, formed a combination of circumstances very remarkable, she was irresistibly restrained from mentioning them ; secretly determining, however, never again to visit the fishing-house without Monsieur or Madame St. Aubert.

They returned pensively to the chateau, Emily musing on the incident which had just occurred ; St. Aubert reflecting with placid gratitude on the blessings he possessed ; and Madame St. Aubert somewhat disturbed and perplexed by the loss of her daughter's picture. As they drew near the house they observed an unusual bustle about it ; the sound of voices was distinctly heard ; servants and horses were seen passing between the trees ; and at length the wheels of a carriage rolled along. Having come within view of the front of the chateau, a landau with smoking horses appeared on the little lawn before it. St. Aubert perceived the liveries of his brother-in-law, and in the parlour he found Monsieur and Madame Quesnel already entered. They had left Paris some days before, and were on the way to their estate, only ten leagues distant from La Vallée, and which Monsieur Quesnel had purchased several years before of St. Aubert. This gentleman was the only brother of Madame St. Aubert ; but the ties of relationship having never been strengthened by congeniality of character, the intercourse between them had not been frequent. M. Quesnel had lived altogether in the world : his aim had been consequence ; splendour was the object of his taste ; and his address and knowledge of character had carried him forward to the attainment of almost all that he had courted. By a man of such a disposition, it is not surprising that the virtues of St. Aubert should be overlooked ; or that his pure taste, simplicity, and moderated wishes, were considered as marks of a weak intellect and of confined views. The marriage of his sister with St. Aubert had been mortifying to his ambition ; for he had designed that the matrimonial connection she formed should assist him to attain the consequence which he so much desired ; and some offers were made her by persons whose rank and fortune flattered his warmest hope. But his sister, who was then addressed also by St. Aubert, perceived, or thought she perceived, that happiness and splendour were not the same ; and she did not hesitate to forego the last for the attainment of the former. Whether Monsieur Quesnel thought them the same or not, he would readily have sacrificed his sister's peace to the gratification of his own ambition ; and, on her marriage with St. Aubert, expressed in private his contempt of her spiritless conduct, and of the connection which it permitted. Madame St. Aubert, though she concealed this insult from her husband, felt, perhaps for the first time, resentment lighted in her heart ; and though a regard for her own dignity, united with considerations of prudence, restrained her expression of this resentment, there was ever after a mild reserve in her manner towards M. Quesnel, which he both understood and felt.

In his own marriage he did not follow his sister's example. His lady was an Italian, and an heiress, by birth ; and, by nature and education, was a vain and frivolous woman.

They now determined to pass the night with St. Aubert ; and as the chateau was not large enough to accommodate their servants, the latter were dismissed to the neighbouring village. When the first compliments were over, and the arrangements for the night made, M. Quesnel began the display of his intelligence and connections ; while St. Aubert, who had been long enough in retirement to find these topics recommended by their novelty, listened with a degree of patience and attention which his guest mistook for the humility of wonder. The latter, indeed, described the few festivities which the turbulence of that period permitted to the court of Henry the Third, with a minuteness that somewhat recompensed for his ostentation ; but when he came to speak of the character of the Duke of Joyeuse, of a secret treaty which he knew to be negotiating with the Porte, and of the light in which Henry of Navarre was received, M. St. Aubert recollected enough of his former experience to be assured that his guest could be only of an inferior class of politicians ; and that, from the importance of the subjects upon which he committed himself, he could not be of the rank to which he pretended to belong. The opinions delivered by M. Quesnel were such as St. Aubert forbore to reply to ; for he knew that his guest had neither humanity to feel, not discernment to perceive, what is just.

Madame Quesnel, meanwhile, was expressing to Madame St. Aubert her astonishment that she could bear to pass her life in this remote corner of the world, as she called it, and describing, from a wish probably of exciting envy, the splendour of the balls, banquets, and processions, which had just been given by the court in honour of the nuptials of the Duke de Joyeuse with Margaretta of Lorrain, the sister of the Queen. She described with equal minuteness the magnificence she had seen, and that from which she had been excluded ; while Emily's vivid fancy, as she listened with the ardent curiosity of youth, heightened the scenes she heard of ; and Madame St. Aubert, looking on her family, felt, as a tear stole to her eye, that though splendour may grace happiness, virtue only can bestow it.

'It is now twelve years, St. Aubert,' said M. Quesnel, 'since I purchased your family estate.'

'Somewhere thereabout,' replied St. Aubert, suppressing a sigh.

'It is near five years since I have been there,' resumed Quesnel ; 'for Paris and its neighbourhood is the only place in the world to live in ; and I am so immersed in politics, and have so many affairs of moment on my hands, that I find it difficult to steal away even for a month or two.' St. Aubert remaining silent, M. Quesnel proceeded : 'I have sometimes wondered how you, who have lived in the capital and have been accustomed to company, can exist elsewhere, especially in so remote a country as this, where you can neither hear nor see anything, and can, in short, be scarcely conscious of life.'

'I live for my family and myself,' said St. Aubert : 'I am now contented to know only happiness ; formerly I knew life.'

'I mean to expend thirty or forty thousand livres on improvements,' said M. Quesnel, without seeming to notice the words of St. Aubert ; 'for I design, next summer, to bring here my friends, the Duke de Durefort and the Marquis Ramont, to pass a month or two with me.' To St. Aubert's inquiry, as to these intended improvements, he replied that 'he should take down the whole east wing of the chateau, and raise upon the site a set of stables.' 'Then I shall build,' said he, 'a *salle à manger*, a *salon*, a *salle au commune*, and a number of rooms for servants, for at present there is not accommodation for a third part of my own people.'

'It accommodated our father's household,' said St. Aubert, grieved that the old mansion was to be thus improved, 'and that was not a small one.'

'Our notions are somewhat enlarged since those days,' said M. Quesnel : 'what was then thought a decent style of living would not now be endured.' Even the calm St. Aubert blushed at these words ; but his anger soon yielded to contempt. 'The ground about the chateau is encumbered with trees ; I mean to cut some of them down.'

'Cut down the trees too !' said St. Aubert.

'Certainly. Why should I not ? they interrupt my prospects. There is a chestnut which spreads its branches before the whole south side of the chateau, and which is so ancient that they tell me the hollow of its trunk will hold a dozen men ; your enthusiasm will scarcely contend that there can be either use or beauty in such a sapless old tree as this.'

'Good God !' exclaimed St. Aubert, 'you surely will not destroy that noble chestnut, which has flourished for centuries, the glory of the estate ! It was in its maturity when the present mansion was built. How often, in my youth, have I climbed among its broad branches, and sat embowered amidst a world of leaves, while the heavy shower has pattered above, and not a rain-drop reached me ! How often have I sat with my book in my hand, sometimes reading, and sometimes looking out between the branches upon the wide landscape, and setting sun, till twilight came, and brought the birds home to their little nests among the leaves ! How often——but pardon me,' added St. Aubert, recollecting that he was speaking to a man who could neither comprehend nor allow for his feelings, ' I am talking of times and feelings as old-fashioned as the taste that would spare that venerable tree.'

' It will certainly come down,' said M. Quesnel : ' I believe I shall plant some Lombardy poplars among the clumps of chestnut that I shall leave of the avenue : Madame Quesnel is partial to the poplar, and tells me how much it adorns a villa of her uncle not far from Venice.'

' On the banks of the Brenta, indeed !' continued St. Aubert, ' where its spiry form is intermingled with the pine and the cypress, and where it plays over light and elegant porticoes and colonnades, it unquestionably adorns the scene ; but among the giants of the forest, and near a heavy Gothic mansion——'

' Well, my good sir,' said M. Quesnel, ' I will not dispute with you ; you must return to Paris before our ideas can at all agree. But *à propos* of Venice, I have some thought of going thither next summer ; events may call me to take possession of that same villa, too, which they tell me is the most charming that can be imagined. In that case I shall leave the improvements I mention to another year ; and I may perhaps be tempted to stay some time in Italy.'

Emily was somewhat surprised to hear him talk of being tempted to remain abroad, after he had mentioned his presence to be so necessary at Paris, that it was with difficulty he could steal away for a month or two ; but St. Aubert understood the self-importance of the man too well to wonder at this trait ; and the possibility that these projected improvements might be deferred, gave him a hope that they might never take place.

Before they separated for the night, M. Quesnel desired to speak with St. Aubert alone ; and they retired to another room, where they remained a considerable time. The subject of this conversation was not known : but, whatever it might be, St. Aubert, when he returned to the supper-room, seemed much disturbed ; and a shade of sorrow sometimes fell upon his features that alarmed Madame St. Aubert. When they were alone, she was tempted to inquire the occasion of it ; but the delicacy of mind, which had ever appeared in his conduct, restrained her : she considered, that, if St. Aubert wished her to be acquainted with the subject of his concern, he would not wait for her inquiries.

On the following day, before M. Quesnel departed, he had a second conference with St. Aubert.

The guests, after dining at the chateau, set out in the cool of the day for Epourville, whither they gave him and Madame St. Aubert a pressing invitation, prompted rather by the vanity of displaying their splendour, than by a wish to make their friends happy.

Emily returned with delight, to the liberty which their presence had restrained—to her books, her walks, and the rational conversation of M. and Madame St. Aubert, who seemed to rejoice no less that they were delivered from the shackles which arrogance and frivolity had imposed.

Madame St. Aubert excused herself from sharing their usual evening walk, complaining that she was not quite well ; and St. Aubert and Emily went out together.

They chose a walk towards the mountains, intending to visit some old pensioners of St. Aubert, whom, from his very moderate income, he contrived to support ; though it is probable M. Quesnel, with his very large one, could not have afforded this.

After distributing to his pensioners their weekly stipends—listening patiently to the complaints of some, redressing the grievances of others, and softening the discontents of all by the look of sympathy and the smile of benevolence — St. Aubert returned home through the woods,

> . . . . . . where
> At fall of eve, the fairy people throng,
> In various games and revelry to pass
> The summer night as village stories tell.
> THOMSON.

' The evening gloom of woods was always delightful to me,' said St. Aubert, whose mind now experienced the sweet calm which results from the consciousness of having done a beneficent action, and which disposes it to receive pleasure from every surrounding object : ' I remember that in my youth this gloom used to call forth to my fancy a thousand fairy visions and romantic images ; and I own I am not yet wholly insensible of that high enthusiasm which wakes the poet's dream : I can linger with solemn steps under the deep shades, send forward a transforming eye into the distant obscurity, and listen with thrilling delight to the mystic murmuring of the woods.'

' O my dear father,' said Emily, while a sudden tear started to her eye, ' how exactly you describe what I have felt so often, and which I thought nobody had ever felt but myself ! But, hark ! here comes the sweeping 'sound over the wood-tops—Now it dies away. How solemn the stillness that succeeds ! Now the breeze swells again ! It is like the voice of some supernatural being —the voice of the spirit of the woods, that watches over them by night. Ah ! what light is yonder ?—But it is gone !—and now it gleams again, near the root of that large chestnut : look, sir !'

'Are you such an admirer of nature,' said St. Aubert, 'and so little acquainted with her appearances, as not to know that for the glow-worm ? But come,' added he gaily, ' step a little further, and we shall see fairies perhaps ; they are often companions. The glow-worm lends his light, and they in return charm him with music and the dance. Do you see nothing tripping yonder ?'

Emily laughed. 'Well, my dear sir,' said she, 'since you allow of this alliance, I may venture to own I have anticipated you ; and almost dare venture to repeat some verses I made one evening in these very woods.'

'Nay,' replied St. Aubert, ' dismiss the *almost,* and venture quite : let us hear what vagaries fancy has been playing in your mind. If she has given you one of her spells, you need not envy those of the fairies.'

'If it is strong enough to enchant your judgment, sir,' said Emily, 'while I disclose her images, I need *not* envy them. The lines go in a sort of tripping measure, which I thought might suit the subject well enough ; but I fear they are too irregular.'

THE GLOW-WORM.

How pleasant is the green-wood's deep-matted shade
  On a mid-summer's eve, when the fresh rain is
    o'er;
When the yellow beams slope, and sparkle through
    the glade,
  And swiftly in the thin-air the light swallows soar !

But sweeter, sweeter still, when the sun sinks to
    rest,
  And twilight comes on, with the fairies so gay
Tripping through the forest-walk, where flowers,
    unprest,
  Bow not their tall heads beneath their frolic play.

To music's softest sounds they dance away the hour,
  Till moon-light steals down among the trembling
    leaves,
And chequers all the ground, and guides them to
    the bower,
  The long-haunted bower, where the nightingale
    grieves.

Then no more they dance, till her sad song is done,
  But, silent as the night, to her mourning attend ;
And often as her dying notes their pity have won,
  They vow all her sacred haunts from mortals to
    defend.

When down among the mountains sinks the evening
    star,
  And the changing moon forsakes this shadowy
    sphere,
How cheerless would they be, though they fairies
    are,
  If I, with my pale light, came not near !

Yet cheerless though they'd be, they're ungrateful
    to my love !
For often, when the traveller's benighted on his
    way,
And I glimmer in his path, and would guide him
    through the grove,
  They bind me in their magic spells to lead him
    far astray ;

And in the mire to leave him, till the stars are all
    burnt out ;
While in strange-looking shapes they frisk about
    the ground,
And afar in the woods they raise a dismal shout,
  Till I shrink into my cell again for terror of the
    sound !

But, see where all the tiny elves come dancing in a
    ring,
  With the merry merry pipe, and the tabor, and
    the horn,
And the timbrel so clear, and the lute with dulcet
    string ;
  Then round about the oak they go till peeping of
    the morn.

Down yonder glade two lovers steal, to shun the
    fairy queen,
  Who frowns upon their plighted vows, and jealous
    is of me,
That yester-eve I lighted them, along the dewy
    green,
  To seek the purple flower whose juice from all her
    spells can free.

And now to punish me, she keeps afar her jocund
    band,
  With the merry merry pipe, and the tabor, and
    the lute ;
If I creep near yonder oak she will wave her fairy
    wand,
  And to me the dance will cease, and the music all
    be mute.

O ! had I but that purple flower whose leaves her
    charms can foil,
  And knew like fays to draw the juice, and throw
    it on the wind,
I'd be her slave no longer, nor the traveller beguile,
  And help all faithful lovers, nor fear the fairy -
    kind !

But soon the *vapour of the woods* will wander afar,
  And the fickle moon will fade, and the stars dis-
    appear ;
Then cheerless will they be, though they fairies are,
  If I, with my pale light, come not near !

Whatever St. Aubert might think of the stanzas he would not deny his daughter the pleasure of believing that he approved them ; and having given his commendation he sunk into a reverie, and they walked on in silence.

. . . . . A faint erroneous ray,
Glanced from the imperfect surfaces of things,
Flung half an image on the straining eye ;
While waving woods, and villages, and streams,
And rocks, and mountain tops, that long retain
The ascending gleam, are all one swimming scene,
Uncertain if beheld.
                                        THOMSON.

St. Aubert continued silent till he reached the chateau, where his wife had retired to her chamber. The languor and dejection that had lately oppressed her, and which the exertion called forth by the arrival of her guests had suspended, now returned with increased effect. On the following day symptoms of fever appeared ; and St. Aubert, having sent for medical advice, learned that her disorder was a fever of the same nature as that from which he had lately recovered. She had, indeed, taken the infection during her attendance upon him ; and her constitution being too weak to throw out the disease immediately, it had lurked in her veins, and occasioned the heavy languor of which she had complained. St. Aubert, whose anxiety for his wife overcame every other consideration, detained the physician in his house. He remembered the feelings and the reflections that had called a momentary gloom upon his mind, on the day when he had last visited the fishing house in company with Madame St. Aubert, and he now admitted a presentiment that this illness would be a fatal one. But he effectually concealed this from her and from his daughter, whom he endeavoured to reanimate with hopes that her constant assiduities would not be unavailing. The physician, when asked by St. Aubert for his opinion of the disorder, replied that the event of it depended upon circumstances which he could not ascertain. Madame St. Aubert seemed to have formed a more decided one ; but her eyes only gave hints of this. She frequently fixed them upon her anxious friends with an expression of pity and of tenderness, as if she anticipated the sorrow that awaited them, and that seemed to say, it was for their sakes only, for their sufferings, that she regretted life. On the seventh day the disorder was at its crisis. The physician assumed a graver manner, which she observed, and took occasion, when her family had once quitted the chamber, to tell him that she perceived her death was approaching. Do not attempt to deceive me, said she ; I feel that I cannot long survive : I am prepared for the event—I have long, I hope, been preparing for it. Since I have not long to live, do not suffer a mistaken compassion to induce you to flatter my family with false hopes. If you do, their affliction will only be the heavier when it arrives : I will endeavour to teach them resignation by my example.

The physician was affected : he promised to obey her, and told St. Aubert somewhat abruptly that there was nothing to expect. The latter was not philosopher enough to restrain his feelings when he received this information ; but a consideration of the increased affliction which the observance of his grief would occasion his wife, enabled him, after some time, to command himself in her presence. Emily was at first overwhelmed with the intelligence ; then, deluded by the strength of her wishes, a hope sprung up in her mind that her mother would yet recover, and to this she pertinaciously adhered almost to the last hour.

The progress of this disorder was marked, on the side of Madame St. Aubert, by patient suffering and subjected wishes. The composure with which she awaited her death could be derived only from the retrospect of a life governed, as far as human frailty permits, by a consciousness of being always in the presence of the Deity, and by the hope of a higher world. But her piety could not entirely subdue the grief of parting from those whom she so dearly loved. During these her last hours she conversed much with St. Aubert and Emily on the prospect of futurity, and other religious topics. The resignation she expressed, with the firm hope of meeting in a future world the friends she left in this, and the effort which sometimes appeared to conceal her sorrow at this temporary separation, frequently affected St. Aubert so much as to oblige him to leave the room. Having indulged his tears awhile, he would dry them, and return to the chamber with a countenance composed by an endeavour which did but increase his grief.

Never had Emily felt the importance of the lessons which had taught her to restrain her sensibility so much as in these moments, and never had she practised them with a triumph so complete. But when the last was over she sunk at once under the pressure of her sorrow, and perceived that it was hope, as well as fortitude, which had hitherto supported her. St. Aubert was for a time too devoid of comfort himself to bestow any on his daughter.

CHAPTER II.

'I could a tale unfold, whose lightest word
Would harrow up thy soul.'

SHAKESPEARE.

MADAME ST. AUBERT was interred in the neighbouring village church : her husband and daughter attended her to the grave, followed by a long train of the peasantry, who were sincere mourners of this excellent woman.

On his return from the funeral, St. Aubert shut himself in his chamber. When he came forth it was with a serene countenance, though pale in sorrow. He gave orders that his family should attend him. Emily only was absent ; who, overcome with the scene she had just witnessed, had retired to her closet to weep alone. St. Aubert followed her thither : he took her hand in silence, while she continued to weep ; and it was some moments before he could so far command his voice as to speak. It trembled while he said, 'My Emily, I am going to prayers with my family ; you will join us. We must ask support from above. Where else ought we to seek it— where else can we find it ?'

Emily checked her tears, and followed her father to the parlour, where the servants being assembled, St. Aubert read, in a low and solemn voice, the Evening Service, and added a prayer for the soul of the departed. During this his voice often faltered, his tears fell upon the book, and at length he paused. But the sublime emotions of pure devotion gradually elevated his views above this world, and finally brought comfort to his heart.

When the service was ended, and the servants were withdrawn, he tenderly kissed Emily, and said : ' I have endeavoured to teach you, from your earliest youth, the duty of self-command ; I have pointed out to you the great importance of it through life, not only as it preserves us in the various and dangerous temptations that call us from rectitude and virtue, but as it limits the indulgences which are termed virtuous, yet which, extended beyond a certain boundary, are vicious, for their consequence is evil. All excess is vicious; even that sorrow which is amiable in its origin, becomes a selfish and unjust passion if indulged at the expense of our duties : by our duties I mean what we owe to ourselves as well as to others. The indulgence of excessive grief enervates the mind, and almost incapacitates it for again partaking of those various innocent enjoyments which a benevolent God designed to be the sunshine of our lives. My dear Emily, recollect and practise the precepts I have so often given you, and which your own experience has so often shown you to be wise.

' Your sorrow is useless. Do not receive this as merely a common-place remark, but let reason *therefore* restrain sorrow. I would not annihilate your feelings, my child, I would only teach you to command them ; for whatever may be the evils resulting from a too susceptible heart, nothing can be hoped from an insensible one ; that, on the other hand, is all vice—vice, of which the deformity is not softened, or the effect consoled for, by any semblance or possibility of good. You know my sufferings, and are therefore convinced that mine are not the light words which, on these occasions, are so often repeated to destroy even the sources of honest emotion, or which merely display the selfish ostentation of a false philosophy. I will show my Emily that I can practise what I advise. I have said thus much because I cannot bear to see you wasting in useless sorrow for want of that resistance which is due from mind ; and I have not said it till now, because there is a period when all reasoning must yield to nature ; that is past : and another, when excessive indulgence having sunk into habit, weighs down the elasticity of the spirits so as to render conquest nearly impossible ; that is to come. You, my Emily will show that you are willing to avoid it.'

Emily smiled through her tears upon her father: ' Dear sir,' said she, and her voice trembled ; she would have added, ' I will show myself worthy of being your daughter ;' but a mingled emotion of gratitude, affection, and grief overcame her.

St. Aubert suffered her to weep without interruption, and then began to talk on common topics.

The first person who came to condole with St. Aubert was a M. Barreaux, an austere and seemingly unfeeling man. A taste for botany had introduced them to each other, for they had frequently met in their wanderings among the mountains. M. Barreaux had retired from the world, and almost from society, to live in a pleasant chateau on the skirts of the woods near La Valée. He also had been disappointed in his opinion of mankind ; but he did not, like St. Aubert, pity and mourn for them ; he felt more indignation at their vices than compassion for their weaknesses.

St. Aubert was somewhat surprised to see him ; for though he had often pressed him to come to the chateau, he had never till now accepted the invitation : and now he came without ceremony or reserve, entering the parlour as an old friend. The claims of misfortune appeared to have softened down all the ruggedness and prejudices of his heart. St. Aubert unhappy, seemed to be the sole idea that occupied his mind. It was in manners, more than in words, that he appeared to sympathise with his friends ; he spoke little on the subject of their grief ; but the minute attention he gave them, and the modulated voice and softened look that accompanied it, came from his heart, and spoke to theirs.

At this melancholy period St. Aubert was likewise visited by Madame Cheron; his only surviving sister, who had been some years a widow, and now resided on her own estate near Thoulouse. The intercourse between them had not been very frequent. In her condolements, words were not wanting ; she understood not the magic of the look that speaks at once to the soul, or the voice that sinks like balm to the heart : but she assured St. Aubert that she sincerely sympathized with him ; praised the virtues of his late wife, and then offered what she considered to be consolation. Emily wept unceasingly while she spoke ; St. Aubert was tranquil, listened to what she said in silence, and then turned the discourse upon another subject.

At parting, she pressed him and her niece to make her an early visit. ' Change of place will amuse you,' said she ; ' and it is wrong to give way to grief.'

St. Aubert acknowledged the truth of these words of course ; but at the same time felt more reluctant than ever to quit the spot which his past happiness had consecrated. The presence of his wife had sanctified every surrounding scene ; and each day, as it gradually softened the acuteness of his suffering, assisted the tender enchantment that bound him to home.

But there are calls which must be complied with, and of this kind was the visit he paid to his brother-in-law M. Quesnel. An affair of an interesting nature made it necessary that he should delay the visit no longer ; and, wishing to rouse Emily from her dejection, he took her with him to Épourville.

As the carriage entered upon the forest that adjoined his paternal domain, his eyes once more caught, between the chesnut avenue, the turreted corners of the chateau. He sighed to think of what had passed since he was last there, and that it was now the property of a man who neither revered nor valued it. At length he entered the avenue, whose lofty trees had so often delighted him when a boy, and whose melancholy shade was now so congenial with the tone of his spirits. Every feature of the edifice, distinguished by an air of heavy grandeur, appeared successively between the branches of the trees—the broad turret, the arched gateway that led into the courts, the drawbridge, and the dry fossé which surrounded the whole.

The sound of carriage wheels brought a troop of servants to the great gate, where St. Aubert alighted, and from which he led Emily into the Gothic hall, now no longer hung with the arms and ancient banners of the family. These were displaced, and the old wainscoting, and beams that crossed the roof, were painted white. The large table, too, that used to stretch along the upper end of the hall, where the master of the mansion loved to display his hospitality, and whence the peal of laughter and the song of conviviality had so often resounded, was now removed ; even the benches that had surrounded the hall were no longer there. The heavy walls were hung with frivolous ornaments, and everything that appeared denoted the false taste and corrupted sentiments of the present owner.

St. Aubert followed a gay Parisian servant to a parlour, where sat Monsieur and Madame Quesnel, who received him with a stately politeness, and, after a few formal words of condolement, seemed to have forgotten that they ever had a sister.

Emily felt tears swell in her eyes, and then resentment checked them. St. Aubert, calm and deliberate, preserved his dignity without assuming importance, and Quesnel was depressed by his presence without exactly knowing wherefore.

After some general conversation, St. Aubert requested to speak with him alone ; and Emily, being left with Madame Quesnel, soon learned that a large party was invited to dine at the chateau, and was compelled to hear that nothing which was past and irremediable ought to prevent the festivity of the present hour.

St. Aubert, when he was told that company were expected, felt a mixed emotion of disgust and indignation against the insensibility of Quesnel, which prompted him to return home immediately. But he was informed that Madame Cheron had been asked to meet him ; and when he looked at Emily, and considered that a time might come when the enmity of her uncle would be prejudicial to her, he determined not to incur it himself, by conduct which would be resented as indecorous, by the very persons who now showed so little sense of decorum.

Among the visitors assembled at dinner were two Italian gentlemen, of whom one was named Montoni, a distant relation of Madame Quesnel, a man about forty, of an uncommonly handsome person, with features manly and expressive, but whose countenance exhibited, upon the whole, more of the haughtiness of command, and the quickness of discernment, than of any other character.

Signor Cavigni, his friend, appeared to be about thirty—inferior in dignity, but equal to him in penetration of countenance, and superior in insinuation of manner.

Emily was shocked by the salutation with which Madame Cheron met her father.

'Dear brother,' said she, 'I am concerned to see you look so very ill ; do, pray, have advice !'

St. Aubert answered with a melancholy smile, that he felt himself much as usual : but Emily's fears made her now fancy that her father looked worse than he really did.

Emily would have been amused by the new characters she saw, and the varied conversation that passed during dinner, which was served in a style of splendour she had seldom seen before, had her spirits been less oppressed. Of the guests, Signor Montoni was lately from Italy, and he spoke of the commotions which at that period agitated the country ; talked of party-differences with warmth, and then lamented the probable consequences of the tumults. His friend spoke, with equal ardour, of the politics of his country ; praised the government and prosperity of Venice, and boasted of its decided superiority over all the other Italian states. He then turned to the ladies, and talked with the same eloquence of Parisian fashions, the French opera, and French manners ; and on the latter subject he did not fail to mingle what is so particularly agreeable to French taste. The flattery was not detected by those to whom it was addressed, though its effects in producing submissive attention did not escape his observation. When he could disengage himself from the assiduities of the other ladies, he sometimes addressed Emily : but she knew nothing of Parisian fashions, of Parisian operas ; and her modesty, simplicity, and correct manners, formed a decided contrast to those of her female companions.

After dinner, St. Aubert stole from the room to view once more the old chestnut which Quesnel talked of cutting down. As he stood under its shade, and looked up among its branches, still luxuriant, and saw here and there the blue sky trembling between them, the pursuits and events of his early days crowded fast to his mind, with the figures and characters of friends—long since gone from the earth ! and he now felt himself to be almost an insulated being, with nobody but his Emily for his heart to turn to.

He stood lost amid the scenes of years which fancy called up, till the succession closed with the picture of his dying wife ; and he started away, to forget it, if possible, at the social board.

St. Aubert ordered his carriage at an early hour, and Emily observed that he was more than usually silent and dejected on the way home ; but she considered this to be the effect of his visit to a place which spoke so eloquently of former times, nor suspected that he had a cause of grief which he concealed from her.

On entering the chateau she felt more depressed than ever, for she more than ever missed the presence of that dear parent, who, whenever she had been from home, used to welcome her return with smiles and fondness : now all was silent and forsaken !

But what reason and effort may fail to do, time effects : week after week passed away, and each, as it passed, stole something from the harshness of her affliction, till it was mellowed to that tenderness which the feeling heart cherishes as sacred. St. Aubert, on the contrary, visibly declined in health ; though Emily, who had been so constantly with him, was almost the last person who observed it. His constitution had never recovered from the late attack of the fever ; and the succeeding shock it received from Madame St. Aubert's death had produced his present infirmity. His physician now ordered him to travel ; for it was perceptible that sorrow had seized upon his nerves, weakened as they had been by the preceding illness ; a variety of scene, it was probable, would, by amusing his mind, restore them to their proper tone.

For some days Emily was occupied in preparations to attend him ; and he, by endeavours to diminish his expenses at home during the journey—a purpose which determined him at length to dismiss his domestics.

Emily seldom opposed her father's wishes by questions or remonstrances, or she would now have asked why he did not take a servant, and have represented that his infirm health made one almost necessary. But when, on the eve of their departure, she found that he had dismissed Jacques, Francis, and Mary, and detained only Theresa, the old housekeeper, she was extremely surprised, and ventured to ask his reason for having done so.

' To save expenses, my dear,' he replied, ' we are going on an expensive excursion.'

The physician had prescribed the air of Languedoc and Province ; and St. Aubert determined therefore to travel leisurely along the shores of the Mediterranean, towards Provence.

They retired early to their chamber on the night before their departure : but Emily had a few books and other things to collect, and the clock had struck twelve before she had finished, or had remembered that some of her drawing instruments, which she meant to take with her, were in the parlour below. As she went to fetch these, she passed her father's room, and perceiving the door half open, concluded that he was in his study ; for, since the death of Madame St. Aubert, it had been frequently his custom to rise from his restless bed, and go thither to compose his mind. When she was below stairs she looked into this room, but without finding him ; and as she returned to her chamber, she tapped at his door, and receiving no answer, stepped softly in, to be certain whether he was there.

The room was dark, but a light glimmered through some panes of glass that were placed in the upper part of a closet-door.

Emily believed her father to be in the closet, and, surprised that he was up at so late an hour, apprehended he was unwell, and was going to inquire ; but considering that her sudden appearance at this hour might alarm him, she removed her light to the staircase, and then stepped softly to the closet.

On looking through the panes of glass, she saw him seated at a small table, with papers before him, some of which he was reading with deep attention and interest, during which he often wept and sobbed aloud.

Emily, who had come to the door to learn whether her father was ill, was now detained there by a mixture of curiosity and tenderness. She could not witness his sorrow without being anxious to know the subject of it ; and she therefore continued to observe him in silence, concluding that those papers were letters of her late mother.

Presently he kneeled down, and, with a look so solemn as she had seldom seen him assume, and which was mingled with a certain wild expression, that partook more of horror than of any other character, he prayed silently for a considerable time.

When he rose, a ghastly paleness was on his countenance. Emily was hastily retiring ; but she saw him turn again to the papers, and she stopped. He took from among them a small case, and from thence a miniature picture. The rays of light fell strongly upon it, and she perceived it to be that of a lady but not of her mother.

St. Aubert gazed earnestly and tenderly upon this portrait, put it to his lips, and then to his heart, and sighed with a convulsive force.

Emily could scarcely believe what she saw to be real. She never knew till now that he had a picture of any other lady than her mother, much less that he had one which he evidently valued so highly ; but having looked repeatedly, to be certain that it was not the resemblance of Madame St. Aubert, she became entirely convinced that it was designed for that of some other person.

At length St. Aubert returned the picture to its case ; and Emily, recollecting that she was intruding upon his private sorrows, softly withdrew from the chamber.

CHAPTER III.

'O how canst thou renounce the boundless store
Of charms which Nature to her votary yields?
The warbling woodland, the resounding shore,
The pomp of groves, and garniture of fields ;
All that the genial ray of morning gilds,
And all that echoes to the song of even ;
All that the mountain's sheltering bosom shields,
And all the dread magnificence of heaven :
O how canst thou renounce, and hope to be forgiven?
. . . .
These charms shall work thy soul's eternal health,
And love, and gentleness, and joy, impart.'
                                    THE MINSTREL.

ST. AUBERT, instead of taking the more direct road that ran along the feet of the Pyrenees to Languedoc, chose one that, winding over the heights, afforded more extensive views and greater variety of romantic scenery. He turned a little out of his way to take leave of M. Barreaux, whom he found botanizing in the wood near his chateau, and who, when he was told the purpose of St. Aubert's visit, expressed a degree of concern such as his friend had thought it was scarcely possible for him to feel on any similar occasion. They parted with mutual regret.

' If any thing could have tempted me from my retirement,' said M. Barreaux, ' it would have been the pleasure of accompanying you on this little tour. I do not often offer compliments ; you may therefore believe me when I say that I shall look for your return with impatience.'

The travellers proceeded on their journey. As they ascended the heights, St. Aubert often looked back upon his chateau in the plain below ; tender images crowded to his mind ; his melancholy imagination suggested that he should return no more ; and though he checked this wandering thought, still he continued to look, till the haziness of distance blended his home with the general landscape, and St. Aubert seemed to

' Drag at each remove a lengthening chain.'

He and Emily continued sunk in musing silence for some leagues ; from which melancholy reverie Emily first awoke, and her young fancy, struck with the grandeur of the objects around, gradually yielded to delightful impressions. The road now descended into glens, confined by stupendous walls of rock, gray and barren, except where shrubs fringed their summits, or patches of meagre vegetation tinted their recesses, in which the wild goat was frequently browsing. And now the way led to the lofty cliffs, from whence the landscape was seen extending in all its magnificence.

Emily could not restrain her transport as she looked over the pine forests of the mountains, upon the vast plains that (enriched with woods, towns, blushing vines, and plantations of almonds, palms, and olives) stretched along, till their various colours melted in distance into one harmonious hue, that seemed to unite earth with heaven. Through the whole of this glorious scene the majestic Garonne wandered, descending from its source among the Pyrenees, and winding its blue waves towards the Bay of Biscay.

The ruggedness of the unfrequented road often obliged the wanderers to alight from their little carriage ; but they thought themselves amply repaid for this inconvenience by the grandeur of the scenes ; and, while the muleteer led his animals slowly over the broken ground, the travellers had leisure to linger amid these solitudes, and to indulge the sublime reflections, which soften while they elevate the heart, and fill it with the certainty of a present God ! Still the enjoyment of St. Aubert was touched with that pensive melancholy which gives to every object a mellower tint, and breathes a sacred charm over all around.

They had provided against part of the evil to be encountered from a want of convenient inns, by carrying a stock of provisions in the carriage ; so that they might take refreshment on any pleasant spot, in the open air, and pass the nights wherever they should happen to meet with a comfortable cottage. For the mind also they had provided by a work on botany written by M. Barreaux, and by several of the Latin and Italian poets ; while Emily's pencil enabled her to preserve some of those combinations of forms which charmed her at every step.

The loneliness of the road, where only now and then a peasant was seen driving his mule, or some mountaineer children at play among the rocks, heightened the effect of the scenery. St. Aubert was so much struck with it, that he determined, if he could hear of a road, to penetrate further among the mountains, and, bending his way rather more to the south, to emerge into Rousillon, and coast the Mediterranean along part of that country to Languedoc.

Soon after mid-day they reached the summit of one of those cliffs, which, bright with the verdure of palm-trees, adorn, like gems, the tremendous walls of the rocks, and which overlooked the greater part of Gascony and part of Languedoc. Here was shade, and the fresh water of a spring, that, gliding among the turf, under the trees, thence precipitated itself from rock to rock, till its dashing murmurs were lost in the abyss, though its white foam was long seen amid the darkness of the pines below.

This was a spot well suited for rest, and the travellers alighted to dine, while the mules were unharnessed to browse on the savoury herbs that enriched this summit.

It was some time before St. Aubert and Emily could withdraw their attention from the surrounding objects, so as to partake of their little repast. Seated in the shade of the palms, St. Aubert pointed out to her observation the course of the rivers, the situation of great towns, and the boundaries of provinces, which science, rather than the eye, enabled him to describe. Notwithstanding this occupation, when he had talked awhile, he suddenly became silent, thoughtful, and tears often swelled to his eyes ; which Emily observed, and the sympathy of her own heart told her their cause. The scene before them bore some resemblance, though it was on a much grander scale, to a favourite one of the late Madame St. Aubert, within view of the fishing-house. They both observed this, and thought how delighted she would have been with the present landscape, while they knew that her eyes must-never never more open upon this world. St. Aubert remembered the last time of his visiting that spot in company with her, and also the mournfully presaging thoughts which had then arisen in his mind, and were now, even thus soon, realized ! The recollections subdued him, and he abruptly rose from his seat, and walked away to where no eye could observe his grief.

When he returned, his countenance had recovered its usual serenity : he took Emily's hand, pressed it affectionately, without speaking, and soon after called to the muleteer, who sat at a little distance, concerning a road among the mountains towards Rousillon. Michael said there were several that way, but he did not know how far they extended, or even whether they were passable ; and St. Aubert, who did not intend to travel after sun-set, asked what village they could reach about that time. The muleteer calculated that they could easily reach Mateau, which was in their present road ; but that if they took a road that sloped towards the south, towards Rousillon, there was a hamlet, which he thought they could gain before the evening shut in.

St. Aubert, after some hesitation, determined to take the latter course ; and Michael, having finished his meal and harnessed his mules, again set forward—but soon stopped ; and St. Aubert saw him doing homage to a cross that stood on a rock impending over their way. Having concluded his devotions, he smacked his whip in the air, and, in spite of the rough road and the pain of his poor mules (which he had been lately lamenting), rattled, in a full gallop, along the edge of a precipice which it made the eye dizzy to look

down. Emily was terrified almost to fainting ; and St. Aubert, apprehending still greater danger from suddenly stopping the driver, was compelled to sit quietly, and trust his fate to the strength and discretion of the mules, who seemed to possess a greater portion of the latter quality than their master ; for they carried the travellers safely into the valley, and there stopped upon the brink of the rivulet that watered it.

Leaving the splendour of extensive prospects, they now entered this narrow valley, screened by

' Rocks on rocks piled, as if by magic spell ;
  Here scorch'd by lightnings, there with ivy green.'

The scene of barrenness was here and there interrupted by the spreading branches of the larch and cedar, which threw their gloom over the cliff, or athwart the torrent that rolled in the vale. No living creature appeared—except the lizard scrambling among the rocks, and often hanging upon points so dangerous that fancy shrunk from the view of them. This was such a scene as *Salvator* would have chosen, had he then existed, for his canvass. St. Aubert, impressed by the romantic character of the place, almost expected to see banditti start from behind some projecting rock, and he kept his hand upon the arms with which he always travelled.

As they advanced, the valley opened ; its savage features gradually softened, and towards evening they were among heathy mountains stretched in far perspective, along which the solitary sheep-bell was heard, and the voice of the shepherd calling his wandering flocks to the nightly fold. His cabin, partly shadowed by the cork-tree and the ilex, which St. Aubert observed to flourish in higher regions of the air than any other trees, except the fir, was all the human habitation that yet appeared. Along the bottom of this valley the most vivid verdure was spread ; and in the little hollow recesses of the mountains, under the shade of the oak and chesnut, herds of cattle were grazing. Groups of them, too, were often seen reposing on the banks of the rivulet, or laving their sides in the cool stream, and sipping its wave.

The sun was now setting upon the valley— its last light gleamed upon the water, and heightened the rich yellow and purple tints of the heath and broom that overspread the mountains. St. Aubert inquired of Michael the distance to the hamlet he had mentioned, but the man could not with certainty tell ; and Emily began to fear that he had mistaken the road. Here was no human being to assist or direct them : they had left the shepherd and his cabin far behind ; and the scene became so obscured in twilight, that the eye could not follow the distant perspective of the valley, in search of a cottage or a hamlet. A glow of the horizon still marked the west, and this was of some little use to the travellers. Michael seemed endeavouring to keep up his courage by singing; his music, however, was not of a kind to disperse melancholy; he sung, in a sort of chant, one of the most dismal ditties his present auditors had ever heard, and St. Aubert at length discovered it to be a vesper-hymn to his favourite saint.

They travelled on, sunk in that thoughtful melancholy with which twilight and solitude impress the mind. Michael had now ended his ditty; and nothing was heard but the drowsy murmur of the breeze among the woods, and its light flutter as it blew freshly into the carriage. They were at length roused by the sound of fire-arms. St. Aubert called to the muleteer to stop, and they listened. The noise was not repeated; but presently they heard a rustling among the brakes. St. Aubert drew forth a pistol, and ordered Michael to proceed as fast as possible; who had not long obeyed before a horn sounded that made the valleys ring. He looked again from the window, and then saw a young man spring from the bushes into the road, followed by a couple of dogs. The stranger was in a hunter's dress; his gun was slung across his shoulders; the hunter's horn hung from his belt; and in his hand was a small pike, which, as he held it, added to the manly grace of his figure, and assisted the agility of his steps.

After a moment's hesitation, St. Aubert again stopped the carriage, and waited till he came up, that they might inquire concerning the hamlet they were in search of. The stranger informed him that it was only half a league distant; that he was going thither himself, and would readily show the way. St. Aubert thanked him for the offer, and, pleased with his chevalier-like air and open countenance, asked him to take a seat in the carriage; which the stranger, with an acknowledgment, declined, adding that he would keep pace with the mules.

'But I fear you will be wretchedly accommodated,' said he; 'the inhabitants of these mountains are a simple people, who are not only without the luxuries of life, but almost destitute of what in other places are held to be its necessaries.'

'I perceive you are not one of its inhabitants, sir,' said St. Aubert.

'No, sir; I am only a wanderer here.'

The carriage drove on; and the increasing dusk made the travellers very thankful that they had a guide; the frequent glens, too, that now opened among the mountains, would likewise have added to their perplexity. Emily, as she looked up one of these, saw something at a great distance like a bright cloud in the air.

'What light is yonder, sir?' said she.

St. Aubert looked, and perceived that it was the snowy summit of a mountain, so much higher than any around it, that it still reflected the sun's rays, while those below lay in deep shade.

At length the village lights were seen to twinkle through the dusk, and soon after, some cottages were discovered in the valley, or rather were seen by reflection in the stream, on whose margin they stood, and which still gleamed with the evening light.

The stranger now came up; and St. Aubert, on further inquiry, found not only that there was no inn in the place, but not any sort of house of public reception. The stranger, however, offered to walk on, and inquire for a cottage to accommodate them; for which further civility St. Aubert returned his thanks, and said, that, as the village was so near, he would alight and walk with him. Emily followed slowly in the carriage.

On the way St. Aubert asked his companion what success he had had in the chase.

'Not much, sir,' he replied; 'nor do I aim at it: I am pleased with the country, and mean to saunter away a few weeks among its scenes: my dogs I take with me more for companionship than for game: this dress, too, gives me an ostensible business, and procures me that respect from the people which would, perhaps, be refused to a lonely stranger who had no visible motive for coming among them.'

'I admire your taste,' said St. Aubert, 'and if I were a younger man, should like to pass a few weeks in your way exceedingly. I, too, am a wanderer; but neither my plan nor pursuits are exactly like yours. I go in search of health as much as of amusement.' St. Aubert sighed, and paused; and then, seeming to recollect himself, he resumed: 'If I can hear of a tolerable road that shall afford decent accommodation, it is my intention to pass into Rousillon, and along the sea-shore to Languedoc. You, sir, seem to be acquainted with the country, and can, perhaps, give me information on the subject?'

The stranger said that what information he could give was entirely at his service; and then mentioned a road rather more to the east, which led to a town, whence it would be easy to proceed into Rousillon.

They now arrived at the village, and commenced their search for a cottage that would afford a night's lodging. In several which they entered, ignorance, poverty, and mirth seemed equally to prevail; and the owners eyed St. Aubert with a mixture of curiosity and timidity. Nothing like a bed could be found; and he had ceased to inquire for one, when Emily joined him, who observed the languor of her father's countenance, and lamented that he had taken a road so ill provided with the comforts necessary for an invalid. Other cottages which they examined seemed somewhat less savage than the former, consisting of two rooms, if such they could be called—the first of these occupied by mules and pigs; the second by the family, which generally consisted of six or eight children, with their parents, who slept on beds of skins and dried beech leaves spread upon a mud floor. Here light was admitted, and smoke discharged through an aperture in the roof; and here the scent of spirits (for the travelling smugglers who haunted the Pyrenees had made the rude people familiar with the use of liquors) was generally perceptible enough.

Emily turned from such scenes, and looked at her father with anxious tenderness, which the young stranger seemed to observe; for, drawing St. Aubert aside, he made him an offer of his own bed.

'It is a decent one,' said he, when compared with what we have just seen, yet such as in other circumstances I should be ashamed to offer you.'

St. Aubert acknowledged how much he felt himself obliged by this kindness; but refused to accept it till the young stranger would take no denial.

'Do not give me the pain of knowing, sir,' said he, 'that an invalid like you lies on hard skins while I sleep in a bed. Besides, sir, your refusal wounds my pride; I must believe you think my offer unworthy your acceptance. Let me show you the way. I have no doubt my landlady can accommodate this young lady also.'

St. Aubert at length consented, that, if this could be done, he would accept the kindness; though he felt rather surprised that the stranger had proved himself so deficient in gallantry as to administer to the repose of an infirm man rather than to that of a very lovely young woman; for he had not once offered the room for Emily. But she thought not of herself; and the animated smile she gave him told how much she felt herself obliged for the preference of her father.

On their way, the stranger, whose name was Valancourt, stepped on first to speak to his hostess; and she came out to welcome St. Aubert into a cottage much superior to any he had seen. This good woman seemed very willing to accommodate the strangers, who were soon compelled to accept the only two beds in the place. Eggs and milk were the only food the cottage afforded; but against scarcity of provisions St. Aubert had provided; and he requested Valancourt to stay and partake with him of less homely fare—an invitation which was readily accepted; and they passed an hour in intelligent conversation. St. Aubert was much pleased with the manly frankness, simplicity, and keen susceptibility to the grandeur of nature which his new acquaintance discovered; and, indeed, he had often been heard to say, that without a certain simplicity of heart this taste could not exist in any strong degree.

The conversation was interrupted by a violent uproar without, in which the voice of the muleteer was heard above every other sound. Valancourt started from his seat, and went to inquire the occasion; but the dispute continued so long afterwards that St. Aubert went himself, and found Michael quarrelling with the hostess because she had refused to let his mules lie in a little room where he and three of her sons were to pass the night. The place was wretched enough, but there was no other for these people to sleep in; and, with somewhat more of delicacy than was usual among the inhabitants of this wild tract of country, she persisted in refusing to let the animals have the same *bed-chamber* with her children. This was a tender point with the muleteer: his honour was wounded when his mules were treated with disrespect, and he would have received a blow, perhaps, with more meekness. He declared that his beasts were as honest beasts and as good beasts as any in the whole province; and that they had a right to be well treated wherever they went.

'They are as harmless as lambs,' said he, 'if people don't affront them. I never knew them behave themselves amiss above once or twice in my life, and then they had good reason for doing so. Once indeed they kicked at a boy's leg that lay asleep in the stable, and broke it; but I told them they were out there: and by St. Anthony! I believe they understood me, for they never did so again.'

He concluded this eloquent harangue with protesting that they should share with him, go where he would.

The dispute was at length settled by Valancourt, who drew the hostess aside, and desired she would let the muleteer and his beasts have the place in question to themselves, while her sons should have the bed of skins designed for him, for that he would wrap himself in his cloak, and sleep on the bench by the cottage door. But this she thought it her duty to oppose; and she felt it to be her inclination to disappoint the muleteer. Valancourt, however, was positive; and the tedious affair was at length settled.

It was late when St. Aubert and Emily retired to their rooms, and Valancourt to his station at the door, which, at this mild season, he preferred to a close cabin and a bed of skins. St. Aubert was somewhat surprised to find in his room volumes of Homer, Horace, and Petrarch; but the name of Valancourt, written in them, told him to whom they belonged.

CHAPTER IV.

'In truth, he was a strange and wayward wight,
Fond of each gentle and each dreadful scene :
In darkness and in storm he found delight ;
Nor less than when on ocean-wave serene
The southern sun diffused his dazzling sheen.
Even sad vicissitude amused his soul;
And if a sigh would sometimes intervene,
And down his cheeks a tear of pity roll,
A sigh, a tear, so sweet, he wish'd not to control.'
THE MINSTREL.

ST. AUBERT awoke at an early hour, re-freshed by sleep, and desirous to set forward. He invited the stranger to breakfast with him ; and, talking again of the road, Valancourt said that some months past he had travelled as far as Beaujeu, which was a town of some consequence on the way to Rousillon. He recommended it to St. Aubert to take that route ; and the latter determined to do so.

The road from this hamlet, said Valancourt, and that to Beaujeu, part at the distance of about a league and a half from hence : if you will give me leave, I will direct your muleteer so far. I must wander somewhere ; and your company would make this a pleasanter ramble than any other I could take.

St. Aubert thankfully accepted his offer, and they set out together—the young stranger on foot ; for he refused the invitation of St. Aubert to take a seat in his little carriage.

The road wound along the feet of the mountains, through a pastoral valley bright with verdure, and varied with groves of dwarf oak, beech and sycamore, under whose branches herds of cattle reposed. The mountain-ash, too, and the weeping birch, often threw their pendent foliage over the steeps above, where the scanty soil scarcely con-cealed their roots, and where their light branches waved to every breeze that fluttered from the mountains.

The travellers were frequently met at this early hour (for the sun had not yet risen upon the valley) by shepherds driving immense flocks from their folds to feed upon the hills. St. Aubert had set out thus early, not only that he might enjoy the first appearance of sun-rise, but that he might inhale the first pure breath of morning, which above all things is refreshing to the spirits of the invalid. In these regions it was particularly so, where an abundance of wild flowers and aromatic herbs breathed forth their essence on the air.

The dawn, which softened the scenery with its peculiar gray tint, now dispersed, and Emily watched the progress of the day, first trembling on the tops of the highest cliffs, then touching them with splendid light, while their sides and the vale below were still wrapped in dewy mist. Meanwhile the sullen gray of the eastern clouds began to blush, then to redden, and then to glow with a thousand colours, till the golden light darted over all the air, touched the lower points of the mountain's brow, and glanced in long sloping beams upon the valley and its stream. All nature seemed to have awakened from death into life. The spirit of St. Aubert was renovated. His heart was full ; he wept : and his thoughts ascended to the Great Creator.

Emily wished to trip along the turf, so green and bright with dew, and to taste the full delight of that liberty which the izard seemed to enjoy as he bounded along the brow of the cliffs ; while Valancourt often stopped to speak with the travellers, and with social feeling to point out to them the peculiar objects of his admiration.

St. Aubert was pleased with him : Here is the real ingenuousness and ardour of youth, said he to himself ; this young man has never been at Paris.

He was sorry when they came to the spot where the roads parted ; and his heart took a more affectionate leave of him than is usual after so short an acquaintance.

Valancourt talked long by the side of the carriage ; seemed more than once to be going, but still lingered, and appeared to search anxiously for topics of conversation to account for his delay. At length he took leave.

As he went, St. Aubert observed him look with an earnest and pensive eye at Emily, who bowed to him with a countenance full of timid sweetness, while the carriage drove on. St. Aubert, for whatever reason, soon after looked from the window, and saw Valancourt standing upon the bank of the road, resting on his pike with folded arms, and following the carriage with his eyes. He waved his hand, and Valancourt, seeming to awake from his reverie, returned the salute, and started away.

The aspect of the country now began to change, and the travellers soon found them-selves among mountains covered from their bases nearly to their summits with forests of gloomy pine, except where a rock of granite shot up from the vale, and lost its snowy top in the clouds. The rivulet, which had hither-to accompanied them, now expanded into a river ; and flowing deeply and silently along, reflected as in a mirror, the blackness of the impending shades.

Sometimes a cliff was seen lifting its bold head above the woods and the vapours that floated mid-way down the mountains ; and sometimes a face of perpendicular marble rose from the water's edge, over which the larch threw his gigantic arms, here scathed with lightning, and there floating in luxuriant foliage.

They continued to travel over a rough and unfrequented road, seeing now and then at a distance the solitary shepherd, with his dog, stalking along the valley, and hearing only the dashing of torrents, which the woods concealed from the eye, the long sullen murmur of the breeze, as it swept over the pines, or the notes of the eagle and the vulture, which were seen towering round the beetling cliff.

Often, as the carriage moved slowly over uneven ground, St. Aubert alighted, and amused himself with examining the curious plants that grew on the banks of the road, and with which these regions abound; while Emily, wrapt in high enthusiasm, wandered away under the shades, listening in deep silence to the lonely murmur of the woods. Neither villages nor hamlet was seen for many leagues: the goat-herd's or the hunter's cabin, perched among the cliffs of the rocks, were the only human habitations that appeared.

The travellers again took their dinner in the open air, on a pleasant spot in the valley, under the spreading shade of cedars; and then set forward towards Beaujeu.

The road now began to ascend, and, leaving the pine forest behind, wound among rocky precipices. The evening twilight again fell over the scene, and the travellers were ignorant how far they might yet be from Beaujeu.

St. Aubert, however, conjectured that the distance could not be very great, and comforted himself with the prospect of travelling on a more frequented road after reaching that town, where he designed to pass the night.

Mingled woods, and rocks, and heathy mountains, were now seen obscurely through the dusk; but soon even these imperfect images faded in darkness.

Michael proceeded with caution, for he could scarcely distinguish the road: his mules, however, seemed to have more sagacity, and their steps were sure.

On turning the angle of a mountain, a light appeared at a distance, that illumined the rocks and the horizon to a great extent. It was evidently a large fire; but whether accidental or otherwise, there were no means of knowing. St. Aubert thought it was probably kindled by some of the numerous banditti that infested the Pyrenees, and he became watchful and anxious to know whether the road passed near this fire. He had arms with him, which on an emergency might afford some protection, though certainly a very unequal one against a band of robbers, so desperate too as those usually were who haunted these wild regions. While many reflections rose upon his mind, he heard a voice shouting from the road behind, and ordering the muleteer to stop. St. Aubert bade him proceed as fast as possible; but either Michael or his mules were obstinate, for they did not quit the old pace. Horses' feet were now heard: a man rode up to the carriage, still ordering the driver to

stop; and St. Aubert, who could no longer doubt his purpose, was with difficulty able to prepare a pistol for his defence, when his hand was upon the door of the chaise. The man staggered on his horse; the report of the pistol was followed by a groan; and St. Aubert's horror may be imagined, when in the next instant he though he heard the faint voice of Valancourt. He now himself bade the muleteer stop; and, pronouncing the name of Valancourt, was answered in a voice that no longer suffered him to doubt. St. Aubert, who instantly alighted and went to his assistance, found him still sitting on his horse, but bleeding profusely, and appearing to be in great pain, though he endeavoured to soften the terror of St. Aubert by assurances that he was not materially hurt, the wound being only in his arm. St. Aubert, with the muleteer, assisted him to dismount, and he sat down on the bank of the road, where St. Aubert tried to bind up his arm; but his hands trembled so excessively that he could not accomplish it; and Michael being now gone in pursuit of the horse, which, on being disengaged from his rider, had galloped off, he called Emily to his assistance. Receiving no answer, he went to the carriage, and found her sunk on the seat in a fainting fit. Between the distress of this circumstance and that of leaving Valancourt bleeding, he scarcely knew what he did; he endeavoured, however, to raise her, and called to Michael to fetch water from the rivulet that flowed by the road; but Michael was gone beyond the reach of his voice. Valancourt, who heard these calls, and also the repeated name of Emily, instantly understood the subject of his distress; and, almost forgetting his own condition, he hastened to her relief. She was reviving when he reached the carriage; and then, understanding that anxiety for him had occasioned her indisposition, he assured her in a voice that trembled, but not from anguish, that his wound was of no consequence. While he said this, St. Aubert turned round; and perceiving that he was still bleeding, the subject of his alarm changed again, and he hastily formed some handkerchiefs into a bandage. This stopped the effusion of the blood; but St. Aubert, dreading the consequence of the wound, inquired repeatedly how far they were from Beaujeu; when learning that it was at two leagues' distance, his distress increased, since he knew not how Valancourt, in his present state, would bear the motion of the carriage, and perceived that he was already faint from loss of blood. When he mentioned the subject of his anxiety, Valancourt entreated that he would not suffer himself to be thus alarmed on his account, for that he had no doubt he should be able to support himself very well; and then he talked of the accident as a slight one. The muleteer being now returned with

Valancourt's horse, assisted him into the chaise; and as Emily was now revived, they moved slowly on towards Beaujeu.

St. Aubert, when he had recovered from the terror occasioned him by this accident, expressed surprise on seeing Valancourt, who explained his unexpected appearance by saying, 'You, sir, renewed my taste for society; when you had left the hamlet, it did appear a solitude. I determined, therefore, since my object was merely amusement, to change the scene, and I took this road, because I knew it led through a more romantic tract of mountains than the spot I have left. Besides,' added he, hesitating for an instant, I will own —and why should I not?—that I had some hope of overtaking you.'

'And I have made you a very unexpected return for the compliment,' said St. Aubert, who lamented again the rashness which had produced the accident, and explained the cause of his late alarm. But Valancourt seemed anxious only to remove from the minds of his companions every unpleasant feeling relative to himself; and, for that purpose, still struggled against a sense of pain, and tried to converse with gaiety. Emily meanwhile was silent, except when Valancourt particularly addressed her; and there was at those times a tremulous tone in his voice that spoke much.

They were now so near the fire which had long flamed at a distance on the blackness of night, that it gleamed upon the road, and they could distinguish figures moving about the blaze. The way winding still nearer, they perceived in the valley one of those numerous bands of gipsies, which at that period particularly haunted the wilds of the Pyrenees, and lived partly by plundering the traveller. Emily looked with some degree of terror on the savage countenances of these people shown by the fire, which heightened the romantic effect of the scenery, as it threw a red dusky gleam upon the rocks and on the foliage of the trees, leaving heavy masses of shade and regions of obscurity which the eye feared to penetrate.

They were preparing their supper: a large pot stood by the fire, over which several figures were busy. The blaze discovered a rude kind of tent, round which many children and dogs were playing; and the whole formed a picture highly grotesque. The travellers saw plainly their danger. Valancourt was silent, but laid his hand on one of St. Aubert's pistols; St. Aubert drew forth another, and Michael was ordered to proceed as fast as possible. They passed the place, however, without being attacked; the rovers being probably unprepared for the opportunity, and too busy about their supper to feel much interest, at the moment, in anything besides.

After a league and a half more passed in darkness, the travellers arrived at Beaujeu, and drove up to the only inn the place afforded; which, though superior to any they had seen since they entered the mountains, was bad enough.

The surgeon of the town was immediately sent for, if a surgeon he could be called, who prescribed for horses as well as for men, and shaved faces at least as dexterously as he set bones. After examining Valancourt's arm, and perceiving that the bullet had passed through the flesh without touching the bone, he dressed it, and left him with a solemn prescription of quiet, which his patient was not inclined to obey. The delight of ease had now succeeded to pain—for ease may be allowed to assume a positive quality when contrasted with anguish—and his spirits thus re-animated, he wished to partake of the conversation of St. Aubert and Emily, who, released from so many apprehensions, were uncommonly cheerful. Late as it was, however, St. Aubert was obliged to go out with the landlord to buy meat for supper; and Emily, who, during this interval, had been absent as long as she could, upon excuses of looking to their accommodation, which she found rather better than she expected, was compelled to return and converse with Valancourt alone. They talked of the character of the scenes they had passed, of the natural history of the country, of poetry, and of St. Aubert, a subject on which Emily always spoke and listened to with peculiar pleasure.

The travellers passed an agreeable evening; but St. Aubert was fatigued with his journey, and as Valancourt seemed again sensible of pain, they separated soon after supper.

In the morning, St. Aubert found that Valancourt had passed a restless night; that he was feverish, and his wound very painful. The surgeon, when he dressed it, advised him to remain quietly at Beaujeu; advice which was too reasonable to be rejected. St. Aubert, however, had no favourable opinion of this practitioner, and was anxious to commit Valancourt into more skilful hands; but, learning upon inquiry that there was no town within several leagues, which seemed more like to afford better advice, he altered the plan of his journey, and determined to await the recovery of Valancourt, who, with somewhat more ceremony than sincerity, made many objections to this delay.

By order of his surgeon, Valancourt did not go out of the house that day; but St. Aubert and Emily surveyed with delight the environs of the town, situated at the feet of the Pyrenean Alps, that rose some in abrupt precipices, and others swelling with woods of cedar, fir, and cypress, which stretched nearly to their highest summits. The cheerful green of the beech and mountain-ash was sometimes seen, like a gleam of light, amidst the dark verdure of the forest; and sometimes a torrent poured its sparkling flood high among the woods.

Valancourt's indisposition detained the travellers at Beaujeu several days, during which interval St. Aubert had observed his disposition and his talents with the philosophic inquiry so natural to him. He saw a frank and generous nature, full of ardour, highly susceptible of whatever is grand and beautiful, but impetuous, wild, and somewhat romantic. Valancourt had known little of the world. His perceptions were clear, and his feelings just ; his indignation of an unworthy or his admiration of a generous action were expressed in terms of equal vehemence. St. Aubert sometimes smiled at his warmth, but seldom checked it ; and often repeated to himself, ' This young man has never been at Paris.' A sigh sometimes followed this silent ejaculation. He determined not to leave Valancourt till he should be perfectly recovered ; and, as he was now well enough to travel, though not able to manage his horse, St. Aubert invited him to accompany him for a few days in the carriage. This he the more readily did, since he had discovered that Valancourt was of a family of the same name in Gascony, with whose respectability he was well acquainted. The latter accepted the offer with great pleasure, and they again set forward among these romantic wilds towards Rousillon.

They travelled leisurely, stopping wherever a scene uncommonly grand appeared ; frequently alighting to walk to an eminence, whither the mules could not go, from which the prospect opened in greater magnificence ; and often sauntering over hillocks covered with lavender, wild thyme, juniper, and tamarisk, and under the shades of woods, between whose boles they caught the long mountain vista, sublime beyond anything that Emily had ever imagined.

St. Aubert sometimes amused himself with botanising, while Valancourt and Emily strolled on ; he pointing out to her notice the objects that particularly charmed him, and reciting beautiful passages from such of the Latin and Italian poets as he had heard her admire. In the pauses of conversation, when he thought himself not observed, he frequently fixed his eyes pensively on her countenance, which expressed with so much animation the taste and energy of her mind ; and when he spoke again there was a peculiar tenderness in the tone of his voice, that defeated any attempt to conceal his sentiments. By degrees these silent pauses became more frequent ; till Emily, only, betrayed an anxiety to interrupt them ; and she, who had been hitherto reserved, would now talk again, and again, of the woods and the valleys and the mountains, to avoid the danger of sympathy and silence.

From Beaujeu the road had constantly ascended, conducting the travellers into the higher regions of the air, where immense glaciers exhibited their frozen horrors, and eternal snow whitened the summits of the mountains. They often paused to contemplate these stupendous scenes, and, seated on some wild cliff, where only the ilex or the larch could flourish, looked over dark forests of fir, and precipices where human foot had never wandered, into the glen—so deep, that the thunder of the torrent, which was seen to foam along the bottom, was scarcely heard to murmur. Over these crags rose others of stupendous height and fantastic shape ; some shooting into cones ; others impending far over their base, in huge masses of granite, along whose broken ridges was often lodged a weight of snow, that, trembling even to the vibration of a sound, threatened to bear destruction in its course to the vale. Around, on every side, far as the eye could penetrate, were seen only forms of grandeur—the long perspective of mountain tops, tinged with ethereal blue, or white with snow ; valleys of ice, and forests of gloomy fir. The serenity and clearness of the air in these high regions were particularly delightful to the travellers ; it seemed to inspire them with a finer spirit, and diffused an indescribable complacency over their minds. They had no words to express the sublime emotions they felt. A solemn expression characterised the feelings of St. Aubert ; tears often came to his eyes, and he frequently walked away from his companions. Valancourt now and then spoke, to point to Emily's notice some feature of the scene. The thinness of the atmosphere, through which every object came so distinctly to the eye, surprised and deluded her, who could scarcely believe that objects which appeared so near, were in reality so distant. The deep silence of these solitudes was broken only at intervals by the scream of the vultures seen cowering round some cliff below, or by the cry of the eagle sailing high in the air ; except when the travellers listened to the hollow thunder that sometimes muttered at their feet. While, above, the deep blue of the heavens was unobscured by the lightest cloud, half way down the mountains long billows of vapour were frequently seen rolling, now wholly excluding the country below, and now opening, and partially revealing its features. Emily delighted to observe the grandeur of these clouds as they changed in shape and tints, and to watch their various effect on the lower world, whose features, partly veiled, were continually assuming new forms of sublimity.

After traversing these regions for many leagues, they began to descend towards Rousillon, and features of beauty then mingled with the scene. Yet the travellers did not look back without some regret to the sublime objects they had quitted ; though the eye, fatigued with the extension of its powers, was glad to repose on the verdure of woods and pastures, that now hung on the margin of the river below ; to view again the humble cottage shaded by cedars, the playful group of mountaineer children, and the flowery nooks that appeared among the hills.

As they descended, they saw at a distance, on the right, one of the grand passes of the Pyrenees into Spain, gleaming with its battlements and towers to the splendour of the setting rays ; yellow tops of woods colouring the steeps below, while far above aspired the snowy points of the mountains, still reflecting a rosy hue.

St. Aubert began to look out for the little town he had been directed to by the people of Beaujeu, and where he meant to pass the night ; but no habitation yet appeared. Of its distance Valancourt could not assist him to judge, for he had never been so far along this chain of Alps before. There was, however, a road to guide them ; and there could be little doubt that it was the right one ; for, since they had left Beaujeu, there had been no variety of tracks to perplex or mislead.

The sun now gave his last light, and St. Aubert bade the muleteer proceed with all possible dispatch. He found, indeed, the lassitude of illness return upon him, after a day of uncommon fatigue both of body and mind, and he longed for repose. His anxiety was not soothed by observing a numerous train, consisting of men, horses, and loaded mules, winding down the steeps of an opposite mountain, appearing and disappearing at intervals among the woods, so that its numbers could not be judged of. Something bright, like arms, glanced in the setting ray, and the military dress was distinguishable upon the men who were in the van, and on others scattered among the troop that followed. As these wound into the vale, the rear of the party emerged from the woods, and exhibited a band of soldiers. St. Aubert's apprehensions now subsided ; he had no doubt that the train before him consisted of smugglers, who, in conveying prohibited goods over the Pyrenees, had been encountered and conquered by a party of troops.

The travellers had lingered so long among the sublimer scenes of these mountains, that they found themselves entirely mistaken in their calculation that they could reach Montigny at sun-set ; but, as they wound along the valley, they saw, on a rude Alpine bridge that united two lofty crags of the glen, a group of mountaineer children amusing themselves with dropping pebbles into a torrent below, and watching the stones plunge into the water, that threw up its white spray high in the air as it received them, and returned a sullen sound, which the echoes of the mountains prolonged. Under the bridge was seen a perspective of the valley, with its cataract descending among the rocks, and a cottage on the cliff overshadowed with pines. It appeared that they could not be far from some small town. St. Aubert bade the muleteer stop, and then called to the children to inquire if he was near Montigny ; but the distance, and the roaring of the waters, would not suffer his voice to be heard ; and the crags adjoining the bridge were of such tremendous height and steepness, that to have climbed either would have been scarcely practicable to a person unacquainted with the ascent. St. Aubert, therefore, did not waste more moments in delay. They continued to travel long after twilight had obscured the road, which was so broken, that, now thinking it safer to walk than to ride, they all alighted. The moon was rising, but her light was yet too feeble to assist them. While they stepped carefully on, they heard the vesper-bell of a convent. The twilight would not permit them to distinguish anything like a building, but the sounds seemed to come from some woods that overhung an acclivity to the right. Valancourt proposed to go in search of this convent.

'If they will not accommodate us with a night's lodging,' said he, ' they may certainly inform us how far we are from Montigny, and direct us towards it.'

He was bounding forward, without waiting St. Aubert's reply, when the latter stopped him.

'I am very weary,' said St. Aubert, 'and wish for nothing so much as for immediate rest. We will all go to the convent ; your good looks would defeat our purpose ; but when they see mine and Emily's exhausted countenance, they will scarcely deny us repose.'

As he said this, he took Emily's arm within his, and, telling Michael to wait a while in the road with the carriage, they began to ascend towards the convent, guided by the bell of the convent. His steps were feeble, and Valancourt offered him his arm, which he accepted. The moon now threw a faint light over their path, and, soon after, enabled them to distinguish some towers rising above the tops of the woods. Still following the note of the bell, they entered the shade of those woods, lighted only by the moon-beams, that glided down between the leaves, and threw a tremulous uncertain gleam upon the steep track they were winding. The gloom, and the silence that prevailed (except when the bell returned upon the air), together with the wildness of the surrounding scene, struck Emily with a degree of fear, which, however, the voice and conversation of Valancourt somewhat repressed.

When they had been some time ascending, St. Aubert complained of weariness ; and they stopped to rest upon a little green summit, where the trees opened, and admitted the moon-light. He sat down upon the turf, between Emily and Valancourt. The bell had now ceased, and the deep repose of the scene was undisturbed by any sound; for the low dull murmur of some distant torrent might be said to soothe rather than to interrupt the silence. Before them extended the valley they had quitted: its rocks and woods to the left, just silvered by the rays, formed a contrast to the deep shadow that involved the opposite cliffs, whose fringed summits only were tipped with light; while the distant perspective of the valley was lost in the yellow mist of moonlight. The travellers sat for some time wrapt in the complacency which such scenes inspire.

'These scenes,' said Valancourt, at length, 'soften the heart like the notes of sweet music, and inspire that delicious melancholy which no person, who had felt it once, would resign for the gayest pleasures. They waken our best and purest feelings; disposing us to benevolence, pity, and friendship. Those whom I love, I always seem to love more in such an hour as this.' His voice trembled, and he paused.

St. Aubert was silent: Emily perceived a warm tear fall upon the hand he held; she knew the object of his thoughts—hers, too, had for some time been occupied by the remembrance of her mother. He seemed by an effort to rouse himself. 'Yes,' said he, with a half-suppressed sigh, 'the memory of those we love—of times for ever past!—in such an hour as this steals upon the mind like a strain of distant music in the stillness of night— all tender and harmonious as this landscape, sleeping in the mellow moon-light.' After a pause of a moment, St. Aubert added, 'I have always fancied that I thought with more clearness and precision at such an hour, than at any other; and that heart must be insensible in a great degree, that does not soften to its influence. But many such there are.'

Valancourt sighed.

'Are there, indeed, many such?' said Emily.

'A few years hence, my dear Emily,' replied St. Aubert, 'and you may smile at the recollection of that question—if you do not weep with it. But come, I am somewhat refreshed: let us proceed.'

Having emerged from the woods, they saw, upon a turfy hillock above, the convent of which they were in search. A high wall that surrounded it, led them to an ancient gate, at which they knocked; and the poor monk who opened it conducted them into a small adjoining room, where he desired they would wait while he informed the superior of their request.

In this interval several friars came in separately to look at them; and at length the first monk returned, and they followed him to a room where the superior was sitting in an arm-chair, with a large folio volume, printed in black letter, open on a desk before him. He received them with courtesy, though he did not rise from his seat; and, having asked them a few questions, granted their request.

After a short conversation, formal and solemn on the part of the superior, they withdrew to the apartment where they were to sup; and Valancourt, whom one of the inferior friars civilly desired to accompany, went to seek Michael and his mules. They had not descended half way down the cliffs before they heard the voice of the muleteer echoing far and wide.

Sometimes he called on St. Aubert, and sometimes on Valancourt; who having at length convinced him that he had nothing to fear, either for himself or his master, and having disposed of him for the night in a cottage on the skirts of the woods, returned to sup with his friends on such sober fare as the monks thought it prudent to set before them.

While St. Aubert was too much indisposed to share it, Emily, in her anxiety for her father, forgot herself; and Valancourt, silent and thoughtful, yet never inattentive to them, appeared particularly solicitious to accommodate and relieve St. Aubert; who often observed, while his daughter was pressing him to eat, or adjusting the pillow she had placed in the back of his arm-chair, that Valancourt fixed on her a look of pensive tenderness, which she was not displeased to understand.

They separated at an early hour, and retired to their respective apartments.

Emily was shown to hers by a nun of the convent, whom she was glad to dismiss, for her heart was melancholy, and her attention so much abstracted, that conversation with a stranger was painful.

She thought her father daily declining; and attributed his present fatigue more to the feeble state of his frame than to the difficulty of the journey. A train of gloomy ideas haunted her mind, till she fell asleep.

In about two hours after, she was awakened by the chiming of a bell, and then heard quick steps pass along the gallery into which her chamber opened. She was so little accustomed to the manners of a convent, as to be alarmed by this circumstance: her fears ever alive for her father, suggested that he was very ill, and she arose in haste to go to him. Having paused, however, to let the persons in the gallery pass before she opened her door, her thoughts in the mean time recovered from the confusion of sleep, and she understood that the bell was the call of the monks to prayers.

It had now ceased; and all being again still, she forbore to go to St. Aubert's room. Her mind was not disposed for immediate sleep, and the moon-light, that shone into her chamber, invited her to open the casement, and look out upon the country.

It was a still and beautiful night—the sky was unobscured by any cloud, and scarce a leaf of the woods beneath trembled in the air.

As she listened, the midnight hymn of the monks rose softly from a chapel that stood on one of the lower cliffs,—a holy strain that seemed to ascend through the silence of night to heaven ; and her thoughts ascended with it.

From the consideration of His works, her mind rose to the adoration of the Deity, in His goodness and power : wherever she turned her view, whether on the sleeping earth, or to the vast regions of space glowing with worlds beyond the reach of human thought, the sublimity of God and the majesty of His presence appeared.

Her eyes were filled with tears of awful love and admiration ; and she felt that pure devotion, superior to all the distinctions of human systems, which lifts the soul above this world, and seems to expand it into a nobler nature—such devotion as can, perhaps, only be experienced when the mind, rescued for a moment from the humbleness of earthly considerations, aspires to contemplate His power in the sublimity of His works, and His goodness in the infinity of His blessings.

'. . . . . Is it not now the hour,
The holy hour, when, to the cloudless height
Of yon starr'd concave, climbs the full-orb'd moon,
And to this nether world, in solemn stillness,
Gives sign, that, to the listening ear of Heaven,
Religion's voice should plead? The very babe
Knows this, and, 'chance awaked, his little hands
Lifts to the gods, and on his innocent couch
Calls down a blessing.'
                                CARACTACUS.

The midnight chant of the monks soon after dropped into silence ; but Emily remained at the casement watching the setting moon, and the valley sinking into deep shade, and willing to prolong her present state of mind. At length she retired to her mattress, and sunk into tranquil slumber.

———

CHAPTER V.

'. . . . . While in the rosy vale
Love breathed his infant sighs, from anguish free.'
                                THOMSON.

ST. AUBERT, sufficiently restored by a night's repose to pursue his journey, set out in the morning, with his family and Valancourt for Rousillon, which he hoped to reach before night-fall. The scenes through which they now passed were as wild and romantic as any they had yet observed ; with this difference, that beauty, every now and then, softened the landscape into smiles.

Little woody recesses appeared among the mountains, covered with bright verdure and flowers ; or a pastoral valley opened its grassy bosom in the shade of the cliffs, with flocks and herds loitering along the banks of a rivulet that refreshed it with perpetual green.

St. Aubert could not repent the having taken this fatiguing road, though he was this day, also, frequently obliged to alight, to walk along the rugged precipice, and to climb the steep and flinty mountain. The wonderful sublimity and variety of the prospects repaid him for all this ; and the enthusiasm with which they were viewed by his young companions, heightened his own, and awakened a remembrance of all the delightful emotions of his early days, when the sublime charms of nature were first unveiled to him. He found great pleasure in conversing with Valancourt, and in listening to his ingenious remarks : the fire and simplicity of his manners seemed to render him a characteristic figure in the scenes around them ; and St. Aubert discovered in his sentiments the justness and the dignity of an elevated mind unbiassed by intercourse with the world.

He perceived that his opinions were formed, rather than imbibed—were more the result of thought, than of learning : of the world he seemed to know nothing, for he believed well of all mankind ; and this opinion gave him the reflected image of his own heart.

St. Aubert, as he sometimes lingered to examine the wild plants in his path, often looked forward with pleasure to Emily and Valancourt as they strolled on together—he with a countenance of animated delight pointing to her attention some grand feature of the scene ; and she listening and observing with a look of tender seriousness that spoke the elevation of her mind. They appeared like two lovers who had never strayed beyond these their native mountains ; whose situation had secluded them from the frivolities of common life ; whose ideas were simple and grand, like the landscapes among which they moved ; and who knew no other happiness than in the union of pure and affectionate hearts. St. Aubert smiled, and sighed at the romantic picture of felicity his fancy drew, and sighed again to think that nature and simplicity were so little known to the world, as that their pleasures were thought romantic.

'The world,' said he, pursuing this train of thought, 'ridicules a passion which it seldom feels : its scenes, and its interests distract the mind, deprave the taste, corrupt the heart ; and love cannot exist in a heart that has lost the meek dignity of innocence. Virtue and taste are nearly the same ; for virtue is little more than active taste ; and the most delicate affections of each combine in real love. How then are we to look for love in great cities, where selfishness, dissipation, and insincerity supply the place of tenderness, simplicity, and truth?

It was near noon, when the travellers, having arrived at a piece of steep and dangerous road, alighted to walk. The road wound up an ascent that was clothed with wood, and instead of following the carriage, they entered the refreshing shade. A dewy coolness was diffused upon the air, which, with the bright verdure of turf that grew under the trees, the mingled fragrance of flowers and of balm, thyme, and lavender that enriched it, and the grandeur of the pines, beech, and chestnuts that overshadowed them rendered this a most delicious retreat. . Sometimes the thick foliage excluded all view of the country ; at others, it admitted some partial catches of the distant scenery which gave hints to the imagination to picture landscapes more interesting, more impressive than any that had been presented to the eye. The wanderers often lingered to indulge in these reveries of fancy.

The pauses of silence, such as had formerly interrupted the conversations of Valancourt and Emily, were more frequent to-day than ever. Valancourt often dropped suddenly from the most animating vivacity into fits of deep musing ; and there was sometimes an unaffected melancholy in his smile, which Emily could not avoid understanding, for her heart was interested in the sentiment it spoke.

St. Aubert was refreshed by the shades, and they continued to saunter under them, following as nearly as they could guess the direction of the road till they perceived that they had totally lost it. They had continued near the brow of the precipice, allured by the scenery it exhibited, while the road wound far away over the cliff above. Valancourt called loudly to Michael, but heard no voice, except his echoing among the rocks, and his various efforts to regain the road were equally unsuccessful. While they were thus circumstanced, they perceived a shepherd's cabin between the boles of the trees at some distance, and Valancourt bounded on first to ask assistance. When he reached it, he saw only two little children at play on the turf before the door. He looked into the hut, but no person was there ; and the eldest of the boys told him that their father was with his flocks, and their mother was gone down into the vale, but would be back presently. As he stood considering what was further to be done, on a sudden he heard Michael's voice roaring forth most manfully among the cliffs above, till he made their echoes ring. Valancourt immediately answered the call, and endeavoured to make his way through the thicket that clothed the steeps, following the direction of the sound. After much struggle over brambles and precipices, he reached Michael, and at length prevailed with him to be silent, and to listen to him. The road was at a considerable distance from the spot where St. Aubert and Emily were ; the carriage could not easily return to the entrance of the wood ; and since it would be very fatiguing for St. Aubert to climb the long and steep road to the place

where it now stood, Valancourt was anxious to find a more easy ascent by the way he had himself passed.

Meanwhile St. Aubert and Emily approached the cottage, and rested themselves on a rustic bench fastened between two pines which overshadowed it, till Valancourt, whose steps they had observed, should return.

The eldest of the children desisted from his play, and stood still to observe the strangers, while the younger continued his little gambols, and teased his brother to join in them. St. Aubert looked with pleasure upon this picture of infantine simplicity till it brought to his remembrance his own boys, whom he had lost about the age of these, and their lamented mother ; and he sunk into a thoughtfulness ; which Emily observing, she immediately began to sing one of those simple and lively airs he was so fond of, and which she knew how to give with the most captivating sweetness. St. Aubert smiled on her through his tears, took her hand and pressed it affectionately, and then tried to dissipate the melancholy reflections that lingered in his mind.

While she sung, Valancourt approached, who was unwilling to interrupt her, and paused at a little distance to listen. When she had concluded, he joined the party, and told them that he had found Michael, as well as a way by which he thought they could ascend the cliff to the carriage. He pointed to the woody steeps above, which St. Aubert surveyed with an anxious eye. He was already wearied by his walk, and this ascent was formidable to him. He thought, however, it would be less toilsome than the long and broken road, and he determined to attempt it ; but Emily, ever watchful of his ease, proposing that he should rest and dine before they proceeded further, Valancourt went to the carriage for the refreshments deposited there.

On his return, he proposed removing a little higher up the mountain, to where the woods opened upon a grand and extensive prospect ; and thither they were preparing to go, when they saw a young woman join the children, and caress and weep over them.

The travellers, interested by her distress, stopped to observe her. She took the youngest of the children in her arms, and, perceiving the strangers, hastily dried her tears and proceeded to the cottage. St. Aubert, on inquiring the occasion of her sorrow, learned that her husband, who was a shepherd, and lived here in the summer months to watch over the flocks he led to feed upon these mountains, had lost on the preceding night his little all. A gang of gipsies, who had for some time infested the neighbourhood, had driven away several of his master's sheep. 'Jacques,' added the shepherd's wife, ' had saved a little money, and had bought a few sheep with it, and now they must go to his master for those that are stolen ; and what is worse than all, his master, when he comes to know how it is, will trust him no longer with the care of his flocks, for he is a hard man ; and then what is to become of our children ?'

The innocent countenance of the woman, and the simplicity of her manner in relating her grievance, inclined St. Aubert to believe her story ; and Valancourt, convinced that it was true, asked eagerly what was the value of the stolen sheep ; on hearing which he turned away with a look of disappointment. St. Aubert put some money into her hand ; Emily too gave something from her little purse, and they walked towards the cliff ; but Valancourt lingered behind, and spoke to the shepherd's wife, who was now weeping with gratitude and surprise. He inquired how much money was yet wanting to replace the stolen sheep, and found that it was a sum very little short of all he had about him. He was perplexed and distressed.

'This sum, then,' said he to himself, 'would make this poor family completely happy—it is in my power to give it—to make them completely happy ! But what is to become of me?—how shall I contrive to reach home with the little money that will remain ?'

For a moment he stood, unwilling to forego the luxury of raising a family from ruin to happiness, yet considering the difficulties of pursuing his journey with so small a sum as would be left.

While he was in this state of perplexity, the shepherd himself appeared : his children ran to meet him ; he took one of them in his arms, and, with the other clinging to his coat, came forward with a loitering step. His forlorn and melancholy look determined Valancourt at once ; he threw down all the money he had, except a very few louis, and bounded away after St. Aubert and Emily, who were proceeding slowly up the steep. Valancourt had seldom felt his heart so light as at this moment ; his gay spirits danced with pleasure ; every object around him appeared more interesting or beautiful than before. St. Aubert observed the uncommon vivacity of his countenance :

'What has pleased you so much ?' said he.

'O what a lovely day !' replied Valancourt ; 'how brightly the sun shines ! how pure is this air ! what enchanting scenery !'

'It is indeed enchanting,' said St. Aubert, whom early experience had taught to understand the nature of Valancourt's present feelings. 'What pity that the wealthy, who can command such sunshine, should ever pass their days in gloom—in the cold shade of selfishness ! For you, my young friend, may the sun always shine as brightly as at this moment ! may your own conduct always give you the sunshine of benevolence and reason united !'

Valancourt, highly flattered by this compli-

ment, could make no reply but by a smile of gratitude.

They continued to wind under the woods, between the grassy knolls of the mountain, and as they reached the shady summit which he had pointed out, the whole party burst into an exclamation. Behind the spot where they stood, the rock rose perpendicularly in a massy wall to a considerable height, and then branched out into overhanging crags. Their grey tints were well contrasted by the bright hues of the plants and wild flowers that grew in their fractured sides, and were deepened by the gloom of the pines and cedars that waved above. The steeps below, over which the eye passed abruptly to the valley, were fringed with thickets of alpine shrubs ; and lower still appeared the tufted tops of the chestnut woods that clothed their base—among which peeped forth the shepherd's cottage just left by the travellers, with its bluish smoke curling high in the air. On every side appeared the majestic summits of the Pyrenees ; some exhibiting tremendous crags of marble, whose appearance was changing every instant as the varying lights fell upon their surface ; others, still higher, displaying only snowy points, while their lower steeps were covered almost invariably with forests of pine, larch, and oak, that stretched down to the vale. This was one of the narrow valleys that open from the Pyrenees into the country of Rousillon, and whose green pastures and cultivated beauty form a decided and wonderful contrast to the romantic grandeur that environs it. Through a vista of the mountains appeared the lowlands of Rousillon, tinted with the blue haze of distance, as they united with the waters of the Mediterranean ; where, on a promontory which marked the boundary of the shore, stood a lonely beacon, over which were seen circling flights of sea-fowl. Beyond appeared now and then a stealing sail, white with the sun-beam, and whose progress was perceivable by its approach to the light-house. Sometimes, too, was seen a sail so distant, that it served only to mark the line of separation between the sky and the waves.

On the other side of the valley, immediately opposite to the spot where the travellers rested, a rocky pass opened towards Gascony. Here no sign of cultivation appeared. The rocks of granite that screened the glen rose abruptly from their base, and stretched their barren points to the clouds, unvaried with woods, and uncheered even by a hunter's cabin. Sometimes, indeed, a gigantic larch threw its long shade over the precipice, and here and there a cliff reared on its brow a monumental cross, to tell the traveller the fate of him who had ventured thither before. This spot seemed the very haunt of banditti ; and Emily, as she looked down upon it, almost expected to see them stealing out from some hollow cave to look for their prey. Soon after an object not less terrific struck her—a gibbet, standing on a point of rock near the entrance of the pass, and immediately over one of the crosses she had before observed. These were hieroglyphics that told a plain and dreadful story. She forbore to point it out to St. Aubert; but it threw a gloom over her spirits, and made her anxious to hasten forward, that they might with certainty reach Rousillon before nightfall. It was necessary, however, that St. Aubert should take some refreshment; and seating themselves on the short dry turf, they opened the basket of provisions, while

'. . . . . by breezy murmurs cool'd,
Broad o'er *their* heads the verdant cedars wave,
And high palmetos lift their graceful shade.

. . . . *they* draw
Ethereal soul, their drink reviving gales
Profusely breathing from the piney groves,
And vales of fragrance; there at distance hear
The roaring floods and cataracts.'

THOMSON.

St. Aubert was revived by rest, and by the serene air of this summit; and Valancourt was so charmed with all around, and with the conversation of his companions, that he seemed to have forgotten he had any further to go. Having concluded their simple repast, they gave a long farewell look to the scene, and again began to ascend. St. Aubert rejoiced when he reached the carriage, which Emily entered with him; but Valancourt, willing to take a more extensive view of the enchanting country, into which they were about to descend, than he could do from a carriage, loosened his dogs, and once more bounded with them along the banks of the road. He often quitted it for points that promised a wider prospect; and the slow pace at which the mules travelled, allowed him to overtake them with ease. Whenever a scene of uncommon magnificence appeared, he hastened to inform St. Aubert, who, though he was too much tired to walk himself, sometimes made the chaise wait, while Emily went to the neighbouring cliff.

It was evening when they descended the lower Alps that bind Rousillon and form a majestic barrier round that charming country, leaving it open only on the east to the Mediterranean. The gay tints of cultivation once more beautified the landscape; for the lowlands were coloured with the richest hues which a luxuriant climate and an industrious people can awaken into life. Groves of orange and lemon perfumed the air, their ripe fruit glowing among the foliage; while, sloping to the plains, extensive vineyards spread their treasures. Beyond these, woods and pastures, and mingled towns and hamlets, stretched towards the sea, on whose bright surface gleamed many a distant sail; while over the whole scene was diffused the purple glow of evening. This landscape, with the surrounding Alps, did indeed present a

perfect picture of the lovely and the sublime—of 'beauty sleeping in the lap of horror.'

The travellers, having reached the plains, proceeded between hedges of flowering myrtle and pomegranate to the town of Arles, where they proposed to rest for the night. They met with simple but neat accommodation, and would have passed a happy evening, after the toils and the delights of this day, had not the approaching separation thrown a gloom over their spirits. It was St. Aubert's plan to proceed on the morrow to the borders of the Mediterranean, and travel along its shores into Languedoc; and Valancourt, since he was now nearly recovered, and had no longer a pretence for continuing with his new friends, resolved to leave them here. St. Aubert, who was much pleased with him, invited him to go further, but did not repeat the invitation; and Valancourt had resolution enough to forego the temptation of accepting it, that he might prove himself not unworthy of the favour. On the following morning, therefore, they were to part; St. Aubert to pursue his way to Languedoc, and Valancourt to explore new scenes among the mountains, on his return home. During this evening he was often silent and thoughtful; St. Aubert's manner towards him was affectionate, though grave; and Emily was serious, though she made frequent efforts to appear cheerful. After one of the most melancholy evenings they had yet passed together, they separated for the night.

CHAPTER VI.

'I care not, Fortune! what you me deny;
You cannot rob me of free Nature's grace,
You cannot shut the windows of the sky,
Through which Aurora shows her brightening
          face;
You cannot bar my constant feet to trace
The woods and lawns, by living stream, at eve:
Let health my nerves and finer fibres brace,
And I their toys to the great children leave:
Of fancy, reason, virtue, nought can me bereave.'

THOMSON.

IN the morning Valancourt breakfasted with St. Aubert and Emily, neither of whom seemed much refreshed by sleep. The languor of illness still hung over St. Aubert, and to Emily's fears his disorder appeared to be increasing fast upon him. She watched his looks with anxious affection, and their expression was always faithfully reflected in her own.

At the commencement of their acquaintance, Valancourt had made known his name and family. St. Aubert was not a stranger to either; for the family estates, which were now in the possession of an elder brother of Valancourt, were little more than twenty miles distant from La Vallée, and he had sometimes met the elder Valancourt on visits in the neighbourhood. This knowledge had made him more willingly receive his present companion ; for, though his countenance and manners would have won him the acquaintance of St. Aubert, who was very apt to trust to the intelligence of his own eyes with respect to countenances, he would not have accepted these as sufficient introductions to that of his daughter.

The breakfast was almost as silent as the supper of the preceding night ; but their musing was at length interrupted by the sound of the carriage wheels which were to bear away St. Aubert and Emily. Valancourt started from his chair, and went to the window ; it was indeed the carriage, and he returned to his seat without speaking. The moment was now come when they must part. St. Aubert told Valancourt that he hoped he would never pass La Vallée without favouring him with a visit ; and Valancourt, eagerly thanking him, assured him that he never would ; as he said which he looked timidly at Emily, who tried to smile away the seriousness of her spirits. They passed a few minutes in interesting conversation, and St. Aubert then led the way to the carriage, Emily and Valancourt following in silence. The latter lingered at the door several minutes after they were seated, and none of the party seemed to have courage enough to say — Farewell ! At length St. Aubert pronounced the melancholy word, which Emily passed to Valancourt, who returned it with a dejected smile, and the carriage drove on.

The travellers remained for some time in a state of tranquil pensiveness which is not unpleasing.

St. Aubert interrupted it by observing : ' This is a very promising young man ; it is many years since I have been so much pleased with any person, on so short an acquaintance. He brings back to my memory the days of my youth, when every scene was new and delightful ! ' St. Aubert sighed, and sunk again into a reverie ; and as Emily looked back upon the road they had passed, Valancourt was seen, at the door of the little inn, following them with his eyes. He perceived her, and waved his hand ; and she returned the adieu till the winding road shut her from his sight.

' I remember when I was about his age, resumed St. Hubert ; and I thought and felt exactly as he does. The world was opening upon me then ; now—it is closing.'

' My dear sir, do not think so gloomily, said Emily in a trembling voice ; I hope you have many, many years to live—for your own sake—for *my* sake.'

' Ah, my Emily ! replied St. Aubert, for thy sake ! Well—I hope it is so.'

He wiped away a tear that was stealing down his cheek, threw a smile upon his countenance, and said in a cheering voice,

' There is something in the ardour and ingenuousness of youth, which is particularly pleasing to the contemplation of an old man, if his feelings have not been entirely corroded by the world. It is cheering and reviving, like the view of spring to a sick person ; his mind catches somewhat of the spirit of the season, and his eyes are lighted up with the transient sunshine. Valancourt is this spring to me.'

Emily, who pressed her father's hand affectionately, had never before listened with so much pleasure to the praises he bestowed ; no, not even when he had bestowed them on herself.

They travelled on, among vineyards, woods, and pastures, delighted with the romantic beauty of the landscape, which was bounded on one side by the grandeur of the Pyrenees, and on the other by the ocean ; and soon after noon they reached the town of Colioure, situated on the Mediterranean. Here they dined, and rested till towards the cool of day, when they pursued their way along the shores —those enchanting shores ! which extend to Languedoc.

Emily gazed with enthusiasm on the vastness of the sea, its surface varying as the lights and shadows fell, and on its woody banks mellowed with autumnal tints.

St. Aubert was impatient to reach Perpignan, where he expected letters from M. Quesnel ; and it was the expectation of these letters that had induced him to leave Colioure, for his feeble frame had required immediate rest.

After travelling a few miles, he fell asleep ; and Emily, who had put two or three books into the carriage on leaving La Vallée, had now the leisure for looking into them. She sought for one in which Valancourt had been reading the day before, and hoped for the pleasure of retracing a page over which the eyes of a beloved friend had lately passed, of dwelling on the passages which he had admired, and of permitting them to speak to her in the language of his own mind, and to bring himself to her presence. On searching for the book she could find it no where, but in its stead perceived a volume of Petrarch's poems, that had belonged to Valancourt, whose name was written in it, and from which he had frequently read passages to her with all the pathetic expression that characterized the feelings of the author.

She hesitated in believing, what would have been sufficiently apparent to almost any other person, that he had purposely left this book instead of the one she had lost, and that love had prompted the exchange ; but having opened it with impatient pleasure, and observed the lines of his pencil drawn along the various passages he had read aloud, and under others more descriptive of delicate tenderness than he had dared to trust his voice with, the conviction came at length to her mind.

For some moments she was conscious only of being beloved ; then, the recollection of all the variations of tone and countenance with which he had recited these sonnets, and of the soul which spoke in their expression, pressed to her memory, and she wept over the memorial of his affection.

They arrived at Perpignan soon after sunset, where, St Aubert found, as he had expected, letters from M. Quesnel ; the contents of which so evidently and grievously affected him, that Emily was alarmed, and pressed him, as far as her delicacy would permit, to disclose the occasion of his concern : but he answered her only by tears, and immediately began to talk on other topics.

Emily, though she forbore to press the one most interesting to her, was greatly affected by her father's manner, and passed a night of sleepless solicitude.

In the morning they pursued their journey along the coast towards Leucate, another town on the Mediterranean, situated on the borders of Languedoc and Rousillon.

On the way, Emily renewed the subject of the preceding night, and appeared so deeply affected by St. Aubert's silence and dejection, that he relaxed from his reserve.

' I was unwilling, my dear Emily,' said he, to throw a cloud over the pleasure you receive from these scenes, and meant, therefore, to conceal ' for the present some circumstances, with which, however, you must at length have been made acquainted. But your anxiety has defeated my purpose ; you suffer as much from this, perhaps, as you will do from a knowledge of the facts I have to relate.

' M. Quesnel's visit proved an unhappy one to me ; he came to tell me part of the news he has confirmed. You may have heard me mention a M. Motteville of Paris, but you did not know that the chief of my personal property was invested in his hands.

' I had great confidence in him, and I am yet willing to believe that he is not wholly unworthy of my esteem. A variety of circumstances have concurred to ruin him, and—I am ruined with him.'

St. Aubert paused to conceal his emotion.

' The letters I have just received from M. Quesnel,' resumed he,' struggling to speak with firmness, ' inclosed others from Motteville, which confirmed all I dreaded.'

' Must we then quit La Vallée ? ' said Emily, after a long pause of silence.

' That is yet uncertain,' replied St. Aubert ; it will depend upon the compromise Motteville is able to make with his creditors. My income, you know, was never large, and now it will be reduced to little indeed ! It is for you, Emily—for you my child, that I am most afflicted.' His last words faltered.

Emily smiled tenderly upon him through her tears, and then, endeavouring to overcome her emotion,

' My dear father, said she, do not grieve for me or for yourself ; we may yet be happy ; —if La Vallée remains for us, we must be happy. We will retain only one servant, and you shall scarcely perceive the change in your income. Be comforted, my dear sir ; we shall not feel the want of those luxuries which others value so highly, since we never had a taste for them ; and poverty cannot deprive us of many consolations ; it cannot rob us of the affection we have for each other, or degrade us in our own opinion, or in that of any person whose opinion we ought to value.

St. Aubert concealed his face with his handkerchief, and was unable to speak ; but Emily continued to urge to her father the truths which himself had impressed upon her mind.

' Besides, my dear sir, poverty cannot deprive us of intellectual delights. It cannot deprive you of the comfort of affording me examples of fortitude and benevolence, nor me of the delight of consoling a beloved parent. It cannot deaden our taste for the grand and the beautiful, nor deny us the means of indulging it ; for the scenes of nature—those sublime spectacles, so infinitely superior to all artificial luxuries ! are open for the enjoyment of the poor as well as of the rich. Of what, then, have we to complain, so long as we are not in want of necessaries ? Pleasures, such as wealth cannot buy, will still be ours. We retain, then, the sublime luxuries of nature, and lose only the frivolous ones of art.

St. Aubert could not reply ; he caught Emily to his bosom, their tears flowed together ; but—they were not tears of sorrow. After this language of the heart, all other would have been feeble, and they remained silent for some time. Then St. Aubert conversed as before ; for, if his mind had not recovered its natural tranquillity, it at least assumed the appearance of it.

They reached the romantic town of Leucate early in the day ; but St. Aubert was weary, and they determined to pass the night there. In the evening he exerted himself so far as to walk with his daughter to view the environs, that overlook the lake of Leucate, the Mediterranean, part of Rousillon, with the Pyrenees, and a wide extent of the luxuriant province of Languedoc, now blushing with the ripened vintage which the peasants were beginning to gather. St. Aubert and Emily saw the busy groups, caught the joyous song that was wafted on the breeze, and anticipated with apparent pleasure their next day's journey over this gay region. He designed, however, still to wind along the sea-shore. To return home immediately was partly his wish ; but from this he was withheld by a desire to lengthen the pleasure which the journey gave his daughter, and to try the effect of the sea air on his own disorder.

On the following day, therefore, they recommenced their journey through Languedoc, winding the shores of the Mediterranean; the Pyrenees still forming the magnificent back-ground of their prospects, while on their right was the ocean, and on their left, wide extended plains melting into the blue horizon. St. Aubert was pleased, and conversed much with Emily; yet his cheerfulness was sometimes artificial, and sometimes a shade of melancholy would steal upon his countenance and betray him. This was soon chased away by Emily's smile; who smiled, however with an aching heart, for she saw that his misfortunes preyed upon his mind and upon his enfeebled frame.

It was evening when they reached a small village of Upper Languedoc, where they meant to pass the night, but the place could not afford them beds; for here, too, it was the time of the vintage; and they were obliged to proceed to the next post. The languor of illness and of fatigue, which returned upon St. Aubert, required immediate repose, and the evening was now far advanced; but from necessity there was no appeal, and he ordered Michael to proceed.

The rich plains of Languedoc, which exhibited all the glories of the vintage, with the gaieties of a French festival, no longer awakened St. Aubert to pleasure, whose condition formed a mournful contrast to the hilarity and youthful beauty which surrounded him. As his languid eyes moved over the scene, he considered that they would soon, perhaps, be closed for ever on this world.

'Those distant and sublime mountains,' said he secretly, as he gazed on a chain of the Pyrenees that stretched towards the west, 'these luxuriant plains, this blue vault, the cheerful light of day, will be shut from my eyes! The song of the peasant, the cheering voice of man—will no longer sound for me!'

The intelligent eyes of Emily seemed to read what passed in the mind of her father, and she fixed them on his face with an expression of such tender pity as recalled his thoughts from every desultory object of regret, and he remembered only that he must leave his daughter without protection. This reflection changed regret to agony; he sighed deeply, and remained silent, while she seemed to understand that sigh, for she pressed his hand affectionately, and then turned to the window to conceal her tears. The sun now threw a last yellow gleam on the waves of the Mediterranean, and the gloom of twilight spread fast over the scene, till only a melancholy ray appeared on the western horizon, marking the point where the sun had set amid the vapours of an autumnal evening. A cool breeze now came from the shore, and Emily let down the glass; but the air which was refreshing to health, was as chilling to sickness, and St. Aubert desired that the window might be drawn up. Increasing illness made him now more anxious than ever to finish the day's journey, and he stopped the muleteer to inquire how far they had yet to go to the next post.

He replied, 'Nine miles.'

'I feel I am unable to proceed much further,' said St. Aubert; 'inquire, as you go, if there is any house on the road that would accommodate us for the night.'

He sunk back in the carriage, and Michael, cracking his whip in the air, set off, and continued on the full gallop, till St. Aubert, almost fainting, called to him to stop. Emily looked anxiously from the window, and saw a peasant walking at some little distance on the road, for whom they waited till he came up, when he was asked if there was any house in the neighbourhood that accommodated travellers.

He replied, that he knew of none. 'There is a chateau, indeed, among those woods on the right,' added he, 'but I believe it receives nobody, and I cannot show you the way, for I am almost a stranger here.'

St. Aubert was going to ask him some further question concerning the chateau, but the man abruptly passed on. After some consideration, he ordered Michael to proceed slowly to the woods. Every moment now deepened the twilight and increased the difficulty of finding the road. Another peasant soon after passed.

'Which is the way to the chateau in the woods?' cried Michael.

'The chateau in the woods!' exclaimed the peasant—'Do you mean that with the turret yonder?'

'I don't know as for the turret, as you call it,' said Michael, 'I mean that white piece of a building that we see at a distance there, among the trees.'

'Yes, that is the turret; why, who are you, that you are going thither?' said the man with surprise.

St. Aubert, on hearing this odd question, and observing the peculiar tone in which it was delivered, looked out from the carriage.

'We are travellers,' said he, 'who are in search of a house of accommodation for the night; is there any hereabout?'

'None, Monsieur, unless you have a mind to try your luck yonder,' replied the peasant, pointing to the woods; 'but I would not advise you to go there.'

'To whom does the chateau belong?'

'I scarcely know myself, Monsieur.'

'It is uninhabited, then?'

'No, not uninhabited; the steward and housekeeper are there, I believe.'

On hearing this, St. Aubert determined to

proceed to the chateau, and risk the refusal of being accommodated for the night : he therefore desired the countryman would show Michael the way, and bade him expect reward for his trouble. The man was for a moment silent, and then said that he was going on other business, but that the road could not be missed, if they went up an avenue to the right, to which he pointed. St. Aubert was going to speak, but the peasant wished him good-night, and walked on.

The carriage now moved towards the avenue, which was guarded by a gate ; and Michael having dismounted to open it, they entered between rows of ancient oak and chestnut, whose intermingled branches formed a lofty arch above. There was something so gloomy and desolate in the appearance of this avenue and its lonely silence, that Emily almost shuddered as she passed along ; and recollecting the manner in which the peasant had mentioned the chateau, she gave a mysterious meaning to his words, such as she had not suspected when he uttered them. These apprehensions, however, she tried to check, considering that they were probably the effect of a melancholy imagination, which her father's situation, and a consideration of her own circumstances, had made sensible to every impression.

They passed slowly on, for they were now almost in darkness, which, together with the unevenness of the ground, and the frequent roots of old trees that shot up above the soil, made it necessary to proceed with caution. On a sudden Michael stopped the carriage ; and as St. Aubert looked from the window to inquire the cause, he perceived a figure at some distance moving up the avenue. The dusk would not permit him to distinguish what it was, but he bade Michael go on.

'This seems a wild place,' said Michael ; 'there is no house hereabout ; don't your honour think we had better turn back ?'

' Go a little further, and if we see no house then, we will return to the road,' replied St. Aubert.

Michael proceeded with reluctance ; and the extreme slowness of his pace made St. Aubert look again from the window to hasten him, when again he saw the same figure. He was somewhat startled ; probably the gloominess of the spot made him more liable to alarm than usual. However this might be, he now stopped Michael, and bade him call to the person in the avenue.

' Please your honour, he may be a robber,' said Michael.

' It does not please me,' replied St. Aubert, who could not forbear smiling at the simplicity of his phrase ; 'and we will therefore return to the road, for I see no probability of meeting here with what we seek.'

Michael turned about immediately, and was retracing his way with alacrity, when a voice was heard from among the trees on the left. It was not the voice of command or distress ; but a deep hollow tone, which seemed to be scarcely human. The man whipped his mules till they went as fast as possible, regardless of the darkness, the broken ground, and the necks of the whole party ; nor once stopped till he reached the gate which opened from the avenue into the high road, where he went into a more moderate pace.

' I am very ill,' said St. Aubert, taking his daughter's hand.

' You are worse, then, sir !' said Emily, extremely alarmed by his manner ; ' you are worse, and here is no assistance ! Good God ! what is to be done ?'

He leaned his head on her shoulder, while she endeavoured to support him with her arm ; and Michael was again ordered to stop. When the rattling of the wheels had ceased, music was heard on the air : it was to Emily the voice of Hope.

' Oh ! we are near some human habitation !' said she : ' help may soon be had.'

She listened anxiously ; the sounds were distant, and seemed to come from a remote part of the woods that bordered the road ; and as she looked towards the spot whence they issued, she perceived in the faint moonlight something like a chateau. It was difficult, however, to reach this. St. Aubert was now too ill to bear the motion of the carriage ; Michael could not quit his mules ; and Emily, who still supported her father, feared to leave him, and also feared to venture alone to such a distance, she knew not whither, or to whom. Something, however, it was necessary to determine upon immediately : St. Aubert, therefore, told Michael to proceed slowly ; but they had not gone far, when he fainted, and the carriage was again stopped. He lay quite senseless.

' My dear, dear father !' cried Emily in great agony, who began to fear that he was dying ; ' speak, if it is only one word, to let me hear the sound of your voice !'

But no voice spoke in reply. In an agony of terror she bade Michael bring water from the rivulet that flowed along the road ; and having received some in the man's hat, with trembling hands she sprinkled it over her father's face, which, as the moon's rays now fell upon it, seemed to bear the impression of death. Every emotion of selfish fear now gave way to a stronger influence ; and committing St. Aubert to the care of Michael, who refused to go far from his mules, she stepped from the carriage in search of the chateau she had seen at a distance. It was a still moonlight night, and the music, which yet sounded on the air, directed her steps from the high road up a shadowy lane that led to the woods. Her mind was for some time so entirely occupied by anxiety and terror for her father, that she felt none for herself, till the deepening gloom of the overhanging foliage, which now wholly excluded the moonlight, and the wildness of the place, recalled her to a sense of her adventurous situation. The music had ceased, and she had no guide but chance. For a moment she paused in terrified perplexity; till a sense of her father's condition again overcoming every consideration for herself, she proceeded. The lane terminated in the woods; but she looked round in vain for a house or a human being, and as vainly listened for a sound to guide her. She hurried on, however, not knowing whither, avoiding the recesses of the woods, and endeavouring to keep along their margin, till a rude kind of avenue, which opened upon a moonlight spot, arrested her attention. The wildness of this avenue brought to her recollection the one leading to the turreted chateau, and she was inclined to believe that this was a part of the same domain, and probably led to the same point. While she hesitated whether to follow it or not, a sound of many voices in loud merriment burst upon her ear; it seemed not the laugh of cheerfulness but of riot; and she stood appalled. While she paused, she heard a distant voice calling from the way she had come, and not doubting but it was that of Michael, her first impulse was to hasten back; but a second thought changed her purpose—she believed that nothing less than the last extremity could have prevailed with Michael to quit his mules; and fearing that her father was now dying, she rushed forward, with a feeble hope of obtaining assistance from the people in the woods.

Her heart beat with fearful expectation as she drew near the spot whence the voices issued, and she often startled when her steps disturbed the fallen leaves. The sounds led her towards the moonlight glade she had before noticed; at a little distance from which she stopped, and saw between the boles of the trees a small circular level of green turf, surrounded by the woods, on which appeared a group of figures. On drawing nearer, she distinguished these, by their dress, to be peasants, and perceived several cottages scattered round the edge of the woods, which waved loftily over this spot. While she gazed, and endeavoured to overcome the apprehensions that withheld her steps, several peasant girls came out of a cottage; music instantly struck up and the dance began. It was the joyous music of the vintage—the same she had before heard upon the air. Her heart, occupied with terror for her father, could not feel the contrast which this gay scene offered to her own distress. She stepped hastily forwards towards a group of elder persons who were seated at the door of a cottage, and, having explained her situation, entreated their assistance. Several of them rose with alacrity, and, offering any service in their power, followed

Emily, who seemed to move on the wind, as fast as they could towards the road.

When she reached the carriage she found St. Aubert restored to animation. On the recovery of his senses, having heard from Michael whither his daughter was gone, anxiety for her overcame every regard for himself, and he had sent him in search of her. He was, however, still languid; and perceiving himself unable to travel much further, he renewed his inquiries for an inn, and concerning the chateau in the woods.

'The chateau cannot accommodate you, sir,' said a venerable peasant who had followed Emily from the woods; 'it is scarcely inhabited; but if you will do me the honour to visit my cottage, you shall be welcome to the best bed it affords.'

St. Aubert was himself a Frenchman, he therefore was not surprised at French courtesy; but ill as he was, he felt the value of the offer enhanced by the manner which accompanied it. He had too much delicacy to apologize, or to appear to hesitate about availing himself of the peasant's hospitality; but immediately accepted it, with the same frankness with which it was offered.

The carriage again moved slowly on; Michael following the peasants up the lane which Emily had just quitted, till they came to the moon-light glade. St. Aubert's spirits were so far restored by the courtesy of his host and the near prospect of repose, that he looked with a sweet complacency upon the moonlight scene, surrounded by the shadowy woods, through which, here and there, an opening admitted the streaming splendour, discovering a cottage or a sparkling rivulet. He listened, with no painful emotion, to the merry notes of the guitar and tambourine; and though tears came to his eyes when he saw the *débonnaire* dance of the peasants, they were not merely tears of mournful regret. With Emily it was otherwise: immediate terror for her father had now subsided into a gentle melancholy, which every note of joy, by awakening comparison, served to heighten.

The dance ceased on the approach of the carriage, which was a phenomenon in these sequestered woods, and the peasantry flocked round it with eager curiosity. On learning that it brought a sick stranger, several girls ran across the turf, and returned with wine and baskets of grapes, which they presented to the travellers—each with kind contention pressing for a preference.

At length the carriage stopped at a neat cottage; and his venerable conductor having assisted St. Aubert to alight, led him and Emily to a small inner room, illumined only by moon-beams which the open easement admitted. St. Aubert, rejoicing in rest, seated himself in an arm-chair, and his senses were refreshed by the cool and balmy air that lightly waved the embowering honeysuckles, and wafted their sweet breath into the apartment. His host, who was called La Voisin, quitted the room, but soon returned with fruits, cream, and all the pastoral luxury his cottage afforded ; having set down which with a smile of unfeigned welcome, he retired behind the chair of his guest. · St. Aubert insisted on his taking a seat at the table ; and when the fruit had allayed the fever of his palate, and he found himself somewhat revived, he began to converse with his host ; who communicated several particulars concerning himself and his family, which were interesting because they were spoken from the heart, and delineated a picture of the sweet courtesies of family kindness. Emily sat by her father holding his hand ; and while she listened to the old man, her heart swelled with the affectionate sympathy he described, and her tears fell to the mournful consideration that death would probably soon deprive her of the dearest blessing she then possessed. The soft moonlight of an autumnal evening, and the distant music which now sounded a plaintive strain, aided the melancholy of her mind. The old man continued to talk of his family, and St. Aubert remained silent.

'I have only one daughter living,' said La Voisin, 'but she is happily married, and is everything to me. When I lost my wife,' he added with a sigh, 'I came to live with Agnes and her family : she has several children, who are all dancing on the green yonder, as merry as grasshoppers—and long may they be so ! I hope to die among them, Monsieur. I am old now, and cannot expect to live long : but there is some comfort in dying surrounded by one's children.'

'My good friend,' said St. Aubert, while his voice trembled, 'I hope you will long live surrounded by them.'

'Ah, sir ! at my age I must not expect that !' replied the old man, and he paused : 'I can scarcely wish it,' he resumed ; 'for I trust that whenever I die I shall go to heaven, where my poor wife is gone before me : I can sometimes almost fancy I see her, of a still moonlight night, walking among these shades she loved so well. Do you believe, Monsieur, that we shall be permitted to revisit the earth after we have quitted the body ?'

Emily could no longer stifle the anguish of her heart ; her tears fell fast upon her father's hand, which she yet held. He made an effort to speak, and at length said in a low voice :

'I hope we shall be permitted to look down on those we have left on the earth ; but I can only hope it : futurity is much veiled from our eyes, and faith and hope are our only guides concerning it. We are not enjoined to believe that disembodied spirits watch over the friends they have loved, but we may innocently hope it. It is a hope which I will never resign,' continued he, while he wiped the tears from his daughter's eyes : 'it will sweeten the bitter moments of death !'

Tears fell slowly on his cheeks : La Voisin wept too ; and there was a pause of silence. Then La Voisin, renewing the subject, said :

'But you believe, sir, that we shall meet in another world the relations we have loved in this ? I must believe this.'

'Then do believe it,' replied St. Aubert ; 'severe, indeed, would be the pangs of separation, if we believed it to be eternal. Look up, my dear Emily, we shall meet again !' He lifted his eyes towards heaven, and a gleam of moonlight, which fell upon his countenance, discovered peace and resignation stealing on the lines of sorrow.

La Voisin felt that he had pursued the subject too far, and he dropped it saying, 'We are in darkness, I forgot to bring a light.'

'No,' said St. Aubert, 'this is a light I love ; sit down, my good friend. Emily, my love, I find myself better than I have been all day : this air refreshes me. I can enjoy this tranquil hour, and that music which floats so sweetly at a distance. Let me see you smile. Who touches that guitar so tastefully ? Are there two instruments, or is it an echo I hear ?'

It is an echo, Monsieur, I fancy. That guitar is often heard at night, when all is still, but nobody knows who touches it ; and it is sometimes accompanied by a voice so sweet and so sad, that one would almost think the woods were haunted.'

'They certainly are haunted,' said St. Aubert with a smile ; 'but I believe it is by mortals.'

'I have sometimes heard it at midnight, when I could not sleep,' rejoined La Voisin, not seeming to notice this remark, 'almost under my window ; and I never heard any music like it : it has often made me think of my poor wife till I cried. I have sometimes got up to the window, to look if I could see anybody ; but as soon as I opened the casement, all was hushed, and nobody to be seen ; and I have listened and listened, till I have been so timorous that even the trembling of the leaves in the breeze has made me start. They say it often comes to warn people of their death ; but I have heard it these many years, and outlived the warning.' · ,

Emily, though she smiled at the mention of this ridiculous superstition, could not, in the present tone of her spirits, wholly resist its contagion.

'Well, but my good friend,' said St. Aubert, 'has nobody had courage to follow the sounds ? If they had, they would probably have discovered who is the musician.'

'Yes, sir, they have followed them some way into the woods ; but the music has still retreated, and seemed as distant as ever ; and the people have at last been afraid of being led into harm, and would go no further. It is very seldom that I have heard these sounds so early in the evening; they usually come about midnight, when that bright planet, which is rising above the turret yonder, sets below the woods on the left.'

'What turret?' asked St. Aubert, with quickness, 'I see none.'

'Your pardon, monsieur, you do see one indeed, for the moon shines full upon it—up the avenue yonder, a long way off: the chateau it belongs to is hid among the trees.'

'Yes, my dear sir,' said Emily, pointing; 'don't you see something glitter above the dark woods? It is a vane, I fancy, which the rays fall upon.'

'O yes; I see what you mean. And whom does the chateau belong to?'

'The Marquis de Villeroi was its owner,' replied La Voisin emphatically.

'Ah!' said St. Aubert, with a deep sigh, 'are we then so near Le-Blanc?' He appeared much agitated.

'It used to be the Marquis's favourite residence,' resumed La Voisin; 'but he took a dislike to the place, and has not been there for many years. We have heard lately that he is dead, and that it is fallen into other hands.'

St. Aubert, who had sat in deep musing, was roused by the last words. 'Dead!' he exclaimed: 'Good God! when did he die?'

'He is reported to have died about five weeks since,' replied La Voisin. 'Did you know the Marquis, sir?'

'This is very extraordinary!' said St. Aubert, without attending to the question.

'Why is it so, my dear sir?' said Emily, in a voice of timid curiosity.

He made no reply, but sunk again into a reverie; and in a few moments, when he seemed to have recovered himself, asked who had succeeded to the estates.

'I have forgot his title, monsieur,' said La Voisin; 'but my lord resides at Paris chiefly; I hear no talk of his coming hither.'

'The chateau is shut up then still?'

'Why, little better, sir; the old housekeeper and her husband the steward have the care of it, but they live generally in a cottage hard by.'

'The chateau is spacious, I suppose?' said Emily, 'and must be desolate for the residence of only two persons.'

'Desolate enough, mademoiselle,' replied La Voisin: 'I would not pass one night in the chateau for the value of the whole domain.'

'What is that?' said St. Aubert, roused again from thoughtfulness. As his host repeated his last sentence, a groan escaped from St. Aubert, and then, as if anxious to prevent it from being noticed, he hastily asked La Voisin how long he had lived in this neighbourhood. 'Almost from my childhood, sir,' replied his host.

'You remember the late Marchioness, then?' said St. Aubert in an altered voice.

'Ah, monsieur!—that I do well. There are many beside me who remember her.'

'Yes,' said St. Aubert—'and I am one of those.'

'Alas, sir! you remember then a most beautiful and excellent lady. She deserved a better fate.'

Tears stood in St. Aubert's eyes.—'Enough,' said he, in a voice almost stifled by the violence of his emotions—'it is enough, my friend.'

Emily, though extremely surprised by her father's manner, forbore to express her feelings by any question.

La Voisin began to apologize, but St. Aubert interrupted him: 'Apology is quite unnecessary,' said he; 'let us change the topic. You were speaking of the music we just now heard.'

'I was, monsieur—but hark! it comes again; listen to that voice!' They were all silent:

'At last a soft and solemn-breathing sound
Rose, like a stream of rich distilled perfumes,
And stole upon the air; that even Silence
Was took ere she was 'ware, and wish'd she might
Deny her nature, and be never more
Still, to be so displaced.'

MILTON.

In a few moments the voice died into air, and the instrument which had been heard before, sounded in low symphony.

St. Aubert now observed that it produced a tone much more full and melodious than that of a guitar, and still more melancholy and soft than the lute.

They continued to listen, but the sounds returned no more.

'This is strange!' said St. Aubert, at length interrupting the silence.

'Very strange!' said Emily.

'It is so,' rejoined La Voisin: and they were again silent.

After a long pause, 'It is now about eighteen years since I first heard that music,' said La Voisin; 'I remember it was on a fine summer's night, much like this, but later, that I was walking in the woods, and alone. I remember, too that my spirits were very low, for one of my boys was ill, and we feared we should lose him. I had been watching at his bedside all the evening, while his mother slept; for she had sat up with him the night before. I had been watching, and went out for a little fresh air: the day had been very sultry. As I walked under the shades, and mused, I heard music at a distance, and thought it was Claude playing upon his flute, as he often did of a fine evening, at the cottage door. But when I came to a place where the trees opened, (I shall never forget it!) and stood looking up at the north-lights, which shot up the heaven to a great height, I heard all of a sudden such sounds !—they came so as I cannot describe. It was like the music of angels ; and I looked up again, almost expecting to see them in the sky. When I came home, I told what I had heard ; but they laughed at me, and said it must be some of the shepherds playing on their pipes, and I could not persuade them to the contrary. A few nights after, however, my wife herself heard the same sounds, and was as much surprised as I was ; and Father Denis frightened her sadly, by saying that it was music come to warn her of her child's death, and that music often came to houses where there was a dying person.'

Emily, on hearing this, shrunk with a superstitious dread entirely new to her, and could scarcely conceal her agitation from St. Aubert.

'But the boy lived, Monsieur, in spite of Father Denis.'

'Father Denis !' said St. Aubert, who had listened to "narrative old age" with patient attention—'Are we near a convent, then ?'

'Yes, sir ; the convent of St. Clair stands at no great distance—on the sea shore yonder.'

'Ah !' said St. Aubert, as if struck with some sudden remembrance. 'The convent of St. Clair !'

Emily observed the clouds of grief, mingled with a faint expression of horror, gathering on his brow ; his countenance became fixed, and, touched as it now was by the silver whiteness of the moonlight, he resembled one of those marble statues of a monument, which seem to bend in hopeless sorrow over the ashes of the dead, shown

'. . . . . . by the blunted light
That the dim moon through painted casements lends.'
THE EMIGRANTS.

'But, my dear sir,' said Emily, anxious to dissipate his thoughts, ' you forget that repose is necessary to you. If our kind host will give me leave, I will prepare your bed, for I know how you like it to be made.'

St. Aubert, recollecting himself, and smiling affectionately, desired she would not add to her fatigue by that attention ; and La Voisin, whose consideration for his guest had been suspended by the interests which his own narrative had recalled, now started from his seat, and apologising for not having called Agnes from the green, hurried out of the room.

In a few moments he returned with his daughter, a young woman of pleasing countenance, and Emily learned from her, what she had not before suspected—that, for their accommodation, it was necessary part of La Vosin's family should leave their beds. She lamented this circumstance, but Agnes, by her reply, fully proved that she inherited at least a share of her father's courteous hospitality. It was settled that some of her

children and Michael should sleep in the neighbouring cottage.

'If I am better to-morrow, my dear,' said St. Aubert, when Emily returned to him, ' I mean to set out at an early hour, that we may rest during the heat of the day, and will travel towards home. In the present state of my health and spirits I cannot look on a longer journey with pleasure, and I am also very anxious to reach La Vallée.'

Emily, though she also desired to return, was grieved at her father's sudden wish to do so, which she thought indicated a greater degree of indisposition than he would acknowledge.

St Aubert now retired to rest, and Emily to her little chamber, but not to immediate repose ; her thoughts returned to the late conversation concerning the state of departed spirits—a subject at this time particularly affecting to her, when she had every reason to believe that her dear father would ere long be numbered with them. She leaned pensively on the little open casement, and in deep thought fixed her eyes on the heaven, whose blue, unclouded concave was studded thick with stars, the worlds perhaps of spirits, unsphered of mortal mould. As her eyes wandered along the boundless ether her thoughts rose, as before towards the sublimity of the Deity, and to the contemplation of futurity. No busy note of this world interrupted the course of her mind ; the merry dance had ceased, and every cottager had retired to his home. The still air seemed scarcely to breathe upon the woods, and now and then the distant sound of a solitary sheep bell, or of a closing casement, was all that broke on silence. At length even this hint of human being was heard no more. Elevated and enwrapt, while her eyes were often wet with tears of sublime devotion and solemn awe, she continued at the casement till the gloom of midnight hung over the earth, and the planet which La Voisin had pointed out sunk below the woods. She then recollected what he had said concerning this planet and the mysterious music, and as she lingered at the window, half hoping and half fearing that it would return, her mind was led to the remembrance of the extreme emotion her father had shown on mention of the Marquis La Villeroi's death, and of the fate of the marchioness, and she felt strongly interested concerning the remote cause of this emotion. Her surprise and curiosity were indeed the greater, because she did not recollect ever to have heard him mention the name of Villeroi.

No music, however, stole on the silence of the night, and Emily, perceiving the lateness of the hour, returned to a scene of fatigue, remembered that she was to rise early in the morning, and withdrew from the window to repose.

CHAPTER VII.

'. . . . . . Let those deplore their doom,
Whose hope still grovels in this dark sojourn:
But lofty souls can look beyond the tomb,
Can smile at fate, and wonder how they mourn.
Shall Spring to these sad scenes no more return?
Is yonder wave the sun's eternal bed?——
Soon shall the orient with new lustre burn,
And Spring shall soon her vital influence shed,
Again attune the grove, again adorn the mead!'
BEATTIE.

EMILY, called, as she had requested, at an early hour, awoke little refreshed by sleep, for uneasy dreams had pursued her, and marred the kindest blessing of the unhappy. But when she opened her casement, looked out upon the woods, bright with the morning sun, and inspired the pure air, her mind was soothed. The scene was filled with that cheering freshness which seem to breathe the very spirit of health, and she heard only sweet and *picturesque* sounds, if such an expression may be allowed—the matin-bell of a distant convent, the faint murmur of the sea waves, the song of birds, and the far-off low of cattle which she saw coming slowly on between the trunks of the trees. Struck with the circumstances of imagery around her, she indulged the pensive tranquillity which they inspired; and while she leaned on her window, waiting till St. Aubert should descend to breakfast, her ideas arranged themselves in the following lines:

THE FIRST HOUR OF MORNING.

How sweet to wind the forest's tangled shade,
When early twilight, from the eastern bound,
Dawns on the sleeping landscape in the glade,
And fades as Morning spreads her blush around!

When every infant flower, that wept in night,
Lifts its chill head, soft glowing with a tear,
Expands its tender blossom to the light,
And gives its incense to the genial air.

How fresh the breeze that wafts the rich perfume,
And swells the melody of waking birds!
The hum of bees, beneath the verdant gloom!
And woodman's song! and low of distant herds!

Then, doubtful gleams the mountains hoary head,
Seen through the parting foliage from afar,
And, further still; the ocean's misty bed,
With flitting sails, that partial sunbeams share.

But vain the silvan shade, the breath of May,
The voice of music floating on the gale,
And forms that beam through Morning's dewy veil,
If health no longer bid the heart be gay!

O balmy hour! 'tis thine her wealth to give;
Here spread her blush, and bid the parent live!

Emily now heard persons moving below in the cottage, and presently the voice of Michael, who was talking to his mules as he led them forth from a hut adjoining. As she left the room, St. Aubert, who was now risen, met her at the door, apparently as little restored by sleep as herself. She led him downstairs to the little parlour in which they had supped on the preceding night, where they found a neat breakfast set out, while the host and his daughter waited to bid them good-morrow.

'I envy you this cottage, my good friends,' said St. Aubert as he met them; 'it is so pleasant, so quiet, and so neat; and this air that one breathes—if anything could restore lost health, it would surely be this air.'

La Voisin bowed gratefully, and replied, with the gallantry of a Frenchman, 'Our cottage may be envied, sir, since you and mademoiselle have honoured it with your presence.'

St. Aubert gave him a friendly smile for his compliment, and sat down to a table spread with cream, fruit, new cheese, butter, and coffee. Emily, who had observed her father with attention, and thought he looked very ill, endeavoured to persuade him to defer travelling till the afternoon; but he seemed very anxious to be at home, and his anxiety he expressed repeatedly and with an earnestness that was unusual with him. He now said he found himself as well as he had been of late, and that he could bear travelling better in the cool hour of the morning than at any other time. But while he was talking with his venerable host, and thanking him for his kind attentions, Emily observed his countenance change, and before she could reach him he fell back in his chair. In a few moments he recovered from the sudden faintness that had come over him; but felt so ill that he perceived himself unable to set out; and having remained a little while, struggling against the pressure of indisposition, he begged he might be helped upstairs to bed. This request renewed all the terror which Emily had suffered on the preceding evening; but, though scarcely able to support herself under the sudden shock it gave her, she tried to conceal her apprehensions from St. Aubert, and gave her trembling arm to assist him to the door of his chamber.

When he was once more in bed, he desired that Emily, who was then weeping in her own room, might be called; and as she came, he waved his hand for every other person to quit the apartment. When they were alone, he held out his hand to her, and fixed his eyes upon her countenance, with an expression so full of tenderness and grief, that all her fortitude forsook her, and she burst into an agony of tears. St. Aubert seemed struggling to acquire firmness, but was still unable to speak; he could only press her hand, and check the tears that stood trembling in his eyes. At length he commanded his voice.

'My dear child,' said he, trying to smile through his anguish, 'my dear Emily!' and paused again. He raised his eyes to heaven, as if in prayer, and then, in a firmer tone, and with a look in which the tenderness of the father was dignified by the pious solemnity of the saint, he said, 'My dear child, I would soften the painful truth I have to tell you, but I find myself quite unequal to the art. Alas! I would at this moment conceal it from you, but that it would be most cruel to deceive you. It cannot be long before we must part; let us talk of it, that our thoughts and our prayers may prepare us to bear it. His voice faltered, while Emily, still weeping, pressed his hand close to her heart, which swelled with a convulsive sigh; but she could not look up.

'Let me not waste these moments,' said St. Aubert, recovering himself; 'I have much to say. There is a circumstance of solemn consequence which I have to mention, and a solemn promise to obtain from you; when this is done I shall be easier. You have observed, my dear, how anxious I am to reach home, but know not all my reasons for this. Listen to what I am going to say. Yet stay, before I say more, give me this promise, a promise made to your dying father!'

St. Aubert was interrupted. Emily, struck by his last words, as if for the first time, with a conviction of his immediate danger, raised her head: her tears stopped; and, gazing at him for a moment with an expression of unutterable anguish, a slight convulsion seized her, and she sunk senseless in her chair. St. Aubert's cries brought La Voisin and his daughter to the room, and they administered every means in their power to restore her, but, for a considerable time without effect. When she recovered, St. Aubert was so exhausted by the scene he had witnessed, that it was many minutes before he had strength to speak; he was, however, somewhat revived by a cordial which Emily gave him; and being again alone with her, he exerted himself to tranquillise her spirits, and to offer her all the comfort of which her situation admitted. She threw herself into his arms, wept on his neck; and grief made her so insensible to all he said, that he ceased to offer the alleviations which he himself could not, at this moment, feel, and mingled his silent tears with hers. Recalled at length to a sense of duty, she tried to spare her father from further view of her suffering; and quitting his embrace, dried her tears, and said something which she meant for consolation.

'My dear Emily,' replied St. Aubert, 'my dear child, we must look up with humble confidence to that Being, who has protected and comforted us in every danger and in every affliction we have known; to whose eye every moment of our lives has been exposed; He will not, He does not, forsake us now; I feel His consolations in my heart. I shall leave you, my child, still in His care; and though I depart from this world, I shall still be in His presence. Nay, weep not again, my Emily. In death there is nothing new or surprising, since we all know that we are born to die;

and nothing terrible to those who can confide in an all-powerful God. Had my life been spared now, after a very few years, in the course of nature, I must have resigned it: old age, with all its train of infirmity, its privations and its sorrows, would have been mine; and then, at last, death would have come, and called forth the tears you now shed. Rather, my child, rejoice that I am saved from such suffering, and that I am permitted to die with a mind unimpared, and sensible of the comforts of faith and of resignation.'

St. Aubert paused, fatigued with speaking. Emily again endeavoured to assume an air of composure; and, in replying to what he had said, tried to soothe him with the belief that he had not spoken in vain.

When he had reposed a while he resumed the conversation.

'Let me return,' said he, 'to a subject which is very near my heart. I said I had a solemn promise to receive from you; let me receive it now, before I explain the chief circumstance which it concerns; there are others, of which your peace requires that you should rest in ignorance. Promise, then, that you will perform exactly what I shall enjoin.'

Emily, awed by the earnest solemnity of his manner, dried her tears, that had begun again to flow in spite of her efforts to suppress them, and, looking eloquently at St. Aubert, bound herself to do whatever he should require, by a vow, at which she shuddered, yet knew not why.

He proceeded:

'I know you too well, my Emily, to believe that you would break any promise, much less one thus solemnly given; your assurance gives me peace, and the observance of it is of the utmost importance to your tranquillity. Hear, then, what I am going to tell you. The closet which adjoins my chamber at La Vallée, has a sliding board in the floor: you will know it by a remarkable knot in the wood, and by its being the next board, except one, to the wainscot which fronts the door. At the distance of about a yard from that end, nearer the window, you will perceive a line across it, as if the plank had been joined. The way to open it is this: press your foot upon the line; the end of the board will then sink, and you may slide it with ease beneath the other. Below, you will see a hollow place.' St. Aubert paused for breath, and Emily sat fixed in deep attention. 'Do you understand these directions, my dear?' said he. Emily, though scarcely able to speak, assured him that she did.

'When you return home, then,' he added with a deep sigh—

At the mention of her return home, all the melancholy circumstances that must attend this return rushed upon her fancy; she burst into convulsive grief; and St. Aubert himself, affected beyond the resistance of the fortitude which he had at first summoned, wept with her.

After some moments he composed himself. 'My dear child,' said he, 'be comforted. When I am gone, you will not be forsaken—I leave you only in the more immediate care of that providence which has never yet forsaken me. Do not afflict me with this excess of grief; rather teach me by your example to bear my own.' He stopped again; and Emily, the more she endeavoured to restrain her emotion, found it the less possible to do so.

St. Aubert, who now spoke with pain, resumed the subject. 'That closet, my dear, —when you return home, go to it; and beneath the board I have described you will find a packet of written papers. Attend to me now, for the promise you have given particularly relates to what I shall direct. These papers you must burn—and, solemnly I command you, *without examining them.*'

Emily's surprise for a moment overcame her grief, and she ventured to ask why this must be.

St. Aubert replied, that, if it had been right for him to explain his reasons, her late promise would have been unnecessarily exacted. 'It is sufficient for you, my love, to have a deep sense of the importance of observing me in this instance.'

St. Aubert proceeded: 'Under that board you will also find about two hundred louis-d'ors wrapped in a silk purse. Indeed, it was to secure whatever money might be in the chateau, that this secret place was contrived, at a time when the province was overrun by troops of men who took advantage of the tumults and became plunderers.

'But I have yet another promise to receive from you, which is—that you will never, whatever may be your future circumstances, *sell* the chateau.' St. Aubert even enjoined her, whenever she might marry, to make it an article in the contract, that the chateau should always be hers.

He then gave her a more minute account of his present circumstances than he had yet done; adding, 'The two hundred louis, with what money you will now find in my purse, is all the ready money I have to leave you. I have told you how I am circumstanced with M. Motteville at Paris. Ah, my child! I leave you poor—but not destitute,' he added, after a long pause.

Emily could make no reply to anything he now said, but kneeled at the bedside, with her face upon the quilt, weeping over the hands he held there.

After this conversation the mind of St. Aubert appeared to be much more at ease: but exhausted by the effort of speaking, he sunk into a kind of doze; and Emily continued to watch and weep beside him, till a gentle tap at the chamber-door roused her. It was La Voisin, come to say that a confessor from the neighbouring convent was below,

ready to attend St. Aubert. Emily would not suffer her father to be disturbed, but desired that the priest might not leave the cottage.

When St. Aubert awoke from this doze, his senses were confused, and it was some moments before he recovered them sufficiently to know that it was Emily who sat beside him. He then moved his lips, and stretched forth his hand to her; as she received which, she sunk back in her chair, overcome by the impression of death on his countenance. In a few minutes he recovered his voice, and Emily then asked if he wished to see the confessor: he replied that he did: and, when the holy father appeared, she withdrew. They remained alone together above half an hour. When Emily was called in, she found St. Aubert more agitated than when she had left him, and she gazed with a slight degree of resentment at the friar, as the cause of this; who, however, looked mildly and mournfully at her, and turned away. St. Aubert in a tremulous voice said he wished her to join in prayer with him, and asked if La Voisin would do so too. The old man and his daughter came: they both wept, and kneeled with Emily round the bed, while the holy father read in a solemn voice the service for the dying. St. Aubert lay with a serene countenance, and seemed to join fervently in the devotion; while tears often stole from beneath his closed eye-lids, and Emily's sobs more than once interrupted the service.

When it was concluded, and extreme unction had been administered, the friar withdrew. St. Aubert then made a sign for La Voisin to come nearer. He gave him his hand, and was for a moment silent. At length he said in a trembling voice, 'My good friend, our acquaintance has been short, but long enough to give you an opportunity of showing me much kind attention. I cannot doubt that you will extend this kindness to my daughter when I am gone; she will have need of it. I entrust her to your care during the few days she will remain here. I need say no more—you know the feelings of a father, for you have children: mine would be indeed severe, if I had less confidence in you.' He paused.

La Voisin assured him, and his tears bore testimony to his sincerity, that he would do all he could to soften her affliction, and that, if St. Aubert wished it, he would even attend her into Gascony—an offer so pleasing to St. Aubert, that he had scarcely words to acknowledge his sense of the old man's kindness, or to tell him that he accepted it,—The scene that followed between St. Aubert and Emily affected La Voisin so much that he quitted the chamber, and she was again left alone with her father, whose spirits seemed fainting fast: but neither his senses nor his voice yet failed him; and at intervals he employed much of these last awful moments in advising his daughter as to her future conduct. Perhaps he never had thought more justly, or expressed himself more clearly, than he did now.

'Above all, my dear Emily,' said he, 'do not indulge in the pride of fine feeling, the romantic error of amiable minds. Those who really possess sensibility ought early to be taught that it is a dangerous quality, which is continually extracting the excess of misery or delight from every surrounding circumstance. And since, in our passage through this world, painful circumstances occur more frequently than pleasing ones, and since our sense of evil is, I fear, more acute than our sense of good, we become the victims of our feelings, unless we can in some degree command them. I know you will say —for you are young, my Emily—I know you will say that you are contented sometimes to suffer, rather than to give up your refined sense of happiness at others; but when your mind has been long harassed by vicissitude, you will be content to rest, and you will then recover from your delusion: you will perceive that the phantom of happiness is exchanged for the substance; for happiness arises in a state of peace, not of tumult: it is of a temperate and uniform nature, and can no more exist in a heart that is continually alive to minute circumstances, than in one that is dead to feeling. You see, my dear, that though I would guard you against the dangers of sensibility, I am not an advocate for apathy. At your age, I should have said that is a vice more hateful than all the errors of sensibility, and I say so still. I call it a *vice*, because it leads to positive evil. In this, however, it does no more than an ill-governed sensibility, which, by such a rule, might also be called a vice; but the evil of the former is of more general consequence.—I have exhausted myself,' said St. Aubert feebly, 'and have wearied you, my Emily; but on a subject so important to your future comfort, I am anxious to be perfectly understood.'

Emily assured him that his advice was most precious to her, and that she would never forget it, or cease from endeavouring to profit by it. St. Aubert smiled affectionately and sorrowfully upon her.

'I repeat,' said he, 'I would not teach you to become insensible if I could. I would only warn you of the evils of susceptibility, and point out how you may avoid them. Beware, my love, I conjure you, of that self-delusion which has been fatal to the peace of so many persons—beware of priding yourself on the gracefulness of sensibility. If you yield to this vanity, your happiness is lost for ever. Always remember how much more valuable is the strength of sensibility. Do not, however, confound fortitude with apathy—apathy cannot know the virtue. Remember, too, that one act of beneficence—one act of real

usefulness—is worth all the abstract sentiment in the world. Sentiment is a disgrace instead of an ornament, unless it lead us to good actions. The miser, who thinks himself respectable merely because he possesses wealth, and thus mistakes the means of doing good for the actual accomplishment of it, is not more blameable than the man of sentiment without active virtue. You may have observed persons who delight so much in this sort of sensibility to sentiment, which excludes that to the calls of any practical virtue, that they turn from the distressed, and, because their sufferings are painful to be contemplated, do not endeavour to relieve them. How despicable is that humanity which can be contented to pity where it might assuage!'

St. Aubert, some time after, spoke of Madame Cheron, his sister.

'Let me inform you of a circumstance that nearly affects your welfare,' he added. 'We have, you know, had little intercourse for some years, but as she is now your only female relation, I have thought it proper to consign you to her care, as you will see in my will, till you are of age, and to recommend you to her protection afterwards. She is not exactly the person to whom I would have committed my Emily; but I had no alternative, and I believe her to be, upon the whole, a good kind of woman. I need not recommend it to your prudence, my love, to endeavour to conciliate her kindness—you will do this for his sake who has often wished to do so for yours.'

Emily assured him that whatever he requested she would religiously perform to the utmost of her ability. 'Alas! added she, in a voice interrupted by sighs, 'that will soon be all which remains for me. It will be almost my only consolation to fulfil your wishes.'

St. Aubert looked up silently in her face, as if he would have spoken; but his spirit sunk a while, and his eyes became heavy and dull. She felt that look at her heart.

'My dear father!' she exclaimed; and then, checking herself, pressed his hand closer and hid her face with her handkerchief. Her tears were concealed, but St. Aubert heard her convulsive sobs. His spirits returned.

'O, my child!' said he faintly, 'let my consolation be yours. I die in peace; for I know that I am about to return to the bosom of my Father, who will still beg our Father when I am gone. Always trust in Him, my love, and he will support you in these moments, as he supports me.'

Emily could only listen and weep, but the extreme composure of his manner, and the faith and hope he expressed, somewhat soothed her anguish. Yet whenever she looked upon his emaciated countenance, and saw the lines of death beginning to prevail over it—saw his sunk eyes still bent on her, and their heavy lids pressing to a close—there was a pang in her heart, such as defied expression, though it required filial virtue like hers to forbear the attempt.

He desired once more to bless her.

'Where are you, my dear?' said he, as he stretched forth his hands.

Emily had turned to the window that he might not perceive her anguish; she now understood that his sight had failed him.

When he had given her his blessing—and it seemed to be the last effort of expiring life—he sunk back on his pillow. She kissed his forehead—the damps of death had settled there—and, forgetting her fortitude for a moment, her tears mingled with them. St. Aubert lifted up his eyes; the spirit of a father returned to them, but it quickly vanished, and he spoke no more.

St. Aubert lingered till about three o'clock in the afternoon, and thus gradually sinking into death, he expired without a struggle or a sigh.

Emily was led from the chamber by La Voisin and his daughter, who did what they could to comfort her. The old man sat and wept with her. Agnes was more erroneously officious.

W magnate struck ↑

CHAPTER IX.

'O'er him, whose doom thy virtues grieve,
Aërial forms shall sit at eve,
And bend the pensive head.'

COLLINS.

THE monk who had before appeared, returned in the evening to offer consolation to Emily, and brought a kind message from the lady abbess, inviting her to the convent. Emily, though she did not accept the offer, returned an answer expressive of her gratitude. The holy conversation of the friar, whose mild benevolence of manners bore some resemblance to those of St. Aubert, soothed the violence of her grief, and lifted her heart to the Being who, extending through all place and all eternity, looks on the events of this little world as on the shadows of a moment, and beholds equally, and in the same instant, the soul that has passed the gates of death and that which still lingers in the body.

'In the sight of God,' said Emily, 'my dear father now exists as truly as he yesterday existed to me. It is to me only that he is dead—to God and to himself he yet lives!'

The good monk left her more tranquil than she had been since St. Aubert died; and before she retired to her little cabin for the night, she trusted herself so far as to visit the corpse. Silent, and without weeping, she stood by its side. The features, placid and serene, told the nature of the last sensations that had lingered in the now deserted frame. For a moment she turned away, in horror of the stillness in which death had fixed that countenance, never till now seen otherwise than animated; then gazed on it with a

mixture of doubt and awful astonishment. Her reason could scarcely overcome an involuntary and unaccountable expectation of seeing that beloved countenance still susceptible. She continued to gaze wildly; took up the cold hand; spoke—still gazed; and then burst into a transport of grief. La Voisin, hearing her sobs, came into the room to lead her away; but she heard nothing, and only begged that he would leave her.

Again alone, she indulged her tears; and when the gloom of evening obscured the chamber, and almost veiled from her eyes the object of her distress, she still hung over the body; till her spirits at length were exhausted, and she became tranquil. La Voisin again knocked at the door, and entreated that she would come to the common apartment. Before she went she kissed the lips of St. Aubert, as she was wont to do when she bade him good-night. Again she kissed them. Her heart felt as if it would break: a few tears of agony started to her eyes—she looked up to heaven—then at St. Aubert—and left the room.

Retired to her lonely cabin, her melancholy thoughts still hovered round the body of her deceased parent; and when she sunk into a kind of slumber, the images of her waking mind still haunted her fancy. She thought she saw her father approaching her with a benign countenance: then, smiling mournfully and pointing upwards, his lips moved; but instead of words, she heard sweet music borne on the distant air, and presently saw his features glow with the mild rapture of a superior being. The strain seemed to swell louder, and she awoke. The vision was gone; but music yet came to her ear in strains such as angels might breathe. She doubted, listened, raised herself in the bed, and again listened. It was music and not an illusion of her imagination. After a solemn steady harmony, it paused—then rose again in mournful sweetness,—and then died, in a cadence that seemed to bear away the listening soul to heaven. She instantly remembered the music of the preceding night, with the strange circumstances related by La Voisin, and the affecting conversation it had led to concerning the state of departed spirits.

All that St. Aubert had said on that subject now pressed upon her heart, and overwhelmed it. What a change in a few hours! He, who then could only conjecture, was now made acquainted with truth—was himself become one of the departed! As she listened, she was chilled with superstitious awe; her tears stopped; and she rose, and went to the window. All without was obscured in shade: but Emily, turning her eyes from the massy darkness of the woods, whose waving outline appeared on the horizon, saw, on the left, that effulgent planet which the old man had pointed out, setting over the woods. She remembered what he had said concerning it;

and the music now coming at intervals on the air, she unclosed the casement to listen to the strains, that soon gradually sunk to a greater distance, and tried to discover whence they came. The obscurity prevented her from distinguishing any object on the green platform below; and the sounds became fainter and fainter, till they softened into silence. She listened, but they returned no more. Soon after she observed the planet trembling between the fringed tops of the woods, and in the next moment sink behind them. Chilled with a melancholy awe, she retired once more to her bed, and at length forgot for a while her sorrows in sleep.

On the following morning she was visited by a sister of the convent, who came with kind offices and a second invitation from the lady abbess; and Emily, though she could not forsake the cottage while the remains of her father were in it, consented, however painful such a visit must be in the present state of her spirits, to pay her respects to the abbess in the evening.

About an hour before sunset Lá Voisin showed her the way through the woods to the convent, which stood in a small bay of the Mediterranean, crowned by a woody amphitheatre; and Emily, had she been less unhappy, would have admired the extensive sea-view that appeared from the green slope in front of the edifice, and the rich shores, hung with woods and pastures, that extended on either hand. But her thoughts were now occupied by one sad idea; and the features of nature were to her colourless and without form. The bell for vespers struck as she passed the ancient gate of the convent, and seemed the funeral note for St. Aubert :—little incidents affect a mind enervated by sorrow. Emily struggled against the sickening faintness that came over her, and was led into the presence of the abbess, who received her with an air of maternal tenderness—an air of such gentle solicitude and consideration as touched her with an instantaneous gratitude; her eyes were filled with tears; and the words she would have spoken faltered on her lips. The abbess led her to a seat, and sat down beside her; still holding her hand, and regarding her in silence, as Emily dried her tears and attempted to speak.

'Be composed, my daughter,' said the abbess in a soothing voice; 'do not speak yet; I know all you would say. Your spirits must be soothed. We are going to prayers: will you attend our evening service? It is comfortable, my child, to look up in our afflictions to a Father who sees and pities us, and who chastens in his mercy.'

Emily's tears flowed again; but a thousand sweet emotions mingled with them. The abbess suffered her to weep without interruption, and watched over her with a look of benignity that might have characterised the countenance of a guardian angel. Emily, when she became tranquil, was encouraged to speak without reserve, and to mention the motive that made her unwilling to quit the cottage; which the abbess did not oppose even by a hint; but praised the filial piety of her conduct, and added a hope that she would pass a few days at the convent before she returned to La Vallée.

'You must allow yourself a little time to recover from your first shock, my daughter, before you encounter a second; I will not affect to conceal from you how much I know your heart must suffer on returning to the scene of your former happiness. Here you will have all that quiet, and sympathy, and religion can give to restore your spirits. But come,' added she, observing the tears swell in Emily's eyes, 'we will go to the chapel.'

Emily followed to the parlour, where the nuns were assembled; to whom the abbess committed her, saying 'This is a daughter for whom I have much esteem; be a sister to her.' They passed on in a train to the chapel, where the solemn devotion with which the service was performed elevated her mind, and brought to it the comforts of faith and resignation.

Twilight came on before the abbess's kindness would suffer Emily to depart; when she left the convent, with a heart much lighter than she had entered it, and was re-conducted by La Voison through the woods, the pensive gloom of which was in unison with the temper of her mind; and she pursued the little wild path in musing silence, till her guide suddenly stopped, looked round, and then struck out of the path into the high grass, saying he had mistaken the road.

He now walked on quickly; and Emily proceeding with difficulty over the obscured and uneven ground, was left at some distance, till her voice arrested him; who seemed unwilling to stop, and still hurried on.

'If you are in doubt about the way,' said Emily, 'had we not better inquire it at the chateau yonder, between the trees?'

'No,' replied La Voisin; 'there is no occasion. When we reach that brook, ma'amselle,—(you see the light upon the water there, beyond the woods)—when we reach that brook, we shall be at home presently: I don't know how I happened to mistake the path: I seldom come this way after sun-set.

'It is solitary enough,' said Emily, 'but you have no banditti here?'

'No, ma'amselle—no banditti.'

'What are you afraid of then, my good friend?—you are not superstitious?'

'No, not superstitious.—but, to tell you the truth, lady, nobody likes to go near the chateau after dusk.'

'By whom is it inhabited,' said Emily, 'that it is so formidable?'

'Why, ma'amselle, it is scarcely inhabited; for our lord the marquis, and the lord of all these fine woods too, is dead. He had not once been in it for these many years; and his people who have the care of it, live in a cottage close by.'

Emily now understood this to be the chateau which La Voisin had formerly pointed out as having belonged to the Marquis Villeroi, on the mention of which her father had been so much affected.

'Ah! it is a desolate place now,' continued La Voisin; 'and such a grand fine place as I remember it!'

Emily inquired what had occasioned this lamentable change; but the old man was silent: and Emily, whose interest was awakened by the fear he had expressed, and above all by a recollection of her father's agitation, repeated the question, and added, 'If you are neither afraid of the inhabitants, my good friend, nor are superstitious, how happens it that you dread to pass that chateau in the dark?'

'Perhaps, then, I am a little superstitious, ma'amselle; and if you knew what I do, you might be so too. Strange things have happened there. Monsieur, your good father, appeared to have known the late marchioness.'

'Pray inform me what did happen,' said Emily with much emotion.

'Alas! ma'amselle,' answered La Voisin, 'inquire no further: it is not for me to lay open the domestic secrets of my lord.'

Emily, surprised by the old man's words and his manner of delivering them, forbore to repeat her question: a nearer interest, the remembrance of St. Aubert, occupied her thoughts; and she was led to recollect the music she heard on the preceding night, which she mentioned to La Voisin.

'You was not alone, ma'amselle, in this,' he replied; 'I heard it too; but I have so often heard it, at the same hour, that I was scarcely surprised.'

'You doubtless believe this music to have some connection with the chateau,' said Emily suddenly; 'and are therefore superstitious?'

'It may be so, ma'amselle; but there are other circumstances belonging to that chateau which I remember, and sadly too!'

A heavy sigh followed: but Emily's delicacy restrained the curiosity these words revived, and she inquired no further.

On reaching the cottage, all the violence of her grief returned: it seemed as if she had escaped its heavy pressure only while she was removed from the object of it. She passed immediately to the chamber where the remains of her father were laid, and yielded to all the anguish of hopeless grief. La Voisin at length persuaded her to leave the room, and she returned to her own; where, exhausted by the sufferings of the day, she soon fell into deep sleep, and awoke considerably refreshed.

When the dreadful hour arrived in which the remains of St. Aubert were to be taken from her for ever, she went alone to the chamber to look upon his countenance yet once again; and La Voisin, who had waited patiently below stairs till her despair should subside, with the respect due to grief, forbore to interrupt the indulgence of it, till surprise at the length of her stay, and then apprehension, overcame his delicacy, and he went to lead her from the chamber.

Having tapped gently at the door without receiving an answer, he listened attentively; but all was still—no sigh, no sob of anguish was heard. Yet more alarmed by this silence, he opened the door, and found Emily lying senseless across the foot of the bed, near which stood the coffin.

His calls procured assistance, and she was carried to her room, where proper applications at length restored her.

During her state of insensibility, La Voisin had given directions for the coffin to be closed, and he succeeded in persuading Emily to forbear revisiting the chamber.

She, indeed, felt herself unequal to this, and also perceived the necessity of sparing her spirits, and collecting fortitude sufficient to bear her through the approaching scene.

St. Aubert had given a particular injunction that his remains should be interred in the church of the convent of St. Clair, and, in mentioning the north chancel, near the ancient tomb of the Villerois, had pointed out the exact spot where he wished to be laid.

The superior had granted this place for the interment; and thither, therefore, the sad procession now moved; which was met at the gates by the venerable priest, followed by a train of friars.

Every person who heard the solemn chant of the anthem, and the peal of the organ, that struck up when the body entered the church, and saw also the feeble steps and the assumed tranquillity of Emily, gave her involuntary tears. She shed none; but walked, her face partly shaded by a thin black veil, between two persons who supported her, preceded by the abbess, and followed by nuns, whose plaintive voices mellowed the swelling harmony of the dirge.

When the procession came to the grave, the music ceased.

Emily drew the veil entirely over her face, and in a momentary pause between the anthem and the rest of the service, her sobs were distinctly audible.

The holy father began the service: and Emily again commanded her feelings, till the coffin was let down, and she heard the earth rattle on its lid: then, as she shuddered, a groan burst from her heart, and she leaned for support on the person who stood next to her. In a few moments she recovered; and when she heard those affecting and sublime words— 'His body is buried in peace, and his soul returns to him that gave it'—her anguish softened into tears.

The abbess led her from the church into her own parlour, and there administered all the consolations that religion and gentle sympathy can give. Emily struggled against the pressure of grief; but the abbess, observing her attentively, ordered a bed to be prepared, and recommended her to retire to repose. She also kindly claimed her promise to remain a few days at the convent; and Emily, who had no wish to return to the cottage, the scene of all her sufferings, had leisure, now that no immediate care pressed upon her attention, to feel the indisposition which disabled her from immediately travelling.

Meanwhile the maternal kindness of the abbess and the gentle attentions of the nuns, did all that was possible towards soothing her spirits and restoring her health. But the latter was too deeply wounded, through the medium of her mind, to be quickly revived. She lingered for some weeks at the convent under the influence of a slow fever, wishing to return home, yet unable to go thither—often even reluctant to leave the spot where her father's relics were deposited, and sometimes soothing herself with the consideration that, if she died here, her remains would repose beside those of St. Aubert.

In the meanwhile she sent letters to Madame Cheron and to the old housekeeper, informing them of the sad event that had taken place, and of her own situation. From her aunt she received an answer, abounding more in common-place condolement than in traits of real sorrow, which assured her that a servant should be sent to conduct her to La Vallée, for that her own time was so much occupied by company, that she had no leisure to undertake so long a journey.

However Emily might prefer La Vallée to Thoulouse, she could not be insensible of the indecorous and unkind conduct of her aunt in suffering her to return thither, where she had no longer a relation to console and protect her—a conduct which was the more culpable since St. Aubert had appointed Madame Cheron the guardian of his orphan daughter.

Madame Cheron's servant made the attendance of the good La Voisin unnecessary; and Emily, who felt sensibly her obligations to him for all his kind attention to her late father, as well as to herself, was glad to spare him a long, and what, at his time of life, must have been a troublesome journey.

During her stay at the convent the peace and sanctity that reigned within, the tranquil beauty of the scenery without, and the delicate attentions of the abbess and the nuns, were circumstances so soothing to her mind that they almost tempted her to leave a world where she had lost her dearest friends, and devote herself to the cloister in a spot rendered sacred to her by containing the tomb of St. Aubert. The pensive enthusiasm, too, so natural to her temper, had spread a beautiful illusion over the sanctified retirement of a nun, that almost hid from her view the selfishness of its security. But the touches which a melancholy fancy, slightly tinctured with superstition, gave to the monastic scene, began to fade as her spirits revived, and brought once more to her heart an image which had only transiently been banished thence. By this she was silently awakened to hope, and comfort, and sweet affections; visions of happiness gleamed faintly at a distance, and though she knew them to be illusions, she could not resolve to shut them out for ever. It was the remembrance of Valancourt—of his taste, his genius, and of the countenance which glowed with both—that perhaps alone determined her to return to the world. The grandeur and sublimity of the scenes amidst which they had first met had fascinated her fancy, and had imperceptibly contributed to render Valancourt more interesting by seeming to communicate to him somewhat of their own character. The esteem, too, which St. Aubert had repeatedly expressed for him sanctioned this kindness. But though his countenance and manner had continually expressed his admiration of her, he had not otherwise declared it; and even the hope of seeing him again was so distant that she was scarcely conscious of it—still less that it influenced her conduct on this occasion.

It was several days after the arrival of Madame Cheron's servant before Emily was sufficiently recovered to undertake the journey to La Vallée. On the evening preceding her departure she went to the cottage to take leave of La Voisin and his family, and to make them a return for their kindness. The old man she found sitting on a bench at his door, between his daughter and his son-in-law, who was just returned from his daily labour, and who was playing upon a pipe that in tone resembled an oboe. A flask of wine stood beside the old man, and before him a small table with fruit and bread, round which stood several of his grandsons, fine rosy children, who were taking their supper as their mother distributed it. On the edge of the little green that spread before the cottage were cattle and a few sheep reposing under the trees. The landscape was touched with the mellow light of the evening sun, whose long slanting beams played through a vista of the woods, and lighted up the distant turrets of the chateau. She paused a moment, before she emerged from the shade, to gaze upon the happy group before her—on the complacency and ease of healthy age depictured on the countenance of La Voisin; the maternal tenderness of Agnes as she looked upon her children; and the innocency of infantine pleasure reflected in their smiles. Emily looked again at the venerable old man and at the cottage. The memory of her father rose with full force upon her mind, and she hastily stepped forward, afraid to trust herself with a longer pause. She took an affectionate and affecting leave of La Voisin and his family; he seemed to love her as his daughter, and shed tears. Emily shed many. She avoided going into the cottage, since she knew it would revive emotions such as she could not now endure.

One painful scene yet awaited her—for she determined to visit again her father's grave; and that she might not be interrupted or observed in the indulgence of her melancholy tenderness, she deferred her visit till every inhabitant of the convent, except the nun who promised to bring her the key of the church, should be retired to rest.

Emily remained in her chamber till she heard the convent bell strike twelve, when the nun came, as she had appointed, with the key of a private door that opened into the church; and they descended together the narrow winding staircase that led thither.

The nun offered to accompany Emily to the grave, adding—'It is melancholy to go alone at this hour;' but the former, thanking her for the consideration, could not consent to have any witness of her sorrow; and the sister having unlocked the door, gave her the lamp.

'You will remember, sister,' said she, 'that in the east aisle, which you must pass, is a newly-opened grave; hold the light to the ground, that you may not stumble over the loose earth.'

Emily, thanking her again, took the lamp, and, stepping into the church, sister Mariette departed.

But Emily paused a moment at the door: a sudden fear came over her, and she returned to the foot of the staircase, where, as she heard the steps of the nun ascending, and, while she held up the lamp, saw her black veil waving over the spiral balusters, she was tempted to call her back. While she hesitated, the veil disappeared; and in the next moment, ashamed of her fears, she returned to the church. The cold air of the aisles chilled her; and their deep silence and extent, feebly shone upon by the moon-light that streamed through a Gothic window, would at any other time have awed her into superstition; now grief occupied all her attention. She scarcely heard the whispering echoes of her own steps, or thought of the open grave till she found herself almost on its brink. A friar of the convent had been buried there on the preceding evening, and, as she had sat alone in her chamber at twilight, she heard, at a distance, the monks chanting the requiem for his

soul. This brought freshly to her memory the circumstances of her father's death; and as the voices, mingling with a low querulous peal of the organ, swelled faintly, gloomy and affecting visions had arisen upon her mind. Now she remembered them; and turning aside to avoid the broken ground, these recollections made her pass on with quicker steps to the grave of St. Aubert; when, in the moon-light that fell athwart a remote part of the aisle, she thought she saw a shadow gliding between the pillars. She stopped to listen; and not hearing any footstep, believed that her fancy had deceived her, and, no longer apprehensive of being observed, proceeded. St. Aubert was buried beneath a plain marble, bearing little more than his name and the date of his birth and death, near the foot of the stately monument of the Villerois. Emily remained at his grave till a chime that called the monks to early prayers warned her to retire; then she wept over it a last farewell, and forced herself from the spot. After this hour of melancholy indulgence, she was refreshed by a deeper sleep than she had experienced for a long time; and on awaking, her mind was more tranquil and resigned than it had been since St. Aubert's death.

But when the moment of her departure from the convent arrived, all her grief returned: the memory of the dead, and the kindness of the living, attached her to the place; and for the sacred spot where her father's remains were interred, she seemed to feel all those tender affections which we conceive for home. The abbess repeated many kind assurances of regard at their parting, and pressed her to return, if ever she should find her condition elsewhere unpleasant; many of the nuns also expressed unaffected regret at her departure; and Emily left the convent with many tears, and followed by sincere wishes for her happiness.

She had travelled several leagues, before the scenes of the country through which she passed had power to rouse her for a moment from the deep melancholy into which she was sunk; and when they did, it was only to remind her that on the last view of them St. Aubert was at her side, and to call up to her remembrance the remarks he had delivered on similar scenery. Thus, without any particular occurrence, passed the day in languor and dejection. She slept that night at a town on the skirts of Languedoc, and on the following morning entered Gascony.

Toward the close of this day Emily came within view of the plains in the neighbourhood of La Valée, and the well-known objects of former times began to press upon her notice. and, with them, recollections that awakened all her tenderness and grief. Often, while she looked through her tears upon the wild grandeur of the Pyrenees, now varied with the rich lights and shadows of evening, she remembered that, when last she saw them, her father partook with her of the pleasure they inspired. Suddenly some scene which he had particularly pointed out to her would present itself, and the sick languor of despair would steal upon her heart. 'There!' she would exclaim—'there are the very cliffs, there the wood of pines, which he looked at with such delight as we passed this road together for the last time! There, too, under the crag of that mountain, is the cottage, peeping from among the cedars, which he bade me remember, and copy with my pencil! O my father, shall I never see you more!'

As she drew near the chateau, these melancholy memorials of past times multiplied. At length the chateau itself appeared, amid the glowing beauty of St. Aubert's favourite landscape. This was an object which called for fortitude, not for tears: Emily dried hers, and prepared to meet with calmness the trying moment of her return to that home where there was no longer a parent to welcome her, 'Yes, said she; let me not forget the lessons he has taught me! How often he has pointed out the necessity of resisting even virtuous sorrow!—how often we have admired together the greatness of a mind that can at once suffer and reason! O my father! if you are permitted to look down upon your child, it will please you to see that she remembers, and endeavours to practise, the precepts you have given her.

. A turn on the road now allowed a nearer view of the chateau; the chimneys, tipped with light, rising from behind St. Aubert's favourite oaks, whose foliage partly concealed the lower part of the building. Emily could not suppress a heavy sigh. 'This, too, was his favourite hour!' said she, as she gazed upon the long evening shadows stretched athwart the landscape. 'How deep the repose! how lovely the scene!—lovely and tranquil as in former days!'

Again she resisted the pressure of sorrow till her ear caught the gay melody of the dance, which she had so often listened to as she walked with St. Aubert on the margin of the Garonne; when all her fortitude forsook her; and she continued to weep till the carriage stopped at the little gate that opened upon what was now her own territory. She raised her eyes on the sudden stoppage of the carriage, and saw her father's old housekeeper coming to open the gate. Manchon also came running and barking before her, and when his young mistress alighted, fawned and played round her, gasping with joy.

'Dear Ma'amselle!' said Theresa, and paused, and looked as if she would have offered something of condolement to Emily, whose tears now prevented reply. The dog still fawned and ran round her, and then flew towards the carriage with a short quick bark.

'Ah, ma'amselle! my poor master!' said Theresa, whose feelings were more awakened than her delicacy; 'Manchon's gone to look for him.'

Emily sobbed aloud; and on looking towards the carriage, which still stood with the door open, saw the animal spring into it, and instantly leaped out, and then, with his nose on the ground, run round the horses.

'Don't cry so, ma'amselle,' said Theresa; 'it breaks my heart to see you.' The dog now came running to Emily, then returned to the carriage, and then back again to her, whining and discontented. 'Poor rogue!' said Theresa, 'thou hast lost thy master— thou mayest well cry! But come, my dear young lady, be comforted. What shall I get to refresh you?'

Emily gave her hand to the old servant, and tried to restrain her grief, while she made some kind inquiries concerning her health. But she still lingered in the walk which led to the chateau—for within was no person to meet her with the kiss of affection: her own heart no longer palpitated with impatient joy to meet again the well-known smile; and she dreaded to see objects which would recall the full remembrance of her former happiness. She moved slowly towards the door, paused, went on, and paused again. How silent, how forsaken, how forlorn, did the chateau appear! Trembling to enter it, yet blaming herself for delaying what she could not avoid, she at length passed into the hall, crossed it with a hurried step as if afraid to look round, and opened the door of that room which she was wont to call her own. The gloom of evening gave solemnity to its silent and deserted air. The chairs, the tables, every article of furniture, so familiar to her in happier times, spoke eloquently to her heart. She seated herself, without immediately observing it, in a window which opened upon the garden, and where St. Aubert had often sat with her watching the sun retire from the rich and extensive prospect that appeared beyond the groves.

Having indulged her tears for some time, she became more composed; and when Theresa, after seeing the baggage deposited in her lady's room, again appeared, she had so far recovered her spirits as to be able to converse with her.

'I have made up the green bed for you, ma'amselle,' said Theresa, as she set the coffee upon the table: 'I thought you would like it better than your own now,; but I little thought, this day month, that you would come back alone. A-well-a-day! the news almost broke my heart when it did come. Who would have believed that my poor master, when he went from home, would never return again!'

Emily hid her face with her handkerchief, and waved her hand.

'Do taste the coffee,' said Theresa. 'My

dear young lady, be comforted—we must all die. My dear master is a saint above.'

Emily took the handkerchief from her face, and raised her eyes, full of tears, towards heaven. Soon after she dried them, and in a calm but tremulous voice began to inquire concerning some of her late father's pensioners.

'Alas-a-day!' said Theresa, as she poured out the coffee and handed it to her mistress, 'all that could come have been here every day to inquire after you and my master.' She then proceeded to tell, that some were dead whom they had left well; and others, who were ill, had recovered. 'And see, ma'amselle,' added Theresa; 'there is old Mary coming up the garden now; she has looked every day these three years as if she would die, yet she is alive still. She has seen the chaise at the door, and knows you are come home.'

The sight of this poor old woman would have been too much for Emily, and she begged Theresa would go and tell her that she was too ill to see any person that night. 'Tomorrow I shall be better, perhaps; but give her this token of my remembrance.'

Emily sat for some time given up to sorrow. Not an object on which her eye glanced but awakened some remembrance that led immediately to the subject of her grief. Her favourite plants, which St. Aubert had taught her to nurse; the little drawings that adorned the room, which his taste had instructed her to execute; the books that he had selected for her use, and which they had read together; her musical instruments, whose sounds he loved so well, and which he sometimes awakened himself—every object gave new force to sorrow. At length she roused herself from this melancholy indulgence; and summoning all her resolution, stepped forward to go into those forlorn rooms, which, though she dreaded to enter, she knew would yet more powerfully affect her if she delayed to visit them.

Having passed through the green-house her courage for a moment forsook her when she opened the door of the library; and perhaps, the shade which evening and the foliage of the trees near the windows threw across the room, heightened the solemnity of her feelings on entering that apartment where every thing spoke of her father. There was an arm chair in which he used to sit: she shrunk when she observed it; for she had so often seen him seated there, and the idea of him rose so distinctly to her mind, that she almost fancied she saw him before her. But she checked the illusions of a distempered imagination, though she could not subdue a certain degree of awe which now mingled with her emotions. She walked slowly to the chair, and seated herself in it. There was a reading-desk before it, on which lay a book, open, as it had been left by her father. It was some moments before she recovered courage enough to examine it; and when she looked at the open page, she immediately recollected that St. Aubert, on the evening before his departure from the chateau, had read to her some passages from this his favourite author. The circumstances now effected her extremely: she looked at the page, wept and looked again. To her the book appeared sacred and invaluable; and she would not have moved it, or closed the page which he had left open, for the treasures of the Indies. Still she sat before the desk; and could not resolve to quit it, though the increasing gloom, and the profound silence of the apartment, revived a degree of painful awe. Her thoughts dwelt on the probable state of departed spirits; and she remembered the affecting conversation which passed between St. Aubert and La Voisin on the night preceding his death.

As she mused, she saw the door slowly open; and a rustling sound in a remote part of the room startled her. Through the dusk she thought she perceived something move. The subject she had been considering, and the present state of her spirits, which made her imagination respond to every impression of her senses, gave her a sudden terror of something supernatural. She sat for a moment motionless; and then her dissipated reason returning, 'What should I fear?' said she; 'if the spirits of those we love ever return again to us, it is in kindness.'

The silence which again reigned, made her ashamed of her late fears, and she believed that her imagination had deluded her, or that she had heard one of those unaccountable noises which sometimes occur in old houses. The same sound, however, returned; and, distinguishing something moving towards her, and in the next instant press beside her into the chair, she shrieked; but her fleeting senses were instantly recalled, on perceiving that it was Manchon who sat by her, and who now licked her hand affectionately.

Perceiving her spirits unequal to the task she had assigned herself, of visiting the deserted rooms of the chateau this night, when she left the library she walked into the garden, and down to the terrace that overhung the river. The sun was now set; but under the dark branches of the almond trees was seen the saffron glow of the west, spreading beyond the twilight of middle air. The bat flitted silently by; and now and then the mourning note of the nightingale was heard.

The circumstances of the hour brought to her recollection some lines which she had once heard St. Aubert recite on this very spot, and she had now a melancholy pleasure in repeating them.

SONNET.

Now the bat circles on the breeze of eve,
  That creeps, in shuddering fits, along the wave,

And trembles 'mid the woods and through the cave,
Whose lonely sighs the wanderer deceive:

For oft, when Melancholy charms his mind,
  He thinks the Spirit of the rock he hears,
Nor listens, but with sweetly-thrilling fears,
To the low mystic murmurs of the wind!

Now the bat circles; and the twilight-dew
  Falls silent round, and o'er the mountain-cliff,
The gleaming wave, and far discover'd skiff,
Spreads the gray veil of soft, harmonious hue.

So falls o'er Grief the dew of Pity's tear,
Dimming her lonely visions of despair.

Emily, wandering on, came to St. Aubert's favourite plane-tree, where so often, at this hour, they had sat beneath the shade together, and with her dear mother so often had conversed on the subject of a future state. How often, too, had her father expressed the comfort he derived from believing that they should meet in another world! Emily, overcome by these recollections, left the plane-tree; and as she leaned pensively on the wall of the terrace, she observed a group of peasants dancing gaily on the banks of the Garonne, which spread in broad expanse below, and reflected the evening light. What a contrast they formed to the desolate, unhappy Emily! They were gay and *debonnaire*, as they were wont to be when she, too, was gay—when St. Aubert used to listen to their merry music, with a countenance beaming pleasure and benevolence. Emily, having looked for a moment on this sprightly band, turned away, unable to bear the remembrances it excited; but where, alas! could she turn, and not meet new objects to give acuteness to grief!

As she walked slowly towards the house, she was met by Theresa.

'Dear Ma'amselle,' said she, 'I have been seeking you up and down this half-hour, and was afraid some accident had happened to you. How can you like to wander about so in this night air? Do come into the house. Think what my poor master would have said, if he could see you. I am sure, when my dear lady died, no gentleman could take it more to heart than he did; yet you know he seldom shed a tear.'

'Pray, Theresa, cease,' said Emily, wishing to interrupt this ill-judged but well-meaning harangue.

Theresa's loquacity, however, was not to be silenced so easily.

'And when you used to grieve so,' she added, 'he often told you how wrong it was—for that my mistress was happy. And if she was happy, I am sure he is, so too; for the prayers of the poor, they say, reach heaven.' During this speech, Emily had walked silently into the chateau, and Theresa lighted her across the hall into the common sitting-parlour, where she had laid the cloth with one solitary knife and fork for supper. Emily was in the room before she perceived that it

was not her own apartment; but she checked the emotion which inclined her to leave it, and seated herself quietly by the little supper-table. Her father's hat hung upon the opposite wall: while she gazed at it a faintness came over her. Theresa looked at her, and then at the object on which her eyes were settled, and went to remove it; but Emily waved her hand.

'No,' said she, 'let it remain; I am going to my chamber.'

'Nay, Ma'amselle, supper is ready.'

'I cannot take it,' replied Emily; I will go to my room, and try to sleep. To-morrow I shall be better.'

'This is poor doings!' said Theresa. 'Dear lady! do take some food! I have dressed a pheasant, and a fine one it is. Old Monsieur Barreaux sent it this morning; for I saw him yesterday, and told him you were coming; and I know nobody that seemed more concerned, when he heard the sad news than he.'

'Did he?' said Emily, in a tender voice, while she felt her poor heart warmed for a moment by a ray of sympathy.

At length her spirits were entirely overcome, and she retired to her room.

CHAPTER X.

'Can Music's voice, can Beauty's eye,
Can Painting's glowing hand, supply
A charm so suited to my mind,
As blows this hollow gust of wind;
As drops this little weeping rill
Soft tinkling down the moss-grown hill;
While through the west, where sinks the crimson day,
Meek Twilight slowly sails, and waves her banners gray?

                 MASON.

EMILY, some time after her return to La Vallée, received letters from her aunt, Madame Cheron, in which, after some common-place condolement and advice, she invited her to Thoulouse, and added, that, as her late brother had intrusted Emily's education to her, she should consider herself bound to overlook her conduct. Emily, at this time, wished only to remain at La Vallée, in the scenes of her early happiness, now rendered infinitely dear to her, as the residence of those whom she had lost for ever; where she could weep unobserved, retrace their steps, and remember each minute particular of their manners. But she was equally anxious to avoid the displeasure of Madame Cheron.

Though her affection would not suffer her to question, even for a moment, the propriety of St. Aubert's conduct in appointing Madame Cheron for her guardian, she was sensible that this step had made her happiness depend, in a great degree, on the humour of her aunt.

In her reply, she begged permission to remain at present at La Vallée; mentioning the extreme dejection of her spirits, and the necessity she felt for quiet and retirement to restore them. These she knew were not to be found at Madame Cheron's, whose inclinations led her into a life of dissipation, which her ample fortune encouraged. And, having given her answer, she felt somewhat more at ease.

In the first days of her affliction she was visited by Monsieur Barreaux, a sincere mourner for St. Aubert.

'I may well lament my friend,' said he, 'for I shall never meet with his resemblance! If I could have found such a man in what is called society, I should not have left it.'

M. Barreaux's admiration of her father endeared him extremely to Emily; whose heart found almost its first relief in conversing of her parents with a man whom she so much revered, and who, though with such an ungracious appearance, possessed so much goodness of heart and delicacy of mind.

Several weeks passed away in quiet retirement, and Emily's affliction began to soften into melancholy. She could bear to read the books she had before read with her father —to sit in his chair in the library—to watch the flowers his hand had planted—to awaken the tones of that instrument his fingers had pressed, and sometimes even to play his favourite air.

When her mind had recovered from the first shock of afflictions, perceiving the danger of yielding to indolence, and that activity alone could restore its tone, she scrupulously endeavoured to pass all her hours in employment. And it was now that she understood the full value of the education she had received from St. Aubert—for, in cultivating her understanding, he had secured her an asylum from indolence without recourse to dissipation, and rich and varied amusement and information independent of the society from which her situation secluded her. Nor were the good effects of this education confined to selfish advantages; since St. Aubert having nourished every amiable quality of her heart, it now expanded in benevolence to all around her, and taught her, when she could not remove the misfortunes of others, at least to soften them by sympathy and tenderness— a benevolence that taught her to feel for all that could suffer.

Madame Cheron returned no answer to Emily's letter; who began to hope that she should be permitted to remain some time longer in her retirement; and her mind had now so far recovered its strength that she ventured to view the scenes which most powerfully recalled the images of past times. Among these was the fishing-house; and to indulge still more the affectionate melancholy of the visit, she took thither her lute, that she might again hear there the tones to which St. Aubert and her mother had so often delighted to listen. She went alone, and at that still hour of the evening which is so soothing to fancy and to grief.

The last time she had been here she was in company with Monsieur and Madame St. Aubert, a few days preceding that on which the latter was seized with a fatal illness; now, when Emily again entered the woods that surrounded the building, they awakened so forcibly the memory of former times, that her resolution yielded for a moment to excess of grief: she stopped, leaned for support against a tree, and wept for some minutes before she had recovered herself sufficiently to proceed. The little path that led to the building was overgrown with grass, and the flowers which St. Aubert had scattered carelessly along the border were almost choked with weeds—the tall thistle, the foxglove, and the nettle. She often paused to look on the desolate spot, now so silent and forsaken!—and when with a trembling hand she opened the door of the fishing house:

'Ah!' said she, 'everything, everything remains as when I left it last—left it with those who never must return!'

She went to a window that overhung the rivulet, and leaning over it, with her eyes fixed on the current, was soon lost in melancholy reverie. The lute she had brought lay forgotten beside her: the mournful sighing of the breeze as it waved the high pines above, and its softer whispers among the osiers that bowed upon the banks below, was a kind of music more in unison with her feelings; it did not vibrate on the chords of unhappy memory, but was soothing to the heart as the voice of pity. She continued to muse, unconscious of the gloom of evening, and that the sun's last light trembled on the heights above; and would probably have remained so much longer if a sudden footstep, without the building, had not alarmed her attention, and first made her recollect that she was unprotected. In the next moment the door opened, and a stranger appeared, who stopped on perceiving Emily, and then began to apologise for his intrusion. But Emily, at the sound of his voice, lost her fear in a stronger emotion: its tones were familiar to her ear; and, though she could not readily distinguish through the dusk the features of the person who spoke, she felt a remembrance too strong to be distrusted.

He repeated his apology, and Emily then said something in reply; when the stranger, eagerly advancing, exclaimed:

'Good God! can it be?—surely I am not mistaken—Ma'amselle St. Aubert?—is it not?'

'It is indeed,' said Emily, who was confirmed in her first conjecture; for she now distinguished the countenance of Valancourt lighted up with still more than its usual animation. A thousand painful recollections crowded to her mind; and the effort which she made to support herself only served to increase her agitation.

Valancourt meanwhile, having inquired anxiously after her health, and expressed his hopes that M. St. Aubert had found benefit from travelling, learned, from the flood of tears which she could no longer repress, the fatal truth. He led her to a seat, and sat down by her; while Emily continued to weep, and Valancourt to hold the hand which she was unconscious he had taken, till it was wet with tears which grief for St. Aubert and sympathy for herself had called forth.

' I feel,' said he at length, ' I feel how insufficient all attempt at consolation must be on this subject; I can only mourn with you; for I cannot doubt the source of your tears. Would to God I were mistaken !'

Emily could still answer only by tears, till she rose and begged they might leave the melancholy spot; when Valancourt, though he saw her feebleness, could not offer to detain her, but took her arm within his, and led her from the fishing-house. They walked silently through the woods; Valancourt anxious to know yet fearing to ask any particulars concerning St. Aubert, and Emily too much distressed to converse. After some time, however, she acquired fortitude enough to speak of her father, and to give a brief account of the manner of his death; during which recital Valancourt's countenance betrayed strong emotion; and when he heard that St. Aubert had died on the road, and that Emily had been left among strangers, he pressed her hand between his, and involuntarily exclaimed, ' Why was I not there !' but in the next moment recollected himself, for he immediately returned to the mention of her father; till, perceiving that her spirits were exhausted, he gradually changed the subject, and spoke of himself. Emily thus learned that, after they had parted, he had wandered for some time along the shores of the Mediterranean, and had then returned through Languedoc into Gascony, which was his native province, and where he usually resided.

When he had concluded his little narrative, he sunk into a silence which Emily was not disposed to interrupt, and it continued till they reached the gate of the chateau, when he stopped, as if he had known this to be the limit of his walk. Here, saying that it was his intention to return to Estuviere on the following day, he asked her if she would permit him to take leave of her in the morning; and Emily, perceiving that she could not reject an ordinary civility without expressing by her refusal an expectation of something more, was compelled to answer that she should be at home.

She passed a melancholy evening, during which the retrospect of all that had happened since she had seen Valancourt would rise to her imagination, and the scene of her father's death appeared in tints as fresh as if it had passed . on the preceding day. She remembered, particularly the earnest and solemn manner in which he had required her to destroy the manuscript papers; and awakened from the lethargy in which sorrow had held her, she was shocked to think she had not yet obeyed him, and determined that another day should not reproach her with the neglect.

CHAPTER XI.

'. . . . Can such things be,
And overcome us like a summer's cloud,
Without our special wonder ?'
                              MACBETH.

On the next morning Emily ordered a fire to be lighted in the stove of the chamber where St. Aubert used to sleep, and as soon as she had breakfasted went thither to burn the papers. Having fastened the door to prevent interruption, she opened the closet where they were concealed; as she entered which she felt an emotion of unusual awe, and stood for some moments surveying it, trembling, and almost afraid to remove the board. There was a great chair in one corner of the closet, and opposite to it stood the table at which she had seen her father sit, on the evening that preceded his departure, looking over, with so much emotion, what she believed to be these very papers.

The solitary life which Emily had led of late, and the melancholy subjects on which she had suffered her thoughts to dwell, had rendered her at times sensible to the ' thick-coming fancies' of a mind greatly enervated. It was lamentable that her excellent understanding should have yielded, even for a moment, to the reveries of superstition, or rather to those starts of imagination which deceive the senses into what can be called nothing less than momentary madness. Instances of this temporary failure of mind had more than once occurred since her return home —particularly when wandering through this lonely mansion in the evening twilight, she had been alarmed by appearances which would have been unseen in her more cheerful days. To this infirm state of her nerves may be attributed what she imagined when, her eyes glancing a second time on the arm-chair, which stood in an obscure part of the closet, the countenance of her dead father appeared there.

Emily stood fixed for a moment to the floor, after which she left the closet. Her spirits, however, soon returned; she reproached herself with the weakness of thus suffering interruption in an act of serious importance, and again opened the door. By the directions which St. Aubert had given her, she readily found the board he had described, in an opposite corner of the closet, near the window, She distinguished also the line he had mentioned; and pressing it, as he had bade her, it slid down and disclosed the bundle of papers, together with some scattered ones and the purse of louis. With a trembling hand she removed them—replaced the board—paused a moment—and was rising from the floor, when, on looking up, there appeared to her alarmed fancy the same countenance in the chair. The illusion (another instance of the unhappy effect which solitude and grief had gradually produced upon her mind) subdued her spirits. She rushed forward into the chamber, and sunk almost senseless into a chair.

Returning reason soon overcame the dreadful, but pitiable, attack of imagination, and she turned to the papers, though still with so little recollection, that her eyes involuntarily settled on the writing of some loose sheets which lay open; and she was unconscious that she was transgressing her father's strict injunction, till a sentence of dreadful import awakened her attention and her memory together. She hastily put the papers from her; but the words which had roused equally her curiosity and terror, she could not dismiss from her thoughts. So powerfully had they affected her, that she even could not resolve to destroy the papers immediately; and the more she dwelt on the circumstance, the more it inflamed her imagination. Urged by the most forcible, and apparently the most necessary, curiosity to inquire further concerning the terrible and mysterious subject to which she had seen an allusion, she began to lament her promise to destroy the papers. For a moment she even doubted whether it could justly be obeyed, in contradiction to such reasons as there appeared to be for further information; but the delusion was momentary; 'I have given a solemn promise', said she, 'to observe a solemn injunction, and it is not my business to argue, but to obey. Let me hasten to remove the temptation that would destroy my innocence, and imbitter my life with the consciousness of irremediable guilt, while I have strength to reject it.'

Thus re-animated with a sense of her duty, she completed the triumph of her integrity over temptation, more forcible than any she had ever known, and consigned the papers to the flames. Her eyes watched them as they slowly consumed : she shuddered at the recollection of the sentence she had just seen, and at the certainty that the only opportunity of explaining it was then passing away for ever.

It was long after this that she recollected the purse ; and as she was depositing it, unopened, in a cabinet, perceiving that it contained something of a size larger than coin, she examined it. 'His hand deposited them here.' said she, as she kissed some pieces of the coin, and wetted them with her tears—'his hand, which is now dust?' At the bottom of the purse was a small packet ; which having taken out, and unfolded paper after paper. she found to be an ivory case containing the miniature of a—lady ! She started. 'The same,' said she, 'my father wept over !' On examining the countenance. she could recollect no person that it resembled : it was of uncommon beauty ; and was characterized by an expression of sweetness shaded with sorrow and tempered by resignation.

St. Aubert had given no directions concerning this picture, nor had even named it ; she therefore thought herself justified in preserving it. More than once remembering his manner when he had spoken of the Marchioness of Villeroi, she felt inclined to believe that this was her resemblance ; yet there appeared no reason why he should have preserved a picture of that lady, or having preserved it, why he should lament over it in a manner so striking and affecting as she had witnessed on the night preceding his departure.

Emily still gazed on the countenance, examining its features ; but she knew not where to detect the charm that captivated her attention, and inspired sentiments of such love and pity. Dark brown hair played carelessly along the open forehead ; the nose was rather inclined to aquiline ; the lips spoke in a smile, but it was a melancholy one ; the eyes were blue, and were directed upwards, with an expression of peculiar meekness ; while the soft cloud of the brow spoke of the fine sensibility of the temper.

Emily was roused from the musing mood into which the picture had thrown her, by the closing of the garden gate ; and on turning her eyes to the window she saw Valancourt coming towards the chateau. Her spirits agitated by the subjects that had lately occupied her mind, she felt unprepared to see him, and remained a few moments in the chamber to recover herself.

When she met him in the parlour, she was struck with the change that appeared in his air and countenance since they had parted at Rousillon, which twilight, and the distress she suffered on the preceding evening had prevented her from observing. But dejection and languor disappeared for a moment, in the smile that now enlightened his countenance on perceiving her. 'You see,' said he, 'I have availed myself of the permission with which you honoured me—of bidding *you* farewell, whom I had the happiness of meeting only yesterday.'

Emily smiled faintly, and, anxious to say something, asked if he had been long in Gascony.

'A few days only,' replied Valancourt, while a blush passed over his cheek. 'I engaged in a long ramble after I had the misfortune of parting with the friends who had made my wanderings among the Pyrenees so delightful.'

A tear came to Emily's eyes as Valancourt said this, which he observed, and, anxious to draw off her attention from the remembrance that had occasioned it, as well as shocked at his own thoughtlessness, he began to speak on other subjects, expressing his admiration of the chateau and its prospects.

Emily, who felt somewhat embarrassed how to support a conversation, was glad of such an opportunity to continue it on different topics. They walked down to the terrace, where Valancourt was charmed with the river scenery, and the views over the opposite shores of Guienne.

As he leaned on the wall of the terrace, watching the rapid current of the Garonne, 'I was a few weeks ago,' said he, 'at the source of this noble river; I had not then the happiness of knowing you, or I should have regretted your absence—it was a scene so exactly suited to your taste. It rises in a part of the Pyrenees still wilder and more sublime, I think, than any we passed in the way to Rousillon.' He then described its fall among the precipices of the mountains, where its waters, augmented by the streams that descend from the snowy summits around, rush into the Valée d'Aran; between those romantic heights it foams along, pursuing its way to the north-west, till it emerges upon the plains of Languedoc; then, washing the walls of Thoulouse, and turning again to the north-west, it assumes a milder character, as it fertilizes the pastures of Gascony and Guienne in its progress to the Bay of Biscay.

Emily and Valancourt talked of the scenes they had passed among the Pyrenean Alps; as he spoke of which there was often a tremulous tenderness in his voice; and sometimes he expatiated on them with all the fire of genius—sometimes would appear scarcely conscious of the topic, though he continued to speak. This subject recalled forcibly to Emily the idea of her father, whose image appeared in every landscape which Valancourt particularized, whose remarks dwelt upon her memory, and whose enthusiasm still glowed in her heart. Her silence at length reminded Valancourt how nearly his conversation approached to the occasion of her grief, and he changed the subject, though for one scarcely less affecting to Emily. When he admired the grandeur of the plane-tree, that spread its wide branches over the terrace, and under whose shade they now sat, she remembered how often she had sat thus with St. Aubert, and heard him express the same admiration.

'This was a favourite tree with my dear father,' said she: 'he used to love to sit under its foliage, with his family about him, in the fine evenings of summer.'

Valancourt understood her feelings, and was silent: had she raised her eyes from the ground, she would have seen tears in his. He rose, and leaned on the wall of the terrace; from which, in a few moments he returned to his seat; then rose again, and appeared to be greatly agitated; while Emily found her spirits so much depressed, that several of her attempts to renew the conversation were ineffectual. Valancourt again sat down; but was still silent, and trembled. At length he said with a hesitating voice, 'This lovely scene I am going to leave!—to leave you—perhaps for ever! These moments may never return! I cannot resolve to neglect, though I scarcely dare to avail myself of them. Let me, however, without offending the delicacy of your sorrow, venture to declare the admiration I must always feel of your goodness—O! that at some future period I might be permitted to call it love!'

Emily's emotion would not suffer her to reply; and Valancourt, who now ventured to look up, observing her countenance change, expected to see her faint, and made an involuntary effort to support her, which recalled Emily to a sense of her situation, and to an exertion of her spirits. Valancourt did not appear to notice her indisposition, but when he spoke again, his voice told the tenderest love. 'I will not presume,' he added, 'to intrude this subject longer upon your attention at this time; but I may perhaps be permitted to mention, that these parting moments would lose much of their bitterness; if I might be allowed to hope the declaration I have made would not exclude me from your presence in future.'

Emily made an effort to overcome the confusion of her thoughts, and to speak. She feared to trust the preference her heart acknowledged towards Valancourt, and to give him any encouragement for hope, on so short an acquaintance; for though, in this narrow period, she had observed much that was admirable in his taste and disposition, and though these observations had been sanctioned by the opinion of her father, they were not sufficient testimonies of his general worth, to determine her upon a subject so infinitely important to her future happiness as that which now solicited her attention. Yet, though the thought of dismissing Valancourt was so very painful to her that she could scarcely endure to pause upon it, the consciousness of this made her fear the partiality of her judgment, and hesitate still more to encourage that suit for which her own heart too tenderly pleaded. The family of Valancourt, if not his circumstances, had been known to her father, and known to be unexceptionable. Of his circumstances Valancourt himself hinted, as far as delicacy would permit, when he said he had at present little else to offer but a heart that adored her. He had solicited only for a distant hope; and she could not resolve to forbid, though she scarcely dared to permit it. At length she acquired courage to say, that she must think herself honoured by the good opinion of any person whom her father had esteemed.

'And was I, then, thought worthy of his esteem?' said Valancourt, in a voice trembling with anxiety. Then checking himself, he added, 'But pardon the question, I scarcely know what I say. If I might dare to hope that you think me not unworthy such honour, and might be permitted sometimes to inquire after your health, I should now leave you with comparative tranquillity.'

Emily, after a moment's silence, said:

'I will be ingenuous with you, for I know you will understand and allow for my situation: you will consider it as a proof of my—my esteem that I am so. Though I live here in what was my father's house, I live here alone. I have, alas! no longer a parent—a parent, whose presence might sanction your visits. It is unnecessary for me to point out the impropriety of my receiving them.'

'Nor will I affect to be insensible of this,' replied Valancourt, adding mournfully—'But what is to console me for my candour? I distress you; and would now leave the subject if I might carry with me a hope of being some time permitted to renew it—of being allowed to make myself known to your family.'

Emily was again confused, and again hesitated what to reply. She felt most acutely the difficulty—the forlornness of her situation—which did not allow her a single relative, or friend to whom she could turn for even a look that might support and guide her in the present embarrassing circumstances. Madame Cheron, who was her only relative, and ought to have been this friend, was either occupied by her own amusements, or so resentful of the reluctance her niece had shown to quit La Vallée, that she seemed totally to have abandoned her.

'Ah! I see,' said Valancourt after a long pause, during which Emily had begun and left unfinished two or three sentences. 'I see that I have nothing to hope: my fears were too just—you think me unworthy of your esteem. That fatal journey! which I considered as the happiest period of my life—those delightful days were to embitter all my future ones! How often I have looked back to them with hope and fear!—yet never till this moment could I prevail with myself to regret their enchanting influence.'

His voice faltered, and he abruptly quitted his seat and walked on the terrace. There was an expression of despair on his countenance that affected Emily. The pleadings of her heart overcame, in some degree, her extreme timidity; and when he resumed his seat, she said in an accent that betrayed her tenderness:

'You do both yourself and me injustice when you say I think you unworthy of my esteem; I will acknowledge that you have long possessed it, and—and—'

Valancourt waited impatiently for the conclusion of the sentence, but the words died on her lips. Her eyes, however, reflected all the emotions of her heart. Valancourt passed in an instant from the impatience of despair to that of joy and tenderness.

'O Emily!' he exclaimed, 'my own Emily —teach me to sustain this moment! Let me seal it as the most sacred of my life!'

He pressed her hand to his lips; it was cold and trembling; and raising his eyes, he saw the paleness of her countenance. Tears came to her relief, and Valancourt watched in anxious silence over her. In a few moments she recovered herself, and smiling faintly through her tears, said: 'Can you excuse this weakness? My spirits have not yet, I believe, recovered from the shock they lately received.'

'I cannot excuse myself,' said Valancourt. 'But I will forbear to renew the subject which may have contributed to agitate them, now that I can leave you with the sweet certainty of possessing your esteem.'

Then, forgetting his resolution, he again spoke of himself:

'You know not,' said he, 'the many anxious hours I have passed near you lately, when you believed me, if indeed you honoured me with a thought, far away. I have wandered near the chateau, in the still hours of the night, when no eye could observe me. It was delightful to know I was so near you; and there was something particularly soothing in the thought that I watched round your habitation while you slept. These grounds are not entirely new to me. Once I ventured within the fence, and spent one of the happiest and yet most melancholy hours of my life, in walking under what I believed to be your window.'

Emily inquired how long Valancourt had been in the neighbourhood.

'Several days,' he replied. 'It was my design to avail myself of the permission M. St. Aubert had given me. I scarcely know how to account for it; but, although I anxiously wished to do this, my resolution always failed when the moment approached, and I constantly deferred my visit. I lodged in a village at some distance, and wandered with my dogs among the scenes of this charming country, wishing continually to meet you, yet not daring to visit you.'

Having thus continued to converse without perceiving the flight of time, Valancourt at length seemed to recollect himself.

'I must go,' said he mournfully—but it is with the hope of seeing you again, of being permitted to pay my respects to your family: —let me hear this hope confirmed by your voice.'

'My family will be happy to see any friend of my dear father,' said Emily.

Valancourt kissed her hand, and still lingered, unable to depart; while Emily sat silently, with her eyes bent on the ground; and Valancourt, as he gazed on her, considered that it would soon be impossible for him to recall, even to his memory, the exact resemblance of the beautiful countenance he then beheld. At this moment a hasty footstep approached from behind the plane-tree, and turning her eyes, Emily saw Madame Cheron. She felt a blush steal upon her cheek, and her frame trembled with the emotion of her mind; but she instantly rose to meet her visitor.

'So niece,' said Madame Cheron, casting a look of surprise and inquiry on Valancourt —'So, niece, how do you do?—But I need not ask—your looks tell me you have already recovered your loss.'

'My looks do me injustice then, Madame; my loss, I know, can never be recovered.'

'Well, well! I will not argue with you: I see you have exactly your father's disposition; and let me tell you, it would have been much happier for him, poor man! if it had been a different one.'

A look of dignified displeasure, with which Emily regarded Madame Cheron while she spoke, would have touched almost any other heart: she made no other reply; but introduced Valancourt, who could scarcely stifle the resentment he felt, and whose bow Madame Cheron returned with a slight curtsy and a look of supercilious examination. After a few moments he took leave of Emily, in a manner that hastily expressed his pain, both at his own departure and at leaving her to the society of Madame Cheron.

'Who is that young man?' said her aunt, in an accent which equally implied inquisitiveness and censure: some idle admirer of yours, I suppose? But I believed, niece, you had a greater sense of propriety than to have received the visits of any young man in your present unfriended situation. Let me tell you, the world will observe those things; and it will talk—ay, and very freely too.'

Emily, extremely shocked at this coarse speech, attempted to interrupt it; but Madame Cheron would proceed, with all the self-importance of a person to whom power is new.

'It is very necessary you should be under the eye of some person more able to guide you than yourself. I, indeed have not much leisure for such a task. However, since your poor father made it his last request that I should overlook your conduct, I must even take you under my care. But this let me tell you, niece, that unless you will determine to be very conformable to my direction, I shall not trouble myself longer about you.'

Emily made no attempt to interrupt Madame Cheron a second time; grief, and the pride of conscious innocence, kept her silent; till her aunt said,

'I am now come to take you with me to Thoulouse, I am sorry to find that your poor father died, after all, in such indifferent circumstances: however, I shall take you home with me. Ah! poor man! he was always more generous than provident, or he would not have left his daughter dependent on his relations.'

'Nor has he done so, I hope, madam,' said Emily calmly; 'nor did his pecuniary misfortunes arise from that noble generosity which always distinguished him: the affairs of M. de Motteville may, I trust, yet be settled without deeply injuring his creditors, and in the meantime I should be very happy to remain at La Vallée.'

'No doubt you would,' replied Madame Cheron, with a smile of irony; 'and I shall no doubt consent to this, since I see how necessary tranquillity and retirement are to restore your spirits. I did not think you capable of so much duplicity, niece. When you pleaded this excuse for remaining here, I foolishly believed it to be a just one, nor expected to have found with you so agreeable a companion as this M. La Val—— : I forget his name.'

Emily could no longer endure these cruel indignities.

'It was a just one, madam,' said she; 'and now, indeed, I feel more than ever the value of the retirement I then solicited; and if the purport of your visit is only to add insult to the sorrows of your brother's child, she could well have spared it.'

'I see that I have undertaken a very troublesome task,' said Madame Cheron, colouring highly.

'I am sure, madam,' said Emily mildly, and endeavouring to restrain her tears, 'I am sure my father did not mean it to be such. I have the happiness to reflect that my conduct under his eye was such as he often delighted to approve. It would be very painful to me to disobey the sister of such a parent; and, if you believe the task will really be so troublesome, I must lament that it is yours.'

'Well, niece, fine speaking signifies little: I am willing, in consideration of my poor brother, to overlook the impropriety of your late conduct, and to try what your future will be.'

Emily interrupted her to beg she would explain what was the impropriety she alluded to.

'What impropriety!—why that of receiving the visits of a lover unknown to your family,' replied Madam Cheron; not considering the impropriety of which she herself had been guilty, in exposing her niece to the possibility of conduct so erroneous.

A faint blush passed over Emily's countenance; pride and anxiety struggled in her breast; and, till she recollected that appearances did, in some degree, justify her aunt's suspicions, she could not resolve to humble herself so far as to enter into the defence of a conduct which had been so innocent and undesigned on her part. She mentioned the manner of Valancourt's introduction to her father; the circumstance of his receiving the pistol-shot, and of their afterwards travelling together; with the accidental way in which she had met him on the preceding evening. She owned he had declared a partiality for her, and that he had asked permission to address her family.

'And who is this young adventurer, pray?' said Madam Cheron, 'and what are his pretensions?'

'These he must himself explain, madam,' replied Emily. 'Of his family my father was not ignorant, and I believe it is unexceptionable.'

She then proceeded to mention what she knew concerning it.

'Oh, then, this it seems is a younger brother!' exclaimed her aunt, 'and of course a beggar. A very fine tale, indeed! And so my brother took a fancy to this young man after only a few days' acquaintance? But that was so like him! In his youth he was always taking these likes and dislikes, when no other person saw any reason for them at all: nay, indeed, I have often thought the people he disapproved were much more agreeable than those he admired. But there is no accounting for tastes. He was always so much influenced by people's countenances! Now I, for my part, have no notion of this; it is all ridiculous enthusiasm. What has a man's face to do with his character? Can a man of good character help having a disagreeable face?'—which last sentence Madam Cheron delivered with the decisive air of a person who congratulates herself on having made a grand discovery, and believes the question to be unanswerably settled.

Emily, desirous of concluding the conversation, inquired if her aunt would accept some refreshment; and Madame Cheron accompanied her to the chateau, but without desisting from a topic which she discussed with so much complacency to herself and severity to her niece.

'I am sorry to perceive, niece,' said she, in allusion to somewhat that Emily had said concerning physiognomy, 'that you have a great many of your father's prejudices, and among them those sudden predilections for people from their looks. I can perceive that you imagine yourself to be violently in love with this young adventurer, after an acquaintance of only a few days. There was something, too, so charmingly romantic in the manner of your meeting!'

Emily checked the tears that trembled in her eyes, while she said,

'When my conduct shall deserve this severity, madam, you will do well to exercise it; till then, justice, if not tenderness, should surely restrain it. I have never willingly offended you. Now I have lost my parents, you are the only person to whom I can look for kindness: let me not lament more than ever the loss of such parents.'

The last words were almost stifled by her emotions, and she burst into tears. Remembering the delicacy and the tenderness of St. Aubert, the happy, happy days she had passed in these scenes; and contrasting them with the coarse and unfeeling behaviour of Madame Cheron, and with the future hours of mortification she must submit to in her presence—a degree of grief seized her, that almost reached despair. Madame Cheron, more offended by the reproof which Emily's words conveyed, than touched by the sorrow they expressed, said nothing that might soften her grief; but, notwithstanding an apparent reluctance to receive her niece, she desired her company. The love of sway was her ruling passion, and she knew it would be highly gratified by taking into her house a young orphan, who had no appeal from her decisions, and on whom she could exercise without control the capricious humour of the moment.

On entering the chateau, Madame Cheron expressed a desire that she would put up what she thought necessary to take to Thoulouse, as she meant to set off immediately. Emily now tried to persuade her to defer the journey at least till the next day; and at length, with much difficulty, prevailed.

The day passed in the exercise of petty tyranny on the part of Madame Cheron, and in mournful regret and melancholy anticipation on that of Emily; who, when her aunt retired to her apartment for the night, went to take leave of every other room in this her dear native home, which she was now quitting for she knew not how long, and for the world to which she was wholly a stranger. She could not conquer a presentiment, which frequently occurred to her this night—that she should never more return to La Vallée. Having passed a considerable time in what had been her father's study; having selected some of his favourite authors to put up with her clothes, and shed many tears as she wiped the dust from their covers; she seated herself in his chair before the reading-desk, and sat lost in melancholy reflection; till Theresa opened the door to examine, as was her custom before she went to bed, it was all safe. She started on observing her young lady, who bade her come in, and then gave her some directions for keeping the chateau in readiness for her reception at all times.

'Alas-a-day! that you should leave it!' said Theresa: 'I think you would be happier here than where you are going, if one may judge.'

Emily made no reply to this remark. The sorrow Theresa proceeded to express at her departure affected her; but she found some comfort in the simple affection of this poor old servant, to whom she gave such directions as might best conduce to her comfort during her own absence.

Having dismissed Theresa to bed, Emily wandered through every lonely apartment of the chateau, lingering long in what had been her father's bed-room, indulging melancholy yet not unpleasing emotions; and having often returned within the door to take another look at it, she withdrew to her own chamber. From her window she gazed upon the garden below, shown faintly by the moon rising over the tops of the palm-trees; and at length the calm beauty of the night increased a desire of indulging the mournful sweetness of bidding farewell to the beloved shades of her childhood, till she was tempted to descend. Throwing over her the light veil in which she usually walked, she silently passed into the garden, and, hastening towards the distant groves was glad to breathe once more the air of liberty, and to sigh unobserved. The deep repose of the scene, the rich scents that floated on the breeze, the grandeur of the wide horizon and of the clear blue arch, soothed, and gradually elevated her mind to that sublime complacency, which renders the vexations of this world so insignificant and mean in our eyes, that we wonder they have had power for a moment to disturb us. Emily forgot Madame Cheron and all the circumstances of her conduct, while her thoughts ascended to the contemplation of those unnumbered worlds that lie scattered in the depths of ether—thousands of them hid from human eyes, and almost beyond the flight of human fancy. As her imagination soared through the regions of space, and aspired to that Great First Cause which pervades and governs all being, the idea of her father scarcely ever left her; but it was a pleasing idea, since she resigned him to God in the full confidence of a pure and holy faith. She pursued her way through the groves to the terrace, often pausing as memory awakened the pang of affection, and as reason anticipated the exile into which she was going.

And now the moon was high over the woods, touching their summits with yellow light, and darting between the foliage long level beams; while on the apid Garonne below, the trembling radiance was faintly obscured by the lightest vapour. Emily long watched the playing lustre; listened to the soothing murmur of the current, and the yet lighter sounds of the air as it stirred at intervals the lofty palm-trees.

'How delightful is the sweet breath of these groves!' said she. 'This lovely scene! —how often shall I remember and regret it when I am far away; Alas! what events may occur before I see it again! O peaceful, happy shades!—scenes of my infant delights, of parental tenderness now lost for ever!—

why must I leave you? In your retreats I should still find safety and repose. Sweet hours of my childhood—I am now to leave even your last memorials! No objects that would revive your impressions will remain for me!'

Then drying her tears, and looking up, her thoughts rose again to the sublime subject she had contemplated: the same divine complacency stole over her heart, and hushing its throbs, inspired hope and confidence and resignation to the will of the Deity, whose works filled her mind with adoration.

Emily gazed long on the plane-tree, and then seated herself for the last time on the bench under its shade, where she had so often sat with her parents; and where, only a few hours before, she had conversed with Valancourt; at the remembrance of whom, thus revived, a mingled sensation of esteem, tenderness, and anxiety, rose in her breast. With this remembrance occurred a recollection of his late confession—that he had often wandered near her habitation in the night, having even passed the boundary of the garden; and it immediately occurred to her that he might be at this moment in the grounds. The fear of meeting him, particularly after the declaration he had made, and of incurring a censure which her aunt might so reasonably bestow, if it was known that she was met by her lover at this hour, made her instantly leave her beloved plane-tree, and walk towards the chateau. She cast an anxious eye around, and often stopped for a moment to examine the shadowy scene before she ventured to proceed: but she passed on without perceiving any person, till, having reached a clump of almond-trees, not far from the house, she rested to take a retrospect of the garden, and to sigh forth another adieu:—as her eyes wandered over the landscape, she thought she perceived a person emerge from the groves, and pass slowly along a moon-light alley that led between them; but the distance, and the imperfect light, would not suffer her to judge with any degree of certainty whether this was fancy or reality. She continued to gaze for some time on the spot; till on the dead stillness of the air she heard a sudden sound, and in the next instant fancied she distinguished footsteps near her. Wasting not another moment in conjecture, she hurried to the chateau, and, having reached it, retired to her chamber, where as she closed her window she looked upon the garden, and then again thought that she distinguished a figure gliding between the almond-trees she had just left. She immediately withdrew from the casement, and, though much agitated, sought in sleep the refreshment of a short oblivion.

CHAPTER XII.

'. . . I leave that flowery path for aye
Of childhood, where I sported many a day,
Warbling and sauntering carelessly along;
Where every face was innocent and gay;
Each vale romantic; tuneful every tongue—
Sweet, wild, and artless, all.'
                              THE MINSTREL.

AT an early hour the carriage which was to take Emily and Madame Cheron to Thoulouse appeared at the door of the chateau; and Madame was already in the breakfast-room when her niece entered. The repast was silent and melancholy on the part of Emily; and Madame Cheron, whose vanity was piqued on observing her dejection, reproved her in a manner that did not contribute to remove it. It was with much reluctance that Emily's request to take with her the dog, which had been a favourite of her father, was granted. Her aunt, impatient to be gone, ordered the carriage to draw up; and while she passed to the hall door, Emily gave another look into the library, and another farewell glance over the garden, and then followed. Old Theresa stood at the door to take leave of her young lady. 'God for ever keep you, Ma'amselle'!' said she; while Emily gave her hand in silence, and could answer only with a pressure of her hand and a forced smile.

At the gate which led out of the grounds, several of her father's pensioners were assembled to bid her farewell; to whom she would have spoken, if her aunt would have suffered the driver to stop; and having distributed to them almost all the money she had about her, she sunk back in the carriage, yielding to the melancholy of her heart. Soon after, she caught between the steep banks of the road another view of the chateau peeping from among the high trees, and surrounded by green slopes and tufted groves; the Garonne winding its way beneath their shades, sometimes lost among the vineyards, and then rising in greater majesty in the distant pastures. The towering precipices of the Pyrenees, that rose to the south, gave Emily a thousand interesting recollections of her late journey; and these objects of her former enthusiastic admiration now excited only sorrow and regret. Having gazed on the chateau and its lovely scenery till the banks again closed upon them, her mind became too much occupied by mournful reflections to permit her to attend to the conversation which Madame Cheron had begun on some trivial topic; so that they soon travelled in profound silence.

Valancourt, meanwhile, was returned to Estuviere, his heart occupied with the image of Emily; sometimes indulging in reveries of future happiness, but more frequently shrinking with dread of the opposition he might encounter from her family. He was the younger son of an ancient family of Gascony; and having lost his parents at an early period of his life, the care of his education and of his small portion had devolved to his brother the Count de Duvarney, his senior by nearly twenty years. Valancourt had been educated in all the accomplishments of his age, and had an ardour of spirit and a certain grandeur of mind, that gave him particular excellence in the exercises then thought heroic. His little fortune had been diminished by the necessary expenses of his education; but M. La Valancourt the elder seemed to think that his genius and accomplishments would amply supply the deficiency of his inheritance. They offered flattering hopes of promotion in the military profession—in those times almost the only one in which a gentleman could engage without incurring a stain on his name; and La Valancourt was of course enrolled in the army. The general genius of his mind was but little understood by his brother. That ardour for whatever is great and good in the moral world, as well as in the natural one, displayed itself in his infant years; and the strong indignation which he felt and expressed at a criminal or a mean action, sometimes drew upon him the displeasure of his tutor; who reprobated it under the general term of violence of temper; and who, when haranguing on the virtues of mildness and moderation, seemed to forget the gentleness and compassion which always appeared in his pupil towards objects of misfortune.

He had now obtained leave of absence from his regiment, when he made the excursion into the Pyrenees which was the means of introducing him to St. Aubert; and as this permission was nearly expired, he was the more anxious to declare himself to Emily's family, from whom he reasonably apprehended opposition, since his fortune, though with a moderate addition from hers it would be sufficient to support them, would not satisfy the views either of vanity or ambition. Valancourt was not without the latter; but he saw golden visions of promotion in the army, and believed that, with Emily, he could in the meantime be delighted to live within the limits of his humble income. His thoughts were now occupied in considering the means of making himself known to her family to whom, however, he had yet no address; for he was entirely ignorant of Emily's precipitate departure from La Valée, of whom he hoped to obtain it.

Meanwhile the travellers pursued their journey; Emily making frequent efforts to appear cheerful, and too often relapsing into silence and dejection. Madame Cheron attributing her melancholy solely to the circumstance of her being removed to a distance from her lover, and believing that the sorrow which her niece still expressed for the loss of St. Aubert proceeded partly from an affectation of sensibility, endeavoured to make it appear ridiculous to her, that such deep regret continued to be felt so long after the period usually allowed for grief.

At length these unpleasant lectures were interrupted by the arrival of the travellers at Thoulouse; and Emily, who had not been there for many years, and had only a very faint recollection of it, was surprised at the ostentatious style exhibited in her aunt's house and furniture; the more so, perhaps, because it was so totally different from the modest elegance to which she had been accustomed. She followed Madame Cheron through a large hall, where several servants in rich liveries appeared, to a kind of saloon fitted up with more show than taste; and her aunt, complaining of fatigue, ordered supper immediately. 'I am glad to find myself in my own house again,' said she, throwing herself on a large settee, 'and to have my own people about me. I detest travelling: though, indeed, I ought to like it, for what I see abroad always makes me delighted to return to my own chateau. What makes you so silent, child?—what is it that disturbs you now?'

Emily suppressed a starting tear, and tried to smile away the expression of an oppressed heart: she was thinking of *her* home, and felt too sensibly the arrogance and ostentatious vanity of Madame Cheron's conversation. 'Can this be my father's sister!' said she to herself; and then, the conviction that she was so warming her heart with something like kindness towards her, she felt anxious to soften the harsh impression her mind had received of her aunt's character, and to show a willingness to oblige her. The effort did not entirely fail; she listened with apparent cheerfulness while Madame Cheron expatiated on the splendour of her house, told of the numerous parties she entertained, and what she should expect of Emily, whose diffidence assumed the air of reserve, which her aunt, believing it to be that of pride and ignorance united, now took occasion to reprehend. She knew nothing of the conduct of a mind that fears to trust its own powers; which, possessing a nice judgment, and inclining to believe that every other person perceives still more critically, fears to commit itself to censure, and seeks shelter in the obscurity of silence. Emily had frequently blushed at the fearless manners which she had seen admired, and the brilliant nothings which she had heard applauded; yet this applause, so far from encouraging her to imitate the conduct that had won it, rather made her shrink into the reserve that would protect her from such absurdity.

Madame Cheron looked on her niece's diffidence with a feeling very near to contempt, and endeavoured to overcome it by reproof, rather than to encourage it by gentleness.

The entrance of supper somewhat interrupted the complacent discourse of Madame Cheron, and the painful considerations which it had forced upon Emily. When the repast (which was rendered ostentatious by the attendance of a great number of servants, and by a profusion of plate) was over, Madame Cheron retired to her chamber, and a female servant came to show Emily to hers. Having passed up a large staircase, and through several galleries, they came to a flight of back stairs, which led into a short passage in a remote part of the chateau; and there the servant opened the door of a small chamber, which she said was Ma'amselle Emily's; who, once more alone, indulged the tears she had long tried to restrain.

Those who know from experience how much the heart becomes attached even to inanimate objects to which it has been long accustomed —how unwillingly it resigns them—how, with the sensations of an old friend, it meets them after temporary absence, will understand the forlornness of Emily's feelings—of Emily shut out from the only home she had known from her infancy, and thrown upon a scene and among persons, disagreeable for more qualities than their novelty. Her father's favourite dog, now in the chamber, thus seemed to acquire the character and importance of a friend; and as the animal fawned over her when she wept, and licked her hands,

'Ah, poor Manchon!' said she, 'I have nobody now to love me—but you!' and she wept the more.

After some time, her thoughts returning to her father's injunctions, she remembered how often he had blamed her for indulging useless sorrow—how often he had pointed out to her the necessity of fortitude and patience; assuring her, that the faculties of the mind strengthen by exertion, till they finally unnerve affliction, and triumph over it. These recollections dried her tears, gradually soothed her spirits, and inspired her with the sweet emulation of practising precepts which her father had so frequently inculcated.

CHAPTER XIII.

'Some power impart the spear and shield,
At which the wizard passions fly,
By which the giant follies die!'   COLLINS.

MADAME CHERON'S house stood at a little distance from the city of Thoulouse, and was surrounded by extensive gardens, in which Emily, who had arisen early, amused herself with wandering before breakfast. From a terrace, that extended along the highest part of them, was a wide view over Languedoc. On the distant horizon to the south she discovered the wild summits of the Pyrenees, and her fancy immediately painted the green pastures of Gascony at their feet. Her heart pointed to her peaceful home—to the neighbourhood where Valancourt was—where St. Aubert had been; and her imagination, piercing the veil of distance, brought that home to her eyes in all its interesting and romantic beauty. She experienced an inexpressible pleasure in believing that she beheld the country around it, though no feature could be distinguished, except the retiring chain of the Pyrenees; and, inattentive to the scene immediately before her, and to the flight of time, she continued to lean on the window of a pavilion that terminated the terrace, with her eyes fixed on Gascony, and her mind occupied with the interesting ideas which the view of it awakened, till a servant came to tell her breakfast was ready. Her thoughts thus recalled to the surrounding objects, the straight walks, square parterres, and artificial fountains of the garden, could not fail, as she passed through it, to appear the worse, opposed to the negligent graces and natural beauties of the grounds of La Valée, upon which her recollection had been so intensively employed.

'Whither have you been rambling so early?' said Madame Cheron, as her niece entered the breakfast-room; 'I don't approve of these solitary walks.'

And Emily was surprised, when, having informed her aunt that she had been no further than the gardens, she understood these to be included in the reproof.

'I desire you will not walk there again, at so early an hour, unattended,' said Madame Cheron: 'my gardens are very extensive; and a young woman who can make assignations by moonlight at La Valée, is not to be trusted to her own inclinations elsewhere.'

Emily, extremely surprised and shocked, had scarcely power to beg an explanation of these words; and when she did, her aunt absolutely refused to give it; though, by her severe looks and half sentences, she appeared anxious to impress Emily with a belief that she was well informed of some degrading circumstances of her conduct. Conscious innocence could not prevent a blush from stealing over Emily's cheek; she trembled, and looked confusedly, under the bold eye of Madame Cheron, who blushed also; but hers was the blush of triumph, such as sometimes stains the countenance of a person congratulating himself on the penetration which had taught him to suspect another, and who loses both pity for the supposed criminal, and indignation at his guilt, in the gratification of his own vanity.

Emily, not doubting that her aunt's mistake arose from the having observed her ramble in the garden on the night preceding her departure from La Vallée, now mentioned the motive of it; at which Madame Cheron smiled contemptuously, refusing either to accept this explanation, or to give her reasons for refusing it; and soon after she concluded the subject by saying, 'I never trust people's assertions: I always judge of them by their actions. But I am willing to try what will be your behaviour in future.'

Emily, less surprised by her aunt's moderation and mysterious silence, than by the accusation she had received, deeply considered the latter, and scarcely doubted that it was Valancourt whom she had seen at night in the gardens of La Vallée, and that he had been observed there by Madame Cheron; who now, passing from one painful topic only to revive another almost equally so, spoke of the situation of her niece's property in the hands of M. Motteville. While she thus talked with ostentatious pity of Emily's misfortunes, she failed not to inculcate the duties of humility and gratitude, or to render Emily fully sensible of every cruel mortification: who soon perceived that she was to be considered as a dependant, not only by her aunt, but by her aunt's servants.

She was now informed that a large party were expected to dinner; on which account Madame Cheron repeated the lesson of the preceding night, concerning her conduct in company; and Emily wished that she might have courage enough to practise it. Her aunt then proceeded to examine the simplicity of her dress, adding, that she expected to see her attired with gaiety and taste. After which she condescended to show Emily the splendour of her chateau, and to point out the particular beauty, or elegance, which she thought distinguished each of her numerous suites of apartments. She then withdrew to her toilet, the throne of her homage, and Emily to her chamber, to unpack her books, and to try to charm her mind by reading, till the hour of dressing.

When the company arrived, Emily entered the saloon with an air of timidity which all her efforts could not overcome, and which was increased by the consciousness of Madame Cheron's severe observation. Her mourning dress, the mild dejection of her beautiful countenance, and the retiring diffidence of her manner, rendered her a very interesting object to many of the company; among whom she distinguished Signor Montoni and his friend Cavigni, the late visitors at M. Quesnel's; who now seemed to converse with Madame Cheron with the familiarity of old acquaintance, and she to attend to them with particular pleasure.

This Signor Montoni had an air of conscious superiority, animated by spirit and strengthened by talents, to which every person seemed involuntarily to yield. The quickness of his perceptions was strikingly expressed on his countenance; yet that countenance could submit implicitly to occasion; and more than once in this day the triumph of art over nature might have been discerned in it. His visage was long, and rather narrow; yet he was called handsome: and it was, perhaps, the spirit and vigour of his soul, sparkling through his features, that triumphed for him. Emily felt admiration, but not the admiration that leads to esteem; for it was mixed with a degree of fear she knew not exactly wherefore.

Cavigni was gay and insinuating as formerly; and though he paid almost incessant attention to Madame Cheron, he found some opportunities of conversing with Emily, to whom he directed at first the sallies of his wit, but now and then assumed an air of tenderness, which she observed and shrunk from. Though she replied but little, the gentleness and sweetness of her manners encouraged him to talk; and she felt relieved when a young lady of the party, who spoke incessantly, obtruded herself on his notice. This lady, who possessed all the sprightliness of a French woman with all her coquetry, affected to understand every subject—or, rather, there was no affectation in the case; for, never looking beyond the limits of her own ignorance, she believed she had nothing to learn. She attracted notice from all—amused some, disgusted others for a moment, and was then forgotten.

This day passed without any material occurrence; and Emily, though amused by the characters she had seen, was glad when she could retire to the recollections which had acquired with her the character of duties.

A fortnight passed in a round of dissipation and company; and Emily who attended Madame Cheron in all her visits, was sometimes entertained, but oftener wearied. She was struck by the apparent talents and knowledge displayed in the various conversations she listened to; and it was long before she discovered that the talents were, for the most part, those of imposture, and the knowledge nothing more than was necessary to assist them. But what deceived her most, was the air of constant gaiety and good spirits displayed by every visitor, and which she supposed to arise from content as constant, and from benevolence as ready. At length, from the over-acting of some less accomplished than the others, she could perceive that, though contentment and benevolence are the only sure sources of cheerfulness, the immoderate and feverish animation, usually exhibited in large parties, results partly from an insensibility to the cares which benevolence must sometimes derive from the sufferings of others, and partly from a desire to display the appearance of that prosperity which they know will command submission and attention to themselves.

Emily's pleasantest hours were passed in the pavilion of the terrace; to which she retired, when she could steal from observation, with a book to overcome, or a lute to indulge, her melancholy. There, as she sat with her eyes fixed on the far distant Pyrenees, and her thoughts on Valancourt and the beloved scenes of Gascony, she would play the sweet and melancholy songs of her native province—the popular songs she had listened to from her childhood,

One evening, having excused herself from accompanying her aunt abroad, she thus withdrew to the pavilion, with books and her lute. It was the mild and beautiful evening of a sultry day; and the windows, which fronted the west, opened upon all the glory of a setting sun. Its rays illuminated, with strong splendour, the cliffs of the Pyrenees, and touched their snowy tops with a roseate hue, that remained long after the sun had sunk below the horizon, and the shades of twilight had stolen over the landscape. Emily touched the lute with that fine melancholy expression which came from her heart. The pensive hour, and the scene; the evening light on the Garonne, that flowed at no great distance, and whose waves as they passed towards La Vallée, she often viewed with a sigh—these united circumstances disposed her mind to tenderness; and her thoughts were with Valancourt, of whom she had heard nothing since her arrival at Thoulouse; and now that she was removed from him, and in uncertainty, she perceived all the interest he held in her heart. Before she saw Valancourt, she had never met a mind and taste so accordant with her own; and though Madame Cheron told her much of the arts of dissimulation, and that the elegance and propriety of thought, which she so much admired in her lover, were assumed for the purpose of pleasing her, she could scarcely doubt their truth. This possibility, however, faint as it was, was sufficient to harass her mind with anxiety; and she found that few conditions are more painful than that of uncertainty as to the merit of a beloved object—an uncertainty which she would not have suffered, had her confidence in her own opinions been greater.

She was was awakened from her musing by the sound of horses' feet along a road that wound under the windows of the pavilion; and a gentleman passed on horseback, whose resemblance to Valancourt, in air and figure (for the twilight did not permit a view of his features), immediately struck her. She retired hastily from the lattice, fearing to be seen, yet wishing to observe further; while the stranger passed on without looking up; and when she returned to the lattice, she saw him faintly through the twilight, winding under the high trees that led to Thoulouse. This little incident so much disturbed her spirits, that the temple and its scenery were no longer interesting to her, and after walking a while on the terrace she returned to the chateau.

Madame Cheron, whether she had seen a rival admired, had lost at play, or had witnessed an entertainment more splendid than her own, was returned from her visit with a temper more than usually discomposed; and Emily was glad when the hour arrived in which she could retire to the solitude of her own apartment.

On the following morning she was summoned to Madame Cheron, whose countenance was inflamed with resentment; and as Emily advanced, she held out a letter to her.

'Do you know this hand?' said she, in a severe tone, and with a look that was intended to search her heart; while Emily examined the letter attentively, and assured her that she did not.

'Do not provoke me,' said her aunt: 'you do know it: confess the truth immediately. I insist upon your confessing the truth instantly.'

Emily was silent, and turned to leave the room; but Madame called her back.

'Oh! you are guilty, then!' said she: 'you do know the hand!'

'If you were before in doubt of this, Madam,' replied Emily, calmly, 'why did you accuse me of having told a falsehood?'

Madame Cheron did not blush; but her niece did, a moment after, when she heard the name of Valancourt. It was not, however, with the consciousness of deserving reproof; for, if she had ever seen his hand-writing, the present characters did not bring it to her recollection.

'It is useless to deny it,' said Madame Cheron; 'I see in your countenance that you are no stranger to this letter; and I dare say you have received many such from this impertinent young man, without my knowledge, in my own house.'

Emily, shocked at the indelicacy of this accusation still more than by the vulgarity of the former, instantly forgot the pride that had imposed silence, and endeavoured to vindicate herself from the aspersion; but Madame Cheron was not to be convinced.

'I cannot suppose,' she resumed, 'that this young man would have taken the liberty of writing to me, if you had not encouraged him to do so; and I must now—'

'You will allow me to remind you, Madam,' said Emily timidly, 'of some particulars of a conversation we had at La Vallée. I then told you truly, that I had only not forbidden Monsieur Valancourt from addressing my family.'

'I will not be interrupted,' said Madame Cheron, interrupting her niece: 'I was going to say—I—I—I have forgot what I was going to say.—But how happened it that you did not forbid him?' Emily was silent. 'How happened it that you encouraged him to trouble me with this letter?—A young man that nobody knows—an utter stranger in the place—a young adventurer, no doubt, who is

looking out for a good fortune. However, on that point he has mistaken his aim.'

'His family was known to my father,' said Emily modestly, and without appearing to be sensible of the last sentence.

'O! that is no recommendation at all,' replied her aunt, with her usual readiness upon this topic; 'he took such strange fancies to people. He was always judging persons by their countenances, and was continually deceived.'

'Yet it was but now, Madam, that you judged me guilty by my countenance,' said Emily, with a design of reproving Madame Cheron, to which she was induced by this disrespectful mention of her father.

'I called you here,' resumed her aunt colouring, 'to tell you that I will not be disturbed, in my own house, by any letters or visits from young men who may take a fancy to flatter you. This M. de Valantine—I think you call him—has the impertinence to beg I will permit him to pay his respects to me! I shall send him a proper answer. And for you, Emily, I repeat it once for all—if you are not contented to conform to my directions, and to my way of life, I shall give up the task of overlooking your conduct—I shall no longer trouble myself with your education, but shall send you to board in a convent.'

'Dear Madame,' said Emily, bursting into tears and overcome by the rude suspicions her aunt had expressed, 'how have I deserved these reproofs?' She could say no more; and so very fearful was she of acting with any degree of impropriety in the affair itself, that, at the present moment, Madame Cheron might perhaps have prevailed with her to bind herself by a promise to renounce Valancourt for ever. Her mind, weakened by her terrors, would no longer suffer her to view him as she had formerly done; she feared the terror of her own judgment, not that of Madame Cheron; and feared also that, in her former conversation with him at La Vallée, she had not conducted herself with sufficient reserve. She knew that she did not deserve the coarse suspicions which her aunt had thrown out; but a thousand scruples rose to torment her, such as would never have disturbed the peace of Madame Cheron. Thus rendered anxious to avoid every opportunity of erring, and willing to submit to any restrictions that her aunt should think proper, she expressed an obedience; to which Madame Cheron did not give much confidence, and which she seemed to consider as the consequence of either fear or artifice.

'Well then,' said she, 'promise me that you will neither see this young man, nor write to him, without my consent.'

'Dear Madam,' replied Emily, 'can you suppose I would do either, unknown to you?'

'I don't know what to suppose. There is

no knowing how young women will act. It is difficult to place any confidence in them, for they have seldom sense enough to wish for the respect of the world.

'Alas! Madam,' said Emily, 'I am anxious for my own respect; my father taught me the value of that; he said, if I deserved my own esteem, that of the world would follow of course.'

'My brother was a good kind of a man,' replied Madame Cheron, 'but he did not know the world. I am sure I have always felt a proper respect for myself; yet——' She stopped; but she might have added, 'that the world had not always shown respect to her; and this without impeaching its judgment.

'Well!' resumed Madame Cheron, 'you have not given me the promise, though, that I demand.'

Emily readily gave it; and being then suffered to withdraw, she walked into the garden: tried to compose her spirits; and at length arrived at her favourite pavilion at the end of the terrace, where, seating herself at one of the embowered windows that opened upon a balcony, the stillness and seclusion of the scene allowed her to recollect her thoughts, and to arrange them so as to form a clearer judgment of her former conduct. She endeavoured to review with exactness all the particulars of her conversation with Valancourt at La Valée; had the satisfaction to observe nothing that could alarm her delicate pride, and thus to be confirmed in the self-esteem which was so necessary to her peace. Her mind then became tranquil; and she saw Valancourt amiable and intelligent as he had formerly appeared, and Madame Cheron neither the one nor the other. The remembrance of her lover, however, brought with it many very painful emotions, for it by no means reconciled her to the thought of resigning him; and Madame Cheron having already shown how highly she disapproved of the attachment, she foresaw much suffering from the opposition of interests: yet with all this was mingled a degree of delight, which, in spite of reason, partook of hope. She determined, however, that no consideration should induce her to permit a clandestine correspondence, and to observe in her conversation with Valancourt, should they ever meet again, the same nicety of reserve which had hitherto marked her conduct. As she repeated the words—should we ever meet again! she shrunk, as if this was a circumstance which had never before occurred to her, and tears came to her eyes; which she hastily dried, for she heard footsteps approaching, and then the door of the pavilion open, and, on turning, she saw—Valancourt.

An emotion of mingled pleasure, surprise, and apprehension pressed so suddenly upon her heart as almost to overcome her spirits:

the colour left her cheeks; then returned brighter than before; and she was for a moment unable to speak, or to rise from her chair. His countenance was the mirror in which she saw her own emotions reflected, and it roused her to self-command. The joy which had animated his features when he entered the pavilion, was suddenly repressed, as approaching he perceived her agitation, and in a tremulous voice inquired after her health. Recovered from her first surprise, she answered him with a tempered smile; but a variety of opposite emotions still assailed her heart, and struggled to subdue the mild dignity of her manner. It was difficult to tell which predominated—the joy of seeing Valancourt, or the terror of her aunt's displeasure when she should hear of this meeting. After some short and embarrassed conversation, she led him into the gardens, and inquired if he had seen Madame Cheron. 'No,' said he, 'I have not yet seen her, for they told me she was engaged; and as soon as I learned that you were in the gardens I came hither.' He paused a moment in great agitation, and then added—'May I venture to tell you the purport of my visit without incurring your displeasure, and to hope that you will not accuse me of precipitation in now availing myself of the permission you once gave me of addressing your family?' Emily, who knew not what to reply, was spared from further perplexity, and was sensible only of fear, when on raising her eyes, she saw Madame Cheron turn into the avenue. As the consciousness of innocence returned this fear was so far dissipated as to permit her to appear tranquil; and instead of avoiding her aunt, she advanced with Valancourt to meet her. The look of haughty and impatient displeasure with which Madame Cheron regarded them, made Emily shrink; who understood, from a single glance, that this meeting was believed to have been more than accidental. Having mentioned Valancourt's name, she became again too much agitated to remain with them, and returned into the chateau; where she awaited long in a state of trembling anxiety the conclusion of the conference. She knew not how to account for Valancourt's visit to her aunt before he had received the permission he solicited, since she was ignorant of a circumstance which would have rendered the request useless, even if Madame Cheron had been inclined to grant it. Valancourt, in the agitation of his spirits, had forgotten to date his letter; so that it was impossible for Madame Cheron to return an answer! and when we recollected this circumstance, he was perhaps not so sorry for the omission, as glad of the excuse it allowed him for waiting on her before she could send a refusal.

Madame Cheron had a long conversation with Valancourt; and when she returned to the chateau, her countenance expressed ill-humour, but not the degree of severity which Emily had apprehended. 'I have dismissed this young man at last,' said she; 'and I hope my house will never again be disturbed with similar visits. He assures me that your interview was not preconcerted.'—'Dear Madam!' said Emily in extreme emotion, 'you surely did not ask him the question?'

'Most certainly I did: you could not suppose I should be so imprudent as to neglect it.'

'Good God!' exclaimed Emily, 'what an opinion must he form of me, since you, Madam, could express a suspicion of such ill conduct!'

'It is of very little consequence what opinion he may form of you,' replied her aunt, 'for I have put an end to the affair; but I believe he will not form a worse opinion of me for my prudent conduct. I let him see that I was not to be trifled with, and that I had more delicacy than to permit any clandestine correspondence to be carried on in my house.'

Emily had frequently heard Madame Cheron use the word delicacy; but she was now more than usually perplexed to understand how she meant to apply it in this instance, in which her whole conduct appeared to merit the very reverse of the term.

'It was very inconsiderate of my brother,' resumed Madame Cheron, 'to leave the trouble of overlooking your conduct to me. I wish you were well settled in life. But if I find that I am to be further troubled with such visitors as this M. Valancourt, I shall place you in a convent at once: so remember the alternative. This young man has the impertinence to own to me—he owns it!—that his fortune is very small, and that he is chiefly dependent on an elder brother and on the profession he has chosen! He should have concealed these circumstances, at least, if he expected to succeed with me. Had he the presumption to suppose I would marry my niece to a person such as he describes himself?'

Emily dried her tears when she heard of the candid confession of Valancourt; and though the circumstances it discovered were afflicting to her hopes, his artless conduct gave her a degree of pleasure that overcame every other emotion. But she was compelled, even thus early in life, to observe, that good sense and noble integrity are not always sufficient to cope with folly and narrow cunning; and her heart was pure enough to allow her, even at this trying moment, to look with more pride on the defeat of the former, than with mortification on the conquests of the latter.

Madame Cheron pursued her triumph—'He has also thought proper to tell me, that he will receive his dismission from no person but yourself. This favour, however, I have absolutely refused him: he shall learn, that it is quite sufficient that I disapprove him. And I take this opportunity of repeating,—that, if you concert any means of interview unknown to me, you shall leave my house immediately.'

'How little do you know me, madam, that you should think such an injunction necessary!' said Emily, trying to suppress her emotion; 'how little of the dear parents who educated me!'

Madame Cheron now went to dress for an engagement which she had made for the evening; and Emily, who would gladly have been excused from attending her aunt, did not ask to remain at home, lest her request should be attributed to an improper motive. When she retired to her own room, the little fortitude which had supported her in the presence of her relation, forsook her; she remembered only that Valancourt, whose character appeared more amiable from every circumstance that unfolded it, was banished from her presence—perhaps for ever!—and she passed the time in weeping, which, according to her aunt's direction, she ought to have employed in dressing. This important duty was, however, quickly dispatched; though, when she joined Madame Cheron at table, her eyes betrayed that she had been in tears, and drew upon her a severe reproof.

Her efforts to appear cheerful did not entirely fail, when she joined the company at the house of Madame Clairval, an elderly widow lady, who had lately come to reside at Thoulouse on an estate of her late husband. She had lived many years at Paris in a splendid style; had naturally a gay temper; and, since her residence at Thoulouse, had given some of the most magnificent entertainments that had been seen in that neighbourhood.

These excited not only the envy, but the trifling ambition of Madame Cheron; who, since she could not rival the splendour of her festivities, was desirous of being ranked in the number of her most intimate friends. For this purpose she paid her the most obsequious attention, and made a point of being disengaged whenever she received an invitation from Madame Clairval; of whom she talked wherever she went, and derived much self-consequence from impressing a belief on her general acquaintance, that they were on the most familiar footing.

The entertainments of this evening consisted of a ball and supper; it was a fancy ball: and the company danced in groups in the gardens, which were very extensive. The high and luxuriant trees under which the groups assembled, were illuminated with a profusion of lamps, disposed with taste and fancy. The gay and various dresses of the company (some of whom were seated on the turf, conversing at their ease, observing the *cotillons*, taking refreshments, and sometimes

3

touching sportively a guitar); the gallant manners of the gentlemen; the exquisitely capricious air of the ladies; the light fantastic steps of their dances; the musicians, with the lute, the hautboy, and the tabor, seated at the foot of an elm; and the sylvan scenery of woods around; were circumstances that unitedly formed a characteristic and striking picture of French festivity. Emily surveyed the gaiety of the scene with a melancholy kind of pleasure; and her emotion may be imagined, when, as she stood with her aunt looking at one of the groups, she perceived Valancourt —saw him dancing with a young and beautiful lady—saw him conversing with her with a mixture of attention and familiarity such as she had seldom observed in his manner. She turned hastily from the scene, and attempted to draw away Madame Cheron, who was conversing with Signor Cavigni, and neither perceived Valancourt, nor was willing to be interrupted. A faintness suddenly came over Emily, and, unable to support herself, she sat down on a turf bank beneath the trees, where several other persons were seated. One of these, observing the extreme paleness of her countenance, inquired if she was ill, and begged she would allow him to fetch her a glass of water; for which politeness she thanked him, but did not accept it. Her apprehension lest Valancourt should observe her emotion was anxious to overcome it; and she succeeded so far as to recompose her countenance. Madame Cheron was still conversing with Cavigni; and the Count Bauvillers, who had addressed Emily, made some observations upon the scene, to which she answered almost unconsciously; for her mind was still occupied with the idea of Valancourt, to whom it was with extreme uneasiness that she remained so near. Some remarks, however, which the count made upon the dance, obliged her to turn her eyes towards it, and at that moment Valancourt's met hers. Her colour faded again; she felt that she was relapsing into faintness, and instantly averted her looks, but not before she had observed the altered countenance of Valancourt on perceiving her. She would have left the spot immediately, had she not been conscious that this conduct would have shown him more obviously the interest he held in her heart; and having tried to attend to the count's conversation, and to join in it, she at length recovered her spirits. But when he made some observations on Valancourt's partner, the fear of showing that she was interested in the remark would have betrayed it to him, had not the count, while he spoke, looked towards the person of whom he was speaking. 'The lady,' said he, 'dancing with that young chevalier, who appears to be accomplished in every thing but in dancing, is ranked among the beauties of Thoulouse. She is handsome, and her fortune will be very large. I hope she will make a better choice in a partner for life than she has done in a partner for the dance; for I observe he has just put the set into great confusion—he does nothing but commit blunders. I am surprised that, with his air and figure, he has not taken more care to accomplish himself in dancing.'

Emily, whose heart trembled at every word that was now uttered, endeavoured to turn the conversation from Valancourt, by inquiring the name of the lady with whom he danced; but before the count could reply, the dance concluded; and Emily, perceiving that Valancourt was coming towards her, rose, and joined Madame Cheron.

'Here is the Chevalier Valancourt, madam,' said she in a whisper, 'pray let us go.' Her aunt immediately moved on, but not before Valancourt had reached them; who bowed lowly to Madame Cheron, and with an earnest and dejected look to Emily; with whom, notwithstanding all her effort, an air of more than common reserve prevailed. The presence of Madam Cheron prevented Valancourt from remaining, and he passed on with a countenance whose melancholy reproached her for having increased it. Emily was called from the musing fit into which she had fallen, by the Count Bauvillers, who was known to her aunt.

'I have your pardon to beg, Ma'amselle,' said he, 'for a rudeness which you will readily believe was quite unintentional. I did not know that the chevalier was your acquaintance when I so freely criticised his dancing.'

Emily blushed, and smiled; and Madame Cheron spared her the difficulty of replying.

'If you mean the person who has just passed us,' said she, 'I can assure you he is no acquaintance of either mine or Ma'amselle St. Aubert's: I know nothing of him.'

'O! that is the Chevalier Valancourt,' said Cavigni carelessly, and looking back.

'You know him, then?' said Madame Cheron.

'I am not acquainted with him,' replied Cavigni. 'You don't know, then, the reason I have to call him impertinent:—he has had the presumption to admire my niece!'

'If every man deserves the title of impertinent who admires Ma'amselle St. Aubert,' replied Cavigni, 'I fear there are a great many impertinents, and I am willing to acknowledge myself one of the number.'

'O Signor!' said Madame Cheron with an affected smile, 'I perceive you have learnt the art of complimenting since you came to France. But it is cruel to compliment children, since they mistake flattery for truth.'

Cavigni turned away his face for a moment, and then said with a studied air, 'Whom, then, are we to compliment, Madam?—for it would be absurd to compliment a woman of refined understanding: *she* is above all praise.'

As he finished this sentence, he gave Emily a sly look, and the smile that had lurked in his eye stole forth. She perfectly understood it, and blushed for Madame Cheron; who replied,—

'You are perfectly right, Signor; no woman of understanding can endure compliment.'

'I have heard Signor Montoni say,' rejoined Cavigni, 'that he never knew but one woman who deserved it.'

'Well! exclaimed Madame Cheron with a short laugh, and a smile of unutterable complacency; and who could she be?'

'O! replied Cavigni,' it is impossible to mistake her; 'for certainly there is not more than one woman in the world who has both the merit to deserve compliment and the wit to refuse it: most women reverse the cast entirely.'

He looked again at Emily, who again blushed deeper than before for her aunt, and turned from him with displeasure.

'Well, Signor!' said Madame Cheron; 'I protest you are a Frenchman: I never heard a foreigner say anything half so gallant as that!'

'True, Madam,' said the Count, who had been some time silent, and with a low bow; 'but the gallantry of the compliment had been utterly lost, but for the ingenuity that discovered the application.'

Madame Cheron did not perceive the meaning of this too satirical sentence, and she therefore escaped the pain which Emily felt on her account.

'O! here comes Signor Montoni himself,' said her aunt; 'I protest I will tell him all the fine things you have been saying to me.' The Signor, however, passed at this moment into another walk. 'Pray, who is it that has so much engaged your friend this evening?' asked Madame Cheron, with an air of chagrin; 'I have not seen him once.'

'He had a very particular engagement with the Marquis la Rivière,' replied Cavigni, 'which has detained him, I perceive, till this moment, or he would have done himself the honour of paying his respects to you, Madam, sooner, as he commissioned me to say. But, I know not how it is—your conversation is so fascinating, that it can charm even memory, I think; or I should certainly have delivered my friend's apology before.'

'The apology, sir, would have been more satisfactory from himself,' said Madame Cheron; whose vanity was more mortified by Montoni's neglect than flattered by Cavigni's compliment. Her manner at this moment, and Cavigni's late conversation, now awakened a suspicion in Emily's mind, which, notwithstanding that some recollections served to confirm it, appeared preposterous. She thought she perceived that Montoni was paying serious addresses to her aunt, and that she not only accepted them, but was jealously watchful of any appearance of neglect on his part.—That Madame Cheron, at her years, should elect a second husband, was ridiculous, though her vanity made it not impossible; but Montoni, with his discernment, his figure, and pretensions, should make choice of Madame Cheron, appeared most wonderful. Her thoughts, however, did not dwell long on the subject—nearer interest pressed upon them: Valancourt rejected of her aunt, and Valancourt dancing with a gay and beautiful partner, alternately tormented her mind. As she passed along the gardens, she looked timidly forward, half fearing and half hoping that he might appear in the crowd; and the disappointment she felt on not seeing him, told her that she had hoped more than she had feared.

Montoni soon after joined the party. He muttered over some short speech about regret for having been so long detained elsewhere, when he knew he should have the pleasure of seeing Madame Cheron here: and she, receiving the apology with the air of a pettish girl, addressed herself entirely to Cavigni, who looked archly at Montoni, as if he would have said, 'I will not triumph over you too much—I will have the goodness to bear my honours meekly; but look sharp, Signor, or I shall certainly run away with your prize.'

The supper was served in different pavilions in the gardens, as well as in one large saloon of the chateau, and with more of taste than either of splendour or even of plenty. Madame Cheron and her party supped with Madame Clairval in the saloon; and Emily with difficulty disguised her emotion, when she saw Valancourt placed at the same table with herself. There Madame Cheron, having surveyed him with high displeasure, said to some person who sat next to her, 'Pray, who *is* that young man?—'

'It is the Chevalier Valancourt,' was the answer.

'Yes; I am not ignorant of his name; but who is this Chevalier Valancourt, that thus intrudes himself at this table?'

The attention of the person to whom she spoke was called off before she received a second reply. The table at which they sat was very long; and Valancourt being seated, with his partner, near the bottom, and Emily near the top, the distance between them may account for his not immediately perceiving her. She avoided looking to that end of the table; but whenever her eyes happened to glance towards it, she observed him conversing with his beautiful companion; and the observation did not contribute to restore her peace, any more than the accounts she heard of the fortune and accomplishments of this same lady.

Madame Cheron, to whom these remarks were sometimes addressed, because they supported topics for trivial conversation, seemed indefatigable in her attempts to deprecate Valancourt ; towards whom she felt all the petty resentment of a narrow pride. ' I admire the lady,' said she, ' but I must condemn her choice of a partner.'—'Oh, the Chevalier Valancourt is one of the most accomplished young men we have,' replied the lady to whom this remark was addressed. ' It is whispered that Mademoiselle d'Emery and her large fortune are to be his.'

' Impossible !' exclaimed Madame Cheron, reddening with vexation ; ' it is impossible that she can be so destitute of taste ; he has so little the air of a person of condition, that, if I did not see him at the table of Madame Clairval, I should never have suspected him to be one. I have, besides, particular reasons for believing the report to be erroneous.'

' I cannot doubt the truth of it,' replied the lady gravely, disgusted by the abrupt contradiction she had received concerning her opinion of Valancourt's merit.

' You will not, perhaps, doubt it,' said Madame Cheron, when I assure you that it was only this morning that I rejected his suit.'

This was said without any intention of imposing the meaning it conveyed, but simply from a habit of considering herself to be the most important person in every affair that concerned her niece, and because, literally, *she* had rejected Valancourt.

' Your reasons are indeed such as cannot be doubted,' replied the lady with an ironical smile.

' Any more than the discernment of the Chevalier Valancourt,' added Cavigni, who stood by the chair of Madame Cheron, and had heard her arrogate to herself, as he thought, a distinction which had been paid to her niece.

' His discernment *may* be justly questioned, signor,' said Madame Cheron ; who was not flattered by what she understood to be an encomium on Emily.

' Alas !' exclaimed Cavigni, surveying Madame Cheron with affected ecstasy, ' how vain is that assertion, while that face—that shape—that air—combine to refute it ! Unhappy Valancourt ! his discernment has been his destruction.'

Emily looked surprised and embarrassed : the lady who had lately spoken, astonished ; and Madame Cheron, who, though she did not perfectly understand this speech, was very ready to believe herself complimented by it, said, smilingly, 'O Signor, you are very gallant : but those who hear you vindicate the chevalier's discernment, will suppose that I am the object of it.'

' They cannot doubt it', replied Cavigni, bowing low.

' And would not that be very mortifying, signor ?'

' Unquestionably it would,' said Cavigni.

' I cannot endure the thought,' said Madame Cheron.

' It is not to be endured,' replied Cavigni.

' What can be done to prevent so humiliating a mistake ?' rejoined Madame Cheron.

' Alas ! I cannot assist you,' replied Cavigni with a deliberating air. ' Your only chance of refuting the calumny, and of making people understand what you wish them to believe, is to persist in your first assertion ; for, when they are told of the chevalier's want of discernment, it is possible they may suppose he never presumed to distress you with his admiration. But then again, that diffidence, which renders you so insensible to your own perfections, they will consider this ; and Valancourt's taste will not be doubted, though you arraign it. In short, they will, in spite of your endeavours, continue to believe, what might very naturally have occurred to them without any hint of mine, that the chevalier has taste enough to admire a beautiful woman.'

' All this is very distressing !' said Madame Cheron, with a profound sigh.

' May I be allowed to ask what is so distressing ?' said Madame Clairval, who was struck with the rueful countenance and doleful accent with which this was delivered.

' It is a delicate subject,' replied Madame Cheron ; a very mortifying one to me.'

' I am concerned to hear it,' said Madame Clairval. ' I hope nothing has occurred, this evening, particularly to distress you ?'

' Alas, yes ! within this half-hour ; and I know not where the report may end. My pride was never so shocked before. But I assure you the report is totally void of foundation.'

' Good God !' exclaimed Madame Clairval, ' what can be done ? Can you point out any way by which I can assist or console you ?'

' The only way by which you can do either,' replied Madame Cheron, ' is to contradict the report wherever you go.'

' Well ! but pray inform me what I am to contradict.'

' It is so very humiliating, that I know not how to mention it,' continued Madame Cheron : ' but you shall judge. Do you observe that young man seated near the bottom of the table, who is conversing with Mademoiselle d'Emery ?'

' Yes ; I perceive whom you mean.'

' You observe how little he has the air of a person of condition ? I was saying, just now, that I should not have thought him a gentleman, if I had not seen him at this table.'

' Well ! but the report,' said Madame Clairval ; ' let me understand the subject of your distress.'

' Ah ! the subject of my distress !' replied Madame Cheron : ' this person whom nobody knows (I beg pardon, madam, I did not consider what I said), this impertinent young man, having had the presumption to address my niece, has, I fear, given rise to a report that he had declared himself my admirer. Now, only consider how very mortifying such a report must be! You, I know, will feel for my situation. A woman of my condition! Think how degrading even the rumour of such an alliance must be l'

'Degrading indeed! my poor friend,' said Madame Clairval. 'You may rely upon it, I will contradict the report wherever I go.' As she said this, she turned her attention upon another part of the company; and Cavigni, who had hitherto appeared a grave spectator of the scene, now fearing he should be unable to smother the laugh that convulsed him, walked abruptly away.

'I perceive you do not know,' said the lady who sat near Madame Cheron, 'that the gentleman you have been speaking of is Madame Clairval's nephew l'

'Impossible l' exclaimed Madame Cheron; who now began to perceive that she had been totally mistaken in her judgment of Valancourt, and to praise him aloud, with as much servility as she had before censured him with frivolous malignity.

Emily, who during the greater part of this conversation had been so absorbed in thought as to be spared the pain of hearing it, was now extremely surprised by her aunt's praise of Valancourt, with whose relationship to Madame Clairval she was unacquainted; but she was not sorry when Madame Cheron (who though she now tried to appear unconcerned, was really much embarrassed) prepared to withdraw, immediately after supper. Montoni then came to hand Madame Cheron to her carriage, and Cavigni, with an arch solemnity of countenance, followed with Emily; who, as she wished them good-night, and drew up the glass, saw Valancourt among the crowd at the gates. Before the carriage drove off, he disappeared. Madame Cheron forbore to mention him to Emily; and as soon as they reached the chateau, they separated for the night.

On the following morning, as Emily sat at breakfast with her aunt, a letter was brought to her, of which she knew the hand-writing upon the cover; and as she received it with a trembling hand, Madame Cheron hastily inquired from whom it came. Emily, with her leave, broke the seal, and observing the signature of Valancourt, gave it, unread, to her aunt, who received it with impatience; and as she looked it over, Emily endeavoured to read on her countenance its contents. Having returned the letter to her niece, whose eyes asked if she might examine it, 'Yes, read it, child,' said Madame Cheron in a manner less severe than she had expected; and Emily had, perhaps, never before so willingly obeyed her aunt. In this letter Valancourt said little of the interview of the preceding day, but con-

cluded with declaring that he would accept his dismission from Emily only, and with entreating that she would allow him to wait upon her on the approaching evening. When she read this she was astonished at the moderation of Madame Cheron, and looked at her with expectation as she said sorrowfully,—'What am I to say Madame?'

'Why—we must see the young man, I believe,' replied her aunt, 'and hear what he has further to say for himself. You may tell him he may come.' Emily dared scarcely credit what she heard. 'Yet stay,' added Madame Cheron; 'I will tell him so myself.' She called for pen and ink; Emily still not daring to trust the emotions she felt, and almost sinking beneath them. Her surprise would have been less, had she overheard, on the preceding evening, what Madame Cheron had not forgotten—that. Valancourt was the nephew of Madame Clairval.

What were the particulars of her aunt's note Emily did not learn, but the result was a visit from Valancourt in the evening; whom Madame Cheron received alone; and they had a long conversation before Emily was called down. When she entered the room, her aunt was conversing with complacency, and she saw the eyes of Valancourt, as he impatiently rose, animated with hope.

'We have been talking over this affair,' said Madame Cheron. 'The chevalier has been telling me, that the late Monsieur Clairval was the brother of the Countess de Duvarney, his mother. I only wish he had mentioned his relationship to Madame Clairval before: I certainly should have considered that circumstance as a sufficient introduction to my house. Valancourt bowed, and was going to address Emily, but her aunt prevented him. I have, therefore, consented that you shall receive his visits; and though I will not bind myself by any promise, or say that I shall consider him as my nephew, yet I shall permit the intercourse, and shall look forward to any further connection as an event which may possibly take place in a course of years, provided the chevalier rises in his profession, or any circumstance occurs which may make it prudent for him to take a wife. But M. Valancourt will observe, and you too, Emily, that, till that happens, I positively forbid any thoughts of marrying.'

Emily's countenance, during this coarse speech, varied every instant, and towards its conclusion her distress had so much increased that she was on the point of leaving the room. Valancourt meanwhile, scarcely less embarrassed, did not dare to look at her for whom she was thus distressed; but when Madame Cheron was silent, he said—'Flattering, Madam, as your approbation is to me—highly as I am honoured by it—I have yet so much to fear, that I scarcely dare to hope.'—'Pray, sir, explain yourself,' said Madame

Cheron—an unexpected requisition, which embarrassed Valancourt again, and almost overcame him with confusion, at circumstances, on which, had he been only a spectator of the scene, he would have smiled.

'Till I receive Mademoiselle St. Aubert's permission to accept your indulgence,' said he, falteringly—' till she allows me to hope—'

'O! is that all?' interrupted Madame Cheron. 'Well, I will take upon me to answer for her. But, at the same time, sir, give me leave to observe to you, that I am her guardian, and that I expect, in every instance, that my will is hers.'

As she said this, she rose and quitted the room, leaving Emily and Valancourt in a state of mutual embarrassment; and when Valancourt's hopes enabled him to overcome his fears, and to address her with the zeal and sincerity so natural to him, it was a considerable time before she was sufficiently recovered to hear with distinctness his solicitations and inquiries.

The conduct of Madame Cheron in this affair had been entirely governed by selfish vanity. Valancourt, in his first interview, had, with great candour, laid open to her the true state of his present circumstances and his future expectancies, and she, with more prudence than humanity, had absolutely and abruptly refused his suit. She wished her niece to marry ambitiously; not because she desired to see her in possession of the happiness which rank and wealth are usually believed to bestow, but because she desired to partake the importance which such an alliance would give. When, therefore, she discovered that Valancourt was the nephew of a person of so much consequence as Madame Clairval, she became anxious for the connexion, since the prospect it afforded of future fortune and distinction for Emily, promised the exaltation she coveted for herself. Her calculations concerning fortune, in this alliance, were guided rather by her wishes than by any hint of Valancourt, or strong appearance of probability; and when she rested her expectation on the wealth of Madame Clairval, she seemed totally to have forgotten that the latter had a daughter. Valancourt, however, had not forgotten this circumstance; and the consideration of it had made him so modest in his expectations from Madame Clairval, that he had not even named the relationship in the first conversation with Madame Cheron. But whatever might be the future fortune of Emily, the present distinction which the connexion would afford for herself was certain, since the splendour of Madame Clairval's establishment was such as to excite the general envy and partial imitation of the neighbourhood. Thus had she consented to involve her niece in an engagement to which she saw only a distant and uncertain conclusion, with as little consideration of her happiness

as when she had so precipitately forbidden it: for though she herself possessed the means of rendering this union not only certain, but prudent, yet to do so was no part of her present intention.

From this period Valancourt made frequent visits to Madame Cheron, and Emily passed in his society the happiest hours she had known since the death of her father. They were both too much engaged by the present moments to give serious consideration to the future. They loved and were beloved, and saw not that the very attachment which formed the delight of their present days might possibly occasion the sufferings of years. Meanwhile, Madame Cheron's intercourse with Madame Clairval became more frequent than before, and her vanity was already gratified by the opportunity of proclaiming, wherever she went, the attachment that subsisted between her nephew and niece.

Montoni was now also become a daily guest at the chateau, and Emily was compelled to observe that he really was a suitor, and a favoured suitor, to her aunt.

Thus passed the winter months, not only in peace, but in happiness, to Valancourt and Emily; the station of his regiment being so near Thoulouse as to allow this frequent intercourse. The pavilion on the terrace was the favourite scene of their interviews, and there Emily with Madame Cheron would work, while Valancourt read aloud works of genius and taste, listened to her enthusiasm, expressed his own, and caught new opportunities of observing that their minds were formed to constitute the happiness of each other; the same taste, the same noble and benevolent sentiments, animating each.

CHAPTER XIV.

'As when a shepherd of the Hebrid-Isles,
Placed far amid the melancholy main
(Whether it be lone fancy him beguiles,
Or that aërial beings sometimes deign
To stand embodied to our senses plain),
Sees on the naked hill, or valley low,
The whilst in ocean Phœbus dips his wain,
A vast assembly moving to and fro,
Then all at once in air dissolves the wondrous show.'
CASTLE OF INDOLENCE.

MADAME CHERON'S avarice at length yielded to her vanity. Some very splendid entertainments which Madame Clairval had given, and the general adulation which was paid her, made the former more anxious than before to secure an alliance that would so much exalt her in her own opinion and in that of the world. She proposed terms for the immediate marriage of her niece, and offered to give Emily a dower, provided Madame Clairval observed equal terms on the part of her nephew. Madame Clairval listened to the proposal, and, considering that Emily was the apparent heiress of her aunt's wealth, accepted it. Meanwhile Emily knew nothing of the transaction, till Madame Cheron informed her that she must make preparation for the nuptials, which would be celebrated without further delay : then, astonished, and wholly unable to account for this sudden conclusion, which Valancourt had not solicited (for he was ignorant of what had passed between the elder ladies, and had not dared to hope such good fortune), she decisively objected to it. Madame Cheron, however, quite as jealous of contradiction now as she had been formerly, contended for a speedy marriage with as much vehemence as she had formerly opposed whatever had the most remote possibility of leading to it ; and Emily's scruples disappeared, when she again saw Valancourt, who was now informed of the happiness designed for him, and came to claim a promise of it from herself.

While preparations were making for these nuptials, Montoni became the acknowledged lover of Madame Cheron ; and though Madame Clairval was much displeased when she heard of the approaching connexion, and was willing to prevent that of Valancourt with Emily, her conscience told her that she had no right thus to trifle with their peace ; and Madame Clairval, though a woman of fashion, was far less advanced than her friend in the art of deriving satisfaction from distinction and admiration, rather than from conscience.

Emily observed with concern the ascendancy which Montoni had acquired over Madame Cheron, as well as the increasing frequency of his visits ; and her own opinion of this Italian was confirmed by that of Valancourt, who had always expressed a dislike of him. As she was one morning sitting at work in the pavilion, enjoying the pleasant freshness of spring, whose colours were now spread upon the landscape, and listening to Valancourt, who was reading, but who often laid aside the book to converse, she received a summons to attend Madame Cheron immediately, and had scarcely entered the dressing-room, when she observed with surprise the dejection of her aunt's countenance, and the contrasted gaiety of her dress. 'So, niece !' said madame, and she stopped under some degree of embarrassment—' I sent for you ; I—I wished to see you : I have news to tell you : from this hour you must consider the Signor Montoni as your uncle—we were married this morning.'

Astonished—not so much at the marriage, as at the secrecy with which it had been concluded, and the agitation with which it was announced—Emily at length attributed the privacy to the wish of Montoni, rather than of her aunt. His wife, however, intended that the contrary should be believed, and therefore added, 'You see, I wished to avoid a bustle ; but now the ceremony is over, I shall do so no

longer, and I wish to announce to my servants that they must accept the Signor Montoni for their master.' Emily made a feeble attempt to congratulate her on these apparently imprudent nuptials. 'I shall now celebrate my marriage with some splendour,' continued Madame Montoni ; 'and to save time, I shall avail myself of the preparation that has been made for yours, which will of course be delayed a little while Such of your wedding clothes as are ready I shall expect you will appear in, to do honour to this festival. I also wish you to inform Monsieur Valancourt that I have changed my name ; and he will acquaint Madame Clairval. In a few days I shall give a grand entertainment, at which I shall request their presence.'

Emily was so lost in surprise and various thought, that she made Madame Montoni scarcely any reply ; but, at her desire, she returned to inform Valancourt of what had passed. Surprise was not his predominant emotion on hearing of these hasty nuptials ; and when he learned that they were to be the means of delaying his own, and that the very ornaments of the chateau which had been prepared to grace the nuptial-day of his Emily were to be degraded to the celebration of Madame Montoni's, grief and indignation agitated him alternately. He could conceal neither from the observation of Emily ; whose efforts to abstract him from these serious emotions, and to laugh at the apprehensive considerations that assailed him, were ineffectual ; and when at length he took leave, there was an earnest tenderness in his manner that extremely affected her ; she even shed tears, when he disappeared at the end of the terrace, yet knew not exactly why she should do so.

Montoni now took possession of the chateau, and the command of its inhabitants, with the ease of a man who had long considered it to be his own. His friend, Cavigni, who had been extremely serviceable in having paid Madame Cheron the attention and flattery which she required, but from which Montoni too often revolted, had apartments assigned to him, and received from the domestics an equal degree of obedience with the master of the mansion.

Within a few days, Madame Montoni, as she had promised, gave a magnificent entertainment to a very numerous company, among whom was Valancourt, but at which Madame Clairval excused herself from attending. There was a concert, ball, and supper. Valancourt was of course Emily's partner ; and though, when he gave a look to the decorations of the apartments, he could not but remember that they were designed for other festivities than those they now contributed to celebrate, he endeavoured to check his concern, by considering that a little while only would elapse before they would be given to their original destination. During this evening, Madame Montoni danced, laughed, and talked incessantly; while Montoni, silent, reserved, and somewhat haughty, seemed weary of the parade, and of the frivolous company it had drawn together.

This was the first and the last entertainment given in celebration of their nuptials. Montani, though the severity of his temper and the gloominess of his pride prevented him from enjoying such festivities, was extremely willing to promote them. It was seldom that he could meet in any company a man of more address, and still seldomer one of more understanding than himself: the balance of advantage in such parties, or in the connections which might arise from them, must therefore be on his side: and knowing, as he did, the selfish purposes for which they are generally frequented, he had no objection to measure his talents of dissimulation with those of any other competitor for distinction and plunder; but his wife, who, when her own interest was immediately concerned, had sometimes more discernment than vanity, acquired a consciousness of her inferiority to other women in personal attractions, which, uniting with the jealousy natural to the discovery, counteracted his readiness for mingling with all the parties Thoulouse could afford. Till she had, as she supposed, the affections of a husband to lose, she had no motive for discovering the unwelcome truth, and it had never obtruded itself upon her; but now that it influenced her policy, she opposed her husband's inclination for company, with the more eagerness, because she believed him to be really as well received in the female society of the place, as during his addresses to her he had affected to be.

A few weeks only had elapsed since the marriage, when Madame Montoni informed Emily that the signor intended to return to Italy as soon as the necessary preparation could be made for so long a journey. 'We shall go to Venice,' said she, 'where the signor has a fine mansion, and from thence to his estate in Tuscany. Why do you look so grave, child? You, who are so fond of a romantic country and fine views, will doubtless be delighted with this journey.'

'Am I then to be of the party, madam?' said Emily with extreme surprise and emotion.

'Most certainly,' replied her aunt: how could you imagine we should leave you behind? But I see you are thinking of the chevalier: he is not yet, I believe, informed of the journey; but he very soon will be so: Signor Montoni is gone to acquaint Madame Clairval of our journey, and to say that the proposed connection between the families must be thought of no more.'

The unfeeling manner in which Madame Montoni thus informed her niece that she must be separated, perhaps for ever, from the man with whom she was on the point of being united for life, added to the dismay which she must otherwise have suffered at such intelligence. When she could speak, she asked the cause of the sudden change in madame's sentiments towards Valancourt; but the only reply she could obtain was, that the signor had forbade the connection, considering it to be greatly inferior to what Emily might reasonably expect.

'I now leave the affair entirely to the signor,' added Madame Montoni; 'but I must say that M. Valancourt never was a favourite with me; and I was over-persuaded, or I should not have given my consent to the connection. I was weak enough—I am so foolish sometimes!—to suffer other people's uneasiness; and so my better judgment yielded to your affliction. But the signor has very properly pointed out the folly of this; and he shall not have to reprove me a second time. I am determined that you shall submit to those who know how to guide you better than yourself. I am determined that you shall be conformable.'

Emily would have been astonished at the assertions of this eloquent speech, had not her mind been so overwhelmed by the sudden shock it had received that she scarcely heard a word of what was latterly addressed to her. Whatever were the weaknesses of Madame Montoni, she might have avoided to accuse herself with those of compassion and tenderness to the feelings of others, and especially to those of Emily. It was the same ambition, that lately prevailed upon her to solicit an alliance with Madame Clairval's family, which induced her to withdraw from it, now that her marriage with Montoni had exalted her self-consequence, and, with it, her views for her niece.

Emily was, at this time, too much affected to employ either remonstrance or entreaty on this topic; and when, at length, she attempted the latter, her emotion overcame her speech, and she retired to her apartment, to think (if in the present state of her mind to think was possible) upon this sudden and overwhelming subject. It was very long before her spirits were sufficiently composed to permit the reflection; which, when it came, was dark, and even terrible. She saw that Montoni sought to aggrandise himself in his disposal of her and it occurred, that his friend Cavigni was the person for whom he was interested. The prospect of going to Italy was still rendered darker, when she considered the tumultuous situation of that country—then torn by civil commotion; where every petty state was at war with its neighbour, and even every castle liable to the attack of an invader. She considered the person to whose immediate guidance she would be committed, and the vast distance that was to separate her from Valancourt; and, at the recollection of him, every other image vanished from her mind, and every thought was again obscured by grief.

In this perturbed state she passed some hours; and when she was summoned to dinner, she entreated permission to remain in her own apartment: but Madame Montoni was alone, and the request was refused. Emily and her aunt said little during the repast—the one occupied by her griefs, the other engrossed by the disappointment which the unexpected absence of Montoni occasioned; for not only was her vanity piqued by the neglect, but her jealousy alarmed by what she considered as a mysterious engagement. When the cloth was drawn, and they were alone, Emily renewed the mention of Valancourt: but her aunt, neither softened to pity nor awakened to remorse, became enraged that her will should be opposed, and the authority of Montoni questioned, though this was done by Emily with her usual gentleness; who, after a long and torturing conversation, retired in tears.

As she crossed the hall, a person entered it by the great door, whom, as her eyes hastily glanced that way, she imagined to be Montoni; and she was passing on with quicker steps, when she heard the well-known voice of Valancourt.

'Emily, O! my Emily!' cried he in a tone faltering with impatience, while she turned, and, as he advanced, was alarmed at the expression of his countenance and the eager desperation of his air. 'In tears, Emily!—I would speak with you,' said he; 'I have much to say: conduct me where we may converse.—But you tremble—you are ill! Let me lead you to a seat.'

He observed the open door of an apartment, and hastily took her hand to lead her thither; but she attempted to withdraw it, and said, with a languid smile, 'I am better already; if you wish to see my aunt she is in the dining-parlour.'—'I must speak with *you*, my Emily,' replied Valancourt. 'Good God! is it already come to this?—Are you indeed so willing to resign me?—But this is an improper place—I am overheard. Let me entreat your attention, if only for a few minutes.'—When you have seen my aunt,' said Emily.—'I was wretched enough when I came hither,' exclaimed Valancourt: 'do not increase my misery by this coldness—this cruel refusal.'

The despondency with which he spoke this affected her almost to tears; but she persisted in refusing to hear him till he had conversed with Madame Montoni? 'Where is her husband? where, then, is Montoni?' said Valancourt in an altered tone: 'it is he to whom I must speak.'

Emily, terrified for the consequence of the indignation that flashed in his eyes, tremblingly assured him that Montoni was not at home, and entreated he would endeavour to moderate his resentment. At the tremulous accents of her voice his eyes softened instantly from wildness into tenderness. 'You are ill, Emily,' said he—'They will destroy us both! Forgive me, that I dared to doubt your affection.'

Emily no longer opposed him, as he led her into an adjoining parlour. The manner in which he had named Montoni, had so much alarmed her for his own safety, that she was now only too anxious to prevent the consequences of this just resentment. He listened to her entreaties with attention, but replied to them only with looks of despondency and tenderness; concealing as much as possible the sentiments he felt toward Montoni, that he might soothe the apprehensions which distressed her. But she saw the veil he had spread over his resentment; and his assumed tranquillity only alarming her more, she urged, at length, the impolicy of forcing an interview with Montoni, and of taking any measure which might render their separation irremediable. Valancourt yielded to these remonstrances: and her affecting entreaties drew from him a promise, that, however Montoni might persist in his design of disuniting them, he would not seek to redress his wrongs by violence.—'For my sake,' said Emily. 'let the consideration of what I should suffer deter you from such a mode of revenge!'—'For your sake, Emily,' replied Valancourt, his eyes filling with tears of tenderness and grief, while he gazed upon her, 'Yes—yes—I shall subdue myself. But though I have given you my solemn promise to do this, do not expect that I can tamely submit to the authority of Montoni: if I could, I should be unworthy of you. Yet, O Emily! how long may he condemn me to live without you—how long may it be before you return to France!'

Emily endeavoured to soothe him with assurances of her unalterable affection, and by representing that, in little more than a year, she should be her own mistress, as far as related to her aunt, from whose guardianship her age would then release her—assurances which gave little consolation to Valancourt, who considered that she would then be in Italy, and in the power of those whose dominion over her would not cease with their rights: but he affected to be consoled by them. Emily, comforted by the promise she had obtained, and by his apparent composure, was about to leave him, when her aunt entered the room. She threw a glance of sharp reproof upon her niece, who immediately withdrew, and of haughty displeasure upon Valancourt.

'This is not the conduct I should have expected from you, sir,' said she: 'I did not expect to see you in my house, after you had been informed that your visits were no longer agreeable; much less, that you would seek a clandestine interview with my niece, and that she would grant one,'

Valancourt, perceiving it necessary to vindicate Emily from such a design, explained, that the purpose of his own visit had been to request an interview with Montoni! and he then entered upon the subject of it, with the tempered spirit which the sex rather than the respectability of Madame Montoni demanded.

His expostulations were answered with severe rebuke : she lamented again, that her prudence had ever yielded to what she termed compassion ; and added, ' that she was so sensible of the folly of her former consent, that, to prevent the possibility of a repetition, she had committed the affair entirely to the conduct of Signor Montoni.'

The feeling eloquence of Valancourt, however, at length made her sensible, in some measure, of her unworthy conduct ; and she became susceptible to shame, but not remorse; she hated Valancourt, who awakened her to this painful sensation ; and in proportion as she grew dissatisfied with herself, her abhorrence of him increased. This was also the more inveterate, because his tempered words and manner were such as, without accusing her, compelled her to accuse herself, and neither left her hope that the odious portrait was the caricature of his prejudice, nor afforded her an excuse for expressing the violent resentment with which she contemplated it. At length, her anger rose to such a height, that Valancourt was compelled to leave the house abruptly, lest he should forfeit his own esteem by an intemperate reply. He was then convinced, that from Madame Montoni he had nothing to hope; for what, of either pity or justice, could be expected from a person who could feel the pain of guilt without the humility of repentance ?

To Montoni he looked with equal despondency ; since it was nearly evident that this plan of separation originated with him, and it was not probable that he would relinquish his own views to entreaties or remonstrances which he must have foreseen, and have been prepared to resist. Yet, remembering his promise to Emily, and more solicitous concerning his love than jealous of his consequence, Valancourt was careful to do nothing that might unnecessarily irritate Montoni : he wrote to him, therefore, not to demand an interview, but to solicit one ; and having done this, he endeavoured to wait with calmness his reply.

Madame Clairval was passive in the affair. When she gave her approbation to Valancourt's marriage, it was in the belief that Emily would be the heiress of Madame Montoni's fortune ; and though, upon the nuptials of the latter, when she perceived the fallacy of this expectation, her conscience had withheld her from adopting any measure to prevent the union, her benevolence was not sufficiently active to impel her towards any

step that might now promote it. She was, on the contrary, secretly pleased that Valancourt was released from an engagement which she considered to be as inferior, in point of fortune, to his merit, as his alliance was thought by Montoni to be humiliating to the beauty of Emily ; and though her pride was wounded by this rejection of a member of her family, she disdained to show resentment otherwise than by silence.

Montoni, in his reply to Valancourt, said, that as an interview could neither remove the objections of the one, nor overcome the wishes of the other, it would serve only to produce useless altercation between them ; he therefore thought proper to refuse it.

In consideration of the policy suggested by Emily, and of his promise to her, Valancourt restrained the impulse that urged him to the house of Montoni to demand what had been denied to his entreaties : he only repeated his solicitations to see him ; seconding them with all the arguments his situation could suggest. Thus several days passed, in remonstrance on one side, and inflexible denial on the other ; for whether it was fear, or shame, or the hatred which results from both, that made Montoni shun the man he had injured, he was peremptory in his refusal, and was neither softened to pity by the agony which Valancourt's letters portrayed, nor awakened to a repentance of his own injustice by the strong remonstrances he employed. At length, Valancourt's letters were returned unopened ; and then, in the first moments of passionate despair, he forgot every promise to Emily, except the solemn one which bound him to avoid violence, and hastened to Montoni's chateau, determined to see her by whatever other means might be necessary. Montoni was denied ; and Valancourt, when he afterwards inquired for Madame and Ma'amselle St. Aubert, was absolutely refused admittance by the servants. Not choosing to submit himself to a contest with these, he at length departed ; and returning home in a state of mind approaching to phrensy, wrote to Emily of what had passed— expressed without restraint all the agony of his heart—and entreated that, since he must not otherwise hope to see her immediately, she would allow him an interview unknown to Montoni. Soon after he had dispatched this, his passions becoming more temperate, he was sensible of the error he had committed, in having given Emily a new subject of distress in the strong mention of his own suffering, and would have given half the world, had it been his, to recover the letter. Emily, however, was spared the pain she must have received from it, by the suspicious policy of Madame Montoni ; who had ordered that all letters addressed to her niece should be delivered to herself, and who, after having perused this, and indulged the expressions of resentment which Valancourt's mention of Montoni provoked, had consigned it to the flames.

Montoni, meanwhile, every day more impatient to leave France, gave repeated orders for dispatch to the servants employed in preparations for the journey, and to the persons with whom he was transacting some particular business. He preserved a steady silence to the letters in which Valancourt, despairing of greater good, and having subdued the passion that had transgressed against his policy, solicited only the indulgence of being allowed to bid Emily farewell. But when Valancourt learned that she was really to set out in a few days, and that it was designed he should see her no more, forgetting every consideration of prudence, he dared, in a second letter to Emily, to propose a clandestine marriage. This also was transmitted to Madame Montoni ; and the last day of Emily's stay at Thoulouse arrived, without affording Valancourt even a line to soothe his sufferings, or a hope that he should be allowed a parting interview.

During this period of torturing suspense to Valancourt, Emily was sunk into that kind of stupor with which sudden and irremediable misfortune sometimes overwhelms the mind. Loving him with the tenderest affection, and having long been accustomed to consider him as the friend and companion of all her future days, she had no ideas of happiness that were not connected with him. What then must have been her suffering, when thus suddenly they were to be separated, perhaps for ever !— certainly to be thrown into distant parts of the world, where they could scarcely hear of each other's existence ;—and all this in obedience to the will of a stranger (for such was Montoni), and of a person who had but lately been anxious to hasten their nuptials ! It was in vain that she endeavoured to subdue her grief, and resign herself to an event which she could not avoid. The silence of Valancourt afflicted more than it surprised her, since she attributed it to its just occasion ; but when the day preceding that on which she was to quit Thoulouse arrived, and she had heard no mention of his being permitted to take leave of her, grief overcame every consideration that had made her reluctant to speak of him, and she inquired of Madame Montoni whether this consolation had been refused. Her aunt informed her that it had ; adding that, after the provocation she had herself received from Valancourt in their last interview, and the persecution which the signor had suffered from his letters, no entreaties should avail to procure it.—' If the chevalier expected this favour from us,' said she, ' he should have conducted himself in a very different manner : he should have waited patiently, till he knew whether we were disposed to grant it, and not have come and reproved me because I did not think proper to bestow my niece upon him, and then have persisted in troubling the signor because he did not think proper to enter into any dispute about so childish an affair. His behaviour throughout has been extremely presumptuous and impertinent ; and I desire that I may never hear his name repeated, and that you will get the better of those foolish sorrows and whims, and look like other people, and not appear with that dismal countenance as if you were ready to cry ; for though you say nothing, you cannot conceal your grief from my penetration : I can see you are ready to cry at this moment, though I am reproving you for it—ay, even now, in spite of my command.'

Emily, having turned away to hide her tears, quitted the room to indulge them ; and the day was passed in an intensity of anguish, such as she had, perhaps, never known before. When she withdrew to her chamber for the night, she remained in the chair where she had placed herself on entering the room, absorbed in her grief, till long after every member of the family, except herself, was retired to rest. She could not divest herself of a belief that she had parted with Valancourt to meet no more—a belief which did not arise merely from foreseen circumstances ; for though the length of the journey she was about to commence, the uncertainty as to the period of her return, together with the prohibitions she had received, seemed to justify it, she yielded also to an impression, which she mistook for a presentiment, that she was going from Valancourt for ever. How dreadful to her imagination, too, was the distance that would separate them—the Alps, those tremendous barriers ! would rise, and whole countries extend between the regions where each must exist ! To live in adjoining provinces, to live even in the same country, though without seeing him, was comparative happiness to the conviction of this dreadful length of distance.

Her mind was at length so much agitated by the consideration of her state, and the belief that she had seen Valancourt for the last time, that she suddenly became very faint ; and looking round the chamber for something that might revive her, she observed the casements, and had just strength to throw one open, near which she seated herself. The air recalled her spirits, and the still moon-light, that fell upon the elms of a long avenue fronting the window, somewhat soothed them, and determined her to try whether exercise and the open air would not relieve the intense pain that bound her temples. In the chateau all was still : and passing down the great staircase into the hall, from whence a passage led immediately to the garden, she softly, and unheard, as she thought, unlocked the door, and entered the avenue. Emily passed on, with steps now hurried and now faltering, as, deceived by the shadows among the trees, she fancied she saw some person move in the distant perspective, and feared it was a spy of Madame Montoni. Her desire, however, to revisit the pavilion where she had passed so many happy hours with Valancourt, and had admired with him the extensive prospect over Languedoc and her native Gascony, overcame her apprehension of being observed, and she moved on towards the terrace, which, running along the upper garden, commanded the whole of the lower one, and communicated with it by a flight of marble steps that terminated the avenue.

Having reached these steps, she paused a moment to look round; for her distance from the chateau now increased the fear which the stillness and obscurity of the hour had awakened. But perceiving nothing that could justify it, she ascended to the terrace; where the moon-light showed the long broad walk, with the pavilion at its extremity, while the rays silvered the foliage of the high trees and shrubs that bordered it on the right, and the tufted summits of those that rose to a level with the balustrade on the left from the garden below, her distance from the chateau again alarming her, she paused to listen; the night was so calm that no sound could have escaped; but she heard only the plaintive sweetness of the nightingale, with the light shiver of the leaves, and she pursued her way towards the pavilion; having reached which, its obscurity did not prevent the emotion that a fuller view of its well-known scene would have excited. The lattices were thrown back, and showed, beyond their embowered arch, the moon-light landscape, shadowy and soft—its groves and plains extending gradually and indistinctly to the eye; its distant mountains catching a stronger gleam; and the nearer river reflecting the moon, and trembling to her rays.

Emily, as she approached the lattice, was sensible of the features of this scene only as they served to bring Valancourt more immediately to her fancy. 'Ah!' said she with a heavy sigh, as she threw herself into a chair by the window, how often have we sat together on this spot—often have looked upon that landscape! Never, never more shall we view it together!—never, never more, perhaps, shall we look upon each other!'

Her tears were suddenly stopped by terror: a voice spoke near her in the pavilion—she shrieked: it spoke again; and she distinguished the well known tones of Valancourt. It was, indeed, Valancourt who supported her in his arms! For some moments their emotion would not suffer either to speak.—'Emily,' said Valancourt at length, as he pressed her hand in his, 'Emily!'—and he was again silent; but the accent in which he had pronounced her name expressed all his tenderness and sorrow.

'O my Emily!' he resumed after a long pause, 'I do then see you once again, and hear again the sound of that voice! I have haunted this place, these gardens—for many, many nights—with a faint, very faint hope of seeing you. This was the only chance that remained for me; and, thank Heaven! it has at length succeeded—I am not condemned to absolute despair!'

Emily said something, she scarcely knew what, expressive of her unalterable affection, and endeavoured to calm the agitation of his mind; but Valancourt could for some time only utter incoherent expressions of his emotions; and when he was somewhat more composed, he said, 'I came hither soon after sunset, and have been watching in the gardens and in this pavilion ever since; for though I had now given up all hope of seeing you, I could not resolve to tear myself away from a place, so near to you, and should probably have lingered about the chateau till morning dawned. O how heavily the moments have passed! yet with what various emotions have they been marked! as I sometimes thought I heard footsteps, and fancied you were approaching, and then again —perceived only a dead and dreary silence! But when you opened the door of the pavilion, and the darkness prevented my distinguishing with certainty whether it was my love, my heart beat so strongly with hopes and fears that I could not speak. The instant I heard the plaintive accents of your voice, my doubts vanished—but not my fears, till you spoke of me; then, losing the apprehension of alarming you in the excess of my emotion, I could no longer be silent.—O Emily! these are moments in which joy and grief struggle so powerfully for pre-eminence, that the heart can scarcely support the contest!'

Emily's heart acknowledged the truth of this assertion. But the joy she felt on thus meeting Valancourt, at the very moment when she was lamenting that they must probably meet no more, soon melted into grief, as reflection stole over her thoughts, and imagination prompted visions of the future. She struggled to recover the calm dignity of mind which was necessary to support her through this last interview, and which Valancourt found it utterly impossible to attain; for the transports of his joy changed abruptly into those of suffering, and he expressed in the most impassioned language his horror of this separation, and his despair of their ever meeting again. Emily wept silently as she listened to him; and then, trying to command her own distress, and to soothe him, she suggested every circumstance that could lead to hope. But the energy of his fears led him instantly to detect the friendly fallacies which she endeavoured to impose on herself and on him, and also to conjure up illusions too powerful for his reason.

'You are going from me,' said he, 'to a distant country—O how distant! to new society, new friends, new admirers! with people, too, who will try to make you forget me, and to promote new connexions! How can I know this, and not know that you will never return for me—never can be mine?' His voice was stifled by sighs.

'You believe, then,' said Emily, 'that the pangs I suffer proceed from a trivial and temporary interest: you believe——'

• 'Suffer,' interrupted Valancourt, 'suffer for me! O Emily, how sweet, how bitter, are those words! what comfort, what anguish, do they give! I ought not to doubt the steadiness of your affection; yet, such is the inconsistency of real love, that it is always awake to suspicion, however unreasonable—always requiring new assurances from the object of its interest: and thus it is, that I always feel revived, as by a new conviction, when your words tell me I am dear to you; and wanting these, I relapse into doubt, and too often into despondency.'—Then seeming to recollect himself, he exclaimed, 'But what a wretch am I, thus to torture you, and in these moments, too! I, who ought to support and comfort you.'

This reflection overcame Valancourt with tenderness; but, relapsing into despondency, he again felt only for himself, and lamented again this cruel separation, in a voice and words so impassioned that Emily could no longer struggle to repress her own grief, or to soothe his. Valancourt, between these emotions of love and pity, lost the power, and almost the wish, of repressing his agitation: and, in the interval of convulsive sobs, he at one moment kissed away her tears; then told her, cruelly, that possibly she might never weep for him; and then tried to speak more calmly, but only exclaimed, 'O Emily—my heart will break!—I cannot, cannot leave you! Now, I gaze upon that countenance, now I hold you in my arms!—a little while, and all this will appear a dream: I shall look, and cannot see you; shall try to recollect your features, and the impression will be fled from my imagination; to hear the tones of your voice, and even memory will be silent!—I· cannot, cannot leave you!—Why should we confide the happiness of our whole lives to the will of people who have no right to interrupt, and, except giving you to me, have no power to promote it?' O Emily! venture to trust your own heart—venture to be mine for ever!' His voice trembled, and he was silent. Emily continued to weep, and was silent also; when Valancourt proceeded to propose an immediate marriage, and that at an early hour on the following morning she should quit Madame Montoni's house, and be conducted by him to the church of the Augustines, where a friar should await to unite them.

The silence with which she listened to a proposal dictated by love and despair, and enforced at a moment when it seemed scarcely possible for her to oppose it—when her heart was softened by the sorrows of separation that might be eternal, and her reason obscured by the illusions of love and terror—encouraged him to hope that it would not be rejected.—

'Speak, my Emily!' said Valancourt eagerly: 'let me hear your voice, let me hear you confirm my fate.'—She spoke not: her cheek was cold, and her senses seemed to fail her; but she did not faint. To Valancourt's terrified imagination she appeared to be dying: he called upon her name, rose to go to the chateau for assistance, and then, recollecting her situation, feared to go, or to leave her for a moment.

After a few minutes she drew a deep sigh, and began to revive. The conflict she had suffered, between love and the duty she at present owed to her father's sister; her repugnance to a clandestine marriage; her fear of emerging on the world with embarrassments, such as might ultimately involve the object of her affection in misery and repentance—all this various interest was too powerful for a mind already enervated by sorrow, and her reason had suffered a transient suspension. But duty and good sense, however hard the conflict, at length triumphed over affection and mournful presentiment. Above all, she dreaded to involve Valancourt in obscurity and vain regret, which she saw, or thought she saw, must be the too certain consequence of a marriage in their present circumstances; and she acted, perhaps, with somewhat more than female fortitude, when she resolved to endure a present, rather than provoke a distant misfortune.

With a candour that proved how truly she esteemed and loved him, and which endeared her to him, if possible, more than ever, she told Valancourt all her reasons for rejecting his proposals. Those which influenced her concerning his future welfare, he instantly refuted, or rather contradicted; but they awakened tender considerations for her, which the frenzy of passion and despair had concealed before; and love, which had but lately prompted him to propose a clandestine and immediate marriage, now induced him to renounce it. The triumph was almost too much for his heart; for Emily's sake, he endeavoured to stifle his grief; but the swelling anguish would not be restrained:—'O Emily!' said he, 'I must leave you—I *must* leave you —and I know it is for ever!'

Convulsive sobs again interrupted his words, and they wept together in silence; till Emily, recollecting the danger of being discovered, and the impropriety of prolonging an interview which might subject her to censure summoned all her fortitude to utter a last farewell!

'Stay!' said Valancourt, 'I conjure you,

stay, for I have much to tell you. The agitation of mind has hitherto suffered me to speak only on the subject that occupied it : I have forborne to mention a doubt of much importance, partly lest it should appear as if I told it with an ungenerous view of alarming you into a compliance with my late proposal.'

Emily, much agitated, did not leave Valancourt, but she led him from the pavilion ; and as they walked upon the terrace, he proceeded as follows :

'This Montoni—I have heard some strange hints concerning him—are you certain that he is of Madame Quesnel's family, and that his fortune is what it appears to be ?'

'I have no reason to doubt either,' replied Emily in a voice of alarm. 'Of the first, indeed, I cannot doubt ; but I have no certain means of judging of the latter, and I entreat you will tell me all you have heard.'

'That I certainly will ; but it is very imperfect and unsatisfactory information : I gathered it by accident from an Italian, who was speaking to another person of this Montoni. They were talking of his marriage : the Italian said, "that if he was the person he meant, he was not likely to make Madame Cheron happy." He proceeded to speak of him in general terms of dislike, and then gave some particular hints concerning his character, that excited my curiosity, and I ventured to ask him a few questions. He was reserved in his replies ; but after hesitating for some time, he owned that he had understood abroad that Montoni was a man of desperate fortune and character. He said someting of a castle of Montoni's situated among the Apennines, and of some strange circumstances that might be mentioned as to his former mode of life. I pressed him to inform me further ; but I believe the strong interest I felt was visible in my manner, and alarmed him ; for no entreaties could prevail with him to give any explanation of the circumstances he had alluded to, or to mention anything further concerning Montoni. I observed to him, that if Montoni was possessed of a castle in the Apennines, it appeared from such a circumstance that he was of some family, and also seemed to contradict the report that he was a man of entirely broken fortunes. He shook his head, and looked as if he could have said a great deal, but made no reply.

'A hope of learning something more satisfactory, or more positive, detained me in his company a considerable time, and I renewed the subject repeatedly ; but the Italian wrapped himself up in reserve, said—'that what he had mentioned he had caught only from floating reports, and that reports frequently arose from personal malice, and were very little to be depended upon.' I forbore to press the subject further, since it was obvious that he was alarmed for the consequence of what he had already said ; and I was compelled to remain in uncertainty on a point where suspense is almost intolerable. Think, Emily, what I must suffer to see you depart for a foreign country, committed to the power of a man of such doubtful character as is this Montoni ! But I will not alarm you unnecessarily : it is possible, as the Italian said at first, that this is not the Montoni he alluded to ; yet, Emily, consider well before you resolve to commit yourself to him. O ! I must not trust myself to speak—or I shall renounce all the motives which so lately influenced me to resign the hope of your becoming mine immediately.'

Valancourt walked upon the terrace with hurried steps, while Emily remained leaning on the balustrade in deep thought. The information she had just received excited, perhaps, more alarm than it could justify, and raised once more the conflict of contrasted interest. She had never liked Montoni : the fire and keenness of his eye, its proud exultation, its bold fierceness, its sullen watchfulness, as occasion, and even slight occasion, had called forth the latent soul, she had often observed with emotion ; while from the usual expression of his countenance she had always shrunk. From such observations she was the more inclined to believe that it was this Montoni of whom the Italian had uttered his suspicious hints. The thought of being solely in his power, in a foreign land, was terrifying to her ; it was not by terror alone that she was urged to an immediate marriage with Valancourt : the tenderest love had already pleaded his cause, but had been unable to overcome her opinion, as to her duty, her disinterested considerations for Valancourt, and the delicacy which made her revolt from a clandestine union. It was not to be expected that a vague terror would be more powerful than the united influence of love and grief ; but it recalled all their energy, and rendered a second conquest necessary.

With Valancourt, whose imagination was now awake to the suggestion of every passion ; whose apprehensions for Emily had acquired strength by the mere mention of them, and became every instant more powerful as his mind brooded over them—with Valancourt no second conquest was attainable. He thought he saw, in the clearest light, and love assisted the fear, that this journey to Italy would involve Emily in misery : he determined, therefore, to persevere in opposing it, and in conjuring her to bestow upon him the title of her lawful protector.

'Emily !' said he with solemn earnestness, 'this is no time for scrupulous distinctions, for weighing the dubious and comparatively trifling circumstances that may affect our future comfort. I now see much more clearly than before the train of serious dangers you are going to encounter with a man of Montoni's character. Those dark hints of the Italian spoke much, but not more than the idea I have of Montoni's disposition, as exhibited even in his countenance. I think I see, at this moment, all that could have been hinted written there. He is the Italian whom I fear ; and I conjure you, for your own sake as well as for mine, to prevent the evils I shudder to foresee. O Emily l let my tenderness, my arms withhold you from them—give me the right to defend you.'

Emily only sighed ; while Valancourt proceeded to remonstrate, and to entreat, with all the energy that love and apprehension could inspire. But, as his imagination magnified to her the possible evils she was going to meet, the mists of her own fancy began to dissipate, and allowed her to distinguish the exaggerated images which imposed on his reason. She considered that there was no proof of Montoni being the person whom the stranger had meant ; that, even if he was so, the Italian had noticed his character and broken fortunes merely from report ; and that, though the countenance of Montoni seemed to give probability to a part of the rumour, it was not by such circumstances that an implicit belief of it could be justified. These considerations would probably not have arisen so distinctly to her mind, at this time, had not the terrors of Valancourt presented to her such obvious exaggerations of her danger as incited her to distrust the fallacies of passion. But while she endeavoured in the gentlest manner to convince him of his error, she plunged him into a new one : his voice and countenance changed to an expression of dark despair—'Emily l' said he, ' this, this moment is the bitterest that is yet come to me. You do not—cannot love me !—It would be impossible for you to reason thus coolly, thus deliberately, if you did. I, *I* am torn with anguish at the prospect of our separation, and of the evils that may await you in consequence of it ; I would encounter any hazards to prevent it—to save you. No, Emily ! no ! —you cannot love me !'

' We have now little time to waste in exclamation or assertion,' said Emily, endeavouring to conceal her emotion : ' if you are yet to learn how dear you are, and ever must be, to my heart, no assurances of mine can give you conviction.'

The last words faltered on her lips, and her tears flowed fast. These words and tears brought once more, and with instantaneous force, conviction of her love to Valancourt, He could only exclaim, ' Emily ! Emily !' and weep over the hand he pressed to his lips ; but she, after some moments, again roused herself from the indulgence of sorrow and said —' I must leave you : it is late, and my absence from the chateau may be discovered. Think of me—love me—when I am far away : the belief of this will be my comfort !'

' Think of you !—love you !' exclaimed Valancourt.

' Try to moderate these transports,' said Emily ; ' for my sake, try.'

' For your sake !'

' Yes, for my sake,' replied Emily in a tremulous voice : I cannot leave you thus !'

' Then do not leave me !' said Valancourt with quickness. Why should we part, or part for longer than till to-morrow ?'

' I am, indeed I am, unequal to these moments,' replied Emily ; ' you tear my heart ; but I never can consent to this hasty, imprudent proposal !'

' If we could command our time, my Emily, it should not be thus hasty ; we must submit to circumstances.'

' We must, indeed ! I have already told you all my heart. My spirits are gone. You allowed the force of my objections, till your tenderness called up vague terrors, which have given us both unnecessary anguish. Spare me ! do not oblige me to repeat the reasons I have already urged.'

' Spare you !' cried Valancourt. ' I am a wretch, a very wretch, that have felt only for myself !—I, who ought to have shown the fortitude of man, who ought to have supported you; —I have increased your sufferings by the conduct of a child ! Forgive me, Emily ; think of the distraction of my mind, now that I am about to part with all that is dear to me, and forgive me ! When you are gone, I shall recollect with bitter remorse what I have made you suffer, and shall wish in vain that I could see you, if only for a moment, that I might soothe your grief.'

Tears again interrupted his voice, and Emily wept with him. ' I will show myself more worthy of your love,' said Valancourt, at length—' I will not prolong these moments. My Emily ! my own Emily ! never forget me ! God knows when we shall meet again ! I resign you to His care.——O God ! O God ! protect and bless her !'

He pressed her hand to his heart. Emily sunk almost lifeless on his bosom, and neither wept nor spoke. Valancourt, now commanding his own distress, tried to comfort and reassure her ; but she appeared totally unaffected by what he said ; and a sigh which she uttered now and then, was all that proved she had not fainted.

He supported her slowly towards the chateau, weeping, and speaking to her ; but she answered only in sighs, till, having reached the gate that terminated the avenue, she seemed to have recovered her consciousness, and, looking round, perceived how near they were to the chateau. ' We must part here,' said she, stopping. ' Why prolong these moments ? Teach me the fortitude I have forgot.'

Valancourt struggled to assume a composed air. ' Farewell, my love !' said he in a voice of solemn tenderness, 'trust me, we shall meet again—meet for each other—meet to part no more!' His voice faltered, but recovering it, he proceeded in a firmer tone. 'You know not what I shall suffer till I hear from you: I shall omit no opportunity of conveying to you my letters; yet I tremble to think how few may occur. And trust me, love, for your dear sake I will try to bear this absence with fortitude. O how little I have shown to-night!'

'Farewell!' said Emily, faintly. 'When you are gone, I shall think of many things I would have said to you.'

'And I of many, many!' said Valancourt. 'I never left you yet, that I did not immediately remember some question, or some entreaty, or some circumstance concerning my love, that I earnestly wished to mention, and felt wretched because I could not. O Emily! this countenance on which I now gaze, will in a moment be gone from my eyes, and not all the efforts of fancy will be able to recall it with exactness. Oh, what an infinite difference between this moment and the next!— *now*, I am in your presence, can behold you! *then*, all will be a dreary blank,—and I shall be a wanderer, exiled from my only home!'

Valancourt again pressed her to his heart, and held her there in silence, weeping. Tears once again calmed her oppressed mind. They again bade each other farewell, lingered a moment, and then parted. Valancourt seemed to force himself from the spot—he passed hastily up the avenue; and Emily, as she moved slowly towards the chateau, heard his distant steps. She listened to the sounds as they sunk fainter and fainter, till the melancholy stillness of night alone remained, and then hurried to her chamber to seek repose, which, alas! was fled from her wretchedness.

CHAPTER XV.

'Where'er I roam, whatever realms I see,
My heart, untravell'd, still shall turn to thee.'
GOLDSMITH.

THE carriages were at the gates at an early hour. The bustle of the domestics passing to and fro in the galleries awakened Emily from harassing slumbers; her unquiet mind had during the night presented her with terrific images and obscure circumstances concerning her affection and her future life. She now endeavoured to chase away the impressions they had left on her fancy; but from imaginary evils she awoke to the consciousness of real ones. Recollecting that she had parted with Valancourt, perhaps for ever, her heart sickened as memory revived. But she tried to dismiss the dismal forebodings that crowded on her mind, and to restrain the sorrow which she could not subdue—efforts which diffused over the settled melancholy of her coun'enance

an expression of tempered resignation, as a thin veil, thrown over the features of beauty, renders them more interesting by a partial concealment. But Madame Montoni observed nothing in this countenance except its unusual paleness, which attracted her censure. She told her niece that she had been indulging in fanciful sorrows, and begged she would have more regard for decorum, than to let the world see that she could not renounce an improper attachment: at which Emily's pale cheek became flushed with crimson—but it was the blush of pride—and she made no answer. Soon after, Montoni entered the breakfast-room, spoke little, and seemed impatient to be gone.

The windows of this room opened upon the garden. As Emily passed them, she saw the spot where she had parted with Valancourt on the preceding night; the remembrance pressed heavily on her heart, and she turned hastily away from the object that had awakened it.

The baggage being at length adjusted, the travellers entered their carriages; and Emily would have left the chateau without one sigh of regret, had it not been situated in the neighbourhood of Valancourt's residence.

From a little eminence she looked back upon Thoulouse, and the far-seen plains of Gascony, beyond which the broken summits of the Pyrenees appeared on the distant horizon, lighted up by a morning sun. 'Dear pleasant mountains!' said she to herself, 'how long may it be ere I see you again, and how much may happen to make me miserable in the interval! O, could I now be certain that I should ever return to you, and find that Valancourt still lived for me, I should go in peace! He will still gaze on you—gaze, when I am far away!'

The trees that impended over the high banks of the road, and formed a line of the perspective with the distant country, now threatened to exclude the view of them; but the bluish mountains still appeared beyond the dark foliage, and Emily continued to lean from the coach window till at length the closing branches shut them from her sight.

Another object soon caught her attention. She had scarcely looked at a person who walked along the bank, with his hat, in which was the military feather, drawn over his eyes, before at the sound of wheels, he suddenly turned, and she perceived that it was Valancourt himself, who waved his hand, sprung into the road, and through the window of the carriage put a letter into her hand. He endeavoured to smile through the despair that overspread his countenance as she passed on. The remembrance of that smile seemed impressed on Emily's mind for ever. She leaned from the window, and saw him on a knoll of the broken bank, leaning against the high trees that waved over him, and pursuing the carriage with his eyes. He waved his hand, and she continued to gaze till distance confused his figure ; and at length another turn of the road entirely separated him from her sight.

Having stopped to take up Signor Cavigni at a chateau on the road, the travellers, of whom Emily was disrespectfully seated with Madame Montoni's woman in a second carriage, pursued their way over the plains of Languedoc. The presence of this servant restrained Emily from reading Valancourt's letter, for she did not choose to expose the emotions it might occasion to the observation of any person : yet such was her wish to read this his last communication, that her trembling hand was every moment on the point of breaking the seal.

At length they reached the village, where they stayed only to change horses, without alighting ; and it was not till they stopped to dine that Emily had an opportunity of reading the letter. Though she had never doubted the sincerity of Valancourt's affection, the fresh assurances she now received of it revived her spirits ; she wept over his letter in tenderness, laid it by to be referred to when they should be particularly depressed, and then thought of him with much less anguish than she had done since they parted. Among some other requests which were interesting to her, because expressive of his tenderness, and because a compliance with them seemed to annihilate for a while the pain of absence, he entreated she would always think of him at sun-set. ' You will then meet me in thought,' said he : ' I shall constantly watch the sunset ; and I shall be happy in the belief that your eyes are fixed upon the same object with mine, and that our minds are conversing. You know not, Emily, the comfort I promise myself from these moments ; but I trust you will experience it.'

It is unnecessary to say with what emotion Emily, on this evening, watched the declining sun, over a long extent of plains, on which she saw it set without interruption, and sink towards the province which Valancourt inhabited. After this hour, her mind became far more tranquil and resigned than it had been since the marriage of Montoni and her aunt.

During several days the travellers journeyed over the plains of Languedoc ; and then entering Dauphiny, and winding for some time among the mountains of that romantic province, they quitted their carriages and began to ascend the Alps. And here such scenes of sublimity opened upon them, as no colours of language must dare to paint ! Emily's mind was even so much engaged with new and wonderful images, that they sometimes banished the idea of Valancourt, though they more frequently revived it. These brought

to her recollection the prospects among the Pyrenees, which they had admired together, and had believed nothing could excel in grandeur. How often did she wish to express to him the new emotions which this astonishing scenery awakened, and that he could partake of them ! Sometimes too she endeavoured to anticipate his remarks, and almost imagined him present. She seemed to have arisen into another world, and to have left every trifling thought, every trifling sentiment, in that below : those only of grandeur and sublimity now dilated her mind, and elevated the affections of her heart.

With what emotions of sublimity, softened by tenderness, did she meet Valancourt in thought, at the customary hour of sun-set, when, wandering among the Alps, she watched the glorious orb sink amidst their summits, his last tints die away on their snowy points, and a solemn obscurity steal over the scene ! and when the last gleam had faded, she turned her eyes from the west with somewhat of the melancholy regret that is experienced after the departure of a beloved friend ; while these lonely feelings were heightened by the spreading gloom, and by the low sounds heard only when darkness confines attention, which made the general stillness more impressive—leaves shook by the air, the last of the breeze that lingers after sun-set, or the murmur of distant streams.

During the first days of this journey among the Alps, the scenery exhibited a wonderful mixture of solitude and inhabitation of cultivation and barrenness. On the edge of tremendous precipices, and within the hollow of the cliffs, below which the clouds often floated, were seen villages, spires, and convent towers ; while green pastures and vineyards spread their hues at the feet of perpendicular rocks of marble or of granite, whose points, tufted with Alpine shrubs, or exhibiting only massy crags, rose above each other, till they terminated in the snowtopped mountains, whence the torrent fell that thundered along the valley.

The snow was not yet melted on the summit of Mount Cenis, over which the travellers passed ; but Emily, as she looked upon its clear lake and extended plain, surrounded by broken cliffs, saw, in imagination, the verdant beauty it would exhibit when the snows should be gone, and the shepherds, leading up the midsummer flocks from Piedmont to pasture on its flowery summit, should add Arcadian figures to Arcadian landscape.

As she descended on the Italian side, the precipices became still more tremendous, the prospects still more wild and majestic ; over which the shifting lights threw all the pomp of colouring. Emily delighted to observe the snowy tops of the mountains under the passing influence of the day—blushing with mourning, glowing with the brightness of noon, or just tinted with the purple even-

going to begin ; but for my part, I should like to live among these pleasant woods and hills, better than in a town ; and they say, Ma'amselle, we shall see no woods or hills, or fields, at Venice, for that it is built in the very middle of the sea.'

Emily agreed with the talkative Annette, that this young man was making a change for the worse ; and could not forbear silently lamenting that he should be drawn from the innocence and beauty of these scenes, to the corrupt ones of that voluptuous city.

When she was alone, unable to sleep, the landscapes of her native home, with Valancourt, and the circumstances of her departure, haunted her fancy : she drew pictures of social happiness amidst the grand simplicity of nature, such as she feared she had bade farewell to for ever ; and then the idea of this young Piedmontese, thus ignorantly sporting with his happiness, returned to her thoughts ; and glad to escape a while from the pressure of nearer interests, she indulged her fancy in composing the following lines :

THE PIEDMONTESE.

Ah, merry swain ! who laugh'd along the vales,
And with your gay pipe made the mountains ring,
Why leave your cot, your woods, and thymy gales,
And friends beloved, for aught that wealth can
    bring !
He goes to wake o'er moonlight seas the string—
Venetian gold his untaught fancy hails !
Yet oft of home his simple carols sing,
And his steps pause, as the last Alp he scales.
Once more he turns to view his native scene—
Far, far below, as roll the clouds away,
He spies his cabin 'mid the pine-tops green,
The well-known woods, clear brook, and pastures
    gay ;
And thinks of friends and parents left behind,
Of sylvan revels, dance, and festive song ;
And hears the faint reed swelling in the wind,
And his sad sighs the distant notes prolong !
Thus went the swain, till mountain-shadows fell,
And dimm'd the landscape to his aching sight :
And must he leave the vales he loves so well ?
Can foreign wealth, and shows, his heart delight ?
No, happy vales ! your wild rocks still shall hear
His pipe light sounding on the morning breeze ;
Still shall he lead the flocks to streamlet clear,
And watch at eve beneath the western trees.
Away, Venetian gold— your charm is o'er !
And now his swift step seeks the lowland bowers,
Where, through the leaves, his cottage light *once
    more*
Guides him to happy friends and jocund hours.
Ah, merry swain ! that laugh along the vales,
And with your gay pipe make the mountains ring,
Your cot, your wood, your thymy-scented gales,
And friends beloved, more joy than wealth can
    bring.

———

CHAPTER XVI.

Titania. If you will patiently dance in our round,
    And see our moonlight revels, go with us.
        MIDSUMMER NIGHT'S DREAM.

EARLY on the following morning the travellers

set out for Turin. The luxuriant plain that extends from the feet of the Alps to that magnificent city, was not then, as now, shaded by an avenue of trees nine miles in length ; but plantations of olives, mulberry, and palms, festooned with vines, mingled with the pastoral scenery through which the rapid Po, after its descent from the mountains, wandered to meet the humble Doria at Turin. As they advanced towards the city, the Alps, seen at some distance, began to appear in all their awful sublimity ; chain rising over chain in long succession, their higher points darkened by the hovering clouds, sometimes hid, and at others seen shooting up far above them ; while their lower steeps, broken into fantastic forms, were touched with blue and purplish tints, which, as they changed in light and shade, seemed to open new scenes to the eye. To the east stretched the plains of Lombardy, with the towers of Turin rising at a distance ; and beyond, the Apennines bounding the horizon.

The general magnificence of that city, with its vistas of churches and palaces branching from the grand square, each opening to a landscape of the distant Alps or Apennines, was not only such as Emily had never seen in France, but such as she had never imagined.

Montoni, who had been often at Turin, and cared little about views of any kind, did not comply with his wife's request that they might survey some of the palaces ; but staying only till the necessary refreshments could be obtained, they set forward for Venice with all possible rapidity. Montoni's manner during this journey was grave, and even haughty ; and towards Madame Montoni he was more especially reserved ; but it was not the reserve of respect, so much as of pride and discontent. Of Emily he took little notice. With Cavigni his conversations were commonly on political or military topics, such as the convulsed state of their country rendered at this time particularly interesting. Emily observed that, at the mention of any daring exploit, Montoni's eyes lost their sullenness, and seemed instantaneously to gleam with fire ; yet they still retained somewhat of a lurking cunning, and she sometimes thought that their fire partook more of the glare of malice than the brightness of valour, though the latter would well have harmonised with the high chivalric air of his figure, in which Cavigni, with all his gay and gallant manners, was his inferior.

On entering the Milanese, the gentlemen exchanged their French hats for the Italian cap of scarlet cloth embroidered ; and Emily was somewhat surprised to observe that Montoni added to his the military plume, while Cavigni retained only the feather which was usually worn with such caps ; but she at length concluded that Montoni assumed this ensign of a soldier for convenience, as a means of passing with more safety through a country overrun with parties of the military.

Over the beautiful plains of this country the devastations of war were frequently visible. Where the lands had not been suffered to lie uncultivated, they were often tracked with the steps of the spoiler; the vines were torn down from the branches that had supported them, the olives trampled upon the ground, and even the groves of mulberry-trees had been hewn by the enemy to light fires that destroyed the hamlets and villages of their owners. Emily turned her eyes with a sigh from these painful vestiges of contention, to the Alps of the Grison, that overlooked them to the north, whose awful solitudes seemed to offer to persecuted man a secure asylum.

The travellers frequently distinguished troops of soldiers moving at a distance: and they experienced at the little inns on the road the scarcity of provision, and other inconveniences which are a part of the consequence of intestine war; but they had never reason to be much alarmed for their immediate safety, and they passed on to Milan with little interruption of any kind, where they stayed not to survey the grandeur of the city, or even to view its vast cathedral which was then building.

Beyond Milan, the country wore the aspect of a ruder devastation; and though everything seemed now quiet, the repose was like that of death spread over features which retain the impression of the last convulsions.

It was not till they had passed the eastern limits of the Milanese, that the travellers saw any troops since they had left Milan; when, as the evening was drawing to a close, they descried what appeared to be an army winding onward along the distant plains, whose spears and other arms caught the last rays of the sun. As the column advanced through a part of the road contracted between two hillocks, some of the commanders on horse-back were distinguished on a small eminence, pointing and making signals for the march; while several of the officers were riding along the line, directing its progress according to the signs communicated by those above; and others, separating from the vanguard, which had emerged from the pass, were riding carelessly along the plains at some distance to the right of the army.

As they drew nearer, Montoni, distinguishing the feathers that waved in their caps, and the banners and liveries of the bands that followed them, thought he knew this to be the small army commanded by the famous captain Utaldo, with whom, as well as with some of the other chiefs, he was personally acquainted. He therefore gave orders that the carriages should draw up by the side of the road, to await their arrival, and give them the pass. A faint strain of martial music

now stole by, and gradually strengthening as the troops approached, Emily distinguished the drums and trumpets, with the clash of cymbals and of arms that were struck by a small party in time to the march.

Montoni being now certain that these were the bands of the victorious Utaldo, leaned from the carriage window, and hailed their general by waving his cap in the air, which compliment the chief returned by raising his spear and then letting it down again suddenly, while some of his officers, who were riding at a distance from the troops, came up to the carriage and saluted Montoni as an old acquaintance. The captain himself soon after arriving, his bands halted while he conversed with Montoni, whom he appeared much rejoiced to see; and from what he said, Emily understood that this was a victorious army returning into their own principality; while the numerous waggons that accompanied them contained the rich spoils of the enemy, their own wounded soldiers, and the prisoners they had taken in battle, who were to be ransomed when the peace, then negotiating between the neighbouring states, should be ratified. The chiefs on the following day were to separate, and each taking his share of the spoil was to return with his own band to his castle. This was therefore to be an evening of uncommon and general festivity, in commemoration of the victory they had accomplished together, and of the farewell which the commanders were about to take of each other.

Emily, as these officers conversed with Montoni, observed with admiration, tinctured with awe, their high martial air, mingled with the haughtiness of the noblesse of those days, and heightened by the gallantry of their dress, by the plumes towering on their caps, the armorial coat, Persian sash, and ancient Spanish cloak. Utaldo, telling Montoni that his army were going to encamp for the night near a village at only a few miles distance, invited him to turn back and partake of their festivity, assuring the ladies also, that they should be pleasantly accommodated: but Montoni excused himself, adding, that it was his design to reach Verona that evening; and after some conversation concerning the state of the country towards that city, they parted.

The travellers proceeded without any interruption; but it was some hours after sun-set before they arrived at Verona, whose beautiful environs were therefore not seen by Emily till the following morning; when, leaving that pleasant town at an early hour, they set off for Padua, where they embarked on the Brenta for Venice. Here the scene was entirely changed; no vestiges of war, such as had deformed the plains of the Milanese, appeared; on the contrary, all was peace and elegance. The verdant banks of the Brenta exhibited a continued landscape of beauty, gaiety and splendour. Emily gazed with admiration on the villas of the Venetian noblesse, with their cool porticos and colonnades, overhung with poplars and cypresses of majestic height and lively verdure ; on their rich orangeries, whose blossoms perfumed the air ; and on the luxuriant willows, that dipped their light leaves in the wave, and sheltered from the sun the gay parties whose music came at intervals on the breeze. The Carnival did, indeed, appear to extend from Venice along the whole line of these enchanting shores ; the river was gay with boats passing to that city, exhibiting the fantastic diversity of a masquerade in the dresses of the people within them ; and towards evening, groups of dancers frequently were seen beneath the trees.

Cavigni meanwhile informed her of the names of the noblemen to whom the several villas they passed belonged, adding light sketches of their characters, such as served to amuse rather than to inform, exhibiting his own wit instead of the delineation of truth. Emily was sometimes diverted by his conversation ; but his gaiety did not entertain Madame Montoni as it had formerly done ; she was frequently grave, and Montoni retained his usual reserve.

Nothing could exceed Emily's admiration on her first view of Venice, with its islets, palaces, and towers rising out of the sea, whose clear surface reflected the tremulous picture in all its colours. The sun, sinking in the west, tinted the waves and the lofty mountains of Friuli, which skirt the northern shores of the Adriatic, with a saffron glow, while on the marble porticos and colonnades of St. Mark were thrown the rich lights and shades of evening. As they glided on, the grander features of this city appeared more distinctly : its terraces, crowned with airy yet majestic fabrics, touched, as they now were, with the splendour of the setting sun, appeared as if they had been called up from the ocean by the wand of an enchanter, rather than reared by mortal hands.

The sun, soon after, sinking to the lower world, the shadow of the earth stole gradually over the waves, and then up the towering sides of the mountains of Friuli, till it extinguished even the last upward beams that had lingered on their summits, and the melancholy purple of evening drew over them like a thin veil. How deep, how beautiful was the tranquillity that wrapped the scene ! All nature seemed to repose ; the finest emotions of the soul were alone awake. Emily's eyes filled with tears of admiration and sublime devotion, as she raised them over the sleeping world to the vast heavens, and heard the notes of solemn music that stole over the waters from a distance. She listened in still rapture, and no person of the party broke the charm by an inquiry. The sounds seemed to grow on the air ; for so smoothly did the barge

glide along, that its motion was not perceivable, and the fairy city appeared approaching to welcome the strangers. They now distinguished a female voice, accompanied by a few instruments, singing a soft and mournful air and its fine expression, as sometimes it seemed pleading with the impassioned tenderness of love, and then languishing into the cadence of hopeless grief, declared that it flowed from no feigned sensibility. 'Ah !' thought Emily, as she sighed and remembered Valancourt, 'those strains come from the heart !'

She looked round with anxious inquiry ; the deep twilight that had fallen over the scene, admitted only imperfect images to the eye, but at some distance on the sea she thought she perceived a gondola : a chorus of voices and instruments now swelled on the air—so sweet, so solemn ! seemed like the hymn of angels descending through the silence of night ! Now it died away, and fancy almost beheld the holy choir reascending towards heaven ; then again it swelled with the breeze, trembled awhile, and again died into silence. It brought to Emily's recollection some lines of her late father, and she repeated in a low voice,

> ' . . . . Oft I hear,
> Upon the silence of the midnight air,
> Celestial voices swell in holy chorus,
> That bears the soul to heaven !'

The deep stillness that succeeded was as expressive as the strain that had just ceased. It was uninterrupted for several minutes, till a general sigh seemed to release the company from their enchantment. Emily, however, long indulged the pleasing sadness that had stolen upon her spirits ; but the gay and busy scene that appeared, as the barge approached St. Mark's Place, at length roused her attention. The rising moon, which threw a shadowy light upon the terrace, and illumined the porticos and magnificent arcades that crowned them, discovered the various company, whose light steps, soft guitars, and softer voices, echoed through the colonades.

The music they heard before now passed Montoni's barge in one of the gondolas, of which several were seen skimming along the moon-light sea, full of gay parties, catching the cool breeze. Most of these had music, made sweeter by the waves over which it floated, and by the measured sound of oars as they dashed the sparkling tide. Emily gazed, and listened, and thought herself in a fairy scene : even Madame Montoni was pleased ; Montoni congratulated himself on his return to Venice, which he called the first city in the world, and Cavigni was more gay and animated than ever.

The barge passed on to the grand canal, where Montoni's mansion was situated. And here, other forms of beauty and of grandeur, such as her imagination had never painted, were unfolded to Emily in the palaces of Sansovino and Palladio, as she glided along the waves. The air bore no sounds but those of sweetness, echoing along each margin of the canal, and from gondolas on its surface, while groups of masks were seen dancing on the moonlight terraces, and seemed almost to realize the romance of fairy-land.

The barge stopped before the portico of a large house, from whence a servant of Montoni crossed the terrace, and immediately the party disembarked. From the portico they passed a noble hall to a staircase of marble, which led to a saloon fitted up in a style of magnificence that surprised Emily. The walls and ceiling were adorned with historical and allegorical paintings in *fresco*; silver tripods, depending from chains of the same metal, illumined the apartment, the floor of which was covered with Indian mats painted in a variety of colours and devices; the couches and drapery of the lattices were of pale green silk, embroidered and fringed with green and gold. Balcony lattices opened upon the grand canal, whence rose a confusion of voices and of musical instruments, and the breeze that gave freshness to the apartment. Emily, considering the gloomy temper of Montoni, looked upon the splendid furniture of his house with surprise, and remembered the report of his being a man of broken fortune, with astonishment. 'Ah!' said she to herself, 'if Valancourt could but see this mansion, what peace would it give him! He would then be convinced that the report was groundless.'

Madame Montoni seemed to assume the airs of a princess; but Montoni was restless and discontented, and did not even observe the civility of bidding her welcome to her home.

Soon after his arrival, he ordered his gondola, and, with Cavigni, went out to mingle in the scenes of the evening. Madame then became serious and thoughtful. Emily, who was charmed with everything she saw, endeavoured to enliven her; but reflection had not, with Madame Montoni, subdued caprice and ill-humour; and her answers discovered so much of both, that Emily gave up the attempt of diverting her, and withdrew to a lattice, to amuse herself with the scene without, so new and so enchanting.

The first object that attracted her notice was a group of dancers on the terrace below, led by a guitar and some other instruments. The girl who struck the guitar, and another who flourished the tamborine, passed on in a dancing step, and with a light grace and gaiety of heart that would have subdued the goddess of spleen in her worst humour. After these came a group of fantastic figures, some dressed as gondolieri, others as minstrels, while others seemed to defy all description. They sung in parts, their voices accompanied by a few soft instruments. At a little distance from the

portico they stopped, and Emily distinguished the verses of Ariosto. They sung of the wars of the Moors against Charlemagne, and then of the woes of Orlando: afterwards the measure changed, and the melancholy sweetness of Petrarch succeeded. The magic of his grief was assisted by all that Italian expression, heightened by the enchantments of Venetian moon-light, could give.

Emily, as she listened, caught the pensive enthusiasm; her tears flowed silently, while her fancy bore her far away to France and to Valancourt. Each succeeding sonnet, more full of charming sadness than the last, seemed to bind the spell of melancholy: with extreme regret she saw the musicians move on, and her attention followed the strain till the last faint warble died in air. She then remained sunk in that pensive tranquillity which soft music leaves on the mind—a state like that produced by the view of a beautiful landscape by moonlight, or by the recollection of scenes marked with the tenderness of friends lost for ever, and with sorrows which time has mellowed into mild regret. Such scenes are indeed, to the mind, like those faint traces which the memory bears of music that is past.

Other sounds soon awakened her attention: it was the solemn harmony of horns, that swelled from a distance: and observing the gondolas arrange themselves along the margin of the terraces, she threw on her veil, and, stepping into the balcony, discerned in the distant perspective of the canal something like a procession floating on the light surface of the water; as it approached, the horns and other instruments mingled sweetly; and soon after, the fabled deities of the city seemed to have arisen from the ocean; for Neptune, with Venice personified as his queen, came on the undulating waves, surrounded by tritons and sea-nymphs. The fantastic splendour of this spectacle, together with the grandeur of the surrounding palaces, appeared like the vision of a poet suddenly embodied; and the fanciful images which it awakened in Emily's mind, lingered there long after the procession had passed away. She indulged herself in imagining what might be the manners and delights of a sea-nymph, till she almost wished to throw off the habit of mortality, and plunge into the green wave to participate them.

'How delightful,' said she, 'to live amidst the coral bowers and crystal caverns of the ocean, with my sister nymphs, and listen to the sounding waters above, and to the soft shells of the tritons! and then, after sun-set, to skim on the surface of the waves, round wild rocks, and along sequestered shores, where perhaps, some pensive wanderer comes to weep! Then would I soothe his sorrows with my sweet music, and offer him from a shell some of the delicious fruit that hangs round Neptune's palace.'

She was recalled from her reverie to a mere mortal supper, and could not forbear smiling at the fancies she had been indulging, and at her conviction of the serious displeasure which Madame Montoni would have expressed, could she have been made acquainted with them.

After supper, her aunt sat late ; but Montoni did not return, and she at length retired to rest. If Emily had admired the magnificence of the saloon, she was not less surprised on observing the half-furnished and forlorn appearance of the apartments she passed in the way to her chamber, whither she went through long suits of noble rooms, that seemed, from their desolate aspect, to have been unoccupied for many years. On the walls of some were the faded remains of tapestry ; from others painted in *fresco*, the damps had almost withdrawn both colours and design. At length she reached her own chamber, spacious, desolate, and lofty, like the rest, with high lattices that opened towards the Adriatic. It brought gloomy images to her mind ; but the view of the Adriatic soon gave her others more airy, among which was that of the sea-nymph, whose delights she had before amused herself with picturing ; and anxious to escape from serious reflections, she now endeavoured to throw her fanciful ideas into a train, and concluded the hour with composing the following lines :

THE SEA-NYMPH.

Down, down a thousand fathom deep,
Among the sounding seas I go ;
Play round the foot of every steep
Whose cliffs above the ocean grow.

There, within their secret caves,
I hear the mighty rivers roar !
And guide their streams through Neptune's waves,
To bless the green earth's inmost shore !

And bid the freshen'd water's glide,
For fern-crown'd nymphs, of lake or brook,
Through winding woods and pastures wide,
And many a wild, romantic nook.

For this the nymphs at fall of eve
Oft dance upon the flowery banks,
And sing my name, and garlands weave
To bear beneath the wave their thanks.

In coral bowers I love to lie,
And hear the surges roll above,
And through the waters view on high
The proud ships sail, and gay clouds move.

And oft at midnight's stillest hour,
When summer seas the vessel lave,
I love to prove my charmful power
While floating on the moonlight wave.

And when deep sleep the crew has bound,
And the sad lover musing leans
O'er the ship's side, I breathe around
Such strains as speak no mortal means !

O'er the dim waves his searching eye
Sees but the vessel's lengthened shade ;
Above—the moon and azure sky :
Entranced he hears and half afraid !

Sometimes a single note I swell,
That, softly sweet, at distance dies !
Then wake the magic of my shell,
And choral voices round me rise !

The trembling youth, charm'd by my strain,
Calls up the crew, who, silent, bend
O'er the high deck, but list in vain :
My song is hush'd, my wonders end !

Within the mountain's woody bay,
Where the tall bark at anchor rides,
At twilight hour, with tritons gay
I dance upon the lapsing tides !

And with my sister-nymphs I sport,
Till the broad sun looks o'er the floods ;
Then swift we seek our crystal court,
Deep in the wave, 'mid Neptune's woods.

In cool arcades and grassy halls
We pass the sultry hours of noon,
Beyond wherever sunbeam falls,
Weaving sea-flowers in gay festoon.

The while we chant our ditties sweet
To some soft shell that warbles near ;
Join'd by the murmuring currents, fleet,
That glide along our halls so clear.

There the pale pearl and sapphire blue,
And ruby red, and emerald green,
Dart from the domes a changing hue,
And sparry columns deck the scene.

When the dark storm scowls o'er the deep,
And long, long peals of thunder sound,
On some high cliff my watch I keep
O'er all the restless seas around :

Till on the ridgy wave afar
Comes the lone vessel, labouring slow,
Spreading the white foam in the air,
With sail and topmast bending low.

Then, plunge I 'mid the ocean's roar,
My way by quivering lightnings shown,
To guide the bark to peaceful shore,
And hush the sailor's fearful groan.

And if too late I reach its side
To save it from the 'whelming surge,
I call my dolphins o'er the tide,
To bear the crew where isles emerge.

Their mournful spirits soon I cheer,
While round the desert coast I go,
With warbled songs they faintly hear,
Oft as the stormy gust sinks low.

My music leads to lofty groves,
That wild upon the sea-bank wave ;
Where sweet fruits bloom, and fresh spring roves,
And closing boughs the tempest brave.

Then, from the air spirits obey,
My potent voice they love so well,
And on the clouds paint visions gay,
While strains more sweet at distance swell.

And thus the lonely hours I cheat,
Soothing the shipwreck'd sailor's heart,
Till from the waves the storms retreat,
And o'er the east the day-beams dart.

Neptune for this oft binds me fast
To rocks below, with coral chain,
Till all the tempest's overpast,
And drowning seamen cry in vain.

Whoe'er ye are that love my lay,
Come when red sunset tints the wave,
To the still sands, where fairies play ;
There, in cool seas, I love to lave.

CHAPTER XVII.

'He is a great observer, and he looks
Quite through the deeds of men: he loves no
    plays,
. . . . he hears no music;
Seldom he smiles; and smiles in such a sort,
As if he mock'd himself, and scorn'd his spirit
That could be moved to smile at anything.
Such men as he be never at heart's ease,
When they behold a greater than themselves.'
                            JULIUS CÆSAR.

MONTONI and his companion did not return home till many hours after the dawn had blushed upon the Adriatic. The airy groups which had danced all night along the colonnade of St. Mark, dispersed before the morning like so many spirits. Montoni had been otherwise engaged; his soul was little susceptible of light pleasures. He delighted in the energies of the passions; the difficulties and tempests of life, which wreck the happiness of others, roused and strengthened all the powers of his mind, and afforded him the highest enjoyments of which his nature was capable. Without some object of strong interest, life was to him little more than a sleep; and when pursuits of real interest failed, he substituted artificial ones, till habit changed their nature, and they ceased to be unreal. Of this kind was the habit of gaming which he had adopted, first, for the purpose of relieving him from the languor of inaction, but had since pursued with the ardour of passion. In this occupation he had passed the night with Cavigni, and a party of young men who had more money than rank and more vice than either. Montoni despised the greater part of these for the inferiority of their talents rather than for their vicious inclinations, and associated with them only to make them the instruments of his purposes. Among these, however, were some of superior abilities, and a few whom Montoni admitted to his intimacy; but even towards these he still preserved a decisive and haughty air, which, while it imposed submission on weak and timid minds, roused the fierce hatred of strong ones. He had, of course, many and bitter enemies; but the rancour of their hatred proved the degree of his power; and as power was his chief aim, he gloried more in such hatred than it was possible he could in being esteemed. A feeling so tempered as that of esteem, he despised, and would have despised himself also had he thought himself capable of being flattered by it.

Among the few whom he distinguished were the Signors Bertolini, Orsino, and Verezzi. The first was a man of gay temper, strong passions, dissipated, and of unbounded extravagance, but generous, brave, and unsuspicious. Orsino was reserved and haughty; loving power more than ostentation; of a cruel and suspicious temper; quick to feel an injury, and relentless in avenging it; cunning

and unsearchable in contrivance, patient and indefatigable in the execution of his schemes. He had a perfect command of feature and of his passions, of which he had scarcely any, but pride, revenge, and avarice; and in the gratification of these, few considerations had power to restrain him, few obstacles to withstand the depth of his stratagems. This man was the chief favourite of Montoni. Verezzi was a man of some talent, of fiery imagination, and the slave of alternate passions. He was gay, voluptuous, and daring; yet had neither perseverance nor true courage, and was meanly selfish in all his aims. Quick to form schemes, and sanguine in his hope of success, he was the first to undertake, and to abandon, not only his own plans, but those adopted from other persons. Proud and impetuous, he revolted against all subordination; yet those who were acquainted with his character, and watched the turn of his passions, could lead him like a child.

Such were the friends whom Montoni introduced to his family and his table, on the day after his arrival at Venice. There were also of the party a Venetian nobleman, Count Morano, and a Signora Livona, whom Montoni had introduced to his wife as a lady of distinguished merit, and who, having called in the morning to welcome her to Venice, had been requested to be of the dinner party.

Madame Montoni received with a very ill grace the compliments of the signors. She disliked them, because they were the friends of her husband; hated them, because she believed they had contributed to detain him abroad till so late an hour of the preceding morning; and envied them, since, conscious of her own want of influence, she was convinced that he preferred their society to her own. The rank of Count Morano procured him that distinction which she refused to the rest of the company. The haughty sullenness of her countenance and manner, and the ostentatious extravagance of her dress, for she had not yet adopted the Venetian habit, were strikingly contrasted by the beauty, modesty, sweetness, and simplicity of Emily, who observed with more attention than pleasure the party around her. The beauty and fascinating manners of Signora Livona, however, won her involuntary regard; while the sweetness of her accents, and her air of gentle kindness, awakened with Emily those pleasing affections which so long had slumbered.

In the cool of the evening the party embarked in Montoni's gondola, and rowed out upon the sea. The red glow of sun-set still touched the waves, and lingered in the west, where the melancholy gleam seemed slowly expiring, while the dark blue of the upper ether began to twinkle with stars. Emily sat, given up to pensive and sweet emotions. The smoothness of the water over which she glided, its reflected images—a new heaven and trembling stars below the waves, with shadowy outlines of towers and porticos —conspired with the stillness of the hour, interrupted only by the passing wave or the notes of distant music, to raise those emotions to enthusiasm. As she listened to the measured sound of the oars, and to the remote warblings that came in the breeze, her softened mind returned to the memory of St. Aubert and to Valancourt, and tears stole to her eyes. The rays of the moon, strengthening as the shadows deepened, soon after threw a silvery gleam upon her countenance, which was partly shaded by a thick black veil, and touched it with inimitable softness. Hers was the *contour* of a Madonna, with the sensibility of a Magdalen; and the pensive uplifted eye, with the tear that glittered on her cheek, confirmed the expression of the character.

The last strain of distant music now died in air, for the gondola was far upon the waves, and the party determined to have music of their own. The Count Morano, who sat next to Emily, and who had been observing her for some time in silence, snatched up a lute, and struck the chords with the finger of harmony herself, while his voice, a fine tenor, accompanied them in a' rondeau full of tender sadness. To him, indeed, might have been applied that beautiful exhortation of an English poet, had it then existed:

'. . . . . . Strike up, my master,
But touch the strings with a religious softness!
Teach sounds to languish through the night's dull ear
Till Melancholy starts from off her couch,
And Carelessness grows convert to Attention.'

With such powers of expression the Count sung the following

RONDEAU.

Soft as yon silver ray, that sleeps
Upon the ocean's trembling tide;
Soft as the air, that lightly sweeps
Yon sail, that swells in stately pride:

Soft as the surge's stealing note,
That dies along the distant shores,
Or warbled strain, that sinks remote——
So soft the sigh my bosom pours!

True as the wave to Cynthia's ray,
True as the vessel to the breeze,
True as the soul to music's sway,
Or music to Venetian seas:

Soft as yon silver beams, that sleep
Upon the ocean's trembling breast;
So soft, so true, fond Love shall weep,
So soft, so true, with *thee* shall rest.

The cadence with which he returned from the last stanza to a repetiton of the first; the fine modulation in which his voice stole upon the first line, and the pathetic energy with which he pronounced the last, were such as only exquisite taste could give. When he had concluded, he gave the lute with a sigh to Emily, who, to avoid any appearance of affectation, immediately began to play. She sung a melancholy little air, one of the popular songs of her native province, with a simplicity and pathos that made it enchanting. But its well-known melody brought so forcibly to her fancy the scenes and the persons among which she had often heard it, that her spirits were overcome, her voice trembled and ceased —and the strings of the lute were struck with a disordered hand; till, ashamed of the emotion she had betrayed, she suddenly passed on to a song so gay and airy, that the steps of the dance seemed almost to echo to the notes. ' *Bravissimo !*' burst instantly from the lips of her delighted auditors, and she was compelled to repeat the air. Among the compliments that followed, those of the count were not the least audible; and they had not concluded when Emily gave the instrument to Signora Livona, whose voice accompanied it with true Italian taste.

Afterwards, the count, Emily, Cavigni, and the signora sung *canzonettes*, accompanied by a couple of lutes and a few other instruments. Sometimes the instruments suddenly ceased, and the voices dropped from the full swell of harmony into a low chant; then, after a deep pause, they rose by degrees, the instruments one by one striking up, till the loud and full chorus soared again to heaven !

Meanwhile Montoni, who was weary of this harmony, was considering how he might disengage himself from his party, or withdraw with such of it as would be willing to play, to a casino. In a pause of the music he proposed returning to shore; a proposal which Orsino eagerly seconded, but which the count and the other gentlemen as warmly opposed.

Montoni still meditated how he might excuse himself from longer attendance upon the count, for to him only he thought excuse necessary, and how he might get to land, till the gondolieri of an empty boat returning to Venice hailed his people. Without troubling himself longer about an excuse, he seized this opportunity of going thither; and committing the ladies to the care of his friends, departed with Orsino, while Emily, for the first time, saw him go with regret: for she considered his presence a protection, though she knew not what she should fear. He landed at St. Mark's, and hurrying to a casino, was soon lost amidst a crowd of gamesters.

Meanwhile the count having secretly dispatched a servant in Montoni's boat for his own gondola and musicians, Emily heard, without knowing his project, the gay song of gondolieri approaching, as they sat on the stern of the boat, and saw the tremulous gleam of the moon-light wave, which their oars disturbed. Presently she heard the sound of instruments, and then a full symphony swelled on the air; and the boats meeting, the gondolieri hailed each other. The count then explaining himself, the party removed into his gondola, which was embellished with all that taste could bestow.

While they partook of a collation of fruits and ice, the whole band, following at a distance in the other boat, played the most sweet and enchanting strains; and the count, who had again seated himself by Emily, paid her unremitted attention; and sometimes in a low but impassioned voice, uttered compliments she could not misunderstand. To avoid them she conversed with Signora Livona, and her manner to the count assumed a mild reserve, which, though dignified, was too gentle to repress his assiduities; he could see, hear, speak to no person but Emily; while Cavigni observed him now and then with a look of displeasure, and Emily, with one of uneasiness. She now wished for nothing so much as to return to Venice : but it was near midnight before the gondolas approached St. Mark's place, where the voice of gaiety and song was loud. The busy hum of mingling sounds was heard at a considerable distance on the water; and had not a bright moonlight discovered the city, with its terraces and towers, a stranger would almost have credited the fabled wonders of Neptune's court, and believed that the tumult arose from beneath the waves.

They landed at St. Mark's, where the gaiety of the colonnades and the beauty of the night made Madame Montoni willingly submit to the count's solicitations to join the promenade, and afterwards to take a supper with the rest of the party at his casino. If anything could have dissipated Emily's uneasiness, it would have been the grandeur, gaiety, and novelty of the surrounding scene, adorned with Palladio's palaces, and busy with parties of masqueraders.

At length they withdrew to the casino, which was fitted up with infinite taste, and where a splendid banquet was prepared. But here Emily's reserve made the count perceive that it was necessary for his interest to win the favour of Madame Montoni, which, from the condescension she had already shown to him, appeared to be an achievement of no great difficulty. He transferred, therefore, part of his attention from Emily to her aunt, who felt too much flattered by the distinction even to disguise her emotion; and before the party broke up, he had entirely engaged the esteem of Madame Montoni. Whenever he addressed her, her ungracious countenance relaxed into smiles, and to whatever he proposed she assented. He invited her with the rest of the party to take coffee in his box at the opera on the following evening; and Emily heard the invitation accepted, with strong anxiety concerning the means of excusing herself from attending Madame Montoni thither.

It was very late before their gondola was ordered; and Emily's surprise was extreme, when, on quitting the casino, she beheld the broad sun rising out of the Adriatic, while St. Mark's Place was yet crowded with company. Sleep had long weighed heavily on her eyes; but now the fresh sea breeze revived her, and she would have quitted the scene with regret, had not the count been present, performing the duty which he had imposed upon himself, of escorting them home. There they heard that Montoni was not yet returned; and his wife retiring in displeasure to her apartment, at length released Emily from the fatigue of further attendance.

Montoni came home late in the morning, in a very ill humour, having lost considerably at play; and before he withdrew to rest had a private conference with Cavigni, whose manner on the following day seemed to tell that the subject of it had not been pleasing to him.

In the evening Madame Montoni, who during the day had observed a sullen silence towards her husband, received visits from some Venetian ladies, with whose sweet manners Emily was particularly charmed. They had an air of ease and kindness towards the strangers, as if they had been their familiar friends for years; and their conversation was by turns tender, sentimental, and gay. Madame, though she had no taste for such conversation, and whose coarseness and selfishness sometimes exhibited a ludicrous contrast to their excessive refinement, could not remain wholly insensible to the captivations of their manner.

In a pause of conversation, a lady who was called Signora Herminia took up a lute, and began to play and sing with as much easy gaiety as if she had been alone. Her voice was uncommonly rich in tone and various in expression; yet she appeared to be entirely unconscious of its powers, and meant nothing less than to display them. She sung from the gaiety of her heart, as she sat with her veil half thrown back, holding gracefully the lute, under the spreading foliage and flowers of some plants that rose from baskets and interlaced one of the lattices of the saloon. Emily, retiring a little from the company, sketched her figure, with the miniature scenery around her, and drew a very interesting picture, which, though it would not perhaps have borne criticism, had spirit and taste enough to awaken both the fancy and the heart. When she had finished it, she presented it to the beautiful original, who was delighted with the offering, as well as the sentiment it conveyed, and assured Emily, with a smile of captivating sweetness, that she should preserve it as a pledge of her friendship.

In the evening Cavigni joined the ladies, but Montoni had other engagements; and they embarked in the gondola for St. Mark's, where the same gay company seemed to flutter as on the preceding night. The cool breeze, the glassy sea, the gentle sound of its waves, and the sweeter murmur of distant music;

the lofty porticos and arcades, and the happy groups that sauntered beneath them ; these, with every feature and circumstance of the scene, united to charm Emily, no longer teased by the officious attentions of Count Morano. But as she looked upon the moon-light sea undulating along the walls of St. Mark, and, lingering for a moment over those walls, caught the sweet and melancholy song of some gondolier as he sat in his boat below waiting for his master, her softened mind returned to the memory of her home, of her friends, and of all that was dear in her native country.

After walking some time, they sat down at the door of a casino : and while Cavigni was accommodating them with coffee and ice, were joined by Count Morano. He sought Emily with a look of impatient delight, who, remem-bering all the attention he had shown her on the preceding evening, was compelled, as before, to shrink from his assiduities into a timid reserve, except when she conversed with Signora Herminia and the other ladies of her party.

It was near midnight before they withdrew to the opera, where Emily was not so charmed but that, when she remembered the scene she had just quitted, she felt how infinitely inferior all the splendour of art is to the sublimity of nature. Her heart was not now affected, tears of admiration did not start to her eyes, as when she viewed the vast expanse of ocean, the grandeur of the heavens, and listened to the rolling waters, and to the faint music that at intervals mingled with their roar. Remem-bering these, the scene before her faded into insignificance.

Of the evening, which passed on without any particular incident, she wished the con-clusion, that she might escape from the atten-tions of the count ; and as opposite qualities frequently attract each other in our thoughts, thus Emily, when she looked on Count Morano, remembered Valancourt, and a sigh sometimes followed the recollection.

Several weeks passed in the course of cus-tomary visits, during which nothing remark-able occurred. Emily was amused by the manners and scenes that surrounded her, so different from those of France, but where Count Morano, too frequently for her com-fort, contrived to introduce himself. His manner, figure, and accomplishments, which were generally admired, Emily would perhaps have admired also, had her heart been dis-engaged from Valancourt, and had the count forborne to persecute her with officious atten-tions, during which she observed some traits in his character that prejudiced her against whatever might otherwise be good in it.

Soon after his arrival at Venice, Montoni received a packet from M. Quesnel, in which the latter mentioned the death of his wife's uncle, at his villa on the Brenta ; and that, in consequence of this event, he should hasten to take possession of that estate and of other effects bequeathed to him. This uncle was the brother of Madame Quesnel's late mother; Montoni was related to her by the father's side ; and though he could have had neither claim nor expectation concerning these posses-sions, he could scarcely conceal the envy which M. Quesnel's letter excited.

Emily had observed with concern, that, since they left France, Montoni had not even affected kindness towards her aunt, and that, after treating her, at first, with neglect, he now met her with uniform ill-humour and reserve. She had never supposed that her aunt's foibles could have escaped the discern-ment of Montoni, or that her mind or figure were of a kind to deserve his attention. Her surprise, therefore, at this match had been ex-treme ; but since he had made the choice, she did not suspect that he would so openly have discovered his contempt of it. But Montoni, who had been allured by the seeming wealth of Madame Cheron, was now severely dis-appointed by her comparative poverty, and highly exasperated by the deceit she had em-ployed to conceal it, till concealment was no longer necessary. He had been deceived in an affair wherein he meant to be the deceiver ; outwitted by the superior cunning of a woman whose understanding he despised, and to whom he had sacrificed his pride and his liberty, without saving himself from the ruin which had impended over his head. Madame Montoni had contrived to have the greatest part of what she really did possess, settled upon herself : what remained, though it was totally inadequate both to her husband's ex-pectations and to his necessities, he had con-verted into money, and brought with him to Venice, that he might a little longer delude society, and make a last effort to regain the fortunes he had lost.

The hints which had been thrown out to Valancourt concerning Montoni's character and condition were too true ; but it was now left to time and occasion to unfold the circum-stances both of what had, and of what had not been hinted,—and to time and occasion we commit them.

Madame Montoni was not of a nature to bear injuries with meekness, or to resent them with dignity : her exasperated pride displayed itself in all the violence and acrimony of a little, or at least of an ill-regulated mind. She would not acknowledge, even to herself, that she had in any degree provoked contempt by her duplicity ; but weakly persisted in be-lieving that she alone was to be pitied, and Montoni alone to be censured ; for, as her mind had naturally little perception of moral obligation, she seldom understood its force but when it happened to be violated against herself : her vanity had already been severely shocked by a discovery of Montoni's contempt : it remained to be further proved by a discovery of his circumstances. His mansion at Venice, though its furniture discovered a part of the truth to unprejudiced persons, told nothing to those who were blinded by a resolution to believe whatever they wished. Madame Montoni still thought herself little less than a princess, possessing a palace at Venice, and a castle among the Apennines. To the castle di Udolpho, indeed, Montoni sometimes talked of going for a few weeks, to examine into its condition, and to receive some rents ; for it appeared that he had not been there for two years, and that during this period it had been inhabited only by an old servant, whom he called his steward.

Emily listened to the mention of this journey with pleasure ; for she not only expected from it new ideas, but a release from the persevering assiduities of Count Morano. In the country, too, she would have leisure to think of Valancourt, and to indulge the melancholy which his image, and a recollection of the scenes of La Vallée, always blessed with the memory of her parents, awakened. The ideal scenes were dearer and more soothing to her heart, than all the splendour of gay assemblies ; they were a kind of talisman that expelled the poison of temporary evils, and supported her hopes of happy days : they appeared like a beautiful landscape lighted up by a gleam of sunshine, and seen through a perspective of dark and rugged rocks.

But Count Morano did not long confine himself to silent assiduities ; he declared his passion to Emily, and made proposals to Montoni, who encouraged, though Emily rejected him : with Montoni for his friend, and an abundance of vanity to delude him, he did not despair of success. Emily was astonished and highly disgusted at his perseverance, after she had explained her sentiments with a frankness that would not allow him to misunderstand them.

He now passed the greater part of his time at Montoni's, dining there almost daily, and attending madame and Emily wherever they went ; and all this notwithstanding the uniform reserve of Emily, whose aunt seemed as anxious as Montoni to promote this marriage, and would never dispense with her attendance at any assembly where the count proposed to be present.

Montoni now said nothing of his intended journey, of which Emily waited impatiently to hear ; and he was seldom at home but when the count or Signor Orsino was there, for between himself and Cavigni a coolness seemed to subsist, though the latter remained in his house. With Orsino, Montoni was frequently closeted for hours together ; and whatever might be the business upon which they consulted, it appeared to be of consequence, since Montoni often sacrificed to it his favourite passion for play, and remained at home the whole night. There was somewhat of privacy, too, in the manner of Orsino's visits, which

had never before occurred, and which excited not only surprise, but some degree of alarm in Emily's mind, who had unwillingly discovered much of his character when he had most endeavoured to disguise it. After these visits, Montoni was often more thoughtful than usual ; sometimes the deep workings of his mind entirely abstracted him from surrounding objects, and threw a gloom over his visage that rendered it terrible ; at others, his eyes seemed almost to flash fire, and all the energies of his soul appeared to be roused for some great enterprise. Emily observed these written characters of his thoughts with deep interest and not without some degree of awe, when she considered that she was entirely in his power ; but forbore even to hint her fears, or her observations, to Madame Montoni, who discerned nothing in her husband, at these times, but his usual sternness.

A second letter from M. Quesnel announced the arrival of himself and his lady at the villa Miarenti ; stated several circumstances of his good fortune respecting the affair that had brought him into Italy ; and concluded with an earnest request to see Montoni, his wife and niece, at his new estate.

Emily received about the same period a much more interesting letter, and which soothed for a while every anxiety of her heart. Valancourt, hoping she might be still at Venice, had trusted a letter to the ordinary post, that told of his health, and of his unceasing and anxious affection. He had lingered at Thoulouse for some time after her departure, that he might indulge the melancholy pleasure of wandering through the scenes where he had been accustomed to behold her, and had thence gone to his brother's chateau, which was in the neighbourhood of La Vallée. Having mentioned this, he added, ' If the duty of attending my regiment did not require my departure, I know not when I should have resolution enough to quit the neighbourhood of a place which is endeared by the remembrance of you. The vicinity to La Valée has alone detained me thus long at Estuviere : I frequently ride thither early in the morning, that I may wander, at leisure through the day, among scenes which were once your home, where I have been accustomed to see you, and hear you converse. I have renewed my acquaintance with the good old Theresa, who rejoiced to see me, that she might talk of you : I need not say how much this circumstance attached me to her, or how eagerly I listened to her upon her favourite subject. You will guess the motive that first induced me to make myself known to Theresa : it was, indeed, no other than that of gaining admittance into the chateau and gardens which my Emily had so lately inhabited ; here, then, I wander, and meet your image under every shade : but chiefly I love to sit beneath the spreading branches of your favourite plane, where once, Emily, we sat together; where I first ventured to tell you that I loved. O Emily! the remembrance of those moments overcomes me—I sit lost in reverie—I endeavour to see you dimly through my tears, in all the heaven of peace and innocence, such as you then appeared to me; to hear again the accents of that voice, which then thrilled my heart with tenderness and hope. I lean on the wall of the terrace, where we together watched the rapid current of the Garonne below, while I described the wild scenery about its source, but thought only of you. O Emily! are these moments passed for ever—will they never more return?'

In another part of his letter he wrote thus: 'You see my letter is dated on many different days, and, if you look back to the first, you will perceive that I began to write soon after your departure from France. To write was indeed the only employment that withdrew me from my own melancholy, and rendered your absence supportable, or rather it seemed to destroy absence; for, when I was conversing with you on paper, and telling you every sentiment and affection of my heart, you almost appeared to be present. This employment has been from time to time my chief consolation, and I have deferred sending off my packet, merely for the comfort of prolonging it, though it was certain that what I had written, was written to no purpose till you received it. Whenever my mind has been more than usually depressed, I have come to pour forth its sorrows to you, and have always found consolation; and when any little occurrence has interested my heart, and given a gleam of joy to my spirits, I have hastened to communicate it to you, and have received reflected satisfaction. Thus my letter is a kind of picture of my life and of my thoughts for the last month; and thus, though it has been deeply interesting to me while I wrote it, and I dare hope will, for the same reason, be not indifferent to you, yet to other readers it would seem to abound only in frivolities. Thus it is always when we attempt to describe the finer movements of the heart; for they are too fine to be discerned, they can only be experienced, and are therefore passed over by the indifferent observer, while the interested one feels that all description is imperfect and unnecessary, except as it may prove the sincerity of the writer, and soothe his own sufferings. You will pardon all this egotism—for I am a lover.

'I have just heard of a circumstance which entirely destroys all my fairy paradise of ideal delight, and which will reconcile me to the necessity of returning to my regiment; for I must no longer wander beneath the beloved shades where I have been accustomed to meet you in thought—La Vallée is let! I have reason to believe this is without your knowledge, from what Theresa told me this morning, and therefore I mention the circumstance.—She shed tears while she related that she was going to leave the service of her dear mistress, and the chateau where she had lived so many happy years; ''and all this,'' added she, '' without even a letter from Mademoiselle to soften the news; but it is all Monsieur Quesnel's doings, and I dare say she does not even know what is going forward.''

'Theresa added, that she had received a letter from him, informing her the chateau was let; and that as her service would no longer be required, she must quit the place on that day week, when the new tenant would arrive.

'Theresa had been surprised by a visit from M. Quesnel, some time before the receipt of this letter, who was accompanied by a stranger that viewed the premises with much curiosity.'

Towards the conclusion of this letter, which is dated a week after this sentence, Valancourt adds, 'I have received a summons from my regiment, and I join it without regret, since I am shut out from the scenes that are so interesting to my heart. I rode to La Vallée this morning, and heard that the new tenant was arrived, and that Theresa was gone. I should not treat the subject thus familiarly if I did not believe you to be uninformed of this disposal of your house; for your satisfaction I have endeavoured to learn something of the character and fortune of your tenant, but without success. He is a gentleman, they say, and this is all I can hear. The place as I wandered round the boundaries appeared more melancholy to my imagination than I had ever seen it. I wished earnestly to have got admittance, that I might have taken another leave of your favourite plane-tree, and thought of you once more beneath its shade; but I forbore to tempt the curiosity of strangers; the fishing-house in the woods, however, was still open to me; thither I went, and passed an hour, which I cannot even look back upon without emotion. O Emily! surely we are not separated for ever—surely we shall live for each other!'

This letter brought many tears to Emily's eyes; tears of tenderness and satisfaction on learning that Valancourt was well, and that time and absence had in no degree effaced her image from his heart. There were passages in this letter which particularly affected her, such as those describing his visits to La Vallée, and the sentiments of delicate affection that its scenes had awakened. It was a considerable time before her mind was sufficiently abstracted from Valancourt to feel the force of his intelligence concerning La Vallée. That Mons. Quesnel should let it, without even consulting her on the measure, both surprised and shocked her; particularly as it proved the absolute authority he thought himself entitled to exercise in her affairs. It is true, he had proposed before she left France that the chateau should be let during her absence, and to the economical prudence of this she had nothing to object; but the committing what had been her father's villa to the power and caprice of strangers, and the depriving herself of a sure home, should any unhappy circumstances make her look back to her home as an asylum, were considerations that made her, even then, strongly oppose the measure. Her father, too, in his last hour, had received from her a solemn promise never to dispose of La Vallée; and this she considered as in some degree violated if she suffered the place to be let. But it was now evident with how little respect M. Quesnel had regarded these objections, and how insignificant he considered every obstacle to pecuniary advantage. It appeared also, that he had not even condescended to inform Montoni of the step he had taken, since no motive was evident for Montoni's concealing the circumstance from her, if it had been made known to him: this both displeased and surprised her; but the chief subjects of her uneasiness were—the temporary disposal of La Vallée, and the dismission of her father's old and faithful servant,—'Poor Theresa,' said Emily. 'thou hadst not saved much in thy servitude, for thou wast always tender towards the poor, and believedst thou shouldst die in the family, where thy best years had been spent. Poor Theresa!—now art thou turned out in thy old age to seek thy bread!'

Emily wept bitterly as these thoughts passed over her mind, and she determined to consider what could be done for Theresa, and to talk very explicitly to M. Quesnel on the subject; but she much feared that his cold heart could feel only for itself. She determined also to inquire whether he had made any mention of her affairs in his letter to Montoni, who soon gave her the opportunity she sought, by desiring that she would attend him in his study. She had little doubt that the interview was intended for the purpose of communicating to her a part of M. Quesnel's letter concerning the transactions of La Vallée, and she obeyed him immediately. Montoni was alone.

'I have just been writing to Mons. Quesnel,' said he, when Emily appeared, 'in reply to the letter I received from him a few days ago, and I wished to talk to you upon a subject that occupied part of it.'

'I also wished to speak with you on this topic, sir,' said Emily.

'It is a subject of some interest to you, undoubtedly,' rejoined Montoni, 'and I think, you must see it in the light that I do; indeed it will not bear any other. I trust you will agree with me, that any objection founded on sentiment, as they call it, ought to yield to circumstances of solid advantage.'

'Granting this, sir,' replied Emily modestly, 'those of humanity ought surely to be at-

tended to. But I fear it is now too late to deliberate upon this plan, and I must regret that it is no longer in my power to reject it.'

'It is too late,' said Montoni; 'but since it is so, I am pleased to observe that you submit to reason and necessity without indulging useless complaint. I applaud this conduct exceedingly, the more, perhaps, since it discovers a strength of mind seldom observable in your sex. When you are older, you will look back with gratitude to the friends who assisted in rescuing you from the romantic illusions of sentiment, and will perceive that they are only the snares of childhood, and should be vanquished the moment you escape from the nursery. I have not closed my letter, and you may add a few lines to inform your uncle of your acquiescence. You will soon see him, for it is my intention to take you, with Madame Montoni, in a few days, to Miarenti, and you can then talk over the affair.'

Emily wrote on the opposite side of the paper as follows:—

'It is now useless, sir, for me to remonstrate upon the circumstances of which Signor Montoni informs me that he has written. I could have wished, at least, that the affair had been concluded with less precipitation, that I might have taught myself to subdue some prejudices, as the signor calls them, which still linger in my heart. As it is, I submit. In point of prudence, nothing certainly can be objected; but, though I submit, I have yet much to say on some other points of the subject, when I shall have the honour of seeing you. In the mean time I entreat you to take care of Theresa, for the sake of,

'Sir,
"Your affectionate niece,
'EMILY ST. AUBERT.'

Montoni smiled satirically at what Emily had written, but did not object to it; and she withdrew to her own apartment, where she sat down to begin a letter to Valancourt, in which she related the particulars of her journey, and her arrival at Venice, described some of the most striking scenes in the passage over the Alps; her emotions on her first view of Italy; the manners and characters of the people around her, and some few circumstances of Montoni's conduct. But she avoided even naming Count Morano, much more the declaration he had made, since she well knew how tremblingly alive to fear is real love, how jealously watchful of every circumstance that may affect its interest; and she scrupulously avoided to give Valancourt even the slightest reason for believing he had a rival.

On the following day Count Morano dined again at Montoni's. He was in an uncommon flow of spirits, and Emily thought there was somewhat of exultation in his manner of addressing her, which she had never observed before. She endeavoured to repress this by more than her usual reserve, but the cold civility of her air now seemed rather to encourage than depress him. He appeared watchful of an opportunity of speaking with her alone, and more than once solicited this; but Emily always replied, that she could hear nothing from him which he would be unwilling to repeat before the whole company.

In the evening Madame Montoni and her party went out upon the sea, and as the count led Emily to his *zendaletto*, he carried her hand to his lips, and thanked her for the condescension she had shown him. Emily, in extreme surprise and displeasure, hastily withdrew her hand, and concluded that he had spoken ironically; but on reaching the steps of the terrace, and observing by the livery that it was the count's *zendaletto* which waited below, while the rest of the party, having arranged themselves in the gondolas, were moving on, she determined not to permit a separate conversation, and wishing him a good evening, returned to the portico. The count followed to expostulate and entreat; and Montoni, who then came out, rendered solicitation unnecessary, for without condescending to speak, he took her hand, and led her to the *zendaletto*. Emily was not silent; she entreated Montoni, in a low voice, to consider the impropriety of these circumstances, and that he would spare her the mortification of submitting to them; he, however, was inflexible.

'This caprice is intolerable,' said he, 'and shall not be indulged: here is no impropriety in the case.'

At this moment Emily's dislike of Count Morano rose to abhorrence. That he should with undaunted assurance thus pursue her, notwithstanding all she had expressed on the subject of his addresses, and think, as it was evident he did, that her opinion of him, was of no consequence so long as his pretensions were sanctioned by Montoni, added indignation to the disgust which she had felt towards him. She was somewhat relieved by observing that Montoni was to be of the party, who seated himself on one side of her, while Morano placed himself on the other. There was a pause of some moments as the gondolieri prepared their oars, and Emily trembled from the apprehension of the discourse that follow this silence. At length she collected courage to break it herself in the hope of preventing fine speeches from Morano, and reproof from Montoni. To some trivial remark which she made the latter immediately returned a short and disobliging reply; but Morano immediately followed with a general observation, which he contrived to end with a particular compliment; and though Emily passed it without even the notice of a smile, he was not discouraged.

'I have been impatient,' said he, addressing Emily, 'to express my gratitude, to thank you for your goodness; but I must also thank Signor Montoni, who has allowed me this opportunity of doing so.'

Emily regarded the count with a look of mingled astonishment and displeasure.

'Why,' continued he, 'should you wish to diminish the delight of this moment by that air of cruel reserve? Why seek to throw me again into the perplexities of doubt, by teaching your eyes to contradict the kindness of your late declaration? You cannot doubt the sincerity, the ardour of my passion; it is therefore unnecessary, charming Emily! surely unnecessary, any longer to attempt a disguise of your sentiments.'

'If I ever had disguised them, sir,' said Emily with recollected spirit, 'it would certainly be unnecessary any longer to do so. I had hoped, sir, that you would have spared me any further necessity of alluding to them; but since you do not grant this, hear me declare, and for the last time, that your perseverance has deprived you even of the esteem which I was inclined to believe you merited.'

'Astonishing!' exclaimed Montoni: 'this is beyond even my expectation, though I have hitherto done justice to the caprice of the sex! But you will observe, Mademoiselle Emily, that I am no lover, though Count Morano is, and that I will not be made the amusement of your capricious moments. Here is the offer of an alliance which would do honour to any family; yours, you will recollect, is not noble; you long resisted my remonstrances, but my honour is now engaged, and it shall not be trifled with. You shall adhere to the declaration which you have made me an agent to convey to the count.'

'I must certainly mistake you, sir,' said Emily; 'my answers on the subject have been uniform; it is unworthy of you to accuse me of caprice. If you have condescended to be my agent, it is an honour I did not solicit. I myself have constantly assured Count Morano, and you also, sir, that I never can accept the honour he offers me, and I now repeat the declaration.'

The count looked with an air of surprise and inquiry at Montoni, whose countenance also was marked with surprise, but it was surprise mingled with indignation.

'Here is confidence, as well as caprice!' said the latter. 'Will you deny your own words, madam?'

'Such a question is unworthy of an answer, sir,' said Emily blushing; 'you will recollect yourself, and be sorry that you have asked it.'

'Speak to the point,' rejoined Montoni in a voice of increasing vehemence. 'Will you deny your own words? will you deny that you acknowledged, only a few hours ago, that it was too late to recede from your engagements, and that you accept the count's hand?'

'I will deny all this, for no words of mine ever imported it.'

'Astonishing! Will you deny what you wrote to Mons. Quesnel, your uncle? If you do, your own hand will bear testimony against you. What have you now to say?' continued Montoni, observing the silence and confusion of Emily.

'I now perceive, sir, that you are under a very great error, and that I have been equally mistaken.'

'No more duplicity, I entreat; be open and candid, if it be possible.'

'I have always been so, sir; and can claim no merit in such conduct, for I have had nothing to conceal.'

'How is this, signor?' cried Morano with trembling emotion.

'Suspend your judgment, Count,' replied Montoni, 'the wiles of a female heart are unsearchable. Now, madam, your *explanation.*'

'Excuse me, sir, if I withhold my explanation till you appear willing to give me your confidence; assertion at present can only subject me to insult.'

'Your explanation, I entreat you!' said Morano.

'Well, well,' rejoined Montoni, 'I give you my confidence; let us hear this explanation.'

'Let me lead to it, then, by asking a question.'

'As many as you please,' said Montoni contemptuously.

'What, then, was the subject of your letter to Mons. Quesnel?'

'The same that was the subject of your note to him, certainly. You did well to stipulate for my confidence before you demanded that question.'

'I must beg you to be more explicit, sir; what was that subject?'

'What could it be, but the noble offer of Count Morano?' said Montoni.

'Then, sir, we entirely misunderstood each other,' replied Emily.

'We entirely misunderstood each other, too, I suppose,' rejoined Montoni, 'in the conversation which preceded the writing of that note? I must do you the justice to own that you are very ingenious at this same art of misunderstanding.'

Emily tried to restrain the tears that came to her eyes, and to answer with becoming firmness, 'Allow me, sir, to explain myself fully, or to be wholly silent.'

'The explanation may now be dispensed with; it is anticipated. If Count Morano still thinks one necessary, I will give him an honest one: you have changed your intention since our last conversation; and if he can have patience and humility enough to wait till to-morrow, he will probably find it changed again; but as I have neither the patience nor

the humility which you expect from a lover, I warn you of the effect of my displeasure!'

'Montoni, you are too precipitate,' said the count, who had listened to this conversation in extreme anxiety and impatience. 'Signora, I entreat your own explanation of this affair!'

'Signor Montoni has said justly,' replied Emily, 'that all explanation may now be dispensed with; after what has passed I cannot suffer myself to give one. It is sufficient for me, and for you, sir, that I repeat my late declaration; let me hope this is the last time it will be necessary for me to repeat it—I never can accept the honour of your alliance.'

'Charming Emily!' exclaimed the count in an impassioned tone, 'let not resentment make you unjust; let me not suffer for the offence of Montoni.—Revoke——'

'Offence!' interrupted Montoni—'Count, this language is ridiculous, this submission is childish:—Speak as becomes a man, not as the slave of a petty tyrant.'

'You distract me, signor; suffer me to plead my own cause; you have already proved insufficient to it.'

'All conversation on this subject, sir,' said Emily, 'is worse than useless, since it can bring only pain to each of us: if you would oblige me, pursue it no further.'

'It is impossible, madam, that I can thus easily resign the object of a passion which is the delight and torment of my life.—I must still love—still pursue you with unremitting ardour;—when you shall be convinced of the strength and constancy of my passion, your heart must soften into pity and repentance.'

'Is this generous, sir? is this manly? Can it either deserve or obtain the esteem you solicit, thus to continue a persecution from which I have no present means of escaping?'

A gleam of moon-light that fell upon Morano's countenance revealed the strong emotions of his soul; and, glancing on Montoni, discovered the dark resentment which contrasted his features.

'By Heaven, this is too much!' suddenly exclaimed the count; 'Signor Montoni, you treat me ill; it is from you that I shall look for explanation.'

'From me, sir, you shall have it,' muttered Montoni; 'if your discernment is indeed so far obscured by passion, as to make explanation necessary. And for you, madam, you should learn, that a man of honour is not to be trifled with, though you may, perhaps, with impunity, treat a *boy* like a puppet.'

This sarcasm roused the pride of Morano; and the resentment which he had felt at the indifference of Emily being lost in indignation of the insolence of Montoni, he determined to mortify him by defending her.

'This also,' said he, replying to Montoni's last words, 'this also, shall not pass unnoticed. I bid you learn, sir, that you have a stronger

4

enemy than a woman to contend with : I will protect Signora St. Aubert from your threatened resentment. You have misled me, and would revenge your disappointed views upon the innocent.'

'Misled you!' retorted Montoni with quickness; 'is my conduct—my word—' then pausing, while he seemed endeavouring to restrain the resentment that flashed in his eyes, in the next moment he added, in a subdued voice, 'Count Morano, this is a language, a sort of conduct, to which I am not accustomed : it is the conduct of a passionate boy —as such, I pass it over in contempt.'

'In contempt, Signor?'

'The respect I owe myself,' rejoined Montoni, 'requires that I should converse more largely with you upon some points of the subject in dispute. Return with me to Venice, and I will condescend to convince you of your error.'

'Condescend, sir ! but I will not condescend to be so conversed with.'

Montoni smiled contemptuously ; and Emily, now terrified for the consequences of what she saw and heard, could no longer be silent. She explained the whole subject upon which she had mistaken Montoni in the morning, declaring that she understood him to have consulted her solely concerning the disposal of La Vallée, and concluded with entreating that he would write immediately to M. Quesnel, and rectify the mistake.

But Montoni either was, or affected to be, still incredulous ; and Count Morano was still entangled in perplexity. While she was speaking, however, the attention of her auditors had been diverted from the immediate occasion of their resentment, and their passion consequently became less. Montoni desired the count would order his servants to row back to Venice, that he might have some private conversation with him ; and Morano, somewhat soothed by his softened voice and manner, and eager to examine into the full extent of his difficulties, complied.

Emily, comforted by this prospect of release, employed the present moments in endeavouring, with conciliating care, to prevent any fatal mischief between the persons who so lately had persecuted and insulted her.

Her spirits revived, when she heard once more the voice of song and laughter resounding from the grand canal, and at length entered again between its stately piazzas. The *zendaletto* stopped at Montoni's mansion, and the count hastily led her into the hall, where Montoni took his arm, and said something in a low voice, on which Morano kissed the hand he held, notwithstanding Emily's effort to disengage it, and, wishing her a good evening, with an accent and look she could not misunderstand, returned to his *zendaletto* with Montoni.

Emily, in her own apartment, considered with intense anxiety all the unjust and tyrannical conduct of Montoni, the dauntless perseverance of Morano, and her own desolate situation, removed from her friends and country. She looked in vain to Valancourt, confined by his profession to a distant kingdom, as her protector ; but it gave her comfort to know that there was at least one person in the world who would sympathise in her afflictions, and whose wishes would fly eagerly to release her. Yet she determined not to give him unavailing pain by relating the reasons she had to regret the having rejected his better judgment concerning Montoni ; reasons, however, which could not induce her to lament the delicacy and disinterested affection that had made her reject his proposal for a clandestine marriage. The approaching interview with her uncle she regarded with some degree of hope, for she determined to represent to him the distresses of her situation, and to entreat that he would allow her to return to France with him and Madame Quesnel. Then, suddenly remembering that her beloved La Vallée, her only home, was no longer at her command, her tears flowed anew, and she feared that she had little pity to expect from a man who, like M. Quesnel, could dispose of it without deigning to consult with her, and could dismiss an aged and faithful servant, destitute of either support or asylum. But though it was certain that she had herself no longer a home in France, and few, very few friends there, she determined to return, if possible, that she might be released from the power of Montoni, whose particularly oppressive conduct towards herself, and general character as to others, were justly terrible to her imagination. She had no wish to reside with her uncle, M. Quesnel, since his behaviour to her late father, and to herself, had been uniformly such as to convince her, that in flying to him she could only obtain an exchange of oppressors ; neither had she the slightest intention of consenting to the proposal of Valancourt for an immediate marriage, though this would give her a lawful and a generous protector ; for the chief reasons which had formerly influenced her conduct, still existed against it ; while others, which seemed to justify the step, would now be done away ; and his interest, his fame, were at all times too dear to her, to suffer her to consent to a union which, at this early period of their lives, would probably defeat both. One sure and proper asylum, however, would still be open to her in France. She knew that she could board in the convent where she had formerly experienced so much kindness, and which had an affecting and solemn claim upon her heart, since it contained the remains of her late father. Here she could remain in safety and tranquillity till the term for which La Vallée might be let should expire ; or till the arrangement of M. Motteville's affairs enabled her so far to estimate the remains of her fortune, as to judge whether it would be prudent for her to reside there.

Concerning Montoni's conduct with respect to his letters to M. Quesnel she had many doubts; however he might be at first mistaken on the subject, she much suspected that he wilfully persevered in his error, as a means of intimidating her into a compliance with his wishes of uniting her to Count Morano. Whether this was or was not the fact, she was extremely anxious to explain the affair to M. Quesnel, and looked forward with a mixture of impatience, hope, and fear, to her approaching visit.

On the following day Madame Montoni, being alone with Emily, introduced the mention of Count Morano, by expressing her surprise that she had not joined the party on the water the preceding evening, and at her abrupt departure to Venice. Emily then related what had passed, expressed her concern for the mutual mistake that had occurred between Montoni and herself, and solicited her aunt's kind offices in urging him to give a decisive denial 'to the count's further addresses: but she soon perceived that Madame Montoni had not been ignorant of the late conversation, when she introduced the present.

'You have no encouragement to expect from me,' said her aunt, 'in these notions. I have already given my opinion on the subject, and think Signor Montoni right in enforcing, by any means, your consent. If young persons will be blind to their interest, and obstinately oppose it, why, the greatest blessings they can have are friends who will oppose their folly. Pray what pretensions of any kind do you think you have to such a match as is now offered you?'

'Not any whatever, Madam,' replied Emily; 'and therefore, at least, suffer me to be happy in my humility.'

'Nay, niece, it cannot be denied that you have pride enough; my poor brother, your father, had his share of pride too; though let me add, his fortune did not justify it.'

Emily, somewhat embarrassed by the indignation which this malevolent allusion to her father excited, and by the difficulty of rendering her answer as temperate as it should be reprehensive, hesitated for some moments in a confusion which highly gratified her aunt. At length she said, 'My father's pride, Madam, had a noble object—the happiness which he knew could be derived only from goodness, knowledge, and charity. As it never consisted in his superiority, in point of fortune, to some persons, it was not humbled by his inferiority, in that respect, to others. He never disdained those who were wretched by poverty and misfortune; he did sometimes despise persons who, with many opportunities of happiness, rendered themselves miserable by vanity, ignorance, and cruelty. I shall think it my highest glory to emulate such pride.'

'I do not pretend to understand anything of these high-flown sentiments, niece: you have all that glory to yourself: I would teach you a little plain sense, and not have you so wise as to despise happiness.'

'That would indeed not be wisdom, but folly,' said Emily, 'for wisdom can boast no higher attainment than happiness; but you will allow, Madam, that our ideas of happiness may differ. I cannot doubt that you wish me to be happy, but I must fear you are mistaken in the means of making me so.'

'I cannot boast of a learned education, niece, such as your father thought proper to give you, and therefore do not pretend to understand all these fine speeches about happiness; I must be contented to understand only common sense; and happy would it have been for you and your father if that had been included in his education.'

Emily was too much shocked by these reflections on her father's memory, to despise this speech as it deserved.

Madame Montoni was about to speak; but Emily quitted the room, and retired to her own, where the little spirit she had lately exerted yielded to grief and vexation, and left her only to her tears. From every review of her situation she could derive, indeed, only new sorrow. To the discovery that had just been forced upon her, of Montoni's unworthiness, she had now to add that of the cruel vanity for the gratification of which her aunt was about to sacrifice her; of the effrontery and cunning with which, at the time that she meditated the sacrifice, she boasted of her tenderness, or insulted her victim; and of the venomous envy which, as it did not scruple to attack her father's character, could scarcely be expected to withhold from her own.

During the few days that intervened between this conversation and the departure for Miarenti, Montoni did not once address himself to Emily. His looks sufficiently declared his resentment: but that he should forbear to renew a mention of the subject of it, exceedingly surprised her, who was no less astonished that, during three days, Count Morano neither visited Montoni nor was named by him. Several conjectures arose in her mind. Sometimes she feared that the dispute between them had been revived, and had ended fatally to the count. Sometimes she was inclined to hope that weariness, or disgust at her firm rejection of his suit, had induced him to relinquish it; and at others, she suspected that he had now recourse to stratagem, and forbore his visits, and prevailed with Montoni to forbear the repetition of his name, in the expectation that gratitude and generosity would prevail with her to give him the consent which he could not hope from love.

Thus passed the time in vain conjecture and alternate hopes and fears, till the day arrived when Montoni was to set out for the villa of Miarenti, which, like the preceding ones, neither brought the count, nor the mention of him.

Montoni having determined not to leave Venice till towards evening, that he might avoid the heats, and catch the cold breezes of night, embarked about an hour before sunset, with his family, in a barge, for the Brenta. Emily sat alone near the stern of the vessel, and, as it floated slowly on, watched the gay and lofty city lessening from her view, till its palaces seemed to sink in the distant waves, while its loftier towers and domes, illumined by the declining sun, appeared on the horizon, like those far-seen clouds which in more northern climes often linger on the western verge, and catch the last light of a summer's evening. Soon after, even these grew dim, and faded in distance from her sight ; but she still sat gazing on the vast scene of cloudless sky and mighty waters, and listening in pleasing awe to the deep-sounding waves, while, as her eyes glanced over the Adriatic, towards the opposite shores, which were, however, far beyond the reach of sight, she thought of Greece ; and a thousand classical remembrances stealing to her mind, she experienced that pensive luxury which is felt on viewing the scenes of ancient story, and on comparing their present state of silence and solitude with that of their former grandeur and animation. The scenes of the Iliad illapsed in glowing colours to her fancy—scenes, once the haunt of heroes—now lonely, and in ruins ; but which still shone, in the poet's strain, in all their youthful splendour.

As her imagination painted with melancholy touches the deserted plains of Troy, such as they appeared in this after-day, she reanimated the landscape with the following little story :

STANZAS.

O'er Ilion's plains, where once the warrior bled,
And once the poet raised his deathless strain,
O'er Ilion's plains a weary driver led
His stately camels : For the ruin'd fane

Wide round the lonely scene his glance he threw,
For now the red cloud faded in the west,
And twilight o'er the silent landscape drew
Her deepening veil ; eastward his course he prest.

There, on the gray horizon's glimmering bound,
Rose the proud columns of deserted Troy,
And wandering shepherds now a shelter found
Within those walls where princes wont to joy.

Beneath a lofty porch the driver pass'd,
Then, from his camels heaved the heavy load ;
Partook with them the simple, cool repast,
And in short vesper gave himself to God.

From distant lands with merchandise he came,
His all of wealth his patient servants bore ;
Oft deep-drawn sighs his anxious wish proclaim
To reach, again, his happy cottage door ;
For there, his wife, his little children dwell ;
Their smiles shall pay the toil of many an hour ;

E'en now warm tears to expectation swell,
As Fancy o'er his mind extends her power.

A death-like stillness reign'd, where once the song,
The song of heroes, waked the midnight air,
Save, when a solemn murmur roll'd along,
That seem'd to say—For future worlds prepare.

For time's imperious voice was frequent heard
Shaking the marble temple to its fall
(By hands he long had conquer'd ; vainly rear'd),
And distant ruins answer'd to his call.

While Hamet slept, his camels round him lay,
Beneath him, all his store of wealth was piled ;
And here, his cruse and empty wallet lay,
And there, the flute that cheer'd him in the wild.

The robber Tartar on his slumber stole,
For o'er the waste, at eve, he watch'd his train ;
Ah ! who his thirst of plunder shall control ?
Who calls on him for mercy—calls in vain !

A poison'd poniard in his belt he bore,
A crescent sword depended at his side,
The deathful quiver at his back he bore,
And infants—at his very look had died !

The moon's cold beam athwart the temple fell,
And to his sleeping prey the Tartar led ;
But, soft !—a startled camel shook his bell,
Then stretch'd his limbs, and rear'd his drowsy head.

Hamet awoke ! the poniard glitter'd high !
Swift from his couch he sprung, and 'scaped the blow ;
When from an unknown hand the arrows fly,
That lay the ruffian, in his vengeance, low.

He groan'd, he died ! from forth a column'd gate
A fearful shepherd pale and silent crept,
Who, as he watch'd his folded flock star-late,
Had mark'd the robber steal where Hamet slept.

He fear'd his own, and saved a stranger's life !
Poor Hamet clasp'd him to his grateful heart ;
Then, roused his camels for the dusty strife,
And with the shepherd hasten'd to depart.

And now Aurora breathes her freshening gale,
And faintly trembles on the eastern cloud ;
And now the sun from under twilight's veil
Looks gaily forth, and melts her airy shroud.

Wide o'er the level plains his slanting beams
Dart their long lines on Ilion's towered site ;
The distant Hellespont with morning gleams,
And old Scamander winds his waves in light.

All merry sound the camel bells so gay,
And merry beats fond Hamet's heart ; for he,
Ere the dim evening steals upon the day,
His children, wife and happy home shall see.

As Emily approached the shores of Italy she began to discriminate the rich features and varied colouring of the landscape—the purple hills, groves of orange, pine and cypress, shading magnificent villas, and towns rising among vineyards and plantations. The noble Brenta, pouring its broad waves into the sea, now appeared ; and when she reached its mouth, the barge stopped, that the horses might be fastened which were now to tow it up the stream. This done, Emily gave a last look to the Adriatic, and to the dim sail

'. . . . : . that from the sky-mix'd wave
    Dawns on the sight ;'

and the barge slowly glided between the green and luxuriant slopes of the river. The grandeur of the Palladian villas that adorn these shores was considerably heightened by the setting rays, which threw strong contrasts of light and shade upon the porticos and long arcades, and beamed a mellow lustre upon the orangeries and the tall groves of pine and cypress that overhung the buildings. The scent of oranges, of flowering myrtles and other odoriferous plants, was diffused upon the air, and often from these embowered retreats a strain of music stole on the calm, and softened into silence.

The sun now sunk below the horizon, twilight fell over the landscape, and Emily, wrapt in musing silence, continued to watch its features gradually vanishing into obscurity. She remembered her many happy evenings, when with St. Aubert she had observed the shades of twilight steal over a scene as beauful as this, from the gardens of La Vallée; and a tear fell to the memory of her father. Her spirits were softened into melancholy by the influence of the hour, by the low murmur of the wave passing under the vessel, and the stillness of the air, that trembled only at intervals with distant music :—why else should she, at these moments, have looked on her attachment to Valancourt with presages so very afflicting, since she had but lately received letters from him that had soothed for a while all her anxieties? It now seemed to her oppressed mind that she had taken leave of him for ever, and that the countries which separated them would never more be traced by her. She looked upon Count Morano with horror, as in some degree the cause of this; but apart from him, a conviction, if such that may be called which arises from no proof, and which she knew not how to account for, seized her mind—that she should never see Valancourt again. Though she knew that neither Morano's solicitations nor Montoni's commands had lawful power to enforce her obedience, she regarded both with a superstitious dread, that they would finally prevail.

Lost in this melancholy reverie, and shedding frequent tears, Emily was at length roused by Montoni; and she followed him to the cabin, where refreshments were spread, and her aunt was seated alone. The countenance of Madame Montoni was inflamed with resentment that appeared to be the consequence of some conversation she had held with her husband, who regarded her with a kind of sullen disdain; and both preserved for some time a haughty silence. Montoni then spoke to Emily of Mons. Quesnel : 'You will not, I hope, persist in disclaiming your knowledge of the subject of my letter to him.'

'I had hoped, sir, that it was no longer necessary for me to disclaim it,' said Emily; 'I had hoped, from your silence, that you were convinced of your error.'

'You have hoped impossibilities then,' replied Montoni; 'I might as reasonably

have expected to find sincerity and uniformity of conduct in one of your sex, as you to convict me of error in this affair.'

Emily blushed, and was silent; she now perceived too clearly that she had hoped an impossibility : for where no mistake had been committed, no conviction could follow; and it was evident that Montoni's conduct had not been the consequence of mistake, but of design.

Anxious to escape from conversation which was both afflicting and humiliating to her, she soon returned to the deck, and resumed her station near the stern, without apprehension of cold, for no vapour rose from the water, and the air was dry and tranquil; here, at least, the benevolence of nature allowed her the quiet which Montoni had denied her elsewhere. It was now past midnight. The stars shed a kind of twilight, that served to show the dark outline of the shores on either hand, and the gray surface of the river; till the moon rose from behind a high palm-grove, and shed her mellow lustre over the scene. The vessel glided smoothly on; amid the stillness of the hour Emily heard, now and then, the solitary voice of the bargemen on the bank, as they spoke to their horses; while from a remote part of the vessel, with melancholy song,

'. . . . . the sailor soothed,
Beneath the trembling moon, the midnight wave.'

Emily, meanwhile, anticipated her reception by Mons. and Madame Quesnel; considered what she could say on the subject of La Vallée; and then, to withhold her mind from more anxious topics, tried to amuse herself by discriminating the faint-drawn features of the landscape reposing in the moon-light. While her fancy thus wandered, she saw at a distance a building peeping between the moon-light trees, and as the barge approached, heard voices speaking, and soon distinguished the lofty portico of a villa overshadowed by groves of pine and sycamore, which she recollected to be the same that had formerly been pointed out to her as belonging to Madame Quesnel's relative.

The barge stopped at a flight of marble steps, which led up the bank to a lawn. Lights appeared between some pillars beyond the portico. Montoni sent forward his servant, and then disembarked with his family. They found Mons. and Madame Quesnel with a few friends, seated on sofas in the portico, enjoying the cool breeze of the night, and eating fruits and ices, while some of their servants at a little distance on the river's bank were performing a simple serenade. Emily was now accustomed to the way of living in this warm country, and was not surprised to find Mons. and Madame Quesnel in their portico two hours after midnight.

The usual salutations being over, the company seated themselves in the portico, and refreshments were brought them from the adjoining hall, where a banquet was spread, and the servants attended. When the bustle of this meeting had subsided, and Emily had recovered from the little flutter into which it had thrown her spirits, she was struck with the singular beauty of the hall, so perfectly accommodated to the luxuries of the season. It was of white marble, and the roof, rising into an open cupola, was supported by columns of the same material. Two opposite sides of the apartment, terminating in open porticos, admitted to the hall a full view of the gardens and of the river scenery; in the centre a fountain continually refreshed the air, and seemed to heighten the fragrance that breathed from the surrounding orangeries, while its dashing waters gave an agreeable and soothing sound. Etruscan lamps, suspended from the pillars, diffused a brilliant light over the interior part of the hall, leaving the remoter porticos to the softer lustre of the moon.

Mons. Quesnel talked apart to Montoni of his own affairs in his usual strain of self-importance; boasted of his new acquisitions, and then affected to pity some disappointments which Montoni had lately sustained. Meanwhile the latter, whose pride at least enabled him to despise such vanity as this, and whose discernment at once detected, under this assumed pity, the frivolous malignity of Quesnel's mind, listened to him in contemptuous silence till he named his niece, and then they left the portico and walked away into the gardens.

Emily, however, still attended to Madame Quesnel, who spoke of France (for even the name of her native country was dear to her), and she found some pleasure in looking at a person who had lately been in it. That country, too, was inhabited by Valancourt, and she listened to the mention of it with a faint hope that he also would be named. Madame Quesnel, who when she was in France had talked with rapture of Italy; now, that she was in Italy, talked with equal praise of France, and endeavoured to excite the wonder and the envy of her auditors by accounts of places which they had not been happy enough to see. In these descriptions she not only imposed upon them, but upon herself; for she never thought a present pleasure equal to one that was past: and thus the delicious climate, the fragrant orangeries, and all the luxuries which surrounded her, slept unnoticed, while her fancy wandered over distant scenes of a northern country.

Emily listened in vain for the name of Valancourt. Madame Montoni spoke in her turn of the delights of Venice, and of the pleasure she expected from visiting the fine castle of Montoni, on the Apennine; which latter mention at least was merely a retaliating boast,

for Emily well knew that her aunt had no taste for solitary grandeur, and particularly for such as the castle of Udolpho promised. Thus the party continued to converse, and, as far as civility would permit, to torture each other by mutual boasts, while they reclined on sofas in the portico, and were environed with delights both from nature and art, by which any honest minds would have been tempered to benevolence, and happy imaginations would have been soothed into enchantment.

The dawn soon after trembled in the eastern horizon, and the light tints of morning gradually expanding showed the beautifully declining forms of the Italian mountains, and the gleaming landscapes stretched at their feet. Then the sun-beams, shooting up from behind the hills, spread over the scene that saffron tinge which seems to impart repose to all its touches. The landscape no longer gleamed; all its glowing colours were revealed, except that its remoter features were still softened and united in the midst of distance, whose sweet effect was heightened to Emily by the dark verdure of the pines and cypresses that over-arched the foreground of the river.

The market people passing with their boats to Venice now formed a moving picture of the Brenta. Most of these had little painted awnings, to shelter their owners from the sun-beams, which, together with the piles of fruits and flowers displayed beneath, and the tasteful simplicity of the peasant girls who watched the rural treasures, rendered them gay and striking objects. The swift movement of the boats down the current, the quick glance of the oars in the water, and now and then the passing chorus of peasants who reclined under the sail of their little bark, or the tones of some rustic instrument played by a girl as she sat near her sylvan cargo, heightened the animation and festivity of the scene.

When Montoni and M. Quesnel had joined the ladies, the party left the portico for the gardens, where the charming scenery soon withdrew Emily's thoughts from painful objects. The majestic forms and rich verdure of cypresses she had never seen so perfect before: groves of cedar, lemon, and orange, the spiry clusters of the pine and poplar, the luxuriant chestnut and oriental plane, threw all their pomp of shade over these gardens; while bowers of flowering myrtle and other spicy shrubs mingled their fragrance with that of flowers whose vivid and various colouring glowed with increased effect beneath the contrasted umbrage of the groves. The air also was continually refreshed by rivulets, which, with more taste than fashion, had been suffered to wander among the green recesses.

Emily often lingered behind the party to contemplate the distant landscape, that closed a vista, or that gleamed beneath the dark foliage of the fore-ground ; the spiral summits of the mountains, touched with a purple tint, broken and steep above, but shelving gradually to their base ; the open valley, marked by no formed lines of art ; and the tall groves of cypress, pine, and poplar, sometimes embellished by a ruined villa, whose broken columns appeared between the branches of a pine that seemed to droop over their fall.

From other parts of the gardens, the character of the view was entirely changed, and the fine solitary beauty of the landscape shifted for the crowded features and varied colouring of inhabitation.

The sun was now gaining fast upon the sky, and the party quitted the gardens, and retired to repose.

CHAPTER XVIII.

'And poor Misfortune feels the lash of Vice.'
        THOMSON.

EMILY seized the first opportunity of conversing alone with Monsieur Questiel concerning La Vallée. His answers to her inquiries were concise, and delivered with the air of a man who is conscious of possessing absolute power, and impatient of hearing it questioned. He declared that the disposal of the place was a necessary measure ; and that she might consider herself indebted to his prudence for even the small income that remained for her. 'But, however,' added he, ' when this Venetian count (I have forgot his name) marries you, your present disagreeable state of dependence will cease. As a relation to you I rejoice in the circumstance, which is so fortunate for you, and, I may add, so unexpected by your friends.'

For some moments Emily was chilled into silence by this speech ; and when she attempted to undeceive him concerning the purport of the note she had inclosed in Montoni's letter, he appeared to have some private reason for disbelieving her assertion, and for a considerable time persevered in accusing her of capricious conduct. Being at length, however, convinced that she really disliked Morano, and had positively rejected his suit, his resentment was extravagant, and he expressed it in terms equally pointed and inhuman ; for, secretly flattered by the prospect of a connection with a nobleman whose title he had affected to forget, he was incapable of feeling pity for whatever sufferings of his niece might stand in the way of his ambition.

Emily saw at once in his manner all the difficulties that awaited her ; and though no oppression could have power to make her renounce Valancourt for Morano, her fortitude now trembled at an encounter with the violent passions of her uncle.

She opposed his turbulence and indignation only by the mild dignity of a superior mind : but the gentle firmness of her conduct served to exasperate still more his resentment, since it compelled him to feel his own inferiority ; and when he left her, he declared that, if she persisted in her folly, both himself and Morano would abandon her to the contempt of the world.

The calmness she had assumed in his presence failed Emily when alone, and she wept bitterly, and called frequently upon the name of her departed father, whose advice to her from his deathbed she then remembered. 'Alas !' said she, ' I do indeed perceive how much more valuable is the strength of fortitude than the grace of sensibility, and I will also endeavour to fulfil the promise I then made ; I will not indulge in unavailing lamentation, but will try to endure with firmness the oppression I cannot elude.'

Somewhat soothed by the consciousness of performing a part of St. Aubert's last request, and of endeavouring to pursue the conduct which he would have approved, she overcame her tears, and, when the company met at dinner, had recovered her usual serenity of countenance.

In the cool of the evening the ladies took the *fresco* along the bank of the Brenta in Madame Quesnel's carriage. The state of Emily's mind was in melancholy contrast with the gay groups assembled beneath the shades that overhung this enchanting stream. Some were dancing under the trees, and others reclining on the grass taking ices and coffee, and calmly enjoying the effect of a beautiful evening on a luxuriant landscape. Emily, when she looked at the snow-capped Apennines ascending in the distance, thought of Montoni's castle, and suffered some terror lest he should carry her thither for the purpose of enforcing her obedience ; but the thought vanished when she considered that she was as much in his power at Venice as she could be elsewhere.

It was moonlight before the party returned to the villa, where supper was spread in the airy hall which had so much enchanted Emily's fancy on the preceding night. The ladies seated themselves in the portico, till M. Quesnel, Montoni, and other gentlemen should join them at table ; and Emily endeavoured to resign herself to the tranquillity of the hour. Presently, a barge stopped at the steps that led into the gardens, and soon after she distinguished the voices of Montoni and Quesnel, and then that of Morano, who in the next moment appeared. His compliments she received in silence, and her cold air seemed at first to discompose him ; but he soon recovered his usual gaiety of manner, though the officious kindness of M. and Madame Quesnel, Emily perceived, disgusted him. Such a degree of attention she had scarcely believed could be shown by

M. Quesnel, for she had never before seen him otherwise than in the presence of his inferiors or equals.

When she could retire to her own apartment, her mind almost involuntarily dwelt on the most probable means of prevailing with the count to withdraw his suit; and to her liberal mind none appeared more probable, than that of acknowledging to him a prior attachment, and throwing herself upon his generosity for a release. When however, on the following day, he renewed his addresses, she shrunk from the adoption of the plan she had formed. There was something so repugnant to her just pride, in laying open the secret of her heart to such a man as Morano, and in suing to him for compassion, that she impatiently rejected this design, and wondered that she could have paused upon it for a moment. The rejection of his suit she repeated in the most decisive terms she could select, mingling with it a severe censure of his conduct; but though the count appeared mortified by this, he persevered in the most ardent professions of admiration, till he was interrupted and released by the presence of Madame Quesnel.

During her stay at this pleasant villa, Emily was thus rendered miserable by the assiduities of Morano, together with the cruelly exerted authority of M. Quesnel and Montoni, who, with her aunt, seemed now more resolutely determined upon this marriage than they had even appeared to be at Venice. M. Quesnel, finding that both argument and menace were ineffectual in enforcing an immediate conclusion to it, at length relinquished his endeavours, and trusted to the power of Montoni and to the course of events at Venice. Emily, indeed, looked to Venice with hope, for there she would be relieved in some measure from the persecution of Morano, who would no longer be an inhabitant of the same house with herself; and from that of Montoni, whose engagements would not permit him to be continually at home. But amidst the pressure of her own misfortunes, she did not forget those of poor Theresa, for whom she pleaded with courageous tenderness to Quesnel, who promised, in slight and general terms, that she should not be forgotten.

Montoni, in a long conversation with M. Quesnel, arranged the plan to be pursued respecting Emily; and M. Quesnel proposed to be at Venice, as soon as he should be informed that the nuptials were concluded.

It was new to Emily to part with any person with whom she was connected without feelings of regret.; the moment, however, in which she took leave of M. and Madame Quesnel was, perhaps, the only satisfactory one she had known in their presence.

Morano returned in Montoni's barge; and Emily, as she watched her gradual approach to that magic city, saw at her side the only person who occasioned her to view it with less than perfect delight. They arrived there about midnight, when Emily was released from the presence of the count, who with Montoni went to a casino, and she was suffered to retire to her own apartment.

On the following day Montoni, in a short conversation which he held with Emily, informed her that he would no longer be *trifled* with, and that, since her marriage with the count would be so highly advantageous to her that folly only could object to it, and folly of such extent as was incapable of conviction, it should be celebrated without further delay, and, if that was necessary, without her consent.

Emily, who had hitherto tried remonstrance, had now recourse to supplication, for distress prevented her from foreseeing that, with a man of Montoni's disposition, supplication would be equally useless. She afterwards inquired by what right he exerted this unlimited authority over her, a question which her better judgment would have withheld her in a calmer moment from making, since it could avail her nothing, and would afford Montoni another opportunity of triumphing over her defenceless condition.

'By what right!' cried Montoni with a malicious smile; 'by the right of my will; if you can elude that I will not inquire by what right you do so. I now remind you, for the last time, that you are a stranger in a foreign country, and that it is your interest to make me your friend; you know the means: if you compel me to be your enemy—I will venture to tell you that the punishment shall exceed your expectation. You may know *I* am not to be trifled with.'

Emily continued, for some time after Montoni had left her, in a state of despair, or rather stupefaction; a consciousness of misery was all that remained in her mind. In this situation Madame Montoni found her, at the sound of whose voice Emily looked up; and her aunt, somewhat softened by the expression of despair that fixed her countenance, spoke in a manner more kind than she had ever yet done. Emily's heart was touched; she shed tears, and after weeping for some time recovered sufficient composure to speak on the subject of her distress, and to endeavour to interest Madame Montoni in her behalf. But though the compassion of her aunt had been surprised, her ambition was not to be overcome, and her present object was to be the aunt of a countess. Emily's efforts, therefore, were as unsuccessful as they had been with Montoni; and she withdrew to her apartment to think and weep alone. How often did she remember the parting scene with Valancourt, and wish that the Italian had mentioned Montoni's character with less reserve! When her mind, however, had recovered from her first shock of this behaviour, she considered that it would be impossible for him to compel her alliance with Morano, if she persisted in refusing to repeat any part of the marriage ceremony ; and she persevered in her resolution to await Montoni's threatened vengeance, rather than give herself for life to a man whom she must have despised for his present conduct had she never even loved Valancourt ; yet she trembled at the revenge she thus resolved to brave.

An affair, however, soon after occurred, which somewhat called off Montoni's attention from Emily. The mysterious visits of Orsino were renewed with more frequency since the return of the former to Venice. There were others also besides Orsino admitted to these midnight councils, and among them Cavigni and Verezzi. Montoni became more reserved and austere in his manner than ever ; and Emily, if her own interests had not made her regardless of his, might have perceived that something extraordinary was working in his mind.

One night, on which a council was not held, Orsino came in great agitation of spirits, and dispatched his confidential servant to Montoni, who was at a casino, desiring that he would return home immediately ; but charging the servant not to mention his name. Montoni obeyed the summons and, on meeting Orsino, was informed of the circumstances that occasioned his visit and his visible alarm, with some of which, however, he was already acquainted.

A Venetian nobleman who had on a late occasion provoked the hatred of Orsino, had been waylaid and poniarded by hired assassins ; and as the murdered person was of the first connexions, the Senate had taken up the affair. One of the assassins was now apprehended, who had confessed that Orsino was his employer in the atrocious deed ; and the latter, informed of his danger, had now come to Montoni to consult on the measures necessary to favour his escape. He knew that at this time the officers of the police were upon the watch for him all over the city ; to leave it at present, therefore, was impracticable ; and Montoni consented to secrete him for a few days till the vigilance of justice should relax, and then to assist him in quitting Venice. He knew the danger he himself incurred by permitting Orsino to remain in his house ; but such was the nature of his obligations to this man, that he did not think it prudent to refuse him an asylum.

Such was the person whom Montoni admitted to his confidence, and for whom he felt as much friendship as was compatible with his character.

While Orsino remained concealed in his house, Montoni was unwilling to attract public observation by the nuptials of Count Morano ; but this obstacle was in a few days overcome by the departure of his criminal visitor ; and

he then informed Emily that her marriage was to be celebrated on the following morning. To her repeated assurances that it should not take place, he replied by a malignant smile ; and telling her that the count and a priest would be at his house early in the morning, he advised her no further to dare his resentment by opposition to his will and to her own interest. ' I am now going out for the evening,' said he ; 'remember that I shall give your hand to Count Morano in the morning.' Emily having ever since his late threats expected that her trials would at length arrive to this crisis, was less shocked by this declaration than she otherwise would have been, and she endeavoured to support herself by a belief that the marriage could not be valid so long as she refused before the priest to repeat any part of the ceremony. Yet, as the moment of trial approached, her long-harassed spirits shrunk almost equally from the encounter of his vengeance and from the hand of Count Morano. She was not even perfectly certain of the consequence of her steady refusal at the altar, and she trembled more than ever at the power of Montoni, which seemed unlimited as his will ; for she saw that he would not scruple to transgress any law, if by so doing he could accomplish his project.

While her mind was thus suffering, she was informed that Morano asked permission to see her ; and the servant had scarcely departed with an excuse, before she repented that she had sent one. In the next moment, reverting to her former design, and determining to try whether expostulation and entreaty would not succeed where a refusal and a just disdain had failed, she recalled the servant, and, sending a different message, prepared to go down to the count.

The dignity and assumed composure with which she met him, and the kind of pensive resignation that softened her countenance, were circumstances not likely to induce him to relinquish her, serving, as they did, to heighten a passion which had already intoxicated his judgment. He listened to all she said with an appearance of complacency and of a wish to oblige her ; but his resolution remained invariably the same, and he endeavoured to win her admiration by every insinuating art he so well knew how to practise. Being at length assured that she had nothing to hope from his justice, she repeated in a solemn manner her absolute rejection of his suit, and quitted him with an assurance that her refusal would be effectually maintained against every circumstance that could be imagined for subduing it. A just pride had restrained her tears in his presence, but now they flowed from the fulness of her heart. She often called upon the name of her late father and often dwelt with unutterable anguish on the idea of Valancourt.

She did not go down to supper, but remained alone in her apartment, sometimes yielding to the influence of grief and terror, and at others endeavouring to fortify her mind against them, and to prepare herself to meet with composed courage the scene of the following morning, when all the stratagem of Morano and the violence of Montoni would be united against her.

The evening was far advanced, when Madame Montoni came to her chamber with some bridal ornaments which the count had sent to Emily. She had this day purposely avoided her niece; perhaps because her usual insensibility failed her, and she feared to trust herself with a view of Emily's distress; or possibly, though her conscience was seldom audible, it now reproached her with her conduct to her brother's orphan child, whose happiness had been intrusted to her care by a dying father.

Emily could not look at these presents, and made a last, though almost hopeless, effort to interest the compassion of Madame Montoni, who, if she did feel any degree of pity or remorse, successfully concealed it, and reproached her niece with folly in being miserable concerning a marriage which ought only to make her happy. 'I am sure,' said she, 'if I was unmarried, and the count had proposed to me, I should have been flattered by the distinction; and if I should have been so, I am sure, niece, you, who have no fortune, ought to feel yourself highly honoured, and show a proper gratitude and humility towards the count for his condescension. I am often surprised, I must own, to observe how humbly he deports himself to you, notwithstanding the haughty airs you give yourself; I wonder he has patience to humour you so; if I were he, I know I should often be ready to reprehend you, and make you know yourself a little better. I would not have flattered you, I can tell you; for it is this absurd flattery that makes you fancy yourself of so much consequence, that you think nobody can deserve you; and I often tell the count so, for I have no patience to hear him pay you such extravagant compliments, which you believe every word of!'

'Your patience, Madam, cannot suffer more cruelly on such occasions than my own,' said Emily.

'O! that is all mere affectation,' rejoined her aunt. 'I know that his flattery delights you, and makes you so vain that you think you may have the whole world at your feet. But you are very much mistaken; I can assure you, niece, you will not meet with many such suitors as the count: every other person would have turned upon his heel, and left you to repent at your leisure, long ago.'

'O that the count had resembled every other person, then!' said Emily with a heavy sigh.

'It is happy for you that he does not,' rejoined Madame Montoni; 'and what I am now saying is from pure kindness. I am endeavouring to convince you of your good fortune, and to persuade you to submit to necessity with a good grace. It is nothing to me, you know, whether you like this marriage or not, for it must be; what I say, therefore, is from pure kindness: I wish to see you happy, and it is your own fault if you are not so. I would ask you now, seriously and calmly, what kind of a match you can expect, since a count cannot content your ambition?'

'I have no ambition, whatever, Madam,' replied Emily; 'my only wish is to remain in my present station.'

'O! that is speaking quite from the purpose,' said her aunt; 'I see you are still thinking of M. Valancourt. Pray get rid of all those fantastic notions about love, and this ridiculous pride, and be something like a reasonable creature. But, however, this is nothing to the purpose—for your marriage with the count takes place to-morrow, you know, whether you approve it or not. The count will be trifled with no longer.'

Emily made no attempt to reply to this curious speech; she felt it would be mean, and she knew it would be useless. Madame Montoni laid the count's presents upon the table on which Emily was leaning, and then, desiring she would be ready early in the morning, bade her good-night. 'Good-night, Madam,' said Emily, with a deep sigh, as the door closed upon her aunt; and she was left once more to her own sad reflections. For some time she sat so lost in thought, as to be wholly unconscious where she was; at length raising her head, and looking round the room, its glooms and profound stillness awed her. She fixed her eyes on the door through which her aunt had disappeared, and listened anxiously for some sound that might relieve the deep dejection of her spirits; but it was past midnight, and all the family, except the servant who sat up for Montoni, had retired to bed. Her mind, long harassed by distress, now yielded to imaginary terrors; she trembled to look into the obscurity of her spacious chamber, and feared she knew not what; a state of mind which continued so long, that she would have called up Annette, her aunt's woman, had her fears permitted her to rise from her chair and to cross the apartment.

These melancholy illusions at length began to disperse, and she retired to her bed, not to sleep, for that was scarcely possible, but to try at least to quiet her disturbed fancy, and to collect strength of spirits sufficient to bear her through the scene of the approaching morning.

CHAPTER XIX.

'Dark power! with shuddering, meek submitted
    thought,
Be mine to read the visions old
Which thy awakening bards have told,
And, lest they meet my blasted view,
Hold each strange tale devoutly true.
                COLLINS'S ODE TO FEAR.

EMILY was recalled from a kind of slumber, into which she had at length sunk, by a quick knocking at her chamber; she started up in terror. Montoni and Count Morano instantly came to her mind; but having listened in silence for some time, and recognising the voice of Annette, she ventured to open the door. 'What brings you hither so early?' said Emily, trembling excessively.

'Dear ma'amselle!' said Annette, 'do not look so pale. I am quite frightened to see you. Here is a fine bustle below stairs, all the servants running to and fro, and none of them fast enough! Here is a bustle, indeed, all of a sudden, and nobody knows for what!'

'Who is below besides them?' said Emily: 'Annette, do not trifle with me.'

'Not for the world, ma'amselle, I would not trifle for the world; but one cannot help making one's remarks: and there is the signor in such a bustle as I never saw him before; and he has sent me to tell you, ma'am, to get ready immediately.'

'Good God, support me!' cried Emily, almost fainting: 'Count Morano is below, then!'

'No, ma'amselle, he is not below that I know of,' replied Annette; 'only his *excellenza* sent me to desire you would get ready directly to leave Venice, for that the gondolas would be at the steps of the canal in a few minutes; but I must hurry back to my lady, who is just at her wits' end, and knows not which way to turn for haste.'

'Explain, Annette, explain the meaning of all this before you go,' said Emily, so overcome with surprise and timid hope that she had scarcely breath to speak.

'Nay, ma'amselle, that is more than I can do. I only know that the signor is just come home in a very ill humour; that he has had us all called out of our beds, and tells us we are all to leave Venice immediately.'

'Is Count Morano to go with the signor?' said Emily; 'and whither are we going?'

'I know neither, ma'am, for certain; but I heard Ludovico say something about going, after we got to *Terra-firma*, to the signor's castle among the mountains that he talked of.'

'The Apennines!' said Emily eagerly; 'O! then I have little to hope!'

'That is the very place, ma'am. But cheer up, and do not take it so much to heart, and think what a little time you have to get ready in, and how impatient the signor is. Holy St. Mark! I hear the oars on the canal; and now

they come nearer, and now they are dashing at the steps below; it is the gondola, sure enough.'

Annette hastened from the room; and Emily prepared for this unexpected flight, not perceiving that any change in her situation could possibly be for the worse. She had scarcely thrown her books and clothes into her travelling-trunk, when receiving a second summons, she went down to her aunt's dressing-room, where she found Montoni impatiently reproving his wife for delay. He went out soon after, to give some further orders to his people, and Emily then inquired the occasion of this hasty journey; but her aunt appeared to be as ignorant as herself, and to undertake the journey with more reluctance.

The family at length embarked, but neither Count Morano nor Cavigni was of the party. Somewhat revived by observing this, Emily, when the gondolieri dashed their oars in the water, and put off from the steps of the portico, felt like a criminal who receives a short reprieve. Her heart beat yet lighter, when they emerged from the canal into the ocean, and lighter still, when they skimmed past the walls of St. Mark, without having stopped to take the Count Morano.

The dawn now began to tint the horizon, and to break upon the shores of the Adriatic. Emily did not venture to ask any questions of Montoni, who sat, for some time, in gloomy silence, and then rolled himself up in his cloak, as if to sleep, while Madame Montoni did the same: but Emily, who could not sleep, undrew one of the little curtains of the gondola, and looked out upon the sea. The rising dawn now enlightened the mountain tops of Friuli; but their lower sides, and the distant waves that rolled at their feet, were still in deep shadow. Emily, sunk in tranquil melancholy, watched the strengthening light spreading upon the ocean, showing progressively Venice with her islets, and the shores of Italy, along which boats with their pointed Latin sails began to move.

The gondolieri were frequently hailed at this early hour by the market people, as they glided by towards Venice, and the *Lagune* soon displayed a gay scene of innumerable little barks passing from *Terra-firma* with provisions. Emily gave a last look to that splendid city; but her mind was then occupied by considering the probable events that awaited her in the scenes to which she was removing, and with conjectures concerning the motive of this sudden journey. It appeared, upon calmer consideration, that Montoni was removing her to his secluded castle, because he could there with more probability of success attempt to terrify her into obedience: or that, should its gloomy and sequestered scenes fail of this effect, her forced marriage with the count could there be solemnized with the secrecy which was necessary to the honour of Montoni. The little spirit which this reprieve had recalled now began to fail, and when Emily reached the shore, her mind had sunk into all its former depression.

Montoni did not embark on the Brenta, but pursued his way in carriages across the country towards the Apennine; during which journey his manner to Emily was so particularly severe, that this alone would have confirmed her late conjecture, had any such confirmation been necessary. Her senses were now dead to the beautiful country through which she travelled. Sometimes she was compelled to smile at the *naïveté* of Annette, in her remarks on what she saw, and sometimes to sigh, as a scene of peculiar beauty recalled Valancourt to her thoughts, who was indeed seldom absent from them, and of whom she could never hope to hear in the solitude to which she was hastening.

At length the travellers began to ascend among the Apennines. The immense pine-forests which at that period overhung these mountains, and between which the road wound, excluded all view but of the cliffs aspiring above, except that now and then an opening through the dark woods allowed the eye a momentary glimpse of the country below. The gloom of these shades, their solitary silence, except when the breeze swept over their summits, the tremendous precipices of the mountains that came partially to the eye, each assisted to raise the solemnity of Emily's feelings into awe: she saw only images of gloomy grandeur, or of dreadful sublimity, around her; other images, equally gloomy, and equally terrible, gleamed on her imagination. She was going she scarcely knew whither, under the dominion of a person from whose arbitrary disposition she had already suffered so much; to marry, perhaps, a man who possessed neither her affection nor esteem; or to endure, beyond the hope of succour, whatever punishment revenge, and that Italian revenge, might dictate.—The more she considered what might be the motive of the journey, the more she became convinced that it was for the purpose of concluding her nuptials with Count Morano, with the secrecy which her resolute resistance had made necessary to the honour, if not to the safety, of Montoni. From the deep solitudes into which she was emerging, and from the gloomy castle of which she had heard some mysterious hints, her sick heart recoiled in despair, and she experienced that, though her mind was already occupied by peculiar distress, it was still alive to the influence of new and local circumstance; why else did she shudder at the image of this desolate castle?

As the travellers still ascended among the pine-forests, steep rose over steep, the moun-

tains seemed to multiply as they went, and what was the summit of one eminence proved to be only the base of another. At length they reached a little plain, where the drivers stopped to rest the mules, when a scene of such extent and magnificence opened below, as drew even from Madame Montoni a note of admiration. Emily lost for a moment her sorrows in the immensity of nature. Beyond the amphitheatre of mountains that stretched below, whose tops appeared as numerous almost as the waves of the sea, and whose feet were concealed by the forests—extended the *campagna* of Italy, where cities and rivers and woods, and all the glow of cultivation, were mingled in gay confusion. The Adriatic bounded the horizon, into which the Po and the Brenta, after winding through the whole extent of the landscape, poured their fruitful waves. Emily gazed long on the splendours of the world she was quitting, of which the whole magnificence seemed thus given to her sight only to increase her regret on leaving it: for her, Valancourt alone was in that world; to him alone her heart turned, and for him alone fell her bitter tears.

From this sublime scene the travellers continued to ascend among the pines, till they entered a narrow pass of the mountains, which shut out every feature of the distant country, and in its stead exhibited only tremendous crags impending over the road, where no vestige of humanity, or even of vegetation, appeared, except here and there the trunk and scathed branches of an oak, that hung nearly headlong from the rock into which its strong roots had fastened. This pass, which led into the heart of the Apennine, at length opened to day, and a scene of mountains stretched in long perspective, as wild as any the travellers had yet passed. Still vast pine-forests hung upon their base, and crowned the ridgy precipice that rose perpendicularly from the vale, while, above, the rolling mists caught the sun-beams, and touched their cliffs with all the magical colouring of light and shade. The scene seemed perpetually changing, and its features to assume new forms, as the winding road brought them to the eye in different attitudes; while the shifting vapours, now partially concealing their minuter beauties, and now illuminating them with splendid tints, assisted the illusions of the sight.

Though the deep valleys between these mountains were for the most part clothed with pines, sometimes an abrupt opening presented a perspective of only barren rocks, with a cataract flashing from their summit among broken cliffs, till its waters, reaching the bottom, foamed along with louder fury; and sometimes pastoral scenes exhibited their 'green delights' in the narrow vales, smiling amid surrounding horror. There herds and flocks of goats and sheep browsing under the shade of hanging woods, and the shepherd's little cabin reared on the margin of a clear stream, presented a sweet picture of repose.

Wild and romantic as were these scenes, their character had far less of the sublime than had those of the Alps which guard the entrance of Italy. Emily was often elevated, but seldom felt those emotions of indescribable awe which she had so continually experienced in her passage over the Alps.

Towards the close of day the road wound into a deep valley. Mountains, whose shaggy steeps appeared to be inaccessible, almost surrounded it. To the east a vista opened, and exhibited the Apennines in their darkest horrors; and the long perspective of retiring summits rising over each other, their ridges clothed with pines, exhibited a stronger image of grandeur than any that Emily had yet seen. The sun had just sunk below the top of the mountains she was descending, whose long shadow stretched athwart the valley; but his sloping rays, shooting through an opening of the cliffs, touched with a yellow gleam the summits of the forest that hung upon the opposite steeps, and streamed in full splendour upon the towers and battlements of a castle that spread its extensive ramparts along the brow of a precipice above. The splendour of these illumined objects was heightened by the contrasted shade which involved the valley below.

'There,' said Montoni, speaking for the first time in several hours, 'is Udolpho.'

Emily gazed with melancholy awe upon the castle, which she understood to be Montoni's; for, though it was now lighted up by the setting sun, the gothic greatness of its features, and its mouldering walls of dark gray stone, rendered it a gloomy and sublime object. As she gazed, the light died away on its walls, leaving a melancholy purple tint, which spread deeper and deeper as the thin vapour crept up the mountain, while the battlements above were still tipped with splendour. From those, too, the rays soon faded, and the whole edifice was invested with the solemn duskiness of evening. Silent, lonely, and sublime, it seemed to stand the sovereign of the scene, and to frown defiance on all who dared to invade its solitary reign. As the twilight deepened, its features became more awful in obscurity; and Emily continued to gaze, till its clustering towers were alone seen rising over the tops of the woods, beneath whose thick shade the carriages soon after began to ascend.

The extent and darkness of these tall woods awakened terrific images in her mind, and she almost expected to see banditti start up from under the trees. At length the carriages emerged upon a heathy rock, and soon after reached the castle gates, where the deep tone of the portal bell, which was struck upon to give notice of their arrival, increased the fearful emotions that had assailed Emily. While they waited till the servant within should come to open the gates, she anxiously surveyed the edifice: but the gloom that overspread it allowed her to distinguish little more than a part of its outline, with the massy walls of the ramparts, and to know that it was vast, ancient, and dreary. From the parts she saw, she judged of the heavy strength and extent of the whole. The gateway before her, leading into the courts, was of gigantic size, and was defended by two round towers crowned by overhanging turrets embattled, where, instead of banners, now waved long grass and wild plants that had taken root among the mouldering stones, and which seemed to sigh, as the breeze rolled past, over the desolation around them. The towers were united by a curtain pierced and embattled also, below which appeared the pointed arch of a huge portcullis surmounting the gates: from these the walls of the ramparts extended to other towers overlooking the precipice, whose shattered outline, appearing on a gleam that lingered in the west, told of the ravages of war.—Beyond these all was lost in the obscurity of evening.

While Emily gazed with awe upon the scene, footsteps were heard within the gates, and the undrawing of bolts; after which an ancient servant of the castle appeared, forcing back the huge folds of the portal to admit his lord. As the carriage-wheels rolled heavily under the portcullis, Emily's heart sunk, and she seemed as if she was going into her prison; the gloomy court into which she passed, served to confirm the idea; and her imagination, ever awake to circumstance, suggested even more terrors than her reason could justify.

Another gate delivered them into the second court, grass-grown and more wild than the first, where, as she surveyed through the twilight its desolation—its lofty walls overtopped with briony, moss, and nightshade, and the embattled towers that rose above—long suffering and murder came to her thoughts. One of those instantaneous and unaccountable convictions, which sometimes conquer even strong minds, impressed her with its horror. The sentiment was not diminished when she entered an extensive gothic hall, obscured by the gloom of evening, which a light glimmering at a distance through a long perspective of arches only rendered more striking. As a servant brought the lamp nearer, partial gleams fell upon the pillars and the pointed arches, forming a strong contrast with their shadows that stretched along the pavement and the walls.

The sudden journey of Montoni had prevented his people from making any other preparations for his reception than could be had in the short interval since the arrival of the servant who had been sent forward from

Venice; and this, in some measure, may account for the air of extreme desolation that everywhere appeared.

The servant who came to light Montoni bowed in silence, and the muscles of his countenance relaxed with no symptom of joy. Montoni noticed the salutation by a slight motion of his hand, and passed on; while his lady, following, and looking round with a degree of surprise and discontent which she seemed fearful of expressing, and Emily, surveying the extent and grandeur of the hall in timid wonder, approached a marble staircase. The arches here opened to a lofty vault, from the centre of which hung a tripod lamp which a servant was hastily lighting; and the rich fret-work of the roof, a corridor leading into several upper apartments, and a painted window stretching nearly from the pavement to the ceiling of the hall, became gradually visible.

Having crossed the foot of the staircase and passed through an ante-room, they entered a spacious apartment, whose walls, wainscoted with black larch-wood, the growth of the neighbouring mountains, were scarcely distinguishable from darkness itself.

'Bring more light,' said Montoni as he entered.

The servant, setting down his lamp, was withdrawing to obey him; when Madame Montoni observing that the evening air of this mountainous region was cold, and that she should like a fire, Montoni ordered that wood might be brought.

While he paced the room with thoughtful steps, and Madame Montoni sat silently on a couch at the upper end of it waiting till the servant returned, Emily was observing the singular solemnity and desolation of the apartment, viewed as it now was by the glimmer of the single lamp, placed near a large Venetian mirror that duskily reflected the scene, with the tall figure of Montoni passing slowly along, his arms folded, and his countenance shaded by the plume that waved in his hat.

From the contemplation of this scene, Emily's mind proceeded to the apprehension of what she might suffer in it, till the remembrance of Valancourt, far, far distant! came to her heart, and softened it into sorrow. A heavy sigh escaped her: but trying to conceal her tears, she walked away to one of the high windows that opened upon the ramparts, below which spread the woods she had passed in her approach to the castle. But the night shade sat deeply on the mountains beyond and their indented outline alone could be faintly traced on the horizon, where a red streak yet glimmered in the west. The valley between was sunk in darkness.

The scene within, upon which Emily turned on the opening of the door, was scarcely less gloomy. The old servant who had received them at the gates now entered, bending under a load of pine branches, while two of Montoni's Venetian servants followed with lights.

'Your *Excellenza* is welcome to the castle, said the old man, as he raised himself from the hearth, where he had laid the wood; 'it has been a lonely place a long while; but you will excuse it, signor, knowing we had but short notice. It is near two years, come next feast of St. Mark, since your *Excellenza* was within these walls.'

'You have a good memory, old Carlo,' said Montoni; 'it is thereabout; and how hast thou contrived to live so long?'

'A-well-a-day, sir, with much ado; the cold winds that blow through the castle in winter are almost too much for me; and I thought sometimes of asking your *Excellenza* to let me leave the mountains, and go down into the lowlands. But I don't know how it is—I am loth to quit these old walls I have lived in so long.'

'Well, how have you gone on in the castle, since I left it?' said Montoni.

'Why, much as usual, signor; only it wants a good deal of repairing. There is the north tower—some of the battlements have tumbled down, and had liked one day to have knocked my poor wife (God rest her soul!) on the head. Your *Excellenza* must know——'

'Well, but the repairs,' interrupted Montoni.

'Ay, the repairs,' said Carlo: 'a part of the roof of the great hall has fallen in, and all the winds from the mountains rushed through it last winter, and whistled through the whole castle so, that there was no keeping one's self warm, be where one would. There my wife and I used to sit shivering over a great fire in one corner of the little hall, ready to die with cold, and——'

'But there are no more repairs wanted,' said Montoni impatiently.

'O Lord! your *Excellenza*, yes—the wall of the rampart has tumbled down in three places; then, the stairs that led to the west gallery have been a long time so bad that it is dangerous to go up them: and the passage leading to the great oak chamber, that overhangs the north rampart—one night last winter I ventured to go there by myself, and your *Excellenza*——'

'Well, well, enough of this,' said Montoni with quickness: 'I will talk more with thee to-morrow.'

The fire was now lighted; Carlo swept the hearth, placed chairs, wiped the dust from a large marble table that stood near it, and then left the room.

Montoni and his family drew round the fire. Madame Montoni made several attempts at conversation, but his sullen answers repulsed her, while Emily sat endeavouring to acquire courage enough to speak to him. At length, in a tremulous voice, she said, 'May I ask, sir, the motive of this sudden journey?'—After a long pause she recovered sufficient courage to repeat the question.

'It does not suit me to answer inquiries,' said Montoni, 'nor does it become you to make them; time may unfold them all; but I desire I may be no further harassed, and I recommend it to you to retire to your chamber, and to endeavour to adopt a more rational conduct than that of yielding to fancies, and to a sensibility which, to call it by the gentlest name, is only a weakness.'

Emily rose to withdraw. 'Good night, madam,' said she to her aunt with an assumed composure that could not disguise her emotion.

'Good night, my dear,' said Madame Montoni in a tone of kindness which her niece had never before heard from her; and the unexpected endearment brought tears to Emily's eyes. She curtsied to Montoni, and was retiring. 'But you do not know the way to your chamber,' said her aunt. Montoni called the servant, who waited in the anteroom, and bade him send Madame Montoni's woman; with whom, in a few minutes, Emily withdrew.

'Do you know which is my room?' said she to Annette, as they crossed the hall.

'Yes, I believe I do, ma'amselle; but this is such a strange rambling place! I have been lost in it already; they call it the double chamber over the south rampart, and I went up this great staircase to it. My lady's room is at the other end of the castle.'

Emily ascended the marble staircase, and came to the corridor, as they passed through which Annette resumed her chat:—'What a wild lonely place this is, ma'am! I shall be quite frightened to live in it. How often and often have I wished myself in France again! I little thought, when I came with my lady to see the world, that I should ever be shut up in such a place as this, or I would never have left my own country! This way, ma'amselle, down this turning. I can almost believe in giants again, and such like, for this is just like one of their castles; and some night or other, I suppose, I shall see fairies too hopping about in that great old hall, that looks more like a church, with its huge pillars, than anything else.'

'Yes,' said Emily smiling, and glad to escape from more serious thought, 'if we come to the corridor about midnight and look down into the hall, we shall certainly see it illuminated with a thousand lamps, and the fairies tripping in gay circles to the sound of delicious music; for it is in such places as this, you know, that they come to hold their revels. But I am afraid, Annette, you will not be able to pay the necessary penance for such a sight: and if once they hear your voice, the whole scene will vanish in an instant.'

'O! if you will bear me company, ma'amselle, I will come to the corridor this very night, and I promise you I will hold my tongue; it shall not be my fault if the show vanishes.—But do you think they will come?'

'I cannot promise that with certainty, but I will venture to say it will not be your fault if the enchantment should vanish.'

'Well, ma'amselle, that is saying more than I expected of you: but I am not so much afraid of fairies as of ghosts; and they say there are a plentiful many of them about the castle; now I should be frightened to death if I should chance to see any of them. But hush, ma'amselle, walk softly! I have thought several times something passed by me.'

'Ridiculous!' said Emily; 'you must not indulge such fancies.'

'O ma'am; they are not fancies, for aught I know; Benedetto says these dismal galleries and halls are fit for nothing but ghosts to live in; and I verily believe, if I *live* long in them, I shall turn to one myself!'

'I hope,' said Emily, 'you will not suffer Signor Montoni to hear of these weak fears; they would highly displease him.'

'What, do you know then, ma'amselle, all about it!' rejoined Annette. 'No, no, I do know better than to do so; though, if the signor can sleep sound, nobody else in the castle has any right to lie awake, I am sure.'

Emily did not appear to notice this remark.

'Down this passage, ma'amselle; this leads to a back staircase. O! if I see anything, I shall be frightened out of my wits!'

'That will scarcely be possible,' said Emily smiling, as she followed the winding of the passage which opened into another gallery; and then Annette perceiving that she had missed her way while she had been so eloquently haranguing on ghosts and fairies, wandered about through other passages and galleries, till at length, frightened by their intricacies and desolation, she called aloud for assistance: but they were beyond the hearing of the servants, who were on the other side of the castle, and Emily now opened the door of a chamber on the left.

'O! do not go in there, ma'amselle,' said Annette, 'you will only lose yourself further.'

'Bring the light forward,' said Emily, 'we may possibly find our way through these rooms.'

Annette stood at the door in an attitude of hesitation, with the light held up to show the chamber, but the feeble rays spread through not half of it. 'Why do you hesitate?' said Emily; 'let me see whither this room leads.'

Annette advanced reluctantly. It opened into a suite of spacious and ancient apartments, some of which were hung with tapestry, and others wainscoted with cedar and black larch-wood. What furniture there was, seemed to be almost as old as the rooms, and retained an appearance of grandeur, though covered with dust, and dropping to pieces with damp and with age.

'How cold these rooms are, ma'amselle!' said Annette: 'nobody has lived in them for many, many years, they say. Do let us go.'

'They may open upon the great staircase, perhaps,' said Emily, passing on till she came to a chamber hung with pictures, and took the light to examine that of a soldier on horseback in a field of battle.—He was darting his spear upon a man who lay under the feet of the horse, and who held up one hand in a supplicating attitude. The soldier, whose beaver was up, regarded him with a look of vengeance, and the countenance, with that expression, struck Emily as resembling Montoni. She shuddered, and turned from it. Passing the light hastily over several other pictures, she came to one concealed by a veil of black silk. The singularity of the circumstance struck her, and she stopped before it, wishing to remove the veil, and examine what could thus carefully be concealed, but somewhat wanting courage. 'Holy Virgin! what can this mean?' exclaimed Annette, 'This is surely the picture they told me of at Venice.'

'What picture?' said Emily. 'Why, a picture—a picture,' replied Annette hesitatingly '—but I never could make out exactly what it was about either.'

'Remove the veil, Annette.'

'What! I, ma'amselle!—I! not for the world!' Emily, turning round, saw Annette's countenance grow pale. 'And pray what have you heard of this picture to terrify you so, my good girl?' said she. 'Nothing, ma'amselle: I have heard nothing, only let us find our way out.'

'Certainly, but I wish first to examine the picture; take the light, Annette, while I lift the veil. Annette took the light, and immediately walked away with it, disregarding Emily's call to stay, who, not choosing to be left alone in the dark chamber, at length followed her. 'What is the reason of this, Annette?' said Emily, when she overtook her; 'what have you heard concerning that picture, which makes you so unwilling to stay when I bid you?'

'I don't know what is the reason, ma'amselle,' replied Annette, 'nor any thing about the picture; only I have heard there is something very dreadful belonging to it—and that it has been covered up in black *ever since*— and that nobody has looked at it for a great many years—and it somehow has to do with the owner of this castle before Signor Montoni came to the possession of it—and——'

'Well, Annette,' said Emily, smiling, 'I perceive it is as you say—that you know nothing about the picture.'

'No, nothing, indeed, ma'amselle, for they made me promise never to tell :——but——'

'Well,' said Emily, who perceived that she was struggling between her inclination to reveal a secret and her apprehension for the consequence, 'I will inquire no further——'

'No, pray, ma'am, do not.'

'Lest you should tell all,' interrupted Emily.

Annette blushed, and Emily smiled, and they passed on to the extremity of this suite of apartments, and found themselves, after some further perplexity, once more at the top of the marble staircase, where Annette left Emily, while she went to call one of the servants of the castle to show them to the chamber for which they had been seeking.

While she was absent, Emily's thoughts returned to the picture; an unwillingness to tamper with the integrity of a servant had checked her inquiries on this subject, as well as concerning some alarming hints which Annette had dropped respecting Montoni: though her curiosity was entirely awakened, and she had perceived that her questions might easily be answered. She was now, however, inclined to go back to the apartment and examine the picture; but the loneliness of the hour and of the place, with the melancholy silence that reigned around her, conspired with a certain degree of awe, excited by the mystery attending this picture, to prevent her. She determined, however, when daylight should have reanimated her spirits, to go thither and remove the veil. As she leaned from the corridor over the staircase, and her eyes wandered round, she again observed with wonder, the vast strength of the walls, now somewhat decayed, and the pillars of solid marble that rose from the hall and supported the roof.

A servant now appeared with Annette, and conducted Emily to her chamber, which was in a remote part of the castle, and at the very end of the corridor from whence the suite of apartments opened through which they had been wandering. The lonely aspect of her room made Emily unwilling that Annette should leave her immediately, and the dampness of it chilled her with more than fear. She begged Caterina, the servant of the castle, to bring some wood and light a fire.

'Ay, lady, it's many a year since a fire was lighted here,' said Caterina.

'You need not tell us that, good woman,' said Annette; 'every room in the castle feels like a well. I wonder how you contrive to live here: for my part, I wish I was at Venice again.' Emily waved her hand for Caterina to fetch the wood.

'I wonder, ma'am, why they call this the double chamber,' said Annette, while Emily surveyed it in silence, and saw that it was lofty and spacious like the others she had seen, and, like many of them, too, had its walls lined with dark larch-wood. The bed and other furniture was very ancient, and had an air of gloomy grandeur, like all she had seen in the castle. One of the high casements, which she opened, overlooked a rampart, but the view beyond was hid in darkness.

In the presence of Annette, Emily tried to support her spirits, and to restrain the tears which every now and then came to her eyes. She wished much to inquire when Count Morano was expected at the castle; but an unwillingness to ask unnecessary questions, and to mention family concerns to a servant, withheld her. Meanwhile, Annette's thoughts were engaged upon another subject: she dearly loved the marvellous, and had heard of a circumstance, connected with the castle, that highly gratified this taste. Having been enjoined not to mention it, her inclination to tell it was so strong that she was every instant on the point of speaking what she had heard; such a strange circumstance, too, and to be obliged to conceal it, was a severe punishment; but she knew that Montoni might impose one much severer, and she feared to incur it by offending him.

Caterina now brought the wood, and its bright blaze dispelled for a while the gloom of her chamber. She told Annette that her lady had inquired for her; and Emily was once again left to her own reflections. Her heart was not yet hardened against the stern manners of Montoni, and she was nearly as much shocked now, as she had been when she first witnessed them. The tenderness and affection to which she had been accustomed till she lost her parents, had made her particularly sensible to any degree of unkindness, and such a reverse as this no apprehension had prepared her to support.

To call off her attention from subjects that pressed heavily on her spirits, she rose and again examined her room and its furniture. As she walked around it she passed a door that was not quite shut; and perceiving that it was not the one through which she entered, she brought the light forward to discover whither it led. She opened it, and, going forward, had nearly fallen down a steep narrow staircase that wound from it, between two stone walls. She wished to know to what it led, and was the more anxious since it communicated so immediately with her apartment; but in the present state of her spirits she wanted courage to venture into the darkness alone. Closing the door, therefore, she endeavoured to fasten it, but upon further examination perceived that it had no bolts on the chamber side, though it had two on the other. By placing a heavy chair against it, she in. some measure remedied the defect: yet she was still alarmed at the thought of sleeping in this remote room alone, with a door opening she knew not whither, and which could not be

perfectly fastened on the inside. Sometimes she wished to entreat of Madame Montoni that Annette might have leave to remain with her all night; but was deferred by an apprehension of betraying what would be thought childish fears and by an unwillingness to increase the apt terrors of Annette.

Her gloomy reflections were soon after interrupted by a footstep in the corridor, and she was glad to see Annette enter with some supper sent by Madame Montoni. Having a table near the fire, she made the good girl sit down and sup with her; and when their little repast was over, Annette, encouraged by her kindness, and stirring the wood into a blaze, drew her chair upon the hearth, nearer to Emily, and said,—'Did you ever hear, ma'amselle, of the strange accident that made the signor lord of this castle?'

'What wonderful story have you now to tell?' said Emily, concealing the curiosity occasioned by the mysterious hints she had formerly heard on that subject.

'I have heard all about it, ma'amselle,' said Annette, looking round the chamber and drawing closer to Emily; 'Benedetto told me as we travelled together: says he, "Annette, you don't know about this castle here, that we are going to?" "No," says I, "Mr. Benedetto, pray what do you know?" But, ma'amselle, you can keep a secret, or I would not tell you for the world; for I promised never to tell, and they say that the signor does not like to have it talked of.'

'If you promised to keep this secret,' said Emily, 'you do right not to mention it.'

Annette paused a moment, and then said, 'O, but to you, ma'amselle, to you I may tell it safely, I know.'

Emily smiled: 'I certainly shall keep it as faithful as yourself, Annette.'

Annette replied very gravely, that would do, and proceeded—'This castle, you must know, ma'amselle, is very old, and very strong, and has stood out many sieges as they say. Now it was not Signor Montoni's always, nor his father's; no: but, by some law or other, it was to come to the signor if the lady died unmarried.'

'What lady?' said Emily.

'I am not come to that yet,' replied Annette: 'it is the lady I am going to tell you about, ma'amselle: but, as I was saying, this lady lived in the castle, and had everything very ga id about her, as you may suppose, ma'amselle. The signor used often to come to see her, and was in love with her, and offered to marry her: for, though he was somehow related, that did not signify. But she was in love with somebody else, and would not have him, which made him very angry, as they say; and you know, ma'amselle, what an ill-looking gentleman he is when he is angry. Perhaps she saw him in a passion, and therefore would not have him. But, as

I was saying, she was very melancholy and unhappy, and all that, for a long time, and—Holy Virgin! what noise is that? did not you hear a sound, ma'amselle?'

'It was only the wind,' said Emily; 'but do come to the end of your story.'

'As I was saying—O, where was I?—as I was saying—she was very melancholy and unhappy a long while, and used to walk about upon the terrace, there, under the windows, by herself, and cry so! it would have done your heart good to hear her. That is—I don't mean good, but it would have made you cry too, as they tell me.'

'Well, but, Annette, do tell me the substance of your tale.'

'All in good time, ma'am: all this I heard before at Venice, but what is to come I never heard till to-day. This happened a great many years ago, when Signor Montoni was quite a young man. The lady—they called her Signora Laurentini, was very handsome, but she used to be in great passions too, sometimes, as well as the signor. Finding he could not make her listen to him—what does he do, but leave the castle, and never comes near it for a long time! but it was all one to her; she was just as unhappy whether he was here or not, till one evening—Holy St. Peter! ma'amselle,' cried Annette, 'look at that lamp, see how blue it burns!' She looked fearfully round the chamber. 'Ridiculous girl!' said Emily, 'why will you indulge those fancies? Pray let me hear the end of your story, I am weary.'

Annette still kept her eyes on the lamp, and proceeded in a lower voice. 'It was one evening, they say, at the latter end of the year, it might be about the middle of September, I suppose, or the beginning of October; nay, for that matter, it might be November, for that, too, is the latter end of the year; but that I cannot say for certain, because they did not tell me for certain themselves. However, it was at the latter end of the year, this grand lady walked out of the castle into the woods below, as she had often done before, all alone, only her maid was with her. The wind blew cold, and strewed the leaves about, and whistled dismally among those great old chestnut-trees that we passed, ma'amselle, as we came to the castle—for Benedetto showed me the trees as he was talking—the wind blew cold, and her woman would have persuaded her to return: but all would not do, for she was fond of walking in the woods at evening time, and if the leaves were falling about her, so much the better.

'Well, they saw her go down among the woods, but night came, and she did not return; ten o'clock, eleven o'clock, twelve o'clock came, and no lady! Well, the servants thought, to be sure, some accident had befallen her, and they went out to seek her. They searched all night long, but

could not find her, or any trace of her: and, from that day to this, ma'amselle, she has never been heard of.'

'Is this true, Annette?' said Emily in much surprise.

'True, ma'am! said Annette with a look of horror, 'yes, it is true, indeed. But they do say,' she added, lowering her voice, 'they do say, that the signora has been seen several times since walking in the woods and about the castle in the night: several of the old servants, who remained here some time after, declare they saw her; and since then, she has been seen by some of the vassals, who have happened to be in the castle at night. Carlo the [old steward could tell such things, they say, if he would!'

'How contradictory is this, Annette! said Emily; 'you say nothing has been since known of her, and yet she has been seen!'

'But all this was told me for a great secret,' rejoined Annette, without noticing the remark, 'and I am sure, ma'am, you would not hurt either me or Benedetto, so much as to go and tell it again.' Emily remained silent, and Annette repeated her last sentence.

'You have nothing to fear from my indiscretion,' replied Emily; 'and let me advise you, my good Annette, be discreet yourself, and never mention what you have just told me to any other person. Signor Montoni, as you say, may be angry if he hears of it, but what inquiries were made concerning the lady?'

'O! a great deal, indeed, ma'amselle, for the signor laid claim to the castle directly, as being the next heir; and they said, that is, the judges, or the senators, or somebody of that sort, said, he could not take possession of it till so many years were gone by, and then, if after all the lady could not be found, why she would be as good as dead, and the castle would be his own; and so it is his own. But the story went round, and many strange reports were spread, so very strange, ma'amselle, that I shall not tell them.'

'That is stranger still, Annette,' said Emily smiling, and rousing herself from her reverie. 'But when Signora Laurentini was afterwards seen in the castle, did nobody speak to her?'

'Speak—speak to her!' cried Annette with a look of terror; 'no, to be sure.'

'And why not?' rejoined Emily, willing to hear further.

'Holy Mother! speak to a spirit!'

'But what reason had they to conclude it was a spirit, unless they had approached and spoken to it?'

'O ma'amselle, I cannot tell. How can you ask such shocking questions? But nobody ever saw it come in or go out of the castle; and it was in one place now, and then the next minute in quite another part of the castle; and then it never spoke, and if it was alive, what should it do in the castle if it never spoke? Several parts of the castle have never been gone into since, they say for that very reason.'

'What, because it never spoke,' said Emily, trying to laugh away the fears that began to steal upon her.

'No, ma'amselle, no,' replied Annette rather angrily; 'but because something has been seen there. They say, too, there is an old chapel adjoining the west side of the castle, where any time at midnight you may hear such groans!—it makes one shudder to think of them;—and strange sights have been seen there——'

'Pr'ythee, Annette, no more of these silly tales,' said Emily

'Silly tales, ma'amselle! O, but I will tell you one story about this, if you please, that Caterina told me. It was one cold winter's night that Caterina (she often came to the castle then, she says, to keep old Carlo and his wife company, and so he recommended her afterwards to the signor, and she has lived here ever since) —Caterina was sitting with them in the little hall: says Carlo, "I wish we had some of those figs to roast, that lie in the store-closet, but it is a long way off, and I am loth to fetch them; do, Caterina," says he, "for you are young and nimble, do bring us some, the fire is in nice trim for roasting them; they lie," says he, "in such a corner of the store-room, at the end of the north gallery; here, take the lamp," says he, "and mind, as you go up the great staircase, that the wind through the roof does not blow it out." So with that Caterina took the lamp—Hush! ma'amselle, I surely heard a noise.'

Emily, whom Annette had now infected with her own terrors, listened attentively; but everything was still, and Annette proceeded: that is,

"Caterina went to the north gallery, that is, the wide gallery we passed, ma'am, before we came to the corridor, here. As she went with the lamp in her hand, thinking of nothing at all——There, again!' cried Annette suddenly—'I heard it again!—it was not fancy, ma'amselle!'

'Hush!' said Emily, trembling. They listened, and continuing to sit quite still, Emily heard a slow knocking against the wall. It came repeatedly. Annette then screamed loudly, and the chamber slowly opened.—It was Caterina, come to tell Annette that her lady wanted her. Emily, though she now perceived who it was, could not immediately overcome her terror; while Annette, half laughing, half crying, scolded Caterina heartily for thus alarming them; and was also terrified lest what she had told had been overheard.—Emily, whose mind was deeply impressed by the chief circumstance of Annette's relation, was unwilling to be left alone, in the present state of her spirits; but to avoid offending Madame Montoni and be-

traying her own weakness, she struggled to overcome the illusions of fear, and dismissed Annette for the night.

When she was alone, her thoughts recurred to the strange history of Signora Laurentini, and then to her own strange situation, in the wild and solitary mountains of a foreign country, in the castle and the power of a man to whom only a few preceding months she was an entire stranger; who had already exercised an usurped authority over her, and whose character she now regarded with a degree of terror apparently justified by the fears of others. She knew that he had invention equal to the conception, and talents to the execution, of any project, and she greatly feared he had a heart too void of feeling to oppose the perpetration of whatever his interest might suggest. She had long observed the unhappiness of Madame Montoni, and had often been witness to the stern and contemptuous behaviour she received from her husband. To these circumstances, which conspired to give her just cause for alarm, were now added those thousand nameless terrors which exist only in active imaginations, and which set reason and examination equally at defiance.

Emily remembered all that Valancourt had told her, on the eve of her departure from Languedoc, respecting Montoni, and all that he had said to dissuade her from venturing on the journey. His fears had often since appeared to her prophetic—now they seemed confirmed. Her heart, as it gave her back the image of Valancourt, mourned in vain regret; but reason soon came with a consolation, which, though feeble at first, acquired vigour from reflection. She considered that, whatever might be her sufferings, she had withheld from involving him in misfortune, and that whatever her future sorrows could be, she was at least free from self-reproach.

Her melancholy was assisted by the hollow sighings of the wind along the corridor and round the castle. The cheerful blaze of the wood had long been extinguished, and she sat with her eyes fixed on the dying embers, till a loud gust, that swept through the corridor, and shook the doors and casements, alarmed her; for its violence had moved the chair she had placed as a fastening, and the door leading to the private staircase stood half open. Her curiosity and her fears were again awakened. She took the lamp to the top of the steps, and stood hesitating whether to go down; but again the profound stillness and the gloom of the place awed her; and determining to inquire further when daylight might assist the search, she closed the door, and placed against it a stronger guard.

She now retired to her bed, leaving the lamp burning on the table; but its gloomy light, instead of dispelling her fear, assisted it; for, by its uncertain rays, she almost fancied she saw shapes flit past her curtains, and glide into the remote obscurity of her chamber.—The castle clock struck one before she closed her eyes to sleep.

CHAPTER XX.

' I think it is the weakness of mine eyes,
That shapes this monstrous apparition.
It comes upon me!'

JULIUS CÆSAR.

DAYLIGHT dispelled from Emily's mind the glooms of superstition, but not those of apprehension. The Count Morano was the first image that occurred to her waking thoughts, and then came a train of anticipated evils which she could neither conquer nor avoid. She rose, and to relieve her mind from the busy ideas that tormented it, compelled herself to notice external objects. From her casement she looked out upon the wild grandeur of the scene, closed nearly on all sides by alpine steeps, whose tops peeping over each other faded from the eye in misty hues, while the promontories below were dark with woods that swept down to their base, and stretched along the narrow valleys. The rich pomp of these woods was particularly delightful to Emily; and she viewed with astonishment the fortifications of the castle spreading along a vast extent of rock, and now partly in decay, the grandeur of the ramparts below, and the towers and battlements and various features of the fabric above. From these her sight wandered over the cliffs and woods into the valley, along which foamed a broad and rapid stream, seen falling among the crags of an opposite mountain, now flashing in the sunbeams, and now shadowed by over-arching pines, till it was entirely concealed by their thick foliage. Again it burst from beneath this darkness in one broad sheet of foam, and fell thundering into the vale. Nearer, towards the west, opened the mountain vista which Emily had viewed with such sublime emotion on her approach to the castle: a thin dusky vapour, that rose from the valley, overspread its features with a sweet obscurity. As this ascended and caught the sunbeams it kindled into a crimson tint, and touched with exquisite beauty the woods and cliffs over which it passed to the summit of the mountains; then, as the veil drew up, it was delightful to watch the gleaming objects that progressively disclosed themselves in the valley—the green turf—dark woods—little rocky recesses—a few peasants' huts—the foaming stream —a herd of cattle, and various images of pastoral beauty. Then, the pine-forests brightened, and then the broad breast of the mountains, till at length the mist settled round their summit, touching them with a ruddy glow. The features of the vista now

appeared distinctly, and the broad deep shadows that fell from the lower cliffs gave strong effect to the streaming splendour above; while the mountains, gradually sinking in the perspective, appeared to shelve into the Adriatic Sea, for such Emily imagined to be the gleam of bluish light that terminated the view.

Thus she endeavoured to amuse her fancy, and was not unsuccessful. The breezy freshness of the morning, too, revived her. She raised her thoughts in prayer, which she felt almost most disposed to do when viewing the sublimity of nature, and her mind recovered its strength.

When she turned from the casement, her eyes glanced upon the door she had so carefully guarded on the preceding night, and she now determined to examine whither it led; but on advancing to remove the chairs, she perceived that they were already moved a little way. Her surprise cannot be easily imagined, when, in the next minute, she perceived that the door was fastened.—She felt as if she had seen an apparition. The door of the corridor was locked as she had left it, but this door, which could be secured only on the outside, must have been bolted during the night. She became seriously uneasy at the thought of sleeping again in a chamber thus liable to intrusion, so remote too as it was from the family, and she determined to mention the circumstance to Madame Montoni, and to request a change.

After some perplexity she found her way into the great hall, and to the room which she had left on the preceding night, where breakfast was spread, and her aunt was alone; for Montoni had been walking over the environs of the castle, examining the condition of its fortifications, and talking for some time with Carlo. Emily observed that her aunt had been weeping, and her heart softened towards her with an affection that showed itself in her manner rather than in words, while she carefully avoided the appearance of having noticed that she was unhappy. She seized the opportunity of Montoni's absence to mention the circumstance of the door, to request that she might be allowed another apartment, and to inquire again concerning the occasion of their sudden journey. On the first subject her aunt referred her to Montoni, positively refusing to interfere in the affair; on the last she professed utter ignorance.

Emily, then, with a wish of making her aunt more reconciled to her situation, praised the grandeur of the castle and the surrounding scenery, and endeavoured to soften every unpleasing circumstance attending it. But though misfortune had somewhat conquered the asperity of Madame Montoni's temper, and, by increasing her cares for herself, had taught her to feel in some degree for others, the capricious love of rule, which nature had planted and habit had nourished in her heart, was not subdued. She could not now deny herself the gratification of tyrannising over the innocent and helpless Emily, by attempting to ridicule the taste she could not feel.

Her satirical discourse was, however, interrupted by the entrance of Montoni, and her countenance immediately assumed a mingled expression of fear and resentment, while he seated himself at the breakfast-table, as if unconscious of there being any person but himself in the room.

Emily, as she observed him in silence, saw that his countenance was darker and sterner than usual. 'O could I know,' said she to herself, 'what passes in that mind; could I know the thoughts that are known there, I should no longer be condemned to this torturing suspense!' Their breakfast passed in silence, till Emily ventured to request that another apartment might be allotted to her, and related the circumstance which made her wish it.

'I have no time to attend to these idle whims,' said Montoni; 'that chamber was prepared for you, and you must rest contented with it. It is not probable that any person would take the trouble of going to that remote staircase for the purpose of fastening a door. If it was not fastened when you entered the chamber, the wind, perhaps, shook the door and made the bolts slide. But I know not why I should undertake to account for so trifling an occurrence.'

This explanation was by no means satisfactory to Emily, who had observed that the bolts were rusted, and consequently could not be thus easily moved; but she forbore to say so, and repeated her request.

'If you will not release yourself from the slavery of these fears,' said Montoni sternly, 'at least forbear to torment others by the mention of them. Conquer such whims, and endeavour to strengthen your mind. No existence is more contemptible than that which is embittered by fear.' As he said this, his eye glanced upon Madame Montoni, who coloured highly, but was still silent. Emily, wounded and disappointed, thought her fears were, in this instance, too reasonable to deserve ridicule; but perceiving that, however they might oppress her, she must endure them, she tried to withdraw her attention from the subject.

Carlo soon after entered with some fruit.

'Your *Excellenza* is tired after your long ramble,' said he, as he set the fruit upon the table: 'but you have more to see after breakfast. There is a place in the vaulted passage leading to——'

Montoni frowned upon him, and waved his hand for him to leave the room. Carlo stopped, looked down, and then added, as he advanced to the breakfast-table, and took up the basket of fruit:

'I made bold, your *Excellenza*, to bring some cherries here, for my honoured lady and my young mistress. Will your ladyship taste them, madam?' said Carlo, presenting the basket; 'they are very fine ones, though I gathered them myself, and from an old tree that catches all the south sun; they are as big as plums, your ladyship.'

'Very well, old Carlo,' said Madame Montoni; 'I am obliged to you.'

'And the young signora, too, she may like some of them?' rejoined Carlo, turning with the basket to Emily; 'it will do me good to see her eat some.'

'Thank you, Carlo,' said Emily, taking some cherries, and smiling kindly.

'Come, come,' said Montoni impatiently, 'enough of this. Leave the room, but be in waiting: I shall want you presently.'

Carlo obeyed, and Montoni soon after went out to examine further into the state of the castle; while Emily remained with her aunt, patiently enduring her ill-humour, and endeavouring, with much sweetness, to soothe her affliction, instead of resenting its effect.

When Madame Montoni retired to her dressing-room, Emily endeavoured to amuse herself by a view of the castle. Through a folding-door she passed from the great hall to the ramparts, which extended along the brow of the precipice round three sides of the edifice; the fourth was guarded by the high walls of the courts, and by the gateway through which she had passed on the preceding evening. The grandeur of the broad ramparts, and the changing scenery they overlooked, excited her high admiration; for the extent of the terraces allowed the features of the country to be seen in such various points of view that they appeared to form new landscapes. She often paused to examine the gothic magnificence of Udolpho, its proud irregularity, its lofty towers and battlements, its high-arched casements, and its slender watch-tower, perched upon the corners of turrets. Then she would lean on the wall of the terrace, and, shuddering, measure with her eye the precipice below, till the dark summits of the woods arrested it. Wherever she turned, appeared mountain-tops, forests of pine, and narrow glens opening among the Apennines, and retiring from the sight into inaccessible regions.

While she thus leaned, Montoni, followed by two men, appeared ascending a winding path cut in the rock below. He stopped upon a cliff, and, pointing to the ramparts, turned to his followers, and talked with much eagerness of gesticulation.—Emily perceived that one of these men was Carlo, the other was in the dress of a peasant, and he alone seemed to be receiving the directions of Montoni.

She withdrew from the walls, and pursued her walk, till she heard at a distance the sound of carriage-wheels, and then the loud bell of the portal, when it instantly occurred to her that Count Morano was arrived. As she hastily passed the folding-doors from the terrace towards her own apartment, several persons entered the hall by an opposite door. She saw them at the extremities of the arcades, and immediately retreated; but the agitation of her spirits, and the extent and duskiness of the hall, had prevented her from distinguishing the persons of the strangers. Her fears, however, had but one object, and they called up that object to her fancy;—she believed that she had seen Count Morano.

When she thought that they had passed the hall, she ventured again to the door; and proceeded unobserved to her room, where she remained agitated with apprehensions and listening to every distant sound. At length, hearing voices on the rampart, she hastened to her window, and observed Montoni with Signor Cavigni walking below, conversing earnestly, and often stopping and turning towards each other, at which time their discourse seemed to be uncommonly interesting.

Of the several persons who had appeared in the hall, here was Cavigni alone: but Emily's alarm was soon after heightened by the steps of some one in the corridor, who, she apprehended, brought a message from the count. In the next moment Annette appeared.

'Ah! ma'amselle,' said she, 'here is the Signor Cavigni arrived! I am sure I rejoiced to see a Christian person in this place; and then he is so good-natured too, he always takes so much notice of me!—And here is also Signor Verezzi, and who do you think besides, ma'amselle?'

'I cannot guess, Annette; tell me quickly.'

'Nay, ma'am, do guess once.'

'Well, then,' said Emily, with assumed composure, 'it is—Count Morano, I suppose.'

'Holy Virgin!' cried Annette, 'are you ill, ma'amselle? you are going to faint! let me get some water.'

Emily sunk into a chair.

'Stay, Annette,' said she feebly, 'do not leave me—I shall soon be better: open the casement.—The count, you say—he is come, then?'

'Who, I!—the count! No, ma'amselle, I did not say so.'

'He is *not* come then?' said Emily eagerly.

'No, ma'amselle.'

'You are sure of it?'

'Lord bless me!' said Annette, 'you recover very suddenly, ma'am! why, I thought you was dying just now.'

'But the count—you are sure, is not come?'

'O yes, quite sure of that, ma'amselle. Why I was looking out through the grate in the north turret, when the carriages drove into the courtyard, and I never expected to

see such a goodly sight in this dismal old castle! but here are masters and servants, too, enough to make the place ring again. O! I was ready to leap through the rusty old bars for joy!—O! who would ever have thought of seeing a Christian face in this huge dreary house! I could have kissed the very horses that brought them.'

'Well, Annette, well, I am better now.'

'Yes, ma'amselle, I see you are. O! all the servants will lead merry lives here, now; we shall have singing and dancing in the little hall, for the signor cannot hear us there—and droll stories—Ludovico's come, ma'am; yes, there is Ludovico come with them! You remember Ludovico, ma'am—a tall, handsome young man—Signor Cavigni's lacquey—who always wears his cloak with such a grace, thrown round his left arm, and his hat set on so smartly, all on one side and—'

'No,' said Emily, who was wearied by her loquacity.

'What, ma'amselle, don't you remember Ludovico—who rode the Cavaliero's gondola at the last regatta, and won the prize? And who used to sing such sweet verses about Orlandos and about the Black-a-moors, too; and Charly—Charly—magne, yes, that was the name all under my lattice, in the west portico, on the moon-light nights at Venice? O! I have listened to him!—'

'I fear, to thy peril, my good Annette,' said Emily: 'for it seems his verses have stolen thy heart. But let me advise you; if it is so, keep the secret; never let him know it.'

'Ah—ma'amselle!—how can one keep such a secret as that?'

'Well, Annette, I am now so much better that you may leave me.'

'O, but ma'amselle, I forgot to ask—how did you sleep in this dreary old chamber last night?—'As well as usual.'—'Did you hear no noises?'—'None.'—'Nor see anything?'—'Nothing.'—'Well, that is surprising!'—'Not in the least: and tell me why you ask these questions.'

'O, ma'amselle! I would not tell you for the world, nor all I have heard about this chamber, either; it would frighten you so.'

'If that is all, you have frightened me already, and may therefore tell me what you know without hurting your conscience.'

'O Lord! they say the room is haunted, and has been so these many years.'

'It is by a ghost, then, who can draw bolts,' said Emily, endeavouring to laugh away her apprehensions; 'for I left that door open last night and found it fastened this morning.'

Annette turned pale, and said not a word.

'Do you know whether any of the servants fastened this door in the morning, before I rose?'

'No, ma'am, that I will be bound they did

not; but I don't know: shall I go and ask, ma'amselle?' said Annette, moving hastily towards the corridor.

'Stay, Annette, I have other questions to ask; tell me what you have heard concerning this room, and whither that staircase leads.'

'I will go and ask it all directly, ma'am; besides, I am sure my lady wants me. I cannot stay now, indeed, ma'am.'

She hurried from the room without waiting Emily's reply, whose heart lightened by the certainty that Morano was not arrived allowed her to smile at the superstitious terror which had seized on Annette; for though she sometimes felt its influence herself, she could smile at it when apparent in other persons.

Montoni having refused Emily another chamber, she determined to bear with patience the evil she could not remove, and in order to make the room as comfortable as possible, unpacked her books, her sweet delight in happier days, and her soothing resource in the hours of moderate sorrow: but there were hours when even these failed of their effect; when the genius, the taste, the enthusiasm of the sublimest writers were felt no longer.

Her little library being arranged on a high chest, part of the furniture of the room, she took out her drawing utensils, and was tranquil enough to be pleased with the thought of sketching the sublime scenes beheld from her windows; but she suddenly checked this pleasure, remembering how often she had soothed herself by the intention of obtaining amusement of this kind, and had been prevented by some new circumstance of misfortune.

'How can I suffer myself to be deluded by hope,' said she, 'and, because Count Morano is not yet arrived, feel a momentary happiness? Alas! what is it to me, whether he is here to-day or to-morrow, if he comes at all? —and that he will come—it were weakness to doubt.'

To withdraw her thoughts, however, from the subject of her misfortunes, she attempted to read; but her attention wandered from the page, and at length she threw aside the book, and determined to explore the adjoining chambers of the castle. Her imagination was pleased with the view of ancient grandeur, and an emotion of melancholy awe awakened all its powers, as she walked through rooms obscure and desolate, where no footsteps had passed probably for many years, and remembered the strange history of the former possessor of the edifice. This brought to her recollection the veiled picture which had attracted her curiosity on the preceding night, and she resolved to examine it. As she passed through the chambers that led to this, she found herself somewhat agitated; its connexion with the late lady of the castle, and the conversation of Annette, together with the circumstance of the veil, throwing a

mystery over the object that excited a faint degree of terror. But a terror of this nature, as it occupies and expands the mind, and elevates it to high expectation, is purely sublime, and leads us, by a kind of fascination, to seek even the object from which we appear to shrink.

Emily passed on with faltering steps; and having paused a moment at the door before she attempted to open it, she then hastily entered the chamber, and went towards the picture, which appeared to be enclosed in a frame of uncommon size, that hung in a dark part of the room. She paused again, and then with a timid hand lifted the veil; but instantly let it fall—perceiving that what it had concealed was no picture, and before she could leave the chamber she dropped senseless on the floor.

When she recovered her recollection, the remembrance of what she had seen had nearly deprived her of it a second time. She had scarcely strength to remove from the room, and regain her own; and, when arrived there, wanted courage to remain alone. Horror occupied her mind, and excluded for a time all sense of past and dread of future misfortune: she seated herself near the casement because from thence she heard voices, though distant, on the terrace, and might see people pass; and these, trifling as they were, were reviving circumstances. When her spirits had recovered their tone, she considered whether she should mention what she had seen to Madame Montoni; and various and important motives urged her to do so, among which the least was the hope of the relief which an overburdened mind finds in speaking of the subjects of its interest. But she was aware of the terrible consequences which such a communication might lead to; and, dreading the indiscretion of her aunt, at length endeavoured to arm herself with resolution to observe a profound silence on the subject. Montoni and Verezzi soon after passed under the casement, speaking cheerfully, and their voices revived her. Presently the Signors Bertolini and Cavigni joined the party on the terrace; and Emily, supposing that Madame Montoni was then alone, went to seek her; for the solitude of her chamber, and its proximity to that where she had received so severe a shock, again affected her spirit.

She found her aunt in her dressing-room, preparing for dinner. Emily's pale and affrighted countenance alarmed even Madame Montoni; but she had sufficient strength of mind to be silent on the subject that still made her shudder, and which was ready to burst from her lips. In her aunt's apartment she remained till they both descended to dinner. There she met the gentlemen lately arrived, who had a kind of busy seriousness in their looks, which was somewhat unusual with them, while their thoughts seemed too much occupied by some deep interest to suffer them to bestow much attention either on Emily or Madame Montoni. They spoke little, and Montoni less. Emily, as she now looked on him, shuddered. The horror of the chamber rushed on her mind. Several times the colour faded from her cheeks; and she feared that illness would betray her emotions, and compel her to leave the room; but the strength of her resolution remedied the weakness of her frame; she obliged herself to converse, and even tried to look cheerful.

Montoni evidently laboured under some vexation, such as would probably have agitated a weaker mind or a more susceptible heart, but which appeared, from the sternness of his countenance, only to bend up his faculties to energy and fortitude.

It was a comfortless and silent meal. The gloom of the castle seemed to have spread its contagion even over the gay countenance of Cavigni, and with this gloom was mingled a fierceness such as she had seldom seen him indicate. Count Morano was not named, and what conversation there was, turned chiefly upon the wars which at that time agitated the Italian states, the strength of the Venetian armies, and the characters of their generals.

After dinner, when the servants had withdrawn, Emily learned that the cavalier who had drawn upon himself the vengeance of Orsino had since died of his wounds, and that strict search was still making for his murderer. The intelligence seemed to disturb Montoni, who mused, and then inquired where Orsino had concealed himself. His guests, who all, except Cavigni, were ignorant that Montoni had himself assisted him to escape from Venice, replied, that he had fled in the night with such precipitation and secrecy, that his most intimate companions knew not whither. Montoni blamed himself for having asked the question, for a second thought convinced him that a man of Orsino's suspicious temper was not likely to trust any of the persons present with the knowledge of his asylum. He considered himself, however, as entitled to his utmost confidence, and did not doubt that he should soon hear of him.

Emily retired with Madame Montoni, soon after the cloth was withdrawn, and left the cavaliers to their secret councils; but not before the significant frowns of Montoni had warned his wife to depart, who passed from the hall to the ramparts, and walked for some time in silence, which Emily did not interrupt, for her mind was also occupied by interests of its own. It required all her resolution to forbear communicating to Madame Montoni the terrible subject which still thrilled her every horror: and sometimes she was on the point of doing so, merely to obtain the relief of a moment; but she knew how wholly she was in the power of Montoni, and, considering

that the indiscretion of her aunt might prove fatal to them both, she compelled herself to endure a present and an inferior evil, rather than to tempt a future and a heavier one. A strange kind of presentiment frequently on this day occurred to her; it seemed as if her fate rested here, and was by some invisible means connected with this castle.

'Let me not accelerate it,' said she to herself; 'for whatever I may be reserved, let me, at least, avoid self-reproach.'

As she looked on the massy walls of the edifice, her melancholy spirits represented it to be her prison; and she started as at a new suggestion, when she considered how far distant she was from her native country, from her little peaceful home, and from her only friend—how remote was her hope of happiness, how feeble the expectation of again seeing him! Yet the idea of Valancourt, and her confidence in his faithful love, had hitherto been her only solace, and she struggled hard to retain them. A few tears of agony started to her eyes, which she turned aside to conceal.

While she afterwards leaned on the wall of the ramparts, some peasants at a little distance were seen examining a breach, before which lay a heap of stones, as if to repair it, and a rusty old cannon that appeared to have fallen from its station above. Madame Montoni stopped to speak to the men, and inquired what they were going to do. 'To repair the fortifications, your ladyship,' said one of them; a labour which she was somewhat surprised that Montoni should think necessary, particularly as he had never spoken of the castle as of a place at which he meant to reside for any considerable time; but she passed on towards a lofty arch that led from the south to the east rampart, and which adjoined the castle on one side, while on the other it supported a small watch-tower that entirely commanded the deep valley below. As she approached this arch, she saw beyond it, winding along the woody descent of a distant mountain, a long troop of horse and foot, whom she knew to be soldiers only by the glitter of their pikes and other arms, for the distance did not allow her to discover the colour of their liveries. As she gazed the vanguard issued from the woods into the valley; but the train still continued to pour over the remote summit of the mountain, in endless succession; while, in the front, the military uniform became distinguishable, and the commanders, riding first, and seeming by their gestures to direct the march of those that followed, at length approached very near to the castle.

Such a spectacle, in these solitary regions, both surprised and alarmed Madame Montoni, and she hastened towards some peasants who were employed in raising bastions before the south rampart, where the rock was less abrupt than elsewhere. These men could give no satisfactory answers to her inquiries, but, being roused by them, gazed in stupid astonishment upon the long cavalcade. Madame Montoni then, thinking it necessary to communicate further the object of her alarm, sent Emily to say that she wished to speak to Montoni ; an errand her niece did not approve, for she dreaded his frowns, which she knew this message would provoke ; but she obeyed in silence.

As she drew near the apartment in which he sat with his guests, she heard them in earnest and loud dispute ; and she paused a moment, trembling at the displeasure which her sudden interruption would occasion. In the next, their voices sunk altogether.; she then ventured to open the door, and while Montoni turned hastily and looked at her without speaking, she delivered her message.

' Tell Madame Montoni I am engaged,' said he.

Emily then thought it proper to mention the subject of her alarm. Montoni and his companions rose instantly and went to the windows ; but these not affording them a view of the troops, they at length proceeded to the ramparts, where Cavigni conjectured it to be a legion of *condottieri* on their march towards Modena.

One part of the cavalcade now extended along the valley, and another wound among the mountains towards the north, while some troops still lingered on the woody precipices, where the first had appeared, so that the great length of the procession seemed to include a whole army. While Montoni and his family watched its progress, they heard the sound of trumpets and the clash of cymbals in the vale, and then others answering from the heights. Emily listened with emotion to the shrill blast that awoke the echoes of the mountains, and Montoni explained the signals, with which he appeared to be well acquainted, and which meant nothing hostile. The uniforms of the troops, and the kind of arms they bore, confirmed to him the conjecture of Cavigni ; and he had the satisfaction to see them pass by, without even stopping to gaze upon his castle. He did not, however, leave the rampart till the bases of the mountains had shut them from his view, and the last murmur of the trumpet floated away on the wind. Cavigni and Verezzi were inspirited by this spectacle, which seemed to have roused all the fire of their temper ; Montoni turned into the castle in thoughtful silence.

Emily's mind had not yet sufficiently recovered from its late shock to endure the loneliness of her chamber, and she remained upon the ramparts : for Madame Montoni had not invited her to her dressing-room, whither she had gone evidently in low spirits ; and Emily, from her late experience, had lost all wish to explore the gloomy and mysterious recesses of the castle. The ramparts, therefore, were almost her only retreat : and here she lingered till the gray haze of evening was spread over the scene.

The cavaliers supped by themselves, and Madame Montoni remained in her apartment, whither Emily went before she retired to her own. She found her aunt weeping, and in much agitation. The tenderness of Emily was naturally so soothing, that it seldom failed to give comfort to the drooping heart ; but Madame Montoni's was torn, and the softest accents of Emily's voice were lost upon it. With her usual delicacy, she did not appear to observe her aunt's distress ; but it gave an involuntary gentleness to her manners, and an air of solicitude to her countenance, which Madame Montoni was vexed to perceive, who seemed to feel the pity of her niece to be an insult to her pride, and dismissed her as soon as she properly could. Emily did not venture to mention again the reluctance she felt to her gloomy chamber ; but she requested that Annette might be permitted to remain with her until she retired to rest ; and the request was somewhat reluctantly granted. Annette, however, was now with the servants, and Emily withdrew alone.

With light and hasty steps she passed through the long galleries, while the feeble glimmer of the lamp she carried only showed the gloom around her, and the passing air threatened to extinguish it. The lonely silence that reigned in this part of the castle, awed her ; now and then, indeed she heard a faint peal of laughter rise from a remote part of the edifice, where the servants were assembled ; but it was soon lost, and a kind of breathless stillness remained. As she passed the suite of rooms which she had visited in the morning, her eyes glanced fearfully on the door, and she almost fancied she heard murmuring sounds within, but she paused not a moment to inquire.

Having reached her own apartment, where no blazing wood on the hearth dissipated the gloom, she sat down with a book to enliven her attention till Annette should come, and a fire could be kindled. She continued to read till her light was nearly expired ; but Annette did not appear, and the solitude and obscurity of her chamber again affected her spirits, the more so, because of its nearness to the scene of horror that she had witnessed in the morning. Gloomy and fantastic images came to her mind. She looked fearfully towards the door of the staircase, and then examining whether it was still fastened, found that it was so. Unable to conquer the uneasiness she felt at the prospect of sleeping again in this remote and insecure apartment, which some person seemed to have entered during the preceding night, her impatience to see Annette, whom she had bidden to inquire concerning this circumstance, became extremely painful. She wished also to question her as to the object which had excited so much horror in her own mind, and which Annette on the preceding evening had appeared to be in part acquainted with, though her words were very remote from the truth, and it appeared plainly to Emily that the girl had been purposely misled by a false report; above all, she was surprised that the door of the chamber, which contained it, should be left unguarded. Such an instance of negligence almost surpassed belief. But her light was now expiring; the faint flashes it threw upon the walls called up all terrors of fancy, and she rose to find her way to the habitable part of the castle before it was quite extinguished.

As she opened the chamber door, she heard remote voices, and soon after saw a light tissue upon the further end of the corridor, which Annette and another servant approached. 'I am glad you are come,' said Emily: 'what has detained you so long? Pray light me a fire immediately.'

'My lady wanted me, ma'amselle,' replied Annette in some confusion; 'I will go and get the wood.'

'No,' said Caterina, 'that is my business;' and left the room instantly: while Annette would have followed; but being called back, she began to talk very loud, and laugh, and seemed to trust a pause of silence.

Caterina soon returned with the wood: and then, when the cheerful blaze once more animated the room, and this servant had withdrawn, Emily asked Annette whether she had made the inquiry she bade her. 'Yes, ma'amselle,' said Annette, 'but not a soul knows anything about the matter: and old Carlo—I watched him well, for they say he knows strange things—old Carlo looked so as I don't know how to tell; and he asked me again and again if I was sure the door was ever unfastened. "Lord," says I—"am I sure I am alive?" And as for me, ma'am, I am all astounded, as one may say, and would no more sleep in this chamber than I would on the great cannon at the end of the east rampart.'

'And what objection have you to that cannon, more than to any of the rest?' said Emily smiling: 'the best would be rather a hard bed.'

'Yes, ma'amselle, any of them would be hard enough, for that matter; but they do say that something has been seen in the dead of night standing beside the great cannon, as if to guard it.'

'Well! my good Annette, the people who tell such stories are happy in having you for an auditor, for I perceive you believe them all.'

'Dear ma'amselle! I will show you the very cannon; you can see it from these windows!'

'Well,' said Emily, 'but that does not that an apparition guards it.'

'What! not if I show you the very cannon! Dear ma'am, you will believe nothing.'

'Nothing probably upon this subject, but what I see,' said Emily.

'Well, ma'am, but you shall see it, if you will only step this way to the casement.'

Emily could not forbear laughing, and Annette looked surprised. Perceiving her extreme aptitude to credit the marvellous, Emily forbore to mention the subject she had intended, lest it should overcome her with ideal terrors; and she began to speak on a lively topic—the regattas of Venice.

'Ay, ma'amselle, those rowing matches,' said Annette, 'and the fine moon-light nights, are all that are worth seeing in Venice. To be sure that moon is brighter than any I ever saw; and then to hear such sweet music, too, as Ludovico has often and often sung under the lattice by the west portico! Ma'amselle, it was Ludovico that told me about the picture which you wanted so to look at last night, and—'

'What picture?' said Emily, wishing Annette to explain herself.

'O! that terrible picture with the black veil over it.'

'You never saw it, then?' said Emily.

'Who, I!—No, ma'amselle, I never did. But this morning,' continued Annette, lowering her voice and looking round the room, 'this morning, as it was broad day-light, do you know, ma'am, I took a strange fancy to see it, as I had heard such strange hints about it, and I got as far as the door, and should have opened it, if it had not been locked.'

Emily, endeavouring to conceal the emotion this circumstance occasioned, inquired at what hour she went to the chamber, and found that it was soon after herself had been there. She also asked further questions, and the answers convinced her that Annette, and probably her informer, were ignorant of the terrible truth, though in Annette's account something very like the truth now and then mingled with the falsehood. Emily now began to fear that her visits to the chamber had been observed, since the door had been closed so immediately after her departure; and dreaded lest this should draw upon her the vengeance of Montoni. Her anxiety, also, was excited to know whence, and for what purpose, the delusive report, which had been imposed upon Annette, had originated; since Montoni could only have wished for silence and secrecy: but she felt that the subject was too terrible for this lonely hour, and she compelled herself to leave it, to converse with Annette, whose chat, simple as it was, she preferred to the stillness of total solitude.

Thus they sat till near midnight, but not without many hints from Annette that she wished to go. The embers were now nearly burnt out; and Emily heard at a distance the thundering sound of the hall doors, as they were shut for the night. She therefore prepared for rest, but was still unwilling that Annette should leave her. At this instant the great bell of the portal sounded. They listened in fearful expectation, when, after a long pause of silence, it sounded again. Soon after they heard the noise of carriage wheels in the court-yard. Emily sunk almost lifeless in her chair; 'It is the count,' said she.

'What, at this time of night, ma'am!' said Annette: 'no, my dear lady. But, for that matter, it is a strange time of night for anybody to come!'

'Nay, pr'ythee, good Annette, stay not talking,' said Emily in a voice of agony—'go, pr'ythee go, and see who it is.'

Annette left the room, and carried with her the light, leaving Emily in darkness, which a few moments before would have terrified her in this room, but was now scarcely observed by her. She listened and waited in breathless expectation, and heard distant noises, but Annette did not return. Her patience at length exhausted, she tried to find her way to the corridor; but it was long before she could touch the door of the chamber, and when she had opened it, the total darkness without made her fear to proceed. Voices were now heard; and Emily even thought she distinguished those of Count Morano and Montoni. Soon after she heard steps approaching; and then a ray of light streamed through the darkness, and Annette appeared, whom Emily went to meet.

'Yes, ma'amselle,' said she, 'you was right, it is the count, sure enough.'

'It is he,' exclaimed Emily, lifting her eyes towards heaven, and supporting herself by Annette's arm.

'Good Lord! my dear lady, don't be in such a *fluster*, and look so pale, we shall soon hear more.'

'We shall, indeed!' said Emily, moving as fast as she was able towards her apartment. 'I am not well, give me air.' Annette opened a casement, and brought water. The faintness soon left Emily, but she desired Annette would not go till she heard from Montoni.

'Dear ma'amselle! he surely will not disturb you at this time of night; why he must think you are asleep.'

'Stay with me till I am so, then,' said Emily, who felt temporary relief from this suggestion, which appeared probable enough, though her fears had prevented its occurring to her. Annette, with secret reluctance, consented to stay, and Emily was now composed enough to ask her some questions; among others, 'whether she had seen the count.'

'Yes, ma'am, I saw him alight, for I went from hence to the grate in the north turret, that overlooks the inner court-yard, you know. There I saw the count's carriage, and

the count in it, waiting at the great door—for the porter was just gone to bed—with several men on horseback, all by the light of the torches they carried.'

Emily was compelled to smile. 'When the door was opened, the count said something that I could not make out, and then got out, and another gentleman with him, I thought to be sure the signor was gone to bed, and I hastened away to my lady's dressing-room to see what I could hear. But in the way I met Ludovico, and he told me that the signor was up, counselling with his master and the other signors in the room at the end of the north gallery; and Ludovico held up his finger, and laid it on his lips, as much as to say—"There is more going on than you think of, Annette, but you must hold your tongue." And so I did hold my tongue, ma'amselle, and came away to tell you directly.'

Emily inquired who the cavalier was that accompanied the count, and how Montoni received them; but Annette could not inform her.

'Ludovico,' she added, 'had just been to call Signor Montoni's valet, that he might tell him they were arrived, when I met him.'

Emily sat musing for some time; and then her anxiety was so much increased, that she desired Annette would go to the servants' hall, where it was possible she might hear something of the count's intention respecting his stay at the castle.

'Yes, ma'am,' said Annette with readiness; 'but how am I to find the way if I leave the lamp with you?'

Emily said she would light her: and they immediately quitted the chamber. When they had reached the top of the great staircase, Emily recollected that she might be seen by the count; and to avoid the great hall, Annette conducted her through some private passages to a back staircase which led directly to that of the servants.

As she returned towards her chamber, Emily began to fear that she might again lose herself in the intricacies of the castle, and again be shocked by some mysterious spectacle; and though she was already perplexed by the numerous turnings, she feared to open one of the many doors that offered. While she stepped thoughtfully along, she fancied that she heard a low moaning at no great distance, and having paused a moment, she heard it again and distinctly. Several doors appeared on the right hand of the passage. She advanced, and listened. When she came to the second, she heard a voice, apparently in complaint, within, to which she continued to listen, afraid to open the door, and unwilling to leave it. Convulsive sobs followed, and then the piercing accents of an agonizing spirit burst forth. Emily stood appalled, and looked through the gloom that surrounded her, in fearful expectation. The lamentations continued. Pity now began to subdue terror; it was possible she might administer comfort to the sufferer, at least, by expressing sympathy, and she laid her hand on the door. While she hesitated, she thought she knew this voice, disguised as it was by tones of grief. Having therefore set down the lamp in the passage, she gently opened the door, within which all was dark, except that from an inner apartment a partial light appeared; and she stepped softly on. Before she reached it, the appearance of Madame Montoni, leaning on her dressing-table, weeping, and with a handkerchief held to her eyes, struck her, and she paused.

Some person was seated in a chair by the fire, but who it was she could not distinguish. He spoke now and then in a low voice, that did not allow Emily to hear what was uttered; but she thought that Madame Montoni at those times wept the more, who was too much occupied by her own distress to observe Emily; while the latter, though anxious to know what occasioned this, and who was the person admitted at so late an hour to her aunt's dressing-room, forbore to add to her sufferings by surprising her, or to take advantage of her situation by listening to a private discourse. She therefore stepped softly back, and after some further difficulty found the way to her own chamber, where nearer interests at length excluded the surprise and concern she had felt respecting Madame Montoni.

Annette, however, returned without satisfactory intelligence; for the servants, among whom she had been, were either entirely ignorant, or affected to be so, concerning the count's intended stay at the castle. They could talk only of the steep and broken road they had just passed, and of the numerous dangers they had escaped, and express wonder how their lord could choose to encounter all these in the darkness of night; for they scarcely allowed that the torches had served for any other purpose but that of showing the dreariness of the mountains. Annette, finding she could gain no information, left them making noisy petitions for more wood on the fire, and more supper on the table.

'And now, ma'amselle,' added she, 'I am so sleepy!—I am sure if you was so sleepy you would not desire me to sit up with you.'

Emily, indeed, began to think it was cruel to wish it; she had also waited so long without receiving a summons from Montoni, that it appeared he did not mean to disturb her at this late hour, and she determined to dismiss Annette. But when she again looked round her gloomy chamber, and recollected certain circumstances, fear seized her spirits, and she hesitated.

'And yet it were cruel of me to ask you to stay till I am asleep, Annette,' said she; 'for I fear it will be very long before I forget myself in sleep.'

'I daresay it will be very long, ma'amselle,' said Annette.

'But before you go,' rejoined Emily, 'let me ask you—Had Signor Montoni left Count Morano when you quitted the hall?'

'O no, ma'am, they were alone together.'

'Have you been in my aunt's dressing-room since you left me?'

'No, ma'amselle: I called at the door as I passed, but it was fastened; so I thought my lady was gone to bed.'

'Who, then, was with your lady just now?' said Emily, forgetting, in surprise, her usual prudence.

'Nobody, I believe, ma'am,' replied Annette; 'nobody has been with her, I believe, since I left you.'

Emily took no further notice of the subject; and after some struggle with imaginary fears, her good nature prevailed over them so far, that she dismissed Annette for the night. She then sat musing upon her own circumstances and those of Madame Montoni, till her eye rested on the miniature picture which she had found after her father's death among the papers he had enjoined her to destroy. It was open upon the table before her among some loose drawings, having with them been taken out of a little box by Emily some hours before. The sight of it called up many interesting reflections; but the melancholy sweetness of the countenance soothed the emotions which these had occasioned. It was the same style of countenance as that of her late father; and while she gazed on it with fondness on this account, she even fancied a resemblance in the features. But this tranquillity was suddenly interrupted when she recollected the words in the manuscript that had been found with this picture, and which had formerly occasioned her so much doubt and horror. At length she roused herself from the deep reverie into which this remembrance had thrown her; but when she rose to undress, the silence and solitude to which she was left at this midnight hour, for not even a distant sound was now heard, conspired with the impression the subject she had been considering had given to her mind to appal her. Annette's hints, too, concerning this chamber, simple as they were, had not failed to affect her, since they followed a circumstance of peculiar horror which she herself had witnessed, and since the scene of this was a chamber nearly adjoining her own.

The door of the staircase was perhaps a subject of more reasonable alarm; and she now began to apprehend, such was the aptitude of her fears, that this staircase had some private communication with the apartment, which she shuddered even to remember. Determined not to undress, she lay down to sleep in her clothes, with her late father's dog, the faithful *Manchon*, at the foot of the bed, whom she considered as a kind of guard.

Thus circumstanced, she tried to banish reflection; but her busy fancy would still hover over the subjects of her interest, and she heard the clock of the castle strike two before she closed her eyes.

From the disturbed slumber into which she then sunk, she was soon awakened by a noise which seemed to arise within her chamber; but the silence that prevailed, as she fearfully listened, inclined her to believe that she had been alarmed by such sounds as sometimes occur in dreams, and she laid her head again upon the pillow.

A return of the noise again disturbed her; it seemed to come from that part of the room which communicated with the private staircase, and she instantly remembered the odd circumstance of the door having been fastened, during the preceding night, by some unknown hand. Her late alarming suspicion concerning its communication also occurred to her. Her heart became faint with terror. Half-raising herself from the bed, and gently drawing aside the curtain, she looked towards the door of the staircase; but the lamp that burnt on the hearth spread so feeble a light through the apartment, that the remote parts of it were lost in shadow. The noise, however, which she was convinced came from the door, continued. It seemed like that made by the drawing of rusty bolts, and often ceased, and was then renewed more gently, as if the hand that occasioned it was restrained by a fear of discovery. While Emily kept her eyes fixed on the spot, she saw the door move, and then slowly opened, and perceived something enter the room, but the extreme duskiness prevented her distinguishing what it was. Almost fainting with terror, she had yet sufficient command over herself to check the shriek that was escaping from her lips, and letting the curtain drop from her hand, continued to observe in silence the motions of the mysterious form she saw. It seemed to glide along the remote obscurity of the apartment, then paused, and, as it approached the hearth, she perceived, in a stronger light, what appeared to be a human figure. Certain remembrances now struck upon the heart, and almost subdued the feeble remains of her spirit; she continued, however, to watch the figure, which remained for some time motionless; but then, advancing slowly towards the bed, stood silently at the feet, where the curtains, being a little open, allowed her still to see it; terror, however, had now deprived her of the power of discrimination, as well as of that of utterance.

Having continued there a moment, the form retreated towards the hearth, when it took the lamp, surveyed the chamber for a few moments, and then again advanced towards the bed. The light at that instant awakening the dog that had slept at Emily's feet, he barked loudly, and, jumping to the floor, flew at the stranger, who struck the animal smartly with a sheathed sword, and springing towards the bed, Emily discovered—Count Morano!

She gazed at him for a moment in speechless affright; while he, throwing himself on his knee at the bed-side, besought her to fear nothing; and, having thrown down his sword, would have taken her hand, when the faculties that terror had suspended suddenly returned, and she sprung from the bed in the dress which surely a kind of prophetic apprehension had prevented her, on this night, from throwing aside.

Morano rose, followed her to the door through which he had entered, and caught her hand as she reached the top of the staircase, but not before she had discovered by a gleam of a lamp another man half-way down the steps. She now screamed in despair, and, believing herself given up by Montoni, saw, indeed, no possibility of escape.

The count, who still held her hand, led her back into the chamber.

'Why all this terror,' said he in a tremulous voice. 'Hear me, Emily, I come not to alarm you; no, by Heaven! I love you too well—too well for my own peace.'

Emily looked at him for a moment in fearful doubt.

'Then leave me, sir,' said she, 'leave me instantly.'

'Hear me, Emily,' resumed Morano—'Hear me! I love, and am in despair—yes —in despair. How can I gaze upon you, and know that it is, perhaps, for the last time, without suffering all the phrensy of despair? But it shall not be so; you shall be mine, in spite of Montoni and all his villany.'

'In spite of Montoni!' cried Emily eagerly; 'what is it I hear?'

'You hear that Montoni is a villain,' exclaimed Morano with vehemence—'a villain who would have sold you to my love! —who—'

'And is he less who would have bought me?' said Emily, fixing on the count an eye of calm contempt. 'Leave the room, sir, instantly,' she continued in a voice trembling between joy and fear, 'or I will alarm the family, and you may receive that from Signor Montoni's vengeance which I have vainly supplicated from his pity.' But Emily knew that she was beyond the hearing of those who might protect her.

'You can never hope anything from his pity,' said Morano; 'he has used me infamously, and my vengeance shall pursue him. And for you, Emily, for you, he has new plans more profitable than the last, no doubt.'—The gleam of hope which the count's former speech had revived was now nearly extinguished by the latter; and while Emily's countenance betrayed the emotions of her mind, he endeavoured to take advantage of the discovery.

'I lose time,' said he; 'I came not to exclaim against Montoni : I came to solicit, to plead—to Emily ; to tell her all I suffer, to entreat her to save me from despair, and herself fly from destruction. Emily ! the schemes of Montoni are unsearchable, but, I warn you, they are terrible ; he has no principle when interest or ambition leads. Can I love you, and abandon you to his power ? Fly, then, fly from this gloomy prison, with a lover who adores you ! I have bribed a servant of the castle to open the gates, and before to-morrow's dawn you shall be far on the way to Venice.'

Emily, overcome by the sudden shock she had received,—at the moment, too, when she had begun to hope for better days,—now thought she saw destruction surround her on every side. Unable to reply, and almost to think, she threw herself into a chair, pale and breathless. That Montoni had formerly sold her to Morano, was very probable ; that he had now withdrawn his consent to the marriage, was evident from the count's present conduct ; and it was nearly certain that a scheme of stronger interest only could have induced the selfish Montoni to forego a plan which he had hitherto so strenuously pursued. These reflections made her tremble at the hints which Morano had just given, which she no longer hesitated to believe ; and while she shrunk from the new scenes of misery and oppression that might await her in the castle of Udolpho, she was compelled to observe, that almost her only means of escaping them was by submitting herself to the protection of this man, with whom evils more certain and not less terrible appeared—evils upon which she could not endure to pause for an instant.

Her silence, though it was that of agony, encouraged the hopes of Morano, who watched her countenance with impatience, took again the resisting hand she had withdrawn, and, as he pressed it to his heart, again conjured her to determine immediately. 'Every moment we lose will make our departure more dangerous,' said he : 'these few moments lost may enable Montoni to overtake us.'

'I beseech you, sir, be silent,' said Emily faintly : 'I am indeed very wretched, and wretched I must remain. Leave me—I command you, leave me to my fate.'

'Never !' cried the count vehemently : 'let me perish first ! But forgive my violence ! the thought of losing you is madness. You cannot be ignorant of Montoni's character ; you may be ignorant of his schemes—nay, you must be so, or you would not hesitate between my love and his power.'

'Nor do I hesitate,' said Emily.

'Let us go then,' said Morano, eagerly kissing her hand, and rising ; 'my carriage waits below the castle walls.'

'You mistake me, sir,' said Emily. 'Allow me to thank you for the interest you express in my welfare, and allow me to decide by my own choice. I shall remain under the protection of Signor Montoni.'

'Under his protection !' exclaimed Morano proudly—'his *protection !* Emily, why will you suffer yourself to be thus deluded ? I have already told you what you have to expect from his *protection.*'

'And pardon me, sir, if in this instance I doubt mere assertion, and, to be convinced, require something approaching to proof.'

'I have now neither the time nor the means of adducing proof,' replied the count.

'Nor have I, sir, the inclination to listen to it, if you had.'

'But you trifle with my patience and my distress,' continued Morano. ' Is a marriage with a man who adores you so very terrible in your eyes, that you would prefer to it all the misery to which Montoni may condemn you in this remote prison? Some wretch must have stolen those affections which ought to be mine, or you could not thus obstinately persist in refusing an offer that would place you beyond the reach of oppression.'—Morano walked about the room with quick steps and a disturbed air.

'This discourse, Count Morano, sufficiently proves that my affections ought not to be yours,' said Emily mildly ; 'and this conduct, that I should not be placed beyond the reach of oppression, so long as I remained in your power. If you wish me to believe otherwise, cease to oppress me by your presence. If you refuse this, you will compel me to expose you to the resentment of Signor Montoni.'

'Yes, let him come,' cried Morano furiously, 'and brave my resentment ! Let him dare to face once more the man he has so courageously injured ; danger shall teach him morality, and vengeance justice—let him come, and receive my sword in his heart.'

The vehemence with which this was uttered gave Emily new cause of alarm, but her trembling frame refused to support her, and she resumed her seat,—the words died on her lips, and when she looked wistfully towards the door of the corridor, which was locked, she considered it was impossible for her to leave the apartment before Morano would be apprized of, and able to counteract her intention.

Without observing her agitation, he continued to pace the room in the utmost perturbation of spirits. His darkened countenance expressed all the rage of jealousy and revenge ; and a person who had seen his features under the smile of ineffable tenderness, which he so lately assumed, would now scarcely have believed them to be the same.

'Count Morano,' said Emily, at length recovering her voice, 'calm, I entreat you, these transports, and listen to reason, if you will not to pity. You have equally misplaced your love and your hatred. I never could have returned the affection with which you honour me, and certainly have never encouraged it; neither has Signor Montoni injured you, for you must have known that he had no right to dispose of my hand, had he even possessed the power to do so. Leave, then, leave the castle, while you may with safety. Spare yourself the dreadful consequences of an unjust revenge, and the remorse of having prolonged to me these moments of sufferings.'

'Is it for mine or for Montoni's safety that you are thus alarmed?' said Morano coldly, and turning towards her with a look of acrimony.

'For both,' replied Emily in a trembling voice.

'Unjust revenge!' cried the count, resuming the abrupt tones of passion. 'Who, that looks upon that face, can imagine a punishment adequate to the injury he would have done me? Yes, I will leave the castle; but it shall not be alone. I have trifled too long. Since my prayers and my sufferings cannot prevail, force shall. I have people in waiting who shall convey you to my carriage. Your voice will bring no succour; it cannot be heard from this remote part of the castle; submit therefore, in silence, to go with me.'

This was an unnecessary injunction at present; for Emily was too certain that her call would avail her nothing; and terror had so entirely disordered her thoughts, that she knew not how to plead to Morano but sat mute and trembling in the chair, till he advanced to lift her from it; when she suddenly raised herself, and, with a repulsive gesture, and a countenance of forced serenity, said: 'Count Morano, I am now in your power; but you will observe, that this is not the conduct which can win the esteem you appear so solicitous to obtain, and that you are preparing for yourself a load of remorse, in the miseries of a friendless orphan, which can never leave you. Do you believe your heart to be, indeed, so hardened, that you can look without emotion on the suffering to which you would condemn me?—'

Emily was interrupted by the growling of the dog, who now came again from the bed; and Morano looked towards the door of the staircase, where no person appearing, he called aloud, 'Cesario!'

'Emily,' said the count, 'why will you reduce me to adopt this conduct? How much more willingly would I persuade, than compel you to become my wife! but, by heaven! I will not leave you to be sold by Montoni. Yet a thought glances across my mind that brings madness with it. I know not how to name it. It is preposterous—it cannot be.— Yet you tremble—you grow pale! It is! it is so;—you—you—love Montoni!' cried Morano, grasping Emily's wrist, and stamping his foot on the floor.

An involuntary air of surprise appeared on her countenance. 'If you have indeed believed so,' said she, 'believe so still.'

'That look, those words confirm it,' exclaimed Morano furiously. 'No, no, no,

Montoni had a richer prize in view than gold. But he shall not live to triumph over me!— This very instant——'

He was interrupted by the loud barking of the dog.

'Stay, Count Morano,' said Emily, terrified by his words and by the fury expressed in his eyes, 'I will save you from this error.—Of all men, Signor Montoni is not your rival; though, if I find all other means of saving myself vain, I will try whether my voice may not arouse his servants to my succour.'

'Assertion,' replied Morano, 'at such a moment is not to be depended upon. How could I suffer myself to doubt, even for an instant, that he could see you, and not love?— But my first care shall be to convey you from the castle. Cesario! ho,—Cesario!'

A man now appeared at the door of the staircase, and other steps were heard ascending. Emily uttered a loud shriek, as Morano hurried her across the chamber, and at the same moment she heard a noise at the door that opened upon the corridor. The count paused an instant, as if his mind was suspended between love and the desire of vengeance; and in that instant the door gave way, and Montoni, followed by the old steward and several other persons, burst into the room.

'Draw!' cried Montoni to the count; who did not pause for a second bidding, but, giving Emily into the hands of the people that appeared from the staircase, turned fiercely round.

'This in thine heart, villain!' said he, as he made a thrust at Montoni with his sword, who parried the blow, and aimed another; while some of the persons who had followed him into the room endeavoured to part the combatants, and others rescued Emily from the hands of Morano's servants.

'Was it for this, Count Morano,' said Montoni, in a cool sarcastic tone of voice, 'that I received you under my roof, and permitted you, though my declared enemy, to remain under it for the night? Was it that you might repay my hospitality with the treachery of a fiend, and rob me of my niece?'

'Who talks of treachery?' said Morano in a tone of unrestrained vehemence; 'let him that does, show an unblushing face of innocence. Montoni, you are a villain! If there is treachery in this affair, look to yourself as the author of it. If—do I say? I—whom you have wronged with unexampled baseness, whom you have injured almost beyond redress! But why do I use words? Come on, coward, and receive justice at my hands!'

'Coward!' cried Montoni, bursting from the people who held him, and rushing on the count; when they both retreated into the corridor, where the fight continued so desperately, that none of the spectators dared approach them, Montoni swearing that the first who interfered should fall by his sword.

Jealousy and revenge lent all their fury to Morano, while the superior skill and the temperance of Montoni enabled him to wound his adversary, whom his servants now attempted to seize; but he would not be restrained, and, regardless of his wound, continued to fight. He seemed to be insensible both of pain and loss of blood, and alive only to the energy of his passions. Montoni, on the contrary, persevered in the combat with a fierce yet wary valour; he received the point of Morano's sword on his arm; but, almost in the same instant, severely wounded and disarmed him. The count then fell back into the arms of his servant, while Montoni held his sword over him, and bade him ask his life. Morano, sinking under the anguish of his wound, had scarcely replied by a gesture, and by a few words feebly articulated, that he would not—when he fainted; and Montoni was then going to have plunged the sword into his breast as he lay senseless, but his arm was arrested by Cavigni. To the interruption he yielded without much difficulty; but his complexion changed almost to blackness as he looked upon his fallen adversary, and ordered that he should be carried instantly from the castle.

In the meantime Emily, who had been withheld from leaving the chamber during the affray, now came forward into the corridor, and pleaded a cause of common humanity with the feelings of the warmest benevolence, when she entreated Montoni to allow Morano the assistance in the castle which his situation required. But Montoni, who had seldom listened to pity, now seemed rapacious of vengeance, and, with a monster's cruelty, again ordered his defeated enemy to be taken from the castle in his present state, though there were only the woods or a solitary neighbouring cottage to shelter him from the night.

The count's servants having declared that they would not move him till he revived, Montoni stood inactive, Cavigni remonstrating, and Emily, superior to Montoni's menaces, giving water to Morano, and directing the attendants to bind up his wound. At length Montoni had leisure to feel pain from his own hurt, and he withdrew to examine it.

The count, meanwhile, having slowly recovered, the first object that he saw on raising his eyes was Emily bending over him with a countenance strongly expressive of solicitude. He surveyed her with a look of anguish.

'I have deserved this,' said he, 'but not from Montoni. It is from you, Emily, that I have deserved punishment, yet I receive only pity!' He paused, for he had spoken with difficulty. After a moment he proceeded: 'I must resign you, but not to Montoni. Forgive me the sufferings I have already occasioned you! But for that villain—his infamy shall not go unpunished. Carry me from this place,' said he to his servants. 'I am in no condition to travel: you must, therefore, take me to the nearest cottage; for I will not pass the night under his roof, although I may expire on the way from it.'

Cesario proposed to go out and inquire for a cottage that might receive his master before he attempted to remove him: but Morano was impatient to be gone; the anguish of his mind seemed to be even greater than that of his wound; and he rejected with disdain the offer of Cavigni to entreat Montoni that he might be suffered to pass the night in the castle. Cesario was now going to call up the carriage to the great gate, but the count forbade him. 'I cannot bear the motion of a carriage,' said he; 'call some others of my people, that they may assist in bearing me in their arms.'

At length, however, Morano submitted to reason, and consented that Cesario should first prepare some cottage to receive him. Emily, now that he had recovered his senses, was about to withdraw from the corridor, when a message from Montoni commanded her to do so, and also that the count, if he was not already gone, should quit the castle immediately. Indignation flashed from Morano's eyes, and flushed his cheeks.

'Tell Montoni,' said he, 'that I shall go when it suits my own convenience; that I quit the castle he dares to call his, as I would the nest of a serpent, and that this is not the last he shall hear from me. Tell him, I will not leave *another* murder on his conscience if I can help it.'

'Count Morano! do you know what you say?' said Cavigni.

'Yes, Signor, I know well what I say, and he will understand well what I mean. His conscience will assist his understanding on this occasion.'

'Count Morano,' said Verezzi, who had hitherto silently observed him, 'dare again to insult my friend, and I will plunge this sword in your body.'

'It would be an action worthy the friend of a villain!' said Morano, as the strong impulse of his indignation enabled him to raise himself from the arms of his servants; but the energy was momentary, and he sunk back exhausted by the effort.—Montoni's people meanwhile held Verezzi, who seemed inclined even in this instant to execute his threats; and Cavigni, who was not so depraved as to abet the cowardly malignity of Verezzi, endeavoured to withdraw him from the corridor; and Emily, whom a compassionate interest had thus long detained, was now quitting it in new terror, when the supplicating voice of Morano arrested her, and by a feeble gesture he beckoned her to draw nearer. She advanced with timid steps, but the fainting languor of his countenance again awakened her pity and overcame her terror.

'I am going from hence for ever,' said he : 'perhaps I shall never see you again. I would carry with me your forgiveness, Emily ; nay more—I would also carry your good wishes.'

'You have my forgiveness then,' said Emily, 'and my sincere wishes for your recovery.'

'And only for my recovery ?' said Morano with a sigh.

'For your general welfare,' added Emily.

'Perhaps I ought to be contented with this,' he resumed : 'I certainly have not deserved more ; but I would ask you, Emily, sometimes to think of me, and, forgetting my offence, to remember only the passion which occasioned it. I would ask, alas ! impossibilities : I would ask you to love me ! At this moment, when I am about to part with you, and that perhaps for ever, I am scarcely myself. Emily—may you never know the torture of a passion like mine ! What do I say ? O that for me you might be sensible of such a passion !'

Emily looked impatient to be gone. 'I entreat you, count, to consult your own safety,' said she, 'and linger here no longer. I tremble for the consequences of Signor Verezzi's passion, and of Montoni's resentment should he learn that you are still here.'

Morano's face was overspread with a momentary crimson, his eyes sparkled, but he seemed endeavouring to conquer his emotion, and replied in a calm voice, 'Since you are interested for my safety, I will regard it, and be gone. But, before I go, let me again hear you say that you wish me well,' said he, fixing on her an earnest and mournful look.

Emily repeated her assurances. He took her hand, which she scarcely attempted to withdraw, and put it to his lips. 'Farewell, Count Morano !' said Emily ; and she turned to go, when a second message arrived from Montoni, and she again conjured Morano, as he valued his life, to quit the castle immediately. He regarded her in silence, with a look of fixed despair. But she had no time to enforce her compassionate entreaties, and, not daring to disobey the second command of Montoni, she left the corridor to attend him.

He was in the cedar parlour that adjoined the great hall, laid upon a couch, and suffering a degree of anguish from his wound, which few persons could have disguised as he did. His countenance, which was stern, but calm, expressed the dark passion of revenge, but no symptom of pain ; bodily pain, indeed, he had always despised, and had yielded only to the strong and terrible energies of the soul. He was attended by old Carlo, and by Signor Bertolini, but Madame Montoni was not with him.

Emily trembled as she approached and received his severe rebuke, for not having obeyed his first summons ; and perceived, also, that he attributed her stay in the corridor to a motive that had not even occurred to her artless mind.

'This is an instance of female caprice,' said he, 'which I ought to have foreseen. Count Morano, whose suit you obstinately rejected so long as it was countenanced by me, you favour, it seems, since you find I have dismissed him.'

Emily looked astonished. 'I do not comprehend you, sir,' said she, 'you certainly do not mean to imply, that the design of the count to visit the double chamber was founded upon any approbation of mine.'

'To that I reply nothing,' said Montoni ; 'but it must certainly be a more than common interest that made you plead so warmly in his cause, and that could detain you thus long in his presence, contrary to my express order —in the presence of a man whom you have hitherto on all occasions most scrupulously shunned.'

'I fear, sir, it was more than common interest that detained me,' said Emily calmly ; 'for of late I have been inclined to think that of compassion is an uncommon one. But how could I, could *you*, sir, witness Count Morano's deplorable condition, and not wish to relieve it ?'

'You add hypocrisy to caprice,' said Montoni frowning, 'and an attempt at satire to both ; 'but before you undertake to regulate the morals of other persons, you should learn and practise the virtues which are indispensable to a woman—sincerity, uniformity of conduct and obedience.'

Emily, who had always endeavoured to regulate her conduct by the nicest laws, and whose mind was finely sensible not only of what is just in morals but of whatever is beautiful in the female character, was shocked by these words ; yet in the next moment her heart swelled with the consciousness of having deserved praise instead of censure, and she was proudly silent. Montoni, acquainted with the delicacy of her mind, knew how keenly she would feel his rebuke ; but he was a stranger to the luxury of conscious worth, and therefore did not foresee the energy of that sentiment which now repelled his satire. Turning to a servant who had lately entered the room, he asked whether Morano had quitted the castle. The man answered that his servants were then removing him on a couch to a neighbouring cottage. Montoni seemed somewhat appeased on hearing this ; and when Ludovico appeared a few moments after, and said that Morano was gone, he told Emily she might retire to her apartment.

She withdrew willingly from his presence ; but the thought of passing the remainder of the night in a chamber which the door from the staircase made liable to the intrusion of any person, now alarmed her more than ever ; and she determined to call at Madame Montoni's room, and request that Annette might be permitted to be with her.

On reaching the great gallery, she heard voices seemingly in dispute ; and her spirits now apt to take alarm, she paused, but soon distinguished some words of Cavigni and Verezzi, and went towards them in the hope of conciliating their difference. They were alone. Verezzi's face was still flushed with rage ; and as the first object of it was now removed from him, he appeared willing to transfer his resentment to Cavigni, who seemed to be expostulating rather than disputing with him.

Verezzi was protesting that he would instantly inform Montoni of the insult which Morano had thrown out against him, and above all, that wherein he had accused him of murder.

'There is no answering,' said Cavigni, ' for the words of a man in a passion ; little serious regard ought to be paid to them. If you persist in your resolution, the consequences may be fatal to both. We have now more serious interests to pursue than those of a petty revenge.'

Emily joined her entreaties to Cavigni's arguments, and they at length prevailed so far, as that Verezzi consented to retire without seeing Montoni.

On calling at her aunt's apartment, she found it fastened. In a few minutes, however, it was opened by Madame Montoni herself.

It may be remembered, that it was by a door leading into the bed-room from a back passage that Emily had secretly entered a few hours preceding. She now conjectured, by the calmness of Madame Montoni's air, that she was not apprized of the accident which had befallen her husband, and was beginning to inform her of it in the tenderest manner she could, when her aunt interrupted her by saying ' she was acquainted with the whole affair.'

Emily knew, indeed, that she had little reason to love Montoni, but could scarcely have believed her capable of such perfect apathy as she now discovered towards him : having obtained permission, however, for Annette to sleep in her chamber, she went thither immediately.

A track of blood appeared along the corridor leading to it : and on the spot where the count and Montoni had fought the whole floor was stained. Emily shuddered, and leaned on Annette as she passed. When she reached her apartment, she instantly determined, since the door of the staircase had been left open, and that Annette was now with her, to explore whither it led,—a circumstance now materially connected with her own safety. Annette accordingly, half curious and half afraid, proposed to descend the stairs ; but on approaching the door they perceived that it

was already fastened without ; and their care was then directed to the securing it on the inside also, by placing against it as much of the heavy furniture of the room as they could lift. Emily then retired to bed, and Annette continued on a chair by the hearth, where some feeble embers remained.

CHAPTER XXI.

' Of aery tongues, that syllable men's names
On sands and shores and desert wildernesses.'
                                              MILTON.

IT is now necessary to mention some circumstances which could not be related amidst the events of Emily's hasty departure from Venice, or together with those which so rapidly succeeded to her arrival in the castle.

On the morning of her journey, Count Morano had gone at the appointed hour to the mansion of Montoni to demand his bride. When he reached it, he was somewhat surprised by the silence and solitary air of the portico where Montoni's lacqueys usually loitered ; but surprise was soon changed to astonishment, and astonishment to the rage of disappointment, when the door was opened by an old woman, who told his servants that her master and his family had left Venice, early in the morning, for *Terra-firma*. Scarcely believing what his servants told, he left his gondola, and rushed into the hall to inquire further. The old woman, who was the only person left in care of the mansion, persisted in her story, which the silent and deserted apartments soon convinced him was no fiction. He then seized her with a menacing air, as if he meant to wreak all his vengeance upon her, at the same time asking her twenty questions in a breath, and all these with a gesticulation so furious that she was deprived of the power of answering them ; then suddenly letting her go, he stamped about the hall like a madman, cursing Montoni and his own folly.

When the good woman was at liberty, and had somewhat recovered from her fright, she told him all she knew of the affair, which was indeed very little, but enough to enable Morano to discover that Montoni was gone to his castle on the Apennine. Thither he followed, as soon as his servants could complete the necessary preparation for the journey, accompanied by a friend, and attended by a number of his people, determined to obtain Emily or a full revenge on Montoni. When his mind had recovered from the first effervescence of rage, and his thoughts became less obscured, his conscience hinted to him certain circumstances which in some measure explained the conduct of Montoni ; but how the latter could have been led to suspect an intention which he had believed was known only to himself, he could not even guess. On this occasion, however, he had been partly betrayed by that sympathetic intelligence which may be said to exist between bad minds, and which teaches one man to judge what another will do in the same circumstances. Thus it was with Montoni, who had now received indisputable proof of a truth which he had some time suspected—that Morano's circumstances, instead of being affluent, as he had been bidden to believe, were greatly involved. Montoni had been interested in his suit by motives entirely selfish, those of avarice and pride ; the last of which would have been gratified by an alliance with a Venetian nobleman, the former by Emily's estate in Gascony, which he had stipulated, as the price of his favour, should be delivered up to him from the day of her marriage. In the mean time he had been led to suspect the consequence of the count's boundless extravagance ; but it was not till the evening preceding the intended nuptials that he obtained certain information of his distressed circumstances. He did not hesitate then to infer that Morano designed to defraud him of Emily's estate ; and·in this supposition he was confirmed, and with apparent reason, by the subsequent conduct of the count, who, after having appointed to meet on that night for the purpose of signing the instrument which was to secure to him his reward, failed in his engagement. Such a circumstance, indeed, in a man of Morano's gay and thoughtless character, and at a time when his mind was engaged by the bustle of preparation for his nuptials, might have been attributed to a cause less decisive than design : but Montoni did not hesitate an instant to interpret it his own way ; and after vainly waiting the count's arrival for several hours, he gave orders for his people to be in readiness to set off at a moment's notice. By hastening to Udolpho he intended to remove Emily from the reach of Morano, as well as to break off the affair without submitting himself to useless altercation : and if the count meant what he called honourably, he would doubtless follow Emily and sign the writings in question. If this was done, so little consideration had Montoni for her welfare, that he would not have scrupled to sacrifice her to a man of ruined fortune, since by that means he could enrich himself ; and he forbore to mention to her the motive of his sudden journey, lest the hope it might revive should render her more intractable when submission would be required.

With these considerations he had left Venice ; and with others totally different, Morano had soon after pursued his steps across the rugged Apennines. When his arrival was announced at the castle, Montoni did not believe that he would have presumed to show himself, unless he had meant to fulfil his engagement, and he therefore readily admitted him ; but the enraged countenance and expressions of Morano as he entered the apartment, instantly undeceived him ; and when Montoni had explained in part the motives of his abrupt departure from Venice, the count still persisted in demanding Emily and reproaching Montoni, without even naming the former stipulation.

Montoni, at length weary of the dispute, deferred the settling of it till the morrow, and Morano retired with some hope suggested by Montoni's apparent indecision. When, however, in the silence of his own apartment, he began to consider the past conversation, the character of Montoni, and some former instances of his duplicity, the hope which he had admitted vanished, and he determined ·not to neglect the present possibility of obtaining Emily by other means. To his confidential valet he told his design of carrying away Emily, and sent him back to Montoni's servants to find out one among them who might enable him to execute it. The choice of this person he intrusted to the fellow's own discernment, and not imprudently ; for he discovered a man whom Montoni had on some former occasion treated harshly, and who was now ready to betray him. This man conducted Cesario round the castle, through a private passage, to the staircase that led to Emily's chamber ; then showed him a short way out of the building, and afterwards procured him the keys that would secure his retreat. The man was well rewarded for his trouble : how the count was rewarded for his treachery has already appeared.

Meanwhile old Carlo had overheard two of Morano's servants, who had been ordered to be in waiting with the carriage beyond the castle walls, expressing their surprise at their master's sudden and secret departure, for the valet had entrusted them with no more of Morano's designs than it was necessary for them to execute. They, however, indulged themselves in surmises, and in expressing them to each other ; and from these Carlo had drawn a just conclusion. But before he ventured to disclose his apprehensions to Montoni, he endeavoured to obtain further confirmation of them, and for this purpose placed himself, with one of his fellow-servants, at the door of Emily's apartment that opened upon the corridor. He did not watch long in vain, though the growling of the dog had once nearly betrayed him. When he was convinced that Morano was in the room, and had listened long enough to his conversation to understand his scheme, he immediately alarmed Montoni, and thus rescued Emily from the designs of the count.

Montoni on the following morning appeared as usual, except that he wore his wounded arm in a sling ; he went out upon the ramparts, overlooked the men employed in repairing them, gave orders for additional work-

5—2

men, and then came into the castle to give audience to several persons who were just arrived, and who were shown into a private apartment, where he communicated with them for near an hour. Carlo was then summoned, and ordered to conduct the strangers to a part of the castle which in former times had been occupied by the upper servants of the family, and to provide them with every necessary refreshment. When he had done this, he was bidden to return to his master.

Meanwhile the count remained in a cottage in the skirts of the woods below, suffering under bodily and mental pain, and meditating deep revenge against Montoni. His servant, whom he had dispatched for a surgeon to the nearest town, which was, however, at a considerable distance, did not return till the following day; when, his wounds being examined and dressed, the practitioner refused to deliver any positive opinion concerning the degree of danger attending them ; but giving his patient a composing draught, and ordering him to be kept quiet, he remained at the cottage to watch the event.

Emily for the remainder of the late eventful night had been suffered to sleep undisturbed ; and when her mind recovered from the confusion of slumber, and she remembered that she was now released from the addresses of Count Morano, her spirits were suddenly relieved from a part of the terrible anxiety that had long oppressed them : that which remained arose chiefly from a recollection of Morano's assertions concerning the schemes of Montoni. He had said that the plans of the latter concerning Emily were unsearchable, yet that he knew them to be terrible. At the time he uttered this, she almost believed it to be designed for the purpose of prevailing with her to throw herself into his protection, and she still thought it might be chiefly so accounted for : but his assertions had left an impression on her mind, which a consideration of the character and former conduct of Montoni did not contribute to efface. She however checked her propensity to anticipate evil ; and, determined to enjoy this respite from actual misfortune, tried to dismiss thought, took her instruments for drawing, and placed herself at a window to select into a landscape some features of the scenery without.

As she was thus employed, she saw walking on the rampart below the men who had so lately arrived at the castle. The sight of strangers surprised her, but still more of strangers such as these. There was a singularity in their dress, and a certain fierceness in their air, that fixed all her attention. She withdrew from the casement while they passed, but soon returned to observe them further. Their figures seemed so well suited to the wildness of the surrounding objects, that, as they stood surveying the castle, she sketched

them for banditti amid the mountain-view of her picture ; when she had finished which, she was surprised to observe the spirit of her group. But she had copied from nature.

Carlo, when he had placed refreshment before these men in the apartment assigned to them, returned, as he was ordered, to Montoni, who was anxious to discover by what servant the keys of the castle had been delivered to Morano on the preceding night. But this man, though he was too faithful to his master to see him quietly injured, would not betray a fellow-servant even to justice ; he therefore pretended to be ignorant who it was that had conspired with Count Morano, and related, as before, that he had only overheard some of the strangers describing the plot.

Montoni's suspicions naturally fell upon the porter, whom he ordered now to attend. Carlo hesitated, and then with slow steps went to seek him.

Barnardine, the porter, denied the accusation with a countenance so steady and undaunted, that Montoni could scarcely believe him guilty, though he knew not how to think him innocent. At length the man was dismissed from his presence, and, though the real offender, escaped detection.

Montoni then went to his wife's apartment, whither Emily followed soon after ; but, finding them in high dispute, was instantly leaving the room, when her aunt called her back, and desired her to stay.—' You shall be a witness,' said she, ' of my opposition. Now, sir, repeat the command I have so often refused to obey.'

Montoni turned with a stern countenance to Emily, and bade her quit the apartment, while his wife persisted in desiring that she would stay. Emily was eager to escape from this scene of contention, and anxious also to serve her aunt ; but she despaired of conciliating Montoni, in whose eyes the rising tempest of his soul flashed terribly.

' Leave the room,' said he in a voice of thunder. Emily obeyed ; and walking down to the rampart which the strangers had now left, continued to meditate on the unhappy marriage of her father's sister, and on her own desolate situation, occasioned by the ridiculous imprudence of her whom she had always wished to respect and love. Madame Montoni's conduct had, indeed, rendered it impossible for Emily to do either ; but her gentle heart was touched by her distress, and in the pity thus awakened she forgot the injurious treatment she had received from her.

As she sauntered on the rampart, Annette appeared at the hall door, looked cautiously round, and then advanced to meet her.

' Dear Ma'amselle, I have been looking for you all over the castle,' said she. ' If you will step this way I will show you a picture.'

'A picture!' exclaimed Emily, and shuddered.

'Yes, ma'am, a picture of the late lady of this place. Old Carlo just now told me it was her, and I thought you would be curious to see it. As to my lady, you know, ma'amselle, one cannot talk about such things to her.'

'And so,' said Emily smilingly, 'as you must talk of them to somebody—'

'Why, yes, ma'amselle; what can one do in such a place as this if one must not talk? If I was in a dungeon, if they would let me talk—it would be some comfort; nay, I would talk, if it was only to the walls. But come, ma'amselle, we lose time—let me show you the picture.'

'Is it veiled?' said Emily, pausing.

'Dear ma'amselle!' said Annette, fixing her eyes on Emily's face, 'what makes you look so pale?—are you ill?'

'No, Annette, I am well enough, but I have no desire to see this picture. Return into the hall.'

'What, ma'am, not to see the lady of this castle?' said the girl; 'the lady who disappeared so strangely? Well! now, I would have run to the furthest mountain we can see, yonder, to have got a sight of such a picture; and, to speak my mind, that strange story is all that makes me care about this old castle, though it makes me thrill all over, as it were, whenever I think of it.'

'Yes, Annette, you love the wonderful; but do you know that, unless you guard against this inclination, it will lead you into all the misery of superstition?'

Annette might have smiled, in her turn, at this sage observation of Emily, who could tremble with ideal terrors as much as herself, and listen almost as eagerly to the recital of a mysterious story. Annette urged her request.

'Are you sure it is a picture?' said Emily. 'Have you seen it?—Is it veiled?'

'Holy Maria! ma'amselle, yes, no, yes. I am sure it is a picture—I have seen it, and it is not veiled.'

The tone and look of surprise with which this was uttered, recalled Emily's prudence; who concealed her emotion under a smile, and bade Annette lead her to the picture. It was in an obscure chamber adjoining that part of the castle allotted to the servants. Several other portraits hung on the walls, covered like this with dust and cob-web.

'That is it, ma'amselle,' said Annette in a low voice, and pointing. Emily advanced and surveyed the picture. It represented a lady in the flower of youth and beauty; her features were handsome and noble, full of strong expression, but had little of the captivating sweetness that Emily had looked for, and still less of the pensive mildness she loved. It was a countenance which spoke the language of passion rather than that of sentiment; a haughty impatience of misfortune—not the placid melancholy of a spirit injured, yet resigned.

'How many years have passed since this lady disappeared, Annette?' said Emily.

'Twenty years, ma'amselle, or thereabout, as they tell me; I know it is a long while ago.' Emily continued to gaze upon the portrait.

'I think,' resumed Annette, 'the signor would do well to hang it in a better place than this old chamber. Now, in my mind, he ought to place the picture of a lady who gave him all these riches, in the handsomest room in the castle. But he may have good reasons for what he does: and some people do say that he has lost his riches as well as his gratitude. But hush, ma'am, not a word!' added Annette, laying her finger on her lips.—Emily was too much absorbed in thought to hear what she said.

''Tis a handsome lady, I am sure,' continued Annette: 'the signor need not be ashamed to put her in the great apartment, where the veiled picture hangs.' Emily turned round. 'But for that matter, she would be as little seen there as here, for the door is always locked, I find.'

'Let us leave the chamber,' said Emily: 'and let me caution you again, Annette; be guarded in your conversation, and never tell that you know anything of that picture.'

'Holy Mother!' exclaimed Annette, 'it is no secret; why all the servants have seen it already!'

Emily started. 'How is this?' said she— 'Have seen it! When?—how?'

'Dear ma'amselle, there is nothing surprising in that; we had all a little more *curiousness* than you had.'

'I thought you told me the door was kept locked?' said Emily.

'If that is the case, ma'amselle,' replied Annette, looking about her, 'how could we get here?'

'O, you mean *this* picture,' said Emily with returning calmness. 'Well, Annette, here is nothing more to engage my attention; we will go.'

Emily, as she passed to her own apartment, saw Montoni go down to the hall, and she turned into her aunt's dressing-room, whom she found weeping and alone, grief and resentment struggling on her countenance. Pride had hitherto restrained complaint. Judging of Emily's disposition from her own, and from a consciousness of what her treatment of her deserved, she had believed that her griefs would be cause of triumph to her niece, rather than of sympathy; that she would despise, not pity her. But she knew not the tenderness and benevolence of Emily's heart, that had always taught her to forget her own injuries in the misfortunes of her enemy. The sufferings of others, whoever they might be, called forth her ready compassion, which dissipated at once every obscuring cloud to goodness, that passion or prejudice might have raised in her mind.

Madame Montoni's sufferings at length rose above her pride ; and when Emily had before entered the room, she would have told them all, had not her husband prevented her : now that she was no longer restrained by his presence, she poured forth all her complaints to her niece.

' O Emily !' she exclaimed, ' I am the most wretched of women—I am indeed cruelly treated ! Who, with my prospects of happiness, could have foreseen such a wretched fate as this?—who could have thought, when I married such a man as the signor, that I should ever have to bewail my lot ? But there is no judging what is for the best—there is no knowing what is for our good ! The most flattering prospects often change—the best judgments may be deceived—who could have foreseen, when I married the signor, that I should ever repent my *generosity ?*'

Emily thought she might have foreseen it, but this was not a thought of triumph. She placed herself in a chair near her aunt, took her hand, and with one of those looks of soft compassion which might characterise the countenance of a guardian angel, spoke to her in the tenderest accents. But these did not soothe Madame Montoni, whom impatience to talk made unwilling to listen. She wanted to complain, not to be consoled ; and it was by exclamations of complaint only that Emily learned the particular circumstances of her affliction.

' Ungrateful man !' said Madame Montoni, 'he has deceived me in every. respect ; and now he has taken me from my country and friends, to shut me up in this old castle ; and here he thinks he can compel me to do whatever he designs ! But he shall find himself mistaken, he shall find that no threats can alter——But who would have believed, who would have supposed, that a man of his family and apparent wealth had absolutely no-fortune ?—no, scarcely a sequin of his own ! I did all for the best ; I thought he was a man of consequence, of great property, or I am sure I would never have married him,— ungrateful, artful man ! She paused to take breath.'

' Dear madam, be composed,' said Emily : ' the signor may not be so rich as you had reason to expect ; but surely he cannot be very poor, since this castle and the mansion at Venice are his. May I ask what are the circumstances that particularly affect you ?'

' What are the circumstances !' exclaimed Madame Montoni with resentment : ' why, is it not sufficient that he had long ago ruined his own fortune by play, and that he has since lost what I brought him—and that now

he would compel me to sign away my settlement (it was well I had the chief of my property settled on myself!) that he may lose this also, or throw it away in wild schemes which nobody can understand but himself? And, and——is not all this sufficient ?'

' It is indeed,' said Emily ; ' but you must recollect, dear madam, that I knew nothing of all this.'

' Well ; and is it not sufficient,' rejoined her aunt, 'that he is also absolutely ruined, that he is sunk deeply in debt, and that neither this castle nor the mansion at Venice is his own, if all his debts, honourable and dishonourable, were paid.'

' I am shocked by what you tell me, madam,' said Emily.

' And is it not enough,' interrupted Madame Montoni, ' that he has treated me with neglect, with cruelty, because I refused to relinquish my settlements, and, instead of being frightened at his menaces, resolutely defied him, and upbraided him with his shameful conduct ? But I bore all meekly,—you know, niece, I never uttered a word of complaint till now ; no ! That such a disposition as mine should be so imposed upon ! That I, whose only faults are too much kindness, too much generosity, should be chained for life to such a vile, deceitful, cruel monster ! '

Want of breath compelled Madame Montoni to stop. If any such thing could have made Emily smile in these moments, it would have been this speech of her aunt, delivered in a voice very little below a scream, and with a vehemence of gesticulation of countenance that turned the whole into burlesque. Emily saw that her misfortunes did not admit of real consolation, and contemning the commonplace terms of superficial comfort, she was silent ; while Madame Montoni; jealous of her own consequence, mistook this for the silence of indifference or of contempt, and reproached her with a want of duty and feeling.

' O ! I suspected what all this boasted sensibility would prove to be,' rejoined she ; ' I thought it would not teach you to feel either duty or affection for your relations, who have treated you like their own daughter.'

' Pardon me madam,' said Emily mildly, ' it is not natural to me to boast, and if it was, I am sure I would not boast of sensibility—a quality, perhaps, more to be feared than desired.'

' Well, well, niece, I will not dispute with you. But, as I said, Montoni threatens me with violence, if I any longer refuse to sign away my settlements, and this was the subject of our contest when you came into the room before. Now I am determined no power on earth shall make me do this. Neither will I bear all this tamely.- He shall hear his true character from me ; I will tell him all he deserves, in spite of his threats and cruel treatment.'

Emily seized a pause of Madame Montoni's voice to speak. 'Dear madam,' said she, 'but will not this serve to irritate the signor unnecessarily? Will it not provoke the harsh treatment you dread?'

'I do not care,' replied Madame Montoni; 'it does not signify; I will not submit to such usage. You would have me give up my settlements, too, I suppose?'

'No, madam, I do not exactly mean that.'

'What is it you do mean, then?'

'You spoke of reproaching the signor,' said Emily with hesitation.

'Why, does he not deserve reproaches?' said her aunt.

'Certainly he does; but will it be prudent in you, madam, to make them?'

'Prudent!' replied Madame Montoni. 'Is this a time to talk of prudence, when one is threatened with all sorts of violence.'

'It is to avoid that violence that prudence is necessary,' said Emily.

'Of prudence!' continued Madame Montoni, without attending to her; 'of prudence towards a man who does not scruple to break all the common ties of humanity in his conduct to me! And is it for me to consider prudence in my behaviour towards him? I am not so mean.'

'It is for your own sake, not for the signor's, madam,' said Emily modestly, 'that you should consult prudence. Your reproaches, however just, cannot punish him; but they may provoke him to further violence against you.'

'What! would you have me submit then to whatever he commands—would you have me kneel down at his feet, and thank him for his cruelties? Would you have me give up my settlement?'

'How much you mistake me, madam!' said Emily; 'I am unequal to advise you on a point so important as the last: but you will pardon me for saying that, if you consult your own peace, you will try to conciliate Signor Montoni, rather than to irritate him by reproaches.'

'Conciliate, indeed! I tell you, niece, it is utterly impossible: I disdain to attempt it.'

Emily was shocked to observe the perverted understanding and obstinate temper of Madame Montoni; but not less grieved for her sufferings, she looked round for some alleviating circumstance to offer her. 'Your situation is perhaps not so desperate, dear madam,' said Emily, 'as you may imagine. The signor may represent his affairs to be worse than they are, for the purpose of pleading a stronger necessity for his possession of your settlement. Besides, so long as you keep this, you may look forward to it as a resource, at least, that will afford you a competence, should the signor's future conduct compel you to sue for separation.'

Madame Montoni impatiently interrupted her. 'Unfeeling, cruel girl!' said she; 'and

so you would persuade me that I have no reason to complain, that the signor is in very flourishing circumstances, that my future prospects promise nothing but comfort, and that my griefs are as fanciful and romantic as your own! Is it the way to console me to endeavour to persuade me out of my senses and my feelings, because you happen to have no feelings yourself? I thought I was opening my heart to a person who could sympathise in my distress, but I find that your people of sensibility can feel for nobody but themselves! You may retire to your chamber.'

Emily, without replying, immediately left the room, with a mingled emotion of pity and contempt, and hastened to her own, where she yielded to the mournful reflections which a knowledge of her aunt's situation had occasioned. The conversation of the Italian with Valancourt in France again occurred to her. His hints respecting the broken fortunes of Montoni were now completely justified: those also concerning his character appeared not less so, though the particular circumstances connected with his fame, to which the stranger had alluded, yet remained to be explained. Notwithstanding that her own observations, and the words of Count Morano, had convinced her that Montoni's situation was not what it formerly appeared to be, the intelligence she had just received from her aunt on this point struck her with all the force of astonishment, which was not weakened when she considered the present style of Montoni's living, the number of servants he maintained, and the new expenses he was incurring by repairing and fortifying his castle. Her anxiety for her aunt and for herself increased with reflection. Several assertions of Morano, which on the preceding night she had believed were prompted either by interest or by resentment, now returned to her mind with the strength of truth. She could not doubt that Montoni had formerly agreed to give her to the count for a pecuniary reward;—his character and his distressed circumstances justified the belief; these, also, seemed to confirm Morano's assertion, that he now designed to dispose of her, more advantageously for himself, to a richer suitor.

Amidst the reproaches which Morano had thrown out against Montoni, he had said—he would not quit the castle *he dared to call his*, nor willingly leave *another* murder on his conscience—hints which might have no other origin than the passion of the moment: but Emily was now inclined to account for them more seriously, and she shuddered to think that she was in the hands of a man to whom it was even possible they could apply. At length, considering that reflection could neither release her from her melancholy situation nor enable her to bear it with greater fortitude, she tried to divert her anxiety, and took down from her little library a volume of her favourite

Ariosto! But his wild imagery and rich invention could not long enchant her attention; his spells did not reach her heart, and over her sleeping fancy they played without awakening it.

She now put aside the book, and took her lute, for it was seldom that her sufferings refused to yield to the magic of sweet sounds; when they did so, she was oppressed by sorrow, that came from excess of tenderness and regret; and there were times when music had increased such sorrow to a degree that was scarcely endurable; when, if it had not suddenly ceased, she might have lost her reason. Such was the time when she mourned for her father, and heard the midnight strains that floated by her window, near the convent in Languedoc, on the night that followed his death.

She continued to play till Annette brought dinner into her chamber, at which Emily was surprised, and inquired whose order she obeyed. 'My lady's, ma'amselle,' replied Annette: 'the signor ordered her dinner to be carried to her own apartment, and so she has sent you yours. There have been sad doings between them, worse than ever, I think.'

Emily, not appearing to notice what she said, sat down to the little table that was spread for her. But Annette was not to be silenced thus easily. While she waited, she told of the arrival of the men whom Emily had observed on the ramparts, and expressed much surprise at their strange appearance, as well as at the manner in which they had been attended by Montoni's order. 'Do they dine with the signor, then?' said Emily.

'No, ma'amselle, they dined long ago in an apartment at the north end of the castle: but I know not when they are to go, for the signor told old Carlo to see them provided with every thing necessary. They have been walking all about the castle, and asking questions of the workmen on the ramparts. I never saw such strange-looking men in my life, I am frightened whenever I see them.'

Emily inquired if she had heard of Count Morano, and whether he was likely to recover: but Annette only knew that he was lodged in a cottage in the wood below, and that everybody said he must die. Emily's countenance discovered her emotion.

'Dear ma'amselle,' said Annette, 'to see how young ladies will disguise themselves when they are in love! I thought you hated the count, or I am sure I would not have told you; and I am sure you have cause enough to hate him.'

'I hope I hate nobody,' replied Emily, trying to smile; 'but certainly I do not love Count Morano: I should be shocked to hear of any person dying by violent means.'

'Yes, ma'amselle, but it is his own fault.'

Emily looked displeased; and Annette,

mistaking the cause of her displeasure, immediately began to excuse the count in her way. 'To be sure, it was very ungenteel behaviour,' said she, 'to break into a lady's room, and then, when he found his discoursing was not agreeable to her, to refuse to go; and then, when the gentleman of the castle comes to desire him to walk about his business—to turn round, and draw his sword, and swear he'll run him through the body! To be sure, it was very ungenteel behaviour; but then he was disguised in love, and so did not know what he was about.'

'Enough of this,' said Emily, who now smiled without an effort; and Annette returned to a mention of the disagreement between Montoni and her lady. 'It is nothing new,' said she: 'we saw and heard enough of this at Venice, though I never told you of it, ma'amselle.'

'Well, Annette, it was very prudent of you not to mention it then: be as prudent now; the subject is an unpleasant one.'

'Ah, dear ma'amselle!—to see now how considerate you can be about some folks, who care so little about you! I cannot bear to see you so deceived, and I must tell you. But it is all for your own good, and not to spite my lady, though, to speak truth, I have little reason to love her; but——'

'You are not speaking thus of my aunt, I hope, Annette?' said Emily gravely.

'Yes, ma'amselle, but I am though; and if you knew as much as I do, you would not look so angry. I have often and often heard the signor and her talking over your marriage with the count, and she always advised him never to give up to your foolish whims, as she was pleased to call them, but to be resolute, and compel you to be obedient, whether you would or not. And I am sure my heart has ached a thousand times; and I have thought, when she was so unhappy herself, she might have felt a little for other people, and——'

'I thank you for your pity, Annette,' said Emily, interrupting her: 'but my aunt was unhappy then, and that disturbed her temper perhaps, or I think—I am sure—You may take away, Annette, I have done.'

'Dear ma'amselle, you have eat nothing at all! Do try and take a little bit more. Disturbed her temper truly! why her temper is always disturbed, I think. And at Thoulouse I have heard my lady talking of you and M. Valancourt to Madame Merveille and Madame Vaison, often and often, in a very ill-natured way, as I thought, telling them what a deal of trouble she had to keep you in order, and what a fatigue and distress it was to her, and that she believed you would run away with M. Valancourt, if she was not to watch you closely; and that you connived at his coming about the house at night, and——'

'Good God!' exclaimed Emily, blushing

deeply, ' it is surely impossible my aunt could thus have represented me !'

'Indeed, ma'am, I say nothing more than the truth, and not all of that. But I thought, myself, she might have found something better to discourse about, than the faults of her own niece, even if you had been in fault, ma'amselle ! but I did not believe a word of what she said. But my lady does not care what she says against anybody, for that matter.'

' However that may be, Annette,' interrupted Emily recovering her composure, ' it does not become you to speak of the faults of my aunt to me. I know you have meant well, but say no more.—I have quite dined.'

Annette blushed, looked down, and then began slowly to clear the table.

' Is this, then, the reward of my ingenuousness ?' said Emily, when she was alone ; ' the treatment I am to receive from a relation—an aunt—who ought to have been the guardian, not the slanderer of my reputation,—who, as a woman, ought to have respected the delicacy of female honour, and, as a relation, should have protected mine ! But to utter falsehoods on so nice a subject—to repay the openness, and, I may say with honest pride, the propriety of my conduct, with slanders—required a depravity of heart such as I could scarcely have believed existed, such as I weep to find in a relation. O ! what a contrast does her character present to that of my beloved father ! while envy and low cunning form the chief traits of hers, his was distinguished by benevolence and philosophic wisdom ! But now let me only remember, if possible, that she is unfortunate.'

Emily threw her veil over her, and went down to walk upon the ramparts, the only walk, indeed, which was open to her, though she often wished that she might be permitted to ramble among the woods below, and still more, that she might sometimes explore the sublime scenes of the surrounding country. But as Montoni would not suffer her to pass the gates of the castle, she tried to be contented with the romantic views she beheld from the walls. The peasants, who had been employed on the fortifications, had left their work, and the ramparts were silent and solitary. Their lonely appearance, together with the gloom of a lowering sky, assisted the musings of her mind, and threw over it a kind of melancholy tranquillity, such as she often loved to indulge. She turned to observe a fine effect of the sun, as his rays, suddenly streaming from behind a heavy cloud, lighted up the west towers of the castle, while the rest of the edifice was in deep shade, except that, through a lofty Gothic arch adjoining the tower, which led to another terrace, the beams darted in full splendour, and showed the three strangers she had observed in the morning. Perceiving them, she started, and a momentary fear came over her as she looked up the long rampart and saw no other persons. While she hesitated, they approached. The gate at the end of the terrace, whither they were advancing, she knew was always locked, and she could not depart by the opposite extremity without meeting them ; but before she passed them, she hastily drew a thin veil over her face, which did indeed but ill conceal her beauty. They looked earnestly at her, and spoke to each other in bad Italian, of which she caught only a few words ; but the fierceness of their countenances, now that she was near enough to discriminate them, struck her yet more than the wild singularity of their air and dress had formerly done. It was the countenance and figure of him who walked between the other two that chiefly seized her attention, which expressed a sullen haughtiness and a kind of dark watchful villany, and gave a thrill of horror to her heart. All this was so legibly written on his features, as to be seen by a single glance ; for she passed the group swiftly, and her timid eyes scarcely rested on them a moment. Having reached the terrace, she stopped, and perceived the strangers standing in the shadow of one of the turrets, gazing after her, and seemingly, by their action, in earnest conversation. She immediately left the rampart, and retired to her apartment.

In the evening, Montoni sat late, carousing with his guests in the cedar chamber. His recent triumph over Count Morano, or, perhaps, some other circumstance, contributed to elevate his spirits to an unusual height. He filled the goblet often, and gave a loose to merriment and talk. The gaiety of Cavigni, on the contrary, was somewhat clouded by anxiety. He kept a watchful eye upon Verezzi, whom with the utmost difficulty he had hitherto restrained from exasperating Montoni against Morano, by a mention of his late taunting words.

One of the company exultingly recurred to the event of the preceding evening. Verezzi's eyes sparkled. The mention of Morano led to that of Emily, of whom they were all profuse in the praise, except Montoni, who sat silent, and then interrupted the subject.

When the servants had withdrawn, Montoni and his friends entered into close conversation, which was sometimes checked by the irascible temper of Verezzi, but in which Montoni displayed his conscious superiority, by that decisive look and manner which always accompanied the vigour of his thought, and to which most of his companions submitted, as to a power that they had no right to question, though of each other's self-importance they were jealously scrupulous. Amidst this conversation, one of them imprudently introduced again the name of Morano ; and Verezzi, now more heated by wine, disregarded the expressive looks of Cavigni, and gave some dark hints of what had passed on the preceding night. These, however, Montoni did not appear to understand, for he continued silent in his chair, without discovering any emotion, while the choler of Verezzi increasing with the apparent insensibility of Montoni, he at length told the suggestion of Morano, that this castle did not lawfully belong to him, and that he would not willingly leave another murder on his conscience.

'Am I to be insulted at my own table, and by my own friends?' said Montoni with a countenance pale in anger. 'Why are the words of that madman repeated to me?' Verezzi, who had expected to hear Montoni's indignation poured forth against Morano, and answered by thanks to himself, looked with astonishment at Cavigni, who enjoyed his confusion. 'Can you be weak enough to credit the assertions of a madman?' rejoined Montoni, 'or, what is the same thing, a man possessed by the spirit of vengeance? But he has succeeded too well; you believe what he said.'

'Signor,' said Verezzi, 'we believe only what we know.'—'How!' interrupted Montoni sternly : ' produce your proof.'

'We believe only what we know,' repeated Verezzi ; 'and we know nothing of what Morano asserts.' Montoni seemed to recover himself. 'I am hasty, my friends,' said he, 'with respect to my honour ; no man shall question it with impunity—you did not mean to question it. These foolish words are not worth your remembrance, or my resentment. Verezzi, here is to your first exploit.'

'Success to your first exploit,' re-echoed the whole company.

'Noble Signor,' replied Verezzi, glad to find he had escaped Montoni's resentment, 'with my good-will, you shall build your ramparts of gold.'

'Pass the goblet,' cried Montoni.—'We well drink to Signora St. Aubert,' said Cavigni. —'By your leave we will first drink to the lady of the castle,' said Bertolini.—Montoni was silent. 'To the lady of the castle,' said his guests. He bowed his head.

'It much surprises me, signor,' said Bertolini, 'that you have so long neglected this castle ; it is a noble edifice.'

'It suits our purpose,' replied Montoni, 'and *is* a noble edifice. You know not, it seems, by what mischance it came to me.'

'It was a lucky mischance, be it what it may, signor,' replied Bertolini smiling ; 'I would that one so lucky had befallen me.'

Montoni looked gravely at him. 'If you will attend to what I say,' he resumed, 'you shall hear the story.'

The countenances of Bertolini and Verezzi expressed something more than curiosity ; Cavigni, who seemed to feel none, had probably heard the relation before.

'It is now near twenty years,' said Montoni,

'since this castle came into my possession. I inherit it by the female line. The lady, my predecessor, was only distantly related to me ; I am the last of her family. She was beautiful and rich : I wooed her ; but her heart was fixed upon another, and she rejected me. It is probable, however, that she was herself rejected of the person, whoever he might be, on whom she bestowed her favour, for a deep and settled melancholy took possession of her ; and I have reason to believe she put a period to her own life. I was not at the castle at the time ; but as there are some singular and mysterious circumstances attending that event, I shall repeat them.'

'Repeat them!' said a voice.

Montoni was silent ; the guests looked at each other, to know who spoke : but they perceived that each was making the same inquiry. Montoni at length recovering himself, 'We are overheard,' said he ; 'we will finish this subject another time. Pass the goblet.'

The cavaliers looked round the wide chamber.

'Here is no person but ourselves,' said Verezzi : ' pray, signor, proceed.'

'Did you hear anything?' said Montoni.

'We did,' said Bertolini.

'It could be only fancy,' said Verezzi, looking round again. ' We see no person besides ourselves ; and the sound I thought I heard seemed within the room. Pray, signor, go on.'

Montoni paused a moment and then proceeded in a lowered voice, while the cavaliers drew nearer to attend.

'Ye are to know, signors, that the Lady Laurentini had for some months shown symptoms of a dejected mind, nay, of a disturbed imagination. Her mood was very unequal ; sometimes she was sunk in calm melancholy, and at others, as I have been told, she betrayed all the symptoms of frantic madness. It was one night in the month of October, after she had recovered from one of those fits of excess, and had sunk again into her usual melancholy, that she retired alone to her chamber, and forbade all interruption. It was the chamber at the end of the corridor, signors, where we had the affray last night. From that hour she was seen no more.'

'How! seen no more!' said Bertolini ; ' was not her body found in the chamber?'

'Were her remains never found?' cried the rest of the company all together.

'Never!' replied Montoni.

'What reasons were there to suppose she destroyed herself, then?' said Bertolini.

'Aye, what reasons?' said Verezzi. 'How happened it that her remains were never found? Although she killed herself, she could not bury herself.'

Montoni looked indignantly at Verezzi, who began to apologise.

'Your pardon, signor,' said he ; 'I did not

consider that the lady was your relative when I spoke of her so lightly.'

Montoni accepted the apology.

' But the signor will oblige us with the reasons which urged him to believe that the lady commited suicide.'

' Those I will explain hereafter,' said Montoni ; 'at present let me relate a most extraordinary circumstance. This conversation goes no further, signors. Listen, then, to what I am going to say.'

' Listen !' said a voice.

They were all again silent, and the countenance of Montoni changed.

' This is no illusion of the fancy,' said Cavigni, at length breaking the profound silence.

' No,' said Bertolini ; ' I heard it myself, now. Yet here is no person in the room but ourselves !'

' This is very extraordinary,' said Montoni, suddenly rising. ' This is not to be borne ; here is some deception, some trick ; I will know what it means.'

All the company rose from their chairs in confusion.

' It is very odd !' said Bertolini. ' Here is really no stranger in the room. If it is a trick, signor, you will do well to punish the author of it severely.'

' A trick ! what else can it be !' said Cavigni, affecting a laugh.

The servants were now summoned, and the chamber was searched, but no person was found. The surprise and consternation of the company increased. Montoni was discomposed.

' We will leave this room,' said he, ' and the subject of our conversation also ; it is too solemn.'

His guests were equally ready to quit the apartment ; but the subject had roused their curiosity, and they entreated Montoni to withdraw to another chamber and finish it : no entreaties could, however, prevail with him. Notwithstanding his efforts to appear at ease, he was visibly and greatly disordered.

' Why, signor, you are not superstitious,' cried Verezzi, jeeringly ; ' you, who have so often laughed at the credulity of others ?'

' I am not superstitious,' replied Montoni, regarding him with stern displeasure, ' though I know how to despise the common-place sentences which are frequently uttered against superstition. I will inquire further into this affair.' He then left the room ; and his guests, separating for the night, retired to their respective apartments.

CHAPTER XXII.

' He wears the rose of youth upon his cheek.'
SHAKESPEARE.

WE now return to Valancourt, who, it may be remembered, remained at Thoulouse some time after the departure of Emily, restless and miserable. Each morrow that approached he designed should carry him from thence ; yet to-morrow and to-morrow came, and still saw him lingering in the scene of his former happiness. He could not immediately tear himself from the spot where he had been accustomed to converse with Emily, or from the objects they had viewed together, which appeared to him memorials of her affection, as well as a kind of surety for its faithfulness ; and next to the pain of bidding her adieu, was that of leaving the scenes which so powerfully awakened her image. Sometimes he had bribed a servant, who had been left in the care of Madame Montoni's chateau, to permit him to visit the gardens ; and there he would wander for hours together, wrapped in a melancholy not unpleasing. The terrace, and the pavilion at the end of it where he had taken leave of Emily on the eve of her departure from Thoulouse, were his most favourite haunts. There, as he walked, or leaned from the window of the building, he would endeavour to recollect all she had said on that night ; to catch the tones of her voice as they faintly vibrated on his memory ; and to remember the exact expression of her countenance, which sometimes came suddenly to his fancy like a vision ; that beautiful countenance, which awakened, as by instantaneous magic, all the tenderness of his heart, and seemed to tell, with irresistible eloquence—that he had lost her for ever ! At these moments his hurried steps would have discovered to a spectator the despair of his heart. The character of Montoni, such as he had received from hints, and such as his fears represented it, would rise to his view, together with all the dangers it seemed to threaten to Emily and to his love. He blamed himself that he had not urged these more forcibly to her while it might have been in his power to detain her, and that he had suffered an absurd and criminal delicacy, as he termed it, to conquer so soon the reasonable arguments he had opposed to this journey. Any evil that might have attended their marriage seemed so inferior to those which now threatened their love, or even to the sufferings that absence occasioned, that he wondered how he could have ceased to urge his suit till he had convinced her of its propriety ; and he would certainly now have followed her to Italy, if he could have been spared from his regiment for so long a journey. His regiment, indeed, soon reminded him that he had other duties to attend to than those of love.

A short time after his arrival at his brother's house, he was summoned to join his brother officers, and he accompanied a battalion to Paris ; where a scene of novelty and gaiety opened upon him, such as till then he had only a faint idea of. But gaiety disgusted, and company fatigued, his sick mind ; and he became an object of unceasing raillery to his companions, from whom, whenever he could steal an opportunity, he escaped to think of Emily. The scenes around him, however, and the company with whom he was obliged to mingle, engaged his attention, though they failed to amuse his fancy, and thus gradually weakened the habit of yielding to lamentation, till it appeared less a duty to his love to indulge it. Among his brother officers were many who added to the ordinary character of a French soldier's gaiety, some of those fascinating qualities which too frequently throw a veil over folly, and sometimes even soften the features of vice into smiles. To these men the reserved and thoughtful manners of Valancourt were a kind of tacit censure on their own, for which they rallied him when present, and plotted against him when absent; they gloried in the thought of reducing him to their own level, and considering it to be a spirited frolic, determined to accomplish it.

Valancourt was a stranger to the gradual progress of scheme and intrigue, against which he could not be on his guard. He had not been accustomed to receive ridicule, and he could ill endure its sting ; he resented it, and this only drew upon him a louder laugh. To escape from such scenes he fled into solitude, and there the image of Emily met him, and revived the pangs of love and despair. He then sought to renew those tasteful studies which had been the delight of his early years ; but his mind had lost the tranquillity which is necessary for their enjoyment. To forget himself, and the grief and anxiety which the idea of her recalled, he would quit his solitude, and again mingle in the crowd—glad of a temporary relief, and rejoicing to snatch amusement for the moment.

Thus passed weeks after weeks, time gradually softening his sorrow, and habit strengthening his desire of amusement, till the scenes around him seemed to awaken into a new character, and Valancourt to have fallen among them from the clouds.

His figure and address made him a welcome visitor wherever he had been introduced, and he soon frequented the most gay and fashionable circles of Paris. Among these was the assembly of the Countess Lacleur, a woman of eminent beauty and captivating manners. She had passed the spring of youth, but her wit prolonged the triumph of its reign, and they mutually assisted the fame of each other ; for those who were charmed by her loveliness, spoke with enthusiasm of her talents ; and others, who admired her playful imagination, declared that her personal graces were unrivalled. But her imagination was merely playful, and her wit, if such it could be called, was brilliant, rather than just ; it dazzled, and its fallacy escaped the detection of the moment ; for the accents in which she pronounced it, and the smile that accom-

panied them, were a spell upon the judgment of the auditors. Her *petits soupers* were the most tasteful of any in Paris, and were frequented by many of the second class of literati. She was fond of music, was herself a scientific performer, and had frequently concerts at her house. Valancourt, who passionately loved music, and who sometimes assisted at these concerts, admired her execution, but remembered with a sigh the eloquent simplicity of Emily's songs, and the natural expression of her manner, which waited not to be approved by the judgment, but found their way at once to the heart.

Madame *La Comtesse* had often deep play at her house, which she affected to restrain, but secretly encouraged ; and it was well known among her friends, that the splendour of her establishment was chiefly supplied from the profits of her tables. But her *petits soupers* were the most charming imaginable ! Here were all the delicacies of the four quarters of the world, all the wit and the lighter efforts of genius, all the graces of conversation—the smiles of beauty, and the charms of music ; and Valancourt passed the pleasantest, as well as most dangerous, hours in these parties.

His brother, who remained with his family in Gascony, had contented himself with giving him letters of introduction to such of his relations residing at Paris as the latter was not already known to. All these were persons of some distinction ; and as neither the person, mind, nor manners of Valancourt the younger threatened to disgrace their alliance, they received him with as much kindness as their nature, hardened by uninterrupted prosperity, would admit of : but their attentions did not extend to acts of real friendship ; for they were too much occupied by their own pursuits, to feel any interest in his ; and thus he was set down in the midst of Paris, in the pride of youth, with an open unsuspicious temper and ardent affections, without one friend to warn him of the dangers to which he was exposed. Emily, who, had she been present, would have saved him from these evils, by awakening his heart, and engaging him in worthy pursuits, now only increased his danger :—it was to lose the grief which the remembrance of her occasioned, that he first sought amusement ; and for this end he pursued it, till habit made it an object of abstract interest.

There was also a Marchioness Champfort, a young widow, at whose assemblies he passed much of his time. She was handsome, still more artful, gay, and fond of intrigue. The society which she drew round her was less elegant and more vicious than that of the Countess Lacleur ; but as she had address enough to throw a veil, though but a slight one, over the worst part of her character, she was still visited by many persons of what is called distinction. Valancourt was introduced to her parties by two of his brother officers, whose late ridicule he had now forgiven so far, that he could sometimes join in the laugh which a mention of his former manners would renew.

The gaiety of the most splendid court in Europe, the magnificence of the palaces, entertainments, and equipages, that surrounded him—all conspired to dazzle his imagination and reanimate his spirits, and the example and maxims of his military associates to delude his mind. Emily's image, indeed, still lived there ; but it was no longer the friend, the monitor, that saved him from himself, and to which he retired to weep the sweet yet melancholy tears of tenderness. When he had recourse to it, it assumed a countenance of mild reproach, that wrung his soul, and called forth tears of unmixed misery; his only escape from which was to forget the object of it, and he endeavoured therefore to think of Emily as seldom as he could.

Thus dangerously circumstanced was Valancourt, at the time when Emily was suffering at Venice from the persecuting addresses of Count Morano and the unjust authority of Montoni ; at which period we leave him

---

CHAPTER XXIII.

' The image of a wicked, heinous fault
Lives in his eye ; that close aspect of his
Does show the mood of a much-troubled breast.
KING JOHN.

LEAVING the gay scenes of Paris, we return to those of the gloomy Apennine, where Emily's thoughts were still faithful to Valancourt. Looking to him as to her only hope, she recollected with jealous exactness every assurance and every proof she had witnessed of his affection ; read again and again the letters she had received from him ; weighed with intense anxiety the force of every word that spoke of his attachment ; and dried her tears as she trusted in his truth.

Montoni meanwhile had made strict inquiry concerning the strange circumstance of his alarm, without obtaining information ; and was at length obliged to account for it by the reasonable supposition that it was a mischievous trick played off by one of his domestics. His disagreements with Madame Montoni on the subject of her settlements were now more frequent than ever ; he even confined her entirely to her own apartment, and did not scruple to threaten her with much greater severity should she persevere in her refusal.

Reason, had she consulted it, would now have perplexed her in the choice of a conduct to be adopted. It would have pointed out the danger of irritating, by further opposition, a man such as Montoni had proved himself to be, and to whose power she had so entirely committed herself ; and it would also have told her of what extreme importance it was, to reserve for her self those possessions, which would enable her to live independently of Montoni should she ever escape from his immediate control. But she was directed by a more decisive guide then reason—the spirit of revenge, which urged her to oppose violence to violence, and obstinacy to obstinacy.

Wholly confined to the solitude of her apartment, she was now reduced to solicit the society she so lately rejected ; for Emily was the only person, except Annette, with whom she was permitted to converse.

Generously anxious for her peace, Emily therefore tried to persuade when she could not convince, and sought by every gentle means to induce her to forbear that asperity of reply which so greatly irritated Montoni. The pride of her aunt did sometimes soften to the soothing voice of Emily, and there even were moments when she regarded her affectionate attentions with good-will.

The scenes of terrible contention to which Emily was frequently compelled to be witness, exhausted her spirits more than any circumstances that had occurred since her departure from Thoulouse. The gentleness and goodness of her parents, together with the scenes of her early happiness, often stole on her mind, like the visions of a higher world ; while the characters and circumstances now passing beneath her eye excited both terror and surprise. She could scarcely have imagined, that passions so fierce and so various, as those which Montoni exhibited, could have been concentrated in one individual ; yet what more surprised her was, that on great occasions he could bend these passions, wild as they were, to the cause of his interest, and generally could disguise in his countenance their operation on his mind ; but she had seen him too often, when he had thought it unnecessary to conceal his nature, to be deceived on such occasions.

Her present life appeared like the dream of a distempered imagination, or like one of those frightful fictions in which the wild genius of the poets sometimes delighted. Reflection brought only regret, and anticipation terror. How often did she wish to ' steal the lark's wing, and mount the swiftest gale,' that Languedoc and repose might once more be hers !

Of Count Morano's health she made frequent inquiry ; but Annette heard only vague reports of his danger, and that his surgeon had said he would never leave the cottage alive ; while Emily could not but be shocked to think that she, however innocently, might be the means of his death ; and Annette, who did not fail to observe her emotion, interpreted it in her own way.

But a circumstance soon occurred, which entirely withdrew Annette's attention from this subject, and awakened the surprise and curiosity so natural to her. Coming one day to Emily's apartment, with a countenance full of importance, 'What can all this mean, ma'amselle?' said she. 'Would I was once safe in Languedoc again, they should never catch me going on my travels any more! I must think it a fine thing, truly, to come abroad, and see foreign parts! I little thought I was coming to be caged up in an old castle, among such dreary mountains, with the chance of being murdered, or, what is as good, having my throat cut!'

'What can all this mean, indeed, Annette?' said Emily in astonishment.

'Ay, ma'amselle, you may look surprised; but you won't believe it, perhaps, till they have murdered you, too. You would not believe about the ghost I told you of, though I showed you the very place where it used to appear!—You will believe nothing, ma'amselle.'

'Not till you speak more reasonably, Annette; for Heaven's sake, explain your meaning. You spoke of murder!'

'Ay, ma'amselle, they are coming to murder us all, perhaps; but what signifies explaining? —you will not believe.'

Emily again desired her to relate what she had seen or heard.

'O, I have seen enough, ma'am, and heard too much, as Ludovico can prove. Poorsoul! they will murder him, too! I little thought, when he sung those sweet verses under my lattice at Venice—' Emily looked impatient and displeased—'Well, ma'amselle, as I was saying, these preparations about the castle, and these strange-looking people that are calling here every day, and the signor's cruel usage of my lady, and his odd goings on—all these, as I told Ludovico, can bode no good. And he bid me hold my tongue. So, says I "The signor's strangely altered, Ludovico, in this gloomy castle, to what he was in France; there, all so gay! Nobody so gallant to my lady, then; and he could smile, too, upon a poor servant sometimes, and jeer her, too, good-naturedly enough. I remember once, when he said to me as I was going out of my lady's dressing-room—'Annette,' says he—"'

'Never mind what the signor said,' interrupted Emily; 'but tell me, at once, the circumstance which has thus alarmed you.'

'Ay, ma'amselle,' rejoined Annette, 'that is just what Ludovico says;' says he, "Never mind what the signor says to you."—"So I told him what I thought about the signor. "He is so strangely altered," said I : "for now is so haughty, and so commanding, and so chary with my lady; and if he meets one, he'll scarcely look at one, unless it be to frown." "So much the better," says Ludovico, "so much

the better." And to tell you the truth, ma'amselle, I thought this was a very ill-natured speech of Ludovico : but I went on. "And then," says I, "he is always knitting his brows; and if one speaks to him, he does not hear; and then he sits up counselling so, of a night, with other signors—there they are till long past midnight discoursing together!" "Ah, but" says Ludovico, "you don't know what they are counselling about." "No," said I, "but I can guess—it is about my young lady." Upon that, Ludovico burst out a-laughing quite loud ; so he put me in a huff, for I did not like that either I or you, ma'amselle, should be laughed at; and I turned away quick, but he stopped me. "Don't be affronted, Annette," said he, "but I cannot help laughing ;" and with that he laughed again. "What!" says he, "do you think that the signors sit up, night after night, only to counsel about thy young lady? No, no, there is something more in the wind than that. And these repairs about the castle, and these preparations about the ramparts—they are not making about young ladies." "Why, surely," said I, "the signor, my master, is not going to make war?" "Make war!" said Ludovico, "what, upon the mountains and the woods? for here is no living soul to make war upon, that I see." "What are these preparations for, then?" said I ; "why surely nobody is coming to take away my master's castle!" "Then there are so many ill-looking fellows coming to the castle every day," says Ludovico, without answering my question, "and the signor sees them all, and talks with them, and they all stay in the neighbourhood! By holy St. Marco! some of them are the most cut-throat looking dogs I ever set my eyes upon."

'I asked Ludovico again, if he thought they were coming to take away my master's castle ; and he said, No, he did not think they were, but he did not know for certain. "Then, yesterday," said he, (but you must not tell this, ma'amselle)—"yesterday, a party of these men came, and left all their horses in the castle stables, where it seems they are to stay, for the signor ordered them all to be entertained with the best provender in the manger ; but the men are most of them in the neighbouring cottages."

'So, ma'amselle, I came to tell you all this, for I never heard anything so strange in my life. But what can these ill-looking men be come about, if it is not to murder us? and the signor knows this, or why should he be so civil to them? and why should he fortify the castle, and counsel so much with the other signors, and be so thoughtful?'

'Is this all you have to tell, Annette?' said Emily. 'Have you heard nothing else that alarms you?'

'Nothing else, ma'amselle!' said Annette ; 'why is not this enough?'—'Quite enough for my patience, Annette, but not quite enough to convince me we are all to be murdered, though I acknowledge here is sufficient food for curiosity.' She forbore to speak her apprehensions, because she would not encourage Annette's wild terrors; but the present circumstances of the castle both surprised and alarmed her. Annette, having told her tale, left the chamber, on the wing for new wonders.

. In the evening Emily had passed some melancholy hours with Madame Montoni, and was retiring to rest, when she was alarmed by a strange and loud knocking at her chamber-door, and then a heavy weight fell against it, that almost burst it open. She called to know who was there, and receiving no answer, repeated the call; but a chilling silence followed. It occurred to her—for at this moment she could not reason on the probability of circumstances—that some one of the strangers lately arrived at the castle had discovered her apartment, and was come with such intent as their looks rendered too possible—to rob, perhaps to murder her. The moment she admitted this possibility, terror supplied the place of conviction, and a kind of instinctive remembrance of her remote situation from the family heightened it to a degree that almost overcame her senses. She looked at the door which led to the staircase, expecting to see it open, and listening in fearful silence for a return of the noise, till she began to think it had proceeded from this door, and a wish of escaping through the opposite one rushed upon her mind. She went to the gallery door, and then fearing to open it, lest some person might be silently lurking for her without, she stopped, but with her eyes fixed in expectation upon the opposite door of the staircase. As thus she stood, she heard a faint breathing near her, and became convinced that some person was on the other side of the door, which was already locked. She sought for other fastening, but there was none.

While she yet listened, the breathing was distinctly heard, and her terror was not soothed when, looking round her wide and lonely chamber, she again considered her remote situation. As she stood hesitating whether to call for assistance, the continuance of the stillness surprised her; and her spirits would have revived had she not continued to hear the faint breathing, that convinced her the person, whoever it was, had not quitted the door.

At length, worn out with anxiety, she determined to call loudly for assistance from her casement; and was advancing to it, when, whether the terror of her mind gave her ideal sounds, or that real ones did come, she thought footsteps were ascending the private staircase; and expecting to see its doors unclosed, she forgot all other cause of alarm, and retreated towards the corridor. Here

she endeavoured to make her escape, but on opening the door was very nearly falling over a person who lay on the floor without. She screamed, and would have passed, but her trembling frame refused to support her; and the moment in which she leaned against the wall of the gallery allowed her leisure to observe the figure before her, and to recognise the features of Annette. Fear instantly yielded to surprise. She spoke in vain to the poor girl, who remained senseless on the floor, and then, losing all consciousness of her own weakness, hurried to her assistance.

When Annette recovered, she was helped by Emily into the chamber, but was still unable to speak, and looked round her as if her eyes followed some person in the room. Emily tried to soothe her disturbed spirits, and forbore at present to ask her any questions; but the faculty of speech was never long withheld from Annette, and she explained in broken sentences, and in her tedious way, the occasion of her disorder. She affirmed, and with a solemnity of conviction that almost staggered the incredulity of Emily, that she had seen an apparition as she was passing to her bedroom through the corridor.

'I had heard strange stories of that chamber before,' said Annette; 'but as it was so near yours, ma'amselle, I would not tell them to you, because they would frighten you. The servants had told me often and often that it was haunted, and that was the reason why it was shut up; nay, for that matter, why the whole string of these rooms here are shut up. I quaked whenever I went by, and I must say I did sometimes think I heard odd noises within it. But, as I said, as I was passing along the corridor, and not thinking a word about the matter, or even of the strange voice that the signors heard the other night, all of a sudden comes a great light, and, looking behind me, there was a tall figure (I saw it as plainly, ma'amselle, as I see you at this moment), a tall figure gliding along (Oh, I cannot describe how!) into the room that is always shut up, and nobody has the key of it but the the signor, and the door shut directly.'

'Then it doubtless was the signor,' said Emily.

'O no, ma'amselle, it could not be him; for I left him busy a-quarrelling in my lady's dressing-room!'

'You bring me strange tales, Annette,' said Emily: 'it was but this morning that you would have terrified me with the apprehension of murder; and now you would persuade me you have seen a ghost! These wonderful stories come too quickly.'

'Nay, ma'amselle, I will say no more; only if I had not been frightened I should not have fainted dead away so. I ran as fast as I could to get to your door; but what was worst of all, I could not call out; then I thought something must be strangely the matter with me, and directly I dropt down.'

'Was it the chamber where the black veil hangs?' said Emily. 'O no! ma'amselle, it was one nearer to this. What shall I do to get to my room?, I would not go into the corridor again for the whole world! Emily, whose spirits had been severely shocked, and who therefore did not like the thought of passing the night alone, told her she might sleep where she was. 'O! no, ma'amselle,' replied Annette, 'I would not sleep in the room now for a thousand sequins.'

Wearied and disappointed, Emily first ridiculed, though she shared her fears, and then tried to soothe them; but neither attempt succeeded, and the girl persisted in believing and affirming that what she had seen was nothing human. It was not till some time after Emily had recovered her composure that she recollected the steps she had heard on the staircase—a remembrance, however, which made her insist that Annette should pass the night with her, and with much difficulty she at length prevailed, assisted by that part of the girl's fear which concerned the corridor.

Early on the following morning, as Emily crossed the hall to the ramparts, she heard a noisy bustle in the courtyard, and the clatter of horses' hoofs. Such unusual sounds excited her curiosity; and instead of going to the ramparts she went to an upper casement, from whence she saw, in the court below, a large party of horsemen dressed in a singular but uniform habit, and completely, though variously armed. They wore a kind of short jacket composed of black and scarlet, and several of them had a cloak of plain black, which covering the person entirely hung down to the stirrups. As one of these cloaks glanced aside, she saw beneath daggers, apparently of different sizes, tucked into the horseman's belt. She further observed that these were carried in the same manner by many of the horsemen without cloaks, most of whom bore also pikes or javelins. On their heads were the small Italian caps, some of which were distinguished by black feathers. Whether these caps gave a fierce air to the countenance, or that the countenances they surmounted had naturally such an appearance, Emily thought she had never till then seen an assemblage of faces so savage and terrific. While she gazed, she almost fancied herself surrounded by banditti; and a vague thought glanced athwart her fancy—that Montoni was the captain of the group before her, and that this castle was to be the place of rendezvous. The strange and horrible supposition was but ·momentary, though her reason could supply none more probable, and though she discovered among the band the strangers she had formerly noticed with so much alarm, who ·e now distinguished by the black plume.

While she continued gazing, Cavigni, Verezzi, and Bertolini, came forth from the hall habited like the rest, except that they wore hats with a mixed plume of black and scarlet, and that their arms differed from those of the rest of the party. As they mounted their horses, Emily was struck with the exulting joy expressed on the visage of Verezzi, while Cavigni was gay, yet with a shade of thought on his countenance; and as he managed his horse with dexterity, his graceful and commanding figure, which exhibited the majesty of a hero, ·had never appeared to more advantage. Emily, as she observed him, thought he somewhat resembled Valancourt in the spirit and dignity of his person; but she looked in vain for the noble, benevolent countenance—the soul's intelligence, which overspread the features of the latter.

As she was hoping, she scarcely knew why, that Montoni would accompany the party, he appeared at the hall door, but unaccoutred. Having carefully observed the horsemen, conversed awhile with the cavaliers, and bidden them farewell, the band wheeled round the court, and, led by Verezzi, issued forth under the portcullis; Montoni following to the portal, and gazing after them for some time. Emily then retired from the casement, and now, certain of being unmolested, went to walk on the ramparts, from whence she soon after saw the party winding among the mountains to the west, appearing and disappearing between the woods, till distance confused their figures, consolidated their numbers, and only a dingy mass appeared moving along the heights.

Emily observed that no workmen were on the ramparts, and that the repairs of the fortifications seemed to be completed. While she sauntered thoughtfully on, she heard distant footsteps, and, raising her eyes, saw several men lurking under the castle walls, who were evidently not workmen, but looked as if they would have accorded well with the party which was gone. Wondering where Annette had hid herself so long, who might have explained some of the late circumstances, and then considering that Madame Montoni was probably risen, she went to her dressing-room, where she mentioned what had occurred; but Madame Montoni either would not or could not give any explanation of the event. The signor's reserve to his wife on this subject was probably nothing more than usual; yet to Emily it gave an air of mystery to the whole affair, that seemed to ·hint there was danger, if not villany, in his schemes.

Anette presently came, and, as usual, was full of alarm; to her lady's eager inquiries of what she had heard among the servants, she replied:

'Ah, madam! nobody knows what it is all about, but old Carlo; he knows well enough, but I dare say he is as close as his master. Some say the signor is going out to frighten the enemy, as they call it : but where is the enemy ? Then others say, he is going to take away somebody's castle ; but I am sure he has room enough in his own, without taking other people's ; and I am sure I should like it a great deal better, if there were more people to fill it.'

'Ah ! you will soon have your wish, I fear,' replied Madame Montoni.

'No, madam ; but such ill-looking fellows are not worth having. I mean such gallant, smart, merry fellows as Ludovico, who is always telling droll stories, to make one laugh. It was but yesterday, he told me such a *humoursome* tale ! I can't help laughing at it now,—Says he——'

'Well, we can dispense with the story,' said her lady.

'Ah !' continued Annette, 'he sees a great way further than other people ! Now he sees into all the signor's meaning, without knowing a word about the matter.'

'How is that ?' said Madame Montoni.

'Why he says—but he made me promise not to tell, and I would not disoblige him for the world.'

'What is it he made you promise not to tell ?' said her lady sternly. 'I insist upon knowing immediately—what is it he made you promise ?'

'O madam,' cried Annette, 'I would not tell for the universe !'

'I insist upon your telling this instant,' said Madame Montoni.

'O dear madam ! I would not tell for a hundred sequins ! You would not have me forswear myself, madam !' exclaimed Annette.

'I will not wait another moment,' said Madame Montoni. Annette was silent.

'The signor shall be informed of this directly,' rejoined her mistress ; 'he will make you discover all.'

'It is Ludovico who has discovered,' said Annette : 'but for mercy's sake, madam, don't tell the signor, and you shall know all directly.' Madame Montoni said that she would not.

'Well, then, madam, Ludovico says that the signor, my master is—is—that is, he only thinks so, and anybody, you know, madam, is free to think—that the signor, my master, is —is—'

'Is what ?' said her lady impatiently.

'That the signor, my master, is going to be —a great robber—that is—he is going to rob on his own account ;—to be (but I am sure I don't understand what he means)—to be a——captain of——robbers.'

'Art thou in thy senses, Annette ?' said Madame Montoni ; 'or is this a trick to deceive me. Tell me, this instant, what Ludovico *did* say to thee ;—no equivocation ;—this instant—'

'Nay, madam,' cried Annette, 'if this is all that I am to get for having told the secret—' Her mistress thus continued to insist, and Annette to protest, till Montoni himself appeared, who bade the latter leave the room ; and she withdrew, trembling for the fate of her story. Emily also was retiring, but her aunt desired she would stay ; and Montoni had so often made her a witness of their contention, that he no longer had scruples on that account.

'I insist upon knowing this instant, signor, what all this means,' said his wife—'what are all these armed men, whom they tell me of, gone out about ?' Montoni answered her only with a look of scorn ; and Emily whispering something to her, 'It does not signify,' said her aunt : 'I will know ; and I will know, too, what the castle has been fortified for.'

'Come, come,' said Montoni, 'other business brought me here. I must be trifled with no longer. I have immediate occasion for what I demand—those estates must be given up, without further contention ; or I may find a way——'

'They never shall be given up,' interrupted Madame Montoni : 'they never shall enable you to carry on your wild schemes :— but what are these ? I will know. Do you expect the castle to be attacked ? Do you expect enemies ? Am I to be shut up here, to be killed in a siege ?'

'Sign the writing,' said Montoni, 'and you shall know more.'

'What enemy can be coming ?' continued his wife. 'Have you entered into the service of the state ? Am I to be blocked up here to die ?'

'That may possibly happen,' said Montoni, 'unless you yield to my demand : for, come what may, you shall not quit the castle till then.' Madame Montoni burst into loud lamentation, which she suddenly checked, considering that her husband's assertions might only be artifices employed to extort her consent. She hinted this suspicion, and in the next moment told him also, that his designs were not so honourable as to serve the state, and that she believed he had only commenced a captain of banditti, to join the enemies of Venice in plundering and laying waste the surrounding country.

Montoni looked at her for a moment with a steady and stern countenance ; while Emily trembled ; and his wife, for once, thought she had said too much. 'You shall be removed this night,' said he, 'to the east turret : there, perhaps, you may understand the danger of offending a man who has an unlimited power over you.'

Emily now fell at his feet, and with tears of terror supplicated for her aunt, who sat trembling with fear and indignation, now ready to pour forth execrations, and now to join the intercessions of Emily. Montoni, however, soon interrupted these entreaties with a terrible oath ; and as he burst from Emily, leaving his cloak in her hand, she fell to the floor, with a force that occasioned her a severe blow on the forehead. But he quitted the room without attempting to raise her, whose attention was called from herself by a deep groan from Madame Montoni, who continued otherwise unmoved in her chair, and had not fainted. Emily, hastening to her assistance, saw her eyes rolling, and her features convulsed.

Having spoken to her without receiving an answer, she brought water, and supported her head while she held it to her lips; but the increasing convulsions soon compelled Emily to call for assistance. On her way through the hall, in search of Annette, she met Montoni, whom she told what had happened, and conjured to return and comfort her aunt; but he turned silently away with a look of indifference, and went out upon the ramparts. At length she found old Carlo and Annette, and they hastened to the dressing-room, where Madame Montoni had fallen on the floor, and was lying in strong convulsions. Having lifted her into the adjoining room, and laid her on the bed, the force of her disorder still made all their strength necessary to hold her; while Annette trembled and sobbed, and old Carlo looked silently and piteously on, as his feeble hands grasped those of his mistress, till turning his eyes on Emily, he exclaimed, 'Good God! signora, what is the matter!'

Emily looked calmly at him, and saw his inquiring eyes fixed on her; and Annette, looking up, screamed loudly; for Emily's face was stained with blood, which continued to fall slowly from her forehead; but her attention had been so entirely occupied by the scene before her that she had felt no pain from the wound. She now held a handkerchief to her face, and, notwithstanding her faintness, continued to watch Madame Montoni, the violence of whose convulsions was abating, till at length they ceased, and left her in a kind of stupor.

'My aunt must remain quiet,' said Emily. 'Go, good Carlo; if we should want your assistance, I will send for you. In the meantime, if you have an opportunity, speak kindly of your mistress to your master.'

'Alas!' said Carlo, 'I have seen too much! I have little influence with the signor. But do, dear young lady, take some care of yourself; that is an ugly wound, and you look sadly.'

'Thank you, my friend, for your consideration,' said Emily smiling kindly: 'the wound is trifling, it came by a fall.'

Carlo shook his head, and left the room; and Emily, with Annette, continued to watch by her aunt. 'Did my lady tell the signor what Ludovico said, ma'amselle?' asked Annette in a whisper; but Emily quieted her fears on that subject.

'I thought what this quarrelling would come to,' continued Annette; 'I suppose the signor has been beating my lady.'

'No, no, Annette, you are totally mistaken; nothing extraordinary has happened.'

'Why, extraordinary things happen here so often, ma'amselle, that there is nothing in them. Here is another legion of those ill-looking fellows come to the castle this morning.'

'Hush, Annette, you will disturb my aunt; we will talk of that by and by.'

They continued watching silently, till Madame Montoni uttered a low sigh, when Emily took her hand, and spoke soothingly to her; but the former gazed with unconscious eyes, and it was long before she knew her niece. Her first words then inquired for Montoni; to which Emily replied by an entreaty that she would compose her spirits, and consent to be kept quiet, adding, 'that if she wished any message to be conveyed to him, she would herself deliver it.' 'No,' said her aunt faintly, 'no—I have nothing new to tell him. Does he persist in saying I shall be removed from my chamber?'

Emily replied that he had not spoken on the subject since Madame Montoni heard him; and then she tried to divert her attention to some other topic; but her aunt seemed to be inattentive to what she said, and lost in secret thoughts. Emily, having brought her some refreshment, now left her to the care of Annette, and went in search of Montoni, whom she found on a remote part of the rampart, conversing among a group of the men described by Annette. They stood round with their fierce yet subjugated looks, while he, speaking earnestly and pointing to the walls, did not perceive Emily, who remained at some distance waiting till he should be at leisure, and observing involuntarily the appearance of one man, more savage than his fellows, who stood resting on his pike and looking over the shoulders of a comrade at Montoni, to whom he listened with uncommon earnestness. This man was apparently of low condition; yet his looks appeared not to acknowledge the superiority of Montoni, as did those of his companions; and sometimes they even assumed an air of authority, which the decisive manner of the signor could not repress. Some few words of Montoni then passed in the wind; and as the men were separating, she heard him say, 'This evening, then, begin the watch at sun-set.'

'At sun-set, signor,' replied one or two of them, and walked away; while Emily approached Montoni, who appeared desirous of avoiding her: but though she observed this, she had courage to proceed. She endeavoured to intercede once more for her aunt, represented to him her sufferings, and urged the danger of exposing her to a cold apartment in her present state. 'She suffers by her own folly,' said Montoni, 'and is not to be pitied; she knows how she may avoid these sufferings in future—if she is removed to the turret, it will be her own fault. Let her be obedient, and sign the writings you heard of, and I will think no more of it.'

When Emily ventured still to plead, he sternly silenced and rebuked her for interfering in his domestic affairs, but at length dismissed her with this concession—That he would not remove Madame Montoni on the ensuing night, but allow her till the next to consider, whether she would resign her settlements, or be imprisoned in the east turret of the castle; 'where she shall find,' he added, 'a punishment she may not expect.'

Emily then hastened to inform her aunt of this short respite, and of the alternative that awaited her; to which the latter made no reply, but appeared thoughtful, while Emily, in consideration of her extreme languor, wished to soothe her mind by leading it to less interesting topics : and though these efforts were unsuccessful, and Madame Montoni became peevish, her resolution on the contended point seemed somewhat to relax, and Emily recommended, as her only means of safety, that she should submit to Montoni's demand. 'You know not what you advise,' said her aunt. 'Do you understand that these estates will descend to you at my death, if I persist in a refusal?'

'I was ignorant of that circumstance, madam,' replied Emily ; 'but the knowledge of it cannot withhold me from advising you to adopt the conduct, which not only your peace, but I fear your safety requires ; and I entreat that you will not suffer a consideration comparatively so trifling to make you hesitate a moment in resigning them.'

'Are you sincere, niece?'—'Is it possible you can doubt it, madam?' Her aunt appeared to be affected. 'You are not unworthy of these estates, niece, I would wish to keep them for your sake—you show a virtue I did not expect.'

'How have I deserved this reproof, madam?' said Emily sorrowfully.

'Reproof!' replied Madame Montoni : 'I meant to praise your virtue.'

'Alas! here is no exertion of virtue,' rejoined Emily, 'for here is no temptation to be overcome.'

'Yet Monsieur Valancourt—' said her aunt. 'O madam!' interrupted Emily, anticipating what she would have said, 'do not let me glance on that subject ; do not let my mind be stained with a wish so shockingly self-interested. She immediately changed the topic, and continued with Madame Montoni till she withdrew to her apartment for the night.'

At that hour the castle was perfectly still, and every inhabitant of it, except herself, seemed to have retired to rest, As she passed along the wide and lonely galleries, dusky and silent, she felt forlorn and apprehensive of—she scarcely knew what ; but when entering the corridor she recollected the incident of the preceding night, a dread seized her, lest a subject of alarm similar to that which had befallen Annette should occur to her, and which, whether real or ideal, would, she felt, have an almost equal effect upon her weakened spirits. The chamber to which Annette had alluded she did not exactly know, but understood it to be one of those she must pass in the way to her own ; and sending a fearful look forward into the gloom, she stepped lightly and cautiously along, till coming to a door, from whence issued a low sound, she hesitated and paused ; and during the delay of that moment her fears so much increased, that she had no power to move from the spot. Believing that she heard a human voice within, she was somewhat revived ; but in the next moment the door was opened, and a person whom she conceived to be Montoni appeared, who instantly started back and closed it, though not before she had seen by the light that burned in the chamber, another person sitting in a melancholy attitude by the fire. Her terror vanished, but her astonishment only began, which was now aroused by the mysterious secrecy of Montoni's manner, and by the discovery of a person whom he thus visited at midnight, in an apartment which had long been shut up, and of which such extraordinary reports were circulated.

While she thus continued hesitating, strongly prompted to watch Montoni's motions, yet fearing to irritate him by appearing to notice them, the door was again opened cautiously, and as instantly closed as before. She then stepped softly to her chamber, which was the next but one to this, but having put down her lamp, returned to an obscure corner of the corridor, to observe the proceedings of this half-seen person, and to ascertain whether it was indeed Montoni.

Having waited in silent expectation for a few minutes, with her eyes fixed on the door, it was again opened, and the same person appeared, whom she now knew to be Montoni. He looked cautiously around, without perceiving her, then, stepping forward, closed the door and left the corridor. Soon after, Emily heard the door fastened on the inside, and she withdrew to her chamber, wondering at what she had witnessed.

It was now twelve o'clock. As she closed her casement, she heard footsteps on the terrace below, and saw imperfectly through the gloom several persons advancing; who passed under the casement. She then heard the clink of arms, and in the next moment the watch-word ; when recollecting the command she had overheard from Montoni, and the hour of the night, she understood that these men were for the first time relieving guard in the castle. Having listened till all was again still, she retired to sleep.

——

'Signor!' said Emily solemnly, 'this dreadful charge, I would answer with my life, is false. Nay, signor,' she added, observing the severity of his countenance, 'this is no moment for restraint on my part; I do not scruple to tell you that you are deceived, most wickedly deceived, by the suggestion of some person who aims at the ruin of my aunt;—it is impossible that you could yourself have imagined a crime so hideous.'

Montoni, his lips trembling more than before, replied only, 'If you value your own safety,' addressing Emily, 'you will be silent. I shall know how to interpret your remonstrances should you persevere in them.'

Emily raised her eyes calmly to heaven. 'Here is, indeed, then, nothing to hope!' said she.

'Peace!' cried Montoni, 'or you shall find there is something to fear.'

He turned to his wife, who had now recovered her spirits, and who vehemently and wildly remonstrated upon this mysterious suspicion; but Montoni's rage heightened with her indignation; and Emily, dreading the event of it, threw herself between them, and clasped his knees in silence, looking up in his face with an expression that might have softened the heart of a fiend. Whether his was hardened by a conviction of Madame Montoni's guilt, or that a bare suspicion of it made him eager to exercise vengeance, he was totally and alike insensible to the distress of his wife, and to the pleading looks of Emily, whom he made no attempt to raise, but was vehemently menacing both, when he was called out of the room by some person at the door. As he shut the door, Emily heard him turn the lock and take out the key; so that Madame Montoni and herself were now prisoners; and she saw that his designs became more and more terrible. Her endeavours to explain his motives for this circumstance were almost as ineffectual as those to soothe the distress of her aunt, whose innocence she could not doubt; but she at length accounted for Montoni's readiness to suspect his wife, by his own consciousness of cruelty towards her, and for the sudden violence of his present conduct against both, before even his suspicions could be completely formed, by his general eagerness to effect suddenly whatever he was led to desire, and his carelessness of justice, or humanity, in accomplishing it.

Madame Montoni, after some time, again looked round in search of a possibility of escape from the castle, and conversed with Emily on the subject, who was now willing to encounter any hazard, though she forbore to encourage a hope in her aunt, which she herself did not admit. How strongly the edifice was secured, and how vigilantly guarded, she knew too well; and trembled to commit their safety to the caprice of the servant, whose assistance they must solicit. Old Carlo was compassionate, but he seemed to be too much in his master's interest to be trusted by them; Annette could of herself do little, and Emily knew Ludovico only from her report. At present, however, these considerations were useless, Madame Montoni and her niece being shut up from all intercourse, even with the persons whom there might be these reasons to reject.

In the hall, confusion and tumult still reigned. Emily, as she listened anxiously to the murmur that sounded along the gallery, sometimes fancied she heard the clashing of swords; and when she considered the nature of the provocation given by Montoni, and his impetuosity, it appeared probable that nothing less than arms would terminate the contention. Madame Montoni having exhausted all her expressions of indignation, and Emily hers of comfort, they remained silent, in that kind of breathless stillness, which, in nature, often succeeds to the uproar of conflicting elements; a stillness, like the morning that dawns upon the ruins of an earthquake.

An uncertain kind of terror pervaded Emily's mind; the circumstances of the past hour still came dimly and confusedly to her memory; and her thoughts were various and rapid, though without tumult.

From this state of waking visions she was recalled by a knocking at the chamber-door, and, inquiring who was there, heard the whispering voice of Annette.

'Dear madam, let me come in; I have a great deal to say,' said the poor girl.

'The door is locked,' answered her lady.

'Yes, ma'am, but do pray open it.'

'The signor has the key,' said Madame Montoni.

'O blessed Virgin! what will become of us?' exclaimed Annette.

'Assist us to escape,' said her mistress. 'Where is Ludovico?'

'Below in the hall, ma'am, amongst them all, fighting with the best of them!'

'Fighting! Who are fighting?' cried Madame Montoni.

'Why the signor, ma'am, and all the signors, and a great many more.'

'Is any person much hurt?' said Emily in a tremulous voice.—'Hurt! Yes, ma'amselle,—there they lie bleeding, and the swords are clashing, and—O holy saints! Do let me in, ma'am, they are coming this way—I shall be murdered!'

'Fly!' cried Emily, 'fly! we cannot open the door.'

Annette repeated that they were coming, and in the same moment fled.

'Be calm, madam,' said Emily, turning to her aunt, 'I entreat you to be calm; I am not frightened, not frightened in the least—do not you be alarmed.'

'You can scarcely support yourself,' replied

her aunt; 'Merciful God! what is it they mean to do with us?'

'They come, perhaps, to liberate us,' said Emily; 'Signor Montoni perhaps is—is conquered.'

The belief of his death gave her spirits a sudden shock, and she grew faint as she saw him, in imagination, expiring at her feet.

'They are coming!' cried Madame Montoni—'I hear their steps—they are at the door.'

Emily turned her languid eyes to the door, but terror deprived her of utterance. The key sounded in the lock; the door opened, and Montoni appeared, followed by three ruffian-like men. 'Execute your orders,' said he, turning to them, and pointing to his wife, who shrieked, but was immediately carried from the room; while Emily sunk senseless on a couch, by which she had endeavoured to support herself. When she recovered, she was alone, and recollected only that Madame Montoni had been there, together with some unconnected particulars of the preceding transaction, which were, however, sufficient to renew all her terror. She looked wildly round the apartment, as if in search of some means of intelligence concerning her aunt, while neither her own danger, nor an idea of escaping from the room, immediately occurred.

When her recollection was more complete, she raised herself and went, but with only a faint hope, to examine whether the door was unfastened. It was so, and she then stepped timidly out into the gallery, but paused there, uncertain which way she should proceed. Her first wish was to gather some information as to her aunt, and she at length turned her steps to go to the lesser hall, where Annette and the other servants usually waited.

Everywhere, as she passed, she heard, from a distance, the uproar of contention, and the figures and faces which she met, hurrying along the passages, struck her mind with dismay. Emily might now have appeared like an angel of light encompassed by fiends. At length she reached the lesser hall, which was silent and deserted, but, panting for breath, she sat down to recover herself. The total stillness of this place was as awful as the tumult from which she had escaped; but she had now time to recall her scattered thoughts, to remember her personal danger; and to consider of some means of safety. She perceived that it was useless to seek Madame Montoni, through the wide extent and intricacies of the castle, now too, when every avenue seemed to be beset with ruffians; in this hall she could not resolve to stay, for she knew not how soon it might become their place of rendezvous; and though she wished to go to her chamber, she dreaded again to encounter them on the way.

Thus she sat, trembling and hesitating, when a distant murmur broke on the silence, and grew louder and louder, till she distinguished voices and steps approaching. She then rose to go; but the sounds came along the only passage by which she could depart, and she was compelled to await in the hall the arrival of the persons whose steps she heard. As these advanced, she distinguished groans, and then saw a man borne slowly along by four others. Her spirits faltered at the sight, and she leaned against the wall for support. The bearers meanwhile entered the hall, and being too busily occupied to detain, or even notice Emily, she attempted to leave it; but her strength failed, and she again sat down on the bench. A damp chillness came over her; her sight became confused; she knew not what had passed, or where she was, yet the groans of the wounded person still vibrated on her heart. In a few moments the tide of life seemed again to flow; she began to breathe more freely, and her senses revived. She had not fainted, nor had ever totally lost her consciousness, but had contrived to support herself on the bench; still without courage to turn her eyes upon the unfortunate object which remained near her, and about whom the men were yet too much engaged to attend her.

When her strength returned, she rose, and was suffered to leave the hall, though her anxiety, having produced some vain inquiries concerning Madame Montoni, had thus made a discovery of herself. Towards her chamber she now hastened as fast as her steps would bear her; for she still perceived, upon her passage, the sounds of confusion at a distance, and she endeavoured, by taking her way through some obscure rooms, to avoid encountering the persons whose looks had terrified her before, as well as those parts of the castle where the tumult might still rage.

At length she reached her chamber, and, having secured the door of the corridor, felt herself for a moment in safety. A profound stillness reigned in this remote apartment, which not even the faint murmur of the most distant sounds now reached. She sat down near one of the casements; and as she gazed on the mountain-view beyond, the deep repose of its beauty struck her with all the force of contrast, and she could scarcely believe herself so near a scene of savage discord. The contending elements seemed to have retired from their natural spheres, and to have collected themselves into the mind of men, for there alone the tempest now reigned.

Emily tried to tranquillize her spirits; but anxiety made her constantly listen for some sound, and often look out upon the ramparts, where all, however, was lonely and still. As a sense of her own immediate danger had decreased, her apprehension concerning Madame Montoni heightened, who, she remembered, had been fiercely threatened with confinement in the east turret, and it was possible that her husband had satisfied his vengeance with this punishment. She therefore determined, when night should return, and the inhabitants of the castle should be asleep, to explore the way to the turret, which, as the direction it stood in was mentioned, appeared not very difficult to be done. She knew indeed that, although her aunt might be there, she could afford her no assistance, but it might give her some comfort even to know that she was discovered, and to hear the sound of her niece's voice: for herself, any certainty concerning Madame Montoni's fate, appeared more tolerable than this exhausting suspense.

Meanwhile Annette did not appear, and Emily was surprised, and somewhat alarmed for her, whom in the confusion of the late scene, various accidents might have befallen, and it was improbable that she would have failed to come to her apartment, unless something unfortunate had happened.

Thus the hours passed in solitude, in silence, and in anxious conjecturing. Being not once disturbed by a message or a sound, it appeared that Montoni had wholly forgotten her, and it gave her some comfort to find that she could be so unnoticed. She endeavoured to withdraw her thoughts from the anxiety that preyed upon them, but they refused control; she could neither read nor draw, and the tones of her lute were so utterly discordant with the present state of her feelings, that she could not endure them for a moment.

The sun at length set behind the western mountains; his fiery beams faded from the clouds, and then a dun melancholy purple drew over them, and gradually involved the features of the country below. Soon after, the sentinels passed on the rampart to commence the watch.

Twilight had now spread its gloom over every object; the dismal obscurity of her chamber recalled fearful thoughts: but she remembered that, to procure a light, she must pass through a great extent of the castle, and above all, through the halls where she had already experienced so much horror. Darkness indeed in the present state of her spirits made silence and solitude terrible to her; it would also prevent the possibility of her finding her way to the turret, and condemn her to remain in suspense concerning the fate of her aunt; yet she dared not to venture forth for a lamp.

Continuing at the casement, that she might catch the last lingering gleam of evening, a thousand vague images of fear floated on her fancy. 'What if some of these ruffians,' said she, 'should find out the private staircase, and in the darkness of night steal into my chamber!' Then recollecting the mysterious inhabitant of the neighbouring apartment, her terror changed its object. 'He is not a pri-

soner,' said she, 'though he remains in one chamber, for Montoni did not fasten the door when he left it; the unknown person himself did this; it is certain, therefore, he can come out when he pleases.'

She paused; for notwithstanding the terrors of darkness, she considered it to be very improbable, whoever he was, that he could have any interest in intruding upon her retirement; and again the subject of her emotion changed, when, remembering her nearness to the chamber where the veil had formerly disclosed a dreadful spectacle, she doubted whether some passage might not communicate between it and the insecure door of the staircase.

It was now entirely dark, and she left the casement. As she sat with her eyes fixed on the hearth, she thought she perceived a spark of light; it twinkled and disappeared, and then again was visible. At length, with much care, she fanned the embers of a wood fire, that had been lighted in the morning, into flame, and, having communicated it to a lamp which always stood in her room, felt a satisfaction not to be conceived without a review of her situation. Her first care was to guard the door of the staircase, for which purpose she placed against it all the furniture she could move, and she was thus employed for some time, at the end of which she had another instance how much more oppressive misfortune is to the idle than to the busy; for, having then leisure to think over all the circumstances of her present afflictions, she imagined a thousand evils for futurity, and these real and ideal subjects of distress alike wounded her mind.

Thus heavily moved the hours till midnight, when she counted the sullen notes of the great clock as they rolled along the rampart unmingled with any sound except the distant foot-fall of a sentinel who came to relieve guard. She now thought she might venture towards the turret, and having gently opened the chamber door to examine the corridor, and to listen if any person was stirring in the castle, found all around in perfect stillness. Yet no sooner had she left the room than she perceived a light flash on the walls of the corridor, and without waiting to see by whom it was carried, she shrunk back and closed her door. No one approaching, she conjectured that it was Montoni going to pay his midnight visit to her unknown neighbour, and she determined to wait till he should have retired to his own apartment.

When the chimes had tolled another half-hour, she once more opened the door; and perceiving that no person was in the corridor, hastily crossed into a passage that led along the south side of the castle towards the staircase, whence she believed she could easily find her way to the turret. Often pausing on her way, listening apprehensively to the murmurs of the wind, and looking fearfully onward into the gloom of the long passages, she at length reached the staircase; but there her perplexity began. Two passages appeared, of which she knew not how to prefer one, and was compelled at last to decide by chance rather than by circumstances. That she entered opened first into a wide gallery, along which she passed lightly and swiftly; for the lonely aspect of the place awed her, and she started at the echo of her own steps.

On a sudden, she thought she heard a voice, and not distinguishing from whence it came, feared equally to proceed or to return. For some moments she stood in an attitude of listening expectation, shrinking almost from herself, and scarcely daring to look round her. The voice came again: but though it was now near her, terror did not allow her to judge exactly whence it proceeded. She thought, however, that it was the voice of complaint, and her belief was soon confirmed by a low moaning sound, that seemed to proceed from one of the chambers opening into the gallery. It instantly occurred to her that Madame Montoni might be there confined, and she advanced to the door to speak, but was checked by considering that she was perhaps going to commit herself to a stranger, who might discover her to Montoni; for though this person, whoever it was, seemed to be in affliction, it did not follow that he was a prisoner.

While these thoughts passed over her mind, and left her still in hesitation, the voice spoke again, and calling Ludovico, she then perceived it to be that of Annette; on which, no longer hesitating, she went in joy to answer her.

'Ludovico!' cried Annette, sobbing—'Ludovico!'

'It is I,' said Emily, trying to open the door. 'How came you here? Who shut you up?'

'Ludovico!' repeated Annette—'O, Ludovico!'

'It is not Ludovico, it is I—Mademoiselle Emily.'

Annette ceased sobbing, and was silent.

'If you can open the door, let me in,' said Emily; 'here is no person to hurt you.'

'Ludovico!—O, Ludovico!' cried Annette.

Emily now lost her patience; and the fear of being overheard increasing, she was even nearly about to leave the door, when she considered that Annette might possibly know something of the situation of Madame Montoni, or direct her to the turret. At length she obtained a reply, though little satisfactory, to her questions; for Annette knew nothing of Madame Montoni, and only conjured Emily to tell her what was become of Ludovico. Of him she had no information to give, and she again asked who had shut Annette up.

'Ludovico,' said the poor girl, 'Ludovico shut me up. When I ran away from the dressing-room door to-day, I went I scarcely knew where for safety; and in this gallery here, I met Ludovico, who hurried me into this chamber, and locked me up to keep me out of harm, as he said. But he was in such a hurry himself he hardly spoke ten words; but he told me he would come and let me out when all was quiet, and he took away the key with him. Now all these hours have passed, and I have neither seen nor heard a word of him; they have murdered him—I know they have!'

Emily suddenly remembered the wounded person whom she had seen borne into the servants' hall, and she scarcely doubted that he was Ludovico; but she concealed the circumstance from Annette, and endeavoured to comfort her. Then, impatient to learn something of her aunt, she again inquired the way to the turret.

'O! you are not going, ma'amselle,' said Annette; 'for Heaven's sake, do not go and leave me here by myself!'

'Nay, Annette, you do not think I can wait in the gallery all night,' replied Emily. 'Direct me to the turret; in the morning I will endeavour to release you.'

'O holy Mary!' exclaimed Annette, 'am I to stay here by myself all night! I shall be frightened out of my senses, and I shall die of hunger; I have had nothing to eat since dinner!'

Emily could scarcely forbear smiling at the heterogeneous distresses of Annette, though she sincerely pitied them, and said what she could to soothe her. At length she obtained something like a direction to the east turret, and quitted the door, from whence, after many intricacies and perplexities, she reached the steep and winding stairs of the turret, at the foot of which she stopped to rest, and to reanimate her courage with a sense of her duty. As she surveyed this dismal place she perceived a door on the opposite side of the staircase, and anxious to know whether it would lead her to Madame Montoni, she tried to undraw the bolts which fastened it. A fresher air came to her face, as she unclosed the door, which opened upon the east rampart, and the sudden current had nearly extinguished her light, which she now removed to a distance; and again looking out upon the obscure terrace, she perceived only the faint outline of the walls and of some towers, while above, heavy clouds borne along the wind seemed to mingle with the stars and wrap the night in thicker darkness. As she gazed, now willing to defer the moment of certainty, from which she expected only confirmation of evil, a distant footstep reminded her that she might be observed by the men on watch; and hastily closing the door, she took her lamp, and passed up the staircase. Trembling came upon her as she ascended through the gloom. To her melancholy fancy this seemed to be a place of death, and the chilling silence that reigned confirmed its character. Her spirits faltered. 'Perhaps,' said she, 'I am come hither only to learn a dreadful truth, or to witness some horrible spectacle ; I feel that my senses would not survive such an addition of horror.'

The image of her aunt murdered—murdered, perhaps, by the hand of Montoni, rose to her mind ; she trembled, gasped for breath —repented that she had dared to venture hither, and checked her steps. But after she had paused a few minutes, the consciousness of her duty returned as she went on. Still all was silent. At length a track of blood upon a stair caught her eye ; and instantly she perceived that the wall and several other steps were stained. She paused, again struggled to support herself, and the lamp almost fell from her trembling hand. Still no sound was heard, no living being seemed to inhabit the turret : a thousand times she wished herself again in her chamber ; dreaded to inquire further—dreaded to encounter some horrible spectacle—and yet could not resolve, now that she was so near the termination of her efforts, to desist from them. Having again collected courage to proceed, after ascending about half way up the turret she came to another door ; but here again she stopped in hesitation, listened for sounds within, and then summoning all her resolution, unclosed it, and entered a chamber, which, as her lamp shot its feeble rays through the darkness, seemed to exhibit only dew-stained and deserted walls. As she stood examining it, in fearful expectation of discovering the remains of her unfortunate aunt, she perceived something lying in an obscure corner of the room, and struck with a horrible conviction, she became for an instant motionless and nearly insensible. Then with a kind of desperate resolution she hurried towards the object that excited her terror, when, perceiving the clothes of some person on the floor, she caught hold of them, and found in her grasp the old uniform of a soldier, beneath which appeared a heap of pikes and other arms. Scarcely daring to trust her sight, she continued for some moments to gaze on the object of her late alarm ; and then left the chamber, so much comforted and occupied by the conviction that her aunt was not there, that she was going to descend the turret without inquiring further ; when, on turning to do so, she observed upon some steps on the second flight an appearance of blood ; and remembering that there was yet another chamber to be explored, she again followed the windings of the ascent. Still, as she ascended, the track of blood glared upon the stairs.

It led her to the door of a landing-place that terminated them, but she was unable to follow it further. Now that she was so near the sought-for certainty, she dreaded to know

it even more than before, and had not fortitude sufficient to speak, or to attempt opening the door.

Having listened in vain for some sound that might confirm or destroy her fears, she at length laid her hand on the lock, and finding it fastened, called on Madame Montoni ; but only a chilling silence ensued.

'She is dead!' she cried,—'murdered ! her blood is on the stairs !'

Emily grew very faint ; could support herself no longer ; and had scarcely presence of mind to set down the lamp, and place herself on a step.

When her recollection returned, she spoke again at the door, and again attempted to open it ; and having lingered for some time without receiving any answer, or hearing any sound, she descended the turret, and, with all the swiftness her feebleness would permit, sought her own apartment.

As she turned into the corridor, the door of a chamber opened, from whence Montoni came forth ; but Emily, more terrified than ever to behold him, shrunk back into the passage soon enough to escape being noticed, and heard him close the door, which she had perceived was the same she formerly observed. Having here listened to his departing steps till their faint sound was lost in distance, she ventured to her apartment, and, securing it, once again retired to her bed, leaving the lamp burning on the hearth. But sleep was fled from her harassed mind, to which images of horror alone occurred. She endeavoured to think it possible that Madame Montoni had not been taken to the turret ; but when she recollected the former menaces of her husband, and the terrible spirit of vengeance which he had displayed on a late occasion ; when she remembered his general character, the looks of the men who had forced Madame Montoni from her apartment, and the written traces on the stairs of the turret—she could not doubt that her aunt had been carried thither, and could scarcely hope that she had not been carried to be murdered.

The gray of morning had long dawned through her casements before Emily closed her eyes in sleep ; when wearied nature at length yielded her a respite from suffering.

CHAPTER XXV.

'Who rears the bloody hand?'

SAVER.

EMILY remained in her chamber on the following morning, without any notice from Montoni, or seeing a human being, except the armed men who sometimes passed on the terrace below. Having tasted no food since the dinner of the preceding day, extreme faintness made her feel the necessity of quitting the asylum of her apartment to obtain refreshment, and she was also very anxious to procure liberty for Annette. Willing, however, to defer venturing forth as long as possible, and considering whether she should apply to Montoni or to the compassion of some other person, her excessive anxiety concerning her aunt at length overcame her abhorrence of his presence, and she determined to go to him, and to entreat that he would suffer her to see Madame Montoni.

Meanwhile it was too certain, from the absence of Annette, that some accident had befallen Ludovico, and that she was still in confinement: Emily therefore resolved also to visit the chamber where she had spoken to her on the preceding night, and, if the poor girl was yet there, to inform Montoni of her situation.

It was near noon before she ventured from her apartment, and went first to the south gallery, whither she passed without meeting a single person or hearing a sound, except now and then the echo of a distant footstep.

It was unnecessary to call Annette, whose lamentations were audible upon the first approach to the gallery, and who, bewailing her own and Ludovico's fate, told Emily that she should certainly be starved to death if she was not let out immediately. Emily replied that she was going to beg her release of Montoni: but the terrors of hunger now yielded to those of the signor; and when Emily left her, she was loudly entreating that her place of refuge might be concealed from him.

As Emily drew near the great hall, the sounds she heard and the people she met in the passages renewed her alarm. The latter, however, were peaceable, and did not interrupt her, though they looked earnestly at her as she passed, and sometimes spoke. On crossing the hall towards the cedar room, where Montoni usually sat, she perceived on the pavement fragments of swords, some tattered garments stained with blood, and almost expected to have seen among them a dead body; but from such a spectacle she was at present spared. As she approached the room, the sound of several voices issued from within; and a dread of appearing before many strangers, as well as of irritating Montoni by such an intrusion, made her pause and falter from her purpose. She looked up through the long arcades of the hall, in search of a servant who might bear a message; but no one appeared, and the urgency of what she had to request made her still linger near the door. The voices within were not in contention, though she distinguished those of several of the guests of the preceding day; but still her resolution failed whenever she would have tapped at the door, and she had determined to walk in the hall till some person should appear who might call Montoni from the room; when, as she turned from the door, it was suddenly opened by himself. Emily trembled and was confused, while he almost started with surprise, and all the terrors of his countenance unfolded themselves. She forgot all she would have said, and neither inquired for her aunt, nor entreated for Annette, but stood silent and embarrassed.

After closing the door, he reproved her for a meanness of which she had not been guilty, and sternly questioned her what she had overheard; an accusation which revived her recollection so far, that she assured him she had not come thither with an intention to listen to his conversation, but to entreat his compassion for her aunt and for Annette. Montoni seemed to doubt this assertion, for he regarded her with a scrutinizing look; and the doubt evidently arose from no trifling interest. Emily then further explained herself, and concluded with entreating him to inform her where her aunt was placed, and to permit that she might visit her; but he looked upon her only with a malignant smile, which instantaneously confirmed her worst fears for her aunt, and at that moment she had not courage to renew her entreaties.

'For Annette,' said he—'if you go to Carlo, he will release the girl; the foolish fellow who shut her up, died yesterday.'

Emily shuddered——'But my aunt, signor,' said she, 'O tell me of my aunt!'

'She is taken care of,' replied Montoni hastily; 'I have no time to answer idle questions.'

He would have passed on; but Emily, in a voice of agony that could not be wholly resisted, conjured him to tell her where Madame Montoni was; while he paused, and she anxiously watched his countenance, a trumpet sounded, and in the next moment she heard the heavy gates of the portal open, and then the clattering of horses' hoofs in the court, with the confusion of many voices. She stood for a moment hesitating whether she should follow Montoni, who at the sound of the trumpet had passed through the hall; and turning her eyes whence it came, she saw, through the door that opened beyond a long perspective of arches into the courts, a party of horsemen, whom she judged, as well as the distance and her embarrassment would allow, to be the same she had seen depart a few days before. But she staid not to scrutinize; for when the trumpet sounded again, the chevaliers rushed out of the cedar room, and men came running into the hall from every quarter of the castle. Emily once more hurried for shelter to her own apartment. Thither she was still pursued by images of horror. She reconsidered Montoni's manner and words when he had spoken of his wife, and they served only to confirm her most terrible suspicions. Tears refused any longer to relieve her distress; and she had sat for a considerable time absorbed in thought, when a knocking at the chamber door roused her, on opening which she found old Carlo.

'Dear young lady,' said he, 'I have been so flurried, I never once thought of you till just now: I have brought you some fruit and wine, and I am sure you must stand in need of them by this time.'

'Thank you, Carlo,' said Emily; 'this is very good of you. Did the signor remind you of me?'

'No, signora,' replied Carlo, 'his *Excellenza* has business enough on his hands.' Emily then renewed her inquiries concerning Madame Montoni; but Carlo had been employed at the other end of the castle during the time that she was removed, and he had heard nothing since concerning her.

While he spoke, Emily looked steadily at him; for she scarcely knew whether he was really ignorant, or concealed his knowledge of the truth from a fear of offending his master. To several questions concerning the contentions of yesterday he gave very limited answers; but told that the disputes were now amicably settled, and that the signor believed himself to have been mistaken in his suspicions of his guests. 'The fighting was about that, signora,' said Carlo; 'but I trust I shall never see such another day in this castle, though strange things are about to be done.'

On her inquiring his meaning, 'Ah, signora!' added he, 'it is not for me to betray secrets, or tell all I think, but time will tell.'

She then desired him to release Annette; and having described the chamber in which the poor girl was confined, he promised to obey her immediately, and was departing, when she remembered to ask who were the persons just arrived. Her late conjecture was right; it was Verezzi, with his party.

Her spirits were somewhat soothed by this short conversation with Carlo; for in her present circumstances it afforded some comfort to hear the accents of compassion and to meet the look of sympathy.

An hour passed before Annette appeared, who then came weeping and sobbing: 'O Ludovico, Ludovico!' cried she.

'My poor Annette!' said Emily, and made her sit down.

'Who could have foreseen this, ma'amselle? O miserable wretched day—that ever I should live to see it!' and she continued to moan and lament till Emily thought it necessary to check her excess of grief. 'We are continually losing dear friends by death,' said she with a sigh that came from her heart. 'We must submit to the will of Heaven—our tears, alas! cannot recall the dead!'

Annette took the handkerchief from her face.

'You will meet Ludovico in a better world, I hope,' added Emily.

'Yes—yes—ma'amselle,' sobbed Annette; 'but I hope I shall meet him again in this—though he is so wounded!'

'Wounded!' exclaimed Emily; 'does he live?'

'Yes, ma'am, but—but he has a terrible wound, and could not come to let me out. They thought him dead at first, and he has not been rightly himself till within this hour.'

'Well, Annette, I rejoice to hear he lives.'

'Lives! Holy Saints! why he will not die, surely!'

Emily said she hoped not; but this expression of hope Annette thought implied fear, and her own increased in proportion as Emily endeavoured to encourage her. To inquiries concerning Madame Montoni she could give no satisfactory answers.

'I quite forgot to ask among the servants,' ma'amselle,' said she, 'for I could think of nobody but poor Ludovico.'

Annette's grief was now somewhat assuaged, and Emily sent her to make inquiries concerning her lady, of whom, however, she could obtain no intelligence, some of the people she spoke with being really ignorant of her fate, and others having probably received orders to conceal it.

This day passed with Emily in continued grief and anxiety for her aunt; but she was unmolested by any notice from Montoni; and now that Annette was liberated, she obtained food without exposing herself to danger or impertinence.

Two following days passed in the same manner, unmarked by any occurrence, during which she obtained no information of Madame Montoni. On the evening of the second, having dismissed Annette and retired to bed, her mind became haunted by the most dismal images, such as her long anxiety concerning her aunt suggested; and unable to forget herself for a moment, or to vanquish the phantoms that tormented her, she rose from her bed, and went to one of the casements of her chamber to breathe a freer air.

All without was silent and dark, unless that could be called light which was only the faint glimmer of the stars, showing imperfectly the outline of the mountains, the western towers of the castle, and the ramparts below where a solitary sentinel was pacing. What an image of repose did this scene present! The fierce and terrible passions, too, which so often agitated the inhabitants of this edifice, seemed now hushed in sleep;—those mysterious workings that rouse the elements of man's nature into tempest—were calm. Emily's heart was not so; but her sufferings, though deep, partook of the gentle character of her mind. Hers was a silent anguish, weeping yet enduring; not the wild energy of passion, inflaming imagination, bearing down the barriers of reason, and living in a world of its own.

The air refreshed her, and she continued at the casement looking on the shadowy scene, over which the planets burned with a clear light, amid the deep blue ether, as they silently moved in their destined course. She remembered how often she had gazed on them with her dear father, how often he had pointed out their way in the heavens, and explained their laws : and these reflections led to others, which in an almost equal degree awakened her grief and astonishment.

They brought a retrospect of all the strange and mournful events which had occurred since she lived in peace with her parents. And to Emily, who had been so tenderly educated, so tenderly loved, who once knew only goodness and happiness—to her, the late events and her present situation—in a foreign land—in a remote castle—surrounded by vice and violence, seemed more like the visions of a distempered, imagination, than the circumstances of truth. She wept to think of what her parents would have suffered, could they have foreseen the events of her future life.

While she raised her streaming eyes to heaven, she observed the same planet which she had seen in Languedoc, on the night preceding her father's death, rise above the eastern towers of the castle, while she remembered the conversation which had passed concerning the probable state of departed souls ; remembered also the solemn music she had heard, and to which the tenderness of her spirit had, in spite of her reason, given a superstitious meaning. At these recollections she wept again, and continued musing ; when suddenly the notes of sweet music passed on the air. A superstitious dread stole over her ; she stood listening for some moments in trembling expectation, and then endeavoured to re-collect her thoughts, and to reason herself into composure : but human reason cannot establish her laws on subjects lost in the obscurity of imagination, any more than the eye can ascertain the form of objects that only glimmer through the dimness of night.

Her surprise on hearing such soothing and delicious sounds, was at least justifiable ; for it was long, very long, since she had listened to anything like melody. The fierce trumpet and the shrill fife were the only instruments she had heard since her arrival at Udolpho.

When her mind was somewhat more composed, she tried to ascertain from what quarter the sounds proceeded, and thought they came from below ; but whether from a room of the castle, or from the terrace, she could not with certainty judge. Fear and surprise now yielded to the enchantment of a strain that floated on the silent night with the most soft and melancholy sweetness. Suddenly it seemed removed to a distance, trembled faintly, and then entirely ceased.

She continued to listen, sunk in that pleasing repose which soft music leaves on the mind—but it came no more. Upon this strange circumstance her thoughts were long engaged ; for strange it certainly was to hear music at midnight, when every inhabitant of the castle had long since retired to rest, and in a place where nothing like harmony had been heard before, probably for many years. Long suffering had made her spirits peculiarly sensible to terror, and liable to be affected by the illusions of superstition.—It now seemed to her as if her dead father had spoken to her in that strain, to inspire her with comfort and confidence on the subject which had then occupied her mind. Yet reason told her that this was a wild conjecture, and she was inclined to dismiss it ; but, with the inconsistency so natural when imagination guides the thoughts, she then wavered towards a belief as wild. She remembered the singular event connected with the castle, which had given it into the possession of its present owner ; and when she considered the mysterious manner in which its late possessor had disappeared, and that she had never since been heard of, her mind was impressed with a high degree of solemn awe ; so that, though there appeared no clue to connect that event with the late music, she was inclined fancifully to think they had some relation to each other. At this conjecture, a sudden chillness ran through her frame ; she looked fearfully upon the duskiness of her chamber, and the dead silence that prevailed there heightened to her fancy its gloomy aspect.

At length she left the casement ; but her steps faltered as she approached the bed, and she stopped and looked round. The single lamp that burned in her spacious chamber was expiring ; for a moment she shrunk from the darkness beyond ; and then, ashamed of the weakness, which, however, she could not wholly conquer, went forward to the bed, where her mind did not soon know the soothings of sleep. She still mused on the late occurrence, and looked with anxiety to the next night, when at the same hour she determined to watch whether the music returned. 'If those sounds were human,' said she, 'I shall probably hear them again.'

END OF PART I.

BILLING AND SONS, PRINTERS, GUILDFORD, SURREY.

THE

MYSTERIES OF UDOLPHO

A ROMANCE

BY

A N N   R A D C L I F F E

AUTHOR OF "THE ROMANCE OF THE FOREST" AND "THE ITALIAN"

* *

LONDON AND NEW YORK
GEORGE ROUTLEDGE AND SONS
1877

THE MYSTERIES OF UDOLPHO.

CHAPTER XXVI.

'Then, oh, you blessed ministers above,
Keep me in patiénce; and, in ripen'd time,
Unfold the evil which is here wrapt up
In countenance.'
                                SHAKSPEARE.

ANNETTE came almost breathless to Emily's apartment in the morning. 'O ma'amselle!' said she in broken sentences, 'what news I have to tell! I have found out who the prisoner is—but he was no prisoner neither;—he that was shut up in the chamber I told you of. I must think him a ghost forsooth!'

'Who was the prisoner?' inquired Emily, while her thoughts glanced back to the circumstance of the preceding night.

'You mistake, ma'am,' said Annette; 'he was not a prisoner, after all.'

'Who is the person, then?'

'Holy saints!' rejoined Annette; 'how I was surprised; I met him just now, on the rampart below there. I never was so surprised in my life! Ah! ma'amselle! this is a strange place! I should never have done wondering, if I was to live here a hundred years. But, as I was saying, I met him just now on the rampart, and I was thinking of nobody less than of him.'

'This trifling is insupportable,' said Emily; 'pr'ythee, Annette, do not torture my patience any longer.'

'Nay, ma'amselle, guess—guess who it was; it was somebody you know very well.'

'I cannot guess,' said Emily impatiently.

'Nay, ma'amselle, I'll tell you something to guess by—A tall signor, with a longish face, who walks so stately, and used to wear such a high feather in his hat; and used often to look down upon the ground when people spoke to him; and to look at people from under his eyebrows, as it were, all so dark and frowning. You have seen him often and often at Venice, ma'am. Then he was so intimate with the signor, too. And, now I think of it, I wonder what he could be afraid of in this lonely old castle, that he shut himself up for. But he is come abroad now, for I met him on the rampart just this minute.'

I trembled when I saw him, for I always was afraid of him, somehow; but I determined I would not let him see it; so I went up to him, and made him a low curtsy: "You are welcome to the castle, Signor Orsini," said I.'

'O, it was Signor Orsini, then!' said Emily.

'Yes, ma'amselle, Signor Orsini himself, who caused that Venetian gentleman to be killed, and has been popping about from place to place ever since, as I hear.'

'Good God!' exclaimed Emily, recovering from the shock of this intelligence; 'and is he come to Udolpho? He does well to endeavour to conceal himself.'

'Yes, ma'amselle; but if that was all, this desolate place would conceal him, without his shutting himself up in one room. Who would think of coming to look for him here? I am sure I should as soon think of going to look for anybody in the world.'

'There is some truth in that,' said Emily, who would now have concluded it was Orsini's music which she had heard on the preceding night, had she not known that he had neither taste nor skill in the art. But though she was unwilling to add to the number of Annette's surprises, by mentioning the subject of her own, she inquired whether any person in the castle played on a musical instrument.

'O yes, ma'amselle; there is Benedetto plays the great drum to admiration; and then, there is Launcelot the trumpeter; nay, for that matter, Ludovico himself can play on the trumpet;—but he is ill now. I remember once——'

Emily interrupted her; 'Have you heard no other music since you came to the castle? —none last night?'

'Why, did *you* hear any last night, ma'amselle?'

Emily evaded this question by repeating her own.

'Why, no, ma'am,' replied Annette: 'I never heard any music here, I must say, but the drums and the trumpet; and as for last night, I did nothing but dream I saw my late lady's ghost.'

6—2

'Your *late* lady's,' said Emily in a tremulous voice : 'you have heard more, then ! Tell me—tell me all, Annette, I entreat ; tell me the worst at once.'

'Nay, ma'amselle—you know the worst already.'

'I know nothing,' said Emily.

'Yes, you do, ma'amselle : you know that nobody knows anything about her ; and it is plain, therefore, she is gone the way of the first lady of the castle—nobody ever knew anything about her.'

Emily leaned her head upon her hand, and was for some time silent : then, telling Annette she wished to be alone, the latter left the room.

The remark of Annette had revived Emily's terrible suspicion concerning the fate of Madame Montoni ; and she resolved to make another effort to obtain certainty on this subject, by applying to Montoni once more.

When Annette returned, a few hours after, she told Emily that the porter of the castle wished very much to speak with her, for that he had something of importance to say : her spirits had, however, of late been so subject to alarm, that any new circumstance excited it ; and this message from the porter, when her first surprise was over, made her look round for some lurking danger—the more suspiciously, perhaps, because she had frequently remarked the unpleasant air and countenance of this man. She now hesitated whether to speak with him, doubting, even, that this request was only a pretext to draw her into some danger : but a little reflection showed her the improbability of this ; and she blushed at her weak fears.

'I will speak to him, Annette,' said she : 'desire him to come to the corridor immediately.'

Annette departed, and soon after returned.

'Barnardine, ma'amselle,' said she, 'dare not come to the corridor, lest he should be discovered, it is so far from his post ; and he dare not even leave the gates for a moment now : but if you will come to him at the portal, through some roundabout passages he told me of, without crossing the courts, he has that to tell which will surprise you : but you must not come through the courts, lest the signor should see you.'

Emily, neither approving these roundabout passages nor the other part of the request, now positively refused to go. 'Tell him,' said she, 'if he has anything of consequence to impart, I will hear him in the corridor, whenever he has an opportunity of coming thither.'

Annette went to deliver this message, and was absent a considerable time. When she returned—'It won't do, ma'amselle,' said she : 'Barnardine has been considering, all this time, what can be done ; for it is as much as his place is worth to leave his post

now ; but if you will come to the east rampart in the dusk of the evening, he can, perhaps, steal away, and tell you all he has to say.'

Emily was surprised and alarmed at the secrecy which this man seemed to think so necessary, and hesitated whether to meet him —till, considering that he might mean to warn her of some serious danger, she resolved to go.

'Soon after sunset,' said she, 'I will be at the end of the east rampart. But then the watch will be set,' she added, recollecting herself ; 'and how can Barnardine pass unobserved ?'

'That is just what I said to him, ma'am : and he answered me, that he had the key of the gate at the end of the rampart, that leads towards the courts, and could let himself through that way ; and as for the sentinels, there were none at this end of the terrace, because the place is guarded enough by the high walls of the castle and the east turret : and he said, those at the other end were too far off to see him, if it was pretty duskyish.'

'Well,' said Emily, 'I must hear what he has to tell ; and therefore desire you will go with me to the terrace this evening.'

'He desired it might be pretty duskyish, ma'amselle,' repeated Annette, 'because of the watch.'

Emily paused ; and then said she would be on the terrace an hour after sunset ;—'and tell Barnardine,' she added, 'to be punctual to the time ; for that I, also, may be observed by Signor Montoni.—Where is the signor ? I would speak with him.'

'He is in the cedar chamber, ma'am, counselling with the other signors. He is going to give them a sort of treat to-day, to make up for what passed at the last, I suppose ; the people are all very busy in the kitchen.'

Emily now inquired if Montoni expected any new guests ; and Annette believed that he did not. 'Poor Ludovico !' added she : 'he would be as merry as the best of them, if he was well. But he may recover yet : Count Morano was wounded as bad as he, and he is got well again, and is gone back to Venice.'

'Is he so ?' said Emily ; 'when did you hear this ?'

'I heard it last night, ma'amselle ; but I forgot to tell it.'

Emily asked some further questions ; and then, desiring Annette would observe, and inform her when Montoni was alone, the girl went to deliver her message to Barnardine.

Montoni was however so much engaged during the whole day, that Emily had no opportunity of seeking a release from her terrible suspense concerning her aunt. Annette was employed in watching his steps, and in attending upon Ludovico, whom she, assisted by Caterina, nursed with the utmost care ; and Emily was of course left much alone. Her thoughts often dwelt on the message of the porter, and were employed in conjecturing the subject that occasioned it ; which she sometimes imagined concerned the fate of Madame Montoni ; at others, that it related to some personal danger which threatened herself. The cautious secrecy which Barnardine observed in his conduct, inclined her to believe the latter.

As the hour of appointment drew near, her impatience increased. At length the sun set : she heard the passing steps of the sentinels going to their posts, and waited only for Annette to accompany her to the terrace ; who soon after came, and they descended together. When Emily expressed apprehensions of meeting Montoni or some of his guests—' O ! there is no fear of that, ma'amselle,' said Annette ; ' they are all set in to feasting yet ; and that Barnardine knows.'

They reached the first terrace, where the sentinels demanded who passed ; and Emily, having answered, walked on to the east rampart ; at the entrance of which they were again stopped ; and having again replied, were permitted to proceed. But Emily did not like to expose herself to the discretion of these men at such an hour ; and impatient to withdraw from the situation, she stepped hastily on in search of Barnardine. He was not yet come. She leaned pensively on the wall of the rampart, and waited for him. The gloom of twilight sat deep on the surrounding objects, blending in soft confusion the valley, the mountains, and the woods, whose tall heads stirred by the evening breeze gave the only sounds that stole on silence—except a faint, faint chorus of distant voices that arose from within the castle.

' What voices are those ?' said Emily as she fearfully listened.

' It is only the signor and his guests carousing,' replied Annette.

' Good God !' thought Emily, ' can this man's heart be so gay when he has made another being so wretched ?—if, indeed, my aunt is yet suffered to feel her wretchedness ! O ! whatever are my own sufferings, may my heart never, never be hardened against those of others !'

She looked up with a sensation of horror to the east turret, near which she then stood. A light glimmered through the grates of the lower chamber, but those of the upper one were dark. Presently she perceived a person moving with a lamp across the lower room : but this circumstance revived no hope concerning Madame Montoni, whom she had vainly sought in that apartment, which had appeared to contain only soldiers' accoutrements : Emily, however, determined to attempt the outer door of the turret as soon as Barnardine should withdraw ; and, if it was unfastened, to make another effort to discover her aunt.

The moments passed, but still Barnardine did not appear ; and Emily, becoming uneasy, hesitated whether to wait any longer. She would have sent Annette to the portal to hasten him, but feared to be left alone : for it was now almost dark, and a melancholy streak of red, that still lingered in the west, was the only vestige of departed day. The strong interest, however, which Barnardine's message had awakened, overcame other apprehensions, and still detained her.

While she was conjecturing with Annette what could thus occasion his absence, they heard a key turn in the lock of the gate near them, and presently saw a man advancing. It was Barnardine ; of whom Emily hastily inquired what he had to communicate, and desired that he would tell her quickly—' for I am chilled with this evening air,' said she.

' You must dismiss your maid, lady,' said the man in a voice the deep tone of which shocked her : ' what I have to tell is to you only.'

Emily, after some hesitation, desired Annette to withdraw to a little distance.—' Now, my friend, what would you say ?'

He was silent a moment, as if considering ; and then said,

' That which would cost me my place, at least, if it came to the signor's ears. You must promise, lady, that nothing shall ever make you tell a syllable of the matter. I have been trusted in this affair ; and if it was known that I betrayed my trust, my life perhaps might answer it : but I was concerned for you, lady ; and I resolved to tell you.' He paused.

Emily thanked him ; assured him that he might repose on her discretion : and entreated him to dispatch.

' Annette told us in the hall how unhappy you was about Signora Montoni, and how much you wished to know what was become of her.'

' Most true,' said Emily eagerly : ' and you can inform me ? I conjure you tell me the worst without hesitation.' She rested her trembling arm upon the wall.

' I can tell you,' said Barnardine, and paused.

Emily had no power to enforce her entreaties.

' I *can* tell you,' resumed Barnardine ;— —but——'

' But what ?' exclaimed Emily, recovering her resolution.

' Here I am, ma'amselle,' said Annette ; who, having heard the eager tone in which Emily pronounced these words, came running towards her.

' Retire !' said Barnardine sternly : ' you are not wanted :' and as Emily said nothing, Annette obeyed.

' I *can* tell you,' repeated the porter ;—' but I know not how :—you was afflicted before—'

'I am prepared for the worst, my friend,' said Emily in a firm and solemn voice ; ' I can support any certainty better than this suspense.'

'Well, signora, if that is the case, you shall hear.—You know, I suppose, that the signor and his lady used sometimes to disagree. It is none of my concerns to inquire what it was about ; but I believe you know it was so.'

'Well,' said Emily, 'proceed.'

'The signor, it seems, had lately been very wroth against her. I saw all, and heard all—a great deal more than people thought for ;—but it was none of my business, so I said nothing. A few days ago, the signor sent for me. "Barnardine," says he, "you are—an honest man : I think I can trust you." I assured his *Excellenza* that he could. "Then," says he—as near as I can remember—"I have an affair in hand which I want you to assist me in." Then he told me what I was to do ; but that I shall say nothing about—it concerned only the signora.'

'O heavens !' exclaimed Emily—' what have you done ?'

Barnardine hesitated, and was silent.

'What fiend could tempt him or you to such an act ?' cried Emily, chilled with horror and scarcely able to support her fainting spirit.

'It was a fiend,' said Barnardine in a gloomy tone of voice. They were now both silent : Emily had - not courage to inquire further, and Barnardine seemed to shrink from telling more. At length he said, ' It is of no use to think of the past. The signor was cruel enough, but he would be obeyed. What signified my refusing ? He would have found others who had no scruple.'

'You have murdered her, then !' said Emily in a hollow and inward voice—' I am talking with a murderer !' Barnardine stood silent ; while Emily turned from him, and attempted to leave the place.

'Stay, lady !' said he. ' You deserve to think so still—since you can believe me capable of such a deed.'

'If you are innocent, tell me quickly,' said Emily in faint accents ; ' for I feel I shall not be able to hear you long.'

'I will tell you no more,' said he, and walked away. Emily had just strength enough to bid him stay, and then to call Annette ; on whose arm she leaned, and they walked slowly up the rampart till they heard steps behind them. It was Barnardine again.

'Send away the girl,' said he, 'and I will tell you more.'

'She must not go,' said Emily : 'what you have to say she may hear.'

'May she so, lady ?' said he. 'You shall know no more then ;' and he was going, though slowly : when Emily's anxiety overcoming the resentment and fear which the man's behaviour had roused, she desired him to stay, and bade Annette retire.

'The signora is alive,' said he, 'for me. She is my prisoner, though : his *Excellenza* has shut her up in the chamber over the great gates of the court, and I have the charge of her. I was going to have told you you might see her —but now——'

Emily, relieved from an unutterable load of anguish by this speech, had now only to ask Barnardine's forgiveness, and to conjure that he would let her visit her aunt.

He complied with less reluctance than she expected ; and told her that if she would repair on the following night, when the signor was retired to rest, to the postern gate of the castle, she should perhaps see Madame Montoni.

Amid all the thankfulness which Emily felt for this concession, she thought she observed a malicious triumph in his manner when he pronounced the last words; but in the next moment she dismissed the thought ; and, having again thanked him, commended her aunt to his pity, and assured him that she herself would reward him, and would be punctual to her appointment : she bade him good-night, and retired, unobserved, to her chamber. It was a considerable time before the tumult of joy, which Barnardine's unexpected intelligence had occasioned, allowed Emily to think with clearness, or to be conscious of the real dangers that still surrounded Madame Montoni and herself. When this agitation subsided, she perceived that her aunt was yet the prisoner of a man to whose vengeance or avarice she might fall a sacrifice : and when she further considered the savage aspect of the person who was appointed to guard Madame Montoni, her doom appeared to be already sealed—for the countenance of Barnardine seemed to bear the stamp of a murderer ; and when she looked upon it, she felt inclined to believe that there was no deed, however black, which he might not be prevailed upon to execute. These reflections brought to her remembrance the tone of voice in which he had promised to grant her request to see his prisoner ; and she mused upon it long, in uneasiness and doubt. Sometimes she even hesitated whether to trust herself with him at the lonely hour he had appointed ; and once, and only once, it struck her, that Madame Montoni might be already murdered, and that this ruffian was appointed to decoy herself to some secret place, where her life also was to be sacrificed to the avarice of Montoni, who then would claim securely the contested estates in Languedoc. The consideration of the enormity of such guilt did, at length, relieve her from the belief of its probability, but not from all the doubts and fears which a recollection of Barnardine's manner had occasioned. From these subjects her thoughts at length passed to others ; and, as the evening advanced, she remembered with somewhat more than surprise the music she had heard on the preceding night, and now awaited its return with more than curiosity.

She distinguished, till a late hour, the distant carousals of Montoni and his companions —the loud contest, the dissolute laugh, and the choral song, that made the halls re-echo. At length she heard the heavy gates of the castle shut for the night, and those sounds instantly sunk into a silence which was disturbed only by the whispering steps of persons passing through the galleries to their remote rooms. Emily now, judging it to be about the time when she had heard the music on the preceding night, dismissed Annette, and gently opened the casement to watch for its return. The planet she had so particularly noticed, at the recurrence of the music, was not yet risen ; but with superstitious weakness she kept her eyes fixed on that part of the hemisphere where it would rise, almost expecting that, when it appeared, the sounds would return. At length it came, serenely bright, over the eastern towers of the castle. Her heart trembled when she perceived it ; and she had scarcely courage to remain at the casement, lest the returning music should confirm her terror, and subdue the little strength she yet retained. The clock soon after struck one ; and knowing this to be about the time when the sounds had occurred, she sat down in a chair near the casement, and endeavoured to compose her spirits ; but the anxiety of expectation yet disturbed them. Everything, however, remained still : she heard only the solitary step of a sentinel, and the lulling murmur of the woods below : and she again leaned from the casement, and again looked, as if for intelligence, to the planet, which was now risen high above the towers.

Emily continued to listen—but no music came. 'Those were surely no mortal sounds!' said she, recollecting their entrancing melody : ' no inhabitant of this castle could utter such : and where is the feeling that could modulate such exquisite expression? We all know that it has been affirmed celestial sounds have sometimes been heard on earth. Father Pierre and Father Antoine declared that they had sometimes heard them in the stillness of night, when they alone were waking to offer their orisons to Heaven. Nay, my dear father himself once said, that soon after my mother's death, as he lay watchful in grief, sounds of uncommon sweetness called him from his bed ; and on opening his window he heard lofty music pass along the midnight air. It soothed him, he said : he looked up with confidence to heaven, and resigned her to his God.'

Emily paused to weep at this recollection. ' Perhaps,' resumed she — ' perhaps those strains I heard were sent to comfort, to encourage me! Never shall I forget those I heard, at this hour, in Languedoc! Perhaps my father watches over me at this moment!' She wept again in tenderness. Thus passed

the hour in watchfulness and solemn thought —but no sounds returned ; and, after remaining at the casement till the light tint of dawn began to edge the mountain-tops, and steal upon the night shade, she concluded that they would not return, and retired reluctantly to repose.

CHAPTER XXVI.

' I will advise you where to plant yourselves,
  Acquaint you with the perfect spy o' the time,
  The moment on't ; for't must be done to-night.'
                                        MACBETH.

EMILY was somewhat surprised, on the following day, to find that Annette had heard of Madame Montoni's confinement in the chamber over the portal, as well as of her purposed visit there on the approaching night. That the circumstance which Barnardine had so solemnly enjoined her to conceal, he had himself told to so indiscreet a hearer as Annette appeared very improbable, though he had now charged her with a message concerning the intended interview. He requested that Emily would meet him, unattended, on the terrace at a little after midnight, when he himself would lead her to the place he had promised ; a proposal from which she immediately shrunk, for a thousand vague fears darted athwart her mind, such as had tormented her on the preceding night, and which she neither knew how to trust nor to dismiss. It frequently occurred to her, that Barnardine might have deceived her concerning Madame Montoni, whose murderer, perhaps, he really was ; and that he had deceived her by order of Montoni, the more easily to draw her into some of the desperate designs of the latter. The terrible suspicion that Madame Montoni no longer lived, thus came, accompanied by one not less dreadful for herself. Unless the crime by which the aunt had suffered was instigated merely by resentment, unconnected with profit, a motive upon which Montoni did not appear very likely to act, its object must be unattained till the niece was also dead, to whom Montoni knew that his wife's estates must descend. Emily remembered the words which had informed her that the contested estates in France would devolve to her if Madame Montoni died without consigning them to her husband : and the former obstinate perseverance of her aunt made it too probable that she had to the last withheld them. At this instant recollecting Barnardine's manner on the preceding night, she now believed what she then had fancied, that it expressed malignant triumph. She shuddered at the recollection which confirmed her fears, and determined not to meet him on the terrace. Soon after, she was inclined to consider these suspicions as the extravagant exaggerations of a timid and harassed mind, and could not believe Montoni liable to such preposterous depravity as that of destroying from one motive his wife and her niece. She blamed herself for suffering her romantic imagination to carry her so far beyond the bounds of probability, and determined to endeavour to check its rapid flights lest they should sometimes extend into madness. Still, however, she shrunk from the thought of meeting Barnardine on the terrace at midnight ; and still the wish to be relieved from this terrible suspense concerning her aunt, to see her, and to soothe her sufferings, made her hesitate what to do.

' Yet how is it possible, Annette, I can pass to the terrace at that hour ?' said she, recollecting herself ; ' the sentinels will stop me, and Signor Montoni will hear of the affair.'

' O ma'amselle ! that is well thought of,' replied Annette. ' That is what Barnardine told me about. He gave me this key, and bade me say it unlocks the door at the end of the vaulted gallery that opens near the end of the east rampart, so that you need not pass any of the men on watch. He bade me say too, that his reason for requesting you to come to the terrace was because he could take you to the place you want to go to without opening the great doors of the hall, which grate so heavily.'

Emily's spirits were somewhat calmed by this explanation, which seemed to be honestly given to Annette. ' But why did he desire I would come alone, Annette ?' said she.

' Why that was what I asked him myself, ma'amselle. Says I, " Why is my young lady to come alone ?—Surely I may come with her ?—What harm can *I* do ?" But he said, " No—no—I tell you not," in his gruff way. " Nay," says I, " I have been trusted in as great affairs as this, I warrant, and it's a hard matter if I can't keep a secret now." Still he would say nothing but " No—no—no." " Well," says I, " if you will only trust me, I will tell you a great secret, that was told me a month ago, and I have never opened my lips about it yet—so you need not be afraid of telling me." But all would not do. Then, ma'amselle, I went so far as to offer him a beautiful new sequin, that Ludovico gave me for a keepsake, and I would not have parted with it for all St. Marco's Place ; but even that would not do ! Now what can be the reason of this ? But I know, you know, ma'am, who you are going to see.'

' Pray did Barnardine tell you this ?'

' He ! No, ma'amselle, that he did not.'

Emily inquired who did ; but Annette showed that she *could* keep a secret.

During the remainder of the day Emily's mind was agitated with doubts and fears and contrary determinations, on the subject of meeting this Barnardine on the rampart, and submitting herself to his guidance she scarcely knew whither. Pity for her aunt, and anxiety for herself, alternately swayed her determination, and night came before she had decided upon her conduct. She heard the castle clock strike eleven—twelve — and yet her mind wavered. The time, however, was now come when she could hesitate no longer : and then the interest she felt for her aunt overcame other considerations ; and bidding Annette follow her to the outer door of the vaulted gallery, and there await her return, she descended from her chamber. The castle was perfectly still ; and the great hall, where so lately she had witnessed a scene of dreadful contention, now returned only the whispering footsteps of the two solitary figures gliding fearfully between the pillars, and gleamed only to the feeble lamp they carried. Emily, deceived by the long shadows of the pillars and by the catching lights between, often stopped, imagining she saw some person moving in the distant obscurity of the perspective ; and as she passed these pillars, she feared to turn her eyes towards them, almost expecting to see a figure start out from behind their broad shaft. She reached, however, the vaulted gallery without interruption, but unclosed its outer door with a trembling hand ; and charging Annette not to quit it, and to keep it a little open, that she might be heard if she called, she delivered to her the lamp, which she did not dare to take herself, because of the men on watch, and, alone, stepped out upon the dark terrace. Everything was so still, that she feared lest her own light steps should be heard by the distant sentinels ; and she walked cautiously towards the spot where she had before met Barnardine, listening for a sound, and looking onward through the gloom in search of him. At length she was startled by a deep voice that spoke near her, and she paused, uncertain whether it was his, till it spoke again, and she then recognised the hollow tones of Barnardine, who had been punctual to the moment, and was at the appointed place resting on the rampart wall. After chiding her for not coming sooner, and saying that he had been waiting nearly half an hour, he desired Emily, who made no reply, to follow him to the door through which he had entered the terrace.

While he unlocked it, she looked back to that she had left, and observing the rays of the lamp stream through a small opening, was certain that Annette was still there. But her remote situation could little befriend Emily, after she had quitted the terrace ; and when Barnardine unclosed the gate, the dismal aspect of the passage beyond, shown by a torch burning on the pavement, made her shrink from following him alone, and she refused to go, unless Annette might accompany her. This, however, Barnardine absolutely refused to permit, mingling at the same time with his refusal such artful circumstances to heighten the pity and curiosity of Emily towards her aunt, that she at length consented to follow him alone to the portal.

He then took up the torch, and led her along the passage, at the extremity of which he unlocked another door, whence they descended a few steps into a chapel, which, as Barnardine held up the torch to light her, Emily observed to be in ruins ; and she immediately recollected a former conversation of Annette concerning it, with very unpleasant emotions. She looked fearfully on the almost roofless walls green with damps, and on the gothic points of the windows where the ivy and the briony had long supplied the place of glass, and ran mantling among the broken capitals of some columns that had once supported the roof. Barnardine stumbled over the broken pavement, and his voice, as he uttered a sudden oath, was returned in hollow echoes that made it more terrific. Emily's heart sunk ; but she still followed him, and he turned out of what had been the principal aisle of the chapel. 'Down these steps, lady,' said Barnardine, as he descended a flight which appeared to lead into the vaults ; but Emily paused on the top, and demanded in a tremulous tone whither he was conducting her.

'To the portal,' said Barnardine.

'Cannot we go through the chapel to the portal ?' said Emily.

'No, signora, that leads to the inner court, which I don't choose to unlock. This way, and we shall reach the outer court presently.'

Emily still hesitated ; fearing not only to go on, but, since she had gone thus far, to irritate Barnardine by refusing to go further.

'Come, lady,' said the man, who had nearly reached the bottom of the flight, 'make a little haste ; I cannot wait here all night.'

'Whither do these steps lead ?' said Emily, yet pausing.

'To the portal,' repeated Barnardine in an angry tone ; 'I will wait no longer.' As he said this, he moved on with the light : and Emily, fearing to provoke him by further delay, reluctantly followed. From the steps they proceeded through a passage adjoining the vaults, the walls of which were dropping with unwholesome dews, and the vapours that crept along the ground made the torch burn so dimly, that Emily expected every moment to see it extinguished ; and Barnardine could scarce find his way. As they advanced, these vapours thickened ; and Barnardine believing the torch expiring, stopped for a moment to trim it. As he then rested against a pair of iron gates that opened from the passage, Emily saw by uncertain flashes of light the vaults beyond, and near her heaps of earth that seemed to surround an open grave. Such an object in such a scene would at any time have disturbed her ; but now she was shocked by an instantaneous presentiment that this was the grave of her unfortunate aunt, and that the treacherous Barnardine was leading herself to destruction. The obscure and terrible place to which he had conducted her seemed to justify the thought; it was a place suited for murder, a receptacle for the dead, where a deed of horror might be committed, and no vestige appear to proclaim it. Emily was so overwhelmed with terror, that for a moment she was unable to determine what conduct to pursue. She then considered that it would be vain to attempt an escape from Barnardine by flight, since the length and intricacy of the way she had passed would soon enable him, who was acquainted with the turnings, to overtake her, and whose feebleness would not suffer her to run long with swiftness. She feared equally to irritate him by a disclosure of her suspicions, which a refusal to accompany him further certainly would do ; and since she was already as much in his power as it was possible she could be, if she proceeded, she at length determined to suppress, as far as she could, the appearance of apprehension, and to follow silently whither he designed to lead her. Pale with horror and anxiety, she now waited till Barnardine had trimmed the torch ; and as her sight glanced again upon the grave, she could not forbear inquiring for whom it was prepared. He took his eyes from the torch, and fixed them upon her face without speaking. She faintly repeated the question ; but the man, shaking the torch, passed on : and she followed, trembling, to a second flight of steps, having ascended which, a door delivered them into the first court of the castle. As they crossed it, the light showed the high black walls around them, fringed with long grass and dank weeds that found a scanty soil among the mouldering stones ; the heavy buttresses, with here and there between them a narrow grate, that admitted a freer circulation of air to the court ; the massy iron gates that led to the castle, whose clustering turrets appeared above ; and, opposite, the huge towers and arch of the portal itself. In this scene, the large uncouth person of Barnardine bearing the torch formed a characteristic figure. This Barnardine was wrapt in a long dark cloak, which scarcely allowed the kind of half-boots, or sandals, that were laced upon his legs, to appear, and showed only the point of a broad sword, which he usually wore, slung in a belt across his shoulders. On his head was a heavy flat velvet cap, somewhat resembling a turban, in which was a short feather ; the visage beneath it showed strong features, and a countenance furrowed with the lines of cunning and darkened by habitual discontent.

The view of the court, however, reanimated Emily, who, as she crossed silently towards the portal, began to hope that her own fears, and not the treachery of Barnardine, had deceived her. She looked anxiously up at the first casement, that appeared above the lofty arch of the portcullis; but it was dark, and she inquired whether it belonged to the chamber where Madame Montoni was confined. Emily spoke low, and Barnardine perhaps did not hear her question, for he returned no answer; and they soon after entered the postern door of the gateway, which brought them to the foot of a narrow staircase that wound up one of the towers.

'Up this staircase the signora lies,' said Barnardine.

'Lies!' repeated Emily faintly, as she began to ascend.

'She lies in the upper chamber,' said Barnardine.

As they passed up, the wind, which poured through the narrow cavities in the wall, made the torch flare, and it threw a stronger gleam upon the grim and sallow countenance of Barnardine, and discovered more fully the desolation of the place—the rough stone walls, the spiral stairs black with age, and a suit of ancient armour, with an iron visor, that hung upon the walls, and appeared a trophy of some former victory.

Having reached a landing-place, 'You may wait here, lady,' said he, applying a key to the door of a chamber, 'while I go up and tell the signora you are coming.'

'That ceremony is unnecessary,' replied Emily; 'my aunt will rejoice to see me.'

'I am not sure of that,' said Barnardine, pointing to the room he had opened; 'Come in here, lady, while I step up.'

Emily, surprised and somewhat shocked, did not dare to oppose him further; but, as he was turning away with the torch, desired he would not leave her in darkness. He looked around, and, observing a tripod lamp that stood on the stairs, lighted and gave it to Emily, who stepped forward into a large old chamber, and he closed the door. As she listened anxiously to his departing steps, she thought he descended, instead of ascending, the stairs: but the gusts of wind that whistled round the portal would not allow her to hear distinctly any other sound. Still, however, she listened, and perceiving no step in the room above, where he had affirmed Madame Montoni to be, her anxiety increased though she considered that the thickness of the floor in this strong building might prevent any sound reaching her from the upper chamber. The next moment, in a pause of the wind, she distinguished Barnardine's step descending to the court, and then thought she heard his voice; but the rising gust again overcoming other sounds, Emily, to be certain on this point, moved softly to the door, which, on attempting to open it, she discovered was fastened. All the horrid apprehensions that had lately assailed her, returned at this instant with redoubled force; and no longer appeared like the exaggerations of a timid spirit, but seemed to have been sent to warn her of her fate. She now did not doubt that Madame Montoni had been murdered, perhaps in this very chamber; or that she herself was brought hither for the same purpose. The countenance, the manners, and the recollected words of Barnardine when he had spoken of her aunt, confirmed her worst fears. For some moments she was incapable of considering of any means by which she might attempt an escape. Still she listened, but heard footsteps neither on the stairs nor in the room above; she thought, however, that she again distinguished Barnardine's voice below, and went to a grated window, that opened upon the court, to inquire further. Here she plainly heard his hoarse accents mingling with the blast that swept by, but they were lost again so quickly that their meaning could not be interpreted; and then the light of a torch, which seemed to issue from the portal below, flashed across the court, and the long shadow of a man, who was under the archway, appeared upon the pavement. Emily, from the hugeness of this sudden portrait, concluded it to be that of Barnardine: but other deep tones which passed in the wind soon convinced her he was not alone, and that his companion was not a person very liable to pity.

When her spirits had overcome the first shock of her situation, she held up the lamp to examine if the chamber afforded a possibility of an escape. It was a spacious room, whose walls, wainscoted with rough oak, showed no casement but the grated one which Emily had left, and no other door than that by which she had entered. The feeble rays of the lamp, however, did not allow her to see at once its full extent; she perceived no furniture, except, indeed, an iron chair fastened in the centre of the chamber, immediately over which, depending on a chain from the ceiling, hung an iron ring. Having gazed upon these for some time with wonder and horror, she next observed iron bars below, made for the purpose of confining the feet, and on the arms of the chair were rings of the same metal. As she continued to survey them, she concluded that they were instruments of torture; and it struck her that some poor wretch had once been fastened in this chair, and had there been starved to death. She was chilled by the thought; but what was her agony when, in the next moment, it occurred to her that her aunt might have been one of these victims, and that she herself might be the next! An acute pain seized her head, she was scarcely able to hold the lamp; and, looking round for support, was seating herself, unconsciously, in the iron chair itself: but suddenly perceiving where she was, she started from it in horror, and sprung towards a remote end of the room. Here again she looked round for a seat to sustain her, and perceived only a dark curtain, which, descending from the ceiling to the floor, was drawn along the whole side of the chamber. Ill as she was, the appearance of this curtain struck her, and she paused to gaze upon it in wonder and apprehension.

It seemed to conceal a recess of the chamber; she wished, yet dreaded, to lift it, and to discover what it veiled; twice she was withheld by a recollection of the terrible spectacle her daring hand had formerly unveiled in an apartment of the castle, till, suddenly conjecturing that it concealed the body of her murdered aunt, she seized it in a fit of desperation, and drew it aside. Beyond appeared a corpse stretched on a kind of low couch which was crimsoned with human blood, as was the floor beneath. The features, deformed by death, were ghastly and horrible, and more than one livid wound appeared in the face. Emily, bending over the body, gazed, for a moment, with an eager, frenzied eye; but, in the next, the lamp dropped from her hand, and she fell senseless at the foot of the couch.

When her senses returned, she found herself surrounded by men, among whom was Barnardine, who were lifting her from the floor, and then bore her along the chamber. She was sensible of what passed; but the extreme languor of her spirits did not permit her to speak, or move, or even to feel any distinct fear. They carried her down the staircase by which she had ascended; when having reached the archway they stopped, and one of the men, taking the torch from Barnardine, opened a small door that was cut in the great gate, and as he stepped out upon the road, the light he bore showed several men on horseback in waiting. Whether it was the freshness of the air that revived Emily, or that the objects she now saw roused the spirit of alarm, she suddenly spoke, and made an ineffectual effort to disengage herself from the grasp of the ruffians who held her.

Barnardine, meanwhile, called loudly for the torch, while distant voices answered, and in the same instant a light flashed upon the court of the castle. Again he vociferated for the torch, and the men hurried Emily through the gate. At a short distance, under the shelter of the castle walls, she perceived the fellow who had taken the light from the porter, holding it to a man busily employed in altering the saddle of a horse, round which were several horsemen looking on, whose harsh features received the full glare of the torch; while the broken ground beneath them, the opposite walls, with the tufted shrubs that overhung their summits, and an embattled watch-tower above, were reddened with the gleam, which fading gradually away, left the remoter ramparts and the woods below to the obscurity of night.

'What do you waste time for, there?' said Barnardine with an oath, as he approached the horsemen. 'Despatch—despatch!'

'The saddle will be ready in a minute,' replied the man who was buckling it, at whom Barnardine now swore again for his negligence; and Emily, calling feebly for help, was hurried towards the horses, while the ruffians disputed on which to place her, the one designed for her not being ready. At this moment a cluster of lights issued from the great gates, and she immediately heard the shrill voice of Annette above those of several other persons who advanced. In the same moment she distinguished Montoni and Cavigni, followed by a number of ruffian-faced fellows, to whom she no longer looked with terror, but with hope; for at this instant she did not tremble at the thought of any dangers that might await her within the castle, whence so lately, and so anxiously, she had wished to escape. Those without threatened her from without had engrossed all her apprehensions.

A short contest ensued between the parties, in which that of Montoni, however, were presently victors; and the horsemen, perceiving that numbers were against them, and being, perhaps, not very warmly interested in the affair they had undertaken, galloped off, while Barnardine had run far enough to be lost in the darkness, and Emily was led back into the castle. As she re-passed the courts, the remembrance of what she had seen in the portal chamber came with all its horror to her mind; and when, soon after, she heard the gate close that shut her once more within the castle walls, she shuddered for herself, and, almost forgetting the danger she had escaped, could scarcely think that anything less precious than liberty and peace was to be found beyond them.

Montoni ordered Emily to await him in the cedar parlour, whither he soon followed, and then sternly questioned her on this mysterious affair. Though she now viewed him with horror, as the murderer of her aunt, and scarcely knew what she said to his impatient inquiries, her answers and her manner convinced him that she had not taken a voluntary part in the late scheme, and he dismissed her upon the appearance of his servants, whom he had ordered to attend, that he might inquire further into the affair, and discover those who had been accomplices in it.

Emily had been some time in her apartment before the tumult of her mind allowed her to remember several of the past circumstances. Then, again, the dead form which the curtain in the portal-chamber had disclosed, came to her fancy, and she uttered a groan, which terrified Annette the more, as Emily forbore to satisfy her curiosity on the subject of it;

for she feared to trust her with so fatal a secret, lest her indiscretion should call down the immediate vengeance of Montoni on herself.

Thus compelled to bear within her own mind the whole horror of the secret that oppressed it, her reason seemed to totter under the intolerable weight. She often fixed a wild and vacant look on Annette, and, when she spoke, either did not hear her or answered from the purpose. Long fits of abstraction succeeded; Annette spoke repeatedly, but her voice seemed not to make any impression on the sense of the long-agitated Emily, who sat fixed and silent, except that now and then she heaved a heavy sigh, but without tears.

Terrified at her condition, Annette at length left the room to inform Montoni of it, who had just dismissed his servants, without having made any discoveries on the subject of his inquiry. The wild description which this girl now gave of Emily, induced him to follow her immediately to the chamber.

At the sound of his voice Emily turned her eyes, and a gleam of recollection seemed to shoot athwart her mind; for she immediately rose from her seat, and moved slowly to a remote part of the room. He spoke to her in accents somewhat softened from their usual harshness, but she regarded him with a kind of half curious, half terrified look, and answered only ' Yes,' to whatever he said. Her mind still seemed to retain no other impression than that of fear.

Of this disorder Annette could give no explanation ; and Montoni, having attempted for some time to persuade Emily to talk, retired after ordering Annette to remain with her during the night, and to inform him in the morning of her condition.

When he was gone, Emily again came forward, and asked who it was that had been there to disturb her. Annette said it was the signor—Signor Montoni. Emily repeated the name after her several times, as if she did not recollect it, and then suddenly groaned, and relapsed into abstraction. With some difficulty Annette led her to the bed, which Emily examined with an eager, phrensied eye, before she lay down ; and then, pointing with a shuddering emotion to Annette, who, now more terrified, went towards the door, that she might bring one of the female servants to pass the night with them : but Emily, observing her going, called her by name, and then, in the naturally plaintive tone of her voice, begged that she, too, would not forsake her.—' For since my father died,' added she sighing, ' everybody forsakes me.'

' Your father, ma'amselle !' said Annette, ' he was dead before you knew me.'

' He was, indeed !' rejoined Emily ; and her tears began to flow. She now wept silently and long ; after which, becoming quite calm, she at length sunk to sleep,

Annette having had discretion enough not to interrupt her tears. This girl, as affectionate as she was simple, lost in these moments all her former fears of remaining in the chamber, and watched alone by Emily during the whole night.

CHAPTER XXVII.

'. . . . . Unfold
What worlds, or what vast regions, hold
The immortal mind, that hath forsook
Her mansion in this fleshly nook !'
                         IL PENSEROSO.

EMILY'S mind was refreshed by sleep. On waking in the morning, she looked with a surprise on Annette, who sat sleeping in a chair beside the bed, and then endeavoured to recollect herself ; but the circumstances of the preceding night were swept from her memory, which seemed to retain no trace of what had passed, and she was still gazing with surprise on Annette, when the latter awoke.

' O dear ma'amselle ! do you know me ?' cried she.

' Know you ! certainly,' replied Emily ; ' you are Annette ; but why are you sitting by me thus ?'

' O you have been very ill, ma'amselle,— very ill indeed ! and I am sure I thought—'

' This is very strange !' said Emily, still trying to recollect the past,—' But I think I do remember that my fancy has been haunted by frightful dreams. Good God !' she added, suddenly starting, ' surely it was nothing more than a dream.'

She fixed a terrible look upon Annette, who, intending to quiet her, said, ' Yes, ma'amselle, it was more than a dream, but it is all over now.'

' She *is* murdered, then !' in an inward voice, and shuddering instantaneously. Annette screamed ; for being ignorant of the circumstance to which Emily referred, she attributed her manner to a disordered fancy ; but when she had explained to what her own speech alluded, Emily, recollecting the attempt that had been made to carry her off, asked if the contriver of it had been discovered. Annette replied that he had not, though he might easily be guessed at ; and then told Emily she might thank her for her deliverance, who, endeavouring to command the emotion which the remembrance of her aunt had occasioned, appeared calmly to listen to Annette, though, in truth, she heard scarcely a word that was said.

' And so, ma'amselle,' continued the latter, ' I was determined to be even with Barnardine for refusing to tell me the secret, by finding it out myself ; so I watched you on the terrace, and as soon as he had opened the door at the end, I stole out from the castle, to try to follow you ; for, says I, " I am sure no good can be planned, or why all this secrecy?" So, sure enough, he had not bolted the door after him; and when I opened it, I saw by the glimmer of the torch, at the other end of the passage, which way you were going. I followed the light, at a distance, till you came to the vaults of the chapel, and there I was afraid to go further, for I had heard strange things about these vaults. But then, again, I was afraid to go back, all in darkness, by myself; so by the time Barnardine had trimmed the light, I had resolved to follow you; and I did so, till you came to the great court, and there I was afraid he would see me; so I stopped at the door again, and watched you across to the gates, and when you was gone up the stairs, I whipt after. There, as I stood under the gate-way, I heard horses' feet without, and several men talking; and I heard them swearing at Barnardine for not bringing you out; and just then he had like to have caught me, for he came down the stairs again, and I had hardly time to get out of his way. But I had heard enough of his secret now, and I determined to be even with him, and to save you, too, ma'amselle, for I guessed it to be some new scheme of Count Morano, though he was gone away. I ran into the castle, but I had hard work to find my way through the passage under the chapel; and what is very strange, I quite forgot to look for the ghosts they had told me about, though I would not go into that place again by myself for the world! Luckily the signor and Signor Cavigni were up, so we had soon a train at our heels, sufficient to frighten that Barnardine and his rogues altogether.'

Annette ceased to speak, but Emily still appeared to listen. At length she said suddenly, 'I think I will go to him myself;—where is he?'

Annette asked who was meant.

'Signor Montoni,' replied Emily. 'I would speak with him;' and Annette, now remembering the order he had given on the preceding night, respecting her young lady, rose, and said she would seek him herself.

This honest girl's suspicions of Count Morano were perfectly just; Emily, too, when she thought on the scheme, had attributed it to him; and Montoni, who had not a doubt on this subject also, began to believe that it was by the direction of Morano that poison had formerly been mingled with his wine.

The professions of repentance which Morano had made to Emily, under the anguish of his wound, were sincere at the moment he offered them: but he had mistaken the subject of his sorrow; for while he thought he was condemning the cruelty of his late design, he was lamenting only the state of suffering to which it had reduced him. As these sufferings abated, his former views revived, till his health being re-established, he again found

himself ready for enterprise and difficulty. The porter of the castle, who had served him on a former occasion, willingly accepted a second bribe; and, having concerted the means of drawing Emily to the gates, Morano publicly left the hamlet, whither he had been carried after the affray, and withdrew with his people to another at several miles distance. From thence, on a night agreed upon by Barnardine, who had discovered, from the thoughtless prattle of Annette, the most probable means of decoying Emily, the count sent back his servants to the castle, while he awaited her arrival at the hamlet, with an intention of carrying her immediately to Venice. How this his second scheme was frustrated, has already appeared; but the violent and various passions with which this Italian lover was now agitated, on his return to that city, can only be imagined.

Annette having made her report to Montoni of Emily's health and of her request to see him, he replied that she might attend him in the cedar-room in about an hour. It was on the subject that pressed so heavily on her mind, that Emily wished to speak to him; yet she did not distinctly know what good purpose this could answer, and sometimes she even recoiled in horror from the expectation of his presence. She wished also to petition, though she scarcely dared to believe the request would be granted, that he would permit her, since her aunt was no more, to return to her native country.

As the moment of interview approached, her agitation increased so much, that she almost resolved to excuse herself under what could scarcely be called a pretence of illness; and when she considered what could be said either concerning herself or the fate of her aunt, she was equally hopeless as to the event of the entreaty, and terrified as to its effect upon the vengeful spirit of Montoni. Yet, to pretend ignorance of her death appeared, in some degree, to be sharing its criminality; and, indeed, this event was the only ground on which Emily could rest her petition for leaving Udolpho.

While her thoughts thus wavered, a message was brought, importing that Montoni could not see her till the next day; and her spirits were then relieved for a moment from an almost intolerable weight of apprehension. Annette said, she fancied the chevaliers were going out to the wars again, for the courtyard was filled with horses, and she heard that the rest of the party who went out before were expected at the castle. 'And I heard one of the soldiers, too,' added she, 'say to his comrade, that he would warrant they'd bring home a rare deal of booty. So thinks I, if the signor can, with a safe conscience, send his people out a-robbing—why it is no business of mine; I only wish I was once safe out of this castle; and, if it had not been for poor

Ludovico's sake, I would have let Count Morano's people run away with us both, for it would have been serving you a good turn, ma'amselle, as well as myself.'

Annette might have continued thus talking for hours, for any interruption she would have received from Emily, who was silent, inattentive, absorbed in thought, and passed the whole of this day in a kind of solemn tranquillity, such as is often the result of faculties overstrained by suffering.

When night returned, Emily recollected the mysterious strains of music that she had lately heard, in which she still felt some degree of interest, and of which she hoped to hear again the soothing sweetness. The influence of superstition now gained on the weakness of her long-harassed mind ; she looked with enthusiastic expectation to the guardian spirit of her father, and having dismissed Annette for the night, determined to watch alone for their return. It was not yet, however, near the time when she had heard the music on a former night ; and anxious to call off her thoughts from distressing subjects, she sat down with one of the few books that she had brought from France ; but her mind, refusing control, became restless and agitated, and she went often to the casement to listen for a sound. Once, she thought she heard a voice ; but then, everything without the casement remaining still, she concluded that her fancy had deceived her.

Thus passed the time till twelve o'clock, soon after which the distant sounds that murmured through the castle ceased, and sleep seemed to reign over all. Emily then seated herself at the casement, where she was soon recalled from the reverie into which she sunk, by very unusual sounds, not of music, but like the low mourning of some person in distress. As she listened, her heart faltered in terror, and she became convinced that the former sound was more than imaginary. Still, at intervals, she heard a kind of feeble lamentation, and sought to discover whence it came. There were several rooms underneath, adjoining the rampart, which had been long shut up ; and as the sound probably rose from one of these, she leaned from the casement to observe whether any light was visible there. The chambers, as far as she could perceive, were quite dark, but at a little distance, on the rampart below, she thought she saw something move.

The faint twilight which the stars shed, did not enable her to distinguish what it was ; but she judged it to be a sentinel on watch ; and she removed her light to a remoter part of the chamber, that she might escape notice during her further observation.

The same object still appeared. Presently it advanced along the rampart towards her window, and she then distinguished something like a human form ; but the silence

with which it moved convinced her it was no sentinel. As it drew near, she hesitated whether to retire ; a thrilling curiosity inclined her to stay, but a dread of she scarcely knew what warned her to withdraw.

While she paused, the figure came opposite to her casement, and was stationary. Everything remained quiet ; she had not heard even a footfall ; and the solemnity of this silence, with the mysterious form she saw, subdued her spirits, so that she was moving from the casement, when, on a sudden, she observed the figure start away, and glide down the rampart, after which it was soon lost in the obscurity of night. Emily continued to gaze for some time on the way it had passed, and then retired within her chamber, musing on this strange circumstance, and scarcely doubting that she had witnessed a supernatural appearance.

When her spirits recovered composure, she looked round for some other explanation. Remembering what she had heard of the daring enterprises of Montoni, it occurred to her that she had just seen some unhappy person, who, having been plundered by his banditti, was brought hither a captive ; and that the music she had formerly heard, came from him. Yet, if they had plundered him, it still appeared improbable that they should have brought him to the castle ; and it was also more consistent with the manners of banditti to murder those they rob, than to make them prisoners. But what more than any other circumstance contradicted the supposition that it was a prisoner, was, that it wandered on the terrace without a guard ; a consideration which made her dismiss immediately her first surmise.

Afterwards she was inclined to believe that Count Morano had obtained admittance into the castle ; but she soon recollected the difficulties and dangers that must have opposed such an enterprise, and that if he had so far succeeded, to come alone and in silence to her casement at midnight, was not the conduct he would have adopted, particularly since the private staircase communicating with her apartment was known to him ; neither would he have uttered the dismal sounds she had heard.

Another suggestion represented that this might be some person who had designs upon the castle ; but the mournful sounds destroyed also that probability. Thus, inquiry only perplexed her. Who, or what, it could be that haunted this lonely hour, complaining in such doleful accents and in such sweet music (for she was still inclined to believe that the former strains and the late appearance were connected), she had no means of ascertaining ; and imagination again assumed her empire, and roused the mysteries of superstition.

She determined, however, to watch on the following night, when her doubts might perhaps be cleared up ; and she almost resolved to address the figure, if it should appear again.

CHAPTER XXVIII.

'Such are those thick and gloomy shadows damp,
Oft seen in charnel-vaults and sepulchres,
Lingering, and sitting by a new-made grave.'
MILTON.

ON the following day Montoni sent a second excuse to Emily, who was surprised at the circumstance. 'This is very strange!' said she to herself: 'his conscience tells him the purport of my visit, and he defers it to avoid an explanation.' She now almost resolved to throw herself in his way, but terror checked the intention ; and this day passed as the preceding one, with Emily, except that a degree of awful expectation, concerning the approaching night, now somewhat disturbed the dreadful calmness that had pervaded her mind.

Towards evening the second part of the band which had made the first excursion among the mountains returned to the castle, where as they entered the courts, Emily, in her remote chamber, heard their loud shouts and strains of exultation, like the orgies of furies over some horrid sacrifice. She even feared they were about to commit some barbarous deed ; a conjecture from which, however, Annette soon relieved her, by telling that the people were only exulting over the plunder they had brought with them. This circumstance still further confirmed her in the belief that Montoni had really commenced to be a captain of banditti, and meant to retrieve his broken fortunes by the plunder of travellers ! Indeed, when she considered all the circumstances of his situation—in an armed and almost inaccessible castle, retired far among the recesses of wild and solitary mountains, along whose distant skirts were scattered towns and cities, whither wealthy travellers were continually passing—this appeared to be the situation of all others most suited for the success of schemes of rapine ; and she yielded to the strange thought, that Montoni was become a captain of robbers. His character also, unprincipled, dauntless, cruel, and enterprising, seemed to fit him for the situation. Delighting in the tumult and in the struggles of life, he was equally a stranger to pity and to fear ; his very courage was a sort of animal ferocity ; not the noble impulse of a principle such as inspirits the mind against the oppressor in the cause of the oppressed ; but a constitutional hardiness of nerve that cannot feel, and that, therefore, cannot fear.

Emily's supposition, however natural, was in part erroneous ; for she was a stranger to the state of this country, and to the circumstances under which its frequent wars were partly conducted. The revenues of the many states of Italy being at that time insufficient to the support of standing armies, even during the short periods which the turbulent habits both of the governments and the people permitted to pass in peace, an order of men arose not known in our age, and but faintly described in the history of their own. Of the soldiers disbanded at the end of every war, few returned to the safe but unprofitable occupations then usual in peace. Sometimes they passed into other countries, and mingled with armies which still kept the field. Sometimes they formed themselves into bands of robbers, and occupied remote fortresses, where their desperate character, the weakness of the governments which they offended, and the certainty that they could be recalled to the armies when their presence should be again wanted, prevented them from being much pursued by the civil power ; and sometimes they attached themselves to the fortunes of a popular chief, by whom they were led into the service of any state which could settle with him the price of their valour. From this latter practice arose their name—*Condottieri ;* a term formidable all over Italy, for a period which concluded in the earlier part of the seventeenth century, but of which it is not so easy to ascertain the commencement.

Contests between the smaller states were then, for the most part, affairs of enterprise alone ; and the probabilities of success were estimated, not from the skill but from the personal courage of the general and the soldiers. The ability which was necessary to the conduct of tedious operations, was little valued. It was enough to know how a party might be led towards their enemies with the greatest secrecy, or conducted from them in the compactest order. The officer was to precipitate himself into a situation where, but for his example, the soldiers might not have ventured ; and as the opposed parties knew little of each other's strength, the event of the day was frequently determined by the boldness of the first movements. In such services the *Condottieri* were eminent ; and in these, where plunder always followed success, their characters acquired a mixture of intrepidity and profligacy which awed even those whom they served.

When they were not thus engaged, their chief had usually his own fortress, in which, or in its neighbourhood, they enjoyed an irksome rest ; and though their wants were at one time partly supplied from the property of the inhabitants, the lavish distribution of their plunder at others prevented them from being obnoxious ; and the peasants of such districts gradually shared the character of their warlike visitors. The neighbouring governments sometimes professed, but seldom endeavoured, to suppress these military communities; both because it was difficult to do so, and because a disguised protection of them ensured for the service of their wars a body of men who could not otherwise be so cheaply maintained or so perfectly qualified. The commanders sometimes even relied so far upon this policy of the several powers as to frequent their capitals; and Montoni, having met them in the gaming parties of Venice and Padua, conceived a desire to emulate their characters before his ruined fortunes tempted him to adopt their practices. It was for the arrangement of his present plan of life that the midnight councils were held at his mansion in Venice, and at which Orsino and some other members of the present community then assisted with suggestions which they had since executed with the wreck of their fortunes.

On the return of night, Emily resumed her station at the casement. There was now a moon; and as it rose over the tufted woods, its yellow light served to show the lonely terrace and the surrounding objects more distinctly than the twilight of the stars had done, and promised Emily to assist her observations, should the mysterious form return. On this subject she again wavered in conjecture, and hesitated whether to speak to the figure, to which a strong and almost irresistible interest urged her; but terror, at intervals, made her reluctant to do so.

'If this is a person who has designs upon the castle,' said she, 'my curiosity may prove fatal to me; yet the mysterious music and the lamentations I heard, must surely have proceeded from him: if so, he cannot be an enemy.'

She then thought of her unfortunate aunt, and shuddering with grief and horror, the suggestions of imagination seized her mind with all the force of truth, and she believed that the form she had seen was supernatural. She trembled, breathed with difficulty, an icy coldness touched her cheeks, and her fears for awhile overcame her judgment. Her resolution now forsook her, and she determined, if the figure should appear, not to speak to it.

Thus the time passed as she sat at her casement, awed by expectation and by the gloom and stillness of midnight; for she saw obscurely in the moonlight only the mountains and woods, a cluster of towers that formed the west angle of the castle, and the terrace below; and heard no sound except now and then the lonely watchword passed by the sentinels on duty, and afterwards the steps of the men who came to relieve guard, and whom she knew at a distance on the rampart by their pikes that glittered in the moonbeam and then by the few short words in which they hailed their fellows of the night. Emily retired within her chamber while they

passed the casement. When she returned to it, all was again quiet. It was now very late; she was wearied with watching, and began to doubt the reality of what she had seen on the preceding night; but she still lingered at the window, for her mind was too perturbed to admit of sleep. The moon shone with a clear lustre that afforded her a complete view of the terrace; but she saw only a solitary sentinel pacing at one end of it; and at length, tired with expectation, she withdrew to seek rest.

Such, however, was the impression left on her mind by the music and the complaining she had formerly heard, as well as by the figure which she fancied she had seen, that she determined to repeat the watch on the following night.

Montoni on the next day took no notice of Emily's appointed visit; but she, more anxious than before to see him, sent Annette to inquire at what hour he would admit her. He mentioned eleven o'clock, and Emily was punctual to the moment; at which she called up all her fortitude to support the shock of his presence, and the dreadful recollections it enforced. He was with several of his officers in the cedar room; on observing whom she paused; and her agitation increased while he continued to converse with them, apparently not observing her, till some of his officers turning round saw Emily, and uttered an exclamation. She was hastily retiring when Montoni's voice arrested her, and in a faltering accent she said, 'I would speak with you, Signor Montoni, if you are at leisure.'

'These are my friends,' he replied; 'whatever you would say they may hear.'

Emily, without replying, turned from the rude gaze of the chevaliers; and Montoni then followed her to the hall, whence he led her to a small room, of which he shut the door with violence. As she looked on his dark countenance, she again thought she saw the murderer of her aunt; and her mind was so convulsed with horror, that she had not power to recall thought enough to explain the purport of her visit; and to trust herself with the mention of Madame Montoni was more than she dared.

Montoni at length impatiently inquired what she had to say. 'I have no time for trifling,' he added, 'my moments are important.'

Emily then told him that she wished to return to France, and came to beg that he would permit her to do so.—But when he looked surprised, and inquired for the motive of the request, she hesitated, became paler than before, trembled, and had nearly sunk at his feet. He observed her emotion with apparent indifference, and interrupted the silence by telling her he must be gone. Emily, however, recalled her spirits sufficiently to enable her to repeat her request. And when

Montoni absolutely refused it, her slumbering mind was roused.

'I can no longer remain here with propriety, sir,' said she, 'and I may be allowed to ask by what right you detain me?'

'It is my will that you remain here,' said Montoni, laying his hand on the door to go; 'let that suffice you.'

Emily, considering that she had no appeal from this will, forbore to dispute his right, and made a feeble effort to persuade him to be just. 'While my aunt lived, sir,' said she in a tremulous voice, 'my residence here was not improper: but now that she is no more, I may surely be permitted to depart. My stay cannot benefit you, sir, and will only distress me.'

'Who told you that Madame Montoni was dead?' said Montoni with an inquisitive eye. Emily hesitated, for nobody had told her so, and she did not dare to avow the having seen that spectacle in the portal-chamber which had compelled her to the belief.

'Who told you so?' he repeated more sternly.

'Alas! I know it too well,' replied Emily: 'spare me on this terrible subject.'

She sat down on a bench to support herself.

'If you wish to see her,' said Montoni, 'you may; she lies in the east turret.'

He now left the room without awaiting her reply, and returned to the cedar chamber, where such of the chevaliers as had not before seen Emily began to rally him on the discovery they had made; but Montoni did not appear disposed to bear this mirth, and they changed the subject.

Having talked with the subtle Orsino on the plan of an excursion which he meditated for a future day, his friend advised that they should lie in wait for the enemy; which Verezzi impetuously opposed, reproached Orsino with want of spirit, and swore that if Montoni would let him lead on fifty men, he would conquer all that should oppose him.

Orsino smiled contemptuously; Montoni smiled too, but he also listened. Verezzi then proceeded with vehement declamation and assertion, till he was stopped by an argument of Orsino, which he knew not how to answer better than by invective. His fierce spirit detested the cunning caution of Orsino, whom he constantly opposed, and whose inveterate though silent hatred he had long ago incurred. And Montoni was a calm observer of both, whose different qualifications he knew, and how to bend their opposite character to the perfection of his own designs. But Verezzi in the heat of opposition, now did not scruple to accuse Orsino of cowardice; at which the countenance of the latter, while he made no reply, was overspread with a livid paleness; and Montoni, who watched his lurking eye, saw him put his hand hastily into his bosom. But Verezzi, whose face glowing with crimson formed a striking contrast to the complexion of Orsino, remarked not the action, and continued boldly declaiming against cowards to Cavigni, who was slyly laughing at his vehemence, and at the silent mortification of Orsino, when the latter, retiring a few steps behind, drew forth a stiletto to stab his adversary in the back. Montoni arrested his half-extended arm, and with a significant look made him return the poniard into his bosom, unseen by all except himself; for most of the party were disputing at a distant window, on the situation of a dell where they meant to form an ambuscade.

When Verezzi had turned round, the deadly hatred expressed on the features of his opponent, raising, for the first time, a suspicion of his intention, he laid his hand on his sword, and then, seeming to recollect himself, strode up to Montoni.

'Signor,' said he, with a significant look at Orsino, 'we are not a band of assassins; if you have business for brave men, employ me on this expedition; you shall have the last drop of my blood: if you have any work for cowards—keep him,' pointing to Orsino, 'and let me quit Udolpho.'

Orsino, still more incensed, again drew forth his stiletto, and rushed towards Verezzi, who at the same instant advanced with his sword, when Montoni and the rest of the party interfered and separated them.

'This is the conduct of a boy,' said Montoni to Verezzi, 'not of a man: be more moderate in your speech.'

'Moderation is the virtue of cowards,' retorted Verezzi; 'they are moderate in every thing—but in fear.'

'I accept your words,' said Montoni, turning upon him with a fierce and haughty look, and drawing his sword out of the scabbard.

'With all my heart,' cried Verezzi, 'though I did not mean them for you.'

He directed a pass at Montoni: and while they fought, the villain Orsino made another attempt to stab Verezzi, and was again prevented.

The combatants were at length separated: and, after a very long and violent dispute, reconciled. Montoni then left the room with Orsino, whom he detained in private consultation for a considerable time.

Emily, meanwhile, stunned by the last words of Montoni, forgot, for the moment, his declaration that she should continue in the castle, while she thought of her unfortunate aunt, who, he had said, was laid in the east turret. In suffering the remains of his wife to lie thus long unburied, there appeared a degree of brutality more shocking than she had suspected even Montoni could practise.

After a long struggle she determined to accept his permission to visit the turret, and to take a last look of her ill-fated aunt : with this design she returned to her chamber, and, while she waited for Annette to accompany her, endeavoured to acquire fortitude sufficient to support her through the approaching scene; for, though she trembled to encounter it, she knew that to remember the performance of this last act of duty would hereafter afford her consoling satisfaction.

Annette came, and Emily mentioned her purpose, from which the former endeavoured to dissuade her, though without effect, and Annette was with much difficulty prevailed upon to accompany her to the turret ; but no consideration could make her promise to enter the chamber of death.

They now left the corridor, and having reached the foot of the staircase, which Emily had formerly ascended, Annette declared she would go no further, and Emily proceeded alone. When she saw the track of blood which she had before observed, her spirits fainted, and being compelled to rest on the stairs, she almost determined to proceed no further. The pause of a few moments restored her resolution, and she went on.

As she drew near the landing-place upon which the upper chamber opened, she remembered that the door was formerly fastened, and apprehended that it might still be so. In this expectation, however she was mistaken ; for the door opened at once into a dusky and silent chamber, round which she fearfully looked, and then slowly advanced, when a hollow voice spoke. Emily, who was unable to speak, or to move from the spot, uttered no sound of terror. The voice spoke again ; and then, thinking that it resembled that of Madame Montoni, Emily's spirits were instantly roused ; she rushed towards a bed that stood in a remote part of the room, and drew aside the curtains. Within, appeared a pale and emaciated face. She started back, then again advanced, shuddered as she took up the skeleton hand that lay stretched upon the quilt ; then let it drop, and then viewed the face with a long unsettled gaze. It was that of Madame Montoni, though so changed by illness that the resemblance of what it had been could scarcely be traced in what it now appeared. She was still alive, and, raising her heavy eyes, she turned them on her niece.

'Where have you been so long ?' said she in the same hollow tone ; 'I thought you had forsaken me.'

'Do you indeed live,' said Emily, at length, 'or is this but a terrible apparition?' She received no answer, and again she snatched up the hand. 'This is substance,' she exclaimed ; 'but it is cold—cold as marble !' She let it fall. 'O, if you really live, speak !' said Emily in a voice of desperation, 'that I may not lose my senses—say you know me !'

'I do live,' replied Madame Montoni, 'but —I feel that I am about to die.'

Emily clasped the hand she held, more eagerly, and groaned. They were both silent for some moments. Then Emily endeavoured to soothe her, and inquired what had reduced her to this present deplorable state.

Montoni, when he removed her to the turret under the improbable suspicion of having attempted his life, had ordered the men employed on the occasion to observe a strict secrecy concerning her. To this he was influenced by a double motive. He meant to debar her from the comfort of Emily's visits, and to secure an opportunity of privately despatching her, should any new circumstances occur to confirm the present suggestions of his suspecting mind. His consciousness of the hatred he deserved, it was natural enough should at first lead him to attribute to her the attempt that had been made upon his life ; and though there was no other reason to believe that she was concerned in that atrocious design, his suspicions remained ; he continued to confine her in the turret, under a strict guard ; and, without pity or remorse, had suffered her to lie, forlorn and neglected, under a raging fever, till it had reduced her to the present state.

The track of blood which Emily had seen on the stairs, had flowed from the unbound wound of one of the men employed to carry Madame Montoni, and which he had received in the late affray. At night these men, having contented themselves with securing the door of their prisoner's room, had retired from guard ; and then it was that Emily, at the time of her first inquiry, had found the turret so silent and deserted.

When she had attempted to open the door of the chamber, her aunt was sleeping, and this occasioned the silence which had contributed to delude her into a belief that she was no more ; yet had her terror permitted her to persevere longer in the call, she would probably have awakened Madame Montoni, and have been spared much suffering. The spectacle in the portal chamber, which afterwards confirmed Emily's horrible suspicion, was the corpse of a man who had fallen in the affray, and the same which had been borne into the servants' hall, where she took refuge from the tumult. This man had lingered under his wounds for some days ; and, soon after his death, his body had been removed, on the couch on which he died, for interment in the vault beneath the chapel, through which Emily and Barnardine had passed to the chamber.

Emily, after asking Madame Montoni a thousand questions concerning herself, left her, and sought Montoni ; for the more solemn interest she felt for her aunt, made her now regardless of the resentment her remonstrances might draw upon herself, and of the improbability of his granting what she meant to entreat.

'Madame Montoni is now dying, sir,' said Emily, as soon as she saw him. 'Your resentment, surely, will not pursue her to the last moment ! Suffer her to be removed from that forlorn room to her own apartment, and to have necessary comforts administered.'

'Of what service will that be, if she is dying ?' said Montoni, with apparent indifference.

'The service, at least, of saving you, sir, from a few of those pangs of conscience you must suffer, when you shall be in the same situation,' said Emily with imprudent indignation : of which Montoni soon made her sensible, by commanding her to quit his presence. Then, forgetting her resentment, and impressed only by compassion for the piteous state of her aunt dying without succour, she submitted to humble herself to Montoni, and to adopt every persuasive means that might reduce him to relent towards his wife.

For a considerable time he was proof against all she said, and all she looked ; but at length the divinity of pity, beaming in Emily's eyes, seemed to touch his heart. He turned away, ashamed of his better feelings, half sullen and half relenting ; but finally consented that his wife should be removed to her own apartment, and that Emily should attend her. Dreading equally that this relief might arrive too late, and that Montoni might retract his concession, Emily scarcely stayed to thank him for it ; but, assisted by Annette, she quickly prepared Madame Montoni's bed, and they carried her a cordial that might enable her feeble frame to sustain the fatigue of a removal.

Madame was scarcely arrived in her own apartment, when an order was given by her husband that she should remain in the turret ; but Emily, thankful that she had made such despatch, hastened to inform him of it, as well as that a second removal would instantly prove fatal ; and he suffered his wife to continue where she was.

During this day, Emily never left Madame Montoni, except to prepare such little nourishing things as she judged necessary to sustain her, and which Madame Montoni received with quiet acquiescence, though she seemed sensible that they could not save her from approaching dissolution, and scarcely appeared to wish for life. Emily meanwhile watched over her with the most tender solicitude, no longer seeing her imperious aunt in the poor object before her, but the sister of her late beloved father, in a situation that called for all her compassion and kindness. When night came, she determined to sit up with her aunt ; but this the latter positively forbade, commanding her to retire to rest, and Annette alone to remain in her chamber,

Rest was, indeed, necessary to Emily, whose spirits and frame were equally wearied by the occurrences and exertions of the day ; but she would not leave Madame Montoni till after the turn of midnight, a period then thought so critical by the physicians.

Soon after twelve, having enjoined Annette to be wakeful, and to call her should any change appear for the worse, Emily sorrowfully bade Madame Montoni good-night and withdrew to her chamber. Her spirits were more than usually depressed by the piteous condition of her aunt, whose recovery she scarcely dared to expect. To her own misfortunes she saw no period, inclosed as she was, in a remote castle, beyond the reach of any friends, had she possessed such, and beyond the pity even of strangers ; while she knew herself to be in the power of a man capable of any action which his interest or his ambition might suggest.

Occupied by melancholy reflections and by anticipations as sad, she did not retire immediately to rest, but leaned thoughtfully on her open casement. The scene before her of woods and mountains reposing in the moonlight, formed a regretted contrast with the state of her mind ; but the lonely murmur of these woods, and the view of this sleeping landscape, gradually soothed her with emotions, and softened her to tears.

She continued to weep, for some time, lost to everything but to a gentle sense of her misfortunes. When she at length took the handkerchief from her eyes, she perceived, before her, on the terrace below, the figure she had formerly observed, which stood fixed and silent immediately opposite to her casement. On perceiving it, she started back, and terror for some time overcame curiosity ; at length she returned to the casement, and still the figure was before it, which she now compelled herself to observe ; but was utterly unable to speak, as she had formerly intended. The moon shone with a clear light, and it was perhaps the agitation of her mind that prevented her distinguishing, with any degree of accuracy, the form before her. It was still stationary, and she began to doubt, whether it was really animated.

Her scattered thoughts were now so far returned, as to remind her that her light exposed her to dangerous observation, and she was stepping back to remove it, when she perceived the figure move, and then wave what seemed to be its arm, as if to beckon her ; and while she gazed, fixed in fear, it repeated the action. She now attempted to speak, but the words died on her lips, and she went from the casement to remove her light ; as she was doing which, she heard from without a faint groan. Listening, but not daring to return, she presently heard it repeated.

'Good God ! what can this mean ?' said she.

Again she listened, but the sound came no more ; and after a long interval of silence, she recovered courage enough to go to the casement, when she again saw the same appearance ! It beckoned again, and again uttered a low sound.

'That groan was surely human !' said she. 'I *will* speak.—Who is it,' cried Emily in a faint voice, 'that wanders at this late hour ?'

The figure raised its head, but suddenly started away, and glided down the terrace. She watched it for a long while passing swiftly in the moonlight, but heard no footstep, till a sentinel from the other extremity of the rampart walked slowly along. The man stopped under her window, and, looking up, called her by name. She was retiring precipitately ; but a second summons inducing her to reply, the soldier then respectfully asked if she had seen anything pass. On her answering that she had, he said no more ; but walked away down the terrace, Emily following him with her eyes, till he was lost in the distance. But, as he was on guard, she knew he could not go beyond the rampart, and therefore resolved to wait his return.

Soon after, his voice was heard at a distance, calling loudly ; and then a voice still more distant answered, and in the next moment the watchword was given, and passed along the terrace. As the soldiers moved hastily under the casement, she called to inquire what had happened, but they passed without regarding her.

Emily's thoughts returning to the figure she had seen, 'It cannot be a person who has designs upon the castle,' said she ; 'such a one would conduct himself very differently. He would not venture where sentinels were on watch, nor fix himself opposite to a window where he perceived he must be observed : much less would he beckon, or utter a sound of complaint. Yet it cannot be a prisoner, for how could he obtain the opportunity to wander thus ?'

If she had been subject to vanity, she might have supposed this figure to be some inhabitant of the castle, who wandered under the casement in the hope of seeing her, and of being allowed to declare his admiration : but this opinion never occurred to Emily ; and if it had, she would have dismissed it as improbable, on considering that, when the opportunity of speaking had occurred, it had been suffered to pass in silence ; and that, even at the moment in which she had spoken, the form had abruptly quitted the place.

While she mused, two sentinels walked up the rampart in earnest conversation, of which she caught a few words, and learned from these that one of their comrades had fallen down senseless. Soon after, three other soldiers appeared slowly advancing from the bottom of the terrace, but she heard only a low voice, that came at intervals. As they drew near, she perceived this to be the voice of him who walked in the middle, apparently supported by his comrades, and she again called to them, inquiring what had happened. At the sound of her voice they stopped, and looked up, while she repeated her question, and was told that Roberto, their fellow of the watch, had been seized with a fit, and that [his cry as he fell had caused a false alarm.

'Is he subject to fits ?' said Emily.

'Yes, signora,' replied Roberto ; 'but if I had not, what I saw was enough to have frightened the Pope himself.'

'What was it ?' inquired Emily trembling.

'I cannot tell what it was, lady, or what I saw, or how it vanished,' replied the soldier, who seemed to shudder at the recollection.

'Was it the person whom you followed down the rampart, that has occasioned you this alarm ?' said Emily, endeavouring to conceal her own.

'Person !' exclaimed the man,—' it was the Devil, and this is not the first time I have seen him !'

'Nor will it be the last,' observed one of his comrades, laughing.

'No, no, I warrant not,' said another.

'Well,' rejoined Roberto, 'you may be as merry now as you please ; you was none so jocose the other night, Sebastian, when you was on watch with Launcelot.'

'Launcelot need not talk of that,' replied Sebastian ; 'let him remember how he stood trembling, and unable to give the *word*, till the man was gone. If the man had not come so silently upon us, I would have seized him, and soon made him tell who he was.'

'What man ?' inquired Emily.

'It was no man, lady,' said Launcelot, who stood by, ' but the Devil himself, as my comrade says. What man, who does not live in the castle, could get within the walls at midnight ? Why I might just as well pretend to march to Venice, and get among all the senators when they are counselling ; and I warrant I should have more chance of getting out again alive, than any fellow that we should catch within the gates after dark. So I think I have proved plainly enough that this can be nobody that lives out of the castle ; and now I will prove that it can be nobody that lives in the castle—for, if he did—why should he be afraid to be seen? So after this, I hope nobody will pretend to tell me it was anybody. No, I say again, by holy Pope ! it was the Devil, and Sebastian, there, knows this is not the first time we have seen him.'

'When did you see the figure then, before ?' said Emily, half smiling ; who, though she thought the conversation somewhat too much, felt an interest which would not permit her to conclude it.

'About a week ago, lady,' said Sebastian, taking up the story.

'And where?'

'On the rampart, lady, higher up.'

'Did you pursue it, that it fled?'

'No, signora. Launcelot and I were on watch together, and everything was so still you might have heard a mouse stir, when suddenly Launcelot says—"Sebastian! do you see nothing?" I turned my head a little to the left, as it might be—thus. "No," says I. "Hush!" said Launcelot,—"look yonder —just by the last cannon on the rampart!" I looked, and then thought I did see something move; but there being no light but what the stars gave, I could not be certain. We stood quite silent, to watch it, and presently saw something pass along the castlewall, just opposite to us!'

'Why did you not seize it then?' cried a soldier, who had scarcely spoken till now.

'Aye, why did you not seize it?' said Roberto.

'You should have been there to have done that,' replied Sebastian: 'you would have been bold enough to have taken it by the throat, though it had been the Devil himself; we could not take such a liberty, perhaps, because we are not so well acquainted with him as you are. But, as I was saying, it stole by us so quickly, that we had not time to get rid of our surprise before it was gone. Then, we knew it was in vain to follow. We kept constant watch all that night, but we saw it no more. Next morning we told some of our comrades, who were on duty on other parts of the ramparts, what we had seen; but they had seen nothing, and laughed at us, and it was not till to-night that the same figure walked again.'

'Where did you lose it, friend?' said Emily to Roberto.

'When I left you, lady,' replied the man, 'you might see me go down the rampart, but it was not till I reached the east terrace that I saw anything. Then, the moon shining bright, I saw something like a shadow flitting before me, as it were, at some distance. I stopped, when I turned the corner of the east tower, where I had seen this figure not a moment before,—but it was gone! As I stood looking through the old arch which leads to the east rampart, and where I am sure it had passed, I heard, all of a sudden, such a sound! —It was not like a groan, or a cry, or a shout, or anything I ever heard in my life. I heard it only once, and that was enough for me; for I know nothing that happened after, till I found my comrades here about me.'

'Come,' said Sebastian, 'let us go to our posts—the moon is setting. Good-night, lady!'

'Aye, let us go,' rejoined Roberto. 'Goodnight, lady,'

'Good-night: the Holy Mother guard you!' said Emily, as she closed her casement, and retired to reflect upon the strange circumstance that had just occurred, connecting which with what had happened on former nights, she endeavoured to derive from the whole something more positive than conjecture. But her imagination was inflamed, while her judgment was not enlightened, and the terrors of superstition again pervaded her mind.

CHAPTER XXIX.

'There is one within,
Beside the things that we have heard and seen,
Recounts most horrid sights seen by the watch.'
JULIUS CÆSAR.

IN the morning Emily found Madame Montoni nearly in the same condition as on the preceding night; she had slept little, and that little had not refreshed her; she smiled on her niece, and seemed cheered by her presence, but spoke only a few words, and never named Montoni, who, however, soon after entered the room. His wife, when she understood that he was there, appeared much agitated, but was entirely silent, till Emily rose from a chair at the bedside, when she begged in a feeble voice that she would not leave her.

The visit of Montoni was not to soothe his wife, whom he knew to be dying, or to console or to ask her forgiveness, but to make a last effort to procure that signature which would transfer her estates in Languedoc, after her death to him rather than to Emily. This was a scene that exhibited on his part his usual inhumanity, and on that of Madame Montoni, a persevering spirit contending with a feeble frame; while Emily repeatedly declared to him her willingness to resign all claim to those estates, rather than that the last hours of her aunt should be disturbed by contention. Montoni, however, did not leave the room till his wife, exhausted by the obstinate dispute, had fainted; and she lay so long insensible that Emily began to fear that the spark of life was extinguished. At length she revived; and looking feebly up at her niece, whose tears were falling over her, made an effort to speak; but her words were unintelligible, and Emily again apprehended she was dying. Afterwards, however, she recovered her speech, and, being somewhat restored by a cordial, conversed for a considerable time on the subject of her estates in France with clearness and precision. She directed her niece where to find some papers relative to them, which she had hitherto concealed from the search of Montoni, and earnestly charged her never to suffer these papers to escape her.

Soon after this conversation Madame Montoni sunk into a doze, and continued slumbering till evening, when she seemed better than she had been since her removal from the turret. Emily never left her for a moment till long after midnight, and even then would not have quitted the room, had not her aunt entreated that she would retire to rest. She then obeyed the more willingly, because her patient appeared somewhat recruited by sleep; and giving Annette the same injunction as on the preceding night, she withdrew to her own apartment. But her spirits were wakeful and agitated; and finding it impossible to sleep, she determined to watch once more for the mysterious appearance that had so much interested and alarmed her.

It was now the second watch of the night; and about the time when the figure had before appeared, Emily heard the passing footsteps of the sentinels on the rampart, as they changed guard; and when all was again silent, she took her station at the casement, leaving her lamp in a remote part of the chamber, that she might escape notice from without. The moon gave a faint and uncertain light, for heavy vapours surrounded it, and often rolling over the disc, left the scene below in total darkness. It was in one of these moments of obscurity that she observed a small and lambent flame moving at some distance on the terrace. While she gazed, it disappeared; and the moon again emerging from the lurid and heavy thunder clouds, she turned her attention to the heavens, where the vivid lightnings darted from cloud to cloud, and flashed silently on the woods below. She loved to catch in the momentary gleam the gloomy landscape. Sometimes a cloud opened its light upon a distant mountain; and, while the sudden splendour illumined all its recesses of rock and wood, the rest of the scene remained in deep shadow; at others, partial features of the castle were revealed by the glimpse—the ancient arch leading to the east rampart, the turret above, or the fortifications beyond; and then, perhaps, the whole edifice, with all its towers, its dark massy walls and pointed casements, would appear, and vanish in an instant.

Emily, looking up again on the rampart, perceived the flame she had seen before; it moved onward; and soon after she thought she heard a footstep. The light appeared and disappeared frequently, while, as she watched, it glided under her casements, and at the same instant she was certain that a footstep passed, but the darkness did not permit her to distinguish any object except the flame. It moved away, and then, by a gleam of lightning, she perceived some person on the terrace. All the anxieties of the preceding night returned. This person advanced, and the playing flame alternately appeared and vanished. Emily wished to speak, to end her

doubts whether this figure were human or supernatural; but her courage failed as often as she attempted utterance, till the light moved again under the casement, and she faintly demanded who passed.

'A friend,' replied a voice.

'What friend,' said Emily, somewhat encouraged; 'who are you, and what is that light you carry?'

'I am Anthonio, one of the signor's soldiers,' replied the voice.

'And what is that tapering light you bear?' said Emily; 'see how it starts upwards,— and now it vanishes!'

'This light, lady,' said the soldier, 'has appeared to-night as you see it, on the point of my lance, and ever since I have been on watch; but what it means I cannot tell.'

'This is very strange,' said Emily.

'My fellow-guard,' continued the man, 'has the same flame on his arms; he says he has sometimes seen it before. I never did; I am but lately come to the castle, for I have not been long a soldier.'

'How does your comrade account for it?' said Emily.

'He says it is an omen, lady, and bodes no good.'

'And what harm can it bode?' rejoined Emily.

'He knows not so much as that, lady.'

Whether Emily was alarmed by this omen, or not, she certainly was relieved from much terror by discovering this man to be only a soldier on duty, and it immediately occurred to her that it might be he who had occasioned so much alarm on the preceding night. There were, however, some circumstances that still required explanation. As far as she could judge by the faint moon-light that had assisted her observation, the figure she had seen did not resemble this man either in shape or size; besides, she was certain it had carried no arms. The silence of its steps, if steps it had, the moaning sounds, too, which it had uttered, and its strange disappearance, were circumstances of mysterious import, that did not apply, with probability, to a soldier engaged in the duty of his guard.

She now inquired of the sentinel, whether he had seen any person, besides his fellow-watch, walking on the terrace about midnight; and then briefly related what she had herself observed.

'I was not on guard that night, lady,' replied the man, 'but I heard of what happened. There are amongst us who believe strange things. Strange stories, too, have long been told of this castle, but it is no business of mine to repeat them; and, for my part, I have no reason to complain, our chief does nobly by us.'

'I commend your prudence,' said Emily. 'Good-night, and accept this from me,' she added, throwing him a small piece of coin, and then closing the casement to put an end to the discourse.

When he was gone, she opened it again, listened with a gloomy pleasure to the distant thunder that began to murmur among the mountains, and watched the arrowy lightnings which broke over the remoter scene. The pealing thunder rolled onward, and then, reverberated by the mountains, other thunder seemed to answer from the opposite horizon ; while the accumulating clouds entirely concealing the moon, assumed a red sulphureous tinge that foretold a violent storm.

Emily remained at her casement, till the vivid lightning, that now every instant revealed the wide horizon and the landscape below, made it no longer safe to do so, and she went to her couch ; but, unable to compose her mind to sleep, still listened in silent awe to the tremendous sounds that seemed to shake the castle to its foundation.

She had continued thus for a considerable time, when amidst the uproar of the storm she thought she heard a voice ; and raising herself to listen, saw the chamber door open, and Annette enter with a countenance of wild affright.

'She is dying, ma'amselle ; my lady is dying !' said she.

Emily started up, and ran to Madame Montoni's room. When she entered, her aunt appeared to have fainted, for she was quite still and insensible ; and Emily, with a strength of mind that refused to yield to grief while any duty required her activity, applied every means that seemed likely to restore her. But the last struggle was over—she was gone for ever.

When Emily perceived that all her efforts were ineffectual, she interrogated the terrified Annette, and learned that Madame Montoni had fallen into a doze soon after Emily's departure, in which she had continued until a few minutes before her death.

'I wondered, ma'amselle,' said Annette, 'what was the reason my lady did not seem frightened at the thunder, when I was so terrified ; and I went often to the bed to speak to her, but she appeared to be asleep ; till presently I heard a strange noise, and, going to her, saw she was dying.'

Emily at this recital shed tears. She had no doubt but that the violent change in the air, which the tempest produced, had effected this fatal one on the exhausted frame of Madame Montoni.

After some deliberation she determined that Montoni should not be informed of this event till the morning ; for she considered that he might perhaps utter some inhuman expressions, such as in the present temper of her spirits she could not bear. With Annette alone, therefore, whom she encouraged by her own example, she performed some of the last solemn offices for the dead, and compelled herself to watch during the night by the body of her deceased aunt. During this solemn period, rendered more awful by the tremendous storm that shook the air, she frequently addressed herself to Heaven for support and protection ; and her pious prayers, we may believe, were accepted of the God that giveth comfort.

CHAPTER XXX.

'The midnight clock has toll'd ; and hark, the bell
Of death beats slow ! heard ye the note profound ?
It pauses now ; and now with rising knell
Flings to the hollow gale its sullen sound.'
    MASON.

WHEN Montoni was informed of the death of his wife, and considered that she had died without giving him the signature so necessary to the accomplishment of his wishes, no sense of decency restrained the expression of his resentment. Emily anxiously avoided his presence, and watched during two days and two nights, with little intermission, by the corpse of her late aunt. Her mind, deeply impressed with the unhappy fate of this object, she forgot all her faults, her unjust and imperious conduct to herself ; and remembering only her sufferings, thought of her only with tender compassion. Sometimes, however, she could not avoid musing upon the strange infatuation that had proved so fatal to her aunt, and had involved herself in a labyrinth of misfortune from which she saw no means of escaping,—the marriage with Montoni. But when she considered this circumstance, it was more in sorrow than in anger, more for the purpose of indulging lamentation, than reproach.

In her pious cares she was not disturbed by Montoni, who not only avoided the chamber where the remains of his wife were laid, but that part of the castle adjoining to it, as if he had apprehended a contagion in death. He seemed to have given no orders respecting the funeral, and Emily began to fear he meant to offer a new insult to the memory of Madame Montoni ; but from this apprehension she was relieved, when, on the evening of the second day, Annette informed her that the interment was to take place that night. She knew that Montoni would not attend ; and it was so very grievous to her to think that the remains of her unfortunate aunt would pass to the grave without one relative or friend to pay them the last decent rites, that she determined to be deterred by no considerations for herself, from observing this duty. She would otherwise have shrunk from the circumstance of following them to the cold vault, to which they were to be carried by men whose air and countenances seemed to stamp them for murderers ; at the midnight hour of silence and privacy, which Montoni had chosen for committing, if possible, to oblivion the reliques of a woman whom his harsh conduct had at least contributed to destroy.

Emily, shuddering with emotions of horror and grief, assisted by Annette, prepared the corpse for interment ; and having wrapt it in cerements and covered it with a winding-sheet, they watched beside it till past midnight, when they heard the approaching footsteps of the men who were to lay it in its earthy bed. It was with difficulty that Emily overcame her emotion, when the door of the chamber being thrown open, their gloomy countenances were seen by the glare of the torch they carried, and two of them, without speaking, lifted the body on their shoulders, while the third, preceding them with the light, descended through the castle towards the grave, which was in the lower vault of the chapel within the castle walls.

They had to cross two courts towards the east wing of the castle, which, adjoining the chapel, was, like it, in ruins ; but the silence and gloom of these courts had now little power over Emily's mind, occupied as it was with more mournful ideas ; and she scarcely heard the low and dismal hooting of the night-bird that roosted among the ivied battlements of the ruin, or perceived the still flittings of the bat which frequently crossed her way. But when, having entered the chapel and passed between the mouldering pillars of the aisles, the bearers stopped at a flight of steps that led down to a low arched door, and, their comrade having descended to unlock it, she saw imperfectly the gloomy abyss beyond—saw the corpse of her aunt carried down these steps, and the ruffian-like figure that stood with a torch at the bottom to receive it—all her fortitude was lost in emotions of inexpressible grief and terror. She turned to lean upon Annette, who was cold and trembling like herself, and she lingered so long on the summit of the flight, that the gleam of the torch began to die away on the pillars of the chapel, and the men were almost beyond her view. Then, the gloom around her awakening other fears, and a sense of what she considered to be her duty overcoming her reluctance, she descended to the vaults, following the echo of footsteps and the faint ray that pierced the darkness, till the harsh grating of a distant door, that was opened to receive the corpse, again appalled her.

After the pause of a moment she went on, and, as she entered the vaults, saw between the arches, at some distance, the men lay down the body near the edge of an open grave, where stood another of Montoni's men, and a priest whom she did not observe till he began the burial service ; then lifting her eyes from the ground, she saw the venerable figure of the friar, and heard him in a low voice, equally solemn and affecting, perform the service for the dead. At the moment in which they let down the body into the earth, the scene was such as only the dark pencil of a Domenichino, perhaps, could have done justice to. The fierce features and wild dress of the *condottieri* bending with their torches over the grave into which the corpse was descending, were contrasted by the venerable figure of the monk wrapt in long black garments, his cowl thrown back from his pale face, on which the light gleaming strongly showed the lines of affliction softened by piety, and the few gray locks which time had spared on his temples : while beside him stood the softer form of Emily, who leaned for support upon Annette ; her face half averted, and shaded by a thin veil that fell over her figure ; and her mild and beautiful countenance fixed in grief so solemn as admitted not of tears, while she thus saw committed untimely to the earth her last relative and friend. The gleams thrown between the arches of the vaults, where, here and there, the broken ground marked the spots in which other bodies had been recently interred, and the general obscurity beyond, were circumstances that alone would have led on the imagination of a spectator to scenes more horrible than even that which was pictured at the grave of the misguided and unfortunate Madame Montoni.

When the service was over, the friar regarded Emily with attention and surprise, and looked as if he wished to speak to her, but was restrained by the presence of the *condottieri*, who, as they now led the way to the courts, amused themselves with jokes upon his holy order, which he endured in silence, demanding only to be conducted safely to his convent, and to which Emily listened with concern and even horror. When they reached the court, the monk gave her his blessing, and, after a lingering look of pity, turned away to the portal, whither one of the men carried a torch ; while Annette, lighting another, preceded Emily to her apartment. The appearance of the friar, and the expression of tender compassion with which he had regarded her, had interested Emily, who, though it was at her earnest supplication that Montoni had consented to allow a priest to perform the last rites for his deceased wife, knew nothing concerning this person, till Annette now informed her that he belonged to a monastery situated among the mountains at a few miles distance. The superior, who regarded Montoni and his associates not only with aversion but with terror, had probably feared to offend him by refusing his request, and had therefore ordered a monk to officiate at the funeral, who, with the meek spirit of a Christian, had overcome his reluctance to enter the walls of such a castle, by the wish of performing what he considered to be his duty ; and, as the chapel was built on consecrated ground, had not objected to commit to it the remains of the late unhappy Madame Montoni.

Several days passed with Emily in total seclusion, and in a state of mind partaking both of terror for herself and grief for the departed. She at length determined to make other efforts to persuade Montoni to permit her to return to France. Why he should wish to detain her, she could scarcely dare to conjecture ; but it was too certain that he did so, and the absolute refusal he had formerly given to her departure allowed her little hope that he would now consent to it. But the horror which his presence inspired, made her defer from day to day the mention of this subject ; and at last she was awakened from her inactivity only by a message from him, desiring her attendance at a certain hour. She began to hope he meant to resign, now that her aunt was no more, the authority that he had usurped over her ; till she recollected that the estates, which had occasioned so much contention, were now hers ; and she then feared Montoni was about to employ some stratagem for obtaining them, and that he would detain her his prisoner till he succeeded. This thought, instead of overcoming her with despondency, roused all the latent powers of her fortitude into action ; and the property which she would willingly have resigned to secure the peace of her aunt, she resolved that no common sufferings of her own should ever compel her to give to Montoni. For Valancourt's sake also she determined to preserve these estates, since they would afford that competency by which she hoped to secure the comfort of their future lives. As she thought of this, she indulged the tenderness as often, and anticipated the delight of that moment when, with affectionate generosity, she might tell him they were his own. She saw the smile that lighted up his features—the affectionate regard, which spoke at once his joy and thanks ; and at this instant she believed she could brave any sufferings which the evil spirit of Montoni might be preparing for her. Remembering then, for the first time since her aunt's death, the papers relative to the estates in question, she determined to search for them as soon as her interview with Montoni was over.

With these resolutions she met him at the appointed time, and waited to hear his intention before she renewed her request. With him were Orsino and another officer, and both were standing near a table covered with papers, which he appeared to be examining.

'I sent for you, Emily,' said Montoni, raising his head, 'that you might be a witness in some business which I am transacting with my friend Orsino. All that is required of you will be to sign your name to this paper :' he then took one up, hurried unintelligibly over some lines, and, laying it before her on the table, offered her a pen. She took it, and

was going to write—when the design of Montoni came upon her mind like a flash of lightning ; she trembled, let the pen fall, and refused to sign what she had not read. Montoni affected to laugh at her scruples, and, taking up the paper again, pretended to read ; but Emily, who still trembled on perceiving her danger, and was astonished that her own credulity had so nearly betrayed her, positively refused to sign any paper whatever. Montoni, for some time, persevered in affecting to ridicule this refusal ; but when he perceived by her steady perseverance that she understood his design, he changed his manner, and bade her follow him to another room. There he told her that he had been willing to spare himself and her the trouble of useless contest, in an affair where his will was justice, and where she should find it a law ; and had therefore endeavoured to persuade, rather than to compel, her to the practice of her duty.

'I, as the husband of the late Signora Montoni,' he added, 'am the heir of all she possessed ; the estates, therefore, which she refused to me in her life-time, can no longer be withheld, and, for your own sake, I would undeceive you respecting a foolish assertion she once made to you in my hearing—that these estates would be yours, if she died without resigning them to me. She knew at that moment she had no power to withhold them from me after her decease ; and I think you have more sense than to provoke my resentment by advancing an unjust claim. I am not in the habit of flattering, and you will therefore receive as sincere the praise I bestow, when I say that you possess an understanding superior to that of your sex ; and that you have none of those contemptible foibles that frequently mark the female character—such as avarice and the love of power, which latter makes women delight to contradict and to tease when they cannot conquer. If I understand your disposition and your mind, you hold in sovereign contempt these common failings of your sex.'

Montoni paused ; and Emily remained silent and expecting ; for she knew him too well, to believe he would condescend to such flattery, unless he thought it would promote his own interest ; and though he had forborne to name vanity among the foibles of women, it was evident that he considered it to be a predominant one, since he designed to sacrifice to hers the character and understanding of her whole sex.

'Judging as I do,' resumed Montoni, 'I cannot believe you will oppose where you know you cannot conquer, or, indeed, that you would wish to conquer, or be avaricious of any property, when you have not justice on your side. I think it proper, however, to acquaint you with the alternative. If you have a just opinion of the subject in question, you shall be allowed a safe conveyance to France, within a short period; but, if you are so unhappy as to be misled by the late assertion of the signora, you shall remain my prisoner till you are convinced of your error.'

Emily calmly said,

'I am not so ignorant, signor, of the laws on this subject, as to be misled by the assertion of any person. The law, in the present instance, gives me the estates in question, and my own hand shall never betray my right.'

'I have been mistaken in my opinion of you, it appears,' rejoined Montoni sternly. 'You speak boldly, and presumptuously, upon a subject which you do not understand. For once, I am willing to pardon the conceit of ignorance; the weakness of your sex, too, from which, it seems, you are not exempt, claims some allowance; but if you persist in this strain—you have every thing to fear from my justice.'

'From your justice, signor,' rejoined Emily, 'I have nothing to fear—I have only to hope.'

Montoni looked at her with vexation, and seemed considering what to say. 'I find that you are weak enough,' he resumed, 'to credit the idle assertion I alluded to! For your own sake I lament this; as to me, it is of little consequence. Your credulity can punish only yourself; and I must pity the weakness of mind which leads you to so much suffering as you are compelling me to prepare for you.'

'You may find, perhaps, signor,' said Emily with mild dignity, 'that the strength of my mind is equal to the justice of my cause; and that I can endure with fortitude, when it is in resistance of oppression.'

'You speak like a heroine,' said Montoni contemptuously; 'we shall see whether you can suffer like one.'

Emily was silent, and he left the room.

Recollecting that it was for Valancourt's sake she had thus resisted, she now smiled complacently upon the threatened sufferings, and retired to the spot which her aunt had pointed out as the repository of the papers relative to the estates, where she found them as described; and, since she knew of no better place of concealment than this, returned them without examining their contents, being fearful of discovery while she should attempt a perusal.

To her own solitary chamber she once more returned, and there thought again of the late conversation with Montoni and of the evil she might expect from opposition to his will. But his power did not appear so terrible to her imagination as it was wont to do: a sacred pride was in her heart, that taught it to swell against the pressure of injustice, and almost to glory in the quiet sufferance of ills, in a cause which had also the interest of Valancourt for its object. For the first time she felt the full extent of her own superiority to Montoni, and despised the authority which, till now, she had only feared.

As she sat musing, a peal of laughter rose from the terrace, and on going to the casement, she saw, with inexpressible surprise, three ladies, dressed in the gala habit of Venice, walking with several gentlemen below. She gazed in an astonishment that made her remain at the window, regardless of being observed, till the group passed under it; and one of the strangers looking up, she perceived the features of Signora Livona, with whose manners she had been so much charmed the day after her arrival at Venice, and who had been there introduced at the table of Montoni. This discovery occasioned her an emotion of doubtful joy; for it was a matter of joy and comfort to know that a person of a mind so gentle as that of Signora Livona seemed to be was near her; yet there was something so extraordinary in her being at this castle, circumstanced as it now was, and evidently, by the gaiety of her air, with her own consent, that a very painful surmise arose concerning her character. But the thought was so shocking to Emily, whose affection the fascinating manners of the signora had won, and appeared so improbable, when she remembered these manners, that she dismissed it almost instantly.

On Annette's appearance, however, she inquired concerning these strangers; and the former was as eager to tell, as Emily was to learn.

'They are just come, ma'amselle,' said Annette, 'with two signors from Venice, and I was glad to see such Christian faces once again. But what can they mean by coming here? They must surely be stark mad to come freely to such a place as this! Yet they do come freely, for they seem merry enough, I am sure.'

'They were taken prisoners, perhaps?' said Emily.

'Taken prisoners!' exclaimed Annette; 'no, indeed, ma'amselle, not they, I remember one of them very well at Venice: she came two or three times to the signor's, you know, ma'amselle; and it was said, but I did not believe a word of it—it was said that the signor liked her better than he should do. "Then why," says I, "bring her to my lady?" "Very true," said Ludovico; but he looked as if he knew more too.'

Emily desired Annette would endeavour to learn who these ladies were, as well as all she could concerning them; and she then changed the subject, and spoke of distant France.

'Ah, ma'amselle! we shall never see it more!' said Annette, almost weeping.—'I must come on my travels, forsooth!'

Emily tried to soothe and to cheer her, with a hope in which she scarcely herself indulged.

'How—how, ma'amselle, could you leave France, and leave Mons. Valancourt, too?' said Annette, sobbing. 'I—I—am sure, if Ludovico had been in France, I would never have left it,'

'Why do you lament quitting France, then?' said Emily, trying to smile; 'since, if you had remained there, you would not have found Ludovico?'

'Ah, ma'amselle! I only wish I was out of this frightful castle, serving you in France, and I would care about nothing else!'

'Thank you, my good Annette, for your affectionate regard: the time will come, I hope, when you may remember the expression of that wish with pleasure.'

Annette departed on her business; and Emily sought to lose the sense of her own cares, in the visionary scenes of the poet; but she had again to lament the irresistible force of circumstances over the taste and powers of the mind; and that it requires a spirit at ease, to be sensible even to the abstract pleasures of pure intellect. The enthusiasm of genius, with all its pictured scenes, now appeared cold and dim. As she mused upon the book before her, she involuntarily exclaimed, 'Are these, indeed, the passages that have so often given me exquisite delight? Where did the charm exist?—Was it in my mind, or in the imagination of the poet? It lived in each,' said she, pausing. 'But the fire of the poet is in vain, if the mind of his reader is not tempered like his own, however it may be inferior to his in power.'

Emily would have pursued this train of thinking, because it relieved her from more painful reflection; but she found again, that thought cannot always be controlled by will, and hers returned to the consideration of her own situation.

In the evening, not choosing to venture down to the ramparts, where she would be exposed to the rude gaze of Montoni's associates, she walked for air in the gallery adjoining her chamber; on reaching the further end of which she heard distant sounds of merriment and laughter. It was the wild uproar of riot, not the cheering gaiety of tempered mirth; and seemed to come from that part of the castle where Montoni usually was. Such sounds at this time, when her aunt had been so few days dead, particularly shocked her, consistent as they were with the late conduct of Montoni.

As she listened, she thought she distinguished female voices mingling with the laughter, and this confirmed her worst surmise concerning the character of Signora Livona and her companions. It was evident that they had not been brought hither by compulsion; and she beheld herself in the remote wilds of the Apennine, surrounded by men whom she considered to be little less than ruffians, and their worst associates, amid scenes of vice from which her soul recoiled in horror. It was at this moment, when the scenes of the present and the future opened to her imagination, that the image of Valancourt failed in its influence, and her resolution shook with dread. She thought she understood all the horrors which Montoni was preparing for her, and shrunk from an encounter with such remorseless vengeance as he could inflict. The disputed estates she now almost determined to yield at once, whenever he should again call upon her, that she might regain safety and freedom; but then, the remembrance of Valancourt would steal to her heart, and plunge her into the distractions of doubt.

She continued walking in the gallery till evening threw its melancholy twilight through the painted casements, and deepened the gloom of the oak wainscoting around her; while the distant perspective of the corridor was so much obscured, as to be discernible only by the glimmering window that terminated it.

Along the vaulted halls and passages below, peals of laughter echoed faintly, at intervals, to this remote part of the castle, and seemed to render the succeeding stillness more dreary. Emily, however, unwilling to return to her more forlorn chamber, whither Annette was not yet come, still paced the gallery. As she passed the door of the apartment, where she had once dared to lift the veil which discovered to her a spectacle so horrible, that she had never after remembered it but with emotions of indescribable awe, this remembrance suddenly recurred. It now brought with it reflections more terrible than it had yet done, which the late conduct of Montoni occasioned; and hastening to quit the gallery while she had power to do so, she heard a sudden step behind her. It might be that of Annette; but turning fearfully to look, she saw through the gloom a tall figure following her, and all the horrors of that chamber rushed upon her mind. In the next moment she found herself clasped in the arms of some person, and heard a deep voice murmur in her ear.

When she had power to speak, or to distinguish articulated sounds, she demanded who detained her.

'It is I,' replied the voice—'Why are you thus alarmed?'

She looked on the face of the person who spoke; but the feeble light that gleamed through the high casement at the end of the gallery, did not permit her to distinguish the features.

'Whoever you are,' said Emily in a trembling voice, 'for Heaven's sake let me go!'

'My charming Emily,' said the man, 'why will you shut yourself up in this obscure place, when there is so much gaiety below? Return with me to the cedar parlour, where you will be the fairest ornament of the party; —you shall not repent the exchange.'

Emily disdained to reply, and still endeavoured to liberate herself.

'Promise that you will come,' he continued,

'and I will release you immediately; but first give me a reward for so doing.'

'Who are you?' demanded Emily, in a tone of mingled terror and indignation, while she still struggled for liberty—'who are you, that have the cruelty thus to insult me?'

'Why call me cruel?' said the man; 'I would remove you from this dreary solitude to a merry party below. Do you not know me?'

Emily now faintly remembered that he was one of the officers who were with Montoni when she attended him in the morning.—'I thank you for the kindness of your intention,' she replied, without appearing to understand him, 'but I wish for nothing so much as that you would leave me.'

'Charming Emily!' said he, 'give up this foolish whim for solitude, and come with me to the company, and eclipse the beauties who make part of it; you, only, are worthy of my love.' He attempted to kiss her hand; but the strong impulse of her indignation gave her power to liberate herself, and she fled towards the chamber. She closed the door before he reached it; having secured which, she sunk in a chair, overcome by terror and by the exertion she had made, while she heard his voice and his attempts to open the door, without having the power to raise herself. At length, she perceived him depart, and had remained listening for a considerable time, and was somewhat revived by not hearing any sound, when suddenly she remembered the door of the private staircase, and that he might enter that way, since it was fastened only on the other side. She then employed herself in endeavouring to secure it in the manner she had formerly done. It appeared to her, that Montoni had already commenced his scheme of vengeance, by withdrawing from her his protection, and she repented of the rashness that made her brave the power of such a man. To retain the estates seemed to be now utterly impossible; and to preserve her life, perhaps her honour, she resolved, if she should escape the horrors of this night, to give up all claims to the estates on the morrow, provided Montoni would suffer her to depart from Udolpho.

When she had come to this decision, her mind became more composed, though she still anxiously listened, and often startled at ideal sounds that appeared to issue from the staircase.

Having sat in darkness for some hours, during all which time Annette did not appear, she began to have serious apprehensions for her: but, not daring to venture down into the castle, was compelled to remain in uncertainty as to the cause of this unusual absence.

Emily often stole to the staircase-door to listen if any step approached, but still no sound alarmed her: determining, however, to watch during the night, she once more rested on her dark and desolate couch, and bathed the pillow with innocent tears. She thought of her deceased parents and then of the absent Valancourt, and frequently called upon their names; for the profound stillness that now reigned was propitious to the musing sorrow of her mind.

While she thus remained, her ear suddenly caught the notes of distant music, to which she listened attentively; and soon perceiving this to be the instrument she had formerly heard at midnight, she rose, and stepped softly to the casement, to which the sounds appeared to come from a lower room.

In a few moments their soft melody was accompanied by a voice so full of pathos, that it evidently sang not of imaginary sorrows. Its sweet and peculiar tones she thought she had somewhere heard before; yet, if this was not fancy, it was, at most, a very faint recollection. It stole over her mind, amidst the anguish of her present suffering, like a celestial strain, soothing, and reassuring her :—'Pleasant as the gale of spring, that sighs on the hunter's ear when he awakens from dreams of joy, and has heard the music of the spirits of the hill.'*

But her emotion can scarcely be imagined, when she heard sung, with the taste and simplicity of true feeling, one of the popular airs of her native province, to which she had so often listened with delight when a child, and which she had so often heard her father repeat! to this well-known song, never, till now, heard but in her native country, her heart melted, while the memory of past times returned. The pleasant, peaceful scenes of Gascony, the tenderness and goodness of her parents, the taste and simplicity of her former life—all rose to her fancy, and formed a picture so sweet and glowing, so strikingly contrasted with the scenes, the characters, and the dangers, which now surrounded her—that her mind could not bear to pause upon the retrospect, and shrunk at the acuteness of its own sufferings.

Her sighs were deep and convulsed; she could no longer listen to the strain that had so often charmed her to tranquillity, and she withdrew from the casement to a remote part of the chamber. But she was not yet beyond the reach of the music; she heard the measure change, and the succeeding air called her again to the window, for she immediately recollected it to be the same she had formerly heard in the fishing-house in Gascony. Assisted, perhaps, by the mystery which had then accompanied this strain, it had made so deep an impression on her memory, that she had never since entirely forgotten it; and the manner in which it was now sung, convinced her, however unaccountable the circumstance appeared, that this was the same voice she had then heard. Surprise soon yielded to other emotions; a thought darted like lightning

* Ossian.

upon her mind, which discovered a train of hopes that revived all her spirits. Yet these hopes were so new, so unexpected, so astonishing, that she did not dare to trust, though she could not resolve to discourage them. She sat down by the casement, breathless, and overcome with the alternate emotions of hope and fear : then rose again, leaned from the window, that she might catch a nearer sound, listened, now doubting and then believing, softly exclaimed the name of Valancourt, and then sunk again into the chair. Yes, it was possible that Valancourt was near her, and she recollected circumstances that induced her to believe it was his voice she had just heard. She remembered he had more than once said that the fishing-house, where she had formerly listened to this voice and air, and where she had seen pencilled sonnets addressed to herself, had been his favourite haunt before he had been made known to her ; there, too, she had herself unexpectedly met him. It appeared, from these circumstances, more than probable that he was the musician who had formerly charmed her attention, and the author of the lines which had expressed such tender admiration ; who else, indeed, could it be ? She was unable, at that time, to form a conjecture as to the writer ; but since her acquaintance with Valancourt, whenever he had mentioned the fishing-house to have been known to him, she had not scrupled to believe that he was the author of the sonnets.

As these considerations passed over her mind, joy, fear, and tenderness contended at her heart ; she leaned again from the casement, to catch the sounds which might confirm or destroy her hope, though she did not recollect to have ever heard him sing : but the voice and the instrument now ceased.

She considered for a moment whether she should venture to speak : then, not choosing, lest it should be he, to mention his name, and yet too much interested to neglect the opportunity of inquiring, she called from the casement, ' Is that song from Gascony ?' Her anxious attention was not cheered by any reply ; everything remained silent. Her impatience increasing with her fears, she repeated the question ; but still no sound was heard, except the sighing of the wind among the battlements above ; and she endeavoured to console herself with a belief that the stranger, whoever he was, had retired, before she had spoken, beyond the reach of her voice, which, it appeared certain, had Valancourt heard and recognised, he would instantly have replied to. Presently, however, she considered that a motive of prudence, and not an accidental removal, might occasion his silence : but the surmise that led to this reflection, suddenly changed her hope and joy to terror and grief ; for, if Valancourt were in the castle, it was too probable that he was here a

prisoner, taken with some of his countrymen, many of whom were at that time engaged in the wars of Italy, or intercepted in some attempt to reach her. Had he even recollected Emily's voice, he would have feared, in these circumstances, to reply to it in the presence of the men who guarded his prison.

What so lately she had eagerly hoped, she now believed she dreaded :—dreaded to know that Valancourt was near her ; and while she was anxious to be relieved from her apprehension for his safety, she still was unconscious that a hope of soon seeing him struggled with the fear.

She remained listening at the casement till the air began to freshen, and one high mountain in the east to glimmer with the morning ; when, wearied with anxiety, she retired to her couch, where she found it utterly impossible to sleep ; for joy, tenderness, doubt, and apprehension, distracted her during the whole night. Now she rose from the couch, and opened the casement to listen ; then she would pace the room with impatient steps, and at length return with despondence to her pillow. Never did hours appear to move so heavily, as those of this anxious night ; after which she hoped that Annette might appear, and conclude her present state of torturing suspense.

CHAPTER XXXI.

. . . . Might we but hear
The folded flocks penn'd in their wattled cotes,
Or sound of pastoral reed with oaten stops,
Or whistle from the lodge, or village cock
Count the night watches to his feathery dames,
'Twould be some solace yet, some little cheering
In this close dungeon of innumerous boughs.'
                                                MILTON.

IN the morning Emily was relieved from her fears for Annette, who came at an early hour. ' Here were fine doings in the castle last night, ma'amselle,' said she, as soon as she entered the room,—' fine doings, indeed ! Was you not frightened, ma'amselle, at not seeing me ?'

' I was alarmed both on your account and on my own,' replied Emily.—' What detained you ?'

' Aye, I said so, I told him so ; but it would not do. It was not my fault, indeed, ma'amselle, for I could not get out. That rogue Ludovico locked me up again.'

' Locked you up !' said Emily, with displeasure. ' Why do you permit Ludovico to lock you up ?'

' Holy Saints !' exclaimed Annette, ' How can I help it ! If he will lock the door, ma'amselle, and take away the key, how am I to get out, unless I jump through the window ? But that I should not mind so much, if the casements here were not all so high; one can hardly scramble up to them on the inside, and one should break one's neck, I suppose, going down on the outside. But you know, I daresay, ma'am, what a hurly-burly the castle was in last night; you must have heard some of the uproar.'

'What, were they disputing, then?' said Emily.

'No, ma'amselle, not fighting, but almost as good, for I believe there was not one of the signors sober; and what is more, not one of those fine ladies sober, either. I thought, when I saw them first, that all those fine silks and fine veils,—why ma'amselle, their veils were worked with silver! and fine trimmings——boded no good——I guessed what they were!'

'Good God!' exclaimed Emily, 'what will become of me?'

'Aye, ma'am, Ludovico said much the same thing of me. "Good God!" said he, "Annette, what is to become of you, if you are to go running about the castle among all these drunken signors?" "O!" says I, "for that matter, I only want to go to my young lady's chamber, and I have only to go, you know, along the vaulted passage and across the great hall and up the marble staircase and along the north gallery and through the west wing of the castle, and I am in the corridor in a minute." "Are you so?" says he; "and what is to become of you if you meet any of those noble cavaliers in the way?" "Well," says I, "if you think there is danger then, go with me, and guard me; I am never afraid when you are by." "What!" says he, "when I am scarcely recovered of one wound, shall I put myself in the way of getting another? for if any of the cavaliers meet you, they will fall a-fighting with me directly. No, no," says he, "I will cut the way shorter, than through the vaulted passage, and up the marble staircase, and along the north gallery, and through the west wing of the castle, for you shall stay here, Annette; you shall not go out of this room to-night." So with that, I says——'

'Well, well,' said Emily impatiently, and anxious to inquire on another subject—'so he locked you up?'

'Yes, he did, indeed, ma'amselle, notwithstanding all I could say to the contrary; and Caterina and I and he stayed there all night. And in a few minutes after I was not so vexed, for there came Signor Verezzi roaring along the passage like a mad bull, and he mistook Ludovico's hall for old Carlo's; so he tried to burst open the door, and called out for more wine, for that he had drunk all the flasks dry, and was dying of thirst. So we were all as still as night, that he might suppose there was nobody in the room; but the signor was as cunning as the best of us, and kept calling out at the door. "Come forth, my ancient hero!" said he "here is no enemy at the gate, that you

need hide yourself: come forth, my valorous Signor Steward!" Just then old Carlo opened his door, and he came with a flask in his hand; for as soon as the signor saw him, he was as tame as could be, and followed him away as naturally as a dog does a butcher with a piece of meat in his basket. All this I saw through the key-hole. "Well, Annette," said Ludovico jeeringly, "shall I let you out now?" "O no," says I, "I would not——"'

'I have some questions to ask you on another subject,' interrupted Emily, quite wearied by this story. 'Do you know whether there are any prisoners in the castle, and whether they are confined at this end of the edifice?'

'I was not in the way, ma'amselle,' replied Annette, 'when the first party came in from the mountains, and the last party is not come back yet, so I don't know whether there are any prisoners; but it is expected back to-night, or to-morrow, and I shall know then, perhaps.'

Emily inquired if she had ever heard the servants talk of prisoners.

'Ah, ma'amselle!' said Annette archly, 'now, I daresay you are thinking of Monsieur Valancourt, and that he may have come among the armies, which, they say, are come from our country, to fight against this state, and that he has met with some of *our* people, and is taken captive. O Lord! how glad I should be, if it was so!'

'Would you, indeed, be glad?' said Emily in a tone of mournful reproach.

'To be sure I should, ma'am,' replied Annette; 'and would you not be glad, too, to see Signor Valancourt? I don't know any chevalier I like better, I have a very great regard for the signor, truly.'

'Your regard for him cannot be doubted,' said Emily, 'since you wish to see him a prisoner.'

'Why no, ma'amselle, not a prisoner either; but one must be glad to see him you know. And it was only the other night I dreamt—I saw him drive into the castle-yard all in a coach and six, and dressed out, with a laced coat and a sword, like a lord as he is.'

Emily could not forbear smiling at Annette's ideas of Valancourt, and repeated her inquiry, whether she had heard the servants talk of prisoners.

'No, ma'amselle,' replied she, 'never; and lately they have done nothing but talk of the apparition that has been walking about of a night on the ramparts, and that frightened the sentinels into fits. It came among them like a flash of fire, they say, and they all fell down in a row, till they came to themselves again; and then it was gone, and nothing to be seen but the old castle walls; so they helped one another up again as fast as they could. You would not believe, ma'amselle, though I showed you the very cannon where it used to appear.'

And are you, indeed, so simple, Annette,' said Emily, smiling at this curious exaggeration of the circumstances she had witnessed, 'as to credit these stories?'

'Credit them, ma'amselle! why all the world could not persuade me out of them. Roberto and Sebastian, and half a dozen more of them went into fits! To be sure there was no occasion for that; I said myself there was no need of that, for says I, when the enemy comes, what a pretty figure they will cut, if they are to fall down in fits, all of a row! The enemy won't be so civil, perhaps, as to walk off like the ghost, and leave them to help one another up, but will fall to, cutting and slashing, till he makes them all rise up dead men. No, no, says I, there is reason in all things; though I might have fallen down in a fit, that was no rule for them being, because it was no business of mine to look gruff and fight battles.

Emily endeavoured to correct the superstitious weakness of Annette, though she could not entirely subdue her own; to which the latter only replied, 'Nay, ma'amselle, you will believe nothing; you are almost as bad as the signor himself, who was in a great passion when they told him of what had happened, and swore that the first man who repeated such nonsense should be thrown into the dungeon under the east turret. This was a hard punishment, too, for only talking nonsense, as he called it; but I daresay he had other reasons for calling it so, than you have, ma'am.'

Emily looked displeased, and made no reply. As she mused upon the recollected appearance, which had lately so much alarmed her, and considered the circumstances of the figure having stationed itself opposite to her casement, she was for a moment inclined to believe it was Valancourt whom she had seen. Yet, if it was he, why did he not speak to her, when he had the opportunity of doing so—and, if he was a prisoner in the castle, and he could be here in no other character, how could he obtain the means of walking abroad on the rampart? Thus she was utterly unable to decide, whether the musician and the form she had observed were the same, or, if they were, whether this was Valancourt. She, however, desired that Annette would endeavour to learn whether any prisoners were in the castle, and also their names.

'O dear, ma'amselle!' said Annette, 'I forgot to tell you what you bade me ask about—the ladies, as they call themselves, who are lately come to Udolpho. Why that Signora Livona, that the signor brought to see my late lady at Venice, is his mistress now, and was little better then, I dare say. And Ludovico says (but pray be secret, ma'am) that his *Excellenza* introduced her only to impose upon the world, that had begun to make free with her character. So when

people saw my lady notice her, they thought what they had heard must be scandal. The other two are the mistresses of Signor Verezzi and Signor Bertolini; and Signor Montoni invited them all to the castle; and so, yesterday, he gave a great entertainment; and there they were, all drinking Tuscany wine and all sorts, and laughing and singing, till they made the castle ring again. But I thought they were dismal sounds, so soon after my poor lady's death too; and they brought to my mind what she would have thought, if she had heard them—"but she cannot hear them now, poor soul!" said I.'

Emily turned away to conceal her emotion, and then desired Annette to go and make inquiry concerning the prisoners that might be in the castle, but conjured her to do it with caution, and on no account to mention her name, or that of Monsieur Valancourt.

'Now I think of it, ma'amselle,' said Annette, 'I do believe there are prisoners, for I overheard one of the signor's men, yesterday, in the servants' hall, talking something about ransoms, and saying what a fine thing it was for his *Excellenza* to catch up men, and they were as good booty as any other, because of the ransoms. And the other man was grumbling, and saying it was fine enough for the signor, but none so fine for his soldiers, "because," said he, "we don't go shares there."'

This information heightened Emily's impatience to know more, and Annette immediately departed on her inquiry.

The late resolution of Emily to resign her estates to Montoni, now gave way to new considerations; the possibility that Valancourt was near her, revived her fortitude, and she determined to brave the threatened vengeance, at least, till she could be assured whether he was really in the castle. She was in this temper of mind, when she received a message from Montoni, requiring her attendance in the cedar parlour, which she obeyed with trembling, and on her way thither endeavoured to animate her fortitude with the idea of Valancourt.

Montoni was alone. 'I sent for you,' said he, 'to give you another opportunity of retracting your late mistaken assertions concerning the Languedoc estates. I will condescend to advise where I may command.—If you are really deluded by an opinion that you have any right to these estates, at least do not persist in the error—an error which you may perceive, too late, has been fatal to you. Dare my resentment no further, but sign the papers.'

'If I have no right in these estates, sir,' said Emily, 'of what service can it be to you, that I should sign any papers concerning them? If the lands are yours by law, you certainly may possess them without my interference or my consent.'

'I will have no more argument,' said Montoni, with a look that made her tremble. 'What had I but trouble to expect, when I condescended to reason with a baby! But I will be trifled with no longer: let the recollection of your aunt's sufferings, in consequence of her folly and obstinacy, teach you a lesson.—Sign the papers.'

Emily's resolution was for a moment awed: —she shrunk at the recollections he revived, and from the vengeance he threatened; but then, the image of Valancourt, who so long had loved her, and who was now, perhaps, so near her, came to her heart, and, together with the strong feelings of indignation, with which she had always from her infancy regarded an act of injustice, inspired her with a noble, though imprudent courage.

'Sign the papers,' said Montoni, more impatiently than before.

'Never, sir,' replied Emily, 'that request would have proved to me the injustice of your claim, had I even been ignorant of my right.'

Montoni turned pale with anger, while his quivering lip and lurking eye made her almost repent the boldness of her speech.

'Then all my vengeance falls upon you,' he exclaimed with a horrible oath. 'And think not it shall be delayed. Neither the estates in Languedoc nor Gascony shall be yours; you have dared to question my right—now dare to question my power. I have a punishment which you think not of: it is terrible! This night—this very night——'

'This night!' repeated another voice.

Montoni paused, and turned half round; but, seeming to recollect himself, he proceeded in a lower tone.

'You have lately seen one terrible example of obstinacy and folly; yet this, it appears, has not been sufficient to deter you.—I could tell you of others——I could make you tremble at the bare recital.'

He was interrupted by a groan, which seemed to rise from underneath the chamber they were in; and, as he threw a glance round it, impatience and rage flashed from his eyes, yet something like a shade of fear passed over his countenance. Emily sat down in a chair near the door, for the various emotions she had suffered now almost overcame her; but Montoni seized scarcely an instant, and, commanding his features, resumed his discourse in a lower, yet sterner voice.

'I say, I could give you other instances of my power and of my character, which it seems you do not understand, or you would not defy me.—I could tell you, that when once my resolution is taken.——But I am talking to a baby. Let me, however, repeat, that terrible as are the examples I could recite, the recital could not now benefit you: for, though your repentance would put an immediate end to opposition, it would not now appease my indignation—I will have vengeance as well as justice.'

Another groan filled the pause which Montoni made.

'Leave the room instantly!' said he, seeming not to notice this strange occurrence. Without power to implore his pity, she rose to go, but found that she could not support herself; awe and terror overcame her, and she sunk again into the chair.

'Quit my presence!' cried Montoni. 'This affectation of fear ill becomes the heroine who has just dared to brave my indignation.'

'Did you hear nothing, signor?' said Emily trembling, and still unable to leave the room.

'I heard my own voice,' rejoined Montoni sternly.

'And nothing else?' said Emily, speaking with difficulty.—'There again! Do you hear nothing now?'

'Obey my order,' repeated Montoni. 'And for these fool's tricks—I will soon discover by whom they are practised.'

Emily again rose, and exerted herself to the utmost to leave the room, while Montoni followed her; but instead of calling aloud to his servants to search the chamber, as he had formerly done on a similar occurrence, passed to the ramparts.

As in her way to the corridor she rested for a moment at an open casement, Emily saw a party of Montoni's troops winding down a distant mountain, whom she noticed no further than as they brought to her mind the wretched prisoners they were perhaps bringing to the castle. At length having reached her apartment, she threw herself upon the couch, overcome with the new horrors of her situation. Her thoughts lost in tumult and perplexity, she could neither repent of nor approve her late conduct; she could only remember that she was in the power of a man who had no principle of action—but his will: and the astonishment and terrors of superstition, which had for a moment so strongly assailed her, now yielded to those of reason.

She was at length roused from the reverie which engaged her, by a confusion of distant voices, and a clattering of hoofs, that seemed to come on the wind, from the courts. A sudden hope that some good was approaching seized her mind, till she remembered the troops she had observed from the casement, and concluded this to be the party which Annette had said were expected at Udolpho.

Soon after, she heard voices faintly from the halls, and the noise of horses' feet sunk away in the wind; silence ensued. Emily listened anxiously for Annette's step in the corridor; but a pause of total stillness continued, till again the castle seemed to be all tumult and confusion. She heard the echoes of many footsteps passing to and fro in the halls and avenues below, and then busy tongues were loud on the rampart. Having hurried to her casement, she perceived Montoni with some of his officers leaning on the walls, and pointing from them ; while several soldiers were employed at the further end of the rampart about some cannon; and she continued to observe them, careless of the passing time.

Annette at length appeared, but brought no intelligence of Valancourt ; 'for, ma'amselle,' said she, 'all the people pretend to know nothing about any prisoners. But here is a fine piece of business ! The rest of the party are just arrived, ma'am ; they came scampering in, as if they would have broken their necks ; one scarcely knew whether the man or his horse would get within the gates first. And they have brought word—and such news ! they have brought word that a party of the enemy, as they call them, are coming towards the castle ; so we shall have all the officers of justice, I suppose, besieging it ! all those terrible-looking fellows one used to see at Venice.'

'Thank God !' exclaimed Emily, fervently ; 'there is yet a hope left for me, then !'

'What mean you, ma'amselle? Do you wish to fall into the hands of those sad-looking men? Why I used to shudder as I passed them, and should have guessed what they were, if Ludovico had not told me.'

'We cannot be in worse hands than at present,' replied Emily, unguardedly ; 'but what reason have you to suppose these are officers of justice?'

'Why *our* people, ma'am, are all in such a fright and a fuss ; and I don't know anything but the fear of justice that could make them so. I used to think nothing on earth could fluster them, unless, indeed, it was a ghost, or so ; but now, some of them are for hiding down in the vaults under the castle ; but you must not tell the signor this, ma'amselle, and I overheard two of them talking——Holy Mother ! what makes you look so sad, ma'amselle? You don't hear what I say !'

'Yes, I do, Annette ; pray proceed.'

'Well, ma'amselle, all the castle is in such hurly-burly.: some of the men are loading the cannon, and some are examining the great gates, and the walls all round, and are hammering and patching up, just as if those repairs had never been made, that were so long about. But what is to become of me and you, ma'amselle, and Ludovico? O ! when I hear the sound of the cannon I shall die with fright : if I could but catch the great gate open for one minute, I would be even with it for shutting me within these walls so long !— it should never see me again.'

Emily caught the latter words of Annette. 'O ! if you could find it open, but for one moment !' she exclaimed, 'my peace might yet be saved !' The heavy groan she uttered, and the wildness of her look, terrified Annette still more than her words ; who entreated Emily to explain the meaning of them, to whom it suddenly occurred that Ludovico might be of some service, if there should be a possibility of escape, and who repeated the substance of what had passed between Montoni and herself, but conjured her to mention this to no person except to Ludovico. 'It may perhaps be in his power,' she added, 'to effect our escape. Go to him, Annette, tell him what I have to apprehend, and what I have already suffered ; but entreat him to be secret, and to lose no time in attempting to release us. If he is willing to undertake this, he shall be amply rewarded. I cannot speak with him myself, for we might be observed, and then effectual care would be taken to prevent our flight. But be quick, Annette, and, above all, be discreet—I will await your return in this apartment.'

The girl, whose honest heart had been much affected by the recital, was now as eager to obey as Emily was to employ her, and she immediately quitted the room.

Emily's surprise increased, as she reflected upon Annette's intelligence. 'Alas !' said she, 'what can the officers of justice do against an armed castle? these cannot be such.' Upon further consideration, however, she concluded, that Montoni's bands having plundered the country round, the inhabitants had taken arms, and were coming with the officers of police and a party of soldiers to force their way into the castle. 'But they know not,' thought she, 'its strength, or the armed numbers within it. Alas ! except from flight, I have nothing to hope !'

Montoni, though not precisely what Emily apprehended him to be—a captain of banditti —had employed his troops in enterprises not less daring, or less atrocious, than such a character would have undertaken. They had not only pillaged, whenever opportunity offered, the helpless traveller, but had attacked and plundered the villas of several persons, which, being situated among the solitary recesses of the mountains, were totally unprepared for resistance. In these expeditions the commanders of the party did not appear, and the men, partly disguised, had sometimes been mistaken for common robbers, and, at others, for bands of the foreign enemy, who at that period invaded the country. But though they had already pillaged several mansions, and brought home considerable treasures, they had ventured to approach only one castle, in the attack of which they were assisted by other troops of their own order ; from this, however, they were vigorously repulsed, and pursued by some of the foreign enemy, who were in league with the besieged. Montoni's troops fled precipitately towards Udolpho, but were so closely tracked over the mountains, that when they reached one of the heights in the neighbourhood of the castle, and looked back upon the road, they perceived the enemy winding among the cliffs

below, and not more than a league distant.
Upon this discovery they hastened forward
with increased speed, to prepare Montoni for
the enemy : and it was their arrival which had
thrown the castle into such confusion and
tumult.

As Emily awaited anxiously some information from below, she now saw from her casements a body of troops pour over the neighbouring heights ; and though Annette had
been gone a very short time and had a
difficult and dangerous business to accomplish,
her impatience for intelligence became painful :
she listened ; opened her door, and often went
out upon the corridor to meet her.

At length she heard a footstep approach her
chamber ; and opening the door, saw not
Annette, but old Carlo ! New fears rushed
upon her mind. He said he came from the
signor, who had ordered him to inform her
that she must be ready to depart from
Udolpho immediately, for that the castle was
about to be besieged ; and that mules were
preparing to convey her, with her guides, to a
place of safety.

'Of safety !' exclaimed Emily thoughtlessly ; 'has, then, the signor so much consideration for me ?'

Carlo looked upon the ground, and made
no reply. A thousand opposite emotions
agitated Emily successively, as she listened to
old Carlo ; those of joy, grief, distrust and
apprehension, appeared and vanished from
her mind with the quickness of lightning.
One moment it seemed impossible that Montoni could take this measure merely for her
preservation ; and so very strange was his
sending her from the castle at all, that she
could attribute it only to the design of carrying into execution the new scheme of vengeance with which he had menaced her. In
the next instant it appeared so desirable to
quit the castle, under any circumstances, that
she could not but rejoice in the prospect,
believing that change must be for the better,
till she remembered the probability of Valancourt being detained in it ; when sorrow and
regret usurped her mind, and she wished
much more fervently than she had yet done, that
it might not be his voice which she had heard.

Carlo having reminded her that she had no
time to lose, for that the enemy were within
sight of the castle, Emily entreated him to inform her whither she was to go ; and after
some hesitation, he said he had received no
orders to tell ; but on her repeating the
question, replied that he believed she was to
be carried into Tuscany.

'To Tuscany !' exclaimed Emily—'and
why thither ?'

Carlo answered that he knew nothing further than that she was to be lodged in a
cottage on the borders of Tuscany, at the feet
of the Apennines—'not a day's journey distant,' said he.

Emily now dismissed him, and with trembling hands prepared the small package that
she meant to take with her ; while she was
employed about which, Annette returned.

'O ma'amselle,' said she, 'nothing can be
done ! Ludovico says the new porter is more
watchful even than Barnardine was, and we
might as well throw ourselves in the way of a
dragon as in his. Ludovico is almost as
broken-hearted as you are, ma'am, on my
account, he says ; and I am sure I shall never
live to hear the cannon fire twice !'

She now began to weep, but revived upon
hearing of what had just occurred, and entreated Emily to take her with her.

'That I will do most willingly,' replied
Emily, 'if Signor Montoni permits it :' to
which Annette made no reply, but ran out of
the room, and immediately sought Montoni,
who was on the terrace surrounded by his
officers, where she began her petition. He
sharply bade her go into the castle, and absolutely refused her request. Annette, however,
not only pleaded for herself, but for Ludovico :
and Montoni had ordered some of his men to
take her from his presence before she would
retire.

In an agony of disappointment she returned
to Emily, who forboded little good towards
herself from this refusal to Annette, and who,
soon after, received a summons to repair to
the great court, where the mules, with their
guides were in waiting. Emily here tried in
vain to soothe the weeping Annette, who persisted in saying that she should never see her
dear young lady again ; a fear which her mistress secretly thought too well justified, but
which she endeavoured to restrain, while with
apparent composure she bade this affectionate
servant farewell. Annette, however, followed
to the courts, which were now thronged with
people busy in preparation for the enemy ;
and having seen her mount her mule, and depart with her attendants through the portal,
turned into the castle and wept again.

Emily, meanwhile, as she looked back upon
the gloomy courts of the castle, no longer
silent as when she had first entered them, but
resounding with the noise of preparation for
their defence, as well as crowded with soldiers
and workmen hurrying to and fro ; and when
she passed once more under the huge portcullis which had formerly struck her with
terror and dismay, and, looking round, saw no
walls to confine her steps—felt, in spite of anticipation, the sudden joy of a prisoner who
unexpectedly finds himself at liberty. This
emotion would not suffer her now to look im-
partially on the dangers that awaited her
without ; on mountains infested by hostile
parties, who seized every opportunity for
plunder ; and on a journey commenced under
the guidance of men whose countenances certainly did not speak favourably of their dispositions. In the present moments, she

could only rejoice that she was liberated from those walls which she had entered with such dismal forebodings ; and, remembering the superstitious presentiment which had then seized her, she could now smile at the impression it had made upon her mind.

As she gazed, with these emotions, upon the turrets of the castle rising high over the woods among which she wound, the stranger, whom she believed to be confined there, returned to her remembrance ; and anxiety and apprehension, lest he should be Valancourt, again passed like a cloud upon her joy. She recollected every circumstance concerning this unknown person, since the night when she had first heard him play the song· of her native province ;—circumstances which she had so often recollected and compared before, without extracting from them anything like conviction, and which still only prompted her to believe that Valancourt was a prisoner at Udolpho. It was possible, however, that the men who were her conductors might afford her information on this subject ; but fearing to question them immediately, lest they should be unwilling to discover any circumstance to her in the presence of each other, she watched for an opportunity of speaking with them separately.

Soon after, a trumpet echoed faintly from a distance ; the guides stopped, and looked towards the quarter whence it came ; but the thick woods which surrounded them excluding all view of the country beyond, one of the men rode on to the point of an eminence that afforded a more extensive prospect, to observe how near the enemy, whose trumpet he guessed this to be, were advanced ; the other, meanwhile, remained with Emily, and to him she put some questions concerning the stranger at Udolpho. Ugo, for this was his name, said that there were several prisoners in the castle ; but he neither recollected their persons, nor the precise time of their arrival, and could therefore give her no information. There was a surliness in his manner, as he spoke, that made it probable he would not have satisfied her inquiries, even if he could have done so.

Having asked him what prisoners had been taken, about the time, as nearly as she could remember, when she had first heard the music, 'All that week,' said Ugo, 'I was out with a party on the mountains, and knew nothing of what was doing at the castle. We had enough upon our hands, we had warm work of it.'

Bertrand, the other man, being now returned, Emily inquired no further ; and when he had related to his companion what he had seen, they travelled on in deep silence ; while Emily often caught between the opening woods partial glimpses of the castle above— the west towers, whose battlements were now crowded with archers, and the ramparts below, where soldiers were seen hurrying along, or busy upon the walls, preparing the cannon.

Having emerged from the woods, they wound along the valley in an opposite direction to that from whence the enemy were approaching. Emily had now a full view of Udolpho, with its grey walls, towers and terraces, high over-topping the precipices and the dark woods, and glittering partially with the arms of the *condottieri*, as the sun's rays, streaming through an autumnal cloud, glanced upon a part of the edifice, whose remaining features stood in darkened majesty. She continued to gaze through her tears, upon walls that perhaps confined Valancourt, and which now, as the cloud floated away, were lighted up with sudden splendour, and then, as suddenly, were shrouded in gloom ; while the passing gleam fell on the wood-tops below, and heightened the first tints of autumn that had begun to steal upon the foliage. The winding mountains at length shut Udolpho from her view, and she turned with mournful reluctance to other objects. The melancholy sighing of the wind among the pines that waved high over the steeps, and the distant thunder of a torrent, assisted her musings, and conspired, with the wild scenery around, to diffuse over her mind emotions solemn, yet not unpleasing, but which were soon interrupted by the distant roar of cannon echoing among the mountains. The sounds rolled along the wind, and were repeated in faint and fainter reverberation, till they sunk in sullen murmurs. This was a signal that the enemy had reached the castle, and fear for Valancourt again tormented Emily. She turned her anxious eye towards that part of the country where the edifice stood, but the intervening heights concealed it from her view ; still, however, she saw the tall head of a mountain which immediately fronted her late chamber, and on this she fixed her gaze, as if it could have told her of all that was passing in the scene it overlooked. The guides twice reminded her that she was losing time, and that they had far to go, before she could turn from this interesting object ; and even when she again moved onward, she often sent a look back, till only its blue point, brightening in a gleam of sunshine, appeared peeping over other mountains.

The sound of the cannon affected Ugo, as the blast of the trumpet does the war-horse ; it called forth all the fire of his nature ; he was impatient to be in the midst of the fight, and uttered frequent execrations against Montoni for having sent him to a distance. The feelings of his comrade seemed to be very opposite, and adapted rather to the cruelties than to the dangers of war.

Emily asked frequent questions concerning the place of her destination, but could only learn that she was going to a cottage in Tuscany ; and whenever she mentioned the subject, she fancied she perceived, in the countenances of these men, an expression of malice and cunning that alarmed her.

It was afternoon when they had left the castle. During several hours, they travelled through regions of profound solitude, where no bleat of sheep, or bark of watch-dog, broke on silence, and they were now too far off to hear even the faint thunder of the cannon. Towards evening, they wound down precipices black with forests of cypress, pine, and cedar, into a glen so savage and secluded that, if Solitude ever had local habitation, this might have been 'her place of dearest residence.' To Emily it appeared a spot exactly suited for the retreat of banditti, and in her imagination she already saw them lurking under the brow of some projecting rock, whence their shadows, lengthened by the setting sun, stretched across the road, and warned the traveller of his danger. She shuddered at the idea; and looking at her conductors, to observe whether they were armed, thought she saw in them the banditti she dreaded!

It was in this glen that they proposed to alight, 'For,' said Ugo, 'night will come on presently, and then the wolves will make it dangerous to stop.' This was a new subject of alarm to Emily, but inferior to what she suffered from the thought of being left in these wilds, at midnight, with two such men as her present conductors. Dark and dreadful hints of what might be Montoni's purpose in sending her hither, came to her mind. She endeavoured to dissuade the men from stopping, and inquired with anxiety how far they had yet to go.

'Many leagues yet,' replied Bertrand, 'As for you, signora, you may do as you please about eating, but for us, we will make a hearty supper while we can; we shall have need of it, I warrant, before we finish our journey. The sun's going down apace; let us alight under that rock yonder.'

His comrade assented, and turning the mules out of the road, they advanced towards a cliff overhung with cedars, Emily following in trembling silence. They lifted her from her mule, and having seated themselves on the grass at the foot of the rocks, drew some homely fare from a wallet, of which Emily tried to eat a little, the better to disguise her apprehensions.

The sun was now sunk behind the high mountains in the west, upon which a purple haze began to spread, and the gloom of twilight to draw over the surrounding objects. To the low and sullen murmur of the breeze passing among the woods, she no longer listened with any degree of pleasure, for it conspired with the wildness of the scene and the evening hour to depress her spirits.

Suspense had so much increased her anxiety as to the prisoner at Udolpho, that finding it impracticable to speak alone with Bertrand on that subject, she renewed her questions in the presence of Ugo; but he either was, or pretended to be, entirely ignorant concerning the stranger. When he had dismissed the question, he talked with Ugo on some subject which led to the mention of Signor Orsino, and of the affair that had banished him from Venice; respecting which Emily had ventured to ask a few questions. Ugo appeared to be well acquainted with the circumstances of that tragical event, and related some minute particulars that both shocked and surprised her; for it appeared very extraordinary how such particulars could be known to any, but to persons present when the assassination was committed.

'He was of rank,' said Bertrand, 'or the state would not have troubled itself to inquire after his assassins. The signor has been lucky hitherto; this is not the first affair of the kind he has had upon his hands; and to be sure, when a gentleman has no other way of getting redress—why he must take this.'

'Aye,' said Ugo, 'and why is not this as good as another? This is the way to have justice done at once, without more ado. If you go to law, you must stay till the judges please, and may lose your cause at last. Why the best way, then, is to make sure of your right, while you can, and execute justice yourself.'

'Yes, yes,' rejoined Bertrand, 'if you wait till justice is done you—you may stay long enough. Why if I want a friend of mine properly served, how am I to get my revenge? Ten to one they tell me he is in the right, and I am in the wrong. Or, if a fellow has got possession of property which I think ought to be mine, why I may wait till I starve, perhaps, before the law will give it me; and then, after all, the judge may say—the estate is his. What is to be done then?—Why the case is plain enough, I must take it at last.'

Emily's horror at this conversation was heightened by a suspicion that the latter part of it was pointed against herself, and that these men had been commissioned by Montoni to execute a similar kind of *justice* in his cause.

'But I was speaking of Signor Orsino,' resumed Bertrand; 'he is one of those who love to do justice at once. I remember, about ten years ago, the signor had a quarrel with a cavaliero of Milan. The story was told me then, and it is still fresh in my head. They quarrelled about a lady that the signor liked, and she was perverse enough to prefer the gentleman of Milan, and even carried her whim so far as to marry him. This provoked the signor, as well it might, for he had tried to talk reason to her a long while, and used to send people to serenade her under her windows of a night; and used to make verses about her, and would swear she was the handsomest lady in Milan.—But all would not do—nothing would bring her to reason ; and, as I said, she went so far as to marry this other cavaliero. This made the signor wroth, with a vengeance : he resolved to be even with her though ; and he watched his opportunity, and did not wait long, for soon after the marriage they set out for Padua, nothing doubting, I warrant, of what was preparing for them. The cavaliero thought, to be sure, he was to be called to no account, but was to go off triumphant ; but he was soon made to know another sort of story.'

'What, then the lady had promised to have Signor Orsino ?' said Ugo.

' Promised ! No,' replied Bertrand, ' she had not wit enough even to tell him she liked him, as I heard, but the contrary, for she used to say, from the first, she never meant to have him. And this was what provoked the signor so ; and with good reason, for who likes to be told that he is disagreeable? and this was saying as good. It was enough to tell him this ; she need not have gone and married another.'

'What, she married, then, on purpose to plague the signor ?' said Ugo.

' I don't know as for that,' replied Bertrand : ' they said, indeed, that she had had a regard for the other gentleman a great while ; but that is nothing to the purpose, she should not have married him, and then the signor would not have been so much provoked. She might have expected what was to follow : it was not to be supposed he would bear her ill usage tamely, and she might thank herself for what happened. But, as I said, they set out for Padua, she and her husband, and the road lay over some barren mountains like these. This suited the signor's purpose well. He watched the time of their departure, and sent his men after them, with directions what to do. They kept their distance till they saw their opportunity, and this did not happen till the second day's journey, when, the gentleman having sent his servants forward to the next town, may-be to have horses in readiness, the signor's men quickened their pace, and overtook the carriage in a hollow between two mountains, where the woods prevented the servants from seeing what passed, though they were then not far off. When we came up, we fired our tromboni, but missed.'

Emily turned pale at these words, and then hoped she had mistaken them ; while Bertrand proceeded :

' The gentleman fired again ; but he was soon made to alight : and it was as he turned to call his people that he was struck. It was the most dexterous feat you ever saw—he was struck in the back with three stilettos at once. He fell, and was dispatched in a minute ; but the lady escaped ; for the servants had heard the firing, and came up before she could be taken care of. " Bertrand," said the signor, when his men returned——'

' Bertrand !' exclaimed Emily, pale with horror, on whom not a syllable of this narrative had been lost.

' Bertrand, did I say ?' rejoined the man with some confusion—' No, Giovanni. But I have forgot where I was ;—" Bertrand," said the signor—'

' Bertrand again !' said Emily in a faltering voice, ' why do you repeat that name ?'

Bertrand swore. ' What signifies it,' he proceeded, ' what the man was called—Bertrand or Giovanni,—or Roberto ; it's all one for that. You have put me out twice with that—question. Bertrand or Giovanni—or what you will—" Bertrand," said the signor, " if your comrades had done their duty as well as you, I should not have lost the lady. Go, my honest fellow, and be happy with this." He gave him a purse of gold—and little enough too, considering the service he had done him.'

' Aye, aye,' said Ugo, ' little enough—little enough.'

Emily now breathed with difficulty, and could scarcely support herself. When first she saw these men, their appearance and their connexion with Montoni had been sufficient to impress her with distrust ; but now, when one of them had betrayed himself to be a murderer, and she saw herself at the approach of night under his guidance, among wild and solitary mountains, and going she scarcely knew whither, the most agonizing terror seized her, which was the less supportable from the necessity she found herself under of concealing all symptoms of it from her companions. Reflecting on the character and the menaces of Montoni, it appeared not improbable that he had delivered her to them, for the purpose of having her murdered, and of thus securing to himself, without further opposition or delay, the estates for which he had so long and so desperately contended. Yet, if this was his design, there appeared no necessity for sending her to such a distance from the castle ; for if any dread of discovery had made him unwilling to perpetrate the deed there, a much nearer place might have sufficed for the purpose of concealment. These considerations, however, did not immediately occur to Emily, with whom so many circumstances conspired to rouse terror, that she had no power to oppose it, or to inquire coolly into its grounds ; and if she had done so, still there were many appearances which would too well have justified her most terrible apprehensions. She did not dare to speak to her conductors, at the sound of whose voices she trembled ; and when, now and then, she stole a glance at them, their countenances, seen imperfectly through the gloom of evening, served to confirm her fears.

The sun had now been set some time ; heavy clouds, whose lower skirts were tinged with sulphureous crimson, lingered in the west, and threw a reddish tint upon the pine forests, which sent forth a solemn sound as the breeze rolled over them. The hollow moan struck upon Emily's heart, and served to render more gloomy and terrific every object around her,—the mountains, shaded in twilight—the gleaming torrent, hoarsely roaring—the black forests, and the deep glen, broken into rocky recesses, high overshadowed by cypress and sycamore, and winding into long obscurity. To this glen, Emily, as she sent forth her anxious eye, thought there was no end : no hamlet, or even cottage, was seen, and still no distant bark of watch-dog, or even faint far-off halloo came on the wind. In a tremulous voice she now ventured to remind the guides that it was growing late, and to ask again how far they had to go : but they were too much occupied by their own discourse to attend to her question, which she forbore to repeat, lest it should provoke a surly answer. Having however, soon after, finished their supper, the men collected the fragments into their wallet, and proceeded along this winding glen in gloomy silence ; while Emily again mused upon her own situation, and concerning the motives of Montoni for involving her in it. That it was for some evil purpose towards herself she could not doubt ; and it seemed that, if he did not intend to destroy her, with a view of immediately seizing her estates, he meant to reserve her awhile in concealment, for some more terrible design, for one that might equally gratify his avarice, and still more his deep revenge. At this moment, remembering Signor Brochio and his behaviour in the corridor a few preceding nights, the latter supposition, horrible as it was, strengthened in her belief. Yet, why remove her from the castle, where deeds of darkness had, she feared, been often executed with secrecy ?—from chambers, perhaps,

'With many a foul and midnight murder stain'd !'

The dread of what she might be going to encounter was now so excessive, that it sometimes threatened her senses ; and often as she went, she thought of her late father and of all he would have suffered, could he have foreseen the strange and dreadful events of her future life ; and how anxiously he would have avoided that fatal confidence, which committed his daughter to the care of a woman so weak as was Madame Montoni. So romantic and improbable, indeed, did her present situation appear to Emily herself, particularly when she compared it with the repose and beauty of her early days, that there were moments when she could almost have believed herself the victim of frightful visions glaring upon a disordered fancy.

Restrained by the presence of her guides from expressing her terrors, their acuteness was at length lost in gloomy despair. The dreadful view of what might await her hereafter, rendered her almost indifferent to the surrounding dangers. She now looked with little emotion on the wild dingles, and the gloomy road and mountains, whose outlines only were distinguishable through the dusk ;—objects, which but lately had affected her spirits so much, as to awaken horrid views of the future, and to tinge these with their own gloom.

It was now so nearly dark, that the travellers, who proceeded only by the slowest pace, could scarcely discern their way. The clouds, which seemed charged with thunder, passed slowly along the heavens, showing at intervals the trembling stars ; while the groves of cypress and sycamore that overhung the rocks, waved high in the breeze as it swept over the glen, and then rushed among the distant woods. Emily shivered as it passed.

'Where is the torch ?' said Ugo, ' it grows dark.'

'Not so dark yet,' replied Bertrand, ' but we may find our way ; and 'tis best not light the torch before we can help, for it may betray us, if any straggling party of the enemy is abroad.'

Ugo muttered something which Emily did not understand, and they proceeded in darkness, while she almost wished that the enemy might discover them ; for from change there was something to hope, since she could scarcely imagine any situation more dreadful than her present one.

As they moved slowly along, her attention was surprised by a thin tapering flame that appeared, by fits, at the point of the pike which Bertrand carried, resembling what she had observed on the lance of the sentinel the night Madame Montoni died, and which he had said was an omen. The event immediately following, it appeared to justify the assertion, and a superstitious impression had remained on Emily's mind, which the present appearance confirmed. She thought it was an omen of her own fate, and watched it successively vanish and return, in gloomy silence, which was at length interrupted by Bertrand.

'Let us light the torch,' said he, ' and get under shelter of the woods ;—a storm is coming on—look at my lance.'

He held it forth, with the flame tapering at its point.*

'Aye,' said Ugo, ' you are not one of those that believe in omens : we have left cowards at the castle, who would turn pale at such a sight. I have often seen it before a thunderstorm, it is an omen of that, and one is coming now, sure enough. The clouds flash fast already.'

Emily was relieved by this conversation from some of the terrors of superstition : but those of reason increased, as, waiting while Ugo searched for a flint to strike fire, she watched the pale lightning gleam over the woods they were about to enter, and illumine

* See the Abbé Berthelon on Electricity.

the harsh countenances of her companions. Ugo could not find a flint, and Bertrand became impatient, for the thunder sounded hollowly at a distance, and the lightning was more frequent. Sometimes it revealed the nearer recesses of the woods, or, displaying some opening in their summits, illumined the ground beneath with partial splendour, the thick foliage of the trees preserving the surrounding scene in deep shadow.

At length Ugo found a flint, and the torch was lighted. The men then dismounted, and, having assisted Emily, led the mules towards the woods that skirted the glen on the left, over broken ground, frequently interrupted with brush-wood and wild plants, which she was often obliged to make a circuit to avoid.

She could not approach these woods without experiencing keener sense of her danger. Their deep silence, except when the wind swept among their branches, and impenetrable gloom shown partially by the sudden flash, and then by the red glare of the torch, which served only to make darkness visible, were circumstances that contributed to renew all her most terrible apprehensions; she thought, too, that at this moment the countenances of her conductors displayed more than their usual fierceness, mingled with a kind of lurking exultation, which they seemed endeavouring to disguise. To her affrighted fancy it occurred that they were leading her into these woods to complete the will of Montoni by her murder. The horrid suggestion called a groan from her heart, which surprised her companions, who turned round quickly towards her, and she demanded why they led her thither, beseeching them to continue their way along the open glen, which she represented to be less dangerous than the woods in a thunder-storm.

'No, no,' said Bertrand, 'we know best where the danger lies. See how the clouds open over our heads. Besides, we can glide under cover of the woods with less hazard of being seen, should any of the enemy be wandering this way. By holy St. Peter and all the rest of them, I've as stout a heart as the best, as many a poor devil could tell, if he were alive again—but what can we do against numbers?'

'What are you whining about?' said Ugo contemptuously—'Who fears numbers? Let them come, though they were as many as the signor's castle could hold: I would show the knaves what fighting is. For you—I would lay you quietly in a dry ditch, where you might peep out, and see me put the rogues to flight.—Who talks of fear?'

Bertrand replied, with a horrible oath, that he did not like such jesting; and a violent altercation ensued, which was at length silenced by the thunder, whose deep volley was heard afar, rolling onward till it burst over their heads in sounds that seemed to shake the earth to its centre. The ruffians paused, and looked upon each other. Between the boles of the trees the blue lightning flashed and quivered along the ground, while, as Emily looked under the boughs, the mountains beyond frequently appeared to be clothed in livid flame. At this moment, perhaps, she felt less fear of the storm than did either of her companions, for other terrors occupied her mind.

The men now rested under an enormous chestnut tree, and fixed their pikes in the ground at some distance; on the iron points of which Emily repeatedly observed the lightning play, and then glide down them into the earth.

'I would we were well in the signor's castle!' said Bertrand, 'I know not why he should send us on this business. Hark! how it rattles above, there! I could almost find in my heart to turn priest, and pray. Ugo has got a rosary!'

'No,' replied Ugo, 'I leave it to cowards like thee, to carry rosaries—I carry a sword.'

'And much good may it do thee in fighting against the storm!' said Bertrand.

Another peel which was reverberated in tremendous echoes among the mountains, silenced them for a moment. As it rolled away, Ugo proposed going on. 'We are only losing time here,' said he, 'for the thick boughs of the wood will shelter us as well as this chestnut tree.'

They again led the mules forward, between the boles of the trees, and over pathless grass that concealed their high knotted roots. The rising wind was now heard contending with the thunder, as it rushed furiously among the branches above, and brightened the red flame of the torch, which threw a stronger light forward among the woods, and showed their gloomy recesses to be suitable resorts for the wolves, of which Ugo had formerly spoken.

At length the strength of the wind seemed to drive the storm before it, for the thunder rolled away into distance, and was only faintly heard. After travelling through the woods for nearly an hour, during which the elements seemed to have returned to repose, the travellers, gradually ascending from the glen, found themselves upon the open brow of a mountain, with a wide valley extending in misty moonlight at their feet, and above, the blue sky trembling through the few thin clouds that lingered after the storm, and were sinking slowly to the verge of the horizon.

Emily's spirits, now that she had quitted the woods, began to revive; for she considered that if these men had received an order to destroy her, they would probably have executed their barbarous purpose in the solitary wild from whence they had just emerged, where the deed would have been shrouded from every human eye. Reassured by this reflection, and by the quiet demeanour of her guides, Emily, as they proceeded silently in a kind of sheep track that wound along the skirts of the woods, which ascended on the right, could not survey the sleeping beauty of the vale, to which they were declining, without a momentary sensation of pleasure. It seemed varied with woods, pastures, and sloping grounds, and was screened to the north and the east by an amphitheatre of the Apennines, whose outline on the horizon was here broken into varied and elegant forms; to the west and the south the landscape extended indistinctly into the low lands of Tuscany.

'There is the sea yonder,' said Bertrand,—as if he had known that Emily was examining the twilight view,—'yonder in the west, though we cannot see it.'

Emily already perceived a change in the climate, from that of the wild and mountainous tract she had left; and as she continued descending, the air became perfumed by the breath of a thousand nameless flowers among the grass, called forth by the late rain. So soothingly beautiful was the scene around her, and so strikingly contrasted to the gloomy grandeur of those to which she had long been confined, and to the manners of the people who moved among them, that she could almost have fancied herself again at La Vallée; and, wondering why Montoni had sent her thither, could scarcely believe that he had selected so enchanting a spot for any cruel design. It was, however, probably not the spot, but the persons who happened to inhabit it, and to whose care he could safely commit the execution of his plans, whatever they might be that had determined his choice.

She now ventured again to inquire whether they were near the place of their destination, and was answered by Ugo, that they had not far to go. 'Only to the wood of chestnuts in the valley yonder,' said he, 'there, by the brook that sparkles with the moon ; I wish I was once at rest there, with a flask of good wine and a slice of Tuscany bacon.'

Emily's spirits revived when she heard that the journey was so nearly concluded, and saw the wood of chestnuts in an open part of the vale, on the margin of the stream.

In a short time they reached the entrance of the wood, and perceived between the twinkling leaves a light streaming from a distant cottage window. They proceeded along the edge of the brook to where the trees, crowding over it, excluded the moonbeams ; but a long line of light, from the cottage above, was seen on its dark tremulous surface. Bertrand now stepped on first, and Emily heard him knock, and call loudly at the door. As she reached it, the small upper casement, where the light appeared, was unclosed by a man, who, having inquired what they wanted, immediately descended, let them into a neat rustic cot,

and called up his wife to set refreshments before the travellers. As this man conversed, rather apart, with Bertrand, Emily anxiously surveyed him. He was a tall but not robust peasant, of sallow complexion, and had a shrewd and cunning eye ; his countenance was not of a character to win the ready confidence of youth, and there was nothing in his manner that might conciliate a stranger.

Ugo called impatiently for supper, and in a tone as if he knew his authority here to be unquestionable. 'I expected you here an hour ago,' said the peasant, 'for I have had Signor Montoni's letter these three hours, and I and my wife had given you up, and gone to bed. How did you fare in the storm?'

'Ill enough,' replied Ugo, 'ill enough, and we are likely to fare ill enough here, too, unless you will make more haste. Get us more wine, and let us see what you have to eat.'

The peasant placed before them all that his cottage afforded—ham, wine, figs, and grapes of such size and flavour as Emily had seldom tasted.

After taking refreshment, she was shown by the peasant's wife to her little bed-chamber, where she asked some questions concerning Montoni ; to which the woman, whose name was Dorina, gave reserved answers, pretending ignorance of his *Excellenza's* intention in sending Emily hither, but acknowledging that her husband had been apprized of the circumstance. Perceiving that she could obtain no intelligence concerning her destination, Emily dismissed Dorina, and retired to repose : but all the busy scenes of the past and the anticipated ones of the future came to her anxious mind, and conspired with the sense of her new situation to banish sleep.

CHAPTER XXXII.

'Was nought around but images of rest,
Sleep-soothing groves and quiet lawns between,
And flowery beds that slumbrous influence kest,
From poppies breathed, and banks of pleasant green,
Where never yet was creeping creature seen.
Meantime unnumber'd glitt'ring streamlets play'd,
And hurled everywhere their water's sheen,
That, as they bicker'd through the sunny glade,
Though restless still themselves, a lulling murmur made.'

                                        THOMSON.

WHEN Emily, in the morning, opened her casement, she was surprised to observe the beauties that surrounded it. The cottage was nearly embowered in the woods, which were chiefly of chestnut intermixed with some cypress, larch, and sycamore. Beneath the dark and spreading branches appeared to the north and to the east the woody Apennines, rising in majestic amphitheatre, not black with pines, as she had been accustomed to see them, but their loftiest summits crowned with ancient forests of chestnut, oak, and oriental plane, now animated with the rich tints of autumn, and which swept downward to the valley uninterruptedly, except where some bold rocky promontory looked out from among the foliage, and caught the passing gleam. Vineyards stretched along the feet of the mountains, where the elegant villas of the Tuscan nobility frequently adorned the scene, and overlooked slopes clothed with groves of olive, mulberry, orange, and lemon. The plain to which these declined, was coloured with the riches of cultivation, whose mingled hues were mellowed into harmony by an Italian sun. Vines, their purple clusters blushing between the russet foliage, hung in luxuriant festoons from the branches of standard fig and cherry trees, while pastures of verdure, such as Emily had seldom seen in Italy, enriched the banks of a stream that, after descending from the mountains, wound along the landscape, which it reflected, to a bay of the sea. There, far in the west, the waters, fading into the sky, assumed a tint of the faintest purple, and the line of separation between them was now and then discernible only by the progress of a sail, brightened with the sunbeam, along the horizon.

The cottage, which was shaded by the woods from the intenser rays of the sun, and was open only to his evening light, was covered entirely with vines, fig-trees, and jessamine whose flowers surpassed in size and fragrance any that Emily had seen. These ripening clusters of grapes hung round her little casement. The turf, that grew under the woods, was inlaid with a variety of wild flowers and perfumed herbs, and on the opposite margin of the stream, whose current diffused freshness beneath the shades, rose a grove of lemon and orange trees. This, though nearly opposite to Emily's window, did not interrupt her prospect, but rather heightened, by its dark verdure, the effect of the perspective; and to her this spot was a bower of sweets, whose charms communicated imperceptibly to her mind somewhat of their own serenity.

She was soon summoned to breakfast by the peasant's daughter, a girl of about seventeen, of a pleasant countenance, which, Emily was glad to observe, seemed animated with the pure affections of nature, though the others that surrounded her expressed, more or less, the worst qualities—cruelty, ferocity, cunning, and duplicity; of the latter style of countenance, especially, were those of the peasant and his wife. Maddelina spoke little; but what she said was in a soft voice, and with an air of modesty and complacency that interested Emily, who breakfasted at a separate table with Dorina, while Ugo and Bertrand were taking a repast of Tuscany bacon and wine

with their host, near the cottage door; when they had finished which, Ugo, rising hastily, inquired for his mule, and Emily learned that he was to return to Udolpho, while Bertrand remained at the cottage; a circumstance which, though it did not surprise, distressed her.

When Ugo was departed, Emily proposed to walk in the neighbouring woods; but on being told that she must not quit the cottage without having Bertrand for her attendant, she withdrew to her own room. There, as her eyes settled on the towering Apennines, she recollected the terrific scenery they had exhibited, and the horrors she had suffered, on the preceding night, particularly at the moment when Bertrand had betrayed himself to be an assassin; and these remembrances awakened a train of images, which, since they abstracted her from a consideration of her own situation, she pursued for some time, and then arranged in the following lines; pleased to have discovered any innocent means by which she could beguile an hour of misfortune.

THE PILGRIM.*

Slow o'er the Apennine, with bleeding feet,
A patient pilgrim wound his lonely way,
To deck the Lady of Loretto's seat,
With all the little wealth his zeal could pay.
From mountain-tops cold died the evening ray,
And, stretch'd in twilight, slept the vale below;
And now the last, last purple streaks of day
Along the melancholy West fade slow.
High o'er his head the restless pines complain,
As on their summit rolls the breeze of night;
Beneath, the hoarse stream chides the rocks in
    vain:
The Pilgrim pauses on the dizzy height.
Then to the vale his cautious step he press'd,
For there a hermit's cross was dimly seen,
Cresting the rock, and there his limbs might rest,
Cheer'd in the good man's cave, by faggot's sheen,
On leafy beds, nor guile his sleep molest.
Unhappy Luke! he trusts a treacherous clue!
Behind the cliff the lurking robber stood:
No friendly moon his giant shadow threw
Athwart the road, to save the Pilgrim's blood;
On as he went a vesper hymn he sang,
The hymn that nightly sooth'd him to repose.
Fierce on his harmless prey the ruffian sprang!
The Pilgrim bleeds to death, his eye-lids close.
Yet his meek spirit knew no vengeful care,
But, dying, for his murderer breathed—a sainted
    prayer!

Preferring the solitude of her room to the company of the person below stairs, Emily dined above, and Maddelina was suffered to attend her, from whose simple conversation she learned that the peasant and his wife were old inhabitants of this cottage, which had been purchased for them by Montoni in reward of some service rendered him many years before by Marco, to whom Carlo, the steward at the castle, was nearly related.

* This poem and that entitled 'The Traveller' have already appeared in a periodical publication.

'So many years ago, signora,' added Madde-lina, 'that I know nothing about it; but my father did the signor a great good, for my mother has often said to him, this cottage was the least he ought to have had.'

To the mention of this circumstance Emily listened with a painful interest, since it ap-peared to give a frightful colour to the cha-racter of Marco, whose service, thus rewarded by Montoni, she could scarcely doubt had been criminal; and, if so, had too much reason to believe that she had been committed into his hands for some desperate purpose. 'Did you ever hear how many years it is,' said Emily, who was considering of Signora Laurentini's disappearance from Udolpho, 'since your father performed the service you spoke of?'

'It was a little before he came to live at the cottage, signora,' replied Maddelina, 'and that is about eighteen years ago.'

This was near the period when Signora Laurentini had been said to disappear; and it occurred to Emily that Marco had assisted in that mysterious affair, and, perhaps, had been employed in a murder! This horrible suggestion fixed her in such profound reverie, that Maddelina quitted the room unperceived by her; and she remained unconscious of all around her for a considerable time. Tears at length came to her relief; after indulging which, her spirits becoming calmer, she ceased to tremble at a view of evils that might never arrive; and had sufficient resolution to endeavour to withdraw her thoughts from the contemplation of her own interests. Remem-bering the few books which even in the hurry of her departure from Udolpho she had put into her little package, she sat down with one of them at her pleasant casement, whence her eyes often wandered from the page to the landscape, whose beauty gradually soothed her mind into gentle melancholy.

Here she remained alone till evening, and saw the sun descend the western sky, through all his pomp of light and shadow upon the mountains, and gleam upon the distant ocean and the stealing sails, as he sunk amidst the waves. Then, at the musing hour of twilight, her softened thoughts returned to Valan-court; she again recollected every circum-stance connected with the midnight music, and all that might assist her conjecture con-cerning his imprisonment at the castle; and becoming confirmed in the supposition that it was his voice she had heard there, she looked back to that gloomy abode with emo-tions of grief and momentary regret.

Refreshed by the cool and fragrant air, and her spirits soothed to a state of gentle melan-choly by the still murmur of the brook below and of the woods around, she lingered at her casement long after the sun had set, watch-ing the valley sinking into obscurity, till only the grand outline of the surrounding moun-tains, shadowed upon the horizon, remained visible. But a clear moonlight that suc-ceeded, gave to the landscape what time gives to the scenes of past life, when it softens all their harsher features, and throws over the whole the mellowing shade of distant con-templation. The scenes of La Vallée in the early morn of her life, when she was protected and beloved by parents equally loved, ap-peared in Emily's memory tenderly beautiful, like the prospect before her, and awakened mournful comparisons. Unwilling to en-counter the coarse behaviour of the peasant's wife, she remained supperless in her room, while she wept again over her forlorn and perilous situation, a review of which entirely overcame the small remains of her fortitude; and reducing her to temporary despondence, she wished to be released from the heavy load of life that had so long oppressed her, and prayed to Heaven to take her, in its mercy, to her parents.

Wearied with weeping, she at length lay down on her mattress and sunk to sleep, but was soon awakened by a knocking at her chamber-door, and, starting up in terror, she heard a voice calling her. The image of Bertrand with a stiletto in his hand appeared to her alarmed fancy, and she neither opened the door nor answered, but listened in pro-found silence, till, the voice repeating her name in the same low tone, she demanded who called. 'It is I, signora,' replied the voice, which she now distinguished to be Maddelina's, 'pray open the door——Don't be frightened, it is I.'

'And what brings you here so late, Madde-lina?' said Emily, as she let her in.

'Hush! signora, for Heaven's sake, hush! —if we are overheard I shall never be for-given. My father and mother and Bertrand are all gone to bed,' continued Maddelina, as she gently shut the door and crept forward, and I have brought you some supper, for you had none, you know, signora, below stairs. Here are some grapes and figs, and half a cup of wine.'

Emily thanked her, but expressed appre-hension lest this kindness should draw upon her the resentment of Dorina, when she per-ceived the fruit was gone. 'Take it back, therefore, Maddelina,' added Emily; 'I shall suffer much less from the want of it, than I should do, if this act of good-nature were to subject you to your mother's displeasure.'

'O signora, there is no danger of that,' replied Maddelina, 'my mother cannot miss the fruit, for I saved it from my own supper. You will make me very unhappy if you refuse to take it, signora.' Emily was so much affected by this instance of the good girl's generosity, that she remained for some time unable to reply; and Maddelina watched her in silence, till, mistaking the cause of her emotion, she said, 'Do not weep so, signora!

My mother, to be sure, is a little cross sometimes, but then it is soon over,—so don't take it so much to heart. She often scolds me, too ; but then I have learned to bear it ; and when she has done, if I can but steal out into the woods, and play upon my sticcado, I forget it all directly.'

Emily, smiling through her tears, told Maddelina that she was a good girl, and then accepted her offering. She wished anxiously to know whether Bertrand and Dorina had spoken of Montoni, or of his designs concerning herself, in the presence of Maddelina, but disdained to tempt the innocent girl to a conduct so mean as that of betraying the private conversation of her parents. When she was departing Emily requested that she would come to her room as often as she dared without offending her mother ; and Maddelina, after promising that she would do so, stole softly back again to her own chamber.

Thus several days passed, during which Emily remained in her own room, Maddelina attending her only at her repast, whose gentle countenance and manners soothed her more than any circumstance she had known for many months. Of her pleasant embowered chamber she now became fond, and began to experience at it those feelings of security which we naturally attach to home. In this interval also her mind, having been undisturbed by any new circumstance of disgust or alarm, recovered its tone sufficiently to permit her enjoyment of her books, among which she found some unfinished sketches of landscapes, several blank sheets of paper, with her drawing instruments ; and she was thus enabled to amuse herself with selecting some of the lovely features of the prospect that her window commanded, and combining them in scenes to which her tasteful fancy gave a last grace. In these little sketches she generally placed interesting groups characteristic of the scenery they animated, and often contrived to tell, with perspicuity, some simple and affecting story, when, as a tear fell over the pictured griefs which her imagination drew, she would forget, for a moment, her real sufferings. Thus innocently she beguiled the heavy hours of misfortune, and with meek patience awaited the events of futurity.

A beautiful evening, that had succeeded to a sultry day, at length induced Emily to walk, though she knew that Bertrand must attend her, and, with Maddelina for her companion, she left the cottage followed by Bertrand, who allowed her to choose her own way. The hour was cool and silent, and she could not look upon the country around her without delight. How lovely, too, appeared the brilliant blue that coloured all the upper regions of air, and, thence fading downward, was lost in the saffron glow of the horizon ! Nor less so were the varied shades and warm colouring of the Apennines, as the evening sun threw his flaming rays athwart their broken surface. Emily followed the course of the stream under the shades that overhung its grassy margin. On the opposite banks the pastures were animated with herds of cattle of a beautiful cream-colour ; and beyond were groves of lemon and orange, with fruit glowing on the branches, frequent almost as the leaves which partly concealed it. She pursued her way towards the sea, which reflected the warm glow of sunset, while the cliffs that rose over its edge were tinted with the last rays. The valley was terminated on the right by a lofty promontory, whose summit, impending over the waves, was crowned with a ruined tower, now serving for the purpose of a beacon, whose shattered battlements and the extended wings of some sea-fowl that circled near it, were still illumined by the upward beams of the sun, though his disc was now sunk beneath the horizon ; while the lower part of the ruin, the cliff on which it stood, and the waves at its foot were shaded with the first tints of twilight.

Having reached this headland, Emily gazed with solemn pleasure on the cliffs that extended on either hand along the sequestered shores, some crowned with groves of pine, and others exhibiting only barren precipices of greyish marble, except where the crags were tufted with myrtle and other aromatic shrubs. The sea slept in a perfect calm ; its waves, dying in murmurs on the shores, flowed with the gentlest undulation, while its clear surface reflected in softened beauty the vermeil tints of the west. Emily, as she looked upon the ocean, thought of France and of past times, and she wished, oh ! how ardently and vainly wished ! that its waves would bear her to her distant native home !

'Ah ! that vessel,' said she, ' that vessel which glides along so stately, with its tall sails reflected in the water, is perhaps bound for France ! Happy—happy bark !' She continued to gaze upon it, with warm emotion, till the grey of twilight obscured the distance, and veiled it from her view. The melancholy sound of the waves at her feet assisted the tenderness that occasioned her tears ; and this was the only sound that broke upon the hour, till, having followed the windings of the beach for some time, a chorus of voices passed her on the air. She paused a moment, wishing to hear more, yet fearing to be seen, and for the first time looked back to Bertrand, as her protector, who was following at a short distance in company with some other person. Reassured by this circumstance, she advanced towards the sounds, which seemed to arise from behind a high promontory that projected athwart the beach. There was now a sudden pause in the music, and then one female voice was heard to sing in a kind of chant. Emily quickened her steps, and winding round the rock saw, within the sweeping bay beyond, which was hung with woods from the borders of the beach to the very summit of the cliffs, two groups of peasants, one seated beneath the shades, and the other standing on the edge of the sea, round the girl who was singing, and who held in her hand a chaplet of flowers, which she seemed about to drop into the waves.

Emily, listening with surprise and attention, distinguished the following invocation, delivered in the pure and elegant tongue of Tuscany, and accompanied by a few pastoral instruments.

TO A SEA-NYMPH.

O nymph! who lovest to float on the green wave,
When Neptune sleeps beneath the moon-light hour,
Lull'd by the music's melancholy power,
O nymph, arise from out thy pearly cave!

For Hesper beams amid the twilight shade,
And soon shall Cynthia tremble o'er the tide,
Gleam on these cliffs, that bound the ocean's pride,
And lonely silence all the air pervade.

Then let thy tender voice at distance swell,
And steal along this solitary shore,
Sink on the breeze, till dying—heard no more—
Thou wakest the sudden magic of thy shell.

While the long coast in echo sweet replies,
Thy soothing strains the pensive heart beguile,
And bid the visions of the future smile,　·
O nymph! from out thy pearly cave—arise!

　　　　(Chorus) *Arise!*
　　　　(Semi-chorus) *Arise!*

The last words being repeated by the surrounding group, the garland of flowers was thrown into the waves, and the chorus, sinking gradually into a chant, died away in silence.

'What can this mean, Maddelina?' said Emily, awakening from the pleasing trance into which the music had lulled her. 'This is the eve of a festival, signora,' replied Maddelina, 'and the peasants then amuse themselves with all kinds of sports.'

'But they talked of a sea-nymph,' said Emily : 'how came these good people to think of a sea-nymph?'

'O, signora,' rejoined Maddelina, mistaking the reason of Emily's surprise, 'nobody *believes* in such things, but our old songs tell of them, and when we are at our sports we sometimes sing to them, and throw garlands into the sea.'

Emily had been early taught to venerate Florence as the seat of literature and of the fine arts ; but that its taste for classic story should descend to the peasants of the country, occasioned her both surprise and admiration. The Arcadian air of the girls next attracted her attention. Their dress was a very short full petticoat of light green, with a bodice of white silk ; the sleeves loose, and tied up at the shoulders with ribbons and bunches of flowers. Their hair, falling in ringlets on their necks, was also ornamented with flowers, and with a small straw hat,

which, set rather backward and on one side of the head, gave an expression of gaiety and smartness to the whole figure. When the song had concluded, several of these girls approached Emily, and, inviting her ·to sit down among them, offered her, and Maddelina, whom they knew, grapes and figs.

Emily accepted their courtesy, much pleased with the gentleness and grace of their manners, which appeared to be perfectly natural to them ; and when Bertrand, soon after, approached, and was hastily drawing her away, a peasant, holding up a flask, invited him to drink ; a temptation which Bertrand was seldom very valiant in resisting.

'Let the young lady join in the dance, my friend,' said the peasant, 'while we empty this flask ; they are going to begin directly. Strike up! my lads, strike up your tambourines and merry flutes !'

They sounded gaily ; and the younger peasants formed themselves into a circle, which Emily would readily have joined, had her spirits been in unison with her mirth. Maddelina, however, tripped it lightly ; and Emily, as she looked on the happy group, lost the sense of her misfortunes in that· of a benevolent pleasure. But the pensive melancholy of her mind returned, as she sat rather apart from the company, listening to the mellow music, which the breeze softened as it bore it away, and watching the moon stealing its tremulous light over the waves and on the woody summits of the trees that wound along these Tuscan shores.

Meanwhile Bertrand was so well pleased with his first flask, that he very willingly commenced the attack on the second, and it was late before Emily, not without some apprehension, returned to the cottage.

After this evening she frequently walked with Maddelina, but was never unattended by Bertrand ; and her mind became by degrees as tranquil as the circumstances of her situation would permit. The quiet in which she was suffered to live, encouraged her to hope that she was not sent hither with an evil design ; and had it not appeared probable that Valancourt was at this time an inhabitant of Udolpho, she would have wished to remain at the cottage till an opportunity should offer of returning to her native country. But concerning Montoni's motive for sending her into Tuscany she was more than ever perplexed, nor could she believe that any consideration for her safety had influenced him on this occasion.

She had been some time at the cottage before she recollected that, in the hurry of leaving Udolpho, she had forgotten the papers committed to her by her late aunt, relative to the Languedoc estates ; but, though this remembrance occasioned her much uneasiness, she had some hope that, in the obscure place where they were deposited, they would escape the detection of Montoni.

———

CHAPTER XXXIII.

'My tongue hath but a heavier tale to say.
I play the torturer, by small and small,
To lengthen out the worst that must be spoken.'
RICHARD II.

WE now return for a moment to Venice, where Count Morano was suffering under an accumulation of misfortunes. Soon after his arrival in that city he had been arrested by order of the senate, and, without knowing of what he was suspected, was conveyed to a place of confinement, whither the most strenuous inquiries of his friends had been unable to trace him. Who the enemy was that had occasioned him this calamity he had not been able to guess, unless, indeed, it was Montoni, on whom his suspicions rested, and not only with much apparent probability, but with justice.

In the affair of the poisoned cup, Montoni had suspected Morano; but being unable to obtain the degree of proof which was necessary to convict him of a guilty intention, he had recourse to means of other revenge than he could hope to obtain by prosecution. He employed a person in whom he believed he might confide, to drop a letter of accusation into the *denunzie secrete*, or lions' mouths, which are fixed in a gallery of the doge's palace, as receptacles for anonymous information concerning persons who may be disaffected towards the state. As, on these occasions, the accuser is not confronted with the accused, a man may falsely impeach his enemy, and accomplish an unjust revenge, without fear of punishment or detection. That Montoni should have recourse to these diabolical means of ruining a person whom he suspected of having attempted his life, is not in the least surprising. In the letter which he had employed as the instrument of his revenge, he accused Morano of designs against the state, which he attempted to prove, with all the plausible simplicity of which he was master; and the senate, with whom a suspicion was, at that time, almost equal to a proof, arrested the count in consequence of this accusation; and, without even hinting to him his crime, threw him into one of those secret prisons which were the terror of the Venetians, and in which persons often languished, and sometimes died, without being discovered by their friends. Morano had incurred the personal resentment of many members of the state; his habits of life had rendered him obnoxious to some; and his ambition, and the bold rivalship which he discovered on several public occasions,—to others; and it was not to be expected that mercy would soften the rigour of a law which was to be dispensed from the hands of his enemies.

Montoni, meantime, was beset by dangers of another kind. His castle was besieged by troops who seemed willing to dare everything, and to suffer patiently any hardships in pursuit of victory. The strength of the fortress, however, withstood their attack; and this, with the vigorous defence of the garrison and the scarcity of provision on these wild mountains, soon compelled the assailants to raise the siege.

When Udolpho was once more left to the quiet possession of Montoni, he dispatched Ugo into Tuscany for Emily, whom he had sent, from considerations of her personal safety, to a place of greater security than a castle which was, at that time, liable to be overrun by his enemies. Tranquillity being once more restored to Udolpho, he was impatient to secure her again under his roof, and had commissioned Ugo to assist Bertrand in guarding her back to the castle. Thus compelled to return, Emily bade the kind Maddelina farewell, with regret; and after about a fortnight's stay in Tuscany, where she had experienced an interval of quiet which was absolutely necessary to sustain her long-harassed spirits, began once more to ascend the Apennines, from whose heights she gave a long and sorrowful look to the beautiful country that extended at their feet, and to the distant Mediterranean, whose waves she had so often wished would bear her back to France. The distress she felt on her return towards the place of her former sufferings, was, however, softened by a conjecture that Valancourt was there; and she found some degree of comfort in the thought of being near him, notwithstanding the consideration that he was probably a prisoner.

It was noon when she had left the cottage, and the evening was closed long before she came within the neighbourhood of Udolpho. There was a moon, but it shone only at intervals, for the night was cloudy; and lighted by the torch which Ugo carried, the travellers passed silently along, Emily musing on her situation, and Bertrand and Ugo anticipating the comforts of a flask of wine and a good fire, for they had perceived for some time the difference between the warm climate of the lowlands of Tuscany and the nipping air of these upper regions. Emily was at length roused from her reverie by the far-off sound of the castle-clock, to which she listened not without some degree of awe, as it rolled away on the breeze. Another and another note succeeded, and died in sullen murmur among the mountains:—to her mournful imagination it seemed a knell measuring out some fatal period for her.

'Aye, there is the old clock,' said Bertrand, 'there he is still; the cannons have not silenced him!'

'No,' answered Ugo, 'he crowed as loud as the best of them in the midst of it all. There he was roaring out in the hottest fire I have seen this many a day! I said that some of them would have a hit at the old fellow, but he escaped, and the tower too.'

The road winding round the base of a mountain, they now came within view of the castle, which was shown in the perspective of the valley by a gleam of moonshine, and then vanished in shade; while even a transient view of it had awakened the poignancy of Emily's feelings. Its massy and gloomy walls gave her terrible ideas of imprisonment and suffering: yet, as she advanced, some degree of hope mingled with her terror; for though this was certainly the residence of Montoni, it was possibly also that of Valancourt, and she could not approach a place where he might be, without experiencing somewhat of the joy of hope.

They continued to wind along the valley, and soon after she saw again the old walls and moonlit towers rising over the woods; the strong rays enabled her also to perceive the ravages which the siege had made—with the broken walls and shattered battlements; for they were now at the foot of the steep on which Udolpho stood. Massy fragments had rolled down among the woods through which the travellers now began to ascend, and there mingled with the loose earth and pieces of rock they had brought with them. The woods, too, had suffered much from the batteries above, for here the enemy had endeavoured to screen themselves from the fire of the ramparts. Many noble trees were levelled with the ground, and others, to a wide extent, were entirely stripped of their upper branches. 'We had better dismount,' said Ugo, 'and lead the mules up the hill, or we shall get into some of the holes which the balls have left: here are plenty of them. Give me the torch,' continued Ugo, after they had dismounted, 'and take care you don't stumble over anything that lies in your way, for the ground is not yet cleared of the enemy.'

'How!' exclaimed Emily, 'are any of the enemy here, then?'

'Nay, I don't know for that, now,' he replied; 'but when I came away I saw one or two of them lying under the trees.'

As they proceeded, the torch threw a gloomy light upon the ground, and far among the recesses of the woods, and Emily feared to look forward, lest some object of horror should meet her eye. The path was often strewn with broken heads of arrows, and with shattered remains of armour such as at that period was mingled with the lighter dress of the soldiers. 'Bring the light hither,' said Bertrand, 'I have stumbled over something that rattles loud enough.' Ugo holding up the torch, they perceived a steel breast-plate on the ground, which Bertrand raised, and they

saw that it was pierced through, and that the lining was entirely covered with blood; but upon Emily's earnest entreaties that they would proceed, Bertrand, uttering some joke upon the unfortunate person to whom it had belonged, threw it hard upon the ground, and they passed on.

At every step she took, Emily feared to see some vestige of death. Coming soon after to an opening in the woods, Bertrand stopped to survey the ground, which was encumbered with massy trunks and branches of the trees that had so lately adorned it, and seemed to have been a spot particularly fatal to the besiegers; for it was evident, from the destruction of trees, that here the hottest fire of the garrison had been directed. As Ugo again held forth the torch, steel glittered between the fallen trees, the ground beneath was covered with broken arms, and with the torn vestments of soldiers, whose mangled forms Emily almost expected to see; and she again entreated her companions to proceed, who were, however, too intent in their examination to regard her, and she turned her eyes from this desolated scene to the castle above, where she observed lights gliding along the ramparts. Presently the castle-clock struck twelve, and then a trumpet sounded, of which Emily inquired the occasion.

'O! they are only changing watch,' replied Ugo.—'I do not remember this trumpet,' said Emily; 'it is a new custom.'—'It is only an old one revived, lady; we always use it in time of war. We have sounded it, at midnight, ever since the place was besieged.'

'Hark!' said Emily, as the trumpet sounded again; and in the next moment she heard a faint clash of arms, and then the watch-word passed along the terrace above, and was answered from a distant part of the castle; after which all was again still. She complained of cold, and begged to go on. 'Presently, lady,' said Bertrand, turning over some broken arms with the pike he usually carried. 'What have we here?'

'Hark!' cried Emily, 'what noise was that?'

'What noise was it?' said Ugo, starting up and listening.

'Hush!' repeated Emily. 'It surely came from the ramparts above;' and on looking up, they perceived a light moving along the walls, while in the next instant, the breeze swelling, the voice sounded louder than before.

'Who goes yonder?' cried a sentinel of the castle. 'Speak, or it will be the worse for you.' Bertrand uttered a shout of joy. 'Ha! my brave comrade, is it you?' said he, and he blew a shrill whistle, which signal was answered by another from the soldier on watch; and the party then passing forward, soon after emerged from the woods upon the broken road that led immediately to the castle gates, and Emily saw with renewed terror the whole of that stupendous structure. 'Alas!' said she to herself, 'I am going again into my prison!'

'Here has been warm work, by St. Marco!' cried Bertrand, waving the torch over the ground; 'the balls have torn up the earth here with a vengeance.'

'Aye,' replied Ugo, 'they were fired from that redoubt yonder, and rare execution they did. The enemy made a furious attack upon the great gates; but they might have guessed they could never carry it there; for, besides the cannon from the walls, our archers on the two round towers showered down upon them at such a rate, that, by holy Peter! there was no standing it. I never saw a better sight in my life; I laughed till my sides ached, to see how the knaves scampered. Bertrand, my good·fellow, thou shouldst have been among them: I warrant thou wouldst have won the race!'

'Hah! you are at your old tricks again,' said Bertrand in a surly tone. 'It is well for thee thou art so near the castle; thou knowest I have killed my man before now.' Ugo replied only by a laugh, and then gave some further account of the siege; to which as Emily listened, she was struck by the strong contrast of the present scene with that which had so lately been acted here.

The mingled uproar of cannon, drums, and trumpets, the groans of the conquered, and the shouts of the conquerors, were now sunk into a silence so profound, that it seemed as if death had triumphed alike over the vanquished and the victor. The shattered condition of one of the towers of the great gates by no means confirmed the *valiant* account just given by Ugo of the scampering party, who, it was evident, had not only made a stand, but had done much mischief before they took to flight; for this tower appeared, as far as Emily could judge by the dim moonlight that fell upon it, to be laid open, and the battlements were nearly demolished. While she gazed, a light glimmered through one of the lower loop-holes, and disappeared; but in the next moment she perceived through the broken wall a soldier, with a lamp, ascending the narrow staircase that wound within the tower; and remembering that it was the same she had passed up on the night when Barnardine had deluded her with a promise of seeing Madame Montoni, fancy gave her somewhat of the terror she had then suffered. She was now very near the gates, over which the soldier having opened the door of the portal-chamber, the lamp he carried gave her a dusky view of that terrible apartment, and she almost sunk under the recollected horrors of the moment when she had drawn aside the curtain and discovered the object it was meant to conceal.

'Perhaps,' said she to herself, 'it is now used for a similar purpose; perhaps that soldier goes, at this dead hour, to watch over the corpse of his friend!' The little remains of her fortitude now gave way to the united force of remembered and anticipated horrors, for the melancholy fate of Madame Montoni appeared to foretell her own. She considered that, though she relinquished the Languedoc estates, if she relinquished them, would satisfy Montoni's avarice, they might not appease his vengeance, which was seldom pacified but by a terrible sacrifice; and she even thought that, were she to resign them, the fear of justice might urge him either to detain her a prisoner or to take away her life.

They were now arrived at the gates, where Bertrand, observing the light glimmer through a small casement of the portal-chamber, called aloud; and the soldier, looking out, demanded who was there. 'Here, I have brought you a prisoner,' said Ugo, 'open the gate, and let us in.'

'Tell me, first, who it is that demands entrance,' replied the soldier. 'What! my old comrade,' cried Ugo, 'don't you know me? not know Ugo? I have brought home a prisoner here, bound hand and foot—a fellow who has been drinking Tuscany wine, while we here have been fighting.'

'You will not rest till you meet with your match,' said Bertrand sullenly. 'Hah! my comrade, is it you?' said the soldier—'I'll be with you directly.'

Emily presently heard his steps descending the stairs within, and then the heavy chain fall, and the bolts undraw of a small postern door, which he opened to admit the party. He held the lamp low, to show the step of the gate, and she found herself once more beneath the gloomy arch, and heard the door close that seemed to shut her from the world for ever. In the next moment she was in the first court of the castle, where she surveyed the spacious and solitary area with a kind of calm despair; while the dead hour of the night, the gothic gloom of the surrounding buildings, and the hollow and imperfect echoes which they returned as Ugo and the soldier conversed together, assisted to increase the melancholy forebodings of her heart. Passing on to the second court, a distant sound broke feebly on the silence, and gradually swelling louder as they advanced, Emily distinguished voices of revelry and laughter, but they were to her far other than sounds of joy. 'Why, you have got some Tuscany wine among you, here,' said Bertrand, 'if one may judge by the uproar that is going forward. Ugo has taken a larger share of that than of fighting, I'll be sworn. Who is carousing at this late hour?'

'His *Excellenza* and the signors,' replied the soldier: 'it is a sign you are a stranger at the castle, or you would not need to ask the question. They are brave spirits that do without sleep—they generally pass the night in good cheer; would that we, who keep the watch, had a little of it! It is cold work, pacing the ramparts so many hours of the night, if one has no good liquor to warm one's heart.'

'Courage, my lad, courage ought to warm your heart,' said Ugo. 'Courage!' replied the soldier sharply, with a menacing air, which Ugo perceiving prevented his saying more, by returning to the subject of the carousal. 'This is a new custom,' said he; 'when I left the castle, the signors used to sit up counselling.'

'Aye, and for that matter, carousing too,' said Bertrand; 'but since the siege, they have done nothing but make merry: and if I was they,' I would settle accounts with myself, for all my hard fighting, the same way.'

They had now crossed the second court, and reached the hall door, when the soldier, bidding them good-night, hastened back to his post; and while they waited for admittance, Emily considered how she might avoid seeing Montoni, and retire unnoticed to her former apartment, for she shrunk from the thought of encountering either him or any of his party at this hour. The uproar within the castle was now so loud, that, though Ugo knocked repeatedly at the hall-door, he was not heard by any of the servants, a circumstance which increased Emily's alarm, while it allowed her time to deliberate on the means of retiring unobserved; for though she might perhaps pass up the great staircase unseen, it was impossible she could find the way to her chamber without a light, the difficulty of procuring which, and the danger of wandering about the castle without one, immediately struck her. Bertrand had only a torch, and she knew that the servants never brought a taper to the door, for the hall was sufficiently lighted by the large tripod lamp which hung in the vaulted roof; and while she should wait till Annette could bring a taper, Montoni or some of his companions might discover her.

The door was now opened by Carlo; and Emily, having requested him to send Annette immediately with a light to the great gallery, where she determined to await her, passed on with hasty steps towards the staircase; while Bertrand and Ugo, with the torch, followed old Carlo to the servants' hall, impatient for supper and the warm blaze of a wood fire. Emily, lighted only by the feeble rays which the lamp above threw between the arches of this extensive hall, endeavoured to find her way to the staircase, now hid in obscurity; while the shouts of merriment that burst from a remote apartment served, by heightening her terror, to increase her perplexity, and she expected every instant to see the door of that room open, and Montoni and his companions issue forth. Having at length reached the staircase, and found her way to the top, she seated herself on the last stair to await the arrival of Annette; for the profound darkness of the gallery deterred her from proceeding further;

and while she listened for her footstep, she heard only distant sounds of revelry, which rose in sullen echoes from among the arcades below. Once she thought she heard a low sound from the dark gallery behind her; and turning her eyes, fancied she saw something luminous move in it; and since she could not at this moment subdue the weakness that caused her fears, she quitted her seat, and crept softly down a few stairs lower.

Annette not yet appearing, Emily now concluded that she was gone to bed, and that nobody chose to call her up; and the prospect that presented itself, of passing the night in darkness in this place, or in some other equally forlorn (for she knew it would be impracticable to find her way through the intricacies of the galleries to her chamber), drew tears of mingled terror and despondency from her eyes.

While thus she sat, she fancied she heard again an odd sound from the gallery, and she listened, scarcely daring to breathe, but the increasing voices below overcame every other sound. Soon after, she heard Montoni and his companions burst into the hall, who spoke as if they were much intoxicated, and seemed to be advancing towards the staircase. She now remembered that they must come this way to their chambers, and, forgetting all the terrors of the gallery, hurried towards it with an intention of secreting herself in some of the passages that opened beyond, and of endeavouring, when the signors were retired, to find her way to her own room, or to that of Annette, which was in a remote part of the castle.

With extended arms she crept along the gallery, still hearing the voices of persons below, who seemed to stop in conversation at the foot of the staircase; and then pausing for a moment to listen, half fearful of going further into the darkness of the gallery, where she still imagined, from the noise she had heard, that some person was lurking—'They are already informed of my arrival,' said she, 'and Montoni is coming himself to seek me! In the present state of his mind, his purpose must be desperate.' Then, recollecting the scene that had passed in the corridor on the night preceding her departure from the castle, 'O Valancourt!' said she, 'I must then resign you for ever. To brave any longer the injustice of Montoni, would not be fortitude, but rashness.' Still the voices below did not draw nearer, but they became louder, and she distinguished those of Verezzi and Bertolini above the rest, while the few words she caught made her listen more anxiously for others. The conversation seemed to concern herself; and having ventured to step a few paces nearer to the staircase, she discovered that they were disputing about her, each seeming to claim some former promise of Montoni, who appeared, at first, inclined to appease and to persuade them to return to their wine, but afterwards to be weary of the dispute, and saying that he left them to settle it as they could, was returning with the rest of the party to the apartment he had just quitted. Verezzi then stopped him. 'Where is she, signor?' said he in a voice of impatience: 'tell us where she is.' 'I have already told you that I do not know,' replied Montoni, who seemed to be somewhat overcome with wine; 'but she is most probably gone to her apartment.' Verezzi and Bertolini now desisted from their inquiries, and sprang to the staircase together; while Emily, who during this discourse had trembled so excessively that she had with difficulty supported herself, seemed inspired with new strength the moment she heard the bound of their steps, and ran along the gallery, dark as it was, with the fleetness of a fawn. But long before she reached its extremity, the light which Verezzi carried, flashed upon the walls; both appeared, and, instantly perceiving Emily, pursued her. At this moment, Bertolini, whose steps though swift were not steady, and whose impatience overcame what little caution he had hitherto used, stumbled, and fell at his length. The lamp fell with him, and was presently expiring on the floor; but Verezzi, regardless of saving it, seized the advantage this accident gave him over his rival, and followed Emily, to whom, however, the light had shown one of the passages that branched from the gallery, and she instantly turned into it. Verezzi could just discern the way she had taken, and this he pursued: but the sound of her steps soon sunk in distance; while he, less acquainted with the passage, was obliged to proceed through the dark with caution, lest he should fall down a flight of steps, such as in this extensive old castle frequently terminated an avenue. This passage at length brought Emily to the corridor into which her own chamber opened; and not hearing any footstep, she paused to take breath, and consider what was the safest design to be adopted. She had followed this passage merely because it was the first that appeared, and now that she had reached the end of it was as perplexed as before. Whither to go, or how further to find her way in the dark, she knew not; she was aware only that she must not seek her apartment, for there she would certainly be sought; and her danger increased every instant while she remained near it. Her spirits and her breath, however, were so much exhausted, that she was compelled to rest for a few minutes at the end of a passage, and still she heard no steps approaching. As thus she stood, light glimmered under an opposite door of the gallery, and from its situation, she knew that it was the door of that mysterious chamber where she had made a discovery so shocking that she never remembered it but with the utmost horror. That there should be light in this chamber, and at this hour, excited

her strong surprise, and she felt a momentary terror concerning it, which did not permit her to look again, for her spirits were now in such a state of weakness, that she almost expected to see the door slowly open and some horrible object appear at it. Still she listened for a step along the passage, and looked up it, where not a ray of light appearing, she concluded that Verezzi had gone back for the lamp; and believing that he would shortly be there, she again considered which way she should go, or rather which way she could find in the dark.

A faint ray still glimmered under the opposite door; but so great, and perhaps so just, was her horror of that chamber, that she would not again have tempted its secrets, though she had been certain of obtaining the light so important to her safety. She was still breathing with difficulty, and resting at the end of the passage, when she heard a rustling sound, and then a low voice so very near her that it seemed close to her ear; but she had presence of mind to check her emotions, and to remain quite still; in the next moment she perceived it to be the voice of Verezzi, who did not appear to know that she was there, but to have spoken to himself. 'The air is fresher here,' said he: 'this should be the corridor.' Perhaps he was one of those heroes whose courage can defy an enemy better than darkness, and he tried to rally his spirits with the sound of his own voice. However this might be, he turned to the light, and proceeded with the same stealing steps towards Emily's apartment, apparently forgetting that in darkness she could easily elude his search, even in her chamber; and, like an intoxicated person, he followed pertinaciously the one idea that had possessed his imagination.

The moment she heard his steps steal away, she left her station, and moved softly to the other end of the corridor, determined to trust again to chance, and to quit it by the first avenue she could find: but before she could effect this, light broke upon the walls of the gallery, and looking back, she saw Verezzi crossing it towards her chamber. She now glided into a passage that opened on the left, without, as she thought, being perceived; but in the next instant, another light glimmering at the further end of this passage threw her into new terror. While she stopped and hesitated which way to go, the pause allowed her to perceive that it was Annette who advanced, and she hurried to meet her; but her imprudence again alarmed Emily, on perceiving whom she burst into a scream of joy, and it was some minutes before she could be prevailed with to be silent, or to release her mistress from the ardent clasp in which she held her. When, at length, Emily made Annette comprehend her danger, they hurried towards Annette's room, which was in a distant part of the castle. No, apprehension, however, could yet silence the latter. 'Oh, dear ma'amselle,' said she as they passed along, 'what a terrified time have I had of it! Oh! I thought I should have died a hundred times! I never thought I should live to see you again! and I never was so glad to see anybody in my whole life, as I am to see you now.' 'Hark!' cried Emily, 'we are pursued; that was the echo of steps!' 'No, ma'amselle,' said Annette, 'it was only the echo of a door shutting; sound runs along these vaulted passages so, that one is continually deceived by it: if one does but speak or cough, it makes a noise as loud as a cannon.' 'Then there is the greater necessity for us to be silent,' said Emily: 'Pr'ythee say no more till we reach your chamber.' Here, at length, they arrived without interruption; and Annette having fastened the door, Emily sat down on her little bed, to recover breath and composure. To her inquiry whether Valancourt was among the prisoners in the castle, Annette replied that she had not been able to hear, but that she knew there were several persons confined. She then proceeded, in her tedious way, to give an account of the siege, or rather a detail of her terrors and various sufferings during the attack. 'But,' added she, 'when I heard the shouts of victory from the ramparts, I thought we were all taken, and gave myself up for lost, instead of which, *we* had driven the enemy away. I went then to the north gallery, and saw a great many of them scampering away among the mountains; but the rampart walls were all in ruins, as one may say, and there was a dismal sight to see down among the woods below, where the poor fellows were lying in heaps, but were carried off presently by their comrades. While the siege was going on, the signor was here, and there, and everywhere, at the same time, as Ludovico told me, for he would not let·me see anything hardly, and locked me up, as he had often done before, in a room in the middle of the castle, and used to bring me food, and come and. talk with me as often as he could; and I must say, if it had not been for Ludovico I should have died outright.'

'Well, Annette,' said Emily, 'and how have affairs gone on since the siege?'

'O! sad hurly-burly doing, ma'amselle,' replied Annette; 'the signors have done nothing but sit and. drink and game ever since. They sit up all night, and play among themselves for all those riches and fine things they brought in some time since, when they used to go out a-robbing, or as good, for days together; and then they have dreadful quarrels about who loses and who wins. That fierce Signor Verezzi is always losing, as they tell me, and Signor Orsino wins from him, and thus makes him very wroth, and they have had several hard set-to's about it. Then, all

those fine ladies are at the castle still; and I declare I am frighted whenever I meet any of them in the passages——'

'Surely, Annette,' said Emily, starting, 'I heard a noise: listen.——' After a long pause, 'No, ma'amselle,' said Annette, 'it was only the wind in the gallery; I often hear it, when it shakes the old doors at the other end. But won't you go to bed, ma'amselle? you surely will not set up starving, all night.' Emily now laid herself down on the mattress, and desired Annette to leave the lamp burning on the hearth; having done which, the latter placed herself beside Emily, who, however, was not suffered to sleep, for she again thought she heard a noise from the passage; and Annette was again trying to convince her that it was only the wind, when footsteps were distinctly heard near the door. Annette was now starting from the bed; but Emily prevailed with her to remain there, and listened with her in a state of terrible expectation. The steps still loitered at the door, when presently an attempt was made on the lock, and in the next instant a voice called. 'For Heaven's sake, Annette, do not answer,' said Emily softly, 'remain quite still: but I fear we must extinguish the lamp, or its glare will betray us.' 'Holy Virgin!' exclaimed Annette, forgetting her discretion, 'I would not be in darkness now for the whole world.' While she spoke, the voice became louder than before, and repeated Annette's name; 'Blessed Virgin!' cried she suddenly, 'it is only Ludovico.' She rose to open the door, but Emily prevented her, till they should be more certain that it was he alone; with whom Annette, at length, talked for some time, and learned that he was come to inquire after herself, whom he had let out of her room to go to Emily, and that he was now returned to lock her in again. Emily, fearful of being overheard if they conversed any longer through the door, consented that it should be opened, and a young man appeared, whose open countenance confirmed the favourable opinion of him which his care of Annette had already prompted her to form. She entreated his protection, should Verezzi make this requisite; and Ludovico offered to pass the night in an old chamber adjoining, that opened from the gallery, and on the first alarm to come to their defence.

Emily was much soothed by this proposal; and Ludovico, having lighted his lamp, went to his station, while she once more endeavoured to repose on her mattress. But a. variety of interests pressed upon her attention, and prevented sleep. She thought much on what Annette had told her of the dissolute manners of Montoni and his associates, and more of his present conduct towards herself, and of the danger from which she had just escaped. From the view of her present situation she shrunk, as from a new picture of terror. She saw herself in a castle inhabited by vice and violence, seated beyond the reach of law or justice, and in the power of a man whose perseverance was equal to every occasion, and in whom passions, of which revenge was not the weakest, entirely supplied the place of principles. She was compelled once more to acknowledge, that it would be folly, and not fortitude, any longer to dare his power : and resigning all hopes of future happiness with Valancourt, she determined that on the following morning she would compromise with Montoni, and give up her estates, on condition that he would permit her immediate return to France. Such considerations kept her waking for many hours ; but the night passed without further alarm from Verezzi.

On the next morning Emily had a long conversation with Ludovico, in which she heard circumstances concerning the castle, and received hints of the designs of Montoni that considerably increased her alarm. On expressing her surprise, that Ludovico, who seemed to be so sensible of the evils of his situation, should continue in it, he informed her that it was not his intention to do so, and she then ventured to ask him if he would assist her to escape from the castle. Ludovico assured her of his readiness to attempt this, but strongly represented the difficulties of the enterprise, and the certain destruction which must ensue should Montoni overtake them before they had passed the mountains ; he, however, promised to be watchful of every circumstance that might contribute to the success of the attempt, and to think upon some plan of departure.

Emily now confided to him the name of Valancourt, and begged he would inquire for such a person among the prisoners in the castle ; for the faint hope which this conversation awakened, made her now recede from her resolution of an immediate compromise with Montoni. She determined, if possible, to delay this till she heard further from Ludovico ; and, if his designs were found to be impracticable, to resign the estates at once. Her thoughts were on this subject, when Montoni, who was now recovered from the intoxication of the preceding night, sent for her, and she immediately obeyed the summons. He was alone. ' I find,' said he, ' that you were not in your chamber last night ; where were you ?' Emily related to him some circumstances of her alarm, and entreated his protection from a repetition of them. ' You know the terms of my protection,' said he : ' if you really value this, you will secure it.' His open declaration, that he would only conditionally protect her while she remained a prisoner in the castle, showed Emily the necessity of an immediate compliance with his terms ; but she first demanded whether he would permit her immediately to depart, if she gave up her claim to the contested estates. In a very solemn manner he then assured her

that he would ; and immediately laid before her a paper, which was to transfer the right of those estates to himself.

She was for a considerable time unable to sign it, and her heart was torn with contending interests, for she was about to resign the happiness of all her future years—the hope which had sustained her in so many hours of adversity.

After hearing from Montoni a recapitulation of the conditions of her compliance, and a remonstrance that his time was valuable, she put her hand to the paper ; when she had done which, she fell back in her chair, but soon recovered, and desired that he would give orders for her departure, and that he would allow Annette to accompany her. Montoni smiled. ' It was necessary to deceive you,' said he—' there was no other way of making you act reasonably : you shall go, but it must not be at present. I must first secure these estates by possession ; when that is done, you may return to France if you will.'

The deliberate villany with which he violated the solemn engagement he had just entered into, shocked Emily as much as the certainty that she had made a fruitless sacrifice, and must still remain his prisoner. She had no words to express what she felt, and knew that it would have been useless if she had. As she looked piteously at Montoni, he turned away, and at the same time desired she would withdraw to her apartment ; but, unable to leave the room, she sat down in a chair near the door, and sighed heavily. She had neither words nor tears.

' Why will you indulge this childish grief ?' said he. ' Endeavour to strengthen your mind to bear patiently what cannot be now avoided ; you have no real evil to lament ; be patient, and you will be sent back to France. At present retire to your apartment.'

' I dare not go, sir,' said she, ' where I shall be liable to the intrusion of Signor Verezzi.' ' Have I not promised to protect you ?' said Montoni. ' You have promised, sir,—' replied Emily, after some hesitation. ' And is not my promise sufficient ?' added he sternly. ' You will recollect your former promise, signor,' said Emily trembling, ' and may determine for me whether I ought to rely upon this.' ' Will you provoke me to declare to you that I will not protect you then ?' said Montoni in a tone of haughty displeasure. ' Withdraw to your chamber before I retract my promise ; you have nothing to fear there.' ' If that will satisfy you I will do it immediately.' Emily left the room, and moved slowly into the hall, where the fear of meeting Verezzi or Bertolini made her quicken her steps, though she could scarcely support herself ; and soon after she reached once more her own apartment. Having looked fearfully round her to examine if any person was there, and having searched every part of it, she fastened the door, and sat down by one of the casements. Here, while she looked out for some hope to support her fainting spirits, which had been so long harassed and oppressed, that, if she had not now struggled much against misfortune, they would have left her perhaps for ever, she endeavoured to believe that Montoni did really intend to permit her return to France as soon as he had secured her property, and that he would, in the mean time, protect her from insult : but her chief hope rested with Ludovico, who, she doubted not, would be zealous in her cause, though he seemed almost in despair of success in it. One circumstance, however, she had to rejoice in. Her prudence, or rather her fears, had saved her from mentioning the name of Valancourt to Montoni, which she was several times on the point of doing before she signed the paper, and of stipulating for his release, if he should be really a prisoner in the castle. Had she done this, Montoni's jealous fears would now probably have loaded Valancourt with new severities, and have suggested the advantage of holding him a captive for life.

Thus passed the melancholy day, as she had before passed many in the same chamber. When night drew on, she would have withdrawn herself to Annette's bed, had not a particular interest inclined her to remain in this chamber, in spite of her fears : for when the castle should be still, and the customary hour arrived, she determined to watch for the music she had formerly heard. Though its sounds might not enable her positively to determined whether Valancourt was there, they would perhaps strengthen her opinion that he was, and impart the comfort so necessary to her present support. But, on the other hand, if all should be silent ! She hardly dared to suffer her thoughts to glance that way, but waited with impatient expectation the approaching hour.

The night was stormy ; the battlements of the castle appeared to rock in the wind, and at intervals long groans seemed to pass on the air, such as those which often deceive the melancholy mind in tempests and amidst scenes of desolation. Emily heard, as formerly, the sentinels pass along the terrace to their posts, and looking out from her casement, observed that the watch was doubled ; a precaution which appeared necessary enough, when she threw her eyes on the walls, and saw their shattered condition. The well-known sounds of the soldiers' march, and of their distant voices, which passed her in the wind, and were lost again, recalled to her memory the melancholy sensation she had suffered when she formerly heard the same sounds, and occasioned almost involuntary comparisons between her present and her late situation. But this was no subject for congratulation, and she wisely checked the course of her thoughts, while, as the hour was not yet come in which she had been accustomed to hear the music,

she closed the casement, and endeavoured to await it in patience. The door of the staircase she tried to secure, as usual, with some of the furniture of the room ; but this expedient her fears now represented to her to be very inadequate to the power and perseverance of Verezzi ; and she often looked at a large and heavy chest that stood in the chamber, with wishes that she and Annette had strength to move it. While she blamed the long stay of this girl, who was still with Ludovico and some other of the servants, she trimmed her wood fire, to make the room appear less desolate, and sat down beside it with a book, which her eyes perused, while her thoughts wandered to Valancourt and her own misfortunes. As she sat thus, she thought, in a pause of the wind, she distinguished music, and went to the casement to listen, but the loud swell of the gust overcame every other sound. When the wind sunk again, she heard distinctly, in the deep pause that succeeded, the sweet strings of a lute ; but again the rising tempest bore away the notes, and again was succeeded by a solemn pause. Emily, trembling with hope and fear, opened her casement to listen, and to try whether her own voice could be heard by the musician ; for to endure any longer this state of torturing suspense concerning Valancourt, seemed to be utterly impossible. There was a kind of breathless stillness in the chambers that permitted her to distinguish from below the tender notes of the very lute she had formerly heard, and with it a plaintive voice, made sweeter by the low rustling sound that now began to creep along the wood-tops till it was lost in the rising wind. Their tall heads then began to wave, while, through a forest of pine on the left, the wind, groaning heavily, rolled onward over the woods below, bending them almost to their roots ; and as the long-resounding gale swept away, other woods, on the right, seemed to answer the 'loud lament ;' then others, further still, softened it into a murmur that died into silence. Emily listened with mingled awe and expectation, hope and fear ; and again the melting sweetness of the lute was heard, and the same solemn-breathing voice. Convinced that these came from an apartment underneath, she leaned far out of her window, that she might discover whether any light was there ; but the casements below, as well as those above, were sunk so deep in the thick walls of the castle, that she could not see them, or even the faint ray that probably glimmered through their bars. She then ventured to call ; but the wind bore her voice to the other end of the terrace, and then the music was heard as before, in the pause of the gust. Suddenly, she thought she heard a noise in her chamber, and she drew herself within the casement ; but in a moment after, distinguishing Annette's voice at the door, she concluded it was her she had heard before, and she let her in,

'Move softly, Annette, to the casement,' said she, 'and listen with me; the music is returned.' They were silent, till, the measure changing, Annette exclaimed, 'Holy Virgin! I know that song well; it is a French song, one of the favourite songs of my dear country. This was the ballad Emily had heard on a former night, though not the one she had first listened to from the fishing-house in Gascony. 'O! it is a Frenchman that sings,' said Annette: 'it must be Monsieur Valancourt.' 'Hark, Annette, do not speak so loud,' said Emily, 'we may be overheard.' 'What! by the chevalier?' said Annette. 'No,' replied Emily mournfully, 'but by somebody who may report us to the signor. What reason have you to think it is Monsieur Valancourt who sings? But hark! now the voice swells louder! Do you recollect those tones? I fear to trust my own judgment.' 'I never happened to hear the chevalier sing, mademoiselle,' replied Annette, who, as Emily was disappointed to perceive, had no stronger reason for concluding this to be Valancourt, than that the musician must be a Frenchman. Soon after, she heard the song of the fishing-house, and distinguished her own name, which was repeated so distinctly that Annette heard it also. She trembled, sunk into a chair by the window, and Annette called aloud, 'Monsieur Valancourt! Monsieur Valancourt!' while Emily endeavoured to check her; but she repeated the call more loudly than before, and the lute and the voice suddenly stopped. Emily listened for some time in a state of intolerable suspense; but no answer being returned, 'It does not signify, mademoiselle,' said Annette; 'it is the chevalier, and I will speak to him.' 'No, Annette,' said Emily; 'I think I will speak myself; if it is he, he will know my voice, and speak again.' 'Who is it,' said she, 'that sings at this late hour?'

A long silence ensued; and having repeated the question, she perceived some faint accents mingling in the blast that swept by; but the sounds were so distant, and passed so suddenly, that she could scarcely hear them, much less distinguish the words they uttered, or recognise the voice. After another pause, Emily called again; and again they heard a voice, but as faintly as before; and they perceived that there were other circumstances, besides the strength and direction of the wind, to contend with; for the great depth at which the casements were fixed in the castle walls, contributed still more than the distance to prevent articulate sounds from being understood, though general ones were easily heard. Emily, however, ventured to believe, from the circumstance of her voice alone having been answered, that the stranger was Valancourt, as well as that he knew her; and she gave herself up to speechless joy. Annette, however, was not speechless. She renewed her calls, but received no answer; and Emily,

fearing that a further attempt, which certainly was at present highly dangerous, might expose them to the guards of the castle, while it could not perhaps terminate her suspense, insisted on Annette's dropping the inquiry for this night, though she determined herself to question Ludovico on the subject in the morning more urgently than she had yet done. She was now enabled to say, that the stranger whom she had formerly heard was still in the castle, and to direct Ludovico to that part of it in which he was confined.

Emily, attended by Annette, continued at the casement for some time, but all remained still; they heard neither lute nor voice again; and Emily was now as much oppressed by anxious joy, as she lately was by a sense of her misfortunes. With hasty steps she paced the room, now half-calling on Valancourt's name, then suddenly stopping, and now going to the casement and listening, where, however, she heard nothing but the solemn waving of the woods. Sometimes her impatience to speak to Ludovico prompted her to send Annette to call him; but a sense of the impropriety of this at midnight restrained her. Annette meanwhile, as impatient as her mistress, went as often to the casement to listen, and returned almost as much disappointed. She at length mentioned Signor Verezzi, and her fear lest he should enter the chamber by the staircase door. 'But the night is now almost past, mademoiselle,' said she, recollecting herself; 'there is the morning light beginning to peep over those mountains yonder, in the east.'

Emily had forgotten till this moment that such a person existed as Verezzi, and all the danger that had appeared to threaten her; but the mention of his name renewed her alarm, and she remembered the old chest that she had wished to place against the door, which she now, with Annette, attempted to move, but it was so heavy that they could not lift it from the floor. 'What is in this great old chest, mademoiselle,' said Annette, 'that makes it so weighty?' Emily having replied that she found it in the chamber when she first came to the castle, and had never examined it—'Then I will, mademoiselle,' said Annette, and she tried to lift the lid; but this was held by a lock, for which she had no key, and which, indeed, appeared from its peculiar construction to open with a spring. The morning now glimmered through the casements, and the wind had sunk into a calm. Emily looked out upon the dusky woods, and on the twilight mountains, just stealing on the eye, and saw the whole scene, after the storm, lying in profound stillness, the woods motionless, and the clouds above, through which the dawn trembled, scarcely appearing to move along the heavens. One soldier was pacing the terrace beneath with measured steps; and two, more distant, were sunk asleep on the walls, wearied with the night's watch. Having inhaled for a while the pure spirit of the air, and of vegetation, which the late rains had called forth ; and having listened, once more, for a note of music, she now closed the casement and retired to rest.

CHAPTER XXXIV.

'Thus on the chill Lapponian's dreary land,
  For many a long month lost in snow profound,
When Sol from Cancer sends the seasons bland,
  And in their northern cave the storms hath bound ;
From silent mountains, straight, with startling
      sound,
Torrents are hurl'd, green hills emerge, and lo,
  The trees with foliage, cliffs with flowers are
      crown'd ;
Pure rills through vales of verdure warbling go ;
  And wonder, love, and joy, the peasant's heart
      o'erflow.'   BEATTIE.

SEVERAL of her succeeding days passed in suspense, for Ludovico could only learn from the soldiers that there was a prisoner in the apartment described to him by Emily, and that he was a Frenchman, whom they had taken in one of the skirmishes with a party of his countrymen. During this interval, Emily escaped the persecutions of Bertolini and Verezzi, by confining herself to her apartment ; except that sometimes, in an evening, she ventured to walk in the adjoining corridor. Montoni appeared to respect his last promise, though he had profaned his first ; for to his protection only could she attribute her present repose ; and in this she was now secure, that she did not wish to leave the castle till she could obtain some certainty concerning Valancourt ; for which she waited, indeed, without any sacrifice of her own comfort, since no circumstance had occurred to make her escape probable.

On the fourth day Ludovico informed her that he had hopes of being admitted to the presence of the prisoner ; it being the turn of a soldier with whom he had been for some time familiar, to attend him on the following night. He was not deceived in his hope ; for, under pretence of carrying in a pitcher of water, he entered the prison, though his prudence having prevented him from telling the sentinel the real motive of his visit, he was obliged to make his conference with the prisoner a very short one.

Emily awaited the result in her own apartment, Ludovico having promised to accompany Annette to the corridor in the evening ; where, after several hours impatiently counted, he arrived. Emily having then uttered the name of Valancourt, could articulate no more, but hesitated in trembling expectation. 'The chevalier would not intrust me with his name, signora,' replied Ludovico ; 'but when I just mentioned yours, he seemed overwhelmed with joy, though he was not so much surprised as I expected.'

'Does he then remember me ?' she exclaimed.

'O ! it is Monsieur Valancourt,' said Annette, and looked impatiently at Ludovico, who understood her look, and replied to Emily : 'Yes, lady, the chevalier does indeed remember you, and I am sure has a very great regard for you, and I made bold to say you had for him. He then inquired how you came to know he was in the castle, and whether you ordered me to speak to him. The first question I could not answer, but the second I did ; and then he went off into his ecstasies again. I was afraid his joy would have betrayed him to the sentinel at the door.'

'But how does he look, Ludovico ?' interrupted Emily : 'is he not melancholy and ill with his long confinement ?'—'Why, as to melancholy, I saw no symptom of that, lady, while I was with him, for he seemed in the finest spirits I ever saw anybody in, in all my life. His countenance was all joy, and if one may judge from that, he was very well ; but I did not ask him.' 'Did he send me no message ?' said Emily. 'O yes, signora, and something besides,' replied Ludovico, who searched his pockets. 'Surely I have not lost it !' added he. 'The chevalier said he would have written, madam, if he had had pen and ink, and was going to have sent a very long message, when the sentinel entered the room, but not before he had given me this.' Ludovico then drew forth a miniature from his bosom, which Emily received with a trembling hand, and perceived to be a portrait of herself —the very picture which her mother had lost so strangely in the fishing-house at La Vallée.

Tears of mingled joy and tenderness flowed to her eyes, while Ludovico proceeded——
'"Tell your lady," said the chevalier as he gave me the picture, "that this has been my companion and only solace in all my misfortunes. Tell her that I have worn it next my heart, and that I send it her as the pledge of an affection which can never die ; that I would not part with it, but to her, for the wealth of worlds ; and that I now part with it, only in the hope of soon receiving it from her hands. Tell her——" Just then, signora, the sentinel came in, and the chevalier said no more : but he had before asked me to contrive an interview for him with you ; and when I told him how little hope I had of prevailing with the guard to assist me, he said that was not perhaps of so much consequence as I imagined, and bade me contrive to bring back your answer, and he would inform me of more than he chose to do then. So this, I think, lady, is the whole of what passed.'

'How, Ludovico, shall I reward you for your zeal ?' said Emily : 'but indeed I do not now possess the means. When can you see the chevalier again ?' 'That is uncertain, signora,' replied he : 'it depends upon who stands guard next ; there are not more than one or two among them, from whom I would dare to ask admittance to the prison-chamber.'

-'I need not bid you remember, Ludovico,' resumed Emily, 'how very much interested I am in your seeing the chevalier soon ; and when you do so, tell him that I have received the picture, and with the sentiments he wished. Tell him I have suffered much, and still suffer.'—She paused. 'But shall I tell him you will see him, lady?' said Ludovico. 'Most certainly I will,' replied Emily. 'But when, signora, and where?' 'That must depend upon circumstances,' returned Emily : 'the place and the hour must be regulated by his opportunities.'

'As to the place, mademoiselle,' said Annette, 'there is no other place in the castle, besides this corridor, where *we* can see him in safety, you know ; and as for the hour—it must be when all the signors are asleep, if that ever happens !' 'You may mention these circumstances to the chevalier, Ludovico,' said she, checking the flippancy of Annette ; : and leave them to his judgment and opportunity. Tell him my heart is unchanged. But, above all, let him see you again as soon as possible ; and, Ludovico, I think it is needless to tell you I shall very anxiously look for you.' Having then wished her good night, Ludovico descended the staircase, and Emily retired to rest, but not to sleep, for joy now rendered her as wakeful as she had ever been from grief. Montoni and his castle had all vanished from her mind, like the frightful vision of a necromancer, and she wandered once more in fairy scenes of unfading happiness :

'. . . . . as when, beneath the beam
Of summer moons, the distant woods among,
Or by some flood all silver'd with the gleam,
The soft embodied Fays through airy portals
stream.'

A week elapsed before Ludovico again visited the prison ; for the sentinels during that period were men in whom he could not confide, and he feared to awaken curiosity by asking to see their prisoner. In this interval he communicated to Emily terrific reports of what was passing in the castle ; of riots, quarrels, and of carousals more alarming than either ; while, from some circumstances which he mentioned, she not only doubted whether Montoni meant ever to release her, but greatly feared that he had designs concerning her —such as she had formerly dreaded. Her name was frequently mentioned in the conversations which Bertolini and Verezzi held together, and at those times they were frequently in contention. Montoni had lost large sums to Verezzi, so that there was a dreadful possibility of his designing her to be a substitute for the debt ; but as she was ignorant that he had formerly encouraged the hopes of Bertolini also, concerning herself, after the latter had done him some signal service, she knew not how to account for these contentions between Bertolini and Ve-

rezzi. The cause of them, however, appeared to be of little consequence ; for she thought she saw destruction approaching in many forms, and her entreaties to Ludovico to contrive an escape, and to see the prisoner again, were more urgent than ever.

At length, he informed her that he had again visited the chevalier, who had directed him to confide in the guard of the prison, from whom he had already received some instances of kindness, and who had promised to permit his going into the castle for half an hour on the ensuing night, when Montoni and his companions should be engaged at their carousals. 'This was kind, to be sure,' added Ludovico : 'but Sebastian knows he runs no risk in letting the chevalier out, for if he can get beyond the bars and iron doors of the castle, he must be cunning indeed. But the chevalier desired me, signora, to go to you immediately, and to beg you would allow him to visit you this night, if it was only for a moment, for that he could no longer live under the same roof without seeing you : the hour,' he said, he could not mention, for it must depend on circumstances (just as you said, signora) ; and the place he desired you would appoint, as knowing which was best for your own safety.'

Emily was now so much agitated by the near prospect of meeting Valancourt, that it was some time before she could give any answer to Ludovico, or consider of the place of meeting ; when she did, she saw none that promised so much security as the corridor near her own apartment, which she was checked from leaving, by the apprehension of meeting any of Montoni's guests on their way to their rooms ; and she dismissed the scruples which delicacy opposed, now that a serious danger was to be avoided by encountering them. It was settled, therefore, that the chevalier should meet her in the corridor, at that hour of the night which Ludovico, who was to be upon the watch, should judge safest : and Emily, as may be imagined, passed this interval in a tumult of hope and joy, anxiety and impatience. Never since her residence in the castle had she watched with so much pleasure the sun set behind the mountains, and twilight shade and darkness veil the scene, as on this evening. She counted the notes of the great clock, and listened to the steps of the sentinels as they changed the watch, only to rejoice that another hour was gone. 'O Valancourt !' said she, 'after all I have suffered ; after our long, long separation, when I thought I should never—never see you more—we are still to meet again ! O ! I have endured grief, and anxiety, and terror, and let me then not sink beneath this joy !' These were moments when it was impossible for her to feel emotions of regret or melancholy for any ordinary interests—even the reflection that she had resigned the estates which would have been a provision for herself and Valancourt for life, threw only a light and transient shade upon her spirits. The idea of Valancourt, and that she should see him so soon, alone occupied her heart.

At length the clock struck twelve; she opened the door to listen if any noise was in the castle, and heard only distant shouts of riot and laughter echoed feebly along the gallery. She guessed that the signor and his guests were at the banquet. 'They are now engaged for the night,' said she; 'and Valancourt will soon be here.'—Having softly closed the door, she paced the room with impatient steps, and often went to the casement to listen for the lute; but all was silent; and her agitation every moment increasing, she was at length unable to support herself, and sat down by the window. Annette, whom she detained, was in the mean time as loquacious as usual; but Emily heard scarcely anything she said; and having at length risen to the casement, she distinguished the chords of the lute struck with an expressive hand, and then the voice she had formerly listened to accompanied it.

'Now rising love they fann'd, now pleasing dole
They breathed in tender musings through the
    heart;
And now a graver, sacred strain they stole,
As when seraphic hands an hymn impart!

Emily wept in doubtful joy and tenderness; and when the strain ceased, she considered it as a signal that Valancourt was about to leave the prison. Soon after she heard steps in the corridor;—they were the light quick steps of hope; she could scarcely support herself as they approached; but, opening the door of the apartment, she advanced to meet Valancourt, and in the next moment sunk in the arms of a stranger. His voice—his countenance instantly convinced her, and she fainted away.

On reviving, she found herself supported by the stranger, who was watching over her recovery with a countenance of ineffable tenderness and anxiety. She had no spirits for reply, or inquiry; she asked no questions, but burst into tears, and disengaged herself from his arms; when the expression of his countenance changed to surprise and disappointment, and he turned to Ludovico for an explanation. Annette soon gave the information, which Ludovico could not. 'O, sir!' said she, in a voice interrupted with sobs; 'O, sir, you are not the other chevalier. We expected Monsieur Valancourt, but you are not he! O Ludovico! how could you deceive us so? my poor lady will never recover it—never!' The stranger, who now appeared much agitated, attempted to speak, but his words faltered; and then striking his hand against his forehead, as if in sudden despair, he walked abruptly to the other end of the corridor.

Suddenly Annette dried her tears, and spoke to Ludovico. 'But perhaps,' said she, 'after all, the other chevalier is not this: perhaps the chevalier Valancourt is still below.' Emily raised her head. 'No,' replied Ludovico, 'Monsieur Valancourt never was below, if this gentleman is not he.——If you, sir,' said Ludovico, addressing the stranger, 'would but have had the goodness to trust me with your name, this mistake had been avoided.' 'Most true,' replied the stranger, speaking in broken Italian; 'but it was of the utmost consequence to me that my name should be concealed from Montoni.—Madam,' added he, then addressing Emily in French, 'will you permit me to apologise for the pain I have occasioned you, and to explain to you alone my name, and the circumstance that has led me into this error? I am of France;—I am your countryman;—we are met in a foreign land.' Emily tried to compose her spirits; yet she hesitated to grant his request. At length, desiring that Ludovico would wait on the staircase, and detaining Annette, she told the stranger that her woman understood very little of Italian, and begged he would communicate what he wished to say in that language.—Having withdrawn to a distant part of the corridor, he said, with a long-drawn sigh, 'You, Madam, are no stranger to me, though I am so unhappy as to be unknown to you.— My name is Du Pont; I am of France, of Gascony, your native province, and have long admired,—and why should I affect to disguise it?—have long loved you.' He paused, but in the next moment proceeded. 'My family, madam, is probably not unknown to you, for we lived within a few miles of La Vallée, and I have sometimes had the happiness of meeting you on visits in the neighbourhood. I will not offend you by repeating how much you interested me; how much I loved to wander in the scenes you frequented; how often I visited your favourite fishing-house, and lamented the circumstance which at that time forbade me to reveal my passion. I will not explain how I surrendered to temptation, and became possessed of a treasure which was to me inestimable; a treasure, which I committed to your messenger a few days ago, with expectations very different from my present ones. I will say nothing of these circumstances, for I know they would avail me little; let me only supplicate for your forgiveness, and the picture which I so unwarily returned. Your generosity will pardon the theft, and restore the prize. My crime has been my punishment; for the portrait I stole has contributed to nourish a passion which must still be my torment.'

Emily now interrupted him. 'I think, sir, I may leave it to your integrity to determine, whether, after what has just appeared concerning Mons. Valancourt, I ought to return the picture. I think you will acknowledge that this would not be generosity; and you will allow me to add, that it would be doing myself an injustice. I must consider myself honoured by your good opinion, but—and she hesitated—the mistake of this evening makes it unnecessary for me to say more.'

'It does, madam,—alas! it does!' said the stranger, who, after a long pause, proceeded. —'But you will allow me to show my disinterestedness, though not my love, and will accept the services I offer. Yet, alas! what services can I offer? I am myself a prisoner, a sufferer like you. But dear as liberty is to me, I would not seek it through half the hazards I would encounter to deliver you from this recess of vice. Accept the offered services of a friend ; do not refuse me the reward of having at least attempted to deserve your thanks.

'You deserve them already, sir,' said Emily ; 'the wish deserves my warmest thanks. But you will excuse me for reminding you of the danger you incur by prolonging this interview. It will be a great consolation to me, to remember, whether your friendly attempts to release me succeed or not, that I have a countryman who would so generously protect me.'—Monsieur du Pont took her hand, which she but feebly attempted to withdraw, and pressed it respectfully to his lips. 'Allow me to breathe another fervent sigh for your happiness,' said he, 'and to applaud myself for an affection which I cannot conquer.' As he said this, Emily heard a noise from her apartment, and, turning round, saw the door from the staircase open, and a man rush into her chamber. 'I will teach you to conquer it,' cried he, as he advanced into the corridor, and drew a stiletto, which he aimed at Du Pont, who was unarmed, but who stepping back, avoided the blow, and then sprung upon Verezzi, from whom he wrenched the stiletto. While they struggled in each other's grasp, Emily, followed by Annette, ran further into the corridor, calling on Ludovico, who was, however, gone from the staircase ; and as she advanced, terrified and uncertain what to do, a distant noise that seemed to arise from the hall, reminded her of the danger she was incurring ; and sending Annette forward in search of Ludovico, she returned to the spot where Du Pont and Verezzi were still struggling for victory. It was her own cause which was to be decided with that of the former, whose conduct independently of this circumstance, would, however, have interested her in his success, even had she not disliked and dreaded Verezzi. She threw herself in a chair, and supplicated them to desist from further violence, till at length Du Pont forced Verezzi to the floor, where he lay stunned by the violence of his fall ; and she then entreated Du Pont to escape from the room, before Montoni or his party should appear : but he still refused to leave her unprotected ; and while Emily, now more terrified for him than for herself, enforced the entreaty, they heard steps ascending the private staircase.

'O you are lost!' cried she ; 'these are Montoni's people.' Du Pont made no reply, but supported Emily, while with a steady though eager countenance he waited their appearance, and in the next moment Ludovico alone mounted the landing-place. Throwing a hasty glance round the chamber, 'Follow me,' said he, 'as you value your lives ; we have not an instant to lose!'

Emily inquired what had occurred, and whither they were to go.

'I cannot stay to tell you now, signora,' replied Ludovico : 'fly! fly!'

She immediately followed him, accompanied by Monsieur du Pont, down the staircase, and along a vaulted passage, when suddenly she recollected Annette, and inquired for her. 'She awaits us further on, signora,' said Ludovico, almost breathless with haste : 'the gates were open, a moment since, to a party just come in from the mountains ; they will be shut, I fear, before we can reach them! Through this door, signora,' added Ludovico, holding down the lamp ; 'take care, here are two steps.'

Emily followed, trembling still more than before she had understood that her escape from the castle depended on the present moment ; while Du Pont supported her, and endeavoured, as they passed along, to cheer her spirits.

'Speak low, signor,' said Ludovico, 'these passages send echoes all round the castle.'

'Take care of the light,' cried Emily, 'you go so fast that the air will extinguish it.'

Ludovico now opened another door, where they found Annette ; and the party then descended a short flight of steps into a passage, which, Ludovico said, led round the inner court of the castle, and opened into the outer one. As they advanced, confused and tumultuous sounds, that seemed to come from the inner court, alarmed Emily. 'Nay, signora,' said Ludovico, 'our only hope is in that tumult ; while the signor's people are busied about the men who are just arrived, we may perhaps pass unnoticed through the gates. But hush!' he added, as they approached the small door that opened into the outer court ; 'if you will remain here a moment, I will go to see whether the gates are open, and anybody is in the way. Pray extinguish the light, signor, if you hear me talking,' continued Ludovico, delivering the lamp to Du Pont, 'and remain quite still.'

Saying this, he stepped out upon the court, and they closed the door, listening anxiously to his departing steps. No voice, however, was heard in the court which he was crossing, though a confusion of many voices yet issued from the inner one. 'We shall soon be beyond the walls,' said Du Pont, softly, to Emily ; 'support yourself a little longer, madam, and all will be well.'

But soon they heard Ludovico speaking loud, and the voice also of some other person, and Du Pont immediately extinguished the lamp. 'Ah! it is too late !' exclaimed Emily—'what is to become of us?' They listened again, and then perceived that Ludovico was talking with a sentinel, whose voices were heard also by Emily's favourite dog, that had followed her from the chamber, and now barked loudly. 'This dog will betray us !' said Du Pont, 'I will hold him.' 'I fear he has already betrayed us !' replied Emily. Du Pont, however, caught him up, and again listening to what was going on without, they heard Ludovico say, 'I'll watch the gates the while.'

'Stay a minute,' replied the sentinel, 'and you need not have the trouble ; for the horses will be sent round to the outer stables, then the gates will be shut, and I can leave my post.' 'I don't mind the trouble, comrade,' said Ludovico, 'you will do such another good turn for me, some time. Go—go, and fetch the wine ; the rogues that are just come in will drink it all else.'

The soldier hesitated, and then called aloud to the people in the second court to know why they did not send out the horses, that the gates might be shut ; but they were too much engaged to attend to him, even if they had heard his voice.

'Aye—aye,' said Ludovico, 'they know better than that ; they are sharing it all among them. If you wait till the horses come out, you must wait till the wine is drunk. I have had my share already ; but, since you do not care about yours, I see no reason why I should not have that too.'

'Hold, hold ; not so fast,' cried the sentinel ; 'do watch then for a moment ; I'll be with you presently.'

'Don't hurry yourself,' said Ludovico coolly ; 'I have kept guard before now. But you may leave me your trombone *, that if the castle should be attacked, you know, I may be able to defend the pass like a hero.'

'There, my good fellow,' returned the soldier ; 'there, take it—it has seen service, though it could do little in defending the castle. I'll tell you a good story, though, about this trombone.'

'You'll tell it better when you have had the wine,' said Ludovico. 'They are coming out from the court already.'

'I'll have the wine, though,' said the sentinel, running off : 'I won't keep you a minute.'

'Take your time, I am in no haste,' replied Ludovico, who was already hurrying across the court when the soldier came back. 'Whither so fast, friend—whither so fast?' said the latter. 'What ! is this the way you keep watch? I must stand to my post myself, I see.'

'Aye, well,' replied Ludovico, 'you have saved me the trouble of following you further ; for I want to tell you, if you have a mind to drink the Tuscany wine, you must go to Sebastian, he is dealing it out ; the other

* A kind of blunderbuss.

that Fredrico has, is not worth having. But you are not likely to have any, I see, for they are all coming out.'

'By St. Peter, so they are,' said the soldier, and again ran off ; while Ludovico, once more at liberty, hastened to the door of the passage, where Emily was sinking under the anxiety this long discourse had occasioned ; but on his telling them the court was clear, they followed him to the gates, without waiting another instant ; yet not before he had seized two horses that had strayed from the second court, and were picking a scanty meal along the grass which grew between the pavement of the first.

They passed without interruption the dreadful gates, and took the road that led down among the woods, Emily, Monsieur du Pont, and Annette on foot, and Ludovico, who was mounted on one horse, leading the other. Having reached them, they stopped while Emily and Annette were placed on horseback with their two protectors ; when, Ludovico leading the way, they set off as fast as the broken road, and the feeble light which a rising moon threw among the foliage, would permit.

Emily was so much astonished by this sudden departure, that she scarcely dared to believe herself awake ; and she yet much doubted whether this adventure would terminate in escape—a doubt which had too much probability to justify it ; for before they quitted the woods, they heard shouts in the wind, and, on emerging from them, saw lights moving quickly near the castle above. Du Pont whipped his horse, and with some difficulty compelled him to go faster.

'Ah ! poor beast,' said Ludovico, 'he is weary enough ; he has been out all day : but, Signor, we must fly for it, now ; for yonder are the lights coming this way.'

Having given his own horse a lash, they now both set off on a full gallop ; and when they again looked back, the lights were so distant as scarcely to be discerned, and the voices were sunk into silence. The travellers then abated their pace ; and, consulting whither they should direct their course, it was determined they should descend into Tuscany, and endeavour to reach the Mediterranean, where they could readily embark for France. Thither Du Pont meant to attend Emily, if he should learn that the regiment he had accompanied into Italy was returned to his native country.

They were now in the road which Emily had travelled with Ugo and Bertrand ; but Ludovico, who was the only one of the party acquainted with the passes of these mountains, said that a little further on, a byroad branching from this, would lead them down into Tuscany with very little difficulty ; and that at a few leagues distance was a small town where necessaries could be procured for their journey.

'But I hope,' added he, 'we shall meet with no straggling parties of banditti; some of them are abroad, I know. However, I have got a good trombone, which will be of some service if we should encounter any of those brave spirits. You have no arms, signor?' 'Yes,' replied Du Pont; 'I have the villain's stilleto, who would have stabbed me. But let us rejoice in our escape from Udolpho, nor torment ourselves with looking out for dangers that may never arrive.'

The moon was now risen high over the woods that hung upon the sides of the narrow glen through which they wandered, and afforded them light sufficient to distinguish their way, and to avoid the loose and broken stones that frequently crossed it. They now travelled leisurely, and in profound silence; for they had scarcely yet recovered from the astonishment into which this sudden escape had thrown them. Emily's mind, especially, was sunk, after the various emotions it had suffered, into a kind of musing stillness, which the reposing beauty of the surrounding scene, and the creeping murmur of the night-breeze among the foliage above, contributed to prolong. She thought of Valancourt and of France with hope; and she would have thought of them with joy, had not the first events of this evening harrassed her spirits too much to permit her now to feel so lively a sensation. Meanwhile, Emily was alone the object of Du Pont's melancholy consideration; yet, with the despondency he suffered, as he mused on his recent disappointment, was mingled a sweet pleasure, occasioned by her presence, though they did not now exchange a single word. Annette thought of this wonderful escape, of the bustle in which Montoni and his people must be, now that their flight was discovered; of her native country, whither she hoped she was returning; and of her marriage with Ludovico, to which there no longer appeared any impediment, for poverty she did not consider such. Ludovico, on his part, congratulated himself on having rescued his Annette and *Signora* Emily from the danger that had surrounded them; on his own liberation from people whose manners he had long detested; on the freedom he had given to Monsieur du Pont; on his prospect of happiness with the object of his affections; and not a little on the address with which he had deceived the sentinel, and conducted the whole of this affair.

Thus, variously engaged in thought, the travellers passed on silently for above an hour, a question being only now and then asked by Du Pont concerning the road, or a remark uttered by Annette respecting objects seen imperfectly in the twilight. At length lights were perceived twinkling on the side of a mountain, and Ludovico had no doubt that they proceeded from the town he had mentioned; while his companions, satisfied by this assur-

ance, sunk again into silence. Annette was the first who interrupted this. 'Holy Peter!' said she, 'what shall we do for money on our journey? for I know neither I nor my lady have a single sequin; the signor took care of that!'

This remark produced a serious inquiry, which ended in as serious an embarrassment, for Du Pont had been rifled of nearly all his money when he was taken prisoner; the remainder he had given to the sentinel who had enabled him occasionally to leave the prison chamber; and Ludovico, who had for some time found a difficulty in procuring any part of the wages due to him, had now scarcely cash sufficient to procure necessary refreshment at the first town in which they should arrive.

Their poverty was the more distressing, since it would detain them among the mountains, where, even in a town, they could scarcely consider themselves safe from Montoni. The travellers, however, had only to proceed and dare the future; and they continued their way through lonely wilds and dusky valleys, where the overhanging foliage now admitted and then excluded the moonlight; wilds so desolate, that they appeared on the first glance as if no human being had ever trod them before. Even the road in which the party were did but slightly contradict this error; for the high grass and other luxuriant vegetation with which it was overgrown, told how very seldom the foot of a traveller had passed it.

At length, from a distance was heard the faint tinkling of a sheep-bell, and soon after the bleat of flocks; and the party then knew that they were near some human habitation; for the light which Ludovico had fancied to proceed from a town had long been concealed by intervening mountains. Cheered by this hope, they quickened their pace along the narrow pass they were winding, and it opened upon one of those pastoral valleys of the Apennines which might be painted for a scene of Arcadia, and whose beauty and simplicity are finely contrasted by the grandeur of the snowtopt mountains above.

The morning light now glimmering in the horizon, showed faintly, at a little distance upon the brow of a hill which seemed to peep from 'under the opening eye-lids of the morn,' the town they were in search of, and which they soon after reached. It was not without some difficulty that they there found a house which could afford shelter for themselves and their horses; and Emily desired they might not rest longer than was necessary for refreshment. Her appearance excited some surprise; for she was without a hat, having had time only to throw on her veil before she left the castle; a circumstance that compelled her to regret again the want of money, without which it was impossible to procure this necessary article of dress.

Ludovico, on examining his purse, found it even insufficient to supply present refreshment ; and Du Pont at length ventured to inform the landlord, whose countenance was simple and honest, of their exact situation, and requested that he would assist them to pursue their journey ; a purpose which he promised to comply with, as far as he was able, when he learned they were prisoners escaping from Montoni, whom he had too much reason to hate. But though he consented to lend them fresh horses to carry them to the next town, he was too poor himself to trust them with money ; and they were again lamenting their poverty, when Ludovico, who had been with his tired horses to the hovel which served for a stable, entered the room half frantic with joy, in which his auditors soon participated. On removing the saddle from one of the horses, he had found beneath it a small bag, containing, no doubt, the booty of one of the *Condottieri*, who had returned from a plundering excursion just before Ludovico left the castle, and whose horse, having strayed from the inner court while his master was engaged in drinking, had brought away the treasure which the ruffian had considered the reward of his exploit.

On counting over this, Du Pont found that it would be more than sufficient to carry them all to France, where he now determined to accompany Emily, whether he should obtain intelligence of his regiment or not ; for though he had as much confidence in the integrity of Ludovico as his small knowledge of him allowed, he could not endure the thought of committing her to his care for the voyage ; nor, perhaps, had he resolution enough to deny himself the dangerous pleasure which he might derive from her presence.

He now consulted them concerning the seaport to which they should direct their way ; and Ludovico, better informed of the geography of the country, said that Leghorn was the nearest port of consequence, which Du Pont knew also to be the most likely of any in Italy to assist their plan, since from thence vessels of all nations were continually departing. Thither, therefore, it was determined that they should proceed.

Emily having purchased a little straw hat, such as was worn by the peasant girls of Tuscany, and some other little necessary equipments for the journey, and the travellers having exchanged their tired horses for others better able to carry them, recommenced their joyous way as the sun was rising over the mountains ; and after travelling through the romantic country for several hours, began to descend into the vale of Arno. And here Emily beheld all the charms of sylvan and pastoral landscape united, adorned with the elegant villas of the Florentine nobles, and diversified with the various riches of cultivation. How vivid the shrubs that embowered the slopes, with the woods that stretched amphitheatrically along the mountains ! and, above all, how elegant the outline of these waving Apennines, now softening from the wildness which their interior regions exhibited ! At a distance, in the east, Emily discovered Florence with its towers rising on the brilliant horizon, and its luxuriant plain spreading to the feet of the Apennines, speckled with gardens and magnificent villas, or coloured with groves of orange and lemon, with vines, corn, and plantations of olives and mulberry ; while, to the west, the vale opened to the waters of the Mediterranean ; so distant, that they were known only by a bluish line that appeared upon the horizon, and by the light marine vapour which just stained the ether above.

With a full heart Emily hailed the waves that were to bear her back to her native country, the remembrance of which, however, brought with it a pang ; for she had there no home to receive, no parents to welcome her, but was going, like a forlorn pilgrim, to weep over the sad spot where he who *was* her father lay interred. Nor were her spirits cheered when she considered how long it would probably be before she should see Valancourt, who might be stationed with his regiment in a distant part of France, and that, when they did meet, it would be only to lament the successful villainy of Montoni ; yet, still she would have felt inexpressible delight at the thought of being once more in the same country with Valancourt, had it even been certain that she could not see him.

The intense heat, for it was now noon, obliged the travellers to look out for a shady recess, where they might rest for a few hours ; and the neighbouring thickets abounding with wild grapes, raspberries, and figs, promised them grateful refreshment. Soon after, they turned from the road into a grove whose thick foliage entirely excluded the sunbeams, and where a spring, gushing from the rock, gave coolness to the air ; and having alighted and turned the horses to graze, Annette and Ludovico ran to gather fruit from the surrounding thickets, of which they soon returned with an abundance. The travellers, seated under the shade of a pine and cypress grove, and on turf enriched with such a profusion of fragrant flowers as Emily had scarcely ever seen, even among the Pyrenees, took their simple repast, and viewed with new delight, beneath the dark umbrage of gigantic pines, the glowing landscape stretching to the sea.

Emily and Du Pont gradually became thoughtful and silent ; but Annette was all joy and loquacity ; and Ludovico was gay, without forgetting the respectful distance which was due to his companions. The repast being over, Du Pont recommended Emily to endeavour to sleep during these sultry hours, and desiring the servants would do the same, said he would watch the while; but Ludovico wished to spare him this trouble; and Emily and Annette, wearied with travelling, tried to repose, while he stood guard with his trombone.

When Emily, refreshed by slumber, awoke, she found the sentinel asleep on his post, and Du Pont awake, but lost in melancholy thought. As the sun was yet too high to allow them to continue their journey, and as it was necessary that Ludovico, after the toils and trouble he had suffered, should finish his sleep, Emily took this opportunity of inquiring by what accident Du Pont became Montoni's prisoner; and he, pleased with the interest this inquiry expressed, and with the excuse it gave him for talking to her of himself, immediately answered her curiosity.

'I came into Italy, madam, said Du Pont, 'in the service of my country. In an adventure among the mountains, our party engaging with the bands of Montoni, was routed, and I, with a few of my comrades, was taken prisoner. When they told me whose captive I was, the name of Montoni struck me; for I remembered that Madame Cheron, your aunt, had married an Italian of that name, and that you had accompanied them into Italy. It was not, however, till some time after, that I became convinced that this was the same Montoni, or learned that you, madam, was under the same roof with myself. I will not pain you by describing what were my emotions upon this discovery, which I owned to a sentinel, whom I had so far won my interest, that he granted me many indulgences, one of which was very important to me, and somewhat dangerous to himself; but he persisted in refusing to convey any letter, or notice of my situation, to you; for he justly dreaded a discovery, and the consequent vengeance of Montoni. He however enabled me to see you more than once. You are surprised, madam: and I will explain myself. My health and spirits suffered extremely from want of air and exercise; and at length I gained so far upon the pity, or the avarice of the man, that he gave me the means of walking on the terrace.

Emily now listened with very anxious attention to the narrative of Du Pont, who proceeded:

' In granting this indulgence, he knew that he had nothing to apprehend from a chance of my escaping from a castle which was vigilantly guarded, and the nearest terrace of which rose over a perpendicular rock: he showed me also,' continued Du Pont, 'a door concealed in the cedar wainscot of the apartment where I was confined, which he instructed me how to open; and which, leading into a passage formed within the thickness of the wall that extended far along the castle, finally opened in an obscure corner of the eastern rampart. I have since been informed that there are many passages of the same kind concealed within the prodigious walls of that edifice, and which were undoubtedly contrived for the purpose of facilitating escapes in time of war. Through this avenue, at the dead of night, I often stole to the terrace, where I walked with the utmost caution, lest my steps should betray me to the sentinels on duty in distant parts; for this end of it, being guarded by high buildings, was not watched by soldiers. In one of these midnight wanderings I saw light in a casement that overlooked the rampart, and which, I observed, was immediately over my prison chamber. It occurred to me, that you might be in that apartment; and with the hope of seeing you, I placed myself opposite to the window.

Emily, remembering the figure that had formerly appeared on the terrace, and which had occasioned her so much anxiety, exclaimed, ' It was you, then, Monsieur du Pont, who occasioned me much foolish terror! My spirits were at that time so much weakened by long suffering, that they took alarm at every hint.' Du Pont, after lamenting that he had occasioned her any apprehension, added: 'As I rested on the wall opposite to your casement, the consideration of your melancholy situation, and of my own, called from me involuntary sounds of lamentation, which drew you, I fancy, to the casement: I saw there a person whom I believed to be you. O! I will say nothing of my emotion at that moment; I wished to speak, but prudence restrained me, till the distant footstep of the sentinel compelled me suddenly to quit my station.

' It was some time before I had another opportunity of walking, for I could only leave my prison when it happened to be the turn of one man to guard me; meanwhile I became convinced, from some circumstances related by him, that your apartment was over mine; and when again I ventured forth, I returned to your casement, where again I saw you, but without daring to speak. I waved my hand, and you suddenly disappeared; then it was that I forgot my prudence, and yielded to lamentation; again you appeared—you spoke —I heard the well-known accent of your voice! and at that moment my discretion would have forsaken me again, had I not heard also the approaching steps of a soldier, when I instantly quitted the place, though not before the man had seen me. He followed down the terrace, and gained so fast upon me that I was compelled to make use of a stratagem, ridiculous enough, to save myself. I had heard of the superstition of many of these men, and I uttered a strange noise, with a hope that my pursuer would mistake it for something supernatural, and desist from pursuit. Luckily for myself, I succeeded; the man, it seems, was subject to fits, and the terror he suffered threw him into one, by which accident I secured my retreat. A sense of the danger I had escaped, and the increased watchfulness which my appearance had occasioned among the sentinels, deterred me ever after from walking on the terrace; but in the stillness of night I frequently beguiled myself with an old lute, procured for me by a soldier, which I sometimes accompanied with my voice, and sometimes, I will acknowledge, with a hope of making myself heard by you: but it was only a few evenings ago that this hope was answered; I then thought I heard a voice in the wind, calling me; yet even then, I feared to reply, lest the sentinel at the prison-door should hear me. Was I right, madam, in this conjecture—was it you who spoke?'

'Yes,' said Emily with an involuntary sigh; 'you was right indeed.'

Du Pont, observing the painful emotions which this question revived, now changed the subject. 'In one of my excursions through the passage which I have mentioned, I overheard a singular conversation,' said he.

'In the passage!' said Emily with surprise.

'I heard it in the passage,' said Du Pont; 'but it proceeded from an apartment adjoining the wall, within which the passage wound, and the shell of the wall was there so thin, and was also somewhat decayed, that I could distinctly hear every word spoken on the other side. It happened that Montoni and his companions were assembled in the room, and Montoni began to relate the extraordinary history of the lady his predecessor in the castle. He did, indeed, mention some very surprising circumstances, and whether they were strictly true, his conscience must decide; I fear it will determine against him. But you, madam, have doubtless heard the report, which he designs should circulate, on the subject of that lady's mysterious fate.'

'I have, sir,' replied Emily, and I perceive that you doubt it.'

'I doubted it before the period I am speaking of,' rejoined Du Pont; 'but some circumstances, mentioned by Montoni, greatly contributed to my suspicions. The account I then heard almost convinced me that he was a murderer. I trembled for you; the more so that I had heard the guests mention your name in a manner that threatened your repose; and, knowing that the most impious men are often the most superstitious, I determined to try whether I could not awaken their consciences, and awe them from the commission of the crime I dreaded. I listened closely to Montoni, and in the most striking passages of his story I joined my voice, and repeated his last words in a disguised and hollow tone.'

'But was you not afraid of being discovered?' said Emily.

'I was not,' replied Du Pont; 'for I knew that if Montoni had been acquainted with the secret of this passage, he would not have confined me in the apartment to which it led. I knew also, from better authority, that he was ignorant of it. The party for some time appeared inattentive to my voice; but at length were so much alarmed that they quitted the apartment; and having heard Montoni order his servants to search it, I returned to my prison, which was very distant from this part of the passage.'

'I remember perfectly to have heard of the conversation you mention,' said Emily; 'it spread a general alarm among Montoni's people, and I will own I was weak enough to partake of it.'

Monsieur du Pont and Emily thus continued to converse of Montoni, and then of France, and of the plan of their voyage; when Emily told him that it was her intention to retire to a convent in Languedoc, where she had been formerly treated with much kindness, and from thence to write to her relation Monsieur Quesnel, and inform him of her conduct. There she designed to wait till La Vallée should again be her own, whither she hoped her income would some time permit her to return; for Du Pont now taught her to expect that the estate, of which Montoni had attempted to defraud her, was not irrecoverably lost, and he again congratulated her on her escape from Montoni, who he had not a doubt meant to have detained her for life. The possibility of recovering her aunt's estates for Valancourt and herself, lighted up a joy in Emily's heart, such as she had not known for many months; but she endeavoured to conceal this from Monsieur du Pont, lest it should lead him to painful remembrance of his rival.

They continued to converse till the sun was declining in the west, when Du Pont awoke Ludovico, and they set forward on their journey. Gradually descending the lower slopes of the valley, they reached the Arno, and wound along its pastoral margin for many miles, delighted with the scenery around them, and with the remembrances which its classic waves revived. At a distance they heard the gay song of the peasants among the vineyards, and observed the setting sun tint the waves with yellow lustre, and twilight draw a dusky purple over the mountains, which at length deepened into night. Then the *lucciola*, the fire-fly of Tuscany, was seen to flash its sudden sparks among the foliage, while the *cicala*, with its shrill note, became more clamorous than even during the noon-day heat, loving best the hour when the English beetle, with less offensive sound,

'. . . . . winds
His small but sullen horn,
As oft he rises 'midst the twilight path,
Against the pilgrim borne in heedless hum.' *

* Collins.

The travellers crossed the Arno by moonlight, at a ferry; and learning that Pisa was distant only a few miles down the river, they wished to have proceeded thither in a boat; but as none could be procured, they set out on their wearied horses for that city. As they approached it, the vale expanded into a plain variegated with vineyards, corn, olives, and mulberry groves; but it was late before they reached its gates, where Emily was surprised to hear the busy sound of footsteps, and the tones of musical instruments, as well as to see the lively groups that filled the streets, and she almost fancied herself again at Venice; but here was no moonlight sea—ho gay gondolas dashing the waves—no *Palladian* palaces, to throw enchantment over the fancy, and lead it into the wilds of fairy story. The Arno rolled through the town, but no music trembled from balconies over its waters; it gave only the busy voices of sailors on board vessels just arrived from the Mediterranean; the melancholy heaving of the anchor, and the boatswain's shrill whistle;—sounds which, since that period, have there sunk into silence. They then served to remind Du Pont that it was probable he might hear of a vessel sailing soon to France from this port, and thus be spared the trouble of going to Leghorn. As soon as Emily had reached the inn, he went therefore to the quay, to make his inquiries; but, after all the endeavours of himself and Ludovico, they could hear of no bark destined immediately for France, and the travellers returned to their resting-place. Here also Du Pont endeavoured to learn where his regiment then lay, but could acquire no information concerning it. The travellers retired early to rest, after the fatigues of this day, and on the following, rose early; and without pausing to view the celebrated antiquities of the place, or the wonders of its hanging tower, pursued their journey, in the cooler hours, through a charming country rich with wine, and corn, and oil. The Apennines, no longer awful, or even grand, here softened into the beauty of sylvan and pastoral landscape: and Emily, as she descended them, looked down delighted on Leghorn, and its spacious bay filled with vessels and crowned with these beautiful hills.

She was no less surprised and amused, on entering this town, to find it crowded with persons in the dresses of all nations; a scene which reminded her of a Venetian masquerade, such as she had witnessed at the time of the Carnival: but here was bustle without gaiety, and noise instead of music; while elegance was to be looked for only in the waving outlines of the surrounding hills.

Monsieur Du Pont, immediately on their arrival, went down to the quay, where he heard of several French vessels, and of one that was to sail in a few days for Marseilles; from whence another vessel could be procured, without difficulty, to take them across the Gulf of Lyons, towards Narbonne, on the coast, not many leagues from which city he understood the convent was seated to which Emily wished to retire. He therefore immediately engaged with the captain to take them to Marseilles, and Emily was delighted to hear that her passage to France was secured. Her mind was now relieved from the terror of pursuit; and the pleasing hope of soon seeing her native country—that country which held Valancourt—restored to her spirits a degree of cheerfulness such as she had scarcely known since the death of her father. At Leghorn, also, Du Pont heard of his regiment, and that it had embarked for France; a circumstance which gave him great satisfaction, for he could now accompany Emily thither, without reproach to his conscience or apprehension of displeasure from his commander. During these days he scrupulously forbore to distress her by a mention of his passion; and she was compelled to esteem and pity, though she could not love him. He endeavoured to amuse her by showing the environs of the town; and they often walked together on the sea-shore, and on the busy quays, where Emily was frequently interested by the arrival and departure of vessels, participating in the joy of meeting friends, and sometimes shedding a sympathetic tear to the sorrow of those that were separating. It was after having witnessed a scene of the latter kind, that she arranged the following stanzas:

THE MARINER.

Soft came the breath of spring; smooth flow'd the
  tide;
And blue the heaven in its mirror smiled;
The white sail trembled, swell'd, expanded wide,
The busy sailors at the anchor toil'd.

With anxious friends, that shed the parting tear,
The deck was throng'd—how swift the moments fly!
The vessel heaves, the farewell signs appear;
Mute is each tongue, and eloquent each eye.

The last dread moment comes!—The sailor youth
Hides the big drop, and smiles amid his pain,
Soothes his sad bride, and vows eternal truth,
Farewell, my love—we shall—shall meet again!

Long on the stern, with waving hand, he stood;
The crowded shore sinks, lessening, from his view,
As gradual glides the bark along the flood;
His bride is seen no more—Adieu!—adieu!

The breeze of eve moans low, her smile is o'er,
Dim steals her twilight down the crimson'd west:
He climbs the top-most mast, to seek once more
The far-seen coast, where all his wishes rest.

He views its dark line on the distant sky,
And Fancy leads him to his little home;
He sees his weeping love, he hears her sigh,
He soothes her griefs, and tells of joys to come.

Eve yields to night, the breeze to wintry gales,
In one vast shade the seas and shores repose;
He turns his aching eyes,—his spirit fails,
The chill tear falls;—sad to the deck he goes!

The storm of midnight swells, the sails are furl'd,
Deep sounds the lead, but finds no friendly shore;
Fast o'er the waves the wretched bark is hurl'd,
' O Ellen, Ellen! we must meet no more !'

Lightnings, that show the vast and foamy deep,
The rending thunders, as they onward roll,
The loud, loud winds, that o'er the billows sweep—
Shake the firm nerve, appal the bravest soul!

Ah ! what avails the seamen's toiling care !—
The straining cordage bursts, the mast is riven ;
The sounds of terror groan along the air,
Then sink afar; the bark on rocks is driven !

Fierce o'er the wreck the whelming waters pass'd,
The helpless crew sunk in the roaring main !
Henry's faint accents trembled in the blast—
' Farewell, my love !—we ne'er shall meet again !'

Oft, at the calm and silent evening hour,
When summer-breezes linger on the wave,
A melancholy voice is heard to pour
Its lonely sweetness o'er poor Henry's grave ;—

And oft, at midnight, airy strains are heard
Around the grove where Ellen's form is laid ;
Nor is the dirge by village maidens fear'd,
For lovers' spirits guard the holy shade !

CHAPTER XXXV.

'. . . . . Oh ! the joy
Of young ideas painted on the mind
In the warm glowing colours fancy spreads
On objects not yet known, when all is new,
And all is lovely !'

          SACRED DRAMAS.

WE now return to Languedoc, and to the mention of Count de Villefort, the nobleman who succeeded to an estate of the Marquis de Villeroi situated near the monastery of St. Claire. It may be recollected, that this chateau was uninhabited when St. Aubert and his daughter were in the neighbourhood, and that the former was much affected on discovering himself to be so near Chateau-le-Blanc, a place concerning which the good old La Voisin afterwards dropped some hints that had alarmed Emily's curiosity.

It was in the year 1584, the beginning of that in which St. Aubert died, that Francis Beauveau, Count de Villefort, came into possession of the mansions and extensive domain called Chateau-le-Blanc, situated in the province of Languedoc, on the shore of the Mediterranean. This estate, which during some centuries had belonged to his family, now descended to him on the decease of his relative the Marquis de Villeroi, who had been latterly a man of reserved manners and austere character ; circumstances which, together with the duties of his profession, that often called him into the field, had prevented any degree of intimacy with his cousin, the Count de Villefort. For many years they had known little of each other, and the count received the first intelligence of his death, which happened in a distant part of France, together with the instruments that gave him possession of the domain of Chateau-le-Blanc ; but it was not till the following year that he determined to visit that estate, when he designed to pass the autumn there. The scenes of Chateau-le-Blanc often came to his remembrance, heightened by the touches which a warm imagination gives to the recollection of early pleasures; for many years before, in the lifetime of the Marchioness, and at that age when the mind is particularly sensible to impressions of gaiety and delight, he had once visited this spot ; and though he had passed a long intervening period amidst the vexations and tumults of public affairs, which too frequently corrode the heart and vitiate the taste, the shades of Languedoc and the grandeur of its distant scenery had never been remembered by him with indifference.

During many years the chateau had been abandoned by the late Marquis, and, being inhabited only by an old steward and his wife, had been suffered to fall much into decay. To superintend the repairs that would be requisite to make it a comfortable residence, had been a principal motive with the count for passing the autumnal months in Languedoc ; and neither the remonstrances nor the tears of the countess, for on urgent occasions she could weep, were powerful enough to overcome his determination. She prepared therefore, to obey the command which she could not conquer, and to resign the gay assemblies of Paris—where her beauty was generally unrivalled, and won the applause to which her wit had but feeble claim—for the twilight canopy of woods, the lonely grandeur of mountains, and the solemnity of gothic halls, and of long, long galleries which echoed only the solitary step of a domestic, or the measured clink that ascended from the great clock—the ancient monitor of the hall below. From these melancholy expectations she endeavoured to relieve her spirits by recollecting all that she had ever heard concerning the joyous vintage of the plains of Languedoc ! but there, alas ! no airy forms would bound to the gay melody of Parisian dances, and a view of the rustic festivities of peasants could afford little pleasure to a heart, in which even the feelings of ordinary benevolence had long since decayed under the corruptions of luxury.

The count had a son and a daughter, the children of a former marriage, who he designed should accompany him to the south of France ; Henri, who was in his twentieth year, was in the French service ; and Blanche, who was not yet eighteen, had been hitherto confined to the convent, where she had been placed immediately on her father's second marriage. The present countess, who had neither sufficient ability nor inclination to superintend the education of her daughter-in-law, had advised this step ; and the dread of superior beauty had since urged her to employ every art that might prevail on the count to prolong the period of Blanche's seclusion ; it was therefore with extreme mortification that she now understood he would no longer submit on this subject ; yet it afforded her some consolation to consider that, though the Lady Blanche would emerge from the convent, the shades of the country would for some time veil her beauty from the public eye.

On the morning which commenced the journey, the postilions stopped at the convent, by the count's order, to take up Blanche, whose heart beat with delight at the prospect of novelty and freedom now before her. As the time of her departure drew nigh, her impatience had increased ; and the last night, during which she counted every note of every hour, had appeared the most tedious of any she had ever known. The morning light at length dawned ; the matin-bell rang ; she heard the nuns descending from their chambers, and she started from a sleepless pillow, to welcome the day which was to emancipate her from the severities of a cloister, and introduce her to a world where pleasure was ever smiling, and goodness ever blessed—where, in short, nothing but pleasure and goodness reigned! When the bell of the great gate rang, and the sound was followed by that of carriage-wheels, she ran, with a palpitating heart, to her lattice, and perceiving her father's carriage, in the court below, danced, with airy steps, along the gallery, where she was met by a nun with a summons from the abbess. In the next moment she was in the parlour, and in the presence of the countess, who now appeared to her as an angel that was to lead her into happiness. But the emotions of the countess, on beholding her, were not in unison with those of Blanche, who had never appeared so lovely as at this moment, when her countenance, animated by the lightening smile of joy, glowed with the beauty of happy innocence.

After conversing for a few minutes with the abbess, the countess rose to go. This was the moment which Blanche had anticipated with such eager expectation, the summit from which she looked down upon the fairy land of happiness, and surveyed all its enchantment ;—was it a moment, then, for tears of regret? Yet it was so. She turned with an altered and dejected countenance to her young companions, who were come to bid her farewell, and wept! Even my lady abbess, so stately and so solemn, she saluted with a degree of sorrow which an hour before she would have believed it impossible to feel, and which may be accounted for by considering how reluctantly we all part, even with unpleasing objects, when the separation is consciously for ever. Again she kissed the poor nuns, and then followed the countess from that spot with tears, which she expected to leave only with smiles.

But the presence of her father, and the variety of objects on the road, soon engaged her attention, and dissipated the shade which tender regret had thrown upon her spirits. Inattentive to a conversation which was passing between the countess and a Mademoiselle Bearn, her friend Blanche sat, lost in pleasing reverie, as she watched the clouds floating silently along the blue expanse, now veiling the sun and stretching their shadows along the distant scene, and then disclosing all his brightness. The journey continued to give Blanche inexpressible delight, for new scenes of nature were every instant opening to her view, and her fancy became stored with gay and beautiful imagery.

It was on the evening of the seventh day that the travellers came within view of the Chateau-le-Blanc, the romantic beauty of whose situation strongly impressed the imagination of Blanche, who observed with sublime astonishment the Pyrenean mountains, which had been seen only at a distance during the day, now rising within a few leagues, with their wild cliffs and immense precipices, which the evening clouds, floating round them, now disclosed, and again veiled. The setting rays, that tinged their snowy summits with a roseate hue, touched their lower points with various colouring, while the bluish tints that pervaded their shadowy recesses gave the strength of contrast to the splendour of light. The plains of Languedoc, blushing with the purple vine, and diversified with groves of mulberry, almond, and olives, spread far to the north and east : to the south appeared the Mediterranean, clear as crystal, and blue as the heavens it reflected, bearing on its bosom vessels, whose white sails caught the sunbeam, and gave animation to the scene. On a high promontory, washed by the waters of the Mediterranean, stood her father's mansion, almost secluded from the eye by woods of intermingled pine, oak, and chestnut, which crowned the eminence, and sloped towards the plains on one side ; while on the other they extended to a considerable distance along the sea-shores.

As Blanche drew nearer, the Gothic features of this ancient mansion successively appeared —first an embattled turret rising above the trees—then the broken arch of an immense gate-way retiring beyond them ; and she almost fancied herself approaching a castle, such as is often celebrated in early story, where the knights look out from the battlements on some champion below, who, clothed in black armour, comes, with his companions, to rescue the fair lady of his love from the oppression of his rival ; a sort of legends to which she had once or twice obtained access in the library of her convent, that, like many others belonging to the monks, was stored with these relics of romantic fiction.

The carriages stopped at a gate which led into the domain of the chateau, but which was now fastened; and the great bell, that had formerly served to announce the arrival

8

of strangers, having long since fallen from its station, a servant climbed over a ruined part of the adjoining wall, to give notice to those within of the arrival of their lord.

As Blanche leaned from the coach window, she resigned herself to the sweet and gentle emotions which the hour and the scenery awakened. The sun had now left the earth, and twilight began to darken the mountains ; while the distant waters, reflecting the blush that still glowed in the west, appeared like a line of light skirting the horizon. The low murmur of waves breaking on the shore came in the breeze, and now and then the melancholy dashing of oars was feebly heard from a distance. She was suffered to indulge her pensive mood, for the thoughts of the rest of the party were silently engaged upon the subjects of their several interests. Meanwhile the countess, reflecting with regret upon the gay parties she had left at Paris, surveyed with disgust what she thought the gloomy woods and solitary wildness of the scene ; and shrinking from the prospect of being shut up in an old castle, was prepared to meet every object with displeasure. The feelings of Henri were somewhat similar to those of the countess ; he gave a mournful sigh to the delights of the capital, and to the remembrance of a lady, who, he believed, had engaged his affections, and who had certainly fascinated his imagination ; but the surrounding country, and the mode of life on which he was entering, had for him at least the charm of novelty, and his regret was softened by the gay expectations of youth.

The gates being at length unbarred, the carriage moved slowly on under spreading chestnuts that almost excluded the remains of day, following what had been formerly a road, but which now, overgrown with luxuriant vegetation, could be traced only by the boundary formed by trees on either side, and which wound for near half a mile among the woods before it reached the chateau. This was the very avenue that St. Aubert and Emily had formerly entered, on their first arrival in the neighbourhood, with the hope of finding a house that would receive them for the night, and had so abruptly quitted on perceiving the wildness of the place. and a figure which the postilion had fancied was a robber.

'What a dismal place is this !' exclaimed the countess as the carriage penetrated the deeper recesses of the woods. Surely, my lord, you do not mean to pass all the autumn in this barbarous spot ! One ought to bring hither a cup of the waters of Lethe, that the remembrance of pleasanter scenes may not heighten at least the natural dreariness of these.'

'I shall be governed by circumstances, madam,' said the count ; ' this barbarous spot was inhabited by my ancestors.'

The carriage now stopped at the chateau, where at the door of the great hall appeared the old steward and the Parisian servants who had been sent to prepare the chateau, waiting to receive their lord. Lady Blanche now perceived that the edifice was not built entirely in the Gothic style, but that it had additions of a more modern date ; the large and gloomy hall, however, into which she now entered, was entirely Gothic ; and sumptuous tapestry, which it was now too dark to distinguish, hung upon the walls, and depictured scenes from some of the ancient Provençal romances. A vast Gothic window, embroidered with *clematis* and eglantine, that ascended to the south, led the eye, now that the casements were thrown open, through this verdant shade, over a sloping lawn to the tops of dark woods that hung upon the brow of the promontory. Beyond appeared the waters of the Mediterranean, stretching far to the south and to the east, where they were lost in the horizon ; while to the north-east they were bounded by the luxuriant shores of Languedoc and Provence, enriched with wood, and gay with vines and sloping pasture ; and to the south-west, by the majestic Pyrenees, now fading from the eye beneath the gradual gloom.

Blanche, as she crossed the hall, stopped a moment to observe this lovely prospect, which the evening twilight obscured, yet did not conceal. But she was quickly awakened from complacent delight, which this scene had diffused upon her mind, by the countess, who, discontented with every object around, and impatient for refreshment and repose, hastened forward to a large parlour, whose cedar wainscot, narrow pointed casements, and dark ceiling of carved cypress wood, gave it an aspect of peculiar gloom, which the dingy green velvet of the chairs and couches, fringed with tarnished gold, had once been designed to enliven.

While the countess inquired for refreshment, the count, attended by his son, went to look over some part of the chateau ; and Lady Blanche reluctantly remained to witness the discontent and ill humour of her stepmother.

' How long have you lived in this desolate place ?' said her ladyship to the old housekeeper, who came to pay her duty. ' Above twenty years your ladyship, on the next feast of St. Jerome.'

' How happened it that you have lived here so long, and almost alone, too ? I understood that the chateau had been shut up for some years ?'

' Yes, madam, it was for many years after my late lord, the count, went to the wars ; but it is above twenty years since I and my husband came into his service. The place is so large, and has of late been so lonely, that we were lost in it, and after some time we went to live in a cottage at the end of the woods, near some of the tenants, and came to look after the chateau every now and then.

'hen my lord returned to France from the urs, he took a dislike to the place, and never me to live here again, and so he was satisfied ith our remaining at the cottage. Alas— as ! how the chateau is changed from what once was ! What delight my late lady ,ed to take in it ! I well remember when e came here a bride, and how fine it was. ow it has been neglected so long, and is ne into such decay ! I shall never see those tys again.

The countess appearing to be somewhat fended by the thoughtless simplicity with hich the old woman regretted former times, orothée added—' But the chateau will now : inhabited, and cheerful again ; not all the orld could tempt me to live in it alone.'

' Well, the experiment will not be made, I ·lieve,' said the countess, displeased that her vn silence had been unable to awe the quacity of this rustic old housekeeper, now ared from further attendance by the entrance the count, who said he had been viewing art of the chateau, and found that it would quire considerable repairs and some alte- tions before it would be perfectly comfortable a place of residence. ' I am sorry to hear my lord,' replied the countess.' ' And ay sorry, madam ?' ' Because the place ll i'll repay your trouble ; and were it even paradise, it would be insufferable at such a stance from Paris.'

The count made no reply, but walked ruptly to a window. ' There are windows, y lord, but they neither admit entertainment or light ; they show only a scene of savage iture.'

' I am at a loss, madam,' said the count, o conjecture what you mean by savage iture. Do those plains, or those woods, or at fine expanse of water deserve the name ?' ' Those mountains certainly do, my lord,' joined the countess, pointing to the Pyre- es ; ' and this chateau, though not a work · rude nature, is, to my taste at least, one of ıvage art.' The count coloured highly. This place, madam, was the work of my acestors,' said he ; ' and you must allow me · say, that your present conversation dis- overs neither good taste nor good manners.' lanche, now shocked at an altercation which ppeared to be increasing to a serious dis- greement, rose to leave the room, when her iother's woman entered it, and the countess, nmediately desiring to be shown to her own partment, withdrew, attended by Made- ioiselle Bearn.

Lady Blanche, it being not yet dark, took iis opportunity of exploring new scenes ; and aving the parlour, she passed from the hall ito a wide gallery, whose walls were deco- ited by marble pilasters, which supported an rched roof composed of a rich mosaic work. 'hrough a distant window, that seemed to rminate the gallery, were seen the purple

clouds of evening, and a landscape whose features, thinly veiled in twilight, no longer appeared distinctly, but, blended into one grand mass, stretched to the horizon, coloured only with a tint of solemn gray.

The gallery terminated in a saloon, to which the window she had seen through an open door belonged ; but the increasing dusk per- mitted her only an imperfect view of this apartment, which seemed to be magnificent, and of modern architecture ; though it had been either suffered to fall into decay or had never been properly finished. The windows, which were numerous and large, descended low, and afforded a very extensive, and, what Blanche's fancy represented to be, a very lovely prospect ; and she stood for some time surveying the gray obscurity, and depicturing imaginary woods and mountains, valleys and rivers, on this scene of night ; her solemn sensations rather assisted, than interrupted, by the distant bark of a watch-dog, and by the breeze as it trembled upon the light foliage of the shrubs. Now and then appeared for a moment, among the woods, a cottage light ; and at length was heard afar off the evening bell of a convent, dying on the air. When she withdrew her thoughts from these subjects of fanciful delight, the gloom and silence of the saloon somewhat awed her ; and having sought the door of the gallery, and pursued for a considerable time a dark passage, she came to a hall, but one totally different from that she had formerly seen. By the twilight admitted through an open portico she could just distinguish this apartment to be of very light and airy architecture, and that it was paved with white marble, pillars of which sup- ported the roof that rose into arches built in the Moorish style. While Blanche stood on the steps of this portico, the moon rose over the sea, and gradually disclosed in partial light the beauties of the eminence on which she stood, whence a lawn, now rude and over- grown with high grass, sloped to the woods, that, almost surrounding the chateau, extended in a grand sweep down the southern sides of the promontory to the very margin of the ocean. Beyond the woods on the north side appeared a long tract of the plains of Lan- guedoc ; and to the east, the landscape she had before dimly seen, with the towers of a monastery illumined by the moon, rising over dark groves.

The soft and shadowy tints that overspread the scene, the waves undulating in the moon- light, and their low and measured murmurs on the beach were circumstances that united to elevate the unaccustomed mind of Blanche to enthusiasm.

' And have I lived in this glorious world so long,' said she, ' and never till now beheld such a prospect — never experienced these delights ! Every peasant girl on my father's domain has viewed from her infancy the face of nature, has ranged at liberty her romantic wilds ; while I have been shut in a cloister from the view of these beautiful appearances, which were designed to enchant all eyes and awaken all hearts. How can the poor nuns and friars feel the full fervour of devotion if they never see the sun rise or set ! Never till this evening did I know what true devotion is ; for never before did I see the sun sink below the vast earth ! To-morrow, for the first time in my life, I will see it rise. O who would live in Paris, to look upon black walls and dirty streets, when, in the country, they might gaze on the blue heavens and all the green earth !'

This enthusiastic soliloquy was interrupted by a rustling noise in the hall : and while the loneliness of the place made her sensible to fear, she thought she perceived something moving between the pillars. For a moment she continued silently observing it, till, ashamed of her ridiculous apprehensions, she collected courage enough to demand who was there. 'O my young lady, is it you?' said the old housekeeper, who was come to shut the windows. The manner in which she spoke this, with a faint breath, rather surprised Blanche, who said, 'You seemed frightened, Dorothée, what is the matter?'

'No, not frightened, ma'amselle,' replied Dorothée, hesitating, and trying to appear composed ; 'but I am old, and—a little matter startles me.' The lady Blanche smiled at the distinction. 'I am glad that my lord the count is come to live at the chateau, ma'amselle,' continued Dorothée ; 'for it has been many a year deserted, and dreary enough ; now the place will look a little as it used to do when my poor lady was alive. Blanche inquired how long it was since the marchioness died?' 'Alas, my lady !' replied Dorothée, 'so long —that I have ceased to count the years ! The place, to my mind, has mourned ever since ; and I am sure my lord's vassals have. But you have lost yourself, ma'amselle—shall I show you to the other side of the chateau?'

Blanche inquired how long this part of the edifice had been built. 'Soon after my lord's marriage, ma'am,' replied Dorothée. 'The place was large enough without this addition, for many rooms of the old building were even then never made use of, and my lord had a princely household too ; but he thought the ancient mansion gloomy, and gloomy enough it is !' Lady Blanche now desired to be shown to the inhabited part of the chateau ; and as the passages were entirely dark, Dorothée conducted her along the edge of the lawn to the opposite side of the edifice where, a door opening into the great hall, she was met by Mademoiselle Bearn. 'Where have you been so long?' said she ; 'I had begun to think some wonderful adventure had befallen you, and that the giant of

this enchanted castle, or the ghost which no doubt haunts it, had conveyed you through a trap-door into some subterranean vault, whence you was never to return.'

'No,' replied Blanche laughingly, 'you seem to love adventures so well, that I leave them for you to achieve.'

'Well, I am willing to achieve them, provided I am allowed to describe them.'

'My dear Mademoiselle Bearn,' said Henri, as he met her at the door of the parlour, 'no ghost of these days would be so savage as to impose silence on you. Our ghosts are more civilised than to condemn a lady to a purgatory severer even than their own, be it what it may.'

Mademoiselle Bearn replied only by a laugh ; and the count now entering the room, supper was served, during which he spoke little, frequently appeared to be abstracted from the company, and more than once remarked that the place was greatly altered since he had last seen it. Many years have intervened since that period,' said he ; 'and though the grand features of the scenery admit of no change, they impress me with sensations very different from those I formerly experienced.'

'Did these scenes, sir,' said Blanche, 'ever appear more lovely than they do now? To me this seems hardly possible.' The count, regarding her with a melancholy smile, said, 'They once were as delightful to me as they are now to you ; the landscape is not changed, but time has changed me ; from my mind the illusion which gave spirit to the colouring of nature, is fading fast ! If you live, my dear Blanche, to revisit this spot at the distance of many years, you will perhaps remember and understand the feelings of your father.'

Lady Blanche, affected by these words, remained silent ; she looked forward to the period which the count anticipated ; and considering that he now spoke would then probably be no more, her eyes, bent to the ground, were filled with tears. She gave her hand to her father, who, smiling affectionately, rose from his chair, and went to a window to conceal his emotion.

The fatigues of the day made the party separate at an early hour ; when Blanche retired through a long oak gallery to her chamber, whose spacious and lofty walls, high antiquated casements, and, what was the effect of these, its gloomy air, did not reconcile her to its remote situation in this ancient building. The furniture also was of ancient date ; the bed was of blue damask trimmed with tarnished gold lace, and its lofty tester rose in the form of a canopy, whence the curtains descended, like those of such tents as are sometimes represented in old pictures, and, indeed, much resembling those exhibited on the faded tapestry with which the chamber was hung. To Blanche, every object here was matter of curiosity ; and, taking the light from her woman to examine the tapestry, she perceived that it represented scenes from the walls of Troy, though the almost colourless worsted now mocked the glowing actions they once had painted. She laughed at the ludicrous absurdity she observed, till recollecting that the hands which had woven it were, like the poet whose thoughts of fire they had attempted to express, long since mouldered into dust, a train of melancholy ideas passed over her mind, and she almost wept.

Having given her woman a strict injunction to awaken her before sun-rise, she dismissed her; and then, to dissipate the gloom which reflection had cast upon her spirits, opened one of the high casements, and was again cheered by the face of living nature. The shadowy earth, the air, the ocean—all was still. Along the deep serene of the heavens a few light clouds floated slowly, through whose skirts the stars now seemed to tremble, and now to emerge with purer splendour. Blanche's thoughts arose involuntarily to the Great Author of the sublime objects she contemplated, and she breathed a prayer of finer devotion than any she had ever uttered beneath the vaulted roof of a cloister. At this casement she remained till the glooms of midnight were stretched over the prospect. She then retired to her pillow, and, ' with gay visions of to-morrow,' to those sweet slumbers which health and happy innocence only know.

' To-morrow, to fresh woods and pastures new.'

CHAPTER XXXVI.

' What transport to retrace our early plays,
Our easy bliss, when each thing joy supplied,
The woods, the mountains, and the warbling maze
Of the wild brooks !'

THOMSON.

BLANCHE'S slumbers continued till long after the hour which she had so impatiently anticipated ; for her woman, fatigued with travelling, did not call her till breakfast was nearly ready. Her disappointment, however, was instantly forgotten, when on opening the casement she saw on the one hand, the wide sea sparkling in the morning rays, with its stealing sails and glancing oars ; and on the other, the fresh woods, the plains far-stretching, and the blue mountains, all glowing with the splendour of the day.

As she inspired the pure breeze, health spread a deeper blush upon her countenance, and pleasure danced in her eyes.

' Who could first invent convents?' said she, ' and who could first persuade people to go into them ? and to make religion a pretence, too, where all that should inspire it is so carefully shut out? God is best pleased with the homage of a grateful heart ; and when we view his glories, we feel most grateful. I

never felt so much devotion, during the many dull years I was in the convent, as I have done in the few hours that I have been here, where I need only look on all around me—to adore God in my inmost heart !

Saying this she left the window, bounded along the gallery, and in the next moment was in the breakfast-room, where the count was already seated. The cheerfulness of a bright sunshine had dispersed the melancholy glooms of his reflections, a pleasant smile was on his countenance, and he spoke in an enlivening voice to Blanche, whose heart echoed back the tones. Henri, and soon after the countess with Mademoiselle Bearn appeared, and the whole party seemed to acknowledge the influence of the scene ; even the countess was so much re-animated as to receive the civilities of her husband with complacency, and but once forgot her good-humour, which was when she asked whether they had any neighbours who were likely to make *this barbarous spot* more tolerable, and whether the count believed it possible for her to exist here without some amusement.

Soon after breakfast the party dispersed. The count, ordering his steward to attend him in the library, went to survey the condition of his premises, and to visit some of his tenants ; Henri hastened with alacrity to the shore to examine a boat that was to bear them on a little voyage in the evening, and to superintend the adjustment of a silk awning ; while the countess, attended by Mademoiselle Bearn, retired to an apartment on the modern side of the chateau, which was fitted up with airy elegance : and as the windows opened upon balconies that fronted the sea, she was there saved from a view of the *horrid* Pyrenees. Here, while she reclined on a sofa, and, casting her languid eyes over the ocean, which appeared beyond the wood-tops, indulged in the luxuries of *ennui*, her companion read aloud a sentimental novel on some fashionable system of philosophy, for the countess was herself somewhat of a *philosopher*, especially as to *infidelity* ; and among a certain circle her opinions were waited for with impatience, and received as doctrines.

The Lady Blanche, meanwhile, hastened to indulge, amidst the wild wood-walks around the chateau, her new enthusiasm, where, as she wandered under the shades, her gay spirits gradually yielded to pensive complacency. Now she moved with solemn steps beneath the gloom of thickly interwoven branches, where the fresh dew still hung upon every flower that peeped from among the grass ; and now tripped sportively along the path on which the sun-beams darted and the chequered foliage trembled—where the tender greens of the beech, the acacia, and the mountain-ash, minging with the solemn tints of the cedar, the pine, and cypress, exhibited as fine a contrast of colouring as the majestic oak and oriental plane did of form, to the feathery lightness of the cork-tree, and the waving grace of the poplar.

Having reached a rustic seat within a deep recess of the woods, she rested a-while; and as her eyes caught through a distant opening a glimpse of the blue waters of the Mediterranean, with a white sail gliding on its bosom, or of the broad mountain glowing beneath the mid-day sun, her mind experienced somewhat of that exquisite delight which awakens the fancy and leads to poetry. The hum of bees alone broke the stillness around her, as, with other insects of various hues, they sported gaily in the shade, or sipped sweets from the fresh flowers: and while Blanche watched a butterfly flitting from bud to bud, she indulged herself in imagining the pleasures of its short day, till she had composed the following stanzas:

THE BUTTERFLY TO HIS LOVE.

What bowery dell, with fragrant breath,
  Courts thee to stay thy airy flight;
Nor seek again the purple heath,
  So oft the scene of gay delight?

Long I've watch'd i' the lily's bell,
  Whose whiteness stole the morning's beam,
No fluttering sounds thy coming tell,
  No waving wings at distance gleam.

But fountain fresh, nor breathing grove,
  Nor sunny mead, nor blossom'd tree,
So sweet as lily's cell shall prove,—
  The bower of constant love and me.

When April buds begin to blow,
  The primrose, and the harebell blue,
That on the verdant moss-bank grow,
  With violet cups that weep in dew;

When wanton gales breathe through the shade,
  And shake the blooms, and steal their sweets,
And swell the song of every glade,
  I range the forest's green retreats:

There, through the tangled wood-walks play,
  Where no rude urchin paces near,
Where sparely peeps the sultry day,
  And light dews freshen all the air.

High on a sun-beam oft I sport,
  O'er bower and fountain, vale and hill,
Oft every blushing floweret court,
  That hangs its head o'er winding rill.

But these I'll leave to be thy guide,
  And show thee where the jasmine spreads
Her snowy leaf, where May-flowers hide,
  And rose-buds rear their peeping heads.

With me the mountain's summit scale,
  And taste the wild-thyme's honey'd bloom,
Whose fragrance, floating on the gale,
  Oft leads me to the cedar's gloom.

Yet, yet, no sound comes in the breeze!
  What shade thus dares to tempt thy stay?
Once, me alone thou wish'd to please,
  And with me only thou would'st stray.

But, while thy long delay I mourn,
  And chide the sweet shades for their guile,
Thou mayst be true, and they forlorn,
  And fairy favours court thy smile.

The tiny queen of fairy-land,
  Who knows thy speed, hath sent thee far,
To bring, or ere the night-watch stand,
  Rich essence for her shadowy car·

Perchance her acorn-cups to fill
  With nectar from the Indian rose,
Or gather, near some haunted rill,
  May-dews, that lull to sleep Love's woes;

Or o'er the mountains bade thee fly,
  To tell her fairy love to speed,
When evening steals upon the sky,
  To dance along the twilight mead.

But now I see thee sailing low,
  Gay as the brightest flowers of spring,
Thy coat of blue and jet I know,
  And well thy gold and purple wing.

Borne on the gale, thou com'st to me;
  O! welcome, welcome to my home!
In lily's cell we'll live in glee,
  Together o'er the mountains roam!

When Lady Blanche returned to the chateau, instead of going to the apartment of the countess, she amused herself with wandering over that part of the edifice which she had not yet examined, of which the most ancient first attracted her curiosity: for though what she had seen of the modern was gay and elegant, there was something in the former more interesting to her imagination. Having passed up the great staircase and through the oak gallery, she entered upon a long suite of chambers, whose walls were either hung with tapestry or wainscoted with cedar, the furniture of which looked almost as ancient as the rooms themselves; the spacious fire-places, where no mark of social cheer remained, presented an image of cold desolation; and the whole suite had so much the air of neglect and desertion, that it seemed as if the venerable persons whose portraits hung upon the walls had been the last to inhabit them.

On leaving these rooms, she found herself in another gallery, one end of which was terminated by a back staircase, and the other by a door that seemed to communicate with the north side of the chateau, but which, being fastened, she descended the staircase, and, opening a door in the wall a few steps down, found herself in a small square room that formed part of the west turret of the castle. Three windows presented each a separate and beautiful prospect: that to the north overlooking Languedoc; another to the west, the hills ascending towards the Pyrenees, whose awful summits crowned the landscape; and a third, fronting the south, gave the Mediterranean, and a part of the wild shores of Roussillon, to the eye.

Having left the turret and descended the narrow staircase, she found herself in a dusky passage, where she wandered, unable to find her way, till impatience yielded to apprehension, and she called for assistance. Presently steps approached and light glimmered through a door at the other extremity of the passage, which was opened with caution by some person who did not venture beyond it, and whom Blanche observed in silence, till the door was closing, when she called aloud, and, hastening towards it, perceived the old housekeeper.

'Dear ma'amselle : is it you?' said Dorothée. ' How could you find your way hither?' Had Blanche been less occupied by her own fears, she would probably have observed the strong expressions of terror and surprise on Dorothée's countenance, who now led her through a long succession of passages and rooms, that looked as if they had been uninhabited for a century, till they reached that appropriated to the housekeeper, where Dorothée entreated she would sit down and take refreshment. Blanche accepted the sweetmeats offered to her, mentioned her discovery of the pleasant turret, and her wish to appropriate it to her own use. Whether Dorothée's taste was not so sensible to the beauties of landscape as her young lady's, or that the constant view of lovely scenery had deadened it, she forbore to praise the subject of Blanche's enthusiasm, which, however, her silence did not repress. To Lady Blanche's inquiry of whither the door she had found fastened led, she replied, that it opened to a suite of rooms which had not been entered during many years ; 'for,' added she, ' my late lady died in one of them, and I could never find in my heart to go into them since.'

Blanche, though she wished to see those chambers, forbore, on observing that Dorothée's eyes were filled with tears, to ask her to unlock them, and soon after went to dress for dinner, at which the whole party met in good spirits and good humour, except the countess, whose vacant mind, overcome by the langour of idleness, would neither suffer her to be happy herself, or to contribute to the happiness of others. Mademoiselle Bearn, attempting to be witty, directed her *badinage* against Henri ; who answered because he could not well avoid it, rather than from any inclination to notice her, whose liveliness sometimes amused, but whose conceit and insensibility often disgusted him.

The cheerfulness with which Blanche rejoined the party vanished on her reaching the margin of the sea ; she gazed with apprehension upon the vast expanse of waters which, at a distance, she had beheld only with delight and astonishment ; and it was by a strong effort that she so far overcame her fears as to follow her father into the boat.

As she silently surveyed the vast horizon bending round the distant verge of the ocean, an emotion of sublimest rapture struggled to overcome a sense of personal danger. A light breeze played on the water and on the silk awning of the boat, and waved the foliage of the receding woods that crowned the cliffs for many miles, and which the count surveyed with the pride of conscious property, as well as with the eye of taste.

At some distance among these woods stood a pavilion, which had once been the scene of social gaiety, and which its situation still made one of romantic beauty. Thither the count

had ordered coffee and other refreshments to be carried ; and thither the sailors now steered their course, following the windings of the shore round many a woody promontory and circling bay ; while the pensive tones of horns and other wind instruments, played by the attendants in a distant boat, echoed among the rocks, and died along the waves. Blanche had now subdued her fears ; a delightful tranquillity stole over her mind, and held her in silence ; and she was too happy to remember even the convent, or her former sorrows, as subjects of comparison with her present felicity.

The countess felt less unhappy than she had done since the moment of her leaving Paris ; for her mind was now under some degree of restraint. She feared to indulge its wayward humours, and even wished to recover the count's good opinion. On his family, and on the surrounding scene, he looked with tempered pleasure and benevolent satisfaction, while his son exhibited the gay spirits of youth, anticipating new delights, and regretless of those that were passed.

After near an hour's rowing, the party landed, and ascended a little path overgrown with vegetation. At a little distance from the point of the eminence, within the shadowy recess of the woods, appeared the pavilion, which Blanche perceived, as she caught a glimpse of its portico between the trees, to be built of variegated marble. As she followed the countess, she often turned her eyes with rapture towards the ocean, seen beneath the dark foliage far below, and from thence upon the deep woods, whose silence and impenetrable gloom awakened emotions more solemn, but scarcely less delightful.

The pavilion had been prepared, as far as was possible on a very short notice, for the reception of its visitors ; but the faded colours of its painted walls and ceiling, and the decayed drapery of its once magnificent furniture, declared how long it had been neglected and abandoned to the empire of the changing seasons. While the party partook of a collation of fruit and coffee, the horns, placed in a distant part of the woods where an echo sweetened and prolonged their melancholy tones, broke softly on the stillness of the scene. This spot seemed to attract even the admiration of the countess ; or perhaps it was merely the pleasure of planning furniture and decorations, that made her dwell so long on the necessity of repairing and adorning it ; while the count, never happier than when he saw her mind engaged by natural and simple objects, acquiesced in all her designs concerning the pavilion. The paintings on the walls and coved ceiling were to be renewed ; the canopies and sofas were to be light green damasks ; marble statues of wood-nymphs bearing on their heads baskets of living flowers were to adorn the recesses between the windows, which, descending to the ground, were to admit to every part of the room (and it was of octagonal form) the various landscape. One window opened upon a romantic glade, where the eye roved among woody recesses, and the scene was bounded only by a lengthened pomp of groves; from another the woods receding disclosed the distant summits of the Pyrenees; a third fronted an avenue, beyond which the gray towers of Chateau-le-Blanc and the picturesque part of its ruin were seen partially among the foliage; while a fourth gave, between the trees, a glimpse of the green pastures and villages that diversify the banks of the Aude. The Mediterranean, with the bold cliffs that overlooked its shores, were the grand objects of a fifth window; and the others gave, in different points of view, the wild scenery of the woods.

After wandering for some time in these, the party returned to the shore, and embarked; and, the beauty of the evening tempting them to extend their excursion, they proceeded further up the bay. A dead calm had succeeded the light breeze that wafted them hither, and the men took to their oars. Around, the waters were spread into one vast expanse of polished mirror, reflecting the gray cliffs and feathery woods that overhung its surface, the glow of the western horizon, and the dark clouds that came slowly from the east. Blanche loved to see the dipping oars imprint the water, and to watch the spreading circles they left, which gave a tremulous motion to the reflected landscape, without destroying the harmony of its features.

Above the darkness of the woods, her eye now caught a cluster of high towers touched with the splendour of the setting rays; and soon after, the horns being then silent, she heard the faint swell of choral voices from a distance. 'What voices are those upon the air?' said the count, looking round and listening;—but the strain had ceased. 'It seemed to be a vesper hymn which I have often heard in my convent,' said Blanche.

'We are near the monastery, then,' observed the count; and the boat soon after doubling a lofty headland, the monastery of St. Claire appeared, seated near the margin of the sea; where the cliffs suddenly sinking formed a low shore within a small bay almost encircled with woods, among which partial features of the edifice were seen—the great gate and Gothic window of the hall, the cloisters, and the side of a chapel more remote; while a venerable arch, which had once led to a part of the fabric now demolished, stood a majestic ruin, detached from the main building, beyond which appeared a grand perspective of the woods. On the grey walls the moss had fastened, and round the pointed windows of the chapel the ivy and the briony hung in many a fantastic wreath.

All without was silent and forsaken: but while Blanche gazed with admiration on this venerable pile, whose effect was heightened by the strong lights and shadows thrown athwart it by a cloudy sunset, a sound of many voices, slowly chanting, arose from within. The count bade his men rest on their oars. The monks were singing the hymn of vespers, and some female voices mingled with the strain; which rose, by soft degrees, till the high organ and the choral sounds swelled into full and solemn harmony. The strain soon after dropped into sudden silence, and was renewed in a low and still more solemn key; till at length the holy chorus died away, and was heard no more.—Blanche sighed; tears trembled in her eyes; and her thoughts seemed wafted with the sounds to heaven. While a rapt stillness prevailed in the boat, a train of friars, and then of nuns veiled in white, issued from the cloisters, and passed under the shade of the woods to the main body of the edifice.

The countess was the first of her party to awaken from this pause of silence.

'These dismal hymns and friars make one quite melancholy,' said she; 'twilight is coming on: pray let us return, or it will be dark before we get home.'

The count, looking up, now perceived that the twilight of evening was anticipated by an approaching storm. In the east a tempest was collecting: a heavy gloom came on, opposing and contrasting the glowing splendour of the setting sun: the clamorous sea-fowl skimmed in fleet circles upon the surface of the sea, dipping their light pinions in the wave, as they fled away in search of shelter. The boatmen pulled hard at their oars. But the thunder that now muttered at a distance, and the heavy drops that began to dimple the water, made the count determine to put back to the monastery for shelter; and the course of the boat was immediately changed. As the clouds approached the west, their lurid darkness changed to a deep ruddy glow, which, by reflection, seemed to fire the tops of the woods and the shattered towers of the monastery.

The appearance of the heavens alarmed the countess and Mademoiselle Bearn; whose expressions of apprehension distressed the count, and perplexed his men; while Blanche continued silent—now agitated with fear, and now with admiration, as she viewed the grandeur of the clouds, and their effect on the scenery, and listened to the long, long peals of thunder that rolled through the air.

The boat having reached the lawn before the monastery, the count sent a servant to announce his arrival, and to entreat shelter of the superior; who soon after appeared at the great gate attended by several monks; while the servant returned with a message expressive at once of hospitality and pride—but of pride disguised in submission. The party immediately disembarked ; and having hastily crossed the lawn—for the shower was now heavy—were received at the gate by the superior ; who, as they entered, stretched forth his hand and gave his blessing ; and they passed into the great hall, where the lady-abbess waited, attended by several nuns clothed, like herself, in black, and veiled in white. The veil of the abbess was, however, thrown half back, and discovered a counten-ance whose chaste dignity was sweetened by the smile of welcome with which she addressed the countess ; whom she led with Blanche and Mademoiselle Bearn into the convent parlour, while the count and Henri were con-ducted by the superior to the refectory.

The countess, fatigued and discontented, received the politeness of the abbess with care-less haughtiness, and had followed her with indolent steps to the parlour ; over which the painted casements, and wainscot of larch wood, threw at all times a melancholy shade, and where the gloom of evening now loured almost to darkness.

While the lady abbess ordered refreshment, and conversed with the countess, Blanche withdrew to a window ; the lower panes of which being without painting, allowed her to observe the progress of the storm over the Mediterranean ; whose dark waves, that had so lately slept, now came boldly swelling in long succession to the shore, where they burst in white foam, and threw up a high spray over the rocks. A red sulphureous tint overspread the long line of clouds that hung above the western horizon ; beneath whose dark skirts the sun looking out illumined the distant shores of Languedoc, as well as the tufted summits of the nearer woods, and shed a partial gleam on the western waves. The rest of the scene was in deep gloom, except where a sunbeam, darting between the clouds, glanced on the white wings of the sea-fowl that circled high among them, or touched the swelling sail of a vessel which was seen labouring in the storm. Blanche for some time anxiously watched the progress of the bark as it threw the waves in foam around it ; and, as the lightnings flashed, looked to the opening heavens with many a sigh for the fate of the poor mariners.

The sun at length set, and the heavy clouds which had long impended, dropped over the splendour of his course ; the vessel, however, was yet dimly seen ; and Blanche continued to observe it, till the quick succession of flashes, lighting up the gloom of the whole horizon, warned her to retire from the window, and she joined the abbess ; who, having exhausted all her topics of conversation with the coun-tess, had now leisure to notice her.

But their discourse was interrupted by tre-mendous peals of thunder ; and the bell of the monastery soon after ringing out, sum-moned the inhabitants to prayer. As Blanche passed the windows she gave another look to the ocean ; where, by the momentary flash that illumined the vast body of the waters, she distinguished the vessel she had observed before, -amidst a sea of foam, breaking the billows—the mast now bowing to the waves and then rising high in air.

She sighed fervently as she gazed, and then followed the lady abbess and the countess to the chapel. Meanwhile some of the count's servants, having gone by land to the chateau for carriages, returned soon after vespers had concluded ; when, the storm being somewhat abated, the count and his family returned home. Blanche was surprised to discover how much the windings of the shore had deceived her concerning the distance of the chateau from the monastery ; whose vesper-bell she had heard on the preceding evening from the windows of the west saloon, and whose towers she would also have seen from thence, had not twilight veiled them.

On their arrival at the chateau, the countess, affecting more fatigue than she really felt, withdrew to her apartment, and the count, with his daughter and Henri, went to the supper-room ; where they had not been long when they heard, in a pause of the gust, a firing of guns ; which the count understand-ing to be signals of distress from some vessel in the storm, went to a window that opened towards the Mediterranean, to observe further ; but the sea was now involved in utter dark-ness, and the loud howlings of the tempest had again overcome every other sound. Blanche, remembering the bark which she had before seen, now joined her father with trembling anxiety. In a few moments the report of guns was again borne along the wind, and as suddenly wafted away ; a tre-mendous burst of thunder followed ; and in the flash that had preceded it, and which seemed to quiver over the whole surface of the waters, a vessel was discovered, tossing amidst the white foam of the waves, at some distance from the shore. Impenetrable dark-ness again involved the scene ; but soon a second flash showed the bark, with one sail unfurled, driving towards the coast. Blanche hung upon her father's arm with looks full of the agony of united terror and pity ; which were unnecessary to awaken the heart of the count, who gazed upon the sea with a piteous expression, and, perceiving that no boat could live in the storm, forbore to send one ; but he gave orders to his people to carry torches out upon the cliff—hoping they might prove a kind of beacon to the vessel, or at least warn the crew of the rocks they were approaching. While Henri went out to direct on what part of the cliffs the lights should appear, Blanche remained with her father at the window, catching every now and then, as the lightnings flashed, a glimpse of the vessel ; and she soon saw with reviving hope the torches flaming on the blackness of night, and, as they waved over the cliffs, casting a red gleam on the gasping billows. When the firing of guns was repeated, the torches were tossed high in the air, as if answering the signal, and the firing was then redoubled; but though the wind bore the sound away, she fancied, as the lightnings glanced, that the vessel was much nearer the shore.

The count's servants were now seen running to and fro on the rocks: some venturing almost to the points of the crags, and bending over, held out their torches fastened to long poles: while others, whose steps could be traced only by the course of the lights, descended the steep and dangerous path that wound to the margin of the sea, and with loud halloos hailed the mariners; whose shrill whistle, and then feeble voices, where heard at intervals mingling with the storm. Sudden shouts from the people on the rocks increased the anxiety of Blanche to an almost intolerable degree; but her suspense concerning the fate of the mariners was soon over, when Henri, running breathless into the room, told that the vessel was anchored in the bay below, but in so shattered a condition, that it was feared she would part before the crew could disembark. The count immediately gave orders for his own boats to assist in bringing them to shore, and that such of these unfortunate strangers as could not be accommodated in the adjacent hamlet, should be entertained at the chateau. Among the latter were Emily St. Aubert, Monsieur du Pont, Ludovico, and Annette; who, having embarked at Leghorn, and reached Marseilles, were from thence crossing the Gulf of Lyons when this storm overtook them. They were received by the count with his usual benignity; who, though Emily wished to have proceeded immediately to the monastery of St. Claire, would not allow her to leave the chateau that night; and, indeed, the terror and fatigue she had suffered would scarcely have permitted her to go farther.

In Monsieur du Pont the count discovered an old acquaintance, and much joy and congratulation passed between them; after which Emily was introduced by name to the count's family, whose hospitable benevolence dissipated the little embarrassment which her situation had occasioned her; and the party were soon seated at the supper-table. The unaffected kindness of Blanche, and the lively joy she expressed on the escape of the strangers, for whom her pity had been so much interested, gradually revived Emily's languid spirits; and Du Pont, relieved from his terrors for her and for himself, felt the full contrast between his late situation on a dark and tremendous ocean, and his present one in a cheerful mansion, where he was surrounded with plenty, elegance, and smiles of welcome.

Annette, meanwhile, in the servants' hall was telling of all the dangers she had encountered, and congratulating herself so heartily upon her own and Ludovico's escape, and on her present comforts, that she often made all that part of the chateau ring with merriment and laughter. Ludovico's spirits were as gay as her own; but he had discretion enough to restrain them, and tried to check hers, though in vain; till her laughter at length ascended to *my lady's* chamber; who sent to inquire what occasioned so much uproar in the chateau, and to command silence.

Emily withdrew early to seek the repose she so much required; but her pillow was long a sleepless one. On this her return to her native country, many interesting remembrances were awakened; all the events and sufferings she had experienced since she quitted it, came in long succession to her fancy, and were chased only by the image of Valancourt; with whom to believe herself once more in the same land, after they had been so long and so distantly separated, gave her emotions of indescribable joy; but which afterwards yielded to anxiety and apprehension, when she considered the long period that had elapsed since any letter had passed between them, and how much might have happened in this interval to affect her future peace. But the thought that Valancourt might be now no more, or, if living, might have forgotten her, was so very terrible to her heart, that she would scarcely suffer herself to pause upon the possibility. She determined to inform him on the following day of her arrival in France; which it was scarcely possible he could know but by a letter from herself: and after soothing her spirits with the hope of soon hearing that he was well and unchanged in his affections, she at length sunk to repose.

CHAPTER XXXVII.

'Oft woo'd the gleam of Cynthia, silver bright,
In cloisters dim, far from the haunts of Folly,
With Freedom by my side, and soft-eyed Melancholy.'

GRAY.

THE Lady Blanche was so much interested for Emily, that upon hearing she was going to reside in the neighbouring convent, she requested the count would invite her to lengthen her stay at the chateau. 'And you know, my dear sir,' added Blanche, 'how delighted I shall be with such a companion; for at present I have no friend to walk or to read with, since Mademoiselle Bearn is my mamma's friend only.'

The count smiled at the youthful simplicity with which his daughter yielded to first impressions; and though he chose to warn her of their danger, he silently applauded the benevolence that could thus readily expand in confidence to a stranger. He had observed Emily with attention on the preceding evening, and was as much pleased with her as it was possible he could be with any person on so short an acquaintance ; the mention made of her by Mons. du Pont had also given him a favourable impression of Emily ; but, extremely cautious as to those whom he introduced to the intimacy of his daughter, he determined, on hearing that the former was no stranger at the convent of St. Claire, to visit the abbess ; and, if her account corresponded with his wish, to invite Emily to pass some time at the chateau. On this subject he was influenced by a consideration of the Lady Blanche's welfare, still more than by either a wish to oblige her, or to befriend the orphan Emily, in whom, however, he felt considerably interested.

On the following morning Emily was too much fatigued to appear ; but Mons. du Pont was at the breakfast-table when the count entered the room ; who pressed him, as his former acquaintance, and the son of a very old friend, to prolong his stay at the chateau —an invitation which Du Pont willingly accepted, since it would allow him to be near Emily ; and though he was not conscious of encouraging a hope that she would ever return his affection, he had not fortitude enough to attempt, at present, to overcome it.

Emily, when she was somewhat recovered, wandered with her new friend over the grounds belonging to the chateau, as much delighted with the surrounding views, as Blanche, in the benevolence of her heart, had wished ; from thence she perceived, beyond the woods, the towers of the monastery, and remarked that it was to this convent she designed to go.

'Ah !' said Blanche with surprise, ' I am but just released from a convent, and would you go into one ? If you could know what pleasure I feel in wandering here at liberty, and in seeing the sky, and the fields, and the woods all around me, I think you would not.' Emily, smiling at the warmth with which the Lady Blanche spoke, observed, 'that she did not mean to confine herself to a convent for life.'

'No, you may not intend it now,' said Blanche ; ' but you do not know to what the nuns may persuade you to consent : I know how kind they will appear, and how happy, for I have seen too much of their art.'

When they returned to the chateau, Lady Blanche conducted Emily to her favourite turret : and from thence they rambled through the ancient chambers, which Blanche had visited before. Emily was amused by observing the structure of these apartments, and the fashion of their old, but still magnificent furniture, and by comparing them with those of the castle of Udolpho, which were yet more antique and grotesque. She was also interested by Dorothée the housekeeper, who attended them ; whose appearance was almost as antique as the objects around her, and who seemed no less interested by Emily ; on whom she frequently gazed with so much deep attention, as scarcely to hear what was said to her.

While Emily looked from one of the casements, she perceived, with surprise, some objects that were familiar to her memory— the fields and woods with the gleaming brook, which she had passed with La Voisin, one evening, soon after the death of Mons. St. Aubert, in her way from the monastery to the cottage ; and she now knew this to be the chateau which he had then avoided, and concerning which he had dropped some remarkable hints.

Shocked by this discovery, yet scarcely knowing why, she mused for some time in silence. and remembered the emotion which her father had betrayed on finding himself so near this mansion, and some other circumstances of his conduct, that now greatly interested her. The music, too, which she had formerly heard, and respecting which La Voisin had given such an odd account, occurred to her ; and desirous of knowing more concerning it, she asked Dorothée whether it returned at midnight, as usual, and whether the musician had yet been discovered.

'Yes, ma'amselle,' replied Dorothée : 'that music is still heard ; but the musician has never been found out, nor ever will, I believe ; though there are some people who can guess.'

'Indeed !' said Emily : 'then why do they not pursue the inquiry ?'

'Ah, young lady ! inquiry enough has been made—but who can pursue a spirit ?'

Emily smiled, and remembering how lately she had suffered herself to be led away by superstition, determined now to resist its contagion ; yet, in spite of her efforts, she felt awe mingled with her curiosity on this subject ; and Blanche, who had hitherto listened in silence, now inquired what this music was, and how long it had been heard.

'Ever since the death of my Lady, madam,' replied Dorothée.

'Why, the place is not haunted, surely ?' said Blanche, between jesting and seriousness.

'I have heard that music almost ever since my dear lady died,' continued Dorothée, 'and never before then. But that is nothing to some things I could tell of.'

'Do, pray, tell them then,' said Lady Blanche, now more in earnest than in jest : 'I am much interested ; for I have heard sister Henriette and sister Sophie, in the convent, tell of such strange appearances which they themselves had witnessed.'

'You never heard, my lady, I suppose, what made us leave the chateau, and go and live in a cottage ?' said Dorothée. 'Never !' replied Blanche with impatience.

'Nor the reason that my lord the Marquis——'
Dorothée checked herself, hesitated, and then endeavoured to change the topic; but the curiosity of Blanche was too much awakened to suffer the subject thus easily to escape her, and she pressed the old housekeeper to proceed with her account: upon whom, however, no entreaties could prevail; and it was evident that she was alarmed for the imprudence into which she had already betrayed herself.

'I perceive,' said Emily smiling, 'that all old mansions are haunted; I am lately come from a place of wonders; but unluckily, since I left it, I have heard almost all of them explained.'

Blanche was silent; Dorothée looked grave, and sighed; and Emily felt herself still inclined to believe more of the wonderful than she chose to acknowledge. Just then she remembered the spectacle she had witnessed in a chamber of Udolpho, and, by an odd kind of coincidence, the alarming words that had met her in the MS. papers which she had destroyed in obedience to the command of her father; and she shuddered at the meaning they seemed to impart, almost as much as at the horrible appearance disclosed by the black veil.

The Lady Blanche, meanwhile, unable to prevail with Dorothée to explain the subject of her late hints, had desired, on reaching the door that terminated the gallery, and which she found fastened on the preceding day, to see the suite of rooms beyond. 'Dear young lady,' said the housekeeper, 'I have told you my reason for not opening them: I have never seen them since my dear lady died; and it would go hard with me to see them now. Pray, madam, do not ask me again.'

'Certainly I will not,' replied Blanche, 'if that is really your objection.'

'Alas! it is,' said the old woman; 'we all loved her well, and I shall always grieve for her. Time runs round!—it is now many years since she died; but I remember everything that happened then, as if it was but yesterday. Many things that have passed of late years are gone quite from my memory; while those so long ago I can see as if in a glass.' She paused; but afterwards, as they walked up the gallery, added of Emily, 'This young lady sometimes brings the late marchioness to my mind: I can remember when she looked just as blooming, and very like her when she smiles. Poor lady! how gay she was when she first came to the chateau!'

'And was she not gay afterwards?' said Blanche.

'Dorothée shook her head; and Emily observed her with eyes strongly expressive of the interest she now felt. 'Let us sit down in this window,' said the Lady Blanche, on reaching the opposite end of the gallery; 'and pray, Dorothée, if it is not painful to you, tell us something more about the marchioness: I

should like to look into the glass you spoke of just now, and see a few of the circumstances which you say often pass over it.'

'No, my lady,' replied Dorothée: 'if you knew as much as I do, you would not; for you would find there a dismal train of them. I often wish I could shut them out, but they will rise to my mind. I see my dear lady on her death-bed—her very look—and remember all she said:—it was a terrible scene!'

'Why was it so terrible?' said Emily with emotion.

'Ah, dear young lady! is not death always terrible?' replied Dorothée.

To some further inquiries of Blanche, Dorothée was silent; and Emily, observing the tears in her eyes, forbore to urge the subject, and endeavoured to withdraw the attention of her young friend to some object in the gardens; where the count with the countess and Monsieur du Pont appearing, they went down to join them.

When he perceived Emily, he advanced to meet her, and presented her to the countess in a manner so benign, that it recalled most powerfully to her mind the idea of her late father; and she felt more gratitude to him than embarrassment towards the countess: who, however, received her with one of those fascinating smiles which her caprice sometimes allowed her to assume, and which was now the result of a conversation the count had held with her concerning Emily. Whatever this might be, or whatever had passed in his conversation with the lady abbess, whom he had just visited, esteem and kindness were strongly apparent in his manner when he addressed Emily; who experienced that sweet emotion which arises from the consciousness of possessing the approbation of the good; for to the count's worth she had been inclined to yield her confidence almost from the first moment in which she had seen him.

Before she could finish her acknowledgments for the hospitality she had received, and mention her design of going immediately to the convent, she was interrupted by an invitation to lengthen her stay at the chateau; which was pressed by the count and the countess, with an appearance of such friendly sincerity that though she much wished to see her old friends at the monastery, and to sigh once more over her father's grave, she consented to remain a few days at the chateau.

To the abbess, however, she immediately wrote mentioning her arrival in Languedoc, and her wish to be received into the convent as a boarder: she also sent letters to Monsieur Quesnel, and to Valancourt, whom she merely informed of her arrival in France; and, as she knew not where the latter might be stationed, she directed her letter to his brother's seat in Gascony.

In the evening Lady Blanche and Monsieur du Pont walked with Emily to the cottage of

La Voisin; which she had now a melancholy pleasure in approaching; for time had softened her grief for the loss of St. Aubert, though it could not annihilate it, and she felt a soothing sadness in indulging the recollections which this scene recalled. La Voisin was still living, and seemed to enjoy as much as formerly the tranquil evening of a blameless life. He was sitting at the door of his cottage, watching some of his grandchildren playing on the grass before him, and now and then, with a laugh or a commendation, encouraging their sports. He immediately recollected Emily, whom he was much pleased to see; and she was as rejoiced to hear that he had not lost one of his family since her departure.

'Yes, ma'amselle,' said the old man, 'we all live merrily together still, thank God! and I believe there is not a happier family to be found in Languedoc than ours.'

Emily did not trust herself in the chamber where St. Aubert died; and after half an hour's conversation with La Voisin and his family, she left the cottage.

During these the first days of her stay at Chateau-le-Blanc, she was often affected by observing the deep but silent melancholy which at times stole over Du Pont; and Emily, pitying the self-delusion which disarmed him of the will to depart, determined to withdraw herself as soon as the respect she owed the Count and Countess De Villefort would permit. The dejection of his friend soon alarmed the anxiety of the count; to whom Du Pont at length confided the secret of his hopeless affection; which, however, the former could only commiserate, though he secretly determined to befriend his suit, if an opportunity of doing so should ever occur. Considering the dangerous situation of Du Pont, he but feebly opposed his intention of leaving Chateau-le-Blanc on the following day, but drew from him a promise of a longer visit when he could return with safety to his peace. Emily herself, though she could not encourage his affection, esteemed him, both for the many virtues he possessed and for the services she had received from him; and it was not without tender emotions of gratitude and pity, that she now saw him depart for his family seat in Gascony; while he took leave of her with a countenance so expressive of love and grief, as to interest the count more warmly in his cause than before.

In a few days Emily also left the chateau; but not before the count and countess had received her promise to repeat her visit very soon; and she was welcomed by the abbess with the same maternal kindness she had formerly experienced, and by the nuns with much expression of regard. The well-known scenes of the convent occasioned her many melancholy recollections; but with these were mingled others, that inspired gratitude for having escaped the various dangers that had

pursued her since she quitted it, and for the good which she yet possessed, and though she once more wept over her father's grave with tears of tender affection, her grief was softened from its former acuteness.

Some time after her return to the monastery, she received a letter from her uncle Monsieur Quesnel, in answer to information that she had arrived in France, and to her inquiries concerning such of her affairs as he had undertaken to conduct during her absence, especially as to the period for which La Vallée had been let: whither it was her wish to return, if it should appear that her income would permit her to do so. The reply of Monsieur Quesnel was cold and formal as she expected, expressing neither concern for the evils she had suffered, nor pleasure that she was now removed from them; nor did he allow the opportunity to pass of reproving her for her rejection of Count Morano, whom he affected still to believe a man of honour and fortune; nor of vehemently declaiming against Montoni, to whom he had always, till now, felt himself to be inferior. On Emily's pecuniary concerns he was not very explicit: he informed her, however, that the term for which La Vallée had been engaged was nearly expired; but, without inviting her to his own house, added, that her circumstances would by no means allow her to reside there, and earnestly advised her to remain for the present in the convent of St. Claire. To her inquiries respecting poor old Theresa, her late father's servant, he gave no answer. In the postscript to his letter, Monsieur Quesnel mentioned M. Motteville, in whose hands the late St. Aubert had placed the chief of his personal property, as being likely to arrange his affairs nearly to the satisfaction of his creditors, and that Emily would recover much more of her fortune than she had formerly reason to expect. The letter also inclosed to Emily an order upon a merchant at Narbonne for a small sum of money.

The tranquillity of the monastery, and the liberty she was suffered to enjoy in wandering among the woods and shores of this delightful province, gradually restored her spirits to their natural tone; except that anxiety would sometimes intrude concerning Valancourt, as the time approached when it was possible that she might receive an answer to her letter.

CHAPTER XXXVIII.

'As when a wave, that from a cloud impends,
And swell'd with tempests, on the ship descends,
White are the decks with foam; the winds, aloud,
Howl o'er the masts and sing through every shroud;
Pale, trembling, tired, the sailors freeze with fears;
And instant death on every wave appears.'
POPE'S HOMER.

THE Lady Blanche, meanwhile, who was left much alone, became impatient for the company of her new friend, whom she wished to observe sharing in the delight she received from the beautiful scenery around. She had now no person to whom she could express her admiration and communicate her pleasures; no eye that sparkled to her smile, or countenance that reflected her happiness; and she became spiritless and pensive. The count, observing her dissatisfaction, readily yielded to her entreaties, and reminded Emily of her promised visit. But the silence of Valancourt which was now prolonged far beyond the period when a letter might have arrived from Estuvière, oppressed Emily with severe anxiety, and, rendering her averse to society, she would willingly have deferred her acceptance of this invitation till her spirits should be relieved. The count and his family, however, pressed to see her; and as the circumstances that prompted her wish for solitude could not be explained, there was an appearance of caprice in her refusal, which she could not persevere in without offending the friends whose esteem she valued. At length, therefore, she returned upon a second visit to Chateau-le-Blanc. Here the friendly manner of Count de Villefort encouraged Emily to mention to him her situation respecting the estates of her late aunt, and to consult him on the means of recovering them. He had little doubt that the law would decide in her favour; and, advising her to apply to it, offered, first, to write to an advocate at Avignon, on whose opinion he thought he could rely. His kindness was gratefully accepted by Emily; who, soothed by the courtesy she daily experienced, would have been once more happy, could she have been assured of Valancourt's welfare and unaltered affection. She had now been above a week at the chateau without receiving intelligence of him; and though she knew that, if he was absent from his brother's residence, it was scarcely probable her letter had yet reached him, she could not forbear to admit doubts and fears that destroyed her peace. Again she would consider of all that might have happened in the long period since her first seclusion at Udolpho; and her mind was sometimes so overwhelmed with an apprehension that Valancourt was no more, or that he lived no longer for her, that the company even of Blanche became intolerably oppressive; and she would sit alone in her apartment for hours together, when the engagements of the family allowed her to do so without incivility.

In one of these solitary hours, she unlocked a little box which contained some letters of Valancourt, with some drawings she had sketched during her stay in Tuscany; the latter of which were no longer interesting to her; but in the letters she now with melancholy indulgence meant to retrace the tenderness that had so often soothed her, and rendered her, for a moment, insensible of the distance which separated her from the writer.

But their effect was now changed: the affection they expressed appealed so forcibly to her heart, when she considered that it had, perhaps, yielded to the powers of time and absence, and even the view of the hand-writing recalled so many painful recollections, that she found herself unable to go through the first she had opened; and sat musing, with her cheek resting on her arm, and tears stealing from her eyes, when old Dorothée entered the room, to inform her that dinner would be ready an hour before the usual time. Emily started on perceiving her, and hastily put up the papers; but not before Dorothée had observed both her agitation and her tears.

'Ah, ma'amselle!' said she, 'you, who are so young,—have you reason for sorrow?'

Emily tried to smile, but was unable to speak.

'Alas, dear young lady! when you come to my age, you will not weep at trifles;—and surely you have nothing serious to grieve you?'

'No, Dorothée; nothing of any consequence,' replied Emily. Dorothée, now stooping to pick up something that had dropped from among the papers, suddenly exclaimed, —'Holy Mary! what is it I see?' and then, trembling, sat down in a chair that stood by the table.

'What is it you do see?' said Emily, alarmed by her manner, and looking round the room.

'It is herself!' said Dorothée; 'her very self! just as she looked a little before she died!'

Emily, still more alarmed, began now to fear that Dorothée was seized with sudden phrensy; but entreated her to explain herself.

'That picture!' said she; 'where did you find it, lady?—it is my blessed mistress herself!'

She laid on the table the miniature which Emily had so long ago found among the papers her father had enjoined her to destroy, and over which she had once seen him shed such tender and affecting tears; and, recollecting all the various circumstances of his conduct, that had long perplexed her, her emotions increased to an excess which deprived her of all power to ask the questions she trembled to have answered; and she could only inquire, whether Dorothée was certain the picture resembled the late marchioness?

'O, ma'amselle!' said she, 'how came it to strike me so the instant I saw it, if it was not my lady's likeness? Ah!' added she, taking up the miniature, 'these are her own blue eyes—looking so sweet and so mild! and there is her very look, such as I have often seen it, when she had sat thinking for a long while; and then the tears would often steal down her cheeks,—but she never would complain! It was that look, so meek, as it were, and resigned, that used to break my heart, and make me love her so!'

'Dorothée!' said Emily solemnly, I am

interested in the cause of that grief—more so, perhaps, than you may imagine ; and I entreat that you will no longer refuse to indulge my curiosity—it is not a common one.'

As Emily said this, she remembered the papers with which the picture had been found, and had scarcely a doubt that they had concerned the Marchioness de Villeroi : but with this supposition came a scruple, whether she ought to inquire further on a subject which might prove to be the same that her father had so carefully endeavoured to conceal. Her curiosity concerning the marchioness, powerful as it was, it is probable she would now have resisted, as she had formerly done on unwarily observing the few terrible words in the papers, which had never since been erased from her memory, had she been certain that the history of that lady was the subject of those papers, or that such simple particulars only as it was probable Dorothée could relate, were included in her father's command. What was known to her, could be no secret to many other persons ; and since it appeared very unlikely that St. Aubert should attempt to conceal what Emily might learn by ordinary means, she at length concluded that, if the papers had related to the story of the marchioness, it was not those circumstances of it which Dorothée could disclose, that he had thought sufficiently important to wish to have concealed : she therefore no longer hesitated to make the inquiries that might lead to the gratification of her curiosity.

'Ah, ma'amselle !' said Dorothée, 'it is a sad story, and cannot be told now ;—but what am I saying?—I never will tell it. Many years have passed since it happened ; and I never loved to talk of the marchioness to any body but my husband. He lived in the family at that time, as well as myself, and he knew many particulars from me which nobody else did ; for I was about the person of my lady in her last illness, and saw and heard as much, or more than my lord himself. Sweet saint ! how patient she was ! When she died, I thought I could have died with her.'

'Dorothée,' said Emily, interrupting her, 'what you shall tell, you may depend upon it, shall never be disclosed by me. I have, I repeat it, particular reasons for wishing to be informed on this subject, and am willing to bind myself, in the most solemn manner, never to mention what you shall wish me to conceal.'

Dorothée seemed surprised at the earnest- ness of Emily's manner, and, after regard- ing her for some moments in silence, said, 'Young lady ! that look of yours pleads for you—it is so like my dear mistress's, that I can almost fancy I see her before me : if you were her daughter, you could not remind me of her more. But dinner will be ready ; had you not better go down?'

'You will first promise to grant my request,' said Emily

'And ought not you first to tell me, ma'amselle, how this picture fell into your hands, and the reasons you say you have for curiosity about my lady ?'

'Why, no, Dorothée,' replied Emily, recol- lecting herself ; 'I have also particular reasons for observing silence on these subjects, at least till I know further ; and remember I do not promise ever to speak upon them : therefore, do not let me induce you to satisfy my curiosity, from an expectation that I shall gratify yours. What I may judge proper to conceal does not concern myself alone, or I should have less scruple in revealing it : let a confidence in my honour alone persuade you to disclose what I request.'

'Well, lady !' replied Dorothée after a long pause, during which her eyes were fixed upon Emily, 'you seem so much interested—and this picture, and that face of yours, make me think you have some reason to be so,—that I will trust you, and tell some things that I never told before to anybody but my husband, though there are people who have suspected as much. I will tell you the particulars of my lady's death, too, and some of my own sus- picions ; but you must first promise me, by all the saints———'

Emily, interrupting her, solemnly promised never to reveal what should be confided to her, without Dorothée's consent.

'But there is the horn, ma'amselle, sound- ing for dinner,' said Dorothée : 'I must be gone.'

'When shall I see you again ?' inquired Emily.

Dorothée mused, and then replied, 'Why, madam, it may make people curious, if it is known I am so much in your apartment ; and that I should be sorry for ; so I will come when I am least likely to be observed. I have little leisure in the day, and I shall have a good deal to say ; so, if you please ma'am, I will come when the family are all in bed.'

'That will suit me very well,' replied Emily ; 'remember then, to-night——'

'Aye, that is well remembered,' said Dorothée : 'I fear I cannot come to-night, madam ; for there will be the dance of the vintage, and it will be late before the servants go to rest ; for when they once set in to dance, they will keep it up, in the cool of the air, till morning : at least, it used to be so in my time.'

'Ah ! is it the dance of the vintage ?' said Emily with a deep sigh, remembering that it was on the evening of this festival, in the pre- ceding year, that St. Aubert and herself had arrived in the neighbourhood of Chateau-le- Blanc. She paused a moment, overcome by the sudden recollection ; and then, recovering herself, added—' But this dance is in the open woods ; you, therefore, will not be wanted, and can easily come to me.'

Dorothée replied that she had been accustomed to be present at the dance of the vintage, and she did not wish to be absent now : ' But if I can get away, madam, I will,' said she.

Emily then hastened to the dining-room, where the count conducted himself with the courtesy which is inseparable from true dignity, and of which the countess frequently practised little, though her manner to Emily was an exception to her usual habit. But if she retained few of the ornamental virtues, she cherished other qualities which she seemed to consider invaluable : she had dismissed the grace of modesty ; but then she knew perfectly well how to manage the stare of assurance : her manners had little of the tempered sweetness which is necessary to render the female character interesting ; but she could occasionally throw into them an affectation of spirits which seemed to triumph over every person who approached her. In the country, however, she generally affected an elegant languor, that persuaded her almost to faint when her favourite read to her a story of fictitious sorrow ; but her countenance suffered no change when living objects of distress solicited her charity, and her heart beat with no transport to the thought of giving them instant relief : she was a stranger to the highest luxury of which, perhaps, the human mind can be sensible—for her benevolence had never yet called smiles upon the face of misery.

In the evening, the count with all his family, except the countess and Mademoiselle Bearn, went to the woods to witness the festivity of the peasants. The scene was in a glade; where the trees, opening, formed a circle round the turf they highly overshadowed. Between their branches, vines loaded with ripe clusters were hung in gay festoons ; beneath were tables with fruit, wine, cheese, and other rural fare, and seats for the count and his family. At a little distance were benches for the elder peasants ; few of whom, however, could forbear to join the jocund dance, which began soon after sunset ; when several of sixty tripped it with almost as much glee and airy lightness as those of sixteen.

The musicians, who sat carelessly on the grass at the foot of a tree, seemed inspired by the sound of their own instruments, which were chiefly flutes and a kind of long guitar. Behind stood a boy flourishing a tambourine, and dancing a solo, except that, as he sometimes gaily tossed the instrument, he tripped among the other dancers : when his antic gestures called forth a broader laugh, and heightened the rustic spirit of the scene.

The count was highly delighted with the happiness he witnessed, to which his bounty had largely contributed ; and the Lady Blanche joined the dance with a young gentleman of her father's party. Du Pont requested Emily's hand ; but her spirits were too much depressed to permit her to engage in the present festivity, which called to her remembrance that of the preceding year, when St. Aubert was living, and of the melancholy scenes which had immediately followed it.

Overcome by these recollections, she at length left the spot and walked slowly into the woods, where the softened music, floating at a distance, soothed her melancholy mind. The moon threw a mellow light among the foliage ; the air was balmy and cool ; and Emily, lost in thought, strolled on without observing whither, till she perceived the sound sinking afar off, and an awful stillness around her, except that, sometimes, the nightingale beguiled the silence with

' Liquid notes, that close the eye of day.'

At length she found herself near the avenue which, on the night of her father's arrival, Michael had attempted to pass in search of a house, which was still nearly as wild and desolate as it had then appeared ; for the count had been so much engaged in directing other improvements, that he had neglected to give orders concerning this extensive approach : and the road was yet broken, and the trees overloaded with their own luxuriance.

As she stood surveying it, and remembering the emotions which she had formerly suffered there, she suddenly recollected the figure that had been seen stealing among the trees, and which had returned no answer to Michael's repeated calls ; and she experienced somewhat of the fear that had then assailed her, for it did not appear improbable that these deep woods were occasionally the haunt of banditti ; she therefore turned back ; and was hastily pursuing her way to the dancers, when she heard steps approaching from the avenue ; and being still beyond the call of the peasants on the green, for she could neither hear their voices nor their music, she quickened her pace : but the persons following gained fast upon her ; and at length distinguishing the voice of Henri, she walked leisurely till he came up. He expressed some surprise at meeting her so far from the company : and on her saying that the pleasant moonlight had beguiled her to walk further than she intended, an exclamation burst from the lips of his companion, and she thought she heard Valancourt speak ! It was indeed he ! and the meeting was such as may be imagined, between persons so affectionate, and so long separated, as they had been.

In the joy of these moments Emily forgot all her past sufferings ; and Valancourt seemed to have forgotten that any person but Emily existed ; while Henri was a silent and astonished spectator of the scene.

Valancourt asked a thousand questions concerning herself and Montoni, which there was no time to answer ; but she learned that her letter had been forwarded to Paris, while he was on the way to Gascony; where, however, at length, it informed him of her arrival in France; and he had immediately set out for Languedoc. On reaching the monastery whence she had dated this letter, he found, to his extreme disappointment, that the gates were already closed for the night; and believing that he should not see Emily till the morrow, he was returning to his little inn, with the intention of writing to her, when he was overtaken by Henri, with whom he had been intimate at Paris, and was led to her, whom he was secretly lamenting that he should not see till the following day.

Emily, with Valancourt and Henri, now returned to the green; where the latter presented Valancourt to the count; who, she fancied, received him with less than his usual benignity, though it appeared that they were not strangers to each other. He was invited, however, to partake of the diversions of the evening; and when he had paid his respects to the count, and while the dancers continued their festivity, he seated himself by Emily, and conversed without restraint. The lights which were hung among the trees under which they sat, allowed her a more perfect view of the countenance she had so frequently in absence endeavoured to recollect, and she perceived with some regret that it was not the same as when last she saw it. There was all its wonted intelligence and fire; but it had lost much of the simplicity, and somewhat of the open benevolence, that used to characterise it. Still, however, it was an interesting countenance; but Emily thought she perceived, at intervals, anxiety contract, and melancholy fix, the features of Valancourt: sometimes, too, he fell into a momentary musing, and then appeared anxious to dissipate thought; while at others, as he fixed his eyes on Emily, a sudden kind of horror seemed to cross his mind. In her he perceived the same goodness and beautiful simplicity that had charmed him on their first acquaintance. The bloom of her countenance was somewhat faded, but all its sweetness remained; and it was rendered more interesting than ever, by the faint expression of melancholy that sometimes mingled with her smile.

At his request she related the most important circumstances that had occurred to her since she left France; and emotions of pity and indignation alternately prevailed in his mind, when he heard how much she had suffered from the villany of Montoni. More than once, when she was speaking of his conduct, of which the guilt was rather softened than exaggerated by her representation, he started from his seat and walked away, apparently overcome as much by self-accusation as by resentment. Her sufferings alone were mentioned in the few words which he could address to her; and he listened not to the account, which she was careful to give as distinctly as possible, of the present loss of Madame Montoni's estates, and of the little reason there was to expect their restoration. At length Valancourt remained lost in thought, and then some secret cause seemed to overcome him with anguish. Again he abruptly left her. When he returned she perceived that he had been weeping, and tenderly begged that he would compose himself. 'My sufferings are all passed now,' said she: 'for I have escaped from the tyranny of Montoni; and I see you well—let me also see you happy.'

Valancourt was more agitated than before. 'I am unworthy of you, Emily,' said he; 'I am unworthy of you;'—words by his manner of uttering which Emily was then more shocked than by their import. She fixed on him a mournful and inquiring eye. 'Do not look thus on me,' said he, turning away, and pressing her hand: 'I cannot bear those looks.'

'I would ask,' said Emily in a gentle but agitated voice, 'the meaning of your words, but I perceive that the question would distress you now. Let us talk on other subjects. To-morrow, perhaps, you may be more composed. Observe those moonlight woods, and the towers which appear obscurely in the perspective. You used to be a great admirer of landscape; and I have heard you say that the faculty of deriving consolation under misfortune, from the sublime prospects which neither oppression nor poverty withholds from us, was the peculiar blessing of the innocent.' Valancourt was deeply affected. 'Yes,' replied he; 'I had once a taste for innocent and elegant delights—I had once an uncorrupted heart!' Then checking himself, he added, 'Do you remember our journey together in the Pyrenees?'

'Can I forget it?' said Emily.'———'Would that I could!' he replied;—'that was the happiest period of my life; I then loved, with enthusiasm, whatever was truly great or good.' It was some time before Emily could repress her tears, and try to command her emotions. 'If you wish to forget that journey,' said she, 'it must certainly be my wish to forget it also.' She paused, and then added, 'You make me very uneasy; but this is not the time for further inquiry. Yet how can I bear to believe, even for a moment, that you are less worthy of my esteem than formerly? I have still sufficient confidence in your candour to believe that, when I shall ask for an explanation, you will give it me.' 'Yes,' said Valancourt; 'yes, Emily; I have not yet lost my candour: if I had, I could better have disguised my emotions on learning what were your sufferings—your virtues; while I—but I will say no more. I did not mean to have said even so much—I have been surprised into the self-accusation. Tell me, Emily, that you will not forget that journey—will not wish to forget it—and I shall be tranquil. I would not lose the remembrance of it for the whole earth.'

'How contradictory is this!' said Emily; 'but we may be overheard. My recollection of it shall depend upon yours: I will endeavour to forget, or to recollect it, as you may do. Let us join the count.' 'Tell me first,' said Valancourt, 'that you forgive the uneasiness I have occasioned you this evening, and that you will still love me.' 'I sincerely forgive you,' replied Emily. 'You best know whether I shall continue to love you, for you know whether you deserve my esteem. At present, I will believe that you do. It is unnecessary to say,' added she, observing his dejection, 'how much pain it would give me to believe otherwise.—The young lady who approaches is the count's daughter.'

Valancourt and Emily now joined the Lady Blanche, and the party soon after sat down with the count, his son, and the Chevalier du Pont, at a banquet spread under a gay awning beneath the trees. At a table also were seated several of the most venerable of the count's tenants; and it was a festive repast—to all but Valancourt and Emily. When the count retired to the chateau, he did not invite Valancourt to accompany him; who, therefore, took leave of Emily, and retired to his solitary inn for the night: meanwhile, she soon withdrew to her own apartment, where she mused, with deep anxiety and concern, on his behaviour, and on the count's reception of him. Her attention was thus so wholly engaged, that she forgot Dorothée and her appointment, till morning was far advanced; when, knowing that the good old woman would not come, she retired for a few hours to repose.

On the following day, when the count had accidentally joined Emily in one of the walks, they talked of the festival of the preceding evening; and this led him to a mention of Valancourt. 'That is a young man of talent,' said he; 'you were formerly acquainted with him, I perceive?' Emily said that she was. 'He was introduced to me at Paris,' said the count, 'and I was much pleased with him on our first acquaintance.' He paused, and Emily trembled, between the desire of hearing more and the fear of showing the count that she felt an interest on the subject. 'May I ask,' said he at length, 'how long you have known Monsieur Valancourt?' 'Will you allow me to ask your reason for the question, sir?' said she; 'and I will answer it immediately.' 'Certainly,' said the count; 'that is but just: I will tell you. I cannot but perceive that Monsieur Valancourt admires you. In that, however, there is nothing extraordinary: every person who sees you must do the same. I am above using common-place compliments: I speak with sincerity. What I fear, is, that he is a favoured admirer!'——'Why do you fear it, sir?' said Emily, endeavouring to conceal

her emotion.—'Because,' replied the count, 'I think him not worthy of your favour.' Emily, greatly agitated, entreated further explanation. 'I will give it,' said he, 'if you will believe that nothing but a strong interest in your welfare could induce me to hazard that assertion.'—'I must believe so, sir,' replied Emily.

'But let us rest under these trees,' continued the count, observing the paleness of her countenance: 'here is a seat—you are fatigued.' They sat down; and the count proceeded—'Many young ladies, circumstanced as you are, would think my conduct on this occasion, and on so short an acquaintance, impertinent, instead of friendly. From what I have observed of your temper and understanding, I do not fear such a return from you: our acquaintance has been short, but long enough to make me esteem you, and feel a lively interest in your happiness. You deserve to be very happy, and I trust you will be so.' Emily sighed softly, and bowed her thanks. The count paused again. 'I am unpleasantly circumstanced,' said he; 'but an opportunity of rendering you important service shall overcome inferior considerations. Will you inform me of the manner of your first acquaintance with the Chevalier Valancourt, if the subject is not too painful?'

Emily briefly related the accident of their meeting in the presence of her father; and then so earnestly entreated the count not to hesitate in declaring what he knew, that he perceived the violent emotion against which she was contending, and, regarding her with a look of tender compassion, considered how he might communicate his information with the least pain to his anxious auditor.

'The chevalier and my son,' said he, 'were introduced to each other at the table of a brother officer; at whose house I also met him, and invited him to my own whenever he should be disengaged. I did not then know that he had formed an acquaintance with a set of men, a disgrace to their species, who live by plunder, and pass their lives in continual debauchery. I knew several of the chevalier's family resident at Paris, and considered them as sufficient pledges for his introduction to my own. But you are ill; I will leave the subject.' 'No, sir,' said Emily; 'I beg you will proceed: I am only distressed.'—'Only!' said the count with emphasis. 'However, I will proceed. I soon learned that these, his associates, had drawn him into a course of dissipation, from which he appeared to have neither the power nor the inclination to extricate himself. He lost large sums at the gaming-table; he became infatuated with play; and was ruined. I spoke tenderly of this to his friends, who assured me that they had remonstrated with him till they were weary. I afterwards learned that, in consideration of his talents for play, which were generally successful when unopposed by the icks of villany—that in consideration of ese, the party had initiated him into the crets of their trade, and allotted him a share their profits.'—'Impossible!' said Emily ddenly ;—'but pardon me, sir, I scarcely now what I say ;—allow for the distress of y mind. I must, indeed I must, believe that u have not been truly informed : the cheva-r had doubtless enemies who misrepresented m.'—'I should be most happy to believe ,' replied the count ; 'but I cannot. No-ing short of conviction, and a regard for ur welfare, could have urged me to repeat ese unpleasant reports.'

Emily was silent. She recollected Valan-urt's sayings on the preceding evening, iich discovered the pangs of self-reproach, d seemed to confirm all that the count had ated. Yet she had not fortitude enough to re conviction ; her heart was overwhelmed th anguish at the mere suspicion of his guilt, d she could not endure a belief of it. After ong silence the count said, ' I perceive, and 1 allow for your want of conviction. It is cessary I should give some proof of what I ve asserted ; but this I cannot do, without bjecting one who is very dear to me to dan-r.'—'What is the danger you apprehend, ?' said Emily. 'If I can prevent it, you y safely confide in my honour.'—'On your nour I am certain I can rely,' said the nt ; 'but can I trust your fortitude? Do 1 think you can resist the solicitation of a oured admirer when he pleads in affliction the name of one who has robbed him of a ssing?'—'I shall not be exposed to such a iptation, sir,' said Emily with modest pride ; r I cannot favour one whom I must no ger esteem. I, however, readily give my rd.' Tears in the meantime contradicted ' first assertion ; and she felt that time and ort only could eradicate an affection which i been formed on virtuous esteem, and rished by habit and difficulty.

I will trust you then,' said the count ; 'for viction is necessary to your future peace, I cannot, I perceive, be obtained without confidence. My son has too often been an -witness of the chevalier's ill conduct ; he s very near being drawn in by it : he was, eed, drawn in to the commission of many ies, but I rescued him from guilt and de-iction. Judge then, Mademoiselle St. Au-t, whether a father, who had nearly lost only son by the example of the chevalier, not, from conviction, reason to warn se whom he esteems against trusting their piness in such hands. I have myself seen chevalier engaged in deep play with men om I almost shuddered to look upon. If still doubt, I will refer you to my son.'

I must not doubt what you have yourself iessed,' replied Emily, sinking with grief ; what you assert. But the chevalier has, haps, been drawn only into a transient folly, which he may never repeat. If you had known the justness of his former principles, you would allow for my present incredulity.'

'Alas!' observed the count, 'it is difficult to believe that which will make us wretched. But I will not soothe you by flattering and false hopes. We all know how fascinating the vice of gaming is, and how difficult it is also to conquer habit. The chevalier might, perhaps, reform for a while ; but he would soon relapse into dissipation—for I fear not only the bonds of habit would be powerful, but that his morals are corrupted. And—why should I conceal from you that play is not his only vice ?—he appears to have a taste for every vicious pleasure.'

The count hesitated, and paused ; while Emily endeavoured to support herself, as with increasing perturbation she expected what he might further say. A long pause of silence ensued, during which he was visibly agitated. At length he said, 'It would be a cruel delicacy that could prevail with me to be silent—and I will inform you that the che-valier's extravagance has brought him twice into the prisons of Paris ; from whence he was last extricated, as I was told upon authority which I cannot doubt, by a well-known Parisian countess, with whom he continued to reside when I left Paris.'

He paused again: and, looking at Emily, perceived her countenance change, and that she was falling from the seat : he caught her ; but she had fainted, and he called loud for aid. They were, however, beyond the hear-ing of his servants at the chateau, and he feared to leave her while he went thither for assistance, yet knew not how otherwise to obtain it ; till a fountain at no great distance caught his eye, and he endeavoured to support Emily against the tree under which she had been sitting, while he went thither for water. Again was he perplexed, for he had nothing near him in which water could be brought ; but while, with increased anxiety, he watched her, he thought he perceived in her coun-tenance symptoms of returning life.

It was long, however, before she revived, and then she found herself supported—not by the count—but by Valancourt, who was ob-serving her with looks of earnest apprehension, and who now spoke to her in a tone tremulous with his anxiety. At the sound of his well-known voice, she raised her eyes ; but presently closed them, and a faintness again came over her.

The count, with a look somewhat stern, waved him to withdraw ; but he only sighed heavily, and called on the name of Emily, as he again held the water that had been brought to her lips. On the count's repeating his action, and accompanying it with words, Valancourt answered him with a look of deep resentment, and refused to leave the place till she should revive, or to resign her for a mo-

Yes, you are still my own Emily——let me believe those tears that tell me so!'

Emily now made an effort to recover her firmness, and, hastily drying them, 'Yes,' said she, 'I do pity you—I weep for you—but ought I to think of you with affection? You may remember that yester evening I said I had still sufficient confidence in your candour to believe, that when I should request an explanation of your words ' you would give it. This explanation is now unnecessary, I understand them too well : but prove, at least, that your candour is deserving of the confidence I give it, when I ask you, whether you are conscious of being the same estimable Valancourt—whom I once loved.'

'Once loved !' cried he—' the same—the same !' He paused in extreme emotion, and then added, in a voice at once solemn and dejected,—' No—I am not the same !—I am lost—I am no longer worthy of you !'

He again concealed his face. Emily was too much affected by this honest confession to reply immediately ; and while she struggled to overcome the pleadings of her heart, and to act with the decisive firmness which was necessary for her future peace, she perceived all the danger of trusting long to her resolution in the presence of Valancourt, and was anxious to conclude an interview that tortured them both : yet when she considered that this was probably their last meeting, her fortitude sunk at once, and she experienced only emotions of tenderness and of despondency.

Valancourt, meanwhile, lost in those of remorse and grief, which he had neither the power nor the will to express, sat insensible almost of the presence of Emily, his features still concealed, and his breast agitated by convulsive sighs.

'Spare me the necessity,' said Emily, recollecting her fortitude, ' spare me the necessity of mentioning those circumstances of your conduct which oblige me to break our connection for ever. We must part—I now see you for the last time.'

'Impossible !' cried Valancourt, roused from his deep silence ; ' You cannot mean what you say !—you cannot mean to throw me from you for ever !'

'We must part,' repeated Emily with emphasis—' and that for ever ! Your own conduct has made this necessary.'

'This is the count's determination,' said he haughtily, ' not yours, and I shall inquire by what authority he interferes between us.' He now rose, and walked about the room in great emotion.

'Let me save you from this error,' said Emily not less agitated—' it is my determination, and, if you reflect a moment on your late conduct, you will perceive that my future peace requires it.'

' Your future peace requires that we should part—part for ever !' said Valancourt : ' How little did I ever expect to hear you say so !'

'And how little did I expect that it would be necessary for me to say so !' rejoined Emily, while her voice softened into tenderness, and her tears flowed again.—'That you —you, Valancourt, would ever fall from my esteem !'

He was silent a moment, as if overwhelmed by the consciousness of no longer deserving this esteem, as well as the certainty of having lost it ; and then, with impassioned grief, lamented the criminality of his late conduct, and the misery to which it had reduced him, till, overcome by a recollection of the past and a conviction of the future, he burst into tears, and uttered only deep and broken sighs.

The remorse he had expressed, and the distress he suffered, could not be witnessed by Emily with indifference ; and had she not called to her recollection all the circumstances of which Count de Villefort had informed her, and all he had said of the danger of confiding in repentance formed under the influence of passion, she might perhaps have trusted to the assurances of her heart, and have forgotten his misconduct in the tenderness which that repentance excited.

Valancourt, returning to the chair beside her, at length said, in a subdued voice, ' 'Tis true, I am fallen—fallen from my own esteem ! but could you, Emily, so soon, so suddenly resign, if you had not before ceased to love me, or, if your conduct was not governed by the designs, I will say the selfish designs, of another person? Would you not otherwise be willing to hope for my reformation—and could you bear, by estranging me from you, to abandon me to misery—to myself !'—Emily wept aloud.—' No, Emily—no—you would not do this if you still loved me. You would find your own happiness in saving mine.'

' There are too many probabilities against that hope,' said Emily, ' to justify me in trusting the comfort of my whole life to it. May I not also ask, whether you could wish me to do this if you really loved me ?'

' Really loved you !' exclaimed Valancourt —' is it possible you can doubt my love? Yet it is reasonable that you should do so, since you see that I am less ready to suffer the horror of parting with you, than that of involving you in my ruin. Yes, Emily—I am ruined—irreparably ruined—I am involved in debts which I can never discharge !' Valancourt's look, which was wild as he spoke this, soon settled into an expression of gloomy despair ; and Emily, while she was compelled to admire his sincerity, saw, with unutterable anguish, new reasons for fear in the suddenness of his feelings, and the extent of the misery in which they might involve him. After some minutes, she seemed to contend

;ainst her grief, and to struggle for fortitude conclude the interview. 'I will not pro-ng these moments,' said she, 'by a conversa-on which can answer no good purpose. ılancourt, farewell.'

'You are not going?' said he wildly, inter-pting her—'You will not leave me thus-u will not abandon me even before my mind s suggested any possibility of compromise tween the last indulgence of my despair and e endurance of my loss!' Emily was terri-d by the sternness of his look, and said in oothing voice, 'You have yourself acknow-lged that it is necessary we should part :—if u wish that I should believe you love me, u will repeat the acknowledgement.'—fever, never,' cried he—'I was distracted en I made it. O! Emily—this is too much; hough you are not deceived as to my faults, a must be deluded into this exasperation iinst them. The count is the barrier ween us ; but he shall not long remain so.' You are indeed distracted,' said Emily, ie count is not your enemy; on the con-ry he is my friend, and that might in some ree induce you to consider him as yours.' Your friend!' said Valancourt hastily : ow long has he been your friend, that he so easily make you forget your lover? is it he who recommended to your favour Monsieur du Pont, who, you say, accom-ied you from Italy, and who, I say, has en your affections? But I have no right question you ;—you are your own mistress. Pont, perhaps, may not long triumph over fallen fortunes!' Emily, more frightened a before by the frantic looks of Valan-rt, said in a tone scarcely audible, 'For iven's sake be reasonable—be composed ! nsieur du Pont is not your rival, nor is the nt his advocate. You have no rival ; nor, :pt yourself, an enemy. My heart is ng with anguish, which must increase le your frantic behaviour shows me more a ever, that you are no longer the Valan--t I have been accustomed to love.'

:e made no reply, but sat with his arms ed on the table, and his face concealed by ands ; while Emily stood silent and trem-3, wretched for herself, and dreading to e him in this state of mind.

O excess of misery!' he suddenly ex-ned, 'that I can never lament my suffer-, without accusing myself, nor remember without recollecting the folly and the by which I have lost you ! Why was I ed to Paris, and why did I yield to allure-ts, which were to make me despicable for ? O! why cannot I look back, without ruption, to those days of innocence and e, the days of our early love?'—The llection seemed to melt his heart, and the :y of despair yielded to tears. After a pause, turning towards her and taking ıand, he said, in a softened voice, 'Emily,

can you bear that we should part—can you resolve to give up a heart that loves you like mine—a heart which, though it has erred—widely erred—is not irretrievable from error, as, you well know, it never can be retrievable from love?' Emily made no reply but with her tears. 'Can you,' continued he, 'can you forget all our former days of happiness and confidence—when I had not a thought that I might wish to conceal it from you—when I had no taste—no pleasures, in which you did not participate?'

'O do not lead me to the remembrance of those days,' said Emily, unless you can teach me to be insensible to the present. I do not mean to reproach you ; if I did, I should be spared these tears ; but why will you render your present sufferings more conspicuous, by contrasting them with your former virtues?'

'Those virtues,' said Valancourt, 'might perhaps again be mine, if your affection, which nurtured them, was unchanged : but I fear, indeed—I see that you can no longer love ; else the happy hours which we have passed together would plead for me, and you could not look back upon them unmoved. Yet why should I torture myself with the re-membrance—why do I linger here? Am I not ruined—would it not be madness to involve you in my misfortunes, even if your heart was still my own? I will not distress you further. Yet, before I go, added he in a solemn voice, let me repeat, that whatever may be my destiny—whatever I may be doomed to suffer, I must always love you—most fondly love you ! I am going, Emily, I am going to leave you—to leave you for ever!' As he spoke the last words, his voice trembled, and he threw himself again into the chair from which he had risen. Emily was utterly unable to leave the room, or to say farewell. All impression of his criminal conduct and almost of his follies was obliterated from her mind, and she was sensible only of pity and grief.

'My fortitude is gone,' said Valancourt at length ; 'I can no longer even struggle to re-call it. I cannot now leave you—I cannot bid you an eternal farewell : say, at least, that you will see me once again.' Emily's heart was somewhat relieved by the request, and she endeavoured to believe that she ought not to refuse it. Yet she was embarrassed by recollecting that she was a visitor in the house of the count, who could not be pleased by the return of Valancourt. Other considera-tions, however, soon overcame this ; and she granted his request, on the condition that he would neither think of the count as his enemy, nor Du Pont as his rival. He then left her, with a heart so much lightened by this short respite, that he almost lost every former sense of misfortune.

Emily withdrew to her own room that she might compose her spirits and remove the traces of her tears, which would encouragthe censorious remarks of the countess and her favourite, as well as excite the curiosity of the rest of the family. She found it, however, impossible to tranquillize her mind, from which she could not expel the remembrance of the late scene with Valancourt, or the consciousness that she was to see him again on the morrow. This meeting now appeared more terrible to her than the last; for the ingenuous confession he had made of his ill conduct and his embarrassed circumstances, with the strength and tenderness of affection which this confession discovered, had deeply impressed her, and, in spite of all she had heard and believed to his disadvantage, her esteem began to return. It frequently appeared to her impossible that he could have been guilty of the depravities reported of him, which, if not inconsistent with his warmth and impetuosity, were entirely so with his candour and sensibility. Whatever was the criminality which had given rise to the reports, she could not now believe them to be wholly true, nor that his heart was finally closed against the charms of virtue. The deep consciousness which he felt, as well as expressed, of his errors, seemed to justify the opinion; and, as she understood not the instability of youthful dispositions, when opposed by habit, and that professions frequently deceive those who make, as well as those who hear them, she might have yielded to the flattering persuasions of her own heart and the pleadings of Valancourt, had she not been guided by the superior prudence of the count. He represented to her in a clear light the danger of her present situation, that of listening to promises of amendment made under the influence of strong passion, and the slight hope which could attach to a connexion, whose chance of happiness rested upon the retrieval of ruined circumstances and the reform of corrupted habits. On these accounts he lamented that Emily had consented to a second interview; for he saw how much it would shake her resolution, and increase the difficulty of her conquest.

Her mind was now so entirely occupied by nearer interests, that she forgot the old housekeeper, and the promised history which so lately had excited her curiosity, but which Dorothée was probably not very anxious to disclose; for night came, the hours passed, and she did not appear in Emily's chamber. With the latter it was a sleepless and dismal night: the more she suffered her memory to dwell on the late scene with Valancourt, the more her resolution declined; and she was obliged to recollect all the arguments which the count had made use of to strengthen it, and all the precepts which she had received from her deceased father on the subject of self-command, to enable her to act with prudence and dignity on this the most severe occasion of her life. There were moments when all her fortitude forsook her; and when, remembering the confidence of former times, she thought it impossible that she could renounce Valancourt. His reformation then appeared certain; the arguments of Count de Villefort were forgotten; she readily believed all she wished, and was willing to encounter any evil, rather than that of an immediate separation.

Thus passed the night in ineffectual struggles between affection and reason, and she rose in the morning with a mind weakened and irresolute, and a frame trembling with illness.

—

CHAPTER XL.

'Come, weep with me;—past hope, past cure, past help.'
                                ROMEO AND JULIET.

VALANCOURT, meanwhile, suffered the tortures of remorse and despair. The sight of Emily had renewed all the ardour with which he first loved her, and which had suffered a temporary abatement from absence and the passing scenes of busy life. When, on the receipt of her letter, he set out for Languedoc, he then knew that his own folly had involved him in ruin, and it was no part of his design to conceal this from her. But he lamented only the delay which his ill conduct must give to their marriage, and did not foresee that the information could induce her to break their connexion for ever. While the prospect of this separation overwhelmed his mind, before stung with self-reproach, he awaited their second interview in a state little short of distraction, yet was still inclined to hope that his pleadings might prevail upon her not to exact it. In the morning he sent to know at what hour she would see him; and his note arrived when she was with the count, who had sought an opportunity of again conversing with her of Valancourt; for he perceived the extreme distress of her mind, and feared more than ever that her fortitude would desert her. Emily having dismissed the messenger, the count returned to the subject of their late conversation, urging his fear of Valancourt's entreaties, and again pointing out to her the lengthened misery that must ensue if she should refuse to encounter some present uneasiness. His repeated arguments could, indeed, alone have protected her from the affection she still felt for Valancourt, and she resolved to be governed by them.

The hour of interview at length arrived. Emily went to it at least with composure of manner; but Valancourt was so much agitated, that he could not speak for several minutes, and his first words were alternately those of lamentation, entreaty, and self-reproach. Afterwards he said, 'Emily, I have loved you—I do love you better than my life; but I am ruined by my own conduct. Yet

I would seek to entangle you in a connexion that must be miserable for you, rather than subject myself to the punishment which is my due—the loss of you. I am a wretch, but I will be a villain no longer. I will not endeavour to shake your resolution by the pleadings of a selfish passion. I resign you, Emily, and will endeavour to find consolation in considering that, though I am miserable, you, at least, may be happy. The merit of the sacrifice is, indeed, not my own, for I should never have attained strength of mind to surrender you, if your prudence had not demanded it.'

He paused a moment, while Emily attempted to conceal the tears which came to her eyes. She would have said, 'You speak now as you were wont to do;' but she checked herself.—'Forgive me, Emily,' said he, 'all the sufferings I have occasioned you, and sometimes, when you think of the wretched Valancourt, remember that his only consolation would be to believe, that you are no longer unhappy by his folly.' The tears now fell fast upon her cheek, and he was relapsing into the phrensy of despair, when Emily endeavoured to recall her fortitude, and to terminate an interview which only seemed to increase the distress of both. Perceiving her tears, and that she was rising to go, Valancourt struggled once more to overcome his own feelings and to soothe hers. 'The remembrance of this sorrow,' said he, 'shall in future be my protection. O! never again will example or temptation have power to seduce me to evil, exalted as I shall be by the recollection of your grief for me.'

Emily was somewhat comforted by this assurance. 'We are now parting for ever,' said she; 'but, if my happiness is dear to you, you will always remember, that nothing can contribute to it more than to believe that you have recovered your own esteem.' Valancourt took her hand—his eyes were covered with tears, and the farewell he would have spoken was lost in sighs. After a few moments Emily said with difficulty and emotion, 'Farewell, Valancourt, may you be happy!' She repeated her farewell, and attempted to withdraw her hand; but he still held it, and bathed it with his tears. 'Why prolong these moments?' Emily said in a voice scarcely audible; 'they are too painful to us both.' 'This is too—too much!' exclaimed Valancourt, resigning her hand and throwing himself into a chair, where he covered his face with his hands, and was overcome for some moments by convulsive sighs. After a long pause, during which Emily wept in silence, and Valancourt seemed struggling with his grief, she again rose to take leave of him. Then, endeavouring to recover his composure,—' I am again afflicting you,' said he, ' but let the anguish I suffer plead for me.' He then added in a solemn voice, which frequently trembled with the agitation of his

heart, 'Farewell, Emily, you will always be the only object of my tenderness. Sometimes you will think of the unhappy Valancourt, and it will be with pity, though it may not be with esteem. O! what is the whole world to me, without your esteem!' He checked himself— 'I am falling again into the error I have just lamented: I must not intrude longer upon your patience, or I shall relapse into despair.'

He once more bade Emily adieu, pressed her hands to his lips, looked at her for the last time, and hurried out of the room.

Emily remained in the chair where he had left her, oppressed with a pain at her heart which scarcely permitted her to breathe, and listening to his departing steps sinking fainter and fainter as he crossed the hall. She was at length roused by the voice of the countess in the garden; and her attention being then awakened, the first object which struck her sight was the vacant chair where Valancourt had sat. The tears which had been for some time repressed by the kind of astonishment that followed his departure, now came to her relief, and she was at length sufficiently composed to return to her own room.

CHAPTER XLI.

'This is no mortal business, nor no'sound
That the earth owes ! . . . .'
                              SHAKESPEARE.

WE now return to the mention of Montoni, whose rage and disappointment were soon lost in nearer interests than any which the unhappy Emily had awakened. His depredations having exceeded their usual limits, and reached an extent, at which neither the timidity of the then commercial senate of Venice, nor their hope of his occasional assistance, would permit them to connive,—the same effort, it was resolved, should complete the suppression of his power and the correction of his outrages. While a corps of considerable strength was upon the point of receiving orders to march for Udolpho, a young officer, prompted partly by resentment for some injury received from Montoni, and partly by the hope of distinction, solicited an interview with the minister who directed the enterprise. To him he represented that the situation of Udolpho rendered it too strong to be taken by open force, except after some tedious operations; that Montoni had lately shown how capable he was of adding to its strength all the advantages which could be derived from the skill of a commander; that so considerable a body of troops as that allotted to the expedition could not approach Udolpho without his knowledge; and that it was not for the honour of the republic to have a large part of its regular force employed, for such a time as the siege of Udolpho would require, upon the attack of a handful of banditti. The object of the expedition, he thought, might be accomplished much more safely and speedily by mingling contrivance with force. It was possible to meet Montoni and his party without their walls, and to attack them then ; or, by approaching the fortress with the secrecy consistent with the march of smaller bodies of troops, to take advantage either of the treachery or negligence of some of his party, and to rush unexpectedly upon the whole, even in the castle of Udolpho.

This advice was seriously attended to, and the officer who gave it received the command of the troops demanded for his purpose. His first efforts were accordingly those of contrivance alone. In the neighbourhood of Udolpho he waited till he had secured the assistance of the *condottieri*, of whom he found none that he addressed unwilling to punish their imperious master, and to secure their own pardon from the senate. He learned also the number of Montoni's troops, and that it had been much increased since his late successes. The conclusion of his plan was soon effected. Having returned with his party, who received the watchword and other assistance from their friends within, Montoni and his officers were surprised by one division, who had been directed to their apartment, while the other maintained the slight combat which preceded the surrender of the whole garrison.—Among the persons seized with Montoni, was Orsino, the assassin, who had joined him on his first arrival at Udolpho, and whose concealment had been made known to the senate by Count Morano, after the unsuccessful attempt of the latter to carry off Emily. It was indeed partly for the purpose of capturing this man, by whom one of the senate had been murdered, that the expedition was undertaken; and its success was so acceptable to them, that Morano was instantly released, notwithstanding the political suspicions which Montoni, by his secret accusation, had excited against him. The celerity and ease with which this whole transaction was completed, prevented it from attracting curiosity, or even from obtaining a place in any of the published records of that time ; so that Emily, who remained in Languedoc, was ignorant of the defeat and signal humiliation of her late persecutor.

Her mind was now occupied with sufferings which no effort of reason had yet been able to control. Count de Villefort, who had sincerely attempted whatever benevolence could suggest for softening them, sometimes allowed her the solitude she wished for ; sometimes led her into friendly parties, and constantly protected her as much as possible from the shrewd inquiries and critical conversation of the countess. He often invited her to make excursions with him and his daughter, during which he conversed entirely on questions suitable to her taste, without appearing to con-

sult it, and thus endeavoured gradually to withdraw her from the subject of her grief, and to awake other interests in her mind. Emily, to whom he appeared as the enlightened friend and protector of her youth, soon felt for him the tender affection of a daughter, and her heart expanded to her young friend Blanche as to a sister, whose kindness and simplicity compensated for the want of more brilliant qualities. It was long before she could sufficiently abstract her mind from Valancourt to listen to the story promised by old Dorothée, concerning which her curiosity had once been so deeply interested ; but Dorothée at length reminded her of it, and Emily desired that she would come that night to her chamber.

Still her thoughts were employed by considerations which weakened her curiosity ; and Dorothée's tap at the door, soon after twelve, surprised her as much as if it had not been appointed. 'I am come at last, lady,' said she ; 'I wonder what it is that makes my old limbs shake so to-night : I thought once or twice I should have dropped as I was a-coming.' Emily seated her in a chair, and desired that she would compose her spirits before she entered upon the subject that had brought her thither. 'Alas!' said Dorothée, 'it is thinking of that, I believe, which has disturbed me so. In my way hither, too, I passed the chamber where my dear lady died, and everything was so still and gloomy about me, that I almost fancied I saw her as she appeared upon her death-bed.'

Emily now drew her chair near to Dorothée, who went on : 'It is about twenty years since my lady marchioness came a bride to the chateau. O! I well remember how she looked when she came into the great hall, where we servants were all assembled to welcome her, and how happy my lord the marquis seemed. Ah! who would have thought then?—But, as I was saying, ma'amselle, I thought the marchioness, with all her sweet looks, did not look happy at heart ; and so I told my husband, and he said it was all fancy : so I said no more, but I made my remarks for all that. My lady marchioness was then about your age, and, as I have often thought, very like you. Well ! my lord the marquis kept open house for a long time, and gave such entertainments, and there was such gay doings, as have never been in the chateau since. I was younger, ma'amselle, then, than I am now, and was as gay as the best of them. I remember I danced with Philip the butler, in a pink gown with yellow ribbons, and a coif, not such as they wear now, but plaited high with ribbons all about it. It was very becoming truly :—my lord the marquis noticed me. Ah! he was a good-natured gentleman then—who would have thought that he——'

'But the marchioness, Dorothée,' said Emily ; 'you was telling me of her.'

O yes, my lady marchioness;—I thought did not seem happy at heart; and once, after the marriage, I caught her crying er chamber; but when she saw me she I her eyes, and pretended to smile. I did dare then to ask what was the matter; he next time I saw her crying, I did, and seemed displeased—so I said no more. I d out, some time after, how it was. Her r, it seems, had commanded her to marry ord the marquis for his money, and there another nobleman, or else a chevalier, she liked better, and that was very fond r; and she fretted for the loss of him, I '; but she never told me so. My lady 's tried to conceal her tears from the uis; for I have often seen her, after she een so sorrowful, look so calm and sweet he came into the room! But my lord, a sudden, grew gloomy and fretful, very unkind sometimes to my lady, afflicted her very much, as I saw, for ever complained; and she used to try so ly to oblige him, and to bring him into d humour, that my heart has often ached e it. But he used to be stubborn, and her harsh answers; and then, when she it all in vain, she would go to her own and cry so!—I used to hear her in the oom, poor dear lady! but I seldom ven- to go to her. I used sometimes to think ord was jealous. To be sure, my lady reatly admired, but she was too good to ve suspicion. Among the many cheva- hat visited at the chateau, there was one always thought seemed just suited for ly; he was so courteous, yet so spirited; ere was such a grace, as it were, in all l or said. I always observed that when- e had been there, the marquis was more y and my lady more thoughtful; and it into my head that this was the cheva- e ought to have married, but I never learn for certain.'

hat was the chevalier's name, Doro- said Emily.

hy that I will not tell even to you, selle, for evil may come of it. I once from a person, who is since dead, that rchioness was not in law the wife of the is, for that she had before been privately d to the gentleman she was so much d to, and was afterwards afraid to to her father, who was a very stern but this seems very unlikely, and I never uch faith to it. As I was saying, the s was most out of humour, as I thought, he chevalier I spoke of had been at the , and at last his ill treatment of my ade her quite miserable. He would dly any visitors at the castle, and made almost by herself. I was her constant nt, and saw all she suffered; but still er complained.

r matters had gone on thus for near a year, my lady was taken ill, and I thought her long fretting had made her so—but, alas! I fear it was worse than that.'

'Worse, Dorothée!' said Emily: 'can that be possible?'

'I fear it was so, madam; there were strange appearances. But I will only tell what hap- pened. My lord the marquis——'

'Hush, Dorothée, what sounds were those?' said Emily.

Dorothée changed countenance; and while they both listened, they heard on the stillness of the night, music of uncommon sweetness.

'I have surely heard that voice before!' said Emily at length.

'I have often heard it, and at this same hour,' said Dorothée solemnly; and if spirits ever bring music—that is surely the music of one!'

Emily, as the sounds drew nearer, knew them to be the same she had formerly heard at the time of her father's death; and whether it was the remembrance they now revived of that melancholy event, or that she was struck with superstitious awe, it is certain she was so much affected that she had nearly fainted.

'I think I once told you, madam,' said Dorothée, 'that I first heard this music soon after my lady's death: I well remember the night!'

'Hark! it comes again!' said Emily; 'let us open the window, and listen.'

They did so; but soon the sounds floated gradually away into distance, and all was again still: they seemed to have sunk among the woods, whose tufted tops were visible upon the clear horizon, while every other feature of the scene was involved in the night shade, which, however, allowed the eye an indistinct view of some objects in the garden below.

As Emily leaned on the window, gazing with a kind of thrilling awe upon the obscu- rity beneath, and then upon the cloudless arch above, enlightened only by the stars, Dorothée, in a low voice, resumed her narrative.

'I was saying, ma'amselle, that I well remember when first I heard that music. It was one night, soon after my lady's death, that I had sat up later than usual; and I don't know how it was, but I had been thinking a great deal about my poor mistress, and of the sad scene I had lately witnessed. The chateau was quite still, and I was in a chamber at a good distance from the rest of the servants, and this, with the mournful things I had been thinking of, I suppose, made me low-spirited, for I felt very lonely and forlorn, as it were, and listened often, wishing to hear a sound in the chateau; for you know, ma'amselle, when one can hear people moving, one does not so much mind about one's fears. But all the servants were gone to bed, and I sat thinking and thinking, till I was almost afraid to look round the room, and my poor lady's coun- tenance often came to my mind, such as I had seen her when she was dying; and once or twice I almost thought I saw her before me —when suddenly I heard such sweet music! it seemed just at my window, and I shall never forget what I felt. I had not power to move from my chair: but then, when I thought it was my dear lady's voice, the tears came to my eyes. I had often heard her sing in her life-time, and to be sure she had a very fine voice; it had made me cry to hear her, many a time, when she has sat in her oriel of an evening playing upon her lute such sad songs, and singing so—O! it went to one's heart! I have listened in the ante-chamber for the hour together; and she would sometimes sit playing, with the window open, when it was summer time, till it was quite dark; and when I have gone in to shut it, she has hardly seemed to know what hour it was. But, as I said, madam,' continued Dorothee, 'when first I heard the music that came just now, I thought it was my late lady's, and I have often thought so again when I have heard it, as I have done at intervals ever since. Sometimes many months have gone by, but still it has returned.'

'It is extraordinary,' observed Emily, 'that no person has yet discovered the musician.'

'Aye, ma'amselle, if it had been anything earthly it would have been discovered long ago, but who could have courage to follow a spirit? and if they had, what good could it do?—for spirits, *you know*, ma'am, can take any shape, or no shape; and they will be here one minute, and the next, perhaps, in a quite different place!'

'Pray resume your story of the marchioness,' said Emily, 'and acquaint me with the manner of her death.'

'I will, ma'am,' said Dorothee; 'but shall we leave the window?'

'This cool air refreshes me,' replied Emily: 'and I love to hear it creep along the woods, and to look upon this dusky landscape. You were speaking of my lord the marquis, when the music interrupted us.'

'Yes, madam, my lord the marquis became more and more gloomy; and my lady grew worse and worse, till one night she was taken very ill indeed. I was called up, and when I came to her bed-side I was shocked to see her countenance—it was so changed! She looked piteously up at me, and desired I would call the marquis again, for he was not yet come, and tell him she had something particular to say to him. At last he came; and he did, to be sure, seem very sorry to see her, but he said very little. My lady told him she felt herself to be dying, and wished to speak with him alone; and then I left the room, but I shall never forget his look as I went.

'When I returned, I ventured to remind my lord about sending for a doctor, for I supposed he had forgot to do so in his grief; but my lady said it was then too late: but my lord, so far from thinking so, seemed to think

lightly of her disorder—till she was seized with such terrible pains! O, I never shall forget her shriek! My lord then sent off a man and horse for a doctor, and walked about the room and all over the chateau in the greatest distress; and I staid by my dear lady, and did what I could to ease her sufferings. She had intervals of ease, and in one of these she sent for my lord again; when he came I was going, but she desired I would not leave her. O! I shall never forget what a scene passed—I can hardly bear to think of it now? My lord was almost distracted, for my lady behaved with so much goodness, and took such pains to comfort him, that if he ever had suffered a suspicion to enter his head, he must now have been convinced he was wrong. And to be sure he did seem to be overwhelmed with the thought of his treatment of her, and this affected her so much that she fainted away.

'We then got my lord out of the room; he went into his library, and threw himself on the floor, and there he stayed, and would hear no reason that was talked to him. When my lady recovered, she inquired for him; but afterwards said she could not bear to see his grief, and desired we would let her die quietly. She died in my arms, ma'amselle, and she went off as peacefully as a child, for all the violence of her disorder was passed.'

Dorothee paused and wept, and Emily wept with her; for she was much affected by the goodness of the late marchioness, and by the meek patience with which she had suffered.

'When the doctor came,' resumed Dorothee —'alas! he came too late—he appeared greatly shocked to see her, for soon after her death a frightful blackness spread all over her face. When he had sent the attendants out of the room, he asked me several odd questions about the marchioness, particularly concerning the manner in which she had been seized; and he often shook his head at my answers, and seemed to mean more than he chose to say. But I understood him too well. However, I kept my remarks to myself, and only told them to my husband, who bade me hold my tongue. Some of the other servants, however, suspected what I did, and strange reports were whispered about the neighbourhood, but no body dared to make any stir about them. When my lord heard that my lady was dead, he shut himself up, and would see nobody but the doctor, who used to be with him alone sometimes for an hour together: and after that the doctor never talked with me again about my lady. When she was buried in the church of the convent, at a little distance yonder (if the moon was up you might see the towers here, ma'amselle), all my lord's vassals followed the funeral, and there was not a dry eye among them, for she had done a deal of good among the poor. My lord the marquis, I never saw anybody s-melancholy as he was afterwards, and sometimes he would be in such fits of violence, that we almost thought he had lost his senses. He did not stay long at the chateau, but joined his regiment ; and soon after, all the servants, except my husband and I, received notice to go, for my lord went to the wars. I never saw him after ; for he would not return to the chateau, though it is such a fine place ; and never finished those fine rooms he was building on the west side of it ; and it has, in a manner, been shut up ever since, till my lord the count came here.'

'The death of the marchioness appears extraordinary,' said Emily, who was anxious to know more than she dared to speak.

'Yes, madam,' replied Dorothee, 'it was extraordinary : I have told you all I saw, and you may easily guess what I think. I cannot say more, because I would not spread reports that might offend my lord the count.

'You are very right,' said Emily ;—'where did the marquis die?'—'In the North of France, I believe, ma'amselle,' replied Dorothee. 'I was very glad when I heard my lord the count was coming, for this had been a sad desolate place these many years, and we heard such strange noises after my lady's death, that, as I told you before, my husband and I left it for a neighbouring cottage. And now, lady, I have told you all this sad history, and all my thoughts, and you have promised, you know, never to give the least hint about it.'—'I have,' said Emily : 'and I will be faithful to my promise, Dorothee ;—what you have told me has interested me more than you can imagine. I only wish I could prevail upon you to tell me the name of the chevalier whom you thought so deserving of the marchioness.'

Dorothee, however, steadily refused to do this, and then returned to the notice of Emily's likeness to the late marchioness. 'There is another picture of her,' added she, 'hanging in a room of the suite which was shut up. It was drawn, as I have heard, before she was married, and is much more like you than the miniature.' When Emily expressed a strong desire to see this, Dorothee replied, that she did not wish to open those rooms ; but Emily reminded her, that the count had talked the other day of ordering them to be opened, of which Dorothee seemed to consider much ; and then she owned that she should feel less, if she went into them with Emily first, than otherwise ; and at length promised to show the picture.

The night was too far advanced, and Emily was too much affected by the narrative of the scenes which had passed in those apartments, to desire to visit them at this hour ; but she requested that Dorothee would return on the following night, when they were not likely to be observed, and conduct her thither. Besides her wish to examine the portrait, she

felt a thrilling curiosity to see the chamber in which the marchioness had died, and which Dorothee had said remained, with the bed and furniture, just as when the corpse was removed for interment. The solemn emotions which the expectation of viewing such a scene had awakened, were in unison with the present tone of her mind, depressed by severe disappointment. Cheerful objects rather added to, than removed this depression ; but perhaps she yielded too much to her melancholy inclination, and imprudently lamented the misfortune, which no virtue of her own could have taught her to avoid, though no effort of reason could make her look unmoved upon the self-degradation of him whom she had once esteemed and loved.

Dorothee promised to return on the following night with the keys of the chambers ; and then wished Emily good repose, and departed. Emily, however, continued at the window, musing upon the melancholy fate of the marchioness, and listening, in awful expectation, for a return of the music. But the stillness of the night remained long unbroken, except by the murmuring sounds of the woods, as they waved in the breeze, and then by the distant bell of the convent, striking one. She now withdrew from the window ; and as she sat at her bedside, indulging melancholy reveries, which the loneliness of the hour assisted, the stillness was suddenly interrupted, not by music, but by very uncommon sounds, that seemed to come either from the room adjoining her own, or from one below. The terrible catastrophe that had been related to her, together with the mysterious circumstances said to have since occurred in the chateau, had so much shocked her spirits, that she now sunk for a moment under the weakness of superstition. The sounds, however, did not return ; and she retired, to forget in sleep the disastrous story she had heard.

CHAPTER XLII.

'Now is the time of night
That, the graves all gaping wide,
Every one lets forth his spright,
In the church-way path to glide.'
SHAKESPEARE.

ON the next night, about the same hour as before, Dorothee came to Emily's chamber with the keys of that suite of rooms which had been particularly appropriated to the late marchioness. These extended along the north side of the chateau, forming part of the old building ; and as Emily's room was in the south, they had to pass over a great extent of the castle, and by the chambers of several of the family, whose observation Dorothee was anxious to avoid, since it might excite inquiry and raise reports, such as would displease the count. She therefore requested that Emily would wait half an hour before they ventured forth, that they might be certain all the servants were gone to bed. It was nearly one before the chateau was perfectly still, or Dorothee thought it prudent to leave the chamber. In this interval, her spirits seemed to be greatly affected by the remembrance of past events, and by the prospect of entering again upon places where these had occurred, and in which she had not been for so many years. Emily too was affected; but her feelings had more of solemnity, and less of fear. From the silence into which reflection and expectation had thrown them, they at length roused themselves, and left the chamber. Dorothee at first carried the lamp, but her hand trembled so much with infirmity and alarm, that Emily took it from her, and offered her arm to support her feeble steps.

They had to descend the great staircase, and, after passing over a wide extent of the chateau, to ascend another, which led to the suite of rooms they were in quest of. They stepped cautiously along the open corridor that ran round the great hall, and into which the chambers of the count, countess, and the Lady Blanche, opened; and from thence, descending the chief staircase, they crossed the hall itself. Proceeding through the servants' hall, where the dying embers of a wood fire still glimmered on the hearth, and the supper-table was surrounded by chairs that obstructed their passage, they came to the foot of the back staircase. Old Dorothee here paused, and looked around: 'Let us listen,' said she, 'if anything is stirring; ma'amselle, do you hear any voice?' 'None,' said Emily, 'there certainly is no person up in the chateau, besides ourselves.'—'No, ma'amselle,' said Dorothee, 'but I have never been here at this hour before, and, after what I know, my fears are not wonderful.'—'What do you know?' said Emily.—'O ma'amselle, we have no time for talking now; let us go on. That door on the left is the one we must open.'

They proceeded; and having reached the top of the staircase, Dorothee applied the key to the lock. 'Ah,' said she, as she endeavoured to turn it, 'so many years have passed since this was opened, that I fear it will not move.' Emily was more successful, and they presently entered a spacious and ancient chamber.

'Alas!' exclaimed Dorothee, as she entered, 'the last time I passed through this door—I followed my poor lady's corpse!'

Emily, struck by the circumstance, and affected by the dusky and solemn air of the apartment, remained silent; and they passed on through a long suite of rooms, till they came to one more spacious than the rest, and rich in the remains of faded magnificence.

'Let us rest here awhile, madam,' said Dorothee faintly, 'we are going into the chamber where my lady died! that door opens into it. Ah, ma'amselle! why did you persuade me to come?'

Emily drew one of the massy arm-chairs with which the apartment was furnished, and begged Dorothee would sit down, and try to compose her spirits.

'How the sight of this place brings all that passed formerly to my mind!' said Dorothee; 'it seems as if it was but yesterday since all that sad affair happened!'

'Hark! what noise is that?' said Emily.

Dorothee, half starting from her chair, looked round the apartment, and they listened; but, everything remaining still, the old woman spoke again upon the subject of her sorrow: 'This saloon, ma'amselle, was in my lady's time the finest apartment in the chateau, and it was fitted up according to her own taste. All this grand furniture,—but you can now hardly see what it was for the dust, and our light is none of the best—ah! how I have seen this room lighted up in my lady's time! all this grand furniture came from Paris, and was made after the fashion of some in the Louvre there, except those large glasses, and they came from some outlandish place, and that rich tapestry. How the colours are faded already!—since I saw it last!'

'I understood that was twenty years ago,' observed Emily.

'Thereabout, madam,' said Dorothee, 'and well remembered; but all the time between then and now seems as nothing. That tapestry used to be greatly admired at: it tells the stories out of some famous book or other, but I have forgot the name.'

Emily now rose to examine the figures it exhibited, and discovered by verses in the Provençal tongue, wrought underneath each scene, that it exhibited stories from some of the most celebrated ancient romances.

Dorothee's spirits being now more composed, she rose, and unlocked the door that led into the late marchioness's apartment, and Emily passed into a lofty chamber hung round with dark arras, and so spacious, that the lamp she held up did not show its extent; while Dorothee, when she entered, had dropped into a chair, where sighing deeply, she scarcely trusted herself with the view of a scene so affecting to her. It was some time before Emily perceived through the dusk the bed on which the marchioness was said to have died: when, advancing to the upper end of the room, she discovered the high canopied tester of dark green damask, with the curtains descending to the floor in the fashion of a tent, half drawn, and remaining apparently as they had been left twenty years before; and over the whole bedding was thrown a counterpane, or pall, of black velvet, that hung down to the floor. Emily shuddered as

e held the lamp over it, and looked within
e dark curtains, where she almost expected
have seen a human face ; and, suddenly
membering the horror she had suffered upon
scovering the dying Madame Montoni in
e turret chamber of Udolpho, her spirits
nted ; and she was turning from the bed,
ien Dorothee, who had now reached it, ex-
iimed, ' Holy Virgin ! methinks I see my
ly stretched upon that pall—as when last I
w her !'
Emily, shocked by this exclamation, looked
oluntarily again within the curtains, but
: blackness of the pall only appeared ; while
rothée was compelled to support herself
on the side of the bed, and presently tears
ught her some relief.
Ah !' said she, after she had wept awhile,
was here I sat on that terrible night, and
d my lady's hand, and heard her last words,
I saw all her sufferings—*here* she died in
arms !'
Do not indulge these painful recollections,
d Emily ; ' let us go. Show me the picture
i mentioned, if it will not too much affect
i.'
It hangs in the oriel,' rising and going to-
rds a small door near the bed's head,
ich she opened ; and Emily followed with
light into the closet of the late marchio-
s.
Alas ! there she is, ma'amselle,' said Doro-
e, pointing to the portrait of a lady ; ' there
ier very self ! just as she looked when she
ae first to the chateau. You see, madam,
was all-blooming like you, then—and so
n to be cut off !'
Vhile Dorothée spoke, Emily was atten-
ly examining the picture, which bore a
ing resemblance to the miniature, though
expression of the countenance in each was
iewhat different ; but still she thought
perceived something of that pensive
ancholy in the portrait, which so strongly
racterised the miniature.
Pray, ma'amselle, stand beside the picture,
t I may look at you together,' said Doro-
e ; who, when the request was complied
i, exclaimed again at the resemblance.
ily also, as she gazed upon it, thought that
had somewhere seen a person very like it,
ugh she could not now recollect who this
.
n this closet were many memorials of the
arted marchioness ; a robe and several
cles of her dress were scattered upon the
irs, as if they had just been thrown off.
the floor were a pair of black satin slip-
s ; and on the dressing-table a pair of
ves, and a long black veil, which, as Emily
k it up to examine, she perceived was drop-
g to pieces with age.
Ah !' said Dorothée, observing the veil,
y lady's hand laid it there ; it has never
n moved since !'

Emily, shuddering, immediately laid it down
again. ' I well remember seeing her take it off,'
continued Dorothée ; it was on the night before
her death, when she had returned from a
little walk I had persuaded her to take in
the gardens, and she seemed refreshed by it.
I told her how much better she looked, and I
remember what a languid smile she gave me ;
but, alas ! she little thought, or I either, that
she was to die that night.'
Dorothee wept again, and then, taking up
the veil, threw it suddenly over Emily, who
shuddered to find it wrapped round her, descending even to her feet ; and as she endeavoured to throw it off, Dorothee entreated
that she would keep it on for one moment.
' I thought,' added she, ' how like you would
look to my dear mistress, in that veil ;—may
your life, ma'amselle, be a happier one than
hers !'
Emily, having disengaged herself from the
veil, laid it again on the dressing-table, and
surveyed the closet, where every object on
which her eye fixed seemed to speak of the
marchioness. In a large oriel window of
painted glass stood a table with a silver crucifix, and a prayer-book open ; and Emily remembered with emotion what Dorothee had
mentioned concerning her custom of playing
on her lute in this window, before she observed
the lute itself lying on a corner of the table,
as if it had been carelessly placed there by the
hand that had so often awakened it.
' This is a sad, forlorn place !' said Dorothee ; ' for when my dear lady died, I had no
heart to put it to rights, or the chamber
either ; and my lord never came into the
rooms after ; so they remain just as they did
when my lady was removed for interment.'
While Dorothee spoke, Emily was still
looking on the lute, which was a Spanish one,
and remarkably large ; and then, with a hesitating hand, she took it up and passed her
fingers over the chords. They were out of
tune, but uttered a deep and full sound.
Dorothée started at their well-known tones,
and seeing the lute in Emily's hand, said,
' This is the lute my lady marchioness loved
so ! I remember when last she played upon
it—it was on the night that she died. I came
as usual to undress her ; and, as I entered
the bed-chamber, I heard the sound of music
from the oriel, and perceiving it was my lady's,
who was sitting there, I stepped softly to the
door, which stood a little open, to listen ; for
the music—though it was mournful—was so
sweet ! There I saw her, with the lute in her
hand, looking upwards ; and the tears fell
upon her cheeks, while she sung a vesper
hymn, so soft, and so solemn ! and her voice
trembled, as it were : and then she would stop
for a moment, and wipe away her tears, and
go on again, lower than before. O ! I had
often listened to my lady, but never heard any
thing so sweet as this ; it made me cry almost

to hear it. She had been at prayers, I fancy, for there was the book open on the table beside her—aye, and there it lies open still! Pray let us leave the oriel, ma'amselle,' added Dorothee, 'this is a heart-breaking place.'

Having returned into the chamber, she desired to look once more upon the bed; when, as they came opposite to the open door leading to the saloon, Emily, in the partial gleam which the lamp threw into it, thought she saw something glide along into the obscurer part of the room. Her spirits had been much affected by the surrounding scene, or it is probable this circumstance, whether real or imaginary, would not have affected her in the degree it did; but she endeavoured to conceal her emotion from Dorothee, who, however, observing her countenance change, inquired if she was ill.

'Let us go,' said Emily faintly; 'the air of these rooms is unwholesome:' but when she attempted to do so, considering that she must pass through the apartment where the phantom of her terror had appeared, this terror increased; and, too faint to support herself, she sat down on the side of the bed.

Dorothee, believing that she was only affected by a consideration of the melancholy catastrophe which had happened on this spot, endeavoured to cheer her; and then, as they sat together on the bed, she began to relate other particulars concerning it, and this without reflecting that it might increase Emily's emotion, but because they were particularly interesting to herself. 'A little before my lady's death,' said she, 'when the pains were gone off, she called me to her; and stretching out her hand to me, I sat down just there— where the curtain falls upon the bed. How well I remember her look at the time—death was in it!—I can almost fancy I see her now. There she lay, ma'amselle—her face was upon the pillow there! This black counterpane was not upon the bed then; it was laid on after her death, and she was laid out upon it.'

Emily turned to look within the dusky curtains, as if she could have seen the countenance of which Dorothee spoke. The edge of the white pillow only appeared above the blackness of the pall; but, as her eyes wandered over the pall itself, she fancied she saw it move. Without speaking, she caught Dorothee's arm, who, surprised by the action, and by the look of terror which accompanied it, turned her eyes from Emily to the bed, where, in the next moment, she too saw the pall slowly lifted and fall again.

Emily attempted to go, but Dorothee stood fixed, and gazed upon the bed; and at length said—'It is only the wind that waves it, ma'amselle! we have left all the doors open; see how the air waves the lamp too—it is only the wind.'

She had scarcely uttered these words, when the pall was more violently agitated than before; but Emily, somewhat ashamed of her terrors, stepped back to the bed, willing to be convinced that the wind only had occasioned her alarm; when, as she gazed within the curtains, the pall moved again, and in the next moment the apparition of a human countenance rose above it.

Screaming with terror, they both fled, and got out of the chamber as fast as their trembling limbs would bear them, leaving open the doors of all the rooms through which they passed. When they reached the staircase, Dorothee threw open a chamber-door, where some of the female servants slept, and sunk breathless on the bed; while Emily, deprived of all presence of mind, made only a feeble attempt to conceal the occasion of her terror from the astonished servants: and though Dorothee, when she could speak, endeavoured to laugh at her own fright, and was joined by Emily, no remonstrances could prevail with the servants, who had quickly taken the alarm, to pass even the remainder of the night in a room near to these terrific chambers.

Dorothee having accompanied Emily to her own apartment, they then began to talk over, with some degree of coolness, the strange circumstance that had just occurred: and Emily would almost have doubted her own perceptions, had not those of Dorothee attested their truth. Having now mentioned what she had observed in the outer chamber, she asked the housekeeper whether she was certain no door had been left unfastened, by which a person might secretly have entered the apartments? Dorothee replied that she had constantly kept the keys of the several doors in her own possession; that when she had gone her rounds through the castle, as she frequently did, to examine if all was safe, she had tried these doors among them, and had always found them fastened. It was therefore impossible, she added, that any person could have got admittance into the apartments; and if they could—it was very improbable they should have chosen to sleep in a place so cold and forlorn.

Emily observed, that their visit to these chambers had perhaps been watched, and that some person, for a frolic, had followed them into the rooms with a design to frighten them; and while they were in the oriel, had taken the opportunity of concealing himself in the bed.

Dorothee allowed that this was possible, till she recollected that, on entering the apartment, she had turned the key of the outer door; and this, which had been done to prevent their visit being noticed by any of the family who might happen to be up, must effectually have excluded every person except themselves, from the chambers; and she now persisted in affirming that the ghastly countenance she had seen was nothing human, but some dreadful apparition.

Emily was very solemnly affected. Of whatever nature might be the appearance she had witnessed, whether human or supernatural, the fate of the deceased marchioness was a truth not to be doubted; and this unaccountable circumstance, occurring in the very scene of her sufferings, affected Emily's imagination with a superstitious awe, to which, after having detected the fallacies at Udolpho, she might not have yielded, had she been ignorant of the unhappy story related by the housekeeper. Her she now solemnly conjured to conceal the occurrence of this night, and to make light of the terror she had already betrayed, that the count might not be distressed by reports, which would certainly spread alarm and confusion among his family. 'Time,' she added, 'may explain this mysterious affair; meanwhile, let us watch the event with silence.'

Dorothée readily acquiesced: but she now recollected that she had left all the doors of the north suite of rooms open; and, not having courage to return alone to lock even the outer one, Emily, after some effort, so far conquered her own fears, that she offered to accompany her to the foot of the back staircase, and to wait there while Dorothee ascended; whose resolution being re-assured by this circumstance, she consented to go; and they left Emily's apartment together.

No sound disturbed the stillness as they passed along the halls and galleries; but on reaching the foot of the back staircase, Dorothee's resolution failed again. Having, however, paused a moment to listen, and no sound being heard above, she ascended, leaving Emily below; and scarcely suffering her eye to glance within the first chamber, she fastened the door which shut up the whole suite of apartments, and returned to Emily.

As they stepped along the passage leading into the great hall, a sound of lamentation was heard, which seemed to come from the hall itself, and they stopped in new alarm to listen; when Emily presently distinguished the voice of Annette, whom she found crossing the hall, with another female servant, and so terrified by the report which the other maids had spread, that, believing she could be safe only where her lady was, she was going for refuge to her apartment. Emily's endeavours to laugh, or to argue her out of these terrors, were equally vain; and, in compassion for her distress, she consented that she should remain in her room during the night.

CHAPTER XLIII.

'Hail, mildly-pleasing Solitude!
Companion of the wise and good!

. . . .
Thine is the balmy breath of morn,
Just as the dew-bent rose is born.

. . . .
But chief when evening scenes decay,
And the faint landscape swims away,
Thine is the doubtful soft decline,
And that best hour of musing thine.'

THOMSON.

EMILY's injunctions to Annette to be silent on the subject of her terror were ineffectual; and the occurrence of the preceding night spread such alarm among the servants, who now all affirmed that they had frequently heard unaccountable noises in the chateau, that a report soon reached the count, of the north side of the castle being haunted. He treated this, at first, with ridicule; but perceiving that it was productive of serious evil, in the confusion it occasioned among his household, he forbade any person to repeat it, on pain of punishment.

The arrival of a party of his friends soon withdrew his thoughts entirely from this subject; and his servants had now little leisure to brood over it, except indeed in the evenings after supper, when they all assembled in their hall, and related stories of ghosts till they feared to look round the room; started if the echo of a closing door murmured along the passage, and refused to go singly to any part of the castle.

On these occasions Annette made a distinguished figure. When she told not only of all the wonders she had witnessed, but of all that she had imagined, in the castle of Udolpho, with the story of the strange disappearance of Signora Laurentini, she made no trifling impression on the mind of her attentive auditors. Her suspicions concerning Montoni, she would also have freely disclosed, had not Ludovico, who was now in the service of the count, prudently checked her loquacity, whenever it pointed to that subject.

Among the visitors at the chateau was the Baron de Saint Foix, an old friend of the count, and his son, the Chevalier St. Foix, a sensible and amiable young man; who, having in the preceding year seen the Lady Blanche at Paris, had become her declared admirer. The friendship which the count had long entertained for his father, and the equality of their circumstances, made him secretly approve of the connection; but thinking his daughter at this time too young to fix her choice for life, and wishing to prove the sincerity and strength of the chevalier's attachment, he then rejected his suit, though without forbidding his future hope. This young man now came, with the baron his father, to claim the reward of a steady affection, a claim which the count admitted, and which Blanche did not reject.

While these visitors were at the chateau, it

9

became a scene of gaiety and splendour. The pavilion in the woods was fitted up, and frequented in the fine evenings as a supper-room, when the hour usually concluded with a concert, at which the count and countess, who were scientific performers, and the chevaliers Henri and St. Foix, with the Lady Blanche and Emily, whose voices and fine taste compensated for the want of more skilful execution, usually assisted. Several of the count's servants performed on horns and other instruments, some of which, placed at a little distance among the woods, spoke in sweet response to the harmony that proceeded from the pavilion.

At any other period these parties would have been delightful to Emily; but her spirits were now oppressed with a melancholy which she perceived that no kind of what is called amusement had power to dissipate, and which the tender and frequently pathetic melody of these concerts sometimes increased to a very painful degree.

She was particularly fond of walking the woods that hung on a promontory overlooking the sea. Their luxuriant shade was soothing to her pensive mind; and in the partial views which they afforded of the Mediterranean, with its winding shores and passing sails, tranquil beauty was united with grandeur. The paths were rude, and frequently overgrown with vegetation; but their tasteful owner would suffer little to be done to them, and scarcely a single branch to be lopped from the venerable trees. On an eminence, in one of the most sequestered parts of these woods, was a rustic seat formed of the trunk of a decayed oak, which had once been a noble tree, and of which many lofty branches still flourishing united with beech and pines to over-canopy the spot. Beneath their deep umbrage, the eye passed over the tops of other woods to the Mediterranean; and to the left, through an opening, was seen a ruined watch-tower, standing on a point of rock near the sea, and rising from among the tufted foliage.

Hither Emily often came alone in the silence of evening; and soothed by the scenery and by the faint murmur that rose from the waves, would sit till darkness obliged her to return to the chateau. Frequently, also, she visited the watch-tower, which commanded the entire prospect; and when she leaned against its broken walls and thought of Valancourt, she not once imagined, what was so true, that this tower had been almost as frequently his resort as her own, since his estrangement from the neighbouring chateau.

One evening she lingered here to a late hour. She had sat on the steps of the building, watching in tranquil melancholy the gradual effect of evening over the extensive prospect, till the gray waters of the Mediterranean and the massy woods were almost the only features of the scene that remained visible; when, as she gazed alternately on these, and on the mild blue of the heavens, where the first pale star of evening appeared, she personified the hour in the following lines :—

SONG OF THE EVENING HOUR.

Last of the Hours that track the fading Day,
I move along the realms of twilight air,
And hear, remote, the choral song decay
Of sister nymphs, who dance around his car.

Then, as I follow through the azure void,
His partial splendour from my straining eye
Sinks in the depth of space; my only guide
His faint ray dawning on the furthest sky;

Save that sweet lingering strain of gayer Hours,
Whose close my voice prolongs in dying notes,
While mortals on the green earth own its powers,
As downward on the evening gale it floats.

When fades along the west the sun's last beam,
As weary to the nether world he goes,
And mountain summits catch the purple gleam,
And slumbering ocean faint and fainter glows;

Silent upon the globe's broad shade I steal,
And o'er its dry turf shed the cooling dews,
And every fever'd herb and floweret heal,
And all their fragrance on the air diffuse.

Where'er I move a tranquil pleasure reigns;
O'er all the scene the dusky tints I send,
That forests wild and mountains, stretching plains,
And peopled towns, in soft confusion blend.

Wide o'er the world I waft the freshening wind,
Low breathing through the woods and twilight vale,
In whispers soft, that woo the pensive mind
Of him who loves my lonely steps to hail.

His tender oaten reed I watch to hear,
Stealing its sweetness o'er some plaining rill,
Or soothing ocean's wave, when storms are near,
Or swelling in the breeze from distant hill!

I wake the fairy elves, who shun the light;
When from their blossom'd beds they slily peep,
And spy my pale star, leading on the night,—
Forth to their games and revelry they leap;

Send all the prison'd sweets abroad in air,
That with them slumber'd in the floweret's cell;
Then to the shores and moonlight brooks repair,
Till the high larks their matin-carol swell.

The wood-nymphs hail my airs and temper'd shade,
With ditties soft and lightly sportive dance,
On river margin of some bowery glade,
And strew their fresh buds as my steps advance:

But swift I pass, and distant regions trace,
For moonbeams silver all the eastern cloud,
And day's last crimson vestige fades apace;
Down the steep west I fly from midnight's shroud.

The moon was now rising out of the sea. She watched its gradual progress, the extending line of radiance it threw upon the waters, the sparkling oars, the sail faintly silvered, and the wood-tops and the battlements of the watch-tower, at whose foot she was sitting, just tinted with the rays. Emily's spirits were in harmony with this scene. As she sat meditating, sounds stole by her on the air, which she immediately knew to be the music and the voice she had formerly heard at midnight; and the emotion of awe which she felt was not unmixed with terror, when she considered her remote and lonely situation. The sounds drew nearer.

ie would have risen to leave the place; but
cy seemed to come from the way she must
ve taken towards the chateau, and she
nited the event in trembling expectation.
ie sounds continued to approach for some
ie, and then ceased. Emily sat listening.
zing, and unable to move, when she saw a
ure emerge from the shade of the woods,
d pass along the bank, at some little dis-
ice before her. It went swiftly; and her
rits were so overcome with awe, that,
ugh she saw, she did not much observe it.
Having left the spot, with a resolution never
iin to visit it alone at so late an hour, she
gan to approach the chateau, when she
ird voices calling her from the part of the
od which was nearest to it. They were
shouts of the count's servants, who were
t to search for her; and when she entered
supper-room, where he sat with Henri and
nche, he gently reproached her with a look
ich she blushed to have deserved.

The little occurrence deeply impressed her
id; and when she withdrew to her own
m, it recalled so forcibly the circumstances
had witnessed a few nights before, that
had scarcely courage to remain alone.
watched to a late hour; when, no sound
ing renewed her fears, she at length sunk
epose. But this was of short continuance,
she was disturbed by a loud and unusual
se that seemed to come from the gallery
which her chamber opened. Groans
e distinctly heard, and immediately after
ead weight fell against the door, with a
ence that threatened to burst it open. She
ed loudly to know who was there, but reed no answer, though at intervals she still
ight she heard something like a low moan-
Fear deprived her of the power to
re. Soon after she heard footsteps in a
ote part of the gallery; and as they ap-
iched, she called more loudly than before,
he steps paused at her door. She then
nguished the voices of several of the ser-
s, who seemed too much engaged by some
instance without, to attend to her calls;
Annette soon after entering the room for
ir, Emily understood that one of the maids
fainted, whom she immediately desired
i to bring into her room, where she
ited to restore her. When this girl had
vered her speech, she affirmed, that as she
passing up the back staircase, in the way
er chamber, she had seen an appari-
on the second landing-place; she held
amp low,' she said, 'that she might pick
way, several of the stairs being infirm and
decayed, and it was upon raising her
that she saw this appearance. It stood
moment in the corner of the landing-
e which she was approaching, and then,
ng up the stairs, vanished at the door of
ipartment that had been lately opened.
heard afterwards a hollow sound.'

'Then the devil has got the key to that
apartment,' said Dorothee, 'for it could be
nobody but he: I locked the door myself!'

The girl, springing down the stairs and passing up the great staircase, had run, with a faint
scream, till she reached the gallery, where she
fell, groaning, at Emily's door.

Gently chiding her for the alarm she had
occasioned, Emily tried to make her ashamed
of her fears; but the girl persisted in saying
that she had seen an apparition, till she went
to her own room, whither she was accompanied by all the servants present, except
Dorothee, who, at Emily's request, remained
with her during the night. Emily was perplexed, and Dorothee was terrified, and mentioned many occurrences of former times,
which had long since confirmed her superstitions; among these, according to her belief,
she had once witnessed an appearance like
that described, and on the very same spot;
and it was the remembrance of it that had
made her pause, when she was going to ascend
the stairs with Emily, and which had increased
her reluctance to open the north apartments.
Whatever might be Emily's opinions, she did
not disclose them, but listened attentively to all
that Dorothee communicated, which occasioned
her much thought and perplexity.

From this night the terror of the servants
increased to such an excess, that several of
them determined to leave the chateau, and
requested their discharge of the count, who,
if he had any faith in the subjects of their
alarm, thought proper to dissemble it, and,
anxious to avoid the inconvenience that threatened him, employed ridicule, and then argument, to convince them they had nothing to
apprehend from supernatural agency. But
fear had rendered their minds inaccessible to
reason; and it was now that Ludovico proved
at once his courage and his gratitude for the
kindness he had received from the count, by
offering to watch, during a night, in the suite
of rooms reputed to be haunted. 'He feared,'
he said, 'no spirits; and if anything of human
form appeared—he would prove that he
dreaded that as little.'

The count paused upon the offer; while the
servants, who heard it, looked upon one
another in doubt and amazement: and Annette, terrified for the safety of Ludovico,
employed tears and entreaties to dissuade
him from his purpose.

'You are a bold fellow,' said the count,
smiling; 'think well of what you are going to
encounter before you finally determine upon it.
However, if you persevere in your resolution,
I will accept your offer, and your intrepidity
shall not go unrewarded.'

'I desire no reward, your *Excellenza*,'
replied Ludovico, 'but your approbation.
Your *Excellenza* has been sufficiently good
to me already; but I wish to have arms, that I
may be equal to my enemy, if he should appear.'

'Your sword cannot defend you against a ghost,' replied the count, throwing a glance of irony upon the other servants: 'neither can bars nor bolts; for a spirit, you know, can glide through a key-hole as easily as through a door.'

'Give me a sword, my lord count,' said Ludovico, 'and I will lay all the spirits that shall attack me in the Red Sea.'

'Well,' said the count, 'You shall have a sword, and good cheer too; and your brave comrades here will, perhaps, have courage enough to remain another night in the chateau, since your boldness will certainly, for this night at least, confine all the malice of the spectre to yourself.'

Curiosity now struggled with fear in the minds of several of his fellow-servants, and at length they resolved to await the event of Ludovico's rashness.

Emily was surprised and concerned when she heard of his intention, and was frequently inclined to mention what she had witnessed in the north apartments to the count; for she could not entirely divest herself of fears for Ludovico's safety, though her reason represented these to be absurd. The necessity, however, of concealing the secret with which Dorothee had intrusted her, and which must have been mentioned with the late occurrence, in excuse for her having so privately visited the north apartments, kept her entirely silent on the subject of her apprehension; and she tried only to soothe Annette, who held that Ludovico was certainly to be destroyed; and who was much less affected by Emily's consoling efforts than by the manner of old Dorothee, who often, as she exclaimed 'Ludovico,' sighed, and threw up her eyes to Heaven.

CHAPTER XLIV.

'Ye gods of quiet, and of sleep profound !
Whose soft dominion o'er this castle sways,
And all the widely silent places round,
Forgive me, if my trembling pen displays
What never yet was sung in mortal lays.'
THOMSON.

THE count gave orders for the north apartments to be opened and prepared for the reception of Ludovico; but Dorothee, remembering what she had lately witnessed there, feared to obey; and not one of the other servants daring to venture thither the rooms remained shut up till the time when Ludovico was to retire thither for the night, an hour for which the whole household waited with impatience.

After supper, Ludovico, by the order of the count, attended him in his closet, where they remained for near half an hour; and on leaving which, his lord delivered to him a sword.

'It has seen service in mortal quarrels,' said the count jocosely; 'you will use it honourably, no doubt, in a spiritual one. To-morrow let me hear that there is not one ghost remaining in the chateau.'

Ludovico received it with a respectful bow. 'You shall be obeyed, my lord,' said he; 'I will engage that no spectre shall disturb the peace of the chateau after this night.'

They now returned to the supper-room, where the count's guests awaited to accompany him and Ludovico to the door of the north apartments; and Dorothee, being summoned for the keys, delivered them to Ludovico, who then led the way, followed by most of the inhabitants of the chateau. Having reached the back staircase, several of the servants shrunk back, and refused to go further; but the rest followed him to the top of the staircase, where a broad landing-place allowed them to flock round him, while he applied the key to the door, during which they watched him with as much eager curiosity as if he had been performing some magical rite. —Ludovico, unaccustomed to the lock, could not turn it; and Dorothee, who had lingered far behind, was called forward, under whose hand the door opened slowly; and, her eye glancing within the dusky chamber, she uttered a sudden shriek, and retreated. At this signal of alarm the greater part of the crowd hurried down the stairs; and the count, Henri, and Ludovico were left alone to pursue the inquiry, who instantly rushed into the apartment—Ludovico with a drawn sword, which he had just time to draw from the scabbard; the count with the lamp in his hand; and Henri carrying a basket containing provision for the courageous adventurer.

Having looked hastily round the first room, where nothing appeared to justify alarm, they passed on to the second; and here too all being quiet, they proceeded to a third with a more tempered step. The count had now leisure to smile at the discomposure into which he had been surprised, and to ask Ludovico in which room he designed to pass his night.

'There are several chambers beyond these, your *Excellenza*,' said Ludovico, pointing to a door, and in one of them is a bed, they say. I will pass the night there; and when I am weary of watching, I can lie down.'

'Good,' said the count; 'let us go on. You see these rooms show nothing but damp walls and decaying furniture. I have been so much engaged since I came to the chateau, that I have not looked into them till now. Remember, Ludovico, to tell the housekeeper to-morrow, to throw open these windows. The damask hangings are dropping to pieces: I will have them taken down, and this antique furniture removed.'

'Dear sir !' said Henri, 'here is an arm-chair so massy with gilding, that it resembles one of the state chairs at the Louvre, more than anything else.'

'Yes,' said the count, stopping a moment to survey it, 'there is a history belonging to that chair, but I have not time to tell it—let us pass on. This suite runs to a greater extent

an I had imagined : it is many years since
was in them. But where is the bed-room
u speak of, Ludovico?—these are only
te-chambers to the great drawing-room.
remember them in their splendour.'

'The bed, my lord,' replied Ludovico,
hey told me was in a room that opens
yond the saloon, and terminates the suite.'

'O, here is the saloon,' said the count, as
ey entered the spacious apartment in which
mily and Dorothee had rested. He here
ood for a moment, surveying the relics of
ded grandeur which it exhibited—the sump-
ous tapestry—the long and low sofas of
lvet, with frames heavily carved and gilded
the floor inlaid with small squares of fine
arble, and covered in the centre with a piece
very rich tapestry work—the casements of
tinted glass—and the large Venetian mirrors,
a size and quality such as at that period
rance could not make, which reflected on
ery side the spacious apartment. These had
rmerly also reflected a gay and brilliant
ene, for this had been the state-room of
e chateau, and here the marchioness had
ld the assemblies that made part of the
stivities of her nuptials. If the wand of a ma-
cian could have recalled the vanished groups
many of them vanished even from the earth
that once had passed over these polished
irrors, what a varied and contrasted picture
ould they have exhibited with the present !
ow, instead of a blaze of lights, and a
lendid and busy crowd, they reflected only
e rays of the one glimmering lamp, which
e count held up, and which scarcely served
show the three forlorn figures that stood
urveying the room, and the spacious and
usky walls around them.

'Ah !' said the count to Henri, awaking
om his deep reverie, 'how the scene is
hanged since last I saw it ! I was a young
nan then ; and the marchioness was alive and
her bloom ; many other persons were here,
oo, who are now no more ! There stood the
rchestra ; here we tripped in many a sprightly
naze—the walls echoing to the dance ! Now,
hey resound only one feeble voice—and even
hat will, ere long, be heard no more ! My
on, remember that I was once as young as
ourself, and that you must pass away like
hose who have preceded you—like those who,
s they sung and danced in this once gay
partment, forgot that years are made up of
noments, and that every step they took car-
ied them nearer to their graves. But such
eflections are useless, I had almost said cri-
ninal, unless they teach us to prepare for
ternity ; since otherwise they cloud our present happiness, without guiding us to a future
one. But enough of this—let us go on.'

Ludovico now opened the door of the bed-
oom, and the count, as he entered, was struck
with the funereal appearance which the dark
arras gave to it. He approached the bed

with an emotion of solemnity, and, perceiving
it to be covered with the pall of black velvet,
paused : 'What can this mean?' said he, as he
gazed upon it.

'I have heard, my lord,' said Ludovico, as
he stood at the feet looking within the canopied curtains, 'that the Lady Marchioness de
Villeroi died in this chamber, and remained
here till she was removed to be buried ; and
this perhaps, signor, may account for the
pall.'

The count made no reply, but stood for a
few moments engaged in thought, and evidently much affected. Then, turning to
Ludovico, he asked him with a serious air
whether he thought his courage would support him through the night? 'If you doubt
this,' added the count, 'do not be ashamed to
own it ; I will release you from your engagement, without exposing you to the triumphs
of your fellow-servants.'

Ludovico paused ; pride, and something
very like fear, seemed struggling in his breast :
pride, however, was victorious ;—he blushed,
and his hesitation ceased.

'No, my lord,' said he, 'I will go through
with what I have begun ; and I am grateful
for your consideration. On that hearth I will
make a fire, and, with the good cheer in this
basket, I doubt not I shall do well.

'Be it so,' said the count ; 'but how will you
beguile the tediousness of the night, if you do
not sleep?'

'When I am weary, my lord,' replied Ludovico, 'I shall not fear to sleep ; in the
meanwhile I have a book that will entertain
me.'

'Well,' said the count, 'I hope nothing
will disturb you ; but if you should be seriously
alarmed in the night, come to my apartment.
I have too much confidence in your good sense
and courage to believe you will be alarmed on
slight grounds, or suffer the gloom of this
chamber, or its remote situation, to overcome
you with ideal terrors. To-morrow I shall
have to thank you for an important service ;
these rooms shall then be thrown open, and
my people will be convinced of their error.
Good night, Ludovico ; let me see you early
in the morning, and remember what I lately
said to you.'

'I will, my lord ; good night to your *Excellenza*,—let me attend you with the light.'

He lighted the count and Henri through
the chambers to the outer door. On the landing-place stood a lamp, which one of the
affrighted servants had left ; and Henri, as he
took it up, again bade Ludovico good night,
who having respectfully returned the wish,
closed the door upon them, and fastened it.
Then, as he retired to the bed-chamber, he
examined the rooms through which he passed,
with more minuteness than he had done before, for he apprehended that some person
might have concealed himself in them, f-

purpose of frightening him. No one, how-ever, but himself was in these chambers; and leaving open the doors through which he passed, he came again to the great drawing-room, whose spaciousness and silent gloom somewhat awed him. For a moment he stood, looking back through the long suite of rooms he had quitted; and as he turned, perceiving a light and his own figure reflected in one of the large mirrors, he started. Other objects too were seen obscurely on its dark surface; but he paused not to examine them, and re-turned hastily into the bed-room, as he sur-veyed which, he observed the door of the oriel, and opened it. All within was still. On look-ing round, his eye was arrested by the por-trait of the deceased marchioness, upon which he gazed for a considerable time with great attention and some surprise; and then, having examined the closet, he returned into the bed-room, where he kindled a wood fire, the bright blaze of which revived his spirits, which had begun to yield to the gloom and silence of the place, for gusts of wind alone broke at inter-vals this silence. He now drew a small table and a chair near the fire, took a bottle of wine and some cold provision out of his basket, and regaled himself. When he had finished his repast, he laid his sword upon the table, and, not feeling disposed to sleep, drew from his pocket the book he had spoken of.—It was a volume of old Provençal tales. —Having stirred the fire into a brighter blaze, trimmed his lamp, and drawn his chair upon the hearth, he began to read, and his atten-tion was soon wholly occupied by the scenes which the page disclosed.

The count, meanwhile, had returned to the supper-room, whither those of the party who had attended him to the north apartment had retreated, upon hearing Dorothée's scream, and who were now earnest in their inquiries concerning those chambers. The count rallied his guests on their precipitate retreat, and on the superstitious inclination which had occa-sioned it; and this led to the question, Whe-ther the spirit, after it has quitted the body, is ever permitted to revisit the earth; and if it is, whether it was possible for spirits to be-come visible to the sense? The baron was of opinion that the first was probable, and the last was possible; and he endeavoured to justify this opinion by respectable authorities, both ancient and modern, which he quoted. The count, however, was decidedly against him; and a long conversation ensued, in which the usual arguments on these subjects were on both sides brought forward with skill, and discussed with candour, but without con-verting either party to the opinion of his op-ponent. The effect of their conversation on their auditors was various. Though the count had much the superiority of the baron in point of argument, he had considerably fewer ad-herents; for that love, so natural to the human

mind, of whatever is able to distend its faculties with wonder and astonishment, attached the majority of the company to the side of the baron; and though many of the count's propo-sitions were unanswerable, his opponents were inclined to believe this the consequence of their own want of knowledge on so abstracted a sub-ject, rather than that arguments did not exist which were forcible enough to conquer his.

Blanche was pale with attention, till the ridicule in her father's glance called a blush upon her countenance, and she then en-deavoured to forget the superstitious tales she had been told in her convent. Meanwhile, Emily had been listening with deep attention to the discussion of what was to her a very interesting question; and remembering the appearance she had witnessed in the apart-ment of the late marchioness, she was fre-quently chilled with awe. Several times she was on the point of mentioning what she had seen; but the fear of giving pain to the count, and the dread of his ridicule, restrained her; and awaiting in anxious expectation the event of Ludovico's intrepidity, she determined that her future silence should depend upon it.

When the party had separated for the night, and the count retired to his dressing-room, the remembrance of the desolate scenes he had lately witnessed in his own mansion deeply affected him, but at length he was aroused from his reverie and his silence. 'What music is that I hear?' said he suddenly to his valet; 'Who plays at this late hour!'

The man made no reply; and the count con-tinued to listen, and then added, 'That is no common musician; he touches the instrument with a delicate hand—who is it, Pierre?'

'My lord!' said the man hesitatingly.

'Who plays that instrument?' repeated the count.

'Does not your lordship know, then?' said the valet.

'What mean you?' said the count, some-what sternly.

'Nothing, my lord, I meant nothing,' re-joined the man submissively—'only—that mu-sic—goes about the house at midnight often, and I thought your lordship might have heard it before.'

'Music goes about the house at midnight! Poor fellow!—does nobody dance to the mu-sic, too?'

'It is not in the chateau, I believe, my lord; the sounds come from the woods, they say, though they seem so near;—but then a spirit can do anything.'

'Ah, poor fellow!' said the count, 'I per-ceive you are as silly as the rest of them; to-morrow you will be convinced of your ridiculous error. But hark!—what voice is that?'

'Oh, my lord! that is the voice we often hear with the music.'

'Often!' said the count: 'How often, pray? It is a very fine one.'

'Why, my lord, I myself have not heard it
ore than two or three times; but there are
ose who have lived here longer, that have
ard it often enough.'

'What a swell was that!' exclaimed the
unt, as he still listened—'and now what a
ring cadence! This is surely something
ore than mortal!'

'That is what they say, my lord,' said the
ilet; 'they say it is nothing mortal that
ters it; and if I might say my thoughts——'

'Peace!' said the count, and he listened till
e strain died away.

'This is strange!' said he, as he turned from
e window—'Close the casements, Pierre.'

Pierre obeyed, and the count soon after dis-
issed him; but did not so soon lose the re-
embrance of the music, which long vibrated in
s fancy in tones of melting sweetness, while
urprise and perplexity engaged his thoughts.

Ludovico, meanwhile, in his remote cham-
er, heard now and then the faint echo of a
osing door as the family retired to rest, and
ien the hall clock at a great distance strike
velve. 'It is midnight,' said he,—and he
oked suspiciously round the spacious cham-
er. The fire on the hearth was now nearly
xpiring; for, his attention having been en-
aged by the book before him, he had for-
otten everything besides; but he soon added
esh wood, not because he was cold, though
ie night was stormy, but because he was
ieerless; and having again trimmed his
.mp, he poured out a glass of wine, drew
is chair nearer to the crackling blaze, tried to
e deaf to the wind that howled mournfully
t the casements, endeavoured to abstract his
iind from the melancholy that was stealing
pon him, and again took up his book. It
ad been lent to him by Dorothée, who had
ormerly picked it up in an obscure corner of
ie marquis's library, and who, having
pened it and perceived some of the marvels
related, had carefully preserved it for her
wn entertainment, its condition giving her
ome excuse for detaining it from its proper
tation. The damp corner into which it had
illen had caused the cover to be disfigured
nd mouldy, and the leaves to be so dis-
oloured with spots, that it was not without
ifficulty the letters could be traced. The
ctions of the Provençal writers, whether
rawn from the Arabian legends brought by
he Saracens into Spain, or recounting the
hivalric exploits performed by the crusaders
hom the troubadors accompanied to the
'ast, were generally splendid, and always
iarvellous both in scenery and incident; and
: is not wonderful that Dorothée and Ludo-
icó should be fascinated by inventions which
iad captivated the careless imagination in
very rank of society in a former age. Some
of the tales, however, in the book now before
ludovico were of simple structure, and ex-
iibited nothing of the magnificent machinery

and heroic manners which usually characterised the fables of the twelfth century, and
of this description was the one he now happened to open; which in its original style was
of great length, but which may be thus shortly
related. The reader will perceive that it is
strongly tinctured with the superstition of the
times.

THE PROVENÇAL TALE.

'There lived in the province of Bretagne a
noble baron, famous for his magnificence and
courtly hospitalities. His castle was graced
with ladies of exquisite beauty, and thronged
with illustrious knights; for the honours he
paid to feats of chivalry invited the brave of
distant countries to enter his lists, and his
court was more splendid than those of many
princes. Eight minstrels were retained in his
service, who used to sing to their harps romantic fictions taken from the Arabians, or adventures of chivalry that befel knights during the
Crusades, or the martial deeds of the baron,
their lord;—while he, surrounded by his knights
and ladies, banqueted in the great hall of his
castle, where the costly tapestry that adorned
the walls with pictured exploits of his ancestors, the casements of painted glass enriched with armorial bearings, the gorgeous
banners that waved along the roof, the sumptuous canopies, the profusion of gold and
silver that glittered on the sideboards, the
numerous dishes that covered the tables, the
number and gay liveries of the attendants,
with the chivalric and splendid attire of the
guests, united to form a scene of magnificence, such as we may not hope to see in
these *degenerate days*.

'Of the baron the following adventure is
related. One night, having retired late from
the banquet to his chamber, and dismissed
his attendants, he was surprised by the appearance of a stranger of a noble air, but of
a sorrowful and dejected countenance. Believing that this person had been secreted in
the apartment, since it appeared impossible
he could have lately passed the ante-room unobserved by the pages in waiting, who would
have prevented this intrusion on their lord,
the baron, calling loudly for his people, drew
his sword, which he had not yet taken from
his side, and stood upon his defence. The
stranger, slowly advancing, told him that
there was nothing to fear; that he came with
no hostile design, but to communicate to him
a terrible secret, which it was necessary for
him to know.

'The baron, appeased by the courteous
manners of the stranger, after surveying him
for some time in silence, returned his sword
into the scabbard, and desired him to explain
the means by which he had obtained access to
the chamber, and the purpose of this extraordinary visit.

'Without answering either of these

quiries, the stranger said that he could not then explain himself, but that if the baron would follow him to the edge of the forest, at a short distance from the castle walls, he would there convince him that he had something of importance to disclose.

'This proposal again alarmed the baron, who would scarcely believe that the stranger meant to draw him to so solitary a spot at this hour of the night; without harbouring a design against his life ; and he refused to go, observing, at the same time, that if the stranger's purpose was an honourable one, he would not persist in refusing to reveal the occasion of his visit in the apartment where they were.

' While he spoke this, he viewed the stranger still more attentively than before, but observed no change in his countenance, nor any symptom that might intimate a consciousness of evil design. He was habited like a knight, was of a tall and majestic stature, and of dignified and courteous manners. Still, however, he refused to communicate the subject of his errand in any place but that he had mentioned ; and at the same time gave hints concerning the secret he would disclose, that awakened a degree of solemn curiosity in the baron, which at length induced him to consent to the stranger on certain conditions.

' "Sir knight," said he, " I will attend you to the forest, and will take with me only four of my people, who shall witness our conference."

' To this, however, the knight objected.

' "What I would disclose," said he with solemnity, "is to you alone. There are only three living persons to whom the circumstance is known : it is of more consequence to you and your house than I shall now explain. In future years you will look back to this night with satisfaction or repentance, accordingly as you now determine. As you would hereafter prosper—follow me ; I pledge you the honour of a knight, that no evil shall befall you. If you are contented to dare futurity—remain in your chamber, and I will depart as I came."

' "Sir knight," replied the baron, "how is it possible that my future peace can depend upon my present determination ?"

' "That is not now to be told," said the stranger ; "I have explained myself to the utmost. It is late ; if you follow me, it must be quickly ;—you will do well to consider the alternative."

' The baron mused ; and as he looked upon the knight, he perceived his countenance assume a singular solemnity.

[Here Ludovico thought he heard a noise, and he threw a glance round the chamber, and then held up the lamp to assist his observation ; but not perceiving anything to confirm his alarm, he took up the book again, and pursued the story.]

' The baron paced his apartment for some time in silence, impressed by the words of the stranger, whose extraordinary request he feared to grant, and feared also to refuse. At length he said, "Sir knight, you are utterly unknown to me ; tell me yourself,—is it reasonable that I should trust myself alone with a stranger, at this hour, in a solitary forest ? Tell me, at least, who you are, and who assisted to secrete you in this chamber."

' The knight frowned at these latter words, and was a moment silent ; then, with a countenance somewhat stern, he said,

' "I am an English knight ; I am called Sir Bevys of Lancaster.—and my deeds are not unknown at the Holy City, whence I was returning to my native land, when I was benighted in the neighbouring forest."

' "Your name is not unknown to fame," said the baron ; "I have heard of it. (The knight looked haughtily.) But why, since my castle is known to entertain all true knights, did not your herald announce you ? Why did you not appear at the banquet, where your presence would have been welcomed, instead of hiding yourself in my castle, and stealing to my chamber at midnight ?"

' The stranger frowned, and turned away in silence ; but the baron repeated the questions.

' "I come not," said the knight, "to answer inquiries, but to reveal facts. If you would know more, follow me, and again I pledge the honour of a knight that you shall return in safety. Be quick in your determination—I must be gone."

' After some further hesitation, the baron determined to follow the stranger, and to see the result of his extraordinary request : he therefore again drew forth his sword, and, taking up a lamp, bade the knight lead on. The latter obeyed ; and opening the door of the chamber, they passed into the ante-room, where the baron, surprised to find all his pages asleep, stopped, and with hasty violence was going to reprimand them for their carelessness, when the knight waved his hand, and looked so expressively upon the baron, that the latter restrained his resentment, and passed on.

' The knight, having descended a staircase, opened a secret door which the baron had believed was known only to himself, and, proceeding through several narrow and winding passages, came at length to a small gate that opened beyond the walls of the castle. Meanwhile the baron followed in silence and amazement, on perceiving that these secret passages were so well known to a stranger, and felt inclined to return from an adventure that appeared to partake of treachery as well as danger. Then, considering that he was armed, and observing the courteous and noble air of his conductor, his courage returned, he blushed that it had failed him for a moment, and he resolved to trace the mystery to its source.

' He now found himself on the heathy platform before the great gates of his castle, where, on looking up, he perceived lights glimmering in the different casements of the guests, who were retiring to sleep ; and while he shivered in the blast, and looked on the dark and desolate scene around him, he thought of the comforts of his warm chamber rendered cheerful by the blaze of wood, and felt, for a moment, the full contrast of his present situation.

[Here Ludovico paused a moment, and, looking at his own fire, gave it a brightening stir.]

' The wind was strong, and the baron watched his lamp with anxiety, expecting every moment to see it extinguished ; but though the flame wavered, it did not expire, and he still followed the stranger, who often sighed as he went, but did not speak.

' When they reached the borders of the forest, the knight turned and raised his head, as if he meant to address the baron ; but then closing his lips in silence, he walked on.

' As they entered beneath the dark and spreading boughs, the baron, affected by the solemnity of the scene, hesitated whether to proceed, and demanded how much further they were to go. The knight replied only by a gesture ; and the baron, with hesitating steps and a suspicious eye, followed through an obscure and intricate path, till, having proceeded a considerable way, he again demanded whither they were going, and refused to proceed unless he was informed.

' As he said this, he looked at his own sword and at the knight alternately, who shook his head, and whose dejected countenance disarmed the baron, for a moment, of suspicion.

' " A little further is the place whither I would lead you," said the stranger : " no evil shall befall you—I have sworn it on the honour of a knight."

' The baron, re-assured, again followed in silence, and they soon arrived at a deep recess of the forest, where the dark and lofty chesnuts entirely excluded the sky, and which was so overgrown with underwood that they proceeded with difficulty. The knight sighed deeply as he passed, and sometimes paused ; and having at length reached a spot where the trees crowded into a knot, he turned, and with a terrific look, pointing to the ground, the baron saw there the body of a man stretched at its length and weltering in blood ; a ghastly wound was on the forehead, and death appeared already to have contracted the features.

' The baron, on perceiving the spectacle, started in horror, looked at the knight for explanation, and was then going to raise the body, and examine if there were yet any remains of life ; but the stranger, waving his hand, fixed upon him a look so earnest and mournful, as not only much surprised him, but made him desist.

' But what were the baron's emotions, when, on holding the lamp near the features of the corpse, he discovered the exact resemblance of the stranger his conductor, to whom he now looked up in astonishment and inquiry ! As he gazed, he perceived the countenance of the knight change and begin to fade, till his whole form gradually vanished from his astonished sense ! While the baron stood, fixed to the spot, a voice was heard to utter these words :—

[Ludovico started, and laid down the book, for he thought he heard a voice in the chamber, and he looked toward the bed, where, however, he saw only the dark curtains and the pall. He listened, scarcely daring to draw his breath, but heard only the distant roaring of the sea in the storm, and the blast that rushed by the casements ; when, concluding that he had been deceived by its sighings, he took up his book to finish the story.]

' " The body of Sir Bevys of Lancaster, a noble knight of England, lies before you. He was this night way-laid and murdered, as he journeyed from the Holy City towards his native land. Respect the honour of knighthood and the law of humanity ; inter the body in Christian ground, and cause his murderers to be punished. As ye observe or neglect this, shall peace and happiness, or war and misery, light upon you and your house for ever ! "

' The baron, when he recovered from the awe and astonishment into which this adventure had thrown him, returned to his castle, whither he caused the body of Sir Bevys to be removed ; and on the following day it was interred, with the honours of knighthood, in the chapel of the castle, attended by all the noble knights and ladies who graced the court of Baron de Brunne.'

Ludovico, having finished this story, laid aside the book, for he felt drowsy ; and after putting more wood on the fire, and taking another glass of wine, he reposed himself in the arm-chair on the hearth. In his dream he still beheld the chamber where he really was, and once or twice started from imperfect slumbers, imagining he saw a man's face looking over the high back of his arm-chair. This idea had so strongly impressed him, that when he raised his eyes he almost expected to meet other eyes fixed upon his own ; and he quitted his seat, and looked behind the chair, before he felt perfectly convinced that no person was there.

Thus closed the hour.

CHAPTER XLV.

'Enjoy the honey-heavy dew of slumber;
Thou hast no figures, nor no fantasies,
Which busy care draws in the brains of men ;
Therefore thou sleep'st so sound.'
                                    SHAKESPEARE.

THE count, who had slept little during the night, rose early, and anxious to speak with Ludovico, went to the north apartment ; but the outer door having been fastened on the preceding night, he was obliged to knock loudly for admittance. Neither the knocking nor his voice was heard ; but considering the distance of this door from the bedroom, and that Ludovico, wearied with watching, had probably fallen into a deep sleep, the count was not surprised on receiving no answer ; and leaving the door, he went down to walk in his grounds.

It was a grey autumnal morning. The sun, rising over Provence, gave only a feeble light, as his rays struggled through the vapours that ascended from the sea, and floated heavily over the woodtops, which were now varied with many a mellow tint of autumn. The storm was passed, but the waves yet violently agitated, and their course was traced by long lines of foam, while not a breeze fluttered in the sails of the vessels near the shore that were weighing anchor to depart. The still gloom of the hour was pleasing to the count, and he pursued his way through the woods sunk in deep thought.

Emily also rose at an early hour, and took her customary walk along the brow of the promontory that overhung the Mediterranean. Her mind was not now occupied with the occurrences of the chateau, and Valancourt was the subject of her mournful thoughts ; whom she had not yet taught herself to consider with indifference, though her judgment constantly reproached her for the affection that lingered in her heart, after her esteem for him was departed. Remembrance frequently gave her his parting look and the tones of his voice when he had bade her a last farewell ; and some accidental associations now recalling these circumstances to her fancy with peculiar energy, she shed bitter tears at the recollection.

Having reached the watch-tower, she seated herself on the broken steps, and in melancholy dejection watched the waves, half hid in a vapour, as they came rolling towards the shore, and threw up their light spray round the rocks below. Their hollow murmur, and the obscuring mists that came in wreaths up the cliffs, gave a solemnity to the scene which was in harmony with the temper of her mind, and she sat, given up to the remembrance of past times, till this became too painful, and she abruptly quitted the place. On passing the little gate of the watch-tower, she observed letters engraved on the stone postern, which she paused to examine ; and though they

appeared to have been rudely cut with a penknife, the characters were familiar to her : at length, recognising the handwriting of Valancourt she read with trembling anxiety, the following lines, entitled

SHIPWRECK.

'Tis solemn midnight ! On this lonely steep,
Beneath this watch-tower's desolated wall,
Where mystic shapes the wanderer appall,
I rest ; and view below the desert deep,
As through tempestuous clouds the moon's cold
    light
Gleams on the wave. Viewless, the winds of night
With loud mysterious force the billows sweep,
And sullen roar the surges far below.
In the still pauses of the gust I hear
The voice of spirits rising sweet and slow,
And oft among the clouds their forms appear.
But hark ! what shriek of death comes in the gale,
And in the distant ray what glimmering sail
Bends to the storm ?—Now sinks the note of fear !
Ah ! wretched mariners !—no more shall day
Unclose his cheering eye to light you on your way !

From these lines it appeared that Valancourt had visited the tower ; that he had probably been here on the preceding night, for it was such a one as they described, and that he had left the building very lately, since it had not long been light, and without light it was impossible these letters could have been cut. It was thus even probable that he might be yet in the gardens.

As these reflections passed rapidly over the mind of Emily, they called up a variety of contending emotions, that almost overcame her spirits : but her first impulse was to avoid him, and immediately leaving the tower, she returned with hasty steps towards the chateau. As she passed along, she remembered the music she had lately heard near the tower, with the figure which had appeared ; and in this moment of agitation she was inclined to believe that she had then heard and seen Valancourt ; but other recollections soon convinced her of her error. On turning into a thicker part of the woods, she perceived a person walking slowly in the gloom at some little distance ; and, her mind engaged by the idea of him, she started and paused, imagining this to be Valancourt. The person advanced with quicker steps ; and before she could recover recollection enough to avoid him, he spoke, and she then knew the voice of the count, who expressed some surprise on finding her walking at so early an hour, and made a feeble effort to rally her on her love of solitude. But he soon perceived this to be more a subject of concern than of light laughter, and changing his manner, affectionately expostulated with Emily on thus indulging unavailing regret, who, though she acknowledged the justness of all he said, could not restrain her tears while she did so, and he presently quitted the topic. Expressing surprise at not having yet heard from his friend, the advocate at Avignon, in answer to the questions prosed to him respecting the estates of the late dame Montoni, he with friendly zeal endvoured to cheer Emily with hopes of ablishing her claim to them; while she . that the estates could now contribute le to the happiness of a life in which Valanirt had no longer an interest.

When they returned to the chateau, Emily ired to her apartment, and Count de Villet to the door of the north chambers. This s still fastened; but being now determined arouse Ludovico, he renewed his calls more idly than before; after which a total silence sued; and the count, finding all his efforts be heard ineffectual, at length began to fear it some accident had befallen Ludovico, iom terror of an imaginary being might ve deprived of his senses. He therefore t the door with an intention of summoning i servants to force it open, some of whom now heard moving in the lower part of the ateau.

To the count's inquiries, whether they had en or heard Ludovico, they replied, in aff ght, that not one of them had ventured on e north side of the chateau since the preceding night.

'He sleeps soundly then,' said the count, nd is at such a distance from the outer door, iich is fastened, that to gain admittance to e chambers it will be necessary to force it. 'ing an instrument and follow me.'

The servant stood mute and dejected; and was not till nearly all the household were sembled, that the count's orders were eyed. In the meantime, Dorothee was lling of a door that opened from a gallery ading from the great staircase into the last te-room of the saloon; and this being much arer to the bed-chamber, it appeared probble that Ludovico might be easily awakened ' an attempt to open it. Thither, therefore, the unt went: but his voice was as ineffectual at is door as it had proved at the remoter one: id now, seriously interested for Ludovico, e was himself going to strike upon the door ith the instrument, when he observed its ngular beauty, and withheld the blow. It opeared on the first glance to be of ebony, dark and close was its grain, and so high s polish; but it proved to be only of larch ood, of the growth of Provence, then famous r its forests of larch. The beauty of its olished hue, and of its delicate carvings, determined the count to spare this door, and he turned to that leading from the back stairise; which, being at length forced, he ntered the first ante-room, followed by lenri and a few of the most courageous of is servants, the rest awaiting the event f the inquiry on the stairs and landinglace.

All was silent in the chambers through which he count passed; and, having reached the ilgon, he called loudly upon Ludovico; after

which, still receiving no answer, he threw open the door of the bed-room and entered.

The profound stillness within confirmed his apprehensions for Ludovico, for not even the breathings of a person in sleep was heard; and his uncertainty was soon terminated, since, the shutters being all closed, the chamber was too dark for any object to be distinguished in it.

The count bade a servant open them, who, as he crossed the room to do so, stumbled over something and fell to the floor; when his cry occasioned such panic among the few of his fellows who had ventured thus far, that they instantly fled, and the count and Henri were left to finish the adventure.

Henri then sprung across the room, and opening a window-shutter, they perceived that the man had fallen over a chair near the hearth in which Ludovico had been sitting;—for he sat there no longer, nor could he any where be seen by the imperfect light that was admitted into the apartment. The count, seriously alarmed, now opened other shutters, that he might be enabled to examine further; and Ludovico, not yet appearing, he stood for a moment suspended in astonishment, and scarcely trusting his senses, till his eyes glancing on the bed, he advanced to examine whether he was there asleep. No person, however, was in it; and he proceeded to the oriel, where everything remained as on the preceding night, but Ludovico was no where to be found.

The count now checked his amazement, considering that Ludovico might have left the chambers during the night, overcome by the terrors which their lonely desolation and the recollected reports concerning them had inspired. Yet, if this had been the fact, the man would naturally have sought society, and his fellow-servants had all declared they had not seen him; the door of the outer room also had been found fastened with the key on the inside. It was impossible, therefore, for him to have passed through that; and all the outer doors of this suite were found, on examination, to be bolted and locked, with the keys also within them. The count, being then compelled to believe that the lad had escaped through the casements, next examined them; but such as opened wide enough to admit the body of a man were found to be carefully secured either by iron bars or by shutters, and no vestige appeared of any person having attempted to pass them; neither was it probable that Ludovico would have incurred the risk of breaking his neck by leaping from a window, when he might have walked safely through a door.

The count's amazement did not admit of words; but he returned once more to examine the bed-room, where was no appearance of disorder, except that occasioned by the late overthrow of the chair, near which had stoo·

small table; and on this Ludovico's sword, his lamp, the book he had been reading, and the remnant of his flask of wine, still remained. At the foot of the table, too, was the basket with some fragments of provision and wood.

Henri and the servant now uttered their astonishment without reserve; and though the count said little, there was a seriousness in his manner that expressed much. It appeared that Ludovico must have quitted these rooms by some concealed passage, for the count could not believe that any supernatural means had occasioned this event; yet, if there was any such passage, it seemed inexplicable why he should retreat through it; and it was equally surprising, that not even the smallest vestige should appear, by which his progress could be traced. In the rooms everything remained as much in order as if he had just walked out by the common way.

The count himself assisted in lifting the arras with which the bed-chamber, saloon, and one of the ante-rooms were hung, that he might discover if any door had been concealed behind it; but, after a laborious search, none was found: and he at length quitted the apartments, having secured the door of the last ante-chamber, the key of which he took into his own possession. He then gave orders that strict search should be made for Ludovico, not only in the chateau, but in the neighbourhood; and retiring with Henri to his closet, they remained there in conversation for a considerable time; and, whatever was the subject of it, Henri from this hour lost much of his vivacity, and his manners were particularly grave and reserved whenever the topic which now agitated the count's family with wonder and alarm was introduced.

On the disappearing of Ludovico, Baron St. Foix seemed strengthened in all his former opinions concerning the probability of apparitions, though it was difficult to discover what connexion there could possibly be between the two subjects, or to account for this effect, otherwise than by supposing that the mystery attending Ludovico, by exciting awe and curiosity, reduced the mind to a state of sensibility which rendered it more liable to the influence of superstition in general. It is however certain, that from this period the baron and his adherents became more bigoted in their own systems than another, while the terrors of the count's servants increased to an excess that occasioned many of them to quit the mansion immediately, and the rest remained only till others could be procured to supply their places.

The most strenuous search after Ludovico proved unsuccessful; and after several days of indefatigable inquiry, poor Annette gave herself up to despair, and the other inhabitants of the chateau to amazement.

Emily, whose mind had been deeply affected by the disastrous fate of the late marchioness, and with the mysterious connexion which she fancied had existed between her and St. Aubert, was particularly impressed by the late extraordinary event, and much concerned for the loss of Ludovico, whose integrity and faithful services claimed both her esteem and gratitude. She was now very desirous to return to the quiet retirement of her convent; but every hint of this was received with real sorrow by Lady Blanche, and affectionately set aside by the count, for whom she felt much of the respectful love and admiration of a daughter, and to whom, by Dorothee's consent, she at length mentioned the appearance which they had witnessed in the chamber of the deceased marchioness. At any other period he would have smiled at such a relation, and have believed that its object had existed only in the distempered fancy of the relater; but he now attended to Emily with seriousness; and, when she concluded, requested of her a promise that this occurrence should rest in silence. 'Whatever may be the cause and the import of these extraordinary occurrences,' added the count, 'time only can explain them. I shall keep a wary eye upon all that passes in the chateau, and shall pursue every possible means of discovering the fate of Ludovico. Meanwhile, we must be prudent and silent. I will myself watch in the north chambers; but of this we will say nothing till the night arrives when I purpose doing so.'

The count then sent for Dorothee, and required of her also a promise of silence concerning what she had already, or might in future witness of an extraordinary nature: and this ancient servant now related to him the particulars of the Marchioness de Villeroi's death, with some of which he appeared to be already acquainted, while by others he was evidently surprised and agitated. After listening to this narrative, the count retired to his closet, where he remained alone for several hours; and when he again appeared, the solemnity of his manner surprised and alarmed Emily, but she gave no utterance to her thoughts.

On the week following the disappearance of Ludovico, all the count's guests took leave of him, except the baron, his son, Mons. St. Foix, and Emily; the latter of whom was soon after embarrassed and distressed by the arrival of another visitor, Mons. du Pont, which made her determine upon withdrawing to her convent immediately. The delight that appeared in his countenance when he met her, told that he brought back the same ardour of passion which had formerly banished him from Chateau-le-Blanc. He was received with reserve by Emily, and with pleasure by the count, who presented him to her with a smile that seemed intended to plead his cause, and who did not hope the less for his friend, from the embarrassment she betrayed.

But M. du Pont, with truer sympathy, seemed to understand her manner, and his countenance quickly lost its vivacity, and sunk into the languor of despondency.

On the following day, however, he sought an opportunity of declaring the purport of his visit, and renewed his suit; a declaration which was received with real concern by Emily, who endeavoured to lessen the pain she might inflict by a second rejection, with assurances of esteem and friendship: yet she left him in a state of mind that claimed and excited her tenderest compassion; and being more sensible than ever of the impropriety of remaining longer at the chateau, she immediately sought the count, and communicated to him her intention of returning to the convent.

'My dear Emily,' said he, 'I observe with extreme concern the illusion you are encouraging—an illusion common to young and sensible minds. Your heart has received a severe shock; you believe you can never entirely recover it; and you will encourage this belief, till the habit of indulging sorrow will subdue the strength of your mind, and discolour your future views with melancholy regret. Let me dissipate this illusion, and awaken you to a sense of your danger.'

Emily smiled mournfully. 'I know what you would say, my dear sir,' said she, 'and am prepared to answer you. I feel that my heart can never know a second affection; and that I must never hope even to recover its tranquillity—if I suffer myself to enter into a second engagement.'

'I know that you feel all this,' replied the count; 'and I know also that time will overcome these feelings, unless you cherish them in solitude, and, pardon me, with romantic tenderness:—then, indeed, time will only confirm habit. I am particularly empowered to speak on this subject, and to sympathize in your sufferings,' added the count with an air of solemnity, 'for I have known what it is to love, and to lament the object of my love. Yes,' continued he, while his eyes filled with tears, 'I have suffered!—but those times have passed away—long passed! and I can now look back upon them without emotion.'

'My dear sir,' said Emily timidly, 'what mean those tears?—they speak, I fear, another language—they plead for me.'

'They are weak tears, for they are useless ones,' replied the count, drying them; 'I would have you superior to such weakness. These, however, are only faint traces of a grief which, if it had not been opposed by long-continued effort, might have led me to the verge of madness! Judge, then, whether I have not cause to warn you of an indulgence which may produce so terrible an effect, and which must certainly, if not opposed, overcloud the years that might otherwise be happy. M. du Pont is a sensible and amiable man, who has long

been tenderly attached to you; his family and fortune are unexceptionable:—after what I have said, it is unnecessary to add, that I should rejoice in your felicity, and that I think M. du Pont would promote it. Do not weep Emily,' continued the count, taking her hand, 'there *is* happiness reserved for you.'

He was silent a moment; and then added in a firmer voice, 'I do not wish that you should make a violent effort to overcome your feeling; all I at present ask is, that you will check the thoughts that would lead you to a remembrance of the past; that you will suffer your mind to be engaged by present objects; that you will allow yourself to believe it possible you may yet be happy; and that you will sometimes think with complacency of poor Du Pont, and not condemn him to the state of despondency, from which, my dear Emily, I am endeavouring to withdraw you.'

'Ah! my dear sir,' said Emily, while her tears still fell, 'do not suffer the benevolence of your wishes to mislead Mons. du Pont with an expectation that I can ever accept his hand. If I understand my own heart, this never can be; your instruction I can obey in almost every other particular than that of adopting a contrary belief.'

'Leave me to understand your heart,' replied the count with a faint smile. 'If you pay me the compliment to be guided by my advice in other instances, I will pardon your incredulity respecting your future conduct towards Mons. du Pont. I will not even press you to remain longer at the chateau than your own satisfaction will permit; but though I forbear to oppose your present retirement, I shall urge the claims of friendship for your future visits.'

Tears of gratitude mingled with those of tender regret, while Emily thanked the count for the many instances of friendship she had received from him; promised to be directed by his advice upon every subject but one; and assured him of the pleasure with which she should, at some future period, accept the invitation of the countess and himself—if Mons. du Pont was not at the chateau.

The count smiled at this condition. 'Be it so,' said he: 'meanwhile the convent is so near the chateau, that my daughter and I shall often visit you; and if, sometimes, we should dare to bring you another visitor—will you forgive us?'

Emily looked distressed, and remained silent.

'Well,' rejoined the count, 'I will pursue the subject no further, and must now entreat your forgiveness for having pressed it thus far. You will, however, do me the justice to believe that I have been urged only by a sincere regard for your happiness, and that of my amiable friend Mons. du Pont.'

Emily, when she left the count, went to mention her intended departure to the coun' ess, who opposed it with polite expressions of regret ; after which, she sent a note to acquaint the lady abbess that she should return to the convent ; and thither she withdrew on the evening of the following day. M. du Pont, in extreme regret, saw her depart, while the count endeavoured to cheer him with a hope that Emily would some time regard him with a more favourable eye.

She was pleased to find herself once more in the tranquil retirement of the convent, where she experienced a renewal of all the maternal kindness of the abbess, and of the sisterly attentions of the nuns. A report of the late extraordinary occurrence at the chateau had already reached them ; and after supper, on the evening of her arrival, it was the subject of conversation in the convent parlour, where she was requested to mention some particulars of that unaccountable event. Emily was guarded in her conversation on this subject, and briefly related a few circumstances concerning Ludovico, whose disappearance, her auditors almost unanimously agreed, had been effected by supernatural means.

A belief had so long prevailed, said a nun, who was called sister Frances, that the chateau was haunted, that I was surprised when I heard the count had the temerity to inhabit it. Its former possessor, I fear, had some deed of conscience to atone for : let us hope that the virtues of its present owner would preserve him from the punishment due to the errors of the last, if, indeed, he was criminal.

'Of what crime then was he suspected ?' said a Mademoiselle Feydeau, a boarder at the convent.

'Let us pray for his soul !' said a nun, who had till now sat in silent attention. 'If he was criminal, his punishment in this world was sufficient.'

There was a mixture of wildness and solemnity in her manner of delivering this, which struck Emily exceedingly ; but Mademoiselle repeated her question, without noticing the solemn eagerness of the nun.

'I dare not presume to say what was his crime,' replied sister Frances ; 'but I have heard many reports of an extraordinary nature respecting the late Marquis de Villeroi, and among others, that soon after the death of his lady he quitted Chateau-le-Blanc, and never afterwards returned to it. I was not here at the time, so I can only mention it from report ; and so many years have passed since the marchioness died, that few of our sisterhood, I believe, can do more.'.

'But I can,' said the nun, who had before spoken, and whom they called sister Agnes.

'You, then,' said Mademoiselle Feydeau, 'are possibly acquainted with circumstances that enable you to judge whether he was criminal or not, and what was the crime imputed to him.'

'I am,' replied the nun ; 'but who shall dare to scrutinize my thoughts—who shall dare to pluck out my opinion ? God only is his judge, and to that judge he is gone.'

Emily looked with surprise at sister Frances, who returned her a significant glance.

'I only requested your opinion,' said Mademoiselle Feydeau mildly ; 'if the subject is displeasing to you, I will drop it.'

'Displeasing !' said the nun with emphasis : —'we are idle talkers ; we do not weigh the meaning of the words we use ; *displeasing* is a poor word. I will go pray.' As she said this, she rose from her seat, and with a profound sigh quitted the room.

'What can be the meaning of this ?' said Emily, when she was gone.

'It is nothing extraordinary,' replied sister Frances, 'she is often thus : but she has no meaning in what she says. Her intellects are at times deranged. Did you never see her thus before ?'

'Never,' said Emily. 'I have, indeed, sometimes thought that there was the melancholy of madness in her look, but never before perceived it in her speech. Poor soul, I will pray for her !'

'Your prayers then, my daughter, will unite with ours,' observed the lady abbess ; 'she has need of them.'

'Dear lady,' said Mademoiselle Feydeau, addressing the abbess, 'what is your opinion of the late marquis ? The strange circumstances that have occurred at the chateau have so awakened my curiosity, that I shall be pardoned the question. What was his imputed crime, and what the punishment to which sister Agnes alluded ?'

'We must be cautious of advancing our opinion,' said the abbess with an air of reserve mingled with solemnity—'we must be cautious of advancing our opinion on so delicate a subject. I will not take upon me to pronounce that the late marquis was a criminal, or to say what was the crime of which he was suspected ; but, concerning the punishment our daughter Agnes hinted, I know of none he suffered. She probably alluded to the severe one which an exasperated conscience can inflict. Beware, my children, of incurring so terrible a punishment—it is the purgatory of this life ! The late marchioness I knew well ; she was a pattern to such as live in the world ; nay, our sacred order need not have blushed to copy her virtues. Our holy convent received her mortal part ; her heavenly spirit, I doubt not, ascended to its sanctuary !'

As the abbess spoke this, the last bell of vespers struck up, and she rose. 'Let us go, my children,' said she, 'and intercede for the wretched ; let us go and confess our sins, and endeavour to purify our souls for the heaven to which *she* is gone !'

Emily was affected by the solemnity of this

ıortation, and remembering her father,
he heaven to which *he* too is gone!' said
: faintly, as she repressed her sighs, and
lowed the abbess and nuns to the chapel.

———

CHAPTER XLVI.

e thou a spirit of health, or goblin damn'd,
ring with thee airs from heaven, or blasts from
 hell,
e thy intents wicked or charitable,
. . . .
. . . I will speak to thee . . : . .'
       HAMLET.

)UNT DE VILLEFORT at length received a
ter from the advocate at Avignon, encour-
ing Emily to assert her claim to the estates
the late Madame Montoni ; and about the
me time a messenger arrived from the late
. Quesnel, with intelligence that made an
peal to the law on this subject unnecessary,
ıce it appeared that the only person who
uld have opposed her claim was now no
ɔre. A friend of M. Quesnel, who resided
Venice, had sent him an account of the
ath of Montoni, who had been brought to
al with Orsino, as his supposed accomplice
the murder of the Venetian nobleman.
rsino was found guilty, condemned and
ecuted upon the wheel ; but nothing being
scovered to criminate Montoni and his col-
ıgues on this charge, they were all released
:cept Montoni, who, being considered by
e senate as a very dangerous person, was,
r other reasons, ordered again into confine-
ent, where it was said he had died in a doubt-
l and mysterious manner, and not without sus-
cion of having been poisoned. The autho-
ty from which M. Quesnel had received this
formation would not allow him to doubt its
uth ; and he told Emily, that she had now
ɪly to lay claim to the estates of her late
ınt to secure them ; and added, that he
ould himself assist in the necessary forms of
ıis business. The term for which La Vallée
ɪd been let being now also nearly expired,
e acquainted her with the circumstance, and
ɪvised her to take the road thither through
'houlouse, where he promised to meet her,
nd where it would be proper for her to take
ossession of the estates of the late Madame
ɪontoni ; adding that he would spare her any
ifficulties that might occur on that occasion
ɔm the want of knowledge on the subject,
nd that he believed it would be necessary for
er to be at Thoulouse in about three weeks
'om the present time.

An increase of fortune seemed to have
.wakened this sudden kindness in M. Quesnel
owards his niece ; and it appeared that he
ntertained more respect for the rich heiress,
han he had ever felt compassion for the poor
ınd unfriended orphan.

The pleasure with which she received this
intelligence was clouded when she considered
that he, for whose sake she had once regretted
the want of fortune, was no longer worthy of
sharing it with her ; but remembering the
friendly admonition of the count, she checked
this melancholy reflection, and endeavoured
to feel only gratitude for the unexpected good
that now attended her ; while it formed no
inconsiderable part of her satisfaction to know
that La Vallée, her native home, which was endeared to her by its having been the residence
of her parents, would be restored to her possession. There she meant to fix her future
residence ; for, though it could not be compared with the chateau at Thoulouse, either
for extent or magnificence, its pleasant scenes,
and the tender remembrances that haunted
them, had claims upon her heart which she
was not inclined to sacrifice to ostentation.
She wrote immediately to thank M. Quesnel for the active interest he took in her concerns, and to say that she would meet him at
Thoulouse at the appointed time.

When Count de Villefort, with Blanche,
came to the convent to give Emily the advice
of the advocate, he was informed of the contents of M. Quesnel's letter, and gave his
sincere congratulations on the occasion ; but
she observed, that when the first expression of
satisfaction had faded from his countenance,
an unusual gravity succeeded, and she scarcely
hesitated to inquire its cause.

' It has no new occasion,' replied the count ;
' I am harassed and perplexed by the confusion into which my family is thrown by their
foolish superstition. Idle reports are floating
round me, which I can neither admit to be
true nor prove to be false ; and I am also
very anxious about the poor fellow Ludovico,
concerning whom I have not been able to
obtain information. Every part of the chateau, and every part of the neighbourhood
too, has, I believe, been searched, and I
know not what further can be done, since I
have already offered large rewards for the recovery of him. The keys of the north apartment I have not suffered to be out of my
possession since he disappeared, and I mean
to watch in those chambers myself this very
night.'

Emily, seriously alarmed for the count,
united her entreaties with those of the Lady
Blanche, to dissuade him from his purpose.

' What should I fear?' said he. ' I have no
faith in supernatural combats ; and for human
opposition I shall be prepared ; nay, I will
even promise not to watch alone.'

' But who, dear sir, will have courage enough
to watch with you?' said Emily.

' My son,' replied the count. ' If I am not
carried off in the night,' added he smiling,
' you shall hear the result of my adventure to-
morrow.'

The count and Lady Blanche shortly afte

wards took leave of Emily, and returned to the chateau, where he informed Henri of his intention, who, not without some secret reluctance, consented to be the partner of his watch; and when the design was mentioned after supper, the countess was terrified, and the baron and M. Du Pont joined with her in entreating that he would not tempt his fate as Ludovico had done. 'We know not,' added the baron, 'the nature or the power of an evil spirit; and that such a spirit haunts those chambers can now, I think, scarcely be doubted. Beware, my lord, how you provoke his vengeance, since it has already given us one terrible example of its malice. I allow it may be probable that the spirits of the dead are permitted to return to the earth only on occasions of high import; but the present import may be your destruction.'

The count could not forbear smiling: 'Do you think, then, baron,' said he, 'that my destruction is of sufficient importance to draw back to earth the soul of the departed? Alas! my good friend, there is no occasion for such means to accomplish the destruction of any individual. Wherever the mystery rests, I trust I shall this night be able to detect it.' You know I am not superstitious.'

'I know that you are incredulous,' interrupted the baron.

'Well, call it what you will; I mean to say that, though you know I am free from superstition, if anything supernatural has appeared, I doubt not it will appear to me; and if any strange event hangs over my house, or if any extraordinary transaction has formerly been connected with it, I shall probably be made acquainted with it. At all events I will invite discovery; and that I may be equal to a mortal attack, which in good truth, my friend, is what I most expect, I shall take care to be well armed.'

The count took leave of his family for the night with an assumed gaiety, which but ill concealed the anxiety that depressed his spirits, and retired to the north apartments, accompanied by his son, and followed by the baron, M. Du Pont, and some of the domestics, who all bade him good night at the outer door. In these chambers everything appeared as when he had last been here: even in the bedroom no alteration was visible, where he lighted his own fire, for none of the domestics could be prevailed upon to venture thither. After carefully examining the chamber and the oriel, the count and Henri drew their chairs upon the hearth, set a bottle of wine and a lamp before them, laid their swords upon the table, and, stirring the wood into a blaze, began to converse on indifferent topics. But Henri was often silent and abstracted, and sometimes threw a glance of mingled awe and curiosity round the gloomy apartment; while the count gradually ceased to converse, and sat either lost in thought, or reading a

volume of Tacitus, which he had brought to beguile the tediousness of the night.

⁎   ——

CHAPTER XLVII.

'Give thy thoughts no tongue.'
SHAKESPEARE.

THE Baron St. Foix, whom anxiety for his friend had kept awake, rose early to inquire the event of the night; when, as he passed the count's closet, hearing steps within, he knocked at the door, and it was opened by his friend himself. Rejoicing to see him in safety, and curious to learn the occurrences of the night, he had not immediately leisure to observe the unusual gravity that overspread the features of the count, whose reserved answers first occasioned him to notice it. The count, then smiling, endeavoured to treat the subject of his curiosity with levity; but the baron was serious, and pursued his inquiries so closely, that the count at length, resuming his gravity, said, 'Well, my friend, press the subject no further, I entreat you; and let me request also that you will hereafter be silent upon any thing you may think extraordinary in my future conduct. I do not scruple to tell you that I am unhappy, and that the watch of the last night has not assisted me to discover Ludovico; upon every occurrence of the night you must excuse my reserve.'

'But where is Henri?' said the baron with surprise and disappointment at this denial.

'He is well, in his own apartment,' replied the count. 'You will not question him on this topic, since you know my wish.'

'Certainly not,' said the baron, somewhat chagrined, 'since it would be displeasing to you; but methinks, my friend, you might rely on my discretion, and drop this unusual reserve. However, you must allow me to suspect that you have seen reason to become a convert to my system, and are no longer the incredulous knight you lately appeared to be.'

'Let us talk no more upon the subject,' said the count: 'you may be assured that no ordinary circumstance has imposed this silence upon me, towards a friend whom I have called so for near thirty years; and my present reserve cannot make you question either my esteem, or the sincerity of my friendship.'

'I will not doubt either,' said the baron, 'though you must allow me to express my surprise at this silence.'

'To me I will allow it,' replied the count; 'but I earnestly entreat that you will forbear to notice it to my family, as well as every thing remarkable you may observe in my conduct towards them.'

The baron readily promised this; and after conversing for some time on general topics, they descended to the breakfast-room, where he count met his family with a cheerful countenance, and evaded their inquiries by employing light ridicule and assuming an air of uncommon gaiety, while he assured them that they need not apprehend anything from the north chambers, since Henri and himself had been permitted to return from them in safety.

Henri, however, was less successful in disguising his feelings. From his countenance an expression of terror was not entirely faded ; he was often silent and thoughtful ; and when he attempted to laugh at the eager inquiries of Mademoiselle Bearn, it was evidently only an attempt.

In the evening, the count called, as he had promised, at the convent, and Emily was surprised to perceive a mixture of playful ridicule and of reserve in his mention of the north apartment. Of what had occurred there, however, he said nothing ; and when she ventured to remind him of his promise to tell her the result of his inquiries, and to ask if he had received any proof that those chambers were haunted, his look became solemn for a moment : then, seeming to recollect himself, he smiled, and said, ' My dear Emily, do not suffer my lady abbess to infect your good understanding with these fancies : she will teach you to expect a ghost in every dark room.' ' But believe me,' added he with a profound sigh, ' the apparition of the dead comes not on light or sportive errands, to terrify or to surprise the timid.' He paused, and fell into a momentary thoughtfulness, and then added, ' We will say no more on this subject.'

Soon after, he took leave ; and when Emily joined some of the nuns, she was surprised to find them acquainted with a circumstance which she had carefully avoided to mention, and expressing their admiration of his intrepidity in having dared to pass a night in the apartment whence Ludovico had disappeared ; for she had not considered with what rapidity a tale of wonder circulates. The nuns had acquired their information from peasants who brought fruit to the monastery, and whose whole attention had been fixed, since the disappearance of Ludovico, on what was passing in the castle.

Emily listened in silence to the various opinions of the nuns concerning the conduct of the count, most of whom condemned it as rash and presumptuous, affirming that it was provoking the vengeance of an evil spirit, thus to intrude upon its haunts.

Sister Frances contended, that the count had acted with the bravery of a virtuous mind. He knew himself guiltless of aught that should provoke a good spirit, and did not fear the spells of an evil one, since he could claim the protection of a higher power ; of Him who can command the wicked and will protect the innocent.'

' The guilty cannot claim that protection !' said sister Agnes. ' Let the count look to his conduct, that he do not forfeit his claim ! Yet who is he that shall dare to call himself innocent ?—all earthly innocence is but comparative. Yet still how wide asunder are the extremes of guilt, and to what a horrible depth may we fall ! Oh !——'

The nun, as she concluded, uttered a shuddering sigh, that startled Emily, who looking up perceived the eyes of Agnes fixed on hers ; after which the sister rose, took her hand, gazed earnestly upon her countenance for some moments in silence, and then said—

' You are young—you are innocent ! I mean you are yet innocent of any great crime !— But you have passions in your heart,—scorpions : they sleep now—beware how you awaken them !—they will sting you, even unto death !'

Emily, affected by these words, and by the solemnity with which they were delivered, could not suppress her tears.

' Ah ! is it so ?' exclaimed Agnes, her countenance softening from its sternness ; ' so young, and so unfortunate ! We are sisters, then, indeed. Yet there is no bond of kindness among the guilty,' she added, while her eyes resumed their wild expression, 'no gentleness—no peace, no hope ! I knew them all once—my eyes could weep—but now they burn ; for now my soul is fixed and fearless ! —I lament no more !'

' Rather let us repent and pray,' said another nun. ' We are taught to hope that prayer and penitence will work our salvation. There is hope for all who repent !'

' Who repent and turn to the true faith,' observed sister Frances.

' For all but me !' replied Agnes solemnly, who paused, and then abruptly added, ' My head burns ; I believe I am not well. O ! could I strike from my memory all former scenes—the figures that rise up, like furies, to torment me !—I see them when I sleep, and when I am awake : they are still before my eyes ! I see them now—now !'

She stood in a fixed attitude of horror, her straining eyes moving slowly round the room, as if they followed something. One of the nuns gently took her hand, to lead her from the parlour. Agnes became calm, drew her other hand across her eyes, looked again, and, sighing deeply, said, ' They are gone— they are gone ! I am feverish, I know not what I say. I am thus sometimes, but it will go off again ; I shall soon be better—Was not that the vesper-bell ?'

' No,' replied Frances, ' the evening service is passed. Let Margaret lead you to your cell.'

' You are right,' replied sister Agnes, ' I shall be better there. Good night, my sisters ; remember me in your orisons.'

When they had withdrawn, Frances, observing Emily's emotions, said, ' Do not be alarmed, our sister is often thus deranged, though I have not lately seen her so frantic her usual mood is melancholy. This fit has been coming on for several days; seclusion and the customary treatment will restore her.'

'But how rationally she conversed at first!' observed Emily; 'her ideas followed each other in perfect order.'

'Yes,' replied the nun, 'this is nothing new: nay, I have sometimes known her argue not only with method but with acuteness, and then in a moment start off into madness.'

'Her conscience seems afflicted, said Emily; 'did you ever hear what circumstance reduced her to this deplorable condition?'

'I have,' replied the nun, who said no more till Emily repeated the question; when she added in a low voice, and looking significantly towards the other boarders, 'I cannot tell you now; but if you think it worth your while, come to my cell to night, when our sisterhood are at rest, and you shall hear more; but remember we rise to midnight prayers, and come either before or after midnight.'

Emily promised to remember; and the abbess soon after appearing, they spoke no more of the unhappy nun.

The count meanwhile, on his return home, had found M. Du Pont in one of those fits of despondency which his attachment to Emily frequently occasioned him, an attachment that had subsisted too long to be easily subdued, and which had already outlived the opposition of his friends. M. Du Pont had first seen Emily in Gascony during the lifetime of his parent, who, on discovering his son's partiality for Mademoiselle St. Aubert, his inferior in point of fortune, forbade him to declare it to her family, or to think of her more. During the life of his father he had observed the first command, but had found it impracticable to obey the second, and had sometimes soothed his passion by visiting her favourite haunts, among which was the fishing-house, where, once or twice, he addressed her in verse, concealing his name in obedience to the promise he had given his father. There too he played the pathetic air to which she had listened with such surprise and admiration; and there he found the miniature that had since cherished a passion fatal to his repose. During this expedition into Italy, his father died; but he received his liberty at a moment when he was the least enabled to profit by it, since the object that rendered it most valuable was no longer within the reach of his vows. By what accident he discovered Emily, and assisted to release her from a terrible imprisonment, has already appeared, and also the unavailing hope with which he then encouraged his love, and the fruitless efforts that he had since made to overcome it.

The count still endeavoured, with friendly zeal, to soothe him with a belief that patience, perseverance, and prudence, would finally obtain for him happiness and Emily. 'Time,' said he, 'will wear away the melancholy impression which disappointment has left on her mind, and she will be sensible of your merit. Your services have already awakened her gratitude, and your sufferings her pity; and trust me, my friend, in a heart so sensible as hers, gratitude and pity lead to love. When her imagination is rescued from its present delusion, she will readily accept the homage of a mind like yours.'

Du Pont sighed while he listened to these words; and endeavouring to hope what his friend believed, he willingly yielded to an invitation to prolong his visit at the chateau, which we now leave for the monastery of St. Claire.

When the nuns had retired to rest, Emily stole to her appointment with sister Frances, whom she found in her cell, engaged in prayer before a little table, where appeared the image she was addressing, and, above, the dim lamp that gave light to the place. Turning her eyes, as the door opened, she beckoned to Emily to come in, who, having done so, seated herself in silence beside the nun's little mattress of straw, till her orisons should conclude. The latter soon rose from her knees; and taking down the lamp and placing it on the table, Emily perceived there a human skull and bones lying beside an hour-glass: but the nun, without observing her emotion, sat down on the mattress by her, saying, 'Your curiosity, sister, has made you punctual; but you have nothing remarkable to hear in the history of poor Agnes, of whom I avoided to speak in the presence of my lay-sisters, only because I would not publish her crime to them.'

'I shall consider your confidence in me as a favour,' said Emily, 'and will not misuse it.'

'Sister Agnes,' resumed the nun, 'is of a noble family, as the dignity of her air must already have informed you; but I will not dishonour their name so much as to reveal it. Love was the occasion of her crime and of her madness. She was beloved by a gentleman of inferior fortune; and her father, as I have heard, bestowing her on a nobleman whom she disliked, an ill-governed passion proved her destruction. Every obligation of virtue and of duty was forgotten, and she profaned her marriage-vows; but her guilt was soon detected, and she would have fallen a sacrifice to the vengeance of her husband, had not her father contrived to convey her from his power. By what means he did this, I never could learn; but he secreted her in this convent, where he afterwards prevailed with her to take the veil, while a report was circulated in the world that she was dead; and the father, to save his daughter, assisted the rumour, and employed such means as induced her husband to believe she had become a victim to his jealousy. You look surprised,' added the nun, observing Emily's countenance; 'I allow the story is uncommon, but not, I believe, without a parallel.'

'Pray proceed,' said Emily, 'I am interested.'

'The story is already told,' resumed the nun; 'I have only to mention, that the long struggle which Agnes suffered between love, remorse, and a sense of the duties she had taken upon herself in becoming of our order, at length unsettled her reason. At first she was frantic and melancholy by quick alternatives; then she sunk into a deep and settled melancholy, which still, however, has at times been interrupted by fits of wildness, and of late these have again been frequent.'

Emily was affected by the history of the sister, some parts of whose story brought to her remembrance that of the Marchioness de Villeroi, who had also been compelled by her father to forsake the object of her affections, for a nobleman of his choice; but, from what Dorothee had related, there appeared no reason to suppose that she had escaped the vengeance of a jealous husband, or to doubt for a moment the innocence of her conduct. But Emily, while she sighed over the misery of the nun, could not forbear shedding a few tears to the misfortunes of the marchioness; and when she returned to the mention of sister Agnes, she asked Frances if she remembered her in her youth, and whether she was then beautiful.

'I was not here at the time when she took the vows,' replied Frances, 'which is so long ago that few of the present sisterhood, I believe, were witnesses of the ceremony; nay, even our lady mother did not then preside over the convent; but I can remember when sister Agnes was a very beautiful woman. She retains that air of high rank which always distinguished her, but her beauty, you must perceive, is fled; I can scarcely discover even a vestige of the loveliness that once animated her features.'

'It is strange,' said Emily, 'but there are moments when her countenance has appeared familiar to my memory! You will think me fanciful; and I think myself so, for I certainly never saw sister Agnes before I came to this convent, and I must therefore have seen some person whom she strongly resembles, though of this I have no recollection.'

'You have been interested by the deep melancholy of her countenance,' said Frances, 'and its impression has probably deluded your imagination; for I might as reasonably think I perceive a likeness between you and Agnes, as you, that you have seen her anywhere but in this convent, since this has been her place of refuge for nearly as many years as make your age.'

'Indeed!' said Emily.

'Yes,' rejoined Frances; 'and why does that circumstance excite your surprise?'

Emily did not appear to notice this question,

but remained thoughtful for a few moments, and then said, 'It was about that same period that the Marchioness de Villeroi expired.'

'That is an odd remark,' said Frances.

Emily, recalled from her reverie, smiled, and gave the conversation another turn; but it soon came back to the subject of the unhappy nun, and Emily remained in the cell of sister Frances till the midnight bell aroused her; when apologizing for having interrupted the sister's repose till this late hour, they quitted the cell together. Emily returned to her chamber, and the nun, bearing a glimmering taper, went to her devotion in the chapel.

Several days followed, during which Emily saw neither the count, nor any of his family; and when at length he appeared, she remarked, with concern, that his air was unusually disturbed.

'My spirits are harassed,' said he, in answer to her anxious inquiries, 'and I mean to change my residence for a little while, an experiment which I hope will restore my mind to its usual tranquillity. My daughter and myself will accompany the Baron St. Foix to his chateau. It lies in a valley of the Pyrenees that opens towards Gascony, and I have been thinking, Emily, that when you set out for La Vallée we may go part of the way together; it would be a satisfaction to me to guard you towards your home.'

She thanked the count for his friendly consideration, and lamented that the necessity for her going first to Thoulouse would render this plan impracticable. 'But when you are at the baron's residence,' she added, 'you will be only a short journey from La Vallée, and I think, sir, you will not leave the country without visiting me; it is unnecessary to say with what pleasure I should receive you and the Lady Blanche.'

'I do not doubt it' replied the count, 'and I will not deny myself and Blanche the pleasure of visiting you, if your affairs should allow you to be at La Vallée about the time when we can meet you there.'

When Emily said that she should hope to see the countess also, she was not sorry to learn that this lady was going, accompanied by Mademoiselle Bearn, to pay a visit for a few weeks to a family in Lower Languedoc.

The count, after some further conversation on his intended journey and on the arrangement of Emily's, took leave; and many days did not succeed this visit before a second letter from M. Quesnel informed her that he was then at Thoulouse, that La Vallée was at liberty, and that he wished her to set off for the former place, where he awaited her arrival with all possible despatch, since his own affairs pressed him to return to Gascony. Emily did not hesitate to obey him; and having taken an affecting leave of the count's family, in which M. du Pont was still included, and of her friends at the convent, she set out

Thoulouse attended by the unhappy Annette, and guarded by a steady servant of the count.

___

CHAPTER XLVIII.

'Lull'd in the countless chambers of the brain,
  Our thoughts are link'd by many a hidden chain;
  Awake but one, and lo, what myriads rise!
  Each stamps its image as the other flies.
              PLEASURES OF MEMORY.'

EMILY pursued her journey without any accident, along the plains of Languedoc towards the north-west; and on this her return to Thoulouse, which she had last left with Madame Montoni, she thought much on the melancholy fate of her aunt, who but for her own imprudence might now have been living in happiness there! Montoni, too, often rose to her fancy, such as she had seen him in his days of triumph, bold, spirited, and commanding; such also as she had since beheld him in his days of vengeance; and now, only a few short months had passed—and he had no longer the power or the will to afflict;—he had become a clod of earth, and his life was vanished like a shadow! Emily could have wept at his fate, had she not remembered his crimes; for that of her unfortunate aunt she did weep; and all sense of her errors was overcome by the recollection of her misfortunes.

Other thoughts and other emotions succeeded as Emily drew near the well-known scenes of her early love, and considered that Valancourt was lost to her and to himself for ever. At length she came to the brow of the hill, whence, on her departure for Italy, she had given a farewell look to this beloved landscape, amongst whose woods and fields she had so often walked with Valancourt, and where he was then to inhabit, when she would be far, far away! She saw, once more, that chain of the Pyrenees which overlooked La Vallée, rising like faint clouds on the horizon. 'There, too, is Gascony extended at their feet!' said she. 'O my father—my mother! And there too is the Garonne!' she added, drying the tears that obscured her sight—'and Thoulouse, and my aunt's mansion—and the groves in her garden!—O my friends! are ye all lost to me!—must I never, never see you more?' Tears rushed again to her eyes, and she continued to weep, till an abrupt turn in the road had nearly occasioned the carriage to overset, when, looking up, she perceived another part of the well-known scene around Thoulouse; and all the reflections and anticipations which she had suffered at the moment when she bade it last adieu, came with recollected force to her heart. She remembered how anxiously she had looked forward into futurity, which was to decide her happiness concerning Valancourt, and what

depressing fears had assailed her; the very words she had uttered, as she withdrew her last look from the prospect, came to her memory. 'Could I but be certain,' she had then said, 'that I should ever return, and that Valancourt would still live for me—I should go in peace!'

Now, that futurity so anxiously anticipated was arrived: she was returned—but what a dreary blank appeared!—Valancourt no longer lived for her! She had no longer even the melancholy satisfaction of contemplating his image in her heart, for he was no longer the same Valancourt she had cherished there—the solace of many a mournful hour, the animating friend that had enabled her to bear up against the oppression of Montoni—the distant hope that had beamed over her gloomy prospect! On perceiving this beloved idea to be an illusion of her own creation, Valancourt seemed to be annihilated, and her soul sickened at the blank that remained. His marriage with a rival, even his death, she thought she could have endured with more fortitude than this discovery; for then, amidst all her grief, she could have looked in secret upon the image of goodness which her fancy had drawn of him, and comfort would have mingled with her suffering!

Drying her tears, she looked once more upon the landscape which had excited them, and perceived that she was passing the very bank where she had taken leave of Valancourt on the morning of her departure from Thoulouse! and she now saw him through her returning tears, such as he had appeared when she looked from the carriage to give him a last adieu—saw him leaning mournfully against the high trees, and remembered the fixed look of mingled tenderness and anguish with which he had then regarded her. This recollection was too much for her heart, and she sank back in the carriage, nor once looked up till it stopped at the gates of what was now her own mansion.

These being opened, and by the servant to whose care the chateau had been intrusted, the carriage drove into the court, where alighting, she hastily passed through the great hall, now silent and solitary, to a large oak parlour, the common sitting-room of the late Madame Montoni; where, instead of being received by M. Quesnel, she found a letter from him, informing her that business of consequence had obliged him to leave Thoulouse two days before. Emily was, upon the whole, not sorry to be spared his presence, since his abrupt departure appeared to indicate the same indifference with which he had formerly regarded her. This letter informed her, also, of the progress he had made in the settlement of her affairs; and concluded with directions concerning the forms of some business which remained for her to transact. But M. Quesnel's unkindness did not long occupy her thoughts, which returned to the remembrance of the persons she had been accustomed to see in this mansion, and chiefly of the ill-guided and unfortunate Madame Montoni. In the room where she now sat, she had breakfasted with her on the morning of their departure for Italy; and the view of it brought most forcibly to her recollection all she had herself suffered at that time, and the many gay expectations which her aunt had formed respecting the journey before her. While Emily's mind was thus engaged, her eyes wandered unconsciously to a large window that looked upon the garden, and here new memorials of the past spoke to her heart; for she saw extended before her the very avenue in which she had parted with Valancourt on the eve of her journey; and all the anxiety, the tender interest he had shown concerning her future happiness, his earnest remonstrances against her committing herself to the power of Montoni, and the truth of his affection, came afresh to her memory. At this moment it appeared almost impossible that Valancourt could have become unworthy of her regard: and she doubted all that she had lately heard to his disadvantage, and even his own words, which had confirmed Count de Villefort's report of him. Overcome by the recollections which the view of this avenue occasioned, she turned abruptly from the window, and sunk into a chair beside it, where she sat, given up to grief, till the entrance of Annette with coffee aroused her.

'Dear madam, how melancholy this place looks now,' said Annette, 'to what it used to do! It is dismal coming home, when there is nobody to welcome one!'

This was not the moment in which Emily could bear the remark; her tears fell again; and as soon as she had taken the coffee she retired to her apartment, where she endeavoured to repose her fatigued spirits. But busy memory would still supply her with the visions of former times: she saw Valancourt interesting and benevolent, as he had been wont to appear in the days of their early love, and amidst the scenes where she had believed that they should some time pass their years together!—but at length sleep closed these afflicting scenes from her view.

On the following morning serious occupation recovered her from such melancholy reflections,; for, being desirous of quitting Thoulouse, and of hastening on to La Vallée, she made some inquiries into the condition of the estate, and immediately dispatched a part of the necessary business concerning it, according to the directions of Monsieur Quesnel. It required a strong effort to abstract her thoughts from other interests sufficiently to attend to this; but she was rewarded for her exertions by again experiencing that employment is the surest antidote to sorrow.

This day was devoted entirely to business; and among other concerns she employed means to learn the situation of all her poor tenants, that she might relieve their wants, or confirm their comforts.

In the evening, her spirits were so much strengthened that she thought she could bear to visit the gardens where she had so often walked with Valancourt, and knowing that if she delayed to do so their scenes would only affect her the more whenever they should be viewed, she took advantage of the present state of her mind, and entered them.

Passing hastily the gate leading from the court into the gardens, she hurried up the great avenue, scarcely permitting her memory to dwell for a moment on the circumstance of her having here parted with Valancourt, and soon quitted this for other walks less interesting to her heart. These brought her at length to the flight of steps that led from the lower garden to the terrace, on seeing which, she became agitated, and hesitated whether to ascend; but, her resolution returning, she proceeded.

'Ah!' said Emily as she ascended, 'these are the same high trees that used to wave over the terrace, and these the same flowery thickets—the laburnum, the wild rose, and the cerinthe—which were wont to grow beneath them! Ah! and there too, on that bank are the very plants which Valancourt so carefully reared!—O when last I saw them!—She checked the thought, but could not restrain her tears; and after walking slowly on for a few moments, her agitation upon the view of this well-known scene increased so much, that she was obliged to stop, and lean upon the wall of the terrace. It was a mild and beautiful evening. The sun was setting over the extensive landscape, to which his beams, sloping from beneath a dark cloud that overhung the west, gave rich and partial colouring, and touched the tufted summits of the groves that rose from the garden below with a yellow gleam. Emily and Valancourt had often admired together this scene at the same hour; and it was exactly on this spot that, on the night preceding her departure for Italy, she had listened to his remonstrances against the journey, and to the pleadings of passionate affection. Some observations which she made on the landscape brought this to her remembrance, and with it all the minute particulars of that conversation; the alarming doubts he had expressed concerning Montoni, doubts which had since been fatally confirmed; the reasons and entreaties he had employed to prevail with her to consent to an immediate marriage; the tenderness of his love, the paroxysms of his grief, and the conviction he had repeatedly expressed, that they should never meet again in happiness! All these circumstances rose afresh to her mind, and awakened the various emotions she had then suffered. Her tenderness for Valancourt became as powerful as in the moments when she thought that she was parting with him and happiness together, and when the strength of her mind had enabled her to triumph over present suffering rather than to deserve the reproach of her conscience by engaging in a clandestine marriage.— 'Alas!' said Emily, as these recollections came to her mind, 'and what have I gained by the fortitude I then practised?—am I happy now?—He said, we should meet no more in happiness; but, O! he little thought his own misconduct would separate us, and lead to the very evil he then dreaded!'

Her reflections increased her anguish, while she was compelled to acknowledge that the fortitude she had formerly exerted, if it had not conducted her to happiness, had saved her from irretrievable misfortune, from Valancourt himself! But in these moments she could not congratulate herself on the prudence that had saved her; she could only lament, with bitterest anguish, the circumstances which had conspired to betray Valancourt into a course of life so different from that which the virtues, the tastes, and the pursuits of his early years had promised; but she still loved him too well to believe that his heart was even now depraved, though his conduct had been criminal. An observation which had fallen from M. St. Aubert more than once, now recurred to her. 'This young man,'said he, speaking of Valancourt, 'has never been at Paris:' a remark that had surprised her at the time it was uttered, but which she now understood: and she exclaimed sorrowfully, 'O Valancourt! if such a friend as my father had been with you at Paris—your noble, ingenuous nature would not have fallen!'

The sun was now set; and recalling her thoughts from their melancholy subject, she continued her walk; for the pensive shade of twilight was pleasing to her, and the nightingales from the surrounding groves began to answer each other in the long-drawn plaintive note which always touched her heart; while all the fragrance of the flowery thickets that bounded the terrace, was awakened by the cool evening air, which floated so lightly among their leaves, that they scarcely trembled as it passed.

Emily came at length to the steps of the pavilion that terminated the terrace, and where her last interview with Valancourt, before her departure from Thoulouse, had so unexpectedly taken place. The door was now shut, and she trembled while she hesitated whether to open it; but her wish to see again a place which had been the chief scene of her former happiness, at length overcoming her reluctance to encounter the painful regret it would renew, she entered. The room was obscured by a melancholy shade; but through the open lattices, darkened by the hanging foliage of the vines, appeared the dusky landscape, the Garonne reflecting the evening light, and the west still glowing. A chair was placed near one of the balconies, as if some persons had been sitting there; but the other furniture of the pavilion remained exactly as usual, and Emily thought it looked as if it had not once been moved since she set out for Italy. The silent and deserted air of the place added solemnity to her emotions; for she heard only the low whisper of the breeze as it shook the leaves of the vines, and the very faint murmur of the Garonne.

She seated herself in a chair near the lattice, and yielded to the sadness of her heart, while she recollected the circumstances of her parting interview with Valancourt on this spot. It was here, too, that she had passed some of the happiest hours of her life with him, when her aunt favoured the connexion; for here she had often sat and worked, while he conversed or read; and she now well remembered with what discriminating judgment, with what tempered energy, he used to repeat some of the sublimest passages of their favourite authors; how often he would pause to admire with her their excellence, and with what tender delight he would listen to her remarks, and correct her taste.

'And is it possible,' said Emily, as these recollections returned—'is it possible that a mind so susceptible of whatever is grand or beautiful, could stoop to low pursuits, and be subdued by frivolous temptations?'

She remembered how often she had seen the sudden tear start in his eye, and had heard his voice tremble with emotion, while he related any great or benevolent action, or repeated a sentiment of the same character. 'And such a mind,' said she, 'such a heart, were to be sacrificed to the habits of a great city!'

These recollections becoming too painful to be endured, she abruptly left the pavilion, and, anxious to escape from the memorials of her departed happiness, returned towards the chateau. As she passed along the terrace, she perceived a person walking with a slow step and a dejected air, under the trees, at some distance. The twilight, which was now deep, would not allow her to distinguish who it was, and she imagined it to be one of the servants, till the sound of her steps seeming to reach him, he turned half round, and she thought she saw Valancourt!

Whoever it was, he instantly struck among the thickets on the left, and disappeared; while Emily, her eyes fixed on the place whence he had vanished, and her frame trembling so excessively that she could scarcely support herself, remained for some moments unable to quit the spot, and scarcely conscious of existence. With her recollection her strength returned, and she hurried towards the house, where she did not venture to inquire who had been in the gardens, lest she should betray her emotion; and she sat down alone, endeavouring to recollect the figure, air, and features, of the person she had just seen. Her view of him, however, had been so transient, and the gloom had rendered it so imperfect, that she could remember nothing with exactness; yet the general appearance of his figure, and his abrupt departure, made her still believe that this person was Valancourt. Sometimes, indeed, she thought that her fancy, which had been occupied by the idea of him, had suggested his image to her uncertain sight; but this conjecture was fleeting. If it was himself whom she had seen, she wondered much that he should be at Thoulouse, and more, how he had gained admittance into the garden: but as often as her impatience prompted her to inquire whether any stranger had been admitted, she was restrained by an unwillingness to betray her doubts; and the evening was passed in anxious conjecture, and in efforts to dismiss the subject from her thoughts. But these endeavours were ineffectual; and a thousand inconsistent emotions assailed her, whenever she fancied that Valancourt might be near her: now she dreaded it to be true, and now she feared it to be false; and while she constantly tried to persuade herself that she wished the person whom she had seen might not be Valancourt, her heart as constantly contradicted her reason.

The following day was occupied by the visits of several neighbouring families, formerly intimate with Madame Montoni, who came to condole with Emily on her death, to congratulate her upon the acquisition of these estates, and to inquire about Montoni, and concerning the strange reports they had heard of her own situation; all which was done with the utmost decorum, and the visitors departed with as much composure as they had arrived.

Emily was wearied by these formalities, and disgusted by the subservient manners of many persons, who had thought her scarcely worthy of common attention while she was believed to be a dependant on Madame Montoni.

'Surely,' said she, 'there is some magic in wealth, which can thus make persons pay their court to it, when it does not even benefit themselves. How strange it is that a fool or a knave, with riches, should be treated with more respect by the world, than a good man or a wise man in poverty!'

It was evening before she was left alone, and she then wished to have refreshed her spirits in the free air of her garden; but she feared to go thither, lest she should meet again the person whom she had seen on the preceding night, and he should prove to be Valancourt. The suspense and anxiety she suffered on this subject, she found all her efforts unable to control; and her secret wish to see Valancourt once more, though unseen by him, powerfully prompted her to go: but prudence and a delicate pride restrained her; and she determined to avoid the possibility of throwing herself in his way, by forbearing to visit the gardens for several days,

When, after near a week, she again ventured thither, she made Annette her companion, and confined her walk to the lower grounds; but often started as the leaves rustled in the breeze, imagining that some person was among the thickets; and at the turn of every alley she looked forward with apprehensive expectation. She pursued her walk thoughtfully and silently; for her agitation would not suffer her to converse with Annette, to whom, however, thought and silence were so intolerable that she did not scruple at length to talk to her mistress.

'Dear madam,' said she, 'why do you start so? one would think you knew what has happened.'

'What has happened?' said Emily in a faltering voice, and trying to command her emotion.

'The night before last, you know, madam—'

'I know nothing, Annette,' replied her lady in a more hurried voice.

'The night before last, madam, there was a robber in the garden.'

'A robber!' said Emily, in an eager yet doubting tone.

'I suppose he was a robber, madam—what else could he be?'

'Where did you see him, Annette?' rejoined Emily, looking round her, and turning back towards the chateau.

'It was not I that saw him, madam: it was Jean, the gardener. It was twelve o'clock at night; and as he was coming across the court to go the back way into the house, what should he see but somebody walking in the avenue that fronts the garden-gate! So, with that, Jean guessed how it was, and he went into the house for his gun.'

'His gun!' exclaimed Emily.

'Yes, madam, his gun; and then he came out into the court to watch him. Presently he sees him come slowly down the avenue, and lean over the garden-gate, and look up at the house for a long time; and I warrant he examined it well, and settled what window he should break in at.'

'But the gun,' said Emily—'the gun!'

'Yes, madam, all in good time. Presently, Jean says, the robber opened the gate, and was coming into the court, and then he thought proper to ask him his business: so he called out again, and bade him say who he was, and what he wanted. But the man would do neither; but turned upon his heel, and passed into the garden again. Jean knew then well enough how it was, and so he fired after him.'

'Fired!' exclaimed Emily.

'Yes, madam, fired off his gun; but, Holy Virgin! what makes you look so pale, madam? The man was not killed,—I dare say; but if he was, his comrades carried him off: for, when Jean went in the morning to look for the body, it was gone, and nothing to be seen but a track of blood on the ground. Jean followed it, that he might find out where the man got into the garden, but it was lost in the grass, and——'

Annette was interrupted : for Emily's spirits died away, and she would have fallen to the ground, if the girl had not caught her, and supported her to a bench close to them.

When, after a long absence, her senses returned, Emily desired to be led to her apartment ; and though she trembled with anxiety to inquire further on the subject of her alarm, she found herself too ill at present to dare the intelligence which it was possible she might receive of Valancourt. Having dismissed Annette that she might weep and think at liberty, she endeavoured to recollect the exact air of the person whom she had seen on the terrace, and still her fancy gave her the figure of Valancourt. She had, indeed, scarcely a doubt that it was he whom she had seen, and at whom the gardener had fired ; for the manner of the latter person, as described by Annette, was not that of a robber : nor did it appear probable that a robber would have come alone to break into a house so spacious as this.

When Emily thought herself sufficiently recovered to listen to what Jean might have to relate, she sent for him ; but he could inform her of no circumstance that might lead to a knowledge of the person who had been shot, or of the consequence of the wound ; and after severely reprimanding him for having fired with bullets, and ordering diligent inquiry to be made in the neighbourhood for the discovery of the wounded person, she dismissed him, and herself remained in the same state of terrible suspense. All the tenderness she had felt for Valancourt was recalled by the sense of his danger ; and the more she considered the subject, the more her conviction strengthened that it was he who had visited the gardens for the purpose of soothing the misery of disappointed affection amidst the scenes of his former happiness.

'Dear madam,' said Annette when she returned, 'I never saw you so affected before ! I dare say the man is not killed.'

Emily shuddered, and lamented bitterly the rashness of the gardener in having fired.

'I knew you would be angry enough about that, madam, or I should have told you before ; and he knew so too ; for says he, "Annette, say nothing about this to my lady." She lies on the other side of the house, so did not hear the gun, perhaps ; but she would be angry with me, if she knew, seeing there is blood. But then," says he, "how is one to keep the garden clear if one is afraid to fire at a robber when one sees him ?"'

'No more of this,' said Emily, 'pray leave me.'

Annette obeyed, and Emily returned to the agonising considerations that had assailed her before, but which she, at length, endeavoured to soothe by a new remark. 'If the stranger was Valancourt, it was certain he had come alone, and it appeared, therefore, that he had been able to quit the gardens without assistance ; a circumstance which did not seem probable, had his wound been dangerous. With this consideration she endeavoured to support herself during the inquiries that were making by her servants in the neighbourhood ; but day after day came, and still closed in uncertainty concerning this affair ; and Emily, suffering in silence, at length drooped, and sunk under the pressure of her anxiety. She was attacked by a slow fever ; and when she yielded to the persuasion of Annette to send for medical advice, the physicians prescribed little besides air, gentle exercise, and amusement. But how was this last to be obtained? She, however, endeavoured to abstract her thoughts from the subject of her anxiety, by employing them in promoting that happiness in others which she had lost herself ; and when the evening was fine, she usually took an airing, including in her ride the cottages of some of her tenants, on whose condition she made such observations as often enabled her, unasked, to fulfil their wishes.

Her indisposition, and the business she engaged in relative to this estate, had already protracted her stay at Thoulouse beyond the period she had formerly fixed for her departure to La Vallée ; and now she was unwilling to leave the only place where it seemed possible that certainty could be obtained on the subject of her distress. But the time was come when her presence was necessary at La Vallée, a letter from the Lady Blanche now informing her that the count and herself, being then at the chateau of the Baron St. Foix, proposed to visit her at La Vallée, on their way home, as soon as they should be informed of her arrival there. Blanche added, that they made this visit with the hope of inducing her to return with them to Chateau-le-Blanc.

Emily having replied to the letter of her friend, and said that she should be at La Vallée in a few days, made hasty preparations for the journey ; and, in thus leaving Thoulouse, endeavoured to support herself in the belief that, if any fatal accident had happened to Valancourt, she must in this interval have heard of it.

On the evening before her departure, she went to take leave of the terrace and the pavilion. The day had been sultry ; but a light shower that fell just before sunset had cooled the air, and given that soft verdure to the woods and pastures which is so refreshing to the eye ; while the rain drops still trembling on the shrubs, glittered in the last yellow gleam that lighted up the scene, and the air was filled with fragrance exhaled by the late shower from herbs and flowers, and from the earth itself. But the lovely prospect which Emily beheld from the terrace, was no longer viewed with delight. She sighed deeply as her eye wandered over it; and her spirits were in a state of such dejection, that she could not think of her approaching return to La Vallee without tears, and seemed to mourn again the death of her father, as if it had been an event of yesterday. Having reached the pavilion, she seated herself at the open lattice; and while her eyes settled on the distant mountains that overlooked Gascony, still gleaming on the horizon, though the sun had now left the plains below, 'Alas!' said she, 'I return to your long-lost scenes, but shall meet no more the parents that were wont to render them delightful!—no more shall see the smile of welcome, or hear the well-known voice of fondness; all will now be cold and silent in what was once my happy home.'

Tears stole down her cheek, as the remembrance of what that home had been returned to her; but after indulging her sorrow for some time, she checked it, accusing herself of ingratitude in forgetting the friends that she possessed, while she lamented those that were departed; and she at length left the pavilion and the terrace, without having observed a shadow of Valancourt, or of any other person.

CHAPTER XLIX.

'Ah happy hills! ah pleasing shade!
  Ah, fields beloved in vain!
Where once my careless childhood stray'd,
  A stranger yet to pain!
I feel the gales that from you blow
  A momentary bliss bestow,
As, waving fresh their gladsome wing,
My weary soul they seem to soothe.'
                                        GRAY.

ON the following morning Emily left Thououse at an early hour, and reached La Vallee about sunset. With the melancholy she experienced on the review of the place which had been the residence of her parents, and the scene of her earliest delight, was mingled, after the first shock had subsided, a tender and indescribable pleasure. For time had so far blunted the acuteness of her grief, that she now courted every scene that awakened the memory of her friends; in every room where she had been accustomed to see them, they also seemed to live again; and she felt that La Vallée was still her happiest home. One of the first apartments she visited was that which had been her father's library, and here she seated herself in his arm-chair: and while she contemplated, with tempered resignation, the picture of past times, which her memory gave, the tears she shed could scarcely be called those of grief.

Soon after her arrival, she was surprised by a visit from the venerable M. Barreaux, who came impatiently to welcome the daughter of his late respected neighbour to her long-deserted home. Emily was comforted by the presence of an old friend, and they passed an interesting hour in conversing of former times, and in relating some of the circumstances that had occurred to each since they parted.

The evening was so far advanced, when M. Barreaux left Emily, that she could not visit the garden that night; but on the following morning she traced its long-regretted scenes with fond impatience; and, as she walked beneath the groves which her father had planted, and where she had so often sauntered in affectionate conversation with him, his countenance, his smile, even the accent of his voice, returned with exactness to her fancy, and her heart melted to the tender recollections.

This, too, was his favourite season of the year, at which they had often together admired the rich and variegated tints of these woods, and the magical effect of autumnal lights upon the mountains: and now, the view of these circumstances made memory eloquent. As she wandered pensively on, she fancied the following address

TO AUTUMN.

Sweet Autumn! how thy melancholy grace
Steals on my heart, as through these shades I
    wind!
Soothed by thy breathing sigh, I fondly trace
Each lonely image of the pensive mind!
Loved scenes, loved friends—long lost! around
    me rise,
And wake the melting thought, the tender tear!
That tear, that thought, which more than mirth I
    prize—
Sweet as the gradual tint that paints thy year!
Thy farewell smile, with fond regret, I view,
Thy beaming lights, soft gliding o'er the woods,
Thy distant landscape, touch'd with yellow hue,
While falls the lengthen'd gleam; thy winding
    floods,
Now veiled in shade, save where the skiff's white
    sails
Swell to the breeze, and catch thy streaming ray.
But now, e'en now, the partial vision fails,
And the wave smiles, as sweeps the cloud away!
Emblem of life!—Thus chequer'd is its plan,
Thus joy succeeds to grief—thus smiles the varied
    man!

One of Emily's earliest inquiries after her arrival at La Vallée was concerning Theresa, her father's old servant, whom it may be remembered that M. Quesnel had turned from the house, when it was let, without any provision. Understanding that she lived in a cottage at no great distance, Emily walked thither, and, on approaching, was pleased to see that her habitation was pleasantly situated on a green slope, sheltered by a tuft of oaks, and had an appearance of comfort and extreme neatness. She found the old woman within, picking vine-stalks, who on perceiving her young mistress, was nearly overcome with joy. 'Ah! my dear young lady!' said she, 'I thought I should never see you again in this world, when I heard you was gone to that outlandish country. I have been hardly used since you went; I little thought they would have turned me out of my old master's family in my old age!'

Emily lamented the circumstance, and then assured her that she would make her latter days comfortable, and expressed satisfaction on seeing her in so pleasant a habitation.

Theresa thanked her with tears, adding, 'Yes, mademoiselle, it is a very comfortable home, thanks to the kind friend who took me out of my distress when you was too far off to help me, and placed me here! I little thought; ——but no more of that—'

'And who was this kind friend?' said Emily; 'whoever it was, I shall consider him as mine also.'

'Ah! mademoiselle! that friend forbade me to blazon the good deed—I must not say who it was. But how you are altered since I saw you last! You look so pale now, and so thin, too; but then there is my old master's smile. Yes, that will never leave you any more than the goodness that used to make him smile. Alas-a-day! the poor lost a friend indeed when he died!

Emily was affected by this mention of her father, which Theresa observing, changed the subject. 'I heard, mademoiselle,' said she, 'that Madam Cheron married a foreign gentleman, after all, and took you abroad; how does she do?'

Emily now mentioned her death. 'Alas!' said Theresa, 'if she had not been my master's sister, I should never have loved her; she was always so cross. But how does that dear young gentleman do, M. Valancourt? he was a handsome youth, and a good one; is he well, mademoiselle?'

Emily was much agitated.

'A blessing on him!' continued Theresa. 'Ah, my dear young lady, you need not look so shy; I know all about it. Do you think I do not know that he loves you? Why, when you was away, mademoiselle, he used to come to the chateau and walk about it so disconsolate! He would go into every room in the lower part of the house, and sometimes he would sit himself down in a chair, with his arms across, and his eyes on the floor, and there he would sit and think, and think, for the hour together. He used to be very fond of the south parlour, because I told him it used to be yours; and there he would stay, looking at the pictures which I said you drew, and playing upon your lute that hung up by the window, and reading in your books till sunset; and then he must go back to his brother's chateau. And then——'

'It is enough, Theresa,' said Emily. 'How long have you lived in this cottage—and how can I serve you? Will you remain here, or return and live with me?'

'Nay, ma'amselle!' said Theresa, 'do not be so shy to your poor old servant: I am sure it is no disgrace to like such a good young gentleman.'

A deep sigh escaped from Emily.

'Ah! how he did love to talk of you! I loved him for that. Nay, for that matter, he liked to hear me talk, for he did not say much himself. But I soon found out what he came to the chateau about. Then he would go into the garden, and down to the terrace, and sit under that great tree there for the day together with one of your books in his hand; but he did not read much, I fancy; for one day I happened to go that way, and I heard somebody talking. Who can be here? says I: I am sure I let nobody into the garden but the chevalier. So I walked softly to see who it could be; and behold! it was the chevalier himself, talking to himself about you, And he repeated your name, and sighed so! and said he had lost you for ever, for that you would never return for him. I thought he was out of his reckoning there; but I said nothing, and stole away.'

'No more of this trifling,' said Emily, awakening from her reverie; 'it displeases me.'

'But when M. Quesnel let the chateau, I thought it would have broken the chevalier's heart.'

'Theresa,' said Emily seriously, 'you must name the chevalier no more!'

'Not name him, mademoiselle!' cried Theresa: 'what times are come up now? Why I love the chevalier next to my old master and you, mademoiselle.'

'Perhaps your love was not well bestowed, then,' replied Emily, trying to conceal her tears; 'but, however that might be, we shall meet no more.'

'Meet no more!—not well bestowed!' exclaimed Theresa. 'What do I hear? No, mademoiselle, my love was well bestowed, for it was the Chevalier Valancourt who gave me this cottage, and has supported me in my old age ever since M. Quesnel turned me from my master's house.'

'The Chevalier Valancourt!' said Emily, trembling extremely.

'Yes, mademoiselle, he himself, though he made me promise not to tell; but how could one help, when one heard him ill spoken of? Ah! dear young lady, you may well weep if you have behaved unkindly to him, for a more tender heart than his never young gentleman had. He found me out in my distress, when you was too far off to help me; and M. Quesnel refused to do so, and bade me go to service again. Alas! I was too old for that!—The chevalier found me, and bought me this cottage, and gave me money to furnish it, and bade me seek out another poor woman to live with me; and he ordered his brother's steward to pay me every quarter that which has supported me in comfort. Think, then, mademoiselle, whether I have not reason to speak well of the chevalier. And there are others who could have afforded it better than he ; and I am afraid he has hurt himself by his generosity, for quarter-day has gone by long since, and no money for me ! But do not weep so, mademoiselle ; you are not sorry surely to hear of the poor chevalier's goodness ?'

' Sorry !' said Emily, and wept the more.

' But how long is it since you have seen him ?'

' Not this many a day, mademoiselle.'

' When did you hear of him ?' inquired Emily with increased emotion.

' Alas ! never since he went away so suddenly into Languedoc ; and he was but just come from Paris then, or I should have seen him I am sure. Quarter-day is gone by long since, and, as I said, no money for me ; and I begin to fear some harm has happened to him ; and if I was not so far from Estuviere and so lame, I should have gone to inquire before this time ; and I have nobody to send so far.'

Emily's anxiety as to the fate of Valancourt was now scarcely endurable ; and, since propriety would not suffer her to send to the chateau of his brother, she requested that Theresa would immediately hire some person to go to his steward from herself ; and when he asked for the quarterage due to her, to make inquiries concerning Valancourt. But she first made Theresa promise never to mention her name in this affair, nor ever with that of the Chevalier Valancourt ; and her former faithfulness to M. St. Aubert induced Emily to confide in her assurances. Theresa now joyfully undertook to procure a person for this errand ; and then Emily, after giving her a sum of money to supply her with present comforts, returned with spirits heavily oppressed to her home, lamenting more than ever, that a heart possessed of so much benevolence as Valancourt's should have been contaminated by the vices of the world, but affected by the delicate affection which his kindness to her old servant expressed for herself.

CHAPTER L.

' . . . . Light thickens, and the crow
Makes wing to the rocky wood :
Good things of day begin to droop, and drowse,
While night's black agents to their preys do rouse.'
                                        MACBETH.

MEANWHILE Count de Villefort and Lady Blanche had passed a pleasant fortnight at the chateau de St. Foix with the baron and baroness, during which they made frequent excursions among the mountains, and were delighted with the romantic wildness of Pyrenean scenery. It was with regret that the count bade adieu to his old friends, although with the hope of being soon united with them in one family ; for it was settled that M. St. Foix, who now attended them into Gascony, should receive the hand of the Lady Blanche upon their arrival at Chateau-le-Blanc. As the road from the baron's residence to La Vallée was over some of the wildest tracts of the Pyrenees, and where a carriage-wheel had never passed, the count hired mules for himself and his family, as well as a couple of stout guides, who were well armed, informed of all the passes of the mountains, and who boasted too that they were acquainted with every brake and dingle in the way, could tell the names of all the highest points of this chain of Alps, knew every forest that spread along their narrow valleys, the shallowest part of every torrent they must cross, and the exact distance of every goatherd's and hunter's cabin they should have occasion to pass —which last article of learning required no very capacious memory, for such simple inhabitants were but thinly scattered over these wilds.

The count left the Chateau de St. Foix early in the morning, with an intention of passing the night at a little inn upon the mountains, about half-way to La Vallée, of which his guides had informed him ; and though this was frequented chiefly by Spanish muleteers on their route into France, and of course would afford only sorry accommodation, the count had no alternative, for it was the only place like an inn on the road.

After a day of admiration and fatigue, the travellers found themselves, about sunset, in a woody valley overlooked on every side by abrupt heights. They had proceeded for many leagues without seeing a human habitation, and had only heard now and then at a distance the melancholy tinkling of a sheepbell : but now they caught the notes of merry music, and presently saw within a little green recess among the rocks a group of mountaineers tripping through a dance. The count, who could not look upon the happiness any more than on the misery of others with indifference, halted to enjoy this scene of simple pleasure. The group before him consisted of French and Spanish peasants, the inhabitants of a neighbouring hamlet, some of whom were performing a sprightly dance, the women with castanets in their hands, to the sounds of a lute and tamborine, till, from the brisk melody of France, the music softened into a slow movement, to which two female peasants danced a Spanish Pavan.

The count, comparing this with the scenes of such gaiety as he had witnessed at Paris, where false taste painted the features, and, while it vainly tried to supply the glow of nature, concealed the charms of animation—where affectation so often distorted the air, and vice perverted the manners—sighed to

think that natural graces and innocent pleasures flourished in the wilds of solitude, while
they drooped amidst the concourse of polished
society. But the lengthening shadows reminded
the travellers that they had no time to lose ;
and leaving the joyous group, they pursued
their way towards the little inn which was to
shelter them from the night.

The rays of the setting sun now threw a
yellow gleam upon the forests of pine and
chestnut that swept down the lower region of
the mountains, and gave resplendent tints to
the snowy points above. But soon even this
light faded fast, and the scenery assumed a
more tremendous appearance, invested with
the obscurity of twilight. Where the torrent
had been seen, it was now only heard ; where
the wild cliffs had displayed every variety of
form and attitude, a dark mass of mountains
now alone appeared ; and the vale, which far
far below had opened its dreadful chasm, the
eye could no longer fathom. A melancholy
gleam still lingered on the summits of the
highest Alps, overlooking the deep repose of
evening, and seeming to make the stillness of
the hour more awful.

Blanche viewed the scene in silence, and
listened with enthusiasm to the murmur of the
pines that extended in dark lines along the
mountains, and to the faint voice of the izard
among the rocks, that came at intervals on the
air. But her enthusiasm sunk into apprehension,
when, as the shadows deepened, she looked
upon the doubtful precipice that bordered
the road, as well as on the various fantastic
forms of danger that glimmered through the
obscurity beyond it ; and she asked her father
how far they were from the inn, and whether
he did not conceive the road to be dangerous
at this late hour. The count repeated the
first question to the guides, who returned a
doubtful answer, adding, that when it was
darker, it would be safest to rest till the moon
rose. ' It is scarcely safe to proceed now,'
said the count ; but the guides, assuring him
that there was no danger, went on. Blanche,
revived by this assurance, again indulged a
pensive pleasure as she watched the progress
of twilight gradually spreading its tints over
the woods and mountains, and stealing from
the eye every minuter feature of the scene, till
the grand outlines of nature alone remained.
Then fell the silent dews ; and every wild
flower and aromatic plant that bloomed among
the cliffs, breathed forth its sweetness ; then,
too, when the mountain-bee had crept into
its blossomed bed, and the hum of every little
insect that had floated gaily in the sunbeam
was hushed, the sound of many streams, not
heard till now, murmured at a distance.—
The bats alone, of all the animals inhabiting
this region, seemed awake ; and while they
flitted across the silent path which Blanche
was pursuing, she remembered the following
lines which Emily had given her :

TO THE BAT.

' From haunt of man, from day's obtrusive glare,
Thou shroud'st thee in the ruin's ivied tower,
Or in some shadowy glen's romantic bower,
Where wizard forms their mystic charms prepare,
Where horror lurks and ever-boding care.
But, at the sweet and silent evening hour,
When closed in sleep is every languid flower,
Thou lovest to sport upon the twilight air,
Mocking the eye that would thy course pursue,
In many a wanton round ; elastic, gay,
Thou flitt'st athwart the pensive wanderer's way,
As his lone footsteps print the mountain-dew.
From Indian isles thou comest with Summer's car;
Twilight thy love, thy guide her beaming star.'

To a warm imagination, the dubious forms
that float half-veiled in darkness, afford a
higher delight than the most distinct scenery
that the sun can show. While the fancy thus
wanders over landscapes partly of its creation,
a sweet complacency steals upon the mind,

' Refines it all to subtlest feeling,
Bids the tears of rapture roll.'

The distant note of a torrent, the weak
trembling of the breeze among the woods, or
the far-off sound of a human voice now lost
and heard again, are circumstances which
wonderfully heighten the enthusiastic tone of
the mind. The young St. Foix, who saw the
presentations of a fervid fancy, and felt whatever enthusiasm could suggest, sometimes
interrupted the silence which the rest of the
party seemed by mutual consent to preserve,
remarking and pointing out to Blanche the
most striking effects of the hour upon the
scenery ; while Blanche, whose apprehensions
were beguiled by the conversation of her lover,
yielded to the taste so congenial to his, and
they conversed in a low restrained voice, the
effect of the pensive tranquillity which twilight
and the scene inspired, rather than of any
fear that they should be heard. But while
the heart was thus soothed to tenderness, St.
Foix gradually mingled with his admiration
of the country a mention of his affection ;
and he continued to speak and Blanche to
listen, till the mountains, the woods, and the
magical illusions of twilight, were remembered
no more.

The shadows of evening soon shifted to the
gloom of night, which was somewhat anticipated by the vapours that, gathering fast
round the mountains, rolled in dark wreaths
along their sides ; and the guides proposed to
rest till the moon should rise, adding, that
they thought a storm was coming on. As
they looked round for a spot that might afford
some kind of shelter, an object was perceived
obscurely through the dusk, on a point of
rock a little way down the mountain, which
they imagined to be a hunter's or a shepherd's
cabin, and the party with cautious steps proceeded towards it. Their labour, however,
was not rewarded, nor their apprehensions
soothed ; for on reaching the object of their

search, they discovered a monumental cross, which marked the spot to have been polluted by murder.

The darkness would not permit them to read the inscription; but the guides knew this to be a cross raised to the memory of a Count de Beliard, who had been murdered here by a horde of banditti that had infested this part of the Pyrenees a few years before; and the uncommon size of the monument seemed to justify the supposition that it was erected for a person of some distinction. Blanche shuddered as she listened to some horrid particulars of the count's fate, which one of the guides related in a low restrained tone, as if the sound of his own voice frightened him; but while they lingered at the cross, attending to his narrative, a flash of lightening glanced upon the rocks, thunder muttered at a distance, and the travellers, now alarmed, quitted this scene of solitary horror in search of shelter.

Having regained their former track, the guides, as they passed on, endeavoured to interest the count by various stories of robbery, and even of murder, which had been perpetrated in the very places they must unavoidably pass, with accounts of their own dauntless courage and wonderful escapes. The chief guide, or rather he who was the most completely armed, drawing forth one of the four pistols that were tucked into his belt, swore that it had shot three robbers within the year. He then brandished a clasp knife of enormous length, and was going to recount the wonderful execution it had done, when St. Foix, perceiving that Blanche was terrified, interrupted him. The count, meanwhile, secretly laughing at the terrible histories and extravagant boastings of the man, resolved to humour him; and telling Blanche in a whisper his design, began to recount some exploits of his own, which infinitely exceeded any related by the guide.

To these surprising circumstances he so artfully gave the colouring of truth, that the courage of the guides was visibly affected by them, who continued silent long after the count had ceased to speak. The loquacity of the chief hero thus laid asleep, the vigilance of his eyes and ears seemed more thoroughly awakened; for he listened with much appearance of anxiety to the deep thunder which murmured at intervals, and often paused, as the breeze, that was now rising, rushed among the pines. But when he made a sudden halt before a tuft of cork trees that projected over the road, and drew forth a pistol, before he would venture to brave the banditti which might lurk behind it, the count could no longer refrain from laughter.

Having now, however, arrived at a level spot somewhat sheltered from the air by over-hanging cliffs, and by a wood of larch that rose over a precipice on the left, and the guides being yet ignorant how far they were

from the inn, the travellers determined to rest till the moon should rise or the storm disperse. Blanche, recalled to a sense of the present moment, looked on the surrounding gloom with terror; but giving her hand to St. Foix, she alighted, and the whole party entered a kind of cave, if such it could be called, which was only a shallow cavity formed by the curve of impending rocks. A light being struck, a fire was kindled, whose blaze afforded some degree of cheerfulness and no small comfort; for though the day had been hot, the night air of this mountainous region was chilling; a fire was partly necessary also to keep off the wolves with which those wilds were infested.

Provisions being spread upon a projection of the rock, the count and his family partook of a supper, which in a scene less rude would have been thought less excellent. When the repast was finished, St. Foix, impatient for the moon, sauntered along the precipice, to a point that fronted the east; but all was yet wrapt in gloom, and the silence of night was broken only by the murmuring of woods that wavered far below, or by distant thunder, and now and then by the faint voices of the party he had quitted. He viewed with emotions of awful sublimity the long volumes of sulphureous clouds that floated along the upper and middle regions of the air, and the lightnings that flashed from them, sometimes silently, and at others followed by sullen peals of thunder, which the mountains feebly prolonged, while the whole horizon, and the abyss on which he stood, were discovered in the momentary light. Upon the succeeding darkness, the fire which had been kindled in the cave threw a partial gleam, illuminating some points of the opposite rocks, and the summits of pine-woods that hung beetling on the cliffs below, while their recesses seemed to frown in deeper shade.

St. Foix stopped to observe the picture which the party in the cave presented, where the elegant form of Blanche was finely contrasted by the majestic figure of the count, who was seated by her on a rude stone; and each was rendered more impressive by the grotesque habits and strong features of the guides and other attendants, who were in the background of the piece. The effect of the light, too, was interesting: on the surrounding figures it threw a strong though pale gleam, and glittered on their bright arms; while upon the foliage of a gigantic larch, that impended its shade over the cliff above, appeared a red, dusky tint, deepening almost imperceptibly into the blackness of night.

While St. Foix contemplated the scene, the moon, broad and yellow, rose over the eastern summits, from among embattled clouds, and showed dimly the grandeur of the heavens, the mass of vapours that rolled half-way down the precipice beneath, and the doubtful mountains.

'What dreadful pleasure, there to stand sublime,
Like shipwreck'd mariner on desert coast,
And view th' enormous waste of vapour, tost
In billows lengthening to th' horizon round !'
                              THE MINSTREL.

From this romantic reverie he was awakened
by the voices of the guides repeating his name,
which was reverberated from cliff to cliff, till
a hundred tongues seemed to call him ; when
he soon quieted the fears of the count and
the Lady Blanche by returning to the cave.
As the storm, however, seemed approaching,
they did not quit their place of shelter ; and
the count, seated between his daughter and
St. Foix, endeavoured to divert the fears of
the former, and conversed on subjects relating
to the natural history of the scenes among
which they wandered. He spoke of the
mineral and fossil substances found in the
depths of these mountains ; the veins of
marble and granite with which they abounded ; the strata of shells discovered near their
summits, many thousand fathoms above the
level of the sea, and at a vast distance from
its present shore ; of the tremendous chasms
and caverns of the rocks, the grotesque form
of the mountains, and the various phenomena
that seem to stamp upon the world the history
of the deluge. From the natural history he
descended to the mention of events and
circumstances connected with the civil story
of the Pyrenees ; named some of the most
remarkable fortresses which France and Spain
had erected in the passes of these mountains ;
and gave a brief account of some celebrated
sieges and encounters in early times, when
Ambition first frightened Solitude from these
her deep recesses, made her mountains, which
before had echoed only to the torrent's roar,
tremble with the clang of arms, and when
man's first footsteps in her sacred haunts had
left the print of blood !

As Blanche sat attentive to the narrative
that rendered the scenes doubly interesting,
and resigned to solemn emotion, while she
considered that she was on the very ground
once polluted by these events, her reverie was
suddenly interrupted by a sound that came on
the wind—it was the distant bark of a watch-
dog. The travellers listened with eager hope,
and, as the wind blew stronger, fancied that the
sound came from no great distance ; and the
guides having little doubt but that it proceeded from the inn they were in search of,
the count determined to pursue his way. The
moon now afforded a stronger though still an
uncertain light, as she moved among broken
clouds ; and the travellers, led by the sound,
re-commenced their journey along the brow of
the precipice, preceded by a single torch that
now contended with the moon-light ; for the
guides, believing they should reach the inn
soon after sun-set, had neglected to provide
more. In silent caution they followed the
sound, which was heard but at intervals, and

which, after some time, entirely ceased. The
guides endeavoured, however, to point their
course to the quarter whence it had issued ;
but the deep roaring of a torrent soon seized
their attention, and presently they came to a
tremendous chasm of the mountain, which
seemed to forbid all further progress. Blanche
alighted from her mule, as did the count and
St. Foix, while the guides traversed the edge
in search of a bridge, which, however, rude,
might convey them to the opposite side ; and
they at length confessed, what the Count had
begun to suspect, that they had been for some
time doubtful of their way, and were now
certain only that they had lost it.

At a little distance was discovered a rude
and dangerous passage, formed by an enormous pine, which, thrown across the chasm,
united the opposite precipices, and which had
been felled probably by the hunter to facilitate
his chase of the izard or the wolf. The
whole party, the guides excepted, shuddered
at the prospect of crossing this Alpine bridge,
whose sides afforded no kind of defence, and
from which to fall was to die. The guides,
however, prepared to lead over the mules,
while Blanche stood trembling on the brink
and listening to the roar of the waters, which
were seen descending from rocks above overhung with lofty pines, and thence precipitating
themselves into the deep abyss, where their
white surges gleamed faintly in the moonlight. The poor animals proceeded over this
perilous bridge with instinctive caution, neither
frightened by the noise of the cataract, nor deceived by the gloom which the impending
foliage threw athwart their way. It was now
that the solitary torch, which had been
hitherto of little service, was found to be an
inestimable treasure ; and Blanche, terrified,
shrinking, but endeavouring to re-collect all
her firmness and presence of mind, preceded by her lover and supported by her
father, followed the red gleam of the torch in
safety to the opposite cliff.

As they went on, the heights contracted and
formed a narrow pass, at the bottom of which
the torrent they had just crossed was heard
to thunder. But they were again cheered by
the bark of a dog keeping watch, perhaps
over the flocks of the mountains to protect
them from the nightly descent of the wolves.
The sound was much nearer than before ; and
while they rejoiced in the hope of soon reaching a place of repose, a light was seen to
glimmer at a distance. It appeared at a
height considerably above the level of their
path, and was lost and seen again, as if the
waving branches of trees sometimes excluded
and then admitted its rays. The guides hal-
loed with all their strength, but the sound
of no human voice was heard in return ; and
at length, as a more effectual means of making themselves known, they fired a pistol.
But while they listened in anxious expecta-

n, the noise of the explosion was alone
ard echoing among the rocks, and it gra-
ally sunk into silence, which no friendly
at of man disturbed. The light, however,
it had been seen before, now became plainer,
d soon after voices were heard indistinctly
the wind; but upon the guides repeating
: call, the voices suddenly ceased, and the
ht disappeared.

The Lady Blanche was now almost sinking
neath the pressure of anxiety, fatigue, and
prehension; and the united efforts of the
unt and St. Foix could scarcely support her
irits. As they continued to advance, an
ject was perceived on a point of rock
ove, which, the strong rays of the moon
en falling on it, appeared to be a watch-
ver. The count, from its situation and
me other circumstances, had little doubt
at it was such; and believing that the light
d proceeded from thence, he endeavoured
re-animate his daughter's spirits by the
ar prospect of shelter and repose, which,
wever rude the accommodation, a ruined
atch-tower might afford.

'Numerous watch-towers have been erected
long the Pyrenees,' said the count, anxious
ly to call Blanche's attention from the sub-
at of her fears; 'and the method by which
ey give intelligence of the approach of the
emy is, you know, by fires kindled on the
mmits of these edifices. Signals have thus
metimes been communicated from post to
st along a frontier line of several hundred
les in length. Then, as occasion may re-
uire, the lurking armies emerge from their
rtresses and the forests, and march forth to
fend perhaps the entrance of some grand
ss, where, planting themselves on the
ights, they assail the astonished enemies,
to wind along the glen below, with frag-
ents of the shattered cliff, and pour death
d defeat upon them. The ancient forts and
atch-towers overlooking the grand passes of
e Pyrenees are carefully preserved; but
me of those in inferior stations have been
ffered to fall into decay, and are now fre-
ently converted into the more peaceful
bitation of the hunter or the shepherd,
to after a day of toil retires hither, and,
th his faithful dogs, forgets, near a cheer-
l blaze, the labour of the chase, or the
xiety of collecting his wandering flocks,
aile he is sheltered from the nightly storm.'

'But are they always thus peacefully in-
bited?' said the Lady Blanche.

'No,' replied the count; 'they are some-
nes the asylum of French and Spanish
uugglers, who cross the mountains with
ntraband goods from their respective coun-
es; and the latter are particularly numerous,
ainst whom strong parties of the king's
oops are sometimes sent. But the desperate
solution of these adventurers,—who know-
g that if they are taken they must expiate

the breach of the law by the most cruel death,
travel in large parties well armed,—often
daunts the courage of the soldiers. The
smugglers who seek only safety, never engage when they can possibly avoid it; the
military also, who know that in these encounters danger is certain, and glory almost
unattainable, are equally reluctant to fight;
an engagement therefore very seldom happens; but when it does, it never concludes
till after the most desperate and bloody conflict. 'You are inattentive, Blanche,' added the
count: 'I have wearied you with a dull subject;
but see yonder, in the moon-light, is the edifice
we have been in search of, and we are fortunate to be so near it before the storm
bursts.'

Blanche, looking up, perceived that they
were at the foot of the cliff, on whose summit
the building stood, but no light now issued
from it; the barking of the dog too had for
some time ceased; and the guides began to
doubt whether this was really the object of
their search. From the distance at which they
surveyed it, shown imperfectly by a cloudy
moon, it appeared to be of more extent than
a single watch-tower; but the difficulty was
how to ascend the height, whose abrupt acclivities seemed to afford no kind of path-way.

While the guides carried forward the torch
to examine the cliff, the count, remaining with
Blanche and St. Foix at its foot, under the
shadow of the woods, endeavoured again to
beguile the time by conversation, but again
anxiety abstracted the mind of Blanche: and
he then consulted apart with St. Foix, whether
it would be advisable, should a path be found,
to venture to an edifice which might possibly
harbour banditti. They considered that their
own party was not small, and that several of
them were well armed; and after enumerating
the dangers to be incurred by passing the
night in the open wild, exposed perhaps to the
effects of a thunderstorm, there remained not
a doubt that they ought to endeavour to
obtain admittance to the edifice above, at any
hazard respecting the inhabitants it might
harbour: but the darkness, and the dead silence
that surrounded it, appeared to contradict
the probability of its being inhabited at all.

A shout from the guides aroused their attention, after which, in a few minutes, one of the
count's servants returned with intelligence that
a path was found, and they immediately
hastened to join the guides, when they all
ascended a little winding way cut in the rock
among the thickets of dwarf wood, and after
much toil and some danger reached the summit, where several ruined towers surrounded
by a massy wall rose to their view, partially
illumined by the moonlight. The space around
the building was silent, and apparently forsaken: but the count was cautious. 'Step
softly,' said he in a low voice, 'while we
reconnoitre the edifice.'

Having proceeded silently along for some paces, they stopped at a gate whose portals were terrible even in ruins; and, after a moment's hesitation, passed on to the court of entrance, but paused again at the head of a terrace, which, branching from it, ran along the brow of a precipice. Over this rose the main body of the edifice, which was now seen to be not a watch-tower, but one of those ancient fortresses that from age and neglect had fallen to decay. Many parts of it, however, appeared to be still entire: it was built of grey stone, in the heavy Saxon-Gothic style, with enormous round towers, buttresses of proportionable strength, and the arch of the large gate which seemed to open into the hall of the fabric was round, as was that of a window above. The air of solemnity which must so strongly have characterised the pile even in the days of its early strength, was now considerably heightened by its shattered battlements and half-demolished walls, and by the huge masses of ruin scattered in its wide area, now silent and grass-grown. In this court of entrance stood the gigantic remains of an oak, that seemed to have flourished and decayed with the building, which it still appeared frowningly to protect by the few remaining branches, leafless and moss-grown, that crowned its trunk, and whose wide extent told how enormous the tree had been in a former age. This fortress was evidently once of great strength, and from its situation on a point of rock impending over a deep glen, had been of great power to annoy as well as to resist: the count, therefore, as he stood surveying it, was somewhat surprised that it had been suffered, ancient as it was, to sink into ruins, and its present lonely and deserted air excited in his breast emotions of melancholy awe. While he indulged for a moment these emotions, he thought he heard a sound of remote voices steal upon the stillness from within the building, the front of which he again surveyed with scrutinizing eyes, but yet no light was visible. He now determined to walk round the fort, to that remote part of it whence he thought the voices had arisen, that he might examine whether any light could be discerned there, before he ventured to knock at the gate: for this purpose he entered upon the terrace, where the remains of cannon were yet apparent in the thick walls: but he had not proceeded many paces when his steps were suddenly arrested by the loud barking of a dog within, and which he fancied to be the same whose voice had been the means of bringing the travellers thither. It now appeared certain that the place was inhabited; and the count returned to consult again with St. Foix, whether he should try to obtain admittance, for its wild aspect had somewhat shaken his former resolution: but after a second consultation, he submitted to the considerations which before determined him, and which were strengthened by the discovery of the dog that guarded the fort, as well as by the stillness that pervaded it. He therefore ordered one of his servants to knock at the gate; who was advancing to obey him, when a light appeared through the loop-hole of one of the towers, and the count called loudly: but receiving no answer, he went up to the gate himself, and struck upon it with an iron pointed pole which had assisted him to climb the steep. When the echoes had ceased that this blow had awakened, the renewed barking—and there were now more than one dog—was the only sound that was heard. The count stepped back a few paces to observe whether the light was in the tower; and perceiving that it was gone, he returned to the portal, and had lifted the pole to strike again, when again he fancied he heard the murmur of voices within, and paused to listen. He was confirmed in the supposition, but they were too remote to be heard otherwise than in a murmur, and the count now let the pole fall heavily upon the gate, when almost immediately a profound silence followed. It was apparent that the people within had heard the sound, and their caution in admitting strangers gave him a favourable opinion of them. 'They are either hunters or shepherds,' said he, 'who, like ourselves, have probably sought shelter from the night within these walls, and are fearful of admitting strangers, lest they should prove robbers. I will endeavour to remove their fears.' So saying, he called aloud, 'We are friends, who ask shelter from the night.' In a few moments steps were heard within, which approached, and a voice then inquired —'Who calls?' 'Friends,' repeated the count; 'open the gates, and you shall know more.' Strong bolts were now heard to be undrawn, and a man armed with a hunting-spear appeared. 'What is it you want at this hour?' said he. The count beckoned his attendants, and then answered, that he wished to inquire the way to the nearest cabin. 'Are you so little acquainted with these mountains,' said the man, 'as not to know that there is none within several leagues? I cannot show you the way; you must seek it—there's a moon.' Saying this, he was closing the gate, and the count was turning away half disappointed and half afraid, when another voice was heard from above; and on looking up, he saw a light and a man's face at the grate of the portal. 'Stay, friend, you have lost your way?' said the voice. 'You are hunters, I suppose, like ourselves? I will be with you presently.' The voice ceased, and the light disappeared. Blanche had been alarmed by the appearance of the man who had opened the gate, and she now entreated her father to quit the place: but the count had observed the hunter's spear which he carried, and the words from the tower encouraged him to await the event. The gate was soon opened:

:veral men in hunters' habits, who had above what had passed below, ap-
1 ; and having listened some time to the told him he was welcome to rest there
e night. They then pressed him with courtesy to enter, and to partake of
are as they were about to sit down to. ount, who had observed them attentively
they spoke, was cautious and somewhat ious ; but he was also weary, fearful of
approaching storm, and of encountering : heights in the obscurity of night : being
se somewhat confident in the strength umber of his attendants, he, after some
r consideration; determined to accept vitation. With this resolution he called
vants, who advancing round the tower, l which some of them had silently listened
s conference, followed their lord, the Blanche, and St. Foix, into the fort-
The strangers led them on to a and rude hall, partially seen by a fire
lazed at its extremity; round which four n the hunter's dress were seated, and on
arth were several dogs stretched in sleep. : middle of the hall stood a large table,
ver the fire some part of an animal was g. As the count approached, the men
: and the dogs, half raising themselves, l fiercely at the strangers, but on hearing
masters' voices, kept their postures on arth.

nche looked round this gloomy and ous hall ; then at the men, and to her
, who, smiling cheerfully at her, ad-:d himself to the hunters. 'This is an
able hearth,' said he : ' the blaze of the reviving after having wandered so long
se dreary wilds. Your dogs are tired ; success have you had ?'. 'Such as we
y have,' replied one of the men, who seen seated in the hall ; 'we kill our
with tolerable certainty.'—'These are -hunters,' said one of the men who had
ht the count hither, ' that have lost vay, and I have told them there is room-
h in the fort for us all.'—'Very true, rue,' replied his companion : 'what luck
rou had in the chase, brothers?' 'We cilled two izards, and that you will say
tty well.'—'You mistake, friend,' said unt ; 'we are not hunters, but travellers;
you will admit us to hunters' fare we be well contented, and will repay your
ess.'—'Sit down then, brother,' said the men : 'Jacques, lay more fuel on
e, the kid will soon be ready ; bring a or the lady too. Ma'amselle, will you
our brandy ? it is true Barcelona, and as as ever flowed from a keg. Blanche
y smiled, and was going to refuse, when ther prevented her, by taking, with a
humoured air, the glass offered to his ter ; and Monsieur St. Foix, who was
next her, pressed her hand, and gave

her an encouraging look ; but her attention was engaged by a man who sat silently by the fire, observing St. Foix with a steady and earnest eye.

'You lead a jolly life here,' said the count. 'The life of a hunter is a pleasant and a healthy one ; and the repose is sweet which succeeds to your labour.'

'Yes,' replied one of the hosts, ' our life is pleasant enough. We live here only during the summer and autumnal months ; in winter the place is dreary, and the swollen torrents that descend from the heights put a stop to the chase.'

''Tis a life of liberty and enjoyment,' said the count : ' I should like to pass a month in your way very well.'

'We find employment for our guns too,' said a man who stood behind the count : ' here are plenty of birds of delicious flavour, that feed upon the wild thyme and herbs that grow in the valleys. Now I think of it, there is a brace of birds hung up in the stone gallery ; go fetch them, Jaques ; we will have them dressed.'

The count now made inquiry concerning the method of pursuing the chase among the rocks and precipices of these romantic regions, and was listening to a curious detail, when a horn was sounded at the gate. Blanche looked timidly at her father, who continued to converse on the subject of the chase, but whose countenance was somewhat expressive of anxiety, and who often turned his eyes towards that part of the hall nearest the gate. The horn sounded again, and a loud halloo succeeded. 'There are some of our companions returned from their day's labour,' said a man, going lazily from his seat towards the gate ; and in a few minutes two men appeared, each with a gun over his shoulder and pistols in his belt. 'What cheer, my lads? what cheer?' said they, as they approached. 'What luck?' returned their companions : 'have you brought home your supper ? You shall have none else.'

'Hah ! who the devil have you brought home ?' said they in bad Spanish, on perceiving the count's party ; ' are they from France, or Spain ?—where did you meet with them ?'

'They met with us ; and a merry meeting too,' replied his companion aloud in good French. 'This chevalier and his party had lost their way, and asked a night's lodging in the fort.' The others made no reply, but threw down a kind of knapsack, and drew forth several brace of birds. The bag sounded heavily as it fell to the ground, and the. glitter of some bright metal within glanced on the eye of the count, who now surveyed with a more inquiring look the man that held the knapsack. He was a tall, robust figure, of a hard countenance, and had short black hair curling on his neck. Instead of the hunter's dress, he wore a faded military uniform ; san-

10

dals were laced on his broad legs : and a kind of short trowsers hung from his waist. On his head he wore a leather cap, somewhat resembling in shape an ancient Roman helmet ; but the brows that scowled beneath it would have characterised those of the barbarians who conquered Rome, rather than those of a Roman soldier. The count at length turned away his eyes, and remained silent and thoughtful, till, again raising them, he perceived a figure standing in an obscure part of the hall, fixed in attentive gaze on St. Foix, who was conversing with Blanche, and did not observe this ; but the count soon after saw the same man looking over the shoulder of the soldier as attentively at himself. He withdrew his eye when that of the count met it, who felt mistrust gathering fast upon his mind, but feared to betray it in his countenance, and, forcing his features to assume a smile, addressed Blanche on some indifferent subject. When he again looked round, he perceived that the soldier and his companion were gone.

The man who was called Jaques now returned from the stone gallery. 'A fire is lighted there,' said he, 'and the birds are dressing ; the table, too, is spread there, for that place is warmer than this.'

His companions approved of the removal, and invited their guests to follow to the gallery ; of whom Blanche appeared distressed and remained silent, and St. Foix looked at the count, who said he preferred the comfortable blaze of the fire he was then near. The hunters, however, commended the warmth of the other apartment, and pressed his removal with such seeming courtesy, that the count, half doubting and half fearful of betraying his doubts, consented to go. The long and ruinous passages through which they went, somewhat daunted him ; but the thunder, which now burst in loud peals above, made it dangerous to quit this place of shelter, and he forbore to provoke his conductors by showing that · he distrusted them. The hunters led the way with a lamp : the count and St. Foix, who wished to please their hosts by some instances of familiarity, carried each a seat, and Blanche followed with faltering steps. As she passed on, part of her dress caught on a nail in the wall ; and while she stopped, somewhat too scrupulously, to disengage it, the count, who was talking to St. Foix, and neither of whom observed the circumstance, followed their conductor round an abrupt angle of the passage, and Blanche was left behind in darkness. The thunder prevented them from hearing her call ; but, having disengaged her dress, she quickly followed, as she thought, the way they had taken. A light that glimmered at a distance confirmed this belief ; and she proceeded towards an open door whence it issued, conjecturing the room beyond to be the stone gal-

lery the men had spoken of. Hearing voices as she advanced, she paused within a few paces of the chamber, that she might be certain whether she was right ; and from thence, by the light of a lamp that hung from the ceiling, observed four men seated round a table, over which they leaned in apparent consultation. In one of them she distinguished the features of him whom she had observed gazing at St. Foix with such deep attention ; and who was now speaking in an earnest, though restrained voice, till one of his companions seeming to oppose him, they spoke together in a loud and harsher tone. Blanche, alarmed by perceiving that neither her father nor St. Foix was there, and terrified at the fierce countenances and manners of these men, was turning hastily from the chamber to pursue her search of the gallery, when she heard one of the men say :

'Let all dispute end here. Who talks of danger? Follow my advice, and there will be none—secure *them*, and the rest are an easy prey.' Blanche, struck with these words, paused a moment to hear more. 'There is nothing to be got by the rest,' said one of his companions ; 'I am never for blood when I can help it—dispatch the two others, and our business is done : the rest may go.'

'May they so !' exclaimed the first ruffian with a tremendous oath—'What ! to tell how we have disposed of their master, and to send the king's troops to drag us to the wheel ! You was always a choice adviser—I warrant we have not yet forgot St. Thomas's eve, last year.'

Blanche's heart now sunk with horror. Her first impulse was to retreat from the door ; but when she would have gone, her trembling frame refused to support her, and having tottered a few paces to a more obscure part of the passage, she was compelled to listen to the dreadful counsels of those who, she was no longer suffered to doubt, were· banditti. In the next moment she heard the following words : 'Why, you would not murder the whole *gang* !'

'I warrant our lives are as good as theirs,' replied his comrade. 'If we don't kill them, they will hang us : better they should die than we be hanged.'

'Better, better,' cried his comrades.

'To commit murder is a hopeful way of escaping the gallows !' said the first ruffian—'many an honest fellow has run his head into the noose that way, though.' There was a pause for some moments, during which they appeared to be considering.

'Confound those fellows,' exclaimed one of the robbers impatiently, 'they ought to have been here by this time ; they will come back presently with the old story, and no booty ; if they were here, our business would be plain and easy. I see we shall not be able to do business to-night, for our numbers are not equal to the enemy ; and in the morning they

ll be for marching off, and how can we de-
n them without force?'

'I have been thinking of a scheme that will
,' said one of his comrades; 'if we can dis-
tch the two chevaliers silently, it will be
sy to master the rest.'.

'That's a plausible scheme, in good faith!'
d another with a smile of scorn—'If I can
t my way through the prison-wall, I shall
at liberty!—How can we dispatch them
ently ?'

'By poison,' replied his companions.

'Well said! that will do,' said the second
ffian; 'that will give a lingering death too,
d satisfy my revenge. These barons shall take
re how they again tempt our vengeance.'

'I knew the son the moment I saw him,'
d the man whom Blanche had observed
zing on St. Foix, 'though he does not know
:; the father I had almost forgotten.'

'Well, you may say what you will,' said the
rd ruffian, 'but I don't believe he is the
ron; and I am as likely to know as any of
u, for I was one of them that attacked him
th our brave lads that suffered.'

'And was not I another?' said the first
fian. 'I tell you he is the baron; but what
es it signify whether he is or not?—shall we
all this booty go out of our hands? It
iot often we have such luck as this. While
run the chance of the wheel for smuggling
'ew pounds of tobacco, to cheat the king's
inufactory, and of breaking our necks down
: precipices in chase of our food; and now
d then rob a brother smuggler, or a strag-
ng pilgrim, of what scarcely repays us the
wder we fire at them; shall we let such a
ze as this go? Why, they have enough
out them to keep us for——'

I am not for that, I am not for that,' re-
:d the third robber; let us make the most
them. Only, if this is the baron, I should
: to have a flash the more at him, for the
:e of our brave comrades that he brought
the gallows.'

Aye, aye, flash as much as you will,' re-
ied the first man, 'but I tell you the baron
taller man.'

Confound your quibbling,' said the second
fian, 'Shall we let them go or not? If we
y much longer they will take the hint,
l march off without our leave. Let them
who they will, they are rich, or why all
se servants? Did you see the ring he whom
l call the baron had on his finger?—it was a
mond; but he has not got it on now: he saw
looking at it, I warrant, and took it off.'

Aye, and then there is the picture; did you
that? She has not taken that off,' ob-
ved the first ruffian, 'it hangs at her neck;
t had not sparkled so, I should not have
nd it out, for it was almost hid by her
ss: those are diamonds too, and a rare
ny of them there must be to go round such
irge picture.'

'But how are we to manage this business?'
said the second ruffian, 'let us talk of that;
there is no fear of there being booty enough,
but how are we to secure it?'

'Aye, aye,' said his comrades; 'let us talk
of that, and remember no time is to be lost.'

'I am still for poison,' observed the third:
'but consider their number; why there are
nine or ten of them, and armed too; when I
saw so many at the gate, I was not for letting
them in, you know, nor you either.'

'I thought they might be some of our
enemies,' replied the second; 'I did not so
much mind numbers.'

'But you must mind them now,' rejoined
his comrade, 'or it will be worse for you. We
are not more than six, and how can we master
ten by open force? I tell you we must give
some of them a dose, and the rest may then
be managed.'

'I'll tell you a better way,' rejoined the
other impatiently; 'draw closer.'

Blanche, who had listened to this conversation in an agony which it would be impossible
to describe, could no longer distinguish what
was said, for the ruffians now spoke in lowered
voices; but the hope that she might save her
friends from the plot, if she could find her way
quickly to them, suddenly re-animated her
spirits, and lent her strength enough to turn
her steps in search of the gallery. Terror,
however, and darkness conspired against her;
and having moved a few yards, the feeble
light that issued from the chamber no longer
even contended with the gloom, and her foot
stumbling over a step that crossed the passage,
she fell to the ground.

The noise startled the banditti, who became
suddenly silent, and then all rushed to the
passage, to examine whether any person was
there who might have overheard their counsels. Blanche saw them approaching, and
perceived their fierce and eager looks; but
before she could raise herself, they discovered
and seized her; and as they dragged her towards the chamber they had quitted, her
screams drew from them horrible threatenings.

Having reached the room, they began to
consult what they should do with her. 'Let us
first know what she has heard,' said the chief
robber. 'How long have you been in the passage, lady, and what brought you there?'

'Let us first secure that picture,' said one of
his comrades, approaching the trembling
Blanche. 'Fair lady, by your leave, that picture; come, surrender it, or I shall seize it.'

Blanche, entreating their mercy, immediately gave up the miniature, while another of
the ruffians fiercely interrogated her concerning what she had overheard of their conversation; when her confusion and terror too
plainly telling what her tongue feared to confess, the ruffians looked expressively upon one
another, and two of them withdrew to a remote part of the room, as if to consult further

10—2

'These are diamonds by St. Peter!' exclaimed the fellow who had been examining the miniature, 'and here is a very pretty picture too, 'faith; as handsome a young chevalier as you would wish to see by a summer's sun. Lady, this is your spouse, I warrant, for it is the spark that was in your company just now.'

Blanche, sinking with terror, conjured him to have pity on her, and, delivering him her purse, promised to say nothing of what had passed if he would suffer her to return to her friends.

He smiled ironically, and was going to reply, when his attention was called off by a distant noise; and while he listened, he grasped the arm of Blanche more firmly, as if he feared she would escape from him, and she again shrieked for help.

The approaching sounds called the ruffians from the other part of the chamber. 'We are betrayed,' said they; 'but let us listen a moment, perhaps it is only our comrades come in from the mountains, and if so, our work is sure—listen!'

A distant discharge of shot confirmed this supposition for a moment: but in the next, the former sounds drawing nearer, the clashing of swords, mingled with the voices of loud contention and with heavy groans, was distinguished in the avenue leading to the chamber. While the ruffians prepared their arms, they heard themselves called by some of their comrades afar off, and then a shrill horn was sounded without the fortress, a signal, it appeared, they too well understood; for three of them, leaving the Lady Blanche to the care of the fourth, instantly rushed from the chamber.

While Blanche, trembling and nearly fainting, was supplicating for release, she heard amid the tumult that approached, the voice of St. Foix; and she had scarcely renewed her shriek, when the door of the room was thrown open, and he appeared much disfigured with blood, and pursued by several ruffians. Blanche neither saw nor heard any more; her head swam, her sight failed, and she became senseless in the arms of the robber who had detained her.

When she recovered, she perceived, by the gloomy light that trembled round her, that she was in the same chamber; but neither the count, St. Foix, nor any other person appeared, and she continued for some time entirely still, and nearly in a state of stupefaction. But the dreadful images of the past returning, she endeavoured to raise herself, that she might seek her friends; when a sullen groan at a little distance reminded her of St. Foix, and of the condition in which she had seen him enter this room; then, starting from the floor by a sudden effort of horror, she advanced to the place whence the sound had proceeded, where a body was lying stretched upon the pavement, and where, by the glimmering light of a lamp, she discovered the

pale and disfigured countenance of St. Foix. Her horrors at that moment may be easily imagined. He was speechless; his eyes were half closed; and on the hand which she grasped in the agony of despair cold damps had settled. While she vainly repeated his name, and called for assistance, steps approached, and a person entered the chamber, who, she soon perceived, was not the count her father; but what was her astonishment, when, supplicating him to give his assistance to St. Foix, she discovered Ludovico! He scarcely paused to recognise her, but immediately bound up the wounds of the chevalier, and perceiving that he had fainted probably from loss of blood, ran for water; but he had been absent only a few moments, when Blanche heard other steps approaching; and while she was almost frantic with apprehension of the ruffians, the light of a torch flashed upon the walls, and then Count de Villefort appeared with an affrighted countenance, and breathless with impatience, calling upon his daughter. At the sound of his voice she rose, and ran to his arms, while he, letting fall the bloody sword he held, pressed her to his bosom in a transport of gratitude and joy, and then hastily inquired for St. Foix, who now gave some signs of life. Ludovico soon after returning with water and brandy, the former was applied to his lips, and the latter to his temples and hands, and Blanche, at length, saw him unclose his eyes, and then heard him inquire for her: but the joy she felt on this occasion was interrupted by new alarms, when Ludovico said it would be necessary to remove Mons. St. Foix immediately, and added, 'The banditti that are out, my lord, were expected home an hour ago, and they will certainly find us if we delay. That shrill horn, they know, is never sounded by their comrades but on most desperate occasions, and it echoes among the mountains for many leagues round. I have known them brought home by its sound even from the Pied de Melicant. Is anyone standing watch at the great gate, my lord?'

'Nobody,' replied the count; 'the rest of my people are now scattered about, I scarcely know where. Go, Ludovico, collect them together, and look out yourself, and listen if you hear the feet of mules.'

Ludovico then hurried away, and the count consulted as to the means of removing St. Foix, who could not have borne the motion of a mule, even if his strength would have supported him in the saddle.

While the count was telling that the banditti, whom they had found in the fort, were secured in the dungeon, Blanche observed that he was himself wounded, and that his left arm was entirely useless; but he smiled at her anxiety, assuring her the wound was trifling.

The count's servants, except two who kept watch at the gate, now appeared, and soon after Ludovico, 'I think I hear mules coming along the glen, my lord,' said he, 'but the roaring of the torrent below will not let me be certain : however, I have brought what will serve the chevalier,' he added, showing a bear's skin fastened to a couple of long poles, which had been adapted for the purpose of bringing home such of the banditti as happened to be wounded in their encounters. Ludovico spread it on the ground, and, placing the skins of several goats upon it, made a kind of bed, into which the chevalier, who was however now much revived, was gently lifted ; and the poles being raised upon the shoulders of the guides, whose footing among these steeps could best be depended upon, he was borne along with an easy motion. Some of the count's servants were also wounded, but not materially ; and their wounds being bound up, they now followed to the great gate. As they passed along the hall, a loud tumult was heard at some distance, and Blanche was terrified. 'It is only those villains in the dungeon, my lady,' said Ludovico. 'They seem to be bursting it open,' said the count. 'No, my lord,' replied Ludovico, 'it has an iron door ; we have nothing to fear from them ; but let me go first, and look out from the rampart.'

They quickly followed him, and found their mules browsing before the gates, where the party listened anxiously, but heard no sound, except that of the torrent below, and of the early breeze sighing among the branches of the old oak that grew in the court ; and they were now glad to perceive the first tints of dawn over the mountain-tops. When they had mounted their mules, Ludovico, undertaking to be their guide, led them by an easier path than that by which they had formerly ascended into the glen. 'We must avoid that valley to the east, my lord,' said he, 'or we may meet the banditti ; they went out that way in the morning.'

The travellers, soon after, quitted this glen, and found themselves in a narrow valley that stretched towards the north-west. The morning-light upon the mountains now strengthened fast, and gradually discovered the green hillocks that skirted the winding feet of the cliffs, tufted with cork-tree and evergreen oak. The thunder-clouds, being dispersed, had left the sky perfectly serene, and Blanche was revived by the fresh breeze and by the view of verdure which the late rain had brightened. Soon after, the sun arose, when the dripping rocks, with the shrubs that fringed their summits, and many a turfy slope below, sparkled in his rays. A wreath of mist was seen floating along the extremity of the valley ; but the gale bore it before the travellers, and the sunbeams gradually drew it up towards the summit of the mountains. They had proceeded about a league, when St. Foix having complained of extreme faintness, they stopped to give him refreshment, and that the men who bore him might rest. Ludovico had brought from the fort some flasks of rich Spanish wine, which now proved a reviving cordial not only to St. Foix but to the whole party ; though to him it gave only a temporary relief, for it fed the fever that burned in his veins, and he could neither disguise in his countenance the anguish he suffered, nor suppress the wish that he was arrived at the inn where they had designed to pass the preceding night.

While they thus reposed themselves under the shade of the dark green pines, the count desired Ludovico to explain shortly by what means he had disappeared from the north apartment, how he came into the hands of the banditti, and how he had contributed so essentially to serve him and his family, for to him he justly attributed their present deliverance. Ludovico was going to obey him, when suddenly they heard the echo of a pistol-shot from the way they had passed, and they rose in alarm hastily to pursue their route.

CHAPTER LI.

'Ah, why did Fate his steps decoy
In stormy paths to roam,
Remote from all congenial joy !'
BEATTIE.

EMILY, meanwhile, was still suffering anxiety as to the fate of Valancourt ; but Theresa, having at length found a person whom she could intrust on her errand to the steward, informed her that the messenger would return on the following day ; and Emily promised to be at the cottage, Theresa being too lame to attend her.

In the evening, therefore, Emily set out alone for the cottage, with a melancholy foreboding concerning Valancourt, while perhaps the gloom of the hour might contribute to depress her spirits. It was a gray autumnal evening, towards the close of the season ; heavy mists partially obscured the mountains, and a chilling breeze, that sighed among the beech woods, strewed her path with some of their last yellow leaves. These circling in the blast, and foretelling the death of the year, gave an image of desolation to her mind, and in her fancy seemed to announce the death of Valancourt. Of this she had, indeed, more than once, so strong a presentiment, that she was on the point of returning home, feeling herself unequal to an encounter with the certainty she anticipated ; but, contending with her emotions, she so far commanded them as to be able to proceed.

While she walked mournfully on, gazing on the long volumes of vapour that poured upon the sky, and watching the swallows tossed along the wind, now disappearing among tempestuous clouds, and then emerging, for a moment, in circles upon the calmer air, the afflictions and vicissitudes of her late life seemed portrayed in these fleeting images ;—thus had she been tossed upon the stormy sea of misfortune for the last year, with but short intervals of peace, if peace that could be called which was only the delay of evils. And now, when she had escaped from so many dangers, was become independent of the will of those who had oppressed her, and found herself mistress of a large fortune—now, when she might reasonably have expected happiness, she perceived that she was as distant from it as ever. She would have accused herself of weakness and ingratitude in thus suffering a sense of the various blessings she possessed to be overcome by that of a single misfortune, had this misfortune affected herself alone ; but when she had wept for Valancourt even as living, tears of compassion had mingled with those of regret ; and while she lamented a human being degraded to vice, and consequently to misery, reason and humanity claimed these tears, and fortitude had not yet taught her to separate them from those of love. In the present moments, however, it was not the certainty of his guilt, but the apprehension of his death (of a death also, to which she herself, however innocently, appeared to have been in some degree instrumental) that now oppressed her. This fear increased, as the means of certainty it approached ; and when she came within view of Theresa's cottage, she was so much disordered, and her resolution failed her so entirely, that, unable to proceed, she rested on a bank beside the path, where, as she sat, the wind that groaned sullenly among the lofty branches above, seemed to her melancholy imagination to bear the sounds of distant lamentation, and in the pauses of the gust she still fancied she heard the feeble and far-off notes of distress. Attention convinced her that this was no more than fancy ; but the increasing gloom, which seemed the sudden close of day, soon warned her to depart, and with faltering steps she again moved towards the cottage. Through the casement appeared the cheerful blaze of a wood fire, and Theresa, who had observed Emily approaching, was already at the door to receive her.

'It is a cold evening, madam,' said she ; 'storms are coming on, and I thought you would like a fire. Do take this chair by the hearth.'

Emily, thanking her for this consideration, sat down ; and then looking in her face, on which the wood fire threw a gleam, she was struck with its expression, and, unable to speak, sunk back in her chair with a countenance so full of woe that Theresa instantly comprehended the occasion of it, but she remained silent. 'Ah !' said Emily at length, 'it is unnecessary for me to ask the result of your inquiry—your silence and that look sufficiently explain it ;—he is dead !'

'Alas ! my dear young lady,' replied Theresa, while tears filled her eyes, 'this world is made up of trouble ; the rich have their share as well as the poor ! But we must endeavour to bear what heaven pleases.'

'He is dead, then !' interrupted Emily : 'Valancourt is dead !'

'A-well-a-day ! I fear he is ! replied Theresa.

'You fear !' said Emily ; 'do you only fear ?'

'Alas ! yes, madam, I fear he is ! neither the steward nor any of the Epourville family have heard of him since he left Languedoc ; and the count is in great affliction about him, for he says he was always punctual in writing, but that he now has not received a line from him since he left Languedoc ; he appointed to be at home three weeks ago, but he has neither come nor written, and they fear some accident has befallen him. Alas ! that I should ever cry for his death ! I am old, and might have died without being missed ; but he'——Emily was faint, and asked for some water ; and Theresa, alarmed by the voice in which she spoke, hastened to her assistance ; and while she held the water to Emily's lips, continued : 'My dear young mistress, do not take it so to heart ; the chevalier may be alive and well, for all this ; let us hope the best !'

'O no ! I cannot hope,' said Emily ; 'I am acquainted with circumstances that will not suffer me to hope. I am somewhat better now, and can hear what you have to say. Tell me, I entreat, the particulars of what you know.'

'Stay till you are a little better : mademoiselle, you look sadly !'

'O no, Theresa, tell me all, while I have the power to hear it,' said Emily ; 'tell me all, I conjure you !'

'Well, madam, I will then ; but the steward did not say much ; for Richard says he seemed shy of talking about Monsieur Valancourt, and what he gathered was from Gabriel, one of the servants, who said he had heard it from my lord's gentleman.'

'What did he hear ?' said Emily.

'Why, madam, Richard has but a bad memory, and could not remember half of it ; and if I had not asked him a great many questions, I should have heard little indeed. But he says that Gabriel said that he and all the other servants were in great trouble about M. Valancourt, for that he was such a kind young gentleman, they all loved him as well as if he had been their own brother—and now, to think what was become of him ! For he used to be so courteous to them all ; and if any of them had been in fault, M. Valancourt was the first to persuade my lord to forgive them. And then, if any poor family was in distress, M. Valancourt was the first, too, to relieve them, though some folks, not a great way off, could have afforded that better than he. And then, said Gabriel, he was so gentle to everybody, and for all he had such a noble look with him, he never would command, and all about him, as some of your quality people do, and we never minded him the less for that. Nay, says Gabriel, for that matter, we minded him the more, and would all have run to obey him at a word, sooner than if some folks had told us what to do at full length ; aye, and were more afraid of displeasing him, too, than of them that used rough words to us.'

Emily, who no longer considered it to be dangerous to listen to praise bestowed on Valancourt, did not attempt to interrupt Theresa, but sat attentive to her words, though almost overwhelmed with grief.

' My lord,' continued Theresa, ' frets about M. Valancourt sadly ; and the more, because they say he had been rather harsh against him ately. Gabriel said he had it from my lord's valet, that M. Valancourt had *comported* himself wildly at Paris, and had spent a great deal of money, more a great deal than my lord liked, for he loves money better than M. Valancourt, who had been led astray sadly. Nay, for that matter, M. Valancourt had been put into prison at Paris, and my lord, says Gabriel, refused to take him out, and said he deserved to suffer ; and when old Gregoire, the butler, heard of this, he actually bought a walking-stick with him to Paris, to visit his young master ; but the next thing we hear is, that M. Valancourt is coming home. O, it was a joyful day when he came ! but he was sadly altered, and my lord looked very cool upon him, and he was very sad indeed. And soon after, he went away again into Languedoc, and since that time we have never seen him.'

Theresa paused ; and Emily, sighing deeply, remained with her eyes fixed upon the floor, without speaking. After a long pause, she inquired what further Theresa had heard. ' Yet why should I ask ?' she added : ' what you have already told is too much. O Valancourt ! thou art gone—for ever gone ! and I —I have murdered thee !' These words, and the countenance of despair which accompanied them, alarmed Theresa, who began to fear that the shock of the intelligence Emily had just received had affected her senses.

' My dear young lady, be composed,' said she, ' and do not say such frightful words. You murder M. Valancourt !—dear heart !' Emily replied only by a heavy sigh.

' Dear lady, it breaks my heart to see you look so,' said Theresa : ' do not sit with your eyes upon the ground, and all so pale and melancholy ; it frightens me to see you.' Emily was still silent, and did not appear to hear anything that was said to her. ' Besides, mademoiselle,' continued Theresa, ' M. Valancourt may be alive and merry yet, for what we know.'

At the mention of his name Emily raised her eyes, and fixed them in a wild gaze upon Theresa, as if she was endeavouring to understand what had been said. ' Aye, my dear lady,' said Theresa, mistaking the meaning of this considerate air, ' M. Valancourt may be alive and merry yet.'

On the repetition of these words Emily comprehended their import, but instead of producing the effect intended, they seemed only to heighten her distress. She rose hastily from her chair, paced the little room with quick steps, and often sighing deeply, clasped her hands, and shuddered.

Meanwhile, Theresa, with simple but honest affection, endeavoured to comfort her : put more wood on the fire, stirred it up into a brighter blaze, swept the hearth, set the chair, which Emily had left, in a warmer situation, and then drew forth from a cupboard a flask of wine. ' It is a stormy night, madam,' said she, ' and blows cold—do come nearer the fire, and take a glass of this wine : it will comfort you, as it has done me often and often, for it is not such wine as one gets every day ; it is rich Languedoc, and the last of six flasks that M. Valancourt sent me the night before he left Gascony for Paris. They have served me ever since as cordials ; and I never drink it, but I think of him, and what kind words he said to me when he gave them. " Theresa," says he, " you are not young now, and should have a glass of good wine now and then. I will send you a few flasks ; and when you taste them, you will sometimes remember me your friend." Yes—those were his very words—" me, your friend !"' Emily still paced the room, without seeming to hear what Theresa said, who continued speaking. ' And I have remembered him often enough, poor young gentleman !—for he gave me this roof for a shelter, and that which has supported me. Ah ! he is in heaven with my blessed master, if ever saint was ?'

Theresa's voice faltered ; she wept, and set down the flask, unable to pour out the wine. Her grief seemed to recall Emily from her own, who went towards her, but then stopped, and, having gazed on her for a moment, turned suddenly away, as if overwhelmed by the reflection that it was Valancourt whom Theresa lamented.

While she yet paced the room, the still soft note of an oboe, or flute, was heard mingling with the blast, the sweetness of which affected Emily's spirits ; she paused a moment in attention. The tender tones, as they swelled along the wind, till they were lost again in the ruder gust, came with a plaintiveness that touched her heart, and she melted into tears.

' Aye,' said Theresa, drying her eyes, ' there is Richard, our neighbour's son, playing on the oboe ; it is sad enough to hear such sweet music now.' Emily continued to weep without replying. ' He often plays of an evening,' added Theresa, ' and sometimes the young folks dance to the sound of his oboe. But, dear young lady ! do not cry so ;

and pray take a glass of this wine,' continued she, pouring some into a glass, and handing it to Emily, who reluctantly took it.

'Taste it for M. Valancourt's sake,' said Theresa, as Emily lifted the glass to her lips; 'for he gave it me, you know, madam.' Emily's hand trembled, and she spilt the wine as she withdrew it from her lips.

'For whose sake?—who gave the wine?' said she in a faltering voice.

'M. Valancourt, dear lady: I knew you would be pleased with it. It is the last flask I have left.'

Emily set the wine upon the table, and burst into tears; while Theresa, disappointed and alarmed, tried to comfort her; but she only waved her hand, entreated she might be left alone, and wept the more.

A knock at the cottage-door prevented Theresa from immediately obeying her mistress; and she was going to open it, when Emily, checking her, requested she would not admit any person; but afterwards recollecting that she had ordered her servant to attend her home, she said it was only Philippe, and endeavoured to restrain her tears, while Theresa opened the door.

A voice that spoke without drew Emily's attention. She listened, turned her eyes to the door, when a person now appeared; and immediately a bright gleam that flashed from the fire, discovered—Valancourt!

Emily, on perceiving him, started from her chair, trembled, and, sinking into it again, became insensible to all around her.

A scream from Theresa now told that she knew Valancourt, whom her imperfect sight and the duskiness of the place had prevented her from immediately recollecting; but his attention was immediately called from her to the person whom he saw falling from a chair near the fire; and hastening to her assistance —he perceived that he was supporting Emily! The various emotions that seized him upon thus unexpectedly meeting with her, from whom he had believed he had parted for ever, and on beholding her pale and lifeless in his arms —may, perhaps, be imagined, though they could neither be then expressed nor now described, any more than Emily's sensations, when at length she unclosed her eyes, and, looking up, again saw Valancourt. The intense anxiety with which he regarded her was instantly changed to an expression of mingled joy and tenderness, as his eyes met hers, and he perceived that she was reviving. But he could only exclaim, 'Emily!' as he silently watched her recovery, while she averted her eye, and feebly attempted to withdraw her hand; but in these the first moments which succeeded to the pangs his supposed death had occasioned her, she forgot every fault which had formerly claimed indignation; and beholding Valancourt such as he had appeared when he won her early affection, she ex-

perienced emotions of only tenderness and joy. This, alas! was but the sunshine of a few short moments; recollections rose like clouds upon her mind, and, darkening the illusive image that possessed it, she again beheld Valancourt degraded—Valancourt unworthy the esteem and tenderness she had once bestowed upon him: her spirits faltered; and, withdrawing her hand, she turned from him to conceal her grief, while he, yet more embarrassed and agitated, remained silent.

A sense of what she owed to herself restrained her tears, and taught her soon to overcome, in some degree, the emotions of mingled joy and sorrow that contended at her heart as she rose, and, having thanked him for the assistance he had given her, bade Theresa good evening. As she was leaving the cottage, Valancourt, who seemed suddenly awakened as from a dream, entreated, in a voice that pleaded powerfully for compassion, a few moments' attention. Emily's heart, perhaps, pleaded as powerfully; but she had resolution enough to resist both, together with the clamorous entreaties of Theresa, that she would not venture home alone in the dark; and had already opened the cottage-door, when the pelting storm compelled her to obey their requests.

Silent and embarrassed she returned to the fire, while Valancourt, with increasing agitation, paced the room, as if he wished yet feared to speak, and Theresa expressed without restraint her joy and wonder upon seeing him.

'Dear heart! sir,' said she, 'I never was so surprised and overjoyed in my life. We were in great tribulation before you came, for we thought you was dead, and were talking and lamenting about you just when you knocked at the door. My young mistress there was crying, fit to break her heart——'

Emily looked with much displeasure at Theresa; but, before she could speak, Valancourt, unable to repress the emotions which Theresa's imprudent discovery occasioned, exclaimed, 'O my Emily! am I then still dear to you? Did you, indeed, honour me with a thought—a tear? O heavens! you weep—you weep now!'

'Theresa, sir,' said Emily with a reserved air, and trying to conquer her tears, 'has reason to remember you with gratitude, and she was concerned because she had not lately heard of you. Allow me to thank you for the kindness you have shown her, and to say, that since I am now upon the spot, she must not be further indebted to you.'

'Emily!' said Valancourt, no longer master of his emotions, 'is it thus you meet him whom once you meant to honour with your hand—thus you meet him, who has loved you, suffered for you?—Yet what do I say? Pardon me, pardon me, Mademoiselle St. Aubert, I know not what I utter. I have no longer any claim upon your remembrance—I have forfeited every pretension to your esteem, your love. Yes! let me not forget that I once possessed your affections, though to know that I have lost them is my severest affliction. Affliction—do I call it?—that is a term of mildness.'

'Dear heart!' said Theresa, preventing Emily from replying, 'talk of once having her affections! Why, my dear young lady loves you now better than she does any body in the whole world, though she pretends to deny it.'

'This is unsupportable!' said Emily; 'Theresa, you know not what you say. Sir, if you respect my tranquillity, you will spare me from the continuance of this distress.'

'I do respect your tranquillity too much, voluntarily to interrupt it,' replied Valancourt, in whose bosom pride now contended with tenderness; 'and will not be a voluntary intruder. I would have entreated a few moments' attention—yet I know not for what purpose. You have ceased to esteem me; and to recount to you my sufferings will degrade me more, without exciting even your pity. Yet I have been, O Emily! I am indeed very wretched! added Valancourt in a voice that softened from solemnity into grief.'

'What! is my dear young master going out in all this rain?' said Theresa. 'No, he shall not stir a step. Dear! dear! to see how gentlefolks can afford to throw away their happiness! Now, if you were poor people, there would be none of this. To talk of unworthiness, and not caring about one another, when I know there are not such a kindhearted lady and gentleman in the whole province, nor any that love one another so well, if the truth was spoken!'

Emily in extreme vexation, now rose from her chair: 'I must be gone,' said she, 'the storm is over.'

'Stay, Emily! stay Mademoiselle St. Aubert!' said Valancourt, summoning all his resolution; 'I will no longer distress you by my presence. Forgive me, that I did not sooner obey you, and, if you can, sometimes pity one, who in losing you—has lost all hope of peace! May you be happy, Emily, however wretched I remain—happy as my fondest wish would have you!'

His voice faltered with the last words, and his countenance changed, while, with a look of ineffable tenderness and grief, he gazed upon her for an instant, and then quitted the cottage.

'Dear heart! dear heart!' cried Theresa, following to the door, 'why, Monsieur Valancourt! how it rains! what a night is this to turn him out in! Why it will give him his death; and it was but now you was crying, Mademoiselle, because he was dead. Well! young ladies do change their mind in a minute, as one may say!'

Emily made no reply, for she heard not what was said, while, lost in sorrow and thought, she remained in her chair by the fire, with her eyes fixed, and the image of Valancourt still before them.

'M. Valancourt is sadly altered! madam,' said Theresa; 'he looks so thin to what he used to do, and so melancholy, and then he wears his arm in a sling.'

Emily raised her eyes at these words, for she had not observed this last circumstance, and she now did not doubt that Valancourt had received the shot of her gardener at Thoulouse: with this conviction, her pity for him returning, she blamed herself for having occasioned him to leave the cottage during the storm.

Soon after, her servants arrived with the carriage; and Emily having censured Theresa for her thoughtless conversation to Valancourt and strictly charging her never to repeat any hints of the same kind to him, withdrew to her home, thoughtful and disconsolate.

Meanwhile Valancourt had returned to a little inn of the village, where he had arrived only a few moments before his visit to Theresa's cottage, on the way from Thoulouse to the chateau of the Count de Duvarney, where he had not been since he bade adieu to Emily at Chateau-le-Blanc, in the neighbourhood of which he had lingered for a considerable time, unable to summon resolution enough to quit a place that contained the object most dear to his heart. There were times, indeed, when grief and despair urged him to appear again before Emily, and, regardless of his ruined circumstances, to renew his suit. Pride, however, and the tenderness of his affection, which could not long endure the thought of involving her in his misfortunes, at length so far triumphed over passion, that he relinquished this desperate design, and quitted Chateau-le-Blanc. But still his fancy wandered among the scenes which had witnessed his early love; and on his way to Gascony he stopped at Thoulouse, where he remained when Emily arrived, concealing, yet indulging, his melancholy in the gardens where he had formerly passed with her so many happy hours; often recurring with vain regret to the evening before her departure for Italy, when she had so unexpectedly met him on the terrace, and endeavouring to recall to his memory every word and look which had then charmed him, the arguments he had employed to dissuade her from the journey, and the tenderness of their last farewell. In such melancholy recollections he had been indulging, when Emily unexpectedly appeared to him on this very terrace, the evening after her arrival at Thoulouse. His emotions, on thus seeing her, can scarcely be imagined; but he so far overcame the first promptings of love, that he forbore to discover himself, and abruptly quitted the gardens. Still, however, the vision he had seen haunted his mind; he became more wretched than before; and the only solace of his sorrow was to return in the silence of the night, to follow the paths which he believed her steps had pressed during the day, and to watch round the habitation where she reposed. It was in one of these mournful wanderings that he had received by the fire of the gardener, who mistook him for a robber, a wound in his arm, which had detained him at Thoulouse, till very lately, under the hands of a surgeon. There, regardless of himself and careless of his friends, whose late unkindness had urged him to believe that they were indifferent as to his fate, he remained, without informing them of his situation; and now, being sufficiently recovered to bear travelling, he had taken La Vallée in his way to Estuviere, the count's residence, partly for the purpose of hearing of Emily, and of being again near her, and partly for that of inquiring into the situation of poor old Theresa, who he had reason to suppose had been deprived of her stipend, small as it was, and which inquiry had brought him to her cottage when Emily happened to be there.

This unexpected interview, which had at once shown him the tenderness of her love and the strength of her resolution, renewed all the acuteness of the despair that had attended their former separation, and which no effort of reason could teach him, in these moments, to subdue. Her image, her look, the tones of her voice, all dwelt on his fancy, as powerfully as they had lately appeared to his senses, and banished from his heart every emotion except those of love and despair.

Before the evening concluded, he returned to Theresa's cottage, that he might hear her talk of Emily, and be in the place where she had so lately been. The joy felt and expressed by that faithful servant was quickly changed to sorrow, when she observed, at one moment, his wild and phrensied look, and at another, the dark melancholy that overhung him.

After he had listened, and for a considerable time, to all she had to relate concerning Emily, he gave Theresa nearly all the money he had about him, though she repeatedly refused it, declaring that her mistress had amply supplied her wants; and then, drawing a ring of value from his finger, he delivered it to her with a solemn charge to present it to Emily, of whom he entreated, as a last favour, that she would preserve it for his sake, and sometimes, when she looked upon it, remember the unhappy giver.

Theresa wept as she received the ring, but it was more from sympathy than from any presentiment of evil; and before she could reply, Valancourt abruptly left the cottage. She followed him to the door, calling upon his name, and entreating him to return; but she received no answer, and saw him no more.

CHAPTER LII.

'Call up him that left half-told
The story of Cambuscan bold.'
                                    MILTON.

ON the following morning, as Emily sat in the parlour adjoining the library, reflecting on the scene of the preceding night, Annette rushed wildly into the room, and without speaking, sunk breathless into a chair. It was some time before she could answer the anxious inquiries of Emily, as to the occasion of her emotion; but at length she exclaimed, 'I have seen his ghost, madam, I have seen his ghost!'

'Whom do you mean?' said Emily with extreme impatience.

'It came in from the hall, madam,' continued Annette, 'as I was crossing to the parlour.'

'Whom are you speaking of?' repeated Emily—'Who came in from the hall?'

'It was dressed just as I have seen him, often and often,' added Annette. 'Ah! who could have thought——'

Emily's patience was now exhausted; and she was reprimanding her for such idle fancies, when a servant entered the room, and informed her that a stranger without begged leave to speak with her.

It immediately occurred to Emily that this stranger was Valancourt, and she told the servant to inform him that she was engaged, and could not see any person.

The servant having delivered his message, returned with one from the stranger, urging the first request, and saying that he had something of consequence to communicate; while Annette, who had hitherto sat silent and amazed, now started up, and crying, 'It is Ludovico!—it is Ludovico!' ran out of the room. Emily bade the servant follow her, and, if it really was Ludovico, to show him into the parlour.

In a few minutes Ludovico appeared, accompanied by Annette, who, as joy rendered her forgetful of all rules of decorum towards her mistress, would not suffer any person to be heard for some time but herself. Emily expressed surprise and satisfaction on seeing Ludovico in safety; and the first emotions increased, when he delivered letters from Count de Villefort and the Lady Blanche, informing her of their late adventure, and of their present situation at an inn among the Pyrenees, where they had been detained by the illness of Mons. St. Foix and the indisposition of Blanche, who added, that the Baron St. Foix was just arrived to attend his son to his chateau, where he would remain till the perfect recovery of his wounds, and then return to Languedoc, but that her father and herself proposed to be at La Vallée on the following day. She added, that Emily's presence would be expected at the approaching nuptials, and begged she would be prepared to proceed in a few days to Chateau-le-Blanc. For an account of Ludovico's adventure she referred her to himself; and Emily, though much interested concerning the means by which he had disappeared from the north apartments, had the forbearance to suspend the gratification of her curiosity till he had taken some refreshment, and had conversed with Annette, whose joy, on seeing him in safety, could not have been more extravagant had he arisen from the grave.

Meanwhile, Emily perused again the letters of her friends, whose expressions of esteem and kindness were very necessary consolations to her heart, awakened as it was by the late interview to emotions of keener sorrow and regret.

The invitation to Chateau-le-Blanc was pressed with so much kindness by the count and his daughter, who strengthened it by a message from the countess, and the occasion of it was so important to her friend, that Emily could not refuse to accept it; nor, though she wished to remain in the quiet shades of her native home, could she avoid perceiving the impropriety of remaining here alone since Valancourt was again in the neighbourhood. Sometimes, too, she thought that change of scenery and the society of her friends might contribute more than retirement, to restore her to tranquillity.

When Ludovico again appeared, she desired him to give a detail of his adventure in the north apartments, and to tell by what means he became a companion of the banditti, with whom the count had found him.

He immediately obeyed; while Annette, who had not yet had leisure to ask him many questions on the subject, prepared to listen with a countenance of extreme curiosity, venturing to remind her lady of her incredulity concerning spirits in the castle of Udolpho, and of her own sagacity in believing in them; while Emily, blushing at the consciousness of her late credulity, observed that, if Ludovico's adventure could justify Annette's superstition, he had probably not been here to relate it.

Ludovico smiled at Annette, and bowed to Emily, and then began as follows:

'You may remember, madam, that on the night when I sat up in the north chamber, my lord the count and Mons. Henri accompanied me thither, and that while they remained there nothing happened to excite any alarm. When they were gone I made a fire in the bed-room, and not being inclined to sleep, I sat down on the hearth with a book I had brought with me to divert my mind. I confess I did sometimes look round the chamber with something like apprehension——'

'O very like it, I dare say,' interrupted Annette; 'and I dare say too, if the truth was known, you shook from head to foot.' 'Not quite so bad as that,' replied Ludovico smiling; 'but several times, as the wind whistled round the castle and shook the old casements, I did fancy I heard odd noises, and once or twice I got up and looked about me; but nothing was to be seen except the grim figures in the tapestry, which seemed to frown upon me as I looked at them. I had sat thus for above an hour,' continued Ludovico, 'when again I thought I heard a noise, and glanced my eyes round the room to discover what it came from; but, not perceiving anything, I began to read again: and when I had finished the story I was upon, I felt drowsy and dropped asleep. But presently I was awakened by the noise I had heard before, and it seemed to come from that part of the chamber where the bed stood; and then, whether it was the story I had been reading that affected my spirits, or the strange reports that had been spread of these apartments, I don't know; but when I looked towards the bed again, I fancied I saw a man's face within the dusky curtains.'

At the mention of this Emily trembled and looked anxiously, remembering the spectacle she had herself witnessed there with Dorothee.

'I confess, madam, my heart did fail me at that instant,' continued Ludovico; but a return of the noise drew my attention from the bed, and I then distinctly heard a sound like that of a key turning in a lock; but what surprised me more was, that I saw no door where the sound seemed to come from. In the next moment, however, the arras near the bed was slowly lifted, and a person appeared behind it, entering from a small door in the wall. He stood for a moment as if half-retreating, with his head bending under the arras, which concealed the upper part of his face, except his eyes scowling beneath the tapestry as he held it; and then, while he raised it higher, I saw the face of another man behind, looking over his shoulder. I know not how it was, but, though my sword was upon the table before me, I had not the power just then to seize it, but sat quite still, watching them with my eyes half-shut, as if I was asleep. I suppose they thought me so, and were debating what they should do; for I heard them whisper, and they stood in the same posture for the value of a minute, and then I thought I perceived other faces in the duskiness beyond the door, and heard louder whispers.'

'This door surprises me,' said Emily, 'because I understood that the count had caused the arras to be lifted, and the walls examined, suspecting that they might have concealed a passage through which you had departed.'

'It does not appear so extraordinary to me, madam,' replied Ludovico, 'that this door should escape notice, because it was formed in a narrow compartment which appeared to be part of the outward wall; and if the count had not passed over it, he might have thought it was useless to search for a door where it seemed as if no passage could communicate with one; but the truth was, that the passage was formed within the wall itself. But to return to the men whom I saw obscurely beyond the door, and who did not suffer me to remain long in suspense concerning their design. They all rushed into the room, and surrounded me, though not before I had snatched up my sword to defend myself. But what could one man do against four? They soon disarmed me, and, having fastened my arms and gagged my mouth, forced me through the private door, leaving my sword upon the table, to assist, as they said, those who should come in the morning to look for me, in fighting against the ghosts. They then led me through many narrow passages, cut, as I fancied in the walls, for I had never seen them before, and down several flights of steps, till we came to the vaults underneath the castle; and then opening a stone door, which I should have taken for the wall itself, we went through a long passage, and down other steps cut in the solid rock, when another door delivered us into a cave. After turning and twining about for some time, we reached the mouth of it, and I found myself on the sea-beach at the foot of the cliffs, with the chateau above. A boat was in waiting, into which the ruffians got, forcing me along with them, and we soon reached a small vessel that was at anchor, where other men appeared, when, setting me aboard, two of the fellows who had seized me followed, and the other two rowed back to the shore while we set sail. I soon found out what all this meant, and what was the business of these men at the chateau. We landed in Roussillon; and after lingering several days about the shore, some of their comrades came down from the mountains, and carried me with them to the fort, where I remained till my lord so unexpectedly arrived; for they had taken good care to prevent my running away, having blindfolded me during the journey; and if they had not done this, I think I never could have found my road to any town through the wild country we traversed. After I reached the fort, I was watched like a prisoner, and never suffered to go out without two or three companions, and I became so weary of life that I often wished to get rid of it.'

'Well, but they let you talk,' said Annette; 'they did not gag you after they got you away from the chateau, so I don't see what reason there was to be so very weary of living; to say nothing about the chance of seeing me again.'

Ludovico smiled, and Emily also, who inquired what was the motive of these men for carrying him off.

'I soon found out, madam, resumed Ludovico, 'that they were pirates, who had during many years secreted their spoil in the vaults of the castle, which, being near the sea, suited their purpose well. To prevent detection, they had tried to have it believed that the chateau was haunted; and having discovered the private way to the north apartments, which had been shut up ever since the death of the lady marchioness, they easily succeeded. The housekeeper and her husband, who were the only persons that had inhabited the castle for some years, were so terrified by the strange noises they heard in the nights, that they would live there no longer. A report soon went abroad that it was haunted; and the whole country believed this the more readily, I suppose, because it had been said that the lady marchioness had died in a strange way, and because my lord never would return to the place afterwards.'

'But why,' said Emily, 'were not these pirates contented with the cave?—why did they think it necessary to deposit their spoil in the castle?'

'The cave, madam,' replied Ludovico, 'was open to anybody, and their treasures would not long have remained undiscovered there; but in the vaults they were secure so long as the report prevailed of their being haunted. Thus, then, it appears that they brought at midnight the spoil they took on the seas, and kept it till they had opportunities of disposing of it to advantage. The pirates were connected with Spanish smugglers and banditti who live among the wilds of the Pyrenees, and carry on various kinds of traffic, such as nobody would think of; and with this desperate horde of banditti I remained till my lord arrived. I shall never forget what I felt when I first discovered him—I almost gave him up for lost; but I knew that if I showed myself, the banditti would discover who he was, and probably murder us all, to prevent their secret in the chateau being detected. I therefore kept out of my lord's sight, but had a strict watch upon the ruffians, and determined, if they offered him or his family violence, to discover myself and fight for our lives. Soon after, I overheard some of them laying a most diabolical plan for the murder and plunder of the whole party; when I contrived to speak to some of my lord's attendants, telling them what was going forward, and we consulted what was best to be done. Meanwhile, my lord, alarmed at the absence of the Lady Blanche, demanded her; and the ruffians having given same unsatisfactory answer, my lord and Mons. St. Foix became furious; so then we thought it a good time to discover the plot: and, rushing into the chamber, I called out Treachery!—My lord count, defend yourself! His lordship and the chevalier drew their swords directly, and a hard battle we had; but we conquered at last, as, madam, you are already informed of by my lord count.'

'This is an extraordinary adventure,' said

mily, 'and much praise is due, Ludovico, to our prudence and intrepidity. There are some circumstances, however, concerning the north apartments which still perplex me; but perhaps you may be able to explain them. Did you ever hear the banditti relate anything extraordinary of these rooms?'

'No, madam,' replied Ludovico; 'I never heard them speak about the rooms, except to laugh at the credulity of the old housekeeper, who once was very near catching one of the pirates; it was since the count arrived at the chateau,' he said; and he laughed heartily as he related the trick he had played off.

A blush spread over Emily's cheek, and she impatiently desired Ludovico to explain himself.

'Why, my lady,' said he, 'as this fellow was one night in the bed-room, he heard somebody approaching through the next apartment; and not having time to lift up the arras and unfasten the door, he hid himself in the bed just by. There he lay in as great a fright, I suppose——'

'As you was in,' interrupted Annette, 'when you sat up so boldly to watch by yourself.'

'Aye,' said Ludovico, 'in as great a fright as he ever made anybody else suffer: and presently the housekeeper and some other person came up to the bed; when he, thinking they were going to examine it, bethought him, that his only chance of escaping detection was by terrifying them; so he lifted up the counterpane; but that did not do, till he raised his face above it; and then they both set off,' he said, 'as if they had seen the devil; and he got out of the rooms undiscovered.'

Emily could not forbear smiling at this explanation of the deception which had given her so much superstitious terror, and was surprised that she could have suffered herself to be thus alarmed, till she considered that, when the mind has once begun to yield to the weakness of superstition, trifles impress it with the force of conviction. Still, however, she remembered with awe the mysterious music which had been heard at midnight near Chateau-le-Blanc, and she asked Ludovico if he could give any explanation of it; but he could not.

'I only know, madam,' he added, 'that it did not belong to the pirates; for I have heard them laugh about it, and say they believed the devil was in league with them there.'

'Yes, I will answer for it he was,' said Annette, her countenance brightening; 'I was sure all along that he or his spirits had something to do with the north apartments, and now you see, madam, I am right at last.'

'It cannot be denied that his spirits were very busy in that part of the chateau,' replied Emily smiling. 'But I am surprised, Ludovico, that these pirates should persevere in their schemes after the arrival of the count; what could they expect but certain detection?'

'I have reason to believe, madam,' replied Ludovico, 'that it was their intention to persevere no longer than was necessary for the removal of the stores which were deposited in the vaults; and it appeared that they had been employed in doing so from within a short period after the count's arrival; but as they had only a few hours in the night for this business, and were carrying on other schemes at the same time, the vaults were not above half emptied when they took me away. They gloried exceedingly in this opportunity of confirming the superstitious reports that had been spread of the north chambers, were careful to leave everything there as they had found it, the better to promote the deception; and frequently in their jocose moods would laugh at the consternation which they believed the inhabitants of the castle had suffered upon my disappearing; and it was to prevent the possibility of my betraying their secret that they had removed me to such a distance. From that period they considered the chateau as nearly their own; but I found from the discourse of their comrades that, though they were cautious at first in showing their power there, they had once very nearly betrayed themselves. Going one night, as was their custom, to the north chamber to repeat the noises that had occasioned such alarm among the servants, they heard, as they were about to unfasten the secret door, voices in the bedroom. My lord has since told me that himself and M. Henri were then in the apartment, and they heard very extraordinary sounds of lamentation, which it seems were made by these fellows, with their usual design of spreading terror; and my lord has owned he then felt somewhat more than surprise; but as it was necessary to the peace of his family that no notice should be taken, he was silent on the subject, and enjoined silence to his son.'

Emily, recollecting the change that had appeared in the spirits of the count, after the night when he had watched in the north room, now perceived the cause of it; and having made some further inquiries upon this strange affair, she dismissed Ludovico, and went to give orders for the accommodation of her friends on the following day.

In the evening, Theresa, lame as she was, came to deliver the ring with which Valancourt had intrusted her; and when she presented it, Emily was much affected, for she remembered to have seen him wear it often in happier days. She was, however, much displeased that Theresa had received it, and positively refused to accept it herself, though to have done so would have afforded her a melancholy pleasure. Theresa entreated, expostulated, and then described the distress of Valancourt when he had given the ring, and repeated the message with which he had commissioned her to deliver it; and Emily could not conceal the extreme sorrow this recital occasioned her, but wept, and remained lost in thought.

' Alas ! my dear young lady !' said Theresa, ' why should all this be ? I have known you from your infancy, and it may well be supposed I love you as if you was my own, and wish as much to see you happy. M. Valancourt, to be sure, I have not known so long, but then I have reason to love him as though he was my own son. I know how well you love one another, or why all this weeping and wailing ?' Emily waved her hand for Theresa to be silent, who, disregarding the signal, continued : ' And how much you are alike in your tempers and ways, and that, if you were married, you would be the happiest couple in the whole province—then what is there to prevent your marrying ? Dear, dear ! to see how some people fling away their happiness, and then cry and lament about it, just as if it was not their own doing, and as if there was more pleasure in wailing and weeping than in being at peace. Learning, to be sure, is a fine thing ; but if it teaches folks no better than that, why I had rather be without it ; if it would teach them to be happier, I would say something to it ; then it would be learning and wisdom too.'

Age and long services had given Theresa a privilege to talk ; but Emily now endeavoured to check her loquacity, and, though she felt the justness of her remarks, did not choose to explain the circumstances that had determined her conduct towards Valancourt. She therefore only told Theresa that it would much displease her to hear the subject renewed ; that she had reasons for her conduct which she did not think it proper to mention ; and that the ring must be returned, with an assurance that she could not accept it with propriety ; and at the same time she forbade Theresa to repeat any future message from Valancourt, as she valued her esteem and kindness. Theresa was afflicted, and made another attempt, though feeble, to interest her for Valancourt ; but the unusual displeasure expressed in Emily's countenance soon obliged her to desist, and she departed in wonder and lamentation.

To relieve her mind, in some degree, from the painful recollections that intruded upon it, Emily busied herself in preparations for the journey into Languedoc ; and while Annette, who assisted her, spoke with joy and affection of the safe return of Ludovico, she was considering how she might best promote their happiness, and determined, if it appeared that his affection was as unchanged as that of the simple and honest Annette, to give her a marriage-portion, and settle them on some part of her estate. These considerations led her to the remembrance of her father's paternal domain, which his affairs had formerly compelled him to dispose of to M. Quesnel,

and which she frequently wished to regain, because St. Aubert had lamented that the chief lands of his ancestors had passed into another family, and because they had been his birth-place and the haunt of his early years. To the estate at Thoulouse she had no particular attachment, and it was her wish to dispose of this, that she might purchase her paternal domains, if M. Quesnel could be prevailed on to part with them, which, as he talked much of living in Italy, did not appear very improbable.

CHAPTER LIII.

' Sweet is the breath of vernal shower,
  The bees' collected treasures sweet,
  Sweet music's melting fall, but sweeter yet
  The still small voice of gratitude.'
                                                GRAY.

ON the following day, the arrival of her friend revived the drooping Emily, and La Vallée became once more the scene of social kindness and of elegant hospitality. Illness and the terror she had suffered had stolen from Blanche much of her sprightliness, but all her affectionate simplicity remained, and though she appeared less blooming, she was not less engaging than before. The unfortunate adventure on the Pyrenees had made the count very anxious to reach home ; and after a little more than a week's stay at La Vallée, Emily prepared to set out with her friends for Languedoc, assigning the care of her house, during her absence, to Theresa. On the evening preceding her departure, this old servant brought again the ring of Valancourt, and, with tears, entreated her mistress to receive it, for that she had neither seen nor heard of M. Valancourt since the night when he delivered it to her. As she said this, her countenance expressed more alarm than she dared to utter ; but Emily, checking her own propensity to fear, considered that he had probably returned to the residence of his brother, and, again refusing to accept the ring, bade Theresa preserve it till she saw him ; which with extreme reluctance she promised to do.

On the following day, Count de Villefort, with Emily and the Lady Blanche, left La Vallée, and on the ensuing evening arrived at the Chateau-le-Blanc, where the Countess, Henri, and M. du Pont, whom Emily was surprised to find there, received them with much joy and congratulation. She was concerned to observe that the count still encouraged the hopes of his friend, whose countenance declared that his affection had suffered no abatement from absence ; and was much distressed, when, on the second evening after her arrival, the count, having withdrawn her from the Lady Blanche, with whom she was walking, renewed the subject of M. du Pont's hopes. The mildness with which she listened his intercourses at first, deceiving him as to · sentiments, he began to believe that, her ection for Valancourt being overcome, she s at length disposed to think favourably of du Pont ; and, when she afterwards con-.ced him of his mistake, he ventured, in the 'nestness of his wish to promote what he 1sidered to be the happiness of two persons om he so much esteemed, gently to remon-ate with her on thus suffering an ill-placed ection to poison the happiness of her most :uable years.

Observing her silence and the deep dejection her countenance, he concluded with saying, will not say more now, but I will still lieve, my dear Mademoiselle St. Aubert, it you will not always reject a person so ily estimable as my friend Du Pont.'

He spared her the pain of replying by iving her ; and she strolled on, somewhat ipleased with the count for having perse-red to plead for a suit which she had repeat-ly rejected, and lost amidst the melancholy :ollections which this topic had revived, till e had insensibly reached the borders of the pods that screened the monastery of St. are, when perceiving how far she had wan-red, she determined to extend her walk a tle further, and to inquire after the abbess d some of her friends among the nuns.

Though the evening was now drawing to a ose, she accepted the invitation of the friar 10 opened the gate, and, anxious to meet me of her old acquaintance, proceeded to-irds the convent parlour. As she crossed e lawn that sloped from the front of the onastery towards the sea, she was struck ith the picture of repose exhibited by some onks sitting in the cloisters, which extended ider the brow of the woods that crowned is eminence ; where, as they meditated, at is twilight hour, holy subjects, they some-nes suffered their attention to be relieved by ie scene before them, nor thought it profane ι look at nature, now that it had exchanged ie brilliant colours of the day for the sober ie of evening. Before the cloisters, however, read an ancient chestnut, whose ample ranches were designed to screen the full iagnificence of a scene that might tempt the ish to worldly pleasures ; but still, beneath ie dark and spreading foliage, gleamed a ide extent of ocean, and many a passing iil ; while, to the right and left, thick woods ere seen stretching along the winding shores. o much as this had been admitted, perhaps,) give to the secluded votary an image of the angers and vicissitudes of life, and to console im now that he had renounced its pleasures y the certainty of having escaped its evils. As :mily walked pensively along, considering ow much suffering she might have escaped ad she become a votaress of the order, and :mained in this retirement from the time of er father's death, the vesper-bell struck up,

and the monks retired slowly toward the chapel ; while she, pursuing her way, entered the great hall, where an unusual silence seemed to reign. The parlour, too, which opened from it, she found vacant ; but, as the evening bell was sounding, she believed the nuns had withdrawn into the chapel, and sat down to rest for a moment before she returned to the chateau, where, however, the increasing gloom made her now anxious to be.

Not many minutes had elapsed, before a nun, entering in haste, inquired for the abbess, and was retiring without recollecting Emily, when she made herself known, and then learned that a mass was going to be performed for the soul of sister Agnes, who had been declining for some time, and who was now believed to be dying.

Of her sufferings the sister gave a melan-choly account, and of the horrors into which she had frequently started, but which had now yielded to a dejection so gloomy, that neither her prayers, in which she was joined by the sisterhood, nor the assurances of her confessor, had power to recall her from it, or to cheer her mind even with a momentary gleam of comfort.

To this relation Emily listened with extreme concern ; and recollecting the phrensied man-ners and the expressions of horror which she had herself witnessed of Agnes, together with the history that sister Frances had communi-cated, her compassion was heightened to a very painful degree. As the evening was already far advanced, Emily did not now desire to see her, or to join in the mass ; and after leaving many kind remembrances with the nun for her old friends, she quitted the monastery, and returned over the cliffs toward the chateau, meditating upon what she had just heard, till at length she forced her mind upon less interesting subjects.

The wind was high ; and as she drew near the chateau, she often paused to listen to its awful sound as it swept over the billows that beat below, or groaned along the surrounding woods ; and while she rested on a cliff a short distance from the chateau, and looked upon the wide waters seen dimly beneath the last shade of twilight, she thought of the following address

TO THE WINDS.

Viewless, through heaven's vast vault your
    course ye steer,
Unknown from whence ye come, or whither go,
Mysterious powers ! I hear you murmur low,
Till swells your loud gust on my startled ear,
And, awful, seems to say—Some god is near !
I love to list your midnight voices float
In the dread storm, that o'er the ocean rolls,
And, while their charm the angry wave controls,
Mix with its sullen roar, and sink remote.
Then, rising in the pause, a sweeter note,
The dirge of spirits, who your deeds bewail,
A sweeter note oft swells while sleeps the gale.

But soon, ye sightless powers, your rest is o'er;
Solemn and slow, ye rise upon the air,
Speak in the shrouds, and bid the sea-boy fear,
And the faint-warbled dirge is heard no more.
Oh! then I deprecate your awful reign.
The loud lament yet bear not on your breath:
Bear not the crash of bark far on the main,
Bear not the cry of men, who cry in vain,
The crew's dread chorus sinking into death;
Oh! give not these, ye powers! I ask alone,
As rapt I climb these dark romantic steeps,
The elemental war, the billow's moan:
I ask the still, sweet tear, that listening Fancy weeps.

CHAPTER LIV.

' . . . . Unnatural deeds
Do breed unnatural troubles: infected minds
To their deaf pillows will discharge their secrets.
More needs she the divine, than the physician.
　　　　　　　　　　　　MACBETH.

ON the following evening, the view of the convent towers rising among the shadowy woods, reminded Emily of the nun whose condition had so much affected her; and anxious to know how she was, as well as to see some of her former friends, she and the Lady Blanche extended their walk to the monastery. At the gate stood a carriage, which, from the heat of the horses, appeared to have just arrived; but a more than common stillness pervaded the court and the cloisters through which Emily and Blanche passed in their way to the great hall, where a nun, who was passing the staircase, replied to the inquiries of the former, that sister Agnes was still living and sensible, but that it was thought she could not survive the night. In the parlour they found several of the boarders, who rejoiced to see Emily, and told her many little circumstances that had happened in the convent since her departure, and which were interesting to her only because they related to persons whom she had regarded with affection. While they thus conversed, the abbess entered the room, and expressed much satisfaction at seeing Emily; but her manner was unusually solemn, and her countenance dejected. 'Our house,' said she, 'after the first salutations were over, 'is truly a house of mourning—a daughter is now paying the debt of nature.— You have heard, perhaps, that our daughter Agnes is dying?'

Emily expressed her sincere concern.

' Here death presents to us a great and awful lesson,' continued the abbess; 'let us read it, and profit by it; let it teach us to prepare ourselves for the change that awaits us all! You are young, and have it in your power to secure " the peace that passeth all understanding "—the peace of conscience. Preserve it in your youth, that it may comfort you in age; for vain, alas! and imperfect are the good deeds of our latter years, if those of our early life have been evil!'

Emily would have said that good deeds, she hoped, were never vain; but she considered that it was the abbess who spoke, and she remained silent.

'The latter days of Agnes,' resumed the abbess, 'have been exemplary; would they might atone for the errors of her former ones! Her sufferings now, alas! are great; let us believe that they will make her peace hereafter! I have left her with her confessor, and a gentleman whom she has long been anxious to see, and who is just arrived from Paris. They, I hope, will be able to administer the repose which her mind has hitherto wanted.'

Emily fervently joined in the wish.

' During her illness she has sometimes named you,' resumed the abbess; ' perhaps it would comfort her to see you; when her present visitors have left her, we will go to her chamber, if the scene will not be too melancholy for your spirits. But, indeed, to such scenes, however painful, we ought to accustom ourselves, for they are salutary to the soul, and prepare us for what we are ourselves to suffer.'

Emily became grave and thoughtful; for this conversation brought to her recollection the dying moments of her beloved father, and she wished once more to weep over the spot where his remains were buried. During the silence which followed the abbess's speech, many minute circumstances attending his last hours occurred to her—his emotion on perceiving himself to be in the neighbourhood of Chateau-le-Blanc—his request to be interred in a particular spot in the church of this monastery—and the solemn charge he had delivered her, to destroy certain papers without examining them.—She recollected also the mysterious and horrible words in those manuscripts, upon which her eye had involuntarily glanced; and though they now, and indeed whenever she remembered them, revived an excess of painful curiosity concerning their full import and the motives for her father's command, it was ever her chief consolation that she had strictly obeyed him in this particular.

Little more was said by the abbess, who appeared too much affected by the subject she had lately left to be willing to converse, and her companions had been for some time silent from the same cause; when this general reverie was interrupted by the entrance of a stranger, Monsieur Bonnac, who had just quitted the chamber of sister Agnes. He appeared much disturbed, but Emily fancied that his countenance had more the expression of horror than of grief. Having drawn the abbess to a distant part of the room, he conversed with her for some time, during which she seemed to listen with earnest attention, and he to speak with caution and a more than common degree of interest. When he had concluded, he owed silently to the rest of the company, nd quitted the room. The abbess, soon fter, proposed going to the chamber of sister ,gnes; to which Emily consented, though ot without some reluctance, and Lady Blanche :mained with the boarders below.

At the door of the chamber they met the onfessor, whom, as he lifted up his head on 1eir approach, Emily observed to be the ume that had attended her dying father; but e passed on without noticing her, and they ntered the apartment, where, on a mattress, as laid sister Agnes, with one nun watching 1 the chair beside her. Her countenance as so much changed that Emily would :arcely have recollected her, had she not :en prepared to do so; it was ghastly, and: verspread with gloomy horror; her dim and: ollow eyes were fixed on a crucifix which she :ld upon her bosom; and she was so much igaged in thought, as not to perceive the obess and Emily till they stood at the bed-Je. Then, turning her heavy eyes, she fixed em, in wild horror, upon Emily; and, reaming, exclaimed, 'Ah! that vision comes on me in my dying hours!'

Emily started back in terror, and looked for planation to the abbess, who made her a rnal not to be alarmed; and calmly said to gnes, 'Daughter, I have brought Made-oiselle St. Aubert to visit you; I thought u would be glad to see her.'

Agnes made no reply; but still gazing ldly upon Emily, exclaimed, 'It is her very .f! Oh! there is all that fascination in her ok which proved my destruction! What vuld you have?—what is it you come to mand?—Retribution?——It will soon be urs—it is yours already. How many years ve passed since last I saw you! My crime but as yesterday.—Yet I am grown old neath it; while you are still young and ooming—blooming as when you forced me. commit that most abhorred deed! Oh! ald I once forget it!——yet what would t avail?—the deed is done!'

Emily, extremely shocked, would now have : the room; but the abbess, taking her id, tried to support her spirits, and begged : would stay a few moments, when Agnes uld probably be calm, whom now she pried soothe. But the latter seemed to disregard ', while she still fixed her eyes on Emily, 1 added, 'What are years of prayers and entance? they cannot wash out the foul-s of murder!——Yes, murder! Where is —where is he?—Look there—look there—where he stalks along the room! Why you come to torment me now?' continued nes, while her straining eyes were bent on : 'why was not I punished before?—Oh! not frown so sternly! Hah! there again! she herself! Why do you look so piteously on me—and smite me, too? Smile on me! lat groan was that?'

Agnes sunk down apparently lifeless, and Emily, unable to support herself, leaned against the bed, while the abbess and the attendant nun were applying the usual remedies to Agnes. 'Peace,' said the abbess, when Emily was going to speak; 'the delirium is going off; she will soon revive. When was she thus before, daughter?'

'Not of many weeks, madam,' replied the nun: 'but her spirits have been much agitated by the arrival of the gentleman she wished so much to see.'

'Yes,' observed the abbess, 'that has un-doubtedly occasioned this paroxysm of phrensy. When she is better, we will leave her to re-pose.'

Emily very readily consented; but, though she could now give little assistance, she was unwilling to quit the chamber while any might be necessary.

When Agnes recovered her senses, she again fixed her eyes on Emily; but their wild ex-pression was gone, and a gloomy melancholy had succeeded. It was some moments before she recovered sufficient spirits to speak: she then said feebly, 'The likeness is wonderful! it must be something more than fancy. Tell me, I conjure you,' she added, addressing Emily, 'though your name is St. Aubert, are you not the daughter of the marchioness?'

'What marchioness?' said Emily in extreme surprise; for she had imagined, from the calmness of Agnes's manner, that her intel-lects were restored. The abbess gave her a, significant glance, but she repeated the ques-tion.

'What marchioness?' exclaimed Agnes; 'I know but of one—the Marchioness de Villeroi.'

Emily, remembering the emotion of her late father upon the unexpected mention of this lady, and his request to be laid near to the tomb of the Villerois, now felt greatly in-terested, and she entreated Agnes to explain the reason of her question. The abbess would now have withdrawn Emily from the room, who being, however, detained by a strong interest, repeated her entreaties.

'Bring me that casket, sister,' said Agnes: 'I will show her to you: yet you need only look at that mirror, and you will behold her; you surely are her daughter; such striking resemblance is never found but among near relations.'

The nun brought the casket; and Agnes having directed her how to unlock it, she took thence a miniature, in which Emily perceived the exact resemblance of the picture which she had found among her late father's papers. Agnes held out her hand to receive it; gazed upon it earnestly for some moments in silence; and then, with a countenance of deep despair, threw up her eyes to heaven, and prayed in-wardly. When she had finished, she returs-

the miniature to Emily. 'Keep it,' said she; 'I bequeath it to you, for I must believe it is your right. I have frequently observed the resemblance between you; but never, till this day, did it strike upon my conscience so powerfully! Stay, sister, do not remove the casket—there is another picture I would show.'

Emily trembled with expectation, and the abbess again would have withdrawn her. 'Agnes is still disordered,' said she; 'you observe how she wanders. In these moods she says anything, and does not scruple as you have witnessed, to accuse herself of the most horrible crimes.'

Emily, however, thought she perceived something more than madness in the inconsistencies of Agnes, whose mention of the marchioness, and production of her picture, had interested her so much, that she determined to obtain further information, if possible, respecting the subject of it.

The nun returned with the casket; and Agnes pointing out to her a secret drawer, she took from it another miniature. 'Here,' said Agnes, as she offered it to Emily, 'learn a lesson for your vanity, at least; look well at this picture, and see if you can discover any resemblance between what I was and what I am.'

Emily impatiently received the miniature, which her eyes had scarcely glanced upon, before her trembling hands had nearly suffered it to fall—it was the resemblance of the portrait of Signora Laurentini, which she had formerly seen in the castle of Udolpho—the lady who had disappeared in so mysterious a manner, and whom Montoni had been suspected of having caused to be murdered.

'Why do you look so sternly on me?' said Agnes, mistaking the nature of Emily's emotion.

'I have seen this face before,' said Emily at length; 'was it really your resemblance?'

'You may well ask that question,' replied the nun—'but I was once esteemed a striking likeness of me. Look at me well, and see what guilt has made me. I then was innocent; the evil passions of my nature slept.' 'Sister!' added she solemnly, and stretching forth her cold damp hand to Emily, who shuddered at its touch—'Sister! beware of the first indulgence of the passions; beware of the first! Their course, if not checked then, is rapid—their force is uncontrollable—they lead us we know not whither—they lead us perhaps to the commission of crimes, for which whole years of prayer and penitence cannot atone!—Such may be the force of even a single passion, that it overcomes every other, and sears up every other approach to the heart. Possessing us like a fiend, it leads us on to the acts of a fiend, making us insensible to pity and to conscience. And when its purpose is accomplished, like a fiend it

leaves us to the torture of those feelings which its power had suspended—not annihilated—to the tortures of compassion, remorse, and conscience. Then, we awaken as from a dream, and perceive a new world around us—we gaze in astonishment and horror—but the deed is committed; not all the powers of heaven and earth united can undo it—and the spectres of conscience will not fly! What are riches—grandeur—health itself, to the luxury of a pure conscience, the health of the soul;—and what the sufferings of poverty, disappointment, despair—to the anguish of an afflicted one! Oh! how long is it since I knew that luxury! I believed that I had suffered the most agonising pangs of human nature, in love, jealousy and despair—but these pangs were ease compared with the stings of conscience which I have since endured. I tasted too what was called the sweet of revenge—but it was transient, it expired even with the object that provoked it. Remember, sister, that the passions are the seeds of vices as well as of virtues, from which either may spring, accordingly as they are nurtured. Unhappy they who have never been taught the art to govern them!'

'Alas! unhappy!' said the abbess, 'and ill-informed of our holy religion!' Emily listened to Agnes in silent awe, while she still examined the miniature, and became confirmed in her opinion of its strong resemblance to the portrait of Udolpho. 'This face is familiar to me,' said she, wishing to lead the nun to an explanation, yet fearing to discover too abruptly her knowledge of Udolpho.

'You are mistaken,' replied Agnes; 'you certainly never saw that picture before.'

'No,' replied Emily; 'but I have seen one extremely like it.' 'Impossible,' said Agnes, who may now be called the Lady Laurentini.

'It was in the castle of Udolpho,' continued Emily, looking steadfastly at her.

'Of Udolpho?' exclaimed Laurentini: 'of Udolpho in Italy?' 'The same,' replied Emily.'

'You know me then,' said Laurentini, 'and you are the daughter of the marchioness.' Emily was somewhat surprised at this abrupt assertion. 'I am the daughter of the late Mons. St. Aubert,' said she; 'and the lady you name is an utter stranger to me.'

'At least you believe so,' rejoined Laurentini.

Emily asked what reasons there could be to believe otherwise.

'The family-likeness that you bear her,' said the nun. 'The marchioness, it is known, was attached to a gentleman of Gascony, at the time when she accepted the hand of the marquis by the command of her father. Ill-fated, unhappy woman!'

Emily remembering the extreme emotion which St. Aubert had betrayed on the mention of the marchioness, would now have suffered something more than surprise, had her confidence in his integrity been less; as it was, she could not for a moment believe what the words of Laurentini insinuated; yet she still felt strongly interested concerning them, and begged that she would explain them further.

'Do not urge me on that subject,' said the nun, 'it is to me a terrible one! Would that I could blot it from my memory!' She sighed deeply, and, after the pause of a moment, asked Emily by what means she had discovered her name.

'By your portrait in the castle of Udolpho, to which this miniature bears a striking resemblance,' replied Emily.

'You have been at Udolpho, then?' said the nun with great emotion. 'Alas! what scenes does the mention of it revive in my fancy—scenes of happiness—of suffering—and of horror!'

At this moment the terrible spectacle which Emily had witnessed in a chamber of that castle occurred to her; and she shuddered while she looked upon the nun—and recollected her late words—that years of prayer and penitence could not wash out the foulness of murder. She was now compelled to attribute these to another cause than that of delirium. With a degree of horror that almost deprived her of sense, she now believed she looked upon a murderess. All the recollected behaviour of Laurentini seemed to confirm the supposition; yet Emily was still lost in a labyrinth of perplexities, and, not knowing how to ask the questions which might lead to truth, she could only hint them in broken sentences.

'Your sudden departure from Udolpho,'—said she.

Laurentini groaned.

The reports that followed it, continued Emily—'The west chamber—the mournful veil—the object it conceals!—When murders are committed——'

The nun shrieked. 'What! there again!' said she, endeavouring to raise herself, while her starting eyes seemed to follow some object round the room—'Come from the grave—What! Blood—blood too!—There was ·no blood—thou canst not say it!—Nay, do not smile,—do not smile so piteously!'

Laurentini fell into convulsions as she uttered the last words; and Emily, unable any longer to endure the horror of the scene, hurried from the room, and sent some nuns to the assistance of the abbess.

The Lady Blanche and the boarders who were in the parlour now assembled round Emily, and, alarmed by her manner and affrighted countenance, asked a hundred questions, which she avoided answering further, than by saying that she believed sister Agnes was dying. They received this as a sufficient explanation of her terror; and had then leisure to offer restoratives, which at length somewhat revived Emily, whose mind was, however, so much shocked with terrible surmises,

and perplexed with doubts by some words from the nun, that she was unable to converse, and would have left the convent immediately, had she not wished to know whether Laurentini would survive the late attack. After waiting some time, she was informed that, the convulsions having ceased, Laurentini seemed to be reviving; and Emily and Blanche were departing, when the abbess appeared, who, drawing the former aside, said she had something of consequence to say to her, but as it was late, she would not detain her then, and requested to see her on the following day.

Emily promised to visit her, and, having taken leave, returned with the Lady Blanche towards the chateau, on the way to which the deep gloom of the woods made Blanche lament that the evening was so far advanced; for the surrounding stillness and obscurity rendered her sensible of fear, though there was a servant to protect her; while Emily was too much engaged by the horrors of the scene she had just witnessed, to be affected by the solemnity of the shades, otherwise than as they served to promote her gloomy reverie, from which, however, she was at length recalled by the Lady Blanche, who pointed out at some distance in the dusky path they were winding, two persons slowly advancing. It was impossible to avoid them without striking into a still more secluded part of the wood, whither the strangers might easily follow; but all apprehension vanished when Emily distinguished the voice of Mons. du Pont, and perceived that his companion was the gentleman whom she had seen at the monastery, and who was now conversing with so much earnestness as not immediately to perceive their approach. When Du Pont joined the ladies, the stranger took leave; and they proceeded to the chateau, where the count, when he heard of Mons. Bonnac, claimed him for an acquaintance, and, on learning the melancholy occasion of his visit to Languedoc, and that he was lodged at a small inn in the village, begged the favour of Mons. du Pont to invite him to the chateau.

The latter was happy to do so: and the scruples of reserve which made M. Bonnac hesitate to accept the invitation being at length overcome, they went to the chateau, where the kindness of the count and the sprightliness of his son were exerted to dissipate the gloom that overhung the spirits of the stranger. M. Bonnac was an officer in the French service, and appeared to be about fifty; his figure was tall and commanding, his manners had received the last polish, and there was something in his countenance uncommonly interesting; for over features which in youth must have been remarkably handsome, was spread a melancholy that seemed the effect of long misfortune, rather than of constitution or temper.

The conversation he held during suppe·

was evidently an effort of politeness, and there were intervals in which, unable to struggle against feelings that depressed him, he relapsed into silence and abstraction; from which, however, the count sometimes withdrew him in a manner so delicate and benevolent, that Emily, while she observed him, almost fancied she beheld her late father.

The party separated at an early hour; and then, in the solitude of her apartment, the scenes which Emily had lately witnessed returned to her fancy with dreadful energy. That in the dying nun she should have discovered Signora Laurentini, who instead of having been murdered by Montoni, was, as it now seemed, herself guilty of some dreadful crime, excited both horror and surprise in a high degree; nor did the hints which she had dropped respecting the marriage of the Marchioness de Villeroi, and the inquiries she had made concerning Emily's birth, occasion her a less degree of interest, though it was of a different nature.

The history which sister Frances had formerly related, and had said to be that of Agnes, it now appeared was erroneous; but for what purpose it had been fabricated, unless the more effectually to conceal the true story, Emily could not even guess. Above all, her interest was excited as to the relation which the story of the late Marchioness de Villeroi bore to that of her father; for that some kind of relation existed between them, the grief of St. Aubert upon hearing her name, his request to be buried near her, and her picture which had been found among his papers, certainly proved. Sometimes it occurred to Emily that he might have been the lover to whom it was said the marchioness was attached, when she was compelled to marry the Marquis de Villeroi; but that he had afterwards cherished a passion for her, she could not suffer herself to believe for a moment. The papers which he had so solemnly enjoined her to destroy, she now fancied had related to this connexion; and she wished more earnestly than before to know the reasons that made him consider the injunction necessary, which, had her faith in his principles been less, would have led her to believe that there was a mystery in her birth dishonourable to her parents, which those manuscripts might have revealed.

Reflections similar to these engaged her mind during the greater part of the night; and when at length she fell into a slumber, it was only to behold a vision of the dying nun, and to awaken in horrors like those she had witnessed.

On the following morning she was too much indisposed to attend her appointment with the abbess, and before the day concluded she heard that sister Agnes was no more. Mons. Bonnac received this intelligence with concern; but Emily observed that he did not appear so much affected now as on the preceding evening, immediately after quitting the apartment of the nun, whose death was probably less terrible to him than the confession he had been then called upon to witness. However this might be, he was perhaps consoled, in some degree, by a knowledge of the legacy bequeathed him, since his family was large, and the extravagance of some part of it had lately been the means of involving him in great distress, and even in the horrors of a prison; and it was the grief he had suffered from the wild career of a favourite son, with the pecuniary anxieties and misfortunes consequent upon it, that had given to his countenance the air of dejection which had so much interested Emily.

To his friend Mons. du Pont he recited some particulars of his late sufferings, when it appeared that he had been confined for several months in one of the prisons of Paris, with little hope of release, and without the comfort of seeing his wife, who had been absent in the country, endeavouring, though in vain, to procure assistance from his friends. When, at length, she had obtained an order for admittance, she was so much shocked at the change which long confinement and sorrow had made in his appearance, that she was seized with fits, which, by their long continuance, threatened her life.

'Our situation affected those who happened to witness it,' continued Mons. Bonnac: 'and one generous friend, who was in confinement at the same time, afterwards employed the first moments of his liberty in efforts to obtain mine. He succeeded; the heavy debt that oppressed me was discharged; and when I would have expressed my sense of the obligation I had received my benefactor was fled from my search. I have reason to believe he was the victim of his own generosity, and that he returned to the state of confinement from which he had released me; but every inquiry after him was unsuccessful. Amiable and unfortunate Valancourt!'

'Valancourt!' exclaimed Mons. du Pont. 'Of what family?'

'The Valancourts, Count Duvarney,' replied Mons. Bonnac.

The emotion of Mons. du Pont, when he discovered the generous benefactor of his friend to be the rival of his love, can only be imagined; but having overcome his first surprise, he dissipated the apprehension of Mons. Bonnac, by acquainting him that Valancourt was at liberty, and had lately been in Languedoc; after which his affection for Emily prompted him to make some inquiries respecting the conduct of his rival during his stay at Paris, of which M. Bonnac appeared to be well informed. The answers he received were such as convinced him that Valancourt had been much misrepresented; and painful as was the sacrifice, he formed the just design of relinquishing his pursuit of Emily, to a lover who, it now appeared, was not unworthy of the regard with which she honoured him.

The conversation of M. Bonnac discovered that Valancourt, some time after his arrival at Paris, had been drawn into the snares which determined vice had spread for him ; and that his hours had been chiefly divided between the parties of the captivating marchioness, and those gaming assemblies to which the envy or the avarice of his brother-officers had spared no art to seduce him. In these parties he had lost large sums in efforts to recover small ones, and to such losses the Count de Villefort and M. Henri had been frequent witnesses. His resources were at length exhausted ; and the count his brother, exasperated by his conduct, refused to continue the supplies necessary to his present mode of life ; when Valancourt, in consequence of accumulated debts, was thrown into confinement, where his brother suffered him to remain, in the hope that punishment might effect a reform of conduct which had not yet been confirmed by long habit.

In the solitude of his prison Valancourt had leisure for reflection and cause for repentance ; here, too, the image of Emily, which amidst the dissipation of the city had been seen, but never obliterated from his heart, revived, with all the charms of innocence and beauty, to reproach him for having sacrificed his happiness and debased his talents by pursuits which his nobler faculties would formerly have taught him to consider were as tasteless as they were degrading. But though his passions had been seduced, his heart was not depraved, nor had habit riveted the chains that hung heavily on his conscience ; and, as he retained that energy of will which was necessary to burst them, he at length emancipated himself from the bondage of vice, but not till after much effort and severe suffering.

Being released by his brother from the prison where he had witnessed the affecting meeting between Mons. Bonnac and his wife, with whom he had been for some time acquainted, the first use of his liberty formed a striking instance of his humanity and his rashness ; for with nearly all the money just received from his brother, he went to a gaming-house, and gave it as a last stake for a chance of restoring his friend to freedom and to his afflicted family. The event was fortunate ; and while he had awaited the issue of this momentous stake, he made a solemn vow never again to yield to the destructive and fascinating vice of gaming.

Having restored the venerable Mons. Bonnac to his rejoicing family, he hurried from Paris to Estuviere ; and in the delight of having made the wretched happy, forgot for a while his own misfortunes. Soon, however, he remembered that he had thrown away the sum without which he could never hope to marry Emily ; and life, unless passed with her, now scarcely appeared supportable ; for her goodness, refinement, and simplicity of heart, rendered her beauty more enchanting, if possible, to his fancy than it had ever yet appeared. Experience had taught him to understand the full value of the qualities which he had before admired, but which the contrasted characters he had seen in the world made him now adore ; and these reflections increasing the pangs of remorse and regret, occasioned the deep dejection that had accompanied him even into the presence of Emily, of whom he considered himself no longer worthy. To the ignominy of having received pecuniary obligations from the Marchioness Chamfort, or any other lady of intrigue, as the Count de Villefort had been informed, or of having been engaged in the depredating schemes of gamesters, Valancourt had never submitted ; and these were some of such scandals as often mingle with truth against the unfortunate. Count de Villefort had received them from authority which he had no reason to doubt, and which the imprudent conduct he had himself witnessed in Valancourt had certainly induced him the more readily to believe. Being such as Emily could not name to the chevalier, he had no opportunity of refuting them ; and when he had confessed himself to be unworthy of her esteem, he little suspected that he was confirming to her the most dreadful calumnies. Thus the mistake had been mutual, and had remained so, when Mons. Bonnac explained the conduct of his generous but imprudent young friend to Du Pont ; who, with severe justice, determined not only to undeceive the count on this subject, but to resign all hope of Emily. Such a sacrifice as his love rendered this, was deserving of a noble reward ; and Mons. Bonnac, if it had been possible for him to forget the benevolent Valancourt, would have wished that Emily might accept the just Du Pont.

When the count was informed of the error he had committed, he was extremely shocked at the consequence of his credulity ; and the account which Mons. Bonnac gave of his friend's situation while at Paris, convinced him that Valancourt had been entrapped by the schemes of a set of dissipated young men with whom his profession had partly obliged him to associate, rather than by an inclination to vice ; and, charmed by the humanity, and noble though rash generosity which his conduct towards Mons. Bonnac exhibited, he forgave him the transient errors that had stained his youth, and restored him to the high degree of esteem with which he had regarded him during their early acquaintance. But as the last reparation he could now make Valancourt was to afford him an opportunity of explaining to Emily his former conduct, he immediately wrote to request his forgiveness of the unintentional injury he had done him, and to invite him to Chateau-le-Blanc. Motives of delicacy withheld the count from informing Emily of this letter, and of kindness from acquainting her with the discovery respecting Valancourt till his arrival should save her from the possibility of anxiety as to its event; and this precaution spared her even severer inquietude than the count had foreseen, since he was ignorant of the symptoms of despair which Valancourt's late conduct had betrayed.

CHAPTER LV.

'. . . . . But in these cases
We still have judgment here; that we but teach
Bloody instructions, which, being taught, return
To plague the inventor; thus even-handed Justice
Commends the ingredients of our poison'd chalice
To our own lips.'

MACBETH.

SOME circumstances of an extraordinary nature now withdrew Emily from her own sorrows, and excited emotions which partook of both surprise and horror.

A few days following that on which Signora Laurentini died, her will was opened at the monastery, in the presence of the superiors and Mons. Bonnac, when it was found that one third of her personal property was bequeathed to the nearest surviving relative of the late Marchioness de Villeroi, and that Emily was the person.

With the secret of Emily's family the abbess had long been acquainted; and it was in observance of the earnest request of St. Aubert, who was known to the friar that attended him on his death-bed, that his daughter had remained in ignorance of her relationship to the marchioness. But some hints which had fallen from Signora Laurentini during her last interview with Emily, and a confession of a very extraordinary nature given in her dying hours, had made the abbess think it necessary to converse with her young friend on the topic she had not before ventured to introduce; and it was for this purpose that she had requested to see her on the morning that followed her interview with the nun. Emily's indisposition had then prevented the intended conversation; but now, after the will had been examined, she received a summons, which she immediately obeyed, and became informed of circumstances that powerfully affected her. As the narrative of the abbess was, however, deficient in many particulars of which the reader may wish to be informed, and the history of the nun is materially connected with the fate of the Marchioness de Villeroi, we shall omit the conversation that passed in the parlour of the convent, and mingle with our relation a brief history of

LAURENTINI DI UDOLPHO,

who was the only child of her parents, and heiress of the ancient house of Udolpho, in the territory of Venice: It was the first misfortune of her life, and that which led to all her succeeding misery, that the friends who ought to have restrained her strong passions, and mildly instructed her in the art of governing them, nurtured them by early indulgence. But they cherished their own failings in her; for their conduct was not the result of rational kindness; and when they either indulged or opposed the passions of their child, they gratified their own. Thus they indulged her with weakness, and reprehended her with violence; her spirit was exasperated by their vehemence, instead of being corrected by their wisdom; and their oppositions became contests for victory, in which the due tenderness of the parents, and the affectionate duties of the child, were equally forgotten: but as returning fondness disarmed the parents' resentment soonest, Laurentini was suffered to believe that she had conquered, and her passions became stronger by every effort that had been employed to subdue them.

The death of her father and mother in the same year left her to her own discretion, under the dangerous circumstances attendant on youth and beauty. She was fond of company, delighted with admiration, yet disdainful of the opinion of the world, when it happened to contradict her inclinations; had a gay and brilliant wit, and was mistress of all the arts of fascination. Her conduct was such as might have been expected from the weakness of her principles and the strength of her passions.

Among her numerous admirers was the late Marquis de Villeroi, who, on his tour through Italy, saw Laurentini at Venice, where he usually resided, and became her passionate adorer. Equally captivated by the figure and accomplishments of the marquis, who was at that period one of the most distinguished noblemen of the French court, she had the art so effectually to conceal from him the dangerous traits of her character, and the blemishes of her late conduct, that he solicited her hand in marriage.

Before the nuptials were concluded, she retired to the castle of Udolpho, whither the marquis followed, and where her conduct, relaxing from the propriety which she had lately assumed, discovered to him the precipice on which he stood. A minuter inquiry than he had before thought it necessary to make, convinced him that he had been deceived in her character; and she, whom he had designed for his wife, afterwards became his mistress.

Having passed some weeks at Udolpho, he was called abruptly to France, whither he returned with extreme reluctance, for his heart was still fascinated by the arts of Laurentini, with whom, however, he had on various pretences delayed his marriage; but, to reconcile her to this separation, he now gave repeated promises of returning to conclude the nuptials, as soon as the affair which thus suddenly called him to France should permit.

Soothed in some degree by these assurances, she suffered him to depart ; and soon after, her relative, Montoni, arriving at Udolpho, renewed the addresses which she had before refused, and which she now again rejected. Meanwhile her thoughts were constantly with the Marquis de Villeroi, for whom she suffered all the delirium of Italian love, cherished by the solitude to which she confined herself; for she had now lost all taste for the pleasures of society and the gaiety of amusement. Her only indulgences were to sigh and weep over a miniature of the marquis ; to visit the scenes that had witnessed their happiness ; to pour forth her heart to him in writing ; and to count the weeks, the days, which must intervene before the period that he had mentioned as probable for his return. But this period passed without bringing him ; and week after week followed in heavy and almost intolerable expectation. During this interval, Laurentini's fancy, occupied incessantly by one idea, became disordered ; and her whole heart being devoted to one object, life became hateful to her, when she believed that object lost.

Several months passed, during which she heard nothing from the Marquis de Villeroi. and her days were marked at intervals, with the frenzy of passion and the sullenness of despair. She secluded herself from all visitors, and sometimes remained in her apartment for weeks together, refusing to speak to every person, except her favourite female attendant, writing scraps of letters, reading again and again those she had received from the marquis, weeping over his picture, and speaking to it, for many hours, upbraiding, reproaching, and caressing it alternately.

At length a report reached her that the marquis had married in France ; and after suffering all the extremes of love, jealousy, and indignation, she formed the desperate resolution of going secretly to that country, and, if the report proved true, of attempting a deep revenge. To her favourite woman only she confided the plan of her journey ; and she engaged her to partake of it. Having collected her jewels, which, descending to her from many branches of her family, were of immense value, and all her cash, to a very large amount, they were packed in a trunk, which was privately conveyed to a neighbouring town, whither Laurentini, with this only servant, followed, and thence proceeded secretly to Leghorn, where they embarked for France.

When, on her arrival in Languedoc, she found that the Marquis de Villeroi had been married for some months, her despair almost deprived her of reason, and she alternately projected and abandoned the horrible design

of murdering the marquis, his wife, and herself. At length she contrived to throw herself in his way, with an intention of reproaching him for his conduct, and of stabbing herself in his presence ; but when she again saw him who so long had been the constant object of her thoughts and affections, resentment yielded to love ; her resolution failed ; she trembled with the conflict of emotions that assailed her heart, and fainted away.

The marquis was not proof against her beauty and sensibility ; all the energy with which he had first loved returned, for his passion had been resisted by prudence, rather than overcome by indifference ; and since the honour of his family would not permit him to marry her, he had endeavoured to subdue his love ; and had so far succeeded as to select the then marchioness for his wife, whom he loved at first with a tempered and rational affection. But the mild virtues of that amiable lady did not recompense him for her indifference, which appeared, notwithstanding her efforts to conceal it ; and he had for some time suspected that her affections were engaged by another person, when Laurentini arrived in Languedoc. This artful Italian soon perceived that she had regained her influence over him ; and, soothed by the discovery, she determined to live, and to employ all her enchantments to win his consent to the diabolical deed, which she believed was necessary to the security of her happiness. She conducted her scheme with deep dissimulation and patient perseverance ; and having completely estranged the affections of the marquis from his wife, whose gentle goodness and unimpassioned manners had ceased to please, when contrasted with the captivations of the Italian, she proceeded to awaken in his mind the jealousy of pride, for it was no longer that of love, and even pointed out to him the person to whom she affirmed the marchioness had sacrificed her honour ; but Laurentini had first extorted from him a solemn promise to forbear avenging himself upon his rival. This was an important part of her plan ; for she knew that if his desire of vengeance was restrained towards one party, it would burn more fiercely towards the other, and he might then perhaps be prevailed on to assist in the horrible act, which would release him from the only barrier that withheld him from making her his wife.

The innocent marchioness meanwhile observed with extreme grief the alteration in her husband's manners. He became reserved and thoughtful in her presence ; his conduct was austere, and sometimes even rude ; and he left her, for many hours together, to weep for his unkindness, and to form plans for the recovery of his affection. His conduct afflicted her the more, because, in obedience to the command of her father she had accepted his hand, though her affections were engaged to another whose amiable disposition she had reason to believe would have ensured her happiness. This circumstance Laurentini had discovered soon after her arrival in France, and had made ample use of it in assisting her designs upon the marquis, to whom she adduced such seeming proof of his wife's infidelity, that, in the frantic rage of wounded honour, he consented to destroy his wife. A slow poison was administered, and she fell a victim to the jealousy and subtlety of Laurentini, and to the guilty weakness of her husband.

But the moment of Laurentini's triumph, the moment to which she had looked forward for the completion all of her wishes, proved only the commencement of a suffering that never left her to her dying hour.

The passion of revenge, which had in part stimulated her to the commission of this atrocious deed, died even at the moment when it was gratified, and left her to the horrors of unavailing pity and remorse, which would probably have impoisoned all the years she had promised herself with the Marquis de Villeroi, had her expectations of an alliance with him been realised. But he, too, had found the moment of his revenge to be that of remorse as to himself, and detestation as to the partner of his crime; the feeling which he had mistaken for conviction was no more; and he stood astonished and aghast, that no proof remained of his wife's infidelity, now that she had suffered the punishment of guilt. Even when he was informed that she was dying, he had felt suddenly and unaccountably reassured of her innocence; nor was the solemn assurance she made him in her last hour capable of affording him a stronger conviction of her blameless conduct.

In the first horrors of remorse and despair, he felt inclined to deliver up himself, and the woman who had plunged him into this abyss of guilt, into the hands of justice; but when the paroxysm of his suffering was over, his intention changed. Laurentini, however, he saw only once afterwards, and that was to curse her as the instigator of his crime, and to say, that he spared her life only on condition that she passed the rest of her days in prayer and penance. Overwhelmed with disappointment, on receiving contempt and abhorrence from the man for whose sake she had not scrupled to stain her conscience with human blood, and touched with horror of the unavailing crime she had committed, she renounced the world, and retired to the monastery of St. Clair, a dreadful victim to unresisted passion.

The marquis, immediately after the death of his wife, quitted Chateau-le-Blanc, to which he never returned, and endeavoured to lose the sense of his crime amidst the tumult of war, or the dissipations of a capital. But his efforts were vain; a deep dejection hung over

him ever after, for which his most intimate friend could not account; and he at length died, with a degree of horror nearly equal to that which Laurentini had suffered. The physician, who had observed the singular appearance of the unfortunate marchioness after her death, had been bribed to silence; and as the surmises of a few of the servants had proceeded no further than a whisper, the affair had never been investigated. Whether this whisper ever reached the father of the marchioness, and if it did, whether the difficulty of obtaining proof, deterred him from prosecuting the Marquis de Villeroi, is uncertain; but her death was deeply lamented by some part of her family, and particularly by her brother, M. St. Aubert; for that was the degree of relationship which had existed between Emily's father and the marchioness; and there is no doubt that he suspected the manner of her death. Many letters passed between the marquis and him, soon after the decease of his beloved sister, the subject of which was not known, but there is reason to believe they related to the cause of her death; and these were the papers, together with some of the letters of the marchioness, who had confided to her brother the occasion of her unhappiness, which St. Aubert had so solemnly enjoined his daughter to destroy : and anxiety for her peace had probably made him forbid her to inquire into the melancholy story to which they alluded. Such, indeed, had been his affliction on the premature death of this his favourite sister, whose unhappy marriage had from the first excited his tenderest pity, that he never could hear her named, or mention her himself after her death, except to Madame St. Aubert. From Emily, whose sensibility he feared to awaken, he had so carefully concealed her history and name, that she was ignorant, till now, that she ever had such a relative as the Marchioness de Villeroi; and from this motive he had enjoined silence to his only surviving sister, Madame Cheron, who had scrupulously observed his request.

It was over some of the last pathetic letters of the marchioness that St. Aubert was weeping when he was observed by Emily on the eve of her departure from La Vallée, and it was her picture which he had so fondly caressed. Her disastrous death may account for the emotion he had betrayed on hearing her named by La Voisin, and for his request to be interred near the monument of the Villerois, where her remains were deposited, but not those of her husband, who was buried, where he died, in the north of France.

The confessor who attended St. Aubert in his last moments, recollected him to be the brother of the late marchioness, when St. Aubert, from tenderness to Emily, had conjured him to conceal the circumstance, and to request that the abbess, to whose care he particularly recommended her, would do the same; a request which had been exactly observed.

Laurentini, on her arrival in France, had carefully concealed her name and family, and, the better to disguise her real history, had, on entering the convent, caused the story to be circulated which had imposed on sister Frances; and it is probable that the abbess, who did not preside in the convent at the time of her noviciation, was also entirely ignorant of the truth. The deep remorse that seized on the mind of Laurentini, together with the sufferings of disappointed passion, for she still loved the marquis, again unsettled her intellect; and after the first paroxysms of despair were passed, a heavy and silent melancholy had settled upon her spirits, which suffered few interruptions from fits of phrensy till the time of her death. During many years, it had been her only amusement to walk in the woods near the monastery, in the solitary hours of night, and to play upon a favourite instrument, to which she sometimes joined the delightful melody of her voice in the most solemn and melancholy airs of her native country, modulated by all the energetic feeling that dwelt in her heart. The physician who had attended her recommended it to the superior to indulge her in this whim, as the only means of soothing her distempered fancy; and she was suffered to walk in the lonely hours of night, attended by the servant who had accompanied her from Italy; but as the indulgence transgressed against the rules of the convent, it was kept as secret as possible; and thus the mysterious music of Laurentini had combined, with other circumstances, to produce a report that not only the chateau, but its neighbourhood, was haunted.

Soon after her entrance into this holy community, and before she had shown any symptoms of insanity there, she made a will, in which, after bequeathing a considerable legacy to the convent, she divided the remainder of her personal property, which her jewels made very valuable, between the wife of Mons. Bonnac, who was an Italian lady, and her relation, and the nearest surviving relative of the late Marchioness de Villeroi. As Emily St. Aubert was not only the nearest but the sole relative, this legacy descended to her, and thus explained to her the whole mystery of her father's conduct.

The resemblance between Emily and her unfortunate aunt had frequently been observed by Laurentini, and had occasioned the singular behaviour which had formerly alarmed her; but it was in the nun's dying hour, when her conscience gave her perpetually the idea of the marchioness, that she became more sensible than ever of this likeness, and in her phrenzy deemed it no resemblance of the person she had injured, but the original herself. The bold assertion that had followed on the

recovery of her senses, that Emily was the daughter of the Marchioness de Villeroi, arose from suspicion that she was so; for, knowing that her rival, when she married the marquis, was attached to another lover, she had scarcely scrupled to believe that her honour had been sacrificed, like her own, to an unresisted passion.

Of a crime, however, to which Emily had suspected, from her phrensied confession of murder, that she had been instrumental in the castle of Udolpho, Laurentini was innocent; and she had herself been deceived concerning the spectacle that formerly occasioned her so much terror, and had since compelled her, for a while, to attribute the horrors of the nun to a consciousness of a murder committed in that castle.

It may be remembered that in a chamber of Udolpho hung a black veil, whose singular situation had excited Emily's curiosity, and which afterwards disclosed an object that had overwhelmed her with horror; for, on lifting it, there appeared, instead of the picture she had expected, within a recess of the wall, a human figure, of ghastly paleness, stretched at its length, and dressed in the habiliments of the grave. What added to the horror of the spectacle, was, that the face appeared partly decayed and disfigured by worms, which were visible on the features and hands. On such an object it will be readily believed that no person could endure to look twice. Emily, it may be recollected, had, after the first glance, let the veil drop, and her terror had prevented her from ever after provoking a renewal of such suffering as she had then experienced. Had she dared to look again, her delusion and her fears would have vanished together, and she would have perceived that the figure before her was not human, but formed of wax. The history of it is somewhat extraordinary, though not without example in the records of that fierce severity which monkish superstition has sometimes inflicted on mankind. A member of the house of Udolpho having committed some offence against the prerogative of the church, had been condemned to the penance of contemplating, during certain hours of the day, a waxen image, made to resemble a human body in the state to which it is reduced after death. This penance, serving as a memento of the condition at which he must himself arrive, had been designed to reprove the pride of the Marquis of Udolpho, which had formerly so much exasperated that of the Romish church; and he had not only superstitiously observed this penance himself, which he had believed was to obtain a pardon for all his sins, but had made it a condition in his will, that his descendants should preserve the image on pain of forfeiting to the church a certain part of his domain, that they also might profit by the humiliating moral it conveyed. The figure, therefore, had been suffered to retain its station in the wall of the chamber; but his descendants excused themselves from observing the penance to which he had been enjoined.

This image was so horribly natural, that it is not surprising that Emily should have mistaken it for the object it resembled; nor, since she had heard such an extraordinary account concerning the disappearing of the late lady of thé castle, and had such experience of the character of Montoni, that she should have believed this to be the murdered body of the Lady Laurentini, and that he had been the contriver of her death.

The situation in which she had discovered it occasioned her at first much surprise and perplexity; but the vigilance with which the doors of the chamber where it was deposited were afterwards secured, had compelled her to believe that Montoni, not daring to confide the secret of her death to any person, had suffered her remains to decay in this obscure chamber. The ceremony of the veil, however, and the circumstance of the doors having been left open even for a moment, had occasioned her much wonder and some doubts; but these were not sufficient to overcome her suspicion of Montoni; and it was the dread of his terrible vengeance that had sealed her lips in silence concerning what she had seen in the west chamber.

Emily, in discovering the Marchioness de Villeroi to have been the sister of Mons. St. Aubert, was variously affected; but, amidst the sorrow which she suffered for her untimely death, she was released from an anxious and painful conjecture, occasioned by the rash assertion of Signora Laurentini, concerning her birth and the honour of her parents. Her faith in St. Aubert's principles would scarcely allow her to suspect that he had acted dishonourably; and she felt such reluctance to believe herself the daughter of any other than her whom she had always considered and loved as a mother, that she would hardly admit such a circumstance to be possible: yet the likeness which it had frequently been affirmed she bore to the late marchioness, the former behaviour of Dorothee the old housekeeper, the assertion of Laurentini, and the mysterious attachment which St. Aubert had discovered, awakened doubts as to his connection with the marchioness, which her reason could neither vanquish nor confirm. From these, however, she was now relieved, and all the circumstances of her father's conduct were fully explained: but her heart was oppressed by the melancholy catastrophe of her amiable relative, and by the awful lesson which the history of the nun exhibited, the indulgence of whose passions had been the means of leading her gradually to the commission of a crime, from the prophecy of which in her early years she would have recoiled in horror, and exclaimed—that it could not be!—a crime, which whole years of repentance and of the severest penance had not been able to obliterate from her conscience.

CHAPTER LVI.

'. . . . . Then, fresh tears
Stood on her cheek, as doth the honey-dew
Upon a gather'd lily almost wither'd.
           SHAKESPEARE.

AFTER the late discoveries, Emily was distinguished at the chateau by the count and his family as a relative of the house of Villeroi, and received, if possible, more friendly attention than had yet been shown her.

Count de Villefort's surprise at the delay of an answer to his letter, which had been directed to Valancourt at Estuviere, was mingled with satisfaction for the prudence which had saved Emily from a share of the anxiety he now suffered; though, when he saw her still drooping under the effect of his former error, all his resolution was necessary to restrain him from relating the truth, that would afford her a momentary relief. The approaching nuptials of the Lady Blanche now divided his attention with this subject of his anxiety; for the inhabitants of the chateau were already busied in preparations for that event, and the arrival of Mons. St. Foix was daily expected. In the gaiety which surrounded her, Emily vainly tried to participate, her spirits being depressed by the late discoveries, and by the anxiety concerning the fate of Valancourt, that had been occasioned by the description of his manner when he had delivered the ring. She seemed to perceive in it the gloomy wildness of despair; and when she considered to what that despair might have urged him, her heart sunk with terror and grief. The state of suspense, as to his safety, to which she believed herself condemned till she should return to La Vallée, appeared insupportable; and, in such moments, she could not even struggle to assume the composure that had left her mind, but would often abruptly quit the company she was with, and endeavour to soothe her spirits in the deep solitudes of the woods that overbrowed the shore. Here the faint roar of foaming waves that beat below, and the sullen murmur of the wind among the branches around, were circumstances in unison with the temper of her mind; and she would sit on a cliff, or on the broken steps of her favourite watch-tower, observing the changing colours of the evening clouds, and the gloom of twilight draw over the sea, till the white tops of billows, riding towards the shore, could scarcely be discerned amidst the darkened waters. The lines engraved by

Valancourt on this tower, she frequently repeated with melancholy enthusiasm, and then would endeavour to check the recollections and the grief they occasioned, and to turn her thoughts to indifferent subjects.

One evening, having wandered with her lute to this her favourite spot, she entered the ruined tower, and ascended a winding staircase that led to a small chamber which was less decayed than the rest of the building, and whence she had often gazed with admiration on the wide prospect of sea and land that extended below. The sun was now setting on that tract of the Pyrenees which divides Languedoc from Roussillon ; and placing herself opposite to a small grated window, which, like the wood-tops beneath, and the waves lower still, gleamed with the red glow of the west, she touched the chords of her lute in solemn symphony, and then accompanied it with her voice in one of the simple and affecting airs to which, in happier days, Valancourt had often listened in rapture, and which she now adapted to the following lines :

TO MELANCHOLY.

Spirit of love and sorrow—hail !
  Thy solemn voice from far I hear,
Mingling with evening's dying gale :
  Hail, with this sadly-pleasing tear !

O ! at this still, this lonely hour,
  Thine own sweet hour of closing day,
Awake thy lute, whose charmful power
  Shall call up Fancy to obey :

To paint the wild romantic dream
  That meets the poet's musing eye,
As on the bank of shadowy stream
  He breathes to her the fervid sigh.

O lonely spirit ! let thy song
  Lead me through all thy sacred haunt :
The minster's moonlight aisles along,
  Where spectres raise the midnight chaunt !

I hear their dirges faintly swell !
  Then, sink at once in silence drear,
While, from the pillar'd cloister's cell,
  Dimly their gliding forms appear !

Lead where the pine-woods wave on high,
  Whose pathless sod is darkly seen,
As the cold moon with trembling eye,
  Darts her long beams the leaves between.

Lead to the mountain's dusky head,
  Where, far below, in shade profound,
Wide forests, plains, and hamlets spread,
  And sad the chimes of vesper sound.

Or guide me where the dashing oar
  Just breaks the stillness of the vale,
As slow it tracks the winding shore,
  To meet the ocean's distant sail :

To pebbly banks, that Neptune laves
  With measured surges loud and deep,
Where the dark cliff bends o'er the waves,
  And wild the winds of autumn sweep.

There pause at midnight's spectered hour,
  And list the long-resounding gale ;
And catch the fleeting moonlight's power,
  O'er foaming seas and distant sail.

The soft tranquillity of the scene below, where the evening breeze scarcely curled the water, or swelled the passing sail that caught the last gleam of the sun, and where, now and then, a dipping oar was all that disturbed the trembling radiance, conspired with the tender melody of her lute to lull her mind into a state of gentle sadness ; and she sung the mournful songs of past times, till the remembrances they awakened were too powerful for her heart, her tears fell upon the lute, over which she drooped, and her voice trembled, and was unable to proceed.

Though the sun had now sunk behind the mountains, and even his reflected light was fading from their highest points, Emily did not leave the watch-tower, but continued to indulge her melancholy reverie, till a footstep at a little distance startled her, and on looking through the grate she observed a person walking below, whom, however, soon perceiving to be Mons. Bonnac, she returned to the quiet thoughtfulness his step had interrupted. After some time she again struck her lute, and sung her favourite air ; but again a step disturbed her, and, as she paused to listen, she heard it ascending the staircase of the tower. The gloom of the hour, perhaps, made her sensible to some degree of fear, which she might not otherwise have felt ; for only a few minutes before she had seen Mons. Bonnac pass. The steps were quick and bounding, and in the next moment the door of the chamber opened, and a person entered whose features were veiled in the obscurity of twilight ; but his voice could not be concealed, for it was the voice of Valancourt ! At the sound, never heard by Emily without emotion, she started in terror, astonishment, and doubtful pleasure ; and had scarcely beheld him at her feet, when she sunk into a seat, overcome by the various emotions that contended at her heart, and almost insensible to that voice whose earnest and trembling calls seemed as if endeavouring to save her. Valancourt, as he hung over Emily, deplored his own rash impatience in having thus surprised her : for when he arrived at the chateau, too anxious to await the return of the count, who, he understood, was in the grounds, he went himself to seek him, when, as he passed the tower, he was struck by the sound of Emily's voice, and immediately ascended.

It was a considerable time before she revived ; but when her recollection returned, she repulsed his attentions with an air of reserve, and inquired, with as much displeasure as it was possible she could feel in these first moments of his appearance, the occasion of his visit.

'Ah, Emily !' said Valancourt, 'that air, those words—alas ! I have, then, little to hope —when you ceased to esteem me, you ceased also to love me !'

'Most true, sir,' replied Emily, endeavouring to command her trembling voice ; 'and if you had valued my esteem, you would not have given me this new occasion for uneasiness.'

Valancourt's countenance changed suddenly from the anxieties of doubt to an expression of surprise and dismay; he was silent a moment, and then said, 'I had been taught to hope for a very different reception! Is it then true, Emily, that I have lost your regard for ever? Am I to believe that though your esteem for me may return—your affection never can? Can the count have meditated the cruelty which now tortures me with a second death?'

The voice in which he spoke this alarmed Emily as much as his words surprised her, and with trembling impatience she begged that he would explain them.

'Can any explanation be necessary?' said Valancourt: 'do you not know how cruelly my conduct has been misrepresented? that the actions of which you once believed me guilty (and, O Emily! how could you so degrade me in your opinion, even for a moment?)—those actions I hold in as much contempt and abhorrence as yourself? Are you, indeed, ignorant that Count de Villefort has detected the slanders that have robbed me of all I hold dear on earth, and has invited me hither to justify to you my former conduct? It is surely impossible you can be uninformed of these circumstances, and I am again torturing myself with a false hope!'

The silence of Emily confirmed this supposition; for the deep twilight would not allow Valancourt to distinguish the astonishment and doubting joy that fixed her features. For a moment she continued unable to speak; then a profound sigh seemed to give some relief to her spirits, and she said,

'Valancourt! I was till this moment ignorant of all the circumstances you have mentioned; the emotion I now suffer may assure you of the truth of this, and that though I had ceased to esteem, I had not taught myself entirely to forget you.'

'This moment!' said Valancourt in a low voice, and leaning for support against the window—'this moment brings with it a conviction that overpowers me!—I am dear to you, then—still dear to you, my Emily!'

'Is it necessary that I should tell you so?' she replied: 'is it necessary that I should say —these are the first moments of joy I have know since your departure, and that they repay me for all those of pain I have suffered in the interval?'

Valancourt sighed deeply, and was unable to reply; but as he pressed her hand to his lips, the tears that fell over it spoke a language which could not be mistaken, and to which words were inadequate.

Emily, somewhat tranquillized, proposed returning to the chateau; and then, for the first time, recollected that the count had invited Valancourt thither to explain his conduct, and that no explanation had yet been given. But while she acknowledged this, her heart would not allow her to dwell for a moment on the possibility of his unworthiness: his look, his voice, his manner, all spoke the noble sincerity which had formerly distinguished him; and she again permitted herself to indulge the emotions of a joy more surprising and powerful than she had ever before experienced.

Neither Emily nor Valancourt were conscious how they reached the chateau, whether they might have been transferred by the spell of a fairy, for anything they could remember; and it was not till they had reached the great hall that either of them recollected there were other persons in the world besides themselves.

The count then came forth with surprise and with the joyfulness of pure benevolence to welcome Valancourt, and to entreat his forgiveness of the injustice he had done him; soon after which Mons. Bonnac joined this happy group, in which he and Valancourt were mutually rejoiced to meet.

When the first congratulations were over, and the general joy became somewhat more tranquil, the count withdrew with Valancourt to the library, where a long conversation passed between them; in which the latter so clearly justified himself of the criminal parts of the conduct imputed to him, and so candidly confessed and so feelingly lamented the follies which he had committed, that the count was confirmed in his belief of all he had hoped; and while he perceived so many noble virtues in Valancourt, and that experience had taught him to detest the follies which before he had only not admired, he did not scruple to believe that he would pass through life with the dignity of a wise and good man, or to intrust to his care the future happiness of Emily St. Aubert, for whom he felt the solicitude of a parent. Of this he soon informed her, in a short conversation, when Valancourt had left him. While Emily listened to a relation of the services that Valancourt had rendered Mons. Bonnac, her eyes overflowed with tears of pleasure; and the further conversation of Count de Villefort perfectly dissipated every doubt, as to the past and future conduct of him, to whom she now restored, without fear, the esteem and affection with which she had formerly received him.

When they returned to the supper-room, the countess and Lady Blanche met Valancourt with sincere congratulations; and Blanche indeed was so much rejoiced to see Emily returned to happiness, as to forget for a while that Mons. St. Foix was not yet arrived at the chateau, though he had been expected for some hours; but her generous sympathy was soon after rewarded by his appearance. He was now perfectly recovered from the wounds received during his perilous adventure among the Pyrenees, the mention of which served to heighten to the parties who had been involved in it, the sense of their present happiness. New congratulations passed between them, and round the supper-table appeared a group of faces smiling with felicity, but with a felicity which had in each a different character. The smile of Blanche was frank and gay, that of Emily tender and pensive; Valancourt's was rapturous, tender, and gay, alternately: Mons. St. Foix's was joyous; and that of the count, as he looked on the surrounding party, expressed the tempered complacency of benevolence; while the features of the countess, Henri, and Mons. Bonnac, discovered fainter traces of animation. Poor Mons. du Pont did not, by his presence, throw a shade of regret over the company, for when he had discovered that Valancourt was not unworthy of the esteem of Emily, he determined seriously to endeavour at the conquest of his own hopeless affection, and had immediately withdrawn from Chateau-le-Blanc—a conduct which Emily now understood, and rewarded with her admiration and pity.

The count and his guests continued together till a late hour, yielding to the delights of social gaiety and to the sweets of friendship. When Annette heard of the arrival of Valancourt, Ludovico had some difficulty to prevent her going into the supper-room to express her joy, for she declared that she had never been so rejoiced at any *accident* as this, since she had found Ludovico himself,

---

CHAPTER LVII,

'Now my task is smoothly done,
I can fly, or I can run
Quickly to the green earth's end,
Where the bow'd welkin low doth bend;
And, from thence, can soar as soon
To the corners of the moon.'

MILTON.

THE marriages of the Lady Blanche and Emily St. Aubert were celebrated on the same day, and with the ancient baronial magnificence, at Chateau-le-Blanc. The feasts were held in the great hall of the castle, which on this occasion was hung with superb new tapestry, representing the exploits of Charlemagne and his twelve peers: here were seen the Saracens, with their horrible visors advancing to battle; and there were displayed the wild solemnities of incantation, and the necromantic feats exhibited by the magician Jarl before the emperor. The sumptuous banners of the family of Villeroi, which had long slept in dust, were once more unfurled, to wave over the Gothic points of painted casements; and music echoed in many a lingering close, through every winding gallery and colonnade of that vast edifice.

As Annette looked down from the corridor upon the hall, whose arches and windows were illuminated with brilliant festoons of lamps, and gazed on the splendid dresses of the dancers, the costly liveries of the attendants, the canopies of purple velvet and gold, and listened to the gay strains that floated along the vaulted roof, she almost fancied herself in an enchanted palace, and declared that she had not met with any place which charmed her so much, since she read the fairy tales; nay, that the fairies themselves, at their nightly revels in this old hall, could display nothing finer; while old Dorothee, as she surveyed the scene, sighed, and said the castle looked as it was wont to do in the time of her youth.

After gracing the festivities of Chateau-le-Blanc for some days, Valancourt and Emily took leave of their friends, and returned to La Vallée, where the faithful Theresa received them with unfeigned joy, and the pleasant shades welcomed them with a thousand tender and affecting remembrances; and while they wandered together over the scenes so long inhabited by the late Mons. and Madame St. Aubert, and Emily pointed out with pensive affection their favourite haunts, her present happiness was heightened by considering, that it would have been worthy of their approbation, could they have witnessed it.

Valancourt led her to the plane-tree on the terrace, where he had first ventured to declare his love, and where now the remembrance of the anxiety he had then suffered, and the retrospect of all the dangers and misfortunes they had each encountered, since last they sat together beneath its broad branches, exalted the sense of their present felicity, which, on this spot, sacred to the memory of St. Aubert, they solemnly vowed to deserve, as far as possible, by endeavouring to imitate his benevolence,—by remembering, that superior attainments of every sort bring with them duties of superior exertion,—and by affording to their fellow-beings, together with that portion of ordinary comforts which prosperity always owes to misfortune, the example of lives passed in happy thankfulness to God, and, therefore, in careful tenderness to His creatures.

Soon after their return to La Vallée, the brother of Valancourt came to congratulate him on his marriage, and to pay his respects to Emily, with whom he was so much pleased, as well as with the prospect of rational happiness which these nuptials offered to Valancourt, that he immediately resigned to him a part of the rich domain, the whole of which, as he had no family, would of course descend to his brother on his decease.

The estates at Thoulouse were disposed of, and Emily purchased of Mons. Quesnel the ancient domain of her late father, where, having given Annette a marriage portion, she settled her as the housekeeper, and Ludovico as the steward; but since both Valancourt and herself preferred the pleasant and long-loved shades of La Vallée to the magnificence of Epourville, they continued to reside there, passing, however, a few months in the year at the birth-place of St. Aubert, in tender respect to his memory.

The legacy which had been bequeathed to Emily by Signor Laurentini, she begged Valancourt would allow her to resign to Mons. Bonnac; and Valancourt, when she made the request, felt all the value of the compliment it conveyed. The castle of Udolpho, also, descended to the wife of Mons. Bonnac, who was the nearest surviving relation of the house of that name; and thus affluence restored his long oppressed spirits to peace, and his family to comfort.

O! how joyful it is to tell of happiness such as that of Valancourt and Emily; to relate that, after suffering under the oppression of the vicious and the disdain of the weak, they were at length restored to each other—to the beloved landscape of their native country—to the securest felicity of this life, that of aspiring to moral and labouring for intellectual improvement—to the pleasures of enlightened society, and to the exercise of the benevolence which had always animated their hearts; while the bowers of La Vallée became once more the retreat of goodness, wisdom, and domestic blessedness!

O! useful may it be to have shown, that though the vicious can sometimes pour affliction upon the good, their power is transient and their punishment certain; and that innocence, though oppressed by injustice, shall, supported by patience, finally triumph over misfortune!

And if the weak hand that has recorded this tale, has by its scenes, beguiled the mourner of one hour of sorrow, or by its moral, taught him to sustain it—the effort, however humble, has not been vain, nor is the writer unrewarded.

THE END.

BILLING AND SONS, PRINTERS, GUILDFORD, SURREY.

ROUTLEDGE'S SIXPENNY NOVELS.

By CAPTAIN MARRYAT.

The King's Own.	Pacha of Many Tales.	Frank Mildmay.
Peter Simple.	Newton Forster.	Midshipman Easy.
Jacob Faithful.	Japhet in Search of a Father.	The Dog Fiend.

By J. F. COOPER.

The Waterwitch.	Homeward Bound.	Precaution.
The Pathfinder.	The Two Admirals.	Oak Openings.
The Deerslayer.	Miles Wallingford.	The Heidenmauer.
Last of the Mohicans.	The Pioneers.	Mark's Reef.
The Pilot.	Wyandotté.	Ned Myers.
The Prairie.	Lionel Lincoln.	Satanstoe.
Eve Effingham.	Afloat and Ashore.	The Borderers.
The Spy.	The Bravo.	Jack Tier.
The Red Rover.	The Sea Lions.	Mercedes.
	The Headsman.	

By Sir WALTER SCOTT.

Guy Mannering.	Peveril of the Peak.	The Abbot.
The Antiquary.	Heart of Midlothian.	Woodstock.
Ivanhoe.	The Bride of Lammermoor.	Redgauntlet.
The Fortunes of Nigel.		Count Robert of Paris.
Rob Roy.	Waverley.	The Talisman.
Kenilworth.	Quentin Durward.	Surgeon's Daughter.
The Pirate.	St. Ronan's Well.	Fair Maid of Perth.
The Monastery.	Legend of Montrose,	Anne of Geierstein.
Old Mortality.	and Black Dwarf.	The Betrothed.

By VARIOUS AUTHORS.

Robinson Crusoe.	Artemus Ward, his Book.
Uncle Tom's Cabin. *Mrs. Stowe.*	A. Ward among the Mormons.
Colleen Bawn. *Gerald Griffin.*	The Nasby Papers.
The Vicar of Wakefield.	Major Jack Downing.
Sketch Book. *Washington Irving.*	The Biglow Papers.
Tristram Shandy. *Sterne.*	Orpheus C. Kerr.
Sentimental Journey. *Sterne.*	The Wide, Wide World.
The English Opium Eater.	Queechy.
De Quincy.	Gulliver's Travels.
Essays of Elia. *Charles Lamb.*	The Wandering Jew. (3 vols.)
Roderick Random. *Smollett.*	The Mysteries of Paris. (3 vols.)
Autocrat of the Breakfast Table.	The Lamplighter.
Tom Jones. 2 vols. *Fielding.*	Professor at the Breakfast Table.

Published by George Routledge and Sons.

NOVELS AT ONE SHILLING.

By CAPTAIN MARRYAT.

Peter Simple.
The King's Own.
Midshipman Easy.
Rattlin the Reefer.
Pacha of Many Tales.
Newton Forster.

Jacob Faithful.
The Dog-Fiend.
Japhet in Search of a Father.
The Poacher.
The Phantom Ship.

Percival Keene.
Valerie.
Frank Mildmay.
Olla Podrida.
Monsieur Violet.

By W. H. AINSWORTH.

Windsor Castle.
Tower of London.
The Miser's Daughter.
Rookwood.
Old St. Paul's.
Crichton.

Guy Fawkes.
The Spendthrift.
James the Second.
Star Chamber.
Flitch of Bacon.
Lancashire Witches.

Mervyn Clitheroe.
Ovingdean Grange.
St. James's.
Auriol.
Jack Sheppard.

By J. FENIMORE COOPER.

The Pilot.
Last of the Mohicans.
The Pioneers.
The Red Rover.
The Spy.
Lionel Lincoln.
The Deerslayer.
The Pathfinder.
The Bravo.

The Waterwitch.
Two Admirals.
Satanstoe.
Afloat and Ashore.
Wyandotté.
Eve Effingham.
Miles Wallingford.
The Headsman.
The Prairie.

Homeward Bound.
The Borderers.
The Sea Lions.
Heidenmauer.
Precaution.
Oak Openings.
Mark's Reef.
Ned Myers.

By ALEXANDRE DUMAS.

Three Musketeers.
Twenty Years After.
Doctor Basilius.
The Twin Captains.
Captain Paul.
Memoirs of a Physician. 2 vols. (1s. each).
The Chevalier de Maison Rouge.
Queen's Necklace.

Countess de Charny.
Monte Cristo. 2 vols. (1s. each).
Nanon.
The Two Dianas.
The Black Tulip.
Forty - Five Guardsmen.
Taking of the Bastile. 2 vols. (1s. each).
Chicot the Jester.

The Conspirators.
Ascanio. [Savoy.
Page of the Duke of Isabel of Bavaria.
Beau Tancrede.
Regent's Daughter.
Pauline.
Catherine Blum.
Ingénue.
Russian Gipsy.
Watchmaker.

By MRS. GORE.

The Ambassador's Wife.

By JANE AUSTEN.

Northanger Abbey.
Emma.

Pride and Prejudice.
Sense and Sensibility.

Mansfield Park.

By MARIA EDGEWORTH.

Ennui. | Vivian. | The Absentee. | Manœuvring.

Published by George Routledge and Sons.

CPSIA information can be obtained
at www.ICGtesting.com
Printed in the USA
LVOW13s2014180218
567080LV00006B/132/P